# RENDEZ-VOUS

**Fourth Edition**

**Judith A. Muyskens**
UNIVERSITY OF CINCINNATI

**Alice C. Omaggio Hadley**
UNIVERSITY OF ILLINOIS, URBANA-CHAMPAIGN

**Thierry Duchesne**

**Claudine Convert-Chalmers**

New York St. Louis San Francisco Auckland
Bogatá Caracas Lisbon London Madrid
Mexico City Milan Montreal New Delhi
San Juan Singapore Sydney Tokyo Toronto

This is an  book.

ISBN 0-07-044337-8 (Student's Edition)
ISBN 0-07-044338-6 (Teacher's Edition)

Rendez-vous: An Invitation to French



1 2 3 4 5 6 7 8 9 0 VNH VNH 9 0 9 8 7 6 5 4

**Library of Congress Cataloging-in-Publication Data**

Rendez-vous : an invitation to French / Judith A. Muyskens, . . . [et al.]. — 4th ed.
p. cm.
"This is an EBI book"—T.p. verso.
Third ed. by Judith A. Muyskens, Alice C. Omaggio, and Claudine Chalmers.
Includes index.
ISBN 0-07-044337-8
1. French language—Textbooks for foreign speakers—English.
2. French language—Grammar. I. Muyskens, Judith A. II. Muyskens, Judith A. Rendez-vous.
PC2129.E5M87 1994
448.2′421—dc20 93-35951
CIP

Sponsoring editor: Leslie Berriman
Development editor: Suzanne Cowan
Copyeditor: Melissa Gruzs
Editing supervisor: E.A. Pauw
Text designer: Francis Owens
Cover designer: Lorna Lo
Cover illustrator: James Stimpson
Illustrators: David Bohn, Axelle Fortier, Lori Heckleman, Ellen Sasaki, and Katherine Tillotson
Photo researcher: Stephen Forsling
Production supervisor: Diane Renda
Production assistance was provided by Edie Williams (Vargas/Williams/Design), Ann Potter, and Marian Hartsough
Compositor: Black Dot Graphics
Printer and binder: Von Hoffman Press

Because this page cannot legibly accommodate all the copyright notices, credits are listed after the index and constitute an extension of the copyright page.

# Table des matières

| Cultural and Literary Readings | Skills Practice |
|---|---|
|  |

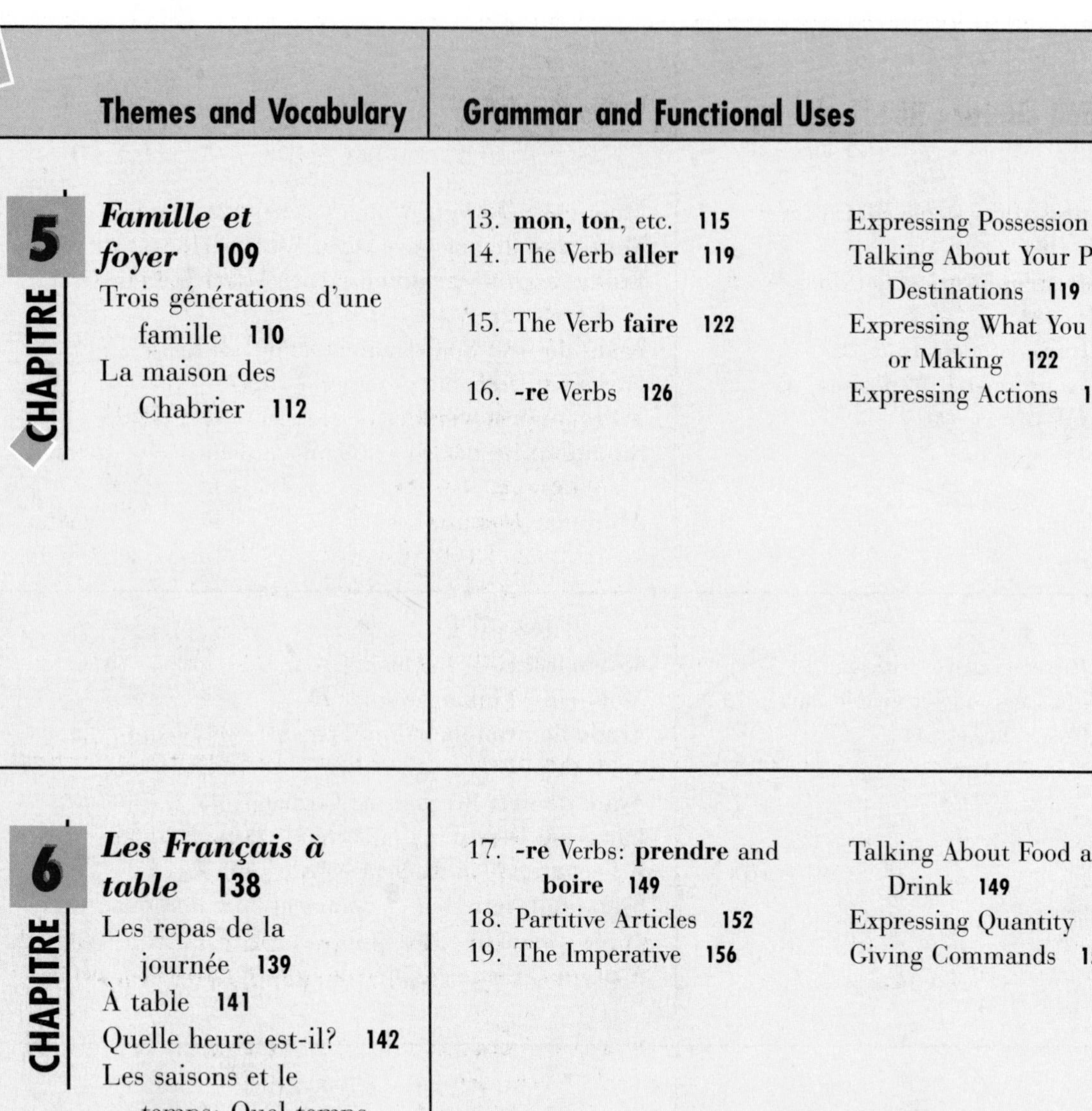

| Cultural and Literary Readings | Skills Practice |
|---|---|
|  |  |
|  |  |

| Cultural and Literary Readings | Skills Practice |
| --- | --- |
|  |

| Cultural and Literary Readings | Skills Practice |
|---|---|
|  |  |
|  |  |

# Preface

Welcome to the fourth edition of *Rendez-vous*, the first-year college and university program designed to promote communicative and interactive use of French. Emphasizing vocabulary before grammar, grammar within a cultural context, and French as it is spoken in authentic, everyday situations, *Rendez-vous* strives to develop proficiency in the four basic language skills (listening, speaking, reading, and writing) while introducing students to the cultural richness and diversity of the French-speaking world.

## Organization of the Fourth Edition

*Rendez-vous* is organized into eighteen chapters. Chapter 1 introduces and practices French expressions commonly used in everyday encounters and gives students the basic tools they need to approach learning French. Chapter 18 is a collection of readings and activities that focus on important issues facing French-speaking people today while reviewing essential first-year skills.

All chapters except Chapters 1 and 18 are organized by the following major sections:

- *Étude de vocabulaire.* A series of visual presentations of thematically linked words and expressions reflect everyday life in French-speaking cultures.
- *Étude de grammaire.* The basic structures of French are introduced contextually through "slice of life" mini-dialogues and then presented through concise English explanations with abundant French examples. Exercises and activities progressing from form-focused and controlled to open-ended and creative follow each grammar point.
- *Étude de prononciation.* Foundations of French pronunciation and spelling are accompanied by reinforcement exercises (through Chapter 7).
- *Mise au point.* A set of review exercises and activities practices each chapter's core vocabulary and grammar structures. **Interactions** contains culminating situations and role-plays.
- *Rencontres.* Accessible, stimulating reading selections (in **Lecture**) are introduced by pre-reading strategies (**Avant de lire**) and followed by a set of step-by-step writing guidelines (**Par écrit**) calculated to enhance students' writing skills while stimulating creative expression of their own ideas. The section culminates with a set of listening comprehension activities (**À l'écoute!**) recorded on the student tape packaged with the student text.
- *Intermède.* This optional section features a situational dialogue (**Situation**), a very practical list of functional expressions (**À propos**), speaking activities and role-plays (**Maintenant à vous!**), and a brief glimpse into the life of a great figure from the French-speaking world (**Portraits**).

## Major Changes in the Fourth Edition

The changes to *Rendez-vous* in the fourth edition are in all major areas: listening, speaking, reading, writing, grammar, and culture.

### Listening

A new listening comprehension tape, packaged with the student text, is coordinated with activities in the text. In the **À l'écoute!** section, students first listen to a passage, which might be a conversation, a radio announcement, an interview, a game show, a weather report, or a story, and then do activities that check their comprehension of the passage. The activities focus on the larger elements in the passage and help students to hone their listening skills.

Two other sections are recorded on the tape packaged with the student text. By listening to the chapter-opening dialogue, **En avant,** students become acquainted with a new chapter's general theme. The true/false and either/or questions on the tape are in English and simply check to see that students have understood the basic content of the brief dialogue. The longer functional dialogue at the end of the chapter, **Situation**, is also recorded on the student tape for additional listening practice. Personalized questions and role-plays that spin off the dialogue appear printed in the text.

Scripts appear at the back of the Instructor's Edition and include the recorded material that does not appear printed in the text, namely, the **À l'écoute!** listening comprehension passages and the **En avant** follow-up questions and answers. Answers to the **À l'écoute!** activities appear at the back of both the student text and Instructor's Edition.

All listening material recorded on the student tape is indicated in the chapters with the listening symbol shown above.

### Speaking

Grammar practice sequences have been organized into two new sections. **Vérifions!** contains controlled, form-focused, and usually single-response exercises. **Parlons-en!** includes open-ended, interactive, and imaginative activities. This new distinction allows students to clearly identify and apply structural principles before moving on to more creative work.

Partner/pair and small-group exercises or activities appear in both **Vérifions!** and **Parlons-en!** and are identified in the chapters by the symbol shown above.

### Reading

The **Lecture** section has been moved forward in all chapters of this edition, out of **Intermède**, to make it more central to the goals of each chapter. Half of the readings in this edition are new, mostly from journalistic or literary sources. Student interest and accessibility were the key criteria that determined selection.

Pre-reading strategy sections (**Avant de lire**) have been strengthened and expanded.

### Writing

In each chapter, **Par écrit** carefully guides students through all stages of writing: from brainstorming and list making to drafting sentences and paragraphs to editing and proofreading and finally to sharing the final written piece with the class. This writing section is the most comprehensive and practical of any found in an introductory French textbook.

### Grammar

Some commonly used grammar structures, such as the conditional used to express polite requests, have been presented as lexical items earlier in the text to give students preliminary practice with these useful expressions. (The conditional paradigm as a whole is then presented later.)

Forms and uses of double-object pronouns have been restored in this edition. Certain points have been streamlined and simplified for greater ease of assimilation.

### Culture

The cultural focus has been significantly extended in this edition. New material is presented on the culture, history, and society of both France (**France-culture**) and the French-speaking world (**Nouvelles francophones**). **En savoir plus**, another new feature, presents practical information about French-speaking countries, such as telling time by the 24-hour clock. **Un peu d'argot**, a non–active vocabulary feature, presents slang words and expressions commonly used among young French-speaking people today. Every chapter ends with **Portraits**, a new photo-based glimpse into the life of an exemplary man or woman in the history of French-speaking cultures.

## Supplementary materials

*Rendez-vous*, fourth edition, is a complete program including the following components:

- A *Workbook* for students' independent study and practice.
- A *Laboratory Manual* that is a guide to speaking practice and engaging listening comprehension activities.
- The *Annotated Instructor's Edition* of the text, which includes marginal notes as well as scripts for the recorded listening comprehension passages.
- The *Instructor's Manual* with theoretical background, practical guidance, and ideas for using *Rendez-vous*.
- The *Testing Program*, which includes three sets of tests for each chapter in addition to mid-terms and final exams.
- A set of *Audiocassettes* for the laboratory program, also available for student purchase.
- A *Tapescript* containing all of the material on the Audiocassettes, available to instructors only.

- The *Listening Comprehension Tape*, packaged with the student text and also available to instructors.
- A set of full-color *Overhead Transparencies* for presenting vocabulary.
- A set of *Slides* from various parts of the French-speaking world, with accompanying commentary and questions for classroom use.
- The *Video to accompany Rendez-vous, fourth edition*, with scenes filmed on location in France tied to the topics of the text.
- The *McGraw-Hill Video Library of Authentic French Materials* including video material from French television.
- The *McGraw-Hill Electronic Language Tutor* (*MHELT 2.0*), available in Macintosh and IBM formats, containing single-response exercises from the text.
- *A Practical Guide to Language Learning: A Fifteen-Week Program of Strategies for Success*, by H. Douglas Brown (San Francisco State University), a brief introduction to the language learning process for beginning language students.
- A *Training Orientation Manual*, offering practical advice for beginning language instructors and coordinators.

All of the components in the *Rendez-vous* program are designed to complement your instruction and to enhance your students' learning experience. Please contact your local McGraw-Hill sales representative for information on the availability and costs of supplementary materials.

## Acknowledgments

The publishers and authors would like to thank again those instructors who participated in the surveys and questionnaires that were essential to the development of the first, second, and third editions of *Rendez-vous* and to thank in particular the instructors listed below who offered thoughts and suggestions for the development of the fourth edition:

Starr Ackley, Albertson College
Joan Adams, Shasta College
Gretchen Buet, Green River Community College
Stephen A. Canfield, Eastern Illinois University
Judy Celli, University of Delaware
Monique Christensen, Texas A & M University, Galveston
Constance Colwell, Presbyterian College
Phyllis Fread, Umpqua Community College
Yvette C. Gerner, Virginia State University
John Gesell, University of Arizona
M. Brooke Hallowell, Wright State University
Karen Harrington, East Tennessee State University
Sylvia Kibart, East Texas State University
Carolyn Lake, Merritt College
Jacques M. Laroche, New Mexico State University
Howard Limoli, Sonoma State University

Janet C. Loy, Taylor University
Derrinita L. Manuel, Bennett College
Judith A. Motiff, Hope College
Sharon O. Nell-Boelsche, Drury College
Diane O'Connell, South Suburban College
Vincent L. Remillard, St. Francis College
Regis Robe, University of South Carolina, Spartanburg
Sylvie Rockmore, Chatham College
Karen S. Rohe, Indiana University Northwest
Enrique Romaguera, University of Dayton
Jose Santos, Bard College
Munir F. Sarkis, Daytona Beach Community College
Kelly Sax, Whitman College
Nigel E. Smith, University of North Carolina, Chapel Hill
Daniela C. Stewart, Everett Community College
Catherine Triantaphilides, University of the Pacific
Martha Wallen, University of Wisconsin, Stout
Janell Watson, Duke University
Michael J. West, Carnegie Mellon University
Anoush Kevorkian Wiggins, Duke University
Mo Xuan, University of Cincinnati
Robert Ziegler, Montana College of Mineral Science and Technology

Many other individuals deserve our thanks. We are indebted to the following people who did in-depth reviews of the fourth edition manuscript as it developed: Jesse Dickson, Miami University of Ohio; Dominick A. DeFilippis, Wheeling Jesuit College; Matuku Ngame, University of Vermont; Lee Anne Smith, Valparaiso University; David Uber, Baylor University.

Our native readers, Hedwige Meyer, of the University of Washington, and Jehanne-Marie Gavarini, did invaluable work checking the naturalness and authenticity of the French throughout the book.

Many thanks to the editing, design, production, and marketing staffs at McGraw-Hill for their expert work: Karen Judd, Phyllis Snyder, Diane Renda, Francis Owens, Lorna Lo, Ann Potter, Edie Williams, Marie Deer, Melissa Gruzs, Nicole Dicop-Hineline, Joan Schoellner, Terri Wicks, Michelle Lyon, and, especially, Liz Pauw, our editing supervisor. Margaret Metz and the marketing and sales staffs at McGraw-Hill are appreciated for their loyal support of *Rendez-vous* through its four editions.

At McGraw-Hill, our development editor, Suzanne Cowan, worked closely on manuscript through all drafts and made numerous invaluable suggestions. Many thanks to Eileen LeVan, who read parts of the manuscript and offered good ideas. Julie Melvin's participation in the final stages is appreciated. We are deeply grateful to our editor, Leslie Berriman, who worked with us to conceptualize the fourth edition and who oversaw every stage of its development through publication. We'd like to offer a final word of thanks to Thalia Dorwick for her continuing support and enthusiasm.

LES PAYS-BAS
L'ANGLETERRE^f
LA BELGIQUE
L'ALLEMAGNE^f
LA MANCHE
LE LUXEMBOURG
Dunkerque
Calais
Boulogne
Lille
la Picardie
Dieppe
Amiens
Cherbourg
Le Havre
Rouen
la Seine
Caen
Reims
Verdun
la Normandie
Paris
la Champagne
la Lorraine
Brest
Versailles
l'Île-de-France^f
Nancy
Strasbourg
Chartres
la Bretagne
Rennes
l'Alsace^f
LES VOSGES^f
le Rhin
Orléans
la Loire
la Loire
Angers
Tours
Blois
Dijon
Besançon
Nantes
la Touraine
Bourges
la Bourgogne
la Saône
LE JURA
LA SUISSE
la Vendée
La Rochelle
L'OCÉAN
ATLANTIQUE^m
le Poitou
Limoges
Clermont-Ferrand
Lyon
la Savoie
L'ITALIE^f
l'Auvergne^f
LE MASSIF
CENTRAL
Grenoble
LES ALPES^f
Bordeaux
la Garonne
le Dauphiné
Le Rhône
Avignon
Nîmes
Arles
la Provence
Nice
MONACO^m
Biarritz
Toulouse
Montpellier
Aix-en-Provence
Cannes
Marseille
St-Tropez
LES PYRÉNÉES^f
Carcassonne
le Languedoc
L'ESPAGNE^f
Perpignan
la Corse
L'ANDORRE^f
Ajaccio
La France
0 50 100 150 MILLES
0 50 100 150 200 250 KILOMÈTRES
LA MER MÉDITERRANÉE
m = masculin f = féminin

L'OCÉAN ARCTIQUE[m]
L'ALASKA
le Yukon
les Territoires du Nord-Ouest[m]
la Colombie-Britannique
LES MONTAGNES ROCHEUSES[f]
le Saskatchewan
l'Alberta[f]
le Manitoba
LA BAIE D'HUDSON
L'OCÉAN ATLANTIQUE[m]
LE CANADA
L'AMÉRIQUE DU NORD[f]
l'Ontario[m]
le Québec
Terre-Neuve[f]
le fleuve St-Laurent
Québec
Montréal
Charlottetown
St-Jean
St-Pierre-et-Miquelon[f] (Fr.)
l'Île du Prince-Édouard[f]
la Nouvelle-Écosse
le Nouveau-Brunswick
Fredericton
la Nouvelle-Angleterre
L'OCÉAN PACIFIQUE[m]
LES ÉTATS-UNIS[m]
la Louisiane
Baton Rouge
La Nouvelle-Orléans
la Guadeloupe
Pointe-à-Pitre
Basse-Terre
la Dominique
Roseau
la Martinique
Fort-de-France
LE MEXIQUE
HAÏTI[m]
Cap-Haïtien
Port-au-Prince
LA MER DES CARAÏBES
L'AMÉRIQUE CENTRALE[f]
LE VENEZUELA
LA COLOMBIE
Cayenne
la Guyane
L'AMÉRIQUE DU SUD[f]
Le français est la langue maternelle majoritaire
Le français est une des langues officielles
Le français est la langue administrative
Présence de la langue française sans statut particulier
Les Amériques[f]
0 100 500 1000 1500 MILLES
0 500 1000 1500 2000 2500 KILOMÈTRES
m = masculin f = féminin

Le français est la langue maternelle majoritaire
Le français est une des langues officielles
Le français est la langue administrative
Présence de la langue française sans statut particulier
L'Europe f
0 50 100 200 300 400 500 MILLES
0 100 200 400 600 800 KILOMÈTRES
m = masculin f = féminin
Reykjavik
L'ISLANDE f
LA SUÈDE
LA FINLANDE
LA NORVÈGE
Oslo
Helsinki
Leningrad
Stockholm
L'ESTONIE f
L'ÉCOSSE f
L'IRLANDE DU NORD f
LA GRANDE-BRETAGNE
LE DANEMARK
LA LETTONIE
Moscou
L'IRLANDE f
Dublin
Copenhague
LA MER BALTIQUE
LA MER DU NORD
LA LITUANIE
LE PAYS DE GALLES
L'ANGLETERRE f
Amsterdam
Londres
LES PAYS BAS m
Berlin
Varsovie
LA COMMUNAUTÉ DES ÉTATS INDÉPENDANTS
Bruxelles
LA BELGIQUE
L'ALLEMAGNE f
Jersey f
Bonn
LA POLOGNE
LE LUXEMBOURG
Luxembourg
Prague
L'OCÉAN ATLANTIQUE m
Paris
LA TCHÉCOSLOVAQUIE
LA FRANCE
Vienne
Berne
Budapest
Lausanne
L'AUTRICHE f
Genève
LA SUISSE
LA HONGRIE
le Val d'Aoste
LA ROUMANIE
LA YOUGOSLAVIE
Belgrade
L'ITALIE f
LA MER TYRRHÉNIENNE
Bucarest
LA MER NOIRE
LE PORTUGAL
MONACO m
L'ANDORRE f
Lisbonne
Madrid
la Corse
LA BULGARIE
Ajaccio
Sofia
L'ESPAGNE f
Rome
Istanbul
Tirana
L'ALBANIE f
LA GRÈCE
LA MER ÉGÉE
LA TURQUIE
LA MER MÉDITERRANÉE
Athènes
L'AFRIQUE f

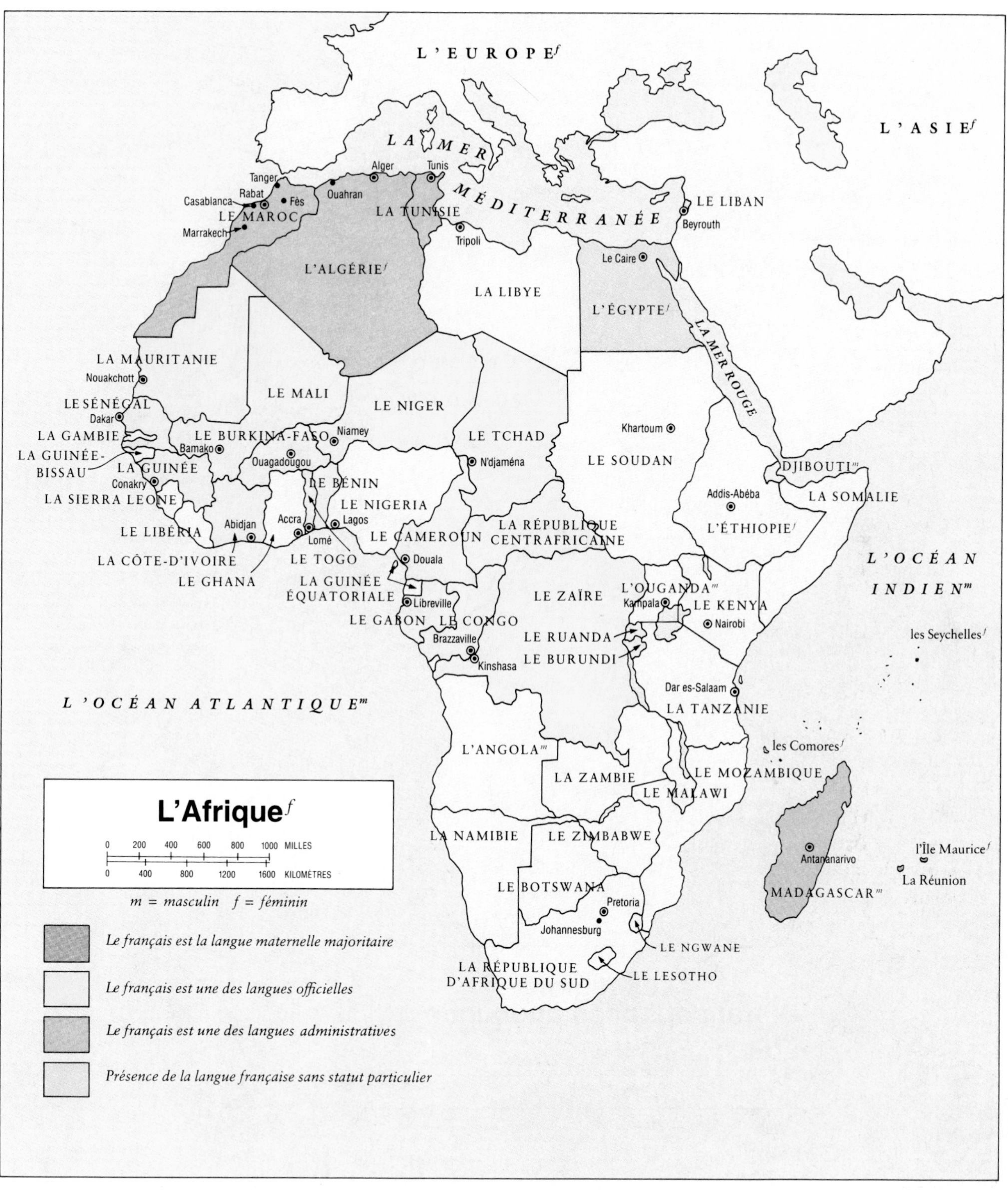

L'EUROPE^f
L'ASIE^f
LA MER MÉDITERRANÉE
LE LIBAN
Beyrouth
Tanger
Rabat
Casablanca
Fès
LE MAROC
Marrakech
Alger
Tunis
Ouahran
LA TUNISIE
Tripoli
L'ALGÉRIE^f
Le Caire
LA LIBYE
L'ÉGYPTE^f
LA MER ROUGE
LA MAURITANIE
Nouakchott
LE MALI
LE NIGER
LE SÉNÉGAL
Dakar
LA GAMBIE
LE BURKINA-FASO
Niamey
Bamako
LA GUINÉE-BISSAU
LA GUINÉE
Ouagadougou
Conakry
LA SIERRA LEONE
LE BÉNIN
LE NIGERIA
LE LIBÉRIA
Abidjan
Accra
Lagos
Lomé
LA CÔTE-D'IVOIRE
LE GHANA
LE TOGO
LE TCHAD
N'djaména
Khartoum
LE SOUDAN
DJIBOUTI^m
Addis-Abéba
LA SOMALIE
L'ÉTHIOPIE^f
LA RÉPUBLIQUE CENTRAFRICAINE
LE CAMEROUN
Douala
LA GUINÉE ÉQUATORIALE
Libreville
LE GABON
LE CONGO
LE ZAÏRE
L'OUGANDA^m
Kampala
LE KENYA
Nairobi
Brazzaville
Kinshasa
LE RUANDA
LE BURUNDI
L'OCÉAN INDIEN^m
les Seychelles^f
L'OCÉAN ATLANTIQUE^m
Dar es-Salaam
LA TANZANIE
les Comores^f
L'ANGOLA^m
LA ZAMBIE
LE MOZAMBIQUE
LE MALAWI
L'Afrique^f
0 200 400 600 800 1000 MILLES
0 400 800 1200 1600 KILOMÈTRES
LA NAMIBIE
LE ZIMBABWE
Antananarivo
MADAGASCAR^m
l'Île Maurice^f
La Réunion
LE BOTSWANA
Pretoria
Johannesburg
LE NGWANE
LA RÉPUBLIQUE D'AFRIQUE DU SUD
LE LESOTHO
m = masculin f = féminin
Le français est la langue maternelle majoritaire
Le français est une des langues officielles
Le français est une des langues administratives
Présence de la langue française sans statut particulier

*m = masculin f = féminin*

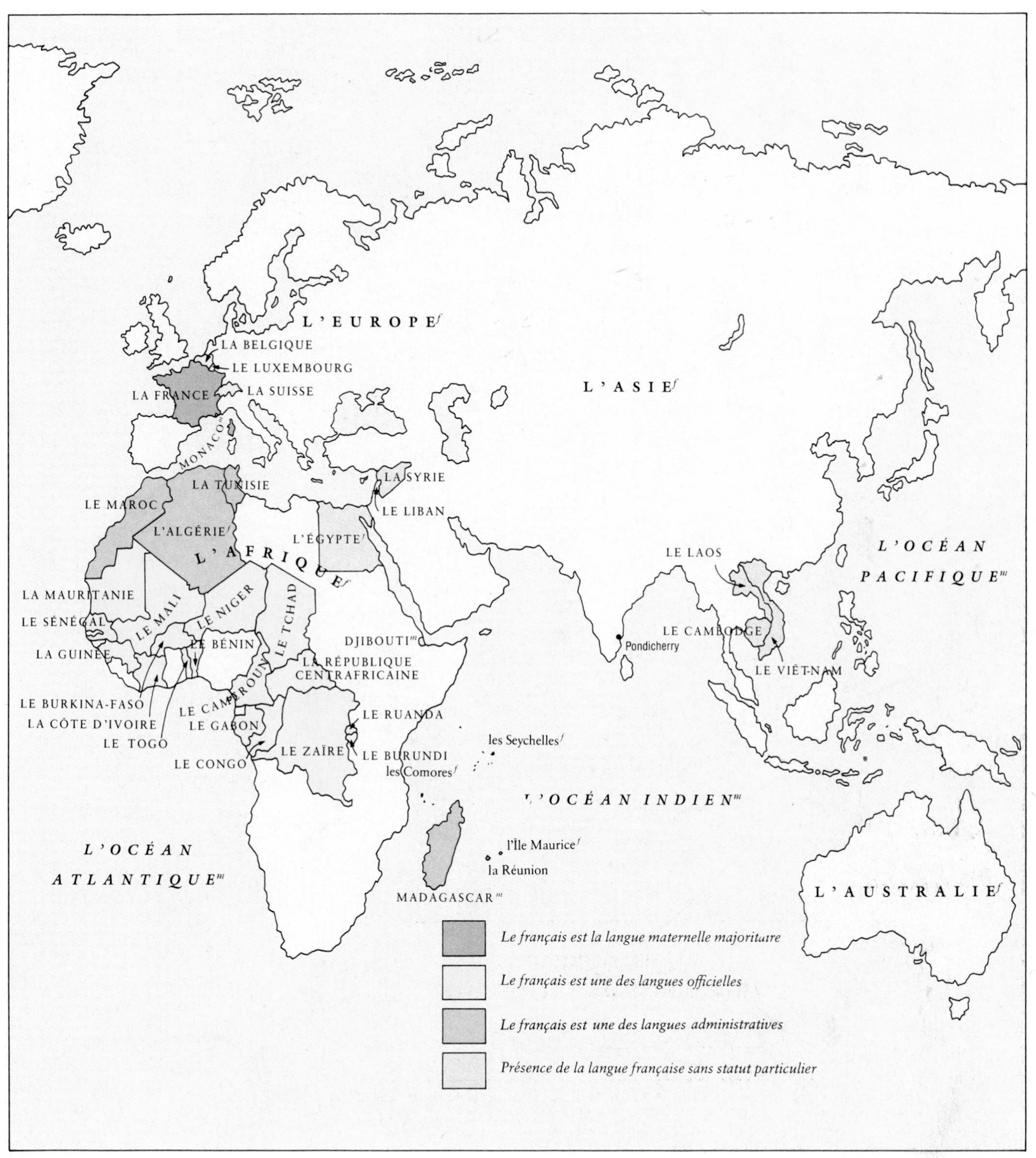

L'EUROPE
LA BELGIQUE
LE LUXEMBOURG
LA SUISSE
LA FRANCE
MONACO
L'ASIE
LA SYRIE
LA TUNISIE
LE MAROC
LE LIBAN
L'ALGÉRIE
L'ÉGYPTE
L'AFRIQUE
LE LAOS
L'OCÉAN PACIFIQUE
LA MAURITANIE
LE MALI
LE NIGER
LE TCHAD
LE SÉNÉGAL
DJIBOUTI
LE CAMBODGE
LE BÉNIN
Pondicherry
LA GUINÉE
LA RÉPUBLIQUE CENTRAFRICAINE
LE VIÊT-NAM
LE BURKINA-FASO
LE CAMEROUN
LA CÔTE D'IVOIRE
LE GABON
LE RUANDA
LE TOGO
les Seychelles
LE ZAÏRE
LE BURUNDI
LE CONGO
les Comores
L'OCÉAN INDIEN
l'Île Maurice
L'OCÉAN ATLANTIQUE
la Réunion
MADAGASCAR
L'AUSTRALIE
Le français est la langue maternelle majoritaire
Le français est une des langues officielles
Le français est une des langues administratives
Présence de la langue française sans statut particulier

CHAPITRE **UN**

# Premier rendez-vous

**En avant**

—Salut Marc, comment ça va?

—Ça va bien, et toi?

—Pas mal.

**Suggestion**: Model pronunciation and have sts. repeat individually or as a group.

**Communicative goals:** greeting people, counting, communicating in class, identifying people and things in the classroom, and telling the day.

**Note**: This chapter presents material appropriate to the *Novice Level* of proficiency, as described in the *ACTFL Guidelines* and tested in the ACTFL/ETS *Oral Proficiency Interview*. The *Novice Level* is characterized by formulaic expressions, typically involving such subjects as greetings, social amenities, common objects, telling time, counting, giving dates, etc.

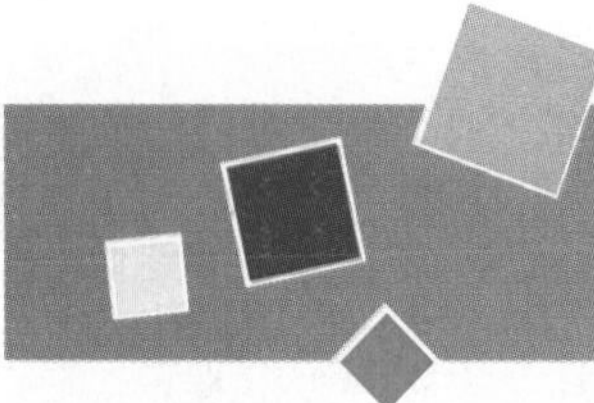

# Première partie

**Summary**: The *En avant* dialogues that open each chapter offer students examples of authentic, spontaneous discourse. These dialogues, accompanied by a brief listening activity, are recorded on the audiocassette packaged with the student text. The recorded material introduces students to the general content and theme of the chapter, gives them easily remembered and useful expressions, and helps to develop their listening skills. Scripts for the follow-up questions that accompany each *En avant* section on tape can be found at the back of the Instructor's Edition. Answers to the follow-up questions appear on tape and with the scripts in the Instructor's Edition.

## Les bonnes manières

1. —Bonjour, Mademoiselle.*
   —Bonjour, Madame.

2. —Bonsoir, Monsieur.
   —Bonsoir, Madame.

3. —Je m'appelle Eric Martin. Et vous, comment vous appelez-vous?
   —Je m'appelle Marie Dupont.

4. —Comment allez-vous?
   —Très bien, merci. Et vous?
   —Pas mal, merci.

5. —Salut, ça va?
   —Oui, ça va bien. Et toi?
   —Comme ci comme ça. (Ça peut aller.)†

6. —Comment? Je ne comprends pas. Répétez, s'il vous plaît.

7. —Oh, pardon! Excusez-moi, Mademoiselle.

8. —Merci beaucoup.
   —De rien.

9. —Au revoir!
   —À bientôt!

---

*Abréviations: Mademoiselle = Mlle  Monsieur = M.  Madame = Mme

†Notice that different greetings are used, depending on the situation: Informal expressions are used among friends and family; formal and professional circumstances require more polite use of language. Compare, for example, drawing number five with number four.

**Note**: The *tu/vous* distinction will be explained in detail in *Grammar Section 3.*

**Suggestions**: (1) Use group repetition to reinforce correct pronunciation. (2) Use these expressions in short, complete dialogues with sts. (3) Shake hands with individual sts. whenever appropriate while activating the exchanges.

## À vous!

**Note**: Direction lines to exs. are in English through Chapter 4. Starting in Chapter 5 they are in French, glossed where necessary.

**Follow-up**: (1) Sts. work in pairs, practicing handshake with appropriate dialogue. (2) Sts. take on fictional identities while performing introductions (political figures, musicians, people known on your campus, etc.).

**A. Répondez, s'il vous plaît.** Give the appropriate response in French.

1. Je m'appelle Maurice Lenôtre. Et vous, comment vous appelez-vous? 2. Bonsoir! 3. Comment allez-vous? 4. Merci. 5. Ça va? 6. Au revoir! 7. Bonjour.

**B. Formel ou informel?** Provide an appropriate expression for each situation. (Decide, first of all, if the situation is formal or informal.)

1.

2.

3.

4.

5.

6.

7.

**Suggestions**: (1) Conduct as individual/group response activity. (2) Have sts. write caption first, then give orally, followed by group repetition.

**Follow-up**: How would you greet your English professor at 10:00 AM? at 8:30 PM? your cousin at noon? What would you say if you were standing in an elevator next to someone you didn't know, but wanted to meet?

## France-culture

*Greetings.* There is almost always some sort of physical contact when the French greet each other. Casual acquaintances or co-workers shake hands briefly when they meet, even if they see each other every day. Friends and relatives exchange two, three, or four kisses on the cheek; the number varies from region to region. Men generally shake hands rather than exchange kisses (**faire la bise**). In conversation, the French tend to stand or sit closer together than the British or Americans do.

**Summary**: Cultural information appears throughout *Rendez-vous*, but is presented especially in two sections: *France-culture* and *Nouvelles francophones*. These sections are in English through Chapter 9 (the first half of the book) and in French thereafter. Exercises based on some of these notes appear in the *Workbook*. *France-culture* aims to make sts. aware that learning about culture is an integral part of learning a language. It presents various aspects of contemporary French culture, not so much in the sense of "classical" culture or the fine arts, but primarily as everyday social customs, practices, attitudes, and tastes. The *Nouvelles francophones* section presents selected aspects of the cultures of French-speaking peoples of the world. Its purpose is to acquaint sts. with the wide variety of nations and groups that share the common heritage of French language.

## Les nombres de 0 à 20

| | | | | | |
|---|---|---|---|---|---|
| 0 | zéro | 7 | sept | 14 | quatorze |
| 1 | un | 8 | huit | 15 | quinze |
| 2 | deux | 9 | neuf | 16 | seize |
| 3 | trois | 10 | dix | 17 | dix-sept |
| 4 | quatre | 11 | onze | 18 | dix-huit |
| 5 | cinq | 12 | douze | 19 | dix-neuf |
| 6 | six | 13 | treize | 20 | vingt |

**Presentation**: Model pronunciation, followed by group response. Point out to sts. the pronunciation of *x* in *deux*, *six*, *dix* when the number is used alone, before a vowel, and before a consonant.

**Suggestions**: For listening comprehension, sts. write the number they hear: 1, 5, 7, 14, 6, 20, 18, 12, etc. or use flash cards with numbers in random order. Sts. say the number as it appears.

Combien? — *How much? How many?*
Combien de (+ *noun*)... ? — *How much . . . ? How many . . . ?*

+ **plus** / **et** — **moins** × **fois** = **font**

### À vous!

**A. Combien?** Give the totals.

1. 卌 卌 III
2. II
3. 卌 II
4. 卌 卌 II
5. 卌 卌 卌 II
6. 卌 卌
7. 卌 卌 卌 IIII
8. IIII
9. 卌 IIII
10. 卌 卌 IIII

**Follow-up**: Ask sts. to count by 2's using even numbers and then odd numbers.

**Additional activity**: *Quel est le plus grand nombre?* 1. *six*, *seize* 2. *deux*, *douze* 3. *treize*, *trois*, etc.

**B. Quel** (*What*) **nombre?** Look at the racing tips and say the number of each horse your instructor mentions by name.

**Note**: See the *IM* (*Instructor's Manual*) for ideas about using authentic materials in class.

**COURSES**[a]
**LES PRONOSTICS D'ETIENNE ROSSO**

**Note**: The numbers to the left in this horse racing program indicate the number the horse wears. The numbers on the right refer to the weight in kilograms of jockey and tack.

**7 PRIX**[b] **DU ROUSSILLON**
(Plat Handicap dédoublé - deuxième épreuve 65.000F 1.600m PD N2)
TRIO URBAIN, Couplés

1 Follow That Star (C. Black)............58
2 Gingerson (D. Lawniczak)..............58
3 Val des Rois (F. Head)....................58
4 Calm Dawn (G. Guignard) E...........57,5
5 Radicofani (D. Boeuf)........................57,5
6 Reach the Beach (Gér. Mossé).....57
7 Naf a Naf (E. Saint-Martin) E........56,5
8 Brillana (F. Sanchez).........................54,5
9 Crystal Feerie (Alain Badel)...........56
10 Geedeep (T. Jarnet)..........................56
11 Le Scoot (C. Nora).............................53,5
12 Saphir d'Avril (P. Bruneau).............53,5
13 Speed Demon (J.-C. Latour)..........52
14 Albanity (S. Guillemin)......................53
15 San Barbero (Y. Talamo)................53
16 Zafar (F. Maerten).............................53
17 Zaburi (Th. Blaise)............................52,5
18 Aula (A.-S. Cruz)................................52
19 Brownsted (O. Benoist)...................52
20 Dominicain (W. Messina).................47,5

[a]Horse races
[b]prize

**C. Problèmes de mathématiques.** Do the following problems with a classmate, and read the solutions out loud.

MODÈLES: 4 + 3 = ? → Quatre et trois font sept. (Quatre plus trois font sept.)
4 − 3 = ? → Quatre moins trois font un.

1. 2 + 5 = ?
2. 6 + 8 = ?
3. 5 + 3 = ?
4. 10 + 1 = ?
5. 9 + 8 = ?
6. 5 − 5 = ?
7. 15 − 9 = ?
8. 13 − 12 = ?
9. 20 − 18 = ?
10. 19 − 15 = ?
11. 10 × 2 = ?
12. 11 × 1 = ?
13. 8 × 2 = ?
14. 6 × 3 = ?
15. 5 × 4 = ?

**Suggestions**: Model the first few problems with whole class. After pair work, use as individual practice.

**Follow-up**: (1) Write additional problems on flashcards or blackboard. Sts. read problems aloud and give answers. (2) Teach *Combien font...?* and give oral problems. (3) Sts. make up additional problems and give them orally. (4) Give a long, continuous problem for fun. For example: 10 + 5 + 4 − 7 − 11 + 6 + 2 + 9 − 1 + 3 = ? (Answer: 20)

## La communication en classe

**Les expressions françaises.** Match each French expression with its English equivalent. Then use the French expressions in the exercise that follows.

1. Répondez.
2. En français, s'il vous plaît.
3. Prenez votre livre.
4. Oui,* c'est exact.
5. Non, ce n'est pas juste, ça.
6. Silence!
7. Est-ce que vous comprenez?
8. Non, je ne comprends pas.*
9. Bravo! Excellent!
10. Je ne sais pas.*
11. Comment dit-on «Cheers!» en français?
12. Écoutez et répétez.
13. Vive le professeur!
14. À bas les examens!
15. Attention!
16. Levez la main.
17. J'ai une question.
18. Allez au tableau.

a. Great! Excellent!
b. Do you understand?
c. How do you say "Cheers!" in French?
d. Raise your hand.
e. I have a question.
f. In French, please.
g. Listen and repeat.
h. Yes, that's correct.
i. Long live (Hurray for) the professor!
j. No, that's not right.
k. Go to the chalkboard.
l. Pay attention! (Be careful! Watch out!)
m. Answer (Respond).
n. Take your book.
o. No, I don't understand.
p. I don't know.
q. Down with exams!
r. Quiet!

**Note**: These phrases are used in normal classroom interaction. Sts. should become familiar with them here and in subsequent activities.

**Suggestion**: Model pronunciation of phrases first before doing ex. Give sts. a few minutes to do the ex. Then do as individual/group response practice.

**Follow-up**: (1) Phrases can be written on index cards, scrambled, then distributed to sts. for rapid response in both English and French. (2) Invite sts. to use phrase number 11 to ask you how to say various English words in French.

**Suggestion**: For listening comprehension practice, say the following commands and questions. Sts. respond with an appropriate action or rejoinder. 1. *Allez au tableau.* 2. *Comment dit-on «hi» en français?* 3. *Prenez votre livre.* 4. *Ouvrez votre livre à la page 5.* 5. *Fermez votre livre.* 6. *Levez la main!* 7. *Dites «hello, how are you?» à (name of classmate).*

### À vous!

**Situations.** Give your personal reaction (in French, please!).

1. You don't understand what the instructor said.
2. You want to know how to say "help!" in French.
3. The exam for the day has been canceled.

**Suggestion**: Solicit individual answers, then use group repetition.

---

*In familiar, informal settings, **oui** may be pronounced **ouais**, **je ne sais pas** may become **shais pas**, and **je ne comprends pas** might be said **j' comprends pas**.

4. You have a question.
5. A classmate mentions that Marseilles is the capital of France.
6. Everyone is talking; you can't hear the professor.

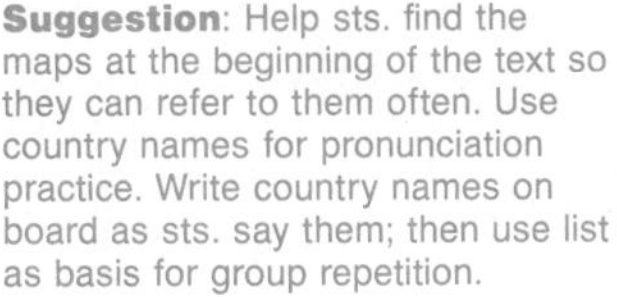
**Suggestion**: Help sts. find the maps at the beginning of the text so they can refer to them often. Use country names for pronunciation practice. Write country names on board as sts. say them; then use list as basis for group repetition.

**Note**: Top 12 languages (source: World Almanac 1992): Chinese (Mandarin), 885 million; Hindi-Urdu (in Pakistan and northern India), 461 million; English, 450 million; Spanish, 352 million; Russian, 294 million; Arabic, 202 million; Bengali, 187 million; Portuguese, 175 million; Malay-Indonesian, 145 million; Japanese, 126 million; French, 122 million; German, 118 million.

# Nouvelles francophones

**Note**: See **Summary** on p. 3.

**Suggestion**: If anyone has visited one of these places, have that st. tell the class about his/her experiences there. If you have slides or photos, bring them to class and give a short cultural lesson. Postcards, newspapers, or magazines from the French-speaking world might also be shown to sts. to enliven discussion.

## The French-speaking world

More than one hundred million people in the world speak French, either as their native language or as a second language used in business or in the workplace. French-speaking countries or regions are found on five continents. Look at the world map at the beginning of the book and find the following places.

- the four European countries where French is one of the principal languages
- three regions on the American continents where French is spoken
- two francophone island nations
- three major North African francophone countries
- five francophone nations on the West African coast
- the largest Central African nation where French is spoken
- three French-speaking Asian nations

Besides the countries shown on the map, French-speaking populations are found in pockets all over the globe. In the United States alone, more than thirteen million people are descendants of French or French-Canadian emigrants. Most live in Louisiana or New England. Many of these Americans still speak or understand French; in numerous ways—through music, food, family customs, habits of thought—their everyday lives reflect their francophone heritage.

# Deuxième partie

## Dans la salle de classe

**Presentation**: Model pronunciation of objects, using group repetition. Stress distinction in pronunciation between nasal *un* and denasalized *une*.
**Follow-up**: Point to objects in your own classroom for review.
**Optional vocabulary**: *la craie*, *le crayon*, *l'affiche*, or objects particular to your classroom.

### À vous!

**A. Qu'est-ce que c'est** (*What is it*)? With a classmate, identify the people and objects in the drawing above.

**Suggestion**: Model dialogue with first two objects, then sts. work in pairs.

MODÈLE: VOUS: L'objet numéro un, qu'est-ce que c'est?*
UN(E) CAMARADE: C'est un (une)... (*It's a . . .* )

**B. Combien?** Look at the classroom above. With a classmate, ask and answer questions about the number of people and objects you see.

MODÈLE: étudiantes → UN(E) CAMARADE: Il y a combien d'étudiantes?†
VOUS: Il y a quatre étudiantes.‡

**Follow-up**: Activate dialogues by pointing to actual classroom objects: *Qu'est-ce que c'est? C'est une porte.*

*The intonation of the voice should drop slightly at the end of this question.
†The intonation of the voice should rise slightly on **combien,** then drop at the end of the sentence.
‡**Il y a** can mean *there are* as well as *there is*. The **s** that makes a word plural is not pronounced.

1. portes
2. fenêtres
3. professeurs
4. étudiants
5. cahiers
6. livres
7. chaises
8. stylos

**Follow-up**: For listening comprehension practice, use a similar drawing on a handout and have sts. place a number on an object according to your description: *L'objet numéro 1, c'est une chaise.* Sts. place a *1* on one of the chairs in the sketch.

**Note**: Point out that most singular and plural forms of nouns sound alike.

**Follow-up**: Use *il y a* to ask about number of persons and objects in actual classroom.

## Les nombres de 20 à 60

| | | | | | |
|---|---|---|---|---|---|
| 20 | vingt | 25 | vingt-cinq | 30 | trente |
| 21 | vingt et un | 26 | vingt-six | 40 | quarante |
| 22 | vingt-deux | 27 | vingt-sept | 50 | cinquante |
| 23 | vingt-trois | 28 | vingt-huit | 60 | soixante |
| 24 | vingt-quatre | 29 | vingt-neuf | | |

**A. Problèmes de mathématiques.**

MODÈLES: 26 + 2 = 28 Vingt-six plus (et) deux font vingt-huit.
49 − 7 = 42 Quarante-neuf moins sept font quarante-deux.
12 × 3 = 36 Douze fois trois font trente-six.

1. 18 + 20 = ?
2. 15 + 39 = ?
3. 41 + 12 = ?
4. 32 + 24 = ?
5. 43 − 16 = ?
6. 60 − 37 = ?
7. 56 − 21 = ?
8. 49 − 27 = ?
9. 2 × 10 = ?
10. 3 × 20 = ?
11. 25 × 2 = ?
12. 15 × 3 = ?

**Suggestions**: (1) Give question *Combien font x et y?* as stimulus for ex. Call on individuals for answers. (2) Do as listening comprehension activity by dictation of problems to sts. whose books are closed or to sts. at the board.

**Additional activity**: *Qu'est-ce qu'il y a dans la salle de classe?* Have sts. say how many of the following various objects there are in the actual classroom: *stylos*, *livres*, *fenêtres*, *étudiants*, *étudiantes*, *cahiers*, *dictionnaires*, *chaises*, *professeurs*, *tables*.

**B. Les numéros de téléphone.** In French, telephone numbers are said in groups of four two-digit numbers. Look in Claire's address book and read out loud some of her most frequently called numbers.

MODÈLE: —L'université de Nantes?
—40.29.07.39

**MES AMIS**

| noms | prénoms | adresses | tél. |
|---|---|---|---|
| Duclos | Alain | 60, blvd. de l'Egalité | 41.48.05.52 |
| Bercegol | Fabienne | 98, avenue Patton | 41.46.42.60 |
| de Bailleux | Bénédicte | 83, rue des Renardières | 41.57.13.44 |
| Koehulein | Valérie | 7, rue de Verneuil | 41.35.21.08 |
| Université | de Nantes | 4400 NANTES | 40.29.07.39 |

**Suggestion**: To exploit realia further, model pronunciation of names and have sts. repeat them.

**Follow-up**: Have sts. work in pairs, with one dictating phone numbers to the other, whose book is closed.

## Quel jour sommes-nous?

**Presentation**: Model pronunciation of days of week and have sts. repeat after your model. Use Ex. A of the following *À vous!* in conjunction with this visual. Practice days of week by asking: *Quel jour sommes-nous? Quels sont les jours du week-end? Quel est votre jour favori? Quel jour détestez-vous?* In presenting new material, answer questions yourself first, giving your opinion, before asking sts. to answer.

La semaine (*week*) de Claire

| | |
|---|---|
| lundi | examen de biologie |
| mardi | examen de chimie |
| mercredi | chez le dentiste |
| jeudi | tennis avec Vincent |
| vendredi | laboratoire |
| samedi | théâtre avec Vincent |
| dimanche | en famille |

In French, the days of the week are not capitalized. The week starts on Monday on the French calendar.

| | |
|---|---|
| —Quel jour sommes-nous (aujourd'hui)? / Quel jour est-ce (aujourd'hui)? | —*What day is it (today)?* |
| —Nous sommes mardi. / C'est mardi. | —*It's Tuesday.* |

### *À vous!*

**A. La semaine de Claire. Quel jour est-ce?** Look at the drawing above.

MODÈLE: Claire est au laboratoire. → Nous sommes vendredi. (C'est vendredi.)

1. Claire va (*goes*) au théâtre avec Vincent.
2. Claire est chez (*at*) le dentiste.
3. Claire a (*has*) un cours de biologie.
4. Claire est en famille.
5. Claire joue au (*is playing*) tennis avec Vincent.
6. Claire a un examen de chimie.

**Suggestion**: Present prepositional phrases (*au cours, au laboratoire, chez le dentiste*, etc.) as fixed forms; sts. are not expected to produce them at this point.

**B. Votre semaine** (*Your week*). Quel jour sommes-nous?

MODÈLE: Vous êtes (*You are*) en famille. → Nous sommes dimanche.

1. Vous êtes au cours de français.
2. Vous êtes au restaurant.
3. Vous êtes au cinéma.
4. Vous êtes au laboratoire.
5. Vous êtes au match de football (*soccer*).

**Additional activity**: Solicit group response, or call on individuals, with class repeating together. *Quel jour sommes-nous?* MODÈLE: *Easter → Nous sommes dimanche.* 1. Thanksgiving 2. Good Friday 3. Labor Day 4. Ash Wednesday 5. Super Bowl

# Troisième partie

## The French Alphabet

| | | | | | | | |
|---|---|---|---|---|---|---|---|
| **a** | a | **h** | hache | **o** | o | **v** | vé |
| **b** | bé | **i** | i | **p** | pé | **w** | double vé |
| **c** | cé | **j** | ji | **q** | ku | **x** | iks |
| **d** | dé | **k** | ka | **r** | erre | **y** | i grec |
| **e** | e | **l** | elle | **s** | esse | **z** | zède |
| **f** | effe | **m** | emme | **t** | té | | |
| **g** | gé | **n** | enne | **u** | u | | |

**Suggestion**: Model pronunciation of the letters. Bring in letters on flash cards. Mix up the letters and have sts. give the letter in French. Spell out places and names and ask sts. to write, guessing the words you have spelled.

**Follow-up**: Play "Hangman," giving a few examples before sts. give their own words.

### À vous!

**A. Devinez.** Spell your name in French. Then spell the name of a city, and see if your classmates can guess what it is.

**B. Inscription.** Several students are signing up for classes. Spell their names and cities for the clerk in registration.

| | |
|---|---|
| DUPONT Isabelle | Paris |
| HUBERT Martine | Lille |
| GUEYE Medoune | Dakar |
| EL AYYADI Allal | Rabat |

## The International Phonetic Alphabet

In English, each letter often represents several sounds. Note the sounds made by the letter *o* in these six words: *cold, cot, corn, love, woman, women*. The same is true in French; the **o**, for example, is pronounced differently in the words **rose** and **robe**. Conversely, in both languages, a single sound can often be spelled in several different ways. Notice, for example, how the sound [f] is spelled in the words ***f**ish*, *al**ph**abet*, and *tou**gh***. Similarly, in French the sound [e], for example, can be spelled in many ways: universit**é**, appel**ez**, cahi**er**.

The discussion of sounds and pronunciation is simplified by the use of the International Phonetic Alphabet (IPA), which assigns a symbol, given in brackets [ ], to each sound in a language. These symbols are used in dictionaries to show pronunciation; they will appear in the pronunciation sections of *Rendez-vous* and the accompanying laboratory program.

The IPA, listing the sounds of the French language, appears on page 11. Each symbol representing a sound is given in the column on the left. In the middle column is the normal spelling of a word or words containing that sound. On the right is the phonetic transcription of that word in the IPA.

| ORAL VOWELS | | | | | |
|---|---|---|---|---|---|
| [a] | madame | [madam] | [o] | au | [o] |
| [i] | dix | [dis] | [ɔ] | porte | [pɔrt] |
| [e] | répétez | [repete] | [ø] | deux | [dø] |
| [ɛ] | merci | [mɛrsi] | [œ] | neuf | [nœf] |
| [u] | jour | [ʒur] | [ə] | de | [də] |
| [y] | salut | [saly] | | | |

| NASAL VOWELS | | | SEMI-VOWELS | | |
|---|---|---|---|---|---|
| [ɑ̃] | en, comment | [ɑ̃], [kɔmɑ̃] | [ɥ] | huit | [ɥit] |
| [ɛ̃] | bien, vingt | [bjɛ̃], [vɛ̃] | [j] | rien | [rjɛ̃] |
| [ɔ̃] | bon, pardon | [bɔ̃], [pardɔ̃] | [w] | moi, oui | [mwa], [wi] |

| CONSONANTS | | | | | |
|---|---|---|---|---|---|
| [b] | bon | [bɔ̃] | [n] | non | [nɔ̃] |
| [ʃ] | chalet | [ʃalɛ] | [p] | plaît | [plɛ] |
| [d] | des | [de] | [r] | revoir | [rəvwar] |
| [f] | photo | [foto] | [k] | comme | [kɔm] |
| [g] | Guy | [gi] | [s] | ça, si | [sa], [si] |
| [ʒ] | je | [ʒ(ə)] | [z] | mademoiselle | [madmwazɛl] |
| [ɲ] | champagne | [ʃɑ̃paɲ] | [t] | Martin | [martɛ̃] |
| [l] | appelle | [apɛl] | [v] | va | [va] |
| [m] | mal | [mal] | | | |

## Pronunciation: Articulation in French

**Articulation.** The articulation of French is physically more tense and energetic than that of English. French sounds, generally produced at the front of the mouth, are never slurred or swallowed.

Pronounce these phrases as your instructor does.

1. Bonjour, ça va?
2. Oui, ça va bien.
3. Comment vous appelez-vous?
4. Je m'appelle Eric Martin.
5. Je ne comprends pas.
6. Répétez, s'il vous plaît.

**Cognates and new sounds.** French and English have many cognates (**mots apparentés**), that is, words spelled similarly with similar meanings. Even though two words may look alike in French and English, they generally do not sound the same. Some sounds will be altogether new to a native speaker of English. You will learn the sounds and intonation patterns of French most easily through attentive listening and imitation.*

Pronounce these cognates as your instructor does.

1. l'attitude
2. la police
3. la balle
4. le bracelet
5. la passion
6. la conclusion
7. l'injustice
8. l'hôpital

**Suggestion**: Most of these examples are cognates, so you may wish to compare American and French pronunciation.

**Pronunciation practice**: Conduct as group repetition first, then solicit individual response, if desired.

**English diphthongs.** A diphthong consists of two vowel sounds pronounced together within the same syllable, such as in the English word *bay*. There is a tendency in English to prolong almost any vowel into a diphthong. In such English words as *rosé, café,* and *entrée*, the final vowel is drawn out into two separate vowel sounds: a long *a* sound and an *ee* sound. In French, each vowel in the words **rosé, café,** and **entrée** is pronounced with a *single*, pure sound.

Pronounce these words as your instructor does.

1. entrée café matinée blasé rosé frappé
2. cage page sage table fable câble sable
3. beau gauche parole rouge

**Summary**: *À l'écoute!* is a listening comprehension section consisting of one or two passages, with follow-up activities, recorded on the audiocassette packaged with the student text. Sts. can listen to the tape and do the activities at home, or you may wish to play selected listening comprehension passages in class and have sts. do the activities together. To ensure that students know how to work with the material, you should do the *À l'écoute!* section with them for the first few chapters. Be sure to let sts. know that they will not understand every word they hear in the listening comprehension passages, as in real life. They should focus globally on the general information in the passages and not be overly concerned about what they do not understand. Scripts of the recorded material appear at the back of the Instructor's Edition. Answers to the listening comprehension activities appear at the back of both the student text and the Instructor's Edition.

## À L'ÉCOUTE!

**Les bonnes manières.** You are going to hear some people greeting each other. First, look at the drawings. Next, listen to the conversations. Then, do the activity. Replay the tape as often as you need to. (See Appendix F for answers.)

Mark a letter (*a* through *e*) under each drawing to indicate which conversation it represents.

1. ____

2. ____

3. ____

4. ____

5. ____

*Several other general aspects of French pronunciation are treated in this chapter and in Chapters 2 through 7 of *Rendez-vous*. Pronunciation is presented and practiced more extensively in the Laboratory Program.

**Summary**: *Vocabulaire* contains chapter words and expressions considered *active*. These are the words and expressions sts. should incorporate into their working vocabulary and be expected to know. Active vocabulary items have been introduced in the following chapter sections:

- *Étude de vocabulaire*
- *Mots-clés*
- Grammar paradigms, verb charts, and example sentences from the grammar sections
- Occasionally, from functional minidialogues that begin grammar sections

The vocabulary list is divided into parts of speech (*Verbes*, *Substantifs*, etc.), *Mots et expressions divers*, and, occasionally, thematic categories (*Expressions avec avoir*, *Expressions interrogatives*, etc.). Words and expressions within each sub-grouping are organized alphabetically.

# Vocabulaire

## Bonnes manières

**À bientôt.** See you soon.
**Au revoir.** Good-bye.
**Bonjour.** Hello. Good day.
**Bonsoir.** Good evening.
**Ça peut aller.** All right, pretty well.
**Ça va?** How's it going?
**Ça va bien.** Fine. (Things are going well.)
**Ça va mal.** Things are going badly.
**Comme ci, comme ça.** So so.
**Comment?** What? (How?)
**Comment allez-vous?** How are you?
**Comment vous appelez-vous?** What's your name?
**De rien.** Not at all, don't mention it, you're welcome.
**Et vous?** And you?
**Excusez-moi.** Excuse me.
**Je m'appelle...** My name is . . .
**Je ne comprends pas.** I don't understand.
**Madame (Mme)** Mrs. (ma'am)
**Mademoiselle (Mlle)** Miss
**Merci.** Thank you.
**Monsieur (M.)** Mr. (sir)
**Pardon.** Pardon (me).
**Pas mal.** Not bad(ly).
**Répétez.** Repeat.
**Salut!** Hi!
**S'il vous plaît.** Please.
**Très bien.** Very well (good).

## La communication en classe

**À bas les examens!** Down with exams!
**Allez au tableau.** Go to the chalkboard.
**Attention!** Pay attention! (Be careful!/Watch out!)
**Bravo! Excellent!** Great! Excellent!
**Comment dit-on «Cheers!» en français?** How do you say "Cheers!" in French?
**Écoutez et répétez.** Listen and repeat.
**En français, s'il vous plaît.** In French, please.
**Est-ce que vous comprenez?** Do you understand?
**J'ai une question.** I have a question.
**Je ne sais pas.** I don't know.
**Levez la main.** Raise your hand.
**Non, ce n'est pas juste, ça.** No, that's not right.
**Non, je ne comprends pas.** No, I don't understand.
**Oui, c'est exact.** Yes, that's correct.
**Prenez votre livre.** Take your book.
**Répondez.** Answer.
**Silence!** Quiet!
**Vive le professeur!** Long live (Hurray for) the professor!

## Dans la salle de classe

**un bureau** a desk
**un cahier** a notebook
**une chaise** a chair
**une craie** a stick of chalk
**un crayon** a pencil
**un étudiant** a (male) student
**une étudiante** a (female) student
**une fenêtre** a window
**un livre** a book
**une porte** a door
**un professeur** a professor, instructor (male or female)
**une salle de classe** a classroom
**un stylo** a pen
**une table** a table
**un tableau** a chalkboard

## Les nombres

**un, deux, trois, quatre, cinq, six, sept, huit, neuf, dix, onze, douze, treize, quatorze, quinze, seize, dix-sept, dix-huit, dix-neuf, vingt, vingt et un, vingt-deux, etc., trente, quarante, cinquante, soixante**

## Les jours de la semaine

**Quel jour sommes-nous/est-ce? Nous sommes...(lundi, mardi, mercredi, jeudi, vendredi, samedi, dimanche).**

## Mots et expressions divers

**aujourd'hui** today
**beaucoup** very much, a lot
**c'est un (une)...** it's a . . .
**combien de** how many
**il y a** there is/are
**il y a... ?** is/are there . . . ?
**non** no
**oui** yes
**Qu'est-ce que c'est?** What is it?
**voici** here is/are
**voilà** there is/are

CHAPITRE **DEUX**

# La vie universitaire

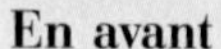

**En avant**

—Est-ce que tu as un cours de maths aujourd'hui?
—Non, mais j'ai un cours de physique et de chimie.
—Moi, je déteste la chimie!

**Communicative goals:** talking about places in and around the university, academic subjects, countries and nationalities, and pastimes; identifying people and things; expressing quantity, actions, and disagreement.

**Suggestion**: Model pronunciation and have sts. repeat individually or as a group.

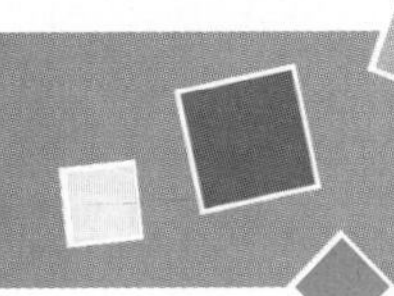

# Étude de vocabulaire

**Summary**: The *Étude de vocabulaire* section presents new words and expressions related to the chapter theme. Most new terms are illustrated through visual displays. Vocabulary items that do not lend themselves to illustration, such as adverbial phrases, abstract concepts, and so on, appear in the *Autres mots utiles* list after the display. New vocabulary terms are practiced after each visual presentation and are recycled throughout the *Étude de grammaire* section, the rest of the chapter, and subsequent chapters.

## Les lieux

Voici l'amphithéâtre (l'amphi).

Voici le restaurant universitaire (le restau-u; le R.U.).

Voici la cité universitaire (la cité-u).

Voici la bibliothèque.

**Summary**: The *En avant* dialogues that open each chapter offer sts. examples of authentic, spontaneous discourse. These dialogues, accompanied by a brief listening activity, are recorded on the audio-cassette packaged with the st. text. The recorded material introduces sts. to the general content and theme of the chapter, gives them easily remembered and useful expressions, and helps to develop their listening skills. Scripts for the follow-up questions that accompany each *En avant* section on tape can be found at the back of the Instructor's Edition. Answers to the follow-up questions appear on tape and with the scripts in the Instructor's Edition.

**A. Une visite.** Where do you find these things?

MODÈLES: Un examen de français? → Dans l'amphithéâtre.
Un coca? → Dans le restaurant universitaire.

1. un dictionnaire?
2. une radio?
3. un café?
4. un livre?
5. une télévision?
6. un cours de français?
7. un sandwich?
8. une encyclopédie?

**Continuation**: *un tableau? un stylo? une fenêtre? un professeur? un bureau?* Solicit individual answers, then use group repetition. You may wish to hold up pictures of objects and ask: *Où trouvez-vous ces choses?*

**B. C'est bizarre? C'est normal?**

MODÈLE: Un match de football dans le restaurant universitaire... → Un match de football dans le restaurant universitaire, c'est bizarre!

1. Un cours de français dans un amphithéâtre...
2. Une radio dans la bibliothèque...
3. Un examen dans la cité universitaire...
4. Un café dans l'amphithéâtre...
5. Un dictionnaire dans la bibliothèque...

**Suggestion**: Have sts. correct any sentence that is *bizarre*.

**Continuation**: Additional sentences may be given orally: *Un professeur dans le restaurant universitaire...; Une télévision dans la bibliothèque...; Une étudiante dans l'amphithéâtre...; Le bureau du professeur dans le restaurant universitaire...*

**Follow-up**: Give sts. a minute to write one or two items to continue this ex. They will read their example for the other sts., who will say: *C'est normal!* or *C'est bizarre!*

## Les matières

À la Faculté des Lettres et Sciences Humaines, on étudie (*one studies*) la littérature, la linguistique, les langues étrangères (*foreign languages*: l'allemand [*German*], l'anglais, le chinois, l'espagnol, l'italien, le japonais), l'histoire, la géographie, la philosophie, la psychologie et la sociologie.

**Suggestion**: Model pronunciation of the fields of study, having sts. repeat after your model. Pay special attention to pronunciation of cognates, especially vowels. Point out to them that *mathématiques* is always plural in French. Sts. may need additional vocabulary to describe their own studies: *l'archéologie, les relations internationales, l'anthropologie, l'électronique, l'architecture, la médecine, l'art dramatique, la peinture, la danse, la psychologie, les sciences politiques, les sciences économiques, la gestion, la publicité, le marketing, l'administration des affaires*, etc.

**Note**: A "third" major French university *faculté* not presented here is *la Faculté de Droit et Sciences Économiques*.

À la Faculté des Sciences, on étudie les mathématiques (les maths), l'informatique (*computer science*), la physique, la chimie (*chemistry*) et les sciences naturelles (la géologie et la biologie).

***Autres mots utiles:***

**le droit** law
**l'économie** economics

**A. Les études et les professions.** Imagine what subjects are necessary for the following professions.

MODÈLE: pour (*for*) la profession de diplomate → On étudie les langues étrangères.

1. pour la profession de psychologue
2. pour la profession de chimiste
3. pour la profession de physicien (*physicist*)
4. pour la profession d'historien
5. pour la profession d'ingénieur

**Suggestion**: Point out that the French word for doctor is *médecin*, not *physicien*.

**Follow-up**: Give the name of a famous person and have sts. indicate which field she or he is or was in: *Marie Curie*, *Margaret Mead*, *Jean-Paul Sartre*, *Alexis de Tocqueville*, *James Joyce*, *Noam Chomsky*, etc.

**B. Les cours** (*courses*) **à l'université.** Look at the following list and say which subjects you are studying this semester (quarter) and which ones you like to study (or don't like to study) in general.

1. J'étudie... (*I'm studying*)
2. J'aime étudier (*I like to study*) (Je n'aime pas [*I don't like*] étudier)...

| | | |
|---|---|---|
| l'espagnol | l'informatique | la littérature |
| la sociologie | la psychologie | la philosophie |
| la biologie | le français | le droit (*law*) |
| la chimie | la géographie | le dessin (*drawing*) |
| l'anglais | la physique | le commerce |
| l'histoire | la musique | la linguistique |
| les maths | le marketing | |

Now name the subjects in your ideal program of study.

**Suggestion**: Ask one st. to act as recorder and report back other sts.' preferences. Encourage sts. to listen carefully and to correct false information about themselves.

**C. Et vos camarades?** Ask a classmate the following questions.

1. Qu'est-ce que tu étudies maintenant (*now*)? (J'étudie...)
2. Tu aimes étudier le français? les maths?... ? (Oui, j'aime/Non, je n'aime pas étudier...)

Now compare the subjects you are taking this semester (quarter) with those of your classmates.

MODÈLE: —Moi (*Me*), j'étudie... et toi (*you*)?
—Moi (aussi [*too*]), j'étudie...

**Suggestion**: Have various sts. choose someone in class to answer this question. Ask for recall by having them tell back what each person answered: *Elle étudie...*

**Follow-up**: Have sts. practice the chapter opening dialogue, using the names of academic disciplines they have learned in this section.

## Un peu d'argot

These lists present **argot** (*slang*) expressions commonly used in informal situations, especially by students and young people. In this text they are presented for recognition only; you do not need to commit them to memory or use them actively in exercises. **Argot** provides a sense of the "flavor" of everyday conversational French, and you may occasionally enjoy integrating it into your exchanges with classmates as you progress

**Summary**: The *Un peu d'argot* sections contain contemporary colloquial and slang expressions. The expressions are presented for student and instructor interest and are not considered to be part of the chapter's active vocabulary.

in your study of the language. Remember, though, that newcomers to French language and culture should use these expressions with caution. Some of them may be considered inappropriate when used with first-time acquaintances or older people, or in business and commercial encounters.

## Le jargon étudiant

| **L'université** | | **Les matières** | |
|---|---|---|---|
| le Bac | le Baccalauréat* | la géo | la géographie |
| la Fac | la Faculté | la philo | la philosophie |
| le prof | le professeur | la psycho | la psychologie |
| l'amphi | l'amphithéâtre | la socio | la sociologie |
| l'exam | l'examen | l'éco | l'économie |

EN CONTEXTE

Moi, je suis (*am*) en **Fac** d'histoire, et toi?
Mon prof de **géo** est (*is*) très sympa (*nice*).
J'ai (*I have*) trois cours en **amphi** aujourd'hui.
Je déteste les **exams**!

**Summary**: *En savoir plus* presents basic facts about French and francophone society and culture. The information generally is expressed in condensed, synthetic form, and can sometimes appear as numerical or statistical data.

## Le système éducatif français

| BAC A | BAC B | BAC C | BAC D | BAC E, F, G, H |
|---|---|---|---|---|
| la philosophie | l'économie | les mathématiques | la chimie<br>les sciences naturelles | les techniques |

| L'UNIVERSITÉ | LES GRANDES ÉCOLES | LES ÉTUDES COURTES (2 ANS) |
|---|---|---|
| La Faculté des Lettres et Sciences Humaines<br>La Faculté de Droit<br>La Faculté des Sciences<br>La Faculté de Médecine | Administration<br>Arts et Manufactures<br>l'École des Mines<br>Lettres et Sciences<br>Polytechnique, etc. | l'IUT (Institut Universitaire de Technologie)<br>le BTS (Brevet de Technicien Supérieur) |

*The "**Bac**" is a nationwide examination administered to all French students completing their last year of **lycée** (roughly equivalent to U.S. high school). Passing the "**Bac**" is a requirement for admission to any French university.

A student who holds a "**Bac**" in a liberal arts subject such as literature, philosophy, history, or economics will generally pursue a university program in **La Faculté des Lettres et Sciences Humaines** or **La Faculté de Droit**. A "**Bac**" in biology, mathematics, natural or physical sciences will usually lead to **La Faculté de Médecine** or **La Faculté des Sciences**. Students who pursue a technical **baccalauréat** (E, F, G, or H) will often enter a two-year program, offered by a specialized institute, leading to a certificate of advanced proficiency in a trade or technical field.

Any student holding a "**Bac**" A through D may theoretically enter one of the **grandes écoles**. These are specialized, semi-private university-level academies. They provide advanced training in a variety of fields to potential leaders at the highest levels of government, business, and industry. Admission to **les grandes écoles** is restricted to a small number of students who must pass highly competitive entrance examinations.

**Presentation**: (1) Find these countries on map with sts. Point out that the names of countries have gender, but do not overemphasize the point, because sts. will not be asked to produce the names. (2) Using pictures of famous people, model the pronunciation of the nationalities, using group repetition. (3) Point out difference in pronunciation of masculine and feminine forms. (4) Point out that all languages are masculine, mentioning that they begin with a lowercase first letter in French. (5) Possible additions to nationalities are *australien(ne)*, *grec(que)*, *iranien(ne)*, *israélien(ne)*, *norvégien(ne)*, *polonais(e)*, *suédois(e)*, *vietnamien(ne)*. Point out to sts. that the countries in West Africa speak a variety of local languages. **Examples**: *ouolof* (*Sénégal*), *bantou* (*Zaïre*), *baoulé* (*Côte-d'Ivoire*).

## Les pays et les nationalités

| LES PAYS | LES NATIONALITÉS | |
|---|---|---|
| | PERSONNES | ADJECTIFS |
| la France | le Français, la Française | français, française |
| l'Angleterre | l'Anglais, l'Anglaise | anglais, anglaise |
| l'Espagne | l'Espagnol, l'Espagnole | espagnol, espagnole |
| l'Italie | l'Italien, l'Italienne | italien, italienne |
| l'Allemagne | l'Allemand, l'Allemande | allemand, allemande |
| la Suisse | le/la Suisse | suisse |
| la Belgique | le/la Belge | belge |
| l'Algérie | l'Algérien, l'Algérienne | algérien, algérienne |
| le Maroc | le Marocain, la Marocaine | marocain, marocaine |
| la Tunisie | le Tunisien, la Tunisienne | tunisien, tunisienne |
| le Liban | le Libanais, la Libanaise | libanais, libanaise |
| le Zaïre | le Zaïrois, la Zaïroise | zaïrois, zaïroise |
| la Côte-d'Ivoire | l'Ivoirien, l'Ivoirienne | ivoirien, ivoirienne |
| le Sénégal | le Sénégalais, la Sénégalaise | sénégalais, sénégalaise |
| les États-Unis | l'Américain, l'Américaine | américain, américaine |
| le Canada | le Canadien, la Canadienne | canadien, canadienne |
| le Québec | le Québécois, la Québécoise | québécois, québécoise |
| le Mexique | le Mexicain, la Mexicaine | mexicain, mexicaine |
| la Chine | le Chinois, la Chinoise | chinois, chinoise |
| le Japon | le Japonais, la Japonaise | japonais, japonaise |
| la Russie | le/la Russe | russe |

The adjective of nationality is identical to the noun except that it is written in lower case. Example: **un Anglais; un étudiant anglais.**

**A. Les villes** (*cities*) **et les nationalités.** What nationality are the following people? Ask a classmate. (Use **un** for males; **une** for females.)

**Continuation**: Have sts. give additional names.

Karim / Tunis

Djamila / Tunis

MODÈLES:

VOUS: Karim habite Tunis. De quelle nationalité est-il?

VOTRE CAMARADE: C'est un (*a, an*) Tunisien.*

VOUS: Djamila habite Tunis. De quelle nationalité est-elle?

VOTRE CAMARADE: C'est une Tunisienne.

1. Gino / Rome

2. Kai / Kyoto

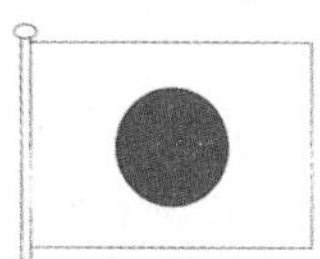

3. Mme Roberge / Montréal

4. Evelyne / Beirut

5. Léopold / Dakar

6. Françoise / Bruxelles

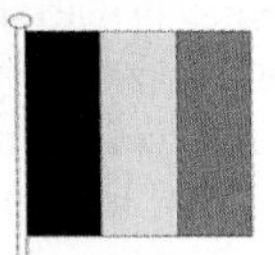

7. Salima / Casablanca

8. Claudine / Genève

---

***C'est un**(**e**)... is used with nationalities to express *He/She is a/an . . .*

**B. D'où sont-ils? Quelles langues parlent-ils?** (*Where are they from? What languages do they speak?*) Look over the names in the left-hand column (corresponding to the people introduced in Exercise A), and the list of languages in the right-hand column below. With a classmate, state the nationality of each person, then the language he or she probably speaks.

MODÈLE: Karim → Karim est tunisien. Il parle arabe et français.

**Suggestion**: Sts. work in pairs.

**Follow-up**: Using a world map, point to important cities and have sts. imagine they live there: *Je parle japonais*. Possibilities: *Tokyo*, *Venise*, *Seattle*, *Rio de Janeiro*, *Québec*, etc.

1. Gino
2. Kai
3. Mme Roberge
4. Evelyne
5. Léopold
6. Françoise
7. Salima
8. Claudine

a. italien
b. français
c. arabe
d. anglais
e. allemand
f. flamand (*Flemish*)
g. japonais

la Suisse - fr./all./romanche

## Les distractions

**Presentation**: (1) Model pronunciation; group repetition. (2) Additional cognate vocabulary: *le volley-ball*, *le ping-pong*, *le football*, *le golf*, *les films policiers*, *les westerns*, *les comédies musicales*, *les films documentaires*.

Julien Fatima Rémi Anne-Laure Marc Thu Sophie Allal

| LA MUSIQUE | LE SPORT | LE CINÉMA |
|---|---|---|
| la musique classique | le tennis | les films d'amour |
| le rock | le jogging | les films d'aventure |
| le jazz | le ski | les films de science-fiction |
| la musique country | le basket-ball | les films d'horreur |
| le rap | le football américain | |

**Préférences.** What do these people like?

MODÈLE: Rémi → Rémi aime le rock.

**Suggestion**: Do as cued-response exercise. You may want to use group repetition after individual responses.

1. Et Thu?
2. Et Sophie?
3. Et Julien?
4. Et Anne-Laure?
5. Et Allal?
6. Et Fatima?
7. Et Marc?

**Follow-up**: Give sts. the name of a famous person in music, sports, or film. They will say *il/elle aime*. For example: *Steven Spielberg*, *Whitney Houston*, *Michael Jordan*, *Gene Siskel*, etc.

# Nouvelles francophones

## The Alliance Française

**Summary**: Cultural information appears throughout *Rendez-vous*, but is presented especially in two sections: *France-culture* and *Nouvelles francophones*. These sections are in English through Chapter 9 (the first half of the book) and French thereafter. Exercises based on some of these notes are in the *Workbook*. The *Nouvelles francophones* section presents selected aspects of the cultures of French-speaking peoples of the world. Its purpose is to acquaint sts. with the wide variety of nations and groups that share the common heritage of French language.

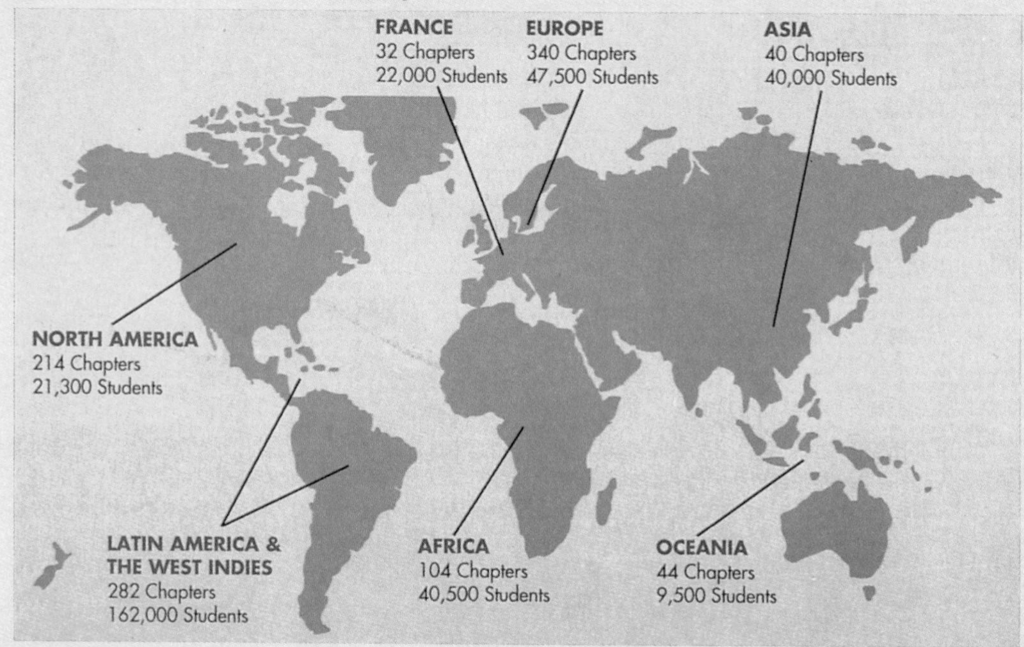

Founded in 1883, this nonprofit association was created to maintain and spread the influence of France all over the world by promoting the French language. The first American chapter was established in San Francisco in 1889. Since then **la vieille dame** (*the old lady*), as it is often called, has become a global network. Today there are 1,300 chapters in 112 countries.

Unlike the Goethe Institut or the British Council, which are affiliated with the respective governments of Germany and the U.K., the **Alliance Française** chapters are autonomous. Each one is established in accordance with the laws of its host country. Funds come from a variety of sources, including membership fees, proceeds from cultural activities, tuition, private contributions, and the French Government.

Today the **Alliance Française** is no longer concerned with spreading the influence of France but works primarily to promote cross-cultural friendships. From language schools, the **Alliance Française** chapters have expanded to become social and cultural centers, presenting films, art exhibits, concerts, plays, and lectures to the general public.

**Summary**: The *Étude de grammaire* section presents the basic structures of the French language. Each grammar point is introduced with a functional minidialogue. Contextualized examples recycle the vocabulary words and expressions of that chapter. Grammar sections in *Rendez-vous* are numbered consecutively throughout the book. **Presentation**: For ideas on presentation of minidialogues, see "*Teaching Strategies*: *Minidialogues and Grammar*" in the *Instructor's Manual*.

# Étude de grammaire

## 1. IDENTIFYING PEOPLE AND THINGS
### Articles and Nouns

**Note**: (1) Point out that all minidialogues are translated at the back of the book, but encourage sts. to get the gist without consulting the translations. (2) Mention that the bookstore would not be a part of the typical French university, but rather an independent establishment off campus.

**Suggestions**: (1) Model pronunciation of dialogue. (2) Ensure that sts. grasp the gist, then use multiple group and individual repetitions. (3) Have sts. do minidialogues in pairs, switching roles. (4) Use questions below minidialogue as dictation, books closed. Sts. can then answer orally or in writing.

### Dans le quartier universitaire

"Functional mini-dialogues" like this one present new grammatical structures in the context of everyday conversations or brief narrative passages. They sometimes use words and expressions that are unfamiliar. If you cannot guess these terms from context, you can find their English equivalents both in the **Lexique français-anglais** (*French-English vocabulary*) in the back of this book, and in the Appendix, where all of the functional mini-dialogues appear in English translation.

Alex, **un étudiant** américain, visite **l'université** avec Mireille, **une étudiante** française.

MIREILLE: Voilà **la bibliothèque, la librairie** universitaire et **le restau-u.**
ALEX: Et y a-t-il aussi **un café**?
MIREILLE: Oui, bien sûr; voici **le café**. C'est le centre de la vie universitaire!
ALEX: En effet! Il y a vingt ou trente personnes ici et seulement **une étudiante** dans **la bibliothèque**!

Complétez la conversation selon le dialogue.

MIREILLE: Voilà ____ bibliothèque et ____ librairie universitaire.
ALEX: Il y a ____ ou ____ personnes ici et ____ étudiante dans ____ bibliothèque.
MIREILLE: C'est normal! ____ café, c'est ____ centre de ____ vie universitaire.

## A. Gender and Forms of the Definite Article

In French, all nouns are either masculine (**masculin**) or feminine (**féminin**) in gender, as are the definite articles that precede them. This applies to nouns designating objects as well as people.

There are three forms of the singular definite article (**le singulier de l'article défini**) in French, corresponding to *the* in English: **le**, **la**, and **l'**.

| MASCULINE | | FEMININE | | MASCULINE OR FEMININE BEGINNING WITH A VOWEL OR MUTE **h** | |
|---|---|---|---|---|---|
| **le** livre | *the book* | **la** femme | *the woman* | **l'**ami | *the friend* (*m.*) |
| **le** cours | *the course* | **la** table | *the table* | **l'**amie | *the friend* (*f.*) |
| | | | | **l'**homme | *the man* (*m.*) |
| | | | | **l'**histoire | *the story* (*f.*) |

**Le** is used with masculine nouns beginning with a consonant (**une consonne**), **la** is used with feminine nouns beginning with a consonant, and **l'** is used with either masculine or feminine nouns beginning with a vowel (**une voyelle**) or with a mute **h**.*

The definite article is used, as in English, to indicate a specified or particular person, place, thing, or idea: **le livre** (*the book*). The definite article also occurs in French with nouns used in a general sense.

| | |
|---|---|
| **le** ski | *skiing* (*in general*) |
| **la** vie | *life* (*in general*) |

**Suggestions**: (1) Point out that Section C presents some ways to identify gender of nouns. (2) Remind sts. to learn article with noun. (3) Give examples in context of nouns used in general sense: *J'aime le ski. J'adore la vie. Je déteste le golf.*

## B. Forms of the Indefinite Article

| MASCULINE | | FEMININE | |
|---|---|---|---|
| **un** ami | *a friend* (*m.*) | **une** amie | *a friend* (*f.*) |
| **un** bureau | *a desk* | **une** librairie | *a bookstore* |
| **un** homme | *a man* | **une** histoire | *a story* |

**Suggestions**: (1) Point out the pronunciation of denasalized *un ami/une amie* and *un homme* versus the *un* in *un bureau.* (2) If you wish, explain that the indefinite article is used for unspecified nouns, while the definite article is used to name a specific person, place, or object, or with nouns used in a general sense.

*In French, **h**'s are either *mute* (*nonaspirate*) or *aspirate*. In **l'homme**, the **h** is called *mute*, which means simply that the word **homme** "elides" with a preceding article (**le** + **homme** = **l'homme**). Most **h**'s in French are of this type. However, some **h**'s are aspirate, which means there is no "elision." **Le héros** (*the hero*) is an example of this. However, in neither case is the **h** pronounced. The **h** is always silent in French.

The singular indefinite article (**le singulier de l'article indéfini**), corresponding to *a* (*an*) in English, is **un** for masculine nouns and **une** for feminine nouns. **Un/Une** can also mean *one*, depending on the context.

| | |
|---|---|
| Voilà **un** café. | *There's a café.* |
| Il y a **une** étudiante. | *There is one student.* |

## C. Identifying the Gender of Nouns

**Suggestion**: Point out that when a noun begins with a vowel, the definite article will not provide a clue to gender. Sts. should make a note of gender, or learn the indefinite article with such nouns.

Since the gender of a noun is not always predictable, it is best to learn the gender along with the noun. For example, learn **un livre** rather than just **livre**. Here are some general guidelines to help you determine gender.

1. Nouns that refer to males are usually masculine. Nouns that refer to females are usually feminine.

   | | |
   |---|---|
   | **l'homme** | *the man* |
   | **la femme** | *the woman* |

2. Sometimes the ending of a noun is a clue to its gender. Some common masculine and feminine endings are:

   | MASCULINE | | FEMININE | |
   |---|---|---|---|
   | **-eau** | le bureau | **-ence** | la différence |
   | **-isme** | le tourisme | **-ion** | la vision |
   | **-ment** | le département | **-ie** | la librairie |
   | | | **-ure** | la littérature |
   | | | **-té** | l'université |

3. Nouns that have come into French from other languages are usually masculine: **le jogging**, **le tennis**, **le Coca-Cola**, **le jazz**, **le basket-ball**.

   **Note**: Exceptions include *la pizza*, *la radio*.

4. The names of languages are masculine. They correspond to the masculine singular form of the nouns of nationality, but they are not capitalized.

   | | |
   |---|---|
   | **l'anglais** | (*the*) *English* (*language*) |
   | **le français** | (*the*) *French* (*language*) |

5. Some nouns that refer to people can be changed from masculine to feminine by changing the noun ending. The feminine form often ends in **-e**.

   | | | |
   |---|---|---|
   | un am**i** *a friend* (*m.*) | → | une am**ie** *a friend* (*f.*) |
   | un étudian**t** *a student* (*m.*) | → | une étudian**te** *a student* (*f.*) |
   | un Américai**n** *an American* (*m.*) | → | une Américai**ne** *an American* (*f.*) |
   | un Alleman**d** *a German* (*m.*) | → | une Alleman**de** *a German* (*f.*) |
   | un Françai**s** *a French man* | → | une Françai**se** *a French woman* |

   Final **t**, **n**, **d**, and **s** are silent in the masculine form. When followed by **-e** in the feminine form, **t**, **n**, **d**, and **s** are pronounced.

**Suggestion**: Model and have sts. repeat masculine and feminine forms.

**Suggestion**: Remind sts. that not all words have both feminine and masculine forms.

**Follow-up**: As a listening comprehension ex., have sts. state gender of word and gender cues they hear: *une Anglaise, un ami, l'Italienne, l'Allemande, l'étudiant, une étudiante, une Espagnole, l'Américaine.*

6. The names of some professions and many nouns that end in **-e** have only one singular form, used to refer to both males and females. Sometimes gender is indicated by the article:

| | |
|---|---|
| **le** touriste | *the tourist* (*m.*) |
| **la** touriste | *the tourist* (*f.*) |

Sometimes even the article is the same for both masculine and feminine.

| | |
|---|---|
| une personne | *a person* (*male or female*) |
| Madame Brunot, **le** professeur | *Mrs. Brunot, the professor* |

**Summary**: Except in Chapters 1 and 18, the practice material in the grammar sections of *Rendez-vous* is divided into two parts. *Vérifions!* contains exs. focusing on form, and usually requiring a single response. (Answers to these exs. appear in the *IM*.) *Parlons-en!* contains exs. and activities that are more communicative and open-ended, often requiring creative thinking from sts. Some exercises and activities in both *Vérifions!* and *Parlons-en!* call for partner/pair or group work.

## Vérifions!

**A. Le, la ou l'? Devinez** (*Guess*)!

1. appartement
2. division
3. allemand
4. tableau
5. Coca-Cola
6. biologie
7. chaise
8. aventure
9. personne
10. tourisme
11. professeur de français
12. homme

**Suggestion**: Use this gender quiz as a preliminary exercise (listening comprehension): Give sts. these words; they respond with *féminin* or *masculin*. 1. *la femme* 2. *une Française* 3. *un touriste* 4. *une comédie* 5. *un étudiant* 6. *une personne* 7. *un stylo* 8. *une fenêtre* 9. *un garçon* 10. *un département*

**Suggestion (A)**: Have sts. give reason for choice of gender by citing rules.

**B. Une réunion de l'Alliance Française.** The **Alliance Française** is hosting a group of people representing many different nationalities and professions at its annual welcome reception this evening. Point out and identify the guests, following the models.

MODÈLES: Henry (Américain) → Voilà Henry, l'Américain.
Danielle (Québécoise) → Voilà Danielle, la Québécoise.

1. Jean-Louis (Français)
2. Franz (Allemand)
3. Pauline (journaliste)
4. Dimitri (Russe)
5. Mme Huet (professeur)
6. Julio (Espagnol)
7. Mathieu (étudiant)
8. Rebecca (Anglaise)
9. Hang (Chinoise)
10. M. Arnaud (poète)

**C. Qu'est-ce que c'est** (*What is it*)?

MODÈLE: 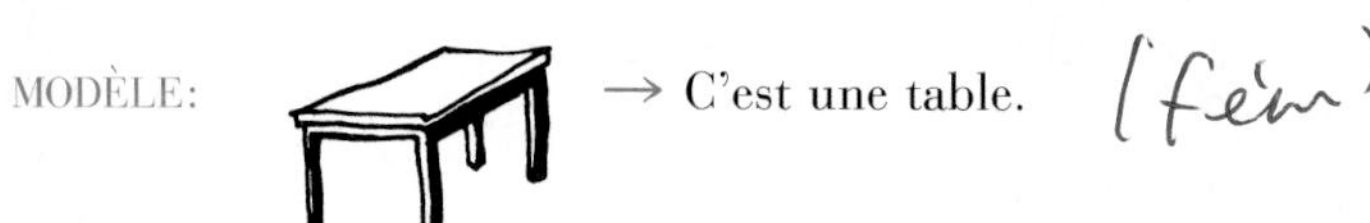 → C'est une table.

**Suggestion**: Model all vocabulary first, using multiple group repetition and individual repetition as desired.

**Follow-up**: Show pictures of other objects or point to other things in classroom.

1. 
2. 
3. 
4. 
5. 
6. 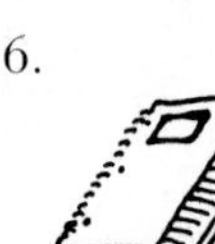
7. 
8. 

**Follow-up**: Have sts. change the definite article to the indefinite article, and vice versa. 1. *le bureau* 2. *une porte* 3. *un crayon* 4. *la table* 5. *une chaise* 6. *le professeur* 7. *un tableau* 8. *un livre* 9. *le cahier* 10. *une fenêtre*

**D. À l'université.** Create sentences using the following words. Then create a different sentence by changing the place.

MODÈLE: étudiante / salle de classe →
Il y a une étudiante dans la salle de classe.
Il y a une étudiante dans la librairie (*bookstore*).

1. tableau / salle de classe
2. meeting / amphithéâtre
3. télévision / laboratoire labo
4. cahier / bureau
5. radio / salle de classe
6. Américaine / restaurant
7. dictionnaire / bibliothèque
8. dictionnaire français / librairie

**Follow-up**: Ask sts. to make up sentences such as *Il y a une télévision dans la salle de classe. Il y a un cahier dans l'amphithéâtre.* Partner will say *C'est logique* or *Ce n'est pas logique*.

## Mots-clés

*Working with a partner:* Many activities in *Rendez-vous* ask you to work with a partner. At first, it may be the student sitting next to you, but try to vary your partners. Choose one when your instructor says **Trouvez un partenaire**. Here are some useful phrases to use.

| | |
|---|---|
| **—Tu as un(e) partenaire?** | *—Do you have a partner?* |
| **—Pas encore.** | *—Not yet.* |
| **—Tu veux qu'on travaille ensemble?** | *—Do you want to work together?* |
| **—Oui, bien sûr. (D'accord.)** | *—Yes, of course.* (*Okay; agreed.*) |

**Summary**: The *Mots-clés* section (lexical items for communication) appears wherever it is useful in each chapter. This feature contains active vocabulary to be used in the activity (activities) it accompanies.

### Parlons-en!

**Interview.** Working with a classmate, ask a question and respond according to your preferences.

MODÈLE: politique (*politics, f.*) →
VOUS: Est-ce que tu aimes la politique?
UN(E) CAMARADE: Oui, j'aime la politique. Vive la politique! (*ou* Non, je déteste la politique. À bas la politique!)

1. rock
2. jogging
3. télévision
4. philosophie
5. opéra
6. gouvernement
7. conformisme
8. cours de français
9. chimie

**Suggestion**: Do model and the first few with whole class. Then have sts. work in pairs. See the section on using pair/group exs. in the *Instructor's Manual*.

# 2. EXPRESSING QUANTITY
## Plural Articles and Nouns

### Un professeur excentrique

LE PROFESSEUR: Voici le système de notation:
zéro pour **les imbéciles**
quatre pour **les médiocres**
huit pour **les génies**
et dix pour le professeur
Il y a **des questions**?

Expliquez le système de notation du professeur: dix pour... ? huit pour... ? quatre pour... ? zéro pour... ?

**Note**: The system of academic grading in France is based on 10 or 20. It is very difficult to receive a score above 8 or 18, depending on scale. *Dix-neuf pour le prof et vingt pour le Bon Dieu!*

| | DEFINITE ARTICLES | | INDEFINITE ARTICLES | |
|---|---|---|---|---|
| | *Singular* | *Plural* | *Singular* | *Plural* |
| *Masculine* | **le** touriste | **les** touristes | **un** étudiant → | **des** étudiants |
| *Feminine* | **la** touriste | | **une** étudiante → | **des** étudiantes |

# A. Plural Forms of Definite and Indefinite Articles

1. The plural form (**le pluriel**) of the definite article is always **les**.

| | |
|---|---|
| le livre, **les** livres | *the book, the books* |
| la femme, **les** femmes | *the woman, the women* |
| l'examen, **les** examens | *the exam, the exams* |

**Suggestion**: Point out the *liaison* in *les examens* versus *les livres*.

2. The plural indefinite article is always **des**.

| | |
|---|---|
| un ami, **des** amis | *a friend, some friends, friends* |
| une question, **des** questions | *a question, some questions, questions* |

**Suggestion**: point out that *des* can mean "some," "several," or "few."

3. Note that in English a plural noun frequently has no article: *friends, questions*. In French, however, a form of the article is almost always used with plural nouns: **les amis**, **des questions**.

## B. Plural of Nouns

**Suggestion**: Point out that oral cues to number are often heard only in article.

1. Most French nouns are made plural by adding an **s*** to the singular, as seen in the preceding examples.

2. Nouns that end in **s**, **x**, or **z** in the singular stay the same in the plural.

| | |
|---|---|
| le cour**s**, les cour**s** | *the course, the courses* |
| un choi**x**, des choi**x** | *a choice, some choices* |
| le ne**z**, les ne**z** | *the nose, the noses* |

3. Nouns that end in **-eau** or **-ieu** in the singular are made plural by adding **x**.

| | |
|---|---|
| le tabl**eau**, les tabl**eaux** | *the board, the boards* |
| le bur**eau**, les bur**eaux** | *the desk, the desks* |
| le l**ieu**, les l**ieux** | *the place, the places* |

4. Nouns that end in **-al** or **-ail** in the singular usually have the plural ending **-aux**.

| | |
|---|---|
| un hôpit**al**, des hôpit**aux** | *a hospital, hospitals* |
| le trav**ail**, les trav**aux** | *the work, tasks* |

**Suggestion**: Point out how one can distinguish singular or plural of these nouns orally in both article and noun form.

5. To refer to a group that includes at least one male, French uses the masculine form.

un étudian**t** et sept étudian**tes** → des étudiants
un Franç**ais** et une Franç**aise** → des Français

**Suggestion**: Have sts. repeat nouns in examples.

### *Vérifions!*

**Suivons** (*Let's follow*) **le guide!** A tour of the university: Give the plural.

MODÈLE: Voilà la salle de classe. → Voilà les salles de classe.

1. Voilà la bibliothèque.
2. Voilà l'amphi(théâtre).
3. Voilà le professeur.
4. Voilà l'étudiant.
5. Voilà le laboratoire de langues.
6. Voilà le bureau.

**Follow-up**: For listening comprehension practice, have sts. indicate whether the following words are *singulier ou pluriel*: *les dictionnaires, des cours, un examen, les livres, l'amphithéâtre, le bureau, un café, des radios, le film, les étudiants, des amis*.

A tour of the neighborhood: Give the plural.

MODÈLE: un Français → Voilà des Français.

7. un hôpital
8. un Anglais
9. une touriste
10. une librairie
11. un restaurant
12. une salle de gymnastique

---

*In French, the final **s** of an article is usually silent, except when followed by a vowel or vowel sound: **des‿étudiants**; **des‿hommes**. In these cases, the **s** is pronounced like the English letter *z*. This linking is called **liaison** (*f.*).

## Parlons-en!

**Continuation**: Expand to a description of the university campus, using vocabulary learned earlier in chapter. Ask questions about campus, such as: *Il y a des amphithéâtres? des salles de cinéma? des cafés? des salles de classe? un restaurant universitaire? des professeurs de mathématiques? une bibliothèque?* (Avoid questions calling for a negative answer.)

**A. Description.** Describe the classroom.

MODÈLE: Dans la salle de classe, il y a des chaises.

Now describe your classroom.

**B. Les études en France.** Skim the following announcement taken from *Le guide pratique d'Angers*. You do not need to understand every word, but try to get a general idea of what it is about. Now look at the highlighted words and try to guess their gender. Use them with **le**, **la**, and **l'**. Discuss with the rest of the class the reasons for your choices. Some of the highlighted words in this announcement are cognates of English words. Can you find others?

### ANGERS accueillera en 1991 plus de 13 000 étudiants sur le campus.

l'Université d'Angers est un ensemble pluridisciplinaire composé de cinq unités de Formation et de Recherche (UFR) et d'un IUT.:

- Droit, Économie et Sciences Sociales,
- Lettres, Langues et Sciences Humaines,
- Sciences de l'Environnement,
- Structures et Matériaux,
- Sciences Médicales et Pharmaceutiques,
- Institut Universitaire de Technologie.

*La Faculté des Lettres* - Photo Université d'Angers.

# 3. EXPRESSING ACTIONS
## -er Verbs

**Rencontre d'amis à la Sorbonne**

XAVIER: Salut, Françoise! **Vous visitez** l'université?
FRANÇOISE: Oui, **nous admirons** la bibliothèque maintenant. Voici Paul, de New York, et Mireille, une amie.
XAVIER: Bonjour, Paul, **tu parles** français?
PAUL: Oui, un petit peu.
XAVIER: Bonjour, Mireille, **tu étudies** ici?
MIREILLE: Oh non! **Je travaille** à la bibliothèque.

**Note**: The minidialogue introduces both subject pronouns and new verb forms (both were previewed in *Étude de vocabulaire* activities). You may prefer to focus on subject pronouns alone before introducing the minidialogue.

Trouvez (*Find*) la forme correcte du verbe dans le dialogue.

1. Vous _____ l'université?
2. Nous _____ la bibliothèque.
3. Tu _____ français?
4. Tu _____ ici?
5. Je _____ à la bibliothèque.

**Follow-up**: Listening. Ask sts. if these statements are true for them. (*oui ou non?*) 1. *Je parle français* (*anglais*). 2. *Nous parlons espagnol* (*français*) *dans cette classe*. 3. *J'étudie à l'université de* _____. 4. *Nous étudions la grammaire française*. 5. *Je travaille le week-end*.

## A. Subject Pronouns and *parler*

**Suggestions**:
A. What pronouns would you use to refer to the following people? 1. *yourself* 2. *yourself and a friend* 3. *your parents* (etc.)
B. What pronouns refer to the following people? 1. *un professeur* 2. *une femme* 3. *des amis* 4. *maman* (etc.)

The subject of a sentence indicates who or what performs the action of the sentence: ***L'étudiant* visite l'université**. A pronoun is a word used in place of a noun: ***Il* visite l'université**.

SUBJECT PRONOUNS AND **parler** (*to speak*)

**Note**: The elided *j'* form will be introduced in Section B.

| *Singular* | | | *Plural* | | |
|---|---|---|---|---|---|
| je | parle | *I speak* | nous | parlons | *we speak* |
| tu | parles | *you speak* | vous | parlez | *you speak* |
| il | parle | *he, it (m.) speaks* | ils | parlent | *they (m., m. + f.) speak* |
| elle | parle | *she, it (f.) speaks* | elles | parlent | *they (f.) speak* |
| on | parle | *one speaks* | | | |

1. **Tu** and **vous**: These are the two ways to say *you* in French. **Tu** is used when speaking to someone you know well—a friend, fellow student, relative, child, or pet. **Vous** is used when speaking to a person you don't know well or when addressing an older person, someone in authority, or anyone else

**Suggestions**: (1) Go over chart, using forms in complete sentences, such as *je parle français*. Do as group repetition drill. (2) Write all forms of verb that are pronounced identically on board first; then present *nous, vous* forms to complete paradigm. Point out that these are sometimes called the "shoe" verbs (because the similarly pronounced conjugations form the shape of a shoe).

with whom you wish to maintain a certain formality. The plural of both **tu** and **vous** is **vous**. The context will indicate whether **vous** refers to one person or to more than one.

| | |
|---|---|
| Michèle, **tu** parles espagnol? | *Michèle, do you speak Spanish?* |
| Maman! Papa! Où êtes-**vous**? | *Mom! Dad! Where are you?* |
| **Vous** parlez bien français, Madame. | *You speak French well, madame.* |
| Pardon, Messieurs (Mesdames, Mesdemoiselles), est-ce que **vous** parlez anglais? | *Excuse me, gentlemen (ladies), do you speak English?* |

**Suggestion**: Ask sts. why examples show *vous* or *tu*. This will reinforce previous material.

2. **Il(s)** and **elle(s)**. The English pronouns *he, she, it,* and *they* are expressed by **il(s)** (referring to masculine nouns) and **elle(s)** (referring to feminine nouns). **Ils** is used to refer to a group that includes at least one masculine noun.

**Suggestion**: Point to two women sts. and ask *ils ou elles*? Do the same with two men, and reinforce as needed.

3. **On.** In English, the words *people, we, one,* or *they* are often used to convey the idea of an indefinite subject. In French, the indefinite pronoun **on** is used, always with the third person singular of the verb.

**Suggestion**: Point out similarity of *on* and English *one*, used for indefinite subjects.

| | |
|---|---|
| Ici **on** parle français. | *One speaks French here.* / *People (They, We) speak French here.* |

**On** is also used frequently in colloquial French instead of **nous**.

Nous parlons français. → **On** parle français.

**Suggestions (B)**: (1) Point out shoe verb formation on board. (2) Remind sts. about *elision* (when a silent *e* or other vowel drops and apostrophe is used). Point out that pronunciation of *s* in two linking words is called *liaison*.

## B. Present Tense of -er Verbs

Most French verbs have infinitives ending in **-er**: **parler** (*to speak*), **aimer** (*to like, to love*), for example. To form the present tense of regular **-er** verbs, add to the stem of the verb, **parl-/aim-** (the infinitive minus the ending **-er**), the endings **-e**, **-es**, **-e**, **-ons**, **-ez**, **-ent**.*

**Presentation**: You may need to explain what an infinitive is, and what conjugating a verb means: An infinitive indicates the action or state, with no reference to who performs it. In English the infinitive is indicated by *to*: *to run*. To conjugate a verb means to change the form of the infinitive to correspond to the subject performing the action. In English, this can be illustrated with the verb *to be* (*I am, you are*, etc.).

| PRESENT TENSE OF **aimer** (*to like, to love*) | | | |
|---|---|---|---|
| j' | aim**e**† | nous | aim**ons** |
| tu | aim**es** | vous | aim**ez** |
| il / elle / on | aim**e** | ils / elles | aim**ent** |

*As you know, final **s** is usually not pronounced in French. Final **z** of the second-person plural and the **ent** of the third-person plural verb form are also silent. Thus **parler** has only three spoken forms: [parl], [parlɔ̃], [parle].

†When a verb begins with a vowel or vowel sound, the pronoun **je** becomes **j'**: **j'aime**, **j'habite**.

**Suggestions**: (1) Model pronunciation of each infinitive several times. Then use the *je* form of each in brief, simple sentences about yourself, repeating several times and

1. Other verbs conjugated like **parler** and **aimer** include:

| | | | |
|---|---|---|---|
| **adorer** | *to love, to adore* | **étudier** | *to study* |
| **aimer mieux** | *to prefer* (*to like better*) | **habiter** | *to live* |
| | | **manger** | *to eat* |
| **chercher** | *to look for* | **regarder** | *to watch, to look at* |
| **danser** | *to dance* | **rêver** | *to dream* |
| **demander** | *to ask for* | **skier** | *to ski* |
| **détester** | *to detest, to hate* | **travailler** | *to work* |
| **donner** | *to give* | **trouver** | *to find* |
| **écouter** | *to listen to* | **visiter** | *to visit* (*a place*) |

pantomiming as appropriate. Transform the base sentence into a simple *vous* question, directed to a st., "coaching" him or her to answer using the *je* form. Example: *danser... danser... J'aime danser. Je danse très bien... Je danse souvent. Et vous, aimez-vous danser? Dansez-vous souvent?* Emphasize infinitives that include English prepositions in their meaning: *chercher* (to look for), *écouter* (to listen to), *regarder* (to look at). (These are difficult for sts.)

2. Note that the present tense (**le présent**) in French has three equivalents in English.

Je **parle** français. { *I speak French.* / *I am speaking French.* / *I do speak French.* }

**Note**: This point should be emphasized strongly.

**Suggestion**: After presenting this idea, ask *Comment dit-on? We are visiting Paris, I'm visiting the Sorbonne* (*la Sorbonne*). *She watches the sts. He does love Paris! You* (*Tu*) *hate Paris.*

3. Some verbs, such as **adorer**, **aimer**, and **détester**, can be followed by an infinitive or a definite article + noun.

| | |
|---|---|
| J'**aime écouter** la radio. | *I like to listen to the radio.* |
| Je **déteste regarder** la télévision. | *I hate to watch television.* |
| J'**adore** le jazz. | *I love jazz.* |

**Suggestion**: Point out the use of present tense questions to indicate near-future action: *Travaillez-vous demain?* (*Are you going to work tomorrow?*)

**Note**: Sts. will usually learn to form simple questions using inversion from hearing you use them.

**Note**: Review use of definite article, if desired. Emphasize use of infinitive after these three verbs.

## *Vérifions!*

**A. Ils... ou Elles...?**

_____ parlent français. _____ parlent italien. _____ parlent espagnol.

**B. Dialogue en classe.** Complete the following dialogue with subject pronouns or forms of **parler**.

LE PROFESSEUR: Ginette, _____[1] parlez français?
GINETTE: Oui, nous _____[2] français.
LE PROFESSEUR: Ici, en classe, on _____[3] français?
JIM: Oui, ici _____[4] parle français.
ROBERT: Marc et Marie, vous _____[5] chinois?
MARC ET MARIE: Oui, _____[6] parlons chinois.
CHRISTINE: Jim, tu _____[7] allemand?
JIM: Oui, _____[8] parle allemand.
MARTINE: Paul parle italien?
ROLAND: Oui, _____[9] parle italien.

**Suggestion**: Use the following oral rapid response exercise as a preliminary activity. Tell sts. to give the corresponding forms.
*je*: *chercher*, *écouter*, *regarder*
*tu*: *manger*, *admirer*, *rêver*
*il*/*elle*: *chanter*, *danser*, etc.

**Suggestions**: (1) Have sts. write out answers to completion ex. first, then give orally. Reinforce by writing forms on board. (2) Have a few sts. write out answers on board. Use group repetition. (3) Do completion exercise on overhead projector. (4) Give practice sentences in English, if necessary, to verify that sts. know what the subject of a sentence is.

**C.** ***Tu* ou *vous*?** Complete the following sentences, using the appropriate pronoun and the correct form of the verb in parentheses.

1. Madame, _____ _____ (habiter) près de (*near*) l'université?
2. Gérard, _____ _____ (chercher) la Faculté des Sciences?
3. Paul et Jacqueline, _____ _____ (visiter) le Quartier latin?
4. Salut, Jeanne! _____ _____ (travailler) ici à la bibliothèque?
5. Richard, _____ _____ (demander) des renseignements (*information*) sur la cité universitaire?

**Suggestion**: Ask different sts. to dictate these sentences to others. May be checked at board or on overhead.

**Additional Activity**: *Qu'est-ce qu'on fait ce soir?* (*What are we doing tonight?*) *Suivez le modèle.* MODÈLE: *Nous travaillons.* → *On travaille?* 1. *Nous parlons de cinéma.* 2. *Nous étudions l'espagnol.* 3. *Nous visitons le quartier universitaire.* 4. *Nous écoutons la radio.* 5. *Nous donnons une soirée.* 6. *Nous regardons la télévision.* 7. *Nous dansons avec les amis de Pierre.*

## Mots-clés

*Telling how often you do things:* Use the following adverbs to tell how often you perform an activity. They usually follow the verb.

| | | | |
|---|---|---|---|
| **toujours** | *always* | **quelquefois** | *sometimes* |
| **souvent** | *often* | **rarement** | *rarely* |
| **en général** | *generally* | **de temps en temps** | *from time to time* |

Je regarde **souvent** la télévision.
Annie et moi, nous dansons **quelquefois** à la discothèque.
**En général**, j'étudie le week-end.

**Suggestion**: Model pronunciation of these adverbs before sts. use them in sentences. If sts. want to express *not* or *never*, teach *ne... pas* (*jamais*) as lexical items; and reinforce when presenting *Grammar Section 4*.

**D. Passe-temps.** Create sentences to describe the activities of these people.

MODÈLE: Olivier / visiter / Marseille → Olivier visite Marseille.

1. Claire / écouter / la radio
2. vous / travailler / beaucoup
3. Philippe et Annie / regarder / toujours / la télé
4. Annie et moi, nous / danser / quelquefois / à la discothèque
5. tu / parler / très bien français

**Follow-up**: For listening comprehension practice, have sts. indicate whether the following sentences are *singulier ou pluriel*. 1. *Elle écoute la radio.* 2. *Ils aiment la musique.* 3. *Il adore Beethoven.* 4. *Elles aiment Bach.* 5. *Elle étudie la musique.*

**Follow-up**: Sts. form sentences with: (*je*) *aimer le français, travailler beaucoup, habiter à Paris*; (*nous*) *écouter le professeur, étudier beaucoup, visiter la librairie*; (*Marie*) *danser bien, adorer le sport, regarder la télévision*; (*ils*) *skier, aimer mieux le jogging, parler avec des amis.*

### Parlons-en!

**A. Portraits.** State the preferences of the following people.

MODÈLE: Mon (*My*) cousin... → Mon cousin aime bien le football, mais (*but*) il aime mieux le basket. Il adore le rock et il déteste le travail!

| | | |
|---|---|---|
| Je... | aimer bien | le tennis |
| Mon (Ma) camarade... | aimer mieux | le jogging |
| Mes parents... | adorer | le cinéma |
| Tu... | détester | la littérature |
| Le professeur... | | les maths |
| ? | | la physique |
| | | ?* |

**Note**: This is called a "sentence builder." Tell sts. that many sentences can be made using each subject and verb with items from column 3. Question marks indicate they can add an answer of their choice.

**Suggestions**: (1) Have sts. work in pairs, taking notes on what their partner says. (2) Have individual sts. give three sentences each. (3) Have sts. write out as homework assignment.

*Throughout *Rendez-vous*, a "?" in an activity means that you are to add an item of your own.

**B. Une interview.** Now interview your instructor.

MODÈLE: aimer mieux danser ou skier →
Vous aimez mieux danser ou skier?

1. aimer mieux la télévision ou le cinéma
2. adorer ou détester regarder la télévision
3. aimer mieux le rock ou la musique classique
4. aimer mieux la musique ou le sport
5. aimer mieux les livres ou l'aventure

**Suggestion**: Sts. recall as many of instructor's responses as possible, stating, for example: *Vous aimez mieux le cinéma, vous...*

**C. Interview.** What do your classmates like? Take turns asking these questions.

1. Tu aimes mieux quels (*which*) cours? Tu détestes quels cours? Tu rêves en classe quelquefois?
2. Tu aimes quel sport?
3. Tu regardes quel programme à la télé?
4. Tu écoutes quelle musique, d'habitude?
5. Qu'est-ce que tu détestes?
6. Qu'est-ce que tu adores?
7. ? Continuez

Dites maintenant quelle réponse vous trouvez (*find*) originale, bizarre.

MODÈLE: Maria déteste la pizza. C'est bizarre!

**Additional activity**: Sts. mention names of celebrities. Their classmates give opinions of them. MODÈLE: *Un(e) étudiant(e): Sting* → *Je déteste Sting.* or *Moi, j'adore Sting.* → *J'aime mieux Janet Jackson.* As sts. are doing ex., take note of what several say and prepare a short *vrai/faux* listening comprehension ex. Examples: *Jessica adore Janet Jackson. Julian déteste Sting.*

## 4. EXPRESSING DISAGREEMENT Negation using *ne... pas*

### La fin d'une amitié?

BERNARD: Avec Martine ça va comme ci comme ça. Elle aime danser, je **n'aime pas** la danse. J'aime skier, elle **n'aime pas** le sport. Elle est étudiante en biologie, je **n'aime pas** les sciences...

MARTINE: Avec Bernard ça va comme ci comme ça. Il **n'aime pas** danser, j'aime la danse. Je **n'aime pas** skier, il aime le sport. Il est étudiant en lettres, je **n'aime pas** la littérature...

1. Martine aime danser? et Bernard?
2. Martine aime le sport? et Bernard?
3. Martine aime la littérature? et Bernard?
4. Martine aime les sciences? et Bernard?

**Suggestion**: To reinforce examples, ask *Aimez-vous danser? Aimez-vous le sport? Aimez-vous la littérature?*

Maintenant posez ces questions à un(e) camarade. (Tu aimes... ?)

To make a sentence negative in French, **ne** is placed before a conjugated verb and **pas** after it.

> Je **parle** chinois. → Je **ne parle pas*** chinois.
> Elles **regardent** souvent la télévision. → Elles **ne regardent pas** souvent la télévision.

**Ne** becomes **n'** before a vowel or a mute **h**.

> Elle aime skier. → Elle **n'a**ime pas skier.
> Nous habitons ici. → Nous **n'h**abitons pas ici.

If a verb is followed by an infinitive, **ne** and **pas** surround the conjugated verb.

> Il aime étudier. → Il **n'aime pas** étudier.

## *Vérifions!*

**A. Opinions et préférences.** Ask a classmate the following questions. He/She will answer according to the model.

MODÈLE: Tu travailles? → Non, je ne travaille pas. (*ou* Oui, je travaille.)

1. Tu étudies la psychologie?
2. Tu skies?
3. Tu détestes les maths?
4. Tu habites à la cité-u?
5. Tu parles russe?
6. Tu manges au restaurant universitaire?
7. Tu danses?
8. Tu aimes le base-ball?

**Note**: Ex. B is based on the minidialogue on page 35.

**B. La fin d'une amitié: Portrait de Bernard.** Here are some more details about Bernard.

Bernard habite à la cité universitaire et, en général, il étudie à la bibliothèque. Après les cours, il parle avec ses amis au café. Le soir (*In the evening*), il écoute la radio, il aime beaucoup le jazz. Il adore le sport, il skie très bien et le week-end, il regarde les matchs de football à la télé.

And Martine? Now tell what Martine doesn't like and doesn't do. Replace **il** with **elle** in the paragraph above and make all the verbs negative. **Martine...**

## *Parlons-en!*

**A. Interview.** Ask a classmate the following questions. He/She will give a personal response.

**Suggestion**: Use in whole class or small group formats.

---

*In rapid conversations in relaxed settings, the **e** in **ne** is often dropped.

> Je ne pense pas (*I don't think so*). Je n'pense pas.

Sometimes you may not hear the **ne** at all.

> J'pense pas.

1. Tu parles italien? russe? chinois? espagnol? anglais?
2. Tu habites quelle (*which*) ville? Paris? New York? Los Angeles? Cincinnati?
3. Tu étudies la littérature? la linguistique? les langues étrangères? la géologie?
4. Tu aimes les examens? les films de science-fiction? les films d'amour? le jazz? la musique country?
5. Le week-end (*On weekends*), tu regardes la télé? Tu écoutes la radio? Tu parles avec tes amis? Tu manges au restaurant?
6. Tu aimes le sport? le football américain? le basket-ball? le base-ball?

Now tell the class five activities that your partner does or does not like to do.

**B. Et vous?** State your preferences by completing the sentences.

**Suggestion**: Have sts. do orally or in writing, whole class or in pairs.

1. J'aime _____, mais je n'aime pas _____.
2. J'adore _____, mais je déteste _____.
3. J'écoute _____, mais je n'écoute pas _____.
4. J'aime _____, mais j'aime mieux _____.
5. Je n'étudie pas _____. J'étudie _____.

## French Vowel Sounds: Oral Vowels

Some French vowel sounds are represented in the written language by a single letter: **a** and **u**, for example. Other vowel sounds have a variety of spellings; the sound [o], for example, can be spelled **o**, **au**, **eau**, or **ô**.

**Summary**: The *Étude de prononciation* section presents guidelines for and examples of French pronunciation. The feature appears through Chapter 7.

Prononcez avec le professeur.

**Follow-up**: Do minimal pair discrimination drills. Sts. write [o] or [ɔ] for words listed in numbers 3 and 4. Read in random order, books closed. They write [e] or [ɛ] for words in 6 and 7, given in random order. They write [y] or [u] for words in 5 and 10 read in random order.

| | IPA SYMBOL | MOST COMMON SPELLING(S) |
|---|---|---|
| 1. ami agréable madame bravo salle classe | [a] | a |
| 2. ici hypocrite typique dîner vive ski | [i] | i î y |
| 3. aussi radio beaucoup chose faux drôle | [o] | eau au ô o |
| 4. objet homme notation normal encore snob | [ɔ] | o |
| 5. utile université musique bureau flûte rue | [y] | u û |
| 6. écouter excusez télévision répéter cité cahier aimer | [e] | é er ez |
| 7. être chaise question treize très examen | [ɛ] | e è ê ei ai |
| 8. Eugène Europe neutron bœufs sérieuse eucalyptus | [ø] | eu œu |
| 9. bœuf déjeuner jeunesse heure jeune professeur | [œ] | eu œu |
| 10. où ouverture tourisme courageux coûte outrage | [u] | ou où oû |

# France-culture

Suggestions: (1) Invite a st. who has studied abroad to talk about his or her experiences. (2) Show slides of several types of French universities. Discuss the old universities versus the new style of campus. (3) Invite someone to your class to discuss the French educational system.

*Student life.* Older French universities are usually located in the center of cities that have grown up around them. There is usually not enough space for more than one or two divisions (**Facultés**) in a particular location. For that reason, there is no campus life, in the American sense of the word. Students do not live at the university. Yet there is a definite student atmosphere in the **quartier universitaire**, the nearby neighborhood—for example, in the famous **Quartier latin** near the Sorbonne, the oldest part of the **Université de Paris**. Students gather to talk in neighborhood **cafés**, which are animated from early morning until well past midnight.

Newer **campus universitaires** in the suburbs (**la banlieue**) resemble American campuses somewhat more. Some residential housing (**la cité universitaire**) is provided on university grounds. There are, however, few facilities for recreation and socializing. Students still prefer to meet at neighboring **cafés** rather than in the university-run **cafétérias** and self-service restaurants.

French universities are state-owned and come under the centralized jurisdiction of the Ministry of Education. Tuition is not charged, and the students pay only a nominal fee of approximately $100.00 a year. Students with a **baccalauréat** degree theoretically have the right to admittance at any university they like, although in reality certain schools have more applicants and are necessarily more competitive.

The French educational system is quite strenuous. Highly competitive exams administered at the end of the first year of a university program allow fewer than half the students to go on to the second year. The others must pass a second exam in the fall or start the first year over again. Those students who make it into the second year have more exams waiting for them before advancement into the third year, at the end of which successful students will earn a **licence**, similar to an American bachelor of arts or bachelor of science degree.

L'université de Jussieu à Paris

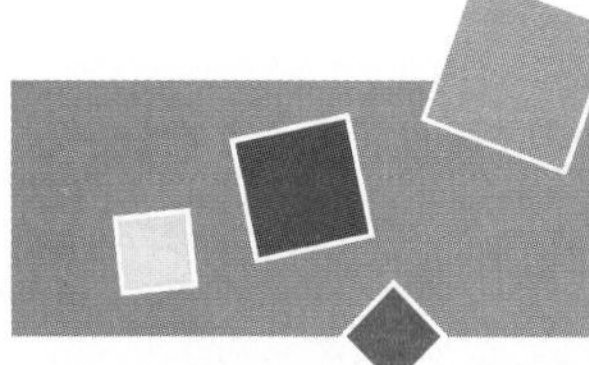

# Mise au point

**Summary**: The *Mise au point* section reviews chapter grammar and vocabulary.

**A. Corrigez.** Look at the picture and change each sentence according to what you see.

MODÈLE: Il y a une chaise. → Il y a des chaises.

1. Il y a un touriste.
2. Il y a des hôpitaux.
3. Voilà un bureau.
4. Il y a un étudiant.
5. Voici des cahiers.
6. Voilà des restaurants universitaires.

**B. Amis par correspondance.** The brochure on page 40 is a brochure from Quebec for students looking for pen pals. Fill it out with as much information as you can. Guess the categories you are unsure of. Pay special attention to the section that asks for **goûts** (*tastes*) **et intérêts particuliers**. Name at least two things you like, using **J'aime...**

NOM ..........................................................................
PRÉNOM ......................................................................
ADRESSE ....................................................................
no rue ou route appartement

..................................................................................
village ou ville comté

..................................................................................
code postal

TÉLÉPHONE .................................................................
SEXE ........................... ÂGE ................................
ÉCOLE[a]
Nom ............................................................................
Adresse .......................................................................
..................................................................................
ANNÉE OU NIVEAU[b] D'ÉTUDES ......................
..................................................................................
GOÛTS OU INTÉRÊTS PARTICULIERS
..................................................................................
..................................................................................

CORRESPONDANT(E) DÉSIRÉ(E)

SEXE ........................... ÂGE ................................

Dans l'impossibilité d'obtenir le correspondant ou la correspondante de ton choix, accepterais-tu indifféremment un garçon ou une fille?
oui .................... NON ................
PAYS[c] 1er choix ....................................
2e choix ....................................
3e choix ....................................

Si tu ne peux obtenir un correspondant ou une correspondante des pays ou régions mentionnés, en accepterais-tu un de n'importe quel[d] pays ou région?
oui .................... NON ................

LANGUE(S) DE CORRESPONDANCE
..................................................................................
..................................................................................
..................................................................................

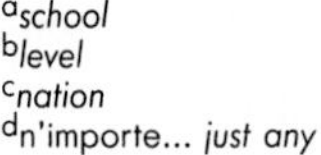
[a]*school*
[b]*level*
[c]*nation*
[d]n'importe... *just any*

## Interactions

**Summary**: *Interactions* is a role-play activity based on the themes, vocabulary, and grammar presented in the chapter. Sts. can prepare their roles at home, or improvise in class along with other sts.

In the second chapter of *Rendez-vous*, you learned how to talk about various aspects of campus life and about your likes and dislikes, as well as how to express actions. Now act out the following situations, using the vocabulary and structures from this chapter.

**Note**: Point out to sts. that this is not a translation ex. but a role-play activity. Tell sts. to choose their roles first and then act out the activity. Have a few groups present their situation to the class. See *Instructor's Manual* for suggestions on using the *Interactions* section.

1. **Rendez-vous.** You run into a friend on campus. Greet him or her. Tell him or her about the courses you like and do not like. Arrange to meet later.

2. **Interprète.** You have been asked to be an interpreter for an exchange student from Africa (your partner). He or she speaks French and Swahili. Introduce yourself. Tell the student that you speak French but not Swahili. Give him or her a tour of the campus. Ask the student what subjects he or she likes best. Get to know the student by telling him or her what you enjoy doing. Ask about his or her favorite activities.

### *Avant de lire* (*Before reading*)

**Contextual guessing.** When you read a text in your own language, you often guess the meanings of unfamiliar words from context. This is equally true when you read a foreign language. Read the following phrase and see if you can guess its meaning.

> Hébergement: à l'hôtel, dans une famille, en résidence universitaire.

The word **hébergement** is new to you, but since you can guess the expressions **hôtel**, **famille**, **résidence universitaire**, you probably guessed that **hébergement** means *lodging*.

Another way to guess from context is by looking at graphic elements such as photos, illustrations, and headings. If you carefully examine the textual and pictorial embellishments that often accompany a text, you will usually find important clues about the content of the passage. Anticipating content helps you recognize the main ideas in the passage as you read.

Remember also to pay close attention to cognates (**les mots apparentés**). Many of them appear in the announcements on p. 42: **cours**, **visa**, **diplômes**, and **excursions**, just to name a few. To practice identifying cognates, underline and then try to guess the meanings of those you find in the following sentence.

> Le campus rassemble la Faculté des Lettres, la résidence universitaire et le restaurant universitaire, la piscine et le gymnase à 10 minutes du centre ville et à 5 minutes des plages.

Before reading **Les universités françaises**, look at the headlines in boldfaced type, and attempt to "get the gist" of the information they convey. Then go through the announcements, underlining all the cognates you can identify. When reading the announcements more carefully, do not stop and

**Summary**: *Rencontres* includes a reading selection (*Lecture*) preceded by a pre-reading section (*Avant de lire*), a guided writing feature (*Par écrit*), and a listening comprehension section (*À l'écoute!*).

**Summary**: *Avant de lire*, which introduces each reading selection in *Rendez-vous*, presents reading strategies and techniques designed to help sts. approach written texts with greater confidence and to acquire the skills necessary to read a foreign language efficiently. Each *Avant de lire* presents a specific strategy followed by a brief "warm-up" exercise or task which prepares sts. for the reading to follow. These pre-reading exercises may be done in class or individually by sts. at home.

**Summary**: *Lecture* is the reading selection that appears in every chapter of *Rendez-vous* except for chapters 1 and 18. (Chapter 18 is entirely devoted to thematic readings and contains several selections.) Many of the readings are drawn from authentic contemporary sources; some are author-written, and others are literary. Each selection is thematically connected to the chapter topic or topics; author-written readings recycle the active vocabulary presented and practiced in the chapter. Unfamiliar words and look up every unfamiliar word. By guessing from the clues already mentioned, you should be able to glean the basic information you need to fill out the form on page 43.

expressions are glossed in the margin. The reading selections follow a progression, through the chapters, from simple "beginner-level" texts to increasingly challenging texts, as sts. expand their vocabulary and gain greater familiarity with complex grammatical and syntactic structures. Each reading selection is followed by a *Compréhension* exercise to verify and expand upon sts. understanding of the text.

**Suggestion**: Discuss reading process in this section. Discuss cognates and, if possible, give practice sentences using more cognates. Have sts. give some cognates they have already learned.

**ALLIANCE FRANÇAISE DE MONTPELLIER**
École internationale de langue et de civilisation françaises

**ÉTÉ 1992**
**juin-juillet-août-septembre**
**3-4 semaines ou plus**

L'école est ouverte toute l'année
**Renseignements, inscriptions**: 6, rue Boussairolles, 34000 MONTPELLIER
Tél.: 67 58 92 74

Cours de langue
Cours intensifs (20 heures par semaine)
4 heures tous les matins
1 h 30 sous forme d'ateliers
(Civilisation. Littérature. Théâtre. Chansons. Grammaire).

I. Cours pour débutants et faux-débutants
II. Cours d'entretien et de perfectionnement (niveaux moyens et avancés)

**PRÉPARATION AUX DIPLÔMES DE L'ALLIANCE FRANÇAISE DE PARIS**

- Diplôme de langue française
- Diplôme Supérieur d'Études Françaises Modernes

Le visa du Ministère de l'Éducation Nationale est apposé sur ces diplômes.
L'Alliance organise des activités socio-culturelles (excursions, visites de musées, théâtre, danse, concerts, festivals).
Hébergement: à l'hôtel, dans une famille, en résidence universitaire.
Restauration: aux restaurants universitaires.
Prix pour 4 semaines: 6 500 F.

Établissement privé d'enseignement supérieur.

**UNIVERSITÉ DE NICE - SOPHIA-ANTIPOLIS**
**Faculté des Lettres, 98 boulevard Herriot - BP 209 - 06204 NICE Cedex 3**

**JUILLET - AOÛT**
3 - 28 JUILLET / 1er AOÛT - 26 AOÛT

**Université Internationale d'Eté**

**COURS**

- Sessions de 2, 3 ou 4 semaines - 23 h. par semaine
- Cours audiovisuels débutants et tous niveaux
- Langue et Civilisation (4 niveaux, sauf débutants)
- Français Economique et Commercial
- Traduction et Conversation en petits groupes
- Séminaires de Pédagogie (observation et discussion, conseils pratiques)
- Possibilité de cours ou séminaires spéciaux pour groupes selon leurs besoins.
- Diplôme d'Université (après examen).

**AUTRES ACTIVITES**

- Conférences et rencontres avec personnalités.
- Ateliers : Musique, Danse, Théâtre, Cuisine, Informatique.
- Visites et Excursions (Riviera, Alpes, Provence)
- Sports : Piscine, tennis, plongée sous-marine, sports de plage.
- Soirées de théâtre, poésie, vidéo, soirées dansantes.

**HEBERGEMENT**

- Logement : en Résidence sur le Campus ou en ville. Pension ou demi-pension.
- Le campus rassemble la Faculté des Lettres, la Résidence et le Restaurant Universitaires, la piscine et le gymnase à 10 minutes du centre ville et à 5 minutes des plages.

**TARIFS**

Exemple :
4 semaines tout compris (sauf excursions) : 7 700 F
4 semaines cours seulement : 3 500 F

**CONTACT**

**Tél. : 93.37.53.94**
**Fax : 93.37.54.66**

## Compréhension

You want to study French this summer in France. In order to choose the school which best suits your needs and interests, do a comparative study of the announcements for the **Alliance Française de Montpellier** and the **Université de Nice-Sophia-Antipolis**. Fill in the boxes with the information you obtain from these announcements.

| | 1 | 2 |
|---|---|---|
| *Nom* | | |
| *Adresse* | | |
| *Prix* (price) *par semaine* | | |
| *Nombre de cours par semaine* | | |
| *Hébergement* | | |
| *Activités proposées* | | |
| *Début* (beginning) *des cours* | | |

Which school do you choose? Explain your preference (in English).

## PAR ÉCRIT

In the **Par écrit** sections of *Rendez-vous*, guidelines are provided to help you organize your ideas and writing through a series of separate steps. Each writing activity will have a general function and a projected audience and goal. Those listed below, for example, present an overview of this chapter's writing project. Look them over before you begin jotting down notes in response to the questions below.

**Function:** Describing (yourself)
**Audience:** A friend or classmate
**Goal:** Write a two-paragraph autobiographical sketch, using the set of questions provided as your guide. Add any relevant information you can. (As an alternative, you may interview another student and write the sketch about him or her.)

**Summary**: *Par écrit* takes a step-by-step approach to writing and aims to develop sts.' writing skills by guiding them through a series of clear, cumulative tasks. See the *Instructor's Manual* for hints on group editing.

**Suggestion**: Composition topics may be done in class or assigned as homework. Read individual paragraphs in class, excluding name of st., for listening comprehension ex. Sts. suggest corrections or guess who wrote paragraph.

PARAGRAPHE 1
Je me présente.

1. Comment vous appelez-vous? 2. Vous habitez à la cité universitaire? dans un appartement? dans une maison (*house*)? 3. Qu'est-ce que vous étudiez? 4. Vous aimez les cours à l'université? 5. Vous aimez (adorez, détestez) le français?

PARAGRAPHE 2
J'aime faire beaucoup de choses. (J'aime la vie active. *ou* J'aime la vie tranquille.)

1. Vous aimez les distractions? le sport? 2. Vous regardez la télévision? Vous écoutez la radio? 3. Vous aimez la musique classique? le jazz? le rock? 4. Qu'est-ce que vous aimez faire avec des amis? 5. Vous aimez discuter au café? flâner (*stroll*) sur le campus? explorer les bibliothèques?

**Steps**

1. Write brief notes in answer to each question before you write out entire sentences. Use these notes as an outline.
2. Write full sentences in response to each question.
3. Organize your work into two paragraphs with a topic sentence introducing the main idea of each. Your first topic sentence could be: **Je me présente.** The second could be: **J'aime faire beaucoup de choses** (*a lot of things*), **J'aime la vie active**, or **J'aime la vie tranquille**.
4. After you have written the first draft, check it for clarity, organization, and smoothness.
5. Have a classmate read the paragraphs to see if what you have written is interesting as well as clear.
6. Finally, make the changes suggested by your classmate if they seem warranted, and check the draft for errors in spelling, punctuation, and grammar. Pay special attention to your verb forms.

**Summary**: *À l'écoute!* is a listening comprehension section consisting of one or two passages, with follow-up activities, recorded on the audiocassette packaged with the st. text. Sts. can listen to the tape and do the activities at home, or you may wish to play selected listening comprehension passages in class and have sts. do the activities together. To ensure that sts. know how to work with the material, you should do the *À l'écoute!* section with them for the first few chapters. Be sure to let sts. know that they will not understand every word they hear in the listening comprehension passages, as in real life. They should focus globally on the general information in the passages and not be overly concerned about what they do not understand. Scripts of the recorded material appear at the back of the Instructor's Edition. Answers to the listening comprehension activities appear at the back of both the student text and the Instructor's Edition.

## À L'ÉCOUTE!

**Les étudiants étrangers.** A journalist is interviewing several foreign students in Paris. First, read through the topics in the chart. Next, listen to the vocabulary followed by the students' remarks. Then, do the activity. Replay the tape as often as you need to. (See Appendix F for answers.)

VOCABULAIRE UTILE

| | | | |
|---|---|---|---|
| **des cinémas** | *movie theaters* | **j'aime mieux** | *I prefer* |
| **partout** | *everywhere* | | |

Draw a line connecting the name of each student with his or her country of origin, field of study, and hobby. (We have drawn the first two lines, to get you started.)

| NOMS | PAYS | ÉTUDES | DISTRACTIONS |
|---|---|---|---|
| Fatima | Canada | philosophie | cinéma |
| François | Tunisie | sociologie | sport |
| Scott | Angleterre | espagnol | café |

**Summary**: *Vocabulaire* contains chapter words and expressions considered *active*. These are the words and expressions sts. should incorporate into their working vocabulary and be expected to know. Active vocabulary items have been introduced in the following chapter sections:

- *Étude de vocabulaire*
- *Mots-clés*
- Grammar paradigms, verb charts, and example sentences from the grammar sections
- Occasionally, from functional minidialogues that begin grammar sections

The vocabulary list is divided into parts of speech (*Verbes*, *Substantifs*, etc.), *Mots et expressions divers*, and, occasionally, thematic categories (*Expressions avec avoir*, *Expressions interrogatives*, etc.). Words and expressions within each sub-grouping are organized alphabetically.

# Vocabulaire

## Verbes

**adorer** to love, adore
**aimer** to like, love
**aimer mieux** to prefer (like better)
**chercher** to look for
**danser** to dance
**détester** to detest
**donner** to give
**écouter** to listen to
**étudier** to study
**habiter** to live
**manger** to eat
**parler** to speak
**regarder** to look at; to watch
**rêver** to dream
**skier** to ski
**travailler** to work
**trouver** to find
**visiter** to visit

## Substantifs

**l'ami(e)** (*m., f.*) friend
**l'amphithéâtre** (*m.*) lecture hall
**la bibliothèque** library
**le café** café; cup of coffee
**le choix** choice
**le cinéma** movies; movie theater
**la cité universitaire (la cité-u)** university dormitory
**le cours** course
**le dictionnaire** dictionary
**l'examen** (*m.*) test, exam
**la faculté** division (*academic*)
**la femme** woman
**le film** film
**l'homme** (*m.*) man
**la librairie** bookstore
**le lieu** place
**la musique** music
**le pays** country
**le quartier** quarter, neighborhood
**la radio** radio
**le restaurant** restaurant
**la soirée** party
**le sport** sport; sports
**la télévision** television
**le travail** work
**l'université** (*f.*) university
**la vie** life
**la ville** city
**la visite** visit

**À REVOIR:** le bureau, le cahier, le livre, la salle de classe, l'étudiant(e), le professeur

## Mots et expressions divers

**à** at, in
**après** after
**avec** with
**d'accord** okay; agreed
**dans** in
**de** of, from
**de temps en temps** from time to time
**en** in
**en général** generally
**et** and
**ici** here
**maintenant** now
**mais** but
**ou** or
**pour** for, in order to
**quelquefois** sometimes
**rarement** rarely
**souvent** often
**toujours** always
**un peu (de)** a little (of)

## Nationalités

**l'Allemand(e), l'Américain(e), l'Anglais(e), le/la Chinois(e), l'Espagnol(e), le/la Français(e), l'Italien(ne), le/la Japonais(e), le/la Russe**

## Les matières

**la biologie, la chimie, le droit** (law), **l'économie** (*f.*), **la géographie, la géologie, l'histoire, l'informatique** (*f.*) (computer science), **les langues étrangères** (*f.*), **la linguistique, la littérature, les mathématiques (les maths)** (*f.*), **la philosophie, la physique, la psychologie, la sociologie**

# Intermède

## SITUATION

### Rendez-vous

**Contexte** *Michel et Julien aiment parler ensemble, mais ils étudient dans des sections° différentes de la Faculté des Lettres.* — departments

**Objectif** *Michel donne rendez-vous à Julien au° café.* — at the

MICHEL: Tiens! Salut, Julien. Comment ça va?
JULIEN: Pas mal. Et toi°? — you
MICHEL: Bof, ça va. Tu travailles à la bibliothèque cet° après-midi? — this
JULIEN: Oui, je prépare une dissertation.° — paper, report
MICHEL: Eh bien alors,° rendez-vous au Métropole à cinq heures°? — Eh... *Well, then* / cinq... *five o'clock*
JULIEN: D'accord.
MICHEL: À tout à l'heure.° — À... *See you later.*
JULIEN: Salut.

**Summary**: *Intermède* is an optional section intended to acquaint students with language expressing and describing "real-life" situations in French. *Situation* is a natural-sounding dialogue recorded on the audiocassette packaged with the student text. It is followed by a selection of highly functional words and expressions (*À propos*) appropriate for use in an actual encounter or situation. *Situation* and *À propos* are followed by a brief set of personalized questions (*Maintenant à vous!*) addressed directly to the student, and sometimes by a simple role-play activity (*Jeu de rôles*). *Intermède* concludes with *Portraits*, brief notes about prominent figures of the French-speaking world.

**Note**: All new vocabulary used in the *Intermède* section is glossed. It is not included in chapter vocabulary lists, and not meant for active learning.

**Suggestion**: Have sts. act out dialogue with handshake. This *Situation* illustrates informal greeting behavior. Sts. at the *Novice* and *Intermediate* levels of oral proficiency should be familiar with this. See *Instructor's Manual* for suggestions.

## À propos

**Summary**: *À propos* presents expressions for communicative use in everyday situations.

### Comment saluer (*to greet*) les amis

| SALUTATIONS | RÉPONSES |
|---|---|
| Salut! | Salut! |
| Tu vas bien? *Are you doing ok?* | Très bien, merci. Et toi? *And you?* |
| Comment vas-tu? *How are you?* | Ça va super bien. *It's going very well.* |
| Comment ça va? *How's it going?* | Ça va! *It's going ok.* |
| | Pas mal. *Not bad.* |
| | Pas terrible. *Not so great.* |
| | Bof, ça peut aller. *Well, it's going ok.* |
| | Ça ne va pas du tout! *It's not going well at all!* |
| Quoi de neuf? *What's new?* | Rien de nouveau. *Nothing new.* |
| | Pas grand-chose. *Not much.* |
| Salut! *Bye!* | Salut! À la prochaine. *Until next time.* |

**Suggestions**: (1) May be presented with the *Situation*. (2) Point out casual nature of language here, and emphasize that it would not be used when addressing those one does not know.

### Comment saluer quelqu'un dans une situation formelle

| SALUTATIONS | RÉPONSES |
|---|---|
| Bonjour! | Bonjour! |
| Comment allez-vous? *How are you?* | Très bien, merci. Et vous? |
| Vous allez bien? *Are you doing well?* | Ça ne va pas du tout.* |
| Au revoir! | Au revoir. À bientôt. *See you soon.* |

## *Maintenant à vous!*

Re-read the **Situation** dialogue, and then answer the following questions.

1. Et vous? Comment ça va? Vous allez bien aujourd'hui?
2. Avez-vous (*Do you have*) rendez-vous avec un ami (une amie) aujourd'hui? Où?
3. Étudiez-vous au café de temps en temps? Où étudiez-vous en général? à la bibliothèque? au lit (*in bed*)? à la discothèque?
4. Aimez-vous préparer les devoirs (*homework*) avec des amis ou préférez-vous travailler seul(e) (*alone*)?

## PORTRAITS

***Jules Ferry*** (1832–93)
A pioneer of public education in France, Jules Ferry served as **Ministre de l'instruction publique et des beaux-arts** (*Minister of Public Education and Fine Arts*) from 1879 to 1883. He was primarily responsible for establishing an educational system that was free, non-religious, and compulsory for all children.

**Summary**: *Portraits* consists of brief notes about prominent figures—painters, designers, writers, scientists, etc.—of the French-speaking world. The short descriptive biographies are accompanied by photos or drawings of the subjects and, where applicable, photos of their works.

*Some expressions can be used in formal or informal situations.

CHAPITRE **TROIS**

# Descriptions

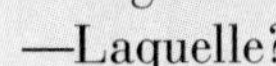

**En avant**

—Regarde comme cette robe est jolie!
—Laquelle?
—La robe noire.
—Moi, j'aime mieux la robe verte, c'est ma couleur préférée.

**Suggestion**: Model pronunciation; have sts. repeat individually or as group.

**Communicative goals:** talking about personalities, clothing, and colors, identifying people and things, describing people and things, getting information, and mentioning a specific place or person.

**Summary**: The *En avant* dialogues that open each chapter offer students examples of authentic,
(continued on p. 49)

# Étude de prononciation

## Quatre personnalités différentes

(*continued from p. 48*)
spontaneous discourse. These dialogues, accompanied by a brief listening activity, are recorded on the audiocassette packaged with the student text. The recorded material introduces students to the general content and theme of the chapter, gives them easily remembered and useful expressions, and helps to develop their listening skills. Scripts for the follow-up questions that accompany each *En avant* section on tape can be found at the back of the Instructor's Edition. Answers to the follow-up questions appear on tape and with the scripts in the Instructor's Edition.

Gilles est un jeune homme { enthousiaste. / idéaliste. / sincère.

Béatrice est une jeune fille { sociable. / sympathique (*nice, likeable*). / dynamique.

**Summary**: The *Étude de vocabulaire* section presents new words and expressions related to the chapter theme. Most new terms are illustrated through visual displays. Vocabulary items that do not lend themselves to illustration, such as adverbial phrases, abstract concepts, and so on, appear in the *Autres mots utiles* list after the display. New vocabulary terms are practiced after each visual presentation and are recycled throughout the *Étude de grammaire* section, the rest of the chapter, and subsequent chapters.

Nathalie est une jeune fille { calme. / réaliste. / raisonnable.

Olivier est un jeune homme { individualiste. / excentrique. / drôle (*funny*).

**Follow-up**: Personalize activity by changing each statement into question, using rising intonation. Example: *Vous aimez parler avec des amis? Oui, je suis sociable.* Or name famous people or members of class. Sts. give adjectives they associate with each. Verify correct adjectives by repeating them in complete sentences (*Oui, Bart Simpson est drôle.*), and making adjectives agree where necessary. Possible names for activity: *Lucy*, *Charlie Brown*, *Snoopy*, *Whoopi Goldberg*, *Arnold Schwarzenegger*, *Madonna*, *Prince*, *Mère Teresa*, *Bill Clinton*, *Hillary Rodham Clinton*, *Al Gore*, *Ruth Bader Ginsberg*.

**A. Qualités.** State the characteristic that corresponds to each statement.

MODÈLE: Béatrice aime parler avec des amis. → C'est une jeune fille sociable.

1. Gilles parle avec sincérité. 2. Nathalie n'aime pas l'extravagance. 3. Olivier est amusant. 4. Béatrice aime l'action. 5. Gilles parle avec enthousiasme. 6. Olivier n'est pas conformiste. 7. Nathalie regarde la vie avec réalisme. 8. Olivier aime l'excentricité. 9. Nathalie n'est pas nerveuse.

**B. Question de personnalité.** State your opinion of the following people by choosing three adjectives to describe them.

**Suggestion:** Do in small groups as an oral or written activity.

**Follow-up**: Give brief (2-3 sentence) descriptions of famous people. Sts. guess who is being described.

**Autres adjectifs possibles:** hypocrite, conformiste, altruiste, antipathique, absurde, optimiste, pessimiste, insociable, calme, égoïste, sincère, modeste, matérialiste...

votre meilleur ami (meilleure amie) (*your best friend*) Il/Elle est...
votre père (*father*)
votre mère (*mother*)
le maire (*mayor*) de votre ville (*city*)
le président américain
Ann Landers
votre camarade de chambre (*roommate*)
Michael Jordan
votre professeur de français
?

**Et vous?** Now describe yourself. Begin your sentence with **Je suis** (*I am*)... **mais je ne suis pas** (*I'm not*)...

## Mots-clés

**Summary**: The *Mots-clés* section (lexical items for communication) appears wherever it is useful in each chapter. This feature contains active vocabulary to be used in the activity (activities) which it accompanies.

*How to qualify your description:* When you first learn a foreign language, you inevitably exaggerate a little because you do not yet know the words to give nuances to your descriptions. The following adverbs may be useful.

| | | | |
|---|---|---|---|
| **très** | *very* | **peu** | *hardly* |
| **assez** | *somewhat* | **un peu** | *a little* |

Jeanne est **très** calme mais Jacques est **un peu** nerveux.
Mon chien (*dog*) est **peu** intelligent mais il est **assez** drôle.

**C. Interview.** Ask a classmate the following questions. Use **très**, **assez**, **peu**, or **un peu** when appropriate.

MODÈLE: Es-tu sociable ou insociable? → Je suis assez sociable.

1. sincère ou hypocrite? 2. excentrique ou conformiste? 3. individualiste ou altruiste? 4. sympathique ou antipathique? 5. calme ou dynamique? 6. réaliste ou idéaliste? 7. raisonnable ou absurde? 8. optimiste ou pessimiste?

**Suggestion**: Can be done by sts. in pairs or small groups. Sts. describe themselves; partners then give a three-sentence summary for rest of class.

Now summarize by stating a few characteristics of your classmate, along with their opposites.

## Un peu d'argot*

| | | |
|---|---|---|
| **vachement** | très | *very* |
| **mignon(ne)** | charmant(e) | *cute* |
| **cool** | décontracté(e) | *cool, relaxed* |
| **marrant(e)** | drôle | *funny* |
| **bosseur/euse** | travailleur/euse | *hardworking* |
| **sympa** | sympathique | *nice* |
| **un copain** | un ami | *a pal (m.)* |
| **une copine** | une amie | *a pal (f.)* |

EN CONTEXTE

SYLVAIN: Sophie, elle est **vachement sympa**.

STEPHANE: Oui, et sa (*her*) **copine**, elle est très **mignonne**.

**Summary**: The *Un peu d'argot* sections contain contemporary colloquial and slang expressions. The expressions are presented for student and instructor interest and are not considered to be part of the chapter's active vocabulary.

**Note**: Most of these terms are part of everyday spoken French; they are simply a little less formal. *Vachement* and *cool*, however, are used only by young people. They should not be used when talking to somebody's boss or parents, or to older people in general.

## Les vêtements

**Presentation**: Bring in clothing or pictures of items of clothing.

**Additional vocabulary**: *un soutien-gorge, des collants, des gants, un slip.*

un imperméable
un jean
un manteau
un blouson
un tailleur
un chemisier
une veste
un veston
une cravate
une chemise
un costume
un pantalon
des chaussures
des chaussettes
des bottes
un pull-over
des tennis
un sac à dos
un maillot de bain
un short
un tee-shirt
un sac à main
une robe
un chapeau
une jupe
des sandales

**Suggestion**: Present clothing vocabulary with questions and answers involving vocabulary known to sts. Point to relevant items as answers are given. For example: *Qu'est-ce qu'il y a sur l'image? Il y a une chemise? Oui, voici une chemise.*

---

*Remember that the words and expressions in **Un peu d'argot** are for recognition only, and are not presented for active use in exercises or activities. Remember, too, that **argot** should be used only in informal situations—with friends and family!

**A. Qu'est-ce qu'ils portent?** Describe what these people are wearing.

1. Bruno porte ____.
2. Mme Dupuy porte ____.
3. Aurélie porte une casquette (*a French cap*), ____.
4. M. Martin porte ____.

Bruno Mme Dupuy Aurélie M. Martin

In general, which articles of clothing are worn only by men? Which are worn only by women? Which by both men and women?

**Note**: May be done in pairs, after model given for whole class.

**Follow-up**: *Quels vêtements sont convenables pour les personnes suivantes: les yuppies? les jeunes BCBG* (*preppies*)? *les chanteurs country-western? les espions* (*ceux qui font de l'espionnage*)? *les punks*?

**B. Un vêtement pour chaque** (*each*) **occasion.** Describe in as much detail as possible what you wear to go . . .

1. à un match de football américain 2. à un concert de rock 3. à une soirée 4. dans un restaurant élégant 5. à l'université 6. à la plage (*beach*)

**Additional activity**: Sts. describe the clothing of persons depicted in photos, magazine ads, slides, etc., taken from target culture, if possible. Ex. may be done orally or in writing. If written, collect descriptions and read in class as you hold up the image described plus two distractors; sts. guess who is described.

## Les couleurs

**Presentation**: Bring in colored construction paper to present the colors initially.

**A. Association.** What colors do you associate with _____?

MODÈLE: Halloween? → Le noir et l'orange.

1. le ski?
2. l'écologie?
3. le pessimisme?
4. l'amour?
5. le jour de la Saint-Valentin?
6. Noël?

**Continuation**: *la salle de classe, le printemps, l'été, la pluie, l'automne, le lundi, la Saint-Patrick, la France, le Canada.*

**Suggestion**: Ask and have sts. ask one another: *Quelle couleur aimez-vous mieux*? Do activity in groups or pairs.

**Additional activity**: *De quelle couleur*? MODÈLE: *une banane* → *Elle*

*est jaune. 1. une rose 2. une orange 3. un rubis 4. un océan 5. un glacier 6. un éléphant*

**B. Descriptions.** Take a few minutes to jot down on a slip of paper what you are wearing. Your instructor will then collect the descriptions, shuffle them, and distribute them at random among the students. Find your partner: the student who most closely matches the description written on the slip of paper you are holding. When you have located him/her, go over and compliment your partner on his/her outfit, using a simple phrase: **J'aime bien ton jean!**; **C'est chic!**; **Comme tu es élégant(e)!** Your partner may respond with a simple **merci**, or may compliment your outfit in turn.

**Follow-up**: *Dictée* and Listening Comprehension A. Dictate items: 1. *une chemise noire* 2. *un imperméable gris* 3. *des chaussures blanches* 4. *un pull* (colors of your university) 5. *une chemise noire et blanche* 6. *un tailleur rouge* B. *Qu'est-ce que vous associez avec...?* (Sts. give items from the *dictée*) 1. *un chanteur* (*country-western*) *célèbre* 2. *un prisonnier* 3. *une équipe de base-ball* 4. *un(e) étudiant(e) de votre université* 5. *la femme du président*

# Christine, Michel et la voiture

Michel est **sur** le banc. Il attend (*is waiting for*) Christine.

Christine arrive. Elle est **dans** la voiture.

Michel est **devant** la voiture.

Christine est **à côté de** la voiture. Michel est **sur** la voiture.

**Note**: Avoid use of *à côté de* with masculine noun.

Michel pousse (*is pushing*) la voiture. Il est **derrière** la voiture.

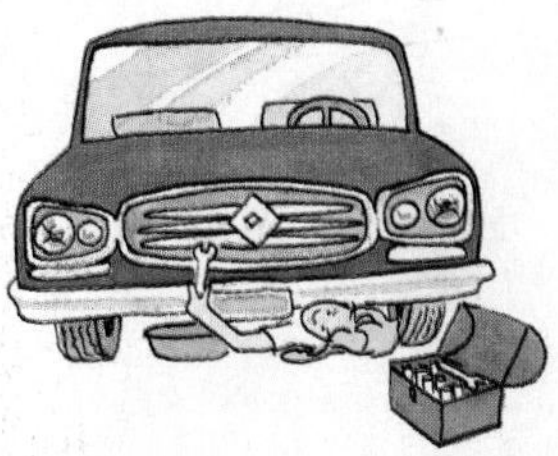

Christine est **sous** la voiture. Elle est **par terre**.

**A. Oui ou non?** Look at the pictures and correct any statements that are wrong.

**Suggestion**: Read sentences and have sts. match them to pictures, covering captions.

1. Christine est assise sur le banc.
2. Michel est dans la voiture.
3. Christine est à côté de la voiture.
4. Michel est derrière la voiture.
5. Michel est devant la voiture.
6. Christine est sous la voiture.
7. Michel est par terre.

**B. Désordre.** Alain has a problem with clutter! Describe his room, using **sur**, **sous**, **devant**, **derrière**, **dans**, and **par terre**.

MODÈLE: Il y a deux livres sous la chaise.

**Follow-up**: Place classroom objects on desk as in drawing. Ask sts. to describe scene. Move objects around several times to elicit different descriptions.

**Additional activity**: For listening comprehension practice, describe a simple scene to sts. and ask them to draw a sketch according to description. Example: *Il y a une table. Derrière la table, il y a deux chaises. À côté de la table, il y a une étudiante. Sur la table, il y a des livres. Sous la table, il y a un chat.* (etc.)

# France-culture

**Summary**: Cultural information appears throughout *Rendez-vous*, but is presented especially in two sections: *France-culture* and *Nouvelles francophones*. These sections are in English through chapter 9 (the first half of the book) and French thereafter. Exercises based on some of these notes are in the *Workbook*. *France-culture* aims to make sts. aware that learning about culture is an integral part of learning a language. It presents various aspects of contemporary French culture, not in the sense of "classical" culture or the fine arts, but primarily understood as everyday social customs, practices, attitudes, and tastes.

*L'esprit critique.* The French often describe themselves as a nation of individualists. One facet of this individualism is their **esprit critique**, the French tendency to call almost everything into question, to take nothing for granted.

The **esprit critique** leads to original and creative thought, but it can also be a source of conflict. Conversations among friends may sound brusque and aggressive to foreigners, as if participants were trying to assert their viewpoints for the pure pleasure of it. As a population, the French enjoy discussion immensely, spending hours—usually around a table—debating everything from politics to food. Defending one's opinions with wit and flair is much admired.

In politics, **l'esprit critique** shows up as a spirit of confrontation rather than compromise. The average French citizen has strong opinions about politics and slightly mistrusts the intentions of politicians—indeed, of any institution or bureaucracy. Criticizing the status quo is a tradition in France. That may account for the popularity of satirical cartoons, which can be found in almost all newspapers and magazines.

What does this cartoon satirize?

**Suggestion**: Discuss the mail and transportation strikes that can disrupt daily life. If possible, bring in other satirical cartoons and **Le Canard enchaîné** as examples of *l'esprit critique*.

**Notes**: (1) You may want to teach the minidialogue inductively by having sts. find verb forms and explain how *être* is conjugated. (2) Explain what an irregular verb is. Use *to be* as an English example, since it has parallel irregularities. Alternatively, have a st. explain the concept of irregular verbs so you can get insight into sts.' current understanding.

# Étude de grammaire

## 5. IDENTIFYING PEOPLE AND THINGS
## The Verb *être*

**Suggestion**: Model pronunciation. Then have sts. read the roles, in small groups or within whole-class format. See *IM* for suggestions on using minidialogue.

**Summary**: The *Étude de grammaire* section presents the basic structures of the French language. Each grammar point is introduced with a functional minidialogue. Contextualized examples recycle the vocabulary words and expressions of that chapter. Grammar sections in *Rendez-vous* are numbered consecutively throughout the book.

### Le génie de Fabrice*

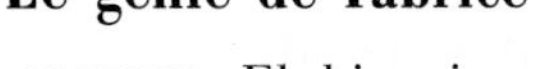

FABRICE: Eh bien, je **suis** prêt à travailler!
MARTINE: Moi aussi, mais où **sont** les livres et le dictionnaire?
FABRICE: Euh... ah oui, regarde, les voilà. Le dictionnaire **est** sous le chapeau et les cahiers **sont** sur le blouson. Maintenant, nous **sommes** prêts.
MARTINE: Tu sais, Fabrice, tu **es** très bon en littérature, mais pour l'organisation, tu **es** nul!
FABRICE: Peut-être, mais le désordre, c'**est** un signe de génie!

Complétez les phrases d'après le dialogue.

1. La chambre de Fabrice est **en ordre / en désordre**.
2. Martine et Fabrice sont étudiants **en lettres / en sciences**.
3. Martine **admire / critique** les talents de Fabrice en littérature.

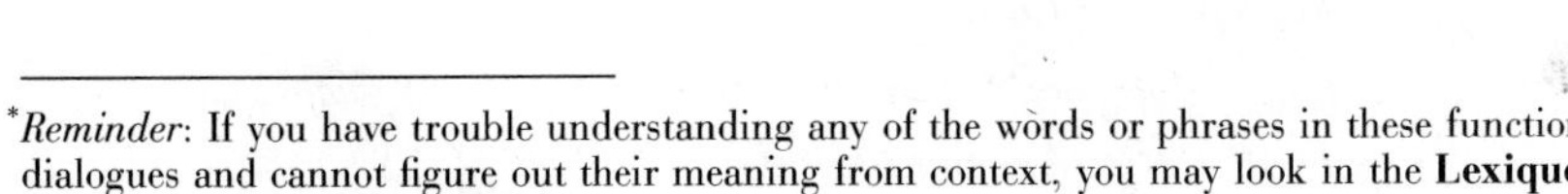

**Reminder*: If you have trouble understanding any of the words or phrases in these functional minidialogues and cannot figure out their meaning from context, you may look in the **Lexique** or in the Appendix, where all minidialogues appear in English.

# A. Forms of être

**Presentation**: Model pronunciation of verb forms, using group repetition. Use complete, simple sentences for modeling: *Je suis intelligent. Tu es sociable. Il est drôle.* (etc.) Point out pronunciation of *vous êtes* and *elles sont*. Stress the [z] and [s] sounds.

| PRESENT TENSE OF **être** (*to be*) | | | |
|---|---|---|---|
| je | **suis** | nous | **sommes** |
| tu | **es** | vous | **êtes** |
| il, elle, on | **est** | ils, elles | **sont** |

# B. The Uses of être

The uses of **être** closely parallel those of *to be*.

Fabrice **est** intelligent. — *Fabrice is intelligent.*
Est-ce que Martine **est** organisée? — *Is Martine organized?*
Nous **sommes** d'accord. — *We agree.*
Fabrice et Martine **sont** à la bibliothèque. — *Fabrice and Martine are at the library.*

In describing someone's nationality, religion, or profession, no article is used with **être**.

—**Je suis anglais. Tu es protestant?** — *—I am English. Are you (a) Protestant?*
—Non, **je suis catholique.** — *—No, I am (a) Catholic.*

—Vous **êtes professeur**? — *—Are you a teacher?*
—Non, je **suis étudiant.** — *—No, I am a student.*

# C. Ce and *il/elle* Used with être

**Suggestion**: In Section C ask a st. to explain what "modified" means. Do a few more transformations on board to show sts. equivalence between *Il/Elle est...* (noun) and *C'est un*(e)... (modified noun). Examples: *Il est professeur. C'est un professeur français. Elle est protestante, et elle est sincère. C'est une protestante sincère.* Ask sts. to give alternative to the following: *C'est un professeur difficile. Il est étudiant, et il est intelligent. Elle est française. C'est une touriste enthousiaste.* Note that sts. rarely learn to produce *c'est* and *il est* correctly in free speech until much later.

1. The indefinite pronoun **ce** (**c'**) is an invariable third-person pronoun. **Ce** has various English equivalents: *this*, *that*, *these*, *those*, *he*, *she*, *they*, and *it*.

   - The expression **c'est** (along with its plural, **ce sont**) is used before modified nouns (*always with an article*) and proper names; it usually answers the questions **Qui est-ce**? or **Qu'est-ce que c'est**?

—Qui est-ce? — *—Who is it?*
—C'est Maxime. C'est un étudiant belge. — *—It's Maxime. He is a Belgian student.*

—Ce sont des Français? — *—Are they French?*
—Non, ce sont des Italiens. — *—No, they are Italian.*

—Qu'est-ce que c'est? — *—What is that?*
—C'est une friperie. — *—That's (It's) a second-hand clothes shop.*

| | |
|---|---|
| —Et ça, qu'est-ce que c'est? | —*And that, over there, what is that?* |
| —Oh ça, c'est une boutique de haute couture. | —*Oh, that's a fashion designer's shop.* |

- **C'est** can also be followed by an adjective, to refer to a general situation or to describe something that is understood in the context of the conversation.

  Le français? C'est facile!
  J'adore la France. C'est magnifique!

2. **Il/Elle est** (and **Ils/Elles sont**) are generally used to describe someone or something already mentioned in the conversation. They are usually followed by an adjective and occasionally by an unmodified noun (*without an article*).

| | |
|---|---|
| —Où est située la friperie? | —*Where is the second-hand clothes shop located?* |
| —Elle est dans la rue Mouffetard. | —*It's on Mouffetard Street.* |
| —Voici Karim. Il est étudiant en biologie. | —*Here is Karim. He is a biology student.* |
| —Est-il français? | —*Is he French?* |
| —Non, il est algérien. | —*No, he is Algerian.* |

## *Vérifions!*

**A. Description.** You have been invited to the home of a French person. Describe the things and people you see, using **devant**, **dans**, **sur**, **sous**, or **derrière**.

Pierre-Louis Daniel

→ Les cafés sont sur la table.
Les garçons (*boys*) sont devant la table.

1. Rémy

2. Cléopâtre

**Summary**: Except in Chapters 1 and 18, the practice material in the grammar sections of *Rendez-vous* is divided into two parts. *Vérifions* contains exs. focusing on form, and usually requiring a single response. (Answers to these exs. appear in the *IM*.) *Parlons-en* contains activities that are more communicative and open-ended, often requiring creative thinking from sts. Many of the *Parlons-en* activities call for partner/pair or group work.

**Suggestion**: Use the following as preliminary exercises. A. Review classroom vocabulary and practice *être*. Hold up or point to objects, asking *Qu'est-ce que c'est*? Elicit plural forms by holding up two books, three pencils, etc.
B. *Identité. Qui est étudiant? Transformez la phrase selon le modèle.* MODÈLE: *Anne est étudiante.* (*je*, *nous*, *Claire-Marine et Hervé*, *tu*, *vous*, *Marc*, *Jeanne-Marie et Catherine*, *Jacques et Pierre*)

**B. Un examen.** Complete the following dialogue between Fabrice and Martine, using the correct form of the verb **être**.

> **Additional activity**: Point to sts. and ask the questions. MODÈLE: *C'est un ami? → Non, ce sont des amis.* 1. *C'est une étudiante?* 2. *C'est une touriste?* 3. *C'est un professeur?* 4. *C'est une Américaine?* 5. *C'est un Anglais?* 6. *C'est une Chinoise?*

FABRICE: Ces livres ____[1] difficiles!
MARTINE: Pas pour toi, tu ____[2] un génie!
FABRICE: Oui, mais le professeur ____[3] très exigeant (*demanding*).
MARTINE: Et il dit toujours (*always says*): «Vous ____[4] une étudiante intelligente, Mademoiselle.»
FABRICE: Nous ____[5] peut-être intelligents, mais moi, je ne ____[6] pas prêt pour l'examen!

**Qui est-ce?** Identify each person described below, on the basis of the dialogue.

1. C'est une personne très exigeante.
   C'est ____.
2. C'est une étudiante intelligente.
   C'est ____.
3. Il n'est pas prêt pour l'examen.
   C'est ____.

**C. Deux étudiants africains à Paris.** Describe this man and woman. Complete each phrase with the appropriate expression in the right-hand column. (Reminder: Use **c'est +** modified nouns; **il/elle est +** adjectives; **il/elle** est **+** unmodified nouns expressing profession, religion, or nationality.)

> **Suggestion**: May be done for written or oral work.
>
> **Note:** Sts. rarely master this distinction at the *Novice Level*.

Voici Barthélémy.

| | |
|---|---|
| C'est... | sénégalais. |
| Il est... | un jeune homme enthousiaste. |
| C'est... | aussi (*also*) un peu timide. |
| Il est... | un étudiant sérieux. |

Sa petite amie s'appelle Fatima.

| | |
|---|---|
| Elle est... | marocaine. |
| C'est... | étudiante en philosophie. |
| Elle est... | une personne sociable et dynamique. |

**D. La France et les Français.** Choose the correct answer, using **c'est** or **ce n'est pas**. Feel free to give an original response.

MODÈLE: le sport préféré des Français: le jogging? le football (*soccer*)? → Ce n'est pas le jogging, c'est le football.

1. un symbole de la France: la rose? la fleur de lys?
2. un président français: Chevalier? Mitterrand?
3. un cadeau (*present*) des Français aux Américains: la Maison-Blanche (*White House*)? la Statue de la Liberté?
4. une ville avec beaucoup de Français: La Nouvelle-Orléans? St. Louis?
5. un pays (*country*) avec beaucoup de Français: le Canada? le Mexique?
6. un génie français: Louis Pasteur? Werner von Braun?
7. parler français: difficile? facile?

> **Suggestion**: Point out pronunciation of *lys* [*lis*]. Draw a *fleur de lys* on the board if sts. are not sure what it is.

### *Parlons-en!*

**Et vous, comment êtes-vous?** Provide a description of yourself.

Je m'appelle ____.
Je suis un(e) ____. (femme / homme / jeune fille / jeune homme)
Je suis ____. (étudiant[e] / professeur)
Je suis ____. (nationalité)
Je suis de ____. (ville [*city*])
Je suis l'ami(e) de ____.
____ et ____ sont mes (*my*) amis.
Maintenant je suis ____. (lieu [*place*])
Je porte ____. (vêtements)

Now describe one of your classmates.

**Suggestion**: Have sts. write out portrait on a 3 × 5 card, deleting their name, but adding any details they choose. Collect cards. Then have a st. select a card from deck and read it aloud. Others guess who is being described.

## 6. DESCRIBING PEOPLE AND THINGS
## Descriptive Adjectives

**Suggestion**: Verify that sts. understand the drawing: *Donnez le nom d'un ordinateur célèbre. Qui dit «Ils sont difficiles à contenter»?* Teach how to use two or more adjectives joined by *et*.

**Rencontres par ordinateur**

| | |
|---|---|
| Il est sociable, | Elle est sociable, |
| charmant, | charmante, |
| sérieux, | sérieuse, |
| beau, | belle, |
| idéaliste, | idéaliste, |
| sportif... | sportive... |

Répondez aux questions suivantes.

1. Il cherche (*is looking for*) une femme sportive? réaliste? extravagante?
2. Il est ordinaire? extraordinaire? réaliste?
3. Elle cherche un homme sociable? drôle? réaliste?
4. Elle est ordinaire? extraordinaire? réaliste?
5. La machine est optimiste?

**Follow-up**: Ask *Est-ce qu'ils sont réalistes?* Then jokingly ask sts. to describe the ideal man or woman.

## A. Position of Descriptive Adjectives

Descriptive adjectives (**les adjectifs qualificatifs**) are used to describe people, places, and things. In French, they normally *follow* the nouns they modify. They may also modify the subject when they follow the verb **être**.

| | |
|---|---|
| un professeur **intéressant** | *an interesting teacher* |
| un ami **sincère** | *a sincere friend* |
| Elle est **sportive**. | *She is sports-minded (likes sports).* |

**Presentation**: Throughout grammar explanation, give or solicit personalized examples from sts. Note that beginning sts. often cannot **hear** the difference between masculine and feminine forms; they usually need to learn to recognize the different sounds before they can produce them.

# B. Agreement of Adjectives*

In French, adjectives must agree in both gender (masculine or feminine) and number (singular or plural) with the nouns they modify. Note the different forms of the adjective **intelligent**:

**Suggestion**: After presenting the concept of gender agreement, try this listening comprehension ex. (which includes only feminine forms with -e). *Masculin ou féminin?* 1. *intelligent* 2. *intelligente* 3. *charmante* 4. *français* 5. *amusant* 6. *amusante* 7. *charmant* 8. *patiente* 9. *américain* 10. *américaine*

| | MASCULINE | FEMININE |
|---|---|---|
| *Singular* | un étudiant intelligent | une étudiante intelligent**e** |
| *Plural* | des étudiants intelligents | des étudiantes intelligent**es** |

1. To create a feminine adjective, an **e** is usually added to the masculine form.

   Alain est persévérant. → Sylvie est persévérant**e**.†

   If the masculine singular form of the adjective ends in an unaccented or silent **-e**, the ending does not change in the feminine singular.

   Paul est optimist**e**. → Claire est optimist**e**.

2. To make an adjective of either gender plural, an **s** is added in most cases.

   Ils sont charmant**s**. Elles sont charmant**es**.

   If the singular form of an adjective already ends in **s** or **x**, the ending does not change in the masculine plural.

   L'étudiant est **français**. → Les étudiants sont **français**.
   Le professeur est **courageux**. → Les professeurs sont **courageux**.

3. If a plural subject contains one or more masculine items or persons, the plural adjective is masculine.

   Sylvie et François sont **français**. Sylvie et Françoise sont **françaises**.

4. Most adjectives of color have both masculine and feminine forms.

   un chemisier **blanc** / **bleu** / **gris** / **noir** / **vert** / **violet**
   une chemise **blanche** / **bleue** / **grise** / **noire** / **verte** / **violette**

   Adjectives of color that end with a silent **e** have the same form for masculine and feminine.

   un pantalon / une robe } **jaune, rose, rouge**

   Two adjectives of color, **marron** and **orange**, are invariable in both gender and number.

   les chemisiers { **marron** / **orange**    les chemises { **marron** / **orange**

**Suggestion**: Illustrate different forms of color adjectives by having sts. describe classroom objects (masculine vs. feminine objects, singular vs. plural objects). Put st. generated examples on board to illustrate grammatical concepts and spelling patterns.

*L'accord des adjectifs

†Remember that final **t**, **d**, and **s**, usually silent in French, are pronounced when **-e** is added.
masculine: **intelligent** [ɛ̃teliʒɑ̃]    feminine: **intelligente** [ɛ̃teliʒɑ̃t]

# C. Descriptive Adjectives with Irregular Forms

| PATTERN | | | SINGULAR | | PLURAL | |
|---|---|---|---|---|---|---|
| *Masc.* | | *Fem.* | *Masc.* | *Fem.* | *Masc.* | *Fem.* |
| -eux | → | **-euse** | courageux | courageuse | courageux | courageuses |
| -eur | → | **-euse** | travailleur | travailleuse | travailleurs | travailleuses |
| -er | → | **-ère** | cher (*expensive*) | chère | chers | chères |
| -if | → | **-ive** | sportif | sportive | sportifs | sportives |
| -il | → | **-ille** | gentil (*nice, pleasant*) | gentille | gentils | gentilles |
| -el | → | **-elle** | intellectuel | intellectuelle | intellectuels | intellectuelles |
| -ien | → | **-ienne** | parisien | parisienne | parisiens | parisiennes |

Other adjectives that follow these patterns include **paresseux/paresseuse** (*lazy*), **naïf/naïve** (*naïve*), **sérieux/sérieuse** (*serious*), **fier/fière** (*proud*), and **canadien/canadienne**. The feminine forms of **beau** (*handsome, beautiful*) and **nouveau** (*new*) are **belle** and **nouvelle**.

**Notes**: (1) Adjectives ending in *-al* are not treated. You may wish to teach the forms of *idéal*, *principal*, *légal*, and *loyal*. Point out the following forms: *idéal*, *idéaux*, *idéale*, *idéales*. Mention the common exception: *finals*. (2) Point out the [j] sound at the end of the feminine form *gentille*.

### Vérifions!

**A. Dans la salle de classe.** Complete the sentences with appropriate adjectives according to their meaning and form.

1. La salle de classe est... (blanche / beau / gentil / orange / petite / chers)
2. Le professeur est... (sérieux / dynamiques / actif / travailleuse / gentils / sportives)
3. Les étudiants sont... (fier / sincères / intelligente / courageux / naturelles / paresseux)
4. Le livre de français est... (longs / intéressant / difficiles / nouveau / amusant / originale)

**Additional vocabulary:** *ambitieux (-euse), impatient(e), généreux (-euse), indépendant(e), (in)discret/(in)discrète*

**Follow-up**: For listening-comprehension practice, ask sts. to number from 1 to 7 on paper, then indicate whether you are talking about *Michel ou Michèle*. (Write names on board and explain that one is male, the other female.) 1. *Michel est gentil.* 2. *Michel est charmant.* 3. *Michèle est travailleuse.* 4. *Michèle est canadienne.* 5. *Michel est sportif.* 6. *Michel est français.* 7. *Michèle est courageuse.*

**B. Le couple idéal.** Patrice and Patricia are soulmates, alike in every respect. Describe Patricia.

MODÈLE: Patrice est français. → Patricia est française.

1. optimiste
2. intelligent
3. charmant
4. fier
5. sérieux
6. parisien
7. naïf
8. gentil
9. sportif
10. courageux
11. travailleur
12. intellectuel

**Suggestion**: Dictate sentences to sts. at board. Have sts. do transformations at board, with remaining sts. doing them at their seats. If desired, change adjectives as well as subjects to expand ex.

**Follow-up:** *Maintenant l'ordinateur parle de Patrice et Patricia. Qu'est-ce qu'il dit?* MODÈLE: *Patrice est français, Patricia aussi est française.* → *Patrice et Patricia sont français.*

**C. Un couple irréconciliable.** But Fabien and Fabienne are as different as night and day! Describe Fabienne.

Fabien est travailleur, patient, sincère, sérieux, sympathique, raisonnable, intéressant, agréable.

Fabienne n'est pas...

**D. De quelle couleur?** State the colors of the following things.

MODÈLE: le drapeau (*flag*) américain →
Le drapeau américain est rouge, blanc et bleu.

1. le drapeau français
2. la mer (= l'océan)
3. l'éléphant (*m.*)
4. la violette
5. la neige (*snow*)
6. le tigre
7. le zèbre
8. les plantes (*f.*)
9. les fleurs (*f.*)

## *Parlons-en!*

**A. Une lettre.** Here is a letter Stéphane just received from his girlfriend. He is desperate! Transform this letter into the one he would have loved to receive by changing the adjectives and some verbs.

**Suggestion**: Point out the slightly different format for letters. Mention that most personal correspondence is handwritten in France.

Angers, le 7 janvier

Stéphane,

Je te déteste. Tu es stupide et antipathique. Tous les jours (*Every day*) tu es nerveux, tu ne rêves pas parce que tu es peu idéaliste, et tu es même (*even*) souvent hypocrite. En plus (*Furthermore*) je trouve que tu es paresseux.

Je ne veux plus te revoir. (*I never want to see you again.*)

Adieu.

Catherine

**B. Les personnes idéales.** Complete these sentences with appropriate adjectives, according to your opinions.

**Suggestion and Continuation**: Have sts. brainstorm and provide as many completions as possible. This may be done first in groups, or as a whole-class activity. Put sts.' answers on board, or have one st. write on board answers given by classmates. Additional examples: *le/la patron(ne); le/la dentiste; le médecin; le président*.

1. L'homme idéal est _____.
2. La femme idéale est _____.
3. Le/La camarade de classe idéal(e) est _____.
4. Le professeur idéal est _____.
5. Le chauffeur de taxi idéal est _____.

**C. Vive la mode!** Look at the people in the ad on page 52. Describe their clothes, including the colors. (Use the verb **porter**.) Then tell the class which items of clothing you like and which you don't like.

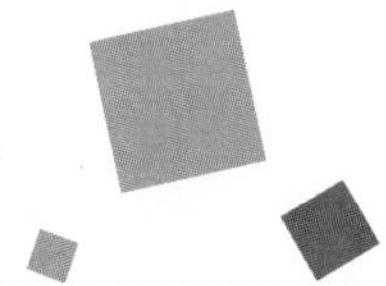

# 7. GETTING INFORMATION
## Yes/No Questions

**Suggestions**: Point out that the French are more animated in discussions than people in the U.S. usually are, often raising their voices and gesticulating vigorously.

### Discussion entre amis

LE TOURISTE: **Est-ce** un accident?
L'AGENT DE POLICE: Non, ce n'est pas un accident.
LE TOURISTE: **Est-ce que** c'est une manifestation?
L'AGENT DE POLICE: Mais, non!
LE TOURISTE: Alors, c'est une dispute?
L'AGENT DE POLICE: Pas vraiment. C'est une discussion animée entre amis.

Voici les réponses. Posez les questions. Elles sont dans le dialogue.

1. Ce n'est pas un accident.
2. Ce n'est pas une manifestation.
3. Ce n'est pas une dispute.

Questions that ask for new information or facts often begin with interrogative words (*who?*, *what?*, and so on). Other questions simply require a *yes* or *no* answer.

**Suggestion**: Model pronunciation of questions in box, having sts. repeat after your model.

## A. Yes/No Questions with No Change in Word Order

**Note:** Make sure sts. understand the difference between yes/no questions and information questions.

Like English, French has more than one type of *yes/no* question.

| | |
|---|---|
| *Statement*: | Vous êtes parisien. |
| *Question with rising intonation*: | Vous êtes parisien? |
| *Tag question with* **n'est-ce pas**: | Vous êtes parisien, **n'est-ce pas**? |
| *Question with* **est-ce que**: | **Est-ce que** vous êtes parisien? |

1. Questions with rising intonation: the pitch of your voice rises at the end of a sentence to create a vocal question mark.

   —Vous ne parlez pas anglais? —*Don't you speak English?*
   —Si,* un peu. —*Yes, a little.*

**Suggestion**: Practice *si* by asking obvious questions: *Vous n'êtes pas américain? Vous n'aimez pas la musique?* etc.

2. Tag questions: when agreement or confirmation is expected, the tag **n'est-ce pas**? is sometimes added to the end of a sentence.†

**Note**: Point out variety of English tags: *Isn't that so? Right? Don't you think?*

*To say *yes* to a negative question, **si** is used, rather than **oui**.
†The question forms are most often used to ask for information. However, when used with present-tense verbs, they may also imply indirect commands; e.g., **Tu étudies ce soir, n'est-ce pas? Tu commences maintenant? Est-ce que tu travailles?** A parent might use these questions to get a child to study.

Il aime la musique, **n'est-ce pas**? — *He loves music, doesn't he?*
Il porte une cravate au concert, **n'est-ce pas**? — *He's wearing a tie to the concert, isn't he?*

3. Questions with **est-ce que**: the statement is preceded by **est-ce que**. This is the easiest and most common way to ask a question in French.

   **Est-ce qu'**elle étudie l'espagnol? — *Is she studying Spanish?*
   **Est-ce qu'**elle arrive après le cours? — *Is she arriving after class?*

   **Est-ce que** is pronounced as one word. Before a vowel, it becomes **est-ce qu'**: **est-ce qu'ils** [ɛskil], **est-ce qu'elles** [ɛskɛl].

**Suggestion**: Mention that although *est-ce que* is the easiest way to form questions, it is not used as much in writing as it is orally.

## B. Yes/No Questions with a Change in Word Order

As in English, questions can be formed in French by inverting the order of subject and verb. However, this syntax creates a rather formal style which is usually confined to written French.

1. Questions with pronoun subjects: the subject pronoun (**ce**, **on**, **il**, and so on) and verb are inverted and hyphenated.

| PRONOUN SUBJECT | |
|---|---|
| *Statement*: | Il est touriste. |
| *Question*: | **Est-il** touriste? |

   Est-ce une dispute? — *Is it a dispute?*
   Aiment-ils les discussions animées? — *Do they like animated discussions?*
   Es-tu d'accord avec nous? — *Do you agree with us?*

   The final **t** of third-person plural verb forms is pronounced when followed by **ils** or **elles**: **aiment-elles**. If a third-person singular verb form ends in a vowel, **-t-** is inserted between the verb and the pronoun.

   **Aime-t-elle** la littérature française? — *Does she like French literature?*
   **Parle-t-on** français ici? — *Is French spoken here?*

   The subject pronoun **je** is seldom inverted. **Est-ce que** is used instead: **Est-ce que je suis en avance** (*early*)?

2. Questions with noun subjects: the third-person pronoun that corresponds to the noun subject follows the verb and is attached to it by a hyphen. The noun subject is retained.

**Note**: You might want to teach inversion with noun subjects for passive recognition only at this point, reentering this type of question formation later in year for active practice.

| NOUN SUBJECT | |
|---|---|
| *Statement*: | Marc est étudiant. |
| | ↓ ↓ |
| *Question*: | **Marc est-il** étudiant? |

Les étudiants français sont-ils travailleurs? — *Are French students hardworking?*

Delphine travaille-t-elle beaucoup? — *Does Delphine work a lot?*

## *Vérifions!*

**A. C'est difficile à croire!** You find it hard to believe what Mireille is telling you about some mutual acquaintances. Express your surprise by turning each statement into a question. (Your intonation should express your disbelief!)

**Suggestion:** In all exs. in this section, encourage sts. to think of other ways to ask same questions. Stress especially easiest ways: rising intonation, tag questions, and *est-ce que*, with inversion using nouns for recognition only at this point.

MODÈLE: Solange est de Paris. → Solange est de Paris?

1. Pascal est aussi de Paris.
2. Solange et Pascal sont parisiens.
3. Roger est le camarade de Pascal.
4. C'est un garçon drôle.
5. Il n'habite pas à Paris.
6. Sandra est canadienne.

Now verify what Mireille has told you by asking someone else. Create questions using **est-ce que**.

MODÈLE: Solange est de Paris. → Est-ce que Solange est de Paris?

**B. Une vaniteuse** (*conceited character*)**.** Laurence n'est pas modeste! Ask rhetorical questions as she would, using the correct adjective forms.

MODÈLE: intelligent → Je suis intelligente, n'est-ce pas?

1. sympathique 2. intéressant 3. gentil 4. sportif

**C. Étudiants à la Sorbonne.** You are writing an article on student life in Paris. Verify the information you have jotted down by expressing your statements as questions.

MODÈLE: Stéphane étudie à la Sorbonne. →
Stéphane étudie-t-il à la Sorbonne?

1. Il est parisien.
2. Vous admirez Stéphane.
3. Stéphane et Carole sont étudiants en philosophie.
4. Ils sont sympa.
5. Carole habite à la cité-u.

## Parlons-en!

**A. Portrait d'un professeur.** Ask your instructor questions about his/her birthplace, personality, tastes, and clothes. Use inversion in your questions.

**Verbes suggérés:** être, aimer, porter, visiter, parler, écouter, habiter, donner, danser, regarder, skier, travailler, étudier...

MODÈLES: Êtes-vous français(e)?
Parlez-vous italien?
Aimez-vous le sport?

Now see if your classmates were listening. Ask a classmate three questions about your instructor.

MODÈLE: VOUS: Est-ce que le professeur parle espagnol?
VOTRE CAMARADE: Non, il/elle ne parle pas espagnol. (*ou* Oui, il/elle parle espagnol.)

**Suggestion (B)**: Bring in other ads for clothing and ask sts. the same kinds of questions. Teach types of fabric by asking sts. which they prefer. A blend = *un mélange*. Ask *C'est un look uniquement français? Quel est le look américain?*

**Follow-up**: Ask sts. to bring in magazine pictures and in small groups describe what people are wearing.

**B. Une publicité.** Look at the following advertisement published in the French magazine *20 ans*, and answer the questions based on it.

1. Est-ce que le cardigan est pour homme ou pour femme?
2. Est-ce que le cardigan est en coton ou en acrylique?
3. Est-ce que le jean pour homme est en coton ou en polyester?
4. Est-ce que la veste est pour homme ou pour femme?
5. Est-ce que les mannequins portent des tennis ou des chaussures?

Maintenant posez des questions générales à un(e) camarade. Utilisez les expressions suivantes: en polyester, en coton, en laine (*wool*), en soie (*silk*), en nylon...

MODÈLE: En général, une cravate est-elle en soie ou en coton?

# 8. MENTIONING A SPECIFIC PLACE OR PERSON The Prepositions *à* and *de*

**Arnaud et Delphine, deux étudiants français typiques**

Ils habitent **à la** cité universitaire.
Ils mangent **au** restaurant universitaire.
Ils jouent **au** volley-ball dans la salle des sports.
Le week-end, ils jouent **aux** cartes avec des amis.
Ils aiment parler **des** professeurs, **de l'**examen d'anglais, **du** cours de littérature française et **de la** vie **à l'**université.

Et vous?

1. Habitez-vous à la cité universitaire?
2. Mangez-vous au restaurant universitaire?
3. Jouez-vous au volley-ball dans la salle des sports?
4. Le week-end, jouez-vous aux cartes?
5. Aimez-vous parler des professeurs? de l'examen de français? du cours de français? de la vie à l'université?

Prepositions (**les prépositions**) are words such as *to, in, under, for,* and so on. In French, they sometimes contract with the following article. The most common French prepositions are **à** and **de**.

## A. Uses of *à* and *de*

1. **À** indicates location or destination. Note that **à** has several English equivalents.

| | |
|---|---|
| Arnaud habite **à** Paris.* | *Arnaud lives in Paris.* |
| Il étudie **à** la bibliothèque. | *He studies at (in) the library.* |
| Ses parents arrivent **à** Paris ce soir. | *His parents are arriving in Paris this evening.* |

**Note**: Articles are not used before names of most cities. Exceptions are *La Nouvelle-Orléans*, *Le Havre*, and *Le Caire*.

With verbs such as **parler**, **donner**, **montrer** (*to show*) and **téléphoner**, **à** introduces the indirect object (usually a person).

| | |
|---|---|
| Arnaud **parle à** un professeur. | *Arnaud is speaking to a professor.* |
| Arnaud **téléphone à** un ami. | *Arnaud is calling a friend.* |
| Il **montre** une photo **à** une camarade. | *He is showing a photo to a friend.* |

**Suggestion:** Urge sts. to learn these verbs that take indirect objects. You may need to explain in more detail what an indirect object is. Using the example "*I gave the ball to Cathy*," ask sts. to point to the direct and indirect objects. Point out that *à + name of person* is the sign for the indirect object in French.

*The preposition **à** expresses location primarily with names of cities. Prepositions used with names of countries are treated in Grammar Section 27.

The preposition *to* is not always used in English, but **à** must be used in French with these verbs.

2. **De** indicates where something or someone comes from.

| | |
|---|---|
| Medhi est **de** Casablanca. | *Medhi is from Casablanca.* |
| Il arrive **de** la bibliothèque. | *He is coming from the library.* |

**De** also indicates possession (expressed by *'s* or *of* in English) and the concept of belonging to, being a part of.

| | |
|---|---|
| Voici la librairie **de** Madame Vernier. | *Here is Madame Vernier's bookstore.* |
| J'aime mieux la librairie **de** l'université. | *I prefer the university bookstore (the bookstore of the university).* |

When used with **parler**, **de** means *about.*

| | |
|---|---|
| Nous parlons **de** la littérature anglaise avec Madame Vernier. | *We're talking about English literature with Madame Vernier.* |

## B. Contractions of *à* and *de* with the Definite Articles *le* and *les*

**Note**: Point out to sts. the pronunciation of *aux* before a consonant and before a vowel (*aux courts de tennis / aux amis*).

| | | | |
|---|---|---|---|
| **à + le = au** | Arnaud arrive **au** cinéma. | **de + le = du** | Arnaud arrive **du** cinéma. |
| **à + les = aux** | Arnaud arrive **aux** courts de tennis. | **de + les = des** | Arnaud arrive **des** courts de tennis. |
| **à + la = à la** | Arnaud arrive **à la** librairie. | **de + la = de la** | Arnaud arrive **de la** librairie. |
| **à + l' = à l'** | Arnaud arrive **à l'**université. | **de + l' = de l'** | Arnaud arrive **de l'**université. |

## C. The Verb *jouer* (*to play*) with the Prepositions *à* and *de*

Martine **joue au tennis.**

Philippe **joue du piano.**

When **jouer** is followed by the preposition **à**, it means *to play* a sport or game. When it is followed by **de**, it means *to play* a musical instrument.

## *Vérifions!*

**A. Camille, une personne très active.** Adapt the following sentences.

1. Camille parle *à la jeune fille*. (touristes, chien, femme)
2. Elle parle *du Café Flore*. (cours de français, musique zydeco, sports français)
3. Camille arrive *de New York*. (bibliothèque, cours d'anglais, restaurant universitaire)
4. Elle aime jouer *au golf*. (le rugby, le violon, la guitare, le hockey, les échecs [*chess*])

**Suggestion**: Do as rapid response drill. Alternatively, dictate sentences to sts. at board (with other sts. writing at their seats) and have sts. do transformations in writing, with group repetition as needed.

**Continuation:** *Camille joue au volley-ball* (*le basket-ball*, *les cartes*, *le tennis*, *le football*). *Elle joue de la guitare* (*le piano*, *la clarinette*, *l'accordéon*, *la flûte*).

**B. Où va-t-on** (*Where do we go*)**?** Answer using the model as a guide.

MODÈLE: Pour écouter une symphonie? → le concert
On va au concert.

| | |
|---|---|
| 1. Pour regarder un film? | l'amphithéâtre |
| 2. Pour jouer au tennis? | la discothèque |
| 3. Pour jouer au volley-ball? | le Quartier latin |
| 4. Pour écouter le professeur? | le cinéma |
| 5. Pour danser? | le café |
| 6. Pour manger? | les courts de tennis |
| 7. Pour visiter la Sorbonne? | la salle de sports |
| 8. Pour parler avec des amis? | le restaurant universitaire |
| | la maison |

**Follow-up**: Draw a simple campus map with locations in the ex. depicted on it. Using the map handout, ask questions such as the following: *Où est la salle de sports? Où est le cinéma?* Ask sts. to give several answers, according to the locations depicted on the map. Sts. will use *à côté de*, *devant*, *derrière*, *près de*, etc. Point out to them that the final *de* in compound prepositions contracts with *le* and *les*.

**C. Les passe-temps.** Complete the following sentences with the verb **jouer à** or **de**. Match the players with the sports or instruments they play.

MODÈLE: Dan Marino → Dan Marino joue au football.

| | |
|---|---|
| 1. Wynton Marsalis | a. le violon |
| 2. Jennifer Capriati | b. le hockey |
| 3. Bruce Springsteen | c. les échecs |
| 4. Midori | d. la trompette |
| 5. Shaquille O'Neal et Christian Laettner | e. le tennis |
| 6. Wayne Gretzky | f. le basket-ball |
| 7. Bobby Fischer | g. la guitare |
| 8. ? | h. ? |

**Suggestion**: See who can find the most names in the shortest time. Show sts. how to prepare a form with activities listed vertically on the left, with plenty of room for names next to each.

## *Parlons-en!*

**A. Trouvez quelqu'un qui...** Find someone in the classroom who does each of the following activities. On a separate piece of paper, note down his or her name next to the activity. See who can complete the list the fastest.

MODÈLE: VOUS: Est-ce que tu joues au tennis?
UN(E) CAMARADE: Oui, je joue au tennis. (*ou* Non, je ne joue pas au tennis.)

jouer de la guitare
jouer au poker
jouer au base-ball
jouer au volley
jouer au bridge
jouer au tennis
aimer les films français
manger à la cafétéria aujourd'hui
aimer le laboratoire de langues
jouer aux cartes

## Mots-clés

*Linking words:* When you first begin to study French, you may think you can speak only in very simple sentences. The following words will help you form more interesting and complicated sentences by linking ideas.

| | | | |
|---|---|---|---|
| **et** | *and* | **mais** | *but* |
| **aussi** | *also* | **si** | *if* |
| **ou** | *or* | **donc** | *therefore* |
| **parce que** | *because* | **alors** | *so* |

Note the different impression linking words make in the following sentences.

- Ma cousine étudie l'espagnol. J'étudie le français. →
  Ma cousine étudie l'espagnol **mais** (**et**) j'étudie le français.
- Je n'aime pas danser. Je ne danse pas ce (*this*) week-end. →
  Je n'aime pas danser, **donc** je ne danse pas ce week-end.
- Je ne suis pas riche. J'achète mes vêtements dans les friperies. →
  Je ne suis pas riche, **alors** j'achète mes vêtements dans les friperies.
- Je ne sais pas (*I don't know*) **si** le professeur aime danser.

**Suggestion**: Provide list of simple sentences for sts. to link several times, to build writing skills. *Example: J'étudie le français. Je parle bien français.* (et) / *J'aime regarder les films. Je n'aime pas aller au cinéma.* (mais) / *Les étudiants aiment bien manger. Ils n'aiment pas la cafétéria sur le campus.* (mais or donc)

**B. Jeu de logique.** Complete the following thoughts logically using a linking word from the **Mots-clés**.

1. Anne est une personne sérieuse et raisonnable _____ elle aime beaucoup les films comiques.
2. Daniel, par contre, est drôle _____ excentrique.
3. Je me demande (*wonder*) _____ Daniel est artiste.
4. Moi, je suis idéaliste, _____ je travaille pour une organisation écologiste.
5. Travaillez-vous _____ vous aimez travailler ou simplement pour gagner de l'argent (*to earn money*)?
6. Êtes-vous sociable _____ préférez-vous des activités solitaires?

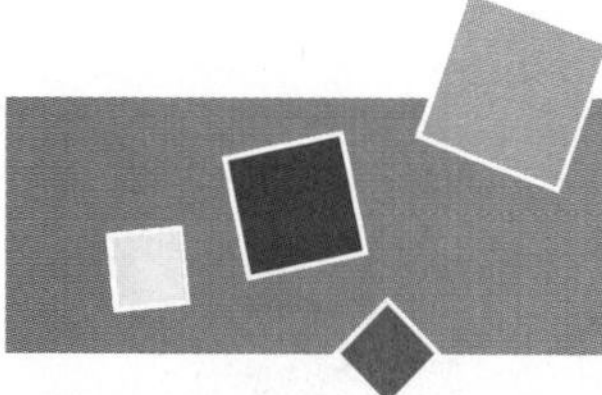

# Étude de prononciation

## French Vowel Sounds: Nasal Vowels

When the letter **n** or **m** follows a vowel or a combination of vowels, it frequently affects the pronunciation of the vowel, giving it a nasal quality. Such vowels are called nasals. The **n** or **m** itself is not pronounced.

Prononcez avec le professeur.

| | IPA SYMBOL | MOST COMMON SPELLINGS |
|---|---|---|
| 1. amphithéâtre employer plan attendez français centre | [ɑ̃] | an am en em |
| 2. onze oncle combien bonjour bon nombre | [ɔ̃] | on om |
| 3. impatient intéressant synthèse sympathique peintre pain faim | [ɛ̃] | im in yn ym ein ain aim |

Note that the vowel is not nasal if the **n** or **m** is followed by a vowel. The **n** or **m** is then pronounced: **banane**, **fine**. The same is true if the **n** or **m** is doubled and then followed by a vowel: **comme**, **Anne**.

Prononcez avec le professeur.

1. un / une
2. dans / Anne
3. Italien / Italienne
4. brun / brune
5. Américain / Américaine
6. fin / fine

**Summary**: The *Étude de prononciation* section presents guidelines for and examples of French pronunciation. The feature appears through Chapter 7.

**Note:** Since [œ̃] is disappearing in modern spoken French, no longer functionally distinguishable from [ɛ̃], we have reduced nasal vowel sounds to three. You may want to reinstate [œ̃], using the words *brun*, *humble*, *opportun*, and *un* as examples.

**Follow-up:** Put the phrase *un bon vin blanc* on the board. Have sts. practice it along with the following words: *oncle*, *employer*, *sympathique*, *américain*, *onze*, *bonjour*, *centre*, *plan*.

**Additional activity**: Have sts. indicate if the vowel is nasalized, by writing *oui* or *non* after each item. 1. *an* 2. *Anne* 3. *bon* 4. *bonne* 5. *une* 6. *un* 7. *fine* 8. *fin* 9. *dune* 10. *dans* 11. *invisible* 12. *inimitable*

# Mise au point

**A. Description: la vie de Martine.** Create complete sentences.

1. Martine / être / étudiante / sérieux / et intéressant
2. elle / habiter / à côté de / bibliothèque
3. elle / jouer / piano
4. nous / jouer / cartes / Martine
5. aujourd'hui / elle / porter / sandales / marron / et / jean / noir
6. chemises / Martine / être / blanc
7. ce / être / jeune fille / simple / mais / excentrique

**Summary**: The *Mise au point* section reviews chapter grammar and vocabulary.

**B. Portraits.** Based on each of the statements in the left-hand column below, create two new sentences using the corresponding adjectives and places.

**Suggestion**: Ask sts. to find as many adjectives as possible in the ad below.

MODÈLE: Nous jouons aux cartes. → Nous sommes calmes et sociables.
→ Nous sommes au café.

| | LES ADJECTIFS | | LES ENDROITS | |
|---|---|---|---|---|
| 1. Nous aimons parler avec des amis. | individualiste | calme | Paris | courts de tennis |
| 2. Elles étudient beaucoup. | sérieux | drôle | café | amphithéâtre |
| 3. Nous dansons beaucoup. | travailleur | fort | cinéma | le Quartier latin |
| 4. Odile est Parisienne. | sportif | excentrique | bibliothèque | |
| 5. Yannick joue au tennis. | idéaliste | à la mode | discothèque | |
| 6. Elles aiment les Talking Heads. | sociable | | maison | |

**C. Le secret des prénoms.** This section from the French magazine *Star club* links people's personalities to their first names. Scan what is said about the name *Manuel*, then complete the following sentences correctly.

**Follow-up**: Use the passage as a model for written homework, and ask sts. to write a simple short description of their first name.

According to the excerpt . . .

1. Men called Manuel have no imagination / a lot of imagination / a little imagination.
2. They have two personalities / no personality / a lot of personality.
3. Their color is pink / red / green.

**LE SECRET DES PRÉNOMS**

**MANUEL**

L'imagination joue un très grand[a] rôle chez ces[b] garçons. Chez eux, on constate souvent une double personnalité : l'une capable d'idées remarquables, et une autre,[c] capable de les mettre en pratique, ce qui est assez rare.[d] Ils peuvent être difficiles à vivre[e] car[f] on ne sait pas toujours à quelle facette[g] de sa personnalité on a affaire.
Couleur : rouge.

[a]chez... *with them*
[b]on... *you notice*
[c]capable... *able to carry them out*
[d]peuvent... *can be hard to live with*
[e]*because*
[f]on... *you don't know*
[g]on... *you're dealing with*

**D. Qui est-ce?** Describe a classmate. The rest of the class guesses who it is.

MODÈLE: Il aime la musique et le tennis, il étudie l'allemand et le français et il n'aime pas danser. Il est de Cincinnati et il habite à la cité universitaire. Il est intelligent, sympathique et sportif. Il porte un pull-over et un jean. Qui est-ce? Son prénom commence par (*with*) M.

# Interactions

**Summary**: *Interactions* is a role-playing activity based on the themes, vocabulary, and grammar presented in the chapter. Sts. can prepare their roles at home, or improvise in class along with other sts.

In Chapter 3, you learned how to ask questions, describe people and things, identify people and things, and talk about where they are. Act out the following situations, using the vocabulary and structures from this chapter.

1. **Journaliste.** You are a reporter for the school newspaper. A classmate plays the role of a visiting celebrity. Find out everything you can about this classmate: likes and dislikes; where she or he likes to go, some personality characteristics.
2. **Emprunt** (*A loan*). Imagine that someone in the class borrowed your French book but you have forgotten his or her name. Describe what he or she was wearing to another classmate, who will try to name the student.

**Suggestion**: Ask several groups to play their roles for the class or have a reporter describe the situations to the whole class.

**Follow-up:** Provide another role-play situation. Using clothing and color vocabulary, sts. can imagine that they are buying clothes in a store.

# Rencontres

## LECTURE

### Avant de lire

**Summary**: *Rencontres* includes a reading selection (*Lecture*) preceded by a pre-reading section (*Avant de lire*), a guided writing feature (*Par écrit*), and a listening comprehension section (*À l'écoute!*).

**Summary**: *Avant de lire*, which introduces each reading selection in *Rendez-vous*, presents reading strategies and techniques designed to help sts. approach written texts with greater confidence, and to acquire the skills necessary to read a foreign language quickly and efficiently. Each *Avant de lire* presents a specific strategy followed by a brief "warm-up" exercise or task which prepares sts. for the reading to follow. These pre-reading exercises may be done in class or individually by sts. at home.

**Recognizing cognates.** You already know that cognates are words similar in form and meaning in two or more languages. The more cognates you recognize, the more quickly and easily you will read French. It will help you to be aware that the endings of many French words correspond to certain English word endings. Here are a few of the most common.

| FRENCH | ENGLISH |
|---|---|
| **-ment** | *-ly* |
| **-iste** | *-ist* |
| **-eux** | *-ous* |
| **-ion** | *-ion* |
| **-ie, -é** | *-y* |
| **-ique** | *-ical* or *-ic* |

What are the English equivalents of the following words?

1. la caractéristique
2. l'unité
3. la transformation
4. la théorie
5. politique
6. typiquement
7. écologiste
8. courageux

**Note:** Instructors are urged to go over the *Avant de lire* section carefully with sts. before assigning reading, which may best be done silently in class. Doing reading during class encourages sts. to read more rapidly, avoiding constant recourse to dictionary. Have sts. talk about their reading strategies and share those strategies that are most successful.

In the following passage, you will also come across a number of examples of **franglais**, English words used in French. Before reading, scan the passage and make two lists, one of the cognates and another of the English words used in French. Remember that in this and subsequent readings, guessable cognates are not glossed. Here, unfamiliar terms that you should be able to guess from context have been underlined.

## À bas la mode et vive le look!

Le chic d'Yves Saint-Laurent ou de Pierre Cardin n'intéresse pas les jeunes Français. La mode, pour eux,° c'est le «look». Quelle est la différence? Le look exprime° des idées personnelles. Les ancêtres du look sont les Hippies de '68. Pour ces° groupes de jeunes le style de vie et les vêtements sont des messages. La jeunesse française d'aujourd'hui est divisée en groupes d'intérêts et d'opinions divers. Chaque groupe a° un code, un langage, un look.

*eux: them*
*exprime: expresses*
*ces: these*
*a: has*

Les punks

Le look: blouson en cuir,° cheveux décolorés° en crête,° lunettes° noires, chaîne de vélo°

Les idées: nihilistes, anarchistes

Les passions: la laideur° calculée, l'agressivité, la provocation

La musique: U2, The Cure, la musique alternative

*leather / bleached*

*en... spiked / glasses / motorbike*

*ugliness*

Les BCBG (bon chic, bon genre)

Le look: britannique, les mocassins, les foulards° Hermès

Les idées: bourgeoises, droite° libérale

Les passions: les grands couturiers,° le bridge, le golf, le tennis

La musique: Madonna, George Michaël

*scarves*

*right (wing)*

*big-name designers*

**Summary**: *Lecture* is the reading selection that appears in every chapter of *Rendez-vous* except for Chapters 1 and 18. (Chapter 18 is entirely devoted to thematic readings and contains several selections.) Many of the readings are drawn from authentic contemporary sources; some are author-written, and others are literary. Each selection is thematically connected to the chapter topic or topics; author-written readings recycle the active vocabulary presented and practiced in the chapter. Unfamiliar words and expressions are glossed in the margin. The reading selections follow a progression, through the chapters, from simple "beginner-level" texts to increasingly challenging texts, as sts. expand their vocabulary and gain greater familiarity with complex grammatical and syntactic structures. Each reading selection is followed by a *Compréhension* exercise to verify and expand upon sts. understanding of the text.

Les branchés

Le look: le jean, le T-shirt

Les idées: américanophiles

Les passions: les États-Unis, le Coca-Cola, les jeeps, le disco

La musique: Bruce Springsteen, Sting, R.E.M.

## Compréhension

Correct any of the following sentences that are wrong.

1. Les jeunes Français adorent la mode chic.
2. La mode chic exprime des idées personnelles.
3. Les ancêtres du look sont Yves Saint-Laurent et Pierre Cardin.
4. La jeunesse française est unifiée.
5. Le look des BCBG est américain.
6. Les branchés sont agressifs.
7. Les punks aiment la musique alternative.

**Follow-up**: Bring in fashion magazines and have sts. give a category for the styles. Discuss the importance of *la mode* in France and the United States.

## PAR ÉCRIT

**Function:** Describing (a person)
**Audience:** Your instructor and classmates
**Goal:** To describe someone in class using the model below.

PARAGRAPHE 1
Julie est une rockeuse. Elle habite à Los Angeles. C'est une jeune fille excentrique mais intéressante. Elle aime parler de musique et de discothèques. Elle n'aime pas parler de cours universitaires. En général, elle porte un pull-over noir, un jean et des chaussettes blanches.

PARAGRAPHE 2
Julie admire R.E.M., The Christians et Guns'n Roses. Elle déteste Madonna. Elle adore danser et écouter la radio. Elle est sociable et optimiste. C'est une personne dynamique.

**Summary**: *Par écrit* takes a step-by-step approach to writing and aims to develop sts.' writing skills by guiding them through a series of clear, cumulative tasks. See the *Instructor's Manual* for hints on group editing.

### Steps

1. Make a list of questions to ask a classmate so that you can gather the same kind of information as is given in the paragraphs above. For example: **Tu habites à Cincinnati? Tu es idéaliste ou réaliste? Tu aimes la musique? Quelle** (*What*) **musique? Tu portes souvent un jean?**
2. As you interview your classmate, jot down the answers in abbreviated form.
3. Next, circle the details you will use to write your composition. Using the model as a guide, write the composition, rounding out the details and adding descriptive information wherever possible. Try to adapt the description to your own writing style.
4. Reread the paragraphs for smoothness and clarity. Rewrite them if they seem unorganized, unfocused, or choppy. Finally, reread the composition, checking for adjective agreement and proper use of the articles **à** and **de**.
5. Be prepared to read your description to your classmates.

**Summary**: *À l'écoute!* is a listening comprehension section consisting of one or two passages, with follow-up activities, recorded on the audiocassette packaged with the student text. Sts. can listen to the tape and do the activities at home, or you may wish to play selected listening comprehension passages in class and have sts. do the activities together. It is recommended in any case that you do the *À l'écoute!* section with students for the first few chapters to be sure that they know how to work with the material. Be sure to let students know that they will not understand every word they hear in the listening comprehension passages, as in real life. They should focus globally on the general information in the passages and not be overly concerned about what they do not understand. Scripts of the recorded material appear at the back of the Instructor's Edition. Answers to the listening comprehension activities appear at the back of both the student text and the Instructor's Edition.

## À L'ÉCOUTE!

**Mon meilleur copain.** Guillaume is talking about his best friend, Patrice. First, look through the activities. Next, listen to the vocabulary and Guillaume's description of Patrice. Then, do the activities. Replay the tape as often as you need to. (See Appendix F for answers.)

VOCABULAIRE UTILE

**vachement** *very* (*slang*)
**cuir** *leather*

**A.** Based on Guillaume's description, circle the drawing of Patrice.

**B.** Now choose the correct answer, based on the description of Patrice.

1. Patrice habite
   a. à Lyon b. à Nice
2. Patrice étudie
   a. l'anglais b. l'espagnol
3. Patrice adore
   a. la musique classique b. le rock
4. Il joue
   a. du piano b. de la guitare
5. Patrice est
   a. intelligent mais un peu paresseux
   b. très intellectuel
6. Patrice porte toujours
   a. un jean et un blouson noir
   b. un costume gris

**Summary**: *Vocabulaire* contains chapter words and expressions considered *active*. These are the words and expressions sts. should incorporate into their working vocabulary and be expected to know. Active vocabulary items have been introduced in the following chapter sections:

- Étude de vocabulaire
- Mots-clés
- Grammar paradigms, verb charts, and example sentences from the grammar sections
- Occasionally, from functional minidialogues that begin grammar sections

The vocabulary list is divided into parts of speech (*Verbes*, *Substantifs*, etc.), *Mots et expressions divers*, and, occasionally, thematic categories (*Expressions avec avoir*, *Expressions interrogatives*, etc.). Words and expressions within each sub-grouping are organized alphabetically.

# Vocabulaire

## Verbes

**arriver** to arrive
**être** to be
**jouer à** to play (*a sport or game*)
**jouer de** to play (*a musical instrument*)
**montrer** to show
**porter** to wear; to carry
**téléphoner à** to telephone

À REVOIR: **regarder, travailler**

## Substantifs

**les cartes** (*f.*) cards
**les échecs** (*m.*) chess
**la jeune fille** girl, young lady
**le jeune homme** young man
**la personne** person
**la voiture** automobile

À REVOIR: **l'ami(e), la bibliothèque, la femme, l'homme, l'université**

## Adjectifs

**beau/belle** beautiful
**cher/chère** expensive
**drôle** funny, odd
**facile** easy
**fier/fière** proud
**gentil(le)** nice, pleasant
**nouveau/nouvelle** new
**paresseux/euse** lazy
**prêt(e)** ready
**sportif/ive** *describes someone who likes physical exercise and sports*
**sympa(thique)** nice
**travailleur/euse** hardworking

À REVOIR: **espagnol(e), français(e), italien(ne)**

## Adjectifs apparentés

**amusant(e), calme, courageux/euse, conformiste, (dés)agréable, différent(e), difficile, dynamique, enthousiaste, excentrique, idéaliste, (im)patient(e), important(e), individualiste, (in)sociable, intellectuel(le), intelligent(e), intéressant(e), naïf/naïve, nerveux/euse, optimiste, parisien(ne), pessimiste, raisonnable, réaliste, sérieux/euse, sincère, snob**

## Prépositions

**à côté de** beside, next to
**derrière** behind
**devant** in front of
**sous** under
**sur** on, on top of

## Les vêtements

**le blouson** windbreaker
**les bottes** (*f.*) boots
**la casquette** French cap
**le chapeau** hat
**les chaussettes** (*f.*) socks
**les chaussures** (*f.*) shoes
**la chemise** shirt
**le chemisier** blouse
**le costume** (*man's*) suit
**la cravate** tie
**l'imperméable** (*m.*) raincoat
**le jean** jeans
**la jupe** skirt
**le maillot de bain** swimsuit
**le manteau** coat
**le pantalon** pants
**le pull-over** sweater
**la robe** dress
**le sac à dos** backpack
**le sac à main** handbag
**les sandales** (*f.*) sandals
**le short** shorts
**le tailleur** woman's suit
**le tee-shirt** T-shirt
**les tennis** (*f.*) tennis shoes
**la veste** sports coat or blazer
**le veston** suit jacket

## Les couleurs

**blanc(he)** white
**bleu(e)** blue
**gris(e)** gray
**jaune** yellow
**marron** (*inv.*) brown
**noir(e)** black
**orange** (*inv.*) orange
**rose** pink
**rouge** red
**vert(e)** green
**violet(te)** violet

## Mots et expressions divers

**alors** so
**assez** somewhat
**aussi** also
**donc** therefore
**eh bien,...** well, . . . (well, then)
**où** where
**par terre** on the ground
**parce que** because
**peu** not very; hardly
**un peu** a little
**quand** when
**qui... ?** who (whom) . . . ?
**si** if
**très** very

# Intermède

## SITUATION

### Au restau-u

**Contexte** *Nous sommes dans un restaurant universitaire d'Aix-en-Provence. Patricia, une étudiante américaine, trouve une place° à la table de Régis.*

**Objectif** *Patricia fait connaissance avec° des étudiants français et francophones.*

RÉGIS: Bonjour! Comment t'appelles-tu?°
PATRICIA: Je m'appelle Patricia. Et toi°?
RÉGIS: Moi, c'est° Régis. Je suis nul en anglais° mais je suis un génie en musique... Voilà Médoune. C'est un pianiste. Il est de Dakar.
PATRICIA: Bonjour, Médoune.
RÉGIS: Et voici Christine. Elle est de Genève et joue très bien au tennis.
PATRICIA: Salut, Christine.
CHRISTINE: Salut. Et toi, Patricia, tu es d'où?

**Note:** Have sts. act out dialogue with appropriate gestures. This *Situation* illustrates informal greeting behavior and accompanying social amenities, with which sts. at the *Novice* and *Intermediate Levels* of oral proficiency should be familiar.

seat

fait... *meets*

Comment... *What's your name?*

*you*

Moi... *Me, I'm* / Je... *I'm very bad at English*

**Summary**: *Intermède* is an optional section intended to acquaint students with language expressing and describing "real-life" situations in French. *Situation* is a natural-sounding dialogue recorded on the audiocassette packaged with the student text. It is followed by a selection of highly functional words and expressions (*À propos*) appropriate for use in an actual encounter or situation. *Situation* and *À propos* are followed by a brief set of personalized questions (*Maintenant à vous!*) addressed directly to the student, and sometimes by a simple role-playing activity (*Jeu de rôles*). *Intermède* concludes with *Portraits*, brief notes about prominent figures of the French-speaking world.
**Note**: All new vocabulary used in the *Intermède* section is glossed. It is not included in chapter vocabulary lists, and not meant for active learning.
**Summary**: *Situation* consists of functional dialogue with follow-up activities. The dialogue is recorded on the cassette tape accompanying students' textbooks.
**Note**: Have students act out dialogue with appropriate gestures. This *Situation* illustrates informal greeting behavior and accompanying social amenities, with which sts. at the *Novice* and *Intermediate Levels* of oral proficiency should be familiar.
**Summary**: *À propos* presents expressions for communicative use in everyday situations.

## À propos

### Comment présenter quelqu'un

**Presentation**: Model pronunciation of these expressions. Have sts. play roles with classmates.

DANS UNE SITUATION INFORMELLE

| **Les présentations** | **Les réponses** |
|---|---|
| Voici Jim. *This is Jim.* | Salut. Bonjour. *Hello.* |
| Ça, c'est Jim. *This is Jim.* | Enchanté(e). *Delighted to meet you.* |
| Je te présente Jim. *I'd like you to meet Jim.* | Très heureux/euse. *Glad to meet you.* |

DANS UNE SITUATION FORMELLE

| **Les présentations** | **Les réponses** |
|---|---|
| Je vous présente Jim Becker. *I would like you to meet Jim Becker.* | Bonjour. *Hello.* |
| | Enchanté(e). *Delighted to meet you.* |
| | Très heureux/euse de faire votre connaissance. *Very happy to make your acquaintance.* |

**Follow-up**: Have sts. imagine that they are introducing the president of the university to the French professor, to a classmate, to their parents.

## *Maintenant à vous!*

**A. Questions personnelles.** Reread the **Situation** dialogue and then answer the following questions.

1. Régis est un génie en musique. Et vous? Préférez-vous les arts? le sport? la mode? les langues étrangères? autre chose?
2. D'où êtes-vous? Habitez-vous une grande ville ou une petite (*small*) ville? En général, aimez-vous les grandes villes ou préférez-vous habiter à la campagne (*in the country*)?
3. De quelle nationalité êtes-vous? D'où sont vos grands-parents? Aimez-vous voyager (*to travel*)? Où aimez-vous voyager?

**B. Jeu de rôles.** Use the expressions in the **Situation** dialogue and **À propos** to play a brief scene with two or three other students. Introduce yourselves (and one another); then tell where you come from, and describe what you are good at or enjoy doing.

## PORTRAITS

### *Coco Chanel (1883–1971)*

Internationally renowned clothing designer Gabrielle (Coco) Chanel revolutionized the fashion industry with her simple, elegant, tailored garments that stressed comfort over showy embellishment. Chanel reigned supreme in the world of Parisian haute couture for nearly sixty years, and established the successful fashion house which still bears her name.

**Summary**: *Portraits* consists of brief notes about prominent figures—painters, designers, writers, scientists, etc.—of the French-speaking world. The short descriptive biographies are accompanied by photos or drawings of the subjects and, where applicable, photos of their works.

CHAPITRE **QUATRE**

# Le logement

**En avant**

—Il est chouette ton studio!

—Oui, il est tout petit, mais il est à moi!

**En avant**: See scripts for follow-up questions recorded on student cassette.

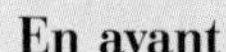

**Communicative goals:** describing lodgings and people; expressing the date; expressing actions, possession, and sensations; expressing the absence of something; and getting information.

# Étude de vocabulaire

## Deux chambres d'étudiants

La chambre d'Agnès est en ordre. Agnès habite dans une maison.

La chambre de Céline est en désordre. Céline habite dans un appartement.

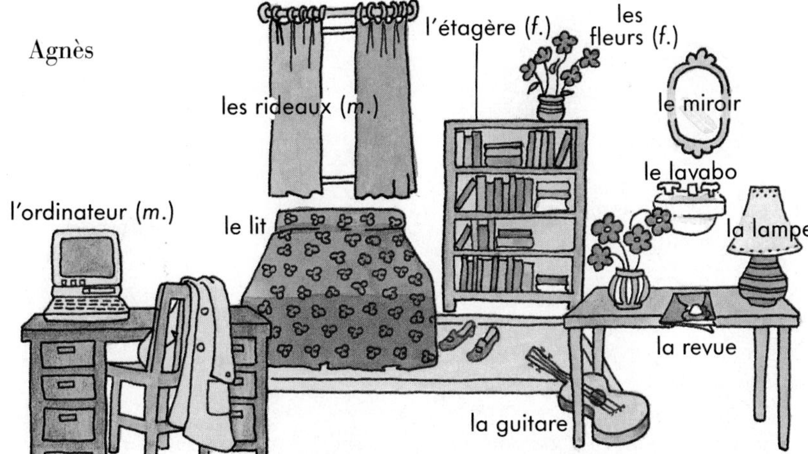

**Suggestions:** (1) Model pronunciation, reinforcing with group and individual work. (2) Have sts. name object(s) that (a) can be held in the hand; (b) make noise; (c) one can sit on; (d) are for studying; (e) are decorative. (3) *Devinettes*: Indicate objects by describing their location: *Elle est sur la table.* Sts. identify: *C'est la revue*. Note that clothing vocabulary can be reentered here. (4) Have sts. give names for visuals you bring in of objects in the room.

***Autres mots utiles:***

**la cassette** cassette tape
**le lecteur de cassettes** cassette deck
**la platine laser** (*ou* **le lecteur de CD**) CD player

**A. Deux chambres**. Describe the two rooms by answering the questions. **Qu'est-ce qu'il y a...**

1. sur le bureau d'Agnès? de Céline?
2. à côté du lit d'Agnès? de Céline?
3. sous la table d'Agnès? de Céline?
4. sur le lit d'Agnès? de Céline?
5. sur l'étagère d'Agnès? de Céline?
6. sous le bureau de Céline?
7. à côté de la radio de Céline?
8. sur le mur d'Agnès? de Céline?
9. par terre (*on the ground*) dans la chambre de Céline?
10. sur la table de Céline?
11. à côté de l'étagère d'Agnès?
12. sur le tapis d'Agnès? de Céline?
13. derrière les étagères d'Agnès et de Céline?

**Follow-up:** Have sts. create a *devinette* as in oral activity described in previous marginal note.

**Additional activity:** *Quels objets dans les chambres d'Agnès et de Céline associez-vous avec les mots suivants?* 1. *Jacques Brel* 2. *Paris-Match* 3. *la fenêtre* 4. *les livres* 5. *la rose* 6. *les murs* 7. *une définition* 8. *Calvin Klein*

**B. L'intrus**. Three items are similar and one is different in each of the following series. Find the items that are out of place.

1. lit / commode / armoire / fleur
2. chaîne stéréo / affiche / guitare / disque
3. lavabo / livre / revue / étagère
4. miroir / affiche / rideaux / revue

**Suggestion:** Do as a listening activity, with sts. writing down the *intrus* as they hear it.

**Follow-up:** Have sts. add another word to each category. Sts. can explain their choices in English. Possibilities: 1. *étagère,* 2. *radio,* 3. *dictionnaire,* 4. *téléphone.*

**C. Préférences**. What do you find in the room of a person who likes the following activities or pursuits?

1. étudier 2. écouter de la musique 3. parler à des amis 4. le sport 5. la mode 6. le cinéma

**Suggestions:** (1) Ask several sts. to give a different answer for each question until possibilities are exhausted. (2) Could be done in pairs or small groups.

**D. La chambre et la personnalité**. A room reveals the personality of its occupant. Describe this room. What does it contain? Which adjectives best describe it (**en ordre**, **en désordre**, **confortable**, **calme**, **simple**...)? Provide as many details as possible about the furniture, objects, colors, and so on.

Then decide...

1. Qui habite cette chambre—un homme? une femme?
2. Quelles sont les préférences de cette personne?
3. D'après vous, comment est la personne qui habite cette chambre? Utilisez trois adjectifs pour décrire sa personnalité.

Il/Elle est _____, _____ et _____.

Now describe your own room, providing as many details as possible. In your opinion, which objects in the room reveal your personality?

**Follow-up:** (1) Use st.-written descriptions for listening comprehension or dictation ex. (2) Call on sts. to remember facts about other sts.' rooms.

## Un peu d'argot

| | |
|---|---|
| **un appart** | un appartement |
| **une piaule** | une chambre |
| **un pieu** | un lit |

EN CONTEXTE

JULIEN: J'habite **un appart** super dans le Quartier latin.

VIRGINIE: Oh, c'est bien. Moi j'ai seulement une petite **piaule**, et mon **pieu** est très dur!

**Note**: *Piaule* and *pieu* have a somewhat negative connotation. They are used mostly by young people and convey something like a place to "crash". Teenagers might also use these terms to talk about their bedrooms while they still live at home. In this case the teenagers' intent would be to show their detachment from the house or family.

**Additional vocabulary:** *âgé(e), jeune, une moustache, une barbe*

## Les amis d'Agnès et de Céline

Lise est grande, belle et dynamique. Elle a (*has*) les yeux verts et les cheveux blonds. (Elle est blonde.)

Déo a les cheveux noirs. Il est beau et charmant. Il est de taille moyenne (*medium height*).

Chantal est aussi de taille moyenne. Elle a les yeux marron et les cheveux courts et roux. (Elle est rousse [*redheaded*].)

Jacques est très sportif. Il est grand, il a les cheveux longs, châtains (*light brown*)* et en désordre.

Thu est très petite et intelligente. Elle a les cheveux noirs et raides.

**Follow-up:** Put four drawings or pictures of people on board, giving each a name. Read a brief description using vocabulary words and have sts. indicate whom you are describing.

**A. Erreur!** Correct any sentences that are wrong.

MODÈLE: Déo a les cheveux châtains. → Mais non, il a les cheveux noirs.

1. Jacques a les cheveux courts. 2. Chantal a les cheveux longs et châtains. 3. Thu a les cheveux noirs. 4. Chantal a les yeux noirs. 5. Lise a les cheveux roux. 6. Déo est très grand. 7. Lise est de taille moyenne. 8. Thu est petite. 9. Déo et Lise sont laids (*ugly*). 10. Chantal est blonde et Lise est rousse.

**Continuation (A)**: Have sts. make up similar short descriptions of people in any visuals you have used in vocabulary presentation.

**B. Personnalités célèbres.** What color hair do the following people have?

MODÈLE: Steve Martin → Steve Martin? Il a les cheveux blancs.

1. Madonna 2. Eddie Murphy 3. Annie, la petite orpheline 4. ?

**Continuation (B)**: Ask sts. to supply more names.

**Follow-up:** Write brief descriptions of some people in Ex. B. Sts. will indicate whom you are describing. Examples: 1. *Il est très amusant. Il est de taille moyenne. C'est un acteur célèbre.* 2. *Elle est rousse. Elle est pauvre, petite et jeune.* 3. *Elle est de taille moyenne. Elle a les cheveux blonds. C'est une actrice.*

---

*literally, *chestnut*; invariable in gender

**C. Et vos camarades de classe?** Describe the hair, eyes, and height of someone in the classroom. Your classmates will guess who it is. (If they have trouble guessing, describe what the person is wearing!)

MODÈLE: Il/Elle a les cheveux longs et noirs, il/elle a les yeux marron et il/elle est de taille moyenne.

Now describe yourself.

MODÈLE: J'ai (*I have*)...
Je suis...

## Quelle est la date d'aujourd'hui?

**Presentation:** Have sts. repeat names of months. You may want to introduce names of seasons at this time and re-introduce them later.

LES MOIS

| | | | |
|---|---|---|---|
| décembre | mars | juin | septembre |
| janvier | avril | juillet | octobre |
| février | mai | août | novembre |

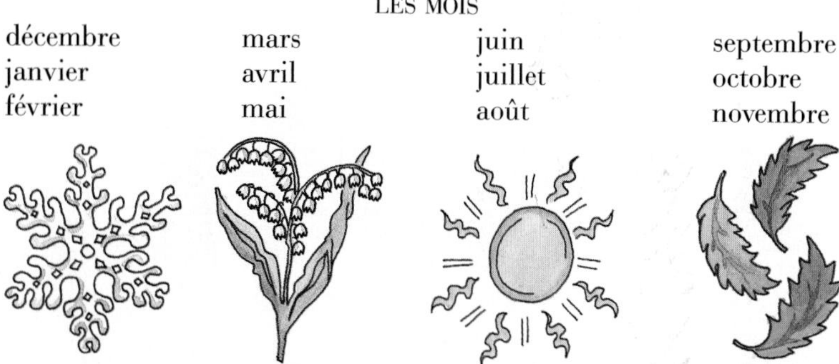

In French, the day is usually followed by the month: **le 21 mars** (abbreviated as 21-3). The day of the month is usually preceded by **le**, meaning *the*. However, the first day of each month is expressed with an ordinal number: **le premier janvier** (**avril**, **septembre**, etc.). The day of the week and the date can be expressed together, as follows. Here are two ways to give the date.

Aujourd'hui, nous sommes mardi, le 20 avril.
Aujourd'hui, nous sommes le 20 avril.

**Suggestion:** Teach *Quelle est la date de ton anniversaire?* Ask sts. to find someone in the class with a birthday in each of the 12 months. Sts. write down the names and months; the first to finish wins.

**Follow-up:** Use pictures of different seasons and have sts. name the months they think are portrayed.

**Note:** *Nous sommes le mardi vingt avril* is also acceptable.

**A. Fêtes** (*Holidays*) **américaines.** What months do you associate with the following holidays?

**Continuation:** Continue with other holidays: *le solstice d'été*, *Hanoukka*, *la fête des rois*, *le Mardi gras*, etc.

What is the date of your family's favorite or most important holiday?

**B. C'est aujourd'hui sa fête** (*name day*). In France, each day of the year is associated with a particular saint. Look over the list of names and dates. Choose six of them, and, with a partner, ask and answer questions about "name days."

**Suggestion:** Use names for pronunciation practice. Comparing pronunciation of cognates illustrates principles of French and English pronunciation clearly.

MODÈLE: VOUS: Quand célèbre-t-on la fête de Didier?
VOTRE CAMARADE: Le vingt-trois mai. Et la fête de Gilbert? (etc.)

## fêtes à souhaiter

**a**

- ADOLPHE 30 juin
- ADRIEN 8 sept
- AGNES 21 janv
- AIME 13 sept
- AIMEE 20 fév
- ALAIN 9 sept
- ALBAN 22 juin
- ALBERT 15 nov
- ALEXANDRE 22 avril
- ALEXIS 17 fév
- ALFRED 15 août
- ALICE 16 déc
- ALINE 20 oct
- ALPHONSE 1 août
- AMAND 6 fév
- ANATOLE 3 fév
- ANDRE 30 nov
- ANGE 5 mai
- ANGELE 27 janv
- ANNE 26 juil
- ANSELME 21 avril
- ANTOINE 17 janv
- ANTOINETTE 28 fév
- ANTONIN 2 mai
- ARISTIDE 31 août
- ARLETTE 17 juil
- ARMAND 8 juin
- ARMEL 16 août
- ARNAUD 10 fév
- ARTHUR 15 nov
- AURORE 13 déc

**b**

- BAUDOUIN 17 oct
- BEATRICE 13 fév
- BENJAMIN 31 mars
- BENOIT 11 juil
- BERNADETTE 18 fév
- BERNARD 20 août
- BERTHE 4 juil
- BERTRAND 6 sept
- BRIGITTE 23 juil

**c**

- CAMILLE 14 juil
- CARINE 7 nov
- CAROLE 17 juil
- CATHERINE 25 nov
- CECILE 22 nov
- CELINE 21 oct
- CHANTAL 12 déc
- CHARLES 2 mars
- CHRISTEL (LE) 24 juil
- CHRISTIAN 12 nov
- CHRISTINE 24 juil
- CHRISTOPHE 21 août
- CLAIRE 11 août
- CLAUDE 6 juin
- CLEMENCE 21 mars
- CLEMENT 23 nov
- CLOTILDE 4 juin
- COLETTE 6 mars
- CORINNE 18 mai
- CYRILLE 18 mars

**d**

- DANIEL 11 déc
- DAVID 29 déc
- DELPHINE 26 nov
- DENIS 9 oct
- DENISE 15 mai
- DIDIER 23 mai
- DOMINIQUE 8 août

**e**

- EDITH 13 sept
- EDMOND 20 nov
- EDOUARD 5 janv
- ELIANE 4 juil
- ELIE 20 juil
- ELISABETH 17 nov
- ELISE 17 nov
- ELOI 1 déc
- EMILE 22 mai
- EMILIENNE 5 janv
- EMMANUEL 25 déc
- ERIC 18 mai
- ERNEST 7 nov
- ESTELLE 11 mai
- ETIENNE 26 déc
- EUGENE 13 juil
- EVA 6 sept
- EVELYNE 27 déc

**f**

- FABIEN 20 janv
- FABRICE 22 août
- FELIX 12 fév
- FERDINAND 30 mai
- FERNAND 27 juin
- FRANÇOIS 4 oct
- FRANÇOISE 12 déc
- FREDERIC 18 juil

**g**

- GABRIEL (LE) 29 sept
- GAEL 17 déc
- GAETAN 7 août
- GASTON 6 fév
- GAUTIER 9 avril
- GENEVIEVE 3 janv
- GEOFFROY 8 nov
- GEORGES 23 avril
- GERALD 5 déc
- GERARD 3 oct
- GERAUD 13 oct
- GERMAIN 31 juil
- GERMAINE 15 juin
- GERVAIS 19 juin
- GHISLAIN 10 oct
- GILBERT 7 juin
- GILBERTE 11 août
- GILLES 1 sept
- GINETTE 3 janv
- GISELE 7 mai
- GODEFROY 8 nov
- GONTRAN 28 mars
- GREGOIRE 3 sept
- GUILLAUME 10 janv
- GUSTAVE 7 oct
- GUY 12 juin

**h**

- HELENE 18 août
- HENRI 13 juil
- HERVE 17 juin
- HONORE 16 mai
- HORTENSE 5 oct
- HUBERT 3 nov
- HUGUES 1 avril

**i**

- IRENE 5 avril
- ISABELLE 22 fév

**j**

- JACINTHE 30 janv
- JACQUELINE 8 fév
- JACQUES 25 juil
- JEAN 24 juin
- JEANNE 30 mai
- JEROME 30 sept
- JOACHIM 26 juil
- JOEL 13 juil
- JOHANNE 30 mai
- JOSEPH 19 mars
- JOSETTE 19 mars
- JOSSELIN 13 déc
- JULES 12 avril
- JULIEN 2 août
- JULIENNE 16 fév
- JULIETTE 30 juil
- JUSTE 14 oct

**k**

- KARINE 7 nov

**l**

- LAETITIA 18 août
- LAURENT 10 août
- LEA 22 mars
- LEON 10 nov
- LILIANE 4 juil
- LINE 20 oct
- LIONEL 10 nov
- LISE 17 nov
- LOIC 25 août
- LOUIS 25 août
- LOUISE 15 mars
- LUC 18 oct
- LUCIE 13 déc
- LUCIEN 8 janv
- LUDOVIC 25 août

**m**

- MADELEINE 22 juil
- MARC 25 avril
- MARCEL 16 janv
- MARCELLE 31 janv
- MARIANNE 9 juil
- MARIANNICK 15 août
- MARIE 15 août
- MARIE-THERESE 7 juin
- MARTHE 29 juil
- MARTIAL 30 juin
- MARTINE 30 janv
- MARYVONNE 15 août
- MATHILDE 14 mars
- MATTHIAS 14 mai
- MATTHIEU 21 sept
- MAURICE 22 sept
- MICHEL 29 sept
- MICHELINE 19 juin
- MIREILLE 15 août
- MONIQUE 27 août
- MURIEL 15 août

**n**

- NATHALIE 27 juil
- NELLY 18 août
- NICOLAS 6 déc
- NICOLE 6 mars
- NOEL 25 déc

**o**

- ODETTE 20 avril
- ODILE 14 déc
- OLIVIER 12 juil

**p**

- PASCAL 17 mai
- PATRICE 17 mars
- PAUL 29 juin
- PAULE 26 janv
- PHILIPPE 3 mai
- PIERRE 29 juin
- PIERRETTE 31 mai

**r**

- RAOUL 7 juil
- RAPHAEL 29 sept
- RAYMOND 7 janv
- REGINE 7 sept
- REGIS 16 juin
- REMI 15 janv
- RENAUD 17 sept
- RENE (E) 19 oct
- RICHARD 3 avril
- ROBERT 30 avril
- RODOLPHE 21 juin
- ROGER 30 déc
- ROLAND 15 sept
- ROLANDE 13 mai
- ROMAIN 28 fév
- RONALD 17 sept
- ROSELINE 17 janv
- ROSINE 11 mars

**s**

- SABINE 29 août
- SAMUEL 20 août
- SANDRINE 2 avril
- SEBASTIEN 20 janv
- SERGE 7 oct
- SIMON 28 oct
- SOLANGE 10 mai
- SOPHIE 25 mai
- STANISLAS 11 avril
- STEPHANE 26 déc
- SUZANNE 11 août
- SYLVAIN 4 mai
- SYLVESTRE 31 déc
- SYLVIE 5 nov

**t**

- TANGUY 19 nov
- THERESE 1 oct
- THIBAUT 8 juil
- THIERRY 1 juil
- THOMAS 3 juil

**v**

- VALENTIN 14 fév
- VALENTINE 25 juil
- VALERIE 28 avril
- VERONIQUE 4 fév
- VICTOR 21 juil
- VINCENT de Paul 27 sept
- VIRGINIE 7 janv
- VIVIANE 2 déc

**w**

- WALTER 9 avril
- WILFRIED 12 oct

**x**

- XAVIER 3 déc

**y**

- YOLANDE 11 juin
- YVES 19 mai
- YVETTE 13 janv
- YVON 19 mai

**C. Le voyageur bien informé.** When traveling it is useful to know the holidays of the countries you visit. Look at the following lists and compare the three countries. (Note that the dates of some holidays vary from country to country.)

**Note:** Realia comes from Air Canada magazine.

**Suisse**

| | |
|---|---|
| **1er janv.** | Nouvel An |
| **2 janv.** | Fête légale |
| **24 mars** | Vendredi saint |
| **26 mars** | Pâques |
| **27 mars** | Lundi de Pâques |
| **4 mai** | Ascension |
| **15 mai** | Lundi de Pentecôte |
| **1er août** | Fête nationale |
| **25 déc.** | Noel |
| **26 déc.** | Lendemain de Noel |

**États-Unis**

| | |
|---|---|
| **1er janv.** | Nouvel An |
| **20 févr.** | Anniversaire de Washington |
| **24 mars** | Vendredi saint |
| **29 mai** | Jour du Souvenir |
| **4 juill.** | Fête de l'Independance |
| **5 sept.** | Fête du Travail |
| **11 nov.** | Fête des Anciens Combattants |
| **23 nov.** | Action de Grâce |
| **25 déc.** | Noel |

**France**

| | |
|---|---|
| **1er janv.** | Nouvel An |
| **27 mars** | Lundi de Pâques |
| **1er mai** | Fête du Travail |
| **4 mai** | Ascension |
| **8 mai** | Armistice |
| **15 mai** | Lundi de Pentecôte |
| **14 juill.** | Fête nationale (Prise de la Bastille) |
| **15 août** | Assomption |
| **1er nov.** | Toussaint |
| **11 nov.** | Jour du Souvenir |
| **25 déc.** | Noel |

1. Quelles fêtes est-ce qu'on célèbre aux États-Unis qui ne sont pas célébrées en France? en Suisse? Donnez la date de ces fêtes.
2. Y a-t-il plus de (*more*) fêtes religieuses en France et en Suisse qu'aux (*than in the*) États-Unis? Nommez-les et donnez leur date.
3. Donnez les dates des fêtes nationales dans les trois pays.
4. Quel est votre jour de fête préféré? Pourquoi (*Why*)?

**Suggestion:** If you have sts. from foreign countries, have them give dates of important national and religious holidays in their country.

**Suggestion:** Sts. think of as many words as they can (in French) that they associate with their own lodgings; they then make a similar word-association chain based on this reading to describe French st. lodging. Using the two sets of chains (or semantic maps) as a point of departure, sts. talk about cultural issues that arise from them. Instructors could also solicit semantic maps around the idea *"logements d'étudiants"* from French native speakers to use for this activity. The activity could be done the night before for homework,

## France-culture

*Student housing.* For financial reasons most French students study in their home towns and live with their families. Foreign students, or French ones who do not live at home, have several choices of housing. They can rent an individual, tiny but inexpensive room in the **cité universitaire**. However, these must be reserved far in advance as there are long waiting lists. Some students rent a studio or an apartment in town, which is expensive, especially in Paris, or a more moderately priced room in a family home. They can find such housing through the **Centre régional des œuvres universitaires et scolaires (C.R.O.U.S.)**, an official social service agency which has a free listing of apartments and rooms, or through newspaper ads.

Lately, the **H.L.M. (habitations à loyers modérés)**, a state agency which owns and manages apartment complexes for low-income families, has reserved some of its apartments for students. Although quite inexpensive, there are few available units. In Paris and other large cities, students can also rent **des chambres de bonne**: rooms on the upper floors of elegant buildings, once used by maids of well-to-do families. These rooms are fairly inexpensive, but their occupants often must share a common bathroom. Occupants may also be prohibited from using the main entrance or elevators of the building, requiring them to climb up and down seven or eight flights.

when sts. read the cultural note. Sts. then share their word association maps in class in small groups, or words from chains can be listed on board. Encourage sts. to think about why lodgings are the way they are in each culture.

Few French students share apartments or houses, preferring to live alone or, at most, with one close friend. Their lodgings may seem quite small by North American standards, and inexpensive accommodations are generally old, lacking the kinds of conveniences—such as laundry and bathtub—which are taken for granted in the United States.

Foreign students go to France from all over the world, but especially from Vietnam, Cambodia, and French-speaking African countries. Most of them live in the **cités universitaires** which reserve rooms for foreigners.

# Étude de grammaire

## 9. EXPRESSING ACTIONS *-ir* Verbs

### À bas les dissertations![*]

Khaled et Naima[†] ont une dissertation d'histoire.

KHALED: Quel sujet **choisis**-tu?
NAIMA: Je ne sais pas, je **réfléchis**. Bon, je **choisis** le premier sujet—l'Empire de Napoléon.
(*Deux jours plus tard.*)
KHALED: Alors, tu es prête?
NAIMA: Attends, je **finis** ma conclusion et j'arrive. Et si je **réussis** à avoir 15 sur 20, on fait la fête!

Vrai ou faux?

1. Naima n'aime pas le premier sujet.
2. Khaled finit sa dissertation après Naima.
3. Naima veut (*wants*) avoir 15 sur 20.

[*] **Dissertation** is the equivalent of a term paper. (A doctoral dissertation in France is **une thèse**.)
[†] About 3.3 million North African Arab immigrants and their French-born children live in France. The presence of these immigrants and descendants of former French territories (Algeria, Morocco and Tunisia) has caused France to rethink its national identity.

You have learned the present-tense conjugation of the largest group of French verbs, those whose infinitives end in **-er**. The infinitives of a second group of verbs end in **-ir**. Notice the addition of **-iss-** between the verb stem and the personal endings in the plural.

**Presentation:** Quickly review forms of a regular *-er* verb (like *parler*) before beginning regular *-ir* verbs. Model pronunciation of verb forms. Compare the pronunciation of double *ss* [s] to single *s* [z] between vowels.

| PRESENT TENSE OF **finir** (*to finish*) | | | |
|---|---|---|---|
| je | fin**is** | nous | fin**issons** |
| tu | fin**is** | vous | fin**issez** |
| il, elle, on | fin**it** | ils, elles | fin**issent** |

The **-is** and **-it** endings of the singular forms of **-ir** verbs are pronounced [i]. The double **s** of the plural forms is pronounced [s].

Other verbs conjugated like **finir** include the following.

**agir** — *to act*
**choisir** — *to choose*
**réfléchir** (**à**)* — *to reflect* (*upon*), *to consider*
**réussir** (**à**) — *to succeed* (*in*)

**Additional vocabulary:** *-ir* verbs: *rougir*, *pâlir*, *grandir*, *punir*, *réagir*, *réussir*

**Note:** Stress the importance of using the preposition *à* after *réfléchir* and *réussir*, and *de* when using *finir* with an infinitive.

J'**agis** toujours avec raison. — *I always act reasonably.*
Nous **choisissons** des affiches. — *We're choosing some posters.*
Elles **réfléchissent aux** questions de Paul. — *They are thinking about Paul's questions.*

The verb **réussir** requires the preposition **à** before an infinitive or before the noun in the expression **réussir à un examen** (*to pass an exam*).

Je **réussis** souvent **à** trouver les réponses. — *I often succeed in finding the answers.*
Marc **réussit** toujours **à** l'examen d'histoire.† — *Marc always passes the history exam.*

The verb **finir** requires the preposition **de** before an infinitive.

En général, je **finis d'**étudier à 8 h 30. — *I usually finish studying at 8:30.*

## Vérifions!

**A. À la bibliothèque.** Read the description of Céline's visit to the library. Then imagine that Céline and Agnès are there together and rewrite the description, using **nous**.

**Suggestion:** May be done orally or in writing. You may want to let sts. work through ex. in writing first and then give answers orally.

*The verb **réfléchir** requires the preposition **à** before a noun when it is used in the sense of *to consider, to think about*, or *to reflect upon something*.

†**Passer un examen** means *to take an exam*, not *to pass* one. French uses **réussir à** (sometimes just **réussir**) **un examen** to express passing an examination.

Je choisis un livre de référence sur la Révolution française. Je réfléchis au sujet. Je réussis à trouver une revue intéressante sur la Révolution. Je finis très tard.

**B. En cours de littérature.** Complete the sentences with appropriate forms of **choisir**, **finir**, **réfléchir** or **réussir.**

1. Le professeur _____ des textes intéressants.
2. Les étudiants _____ avant de répondre aux questions du professeur.
3. Pierre et Anne _____ toujours les devoirs très vite (*fast*).
4. Nous _____ toujours aux examens.
5. Toi, tu _____ souvent sans (*without*) réfléchir.
6. Et moi, je _____ toujours par comprendre (*understanding*) la leçon.*

**Additional activity**: *En français, s'il vous plaît*. 1. Marie-Josée always chooses difficult courses. 2. She thinks about university studies and succeeds in finding dynamic professors. 3. She never acts without thinking (*sans réfléchir*) 4. She finishes studying at 11:00 PM.

### *Parlons-en!*

**Une interview.** Invent questions using the cues below to interview a classmate. For each response your classmate gives, make a comment reacting to what he/she says, and provide your own personal response to the question.

MODÈLE: réussir / aux examens →

VOUS: Est-ce que tu réussis toujours aux examens?
UN(E) CAMARADE: Oui, je réussis toujours aux examens. (*ou* Non, je ne réussis pas toujours aux examens.)
VOUS: Ah, tu es intelligent(e)! Je ne réussis pas toujours aux examens. (*ou* Moi aussi, je réussis quelquefois aux examens, mais pas toujours.)

1. agir / souvent / sans réfléchir
2. finir / exercices / français
3. choisir / cours (difficiles, faciles,...)
4. réfléchir / problèmes (politiques, des étudiants,...)
5. choisir / camarade de chambre / patient (intellectuel, calme,...)
6. ?

## 10. EXPRESSING POSSESSION AND SENSATIONS
## The Verb *avoir*

**Camarades de chambre**

JEAN-PIERRE: Tu **as** une chambre très agréable, et elle **a l'air** tranquille...
FLORENCE: Oui, j'**ai besoin de** beaucoup de calme pour travailler.

*When followed by **par** + infinitive, **finir** means *to end* (*up*).

JEAN-PIERRE: Tu **as** une camarade de chambre sympathique?
FLORENCE: Oui, nous **avons de la chance**: nous aimons toutes les deux le tennis, le calme... et le désordre!

Vrai ou faux?

1. La chambre est calme.
2. Florence aime le calme pour étudier.
3. La camarade de chambre de Florence est ordonnée (*organized*).
4. Elles n'aiment pas le tennis.

**Follow-up:** Ask personalized questions using the verb *avoir* and the theme of the minidialogue. Examples: *Avez-vous une chambre agréable? Avez-vous besoin de calme? Avez-vous un(e) camarade de chambre sympathique?*

## A. Forms of *avoir*

The verb **avoir** is irregular in form.

**Presentation:** Model pronunciation. Note the [z] sound in *nous avons*, *vous avez*, and *elles ont*. Point out the oral distinction between *elles ont* and *elles sont*.

| PRESENT TENSE OF **avoir** (*to have*) | | | |
|---|---|---|---|
| j' | **ai** | nous | **avons** |
| tu | **as** | vous | **avez** |
| il, elle, on | **a** | ils, elles | **ont** |

—J'**ai** un studio agréable. —*I have a nice studio apartment.*

—**Avez**-vous une camarade de chambre sympathique? —*Do you have a pleasant roommate?*

—Oui, elle **a** beaucoup de patience. —*Yes, she has lots of patience.*

**Presentation:** Bring in other pictures to demonstrate expressions. Interject personalized questions to individual sts. using expressions featured.

**Follow-up:** For listening comprehension practice, have sts. indicate whether they hear verb *être* or *avoir* in following sentences: 1. *Elle est contente.* 2. *Nous avons raison.* 3. *Ils sont américains.* 4. *Ils ont de la chance.* 5. *Elle a l'air content.* 6. *Tu es française, n'est-ce pas?* 7. *J'ai de la chance aussi.*

## B. Expressions with *avoir*

Many concepts expressed in French with **avoir** have English equivalents that use *to be*.

**Additional activity:** Ask sts. who in the class has *des disques / une guitare / une clarinette / des cassettes / un piano / une flûte*, etc.

Elle **a chaud**, il **a froid**.

Elles **ont faim**, ils **ont soif**.

Loïc, tu **as tort**. Magalie, tu **as raison**.

Frédéric **a l'air** content. Il **a de la chance**.

L'immeuble **a l'air** moderne.

Jean **a sommeil**.

Ingrid **a besoin d'**une lampe.

**Avez-vous envie de** danser?

Il **a rendez-vous** avec le professeur.

Il **a peur du** chien.

Elle **a honte**.

Isabelle **a quatre ans**.

Note that with **avoir besoin de**, **avoir envie de**, and **avoir peur de**, the preposition **de** is used before an infinitive or a noun.*

## Un peu d'argot

| | |
|---|---|
| **Il a du pot.** | Il a de la chance. |
| **J'en ai marre!** | J'en ai assez! *I'm fed up!* |
| **Tu as la trouille.** | Tu as peur. |

EN CONTEXTE

PATRICE: Sébastien, **il a du pot** en maths. Il a toujours 16 sur 20.
ERIC: Moi, **j'en ai marre** des maths. J'ai toujours 5 sur 20.
PATRICE: Et moi, **j'ai la trouille** du prof.

### *Vérifions!*

**A. Vive la musique!** You and your friends are planning an evening of music and entertainment. Say what each person has to contribute to the occasion.

---

*In Chapter 1, you learned a frequently used **avoir** expression, **il y a**, which means *there is* or *there are*.

MODÈLE: Isaac / une chaîne stéréo → Isaac a une chaîne stéréo.

1. Monique et Marc / des disques
2. vous / une guitare
3. tu / une clarinette
4. je / des cassettes
5. nous / un piano
6. Isabelle / une flûte

**B. Quel âge ont-ils?** A student inquires about the age of the people in the pictures below. Guess how old they are.

**Follow-up:** 1. Have sts. estimate ages of others in class. 2. Bring in pictures of people or give names of famous people and have sts. estimate their ages. 3. Teach *environ*: *Il a environ 40 ans.*

MODÈLE: L'ÉTUDIANT(E): Quel âge a-t-il?
VOUS: Il a deux ou trois ans.

**C. Qu'est-ce que vous avez** (*What's the matter*)**?** For each situation, use an expression with **avoir**.

**Suggestion:** Ask sts. to work in pairs, thinking of many possibilities and providing additional information.

MODÈLE: Pour moi, un Coca-Cola, s'il vous plaît. → J'ai soif.

1. Je porte un pull et un manteau.
2. Il est minuit (*midnight*).
3. J'ouvre (*open*) la fenêtre.
4. Je mange une quiche.
5. Paris est la capitale de la France.
6. Des amis français m'invitent (*invite me*) à Paris.
7. Je gagne (*win*) à la roulette.
8. Attention, un lion!
9. Je casse (*break*) le vase préféré de ma mère.
10. Je vais à la discothèque.
11. Rome est en Belgique.
12. 30 ans? Non, moi...
13. J'ai un examen difficile.
14. Et une limonade, s'il vous plaît.

## Parlons-en!

**A. Désirs et devoirs** (*duties*)**.** All of us have things we want to do and things we have to do. To express these ideas, create complete sentences using the words in each of the three columns, or use words of your own choosing. Take care to use the correct form of **avoir**.

**Suggestion:** May be done orally in small groups or in writing. Ask sts. to report back some of their answers to the class.

| | | |
|---|---|---|
| Je | avoir besoin de | étudier davantage (*more*) |
| Mon meilleur ami (Ma meilleure amie) | avoir envie de | acheter (*to buy*) une voiture |
| Mes parents | | visiter l'Europe |
| Le professeur de français | | danser à la discothèque |
| Mon/Ma camarade de chambre | | jouer au tennis |
| ? | | écouter un concert de rock |
| | | travailler le week-end |
| | | ? |

**B. Conversation.** Ask a classmate the following questions. Then tell the other students the most surprising or unusual fact that you learned about your classmate!

1. De quoi (*what*) as-tu peur? 2. Quel objet bizarre as-tu dans ta chambre? 3. De quoi as-tu besoin pour préparer ton cours de français? 4. De quoi as-tu envie quand tu as faim? quand tu as soif? 5. De quoi as-tu envie maintenant? 6. ?

## 11. EXPRESSING THE ABSENCE OF SOMETHING Indefinite Articles in Negative Sentences

### Le confort étudiant

NATHALIE: Où sont les toilettes*?

ANNE: Désolée, je **n**'ai **pas de** toilettes dans ma chambre. Elles sont dans le couloir.

NATHALIE: Mais tu as une douche?

ANNE: Non, **pas de** toilettes, **pas de** douche, mais j'ai une petite kitchenette et...

NATHALIE: Et une télé?

ANNE: Non, il **n**'y a **pas de** télé, mais j'ai une chaîne stéréo.

Complétez selon le dialogue.

1. Dans sa chambre, Anne n'a ____.
2. Il n'y a pas ____.
3. Elle a une chaîne stéréo mais ____.

In negative sentences, the indefinite article (**un**, **une**, **des**) becomes **de** (**d'**) after **pas**.

**Presentation:** Using simple drawings demonstrating sentences or using sts. as examples may make presentation more interesting. For example: *Maria (une étudiante) a un stylo, mais pas de papier*, etc.

Il a une amie.

Elle porte une casquette.

Il y a des voitures dans la rue.

*In French, **toilettes** is always plural. You can also say **les W.-C.** (*water closet*).

Il n'a pas d'amie.

Elle ne porte pas de casquette.

Il n'y a pas de voitures dans la rue.

—Est-ce qu'il y a **un livre** sur la table? — *Is there a book on the table?*
—Non, il n'y a **pas de livre** sur la table. — *No, there is no book on the table.*

**Note**: Point out that *pas de* is used as a negative expression of quantity to state the absence of something.

—Est-ce qu'il y a **des livres** sur la table? — *Are there any books on the table?*
—Non, il n'y a **pas de livres** sur la table. — *No, there aren't any books on the table.*

**Presentation**: Model pronunciation of sentences so sts. can hear the difference between *des* and *de*.

In negative sentences with **être**, however, the indefinite article does not change.

**—C'est un livre?**
**—Non, ce n'est pas un livre.** (*It's not a book.*)

The definite article (**le**, **la**, **les**) does not change in a negative sentence.

—Elle a **la** voiture aujourd'hui?
—Non, elle n'a pas **la** voiture.

## *Vérifions!*

**A. Une chambre intéressante!** Patrick is not very happy. In his room . . .

MODÈLE: Il y a un ordinateur... mais →
Il y a un ordinateur, mais il n'y a pas de téléphone.

**Additional Activities:** Ask the following questions pertaining to the classroom: *Est-ce qu'il y a une lampe dans la salle de classe? un lavabo? des étagères? une stéréo? des tapis? un miroir? un lit? une télévision?*

1. Il y a une table... mais ____.

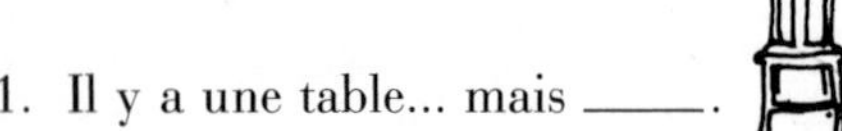

2. Il y a une étagère... mais ____.
3. Il y a une chaîne stéréo... mais ____.

4. Il y a un cahier... mais ____.
5. Il y a une raquette... mais ____. (balle)

**Follow-up:** Dictate the following paragraph and have sts. make each sentence negative. *Nous avons des disques. Ce sont des disques français. C'est un disque de Vanessa Paradis. Il y a un disque de Céline Dion ici. Tu as des disques intéressants.*

**B. Chambre à louer.** The room Christian is inquiring about is very sparsely furnished. Play the roles of Christian and his prospective landlord or landlady, following the example.

MODÈLE: une télé →
CHRISTIAN: Est-ce qu'il y a une télé dans la chambre?
LE/LA PROPRIÉTAIRE: Non, il n'y a pas de télé.

1. un lavabo
2. une armoire
3. des tapis
4. des étagères
5. une commode
6. un lit

## *Parlons-en!*

**A. Une interview.** Interview a classmate.

MODÈLE: ami français →
É1: As-tu un ami français?
É2: Oui, j'ai un ami français. (*ou* Non, je n'ai pas d'ami français, mais j'ai un ami mexicain.)

1. amis individualistes, snobs, blonds, roux 2. livre de français, de russe, d'espagnol 3. cours d'anglais, d'art, d'histoire 4. chaîne stéréo, télévision, disques de _____ 5. guitare, piano 6. chat (*cat*), chien 7. affiches, téléphone, rideaux, armoire 8. appartement, voiture de sport 9. ?

**Suggestions:** (1) On a prepared ditto or on notebook paper, have sts. list items in two columns, according to whether a classmate has the item or not. Then have them compare lengths of lists. (2) Have sts. repeat as much of interview as they can remember without reference to notes. They may repeat the items to their partner by saying: *tu as x, y. Tu n'as pas de z;* or to whole class: *Elle/Il a....*

**B. Sondage: Les Français et la chance.** Here is an opinion poll (**un sondage**) published in the French magazine *Vital.* Read the four opinions below, consider the results, and choose the correct response.

*Question : « Diriez-vous[a] qu'en général... ? »*

| | Ensemble | Hommes | Femmes |
|---|---|---|---|
| | % | % | % |
| • Vous avez une chance insolente[b] | 4 | 4 | 2 |
| • Vous avez beaucoup de chance | 31 | 32 | 31 |
| • Vous n'avez pas tellement[c] de chance | 45 | 45 | 45 |
| • Vous n'avez pas de chance du tout | 11 | 8 | 14 |
| • Ne se prononcent pas[d] | 9 | 11 | 8 |
| | 100 | 100 | 100 |

**4% des Français ont une chance insolente. 11% n'ont pas de chance du tout. Les femmes croient moins à la chance que les hommes.**

[a]*Would you say*
[b]*une... amazing luck*
[c]*pas... not so (much)*
[d]*Ne... No opinion*

**Suggestion:** Ask sts. to cover the numbers in poll and choose the statement that applies to them personally. At the end, tally the responses and compare the percentages with those presented in the magazine.

D'après (*According to*) le sondage,

1. 4% des (hommes / femmes) ont une chance insolente.
2. (14% / 11%) des femmes n'ont pas de chance.
3. (31% / 32%) de tous les Français ont beaucoup de chance.
4. Et 8% des (hommes / femmes) n'ont pas d'opinion.

Now choose the sentence in the poll which describes you best!

# 12. GETTING INFORMATION *où, quand, comment, pourquoi, etc.*

**Presentation:** Model pronunciation. Have half the class take the role of *Mme Gérard* and the other half the role of *Audrey*.

### Chambre à louer

MME GÉRARD: Bonjour, Mademoiselle. **Comment** vous appelez-vous?
AUDREY: Audrey Delorme.
MME GÉRARD: Vous êtes étudiante?
AUDREY: Oui.
MME GÉRARD: **Où** est-ce que vous étudiez?
AUDREY: À la Sorbonne.
MME GÉRARD: C'est très bien, ça. Et **qu'est-ce que** vous étudiez?
AUDREY: La philosophie.
MME GÉRARD: Oh, c'est sérieux, ça. Vous avez **combien d'**heures de cours?
AUDREY: 21 heures par semaine.
MME GÉRARD: Alors, vous avez besoin d'une chambre pas chère?
AUDREY: Oui, c'est ça. **Quand** est-ce que la chambre est disponible?
MME GÉRARD: Aujourd'hui. Elle est à vous.

Vrai ou faux?

1. Audrey est étudiante à Paris.
2. Mme Gérard a l'air gentille.
3. Audrey a besoin d'une chambre pas chère.
4. Audrey étudie les mathématiques.

**Follow-up:** Sts. practice dialogue in pairs. They should be encouraged to answer questions as they please. Interviewers may ask additional questions.

## A. Information Questions with Interrogative Words

Information questions ask for new information or facts. They often begin with interrogative expressions. Here are some of the most common interrogative words in French.

**Note:** It is important that sts. understand the distinction between information questions and yes/no questions.

| | |
|---|---|
| **où** | *where* |
| **quand** | *when* |
| **comment** | *how* |
| **pourquoi** | *why* |
| **combien de** | *how much, how many* |

Information questions may be formed with **est-ce que** or by inverting the subject and verb. The interrogative word is usually placed at the beginning of the question.

**Suggestion:** Remind sts. that *je* is almost never inverted with the verb; *est-ce que* is used instead.

1. These are information questions with **est-ce que**.

   **Où** / **Quand** / **Comment** / **Pourquoi** } **est-ce que** Michel joue du banjo?

   **Combien de** fois par semaine (*times a week*) **est-ce que** Michel joue?

2. These are information questions with a change in word order.*

   PRONOUN SUBJECT

   **Où** / **Quand** / **Comment** / **Pourquoi** } étudie-t-il la musique?

   **Combien d'**instruments a-t-il?

   NOUN SUBJECT

   **Où** / **Quand** / **Comment** / **Pourquoi** } Michel étudie-t-il la musique?

   **Combien d'**instruments Michel a-t-il?

3. These are information questions with noun subject and verb only. With the interrogatives **où**, **quand**, **comment**, and **combien de**, it is possible to ask information questions using only a noun subject and the verb, with no pronoun.

   **Où** / **Quand** / **Comment** } étudie Michel?

   **Combien d'**instruments a Michel?

   However, the pronoun is almost always required with **pourquoi**.

   **Pourquoi** Michel étudie-t-**il**?

## B. Information Questions with Interrogative Pronouns

Some of the most common French interrogative pronouns (**les pronoms interrogatifs**) are **qui**, **qu'est-ce que**, **que**, and **quoi**.

---

*In everyday conversation the French rarely invert the subject and verb when asking questions. Inversion is commonly used in writing, however.

1. **Qui** (*who, whom*) is used in questions inquiring about a person or persons.

| | |
|---|---|
| **Qui** étudie le français? | *Who studies French?* |
| **Qui** regardez-vous? / **Qui** est-ce que vous regardez? | *Whom are you looking at?* |
| **À qui** Michel parle-t-il? / **À qui** est-ce que Michel parle? | *Whom is Michel speaking to?* |

2. **Qu'est-ce que** and **que** (*what*) refer to things or ideas. **Que** requires inversion.

| | |
|---|---|
| **Qu'est-ce que** vous étudiez? / **Qu'**étudiez-vous? | *What are you studying?* |
| **Que** pense-t-il de la chambre? | *What does he think of the room?* |

**Suggestion:** Point out that *qui* can be a subject, a direct object, or the object of a preposition. After this section, sts. are prepared to do Ex. C.

**Suggestion:** Ask sts. to listen to the following paragraph for *who, what, when, where,* and *why* information. Afterwards, they will ask each other those questions about the passage. *Marina habite à la cité universitaire. Elle a une chambre agréable mais petite. Le matin elle est à l'université parce qu'elle a des cours. Elle est très contente parce qu'elle aime la vie universitaire.*

**Suggestion:** Use the following as preliminary exercises: A. *Transformez en questions:* 1. *Michel part.* (*où, quand, comment, pourquoi*) 2. *Marie achète des affiches.* (*qui, qu'est-ce que, combien de*) B. *Posez la question qui convient en utilisant qui ou qui est-ce que.* 1. *Richard veut une nouvelle radio.* 2. *Les Boucher font des achats pour Noël.*

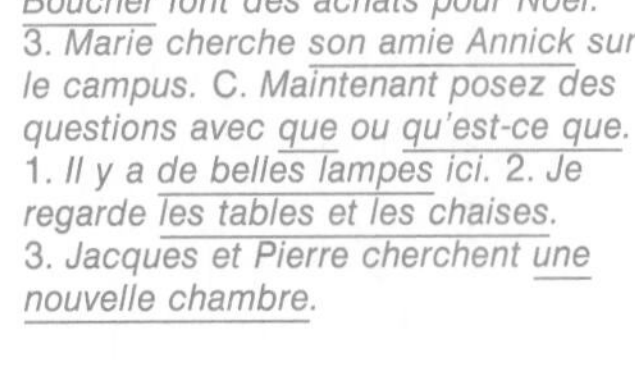

3. *Marie cherche son amie Annick sur le campus.* C. *Maintenant posez des questions avec que ou qu'est-ce que.* 1. *Il y a de belles lampes ici.* 2. *Je regarde les tables et les chaises.* 3. *Jacques et Pierre cherchent une nouvelle chambre.*

## Vérifions!

**A. De l'argent** (*Money*). Monsieur Harpagon doesn't like to spend money. Ask each of his questions using **pourquoi**.

MODÈLE: MME HARPAGON: J'ai besoin d'un manteau.
M. HARPAGON: Pourquoi as-tu besoin d'un manteau?

1. Nous avons besoin d'une étagère. 2. Monique a besoin d'un dictionnaire d'anglais. 3. Paul a besoin d'une voiture. 4. J'ai besoin d'un nouveau tapis.

**B. Une visite chez Camille et Marie-Claude.** Think of a question that corresponds to each statement about Camille and Marie-Claude's new apartment. Use **qu'est-ce que** or **que**.

MODÈLE: Nous visitons le logement de Camille et Marie-Claude. →
Qu'est-ce que vous visitez? (*ou* Que visitez-vous?)

1. Il y a un miroir sur le mur. 2. Je regarde les affiches de Camille. 3. Nous admirons l'ordre de la chambre de Camille. 4. Guy écoute les disques de Marie-Claude. 5. Je trouve des revues intéressantes. 6. Elles cherchent le chat de Camille. 7. Guy n'aime pas les rideaux à fleurs. 8. Nous aimons bien la vue et le balcon.

**C. Les étudiants et le logement.** With a little help from her friends, Brigitte finds a new room. Create a question, using **qui** or **à qui**, that corresponds to each item of information.

1. *Brigitte* cherche un logement. 2. *Mme Boucher* a une petite chambre à louer dans une maison. 3. Jocelyne et Richard parlent de Mme Boucher à *Brigitte*. 4. Brigitte téléphone à *Mme Boucher*. 5. Mme Boucher montre (*shows*) la chambre à *Brigitte*. 6. *Brigitte* loue la chambre de Mme Boucher.

Ce studio a l'air bien. On va le voir après les cours?

**D. Une chambre d'étudiant.** Here is a conversation between two students. Based on Julien's answers, imagine which questions Sabine asks him.

**Suggestions:** comment, où, qu'est-ce que (que), pourquoi, quand, combien de...

MODÈLE: SABINE: Comment est la chambre?
JULIEN: La chambre est *très agréable.*

SABINE: _____?
JULIEN: Il y a *des affiches* et *un miroir* sur le mur.
SABINE: _____?
JULIEN: La lampe est *à côté de la stéréo.*
SABINE: _____?
JULIEN: Il y a *deux* chaises et *une* table.
SABINE: _____?
JULIEN: J'ai une stéréo *parce que j'adore la musique.*
SABINE: _____?
JULIEN: J'écoute de la musique *quand j'étudie.*
SABINE: _____?
JULIEN: La chambre est *petite* mais *confortable.*

## Parlons-en!

**A. Voici les réponses.** Invent appropriate questions for these answers.

MODÈLE: Dans la chambre de Marie-Jo →
Où y a-t-il des affiches de cinéma? Où sont les disques d'Aimé?

1. C'est une revue française. 2. À l'université. 3. Parce que je n'ai pas envie d'étudier. 4. Vingt-quatre étudiants. 5. À midi. 6. Maryse. 7. Très bien. 8. Parce que j'ai faim. 9. Maintenant.

**B. Une interview.** Interview a classmate.

1. D'où es-tu? Comment est ta (*your*) ville?
2. Où habites-tu? Dans une maison, un appartement ou une résidence universitaire? Avec qui? Comment est ta chambre?
3. Est-ce que tu aimes l'université? Pourquoi? Combien de cours as-tu ce semestre? Comment sont tes cours?
4. Comment sont tes camarades? ton/ta camarade de chambre? tes professeurs?
5. Est-ce que tu parles avec tes amis après les cours? Où?

Is your classmate's life very different from yours? What do you have in common? Explain the similarities and differences.

**Additional activity:** *Votre camarade joue le rôle d'un Francophone qui passe une année dans votre université. Vous voulez savoir* (*to know*): 1. where he/she is from 2. where he/she is living and with whom 3. how many courses he/she has 4. which courses he/she prefers 5. whether he/she is working and where 6. his/her feelings about the university or town.

**Suggestions:** (1) Play the role of the French visitor and have sts. ask questions. (2) If possible, invite a French-speaking colleague to come in for five or ten minutes to answer questions of this type. (3) If B is done as a straight interview, ask sts. to report back what they learned.

## Mots-clés

*Giving reasons*: To answer the question *why* (**pourquoi?**), use **parce que**.

Je travaille **parce que** j'ai besoin d'argent.

**C. Êtes-vous curieux/curieuse?** Why is it always the instructor who asks questions? It's your turn to question him/her.

MODÈLES: D'où êtes-vous?
Pourquoi aimez-vous le français?

**Suggestion:** Give sts. a minute to think of questions to ask you. Or have sts. write their questions on cards to be handed in to you.

# Étude de prononciation

## Accent Marks

**Suggestion:** After using group or individual repetition of these words, dictate them to sts. to see whether they place the accents properly.

| NAME | MARK | EXAMPLE | PRONUNCIATION |
|---|---|---|---|
| Accent aigu | **é** | **café** | Letter **é** pronounced [e]. |
| Accent grave | **è**<br>**à, ù** | **très**<br>**là, où** | Letter **è** pronounced [ɛ].<br>Accent mark does not affect pronunciation. Used to distinguish words spelled alike but having different meanings: **la** (*the*) vs. **là** (*there*); **ou** (*or*) vs. **où** (*where*). |
| Accent circonflexe | **ê**<br>**â, û**<br>**ô**<br>**î** | **prêt**<br>**âge, flûte**<br>**hôpital**<br>**dîner** | Letter **ê** pronounced [ɛ].<br>Accent mark does not affect pronunciation.<br>Letter **ô** pronounced [o].<br>Accent mark does not affect pronunciation. |
| Tréma | **ë, ï** | **Noël, naïf** | Indicates that each vowel is pronounced independently of the other: [no-ɛl], [na-if]. |
| Cédille | **ç** | **français** | Letter **ç** pronounced [s]. |

Prononcez avec le professeur. Donnez aussi le nom des accents.

1. à bientôt
2. voilà
3. étudiant
4. Ça va.
5. fenêtre
6. modèle
7. à bas
8. répétez
9. français
10. s'il vous plaît
11. très
12. Noël

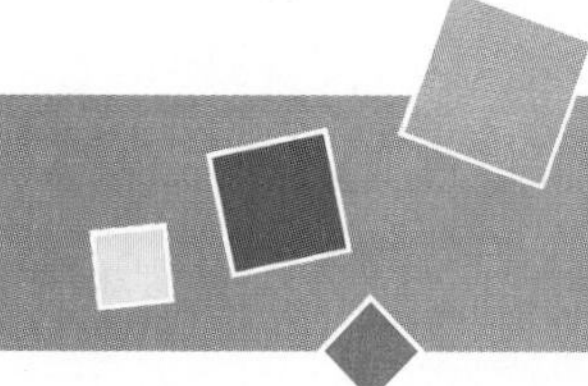

# Mise au point

**A. Logique ou pas logique?** React to your classmate's statements. If they are illogical, correct them according to the model.

MODÈLE: UN(E) CAMARADE: J'ai faim. Je demande un Coca-Cola.
VOUS: Ce n'est pas logique. Tu as soif. Tu demandes un Coca-Cola.

1. Le professeur est très compétent. Il a toujours tort. 2. Ahmed réussit presque toujours (*almost always*) aux examens. Il n'a pas de chance! 3. J'ai envie de trouver un livre. Je cherche le lit. 4. Vingt et trente font soixante? Vous avez raison. 5. Nous désirons louer une chambre. Où trouve-t-on un hôtel?

**B. Une conversation téléphonique.** A friend is talking on the phone. You hear only her answers. What are the questions? In your opinion, with whom is she speaking?

| QUESTIONS | RÉPONSES |
|---|---|
| ? | 1. Non, je n'ai pas faim. |
| ? | 2. Maintenant? Les maths. |
| ? | 3. Avec Jim. |
| ? | 4. Parce qu'il est très fort en maths. |
| ? | 5. Oui, il est très sympa. |

**C. Conversation entre étudiants.** Create complete questions using the words below. A classmate will give personal answers to the questions.

1. où / étudier / tu? / pourquoi / étudier / tu / là?
2. avoir / tu / souvent / tort? / quand / avoir / tu / tort?
3. avoir / tu / faim? / où / aimer / tu / mieux / manger / quand / tu / avoir / faim?
4. à qui / poser / tu / questions / sur / cours universitaires? / pourquoi?
5. combien de disques (cassettes, CD) / avoir / tu? / où / être / ils?
6. combien de frères / sœurs (*brothers* / *sisters*) / avoir / tu? / où / habiter / ils?

**D. Au contraire.** Working with one or more students, practice your argumentative skills by contradicting every statement they make in response to these questions. You may start your sentences with **Au contraire...**, **Moi, je pense que...**, or **Ce n'est pas vrai** (*true*).

MODÈLE: Comment trouvez-vous la vie universitaire? →

É1: La vie universitaire n'est pas très intéressante.
É2: Au contraire, elle est excitante et très, très intéressante.

1. Où trouve-t-on un bon restaurant près de l'université?
2. Qu'est-ce qu'on a envie de faire (*to do*) après un examen difficile?
3. Est-ce que les étudiants ont besoin d'une chaîne stéréo? d'une télévision?
4. Qu'est-ce qu'on a besoin de faire (*to do*) pour réussir dans un cours de langue?
5. Pourquoi a-t-on besoin d'une licence (*degree, equivalent to a B.A.*)?

**Continuation:** Ask several other questions and have sts. contradict each other: *Est-ce que les étudiants ont besoin d'une voiture? Est-ce que les professeurs ont besoin de préparer les cours?*

**E. Une chambre.** Julie, a student living in Quebec, is looking for a room to rent. She is funny and independent, and enjoys having a good time. She is rather untidy, smokes, and has a cat, but no car. Look at this classified ad in the rentals section of the Quebec newspaper *Le Soleil.* In your opinion, which room does Julie choose, and why?

**CHAMBRES**

CHAMBRE plus salon avec pension non-fumeur, sobre, aimant chats, idéal étudiant(e)s 622-9378

ARRIERE CHUL, grande chambre, câble, cuisine, buanderie, salle de bains, fille sérieuse et non fumeuse, 653-8676 après 18h.

CHAMBRE pour personne honnête et propre, 658-3702

PRES CEGEP, université, très propre, meublée, entrée privée, laveuse, sécheuse..., 688-1066

POUR étudiante, Rte de l'Église près Ch. Ste-Foy, entrée privée, frigo, évier, cuisine commune, près de tout, 170$ mois, 653-5948

BELLE grande chambre dans maison neuve, piscine chauffée, laveuse-sécheuse, près d'autobus, fille non-fumeuse 225$ 657-4543

CHAMBRE avec salle de bains, entrée privée, cuisinette et possibilité d'emploi, près CEGEP, université, 687-1912

**Suggestion:** Have sts. play the roles; encourage them to respond naturally to questions and to ask for additional information. At the end, have one or two groups present the skit to the class.

## Interactions

In Chapter 4, you have practiced talking about rooms, describing people, telling what you do and do not have, and asking questions. Act out the following situations, using the vocabulary and structures from this chapter.

1. **Camarade de chambre.** You are interviewing a prospective roommate (your partner). You find out the following information about him or her.

   what his or her name is
   how old he or she is
   what he or she is studying
   what time he or she has class
   whom he or she telephones often
   if he or she likes order or disorder

2. **Nous sommes tous des artistes.** Choose a partner and provide him/her with a physical description of your closest friend. Your partner will draw this friend as exactly as he/she can according to your instructions. Decide if you wish to share the drawing with your friend!

–C'est un impulsif. Quand il a sommeil, il ne réfléchit pas, il dort[a]!

[a]sleeps

3. **Un appartement.** You are moving into an unfurnished apartment. Next door, two French students (your partners) are moving out. Introduce yourself to them, and engage them in conversation. Describe the things you need for your small apartment, in the hope that you might be able to obtain some of them from your departing neighbors.

## LECTURE

### *Avant de lire*

**More on contextual guessing.** Another form of guessing you probably use often when you encounter an unfamiliar word in English is to look at the surrounding context to figure out the meaning of the word. It is usually necessary to read ahead. Often the sentences that follow an unfamiliar phrase or word will clarify the meaning. Look, for example, at the underlined word in this sentence.

> Comme tous les étudiants, Patrice et Sophie louent leur logement. Ils paient 1565 francs de loyer par mois.

When you encounter the word **louent**, you probably do not know what it means, but if you finish the sentence, you will easily guess that it is a verb meaning *rent*. Try the same strategy with the other underlined words in the reading.

## *Le logement*

Patrice et Sophie habitent un petit studio à Lyon. Ils ont une grande pièce avec une petite cuisine équipée. Leur studio n'est pas grand mais il est très agréable. Comme tous les étudiants, Patrice et Sophie louent leur logement. Ils paient 1565 francs de loyer par mois.

**Suggestion:** Before reading in depth, have sts. guess the content by looking at the photographs. Bring in other photos of housing if possible. Ask the sts. to comment on differences between French and American housing.

**Suggestion:** Encourage sts. to skim for specific information rather than reading every word. Comprehension questions require only that they show passive understanding of the article.

L'immeuble° des parents de Patrice est ancien. Mais en France on trouve aussi beaucoup de maisons et d'immeubles modernes, surtout en banlieue.° Dans les villes on construit beaucoup ou on rénove les bâtiments° anciens. Souvent, quand l'immeuble est très beau mais en mauvais état,° on garde seulement° sa façade et on construit derrière un bâtiment neuf.°

Comme beaucoup de personnes qui habitent en ville, les parents de Patrice sont aussi propriétaires d'une maison à la campagne° où ils passent leurs° week-ends et une partie de leurs vacances. Ils organisent souvent des dîners en famille ou entre amis.

*apartment building*
*suburbs*
*buildings*
*mauvais... poor condition / only*
*new*
*country / their*

**Suggestion:** Have sts. compare housing in French university towns to housing in their own towns. If possible, show slides of different types of lodging for sts. Photocopies of housing ads could be used to practice getting and giving information.

**Follow-up:** Bring in *chambre à louer* ads from a French newspaper and have sts. try to read and understand abbreviations. Ask sts. to write an ad for their present housing.

## Compréhension

1. Comment est l'appartement de Patrice et Sophie? Donnez des détails.
2. Où trouve-t-on, en général, des immeubles modernes?
3. Où vont beaucoup de Français le week-end?

## PAR ÉCRIT

**Function:** More on describing (a person)
**Audience:** School newspaper
**Goal:** Write an article about a new exchange student on campus, Izé Bola.
This is how she describes herself:

> «Je m'appelle Izé Bola. J'habite au Zaïre. Je suis aux États-Unis pour améliorer mon anglais. Je me spécialise en sciences. Un jour, je veux° être médecin comme mon père.»

*want*

### Steps

1. Complete the sentences below. Then write two or three other sentences of your own, making inferences from Izé's description of herself and inventing other plausible details.

Izé est étudiante en biologie. Elle veut (*wants*)...
Elle a aussi envie...
Elle a l'air...
Elle a _____ ans.
Elle étudie aux États-Unis parce que...
C'est une jeune fille...
Elle parle...
Elle aime surtout (*especially*)... mais elle n'aime pas du tout...

2. As you write, try to make the subject come alive for your readers. Use the following techniques as you write your first draft.
   - Include vivid and specific details that suggest something about the person's personality—preferences, appearance, taste in clothing.
   - Quote the person, to give an idea of what he or she is like.
   - Arrange each sentence so that the most interesting points stand out. Put them at the beginning or the end, or set them off in a brief sentence contrasted with longer ones that surround it.
3. Reread the draft, checking for organization and smoothness of style. Make any necessary changes. You may ask a classmate to help you.
4. Check the composition again for spelling, punctuation, and grammar errors. Focus especially on your use of verbs.
5. Be prepared to read your composition to a small group of classmates.

## À L'ÉCOUTE!

**À l'écoute!** See scripts for listening passages and follow-up activities recorded on student cassette. Remind students that in the listening comprehension passages (as in real life) they will not understand every word they hear. They should focus globally on the general information in the passages and not be overly concerned about what they do not understand.

**Chambre à louer.** Laurence is looking for a room. She calls Madame Boussard, who has a room to rent. First, read through the activity. Next, listen to the vocabulary and the conversation. Then, do the activity.

VOCABULAIRE UTILE

**qui donnent sur** *that overlook*
**meublé(e)** *furnished*
**je peux la visiter** *I may (may I) visit it*

Circle all the words that describe the room for rent.

1. La chambre est

| | | |
|---|---|---|
| a. petite | d. simple | g. blanche |
| b. grande | e. confortable | |
| c. moderne | f. calme | |

2. Dans la chambre, il y a

| | | |
|---|---|---|
| a. un lavabo | d. deux étagères | g. deux chaises |
| b. un lit | e. une chaîne stéréo | h. une table |
| c. un canapé | f. une armoire | |

# Vocabulaire

## Verbes

**agir** to act
**avoir** to have
**choisir** to choose
**demander** to ask (for)
**finir de** (+ *inf.*) to finish
**louer** to rent
**passer un examen** to take an exam
**réfléchir (à)** to think (about)
**réussir (à)** to succeed (at); to pass (*a test*)

## Substantifs

**l'affiche** (*f.*) poster
**le (la) camarade de chambre** roommate
**le canapé** sofa
**la cassette** cassette tape
**la chaîne stéréo** stereo
**la chambre** room
**les cheveux** (*m.*) hair
**le chien** dog
**la commode** chest of drawers
**le disque** record
**la douche** shower
**l'étagère** (*f.*) shelf
**la fête** holiday; name day
**la fleur** flower
**l'immeuble** (*m.*) apartment building
**la lampe** lamp
**le lavabo** bathroom sink
**le lecteur de cassettes** cassette player
**le lit** bed
**le logement** lodging(s), place of residence
**la maison** house, home
**le miroir** mirror
**le mot** word
**le mur** wall
**l'ordinateur** (*m.*) computer
**la platine laser (le lecteur de CD)** compact disc (CD) player
**le réveil** alarm clock
**la revue** magazine
**le rideau** curtain
**la rue** street
**le tapis** rug
**le téléphone** telephone
**les yeux** (*m.*) eyes

À REVOIR: **le cahier, la casquette, la télévision, la voiture**

## Adjectifs

**autre** other
**blond(e)** blond
**châtain** brown (*hair*)
**court(e)** short (*hair*)
**grand(e)** tall, big
**laid(e)** ugly
**long(ue)** long
**petit(e)** small, short
**raide** straight (*hair*)
**roux** red (*hair*)
**roux/rousse** redheaded
**tranquille** quiet, calm

## Expressions avec *avoir*

**avoir l'air** (+ *adj.*); **avoir l'air (de** + *inf.*) to seem; to look
**avoir (20) ans** to be (20) years old
**avoir besoin de** to need
**avoir chaud** to be warm
**avoir de la chance** to be lucky
**avoir envie de** to want, to feel like
**avoir faim** to be hungry
**avoir froid** to be cold
**avoir honte** to be ashamed
**avoir peur de** to be afraid of
**avoir raison** to be right
**avoir rendez-vous avec** to have a meeting (date) with
**avoir soif** to be thirsty
**avoir sommeil** to be sleepy
**avoir tort** to be wrong

## Expressions interrogatives

**combien (de)... ?, comment... ?, pourquoi... ?, que... ?, qu'est-ce que... ?, ...quoi... ?**

## Mots et expressions divers

**de taille moyenne** of medium height
**en désordre** disorderly, disheveled
**en ordre** orderly
**près de** close to

À REVOIR: **à côté de, derrière, devant, sous, sur**

## Les mois

**janvier** January
**février** February
**mars** March
**avril** April
**mai** May
**juin** June
**juillet** July
**août** August
**septembre** September
**octobre** October
**novembre** November
**décembre** December

# Intermède

## SITUATION

### Pardon...

**Situation:** The *Situation* dialogues are recorded on the student cassette packaged with the student text.

**Contexte** *C'est le premier jour de Karen, une étudiante américaine, à la cité universitaire d'Orléans. Elle pose des questions à une étudiante française.*

**Objectif** *Karen demande des renseignements.*° (information)

KAREN: Pardon, où est le téléphone, s'il te plaît?
MIREILLE: Dans le foyer.
KAREN: Mmm... qu'est-ce que c'est, le foyer?
MIREILLE: Eh bien, c'est la salle, en bas, où il y une télé, une table de ping-pong, un distributeur° (machine) de café et de Coca...
KAREN: Dis-moi, comment est le restaurant universitaire?
MIREILLE: Ça, je ne sais pas. Moi aussi, je suis nouvelle ici. On déjeune ensemble°? (à deux)
KAREN: Bonne idée! J'ai très faim!

## À propos

### Comment demander des renseignements

| | |
|---|---|
| DANS UNE SITUATION INFORMELLE | |
| Pardon, est-ce que tu peux me dire... | *Excuse me, can you tell me . . .* |
| où se trouve... | *where to find (one finds) . . .* |
| où est/sont... | *where is/are . . .* |
| S'il te plaît, est-ce que tu sais... | *Please, do you know . . .* |
| DANS UNE SITUATION FORMELLE | |
| Excusez-moi, Madame/Monsieur, pourriez-vous* m'indiquer (me dire)... / savez-vous... / j'aimerais* savoir... | *Excuse me, ma'am/sir, could you tell me . . . / do you know . . . / I'd like to know . . .* |

*These verbs are in the conditional mood, used to express polite requests.

## *Maintenant à vous!*

**A. Questions personnelles.** Read the **Situation** dialogue again and then answer the following questions.

1. Savez-vous où se trouve le téléphone le plus proche (*near*) de la salle de classe? Dites où il se trouve à un(e) camarade de classe.
2. Quand vous visitez un endroit pour la première fois (*first time*), demandez-vous des renseignements à un passant dans la rue? Avez-vous peur de parler aux inconnus (*strangers*)? Sinon, quel genre de question posez-vous d'habitude (*usually*)? (Où se trouve[nt]...?)
3. Y a-t-il un foyer, ou une salle de récréation, où vous passez quelquefois du temps avec vos camarades? Qu'est-ce qu'il y a dans ce foyer?

**B. Jeu de rôles.** Use the expressions in **À propos** to play a brief scene with another student. He/She is looking for a roommate, and you want to obtain more information. Ask

**Suggestion:** Ask sts. to add other questions.

1. où est la chambre à louer
2. s'il y a un téléphone ou une télévision
3. s'il y a un lavabo ou une douche dans la chambre
4. si la chambre est calme
5. s'il est possible d'avoir des visiteurs le soir
6. si l'immeuble est grand ou petit

After the interview, decide if you are going to rent the room, and explain why or why not.

## PORTRAITS

### *Léopold Sédar Senghor (1906–)*

One of the most famous of the many Africans who have studied in Paris is the Senegalese poet and statesman Léopold Senghor. He graduated from the **Faculté des lettres** of the Sorbonne and taught in a **lycée** (*high school*) in Tours before returning to his native country, where he gained status and experience as a political leader and eventually became president—an office he held from 1960 to 1980. Senghor is also widely regarded as a poet and literary scholar. His poetry celebrates the traditions, land and people of Senegal, as well as the unifying greatness of **négritude** (*the culture and spirit of black people*).

CHAPITRE **CINQ**

# Famille et foyer

**En avant**

—Encore une histoire, s'il te plaît.

—Bon, mais après, vous allez au lit, les enfants!

**Communicative goals:** talking about family and relatives, identifying rooms in a house, expressing possession, talking about plans and destinations, expressing what you are doing or making, and expressing actions.

**En avant:** See scripts for follow-up questions recorded on student cassette.

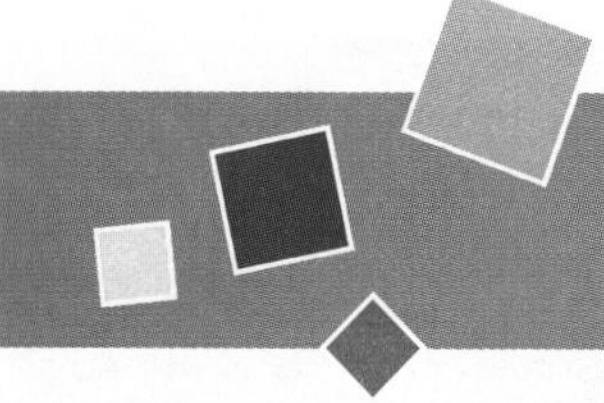

# Étude de vocabulaire

## Trois générations d'une famille

**Presentation:** Bring in pictures of famous families (the royal, Jackson, Kennedy families) to reinforce vocabulary. Once sts. have mastered the new nouns, make illogical statements and have sts. correct you: *Caroline Kennedy est la mère de Jacqueline. Ted Kennedy est le grand-père de John Kennedy, Jr., etc.*

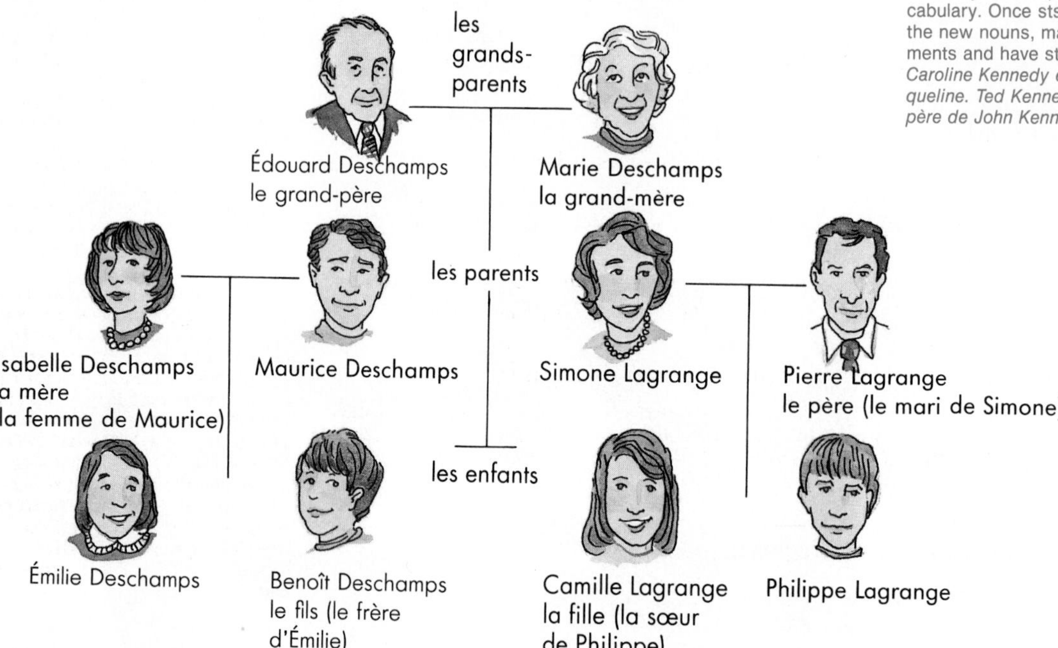


***Autres mots utiles:***

**le petit-enfant** grandchild
**la petite-fille** granddaughter
**le petit-fils** grandson

**le cousin, la cousine** cousin
**le neveu** nephew
**la nièce** niece
**l'oncle** uncle
**la tante** aunt

**le beau-frère** brother-in-law
**la belle-sœur** sister-in-law
**le demi-frère** half brother (or stepbrother)
**la demi-sœur** half sister (or stepsister)
**le beau-père** father-in-law (or stepfather)
**la belle-mère** mother-in-law (or stepmother)

**le parent** parent (or relative)
**l'arrière-grand-parent** great-grandparent

**célibataire** single
**divorcé(e)** divorced
**marié(e)** married

**A. La famille Deschamps.** Étudiez l'arbre généalogique (*family tree*) de la famille Deschamps et répondez aux questions.

1. Comment s'appelle la femme d'Édouard?
2. Comment s'appelle le mari d'Isabelle?
3. Comment s'appelle la tante d'Émilie et de Benoît? Et l'oncle?
4. Combien d'enfants ont les Lagrange? Combien de filles? Combien de fils?
5. Comment s'appelle le frère d'Émilie?
6. Combien de cousins ont Émilie et Benoît? Combien de cousines?
7. Comment s'appelle la grand-mère de Philippe? Et le grand-père?
8. Combien de petits-enfants ont Édouard et Marie? Combien de petites-filles? Combien de petits-fils?
9. Comment s'appelle la sœur de Philippe?
10. Comment s'appellent les parents de Maurice et de Simone?

**B. Masculin, féminin.** Donnez le féminin.

MODÈLE: le frère → la sœur

1. le mari 2. l'oncle 3. le père 4. le fils 5. le grand-père 6. le cousin

**C. Qui sont-ils?** Complétez les définitions suivantes de façon (*manner*) logique.

1. Le frère de mon père est mon _____.
2. La fille de ma tante est ma _____.
3. Le père de ma mère est mon _____.
4. La femme de mon grand-père est ma _____.

Maintenant définissez les personnes suivantes.

5. nièce
6. cousin
7. tante
8. grand-père
9. belle-sœur
10. demi-frère

**D. Conversation: Une famille française.** Avec un(e) camarade, décrivez (*describe*) la famille sur la photo. Donnez le nombre de personnes, et essayez de deviner (*try to guess*) qui sont les personnes et quel âge elles ont. Puis imaginez leur (*their*) profession, leurs goûts (*tastes*), leur personnalité. Donnez le plus de (*as many . . . as*) détails possibles.

**Suggestions:** Voici, voilà, c'est, il/elle a, il/elle aime, il/elle est...

**Suggestion:** May be done in pairs. Spot check some of the answers afterwards.

**Additional activities:** A. *Décrivez la famille Deschamps.* MODÈLE: *Isabelle Deschamps: Maurice Deschamps → Isabelle Deschamps est la femme de Maurice Deschamps.* 1. *Édouard Deschamps: Émilie Deschamps* 2. *Pierre Lagrange: Camille Lagrange* 3. *Isabelle Deschamps: Benoît Deschamps* 4. *Maurice Deschamps: Édouard Deschamps* 5. *Camille Lagrange: Simone Lagrange* 6. *Édouard et Marie Deschamps: Camille Lagrange* B. *Les parents proches. Continuez à décrire la famille Deschamps.* 1. *Simone Lagrange est la tante de Benoît et d'Émilie. Qui est la tante de Philippe et de Camille?* 2. *Pierre Lagrange est l'oncle de Benoît et d'Émilie. Qui est l'oncle de Philippe et de Camille?* 3. *Benoît est le neveu de Simone et de Pierre Lagrange. Qui est le neveu de Maurice Deschamps?* 4. *Émilie est la nièce de Simone et de Pierre Lagrange. Qui est la nièce de Maurice Deschamps?* C. Focus on one family member and review his/her relationship to others in family: *Comment s'appelle la mère de Simone? Qui est le père de Philippe?* D. Sts. invent details about members of the Deschamps family as you ask questions, using *-er* verbs. *Qui travaille? Où travaillent-ils/elles? Qui étudie à l'école primaire? à l'école secondaire?* etc.

**E. Une famille américaine.** Maintenant posez (*ask*) les questions suivantes à votre camarade.

1. As-tu des frères? des sœurs? des demi-frères ou des demi-sœurs? Combien? Comment s'appellent-ils/elles? (Ils/Elles s'appellent... )
2. As-tu des grands-parents? Combien? Habitent-ils avec la famille? dans une maison? dans un appartement?
3. As-tu des cousins ou des cousines? Combien? Habitent-ils/elles près ou loin (*far*) de la famille?
4. Combien d'enfants (de fils ou de filles) désires-tu avoir? Combien d'enfants y a-t-il dans une famille idéale?

**Suggestion:** May be done in pairs or groups of three. Sts. should take notes and report answers.

**Follow-up:** Three or four sts. could be asked to give a short description of the family of one of the other sts. interviewed, while the whole class takes notes. The class then asks instructor questions about information shared. Class members are divided into two teams for this activity. When a team "stumps" the teacher, they get a point. Team with most questions missed by teacher wins.

| | | | |
|---|---|---|---|
| **papa** | le père | **tonton** | l'oncle |
| **maman** | la mère | **tatie** ou **tata** | la tante |
| **papy** ou **pépé** | le grand-père | **le frangin** | le frère |
| **mamie** ou **mémé** | la grand-mère | **la frangine** | la sœur |
| **les vieux** | les parents | | |

EN CONTEXTE

**Mes vieux** aiment passer le dimanche en famille. **Ma frangine** parle de ses cours de physique à **tatie** Isabelle. **Mon frangin** joue aux cartes avec **pépé** et **tonton** Marcel. Et moi, je parle de politique avec **mémé**.

**Note**: *Papa, maman, papy, pépé, mamie, mémé, tonton, tatie* and *tata* are used by people to address their relatives or to talk about them with other relatives. *Les vieux* should only be used in conversation between young people. It conveys the generation gap, as well as teenagers' rebelliousness and sense of superiority over their parents' generation. *Frangin, frangine* are used by youth to talk about their siblings. It does not have any particular connotation or judgment.

## La maison des Chabrier

MAISON À LOUER: 5 pièces—cuisine, salle de bains

**Presentation:** Use magazine pictures in class for identification of rooms and furniture.

**Continuation:** Ask questions such as the following: *Où joue-t-on aux cartes? Où parie-t-on avec des amis? Où est le téléphone?*

la chambre
le couloir
la salle de bains
le balcon
l'arbre
la terrasse
la salle de séjour
la salle à manger
la cuisine
le jardin

***Autres mots utiles:***

**le bureau** study/office
**l'escalier** (*m.*) stairway
**le rez-de-chaussée** ground floor
**le premier (deuxième) étage** second (third) floor (in the U.S.)

**Note:** Sts. often have trouble with the difference between *premier étage* and *first floor*. A drawing on the board may help.

**Additional activity:** *Le plan de la maison. Décrivez la maison des Chabrier.* MODÈLE: *sous / salle de bains* → *La cuisine est sous la salle de bains.* 1. *à côté de / salle de séjour* 2. *sur / salle de séjour* 3. *à côté de / salle de bains* 4. *à côté de / salle à manger* 5. *sous / chambre* 6. *à côté de / maison*

**A. Les pièces de la maison.** Trouvez les pièces d'après (*according to*) les définitions suivantes.

1. la pièce où il y a une table pour manger 2. la pièce où il y a un poste de télévision (*TV set*) 3. la pièce où il y a un lavabo 4. la pièce où on prépare le dîner 5. un lieu de passage 6. la pièce où il y a un lit

**B. Nantes: Propriété à vendre.** Regardez la publicité et choisissez la réponse correcte.

1. La publicité montre une propriété simple / luxueuse (*luxurious*).
2. La propriété a un grand parc / un petit jardin.
3. Il y a plusieurs chambres au rez-de-chaussée / une chambre au rez-de-chaussée.

**Répondez.**

1. À votre avis, quels sont les avantages de cette propriété? Et les inconvénients (*disadvantages*)?
2. Trouvez quelque chose (*something*) sur la photo qui n'est pas mentionné dans le texte.

**Suggestion:** See the *IM* (*Instructor's Manual*) for a discussion of using realia in the classroom. Remind sts. that they do not need to understand every word in the ad. Bring in other housing ads and ask either/or questions about them: *Ces appartements sont-ils grands ou petits?*

**Follow-up:** Ask sts. to describe their ideal apartment.

**LA COQUETTE DE L'OUEST**

A proximité de Nantes se cache[a] derrière de hauts murs[b] une propriété du XV[e] siècle entourée d'un parc paysager[c] de 6 500 mètres carrés. Le bâtiment[d] principal se compose, au rez-de-chaussée, d'un salon, de deux salles à manger, d'une cuisine, d'un bureau et d'une chambre avec salle de bains. Chaque pièce comprend une grande cheminée aux armoiries des seigneurs de Housseau. On accède à l'étage supérieur par un escalier d'époque[e] et on trouve plusieurs chambres avec salle de bains. Belles dépendances aménageables et piscine chauffée.[f] Surface habitable : 500 m². Prix : 5 500 000F. Renseignements : Michel Audonnet, au 40 30 21 95.

[a]se... *hides*
[b]hauts... *high walls*
[c]entourée... *surrounded by a wooded park*
[d]*building*
[e]*original (period)*
[f]piscine... *heated pool*

## Mots-clés

*Chez.* **Chez** is a very commonly used word which generally refers to someone's personal residence and means **à la maison de**. **Chez** can also express a place of business (doctor's office, auto repair shop, tailor's studio, etc.).

| | |
|---|---|
| Tu vas **chez** Eric ce soir? | *Are you going to Eric's tonight?* |
| J'habite **chez** mes parents. | *I live with my parents.* |
| On va **chez** toi ou **chez** moi? | *Are we going to your place or my place?* |
| Moi, je vais **chez** le dentiste et puis **chez** le boucher! | *I'm going to the dentist('s) and then to the butcher('s)!* |

**Additional activity:** Sts. think of as many words as they can (in French) that they associate with their own lodgings; they then make a similar word-association chain based on the Zairian idea of *maison*. Use these chains as a point of departure for a cross-cultural comparison. During the discussion, encourage sts. to think about why houses are designed as they are in a given culture: *tradition*, *climate*, *local resources*, etc.

The activity could be done the night before for homework, when sts. read the cultural note. Sts. then share their word association maps in class in small groups, or words from chains can be listed on board.

## Nouvelles francophones

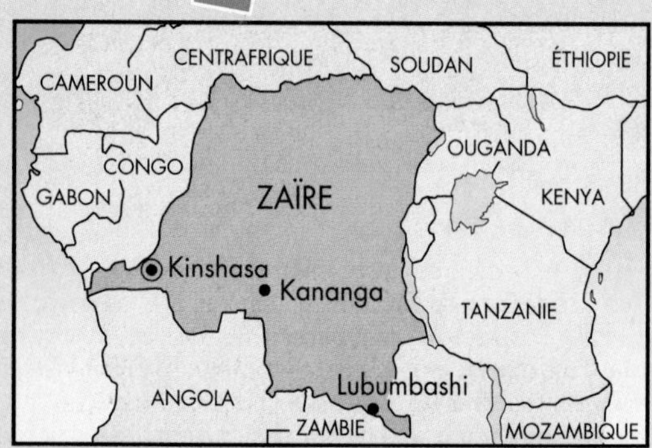

### Zaïre: Another kind of housing

Most of the Zairian population is rural and lives in scattered villages. The style of housing varies regionally, as does the size of the villages. A village with 150 to 200 dwellings is considered large. Houses are constructed of local materials. The walls are built first with trees or poles vertically planted in the ground. They are kept sturdy with branches of palm trees or split bamboo that are placed horizontally on both sides of the walls and tied with vines. Mud clay is then put in the spaces inside the branches and between the poles and is also used to smooth the sides of the walls. The base of the roof is made of lightweight trees that serve as rafters; they are held together with palm-tree branches or bamboo and vines. A special type of dry grass is added for thatching.

In large urban areas one finds a combination of European-style houses, generally made of stucco, and smaller, cement dwellings with tin roofs. Although these modern houses last longer and save the owner from periodically rejuvenating the grass roofs, the traditional house is cooler and less expensive.

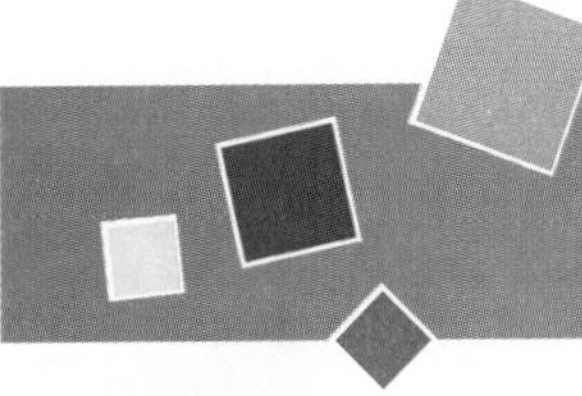

# Étude de grammaire

## 13. EXPRESSING POSSESSION
### *mon, ton, etc.*

**La maison, reflet d'une situation sociale**

Marc, un étudiant à la Sorbonne, fait un petit tour de Paris et de la banlieue avec Thu, une amie vietnamienne. En voiture, il indique à Thu différentes sortes de logement.

**Mon** beau-frère a beaucoup d'argent. Voilà **sa** villa: elle est formidable, n'est-ce pas? **Notre** maison est petite, mais confortable; **ma** famille y est assez heureuse. Ici en banlieue on trouve les grands ensembles où habitent surtout des familles d'ouvriers et d'immigrés. **Leurs** immeubles s'appellent les H.L.M.

Maintenant complétez les phrases selon la description de Marc.

1. Voici les immeubles où habitent beaucoup d'ouvriers et d'immigrés. _____ habitations s'appellent les _____.
2. _____ beau-frère est très riche; _____ villa est grande et élégante.
3. Et voilà la maison de _____ famille. Elle est petite mais _____.

One way to indicate possession in French is to use the preposition **de: la maison *de* Claudine**. Another way to show possession is to use possessive adjectives. In French, possessive adjectives agree in gender and number with the nouns they modify.

| | SINGULAR | | PLURAL |
|---|---|---|---|
| | *Masculine* | *Feminine* | *Masculine and Feminine* |
| my<br>your (**tu**)<br>his, her, its, one's | **mon** père<br>**ton** père<br>**son** père | **ma** mère<br>**ta** mère<br>**sa** mère | **mes** parents<br>**tes** parents<br>**ses** parents |
| our<br>your (**vous**)<br>their | **notre** père<br>**votre** père<br>**leur** père | **notre** mère<br>**votre** mère<br>**leur** mère | **nos** parents<br>**vos** parents<br>**leurs** parents |

**Mon frère** et **ma sœur** aiment le sport. — *My brother and my sister like sports.*
Voilà **notre maison**. — *There's our house.*
Habitez-vous avec **votre sœur** et **vos parents**? — *Do you live with your sister and your parents?*
Ils skient avec **leurs cousins** et **leur oncle**. — *They're skiing with their cousins and their uncle.*

**Presentation:** Model pronunciation, using a short sentence: *Mon père est sympathique. Ma mère est agréable,* etc. Point out the open *o* in *votre* [vɔtrə] and *notre* [nɔtrə].

The forms **mon**, **ton**, and **son** are also used before feminine nouns that begin with a vowel or mute **h**:

affiche (*f.*) → **mon affiche**
amie (*f.*) → **ton amie**
histoire (*f.*) → **son histoire**

Pay particular attention to the use of **sa**, **son**, **ses** (*his, her*). While English has two possessives, corresponding to the sex of the possessor (*his, her*), French has three, corresponding to the gender and number of the noun possessed (**sa**, **son**, **ses**).

Il / Elle } aime **sa** maison. — *He likes his house. She likes her house.*
Il / Elle } aime **son** chien. — *He likes his dog. She likes her dog.*
Il / Elle } aime **ses** livres. — *He likes his books. She likes her books.*

**Note:** Mention that *Elle aime sa maison* can also mean *She likes his house*, but that the French often add *sa maison à elle/à lui* to clarify. The stressed pronouns are presented in a later chapter.

**Suggestion:** Use the following as a preliminary ex.: *Comment dit-on en français? 1. Anne is looking at her mother. 2. Anne is looking at her father. 3. Anne is looking at her parents. 4. Marc is listening to his father. 5. Marc is listening to his mother. 6. Marc is listening to his brothers and sisters.*

## Vérifions!

**A. La curiosité.** Formulez des questions et répondez.

MODÈLES: la lampe de Georges? →
—Est-ce que c'est la lampe de Georges?
—Oui, c'est sa lampe.

les lampes de Georges →
—Est-ce que ce sont les lampes de Georges?
—Non, ce ne sont pas ses lampes.

1. la chambre de Pierre? (oui)
2. la commode d'Yvonne? (non)
3. les affiches de Jean? (non)
4. le piano de Pierre et de Sophie? (oui)
5. les meubles (*furniture*) d'Annick? (non)
6. les bureaux des parents? (oui)

**Follow-up:** Ask sts. to show pictures of family members or objects or show possessions. Ask questions that elicit possessive adjectives.

**B. Casse-tête familial** (*Family puzzle*). Posez rapidement les questions suivantes à un(e) camarade.

MODÈLE: Qui est le fils de ton oncle? → C'est mon cousin.

1. Qui est la mère de ton père?
2. Qui est la fille de ta tante?
3. Qui est la femme de ton oncle?
4. Qui est le père de ton père?
5. Qui est le frère de ta mère?
6. Qui est la sœur de ta mère?

**Follow-up:** Sts. invent questions of their own, trying to stump other sts. For example: *Qui est le frère de mon père?*

**C. À qui est-ce?** Complétez les dialogues suivants avec des adjectifs possessifs: **mon**, **ma**, **mes**, **ton**, **ta**, **tes**, **son**, **sa**, **ses**, **notre**, **nos**, **votre**, **vos**, **leur**, **leurs**. Utilisez chaque (*each*) adjectif seulement une fois (*only once*). Étudiez bien le contexte avant de (*before*) choisir l'adjectif.

1. —Paul et Florence adorent les animaux.
   —Oui, ils ont un chien et deux chats (*cats*): _____ chien s'appelle Marius et _____ chats Minou et Félix.
2. —Tiens, voilà Pierre. Avec qui est-il?
   —Il est avec _____ parents et _____ amie Laure.
   —Et _____ sœur n'est pas là?
   —Non, elle est en vacances au Maroc.
3. —Salut, Alain!
   —Salut, Pierre. Dis, la jolie fille aux cheveux blonds, c'est _____ cousine belge?
   —Oui. Viens (*Come*). Alain, je te présente _____ cousine Sylvie.
   —Enchanté, Mademoiselle.
4. —Pardon, vous êtes Monsieur et Madame Legrand, n'est-ce pas?
   —Oui.
   —Je suis Monsieur Smith, le professeur d'anglais de _____ enfants.
   —Oh, mais ce ne sont pas _____ enfants, ce sont les fils de mon frère Henri. Voici _____ fils.
5. —Tu as de la chance, tu as une famille super! _____ parents sont très sympa! Est-ce que _____ grand-père habite avec vous?
   —Non, mais il est souvent à la maison.

**Suggestion:** Ask pairs of sts. to play the roles in the dialogues, completing the sentences. Ask several sts. to play the roles for the whole class, in order to check responses.

**Additional activity:** *À la maison. Faites les substitutions et les changements nécessaires.* 1. *Avec qui habitez-vous?* → *J'habite avec mon* père. (*sœurs, grand-mère, oncle, amis*) 2. *Qu'est-ce que tu aimes dans ma chambre?* → *J'aime ton chat.* (*affiches, chaîne stéréo, disques, armoire*) 3. *À qui téléphone ma cousine Claire?* → *Elle téléphone à votre* père. (*parents, tante, cousin*) 4. *Avec qui habitent-ils?* → *Ils habitent avec leurs* parents. (*frère, amis, mère, grands-parents*)

## Mots-clés

*Saying how you feel about something*: Often in conversation, you just want to express your personal reaction to something. Here are some useful phrases.

| | |
|---|---|
| Comment trouves-tu la nouvelle maison d'oncle Henri? | *What do you think of Uncle Henry's new house?* |
| Elle est **formidable/superbe/géniale**! | *It's great/superb/cool!* |
| Elle est **super/très chouette**! | *It's super/cute!* |
| Elle est **bien**. | *It's nice.* |
| Elle n'est **pas mal**. | *It's not bad.* |
| Je ne l'aime **pas du tout**. | *I don't like it at all.* |
| Franchement, elle est **affreuse/horrible**! | *Frankly, it's awful!* |

**Suggestion:** Give other questions that elicit these responses: *Comment trouves-tu ma nouvelle robe? Comment trouves-tu mon nouveau tableau? Comment trouves-tu mes nouvelles bottes? ma nouvelle coiffure?* etc.

**Suggestion:** Model pronunciation and encourage sts. to use these adjectives and adverbs in the exercises.

### *Parlons-en!*

**A. Interview.** Posez les questions suivantes à un(e) camarade de classe.

1. Y a-t-il un membre de ta famille (un cousin, une cousine, un neveu, etc.) que tu admires particulièrement? Pourquoi? 2. Comment s'appelle-t-il/elle? 3. Où habite-t-il/elle? Avec qui? Comment est sa maison? 4. Quel est son sport préféré? Sa musique favorite?

Maintenant faites le portrait du parent proche (*close relative*) préféré de votre camarade. Utilisez les mots (les expressions) suivant(e)s: **formidable**, **bien**, **génial**, **pas mal**.

**Follow-up:** Have sts. write short description of their partner's relative and hand it in at end of interview activity. Use this st. material for dictations or listening passages the next class day.

**B. Sondage** (*Poll*) ***Madame Figaro*: Le bonheur** (*happiness*) **dans le monde**; **les Européens plutôt heureux.** Look at the table, assess the information, and express your personal opinion. Rank the different criteria in the table from 1 (most important) to 10 (least important).

**Suggestion:** Before analyzing results, have sts. cover them and circulate to interview classmates quickly. The class responses can be tallied at the end and compared to the results presented.

**IMPORTANT : L'ÉDUCATION DES ENFANTS**
**Sur le plan du bonheur, quel domaine vous semble le plus important ?**

| CRITÈRES / PAYS | FRANCE | BELGIQUE | R.F.A. | ITALIE | ESPAGNE | G.B. | ETATS-UNIS | JAPON |
|---|---|---|---|---|---|---|---|---|
| ÉDUCATION ENFANTS | **8,4** | **8,2** | 7,8 | **8,4** | **8,3** | **7,4** | **7,1** | 6,5 |
| SANTÉ[a] | 8,1 | 8,1 | **8,4** | 8,2 | 7,9 | 7,3 | 7,0 | **8,1** |
| VIE DE FAMILLE | 8,0 | 7,8 | 7,8 | 8,0 | 7,9 | 7,3 | 7,1 | 7,6 |
| QUALITÉ DE VIE | 7,0 | 6,5 | 6,4 | 6,0 | 6,2 | 6,8 | 6,8 | 6,3 |
| JOB | 6,8 | 6,8 | 6,8 | 6,8 | 6,8 | 6,0 | 5,9 | 7,6 |
| VIE AMOUREUSE[b] | 6,5 | 6,7 | 5,7 | 7,5 | 7,1 | 6,3 | 6,1 | 5,7 |
| AMIS[c] | 6,2 | 6,0 | 5,6 | 5,8 | 7,1 | 6,2 | 6,5 | 6,6 |
| NIVEAU DE VIE | 6,1 | 5,7 | 6,1 | 5,6 | 5,4 | 5,9 | 5,9 | 5,8 |
| LOISIRS[d] | 5,5 | 5,7 | 5,0 | 5,8 | 5,7 | 4,7 | 5,3 | 5,2 |
| POLITIQUE | 3,8 | 3,3 | 5,0 | 3,2 | 3,9 | 4,1 | 4,5 | 5,1 |

N.B. : les notes sont données sur 10.

[a]*health*
[b]*love*
[c]*standard*
[d]*leisure activities*

**Selon** (*According to*) **vous:**

Le domaine (*area*) le plus important, c'est ____.
Le domaine le moins important, c'est ____.
Le domaine qui donne le plus de satisfaction, c'est ____.
Le domaine qui donne le moins de satisfaction, c'est ____.

Maintenant regardez les résultats du sondage par catégorie et par pays (*nation*). Choisissez la réponse correcte.

1. Les Français pensent que le plus (*the most*) important, c'est *la santé / l'éducation des enfants / la vie de famille.*
2. Les Japonais pensent que le plus important, c'est *l'éducation des enfants / la vie de famille / la santé.*
3. Les Américains pensent que *le job / la vie amoureuse / la vie de famille* donne le plus de satisfaction.
4. Les Espagnols pensent que *la vie de famille / l'éducation des enfants / la qualité de la vie* donne le plus de satisfaction.

Comparez vos réponses avec les résultats du sondage et les réponses de vos camarades.

Le jardinage est un des passe-temps favoris des Français.

## 14. TALKING ABOUT YOUR PLANS AND DESTINATIONS
## The Verb *aller*

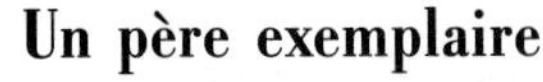

### Un père exemplaire

SIMON: On joue au tennis cet après-midi?
STÉPHANE: Non, je **vais** au jardin zoologique avec Céline.
SIMON: Alors, demain?
STÉPHANE: Désolé, mais demain je **vais** emmener Sébastien chez le dentiste.
SIMON: Quel père exemplaire!

Vrai ou faux? Corrigez les phrases fausses.

1. Stéphane est le grand-père de Céline et Sébastien.
2. Stéphane va aller au zoo avec Céline.
3. Simon va jouer au tennis avec Stéphane.

## A. Forms of *aller*

The verb **aller** is irregular in form.

| PRESENT TENSE OF **aller** (*to go*) | | | |
|---|---|---|---|
| je | **vais** | nous | **allons** |
| tu | **vas** | vous | **allez** |
| il, elle, on | **va** | ils, elles | **vont** |

| | |
|---|---|
| **Allez-vous** à Grenoble pour vos vacances? | *Are you going to Grenoble for your vacation?* |
| Comment **va-t-on** à Grenoble? | *How do you go to (get to) Grenoble?* |

You have already used **aller** in several expressions.

| | |
|---|---|
| Comment **allez-vous**? | *How are you?* |
| Salut, ça **va**? | *Hi, how's it going?* |
| Ça **va** bien (mal). | *Fine (badly). (Things are going fine [badly].)* |

## B. *Aller* + Infinitive: Near Future*

In French, **aller** + *infinitive* is used to express a future event, usually something that is going to happen soon, in the near future. English also uses *to go* + *infinitive* to express actions or events that are going to happen soon.

| | |
|---|---|
| Nous **allons téléphoner** à Paul. | *We're going to call Paul.* |
| Il **va louer** un appartement. | *He's going to rent an apartment.* |
| **Allez**-vous **visiter** la France cet été? | *Are you going to visit France this summer?* |

### *Vérifions!*

**A. Où va-t-on?** La solution est simple!

**Suggestion:** Can be done as a paired writing activity. Several sts. can share their answers with the class at the end.

MODÈLE: J'ai envie de regarder un film. → Alors, je vais au cinéma!

| | |
|---|---|
| 1. Nous avons faim. | à l'hôpital |
| 2. Il a envie de parler français. | dans la salle de séjour |
| 3. Elles ont besoin d'étudier. | à la bibliothèque |
| 4. J'ai soif. | dans la cuisine |
| 5. Tu as sommeil. | aux courts de tennis |
| 6. Vous avez envie de regarder la télévision. | à Paris |
| 7. Nous sommes malades (*sick*). | dans la salle à manger |
| 8. Elle a envie de jouer au tennis. | dans la chambre |

*Le futur proche

## Mots-clés

*Saying when you are going to do something*

| | |
|---|---|
| **tout à l'heure** | *in a while* |
| **tout de suite** | *immediately* |
| **bientôt** | *soon* |
| **demain** | *tomorrow* |
| **la semaine prochaine** | *next week* |
| **dans quatre jours** | *in four days* |
| **ce week-end** | *this weekend* |
| **ce soir/matin** | *this evening/morning* |
| **cet après-midi** | *this afternoon* |

**B. Des projets** (*plans*).

MODÈLE: tu / regarder / programme préféré / soir →
Tu vas regarder ton programme préféré ce soir.

1. je / finir / travail / semaine prochaine
2. nous / écouter / disques de jazz
3. vous / jouer / guitare
4. Frédéric / trouver / livre de français / tout de suite
5. je / choisir / film préféré
6. les garçons / aller au cinéma / voiture / après-midi
7. tu / aller / concert / avec / amis

### *Parlons-en!*

**A. Samedi après-midi.** Qu'est-ce que ces gens vont faire? Regardez les dessins et devinez leur intention.

MODÈLE: Monique a **sa** raquette parce qu'elle (*because she*) **va jouer au tennis**.

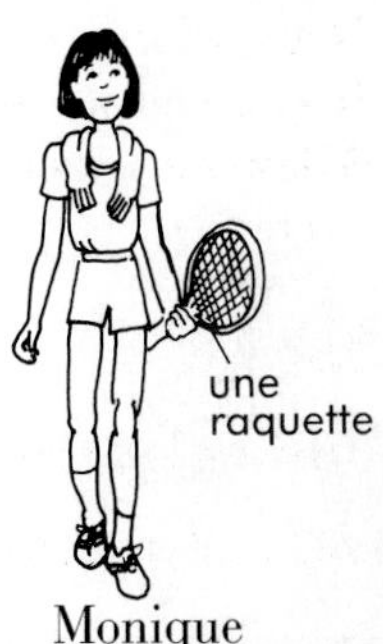

Monique

Saïd

Mme Rosso

M. Cartier

Cyrille

M. Duteil

Marie

Franck

**B. Quels sont vos projets pour le week-end?** Interviewez un(e) camarade de classe. Racontez (*Tell*) à la classe les projets de votre camarade. Est-ce que vous faites (*are doing*) les mêmes choses (*same things*) ce week-end?

**Suggestions**: rester (*stay*) à la maison, écouter la radio (des disques), préparer un dîner (des leçons), regarder un film (la télévision), travailler à la bibliothèque (dans le jardin), aller dans un restaurant extraordinaire, parler avec des amis, finir un livre intéressant...

MODÈLE: aller au cinéma →

VOUS: Vas-tu aller au cinéma?
UN(E) CAMARADE: Oui, je vais aller au cinéma. (*ou* Non, je ne vais pas aller au cinéma.)

**Follow-up:** Have sts. report a few answers to class, or write a short composition on their partner's responses. Sts. can count up number of affirmative sentences to see who is the most active individual in class.

**Follow-up:** Ask sts. to give their *"projets pour demain"* to a small group. They can choose responses from those presented or add other ideas.

# 15. EXPRESSING WHAT YOU ARE DOING OR MAKING
## The Verb *faire*

### Une question d'organisation

SANDRINE: Vous mangez à la cafétéria, ta camarade de chambre et toi?
MARION: Non, Candice et moi, nous sommes très organisées. Elle, elle **fait** les courses et moi, je **fais** la cuisine.
SANDRINE: Et qui **fait** la vaisselle?
MARION: Le lave-vaisselle, bien sûr!

Répondez d'après le dialogue.

1. Qui fait la cuisine?
2. Qui fait la vaisselle?
3. Qui fait les courses?

Et chez vous, en général, qui fait la cuisine? La vaisselle? Les courses?

## A. Forms of faire

*Presentation: Model pronunciation of verb forms in short sentences, taken from dialogue. Example: Je fais la vaisselle après le dîner.*

The verb **faire** is irregular in form.

| PRESENT TENSE OF **faire** (*to do, to make*) | | | |
|---|---|---|---|
| je | **fais** | nous | **faisons** |
| tu | **fais** | vous | **faites** |
| il, elle, on | **fait** | ils, elles | **font** |

Note the difference in the pronunciation of **fais/fait** [fɛ], **faites** [fɛt], and **faisons** [fəzɔ̃].

| | |
|---|---|
| **Je fais** mon lit. | *I make my bed.* |
| **Nous faisons** le café. | *We're making coffee.* |
| **Faites** attention! C'est chaud. | *Watch out! It's hot.* |

## B. Expressions with faire

*Presentation: Model pronunciation of faire expressions. You may want to use expressions in short personalized questions as you present them: Aimez-vous faire la cuisine? Où faites-vous vos devoirs? If possible, bring in pictures demonstrating these actions. You may need to explain what an idiomatic expression is. An idiom (une expression idiomatique) is a group of words that has meaning to the speakers of a language but that does not necessarily appear to make sense when examined word by word. Idiomatic expressions are often different from one language to another. For example, in English, to pull Mary's leg usually means to tease her, not to grab her leg and pull it.*

The verb **faire** is used in many idiomatic expressions.

| | |
|---|---|
| faire attention | *to pay attention to, to watch out (for)* |
| faire la connaissance (de) | *to meet (for the first time), make the acquaintance (of)* |
| faire les courses | *to do errands* |
| faire la cuisine | *to cook* |
| faire ses devoirs | *to do (one's) homework* |
| faire la lessive | *to do the laundry* |
| faire le marché | *to do the shopping, to go to the market* |
| faire le ménage | *to do the housework* |
| faire une promenade | *to take a walk* |
| faire un tour (en voiture) | *to take a walk (a ride)* |
| faire la vaisselle | *to do the dishes* |
| faire un voyage | *to take a trip* |
| Le matin je **fais le marché**, l'après-midi je **fais une promenade** et le soir je **fais la cuisine**. | *In the morning I go to the market, in the afternoon I take a walk, and in the evening I cook.* |

**Faire** is also used to talk about sports: **faire du sport**, **faire du jogging**, **de la voile** (*sailing*), **du ski**, **de l'aérobic**... As you progress in your study of French, you will notice that **faire** is one of the most commonly used verbs.

## *Vérifions!*

**A. Faisons connaissance!** Suivez le modèle.

MODÈLE: je / le professeur d'italien →
Je fais la connaissance du professeur d'italien.

1. tu / la sœur de Louise
2. nous / un cousin
3. Annick / une étudiante sympathique
4. les Levêque / les parents de Simone
5. je / la femme du professeur
6. vous / la nièce de M. de La Tour

**B. Activités du week-end.** Qui fait les activités suivantes? Faites des phrases logiques avec les éléments des deux colonnes.

**Suggestion:** Encourage sts. to use other idiomatic expressions with *faire*.

1. Tu...
2. Pierre...
3. Anne et Monique...
4. Mon frère et moi, nous...
5. Benoît et toi, vous...
6. Non, moi le dimanche, je...

a. faisons du jogging dans le parc
b. ne fais pas le ménage
c. faites vos devoirs de français
d. fais la cuisine pour mes amis
e. font des courses en ville
f. fait du sport avec ses copains

**C. Qu'est-ce qu'ils font?** Faites des phrases complètes. Utilisez des expressions avec **faire**.

**Suggestion:** Bring in magazine pictures of people doing activities that require *faire* expressions and have sts. describe pictures.

1. M. Dupont et son chien...

2. M. Henri... de Mlle Gervais.

3. Vous, vous...

4. Mlle Duval...

5. Ma sœur et moi...

6. Et moi maintenant, je...

## Mots-clés

*Saying how often you usually do things*

| | |
|---|---|
| **tous les jours** | *every day* |
| **une / deux / trois fois par semaine** | *once / twice / three times a week* |
| **le lundi / le vendredi soir** | *on Mondays / on Friday evenings* |
| **le week-end** | *on weekends* |
| **pendant les vacances** | *during vacation* |

### Parlons-en!

**A. Les activités.** Qu'est-ce que vous faites... ? Complétez les phrases suivantes avec des réponses personnelles.

1. Je fais _____ tous les jours. 2. J'aime faire _____. 3. Je suis obligé(e) de faire _____ une fois par semaine. 4. Je déteste faire _____ le week-end. 5. J'adore faire _____ pendant les vacances.

**Suggestion:** Have sts. do in writing first and then solicit variety of answers orally. Ask sts. to recall each other's answers: *X préfère jouer au frisbee le week-end...*

**Sondage.** Maintenant comparez vos réponses avec celles (*those*) de vos camarades. Faites une liste de toutes les activités mentionnées. Ensuite, classez-les selon (*Then rank them according to*) leur popularité.

**B. Mimes.** Form two teams. Out of a hat choose a piece of paper on which an expression with **faire** is written. Mime the expression and the other students will guess it. Each team gets one point when they guess the right expression.

# 16. EXPRESSING ACTIONS
## -re Verbs

### Beauregard au restaurant

JILL: Vous **entendez**?
GÉRARD: Non, qu'est-ce qu'il y a?
JILL: J'**entends** un bruit sous la table.
GENEVIÉVE: Oh ça! C'est Beauregard... Il **attend** le poulet... et il n'aime pas **attendre**...

Trouvez la phrase équivalente dans le dialogue.

1. Écoutez.
2. Quel est le problème?
3. Il n'aime pas patienter (*wait patiently*).

A third group of French verbs has infinitives that end in **-re**, like **vendre** (*to sell*).

**Note:** Point out that all three singular forms sound alike.

**Suggestion:** For listening comprehension practice, have sts. indicate whether they hear a singular or plural verb in the following sentences: 1. *Elles attendent le dessert.* (Solicit two reasons for plural: *liaison* and *d* sound.) 2. *Il rend le poulet au chef.* 3. *Elles perdent leur appétit.* 4. *Il entend le chien.* 5. *Il répond à la question de son ami.*

| PRESENT TENSE OF **vendre** (*to sell*) | | | |
|---|---|---|---|
| je | vends | nous | vend**ons** |
| tu | vends | vous | vend**ez** |
| il, elle, on | vend | ils, elles | vend**ent** |

Other verbs conjugated like **vendre** include the following.

| | |
|---|---|
| **attendre** | *to wait (for)* |
| **descendre** | *to go down (to), to get off* |
| **entendre** | *to hear* |
| **perdre** | *to lose, to waste* |
| **rendre** | *to give back, to return* |
| **rendre visite à** | *to visit (someone)* |
| **répondre à** | *to answer* |

| | |
|---|---|
| **Elle attend** le dessert. | *She's waiting for dessert.* |
| **Nous descendons de** l'autobus. | *We're getting off the bus.* |
| **Le commerçant rend** la monnaie à la cliente. | *The storekeeper gives change back to the customer.* |
| **Je réponds à** sa question. | *I'm answering his question.* |

**Note:** Provide lots of examples with *attendre*, which poses problems because the English equivalent requires a preposition. *Rendre visite à* and *répondre à* also pose problems because of interference from English.

In French, the expression **rendre visite à** means to visit a *person* or *persons*.

**Je rends visite à** mon ami.

The verb **visiter** is used only with places or things.

**Les touristes visitent** les monuments de Paris.

## *Vérifions!*

**A. Tiens** (*You don't say*)! C'est bizarre: tout ce que (*everything that*) fait Jean-Paul, les autres le font aussi. Formez les phrases selon le modèle.

**Additional activity:** *Qu'est-ce qu'on fait maintenant? Changez du singulier au pluriel ou vice versa.* MODÈLE: *Je vends ma guitare.* → *Nous vendons notre guitare.* 1. *Tu rends visite à ton amie Paulette.* 2. *Vous rendez un livre à la bibliothèque.* 3. *J'entends la voiture qui arrive.* 4. *Nous descendons de la voiture.* 5. *Elles perdent du temps au café.* 6. *Il répond aux questions de sa sœur.*

MODÈLE: vendre sa guitare (moi) →
—Jean-Paul vend sa guitare.
—Tiens! Moi aussi, je vends ma guitare.

1. rendre tous (*all*) ses livres à la bibliothèque (nous)
2. attendre une lettre importante (son frère)
3. descendre de l'autobus rue Mouffetard (vous)
4. entendre des bruits bizarres au sous-sol (*in the basement*) (moi)
5. perdre toujours ses lunettes (*glasses*) (toi)
6. répondre à un sondage (*poll*) d'opinion politique (les amis)

**B. Un week-end à Paris.** Complétez l'histoire avec les verbes de la colonne de droite (*right-hand column*).

**Suggestion:** Ask sts. to read the story in pairs, completing the sentences. Afterward, as a comprehension check, ask them to complete items 1–3 about the story.

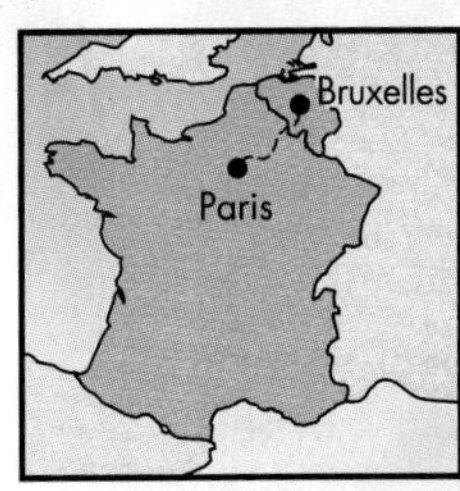


Alain et Marie-Lise habitent à Bruxelles. Aujourd'hui ils _____[1] à Paris en train. Ils vont _____[2] visite à leur cousine Pauline. Les trois cousins ont toujours beaucoup de projets (*plans*) et ne _____[3] pas une minute quand ils sont ensemble (*together*). Alain et Marie-Lise aiment beaucoup Pauline parce qu'elle _____[4] toujours à leurs lettres. Pauline aime aussi ses cousins, et elle _____[5] leur arrivée avec impatience. Elle _____[6] enfin la sonnette (*doorbell*)!

perdre
rendre
descendre
entendre
attendre
répondre

D'après (*according to*) l'histoire,...

1. Alain et Marie-Lise habitent en *France / Suisse / Belgique*.
2. Alain, Marie-Lise et Pauline sont *calmes / actifs / individualistes*.
3. Pauline *déteste / aime* écrire des lettres.

## *Parlons-en!*

**Suggestion:** Use for paired interview.

**Follow-up:** (1) Take tally of results of interviews. *Qui est patient? Qui est normal? Qui n'est pas patient du tout?* (2) Expand answers by asking sts. to say what they do in each situation. Example of expansion with model sentence: *Je prends un taxi.*

**Perdez-vous souvent patience?** Utilisez les questions suivantes pour interviewer un(e) camarade de classe. Il/Elle utilise **souvent**, **pas souvent** ou **toujours** dans sa réponse. Décidez d'après ses réponses s'il (si elle) est **très patient(e)**, **patient(e)**, **normal(e)**, **impatient(e)**, **très impatient(e)**.

MODÈLE:
VOUS: Tu attends l'autobus. Il n'arrive pas. Est-ce que tu perds patience?
UN(E) CAMARADE: Oui, je perds souvent patience.

1. Tu attends un coup de téléphone (*telephone call*). La personne ne téléphone pas. 2. Un ami (Une amie) ne répond pas à tes lettres. 3. Tu perds les clés (*keys*) de ta voiture ou de ton appartement. 4. Tu as rendez-vous avec un ami (une amie). Tu attends longtemps (*for a long time*), mais il/elle n'arrive pas.

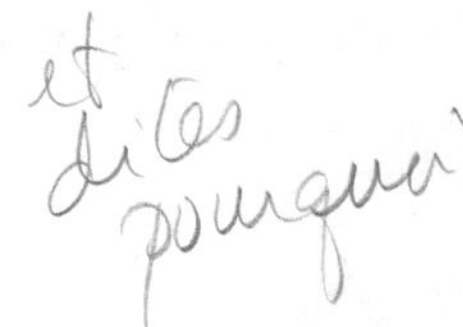

## France-culture

*Family life in France.* The French family is a strong social unit. In general, divorce is less common than in the United States, although the rate is rising. Extended families, in which grandparents and other family members live near one another and see each other frequently, are slightly more common. For all these reasons, the family has a strong influence on an individual's life.

The French government provides significant financial support for families. Both mother and father have the right to a substantial paid leave from work when a child is born. Families with more than two children receive governmental subsidies (**allocations familiales**). State-supported day-care centers (**crèches**) make it possible for parents to work outside the home. Children of unmarried parents receive the same protection and benefits as those of married parents.

Most French people continue to marry, but an increasing number do so only after having lived together (**l'union libre**) for several years. In the early 1990s more than half of the newly married couples had already lived under the same roof before officially saying "yes."

## Étude de prononciation

### Semivowels and Final Consonants

**Semivowels.** The sounds [ɥ], [w], and [j] are called semivowels. They are spelled with the letter groups indicated in the following examples and are pronounced in a single syllable, with no diphthong.

Prononcez avec le professeur.

1. [ɥ] huit fruit cuisine
2. [w] moi moins oui quoi revoir fois
3. [j] bien Marseille science voyage famille

**Final Consonants.** You have noticed that final consonants are generally silent in French. There are, however, a number of exceptions. The final consonant *is* pronounced, for example, in many words that end in the letters **c**, **r**, **f**, and **l**: **le lac**, **le soir**, **le chef**, **l'hôtel**. This rule itself has numerous exceptions: **le tabac**, **le dîner**, **le porc**, and **gentil** all end in a silent consonant. Learn the pronunciation of final consonants by example or by referring to a dictionary.

# Mise au point

**A. Les projets de Séverine et de Karine.** Formez des phrases complètes.

1. Séverine et Karine / aller / finir / études
2. elles / aller / faire / voyage / en France
3. elles / travailler / maintenant / pour payer (*to pay for*) / voyage
4. Séverine / faire / ménage / pour / tante
5. elles / aller / rendre visite à / tante de Séverine / à Paris
6. tante / habiter / près de / Quartier latin
7. elles / aller / être / content / parce que / elles / aller / faire / voyage magnifique

D'après l'histoire, choisissez la réponse la plus logique.

1. Séverine et Karine ont *50 ans / 35 ans / 20 ans*.
2. La tante de Séverine parle *allemand / français / latin*.
3. Pour payer le voyage, Séverine travaille comme *secrétaire / femme de ménage / vendeuse*.

**B. Activités.** Qu'est-ce qu'ils font et qu'est-ce qu'ils vont faire? Expliquez.

MODÈLE: le frère de Loïc et de Sandra →
Maintenant, leur frère fait ses devoirs. Après, il va aller au cinéma.

**Suggestion**: Have sts. write this out and present orally for correction. Show sts. that the seven sentences form a short story. If they write out ex., have them do so in paragraph form rather than with numbered sentences.

**Suggestion**: With books closed, have sts. take down story represented in sentences as dictation.

**Additional activities**: (1) *Conversation. Avec un(e) camarade de classe, reconstituez la conversation.* A: *Demandez à* B *ce qu'il/elle va faire aujourd'hui. (Qu'est-ce que...)* B: *Dites à (Tell)* A *que vous allez au concert.* A: *Demandez à* B *pourquoi il/elle va au concert.* B: *Dites à* A *que vos cousins rendent visite à votre famille et qu'ils ont envie d'aller au concert. Demandez à* A *s'il (si elle) a envie de faire la connaissance de vos cousins.* A: *Dites non à* B *et que vous préférez rester à la maison parce que vous faites vos devoirs.* B: *Dites à* A *que vous allez être en retard (late). Dites au revoir.* A: *Dites au revoir à* B. (2) *Un message. Vous travaillez dans un hôtel. Une touriste anglaise téléphone à l'hôtel, mais la propriétaire est absente. Vous notez son message. Maintenant, donnez le message à la propriétaire en français: 15h45: Mrs. Chesterfield telephones to (pour) answer your letter (lettre, f.). She is going to arrive at 5:00 P.M. with her son and daughter. They are going to wait for their cousins at the hotel. They are going to be six for dinner (à dîner). They prefer to eat in the hotel restaurant and are going to pay for (payer) the rooms in pounds (en livres).*

1. les parents de Loïc et de Sandra

2. le père de Loïc et de Sandra

3. l'oncle de Loïc et de Sandra

**Et vous?** Qu'est-ce que vous faites maintenant? Qu'est-ce que vous allez faire dans une heure?

**C. Questions personnelles.** En français, posez les questions suivantes à un(e) camarade de classe.

1. **La vie en famille:** Who does the dishes? When does he/she do the dishes? Who answers the telephone? Who does the shopping? When?
2. **La famille et les amis:** How many brothers and sisters does he/she have? Do they still (**toujours**) live at home? In what room does he/she talk with his/her friends and classmates? Are his/her parents going to meet his/her friends from the university? Does he/she often visit relatives?
3. **Ce week-end:** Is he/she going to take a trip? Is he/she going to visit friends? Whom? And you, what are you going to do? Where are you going to go?

**Suggestion:** Have sts. take notes on interview and report contents, orally or in writing.

**Follow-up:** Play a game about family members. Ask a st. to tell the truth or lie about how many brothers or sisters she or he has. The other sts. will ask questions (names, ages, professions, physical descriptions) about them to determine whether the st. is telling the truth.

## Interactions

**Suggestion:** Ask sts. to play their roles in groups (three for the first one; two for the second). Ask several sts. to replay the situations for the whole class.

In this chapter of *Rendez-vous*, you have practiced talking about your family and home, expressing possession, and talking about where you are going and your future plans. Act out the following situations, using the vocabulary and structures from these chapters.

**1. Conversation.** You are left alone in a room with a friend's parents (two classmates) while your friend prepares to go out with you. Make polite conversation with them. Talk about your family, your home, where you and your friend will go, and what you will do together this evening.

**2. En retard.** Call your mother, your father, or someone waiting for you (your classmate). Explain to him/her why you will be late. Tell where you are and what you are doing. Mention where you plan to go next and what you plan to do.

**Additional activity:** You run into your professor while walking across campus and must make small talk until you arrive at your destination. Talk about class, what you will do that weekend, your families, and future plans. Be very polite.

# Rencontres

## LECTURE

Presentation: Go over reading hints with sts., helping them notice topic sentences. Ask them to guess how topic sentences might be developed in each paragraph. As they read, they can confirm or refute their guesses.

### *Avant de lire*

**Topic sentences.** Notice that a sentence has been underlined in the first paragraph of the passage below. This is a topic sentence, so called because it expresses the general idea or main point of a paragraph. The other sentences elaborate upon or illustrate the main point. The topic sentence is usually the first one in a paragraph, although it sometimes appears at the end to summarize the ideas presented earlier. It may occasionally appear in the middle, serving as a thread to link ideas together. Can you identify the topic sentence in the third paragraph of the passage?

## Week-ends : les vacances hebdomadaires[a]

***Le dimanche reste un jour exceptionnel.***

Pour la plupart[b] des Français, il est synonyme de fête et de famille, une pause nécessaire dans un emploi du temps généralement chargé.[c] Neuf Français sur dix le passent en famille et il n'est pas rare que trois générations se retrouvent[d]; les jeunes de moins de 35 ans mariés se déplacent fréquemment[e] chez leurs parents pour déjeuner[f] avec eux, avec leurs propres enfants.

**Les Français aiment les dimanches**

- 86 % des Français aiment le dimanche, 11 % peu, 3 % pas du tout.
- Habituellement, 56 % retrouvent la famille, rencontrent des amis, 50 % regardent la télévision, 43 % se promènent, 33 % flânent[g] chez eux, 32 % jardinent ou bricolent,[h] 32 % lisent[i] ou écrivent[j] de la musique, 21 % dorment[k] ou font la sieste, 20 % s'occupent de[l] leurs enfants, 20 % cuisinent[m] ou vont au restaurant, 16 % font du sport, 16 % travaillent, 11 % prennent le temps de prier,[n] 9 % vont au marché ou font les courses, 4 % vont au cinéma.
- Pour 42 % des Français, le dimanche a une signification religieuse, pour 58 % non.
- Pour 76 %, le dimanche est le dernier jour de la semaine, pour 23 % le premier.

Le repas[o] de midi est en effet une étape[p] importante du rituel dominical.[q] 60 % des familles font plus de cuisine le dimanche ; la plupart privilégient la cuisine traditionnelle (poulet, gigot...[r]) et terminent le repas par un gâteau.[s]

Les loisirs[t] dominicaux n'évoluent guère[u]: la famille, les amis et la télévision y tiennent[v] la plus grande place. Mais une autre tradition, celle de la messe,[w] est au contraire en nette diminution[x]; moins d'un quart des ménages[y] se rendent[z] à l'église[aa] le dimanche.

[a]*weekly*
[b]*majority*
[c]un emploi... *a busy timetable*
[d]se... *get together*
[e]se... vont souvent
[f]*to have a midday meal*
[g]*idle their time away*
[h]*do odd jobs*
[i]*read*
[j]*write*
[k]*sleep*
[l]s'occupent... *take care of*
[m]*cook*
[n]*to pray*
[o]*meal*
[p]*step, stage*
[q]du dimanche
[r]poulet... *chicken, leg of lamb*
[s]*cake*
[t]*leisure activities*
[u]n'évoluent... *scarcely change at all*
[v]y... *occupy*
[w]*mass*
[x]en... *clearly in decline*
[y]moins... *less than one quarter of all families*
[z]se... vont
[aa]*church*

## Compréhension

1. En général, est-ce que les Français passent le dimanche en famille?
2. Quelles activités occupent la plus grande place dans les familles françaises?
3. À votre avis, est-ce que la religion a beaucoup d'importance pour les Français? Expliquez.
4. Les Français aiment le dimanche. Et vous, aimez-vous le dimanche? Pourquoi (ou pourquoi pas)?
5. Est-ce que les dimanches sont différents aux États-Unis? Expliquez.

# PAR ÉCRIT

**Function:** Describing (a place)
**Audience:** A classmate or your instructor
**Goal:** Write a description of *home* by answering the following questions: **Qu'est-ce que c'est qu'une maison? Quelle est votre maison idéale? Est-elle bien meublée, simple, etc.? Qu'est-ce qu'on fait à la maison? Avec qui?**

**Steps**

1. Begin by brainstorming what home is for you. Think of any adjectives that describe it, its real or ideal inhabitants, what you do there.
2. Consider the tone you want to adopt. Do you want to describe a specific home in an objective or detached way, or do you want to use a more subjective approach? A detached tone would result from stating in a direct manner what your house is like and what people do there; a more personal

**Suggestion:** Show slides of variety of exteriors and interiors of French homes, if available. If slides are not available, look for magazine pictures showing homes and home plans. Or have a French native speaker give you a description of "home" (perhaps just a word-association chain), and use it to compare what home means to American vs. native French people.

**Additional activity:** Encourage sts. to keep a journal in French for the rest of the semester or year.

and emotional approach would be to choose words, such as **aimer**, **adorer**, and **détester**, that show how you feel about your home and its inhabitants.
3. Decide what vantage point you want to use to describe your home. Do you want to move through a number of rooms and describe what you see or do there? Do you prefer to be a fixed observer, describing your impressions from one point of view, such as from the garden or the living room?
4. Organize your principal ideas and use them to form the paragraphs of your first draft.
5. After you have completed the draft, reread it checking for organization, smoothness of style, and consistency of vantage point.
6. Have a friend reread the draft to see if what you've written is clear.
7. Finally, make the changes suggested by your classmate if you agree that they are warranted, and check the draft for spelling, punctuation, and grammar errors. Focus especially on your use of possessive adjectives and the verbs **faire** and **aller**. Be prepared to read your composition to a small group of classmates.

**Suggestion:** Read a few of the better compositions for the whole class, as listening comprehension practice. See whether sts. can guess who wrote the composition.

## À L'ÉCOUTE!

**À l'écoute!** See scripts for listening passages and follow-up activities recorded on student cassette. Remind students that in the listening comprehension passages (as in real life) they will not understand every word they hear. They should focus globally on the general information in the passages and not be overly concerned about what they do not understand.

**Une grande famille.** Véronique is 15. She is very fond of her family, and is describing it to a friend. First, look at the diagram on the next page. Next, listen to the vocabulary and the names of the people in Véronique's family. Then, listen to Véronique's description. Finally, do the activity.

VOCABULAIRE UTILE

**au lycée** *at the high school*
**une banque** *bank*
**un garçon** *boy*
**unique** *only*
**un atelier** *artist's studio*

LA FAMILLE DE VÉRONIQUE

| | | |
|---|---|---|
| Henri | Raphaël | Franck |
| Virginie | Géraldine | Caroline |
| Georges | Charles | Léa |
| Gérard | Marie | |
| Nicole | Juliette | |
| Josiane | Laurence | |

Fill in the blank boxes with the correct names based on Véronique's description.

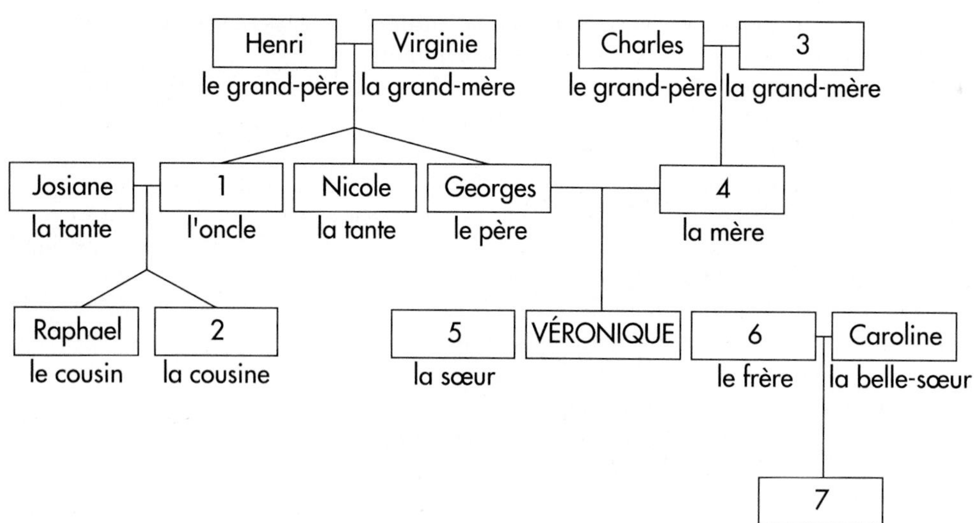


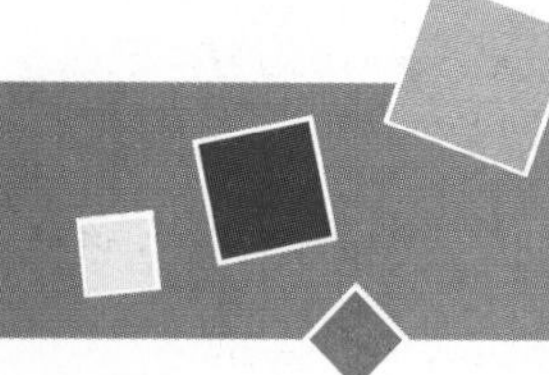

# Vocabulaire

## Verbes

**aller** to go
**aller +** *inf.* to be going (to do something)
**aller mal** to feel bad (ill)
**attendre** to wait for
**descendre à** to go down (south) to
**descendre de** to get down (from), get off
**entendre** to hear
**faire** to do; to make
**perdre** to lose; to waste
**préparer** to prepare
**rendre** to give back; to return; to hand in
**rendre visite à** to visit (*someone*)
**répondre à** to answer
**rester** to stay, remain
**vendre** to sell

À REVOIR: **étudier, habiter, jouer à (de), laver, manger**

## Substantifs

**l'appartement** (*m.*) apartment
**l'arbre** (*m.*) tree
**l'autobus** (*m.*) (city) bus
**le bruit** noise
**le bureau** office
**la famille** family
**le foyer** home
**le premier (deuxième) étage** second (third) floor (in the U.S.)
**les projets** (*m.*) plans
**le rez-de-chaussée** ground floor
**le temps** time
**les vacances** (*f. pl.*) vacation

À REVOIR: **l'affiche** (*f.*), **le chien, la commode, le lavabo, le lit, le logement**

## Adjectifs

**affreux/euse** awful
**célibataire** single (*person*)
**chouette** cute
**divorcé(e)** divorced
**formidable** great
**génial(e)** delightful
**marié(e)** married
**préféré(e)** favorite, preferred
**superbe** superb

## Les parents

**l'arrière-grand-parent** great-grandparent
**le beau-frère** brother-in-law
**le beau-père** father-in-law; stepfather
**la belle-mère** mother-in-law; stepmother
**la belle-sœur** sister-in-law
**le cousin** cousin (*male*)
**la cousine** cousin (*female*)

**le demi-frère** half-brother; stepbrother
**la demi-sœur** half-sister; stepsister
**l'enfant** (*m., f.*) child
**la femme** wife
**la fille** daughter
**le fils** son
**le grand-père** grandfather
**la grand-mère** grandmother
**le grand-parent (les grands-parents)** grandparent
**le mari** husband
**le neveu** nephew
**la nièce** niece
**l'oncle** (*m.*) uncle
**le petit-enfant** grandchild
**la petite-fille** granddaughter
**le petit-fils** grandson
**la sœur** sister
**la tante** aunt

## La maison

**le balcon** balcony
**la chambre** room; bedroom
**le couloir** hall
**la cuisine** kitchen
**l'escalier** (*m.*) stairway
**le jardin** garden
**le meuble** piece of furniture
**la pièce** room
**le poste de télévision** TV set
**la salle à manger** dining room
**la salle de bains** bathroom
**la salle de séjour** living room
**la terrasse** terrace

## Expressions avec *faire*

**faire attention** to be careful, to watch out
**faire la connaissance de** to meet (for the first time), make the acquaintance of
**faire les courses** to do errands
**faire la cuisine** to cook
**faire ses devoirs** to do homework
**faire la lessive** to do the laundry
**faire le marché** to do the shopping, go to the market
**faire le ménage** to do the housework
**faire une promenade** to take a walk
**faire un tour** to take a walk, ride
**faire du sport: faire de l'aérobic** to do aerobics; **du jogging** to run, jog; **du ski** to ski; **du vélo** to go cycling; **de la voile** to go sailing
**faire la vaisselle** to do the dishes
**faire un voyage** to take a trip

## Mots et expressions divers

**alors** then, in that case
**après** after, afterward
**bien** good (*fam.*)
**bientôt** soon
**ce week-end** this weekend
**cet après-midi / ce matin / ce soir** this afternoon / morning / evening
**chez** at the home (establishment) of
**dans quatre jours...** in four days . . .
**demain** tomorrow
**une fois par semaine** once a week
**loin de** far from
**le lundi / le vendredi soir** on Mondays / on Friday evenings
**mal** badly
**pas du tout** not at all
**pendant les vacances** (*f.*) during vacation
**peut-être** maybe
**la semaine prochaine** next week
**tous les jours** every day
**tout à l'heure** in a while
**tout de suite** immediately
**le week-end** on weekends

# Intermède

## SITUATION

### Invitation

**Contexte** *Jennifer et son ami Yannick étudient le marketing à l'université de Montpellier. Yannick et sa famille invitent souvent Jennifer pour le week-end.*

**Objectif** *Jennifer accepte une invitation.*

YANNICK: Jennifer, tu es libre° dimanche?
JENNIFER: Oui, pourquoi?
YANNICK: Eh bien, nous allons pique-niquer en famille. Tu veux venir avec nous?
JENNIFER: Oh, oui, avec plaisir! Qu'est-ce que je peux apporter°?
YANNICK: Je ne sais pas, des fruits ou du chocolat... Ah, et n'oublie° pas ton frisbee!
JENNIFER: Oui, d'accord. Ça va être sympa!

*free*
*to bring*
*forget*

**Situation:** The *Situation* dialogues are recorded on the student cassette packaged with the student text.

**Follow-up:** Change some facts in original situation and have a colleague record it with you for listening comprehension practice.

## À propos

**Suggestion:** Use *À propos* section to supplement the ways in which invitations are accepted and offered.

**Suggestion:** Ask sts. to bring in an ad and role-play, inviting other classmates to this place. Afterward, discuss who had the funniest, most cultural, most bizarre (etc.) invitation.

### Comment inviter des amis

DANS UNE SITUATION INFORMELLE
Tu es libre?
Tu as envie de... ?
Je t'invite à...
Viens donc...
écouter de la musique, faire une promenade, jouer au tennis...

DANS UNE SITUATION FORMELLE
Êtes-vous libre?
Avez-vous envie de... ?
Je vous invite à...
Venez donc...
écouter de la musique, faire une promenade, etc.

### Pour accepter

DANS UNE SITUATION INFORMELLE
Oui, je suis libre.
Bonne idée!
D'accord.
Ça va être sympa(thique)!

DANS UNE SITUATION FORMELLE
Ça me ferait (*would give me*) grand plaisir.
J'accepte avec plaisir.
Je vous remercie (*I thank you*).
C'est gentil.

### Pour refuser poliment

DANS LES SITUATIONS FORMELLES ET INFORMELLES

| | |
|---|---|
| C'est gentil, mais... | je ne suis pas libre. |
| C'est dommage (*too bad*), mais... | je suis pris(e) (*engaged*). |
| Désolé(e), mais... | je ne peux pas (*I can't*). |
| | je suis occupé(e) (*busy*). |
| | j'ai quelque chose de prévu (*something planned*). |

## Maintenant à vous!

**La famille américaine.** Un Français (Une Française) vous pose des questions sur les habitudes des familles américaines. Répondez-lui.

1. En général, les jeunes Américains préfèrent habiter en famille, ou avec des amis?
2. Combien de personnes y a-t-il dans ta famille immédiate? Où habitent tes parents proches (*close*)?
3. Est-ce que vous invitez quelquefois des amis à passer le dimanche en famille avec vous? Qu'est-ce que vous faites: un pique-nique, un tour en voiture, une promenade... ?
4. Aimez-vous passer le dimanche en famille (ou chez des amis)? Est-ce que vous êtes souvent invité(e) dans la famille de vos amis pour le week-end?
5. En général, comment répondez-vous aux invitations?

# PORTRAITS

### Le Corbusier (1887–1965)

Swiss-born Charles-Édouard Jeanneret, commonly known by his pseudonym Le Corbusier, is considered one of the masters of modern architecture. He pioneered the use of simple, geometric lines, and spaces conceived according to strictly functional rather than ornamental principles. Some of Le Corbusier's major structures, which many considered outrageously daring at the time they were built, include la villa Savoye in Passy (France), the Ministry of Culture in Rio de Janeiro (Brazil), and the chapel Notre-Dame de Ronchamp (France), whose forms and planes give it a highly sculptural appearance.

CHAPITRE **SIX**

# Les Français à table

**En avant**

—Ce gâteau a l'air délicieux.

—Merci. Il est très facile à faire. Est-ce que tu veux la recette?

**Communicative goals:** talking about food and drink, telling time, talking about seasons and the weather, expressing quantity, and giving commands.

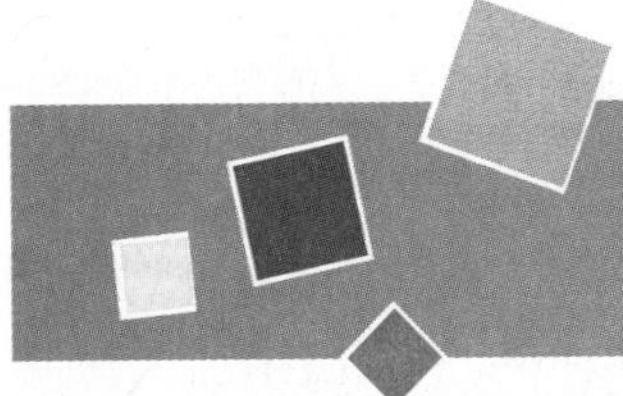

# Étude de vocabulaire

## Les repas de la journée*

**Presentation:** Bring in pictures of the various foods portrayed.

**Note:** Optional words and personalized vocabulary: *l'infusion* (*herb tea*); *la confiture* (*preserves*); *le jus d'orange* (*orange juice*); names of fruits or vegetables requested by sts.

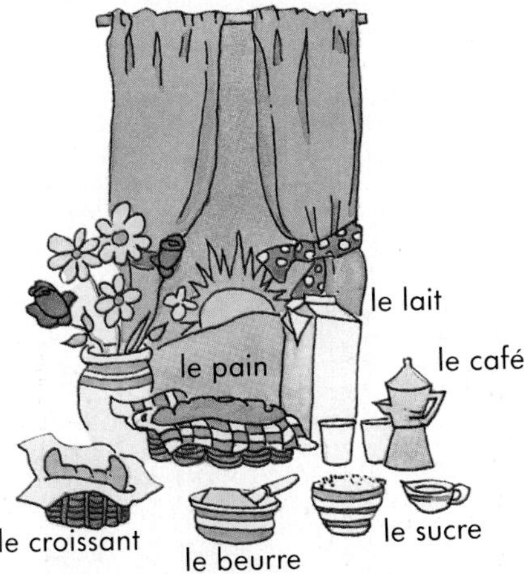


Le matin: le petit déjeuner

À midi: le déjeuner

L'après-midi: le goûter†

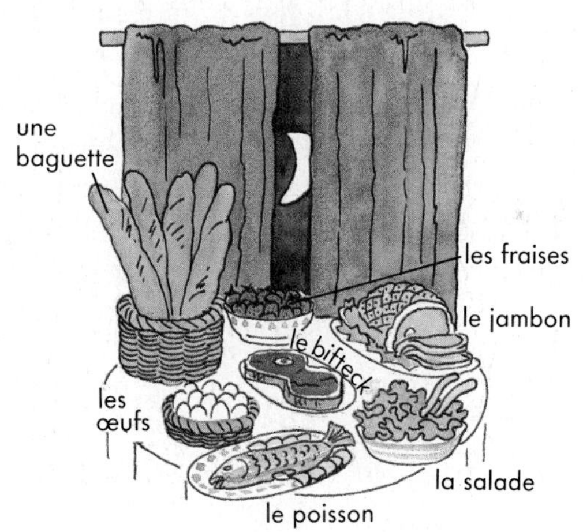


Le soir: le dîner

*Use **la journée** (*the day*) instead of **le jour** when you wish to emphasize the notion of an entire day, or the whole day long, as in the expression "**Quelle journée!**" (*What a day!*).

†**Le goûter** is an occasional afternoon snack: **pain et chocolat pour les enfants; thé ou café et gâteaux pour les adultes**.

***Autres mots utiles:***

**la boisson** drink
**la cuisine** cooking; food
**le fruit** fruit
**le légume** vegetable
**la viande** meat

Additional vocabulary: *les boissons: un café au lait, un thé au lait, un thé au citron, une limonade, un Orangina, un citron pressé, un Coca,* etc.

**A. Catégories.** Ajoutez (*Add*) d'autres aliments dans les catégories mentionnées.

MODÈLE: La mousse au chocolat est *un dessert.* →
Le gâteau, la tarte aux pommes et les fraises sont aussi des desserts.

1. La bière est *une boisson.*
2. La pomme de terre est *un légume.*
3. Le porc* est *une viande.*
4. La banane est *un fruit.*

Maintenant, trouvez l'intrus (*the item that doesn't belong*) et expliquez votre choix.

1. café / fraise / bière / thé / lait
2. haricots verts / salade / carotte / œuf† / pomme de terre
3. bifteck / porc / pain / jambon / poulet
4. sel / gâteau / poivre / sucre / beurre
5. vin / banane / pomme / orange / melon

**Suggestion**: Have sts. do individually first and then solicit answers.

**Additional activities**: A. *Définitions. Suivez le modèle.* MODÈLE: *Le goûter* → *Le goûter est le repas de l'après-midi.* 1. *le petit déjeuner* 2. *le dîner* 3. *le déjeuner*
B. *Plats. Faites une liste des ingrédients nécessaires à chaque plat.* MODÈLE: *une mousse au chocolat* → *le chocolat, le beurre, les œufs*
1. *une soupe* 2. *un café au lait* 3. *une omelette* 4. *une salade de fruits* 5. *un sandwich* 6. *une fondue*

**Suggestion**: Do Part 2, Ex. A as a listening activity, with sts. writing down the *intrus* as they hear it.

**Follow-up**: Have sts. add another word to category that *does* belong. Possibilities: *eau minérale, petits pois, veau, huile, fraises.*

**B. Associations.** Quels mots associez-vous avec... ?

1. une omelette 2. une salade de fruits 3. un régime (*diet*) 4. un bon repas 5. un sandwich 6. un pique-nique

**C. Fiche** (*Form*) **gastronomique.** Demandez à un(e) camarade de classe quelles sont ses préférences et complétez la fiche. Utilisez **quel/quelle**‡ et le verbe **préférer**.

MODÈLE: —Quelle boisson préfères-tu?§
—Je préfère le/la...

boisson ______________
viande ______________
légume ______________
fruit ______________
dessert ______________
repas ______________
plat (*dish*) ______________

**Suggestion**: Could be done as a poll where sts. circulate and interview several class members.

**Note**: You may wish to have sts. turn to the verb *préférer* in the Appendix and model the pronunciation.

Maintenant, avec vos camarades de classe, examinez les différentes fiches et déterminez quels sont les plats et les boissons préférés de la classe.

---

*The **c** at the end of **porc** is silent [pɔr].
†Pronunciation: **un œuf** [œ̃nœf], **des œufs** [dezø].
‡**Quel** (*what, which*) is used before masculine words, **quelle** before feminine words.
§**Préférer**: for **-er** verbs with spelling changes, see Appendix, p. A-24–25.

# À table

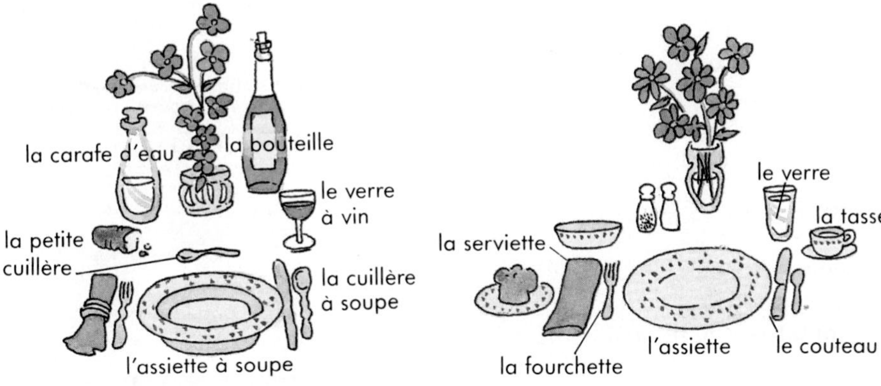


Une table française

Une table américaine

**Note:** Optional words: *La corbeille à pain*, *la nappe*. Distinguish between *l'assiette creuse* and *l'assiette plate*. Distinguish between the use of *plat* and *assiette* for dish.

**Suggestions:** (1) Bring in items to set table. Demonstrate different setting and style of eating in France. (2) Have sts. comment in English about differences in table settings in France and the U.S.

***Autres mots utiles:***

**le bol** wide, bowl-shaped cup

**A. L'objet nécessaire.** Quels objets utilisez-vous?

MODÈLE: le café au lait →
J'utilise un bol pour le café au lait.

1. le vin
2. la viande
3. la soupe
4. la salade
5. le thé
6. la mousse au chocolat

**Suggestion:** Do as rapid response activity, individual response with occasional group repetition. Solicit a variety of answers (*assiette*, *couteau*, etc.)

**Continuation:** *le beurre*, *la tarte aux pommes*, *le lait*, *le fromage*.

**B. L'art de la table.** Mettre le couvert (*Setting the table*) est souvent un art. Regardez la photo tirée du magazine *Gault Millau* et répondez aux questions.

**Follow-up:** Use the Rose technique to practice vocabulary, speaking, and listening: Ask one st. to draw a place setting. She or he will describe it to a partner who will draw without looking at the picture. At the end, sts. confirm comprehension by looking at the first picture.

L'ÉLYSÉE

1. Décrivez ce qu'il y a sur la table. Est-ce une table pour un repas simple ou élégant? Quel est l'objet en papier à gauche (*on the left*)? Où sont la salière et la poivrière (*salt and pepper shakers*)?
2. À votre avis, pourquoi y a-t-il quatre verres?
3. Et chez vous, qu'est-ce qu'on place sur la table au petit déjeuner? au déjeuner? au dîner? pour un repas spécial?

# Un peu d'argot

| | | |
|---|---|---|
| **la bouffe** | la nourriture | *food* |
| **une bouffe** | un repas entre amis | *a dinner party* |
| **bouffer** | manger | *to eat* |
| **la patate** | la pomme de terre | *potato* |
| **le pinard** | le vin | |
| **la flotte** | l'eau | |

EN CONTEXTE

VINCENT: On fait **une bouffe** samedi?
NATHALIE: OK. Je vais faire un poulet rôti (*roasted*).
VINCENT: Super! J'apporte **les patates** et **le pinard**.

**Note**: These terms should be used only among friends or family. None of them is really offensive, but they imply a certain humor and a sense of intimacy.
Literally, *bouffer* means to puff and *flotte* means fleet (*flotter* = to float).

**Presentation:** Model pronunciation of captions with group repetition. Use cardboard clock to show times as they are repeated and to illustrate principles of telling time.

## Quelle heure est-il?

Il est sept heures. Quel repas Vincent prend-il (*is he having*)?

Il est dix heures et demie.* Où est Vincent?

Il est midi. Quel repas prend-il?

Il est deux heures et quart. Où est Vincent?

Il est quatre heures moins le quart. Où Vincent prend-il un café?

Il est huit heures vingt. Qui sert (*is serving*) le dîner?

Il est minuit moins vingt. Est-ce que Vincent étudie toujours?

Il est minuit. Vincent dort (*is sleeping*).

---

*To tell the time on the half hour, **et demie** is used after the feminine noun **heure**(**s**) and **et demi** is used after the masculine nouns **midi** and **minuit**.

| | |
|---|---|
| Il est trois heures **et demie**. | *It's 3:30* (*half past three*). |
| Il est midi **et demi**. | *It's 12:30* (*half past noon*). |

- To ask the time

Excusez-moi, **quelle heure est-il**, s'il vous plaît? — *Excuse me, what time is it, please?*

- To ask at what time something happens

**À quelle heure** commence le film? — *At what time does the movie start?*
À deux heures et demie. — *At two thirty.*
Vers trois heures. — *Around three.*

- To tell the time

In French, the expression **Il est... heure**(**s**) is used to tell time on the hour. *Noon* is expressed by **midi**, *midnight* by **minuit**.

**Il est** une **heure**. — *It is one o'clock.*
**Il est** deux **heures**. — *It is two o'clock.*
**Il est** presque **midi/minuit**. — *It's almost noon/midnight.*

## En savoir plus

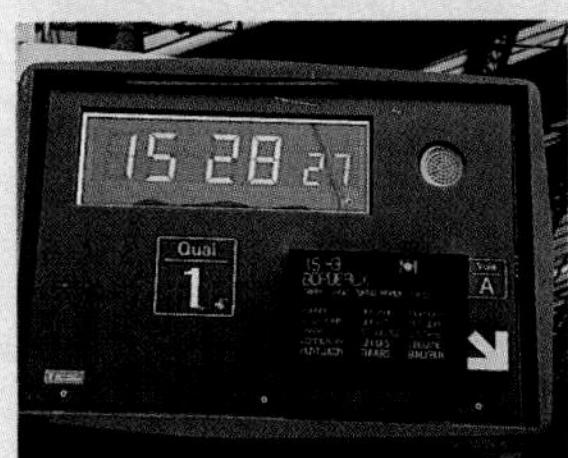

Quelle heure est-il?

### A.M. versus P.M.

In both English and French, the context often makes it clear whether a speaker is talking about A.M. or P.M. In French, **du matin** is used to specify A.M. To indicate P.M., **de l'après-midi** is used for *in the afternoon*, and **du soir** is used for *in the evening* or *at night* (before midnight). Generally, these expressions are used only to tell the time on the hour.

Il est neuf heures **du matin**. — *It's 9 A.M.*
Il est quatre heures **de l'après-midi**. — *It's 4 P.M.*
Il est onze heures **du soir**. — *It's 11 P.M.*

The twenty-four-hour clock is used in official announcements—such as on TV, on the radio, and in train or plane schedules—to avoid ambiguity. Sometimes it is also used to make appointments. When time is expressed in figures, **h** (for hours) is used rather than a colon.

Il est quinze heures trente (15 h 30). — *It's 3:30 P.M.*
Il est vingt-deux heures quarante-cinq (22 h 45). — *It's 10:45 P.M.*

**A.** Quelle heure est-il?

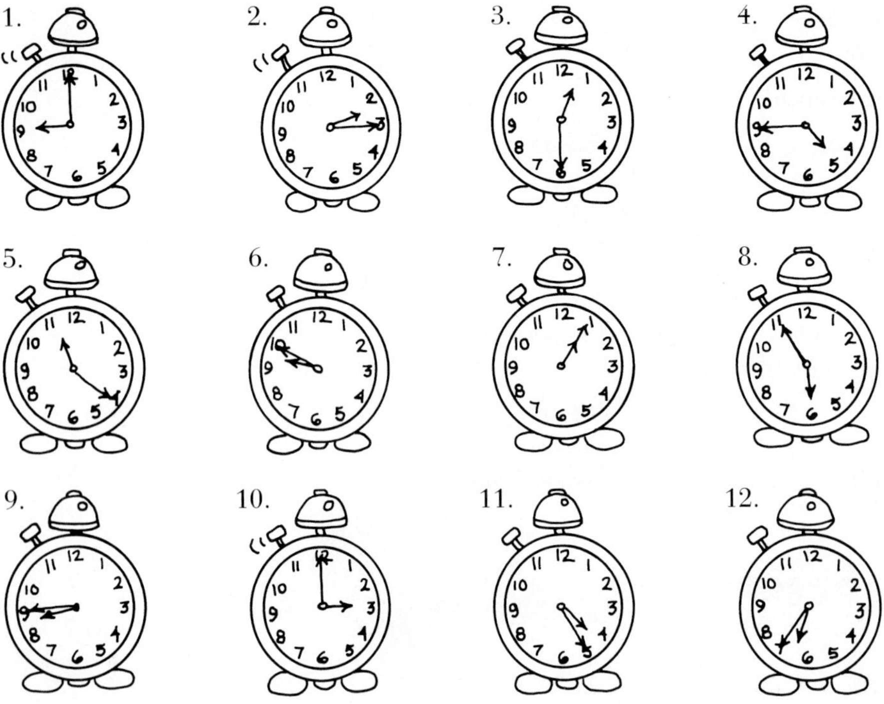

**Suggestion:** Do as whole-class response activity, or in pairs, after first few items are modeled for whole group.

**Suggestion:** Use the following as preliminary listening exs. A. Hold up clock face, arrange hands to show various times and simultaneously pronounce them, correctly or incorrectly. Sts. respond *oui* or *non*.
B. Give the following times and ask sts. to draw the corresponding clock face. Then put the correct answers on the board, for immediate feedback. *Il est...* 1. *9h* 2. *10h30* 3. *11h45* (*midi moins le quart*) 4. *2h15* 5. *24 heures,* etc.

**B.** Quelle heure est-il pour vous? Qu'est-ce que vous faites?

**C. Paris–Genève en TGV.** Imaginez que vous êtes à Paris et que vous voulez (*want*) visiter Genève. Vous décidez de prendre le train. Voici les horaires (*schedules*) du TGV (Train à Grande Vitesse).

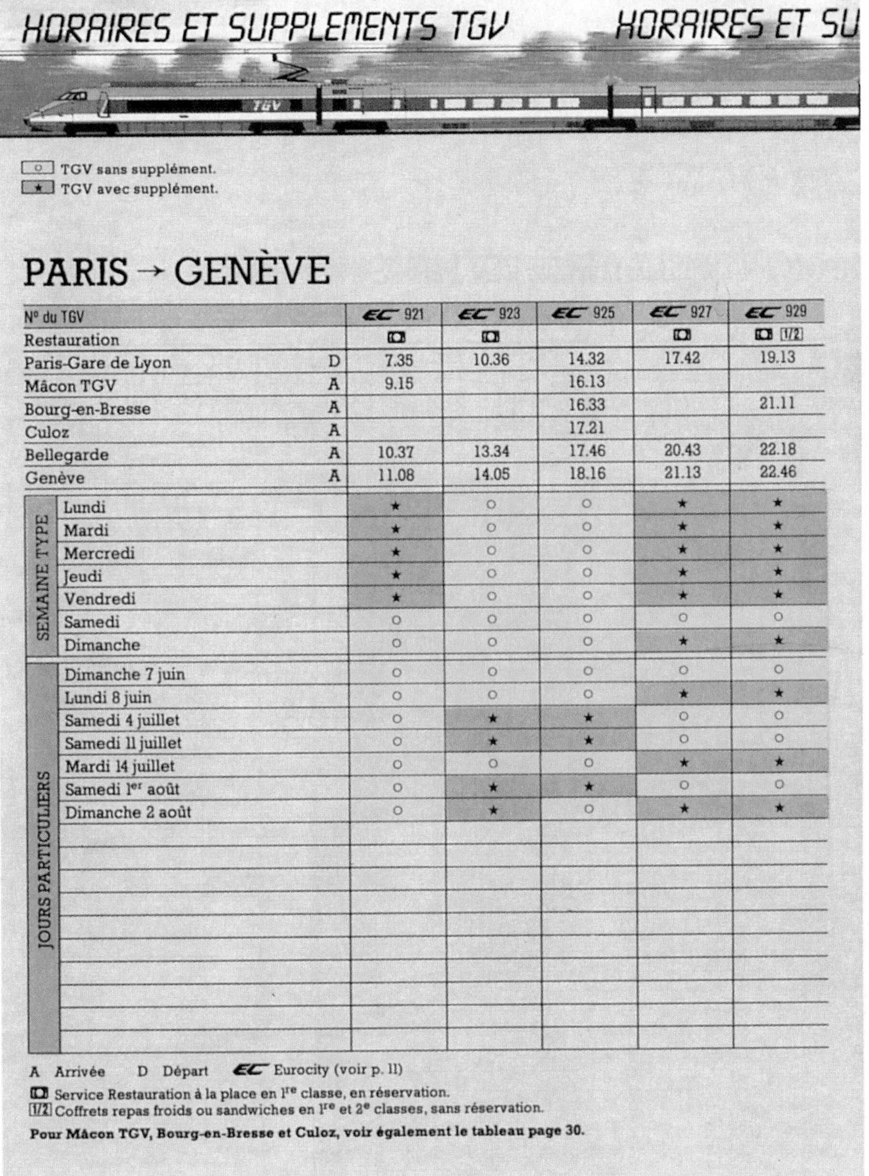


○ TGV sans supplément.
★ TGV avec supplément.

## PARIS → GENÈVE

| N° du TGV | | EC 921 | EC 923 | EC 925 | EC 927 | EC 929 |
|---|---|---|---|---|---|---|
| Restauration | | ▣ | ▣ | | ▣ | ▣ 1/2 |
| Paris-Gare de Lyon | D | 7.35 | 10.36 | 14.32 | 17.42 | 19.13 |
| Mâcon TGV | A | 9.15 | | 16.13 | | |
| Bourg-en-Bresse | A | | | 16.33 | | 21.11 |
| Culoz | A | | | 17.21 | | |
| Bellegarde | A | 10.37 | 13.34 | 17.46 | 20.43 | 22.18 |
| Genève | A | 11.08 | 14.05 | 18.16 | 21.13 | 22.46 |
| SEMAINE TYPE | Lundi | ★ | ○ | ○ | ★ | ★ |
| | Mardi | ★ | ○ | ○ | ★ | ★ |
| | Mercredi | ★ | ○ | ○ | ★ | ★ |
| | Jeudi | ★ | ○ | ○ | ★ | ★ |
| | Vendredi | ★ | ○ | ○ | ★ | ★ |
| | Samedi | ○ | ○ | ○ | ○ | ○ |
| | Dimanche | ○ | ○ | ○ | ★ | ★ |
| JOURS PARTICULIERS | Dimanche 7 juin | ○ | ○ | ○ | ○ | ○ |
| | Lundi 8 juin | ○ | ○ | ○ | ★ | ★ |
| | Samedi 4 juillet | ○ | ★ | ★ | ○ | ○ |
| | Samedi 11 juillet | ○ | ★ | ★ | ○ | ○ |
| | Mardi 14 juillet | ○ | ○ | ○ | ★ | ★ |
| | Samedi 1er août | ○ | ★ | ★ | ○ | ○ |
| | Dimanche 2 août | ○ | ★ | ○ | ★ | ★ |

A Arrivée D Départ EC Eurocity (voir p. 11)
▣ Service Restauration à la place en 1re classe, en réservation.
1/2 Coffrets repas froids ou sandwiches en 1re et 2e classes, sans réservation.
**Pour Mâcon TGV, Bourg-en-Bresse et Culoz, voir également le tableau page 30.**

1. À quelle heure y a-t-il des départs (*departures*) de Paris-Gare de Lyon pour Genève? À quelle heure ces trains arrivent-ils à Genève?
2. À quelle heure y a-t-il des départs le week-end?
3. Regardez l'itinéraire du TGV 925. À quelle heure part-il de Paris? À quelle heure arrive-t-il dans chaque (*each*) ville? Utilisez **du matin**, **de l'après-midi** et **du soir** (14:32 = 2 heures trente-deux, de l'après-midi).
4. Maintenant décidez quel train vous allez prendre et expliquez pourquoi.

**Follow-up:** Have sts. give times in both official and conversational ways. Ask sts. to role-play the situation of buying the ticket for *Genève*. The traveler will explain where she or he is going, the day and time she or he wishes to leave, and how many tickets she or he wishes to purchase. The employee will determine price of the ticket(s), ask if the traveler wants to reserve a seat (seats), and ask for any further information.

## Mots-clés

*Expressing the time in a general way*

| | |
|---|---|
| Il est **tard**. | *It's late.* |
| Il est **tôt**. | *It's early.* |
| Alain prend son repas **de bonne heure**. | *Alain eats early.* |
| M. RENOU: Ne rentre pas **tard** ce soir! | *Don't come home late tonight!* |
| ERIC RENOU: Mais non, je rentre toujours **de bonne heure**. Et demain, je dois partir **tôt**. | *No, I always come home early. And tomorrow I have to leave early.* |

## Les saisons et le temps: Quel temps fait-il?

**En été, à la Martinique,**
il fait du soleil.
il fait chaud.

**En automne, en Bretagne,**
il pleut.
il fait mauvais.

**En hiver, au Québec,**
il neige.
il fait froid.

**Au printemps, en Belgique,**
le temps est nuageux.
il fait frais. (*It's cool*).

***Autres mots utiles:***

**Il fait beau.** It's fine weather.
**Il fait du vent.** It's windy.

**Presentation:** Have sts. repeat seasons and weather expressions after your model. Using an overhead projector or flashcards with pictures like those depicted here, review seasons and weather expressions in random order. Re-enter months of year by asking *Quels sont les mois d'été? Quels sont les mois d'automne?* etc.

# En savoir plus

## Measuring temperature

Throughout Europe, temperature is measured on the Celsius, rather than the Fahrenheit scale. The following chart gives approximate correspondences between the two scales.

| CELSIUS | FAHRENHEIT | CELSIUS | FAHRENHEIT |
|---|---|---|---|
| 100° | 212° | 20° | 68° |
| 37° | 98.6° | 10° | 50° |
| 30° | 86° | 0° | 32° |

**Continuation** (ex. A): *le 1er avril, le 1er janvier.*

**Additional activity:** *Les mois et le temps. Quel temps fait-il ici en janvier? en mars? en juillet? en octobre?*

**Follow-up** (ex. B): Ask sts. to work in small groups to prepare *la météo* of the United States in French, using a weather map from the newspaper. They may pick a *météorologiste* from their group to present the weather to the class.

**A. Les fêtes et le temps.** Donnez la saison et le temps qu'il fait.

MODÈLE: Noël → Nous sommes en hiver et il fait froid.

1. Pâques (*Easter*)
2. Thanksgiving
3. la Saint-Valentin
4. le jour de l'Indépendance américaine
5. Labor Day

**B. La météo.** Regardez le temps prévu (*forecast*) sur l'Alsace et sur l'Europe. Dites (*Say*) si les phrases sont vraies ou fausses, et corrigez les phrases incorrectes.

1. Sur l'Alsace:
   a. Il pleut à Strasbourg.
   b. Il fait très chaud à Colmar.
   c. Le temps est nuageux sur Guebwiller.
2. Sur l'Europe:
   a. Il fait mauvais à Madrid.
   b. Le temps est orageux (*stormy*) sur Stockholm.
   c. Il fait froid à Athènes.

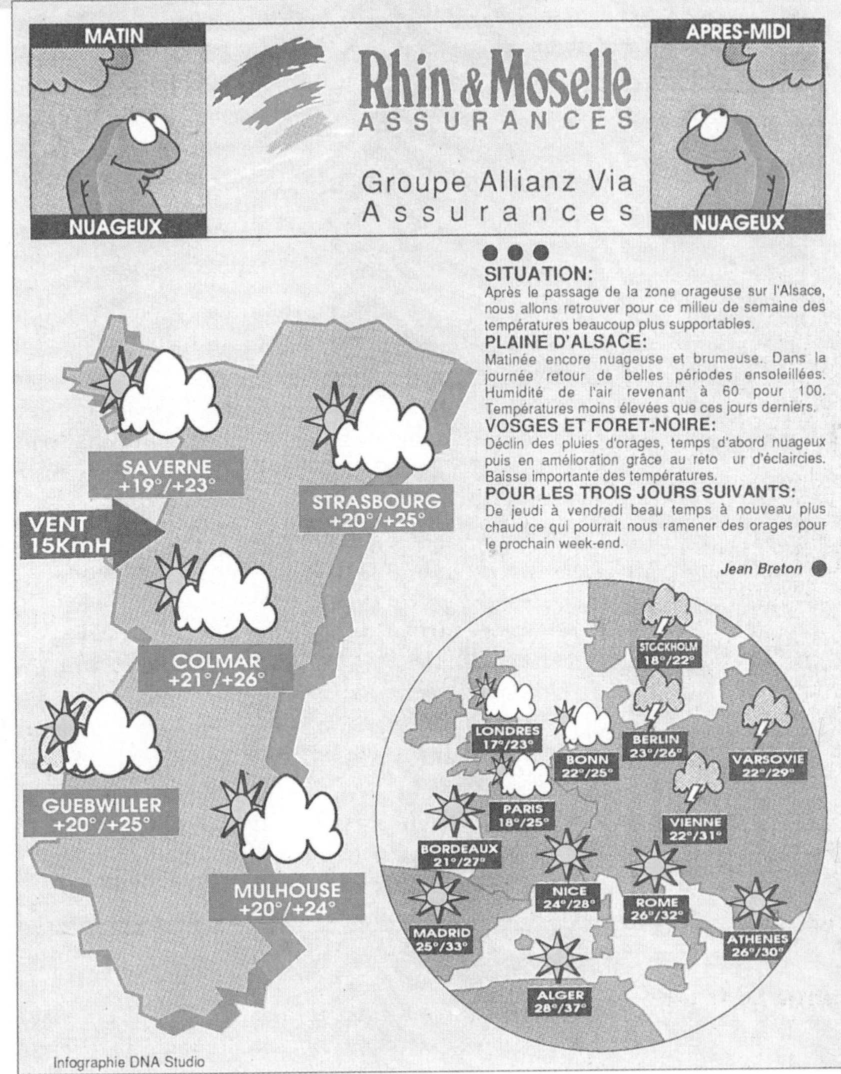

**C. Encore de la météo.** Répondez selon les instructions.

1. Donnez la température approximative qu'il fait à Paris et à Vienne en degrés Fahrenheit.
2. Maintenant décrivez le temps qu'il fait aujourd'hui dans votre ville.

**D. Le temps et les goûts.** Qu'est-ce que vous aimez manger et boire quand... ?

1. il fait très chaud
2. il fait froid et qu'il neige
3. il fait beau et frais
4. il pleut

**Additional activity:** In groups sts. prepare descriptions of a particular state or city, identifying it as one or the other. They mention characteristic weather and appropriate clothing, as well as a few telling characteristics. Each group reads its description to the class, and the others try to guess the place described. If sts. cannot guess immediately, which is probable, allow them to ask five yes/no questions to get more information.

# France-culture

**Suggestion:** If possible, show photos of French meals and ask sts. to guess which meal it is.

*French food.* French home cooking is probably simpler than most foreign visitors imagine. Its excellence comes partly from the high quality of the ingredients used. French consumers spend significantly more on food than American consumers do, and as a group, they seem willing to pay more for high-quality products, although that amount has been declining over the last five years.

Breakfast (**le petit déjeuner**) is simple—usually **tartines** (French bread and butter) or croissants with **café au lait**. The noon meal (**le déjeuner**) has traditionally been the main meal, but many people now take less time for lunch and prefer to have a larger evening meal (**le dîner**). Children usually have a snack (**le goûter**) of bread and chocolate when they come home from school around 4:00 or 5:00. Dinner is served around 7:30 or 8:00.

**Note:** Talk about the custom of bringing a small gift when one is invited for a meal. Talk about the tradition of serving wines with special meals, as well as an *apéritif* and sometimes a *digestif*.

**Suggestion:** Ask sts. at what time they typically eat breakfast, lunch, snack, and dinner (reviewing telling time), and what each meal typically consists of.

Whether served at noon or in the evening, a French meal begins with either an **hors-d'œuvre** or an **entrée** or both. The **hors-d'œuvre** is always a cold dish; it may be coldcuts, eggs in mayonnaise, or some variety of **pâté**. An **entrée** is not a main dish but a light, warm dish—trout, mussels, or **quenelles** (*dumplings*), for example. It is followed by a meat or fish dish, vegetable, salad, cheese, and fresh fruit. Children often drink water, while the rest of the family may have **vin rouge ordinaire**, sometimes diluted with water. After the meal, a cup of strong coffee is generally served.

Bread is laid directly on the tablecloth, beside each plate; it is broken with the fingers and eaten in small pieces. Each course of a French meal is served separately, usually on the same plate (unless the meal is formal).

Meals take longer in France than in the United States, partly because there are so many courses, but also because they are a time for socializing.

Many French chefs are worried about the "Americanization" of French eating habits. They note that the French are beginning to snack rather than eat three regular meals. Some chefs are visiting primary schools in order to educate children about the joys of French cuisine.

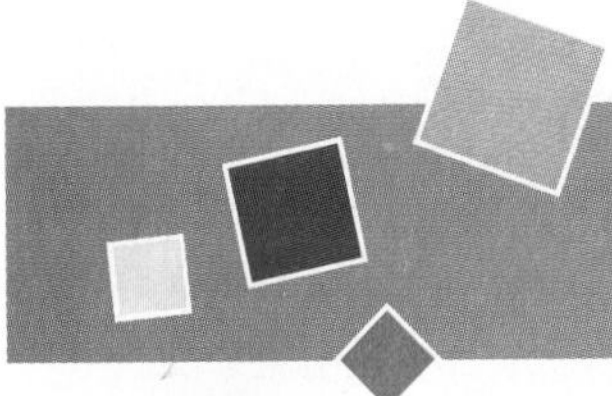

# Étude de grammaire

## 17. TALKING ABOUT FOOD AND DRINK
## *-re* Verbs: *prendre* and *boire*

### Au restaurant

LE SERVEUR: Que **prenez**-vous, Messieurs Dames?
JEAN-MICHEL: Nous **prenons** le poulet à la crème et les légumes.
LE SERVEUR: Et que **buvez**-vous?
JEAN-MICHEL: Je **prends** une bière, et pour mademoiselle une bouteille d'eau minérale, s'il vous plaît.

Maintenant, avec un(e) camarade, faites les substitutions suivantes et jouez à nouveau le dialogue.

le poulet à la crème → le poisson grillé
les légumes → la salade de tomates
une bière → un verre de vin rouge
une bouteille d'eau minérale → une carafe d'eau

**Presentation:** Ask class to provide substitutions orally or in writing. When sts. have created new dialogue, have class repeat new lines in group responses.

## A. *Prendre* and Verbs Like *prendre*

The verb **prendre** is irregular in its plural forms.

| PRESENT TENSE OF **prendre** (*to take*) | | | |
|---|---|---|---|
| je | prends | nous | pren**ons** |
| tu | prends | vous | pren**ez** |
| il, elle, on | prend | ils, elles | pren**nent** |

**Presentation:** Use whole sentences to model pronunciation such as *Je prends du poulet, Tu prends du poisson*, etc.

**Suggestion:** For listening comprehension practice, have sts. say whether verbs are singular or plural. You may want to do this as a *dictée*. *Il prend le poulet à la crème. Elles prennent un sandwich au fromage. Ils prennent de la bière. Elle prend une pizza. Ils comprennent le menu. Elle apprend le français. Ils apprennent à choisir le vin. Ça prend du temps.*

Verbs conjugated like **prendre** are **apprendre** (*to learn*) and **comprendre** (*to understand*).

| | |
|---|---|
| —Qu'est-ce que vous **prenez**? | —*What are you having?* |
| —Je **prends** la salade verte. | —*I'm having the green salad.* |

| | |
|---|---|
| Il **apprend** l'espagnol. | *He's learning (how to speak) Spanish.* |
| Est-ce que tu **comprends** presque toujours le professeur d'espagnol? | *Do you almost always understand the Spanish professor?* |

When an infinitive follows **apprendre**, the preposition **à** must be used also.

| | |
|---|---|
| Ma sœur **apprend à** danser. | *My sister is learning (how) to dance.* |
| **Apprenez**-vous **à** skier? | *Are you learning (how) to ski?* |

Some common expressions with **prendre** include the following.

**Suggestion:** Ask sts. to make up sentences using these expressions.

| | |
|---|---|
| **prendre son temps** | *to take one's time* |
| **prendre un repas** | *to eat a meal* |
| **prendre le petit déjeuner** | *to have breakfast* |
| **prendre un verre** | *to have a drink (usually alcoholic)* |

## B. Boire

The verb **boire** is also irregular in form.

**Note:** Stress pronunciation of [y] in *buvons*.

| PRESENT TENSE OF **boire** (*to drink*) | | | |
|---|---|---|---|
| je | **bois** | nous | **buvons** |
| tu | **bois** | vous | **buvez** |
| il, elle, on | **boit** | ils, elles | **boivent** |

| | |
|---|---|
| Tu **bois** de l'eau minérale. | *You're drinking mineral water.* |
| Nous **buvons** de la bière. | *We're drinking beer.* |

### Vérifions!

**A. Des étudiants modèles.** Lisez les phrases, puis faites les substitutions suivantes: (1) tu, (2) mon meilleur (*best*) ami (ma meilleure amie), (3) mon/ma camarade et moi, (4) je, (5) mes camarades de classe. Faites d'autres substitutions si vous voulez (*want*).

**Suggestion:** Sts. do as dictation at board, transforming sentences after writing the first cue.

1. Vous apprenez le français. 2. Vous comprenez presque (*almost*) toujours le professeur. 3. Pour préparer les examens, vous prenez des livres à la bibliothèque. 4. Pour faire vos devoirs, vous prenez votre temps. 5. Mais malheureusement (*unfortunately*), vous buvez trop de (*too much*) café.

**B. Qu'est-ce qu'on boit?** Choisissez une boisson différente pour chaque situation.

MODÈLE: Il fête son anniversaire (*He's celebrating his birthday*). (il) →
Il boit un verre de champagne.

1. Il fait très chaud. (vous)
2. Il fait froid. (Christian)
3. Il est minuit. (tu)
4. Il est 8 h du matin. (je)
5. Nous sommes au café. (nous)
6. Elles sont au restaurant. (Agnès et Corinne)

**C. Conversations au café.** Vous êtes au café. Les gens (*people*) parlent autour de (*around*) vous. Complétez leurs conversations avec les verbes **prendre**, **apprendre** ou **comprendre**.

1. —Est-ce que tu ____ un café?
   —Non, j'ai soif; je ____ une bouteille d'eau minérale.
2. —Est-ce que tu ____ l'anglais?
   —Oui, j'ai un cours de conversation tous les matins (*every morning*). Et vous deux, qu'est-ce que vous ____ comme (*as*) langue étrangère?
   —Nous, nous ____ l'allemand.
3. —Est-ce que vous ____ toujours le professeur d'histoire?
   —Non, mais les autres (*other*) étudiants ____ tout (*everything*)!

## *Parlons-en!*

**A. La réponse est simple!** Trouvez des réponses aux problèmes suivants. Utilisez les verbes **boire**, **apprendre**, **comprendre** ou **prendre** ou des expressions avec **prendre**.

**Suggestion:** Have sts. write out answers first and then solicit individual responses from class.

**Continuation:** Other possible stimuli: *J'ai mal à la tête. Mon ami a mal à l'estomac. Nous avons très soif.*

MODÈLE: Je désire parler avec un ami. →
Je prends un verre au café avec un ami.

1. J'ai faim. 2. J'ai soif. 3. Je désire bien parler français. 4. Je désire étudier les mathématiques. 5. Je n'aime pas le vin. 6. *À vous de faire une phrase!*

**B. Mission impossible?** Parmi (*Among*) vos camarades, trouvez quelqu'un qui (*someone who*)...

MODÈLE: prend du sucre dans son café →
Est-ce que tu prends du sucre dans ton café?

1. ne prend pas de petit déjeuner
2. prend en général des crêpes (*pancakes*) au petit déjeuner
3. boit cinq tasses de café ou plus par jour
4. boit un verre de lait à chaque (*each*) repas
5. apprend un nouveau sport ce semestre
6. comprend le sens de la vie (*meaning of life*)

Celui qui finit le premier gagne le concours (*Whoever finishes first wins the contest*).

# 18. EXPRESSING QUANTITY Partitive Articles

### Pas de dessert

JULIEN: Qu'est-ce qu'on mange aujourd'hui, maman?
MME TESSIER: Il y a **du poulet** avec **des pommes de terre**.
JULIEN: Et **la mousse au chocolat** dans le frigo, c'est pour ce midi?
MME TESSIER: Ah non, **la mousse**, c'est pour ce soir. Pour ce midi, il y a **des fruits** ou **de la glace au café**.
JULIEN: Je n'aime pas **la glace** et je n'aime pas **les fruits**! Mais j'adore **la mousse**!
MME TESSIER: Non, c'est non!

Et vous? Répondez aux questions suivantes.

1. Mangez-vous souvent **du** poulet?
2. Prenez-vous souvent **des** fruits?
3. Est-ce que vous aimez **la** glace?

## A. The Partitive Articles

**Suggestion:** You may wish to teach concept inductively using a chocolate bar, asking *Aimez-vous le chocolat? Voulez-vous du chocolat? Je prends du chocolat.*

In addition to the definite and indefinite articles, French has a third article, called the partitive (**le partitif**). It has three forms: **du** (*m.*), **de la** (*f.*), and **de l'** (before a vowel or mute h). It agrees in gender with the noun it precedes.

| | |
|---|---|
| Prenez-vous **du** porc? | *Are you having (some) pork?* |
| **de la** salade? | *(some) salad?* |
| **de l'**eau minérale? | *(some) mineral water?* |

The partitive article is used to indicate only a part of an entire quantity, which is measurable but not countable. This idea is sometimes expressed in English by *some* or *any*; usually, however, *some* is not stated directly but only implied. Examples of noncountable nouns (also called *mass nouns*) include **viande**, **chocolat**, **lait**, **sucre**, **glace**, **vin**, **eau**, **beurre**, and **pain**.

| | |
|---|---|
| Avez-vous **du** thé? | *Do you have tea?* |
| Je voudrais **du** sucre. | *I would like (some) sugar.* |
| Mangez-vous **du** poisson? | *Do you eat fish?* |

When the quantity is countable, the indefinite article is used instead.

Je vais préparer **une** tarte aux fraises. — *I'm going to prepare a strawberry tart.*
Elle commande **un** jus de fruits. — *She is ordering a fruit juice.*
Elle achète **des** tomates et **des** haricots verts. — *She is buying tomatoes and green beans.*

**Follow-up:** Dictate following sentences and have sts. explain why partitive or indefinite article is used: *Il y a une assiette, un couteau, une tasse, du beurre, des croissants et du café.*

## B. The Partitive versus the Definite Article

The partitive article is used with such verbs as **prendre**, **boire**, **acheter**, and **manger**, because they refer to consuming or buying a portion of something. One usually has, drinks, buys, and eats a limited amount or number of things, and not all of them. But, after such verbs of preference as **aimer**, **aimer mieux**, **préférer**, **adorer**, and **détester**, the definite article is used, because these verbs express a preference or an aversion to a general category.

Beaucoup de Français mangent **du** fromage après le repas, mais moi, je déteste **le** fromage. — *Many French people eat (some) cheese after a meal, but I hate cheese.*

**Note:** *Rendez-vous* presents the comparison between the partitive and definite articles as soon as possible after explaining the partitive because many sts. grasp the concept of partitive only when they see this contrast. At this early stage, it may be helpful to emphasize the somewhat simplified rule of thumb given: *aimer*, *détester*, *préférer* take the definite article; *boire*, *manger*, *prendre*, *acheter* usually take the partitive article.

**Suggestion:** Point out how each noun in examples refers to divisible or measurable quantities rather than nondivisible, countable nouns. Some grammarians consider that true partitives are used only in singular.

The partitive is also used with abstract qualities attributed to people, while the definite article is used to talk about these qualities in general.

Elle a **du** courage. — *She has (some) courage.*
Elle déteste **l'**hypocrisie. — *She hates hypocrisy.*

## C. The Partitive in Negative Sentences

In negative sentences, partitive articles become **de** (**d'**), except after **être**.

Je bois **du** lait. → Je ne bois **pas de** lait.
Tu prends **de l'**eau. → Tu ne prends **pas d'**eau.
Vous mangez **des** carottes. → Vous ne mangez **pas de** carottes.

The expression **ne... plus** (*no more, not any more*) surrounds the conjugated verb, like **ne... pas**.

Je suis désolé, mais nous **n'**avons **plus** de vin. — *I'm sorry, but we have no more wine.*

## D. The Partitive with Expressions of Quantity

Partitive articles also become **de** (**d'**) after expressions of quantity.

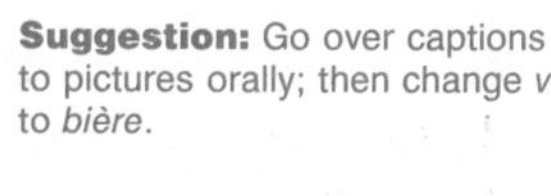
**Suggestion:** Go over captions to pictures orally; then change *vin* to *bière*.

Elle commande **du vin**.

**Combien de verres** commande-t-elle?

Elle commande **un peu de vin**.

Elle commande **beaucoup de vin**.

Elle commande **un verre de vin**.

Elle a **assez de vin**.

Elle boit **trop de vin**.

**Suggestion:** May be done first in small groups or in writing and then reviewed orally with the whole class.

**Continuation:** Hold up pictures of food items from magazines to continue activity.

## Vérifions!

**A. À table!** Qu'est-ce que vous prenez, en général, à chaque repas?

MODÈLE: Au déjeuner, je prends de la pizza. / Je ne prends pas de pizza.

| **Au petit déjeuner...** | **Au déjeuner...** | **Au dîner...** |
|---|---|---|
| du bacon | du poisson | de la soupe |
| des œufs | du poulet | un hamburger |
| des croissants | de la pizza | des frites |
| du café au lait | des spaghettis | du fromage |
| du thé | de la viande | du riz (*rice*) |
| des céréales | des légumes | un bifteck |
| du jus (*juice*) d'orange | un fruit | de la salade |
| ? | ? | ? |

**Additional activities:** A. *À table! Qu'est-ce qu'on mange?* MODÈLE: *le poulet* → *On mange du poulet.* 1. *la salade* 2. *les pommes de terre* 3. *le poisson* 4. *la viande* 5. *le pain* 6. *les fruits* 7. *le melon* 8. *les œufs* 9. *la soupe* 10. *l'omelette* 11. *la tarte aux pommes* 12. *les sandwichs*
B. *Au restaurant. Faites des phrases complètes pour décrire la scène.* 1. *Thibaut / demander / bifteck* 2. *nous / demander / lait* 3. *vous / commander / bière* 4. *Jean-Pierre et Anne / manger / sandwichs.* 5. *le serveur* (waiter) */ avoir / patience / avec nous*

**B. Dîner d'anniversaire** (*birthday*). Avec un(e) camarade vous préparez un dîner surprise pour fêter l'anniversaire d'un ami (d'une amie). Mais avez-vous tous (*all*) les ingrédients nécessaires?

MODÈLE: carottes (assez) / (ne... pas) champignons →
VOTRE CAMARADE: Est-ce que tu as des carottes?
VOUS: Oui, j'ai assez de carottes mais je n'ai pas de champignons.

1. eau minérale (3 bouteilles) / (ne... plus) jus d'orange
2. café (un peu) / (ne... plus) thé
3. fraises (beaucoup) / (ne... pas) melon
4. chocolat (trop) / (ne... pas) marrons glacés (*candied chestnuts*)
5. viande (assez) / (ne... pas) légumes
6. sucre (un bol) / (ne... plus) sel
7. talent pour faire la cuisine (beaucoup) / (ne... pas) patience
8. ?

**Additional activity:** *Conversation. Posez les questions suivantes à un(e) camarade. 1. Combien de repas prends-tu par jour (each day)? Prends-tu ton repas principal le matin? à midi? le soir? Prends-tu peu de temps pour manger? beaucoup de temps? Bois-tu pendant (during) les repas ou entre les repas? Prends-tu du pain avec chaque repas? 2. Qu'est-ce que tu prends au petit déjeuner? des œufs? des céréales? du jambon? du pain et du beurre? des croissants? Qu'est-ce que tu bois au petit déjeuner? du café? du thé? du chocolat? Avec ton café, est-ce que tu prends du sucre? du lait? de la crème?*

## Parlons-en!

**A. Ce que mangent les Français.** Regardez le tableau, étudiez les résultats (*results*) et répondez aux questions.

### Français, ce que vous mangez*

| EN BAISSE[a] | 1965 | 1979 | 1989 | EN HAUSSE[b] | 1965 | 1979 | 1989 |
|---|---|---|---|---|---|---|---|
| Pain (kg) | 84,3 | 51,3 | 44,3 | Agrumes[f] et bananes (kg) | 21,0 | 22,7 | 24,0 |
| Pâtes[c] alimentaires (kg) | 7,6 | 5,5 | 5,7 | Fruits frais métropolitains (kg)[g] | 36,9 | 39,3 | 37,7 |
| Pommes de terre (kg) | 95,2 | 56,2 | 34,7 | | | | |
| Légumes frais (kg) | 72,1 | 65,4 | 59,2 | Porc, lard (kg) | 3,0 | 8,7 | 7,8 |
| Viande de boucherie (kg)[d] | 20,9 | 24,0 | 18,7 | Charcuterie (kg)[h] | 7,0 | 8,7 | 9,0 |
| Œufs (unités) | 169 | 179 | 147 | Volailles (kg)[i] | 12,2 | 13,7 | 13,4 |
| Beurre (kg) | 8,8 | 8,0 | 5,5 | Poissons, crustacés (kg) | 6,6 | 6,8 | 7,7 |
| Huiles alimentaires (litres)[e] | 11,8 | 10,3 | 8,5 | Fromages (kg) | 10,4 | 14,4 | 16,9 |
| Sucre (kg) | 20,9 | 13,4 | 8,6 | Yaourts (unités) | — | 73,3 | 161,5 |
| Vin (litres) | 90,6 | 54,9 | 31,7 | Boissons non alcoolisées (litres) | — | 65,6 | 99,7 |
| Bière (litres) | 20,8 | 16,6 | 11,8 | | | | |

**Quantités consommées à domicile par personne par an. Source INSEE.*

[a] *en... diminishing*
[b] *en... increasing*
[c] *Pasta*
[d] *butcher's shop*
[e] *Huiles... Cooking oils*
[f] *Citrus fruits*
[g] *frais... fresh grown in France (not overseas)*
[h] *Sausage, salami, delicatessen specialties*
[i] *Poultry*

1. Qu'est-ce que les Français aiment mieux: le pain ou les pommes de terre?
2. Est-ce que les Français mangent plus de fromage en 1989 qu'en 1965, ou moins?
3. En 1979, les Français boivent beaucoup moins de vin que de boissons non alcoolisées (moins... que: *less than*). Et en 1989?
4. À votre avis, les Français boivent-ils plus de bière que les Américains, ou vice-versa (le contraire)? (plus... que: *more than*)
5. D'après ce tableau, quelles sont les boissons préférées des Français?
6. À votre avis, est-ce que les Français mangent trop? pas assez?
7. À votre avis, y a-t-il une grande différence entre ce que (*what*) mangent les Français et ce que mangent les Américains? Expliquez.
8. Et vous, qu'est-ce que vous mangez et buvez un peu (beaucoup, trop, pas assez)?

## Mots-clés

*More about expressing likes and dislikes:* You have been expressing your preferences since the beginning of the course. Here are several simple ways to express *intense* likes and dislikes.

> **Moi, j'adore ça! Je suis gourmand(e).** (*I love to eat.*)
> **Je n'aime pas du tout** le bifteck!
> **J'ai horreur des** escargots (*snails*).

**Suggestion:** Give sts. certain food items and have them react, using these expressions: *le foie* (*liver*), *les concombres*, *le chocolat*, *le brocoli*, *les épinards*, *les éclairs*, *la salade*, etc.

**B. Trouvez quelqu'un qui...** Parmi vos camarades de classe, trouvez quelqu'un dans chacune (*each one*) des catégories suivantes. Demandez aussi des renseignements (= informations) supplémentaires. Ensuite, présentez les résultats de l'enquête aux autres membres de la classe. Trouvez quelqu'un qui...

1. est végétarien(ne) (Pourquoi?)
2. ne prend jamais de dessert (Pourquoi?)
3. adore faire la cuisine (Spécialité?)
4. mange très peu (Combien de fois par jour?)
5. apprécie la cuisine exotique (Quels plats?)
6. refuse de manger certains aliments (*foods*) (Lesquels [*Which*] et pourquoi?)
7. a horreur de certains légumes (Lesquels?)
8. aime surtout (*especially*) certaines viandes (Lesquelles?)
9. est gourmand(e)

**Additional activity:** *Conversation et interview.* 1. *Est-ce que vous mangez beaucoup de viande? de poisson? de légumes? de fruits?* 2. *Qu'est-ce que vous aimez manger? Qu'est-ce que vous n'aimez pas manger?* 3. *Qu'est-ce que vous aimez manger au petit déjeuner? au déjeuner? au dîner?* 4. *Qu'est-ce que vous aimez manger comme dessert?* 5. *Est-ce que vous faites souvent la cuisine? Qu'est-ce que vous aimez préparer?* 6. *Imaginez que vous allez faire un pique-nique avec des amis. Qu'est-ce que vous allez apporter?*

## 19. GIVING COMMANDS
## The Imperative

### L'ennemi d'un bon repas

FRANÇOIS: Martine, **passe**-moi le sel, s'il te plaît... (*Martine passe la salade à François.*)
FRANÇOIS: Mais non, enfin! **Écoute** un peu... je te demande le sel!
MARTINE: François, **sois** gentil—**ne parle pas** si fort. Je n'entends plus la télé...

1. Est-ce que François demande la salade?
2. Est-ce que Martine passe le sel à François?
3. Est-ce que Martine écoute François?

## A. Kinds of Imperatives

The imperative is the command form of a verb. There are three forms. Note that subject pronouns are not used with them.

| | | |
|---|---|---|
| **tu** form | **Parle!** | *Speak!* |
| **nous** form | **Parlons!** | *Let's speak!* |
| **vous** form | **Parlez!** | *Speak!* |

## B. Imperative Forms of -er Verbs

The imperatives of regular **-er** verbs are the same as the corresponding present-tense forms, except that the **tu** form does not end in **-s**.

| INFINITIVE | tu | nous | vous |
|---|---|---|---|
| regarder | **Regarde!** | **Regardons!** | **Regardez!** |
| entrer | **Entre!** | **Entrons!** | **Entrez!** |

**Regardez!** Un restaurant russe. *Look! A Russian restaurant.*
**Entrons!** *Let's go in!*

The imperative forms of the irregular verb **aller** follow the pattern of regular **-er** imperatives: **va**, **allons**, **allez**.

## C. Imperative Forms of -re and -ir Verbs

The imperative forms of the **-re** and **-ir** verbs you have learned—even most of the irregular ones—are identical to their corresponding present-tense forms.

| INFINITIVE | tu | nous | vous |
|---|---|---|---|
| attendre | **Attends!** | **Attendons!** | **Attendez!** |
| finir | **Finis!** | **Finissons!** | **Finissez!** |
| faire | **Fais... !** | **Faisons... !** | **Faites... !** |

**Attends! Finis** ton verre! *Wait! Finish your drink!*
**Faites** attention! *Pay attention! (Watch out!)*

## D. Irregular Imperative Forms

The verbs **avoir** and **être** have irregular command forms.

| INFINITIVE | tu | nous | vous |
|---|---|---|---|
| avoir | **Aie... !** | **Ayons... !** | **Ayez... !** |
| être | **Sois... !** | **Soyons... !** | **Soyez... !** |

**Sois** gentil, Michel. — *Be nice, Michel.*
**Ayez** de la patience. — *Have patience.*

## E. Negative Commands

In negative commands, **ne** comes before the verb and **pas** follows it.

**Ne prends pas** de sucre! — *Don't have any sugar!*
**Ne buvons pas** trop de café. — *Let's not drink too much coffee.*
**N'attendez pas** le dessert. — *Don't wait for dessert.*

### *Vérifions!*

**A. Les bonnes manières.** Vous apprenez* les bonnes manières à un enfant.

MODÈLE: ne pas jouer avec ton couteau →
Ne joue pas avec ton couteau!

1. attendre ton père 2. prendre ta serviette 3. finir ta soupe 4. manger tes carottes 5. regarder ton assiette 6. être sage (*good* [*lit.*, *wise*])† 7. ne pas manger de sucre 8. boire ton verre de lait 9. ne pas demander le dessert

Et maintenant donnez les mêmes recommandations à deux enfants.

MODÈLE: ne pas jouer avec ton couteau →
Ne jouez pas avec vos couteaux!

**B. Un job d'été.** Vous travaillez deux semaines comme serveur (serveuse) dans un café. Voici les recommandations du patron (*owner*).

MODÈLE: faire attention aux clients → Faites attention aux clients.

1. être aimable 2. avoir de la patience 3. écouter les clients 4. répondre aux questions 5. ne pas perdre de temps 6. rendre correctement la monnaie (*change*)

**Follow-up:** Have sts. decide whether following commands should be in the affirmative or negative: 1. *faire ses devoirs après le dîner* 2. *jeter* (*throw*) *sa serviette par terre* (*on the floor*) 3. *manger vite* 4. *être poli*(*e*).

**Additional activity:** *Préparatifs.* MODÈLE: *Vous faites le marché.* → *Faites le marché.* 1. *Vous allez vite au marché.* 2. *Nous attendons l'autobus.* 3. *Tu descends de l'autobus.* 4. *Vous achetez du pain frais* (*fresh*). 5. *Nous choisissons un camembert.* 6. *Tu commandes un poulet chaud.* 7. *Tu prends ta fourchette. Maintenant, mettez les phrases précédentes à la forme négative de l'impératif.*

**Follow-up:** Play *Jacques a dit.* For example: *Jacques a dit: Prenez votre livre de français. Prenez votre stylo. Jacques a dit: Regardez le mur. Dites bonjour à votre camarade de classe.*

*__Apprendre__ can also mean *to teach*. The person taught is preceded by **à**. The thing taught can be either a noun or a verb. The verb is also preceded by **à**: **Tu apprends les bonnes manières à un enfant.** (**Tu apprends à l'enfant à avoir de bonnes manières**.)

†Note that the French appeal to a child's wisdom when correcting a child, Americans appeal to a child's moral side when they say "Be good."

Imaginez maintenant trois autres recommandations possibles du patron. Soyez créatif (créative)!

Maintenant vous parlez avec un autre serveur (une autre serveuse) des choses qu'il faut (= il est nécessaire de) faire au travail. Répétez les recommandations du patron.

MODÈLE: faire attention aux clients → Faisons attention aux clients!

### Parlons-en!

**Le robot.** Vous avez un robot qui travaille pour vous. La classe choisit un étudiant (une étudiante) pour jouer le rôle du robot. Donnez cinq ordres en français au robot. Il/Elle est obligé(e) d'obéir.

MODÈLES: Va au tableau!
Prends ton livre de français!
Regarde le mur!

**Suggestion**: You may want to do a set of orders first to show sts. how to create a chain of actions. Have various sts. play the robot.

# Étude de prononciation

## Stress and Intonation

**Stress** (***L'accent***). Stress refers to the emphasis given to a syllable. English speakers tend to emphasize syllables within a word and within a sentence. French rhythmic patterns, however, are based on *evenly* stressed syllables. There is a slight emphasis (called **l'accent final**) on the final syllable of each French word.

Prononcez avec le professeur.

1. le bureau
2. le professeur
3. la différence
4. l'attention
5. l'administration
6. le garçon

**Intonation.** Intonation refers to the variation of the pitch, the rise and fall of the voice (not loudness), in a sentence. Here are three basic French intonation patterns.

**Model intonation:** Use short sentences to provide a context.

1. In *declarative sentences*, the intonation rises within each breath group (group of words produced in one breath) and falls at the end of the sentence, starting with the last breath group.

   Je m'appelle Eric Martin. Bonjour, mademoiselle.

   Il est content de quitter l'université à trois heures.

2. In *yes/no questions*, the intonation rises at the end of the question.

   Ça va? Est-ce que c'est un professeur?

3. In *information questions*, the intonation starts high and falls at the end of the question.

   Comment allez-vous? Qu'est-ce que c'est?

**A. Vos plats préférés.** Quels plats aimez-vous? Quels plats n'aimez-vous pas? Pourquoi? Faites des phrases complètes.

MODÈLES: J'aime les hot-dogs parce qu'ils sont faciles à préparer.
Je n'aime pas le curry indien parce qu'il est épicé (*spicy*).

| **J'aime... / Je n'aime pas...** | **parce que...** |
|---|---|
| les «Big Mac» | difficile(s) à préparer |
| le bifteck et les pommes de terre | facile(s) à préparer |
| le jambon | beaucoup de calories |
| les soupes de légumes | peu de calories |
| les gâteaux au chocolat | beaucoup d'ingrédients |
| les hot-dogs | des ingrédients chimiques |
| les spaghettis | exotique(s) |
| la pizza | dégoûtant(e/s) (*disgusting*) |
| les escargots (*snails*) | cher(s)/chère(s) |
| le curry indien | très sucré(e/s) |
| le canard laqué (*Peking duck*) | nutritif(s)/nutritive(s) |
| le poulet frit à la Kentucky | très snob(s) |
| les éclairs | très américain(e/s) |
| les fruits | très français(e/s) |
| ? | ? |

On est ce qu'on mange. Le/La gourmand(e) aime manger et il/elle mange beaucoup. Le gourmet aime seulement (*only*) la nourriture (*food*) de qualité et ne mange pas beaucoup. Selon vos réponses, êtes-vous gourmand(e) ou gourmet? Pourquoi? À quelles occasions êtes-vous gourmand(e)? À quelles occasions êtes-vous gourmet?

**Suggestions:** (1) Sts. write out at least five sentences, then elicit individual answers. (2) Do exercises orally, calling on several individuals. Have several sts. remember responses of various classmates. (3) Do in pairs.

**B. La nourriture et les boissons.** Complétez le dialogue.

É1: qu'est-ce que vous / prendre / dîner?
É2: on / prendre / jambon / et / salade
É1: manger / vous / assez / fruits?
É2: oui, nous / manger / souvent / poires / et / pommes
É1: prendre / tu / beaucoup / vin?
É2: non / il y a / ne... plus / vin
É1: mes amis / boire / eau minérale
É2: qui / payer (*to pay for*) / repas?
É1: hélas (*alas*) / souvent / moi

**Suggestion:** Give sts. a few minutes to write out and check on overhead.

**Follow-up:** Have sts. play the two roles.

**Additional activity:** *Au marché. Changez chaque verbe du singulier au pluriel ou vice versa. Faites les autres changements nécessaires.*
MODÈLES: *Le client prend de la viande.* → *Les clients prennent de la viande.*
*Bois de la bière.* → *Buvez de la bière.*
1. *Nous apprenons à faire des courses en France.* 2. *Nous allons acheter du fromage.* 3. *Tu achètes du poulet.* 4. *Prends ton temps.* 5. *Ne perds pas patience.* 6. *Prends ton sac.* 7. *Tu paies le commerçant.* 8. *Le commerçant comprend ses clients.* 9. *Le commerçant rend la monnaie.* 10. *Désirez-vous prendre un verre?* 11. *Je bois de l'eau minérale.* 12. *Je mange aussi de la quiche.* 13. *Nous préférons le champagne, mais c'est cher.*

## Mots-clés

*Expressing agreement, disagreement, and surprise*

| | |
|---|---|
| **D'accord.** | *All right.* |
| **Bien sûr que oui (non).** | *But of course. / Of course not.* |
| **Ah bon.** | *Oh, really?* |
| **Mais non! Moi, je préfère...** | *Of course not! I'd rather . . .* |
| **Au contraire, moi, je...** | *On the contrary, I . . .* |
| **Peut-être, mais...** | *Maybe, but . . .* |

**Suggestions:** Ask sts. to use these expressions in Ex. C as they react to the responses in the interview.

**C. Sondage: Préférences gastronomiques.** Interviewez cinq camarades. Ensuite décrivez à la classe leurs préférences gastronomiques et comparez vos résultats avec les résultats des autres enquêteurs (*interviewers*). Puis décidez qui dans la classe aime le plat le plus original, le plus bizarre; qui mange à des heures inhabituelles (*unusual*); qui préfère une boisson peu commune, un restaurant exotique... Y a-t-il d'autres réponses surprenantes (*surprising*)? Expliquez.

**Suggestion:** Have sts. circulate among class members to get five answers to each question. Sts. can take notes as they do their surveys. Limit this activity to ten minutes for interviewing and to five minutes for summary of results.

QUESTIONS SUGGÉRÉES

1. Quel est ton restaurant préféré? Manges-tu souvent au restaurant?
2. Quel est ton repas préféré? Pourquoi?
3. Au petit déjeuner, préfères-tu prendre du café? du thé? du chocolat? du lait? _____? Prends-tu aussi des œufs? des céréales? _____?
4. Que préfères-tu prendre au déjeuner? un sandwich? une omelette? un repas complet? _____?
5. Qu'est-ce que tu bois au déjeuner? du lait? du vin? du Coca-Cola? de l'eau minérale? du café?
6. Qu'est-ce que tu prends au dîner? du jambon? du rôti de bœuf (*roast beef*)? du poisson? _____? Qu'est-ce que tu bois?
7. En général, quel dessert préfères-tu? des fruits? du fromage? du gâteau? _____?

8. Manges-tu les mêmes plats toute l'année? Y a-t-il quelque chose que tu aimes particulièrement en chaque saison?

## Interactions

In this chapter, you have practiced talking about food and drink, giving commands, and telling time. Act out the following situations, using the vocabulary and structures from this chapter.

**Suggestion:** Ask a third st. to listen to the role-play activities. Afterward, he or she will summarize the conversations to the whole class. He or she can make evaluations of the discussion if possible, judging the politeness of the sts. in the first *Interaction* and the advice given in the second one.

1. **Au restaurant universitaire.** While you are eating on campus, you get stuck sitting next to someone (role-played by a classmate) with whom you have nothing in common and whom you do not particularly like. Make small talk about the meal, the weather, the classes, etc. Try to leave as soon as you can.
2. **Conseils.** A French exchange student has recently arrived at your university and wants to know the hours when the campus dining places are open (= *ouvert*) and the kinds of foods they serve. Give him/her some information and simple advice about what and where to eat.

## LECTURE

### Avant de lire

**Finding the main thought in a sentence.** As you know, the normal word order of French syntax is *subject + verb*. Together, the subject and the verb represent the main thought expressed in a sentence. To grasp the meaning of a long sentence, it is useful to begin by isolating the subject and the verb.

**Suggestions:** (1) This is a good time to continue discussion of linking sentences. Remind sts. of the expressions introduced previously (*mais*, *ou*, *donc*, *et*). Mention that the relative pronouns will be formally introduced later. (2) Point out and discuss sentences containing relative pronouns before sts. read passage. (3) Discuss illustrations with sts. as a pre-reading activity. Ask them to describe what they see, if they are reminded of an American holiday, etc.

Two strategies can help you. First, omit words and phrases set off by commas. They are most likely to contain information supplementary to the main thought. Second, delete the relative clauses or clauses introduced by relative pronouns (for example, **qui** and **que**, meaning *who*, *whom*, or *that*). You will learn the relative pronouns later, but you should recognize them for the purpose of reading.

Try to find the subject and verb in the following sentence.

> **Au dessert, on mange la bûche de Noël, un gâteau roulé au chocolat en forme de bûche.**

Once you have identified the subject and the verb (**on mange**), you can reread the sentence, adding more information. What does one eat? Is there a definition of **la bûche de Noël** in the sentence? Set off by a comma to the right of this term is a phrase including the words **gâteau** and **chocolat**, which you learned in this chapter. Set off by a comma at the beginning of the sentence is the word **dessert**. Without English glossing, you still may not know the literal definition of **la bûche**, but you should have understood that it is a chocolate dessert eaten at Christmas time. And that is sufficient to "get the gist" of the sentence.

Apply these strategies to your reading of "Grandes occasions," and remember to scan the glosses and the illustrations first.

# Grandes occasions

En France, les jours de fête sont une occasion pour se réunir° en famille ou entre amis. Pour chaque fête, on mange des plats typiques qui changent° parfois° selon les régions. Voici les fêtes les plus gourmandes° du calendrier français.

*se... to get together*
varient
quelquefois
les plus... où l'on mange bien

Pour la fête des rois,* le 6 janvier, on achète chez le pâtissier° une galette. C'est un gâteau qui contient un petit objet appelé une **fève**. La personne qui trouve la fève dans son morceau° de gâteau est maintenant le roi (ou la reine)° et il choisit sa reine (ou son roi). La famille ou les amis boivent à leur santé.°

*pastry shop*
*piece*
roi... *king* (*or queen*)
*health*

Qui a trouvé la fève?

Les Français adorent la bûche de Noël.

Pâques° est, bien sûr, la fête du chocolat! C'est aussi un grand jour de réunion familiale, à l'église et à table. On fait un grand repas, et au dessert grands et petits mangent des œufs, des cloches,° des poules ou des poissons en chocolat remplis° de bonbons.

*Easter*
*bells / filled*

Noël est peut-être la fête des fêtes. Le Réveillon° de Noël est un grand dîner que l'on prend le plus souvent après la messe° de minuit. Au menu: huîtres, foie gras, dinde aux marrons° et beaucoup de champagne! Au dessert, on mange la bûche° de Noël, un gâteau roulé au chocolat en forme de bûche. Les enfants, bien sûr, attendent avec impatience l'arrivée du Père Noël.

*Midnight supper*
une cérémonie catholique
huîtres... *oysters, pâté, turkey with chestnuts / log*

*This Christian holiday, also called Twelfth-day, commemorates Christ's appearance (in the form of the Magi) to the Gentiles.

## Compréhension

Match the following quotations with the relevant paragraphs in "Grandes occasions."

1. «C'est ma fête préférée parce que j'adore les œufs en chocolat.»
2. «Je suis le roi!»
3. «Nous attendons toujours avec impatience l'arrivée de la bûche.»

**Additional activity:** Have sts. create a word association chain about two holidays in the U.S. Then use these as a basis for comparison of traditions and customs in the two countries.

## PAR ÉCRIT

**Function:** Writing about daily habits
**Audience:** Someone you do not know
**Goal:** Write a passage describing your eating habits. Use the following questions as a guide.

PARAGRAPHE 1
Combien de repas par jour prenez-vous? En général, mangez-vous bien ou mal? Expliquez.

PARAGRAPHE 2
Que prenez-vous au petit déjeuner?

PARAGRAPHE 3
Où mangez-vous à midi? Prenez-vous un repas complet au déjeuner?

PARAGRAPHE 4
Mangez-vous pendant l'après-midi? Qu'est-ce que vous mangez?

PARAGRAPHE 5
Qui prépare le dîner chez vous? Passez-vous beaucoup de temps à table?

PARAGRAPHE 6
Quand invitez-vous des amis à dîner chez vous? À quelle occasion préparez-vous un repas spécial?

### Steps

1. Begin by answering the questions above in rough form.
2. After you have jotted down the answers, write a single sentence that sums up the main point you want to make in each paragraph. (As you structure your paragraphs, keep in mind what you discovered about topic sentences in the **Avant de lire** section in Chapter 5. A topic sentence always expresses a "key idea" which will be developed or supported in the rest of your paragraph.) Write a few topic sentences before you settle on the final one.
3. After you have written the draft, reread it to check for organization and smoothness of style. Have a classmate read it to see if what you have written is clear. Make any necessary changes.

4. Finally, read the composition once more for spelling, punctuation, and grammar errors. Pay particular attention to your use of articles, especially the partitive. Underline the topic sentences before you hand in your composition. Be prepared to read it to a small group of classmates.

**À l'écoute!** See scripts for listening passages and follow-up activities recorded on student cassette. Remind sts. that in the listening comprehension passages (as in real life) they will not understand every word they hear. They should focus globally on the general information in the passages and not be overly concerned about what they do not understand.

## À L'ÉCOUTE!

**La météo.** You will hear a weather forecast for all of France. First, look through the drawings and the activities. Next, listen to the forecast. Then, do the activities.

**A.** Based on the forecast, place the appropriate weather symbol in the correct place on the map of France. Next, write down the temperatures you hear next to the appropriate city.

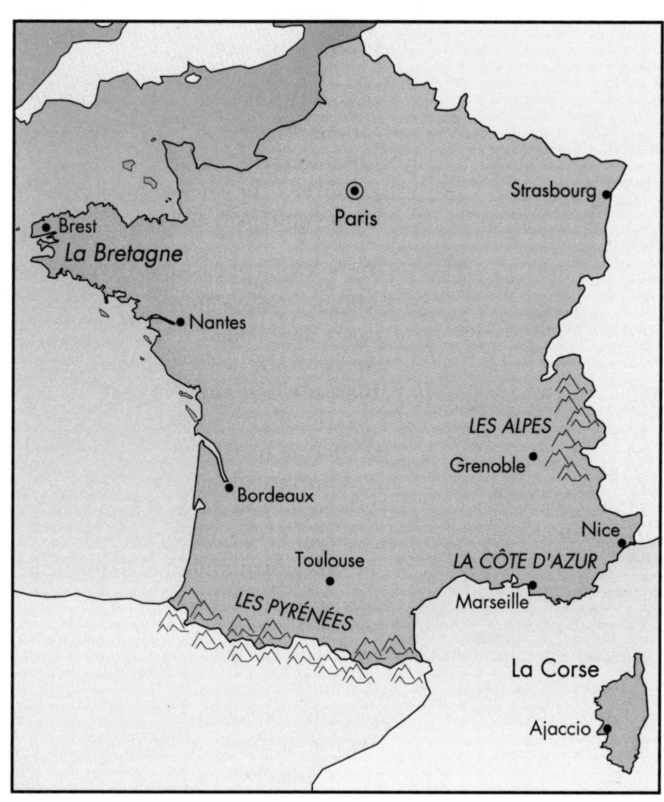


**B. Vrai ou faux?** Now turn on the tape again and listen to short statements about weather. Indicate here whether they are true or false according to current weather conditions in *your area.*

1. _____
2. _____
3. _____
4. _____
5. _____
6. _____
7. _____
8. _____

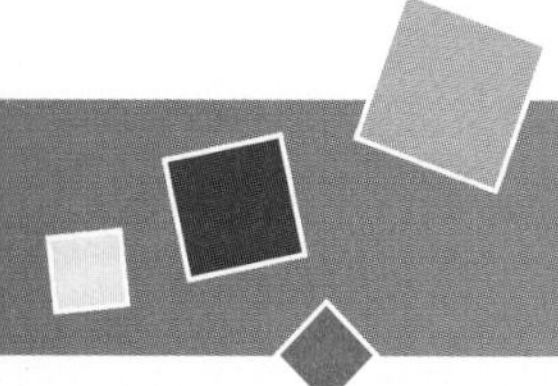

# Vocabulaire

## Verbes

**acheter** to buy
**apprendre** to learn
**boire** to drink
**commander** to order (*in a restaurant*)
**comprendre** to understand
**dîner** to dine, have dinner
**passer** to pass, spend (*time*)
**préférer** to prefer
**prendre** to take; to have (to eat; to order)

À REVOIR: **aimer mieux, préparer**

## Substantifs

**la boisson** drink
**la cuisine** cooking; kitchen
**le déjeuner** lunch
**le dessert** dessert
**le dîner** dinner
**le fruit** fruit
**le goûter** afternoon snack
**le hors-d'œuvre*** appetizer
**la journée** (whole) day
**le légume** vegetable
**le petit déjeuner** breakfast
**le repas** meal
**la viande** meat

## Les provisions

**le beurre** butter
**la bière** beer
**le bifteck** steak
**la carotte** carrot
**le chocolat** chocolate
**la crème** cream
**le croissant** croissant
**l'eau (minérale)** (*f.*) (mineral) water
**la fraise** strawberry
**les frites** (*f.*) French fries
**le fromage** cheese
**le gâteau** cake
**les haricots* verts** (*m.*) green beans
**le jambon** ham
**le lait** milk
**l'œuf** (*m.*) egg
**le pain** bread
**la poire** pear
**le poisson** fish
**le poivre** pepper
**la pomme** apple
**la pomme de terre** potato
**le poulet** chicken
**la salade** salade, lettuce
**le sel** salt
**le sucre** sugar
**la tarte** pie
**le thé** tea
**la tomate** tomato
**le vin** wine

## À table

**l'assiette** (*f.*) plate
**le bol** wide cup
**la bouteille** bottle
**la carafe** carafe
**le couteau** knife
**la cuillère (à soupe)** (soup) spoon
**la fourchette** fork
**la serviette** napkin
**la tasse** cup
**le verre** glass

## L'heure

**Quelle heure est-il?** What time is it?
**Il est... heure(s).** It is . . . o'clock.
**Il est midi.** It's noon.
**Il est minuit.** It's midnight.
**...et demi(e)** half past (the hour)
**...et quart** quarter past (the hour)
**...moins le quart** quarter to (the hour)
**...du matin** in the morning
**...de l'après-midi** in the afternoon
**...du soir** in the evening, at night

À REVOIR: **les chiffres** (*numbers*) **aux pages 4 et 8.**

## Le temps

**Quel temps fait-il?** How's the weather?
**Il fait beau.** It's nice (out).
**Il fait chaud.** It's hot.
**Il fait du soleil.** It's sunny.
**Il fait du vent.** It's windy.
**Il fait frais.** It's cool.
**Il fait froid.** It's cold.
**Il fait mauvais.** It's bad (out).
**Il neige.** It's snowing.
**Il pleut.** It's raining.

## Les saisons

**En été...** In summer . . .
**En automne...** In fall . . .
**En hiver...** In winter . . .
**Au printemps...** In spring . . .

## Mots et expressions divers

**Ah bon.** Oh, really?
**assez de** enough
**Au contraire...** On the contrary . . .
**Bien sûr que oui (non).** Of course (not).
**de bonne heure** early
**J'ai horreur de...** I can't stand . . .
**Je n'aime pas du tout...** I don't like . . . at all
**Je suis gourmand(e).** I like to eat.
**ne... plus** no more
**presque** almost
**tard** late
**tôt** early
**trop de** too much
**vers** around, about (with time expressions)

---

*The initial **h** is aspirate here, which means there is no elision with the article **le**.

# Intermède

## SITUATION

Situation: The *Situation* dialogues are recorded on the student cassette packaged with the student text.

### Non, merci

**Contexte** *Ken, un étudiant américain, passe un semestre à Strasbourg, où il habite dans une famille française. Strasbourg est la ville principale d'Alsace, une province où la cuisine est très riche. Les Alsaciens sont aussi très hospitaliers. Ken découvre° les plaisirs et les dangers d'un repas de week-end en famille!*

**Suggestion:** Have sts. read dialogue to find expressions used to decline tactfully and ask what they would say if accepting the offer.

*discovers*

**Objectif** *Ken essaie de refuser un plat avec tact.*

Une vue pittoresque du vieux Strasbourg

M. GIRARD: Encore un peu de bière, Ken?
KEN: Non, merci.
MME GIRARD: Vous allez bien reprendre un peu de quiche, quand même°?
KEN: Elle est vraiment° délicieuse, mais non, merci.
MARIE-LINE: Tu es au régime?
KEN: Non, mais j'ai déjà beaucoup mangé.
MARIE-LINE: Ken, la cuisine, c'est une expérience culturelle.
MME GIRARD: Mais oui, Ken, faites un sacrifice culturel et prenez de la tarte aux mirabelles:° c'est ma spécialité!
KEN: Alors, je ne peux° pas refuser.

*quand... all the same*
*truly, really*
*plums*
*can*

## À propos

### À table

The following expressions will be useful when you are eating in a French-speaking area.

**Bon appétit!** — *Enjoy your meal;* literally, *good appetite.*

**Santé!**
**À votre santé!**
**À ta santé!** — These expressions meaning *to your health* or *Cheers!* are useful for toasts.

**Suggestion:** These expressions may be used by sts. in skits to practice table manners. Discuss ways in which the French hold knife and fork and where they place their hands during meals.

| | |
|---|---|
| **Je reprendrais bien un peu de...**<br>**Passez-moi... s'il vous plaît.**<br>**Passe-moi... s'il te plaît.** | *May I have another helping of . . .* Say this when you want someone to pass you something. |
| **En voulez-vous encore?**<br>**En veux-tu encore?** | *Do you want some more* (*of a certain dish or drink*)? |
| **S'il vous plaît. / Non, merci.** | *Yes, please. / No, thank you.* |
| **Je n'ai plus faim.** | *I'm full. I've eaten enough.* |
| **C'est délicieux! Je me régale.** | *It's delicious! I'm having a feast.* Say this to compliment the cook. |

## Maintenant à vous!

**A. Questions personnelles.** Relisez (*Reread*) le dialogue, puis répondez aux questions.

1. Est-ce que vous dînez souvent en famille le dimanche? Quels plats sert-on? Qu'est-ce qu'on aime manger chez vous?
2. Qu'est-ce que vous aimez manger quand vous dînez dans un bon restaurant?
3. Est-ce qu'il y a des plats typiques de votre région? Lesquels préférez-vous?

**B. Jeu de rôles: Un repas entre amis.** Avec deux camarades, imaginez une conversation qui prend place (*which takes place*) à table. Utilisez les expressions de l'*À propos*. Puis jouez la scène devant la classe.

# PORTRAITS

### *Édouard Manet:* Déjeuner sur l'herbe (1832–1883)

Édouard Manet's *Déjeuner sur l'herbe* created a scandal in 1863 because of its thoroughly natural depiction of the human body, divorced from any historical, mythological or heroic context. This congenial group of picnickers exercised a profound influence on the Impressionists and helped usher in the modern age of Western painting. It now hangs in the Musée d'Orsay in Paris.

CHAPITRE **SEPT**

# On mange bien en France!

**En avant**

—Bonjour, Madame.

—Bonjour. Je voudrais un kilo de saumon, s'il vous plaît.

—Oui, et avec ceci?

—C'est tout.

—Alors, ça vous fait 65,80 F.

**En avant**: See scripts for follow-up questions recorded on student cassette.

**Communicative goals:** going shopping; ordering in a restaurant; counting above 60; using French currency; pointing out and describing people and things; expressing desire, ability, and obligation; and asking about choices.

**Note**: This chapter treats topics appropriate for Intermediate Level of proficiency.

# Étude de vocabulaire

## Les magasins d'alimentation

**Additional vocab.**: *du riz, des pommes frites, de la pizza, de l'agneau, des pâtes, du yaourt*

**Note**: Point out that one says *à la boucherie* but *chez le boucher*, etc.

**Presentation**: (1) Model pronunciation. (2) Have sts. name foods that are: *sucré, salé, des légumes, des fruits, des produits laitiers, du porc, du bœuf*. Mention that the French do not mix *sucré* and *salé* in the same dish. (3) If available, show slides of French markets of various types, including open-air, supermarkets, and specialty shops. Have sts. name foods and stores seen in slide presentation.

**Les magasins du quartier.** Où allez-vous pour acheter les produits suivants?

MODÈLE: des côtes de bœuf →
Pour acheter des côtes de bœuf, je vais à la boucherie-charcuterie.*

1. des pains au chocolat 2. des pommes de terre 3. des boîtes de thon (*tuna*) à l'huile 4. du poisson frais (*fresh*) 5. du veau 6. une baguette 7. du pâté de canard (*duck*) 8. des crevettes (*shrimp*)

**Follow-up**: One st. chooses a store and names one product that can be bought there. Another repeats the product and names a new one, and so on. Do this for several stores. MODÈLE:—*À la boulangerie-pâtisserie, j'achète un éclair au chocolat.—J'achète un éclair au chocolat et une baguette. —J'achète un éclair au chocolat, une baguette et...*

---

*There are also separate stores: **la boucherie**, **la charcuterie**, **la boulangerie**, **la pâtisserie**. Many of these stores are disappearing as the French increasingly patronize **les supermarchés**.

## L'HIPPO FUTÉ 73,00 F

Salade Hippo
Faux filet grillé (240 g)
sauce poivrade
Pommes allumettes

### LES VINS EN PICHET[a] (31 cl)

| | |
|---|---|
| BORDEAUX ROUGE A.C. | 23,00 F |
| GAMAY DE TOURAINE A.C. | 17,00 F |

### LES ENTRÉES

| | |
|---|---|
| ASSIETTE DU JARDINIER[b] | 29,00 F |
| TERRINE DU CHEF | 27,00 F |
| COCKTAIL DE CREVETTES | 30,00 F |
| SALADE DE SAISON | 13,00 F |

### LES GRILLADES

*avec sauce au choix.*

FAUX FILET MINUTE ........ 59,00 F
*Tellement goûteux qu'il plaît aussi à ceux qui l'aiment «bien cuit».*

T. BONE ........ 89,00 F
*Tranche à l'américaine, avec le filet et le faux filet de part et d'autre de l'os en T. 2 qualités de viande dans le même morceau d'environ 380 g.*

PAVÉ* ........ 69,00 F
*Tranché dans le cœur des rumsteaks, c'est une tranche maigre et épaisse (conseillé pour ceux qui aiment «rouge»).*

ENTRECÔTE* ........ 69,00 F
*Un morceau qui permet à ceux qui aiment «bien cuit» d'apprécier cependant la bonne viande.*

CÔTE «VILLETTE»* ........ 184,00 F
*Pour 2 affamés d'accord sur la même cuisson. 850 grammes environ.*

CÔTES D'AGNEAU[c] ........ 73,00 F

### LES FROMAGES

| | |
|---|---|
| BRIE DE MEAUX AUX NOIX | 23,00 F |
| FROMAGE BLANC NATURE | 15,00 F |

### LES DESSERTS

| | |
|---|---|
| MOUSSE AU CHOCOLAT | 22,00 F |
| TARTE AUX FRUITS | 29,00 F |

### LES SORBETS[d]

| | |
|---|---|
| POIRE | 22,00 F |
| FRUIT DE LA PASSION | 22,00 F |

[a]pitcher
[b]Assiette... *mixed salad*
[c]lamb
[d]sherbets

***Autres mots utiles:***

**l'entrée** (*f.*) first course
**le plat** dish (type of food); course (of a meal)
**le plat principal** main course
**l'addition** (*f.*) check
**le pourboire** tip

**Suggestion**: Look at menu with sts. and ask *Quel est le nom du restaurant? Est-ce un restaurant élégant? cher? Lisez le nom de chaque catégorie de plats. Que signifie probablement grillades? fromages? desserts? Quels plats aimeriez-vous goûter? (J'aimerais goûter... ).*

**A. L'Hippo.** Mettez le dialogue à la page suivante dans le bon ordre. Numérotez de 1 jusqu'à 14.

---

*Pavé, entrecôte, and côte «villette» are different cuts of beef.

LE SERVEUR

_____ —Vous voulez (*want*) de la sauce avec votre entrecôte?
_____ —Vous prenez le menu ou la carte?
_____ —Bien, je vous écoute.
_____ —Bonjour, Madame. Avez-vous choisi (*Have you chosen*)?
_____ —(*plus tard*) Prenez-vous du fromage ou un dessert?
_____ —(*plus tard*) Vous désirez autre chose (*something else*)?
_____ —Et vous prenez du vin?

**Note**: *Rendez-vous* avoids use of *garçon* for *serveur*; the former is now considered demeaning by many French people.

LA CLIENTE

_____ —Oui, je vais prendre un pichet de gamay de Touraine.
_____ —Je vais prendre la carte.
_____ —Oui, j'ai fait mon choix (*I've made my choice*).
_____ —Non merci. Apportez-moi l'addition, s'il vous plaît!
_____ —Non, merci, je suis au régime (*on a diet*).
_____ —Euh, je vais prendre un sorbet à la poire et un café.
_____ —Comme entrée, je vais prendre une assiette du jardinier, et ensuite une entrecôte saignante (*rare*) avec des frites.

**Additional activity**: *Qui est-ce? Est-ce que c'est un client, une cliente, un serveur ou une serveuse?* 1. *Il a faim.* 2. *Elle arrive avec la carte.* 3. *Elle prend le menu à quarante francs.* 4. *Il commande un repas.* 5. *Il prend la commande.* 6. *Il apporte les hors-d'œuvre.* 7. *Elle boit son vin.* 8. *Elle apporte l'addition.* 9. *Il paie l'addition et laisse un pourboire.* 10. *Elle prend le pourboire.*

## En savoir plus

### La carte ou le menu?

**Le menu** in France refers to a full meal including **une entrée** or **un hors-d'œuvre**, **un plat principal**, and **du fromage** or **un dessert**. The price is fixed and the tip is included. Many restaurants have at least two **menus**: an inexpensive one and a more expensive one.

If you want to order a single dish or if you do not like what is offered as the **menu** you can order **à la carte**. **La carte** is more expensive than the **menu** but offers more variety. Apart from the main **carte**, restaurants also have **une carte des vins** and **une carte des desserts**.

**Note**: The beverage is often included (*boisson comprise*) in the cost of the *menu à prix fixe*.

**B. Au restaurant.** Avec un(e) camarade, regardez le menu et la carte de l'Hippo Futé. Jouez les rôles du serveur (de la serveuse) et du client (de la cliente). Notez ce que le client commande.

MODÈLE: LE SERVEUR (LA SERVEUSE): Qu'est-ce que vous prenez comme entrée? (plat principal, boisson...)
LE CLIENT (LA CLIENTE): Je prends le/la*...

Ensuite décrivez le déjeuner ou le dîner de votre camarade à la classe. Commentez ses goûts (*tastes*).

**Follow-up**: After group work, have several sts. describe each meal. Ask class *Qui a le repas le plus* (the most) *intéressant?*

**Additional activity**: *Préférez-vous_____?* 1. *le café ou le thé?* 2. *le porc, le bœuf, le veau ou le poulet?* 3. *la viande ou le poisson?* 4. *le gâteau ou les fruits?* 5. *le pain ou les croissants?* 6. *la tarte aux pommes ou la tarte à la crème?*

*When ordering from a menu, one often uses the definite article, rather than the partitive.

## Un peu d'argot

| | | | |
|---|---|---|---|
| **la bidoche** | la viande | 10 (250; 1000) **balles** | 10 (250; 1000) francs |
| **le frometon** | le fromage | | |
| **la douloureuse** | l'addition | | |

EN CONTEXTE

JEAN-LOUIS: Tu veux prendre **de la bidoche** ou **du frometon**?

LAURENT: Non, je n'ai pas envie de payer **une douloureuse** de plus de cinquante **balles**!

**Note**: *Bidoche* comes from *bidet*, meaning donkey or horse. Thus, there is a reference being made to low-quality meat. The use of *bidoche* signifies either a lack of respect for the food or a desire to be humorous. Along with *frometon*, it should be used only with one's family or peers. *La douloureuse* can be used when one wants to be humorous about an expensive meal in a restaurant. *Balles* is always plural. It should be used only in informal situations.

# Encore des nombres (60, 61, etc.)

| | | | |
|---|---|---|---|
| 60 | soixante | 80 | quatre-vingts |
| 61 | soixante **et** un | 81 | quatre-vingt-un |
| 62 | soixante-deux | 82 | quatre-vingt-deux |
| 63 | soixante-trois | 83 | quatre-vingt-trois |
| 70 | soixante-dix | 90 | quatre-vingt-dix |
| 71 | soixante **et** onze | 91 | quatre-vingt-onze |
| 72 | soixante-douze | 92 | quatre-vingt-douze |
| 73 | soixante-treize | 93 | quatre-vingt-treize |
| | | 100 | cent |

**Presentation**: Review numbers 1 to 60 first. Model pronunciation of numbers 60 to 100. Ask sts. to (1) count from 60 to 100 by 2's, 3's or 5's; (2) tell you numbers on flashcards held up for them, prepared in advance of class and presented in random order; (3) guess number of pennies (candies, other small objects) in a jar by suggesting numbers from 60 to 100. St. guessing right number gets the "prize." Then present numbers 100 to 999 by explaining system briefly.

Note that the number 80 (**quatre-vingts**) takes an **-s**, but that numbers based on it do not: **quatre-vingt-un**, and so on.

| | | | |
|---|---|---|---|
| 101 | cent un | 600 | six cents |
| 102 | cent deux, etc. | 700 | sept cents |
| 200 | deux cents | 800 | huit cents |
| 201 | deux cent un, etc. | 900 | neuf cents |
| 300 | trois cents | 999 | neuf cent quatre-vingt-dix-neuf |
| 400 | quatre cents | 1 000 | mille |
| 500 | cinq cents | 999 999 | ? |

**Note**: Point out to sts. that the French count by tens from 1 to 60 but by twenties from 61 to 100: 61–79, 80–99. Note that *et* is used with the numbers 61 and 71 (as with 21, etc.) but not with 81 and 91. There is no *liaison* in *quatre-vingt-un* [katrə vɛ̃ ɛ̃], *quatre-vingt-huit* [katrə vɛ̃ ɥit], and *quatre-vingt-onze* [katrə vɛ̃ ɔ̃z]. Note also the use in French of a blank space where English uses a comma to indicate thousand(s). A period (*un point*) is sometimes also used. *Deux mille deux cent cinquante* is written either 2 250 or 2.250. The French use the comma (*la virgule*) in decimal numbers only: 3,25 (*three and 25/100*) is said as *trois virgule vingt-cinq*.

Note that the **-s** of **cents** is dropped if it is followed by any other number: **deux cent un**, **sept cent trente-cinq**.

Like **cent**, **mille** (*one thousand*) is expressed without an article. **Mille** is invariable and thus never ends in **s**.

1 004 **mille quatre**
7 009 **sept mille neuf**
9 999 **neuf mille neuf cent quatre-vingt-dix-neuf**

**Suggestion**: Have sts. do this exercise in pairs. Use as listening comp. as follows: Dictate the problem by saying *Combien font... ?* Sts. write down problem and volunteer answer by a show of hands. Problems and answers may be done at board by a few sts. during this ex.

**A. Problèmes de mathématiques.** Inventez six problèmes selon le modèle, puis demandez à un(e) camarade de les résoudre (*solve them*).

MODÈLES: 37 + 42 = ? → Trente-sept plus (et) quarante-deux font soixante-dix-neuf.
96 − 3 = ? → Quatre-vingt-seize moins trois font quatre-vingt-treize.
500 × 24 = ? → Cinq cents fois vingt-quatre font douze mille.

**B. Voyage gastronomique.** Vous passez trois jours en Bretagne avec des amis. Vous cherchez des restaurants dans un guide.

**Suggestion**: Begin by asking sts. what they know about *Bretagne* and its cuisine. Ask sts. to do activity in pairs; ask a few pairs to present their role-play to the class.

**LA DOUANE**
RESTAURANT GASTRONOMIQUE
Jean-Marc PÉRON
*Spécialités* - les langoustines à la diable
- la lotte fumée "à la maison"
- le saint pierre en infusion de gingembre et de citron
- gourmandises aux chocolats
71, avenue Alain Le Lay - CONCARNEAU
Tél. 98 97 30 27 (salle air conditionné)

RESTAURANT VIETNAMIEN
**LE JARDIN D'ASIE**
SPÉCIALITÉS GRILL
(Brochettes : crevettes, porc, poisson, canard)
Ambiance intime
Repas de famille et d'affaires
Prix étudiés
Plats à emporter
*Ouvert midi et soir de 19 H à 23 H*
27, avenue de la Gare - QUIMPER
**Tél. 98 90 46 92**

1. Avec un(e) camarade, choisissez votre restaurant préféré, puis expliquez à la classe les raisons de votre choix (spécialités de la maison, type de cuisine, etc.).
2. Téléphonez pour réserver une table. Jouez les rôles du maître d'hôtel et du client (de la cliente). N'oubliez pas d'indiquer le nombre de personnes, le jour et l'heure de votre réservation. Vous pouvez aussi demander le prix du menu s'il n'est pas indiqué.

MODÈLE: —Allô, c'est bien le 98.97.30.27?
—Oui, c'est le restaurant...
—Je voudrais réserver une table pour...

3. Maintenant votre camarade donne à la classe les détails de votre réservation: jour, heure et nombre de personnes. Allez-vous retrouver d'autres camarades dans un de ces restaurants? Qui?

**Follow-up**: Have sts. name restaurants they all know, asking others to give price of meal, tip, and total price.

**C. La cuisine diététique.** Votre partenaire et vous avez un restaurant français qui sert (*serves*) de la cuisine diététique. Créez (*Create*) un menu avec moins de (*less than*) 1 000 calories. Le menu doit (*must*) avoir...

une entrée ou un hors-d'œuvre
un plat principal (viande + légumes)
un fromage ou un dessert

**Valeur Calorique de quelques aliments**

| Très caloriques | | Caloriques | | Peu caloriques | | Très peu caloriques | |
|---|---|---|---|---|---|---|---|
| Saucisson | 559 | Brie | 271 | Banane | 97 | Poire (*pear*) | 61 |
| Chocolat | 500 | Pain | 259 | Crevettes | 96 | Pomme | 61 |
| Pâté de foie gras | 454 | Côte d'agneau | 256 | Pommes de terre | 89 | Carotte | 43 |
| Biscuits secs | 410 | Filet de porc | 172 | Lait | 67 | Fraise | 40 |
| Macaronis, pâtes | 351 | Œufs | 162 | Artichaut | 64 | Orange | 40 |
| Riz | 340 | Poulet | 147 | | | Champignons | 31 |
| Camembert | 312 | Canard (*duck*) | 135 | | | Tomates | 22 |

**Suggestion**: For odd-numbered clusters of digits, have sts. give single digit first, then two-digit groups.

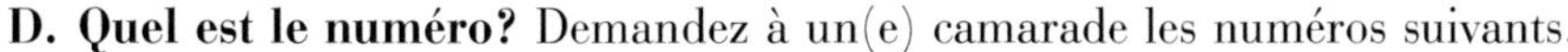

**D. Quel est le numéro?** Demandez à un(e) camarade les numéros suivants.

1. son numéro de sécurité sociale 2. son adresse 3. le numéro de son permis de conduire (*driver's license*) 4. son code postal 5. le numéro de téléphone d'un ami (d'une amie) 6. le numéro de sa carte d'étudiant

## En savoir plus

### La monnaie française

French currency is **le franc** (**fr**). It is divided into **centimes**.

**Presentation**: If possible, bring in coins and bank notes from French-speaking countries.

LES BILLETS (*bills*)
500 francs 50 francs
200 francs 20 francs
100 francs

LES PIÈCES (*coins*)
20 francs
10 francs
5 francs
2 francs
1 franc
50 centimes
20 centimes
10 centimes
5 centimes

There are two common ways of writing prices in French:

48frs50*: quarante-huit francs cinquante. 48,50frs: quarante-huit cinquante.

**Suggestion**: Ask several questions about the banknote: *Décrivez le billet. En quoi est-il différent d'un billet américain? (Les billets français dépeignent tous des personnages célèbres.) À votre avis, qui voit-on sur ce billet—le musicien Debussy ou le philosophe Montesquieu?* (*Debussy*) *Qui est Debussy? Pourquoi est-il célèbre?*

*Sums of money in France can also be written using **F**, **ff**, or a comma in place of **frs** (**francs**): **48F50**, **48ff50**, **48,50**.

**E. Les promotions du mois.** Ce soir vous faites des courses. Vous allez dans un magasin spécialisé en produits surgelés (*frozen*). Vous achetez un plat principal, des légumes et un dessert. Qu'est-ce que vous allez choisir?

**Additional activity**: *Dans votre porte-monnaie. Comptez vos pièces de monnaie selon les modèles.* MODÈLES: 5 F + 50 c → *cinq francs cinquante*; 10 c + 5 c + 1 c → *seize centimes* (1) 50 c + 20 c + 10 c + 5 c + 1 c (2) 50 c + 20 c + 20 c + 5 c + 1 c (3) 50 c + 10 c + 1 c (4) 5 F + 1 F + 50 c + 20 c + 5 c (5) 5 F + 1 F + 1 F + 50 c + 10 c (6) 2 F + 1 F + 10 c + 10 c + 5 c + 1 c (7) 10 F + 1 F + 20 c + 5 c (8) 10 F + 5 F + 2 F + 20 c + 5 c

## Les promotions du mois chez Picard Surgelés

| Produit | Ancien prix | Prix promotion |
|---|---|---|
| **Bifteck bavette** Bigard, 130 g env. Sac de 8. Le kg | ~~75,70~~ | **68,10** |
| **Côtes de porc** première et filet Bigard, 140 g. env. (le kg 32,00 F). Sac de 1,3 kg | ~~46,30~~ | **41,60** |
| **Rôti de veau** épaule, sans barde, Bigard, 1 kg environ. Le kg | ~~58,20~~ | **52,40** |
| **Navarin** (assortiment ragoût) Bigard, morceaux 70 g env. Sac de 1 kg | ~~41,10~~ | **37,00** |
| **Poulet** classe A, sans abats, 1,2 kg environ. Le kg | ~~20,80~~ | **18,70** |
| **Poisson Thaï** au lait de coco, avec riz printanier, Thaïlande, (le kg 58,44 F). Boîte de 450 g | ~~29,20~~ | **26,30** |
| **Chili con carne,** bœuf et légumes avec épices fortes à part, Mexique (le kg 61,42 F). Boîte de 350 g | ~~23,90~~ | **21,50** |
| **Feuilletine de veau** à l'orange, sauce porto, M. Guérard (le kg 92,50 F). Boîte de 440 g | ~~45,20~~ | **40,70** |
| **Cannelloni** (le kg 34,44 F). Boîte de 450 g | ~~18,20~~ | **15,50** |
| **Petits pois doux** extra-fins (le kg 10,00 F). Sac de 2,5 kg | ~~28,40~~ | **25,00** |
| **Haricots mange-tout** mi-fins (le kg 7,76 F). Sac de 2,5 kg | ~~22,10~~ | **19,40** |

| Produit | Ancien prix | Prix promotion |
|---|---|---|
| **Epinards hachés,** tablettes 6 g environ. Sac de 1 kg | ~~8,60~~ | **7,60** |
| **Choux-fleurs** en fleurettes. Sac de 1 kg | ~~12,50~~ | **11,00** |
| **Chou vert,** 2 plaques de 500 g. Sac de 1 kg | ~~13,40~~ | **11,80** |
| **Poivrons** verts et rouges mélangés en dés, Espagne. Sac de 1 kg | ~~13,70~~ | **12,10** |
| **Pommes de terre** en cubes à rissoler, préfrites Sac de 1 kg | ~~9,80~~ | **8,60** |
| **Purée de carottes,** tablettes de 6 g environ. Sac de 1 kg | ~~13,20~~ | **11,60** |
| **Eclairs** (2 café, 2 chocolat) 60 g, Patigel (le kg 53,75 F). Boîte de 4 | ~~15,20~~ | **12,90** |
| **Bavaroise aux myrtilles,** Niemetz, 530 g, 8 parts (le kg 54,15 F). Pièce | ~~33,80~~ | **28,70** |
| **Tarte Tatin,** Ninon, 450 g, 4 parts (le kg 44,22 F). Pièce | ~~23,40~~ | **19,90** |
| **Fraises** entières, France. Sac de 1 kg | ~~23,70~~ | **21,00** |
| **Croissants feuilletés,** pur beurre, cuits, 40-45 g (le kg 38,75 F). Sachet de 12 | ~~21,90~~ | **18,60** |
| **Poire Belle-Hélène,** Miko, 125 ml (le litre 27,40 F). Boîte de 4 | ~~16,10~~ | **13,70** |
| **Crème vanille,** Mövenpick, crème glacée vanille avec crème. Boîte de 1 litre | ~~29,80~~ | **25,30** |

Composez votre menu.

Maintenant calculez le prix réel de ce que vous allez acheter, le prix en promotion que vous allez payer et combien vous allez économiser (*to save*).

**Follow-up**: Have sts. role-play shopping with a friend and choosing the items for their meal. They can use the expressions *plus cher*, *moins cher*, *de bonne qualité*.

| | PRIX AVANT PROMOTION | PRIX EN PROMOTION | DIFFÉRENCE DE PRIX |
|---|---|---|---|
| Plat principal | ________ | ________ | ________ |
| Légumes | ________ | ________ | ________ |
| Dessert | ________ | ________ | ________ |
| Total | ________ | ________ | ________ |

Enfin, donnez votre menu et les résultats de vos calculs à la classe. Qui compose le menu le plus cher (*most expensive*)? le plus original? Qui économise le plus? Combien économise-t-il/elle?

## France-culture

*Shopping for food in France.* Although the **supermarché** is becoming more common in France, some French people still shop in the traditional way—that is, they walk from store to store in their own neighborhoods,

**Suggestion**: Ask sts. to list advantages and disadvantages of shopping in traditional French way.

finding the items that are especially fresh and engaging store owners and other customers in conversation. Shopping in this manner is part of the social fabric of the **quartier**, or neighborhood, and it gives city dwellers the same sense of community found in small towns or villages.

For the foreign visitor, shopping in the traditional French way is fun. To get a "cook's tour" of the great variety of specialty dishes that make up French cuisine, go to **le traiteur**, a shop that provides catering service for gourmet dishes, mostly precooked and ready to go. Although **traiteur** means "delicatessen owner," it is also used to designate the store itself.

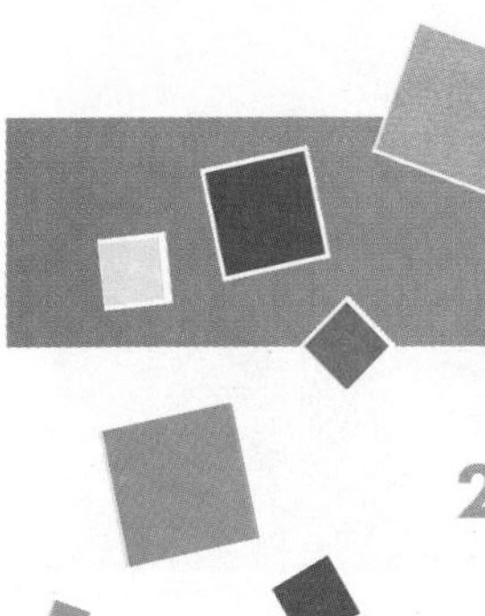

# Étude de grammaire

## 20. POINTING OUT PEOPLE AND THINGS
### Demonstrative Adjectives

**Un dîner entre amis**

BRUNO: **Ce** rôti de bœuf est vraiment délicieux!
ANNE: Merci.
BRUNO: Est-ce que je peux goûter encore un peu de **cette** sauce-**là**?
ANNE: Mais bien sûr.
MARIE: **Ces** haricots verts, hum! Où vas-tu faire tes courses?
ANNE: Rue Contrescarpe.
MARIE: Moi aussi. J'adore **cette** rue, **cette** ambiance de village, **ces** petits magasins...

Répondez.

1. Qu'est-ce que les trois amis mangent?
2. Pourquoi Marie aime-t-elle la rue Contrescarpe?

# A. Forms of Demonstrative Adjectives

**Presentation**: (1) Review rules (Chapter 2) for determining gender of nouns. (2) Use pictures to present the demonstrative adjectives inductively: *Je préfère cette voiture-ci. Et vous, préférez-vous cette voiture-ci ou cette voiture-là? Je préfère cet acteur-là. Et vous?*, etc.

Demonstrative adjectives (*this/that, these/those*) are used to point out or to specify a particular person, object, or idea. They agree with the nouns they modify in gender and number.

| | SINGULAR | PLURAL |
|---|---|---|
| *Masculine* | **ce** magasin<br>**cet** escargot<br>**cet** homme | **ces** magasins<br>**ces** escargots<br>**ces** hommes |
| *Feminine* | **cette** épicerie | **ces** épiceries |

Note that **ce** becomes **cet** before masculine nouns that start with a vowel or mute **h**.

Il n'est pas toujours facile de choisir un dessert devant les vitrines des pâtisseries françaises!

# B. Use of *-ci* and *-là*

In English, *this/these* and *that/those* indicate the relative distance to the speaker. In French, the suffix **-ci** is added to indicate closeness, and **-là**, to indicate greater distance.

—Prenez-vous **ce** gâteau-**ci**?
—Non, je préfère **cet** éclair-**là**.

## *Vérifions!*

**A. Au supermarché.** Qu'est-ce que vous achetez?

MODÈLE: une bouteille d'huile (*oil*) → J'achète cette bouteille d'huile.

1. une boîte de sardines 2. un camembert 3. des tomates 4. une bouteille de vin 5. quatre poires 6. une bouteille d'eau minérale 7. des pommes de terre 8. un éclair au café 9. un artichaut

**Suggestion**: Have sts. do this in pairs, or use sentences for board work.

**B. Exercice de contradiction.** Vous allez faire un pique-nique. Vous faites des courses avec un(e) camarade, mais vous n'êtes pas d'accord! Jouez les rôles.

MODÈLE: pain / baguette →
VOUS: On prend ce pain?
VOTRE CAMARADE: Non, je préfère cette baguette.

1. saucisson / jambon
2. pâté / poulet froid
3. filet de bœuf / rôti de veau
4. haricots verts / boîte de carottes
5. pizza (*f.*) / sandwich
6. pommes / bananes
7. tarte / éclair
8. gâteau / glace
9. jus de fruits / bouteille de vin
10. boîte de sardines / morceau de fromage

**Suggestion**: Do activity in pairs. Have whole class go over a few responses to check small-group work.

**Additional activity**: *À la boulangerie-pâtisserie. Qu'est-ce que vous allez prendre?* (Bring in photos and allow sts. to choose items.) MODÈLE: *tartes* → *Je vais prendre ces tartes.* 1. *éclair* 2. *gâteau* 3. *tarte aux pommes* 4. *baguette* 5. *pain* 6. *croissants chauds*

### Parlons-en!

**Chez le traiteur.** Avec un(e) camarade, jouez les rôles du client et du traiteur. Ajoutez d'autres exemples.

MODÈLE: poulet →
LE CLIENT (LA CLIENTE): Donnez-moi du poulet, s'il vous plaît.
LE TRAITEUR: Ce poulet-ci ou ce poulet-là?
LE CLIENT (LA CLIENTE): Ce poulet-ci. Et donnez-moi aussi un peu de ce fromage.
LE TRAITEUR: Tout de suite, Monsieur (Madame).

1. salade 2. rôti 3. légumes 4. pâté 5. pizza 6. saucisses 7. ?

## 21. EXPRESSING DESIRE, ABILITY, AND OBLIGATION
## The Verbs *vouloir, pouvoir,* and *devoir*

**Le Procope***

MARIE-FRANCE: Tu **veux** du café?
CAROLE: Non, merci, je ne **peux** pas boire de café. Je **dois** faire attention. J'ai un examen aujourd'hui. Si je bois du café, je vais être trop nerveuse.
PATRICK: Je bois du café seulement les jours d'examen. Ça me donne de l'inspiration, comme à Voltaire!

Répétez le dialogue et substituez les nouvelles expressions aux expressions suivantes.

1. café → vin
2. nerveux/euse → lent(e) (*sluggish*)
3. Voltaire → Bacchus†

## A. Present-Tense Forms of vouloir, pouvoir, and devoir

The verbs **vouloir** (*to want*), **pouvoir** (*to be able to*), and **devoir** (*to owe; to have to, to be obliged to*) are all irregular in form.

---

*In the eighteenth century, **Le Procope** was the first place in France to serve coffee. Because coffee was considered a dangerous, subversive beverage, only liberals like Voltaire dared to consume it.
†In classical mythology, Bacchus is the god of wine.

| | vouloir | pouvoir | devoir |
|---|---|---|---|
| je | **veux** | **peux** | **dois** |
| tu | **veux** | **peux** | **dois** |
| il, elle, on | **veut** | **peut** | **doit** |
| nous | **voulons** | **pouvons** | **devons** |
| vous | **voulez** | **pouvez** | **devez** |
| ils, elles | **veulent** | **peuvent** | **doivent** |

**Presentation**: Model pronunciation, emphasizing the [ø] sound in *veux* and *peux*, using short sentences. For example: *Je veux du fromage. Tu peux payer?* etc.

**Voulez**-vous des hors-d'œuvre, Monsieur? — *Do you want some hors d'œuvres, sir?*

Est-ce que nous **pouvons** avoir la salade avant le plat principal? — *Can we have the salad before the entrée?*

Je **dois** laisser un pourboire. — *I must leave a tip.*

## B. Uses of vouloir and devoir

1. **Vouloir bien** means *to be willing to, to be glad to* (*do something*).

   Je **veux bien**. — *I'm willing.* (*I'll be glad to.*)
   Il **veut bien** goûter les escargots. — *He's willing to taste the snails.*

   **Vouloir dire** expresses *to mean.*

   Qu'est-ce que ce mot **veut dire**? — *What does this word mean?*
   Que **veut dire** «pourboire»? — *What does* **pourboire** *mean?*

**Note**: You could mention use of *veuillez* plus infinitive to express polite requests in writing. Teach also *Je voudrais bien*.

2. **Devoir** can express necessity or obligation.

   Je suis désolé, mais nous **devons** partir. — *I'm sorry, but we must leave.*

   **Devoir** can also express probability.

   Elles **doivent** arriver demain. — *They are supposed to arrive tomorrow.*
   Marc n'est pas en cours; il **doit** être malade. — *Marc isn't in class; he must be ill.*

   When not followed by an infinitive, **devoir** means *to owe.*

   Combien d'argent est-ce que tu **dois** à tes amis? — *How much money do you owe (to) your friends?*
   Je **dois** 87F à Henri et 99F à Georges. — *I owe Henri 87 francs and Georges 99 francs.*

## Vérifions!

**A. Le Ritz.** Pour fêter son anniversaire (*to celebrate his birthday*), Stéphane invite ses amis américains Ben et Jessica au restaurant «le Ritz». Complétez leur dialogue. Remplacez les blancs par les verbes **pouvoir**, **devoir** ou **vouloir** selon le contexte et conjuguez ces verbes.

BEN: Qu'est-ce qu'on ____[1] prendre?
STÉPHANE: En entrée vous ____[2] prendre du pâté de lapin, il est excellent. Et comme plat de résistance...
JESSICA: Pardon, que ____[3] dire «plat de résistance»?
STÉPHANE: Bon, c'est le plat principal du repas. Vous ____[4] absolument essayer la truite aux amandes, c'est la spécialité de la maison. En dessert si vous ____[5], vous ____[6] prendre une charlotte aux framboises.
JESSICA: Ce ____[7] être très nourrissant (*rich, fattening*) tout ça, non?
STÉPHANE: Un peu mais ce n'est pas tous les jours mon anniversaire. Tu ____[8] oublier ton régime pour aujourd'hui.

(*Une heure plus tard.*)

STÉPHANE: Bon, on ____[9] y aller. Mes parents ____[10] aller au ciné ce soir et ils ____[11] attendre la voiture. S'il vous plaît, combien je vous ____[12]?
LE SERVEUR: Deux cent soixante-quinze francs, s'il vous plaît.
BEN: Est-ce que nous ____[13] laisser un pourboire?
STÉPHANE: Si tu ____[14] mais ici le service est compris. Cela ____[15] dire qu'on n'est pas obligé.

**Additional activity**: *Au restaurant. Faites les substitutions indiquées.* 1. *Qu'est-ce que vous voulez prendre? (nous, les étudiantes, Paul et vous)* 2. *Tu dois commander maintenant. (ils, nous, elle, je)* 3. *Elle veut bien essayer les huîtres. (je, tu, Marc et Pierre)* 4. *Vous pouvez apporter le plat. (nous, les étudiants, tu)* 5. *Combien est-ce que je dois? (vous, tu, nous, ils, Fernand)* 6. *Qu'est-ce que tu veux dire? (Patrick et Jeanne, vous, elles, la serveuse)* 7. *Elle doit payer cent francs. (je, les étudiants)*

**B. Une soirée compliquée.** Composez un dialogue entre Christiane et François.

CHRISTIANE: je / avoir / faim / et / je / vouloir / manger / maintenant
FRANÇOIS: tu / vouloir / faire / cuisine?
CHRISTIANE: non... / est-ce que / nous / pouvoir / aller / restaurant?
FRANÇOIS: oui, je / vouloir / bien
CHRISTIANE: où / est-ce que / nous / pouvoir / aller?
FRANÇOIS: on / pouvoir / manger / couscous / Chez Bébert
CHRISTIANE: nous / devoir / inviter / Carole
FRANÇOIS: tu / pouvoir / inviter / Jean-Pierre / aussi
CHRISTIANE: ce / soir / ils / devoir / être / cité universitaire?
FRANÇOIS: oui, ils / devoir / préparer / un / examen
CHRISTIANE: un / examen? / mais / nous / aussi, / nous / avoir / un / examen / demain
FRANÇOIS: ce / (ne... pas) être / sérieux / nous / pouvoir / parler / de / ce / examen / restaurant

**Suggestion**: Ask sts. to write individually and then to read resulting dialogue in pairs.

Maintenant donnez une réponse logique d'après le dialogue.

1. François veut aller dans un restaurant ____. (*italien / marocain / antillais*)

2. François pense que (*thinks that*) ce soir Jean-Pierre et Carole doivent ______. (*étudier / travailler / dîner*)
3. À la fin, Christiane et François ______ dîner au restaurant. (*veulent / ne veulent pas*)

**Additional activity:** *Des projets. Racontez les histoires suivantes. Utilisez les verbes vouloir, devoir et ne pas pouvoir, selon le modèle.* MODÈLE: *Jacques / être riche / travailler / aller souvent au cinéma → Jacques veut être riche. Il doit beaucoup travailler. Il ne peut pas aller souvent au cinéma.* 1. *les étudiants / réussir aux examens / écouter le professeur / parler en cours* 2. *Claudine / préparer une mousse au chocolat / employer du sucre, du chocolat et de la crème / employer des huîtres* 3. *l'épicier / avoir beaucoup de clients / être agréable / être désagréable* 4. *Pierre / être serveur / prendre correctement les commandes / boire au restaurant où il travaille*

**Note**: The expression *Il faut* is being taught lexically because of its usefulness when talking about obligations. Here, sts. will learn to use it with the infinitive. It will be presented again with the subjunctive.

## Mots-clés

*Other ways to talk about obligations*: **Devoir** is generally used to talk about what one or several individuals must do. To talk about necessity in a more general way, use **il faut** with an infinitive.

Pour ne pas grossir, **il faut** faire de l'exercice. **Il ne faut pas** manger trop d'aliments riches.

**Il faut** can also be followed by nouns referring to objects, to talk about what is needed.

Pour faire une soupe à l'oignon, **il faut** des oignons, du consommé de bœuf, du gruyère et du pain.

**Il faut** du courage pour goûter des escargots, n'est-ce pas?

### Parlons-en!

**A. Qu'est-ce qu'il faut?** Répondez aux questions avec un(e) camarade et notez vos conclusions. Répondez avec **il faut** + infinitif ou nom.

MODÈLE: Qu'est-ce qu'il faut pour passer une soirée à la française? → Il faut des amis. (*ou* Il faut aimer la bonne cuisine. / Il faut prendre son temps.)

1. pour faire une omelette?
2. pour ne pas grossir (*to gain weight*)?
3. pour s'amuser (*to have fun*) à une soirée à l'américaine?
4. pour se faire «une bonne bouffe (*a big meal*)»?
5. pour passer un bon réveillon (*New Year's Eve*)?

**B. Conversation à trois.** Avec deux autres camarades vous allez préparer un repas pour toute la classe. Qu'est-ce que vous allez préparer? Où pouvez-vous acheter les provisions nécessaires? Comment voulez-vous partager (*to share*) le travail? Utilisez les verbes **pouvoir**, **vouloir** et **devoir**.

**Suggestion**: Have sts. write out their comments before presenting them orally to rest of class. One st. can be note-taker.

**Expressions utiles:** vouloir bien, devoir acheter, devoir commander, devoir essayer de préparer un plat français, pouvoir acheter, pouvoir choisir, pouvoir boire du champagne, devoir demander un pourboire

Après votre conversation, décrivez votre menu à la classe.

# 22. ASKING ABOUT CHOICES The Interrogative Adjective *quel*

**Henri Lefèvre, restaurateur à Albertville**

Dan Bartell, journaliste américain, interroge Henri Lefèvre.

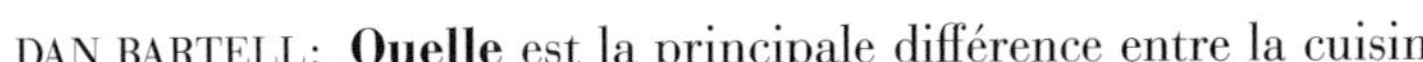

DAN BARTELL: **Quelle** est la principale différence entre la cuisine traditionnelle et la nouvelle cuisine?

HENRI LEFÉVRE: Les sauces, mon ami, les sauces.

DAN BARTELL: Et **quelles** sauces préparez-vous?

HENRI LEFÉVRE: J'aime beaucoup préparer les sauces traditionnelles comme la sauce bordelaise et le beurre blanc.

DAN BARTELL: **Quels** vins achetez-vous pour votre restaurant?

HENRI LEFÉVRE: J'achète surtout des vins rouges de Bourgogne et des vins blancs d'Anjou.

Et vous?

1. Quel est votre plat favori?
2. Quelle boisson préférez-vous?
3. Quelle cuisine préférez-vous?

## A. Forms of the Interrogative Adjective *quel*

You are already familiar with the interrogative adjective **quel** in expressions such as **Quelle heure est-il?** and **Quel temps fait-il? Quel** (**quelle**, **quels**, **quelles**) means *which* or *what*. Its function is to elicit more precise information about a noun that is understood or established in context. It agrees in gender and number with the noun to which it refers.*

| | |
|---|---|
| **Quel** fromage voulez-vous goûter? | *Which* (*What*) *cheese would you like to try?* |
| **À quelle** heure dînez-vous? | (*At*) *what time do you have dinner?* |
| Dans **quels** restaurants aimez-vous manger? | *In what* (*which*) *restaurants do you like to eat?* |
| **Quelles** boissons préférez-vous? | *What* (*Which*) *beverages do you prefer?* |

**Presentation**: Remind sts. that different interrogative forms reflect differences in questioner's expectations about information he or she will receive in response. Questions with inversion and *est-ce que* indicate that the questioner seeks a yes/no answer. Questions with *qu'est-ce que* imply that the questioner is seeking new information. In questions with *quand*, *pourquoi*, and *où*, the questioner seeks information about specific circumstances. In questions with interrogative adjective *quel*(*le*)(*s*), questioner seeks more precise information.

*Note that the pronunciation of all four forms of **quel** is identical, [kɛl], but when the plural form precedes a word beginning with a vowel sound, there is **liaison**: **quels étudiants**, **quelles étudiantes**, [kɛl-ze-ty-djɑ̃(t)].

## B. *Quel* with *être*

**Quel** can also stand alone before the verb **être** followed by the noun it modifies.

| | |
|---|---|
| **Quel est** le prix de ce champagne? | *What's the price of this champagne?* |
| **Quelle est** la différence entre le Perrier et l'eau minérale de Calistoga? | *What's the difference between Perrier (water) and Calistoga (water)?* |

## Mots-clés

*Expressing admiration:* **Quel** is also used in exclamations.

| | |
|---|---|
| **Quel** père exemplaire! | *What an exemplary father!* |
| **Quelle** bonne idée! | *What a great idea!* |

**Suggestion**: Ask sts. to give other exclamations. *Contexts*: in French class, with a young child, in a food store, buying a car, etc.

### *Vérifions!*

**Qui vient dîner?** Mme Guilloux veut organiser un dîner demain soir. Son mari l'interroge (*asks her questions*). Complétez leur dialogue avec **qu'est-ce que, quel**(**le**) ou **qui**.

M. GUILLOUX: _____[1] vas-tu inviter?
MME GUILLOUX: Maxime, Isabelle et Laurence.
M. GUILLOUX: Et _____[2] tu vas préparer?
MME GUILLOUX: Un rôti de bœuf avec des pommes de terre sautées.
M. GUILLOUX: Super! Mais _____[3] va faire les courses?
MME GUILLOUX: Toi, bien sûr.
M. GUILLOUX: Ben voyons! _____[4] vin est-ce que je dois acheter?
MME GUILLOUX: Je ne sais pas. _____[5] tu préfères?
M. GUILLOUX: Un bordeaux rouge.
MME GUILLOUX: Très bien. _____[6] heure est-il?
M. GUILLOUX: 6h30.
MME GUILLOUX: Déjà! _____[7] tu attends? Dépêche-toi (*Hurry up*), les magasins vont bientôt fermer.

**Additional activity**: *Préparatifs. Vous organisez une soirée avec un(e) camarade. Formez des questions complètes en utilisant un adjectif interrogatif.* MODÈLE: *quel / boisson / apporter / tu? → Quelle boisson apportes-tu? 1. quel / viande / préparer / tu? 2. quel légumes / préférer / tu? 3. quel / plat / apporter / tu? 4. quel / salade / préparer / tu? 5. quel / fromage / acheter / tu? 6. quel / fruits / avoir / tu? 7. quel / dessert / choisir / tu? 8. quel / amies / inviter / tu?*

### *Parlons-en!*

**Une interview.** Interrogez vos camarades sur leurs goûts. Utilisez l'adjectif interrogatif **quel** et variez la forme de vos questions.

MODÈLE: sport →
Quel est le sport que tu préfères? (*ou* Quel sport préfères-tu?)

1. boisson
2. légume
3. viande
4. repas
5. distractions
6. disques
7. discothèque (*f.*)
8. programme de télévision
9. livres
10. revues
11. couleur (*f.*)
12. matières
13. vêtements
14. films

**Suggestion**: Have sts. do this in small groups, or dictate questions to sts., with some at board and others at their seats, after which they write a response. Compare responses at board and among members of class.

Quelle est la réponse la plus insolite (*unusual*)? la plus drôle?

## 23. DESCRIBING PEOPLE AND THINGS
### The Placement of Adjectives

**Un nouveau restaurant**

CHLOË: Il y a un **nouveau** restaurant dans le quartier.
VINCENT: Ah bon! Où ça?
CHLOË: À côté de la **petite** épicerie. Il s'appelle «Le **Bon Vieux** Temps».
VINCENT: C'est un **joli** nom. On y va samedi soir?
CHLOË: **Bonne** idée!

Corrigez les phrases incorrectes.

1. Il y a un nouvel hôtel dans le quartier.
2. D'après son nom, ce restaurant prépare des plats traditionnels.
3. Vincent n'aime pas le nom du restaurant.
4. Vincent et Chloé vont au restaurant samedi soir.

## A. Adjectives That Usually Precede the Noun

1. Certain short and commonly used adjectives usually precede the nouns they modify.

| REGULAR | IRREGULAR | IDENTICAL IN MASCULINE AND FEMININE |
|---|---|---|
| **grand**(**e**) *big, tall; great*<br>**joli**(**e**) *pretty*<br>**mauvais**(**e**) *bad*<br>**petit**(**e**) *small, little*<br>**vrai**(**e**) *true* | **beau/belle** *beautiful, handsome*<br>**bon**(**ne**) *good*<br>**faux/fausse** *false*<br>**gentil**(**le**) *nice, kind*<br>**gros**(**se**) *large, fat, thick*<br>**long**(**ue**) *long*<br>**nouveau/nouvelle** *new*<br>**vieux/vieille** *old* | **autre** *other*<br>**chaque** *each, every*<br>**jeune** *young*<br>**pauvre** *poor; unfortunate* |

La cuisine est une **vraie** tradition pour les Français. — *Cooking is a real tradition for the French.*

La **nouvelle** cuisine est très populaire en ce moment. — *The "new cooking" is very popular right now.*

Antoine est un **vieux** restaurant de La Nouvelle-Orléans. — *Antoine is an old restaurant in New Orleans.*

Les **jeunes** clients aiment bien le propriétaire de ce restaurant. — *The young customers like the owner of this restaurant.*

Un restaurant élégant en plein air, en Alsace

**Presentation**: Use the mnemonic device BAGS (beauty, age, goodness, size) to help sts. remember the short adjectives that precede. Use pictures of famous people, and describe them using these adjectives (*C'est un bon acteur*; *C'est un petit homme*; etc.).

2. The adjectives **beau**, **nouveau**, and **vieux** are irregular. They have two masculine forms in the singular.

| SINGULAR | | |
|---|---|---|
| *Masculine* | *Masculine before vowel or mute* **h** | *Feminine* |
| un **beau** livre<br>un **nouveau** livre<br>un **vieux** livre | un **bel** appartement<br>un **nouvel** appartement<br>un **vieil** appartement | une **belle** voiture<br>une **nouvelle** voiture<br>une **vieille** voiture |

| PLURAL | |
|---|---|
| *Masculine* | *Feminine* |
| de **beaux** appartements<br>de **nouveaux** appartements<br>de **vieux** appartements | de **belles** voitures<br>de **nouvelles** voitures<br>de **vieilles** voitures |

## B. Adjectives Preceding Plural Nouns

When an adjective precedes the noun in the plural form, the plural indefinite article **des** generally becomes **de**.*

| | |
|---|---|
| J'ai **des** livres de cuisine. | J'ai **de** nouveaux livres de cuisine. |
| Faisons **des** desserts! | Faisons **de** bons desserts! |

## C. Adjectives That May Precede or Follow Nouns They Modify

The adjectives **ancien/ancienne** (*old; former*), **cher/chère** (*dear; expensive*), **grand(e)**, and **pauvre** may either precede or follow a noun, but their meaning

*In colloquial speech, **des** is often retained before the plural adjective: **Elle trouve toujours *des beaux* fruits**.

depends on their position. Generally, the adjective in question has a literal meaning when it follows the noun and a figurative meaning when it precedes the noun.

| LITERAL SENSE | FIGURATIVE SENSE |
|---|---|
| C'est un homme très **grand**.* *He's a very tall man.* | C'est un très **grand** chef de cuisine. *He's a very great chef.* |
| Les clients **pauvres** ne vont pas à la Tour d'Argent. *Poor (not rich) customers don't go to the Tour d'Argent.* | **Pauvres** clients! Il n'y a plus de champagne! *The poor (unfortunate) customers! There's no more champagne!* |
| Il achète des chaises **anciennes** pour décorer la Tour d'Argent. *He's buying antique chairs to decorate the Tour d'Argent.* | M. Sellier est **l'ancien** maître d'hôtel de la Tour d'Argent. *Mr. Sellier is the former maître d'hôtel of the Tour d'Argent.* |
| C'est un vin très **cher**. *That's a very expensive wine.* | Ma **chère** amie... *My dear friend . . .* |

## D. Placement of More Than One Adjective

When more than one adjective modifies a noun, each adjective precedes or follows the noun as if it were used alone.

C'est une **petite** femme **blonde**.
J'ai de **bons** livres **français**.
C'est un **vieux** restaurant **agréable**.

### *Vérifions!*

**A. Qu'est-ce que vous aimez?** Choisissez parmi ces adjectifs et faites des phrases selon le modèle: beau/belle; grand(e); joli(e); petit(e); vrai(e); bon(ne); nouveau/nouvelle; vieux/vieille; gros(se)

MODÈLE: les desserts → J'aime les **bons** desserts.

1. les restaurants
2. les recettes (*recipes*)
3. les hamburgers
4. les voitures
5. les maisons

**B. Un dîner réussi.** Hervé nous explique comment il fait pour réussir un bon repas. Transformez les noms du singulier au pluriel.

---

*The adjective **grand(e)** is placed *after* the noun to mean *big* or *tall* only in descriptions of people. When it precedes the noun in descriptions of things and places, it means *big, tall, large*: **les grandes fenêtres, un grand appartement, une grande table**.

MODÈLE: J'invite un vrai ami. → J'invite de vrais amis.

D'abord je mets sur la table une belle plante mais je ne mets jamais une fausse assiette en plastique. Je choisis toujours un bon vin. J'essaie (*try*) une nouvelle recette. J'achète un beau pain de campagne. Comme dessert, je prépare un bon gâteau et ensuite je sers un petit verre de liqueur ou un petit digestif (*after-dinner drink*).

**Additional activity**: *Dictée. Faites les substitutions indiquées et les changements nécessaires. 1. Quel beau plat* (assiette, verres, bouteille, dessert) *2. Quel gros bifteck!* (dinde, saucisson, pommes de terre, poires, fraises)

**C. On fait la critique.** Voici la description d'un nouveau restaurant à New York. Complétez les phrases avec les adjectifs entre parenthèses. Faites attention! Les adjectifs ne sont pas toujours dans le bon ordre.

MODÈLE: Le chef fait la cuisine selon *la tradition*... (français, vieux) → Le chef fait la cuisine selon la vieille tradition française.

1. Les clients trouvent *une ambiance*... (bon, français)
2. Vous pouvez dîner sur *une terrasse*... (agréable, grand)
3. On peut commander *un vin*... (rouge, bon)
4. Il y a *du pain*... (vrai, français)
5. Les clients paient *des prix*... (raisonnable, petit)
6. Vous allez parler avec *la propriétaire*... (vieux, sympathique)
7. Les étudiants universitaires sont *des clients*... (agréable, jeune)

## Parlons-en!

**A. Une bonne table.** Lisez ce que le magazine gastronomique *GaultMillau* dit du restaurant l'Auberge du Cheval Blanc à Lembach, en Alsace. Puis remplacez les adjectifs **vieux**, **opulente** et **large** par les adjectifs **ancien**, **pittoresque** et **varié**. Faites attention à la position des nouveaux adjectifs.

**• LEMBACH**

**15/20 Auberge du Cheval Blanc**
Un vieux relais de poste transformé en opulente auberge au large répertoire culinaire : salade aux crustacés, panaché de foie chaud, turbot aux huîtres. Produits magnifiques, exécution impeccable. Menus de 115 F à 265 F.
*4, rue Wissembourg. F. lundi, mardi et du 4 au 22 juil. Jusqu'à 21 h. Tél. : 88 94 41 86.*

Maintenant, avec un(e) camarade, faites la description d'un restaurant de votre région. Ensuite, présentez votre description devant la classe sans nommer le restaurant. Est-ce que les autres membres de la classe peuvent deviner de quel restaurant vous parlez?

**B. Les Parisiens.** Faites la description la plus complète possible de ces personnes.

**Mots utiles: à gauche,** *on the left*; **à droite,** *on the right*

**C. Personnages célèbres.** Avec un(e) camarade, utilisez les mots suivants pour former des phrases complètes. (Attention à l'ordre des adjectifs!)

**Suggestion**: Ask sts. to write out sentences before doing orally. Or have several sts. write their sentences on the board for whole-class reaction.

MODÈLE: Whitney Houston / femme / jeune / dynamique →
Whitney Houston est une jeune femme dynamique.

PERSONNES

| | | |
|---|---|---|
| Charles Barkley | Kristi Yamaguchi | Catherine Deneuve |
| Garfield | Howard Cosell | Gérard Depardieu |
| la princesse Diana | Snoopy | Joe Montana |
| Eddie Murphy | Goldie Hawn | ? |
| Dumbo | Charlie Brown | |

NOMS

| | | |
|---|---|---|
| fille | garçon | éléphant |
| homme | chien | acteur/trice |
| chat | femme | ? |

ADJECTIFS

| | | |
|---|---|---|
| jeune | joli | snob |
| beau | gentil | drôle |
| vieux | agréable | orange |
| grand | rouge | enthousiaste |
| petit | sociable | calme |
| bon | dynamique | désagréable |
| mauvais | sportif | ? |
| gros | gris | |

# Étude de prononciation

## Liaison

**Note**: This is the last pronunciation section in the st. text. Additional practice with pronunciation and phonetics is provided in the laboratory program.

A consonant that occurs at the end of a word is often "linked" to the next word if that word begins with a vowel sound: les‿amis [lɛ za mi]. This linking is called **liaison**. It occurs between words that are already united by meaning or syntax: Ils‿ont‿un‿ami [il zɔ̃ tɛ̃ na mi].

**Liaison** is compulsory in the following cases.

| | |
|---|---|
| between a pronoun and a verb | ils‿ont; ont‿ils |
| between a noun and a preceding adjective | de beaux‿hommes |

| | |
|---|---|
| between a one-syllable preposition and its object | sans‿argent |
| between a short adverb and an adjective | très‿intéressant |
| between an article and a noun or adjective | un‿exercice; les‿autres pays |
| after **est** | c'est‿évident |
| after numbers | huit‿étudiants |

**Liaison** *does not* take place in the following cases.

| | |
|---|---|
| after a singular noun | un étudiant / intéressant |
| after **et** | il parle français et / anglais |
| before an aspirate **h** | un / Hollandais |
| after a name | Jean / est riche |

**Liaison** produces the following sound changes.

| | |
|---|---|
| a final **s** is pronounced [z] | les‿étudiants |
| a final **x** is pronounced [z] | dix‿étudiants |
| a final **z** is pronounced [z] | chez‿elle |
| a final **d** is pronounced [t] | un grand‿homme |
| a final **f** is pronounced [f] or [v]* | neuf‿ans |

**Liaison** and its uses vary according to language level. For example, in a poetic or dramatic reading, or in other very formal situations, most conventional **liaisons** are made. Fewer and fewer are made as the level of language becomes more informal.

**A.** Prononcez avec le professeur.

1. un grand appartement
2. les écoles américaines
3. le jardinier anglais
4. les hors-d'œuvre
5. les deux églises
6. Il est ouvrier et artisan.
7. Elles étaient à la mairie.
8. Vous êtes sans intérêt.
9. Vont-elles au centre-ville?
10. Tu ne m'as pas écouté.
11. C'est horrible!
12. C'est un quartier ancien.

**B.** Prononcez avec le professeur.

1. Vous allez mettre trois assiettes sur la table.
2. Les deux assiettes blanches sont à la cuisine.
3. Vous achetez des oranges et des œufs, n'est-ce pas?
4. Les nouveaux étudiants français mangent des haricots verts.

---

*Final **f** is pronounced [v] before the words **an** (*year*) and **heure** (*hour*) only.

# France-culture

Suggestion: Bring in some French recipes for these and/or other dishes. Distribute them to sts. and explain linguistic conventions used.

*Food in France: regional and international.* Although "fast food" is making inroads into French culture, **la grande cuisine** remains one of France's great traditions. This is due less to sophisticated recipes than to the variety and delicacy of French regional products. Regional cuisine is as diverse as French geography, from the endless variety of **crêpes** and seafood in Brittany to oysters and rich **pâtés de foie gras** in the Bordeaux region; from the **quiche**, fruit desserts, and brandies of Alsace to the heady flavors of garlic, herbs, and fresh tomato and fish dishes of Provence.

Foreign cuisine (especially Chinese and Italian) is also popular in France. Creole cooking is part of the French heritage. With its spicy and exotic flavors, it is highly appreciated, as is North African cooking from Tunisia, Algeria, and Morocco. Lately, West African dishes (especially those from Senegal), along with Senegalese music, have become fashionable among young people.

LE BISTROT A VINS
**LES BACCHANTES**
21, rue Caumartin - 75009 PARIS
Tél. : 42 65 25 35
Face au Cartouche Edouard VII
*Ouvert 7 jours sur 7*
*de midi à minuit*
*Dans une ambiance décontractée, une sélection de vins au verre et à la bouteille, plats du jour, charcuteries régionales, omelettes paysannes, fromages et tartines de Poilane frais.*

RESTAURANT
**Cartouche Edouard VII**
18, rue Caumartin - 75009 PARIS
Tél. : 47 42 08 82
*Ouverture du Lundi au Vendredi*
*au déjeuner, au dîner à partir de 18h45*

*Spécialités des Iles*
**LA CREOLE**
Le célèbre et renommé restaurant antillais
122, bd du Montparnasse 14e. Rés. 43.20.62.12 (Ouvert T.L.J

LA TABLE DE MING
新敦煌
Vous dégusterez des **DIM SUNS**
sans concurrence à Paris (Gault Millau)
Réservation : **42.60.93.88**
17, avenue de l'Opéra, 75001 Paris

**EL MARIACHI**
**RESTAURANT MEXICAIN**
**2 ORCHESTRES**
**DINERS OU CONSOMMATIONS**
62,rue P. Charron 8e(Champs-Elysées)
**45.63.40.88** — Salle clim. Fermé Dim.

# Mise au point

**A. Allons au restaurant!** Marc et Jean vont au restaurant. Avec un(e) camarade, faites des phrases complètes et jouez le dialogue entre les deux amis.

MARC: je / vouloir / aller / restaurant
JEAN: dans / quel / restaurant / vouloir / tu / aller?
MARC: on / ne... pas / pouvoir / passer / trop / temps / restaurant
JEAN: oui / on / devoir / être / université / à / 2 heures
MARC: alors / nous / pouvoir / aller / dans / bistrot
JEAN: je / aller / manger / sandwich
MARC: moi / je / vouloir / aussi / dessert
JEAN: monsieur / addition / s'il vous plaît. Mais / je / ne... pas / avoir / argent
MARC: moi / je / aller / payer / addition / et / laisser / pourboire
JEAN: merci / je / te / devoir / trente-cinq / francs

1. Qui veut un dessert?
2. Qui paie l'addition? Pourquoi?

**Suggestion**: Sts. may dictate answers to a classmate at board.

**B. Vos impressions.** Complétez les phrases suivantes à la forme affirmative ou à la forme négative, selon votre opinion personnelle. Utilisez **devoir**, **pouvoir** ou **vouloir** + infinitif dans chaque phrase.

MODÈLE: Les étudiants _____. → Les étudiants ne doivent pas étudier jusqu'à (*until*) minuit tous les soirs.

1. Le professeur _____.
2. Les parents _____.
3. Mes camarades _____.
4. Les hommes _____.
5. Les femmes _____.
6. Je _____.

**Suggestions**: (1) Dictate incomplete sentences, with as many sts. as possible at board and others at seats. Compare completions provided by a variety of sts. (2) May be done in small groups.

**C. Question de goût.** Modifiez les noms pour expliquer vos goûts à la classe. Vous pouvez utiliser plusieurs adjectifs par phrase. Attention à la place de l'adjectif.

| | SUGGESTIONS |
|---|---|
| 1. J'aime les *restaurants*. | bon / nouveau / cher / intéressant / chinois... |
| 2. Je vais souvent au *restaurant* avec des *amis*. | sympathique / intime / jeune / bon / amusant... |
| 3. Nous buvons souvent du *vin et de la bière*. | californien / français / frais / bon / rouge... |
| 4. Nous prenons quelquefois des *repas* ensemble. | cher / bon / long / agréable / gastronomique... |

**Suggestion**: Use for board work, dictating stimulus sentences and then having sts. transform them with new items.

**D. Une conversation au restaurant.** Vous êtes au restaurant et vous entendez une partie d'une conversation. Imaginez ce que répond l'autre personne.

1. —Et alors, Pascal, tu as très faim? Que veux-tu prendre ce soir comme plat principal?
   —_____
2. —Si tu veux... moi, je préfère le poisson. Et comme boisson? Qu'est-ce que tu veux?
   —_____
3. —C'est une bonne idée. Ce vin est excellent. Et tu prends des légumes?
   —_____

4. —Ah oui? Je déteste ça. Et comme dessert, qu'est-ce que tu prends?
   —_____
5. —Oui, ça va bien avec un bon dîner. Moi, je prends de la tarte aux pommes. Oh, je n'ai pas d'argent! Tu peux payer, n'est-ce pas?
   —(Zut!)...

## Interactions

**Suggestion**: Ask sts. to play the roles in one of the *Interactions* for the whole class, if time allows.

In this chapter, you practiced how to specify, express desire and obligation, and describe people and things. Act out the following situations, using the vocabulary and structures from this chapter.

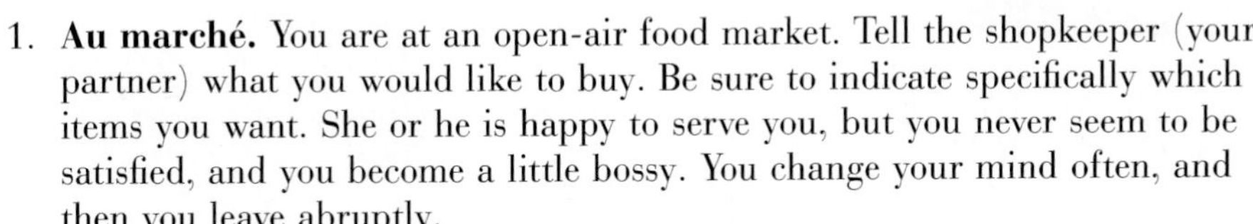

1. **Au marché.** You are at an open-air food market. Tell the shopkeeper (your partner) what you would like to buy. Be sure to indicate specifically which items you want. She or he is happy to serve you, but you never seem to be satisfied, and you become a little bossy. You change your mind often, and then you leave abruptly.
2. **Au restaurant.** You are out to dinner with a special person. You want everything to be perfect. You make everything clear to the head waiter or waitress (your partner). Tell him or her that you want a small table for two, a good waiter or waitress, and a good wine. Ask what meal is good this evening and which dessert is good. Explain that you have no money (**argent** [*m.*]). Jokingly ask if you can do the dishes. Ask if the restaurant accepts credit cards (**accepter des cartes de crédit**). Thank him or her for the help.

# Rencontres

## LECTURE

### *Avant de lire*

**Skimming for the gist.** Skimming is a useful way to approach any new text, particularly in a foreign language. You will usually find it easier to understand more difficult passages once you have a general idea of the content. At this point, you need not be concerned with understanding everything when reading authentic French texts; just try to get the gist, then answer the questions that follow the reading to check your overall comprehension.

The following article appeared in a French magazine, *Bon sens*. Glance at the title and headings. What kind of information do you think the article contains, and how is the information organized?

Next, skim the article to get an impression of the major points. Do not attempt to understand every word. See if you can remember five or six primary pieces of information. Then read the sections that may have appeared most difficult when you skimmed the article, and try to guess their meaning based on the rest of the text.

**Suggestion**: If sts. find the reading difficult, you may want to suggest that they look over the comprehension questions first to help them find the major points. Give sts. encouragement whenever they encounter authentic materials. At the end of the reading, emphasize to sts. that they have just successfully read something from an authentic French source.

***Notre corps, c'est ce qu'on néglige le plus en période d'examens. On mange trop (pour surmonter le stress) ou pas assez (pas le temps d'y penser maintenant), on dort[a] mal même quand on dort beaucoup, on ne bouge plus de sa[b] chaise et, quand on fait du sport pour se défouler,[c] on se fait mal.[d] Attention, ne prenez pas de tels risques!***

## « DIS-MOI[e] CE QUE TU MANGES, JE TE DIRAI[f] QUI TU ES »

L'alimentation est le premier facteur de l'équilibre. Surtout en période de révisions. C'est souvent quand on a particulièrement besoin d'un apport régulier et équilibré de protides, glucides, lipides, éléments minéraux et vitamines, que le stress nous incite à sauter[g] des repas, à négliger notre corps, à grignoter n'importe quoi[h] à n'importe quelle heure, bref: à faire exactement ce qu'il ne faut pas faire.

### *COMMENT MANGER?*

**Régulièrement**

Avant tout, il s'agit de faire de chaque repas une occasion pour se détendre[i]; inutile donc de grignoter deux biscuits diététiques en travaillant, juste pour vous donner bonne conscience.

Fractionnez plutôt[j] vos repas (maximum 5 par jour, dont 2 en-cas[k]), et prenez-les à heures régulières: les repas doivent rythmer votre journée. Et rappelez-vous[l] que le petit déjeuner doit apporter 25% des calories quotidiennes, l'en-cas de 10 heures 10%, le déjeuner 30%, le goûter 5% et le dîner 30%.

[a] *sleeps*
[b] *ne... never gets out of one's*
[c] *se... to unwind*
[d] *se... hurts oneself*
[e] *Tell me*
[f] *te... will tell you*
[g] *to skip*
[h] *grignoter... to snack on just anything*
[i] *se... to relax*
[j] *Fractionnez... Rather, divide up*
[k] *snacks*
[l] *rappelez... remember*

## Compréhension

1. Selon l'article, quels problèmes avons-nous en période d'examens?
2. Pourquoi saute(*skip*)-t-on des repas en période d'examens? Et vous, sautez-vous souvent des repas? Pourquoi?
3. Selon l'auteur, pourquoi doit-on prendre les repas à heures régulières? Quel est votre repas le plus important, en général? Et en période d'examens?
4. Combien de repas par jour prenez-vous d'habitude? À votre avis, est-ce que votre alimentation est équilibrée? Pourquoi?
5. À votre avis, que veut dire le titre de l'article? Qu'est-ce que vous faites pour tenir la forme?

## PAR ÉCRIT

**Function:** More on describing (a place)
**Audience:** A friend or classmate
**Goal:** Write a note to a friend inviting him or her to dinner. To persuade your friend to come, describe your chosen restaurant using the following questions as a guide. **Dans quel restaurant préférez-vous dîner? Mangez-vous souvent dans ce restaurant? Quand? Est-ce qu'il est fréquenté** (*visited*) **par beaucoup de clients? Est-ce que la carte est simple ou complexe? Quel est votre plat préféré? Quelle est la spécialité du chef?** Begin the letter with **Cher** (**Chère**) _____. End with **À bientôt...** (*See you soon . . .* )

**Steps**

1. Write the introduction. Begin with an interesting or amusing thought to attract your reader's attention. You may wish to start out with a question. Some examples are: **Veux-tu prendre un repas magnifique avec un ami (une amie) très sympathique?** ***ou*** **Tu es mon invité**(**e**)**.** Then compose the invitation.
2. Write the body of the note. It should answer the questions posed in the paragraph on **Goal**, above.
3. Write a conclusion, restating your invitation as intriguingly as possible. You may tell an anecdote, briefly describe the restaurant, or set down more specific plans for the place, date, and time of your appointment.
4. Revise your composition after checking the organization of its opening and closing paragraphs. Have a classmate read it to see if what you have written is clear. Revise again if necessary. Finally, reread the composition for spelling, punctuation, and grammar errors. (Focus especially on your use of adjectives!) Be prepared to share your composition with classmates.

**Suggestion**: Use sts.' letters for listening comp. practice. Ask sts. to guess who wrote the letter.

**Follow-up**: Peer-editing. Ask sts. to work in groups of 3 or 4 to edit their compositions.

# À L'ÉCOUTE!

**À l'écoute!**: See scripts for listening passages and follow-up activities recorded on st. cassette. Remind sts. that in the listening comprehension passages (as in real life) they will not understand every word they hear. They should focus globally on the general information in the passages and not be overly concerned about what they do not understand.

**I. Les supermarchés Traffic.** The **Traffic** supermarket chain is advertising some of its products on the radio. First, look at activities A and B. Next, listen to the vocabulary and the ad. Then, do the activities.

VOCABULAIRE UTILE
des promotions *specials* (*sales*)
des prix incroyables *incredible prices*
des produits *products*
ouverts *open*
venez vite! *come quickly!*

**A. Les promotions Traffic.** Draw a line linking each price with the appropriate product, based on the ad.

| | |
|---|---|
| 1. 5frs | a. un litre de jus de pommes |
| 2. 40frs | b. un kilo de jambon |
| 3. 3frs | c. une baguette |
| 4. 2,50frs | d. un kilo d'oranges |

**B.** Place a check mark next to the correct answer.

Les supermarchés Traffic sont ouverts:

1. _____ de 8 heures à 21 heures
2. _____ de 9 heures à 22 heures
3. _____ de 9 heures à 21 heures

**II. Un repas inoubliable** (*unforgettable*)**.** Marise and Thomas, a tourist couple from Belgium, are having dinner in a French restaurant. A waiter is taking their order. First, look at the activity. Next, listen to their conversation. Then, do the activity.

Circle the correct answer.

1. Ils ont une réservation pour
   a. 8h00 b. 7h30
2. Le nom de famille de Thomas est
   a. Bonnet b. Blanchard
3. Marise commande
   a. le poisson b. le filet de bœuf
4. Thomas commande
   a. le steak au poivre b. le saumon
5. Aujourd'hui, c'est
   a. la fête b. dimanche
6. Marise et Thomas dînent dans
   a. un restaurant élégant b. un café

# Vocabulaire

## Verbes

**apporter** to bring; to carry
**devoir** to owe; to have to, be obliged to
**goûter** to taste
**laisser** to leave (behind)
**pouvoir** to be able
**vouloir** to want
  **vouloir bien** to be willing
  **vouloir dire** to mean

À REVOIR: acheter, boire, commander, goûter, préparer, vendre

## Substantifs

**l'addition** (*f.*) bill, check (*in a restaurant*)
**l'argent** (*m.*) money
**la baguette (de pain)** baguette
**le billet** bill (*currency*)
**le bœuf** beef
**la boîte (de conserve)** can (of food)
**la carte** menu
**le centime** 1/100th of a French franc
**la côte** chop
**l'éclair** (*m.*) eclair (*pastry*)
**l'entrée** (*f.*) first course
**le filet** fillet (*beef, fish, etc.*)
**le franc** franc (*currency*)
**la glace** ice cream; ice
**le hors-d'œuvre*** appetizer
**l'huître** (*f.*) oyster
**le jus (de fruits)** (fruit) juice
**le kilo(gramme)** kilo(gram)
**le magasin** store, shop
**le menu** fixed (price) menu
**le morceau** piece
**le pâté de campagne** (country-style) pâté
**la pièce** coin
**le plat** course (*meal*)
**le plat principal** main dish
**le porc** pork
**le pourboire** tip
**le prix** price
**le rôti** roast
**les sardines (à l'huile)** (*f.*) sardines (in oil)
**la saucisse** sausage
**le/la serveur/euse** waiter, waitress
**la sole** sole (*fish*)
**la tranche** slice

À REVOIR: l'assiette (*f.*), la boisson, la cuisine, le déjeuner, le dîner, le fromage, le gâteau, les haricots verts, le pain, le petit déjeuner, la pomme, la pomme de terre, la viande, le vin

## Adjectifs

**ancien(ne)** old, antique; former
**bon(ne)** good
**cher/chère** dear; expensive
**faux/fausse** false
**frais/fraîche** fresh
**jeune** young
**joli(e)** pretty
**mauvais(e)** bad
**nouveau/nouvel/nouvelle** new
**pauvre** poor; unfortunate
**quel(le)** which (*int. adj.*)
**vieux/vieil/vieille** old
**vrai(e)** true

## Les magasins

**la boucherie** butcher shop
**la boulangerie** bakery
**la charcuterie** pork butcher's shop (delicatessen)
**l'épicerie** (*f.*) grocery store
**la pâtisserie** pastry shop; pastry
**la poissonnerie** fish store

## Mots et expressions divers

**cela (ça)** this, that
**ensuite** then, next
**J'aimerais** (+ *infinitive*)... I would like (to) . . .
**Il faut...** It is necessary to / One needs . . .
**même** same; even
**plutôt** instead, rather
**(et) puis** (and) then, next
**Que veut dire...?** What does ______ mean?
**si** so (very); if

---

*The **h** in **hors-d'œuvre** is aspirate, which means that there is no "elision" with the article **le** (i.e. **le hors-d'œuvre**). Note how this is different from **l'huître**, which has a mute **h**. In both cases, the **h** is silent.

# Intermède

## SITUATION

### Déjeuner sur le pouce*

**Contexte** *Nous sommes dans une croissanterie° du Quartier latin où Sébastien et Corinne, deux étudiants québécois, déjeunent sur le pouce, entre deux cours.*

un magasin où on vend des croissants

**Situation**: The *Situation* dialogues are recorded on the st. cassette packaged with the st. text.

**Objectif** *Sébastien et Corinne commandent un repas à emporter* (to take out).

LA SERVEUSE: Vous désirez?
SÉBASTIEN: Un croissant au jambon, s'il vous plaît.
CORINNE: Et pour moi, un croque-monsieur.
LA SERVEUSE: C'est tout?
SÉBASTIEN: Non, je voudrais aussi une crêpe au Grand-Marnier.° Et toi, Corinne?
CORINNE: C'est tout pour moi.
LA SERVEUSE: Et comme boisson?
SÉBASTIEN: Deux cafés, s'il vous plaît.
LA SERVEUSE: C'est pour emporter ou pour manger ici?
CORINNE: Pour emporter.
SÉBASTIEN: Ça fait combien?
LA SERVEUSE: Ça fait trente-sept francs trente... Merci.
SÉBASTIEN: Au revoir, merci.

crêpe... *French-style pancake served with Grand Marnier liqueur*

**Note**: This *Situation* is appropriate to the Intermediate Level of oral proficiency and illustrates the type of behavior and language one needs to order a simple meal. You may want to have sts. role-play this *Situation* using the *À propos* section where more restaurant vocab. is provided.

## À propos

### Au restaurant

Voici d'autres expressions qu'on entend au restaurant.

Le serveur (La serveuse):
- Combien de personnes, s'il vous plaît?
- Comment voulez-vous le bifteck?

Les clients:
- ...saignant (*rare*)
- ...à point (*medium*)
- ...bien cuit (*well done*)
- Je vais prendre...
- Donnez-moi aussi...
- L'addition, s'il vous plaît.
- Le service est-il compris? (*Is the tip included?*)

*__Déjeuner...__ Snack lunch (literally, "lunch on the thumb")

## Maintenant à vous!

**A. Improvisez!** Vous êtes dans une crêperie à Paris pour déjeuner sur le pouce avec des camarades. Un étudiant (Une étudiante) joue le rôle du serveur (de la serveuse). Voici la carte.

Tu veux un hamburger et des frites?

### Crêpes

Prix nets

| | |
|---|---|
| BEURRE ET SUCRE | 11,00 F |
| POMMES (compote) | 14,50 F |
| CITRON | 14,00 F |
| MIEL D'ACADIA | 17,00 F |
| CHOCOLAT CHAUD | 17,00 F |
| CREME DE MARRONS | 17,00 F |
| CONFITURE (fraise, abricot) | 16,00 F |
| CONFITURE (myrtilles) | 17,00 F |
| NOISETTES CHOCOLAT OU CARAMEL | 19,50 F |
| **LA CHOCONOIX** | 20,50 F |
| **COCO CASSIS** (noix de coco et crème de cassis) | 19,50 F |
| CHANTILLY | 18,00 F |
| SIROP D'ERABLE | 18,00 F |
| GRAND MARNIER OU RHUM | 19,50 F |
| **LA CHATELAINE** (Noisettes, chocolat chaud, Chantilly) | 23,00 F |
| **CLAFOUTIS Maison** | 15,50 F |
| **+ Chantilly** | 17,50 F |
| **CREPE TATIN A LA SAUCE NOUGAT** (Pommes morceaux, sauce nougat, Calvados, Chantilly) | 23,50 F |
| L'ARMADA (Poire arrosée de Calvados, chocolat chaud, Chantilly) | 23,50 F |
| **COCKTAIL DE FRUITS AU GRAND MARNIER** | 17,50 F |

**B. Jeu de rôles.** Avec des camarades, créez une scène au restaurant depuis (*from*) l'arrivée des clients jusqu'à leur départ. Voici une description des rôles à jouer.

- Un membre de votre groupe est très gourmand. Il/Elle aime beaucoup manger et mange beaucoup. Commandez le repas d'un vrai gourmand.
- Un autre est un gourmet qui apprécie la bonne cuisine.
- Un autre a peur de grossir (*to gain weight*). Commandez un repas léger en (*light in*) calories.

## PORTRAITS

### *Paul Bocuse (1926–)*

The art of fine cooking has been handed down through generations of the Bocuse family since 1765. Paul Bocuse, one of France's most famous chefs, was a pioneer of **nouvelle cuisine**: a style of cooking based on fresh produce and a minimum of fats. In 1961 he was awarded the formal honor of **meilleur ouvrier** (*best worker*) of France, and in recent years he has gained world renown through his cookbooks and television appearances. Paul Bocuse is the proprietor of a restaurant in Collonges-au-Mont-d'Or, near Lyon, in the Rhône valley.

CHAPITRE **HUIT**

# Vive les vacances!

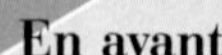

**En avant**

—Que c'est bon, les vacances!

—Oui, on oublie ses problèmes, on peut faire de la voile...

—Et on peut dormir jusqu'à midi!

**Communicative goals:** talking about vacations, discussing sports equipment, expressing dates and actions, talking about the past, expressing how long or how long ago, expressing location, and expressing observations and beliefs.

**En avant**: See scripts for follow-up questions recorded on student cassette.

# Étude de vocabulaire

## Les vacances en France

**Additional vocab.**: *aller à la chasse, faire de la voile, faire du patinage, faire de l'équitation, faire du jogging, jouer au tennis, jouer au golf*

**Suggestion**: Provide sts. with other expressions, depending on how they spend their vacations.

***Autres mots utiles:***

**faire... du cheval** horseback riding
**de la plongée sous-marine** skin diving
**du ski nautique** waterskiing

**faire... du ski de piste** downhill skiing
**du ski de fond** cross-country skiing
**pêcher** to fish
**une randonnée** hike

*Faire de la bicyclette is synonymous with faire de vélo

**A. Où passer les vacances?** Quels sont les avantages touristiques des endroits (*places*) suivants?

1. Qu'est-ce qu'on peut faire dans les montagnes? 2. Dans les lacs? 3. Sur les plages? 4. Sur les routes de campagne? 5. Sur les fleuves? 6. Dans les forêts? 7. À la mer?

Maintenant expliquez où vous voulez passer vos prochaines vacances et quelles activités on peut faire à cet endroit.

**Suggestion**: Have sts. make list in groups and share responses with class.

**Additional activity**: *Vos vacances.* 1. *Où préfères-tu passer les vacances d'été? à la mer? à la montagne? à la campagne?* 2. *Qu'est-ce que tu aimes faire en vacances?* 3. *Où vas-tu aller l'été prochain?*

**B. Activités de vacances.** Qu'est-ce qu'ils font?

1. Que fait un nageur (une nageuse) (*swimmer*)? Où trouve-t-on beaucoup de nageurs?
2. Que fait un campeur (une campeuse) (*camper*)? Où fait-on du camping en France? aux États-Unis?
3. Que fait un skieur (une skieuse) (*skier*)? Où fait-on du ski en France? aux États-Unis?
4. Que fait un cycliste? Où fait-on de la bicyclette en France? aux États-Unis?
5. Combien de nageurs, campeurs, skieurs, cyclistes y a-t-il dans la classe? D'habitude, où passent-ils leurs vacances?

**Suggestions**: Teach sts. to say *dans l'état de...* and ask *Où fait-on du camping aux États-Unis?* etc.

**Additional activity**: *Qu'est-ce qu'ils vont faire?* 1. *Maurice cherche ses skis.* 2. *Claire apporte sa tente.* 3. *Dominique achète une bicyclette.* 4. *Serge loue un bateau.* 5. *Sylvie prend des leçons de natation.* 6. *Les Vasseur achètent de l'huile solaire.*

## Au magasin de sports

**Presentation**: Bring in pictures or examples of these clothing items to teach vocab.

**Additional vocab.**: *un bikini, des sandales, des bottes, des espadrilles*

**A. Achats** (*Purchases*). Complétez les phrases selon l'image.

1. Le jeune homme va acheter des _____. Il va passer ses vacances à Grenoble où il veut _____.
2. La jeune femme veut acheter un _____, une _____ et des _____. Elle va descendre sur la Côte d'Azur (*French Riviera*) où elle va _____ et _____.

**Suggestion**: Could be done for listening comp. by changing statements with blanks into questions. Ask sts. to look at pictures. Instructor reads items and sts. identify pictures.

3. La jeune fille a envie d'acheter des _____ de ski, des chaussures de _____ et un _____ de ski. Sa famille va passer les vacances dans les Alpes où elle va _____.
4. L'homme va acheter un _____ et une _____. Il va _____ dans le nord de la France ce week-end.
5. La vieille dame est très sportive. Elle va acheter un _____ et des _____. Ce week-end, elle va _____ avec son mari dans les Pyrénées.
6. Le vieux monsieur a l'aire patient. Il veut acheter un _____.

**B. L'intrus.** Dans les groupes suivants, trouvez le mot qui ne va pas avec les autres. Expliquez votre choix.

**Suggestions**: (1) Could be done for listening comp. with books closed. (2) After sts. have found odd word, have them try to find one more word that is related in some way to other words.

1. le maillot de bain / les lunettes de soleil / l'huile solaire (*suntan oil*) / l'anorak
2. la tente / le maillot de bain / le sac de couchage / le sac à dos
3. les gants de ski / la serviette de plage / les skis / l'anorak
4. les lunettes de soleil / les chaussures de ski / le short / le maillot de bain

**C. Choix de vêtements.** Qu'est-ce qu'on porte pour faire les activités suivantes?

**Suggestion**: Refer sts. to previous clothing vocab. from Chapter 3 for review.

MODÈLE: pour aller pêcher (*to go fishing*) →
Pour aller pêcher, on porte un chapeau, un vieux pantalon...

**Continuation**: (1) *Pour aller au cinéma*; *pour aller aux offices religieux*; *pour aller danser*. (2) Ask sts. to name one thing they would *not* wear during these activities.

1. pour faire du ski nautique 2. pour aller à la montagne 3. pour faire une promenade dans la forêt 4. pour faire de la bicyclette 5. pour faire du bateau 6. pour faire du ski de fond

**Follow-up**: Bring in a clothing size chart from France to show how sizes are different. Teach *la taille* and *la pointure* (*Je chausse du...* ).

**Et vous?** Décrivez les vêtements que vous portez quand vous faites votre sport favori.

**Suggestion**: Encourage sts. to tell what they know about Tunisia.

**D. Conseils pratiques.** Vous préparez un voyage en Tunisie. Voici les vêtements qu'on vous recommande.

**Note**: Information on Tunisia is from a brochure published by *Le Point Azur*.

***Les vêtements***

*En hiver : quelques pulls, un imperméable et des vêtements de demi-saison.*[a]
*En été : des vêtements légers en fibres naturelles, maillot de bain, lunettes de soleil, chapeau, chaussures aérées,*[b] *tenues*[c] *pratiques pour les excursions. Sans oublier un léger pull pour les soirées et les hôtels climatisés.*[d]

[a] spring or autumn
[b] well-ventilated
[c] dress, clothes
[d] air-conditioned

Une promenade en dromadaire sur la plage de Djerba en Tunisie

1. Selon la brochure, quels vêtements mettez-vous dans votre valise si vous voyagez en hiver? en été? Donnez des exemples.
2. À votre avis, quel temps fait-il en Tunisie en hiver? en été?

Imaginez maintenant que vous travaillez dans une agence de voyages. Quels vêtements allez-vous conseiller à des touristes qui voyagent en Alaska? au Mexique? dans le Grand Canyon? Quels autres achats conseillez-vous (*do you suggest*)?

**Follow-up**: Have sts. play the roles of *agent de voyages* and *voyageur(euse)*.

## Des années importantes

**Presentation**: You may introduce *Quand êtes-vous né(e)?* and *je suis né(e) en...* as lexical items to have sts. practice saying years. Reenter dates and seasons by having sts. guess each other's birthdays. Suggested question sequence: *Est-ce que ton anniversaire est... en automne? au printemps?* etc. *au mois de novembre?* etc. *le 13? le 14?*

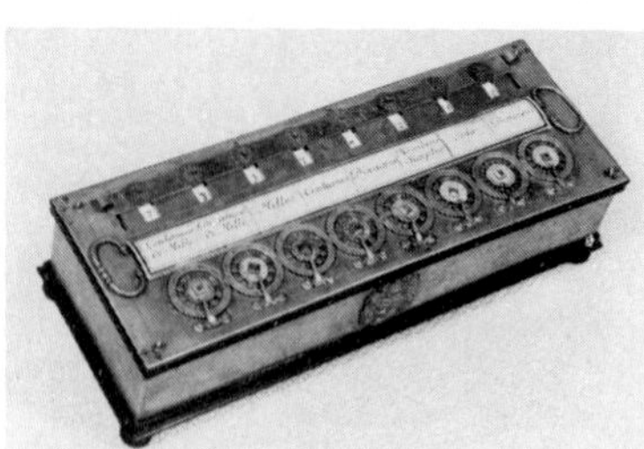

**1642** La machine à calculer inventée par Blaise Pascal en seize cent quarante-deux.

**1783** Le ballon à air chaud inventé par les frères Montgolfier en dix-sept cent quatre-vingt-trois.

**1835** Les procédés de développement des images photographiques inventés par Jacques Daguerre en dix-huit cent trente-cinq.

In French, years are expressed with a multiple of **cent** or with **mil**.*

| | |
|---|---|
| **dix-neuf cents** (**mil neuf cents**) | *1900* |
| **dix-neuf cent quatre-vingt-huit** (**mil neuf cent quatre-vingt-huit**) | *1988* |
| **seize cent quatre** (**mil six cent quatre**) | *1604* |

*__Mille__ is spelled **mil** when years are spelled out. An exception is the year 1000, **l'an mille**, or 2000, **l'an deux mille**.

The preposition **en** is used to express *in* with a year.

**en** dix-neuf cent vingt-trois — *in 1923*

## Mots-clés

*To talk about a decade or an era*

**les années** _____ Aux États-Unis, on appelle **les années vingt** *the roaring twenties.*

**Answers (ex.A)**: (1) g (2) d (3) e (4) f (5) b (6) c (7) a

**Follow-up**: For listening comp. practice, give sts. years orally and have them choose event during that year.

**A. Un peu d'histoire.** Êtes-vous bon(ne) en histoire? Avec un(e) camarade, trouvez la date qui correspond à chaque événement historique. Les événements sont en ordre chronologique!

1. Charlemagne est couronné (*crowned*) empereur d'Occident.
2. Guillaume, duc de Normandie, conquiert (*conquers*) l'Angleterre.
3. Jeanne d'Arc bat (*beats*) les Anglais à Orléans.
4. Prise de la Bastille.
5. Napoléon est couronné empereur des Français.
6. Gustave Eiffel construit la tour Eiffel.
7. Débarquement (*Landing*) anglo-américain en France.

a. 1944
b. 1804
c. 1889
d. 1066
e. 1429
f. 1789
g. l'an 800

**Suggestions (ex. B)**: (1) Give sts. a few moments to do matching exercise silently and then, to check work, ask for oral responses. (2) Dictate dates and have sts. write them in numerals. (3) Because sts. have trouble remembering historical dates, you may ask them to prepare this before coming to class.

**Answers**: (1) d (2) e (3) c (4) a (5) b

**Continuation**: *Maintenant, chaque étudiant(e)* nomme un événement historique. Les autres donnent la date de l'événement en question. Qui est l'historien/l'historienne de la classe? Suggestions: *le voyage autour du monde de Magellan; l'arrivée de Christophe Colomb en Amérique; la rédaction de la Constitution américaine; la vente de la Louisiane aux États-Unis par Napoléon*

**Continuation**: 4. *En quelle année vas-tu aller à Paris? à Montréal? en Europe? en Afrique? en Asie?* 5. *En quelle année tes enfants vont-ils commencer leurs études universitaires?*

**B. Dates inoubliables** (*unforgettable*). Lisez les dates suivantes. Quel événement correspond à chaque date?

MODÈLE: 28.6.19 →
le vingt-huit juin dix-neuf cent dix-neuf: le traité de Versailles*

1. 7.12.41
2. 22.11.63
3. 2.9.45
4. 18.4.06
5. 18.5.80
6. ?

a. Le grand tremblement de terre (*earthquake*) de San Francisco
b. L'éruption du mont Sainte-Hélène (état de Washington)
c. La fin de la Deuxième Guerre mondiale (*WW II*) pour les États-Unis
d. L'attaque de Pearl Harbor
e. L'assassinat de J. F. Kennedy
f. Aujourd'hui

**C. L'avenir** (*The future*). Quels sont vos projets d'avenir? Posez les questions suivantes à un(e) camarade. Ensuite, présentez à la classe une observation sur l'avenir de votre camarade.

1. En quelle année vas-tu obtenir (*obtain*) ton diplôme universitaire?
2. En quelle année vas-tu passer des vacances en France?
3. En quelle année vas-tu avoir 65 ans?

**Follow-up**: Ask sts. to guess year of birth of their partner based on information they have received.

*Le traité de Versailles marque la fin de la Première Guerre mondiale (*World War I*).

# Nouvelles francophones

## Vacations in the Francophone world

If you want to speak French on your vacation without traveling to France, you can choose from many different countries. The Francophone world extends to many parts of the globe, and offers an exciting variety of cultures, landscapes, and climates.

À Montréal, certaines traditions comme la promenade en calèche sont toujours très populaires.

Would you enjoy a large multicultural metropolis? In Montreal, the largest Francophone city after Paris, you will find a fascinating combination of modern, upbeat urban life and old-world tradition. If you prefer mountains, lakes, clean air, and quiet, the alpine areas of Switzerland will be your ideal vacation spot. For an exotic landscape and cultural environment, consider Senegal, in West Africa: there you will find deserts, tropical beaches with coconut trees, and vibrant colors. Other places to vacation in the Francophone world include Guyana, New Caledonia, Egypt, the Ivory Coast, Tahiti, Madagascar, and Vietnam—countries where many people speak French and where French culture has developed many fascinating variants through its interaction with local traditions.

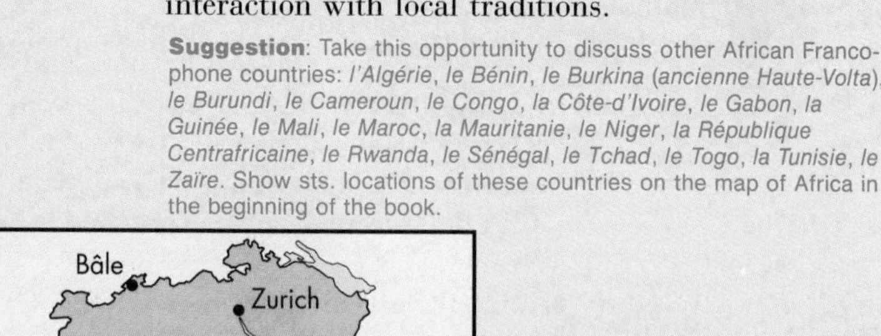

**Suggestion**: Take this opportunity to discuss other African Francophone countries: *l'Algérie*, *le Bénin*, *le Burkina* (*ancienne Haute-Volta*), *le Burundi*, *le Cameroun*, *le Congo*, *la Côte-d'Ivoire*, *le Gabon*, *la Guinée*, *le Mali*, *le Maroc*, *la Mauritanie*, *le Niger*, *la République Centrafricaine*, *le Rwanda*, *le Sénégal*, *le Tchad*, *le Togo*, *la Tunisie*, *le Zaïre*. Show sts. locations of these countries on the map of Africa in the beginning of the book.

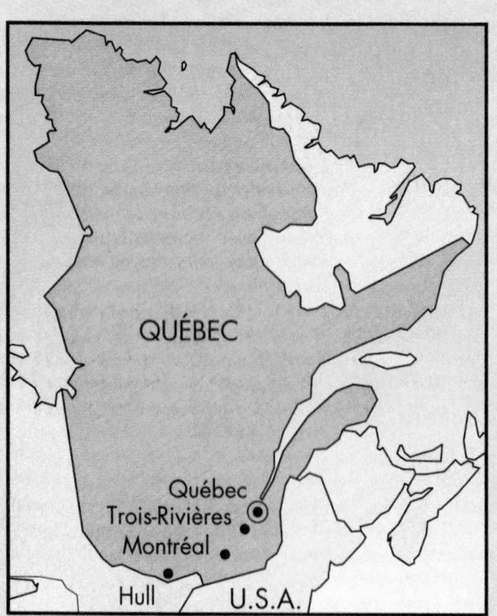



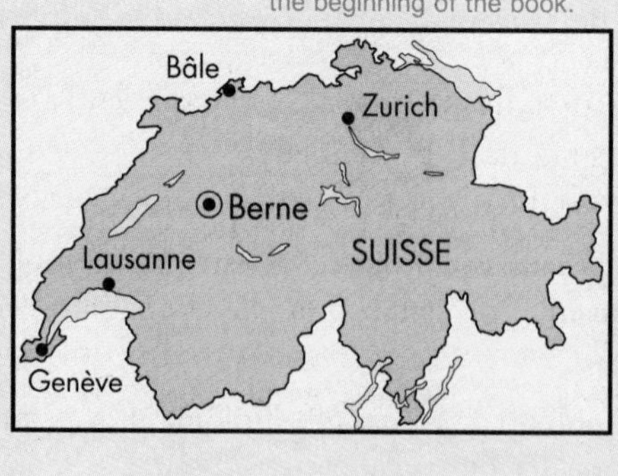



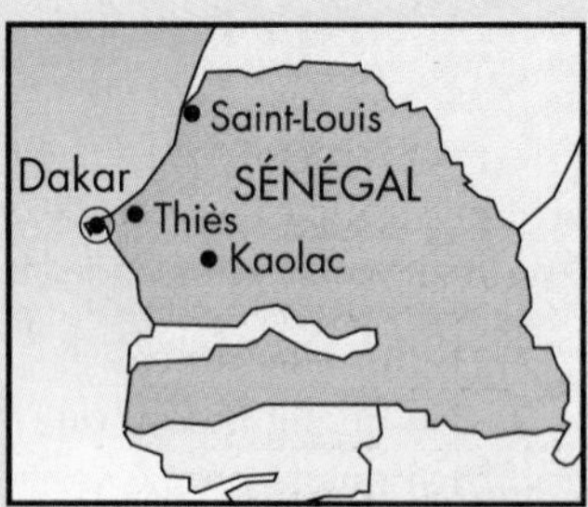

# Étude de grammaire

## 24. EXPRESSING ACTIONS
### *dormir* and Similar Verbs; *venir*

### Les joies de la nature

STÉPHANE: Vous allez où en vacances cet été?

ANNE-LAURE: Cette année on va à la Martinique. On va camper dans un petit village à 30 km de Fort-de-France. Boire du ti'punch,* **sortir** tous les soirs, bronzer à l'ombre des cocotiers... le rêve quoi!† **Viens** avec nous. On **part** le deux août.

STÉPHANE: Non merci, la mer n'est pas pour moi. **Sentir** les odeurs de poisson, **dormir** avec les moustiques, pas question!

ROMAIN: Décidément, tu ne changes pas. Monsieur a besoin de son petit confort. Tant pis pour toi! Nous, on aime **dormir** à la belle étoile, **sentir** le vent de la mer et admirer les étoiles.

Décidez d'après le dialogue si les affirmations suivantes sont probables ou peu probables. Corrigez les phrases improbables.

1. Anne-Laure et Romain ont peur de dormir à la belle étoile.
2. Stéphane adore camper.
3. Romain est romantique.
4. Anne-Laure aime faire la fête (*to party*).
5. Anne-Laure et Romain adorent la nature.

## A. *Dormir* and Verbs Like *dormir*

1. The verbs in the group **dormir** have an irregular conjugation.

| PRESENT TENSE OF **dormir** (*to sleep*) | | | |
|---|---|---|---|
| je | **dors** | nous | **dormons** |
| tu | **dors** | vous | **dormez** |
| il, elle, on | **dort** | ils, elles | **dorment** |

**Presentation**: Point out that the consonant sound of the verb stem is heard in third-person plural but not in singular, which helps listener distinguish singular from plural.

*Creole language for a white rum and lime drink.
†*a dream, huh?* **Quoi** is often added to the end of sentences in informal conversations for emphasis.

| | |
|---|---|
| Je **dors** très bien. | *I sleep very well.* |
| **Dormez**-vous à la belle étoile? | *Do you sleep in the open air (under the stars)?* |
| Nous **dormons** jusqu'à 7h30. | *We sleep until 7:30.* |

2. Verbs conjugated like **dormir** include the following.

| | |
|---|---|
| **partir** | *to leave, to depart* |
| **sentir** | *to feel; to sense; to smell* |
| **servir** | *to serve* |
| **sortir** | *to go out; to take out* |

| | |
|---|---|
| Je **pars** en vacances. | *I'm leaving on vacation.* |
| Ce plat **sent** bon (mauvais). | *This dish smells good (bad).* |
| Nous **servons** le petit déjeuner à 8 heures. | *We serve breakfast at 8:00.* |
| À quelle heure allez-vous **sortir** ce soir? | *What time are you going out tonight?* |

**Suggestion**: Use the following as a listening discrimination ex. *Singulier ou pluriel?* 1. *Ils servent le dîner?* 2. *Elle sent le pain chaud.* 3. *Ils sentent les fleurs sur la table.* 4. *Elle dort après le dîner.* 5. *Ils dorment devant la télé.* 6. *Elles sortent ce soir.* Sts. write *S* or *P* next to each number. Go over exercise, asking sts. to explain their answers.

## B. *Partir* and *sortir*

**Partir** and **sortir** both mean *to leave*, but each is used differently.* **Partir** is either used alone or is followed by a preposition.

| | |
|---|---|
| Je **pars**. | *I'm leaving.* |
| Elle **part de** (**pour**) Cannes. | *She's leaving from (for) Cannes.* |

**Sortir** is also used either alone or with a preposition. In this usage, **sortir** implies leaving an enclosed space.

| | |
|---|---|
| Tu **sors?** | *You're going out?* |
| Elle **sort de** la caravane. | *She's getting out of the camping trailer.* |
| **Sortons de** l'eau! | *Let's get out of the water!* |

**Sortir** can also mean that one is going out for the evening, or it can be used to imply that one person is going out with someone else in the sense of seeing him or her regularly.†

| | |
|---|---|
| Tu **sors** ce soir? | *Are you going out tonight?* |
| Michèle et Édouard **sortent** ensemble. | *Michèle and Édouard are going out together.* |

***Quitter**, a regular **-er** verb, means *to leave somewhere or someone*. It always require a direct object, either a place or a person: **Je quitte Paris. Elle quitte son ami.**

†Dating in the American sense does not exist in France. Young people go out in groups in France until the relationship is serious.

## C. Venir

1. The verb **venir** (*to come*) is irregular.

| PRESENT TENSE OF **venir** (*to come*) | | | |
|---|---|---|---|
| je | **viens** | nous | **venons** |
| tu | **viens** | vous | **venez** |
| il, elle, on | **vient** | ils, elles | **viennent** |

Presentation: Write forms of *venir* on board as you model them, with 3 singular forms and third-person plural first (because stems are alike) and 2 other plural forms last. Draw a "shoe" shape around the 4 forms with identical vowel spelling in stems. Point out that consonant also doubles in third-person plural form and that nasal vowel disappears.

Nous **venons** de Saint-Malo. — *We come from Saint-Malo.*
**Viens** voir la plage! — *Come see the beach!*

**Venir de** plus an infinitive means *to have just* (done something).

Note: Point out that *venir de* is an easy way to indicate a very recent past event.

Je **viens de nager**. — *I have just come from swimming.*
Mes amis **viennent de téléphoner**. — *My friends have just telephoned.*

2. Verbs conjugated like **venir** include the following.

**devenir** — *to become*
**revenir** — *to come back*

Ils **reviennent** de vacances. — *They're coming back from vacation.*

On **devient** expert grâce à l'expérience. — *One becomes expert with (thanks to) experience.*

Suggestion: (Preliminary ex.) *Singulier ou pluriel? 1. Ils partent en vacances demain. 2. Elle vient d'obtenir des brochures. 3. Elle sort de l'agence de voyages. 4. Ils obtiennent un visa. 5. Ils reviennent en voiture.*

### Vérifions!

**A. Tu pars ou tu sors?** Choisissez le verbe correct: **partir** ou **sortir**.

MODÈLE: Alain, Philippe et Claire sont amis. →
Ils **sortent** ensemble tous les week-ends.

1. Luc aime aller au ciné. Il _____ souvent.
2. Caroline et Patrick vont au Canada. Ils _____ demain.
3. Isabelle est à la discothèque. Il fait trop chaud. Elle _____ de la discothèque.
4. Vous avez fini (*have finished*) vos études. Vous _____ en vacances.
5. Je ne veux pas rester seul(e). Je _____ avec mes amis.

**B. Au pays des pharaons** (*pharaohs*). Loïc et Nathalie sont en vacances en Égypte avec le Club Aquarius. Ils envoient (*send*) une carte postale à leur grand-mère. Complétez la carte avec les verbes de la colonne de droite.

Additional activity: *Le programme d'une journée de vacances. Faites les substitutions indiquées et les changements nécessaires. 1. Jean-Marie part pour faire de la bicyclette. (les étudiants, nous, tu) 2. Je sors de la caravane à six heures. (vous, Christine et Marie-France, il) 3. Nous sentons les fleurs. (je, on, Jean-Marie et Chantal) 4. Pierre dort jusqu'à midi. (ils, vous, tu)*

Additional activity: *En français, s'il vous plaît. 1. My family is leaving on vacation today. 2. My cousins are leaving New York. 3. My sister is leaving for Brittany tomorrow. 4. My brother has just bought some skis. 5. He's going out with a friend. 6. Why are you leaving? 7. You're going out with my sister now? 8. Let's leave together. 9. I can't go out. I have to work.*

Chère mamie,

Nous _____[1] d'arriver en Égypte. Le Club Aquarius, c'est le grand confort. Nous _____[2] dans des chambres immenses et tous les matins on _____[3] le petit déjeuner dans la chambre. Demain nous _____[4] pour le temple de Louxor. Nous _____[5] des experts en égyptologie. Nous _____[6] en France dans quatre jours.

À bientôt et grosses bises (*hugs 'n kisses*).

Joïc et Nathalie

servir
partir
devenir
venir
revenir
dormir

Maintenant imaginez que c'est vous qui êtes en Égypte. Reprenez la carte et faites tous les changements nécessaires. Commencez par «Je viens d'...».

## *Parlons-en!*

**A. La curiosité.** Imaginez avec un(e) camarade ce que ces personnes viennent de faire. Donnez trois possibilités pour chaque phrase.

MODÈLE: Albert rentre d'Afrique. →
Il vient de visiter le Sénégal. Il vient de passer une semaine au soleil. Il vient de faire un safari.

**Suggestion**: Give sts. a minute to write sentences and then put them on board or check on overhead.

1. Jennifer part en vacances. 2. Je sors du magasin de sports. 3. Nous revenons de la montagne. 4. Jean-Jacques et Yvon reviennent de la campagne. 5. Marie-Laure rentre du Canada.

**B. Conversation.** Engagez avec un(e) camarade assis(e) loin de vous une conversation basée sur les questions suivantes. Ensuite, faites un commentaire sur les habitudes (*habits*) ou les attitudes de votre camarade.

**Suggestion**: Could be done at end of class hour. Sts. prepare commentary for homework.

1. Pars-tu souvent en voyage? Où vas-tu? Viens-tu d'acheter des vêtements ou d'autres objets nécessaires pour tes vacances? Qu'est-ce que tu viens d'acheter?
2. Sors-tu souvent pendant (*during*) le week-end ou restes-tu à la maison? Sors-tu souvent pendant la semaine? Qu'est-ce que tu portes quand tu sors?
3. Aimes-tu la fin des vacances? Tes ami(e)s sentent-ils/elles une différence quand tu reviens chez toi? Deviens-tu plus calme? nerveux/euse? triste? heureux/euse?

Ski de fond en Vanoise,
Alpes françaises

# 25. TALKING ABOUT THE PAST
## The *passé composé* with *avoir*

### À l'hôtel

**Suggestion**: Ask sts. to play roles.

LE CLIENT: Bonjour, Madame. **J'ai réservé** une chambre pour deux personnes.
L'EMPLOYÉE: Votre nom, s'il vous plaît.
LE CLIENT: Bernard Meunier.
L'EMPLOYÉE: Heu... oui, chambre n° 12, au rez-de-chaussée. Vous **avez demandé** une chambre avec vue sur la mer, c'est bien ça?
LE CLIENT: Oui, c'est exact.
L'EMPLOYÉE: Alors, remplissez cette fiche, s'il vous plaît.

Jouez le dialogue avec un(e) camarade et faites les substitutions suivantes.

Nombre de personnes: une
Nom: votre nom
Vue demandée: la forêt

## A. The *passé composé*

**Suggestion**: Review conjugation of *avoir* before presenting *passé composé* with *avoir*. You may wish to point out that the *passé composé* is the past tense form used most frequently in conversation.

As in English, there are several past tenses in French. The **passé composé**, the compound past tense, is most commonly used to indicate simple past actions. It describes events that began and ended at some point in the past. The **passé composé** of most verbs is formed with the present tense of the auxiliary verb (**le verbe auxiliaire**) **avoir** plus a past participle (**le participe passé**).*

| PASSÉ COMPOSÉ OF **voyager** (*to travel*) | | | |
|---|---|---|---|
| j' | **ai voyagé** | nous | **avons voyagé** |
| tu | **as voyagé** | vous | **avez voyagé** |
| il, elle, on | **a voyagé** | ils, elles | **ont voyagé** |

The **passé composé** has several equivalents in English. For example, **j'ai voyagé** can mean *I traveled*, *I have traveled*, or *I did travel*, according to the context.

*The formation of the **passé composé** with **être** will be treated in Chapter 9.

## B. Formation of the Past Participle

1. To form regular past participles of **-er** and **-ir** verbs, the final **-r** is dropped from the infinitive. For **-er** verbs, an **accent aigu** (´) is added to the final **-e**. For regular past participles of **-re** verbs, the **-re** is dropped and **-u** is added.

| | | |
|---|---|---|
| acheter → **acheté** | J'**ai acheté** de nouvelles valises. | *I bought some new suitcases.* |
| choisir → **choisi** | Tu **as choisi*** la date de ton départ? | *Have you chosen your departure date?* |
| perdre → **perdu** | Nous **avons perdu** nos passeports. | *We lost our passports.* |

**Presentation**: Model pronunciation of past participles.

2. Most irregular verbs have irregular past participles.

- Verbs with past participles ending in **-u**

| | | | |
|---|---|---|---|
| avoir: | **eu** | pleuvoir (*to rain*): | **plu** |
| boire: | **bu** | pouvoir: | **pu** |
| devoir: | **dû** | recevoir: | **reçu** |
| obtenir (*to obtain*): | **obtenu**† | vouloir: | **voulu** |

| | |
|---|---|
| Nous **avons eu** peur. | *We got scared.* |
| Il **a bu** deux verres de vin. | *He drank two glasses of wine.* |
| Nous **avons obtenu** de bons résultats. | *We got (obtained) good results.* |

- Verbs with past participles ending in **-s**

| | |
|---|---|
| apprendre: | **appris** |
| comprendre: | **compris** |
| mettre: | **mis** |
| prendre: | **pris** |

| | |
|---|---|
| Nous **avons pris** le soleil. | *We sat in the sun (sunbathed).* |
| Marc **a appris** à faire du ski. | *Marc learned to ski.* |
| Marc **a mis** ses gants pour faire du ski. | *Marc put his gloves on to ski.* |

- Verbs with past participles ending in **-t**

| | |
|---|---|
| dire: | **dit** |
| écrire: | **écrit** |
| faire: | **fait** |

*In informal and rapid conversation, **tu as choisi** may be pronounced **t'as choisi**.
†**Obtenir** is conjugated like **venir** in the present tense.

Nous **avons fait** une promenade sur la plage. — *We took a walk on the beach.*

Ce matin j'**ai écrit** six cartes postales. — *This morning I wrote six postcards.*

- The past participle of **être** is **été**.

Mes vacances **ont été** formidables. — *My vacation was wonderful.*

**Suggestion**: (*End of presentation, for listening comp.*) Read the following sentences. Sts. indicate whether they hear *passé composé* or *présent*: 1. *Il a plu hier.* 2. *Martine a mis un imperméable.* 3. *Georges lit un livre.* 4. *Il écrit une lettre.* 5. *Nous avons vu Jeanne au cinéma.* 6. *Tu as vu Jeanne aussi?* 7. *Je fais une promenade.*

## C. Negative and Interrogative Sentences in the *passé composé*

In negative sentences, **ne... pas** surrounds the auxiliary verb (**avoir**).

Nous **n'avons pas** voyagé en Suisse. — *We have not traveled to Switzerland.*

Vous **n'avez pas** pris de vacances? — *Didn't you take a vacation?*

In questions with inversion, only the auxiliary verb and the subject are inverted.

Marie **a-t-elle demandé** le prix de la robe? — *Did Marie ask the price of the dress?*

**As-tu oublié** ton passeport? — *Did you forget your passport?*

### *Vérifions!*

**A. Tourisme.** Qu'est-ce qu'ils ont fait pendant les vacances? Faites des phrases complètes au passé composé.

1. tu / nager / dans / fleuve
2. Sylvie / camper / dans / forêt
3. Michèle et Vincent / finir par (*ended up by*) / visiter / Paris
4. je / dormir / sous / tente*
5. ils / perdre / clés (*keys*)
6. Thibaut / faire / bicyclette
7. vous / boire / Coca / au bord (*shore*) de / mer
8. nous / prendre / beaucoup / photos
9. Thérèse et toi, vous / apprendre à / faire du bateau
10. je / prendre / valise

**B. Une carte postale de la neige.** Complétez la carte postale de Marie. Mettez les verbes au passé composé.

**Additional activity**: *À l'hôtel. Faites les substitutions et les changements nécessaires.* 1. *Vous allez dans les Alpes?—Oui, nous avons trouvé un excellent hôtel.* (*je, Marc, ils, elle*) 2. *Avez-vous choisi une chambre?—Oui, j'ai choisi une chambre.* (*nos cousins, nous, Michel et Paul*) 3. *Que cherchez-vous?—Marie a perdu la clé.* (*nous, je, vous, Marc et Michel*)

*In French one says **dormir *sous* la tente**.

Chère Claudine,

J'_____[1] mes vacances d'hiver une semaine avant Noël avec Christine. Nous _____[2] le train jusqu'en Suisse. Nous _____[3] deux semaines à la montagne.

Nous _____[4] de rester à Saint-Moritz. Nous _____[5] du ski et du patin à glace (*ice skating*). Nous _____[6] une fondue délicieuse. Au retour, nous _____[7] visite à des amis à Genève. Notre séjour en Suisse _____[8] inoubliable.

Je t'embrasse,

Marie

prendre
commencer (*begin*)
passer
être
manger
faire
décider
rendre

**C. À Orange.** Thierry pose des questions à ses cousins Chantal et Jean-Claude, qui (*who*) ont visité la ville historique d'Orange. Jouez les rôles avec deux camarades.

**Suggestion**: Do in groups of 3. One st. asks questions and other two alternate answering.

MODÈLE: trouver l'auberge de jeunesse (*youth hostel*) à Orange →
THIERRY: Avez-vous trouvé l'auberge de jeunesse à Orange?
JEAN-CLAUDE: Non, nous n'avons pas trouvé l'auberge de jeunesse à Orange.

1. faire une promenade dans la vieille ville 2. prendre une photo de l'amphithéâtre romain 3. contempler la vieille fontaine 4. étudier les inscriptions romaines 5. apprendre l'histoire de France 6. acheter des cartes postales 7. envoyer une description de la ville à vos parents

## Parlons-en!

**A. Des vacances réussies.** Laurent a passé ses vacances au Maroc. Qu'est-ce qu'il a fait?

**Verbes utiles:** acheter, apprendre, boire, dormir, faire du jogging, jouer au tennis, manger, nager, prendre des photos...

1.

2.

3.

4.

5.

6.

7.

8.

**B. Alternatives.** Qu'est-ce qu'il n'a pas fait?

**Verbes utiles:** aimer; bronzer; faire... du cheval, du ski nautique, une randonnée, de la planche à voile; pêcher...

**Suggestion**: Model pronunciation of these words, and encourage sts. to use them in subsequent activities.

## Mots-clés

*Expressing when you did something in the past*

| | |
|---|---|
| **avant-hier** (*the day before yesterday*) | **Avant-hier,** une amie m'a invité à faire du camping. |
| **hier matin** | **Hier matin**, j'ai fait les préparatifs. |
| **hier après-midi, hier soir** | Nous avons acheté des sacs à dos **hier après-midi**, et nous les avons perdus **hier soir**. |

Use **matinée** and **soirée**, rather than **matin** and **soir**, if you wish to emphasize the duration. They are often used with **toute**.

| | |
|---|---|
| **toute la matinée** (**soirée**) | J'ai passé **toute la matinée** (**soirée**) à acheter des provisions. |

Use **dernier** or **passé** to express *last* (*month, week, etc.*).

| | |
|---|---|
| **la semaine dernière** (**passée**) | J'ai acheté un billet d'avion pour Rome **la semaine dernière**. |
| **l'an dernier** (**passé**) / **l'année dernière** (**passée**) | Nous avons voyagé en Grèce **l'année passée**. |

**C. Interview.** Posez des questions à un(e) camarade sur ses activités du passé. Essayez d'utiliser les expressions des *Mots-clés*. Voici des suggestions.

**Suggestion**: Have sts. do in pairs and report one thing their partners did.

**Le matin**: dormir tard, faire du sport, regarder la télévision, boire du café, prendre un petit déjeuner, ...

**L'après-midi / Le soir**: pique-niquer, skier, jouer aux cartes, étudier une leçon, inviter des amis, ...

**La semaine dernière / L'année dernière**: voyager en Europe, finir une dissertation, travailler dans un magasin, rendre visite à des amis, acheter une nouvelle bicyclette, ...

Puis racontez à la classe ce que votre camarade a fait.

# 26. EXPRESSING HOW LONG OR HOW LONG AGO *depuis, pendant, il y a*

### Question d'entraînement

MONIQUE: **Depuis quand** participes-tu à des compétitions?
FRANÇOISE: **Depuis** 1992. Et toi, **depuis combien de temps** fais-tu de la planche à voile?
MONIQUE: **Depuis** quinze jours seulement!
FRANÇOISE: Moi, j'ai commencé **il y a** huit ans.
MONIQUE: C'est dur, mais c'est formidable! Hier j'ai même pu rester sur la planche **pendant** quatre minutes.

1. Depuis quand Françoise participe-t-elle à des compétitions?
2. Depuis combien de temps Monique fait-elle de la planche à voile?
3. Pendant combien de temps a-t-elle pu rester sur sa planche hier?

## A. *Depuis*

**Depuis** is used with a verb in the present tense to talk about an activity that began in the past and has continued into the present time.

**Presentation and suggestion**: Model pronunciation of sentences. Give personal examples and ask sts. to give some, too. Examples: *J'étudie le français depuis sept ans. Je suis à l'université de X depuis trois ans. Nous étudions le français depuis septembre.*

| | | | |
|---|---|---|---|
| **Depuis quand...** ? / **Depuis combien de temps...** ? | + *present tense* | = | How long . . . ? / For how long . . . ? |
| **Depuis** + *time period* | + *present tense* | = | for (*duration*) |
| **Depuis** + *date* | + *present tense* | = | since |

| | |
|---|---|
| —**Depuis quand** (**Depuis combien de temps**) **jouez**-vous au tennis? | —*(For) how long have you been playing tennis?* |
| —Je **joue** au tennis **depuis deux ans** (**depuis 1992**). | —*I've been playing tennis for two years* (*since 1992*). |

**Suggestion**: (*Listening comp.*:) Ask sts. to indicate whether action took place in past or if it is still going on. 1. *J'étudie le français depuis quatre ans.* 2. *J'ai passé un mois en France.* 3. *J'écris des lettres à mes amis français depuis mon retour.* 4. *Depuis le mois de mai ils habitent à Lyon.*

## B. *Pendant*

**Pendant** expresses the duration of a habitual or repeated action, situation, or event with a definite beginning and end.

**Pendant combien de temps** + *present or past tense* = How long . . . ? For how long . . . ?
**Pendant** + *time period* + *present or past tense* = for (*duration*)

**Pendant combien de temps dormez-vous** chaque nuit? — *How long do you sleep every night?*

—**Pendant combien de temps ont-ils visité** Paris? — *—(For) how long did they visit Paris?*
—**Ils ont visité** Paris **pendant deux semaines**. — *—They visited Paris for two weeks.*

**Note**: You may wish to present *il y a... que* (*Voilà... que*). They could be presented for recognition rather than production.

**Additional activities**: *En français, s'il vous plaît.* 1. *How long have you been at this university?* 2. *How long do you study every day?* 3. *How long have you lived in this town?* 4. *How long have you played the piano?* 5. *How long do you play (practice) each day?* 6. *I've been playing tennis since 1990. Sondage.* Have sts. ask classmates the following questions, or poll the class yourself. Then decide together who has the most sensible habits. 1. *Combien d'heures dors-tu chaque nuit?* 2. *Combien d'heures passes-tu à la bibliothèque le week-end?* 3. *Pendant combien de temps est-ce que tu prépares la leçon de français, en général? Pendant combien de temps as-tu préparé la leçon hier soir?*

## C. Il y a

**Il y a** + *time period* = ago

J'ai acheté ce guide d'Italie **il y a une semaine**. — *I bought this guide to Italy a week ago.*
Avez-vous voyagé en Espagne **il y a deux ans**? — *Did you go to Spain two years ago?*

### Vérifions!

**Expressions de temps.** Complétez les phrases de façon logique, selon vos observations ou vos expériences personnelles.

1. L'été passé, j'ai ____ pendant ____ semaines (mois).
2. Ma famille ____ depuis ____ ans.
3. Il y a deux semaines, mes amis et moi, nous ____.
4. Les étudiants de cette classe ____ depuis ____.
5. Pendant une heure (____ heures), je ____.
6. Je ne ____ depuis le mois de ____.

### Parlons-en!

**Activités.** Demandez à vos camarades depuis quand ou depuis combien de temps ils/elles font les activités suivantes.

MODÈLE: être étudiant(e) →
—Depuis combien de temps est-ce que tu es étudiant(e)?
—Je suis étudiant(e) depuis...

1. étudier le français 2. pratiquer son sport préféré 3. être à l'université 4. avoir son objet préféré 5. habiter à... 6. ?

**Suggestion**: Sts. jot down notes about each interviewee and determine who has the best habits. Then determine results for class as a whole.

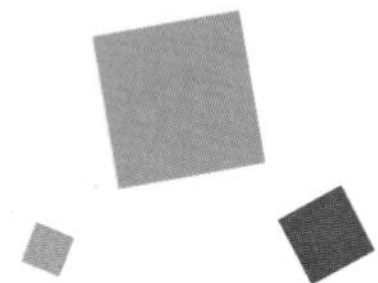

# 27. EXPRESSING LOCATION
## Using Prepositions with Geographical Names

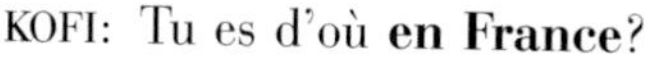

### Bruno au Congo

Bruno est en vacances au Congo. Il a fait la connaissance de Kofi.

KOFI: Tu es d'où **en France**?
BRUNO: **De Marseille**.
KOFI: Ce doit être beau là-bas! Dis, tu as d'autres projets de voyages pour l'avenir?
BRUNO: Ouais, plein.* D'abord l'année prochaine je vais aller **au Mexique** avec ma copine. Et à l'avenir je veux aller **en Russie**, **au Québec**, **au Sénégal** et aussi **en Asie**.
KOFI: Et tu aimerais habiter dans quelle ville?†
BRUNO: **À Vérone en Italie** pour trouver ma Juliette.

Répondez aux questions selon les indications.

1. D'où vient Bruno? (ville, pays) D'où est Kofi? (pays, continent)
2. Où Bruno va-t-il aller l'année prochaine? (pays, continent)
3. Et où veut-il aller à l'avenir? (continents)
4. Où rêve-t-il d'habiter? (ville, pays)

## A. Gender of Geographical Names

In French, most place names that end in **-e** are feminine; most others are masculine. Two exceptions are **le Zaïre** and **le Mexique**. The names of the continents are feminine: **l'Europe**, **l'Afrique**, **l'Asie**, **l'Australie**,‡ **l'Amérique du Nord**, **l'Amérique du Sud**. The names of most states in the United States are masculine: **le Kentucky**, **le Connecticut**. The names of nine states end in **-e** in French and are feminine: **la Californie**, **la Caroline du Nord et du Sud**, **la Floride**, **la Géorgie**, **la Louisiane**, **la Pennsylvanie**, **la Virginie**, **la Virginie occidentale**.

**Presentation**: Use maps, and ask sts. to give the country name using the article to indicate gender. Later you can use these maps to have sts. say *Je vais en/au/aux...*; *Je reviens de/du/des...*

**Note**: Additional countries not mentioned in this section: *l'Argentine, l'Autriche, la Bolivie, la Bulgarie, l'Égypte, l'Indonésie, la Jordanie, la Norvège, la Pologne, la Roumanie, la République Tchèque, la Slovaquie, la Thaïlande, la Turquie, le Venezuela, le Brésil, le Chili, Cuba, le Guatemala, l'Iran, le Kenya, le Liban, le Nicaragua, le Nigeria, le Pakistan, les Pays-Bas, le Panamá, le Soudan*.

## B. *To, in,* and *from* with Geographical Names

1. **Les villes et les îles**. With names of cities and most islands:

---

*Informal speech for **Oui, beaucoup**.

†*And what city would you like to live in?* Note that the speaker uses the conditional tense (*would like*) and direct word order to ask the question. This happens often in informal conversation.

‡To refer to the Pacific islands and Australia as a whole, the French use **l'Océanie** (*f.*).

**à** *to* or *in* **de** (**d'**) *from*

| | |
|---|---|
| Mlle Dupont habite **à Paris**. | *Mlle Dupont lives in Paris.* |
| Ils sont allés **à Cuba**. | *They went to Cuba.* |
| Ils sont **de Marseille**. | *They are from Marseille.* |
| Elles sont parties **d'Hawaï**. | *They left (from) Hawaii.* |

2. **Les pays.**
   a. **masculins.** With masculine countries:

**au** (**aux**) *to* or *in* **du** (**des**) *from*

| | |
|---|---|
| Les Doi habitent **au Japon.** | *The Doi family lives in Japan.* |
| Ils vont arriver **aux États-Unis** demain. | *They're going to arrive in the United States tomorrow.* |
| Es-tu jamais allé **au Mexique**? | *Have you ever been to Mexico?* |
| Quand sont-ils partis **des Pays-Bas**? | *When did they leave the Netherlands (Holland)?* |

   b. **féminins.** With feminine countries:

**en** *to* or *in* **de** (**d'**) *from*

| | |
|---|---|
| Je vais **en Belgique**. | *I'm going to Belgium.* |
| Il revient **de France**. | *He is coming back from France.* |

3. **Les continents.** With names of continents:

**en** *to* or *in* **de** (**d'**) *from*

| | |
|---|---|
| Le prof d'espagnol voyage **en Amérique du Sud**. | *The Spanish professor is traveling in South America.* |
| Il vient **d'Amérique du Nord**. | *He comes from North America.* |

4. **Les états et les régions.**
   a. **masculins.** With names of masculine states or regions*:

**Note**: Point out that the use of prepositions with the names of states in the U.S. varies. Usually, if the state is feminine, it is preceded by *en*. Masculine states beginning with a vowel or vowel sound take *en* and *de*. Otherwise, they are preceded by *au* and *du*. French speakers do not always agree on this point.

**dans le** (**dans l'**) *to* or *in* **du** (**de l'**) *from*

| | |
|---|---|
| Sophie a passé la semaine **dans le Nevada.** | *Sophie spent the week in Nevada.* |
| Elle vient **du Michigan**. | *She comes from Michigan.* |

   b. **féminins.** With names of feminine states or regions:

**en** *to* or *in* **de** (**d'**) *from*

| | |
|---|---|
| Pierre va passer un mois **en Californie.** | *Pierre is going to spend a month in California.* |
| M. Carter est **de Géorgie.** | *Mr. Carter is from Georgia.* |

*Exceptions: The French always say **au Texas**. To distinguish the states of New York and Washington from the cities of the same name, the French say **dans l'état de New York** (**Washington**).

## Vérifions!

**A. Jeu géographique.** Voici quelques villes francophones. Savez-vous dans quels pays elles se trouvent? (Voir les cartes au début du livre.)

MODÈLE: Paris est en France.

| | |
|---|---|
| 1. Rabat | a. Haïti |
| 2. Montréal | b. la Belgique |
| 3. Kinshasa | c. la Tunisie |
| 4. Alger | d. le Zaïre |
| 5. Dakar | e. le Canada |
| 6. Bruxelles | f. la Suisse |
| 7. Tunis | g. le Maroc |
| 8. Abidjan | h. la Côte-d'Ivoire |
| 9. Port-au-Prince | i. l'Algérie |
| 10. Genève | j. le Sénégal |

**Suggestion**: After modeling a few answers, have sts. do activities in pairs for maximum practice. Have sts. come back to whole group periodically to check their answers, or prepare written answer sheets to pass out for correction. If latter idea is used, have 3 sts. in a group, with one st. checking answers of other 2 against key. Sts. may take turns using answer key to monitor work of others.

**B. Retour de vacances.** Voici un groupe de touristes qui rentre de vacances. D'après ce qu'ils ont dans leurs valises, dites d'où ils arrivent.

MODÈLE: une montre
la Suisse → Ils arrivent de Suisse.

| SOUVENIRS | PAYS |
|---|---|
| 1. du parfum | le Cameroun |
| 2. une caméra vidéo ultra-moderne | la Hollande |
| 3. une bouteille de Tequila | l'Italie |
| 4. un masque d'initiation | le Mexique |
| 5. des chaussures en cuir (*leather*) | le Japon |
| 6. un pull en cashmere | l'Écosse |
| 7. du chocolat | le Maroc |
| 8. du café | la Colombie |
| 9. un couscoussier (*couscous maker*) | la Belgique |
| 10. des tulipes | la France |

**Continuation**: *des marrons glacés, des spaghettis, une statue des Pyramides, du whisky, du thé*

**Additional activity**: *Pendant son voyage, votre camarade vous envoie des cartes postales. D'où a-t-il/elle envoyé les cartes postales?* MODÈLE: *Afrique / Maroc* —Cette carte postale vient-elle d'Afrique? —Oui, il/elle a envoyé cette carte du Maroc. 1. *Asie / Japon* 2. *Amérique du Nord / Canada* 3. *Asie / Russie* 4. *Afrique / Égypte* 5. *Asie / Inde* 6. *Amérique du Sud / Brésil* 7. *Europe / Suisse*

## Parlons-en!

**A. Un(e) jeune globe-trotter.** Votre camarade va faire le tour du monde. Vous lui demandez où il/elle va aller.

**Continents:** l'Afrique, l'Océanie, l'Europe, l'Asie, l'Amérique du Nord, l'Amérique du Sud.

**Pays:** l'Algérie, l'Allemagne, l'Australie, le Brésil, le Canada, la Chine, le Danemark, l'Égypte, les États-Unis, la Finlande, la Grèce, l'Inde, l'Italie, le Japon, le Maroc, le Mexique, la Polynésie française, la Norvège, le Viêt-nam...

MODÈLE: —Vas-tu en Asie?
—Oui, je vais en Chine (au Japon... ).

**B. Interview.** Posez les questions à un(e) camarade de classe. Ensuite, racontez sa réponse la plus surprenante à la classe.

1. D'où viens-tu? de quelle ville? de quel état? Et tes parents?
2. Où habitent tes parents? Et le reste de ta famille?
3. Dans quels états as-tu voyagé?
4. Est-ce qu'il y a un état que tu préfères? Pourquoi?
5. Est-ce qu'il y a un état que tu n'aimes pas? Pourquoi?
6. Dans quel état est-ce qu'il y a de beaux parcs? de beaux lacs? de belles montagnes? de grandes villes? de grands déserts?
7. Tu es riche. Où vas-tu passer tes vacances?

**Suggestion**: Sts. ask questions and take brief notes on classmates' answers in order to report information. Ex. may be done in groups of three.

**Follow-up**: Each group reports information about states they come from and states they prefer. Answers are added up to answer final questions of activity.

## 28. EXPRESSING OBSERVATIONS AND BELIEFS
## *voir and croire*

### Où sont les clés?

MICHAËL: Je **crois** que* j'ai perdu les clés de la voiture.
VIRGINIE: Quoi!... Elles doivent être au restaurant.
MICHAËL: Tu **crois**?
VIRGINIE: Je ne suis pas sûre mais on peut aller **voir**.

(*Au restaurant.*)

MICHAËL: Tu as raison. Elles sont là-bas sur la table. Je les **vois**.
VIRGINIE: Ouf! Bon, qu'est-ce qu'on fait maintenant?
MICHAËL: On va **voir** la pyramide du Louvre.

Vrai ou faux?

1. Virginie croit que les clés sont au restaurant.
2. Michaël voit une plante sur la table.
3. Virginie et Michaël sont à Strasbourg.
4. Michaël veut voir la tour Eiffel.

The verbs **voir** (*to see*) and **croire** (*to believe*) are irregular.

| **voir** (*to see*) | | | | **croire** (*to believe*) | | | |
|---|---|---|---|---|---|---|---|
| je | **vois** | nous | **voyons** | je | **crois** | nous | **croyons** |
| tu | **vois** | vous | **voyez** | tu | **crois** | vous | **croyez** |
| il, elle, on | **voit** | ils, elles | **voient** | il, elle, on | **croit** | ils, elles | **croient** |
| *Past participle:* vu | | | | *Past participle:* cru | | | |

| | |
|---|---|
| J'**ai vu** Michèle à la plage la semaine passée. | *I saw Michèle at the beach last week.* |
| Est-ce que tu **crois** cette histoire? | *Do you believe this story?* |
| Je **crois** qu'il va faire beau demain. | *I think the weather is going to be fine tomorrow.* |
| —La capitale de l'Algérie, c'est Alger. | *Algeria's capital city is Algiers.* |
| —Tu **crois**? | *You think so?* / *Are you sure?* |

**Note**: *Croire que* will be treated later.

**Revoir** (*to see again*) is conjugated like **voir**.

| | |
|---|---|
| Je **revois** les Moreau au mois d'août. | *I'm seeing the Moreau family again in August.* |

**Croire à**[*] means *to believe in* a concept or idea.

| | |
|---|---|
| Nous **croyons à** la chance. | *We believe in luck.* |

## Vérifions!

**Alpinisme dans le brouillard** (*fog*). Complétez la conversation avec les verbes **croire** et **voir** au présent, sauf quand le passé composé est indiqué.

**Suggestion**: May be done in groups of 3 as a role-play activity.

JULIE: Tu _____[1] où on est?
ALAIN: Non, je ne _____[2] pas cette montagne sur la carte.
YVES: Vous faites confiance à cette vieille carte?
JULIE: Non, nous _____[3] ce que (*what*) nous a dit le guide.
ALAIN: Elle a beaucoup d'expérience et elle _____[4] que cette route est bonne.
YVES: Moi, je pense qu'elle _____[5] à la chance!
JULIE: Très drôle... mais dis, Alain, tu _____[6] (*passé composé*) Annick, le guide, quelque part?
ALAIN: Oui, j' _____[7] (*passé composé*) le guide, mais il y a environ une heure.
YVES: Cette fois, je _____[8] que nous sommes perdus!

## Parlons-en!

**Suggestion**: If sts. have not traveled recently, they may have to invent the trip.

**A. Conversation.** Avec un(e) camarade, parlez d'un voyage qu'il/elle a fait récemment. Qu'est-ce qu'il/elle a vu? Qui a-t-il/elle vu? Qu'est-ce qu'il/elle veut revoir? Qui veut-il/elle revoir? Ensuite, racontez à la classe l'expérience la plus intéressante (*most interesting*) de votre camarade.

**B. Interview.** Interrogez un(e) camarade sur ses croyances. Est-ce qu'il/elle croit à la chance? à l'amour? au progrès? à une religion? à la perception extra-sensorielle? aux O.V.N.I. (*UFO*)? à _____?... Après l'interview, essayez de

**Suggestion**: Ask sts. to prepare a list of their beliefs in order to help conversation flow more smoothly.

[*]An exception is the expression **croire en Dieu**, *to believe in God*.

définir la personnalité de votre camarade d'après ses réponses. Est-ce qu'il/elle est sceptique? idéaliste? religieux/euse? réaliste? sentimental(e)? superstitieux/euse?

**Follow-up**: Ask sts. to volunteer to describe the beliefs of a classmate.

# Mise au point

**A. Vacances d'été.** Formez des phrases complètes selon les indications.

MARC: où / passer / tu / vacances d'été? (*passé composé*)
PAULE: je / voyager / à la Guadeloupe avec mes parents (*passé composé*). nous / camper / et / prendre le soleil (*passé composé*) / pendant quatre semaines
MARC: nager / vous / beaucoup? (*passé composé*)
PAULE: oui, il y a / plages magnifiques / et / climat / tropical. la Guadeloupe / être / vraiment / beau (*présent*)
MARC: manger / vous / bien? (*passé composé*)
PAULE: oui, / nous / manger / petit / restaurants / et nous / essayer / plats créoles (*passé composé*)

Maintenant, décrivez les vacances de Paule.

- Est-ce qu'elle a passé des vacances superbes ou ennuyeuses?
- Où est-ce qu'elle a dormi?
- Qu'est-ce qui l'a impressionnée le plus?

**Suggestion**: Sts. write out and perform dialogue in pairs.

**Additional activity**: *En français, s'il vous plaît.*
CORINNE: *Two days ago, I met Greg, an American. I'm going out with him (avec lui) this evening.*
SYLVIE: *Oh, how long has he been in Paris?*
CORINNE: *Three days, but he's been traveling in France for four weeks.*
SYLVIE: *You know (Tu sais), I lived in Chicago for a year.*
CORINNE: *How long did you spend in the United States, in all (en tout)?*
SYLVIE: *Two years. I left the United States in 1990. I would like (J'aimerais) to meet a young American.*
CORINNE: *I'm going to ask Greg if he has a friend.*
SYLVIE: *Thank you, Corinne!*

**B. Vos vacances.** Interviewez un(e) camarade sur ses vacances les plus (*the most*) intéressantes. Posez les questions suivantes et encore d'autres de votre invention. Puis décrivez ses vacances à la classe.

1. Où as-tu passé tes vacances les plus intéressantes?
2. Avec qui as-tu voyagé?
3. Combien de temps as-tu passé à cet endroit?
4. Où as-tu logé (*stay*)?
5. Qu'est-ce que tu as fait pendant la journée?
6. Quel temps a-t-il fait?
7. Qu'est-ce que tu as porté comme vêtements?
8. Qu'est-ce que tu as acheté?
9. Qu'est-ce que tu ne vas pas oublier?
10. As-tu envie de retourner au même endroit l'année prochaine (*next*)?

**Suggestions**: (1) Sts. share responses with class. (2) Have sts. write short composition, using questions as guide. Collect and use for dictation or listening comp.

**C. Vacances exotiques au Club Med.** Vous allez passer une semaine de vacances au Club Med en Martinique.* Voici la brochure du village où vous allez.

**Follow-up**: Talk about *la Guadeloupe et Haïti* as well. You may wish to mention *la Polynésie française* (*l'Océanie*) too.

*Note that French speakers say both **à la Martinique** and **en Martinique**.

## MARTINIQUE

# les Boucaniers

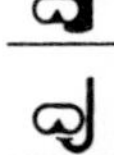

TOUS LES PLAISIRS DE LA MER DES CARAIBES. COULEURS ET PARFUMS DES TROPIQUES.
RYTHMES DE LA "BIGUINE" ET DOUCEUR DU PARLER CREOLE.

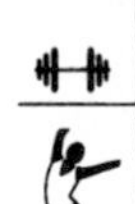

**VILLAGE**
Au sud de la Martinique, à proximité de Sainte-Anne, un village aux teintes pastel entre une vaste cocoteraie et une plage de sable clair. Bungalows climatisés à 2 lits avec salle d'eau. Voltage : 220.

**SPORTS**
Voile : 10 Holders, 1 Laser, 1 Mentor. Ski nautique : 4 bateaux. Plongée bouteille : école d'initiation et de perfectionnement. Plongée libre. Planche à voile Tiga : 15 Fun Cup, 7 Speed, 5 Swift, 3 Jibe. Promenades en mer et pique-niques. Tennis : 7 courts en dur dont 6 éclairés. Basket-ball. Volley-ball. Salle de musculation et mise en forme. Aérobic.

**ET AUSSI...**
Spécialites à la "Maison créole". Boutique Club. Location de voitures. Enfants à partir de 12 ans.

**EXCURSIONS**
Un programme varié d'excursions vous sera proposé sur place.
C.M. - Les Boucaniers -
97227 Pointe Marin - Sainte-Anne - Tél. 596.76.74.52.

1. Quel est le nom du village? 2. Où allez-vous loger? 3. Essayez d'identifier quelles activités représentent les dessins. 4. Quelles activités aimeriez-vous faire?

Imaginez maintenant que vous venez de rentrer de vacances. Décrivez vos vacances à la classe. Commencez par «J'ai passé une semaine en Martinique...».

**Suggestion**: Have sts. tell about their vacation in small groups.

**Suggestions:** vêtements, temps, sports, ambiance, repas, jeux...

## Interactions

In this chapter you practiced talking about vacations, about events in the past, about various geographical locations, and about observations and beliefs. Act out the following situations, using vocabulary and structures from this chapter.

**Additional activity**: *Vous avez économisé assez d'argent pour passer une semaine au Club Méditerranée. Faites vos réservations. Vous téléphonez au représentant local de Club Med qui ne parle pas anglais. Jouez la scène avec un(e) camarade. Demandez quels sports et activités sont inclus.*

1. **En vacances.** You are planning a vacation. Visit a travel agent (your partner). Explain what type of vacation you would like to take and discuss some alternative holiday destinations. Talk about the activities that interest you. The agent will recommend an itinerary and explain why.
2. **Qu'est-ce que j'ai fait?** Think of something you did last evening. Your partner will ask you yes/no questions, to guess what it was. Then exchange roles.

# Rencontres

## LECTURE

### *Avant de lire*

**Reading for global understanding:** The poll (**une enquête**) on pages 226–227 was published in a French women's fitness magazine, *Vital*. It has been abridged and glosses have been added, but it has not been simplified. Your goal as you read through it should be simply to understand as much as you can, without looking words up in the dictionary. Use the strategies you learned in the preceding chapters. Look for cognates. Read for the gist of each question; you do not need to understand every word. Develop your guessing skills; you will use them often, whenever you read in French.

In particular, the following strategies may help.

- If you don't understand something, read ahead. What follows will often clarify an unfamiliar word or phrase. In this poll, the proposed answers will often tell you what the question is about, or the final answer may make clear what the preceding ones were.
- Think about what you expect the question to be, on the basis of your knowledge of the magazine and the interests of its readers: fitness, sports, diet, well-being.
- Skip questions that you really don't understand. You can figure them out later, during class discussion, or with a classmate.

After your first reading, go back and answer as many questions as you can, on the basis of one of your vacations. Skip questions that do not apply to you. Remember that this poll was written for women; you may need to make certain changes if you are a man.

**Note**: You may wish to have sts. give the masculine form of the adjectives before doing the questionnaire.

—En vacances, j'adore faire du vélo sur les petites routes de campagne.

# RACONTEZ VOUS VOS

**En répondant à ce questionnaire, vous allez pouvoir tester vos vacances, tranquillement, sans vous raconter d'histoires. Et savoir si elles ont bien rempli la mission pour laquelle elles sont faites : vous faire vivre[a] un mois, au plus près du bonheur.[b]**

**1 Avez-vous pris des vacances cet été ?**
oui
non

**2 Combien de temps aurez-vous pris cet été ?**
Moins d'une semaine
1 semaine
2 semaines
3 semaines
1 mois
plus d'un mois
c'était suffisant
ce n'était pas assez

**3 Etes-vous encore[c] en vacances en ce moment ?**
oui
non

**4 Etes-vous restée[d] au même endroit pendant toutes vos vacances ?**
oui
non

**5 Si oui, où ?**

| | |
|---|---|
| Mer | en France |
| Montagne | en France |
| Campagne | en France |
| Ville | en France |
| Mer | A l'étranger |
| Montagne | A l'étranger |
| Campagne | A l'étranger |
| Ville | A l'étranger |
| Désert | |
| Pleine mer | |

**6 Si non, pourquoi et comment ?**
*(Précisez-nous s'il s'agissait d'une décision (ne jamais rester au même endroit), d'une obligation (famille, enfants, opportunités), ou bien d'un périple (itinéraire culturel, aventurier, amical, autres...)*

________________________

________________________

________________________

**7 Ces vacances étaient[e] :**
les mêmes que celles de l'an passé
les mêmes que celles de chaque année
différentes
une innovation

**8 Vos vacances, cette année, ont été :**
parfaites
plutôt réussies
un petit peu ratées
décevantes
mieux que celles de l'année dernière
moins bien que celles de l'année dernière
les mêmes

**9 Est-ce vous qui avez décidées ces vacances, lieu, timing, activité ?**
oui
non

**10 Les avez-vous préparées longtemps à l'avance ?**
non
oui
oui, depuis quand ?

**11 Avez-vous vécu :**
dans une maison
dans un hôtel
sous une tente
à la belle étoile
sur un bateau
dans un club
entre deux aéroports et quelques six étoiles
chez des copains

**12 Etiez-vous :**
seule
seule avec lui
avec lui et les enfants
avec les enfants
avec vos parents
dans votre famille
avec des ami (e) s

**13 Avez-vous découvert cette année un endroit dont vous êtes tombé amoureux[f] au point :**
d'y revenir l'année prochain..oui..non
d'avoir envie d'y acheter une maison oui non
d'avoir envie d'y vivre.. oui ..non

**14 La dominante de ces vacances :**

| | |
|---|---|
| Le repos | Les enfants |
| Le sport | L'amour |
| La convivialité | L'aventure |
| La lecture | La réflexion |

La culture (festivals, châteaux, musées...)
Les souvenirs d'enfance
Les affaires (contacts et recontacts)

**15 Après ces vacances, quoi de neuf[g] ?**

| | |
|---|---|
| Du tonus | De la santé |
| De la beauté | De la lucidité |
| Des sentiments | Rien |
| Un cerveau clair | |

**16 Pendant les vacances, avez-vous ?**
minci de...kilos
grossi de...kilos
vous êtes restée stable

**17 Pendant ces vacances, avez-vous ?**
ri[h] tout le temps
bien ri
assez peu ri

**18 En vacances, éprouvez-vous plus que dans l'année un sentiment de :**

| | |
|---|---|
| liberté | beauté |
| santé | bien-être |
| séduction | sensualité |
| dynamisme | vérité |

**19 En rentrant[i] de vacances, vous vous estimez :**
plus jolie
plus performante
plus drôle
plus chaleureuse
plus indulgente
plus détendue
plus amoureuse
plus paisible
plus proche des autres

**20 En vacances, vous avez mangé :**

| | |
|---|---|
| plus léger[j] | plus savoureux |
| plus lourd[k] | plus rigolo |
| plus arrosé | comme d'habitude |

[a] *live*
[b] *happiness*
[c] *still*
[d] Êtes... *Did you stay . . . ?*
[e] *were*
[f] êtes... *fell in love*
[g] quoi... *what's new?*
[h] *laugh*
[i] En... *Coming back*
[j] *light*
[k] *heavy*

# VACANCES

**21 Vous avez, en particulier, forcé sur :**
le poisson, les fruits de mer
les crudités
les fruits
les produits laitiers
le pain
autre chose, quoi ?

**22 Vous avez fait :**
trois repas à horaire fixe
des grignotages suivant l'humeur
un grand petit déjeuner et un dîner
des variations chaque jour

**23 En vacances, vous avez :**
plus faim que pendant l'année
moins faim
le même appétit que d'habitude

**24 Avez-vous dormi**
plus que d'habitude
moins que d'habitude
mieux[l] que d'habitude
comme d'habitude

**25 Pendant ces vacances, avez-vous :**
fait quelque chose que vous n'aviez jamais fait[m] et quoi ?
oui
non
quoi

**26 Avez-vous :**
lu[n] — joué au tennis
nagé — joué au volley
couru — joué au golf
dansé — écrit
fait de la planche à voile
du dériveur
du gros bateau
du deltaplane
de l'escalade
de la marche
joué de la musique
écouté de la musique
brodé
fait de la cuisine

**27 Avez-vous fait la sieste ?**
oui
non

**28 Si vous fumez,[o] avez-vous :**
moins fumé ? — autant ?
davantage ? — vous avez arrêté ?

**29 Pendant ces vacances, avez-vous rencontré :**
un monsieur formidable
une fille sympa
des gens merveilleux

**30 Quelle somme faudrait-il vous donner pour que vous acceptiez l'année prochaine de renoncer à vos vacances d'été ?**

**31 A votre avis, ce qui gâche[p] le plus sûrement les vacances :**
le mauvais temps — la foule
la mauvaise humeur — la solitude
le manque de sous — la monotonie
la promiscuité — les accidents
l'idée de la rentrée — quoi d'autre
les embouteillages

**32 Lorsque vous rentrez de vacances, vous êtes pleine[q] :**
de projets — de désirs
de regrets — de souvenirs

**33 Le plus important en vacances :**
c'est le soleil
c'est d'être amoureuse
c'est d'être bien avec ceux qu'on aime
c'est d'avoir la paix
c'est d'avoir le temps

**34 Attribuez une note de 0 à 20 aux vacances que vous venez de vivre :**

**35 Une bonne fée[r] vous offre les vacances idéales. Racontez :**

______________________
______________________
______________________

On trouve des paysages fantastiques dans les Alpes.

**—Pourquoi sont-ils tous partis en même temps que nous?** (Tetsu)

[l] *better*
[m] n'aviez... *had never done*
[n] *read*
[o] *smoke*
[p] *ruins*
[q] *full*
[r] *fairy*

## Compréhension

Comparez vos réponses avec celles de vos camarades.

1. Qui a donné la meilleure (*best*) note à ses vacances?
2. Où sont allés (*went*) les étudiants qui sont restés aux États-Unis? Quels pays ont visités les étudiants qui ont voyagé à l'étranger (*abroad*)?
3. Quel type de logement a été le plus populaire parmi vos camarades?
4. Qu'est-ce que vos camarades ont fait pendant leurs vacances?
5. Y a-t-il eu une réponse que vous avez trouvée particulièrement intéressante? surprenante? bizarre? amusante?

## PAR ÉCRIT

**Function:** Narrating in the past
**Audience:** Friends
**Goal:** Write a story about a disastrous vacation (**des vacances désastreuses**) that you experienced, or invent such a situation. Use the techniques described below.

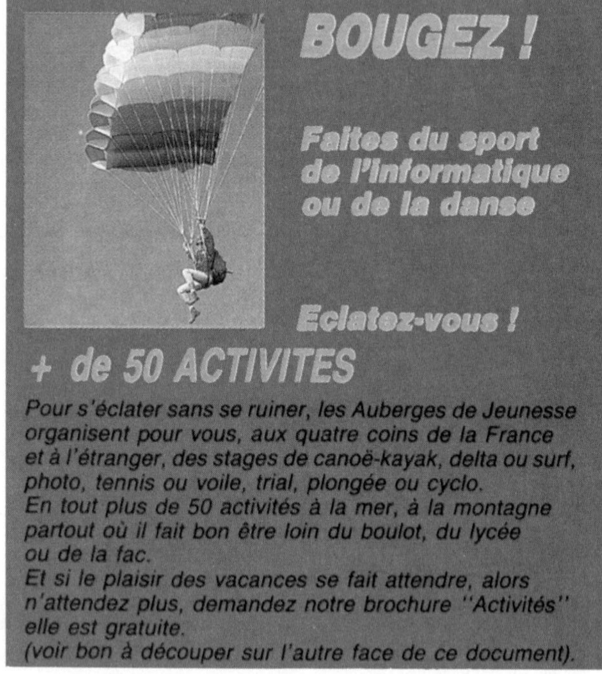


**Steps**

1. Do an outline of your story.
   a. Begin by setting the scene. Describe who was with you, where you were, and the general circumstances.
   b. Outline the complications that affected your plans.
   c. Explain your reactions, and those of your companions, to the adverse circumstances.
   d. Describe how the vacation ended and how the difficulties were resolved.
2. After completing the outline, fill in any details and prepare the first draft.
3. Have a classmate reread the draft to see if what you've written is clear.
4. Finally, make any changes suggested by your classmate that seem warranted and check the draft for spelling, punctuation, and grammar errors. Focus especially on your use of the past tense with **avoir**.

## À L'ÉCOUTE!

**I. Souvenirs de vacances.** This is the first day of class at the **Université de Nice**. Sandrine and Jean-Yves are talking about their vacations. First, read through the activities. Next, listen to the vocabulary followed by the conversation. Then, do the activities.

VOCABULAIRE UTILE
quinze jours *two weeks*
essayer *to try*
j'ai aussi rencontré *I also met*

You will now hear their conversation, followed by a few statements about it. Listen carefully, then do the exercises.

**A. Vrai ou faux?**

1. _____ Jean-Yves a passé du temps à la campagne.
2. _____ Jean-Yves a trouvé très nerveux les gens de campagne.
3. _____ Jean-Yves a fait du sport.
4. _____ Sandrine a passé un mois avec des amis.
5. _____ Sandrine a fait de la planche à voile, mais elle a eu peur.
6. _____ Sandrine a fait du bateau.

**B.** Now determine who could have made the following statements. Mark **S** for Sandrine and **J-Y** for Jean-Yves.

1. _____ Cette année j'ai pris deux semaines de vacances.
2. _____ J'ai rendu visite à ma grand-mère.
3. _____ J'ai beaucoup dormi.
4. _____ J'ai passé des heures au soleil.
5. _____ J'ai loué un bateau.
6. _____ J'ai marché sur la plage.

**II. Géopari**. "Géopari" is a radio quiz show where the contestant is asked questions about geography. First, look at the activity. Next, listen to the vocabulary followed by the conversation. Then, do the activity.

VOCABULAIRE UTILE
se trouve *is (located)*
désolé *sorry*
la plage d'Ipanéma *a beach in Brazil*
dommage *too bad*
vous gagnez *you win*

Circle the correct answer.

1. La ville d'Oslo se trouve
   a. en Suède b. en Belgique c. en Norvège
2. La Maison-Blanche se trouve
   a. aux États-Unis b. au Brésil c. en Suisse
3. Le Taj Mahāl se trouve
   a. au Maroc b. en Inde c. en Chine
4. La plage d'Ipanéma se trouve
   a. à Rio de Janeiro b. à São Paulo c à Brasília

**À l'écoute!** See scripts for listening passages and follow-up activities recorded on student cassette. Remind students that in the listening comprehension passages (as in real life) they will not understand every word they hear. They should focus globally on the general information in the passages and not be overly concerned about what they do not understand.

# Vocabulaire

## Verbes

**bronzer** to get a suntan
**croire** to believe
  **croire à** (**que**) to believe in (that)
**devenir** to become
**dormir** to sleep
**fermer** to close
**fumer** to smoke
**mettre** to put on; to place
**nager** to swim
**obtenir** to obtain, get
**oublier** to forget
**partir** (**à**) (**de**) leave (for) (from)
**pêcher** to fish
**pleuvoir** to rain
**quitter** to leave (someone or someplace)
**revenir** to come back to, return (someplace)
**revoir** to see again
**sentir** to feel; to sense; to smell
**servir** to serve
**sortir** to leave; to go out
**venir** to come
  **venir de** + *inf.* to have just (*done something*)
**voir** to see
**voyager** to travel

**À REVOIR:** porter, pouvoir, rendre visite à, réserver, rester

## Substantifs

**l'achat** (*m.*) purchase
**l'alpinisme** (*m.*) mountaineering
**l'an** (*m.*) year
**l'année** (*f.*) year
**le bateau** (**à voile**) (sail)boat
**la bicyclette** bicycle
  **faire de la...** to go bicycling
**la campagne** country(side)
**le camping** camping
**le cheval** horse
  **faire du...** to go horseback riding
**la clé, clef** key
**l'endroit** (*m.*) place
**l'état** (*m.*) state
**le fleuve** (large) river
**la forêt** forest
**le lac** lake
**la matinée** morning
**la mer** sea, ocean
**le mois** month
**le monde** world
**la montagne** mountain
**la nuit** night
**le parapluie** umbrella
**le pays** country (nation)
**la plage** beach
**la planche à voile** windsurfer
**la plongée sous-marine** skin diving
**la randonnée** hike
**la route** road
**la semaine** week
**le ski de piste** downhill skiing
  **...de fond** cross-country skiing
  **...nautique** waterskiing
**la soirée** evening
**le/la voisin(e)** neighbor

**À REVOIR:** la carte postale, la promenade, les vacances (*f. pl.*)

## Les vêtements et l'équipement sportifs

**l'anorak** (*m.*) (ski) jacket
**les chaussures** (*f.*) **de ski** ski boots
  **...de montagne** hiking boots
**les lunettes** (*f.*) glasses
  **...de ski** ski goggles
  **...de soleil** sunglasses
**le sac de couchage** sleeping bag
**la serviette de plage** beach towel
**le ski** ski
**la tente** tent

**À REVOIR:** la chaussure, le maillot de bain, la robe, le sac à dos

## Expressions temporelles

**les années** (**cinquante**) the decade (era) of (the fifties)
**avant-hier** the day before yesterday
**depuis** since, for
**dernier/ière** last
**hier** yesterday
**il y a** ago
**passé**(**e**) last

## Pays

**l'Algérie** (*f.*) Algeria
**l'Allemagne** (*f.*) Germany
**l'Angleterre** (*f.*) England
**la Belgique** Belgium
**le Brésil** Brazil
**le Canada** Canada
**la Chine** China
**le Congo** Congo
**la Côte-d'Ivoire** Ivory Coast
**l'Espagne** (*f.*) Spain
**les États-Unis** (*m.*) United States
**la France** France
**la Grèce** Greece
**Haïti** (*m.*) Haiti
**l'Italie** (*f.*) Italy
**le Japon** Japan
**le Maroc** Morocco
**le Mexique** Mexico
**le Portugal** Portugal
**le Québec** Quebec
**la Russie** Russia
**le Sénégal** Senegal
**la Suisse** Switzerland
**la Tunisie** Tunisia
**le Zaïre** Zaire

# Intermède

## SITUATION

### Une nuit à l'auberge de jeunesse

**Situation**: The *Situation* dialogues are recorded on the st. cassette packaged with the st. text.

**Contexte** *Sean fait un voyage en France depuis deux mois et il dort chaque nuit dans une auberge de jeunesse. L'avantage? Les auberges sont souvent situées près d'une gare,° elles ne coûtent pas cher et l'ambiance° y est très sympathique. Ici, Sean arrive à l'Auberge de Jeunesse de Caen, en Normandie.*

*train station / atmosphere*

**Objectif** *Sean réserve une place à l'auberge.*

SEAN: Bonjour, Madame, est-ce que vous avez encore de la place?
LA DAME: Oui, il y a de la place dans le petit dortoir.° *sleeping quarters (dormitory)*
SEAN: Ça fait combien, pour une nuit? J'ai une carte° de l'American Youth Hostels... *(membership) card*
LA DAME: Alors, quarante-cinq francs. Vous avez besoin de draps°? *sheets*
SEAN: Non, j'ai mon sac de couchage.
LA DAME: Nous ne servons pas de repas chauds, mais il y a une petite cuisine au rez-de-chaussée.
SEAN: Eh bien, c'est d'accord. Voici quarante-cinq francs.
LA DAME: Merci. Ah, faites bien attention: l'auberge ferme° à vingt-deux heures. Ne rentrez° pas trop tard! *closes* / *return*

## À propos

### Comment choisir une chambre d'hôtel

Je voudrais une chambre pour deux personnes / une chambre à deux lits, s'il vous plaît.
Combien coûte la chambre? / Quel est le prix de la chambre?
Est-ce que le petit déjeuner est compris?
Est-ce qu'il y a une salle de bains dans la chambre?
Est-ce que vous prenez les cartes de crédit / les chèques de voyage?

### *Maintenant à vous!*

**A. Questions personnelles.** Relisez le dialogue, puis répondez aux questions.

1. Avez-vous déjà passé la nuit dans une auberge de jeunesse? Où? D'habitude, où dormez-vous quand vous êtes en voyage?

2. Aimez-vous dormir à la belle étoile? Quels en sont les avantages? les inconvénients? Préférez-vous le camping sauvage ou les terrains de camping (avec douche!)?
3. De quoi a-t-on besoin pour faire du camping? Avez-vous tout le nécessaire? Qu'est-ce que vous devez encore acheter?
4. Descendez-vous de temps en temps dans un hôtel ou motel? Parlez de votre dernier séjour (*stay*) dans un hôtel. Avez-vous bien dormi? Pourquoi (pas)?

**B. Jeu de rôles: Des vacances à Paris.** Avec deux camarades, préparez la scène suivante. Utilisez les expressions de l'*À Propos*. Puis jouez la scène devant la classe.

Vous entrez dans un hôtel de luxe. Vous demandez au/à la réceptionniste une chambre pour une personne. Vous demandez des renseignements sur la chambre. Le réceptionniste vous demande votre nom, adresse, etc. Vous voulez votre petit déjeuner au lit et vous précisez ce que vous désirez.

## PORTRAITS

### *Paul Gauguin (1848–1903)*

Paul Gauguin is one of modern France's most important painters. Originally employed as a stockbroker, he abandoned his profession in 1883 to devote himself exclusively to painting. He left urban civilization behind to paint peasant life in Brittany, and later discovered the brilliant colors of the tropics on Martinique. He finally settled in Tahiti, where he represented the statuesque nobility of the native people in a series of elegant yet simple paintings. Gauguin's painting exploits the expressive power of line and large areas of bright color, a style that influenced such 20th-century painters as Modigliani and Picasso.

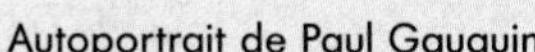

Autoportrait de Paul Gauguin

CHAPITRE **NEUF**

# Voyages et transports

**En avant**

—À quelle heure part ton train pour Marseille?
—À 19h30.
—Si tu veux, je peux te conduire à la gare.
—À cette heure-là? Avec toute la circulation? Non, je vais prendre le métro, il y en a un toutes les cinq minutes.

**Communicative goals:** talking about transportation, talking about the past, expressing wishes and polite requests, and expressing negation.

**En avant**: See scripts for follow-up questions recorded on student cassette.

# Étude de vocabulaire

## Visitez le monde en avion

### À l'aéroport

**A. Bienvenue à bord.** Complétez les phrases d'après le dessin.

1. Si on fume, on veut un siège (*seat*) dans la _____.
2. Le _____ est le conducteur de l'avion.
3. L'_____ apporte les repas.
4. Les personnes très riches voyagent en _____.
5. Quand on est dans la _____, on ne peut pas fumer.
6. Le _____ sert les boissons.
7. On présente une _____ pour monter dans l'avion.
8. Les hommes et les femmes d'affaires voyagent en _____.
9. Les étudiants voyagent en _____.
10. Le _____ 512 part à 13h50.

**B. Quelques pays européens et leurs capitales.** Quel pays trouve-t-on _____? Quelle est sa capitale? (Regardez la carte géographique de l'Europe au début de ce livre.)

**Suggestion**: Use the world map or map of Europe at the beginning of *Rendez-vous* to have sts. point out the countries mentioned.

MODÈLE: au sud-est* de l'Italie →
Au sud-est de l'Italie, on trouve la Grèce. Capitale: Athènes.

*In the words **est** (*east*), **ouest** (*west*), and **sud** (*south*), the final letters are pronounced, i.e., [est], [west], [syd].

| PAYS | CAPITALES |
|---|---|
| 1. au nord-est de l'Espagne | Londres |
| 2. à l'est de la Belgique | Madrid |
| 3. au sud-ouest de la France | Bruxelles |
| 4. à l'ouest de l'Espagne | Berne |
| 5. au nord-ouest de la France | Berlin |
| 6. au sud-est de la France | Rome |
| 7. au nord de l'Italie | Lisbonne |
| 8. au nord de la France | Paris |

**Suggestions**: (1) May be done as whole-class or small-group activity. (2) It may be useful to have sts. fill in names of countries guessed on a blank map.

**Answers**: 1. *France: Paris* 2. *Allemagne: Berlin* 3. *Espagne: Madrid* 4. *Portugal: Lisbonne* 5. *Angleterre: Londres* 6. *Italie: Rome* 7. *Suisse: Berne* 8. *Belgique: Bruxelles*

**C. Devinez!** Maintenant, un(e) de vos camarades décrit la situation géographique d'un pays étranger qu'il/elle a visité (*has visited*) ou d'un pays étranger visité par un ami ou un parent. Essayez de deviner le pays. Puis donnez le nom d'une ville de ce pays.

MODÈLE: VOTRE CAMARADE: Ma cousine Betty a visité un pays au nord-ouest de l'Italie.
VOUS: Ta cousine a-t-elle visité la France?
VOTRE CAMARADE: C'est exact. Elle a visité Lille.

**Voici quelques possibilités:** l'Irlande, l'Écosse (*Scotland*), le Danemark, la Suède, l'Autriche (*Austria*), la Grèce, l'Égypte, l'Afrique du Sud, le Zaïre, Israël, la Jordanie, l'Arabie Saoudite, l'Iran, l'Australie, l'Argentine, le Venezuela, le Nicaragua

## L'Europe en train

### À la gare

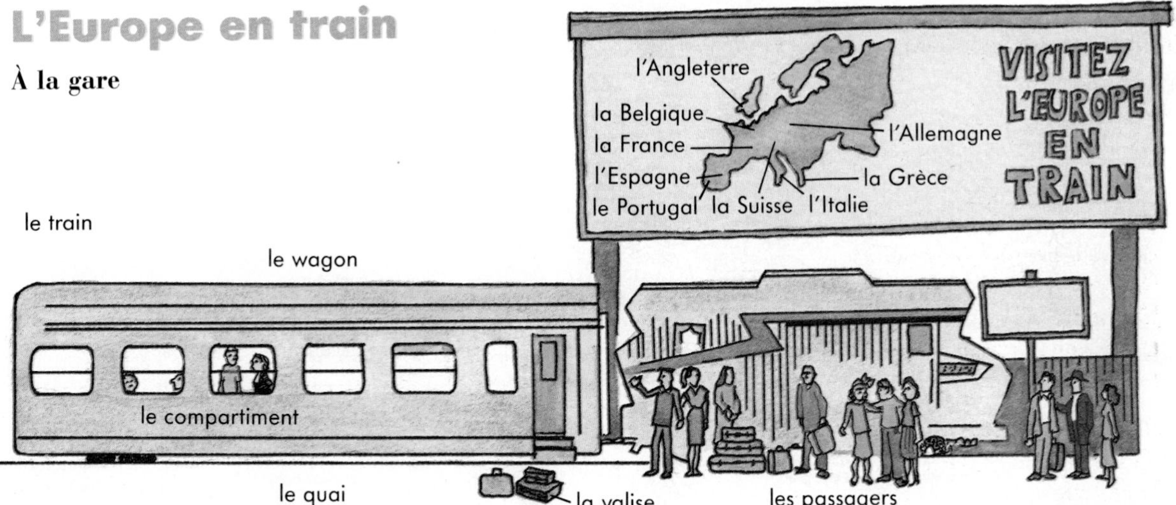


**Additional vocab.**: *le couloir, un wagon-lit, un wagon-restaurant, une voiture-couchettes, un buffet, un billet aller simple, un billet aller-retour, le TGV, réserver des places*

**A. Définitions**

1. Quel véhicule de transport trouve-t-on dans une gare?
2. Comment s'appelle chaque voiture d'un train?
3. Comment s'appellent les personnes qui voyagent?

4. Comment s'appelle la partie du wagon où les passagers sont assis (*seated*)?
5. Où est-ce que les passagers attendent l'arrivée d'un train?

**Follow-up**: Have sts. create simple definitions of vocab. in drawings. Example: *Ce sont les personnes qui voyagent.* (*passengers*) This can also be done in small groups, with each st. receiving a 3 × 5 card with a word he or she is to define for others who try to identify word.

**B. Trains/autos accompagnées.** Pour partir en vacances, beaucoup de Français prennent le train. Lisez la publicité de la SNCF (Société Nationale des Chemins de Fer) puis répondez aux questions.

1. Quel service propose cette publicité?
2. Où se trouve le «coffre» d'une voiture? À quoi sert-il (*What is it for*)?
3. Quel autre véhicule peut-on transporter en train?
4. Comment sont les compartiments?
5. Est-ce que le petit déjeuner est compris dans le prix du voyage?
6. Combien de temps après l'arrivée retrouve-t-on sa voiture?

SNCF

TRAINS AUTOS ACCOMPAGNÉES

1 Chez vous ; le coffre est chargé : plus de souci de valises jusqu'à l'arrivée.

2 Vous arrivez tranquillement à la gare de chargement, vous avez jusqu'à 20 h 15 pour remettre votre voiture ou votre moto

3 Le compartiment est climatisé, la couchette est confortable, vous vous glissez dans vos draps.

4 C'est le plein sommeil, le train roule, votre voiture ou votre moto vous suit.

5 7 h 45 : vous descendez du train ; le petit déjeuner vous attend, il est gratuit.

6 8 h 30 : en forme, vous retrouvez votre voiture ou votre moto. Bonne route !

Un exemple : Paris - Saint-Raphaël.

**Suggestion** (C): Have sts. take notes on partners' answers and report orally or in writing.

**C. Interview.** Demandez à un(e) camarade s'il (si elle) a voyagé en train. A-t-il/elle mangé dans un wagon-restaurant? A-t-il/elle dormi dans un wagon-lit? Quelle ville a-t-il/elle visitée pendant ce voyage? À qui a-t-il/elle rendu visite? Ensuite, racontez à la classe le voyage de votre camarade.

# En route

Jean-Pierre **conduit** sa moto dans les Alpes.

Annick **roule** toujours très vite. Elle a une voiture de sport toute neuve!

Marianne **fait le plein** d'essence à la station-service.

Martine et Annie **traversent** la France en vélo.

**A. Associations.** Quels adjectifs associez-vous avec les moyens de transport suivants? Expliquez les raisons de votre choix.

**Point out**: One says: *en voiture, en autobus, en taxi, à pied, à bicyclette, en métro, par le train, monter dans..., descendre de...*

| | | |
|---|---|---|
| 1. l'avion | a. lent | m. polluant |
| 2. le bateau | b. cher | n. agréable |
| 3. l'autobus | c. rapide | o. monotone |
| 4. la voiture | d. bruyant (*noisy*) | p. luxueux |
| 5. le train | e. dangereux | |
| 6. le camion (*truck*) | f. amusant | |
| 7. le taxi | g. fatigant (*tiring*) | |
| 8. la moto | h. confortable | |
| 9. l'ambulance | i. sûr (*safe*) | |
| 10. l'hélicoptère | j. économique | |
| 11. le métro | k. silencieux | |
| 12. le vélo | l. pratique | |

**B. Moyens de transport.** Quel véhicule conduit-on dans les situations suivantes?

1. Votre famille déménage (*moves*). 2. La classe fait une excursion. 3. Vous êtes sportif/ive. 4. Vous aimez rouler très vite. 5. Vous passez le week-end avec votre famille. 6. Vous arrivez à l'aéroport d'une ville. 7. Vous voulez faire de l'exercice. 8. Quand vous faites le plein, vous payez très peu.

**C. Interview.** Posez les questions suivantes à un(e) camarade.

1. Comment préfères-tu voyager en vacances? Pourquoi? Est-ce que ça dépend de ta destination?
2. Quels moyens de transport préfères-tu prendre en ville?
3. À ton avis, quel moyen de transport est très économique? très rapide? très dangereux? très polluant? très agréable? Quels problèmes de transport y a-t-il dans ta ville ou dans ta région?

# Pour parler de la conduite: le verbe conduire

**Suggestion**: Model pronunciation of *je* and *nous* forms of *conduire*. Encourage answers in short sentences.

| PRESENT TENSE OF **conduire** (*to drive*) | | | |
|---|---|---|---|
| je | condu**is** | nous | condu**isons** |
| tu | condu**is** | vous | condu**isez** |
| il, elle, on | condu**it** | ils, elles | condu**isent** |
| *Past participle:* conduit | | | |

All verbs ending in **-uire** are conjugated like **conduire**.

**Additional verbs**: *produire* (*to produce*), *réduire* (*to reduce*)

| | | |
|---|---|---|
| **construire** | *to construct* | Nous **construisons** une nouvelle ville. |
| **détruire** | *to destroy* | On **détruit** le vieux pour construire du neuf. |
| **traduire** | *to translate* | **Traduis** cette brochure en espagnol. |

**Interview.** Posez les questions suivantes à un(e) camarade de classe. Ensuite, rapportez le fait le plus intéressant à la classe. Utilisez également les expressions de la page 237.

**Suggestion**: Have sts. ask questions in pairs and have a few report answers. As a whole-group activity, sts. ask instructor similar questions.

1. Conduis-tu souvent? Quand tu sors avec des copains (= amis), conduisez-vous ou utilisez-vous les transports en commun?
2. Dans ta famille, qui conduit le plus souvent? Qui ne conduit pas?
3. Aimes-tu conduire? Quelle marque de voiture préfères-tu? Pourquoi? Préfères-tu les voitures américaines ou les voitures fabriquées à l'étranger (*abroad*)?
4. Penses-tu que les voitures détruisent les grandes villes? Est-ce qu'on construit trop d'autoroutes aux États-Unis?
5. Que penses-tu des motos? des bicyclettes?
6. As-tu jamais traversé les États-Unis (ou ton état) en voiture? Quand? Avec qui?

# France-culture

Suggestion: Ask sts. to compare and contrast train systems in the U.S. and France.

*Trains.* Trains are an important form of transportation, much more popular in France than in the United States. Since 1938, French railroads have been controlled by the **Société Nationale des Chemins de Fer français** (**SNCF**), a government-regulated monopoly. You will find the train system to be the most economical and convenient form of transportation in France. Here are some points to keep in mind.

- For long trips, it is possible to reserve a seat or a berth (**couchette**) in a sleeping compartment. If the station seems crowded, or if you are traveling during a French vacation time, be sure to make such a reservation at the ticket window.
- On the door of each train compartment there is a notice that indicates if the seats inside are reserved. If you cannot find an unreserved seat or if you have reserved a seat in advance, seek help from the conductor taking tickets.
- On the platform there is a notice board (**un tableau d'affichage**) that indicates which cars are first class and which are second. You can move from car to car within a given class, but it is often impossible to move from one class to another.
- If you take the **TGV** (**train à grande vitesse**), reservations are required. You can reserve your ticket by phone, by **minitel** (terminal at home) or at the ticket window (**guichet**) until three minutes before departure.

# Étude de grammaire

## 29. TALKING ABOUT THE PAST The *passé composé* with *être*

Suggestion: Have two sts. read roles of *Mme Ferry* and *Stéphanie*. Ask sts. to find paraphrases below the dialogue. Have sts. talk about how *passé composé* is formed with *être*, from examples of italicized verbs.

### Les explications du dimanche matin

MME FERRY: Je voudrais bien savoir où tu **es allée** hier soir! Et à quelle heure **es-tu rentrée**?

STÉPHANIE: Pas tard, maman. Je **suis sortie** avec des copains. On **est allé** prendre un verre chez Laurent, on **est resté** à peu près une heure puis on **est parti** pour aller au ciné. Je **suis revenue** à la maison aussitôt après le ciné.

MME FERRY: Tu es sûre? Parce que ton père **est arrivé** du match de foot à 11h et il n'a pas vu la voiture dans le garage....

Retrouvez la phrase correcte dans le dialogue.

1. À quelle heure es-tu arrivée hier soir?
2. On a bu un verre chez Laurent.
3. On a discuté pendant une heure.
4. On a vu un film.
5. Ton père est rentré à 11h.

## A. The Auxiliary Verb *être*

Most French verbs use a form of **avoir** as an auxiliary verb in the **passé composé**. The **passé composé** of some verbs, however, is generally formed with **être**; one of these verbs is **aller** (*to go*).

**Presentation**: Model pronunciation of past-tense forms of *aller* using simple sentences. Examples: *Je suis allé en France l'année dernière. Où est-ce que vous êtes allé*? (question directed to a st. in class, who answers with *je* form.) *Ah, il est allé en Californie*, etc.

| PASSÉ COMPOSÉ OF **aller** (*to go*) | | | |
|---|---|---|---|
| je | suis allé(**e**) | nous | sommes allé(**e**)**s** |
| tu | es allé(**e**) | vous | êtes allé(**e**)(**s**) |
| il, on | est allé | ils | sont allé**s** |
| elle | est allé**e** | elles | sont allé**es** |

In the **passé composé** with **être**, the past participle always agrees with the subject in gender and number. The following verbs* take **être** in the **passé composé**. The drawing on page 241 lists most of these verbs, organized around the "house of **être**."

**Suggestion**: Have sts. close books after looking at list of verbs and dictate story of *Mme Bernard* in the example sentences on following page for immediate written reinforcement.

**aller: allé** *to go*
**arriver: arrivé** *to arrive*
**descendre: descendu** *to go down; to get off*
**devenir: devenu** *to become*
**entrer: entré** *to enter*
**monter: monté** *to go up; to climb*
**mourir: mort** *to die*
**naître: né** *to be born*
**partir: parti** *to leave*
**passer (par): passé** *to pass (by)*
**rentrer: rentré** *to return; to go home*
**rester: resté** *to stay*
**retourner: retourné** *to return; to go back*
**revenir: revenu** *to come back*
**sortir: sorti** *to go out*
**tomber: tombé** *to fall*
**venir: venu** *to come*

*When **monter**, **descendre**, **sortir**, and **passer** are followed by a direct object, they take **avoir** in the **passé composé**: **elle *a passé* la frontière hier. Nous *avons descendu* la rivière en bateau.**

| | |
|---|---|
| Mme Bernard **est née** en France. | *Mme Bernard was born in France.* |
| Elle **est allée** aux États-Unis en 1940. | *She went to the United States in 1940.* |
| Elle **est arrivée** à New York. | *She arrived in New York.* |
| Elle **est partie** en Californie. | *She left for California.* |
| Elle **est restée** dix ans à San Francisco. | *She stayed in San Francisco for ten years.* |
| Ensuite, elle **est rentrée** en France. | *Then she returned to France.* |
| Elle **est morte** à Paris en 1952. | *She died in Paris in 1952.* |

**Note**: With whole class, talk about all characters' actions in illustration, using *passé composé*. Explain mnemonic devices and how the house serves as a memory aid by providing a total picture, showing all common verbs using *être*. Teach the mnemonic device of *MRS. VANDETRAMPP*: *Monter* (*remonter*), *Rester*, *Sortir*, *Venir* (*revenir*, *devenir*), *Aller*, *Naître*, *Descendre*, *Entrer* (*rentrer*), *Tomber*, *Retourner*, *Arriver*, *Mourir*, *Partir* (*repartir*), *Passer*.

## B. Negative and Interrogative Sentences in the *passé composé*

Word order in negative and interrogative sentences in the **passé composé** with **être** is the same as that for the **passé composé** with **avoir**.

| | |
|---|---|
| Je **ne suis pas** allé en cours. | *I did not go to class.* |
| **Sont-ils** arrivés à l'heure? | *Did they arrive on time?* |

## Vérifions!

**A. Une journée de vacances.** Dites où chaque personne est allée selon ses préférences.

Suggestion: Give sts. a few minutes to write answers before soliciting oral responses.

MODÈLE: Jessica (la musique classique) →
Jessica aime la musique classique. Elle est allée au concert.

1. mon meilleur ami (ma meilleure amie) (la planche à voile)
2. toi (= tu) (le football)
3. le professeur (le plein air, les arbres et les fleurs)
4. nous (les trains)
5. mes parents (cousins... ) (les films)
6. vous (l'art)
7. moi (= je) (le soleil)

a. au cinéma
b. à la gare
c. à la plage
d. au musée
e. au match
f. à la campagne
g. au lac

**B. Week-end en Suisse.** Brigitte et Bernard ont passé le week-end à Genève. Mettez l'histoire au passé composé et faites attention au choix de l'auxiliaire (**avoir** ou **être**).

Suggestion: Have sts. write out or give orally the past-tense rendition of this story. May be done as a short composition, with sts. embellishing story as they wish.

Bernard vient[1] chercher Brigitte pour aller à la gare. Ils montent[2] dans le train. Ils cherchent[3] leur compartiment. Le train part[4] quelques minutes plus tard. Il entre[5] en gare de Genève à midi. Bernard et Brigitte descendent[6] du train et vont[7] tout de suite à l'hôtel. L'après-midi, ils sortent[8] visiter la ville. Le soir ils dînent[9] dans un restaurant élégant. Dimanche Brigitte va[10] au musée et prend[11] beaucoup de photos de la ville. Bernard reste[12] à l'hôtel. Brigitte et Bernard quittent[13] Genève en fin d'après-midi. Ils arrivent[14] à Paris fatigués mais contents de leur week-end.

Qu'est-ce que Brigitte a fait que Bernard n'a pas fait?

**C. Départ en vacances.** Les Dupont, vos voisins, sont partis en vacances ce week-end. Vous racontez maintenant la scène à vos amis. Complétez l'histoire de façon logique et mettez les verbes au passé composé.

**Follow-up**: Ask sts. to invent a similar story, using following stimuli, which can be dictated or handed out: *Ils vont à la montagne. Ils partent à 6h du matin. Ils retournent à 6h30. Ils entrent dans la maison pour chercher des objets oubliés (leurs skis!). Ils montent dans la voiture. Ils partent de nouveau. Un des skis tombe du toit.* Sts. end story as they wish.

Ce matin, mes voisins les Dupont _____[1] en vacances. Ils _____[2] à la mer. À 8 heures, M. Dupont et son fils _____[3] et _____[4] de la maison plusieurs fois avec des sacs et des valises. Mme Dupont _____[5] cinq fois dans la maison pour aller chercher des objets oubliés.

Enfin, trois heures plus tard, toute la famille _____[6] dans la voiture et elle _____[7]. Mais pas de chance, une des valises _____[8] de la galerie (*roof rack*). M. Dupont _____[9] de la voiture pour la remettre sur la galerie et ils _____[10]. Moi, je _____[11] chez moi.

sortir
entrer
partir
retourner
aller
descendre
partir
tomber
repartir
monter
rester

**D. Les voyageurs.** Vos amis ont voyagé en Europe. Vous voulez savoir les détails du voyage. Formulez des questions complètes.

MODÈLE: Jacqueline / partir le 19 juin
Est-elle partie le 19 juin?

1. Raphaël / rester une semaine à Nice 2. toi / arriver hier soir 3. Emma / aller en Italie 4. Marianne et David / passer par la Suisse 5. vous / repartir le 15 août 6. Marie et Flore / revenir en septembre

**Additional activity:** *Projets de voyage. Alice prépare un voyage en Europe. Elle vous pose des questions sur les activités de vos amis. Répondez à la forme négative.* 1. *Marianne est-elle déjà montée dans le Concorde?* 2. *Son vol est-il arrivé à l'heure?* 3. *Sont-ils partis en vacances en train?* 4. *Êtes-vous allé(e) en France récemment?* 5. *Sont-ils restés longtemps en Espagne?* 6. *Es-tu passé(e) par la Suisse?* 7. *Es-tu rentré(e) en bateau?* 8. *Sont-elles revenues à San Francisco en septembre?*

## Parlons-en!

**A. Souvenirs de vacances.** Décrivez les vacances de l'année passée d'un(e) camarade. D'abord (*First*), posez les questions suivantes à votre camarade. Si vous voulez, posez encore d'autres questions. Ensuite, présentez à la classe une description de ses vacances.

1. Quand es-tu parti(e)? Quel moyen de transport as-tu pris? Où es-tu allé(e)? Es-tu resté(e) aux États-Unis ou es-tu allé(e) à l'étranger? As-tu visité un endroit exotique?
2. Es-tu allé(e) voir l'endroit où tes parents sont nés? Où es-tu né(e)?
3. Qu'est-ce que tu as fait pendant les vacances? As-tu rencontré des gens intéressants?
4. Comment es-tu rentré(e)? en avion? par bateau? Es-tu revenu(e) mort(e) de fatigue?
5. Prépares-tu déjà tes vacances de l'année prochaine?

**Suggestion**: Have sts. write description of their partners' vacations as a short *résumé*. Collect them and use as dictation or listening comp. material on a subsequent class day.

**B. Vacances en Afrique.** Vous venez de passer dix jours en Côte-d'Ivoire avec deux autres camarades de classe. Voici une brochure de l'endroit où vous êtes allés.

# LA TAVERNE BASSAMOISE ★

**EXCLUSIF**

**GRAND BASSAM**

*Grand Bassam fut la première capitale de la Côte-d'Ivoire. C'est aujourd'hui une petite ville historique chargée de souvenirs d'un passé encore vivant. Elle est située au bord de la mer, à 43 km environ d'Abidjan.*
*Amateurs de bonne table, d'harmonie, de calme, des vacances sans contrainte dans un établissement qui offre les garanties d'un bon confort dans un cadre agréable, Patrick et Isabelle vous attendent à la Taverne Bassamoise! C'est une exclusivité AIRTOUR.*

**FICHE D'IDENTITÉ:**
- BP 154 Grand Bassam - Tél.: (225) 30.10.62.
- Capacité: 20 chambres et 5 bungalows.

**SITUATION:**
Construit directement en bordure de plage, au milieu d'une belle cocoteraie, de la verdure et des fleurs. Grand Bassam est à 1,5 km, l'aéroport à 25 km, Abidjan à 45 km.

**A VOTRE DISPOSITION:**
- 1 restaurant en terrasse (spécialités européennes et africaines).
- 2 bars.
- 1 salon.
- 1 salon TV vidéo.
- 1 boutique.
- 1 discothèque: «le Mogambo».
- Piscine, bassin pour les enfants.
- Plage aménagée.

**VOTRE CHAMBRE:**
Les chambres de plain-pied, construites au milieu de la verdure et des fleurs, sont avec douche, climatisation et terrasse.
Possibilité de logement en bungalows (plus spacieux) avec supplément.

**VOS REPAS:**
- Demi-pension (dîner obligatoire), pension complète en option.

**EXCURSIONS:**
- **Exclusif: descente du fleuve Comoe en zodiac** (1 jour/1 nuit) 28 000 CFA environ. Logement sur une île dans un campement simple. La cuisine sera confectionnée par les villageois.
- **1 journée en brousse** en Chevrolet 4/4 climatisée: 22 500 CFA environ pique-nique inclus. Visite des plantations de café, cacao, bananes et ananas. Promenade en pirogue sur le fleuve Comoe. Possibilité de baignade dans le fleuve. Visite de villages typiques.

**SPORTS ET LOISIRS:**
**Gratuits:**
- Tennis: 1 court en dur.
- Ping-pong.
- Pétanque.
- Volley-ball.

**Payants:**
Possibilité de sports nautiques sur la lagune proche de l'hôtel. Soirée folklorique avec repas langouste: 5 000 CFA environ.

Choisissez d'abord vos compagnons de voyage. Puis, à l'aide de cette brochure, répondez aux questions suivantes.

1. Où est situé Grand Bassam? 2. Quels sports offre l'hôtel? 3. Que met (*puts*) l'hôtel à votre disposition? 4. Quelles excursions peut-on faire?

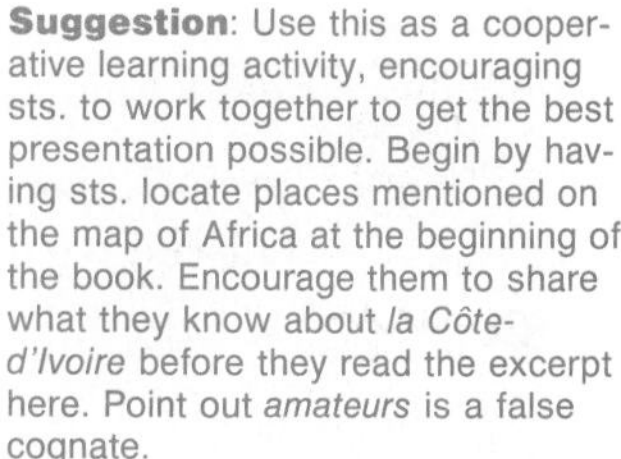

**Suggestion**: Use this as a cooperative learning activity, encouraging sts. to work together to get the best presentation possible. Begin by having sts. locate places mentioned on the map of Africa at the beginning of the book. Encourage them to share what they know about *la Côte-d'Ivoire* before they read the excerpt here. Point out *amateurs* is a false cognate.

Ensuite imaginez ce que vous avez fait tous les trois pendant votre séjour à Grand Bassam. Prenez quelques notes, puis faites une courte (*short*) présentation au reste de la classe (au passé composé, bien sûr!). Attention au choix de l'auxiliaire. Commencez par «Nous sommes allés à Grand Bassam, en Côte-d'Ivoire... »

**Verbes utiles:** rester, dormir, aller, jouer à, regarder, prendre, manger, visiter, faire, nager, danser, descendre, passer, voir, avoir, être...

**C. Profil psychologique.** Posez à un(e) camarade des questions basées sur les éléments donnés. Utilisez le passé composé dans vos questions. Après, faites le portrait psychologique de votre camarade. D'après les réponses de votre camarade, quel caractère a-t-il/elle? Justifiez votre profil psychologique.

**Suggestion**: Have sts. do activity in pairs, with written follow-up. A few sts. then read their *profil* to rest of class.

**Mots utiles:** sociable, (ir)responsable, ponctuel(le), négligent(e), nostalgique, courageux/euse, aventureux/euse, (im)prudent(e), superstitieux/euse...

1. prendre un verre avec des amis hier soir
2. à quelle heure / rentrer
3. à quelle heure / arriver à l'université ce matin
4. entrer dans la salle de classe en retard, à l'heure ou en avance (*early*, or *in advance*)
5. retourner souvent à l'endroit où il/elle est né(e)
6. passer la nuit tout(e) seul(e) dans une forêt
7. monter souvent au sommet d'une montagne
8. descendre souvent dans une grotte (*cave*)
9. refuser de passer sous une échelle (*ladder*)

## 30. EXPRESSING WISHES AND POLITE REQUESTS The Present Conditional

### Un week-end à Londres

JULIE: Est-ce que vous **auriez** des tarifs intéressants en ce moment pour Londres?

L'EMPLOYÉE: Vous tombez bien! Nous avons un vol en promotion à cinq cent cinquante francs aller-retour.

JULIE: Super! Et **pourriez**-vous me réserver une chambre d'hôtel du trois au sept septembre?

L'EMPLOYÉE: Pas de problème! Dans quel coin de Londres **aimeriez**-vous être?
JULIE: Je **voudrais** trouver un hôtel pas trop cher près de Hyde Park.

Quelles phrases de la partie de Julie correspondent aux descriptions suivantes?

1. Julie veut acheter un billet pas cher pour Londres.
2. Elle veut réserver une chambre d'hôtel.
3. Elle veut être près de Hyde Park.

The conditional is used to express wishes or requests. It gives a tone of deference or politeness that makes a request or question less abrupt. For example,

| | |
|---|---|
| Je **voudrais** aller à la Martinique. | *I'd like to go to Martinique.* |
| **Pourriez**-vous m'aider à trouver un vol? | *Could you help me (to) find a flight?* |
| **Auriez**-vous l'horaire des avions? | *Would you have the flight schedule?* |

## Formation of the Conditional

The complete formation of the conditional will be presented in Chapter 15. Only certain forms of some useful verbs will be presented now. They appear in bold type in the following examples.

AVOIR

| | |
|---|---|
| Valérie, tu **aurais** un livre de français à me prêter? | *Valérie, would you have a French book to lend me?* |
| Monsieur, **auriez**-vous la gentillesse de m'aider avec ma valise? | *Sir, would you be so kind as to help me with my suitcase?* |

POUVOIR

| | |
|---|---|
| Excusez-moi, Monsieur. Je **pourrais** vous poser une question? | *Excuse me, sir. Could I ask you a question?* |
| Martine, tu **pourrais** m'aider? | *Martine, could you help me?* |
| **Pourriez**-vous me répondre par écrit? | *Could you answer me in writing?* |

VOULOIR

| | |
|---|---|
| Bonjour, Madame. Je **voudrais** un billet de train pour aller à Lyon. | *Hello, Madam. I would like a train ticket to go to Lyon.* |
| Marc, tu **voudrais** venir avec moi? | *Marc, would you like to come with me?* |
| Mademoiselle, **voudriez**-vous me suivre? | *Miss, would you follow me, please?* |

## Vérifions!

**A. Dans le train.** Vous êtes dans un compartiment de train. Vous entendez ces bribes (*snippets, fragments*) de conversation. Complétez les phrases suivantes de façon logique et utilisez le conditionnel des verbes suivants: **pouvoir**, **vouloir**, **avoir**.

1. _____-vous la gentillesse de fermer la fenêtre?
2. _____-tu me passer mon sac?
3. _____-tu un stylo à me prêter (*lend me*), s'il te plaît?
4. Est-ce que je _____ ouvrir la fenêtre maintenant? J'ai chaud.
5. _____-vous me dire à quelle heure le train arrive à Lyon?
6. _____-vous venir au wagon-restaurant avec nous?
7. Tu _____ peut-être partager (*share*) mon sandwich?

**B. Soyons diplomates** (*diplomatic*). Vous avez un ami (une amie) qui donne des ordres au lieu de (*instead of*) poser des questions poliment. Indiquez-lui (*Tell him/her*) deux façons de demander la même chose, mais poliment. Jouez les rôles avec un(e) camarade selon le modèle.

MODÈLE: L'AMI(E): Dites-moi (*me*) à quelle heure le train part pour Tournus!*

VOUS: Non! Pourriez-vous me dire (*tell me*) à quelle heure le train part pour Tournus? (Je voudrais savoir [*to know*] à quelle heure le train part.)

1. Donnez-moi un billet de première classe!
2. Expliquez-moi pourquoi les places (*seats*) sont si chères.
3. Donnez-moi des places moins chères.
4. Donnez-moi quatre billets de deuxième classe.
5. Indiquez-moi quand le train va arriver.
6. Dites-moi si je dois réserver des places!

## Parlons-en!

**Que dites-vous?** Utilisez les verbes **pouvoir**, **vouloir** ou **avoir** pour exprimer vos besoins dans les situations suivantes. Soyez très poli(e)!

---

*Tournus (ne prononcez pas le -s à la fin) est une petite ville de 7 338 habitants située sur la Saône dans le nord-est de la France.

MODÈLE: Vous ne savez pas la date d'aujourd'hui, mais votre professeur a un calendrier. →
Pourriez-vous me dire la date d'aujourd'hui, s'il vous plaît?

1. Vous avez besoin d'argent. Demandez dix dollars à votre père.
2. Vous êtes perdu(e). Demandez à quelqu'un où est l'université.
3. Vous êtes dans un restaurant où il fait chaud. Vous demandez au serveur d'ouvrir la porte.
4. Vous avez perdu votre livre. Demandez à un(e) camarade de classe si vous pouvez emprunter (*borrow*) son livre.
5. Vous êtes à la gare. Demandez au monsieur / à la dame du guichet de vous vendre un billet de train. Demandez aussi l'heure du prochain train pour Paris.

## 31. EXPRESSING NEGATION
## Affirmative and Negative Adverbs

### Le train à grande vitesse

PATRICIA: Tu as **déjà** voyagé en TGV?
FRÉDÉRIC: Non, **pas encore**. Mais j'ai réservé une place pour samedi prochain. Je vais voir mes parents en Bretagne.
PATRICIA: Est-ce qu'il faut **toujours** réserver à l'avance pour le TGV?
FRÉDÉRIC: Oui, c'est obligatoire. Moi, je **n**'aime **pas du tout** ce système parce que j'ai **toujours** eu horreur de prévoir à l'avance. J'aime partir à la dernière minute, je **ne** fais **jamais de** projets, et je **n**'ai **jamais** eu **d**'agenda.

Trouvez la phrase ou la question équivalente dans le dialogue.

1. Tu n'as pas encore voyagé en TGV?
2. Ne peut-on jamais prendre le TGV sans réservation?
3. Moi, je déteste ce système.

## Ne... jamais, ne... plus, ne... pas encore

1. **Toujours**, **souvent**, and **parfois** are adverbs that generally follow the verb in the present tense. The expression **ne** (**n'**)**... jamais**, constructed like **ne... pas**, is the negative adverb (**l'adverbe de négation**) used to express the fact that an action never takes place.

| | |
|---|---|
| Henri voyage **toujours** en train.* <br> Marie voyage **souvent** en train.* <br> Hélène voyage **parfois** en train. | Je **ne** voyage **jamais** en train. <br> *I never travel by train.* |

Other adverbs also follow this pattern.

| AFFIRMATIVE | NEGATIVE |
|---|---|
| **encore** *still* | **ne** (**n'**)**... plus** *no longer, no more* |
| **déjà** *already* | **ne** (**n'**)**... pas encore** *not yet* |
| Le train est **encore** sur le quai. <br> *The train is still on the platform.* | Le train **n'**est **plus** sur le quai. <br> *The train is no longer on the platform.* |
| Nos valises sont **déjà** là? <br> *Are our suitcases there already?* | Nos valises **ne** sont **pas encore** là. <br> *Our suitcases aren't there yet.* |

2. As with **ne** (**n'**)**... pas**, the indefinite article and the partitive article become **de** (**d'**) when they follow negative verbs.

| AFFIRMATIVE | NEGATIVE |
|---|---|
| Je vois **toujours des Américains** dans l'autocar. <br> *I always see Americans on the tourist bus.* | Je **ne** vois **jamais de Français** dans l'autocar. <br> *I never see (any) French people on the tourist bus.* |
| Avez-vous **encore des billets** à vendre? <br> *Do you still have (some) tickets to sell?* | Non, je **n'ai plus de billets** à vendre. <br> *No, I have no more (I don't have any more) tickets to sell.* |
| Karen a **déjà des amis** en France. <br> *Karen already has (some) friends in France.* | Vincent **n'a pas encore d'amis** aux États-Unis. <br> *Vincent doesn't have any friends in the United States yet.* |

*Sentences whose verbs are modified by **toujours** and **souvent** may also be negated by **ne** (**n'**)**... pas**: **Henri ne voyage pas toujours en train. Il voyage parfois en avion. Marie ne voyage pas souvent en train. Elle préfère conduire sa voiture.**

Definite articles do not change.

Je ne vois jamais **le** contrôleur (*conductor*) dans ce train.
Annick ne prend plus **l'**autoroute à Caen.
On ne voit pas encore **le** sommet de la montagne.

3. In the **passé composé**, the affirmative adverbs are generally placed between the auxiliary and the past participle.

M. Huet **a toujours** (**souvent**, **parfois**) pris l'avion.

Note the interrogative forms of the negative adverbial construction.

| | |
|---|---|
| —Marie **n'a**-t-elle **jamais** voyagé en avion? (Est-ce que Marie a déjà voyagé en avion?) | —*Hasn't Marie ever traveled by plane? (Has she already traveled by plane?)* |
| —Non, elle **n'**a **jamais** voyagé en avion. | —*No, she has never traveled by plane.* |
| —Non, elle **n'**a **pas encore** voyagé en avion. | —*No, she has not yet traveled by plane.* |

4. **Ne... pas du tout** is used instead of **ne... pas** for emphasis.

| | |
|---|---|
| Je **n'**aime **pas du tout** les avions! | *I don't like planes at all!* |
| —As-tu faim? | —*Are you hungry?* |
| **—Pas du tout!** | —*Not at all!* |

> **Note**: Point out that when conjugated verb is followed by an infinitive, negative particles surround conjugated verb, as with *ne... pas*: *Je ne vais plus acheter de billets.* Also, when infinitive itself is being negated, two negative particles precede infinitive directly: *J'ai l'intention de ne plus voyager dans le Sud.*

## *Vérifions!*

**A. Un voyageur nerveux.** Chaque fois qu'il part en vacances, M. Laffont se préoccupe de tout (*worries about everything*). Mme Laffont essaie toujours de le calmer (*calm him down*). Avec un(e) camarade, jouez les rôles de M. et Mme Laffont. Suivez le modèle.

MODÈLE: M. LAFFONT: Tu n'as pas encore trouvé les valises!
MME LAFFONT: Mais si![*] J'ai déjà trouvé les valises.

1. Nous ne faisons jamais de voyages agréables.
2. Il n'y a plus de places dans le train.
3. Il n'y a plus de billets en classe économique.
4. Nous ne sommes pas encore arrivés.
5. Il n'y a jamais de téléphone à la gare.
6. Il n'y a plus de voitures à louer.
7. Tu n'as pas encore trouvé la carte (*map*).
8. Nous ne sommes pas encore sur la bonne route (*the right road*).

> **Additional activity**: *Personnalités opposées. Voici le portrait de Monique. Faites le portrait de Joseph en suivant le modèle.* MODÈLE: *Monique a parfois sommeil en cours. → Joseph n'a jamais sommeil en cours. 1. Monique a déjà des problèmes avec ses études. 2. Elle a souvent envie de changer de cours. 3. Elle a parfois peur des professeurs. 4. Elle a déjà besoin de vacances. 5. Elle croit encore aux miracles.*

[*]Remember that **si** rather than **oui** is used to contradict a negative question or statement.

## Mots-clés

*Ne... que*

The expression **ne** (**n'**)**... que** (**qu'**) is used to indicate a limited quantity of something. It has the same meaning as **seulement** (*only*).

| | |
|---|---|
| Je **n'**ai **qu'**un billet.<br>J'ai **seulement** un billet. | *I have only one ticket.* |
| Il **n'**y a **que** trois trains cet après-midi.<br>Il y a **seulement** trois trains cet après-midi. | *There are only three trains this afternoon.* |
| Hélène **n'**a fait **que** deux réservations.<br>Hélène a fait **seulement** deux réservations. | *Hélène made only two reservations.* |

**B. En voyage.** Dites ce que font ces personnes quand elles sont en voyage. Remplacez **seulement** par **ne... que**.

MODÈLE: Je prends seulement le train. →
Je ne prends que le train.

1. Martin envoie (*sends*) seulement des cartes postales.
2. Vous achetez seulement des souvenirs drôles.
3. Mes cousins mangent seulement dans les fast-food.
4. Tu prends seulement une valise.
5. Nous dormons seulement dans des auberges de jeunesse (*youth hostels*).
6. Sophie regarde seulement les bateaux sur la mer.

### Parlons-en!

**A. Préparatifs de voyage.** Quand vous partez en voyage, faites-vous les choses suivantes **toujours**, **souvent**, **parfois** ou **jamais**?

**Suggestion**: Model one or two items, and then have sts. do activity in pairs for maximum practice.

MODÈLE: arriver à l'aéroport à la dernière minute. →
J'arrive toujours (Je n'arrive jamais) à l'aéroport à la dernière minute.

1. oublier son passeport (sa brosse à dents [*toothbrush*], sa carte de crédit...)
2. prendre son appareil-photo (un guide, une carte...)
3. acheter de nouveaux vêtements (de nouvelles chaussures, de nouvelles lunettes de soleil...)
4. créer un itinéraire (à l'avance, au dernier moment)
5. faire sa valise au dernier moment (la veille [*the day before*], une semaine avant...)
6. ?

**B. Voyages exotiques.** Interviewez vos camarades.

camper dans le Sahara

VOUS: N'as-tu jamais campé dans le Sahara?
VOTRE CAMARADE: Non, je n'ai jamais campé dans le Sahara. (*ou* Si, j'ai campé dans le Sahara [l'été passé, il y a deux ans, etc.].)

1. faire du bateau sur le Nil
2. voir le Sphinx en Égypte
3. faire une expédition dans l'Antarctique
4. passer tes vacances à Tahiti
5. faire de l'alpinisme dans l'Himalaya
6. voir les chutes Victoria (*Victoria Falls*) en Afrique
7. faire un safari-photos au Cameroun
8. ?

Qui dans votre classe a fait le voyage le plus exotique?

## 32. EXPRESSING NEGATION
## Affirmative and Negative Pronouns

### La consigne automatique

SERGE: Il y a **quelque chose** qui ne va pas?
JEAN-PIERRE: Oui, j'ai des ennuis avec la consigne; elle ne marche pas.
SERGE: Ah, ça! Il n'y a **rien** de plus énervant!
JEAN-PIERRE: **Tout le monde** semble toujours trouver une consigne qui marche, sauf moi.
SERGE: Regarde, **quelqu'un** sort ses bagages d'une consigne. Là, tu es sûr qu'elle marche!
JEAN-PIERRE: Excellente idée!

Corrigez les phrases inexactes.

1. Tout va bien pour Jean-Pierre.
2. Il y a quelque chose de plus énervant (*something more exasperating*) qu'une consigne qui ne marche pas.
3. Jean-Pierre et deux autres passagers ne trouvent pas de consigne qui marche.
4. Quand quelqu'un place ses bagages dans une consigne, on est sûr qu'elle marche.

## A. Affirmative Pronouns

**Quelqu'un**[*] (*Someone*), **quelque chose** (*something*), **tout** (*everything, all*), and **tout le monde** (*everybody*) are indefinite pronouns (**des pronoms indéfinis**). All four may serve as the subject of a sentence, the object of a verb, or the object of a preposition.

| | |
|---|---|
| Il y a **quelqu'un** au guichet maintenant. | *Someone is at the ticket counter now.* |
| Vous avez vu **quelqu'un** sur le quai? | *Did you see someone on the platform?* |
| Jacques a parlé avec **quelqu'un** il y a un moment. | *Jacques spoke with someone a moment ago.* |
| **Quelque chose** est arrivé. | *Something has happened.* |
| Marie a acheté **quelque chose** au restaurant de la gare. | *Marie bought something at the station restaurant.* |
| Elle pense à **quelque chose**, mais à quoi? | *She's thinking about something, but what?* |
| **Tout** est possible. | *Everything is possible.* |
| **Tout le monde** est prêt? | *Is everybody ready?* |

## B. Negative Pronouns

1. **Personne** (*No one, Nobody, Not anybody*) and **rien** (*nothing, not anything*) are negative pronouns generally used in a construction with **ne** (**n'**). They can be the subject of a sentence, the object of a verb, or the object of a preposition. As objects of a verb in the **passé composé**, **rien** precedes the past participle, but **personne** is placed after the past participle.

**Note**: Sts. often confuse the *personne... ne* construction with the noun *une personne*.

| | |
|---|---|
| **Personne n**'est monté dans ce train. | *No one boarded this train.* |
| Je **n**'ai vu **personne** sur le quai. | *I didn't see anyone on the platform.* |
| Jacques **ne** parle avec **personne** maintenant. | *Jacques isn't speaking with anyone right now.* |
| **Rien ne** l'intéresse. | *Nothing interests him/her.* |
| Marie **n**'a **rien** acheté au restaurant de la gare. | *Marie didn't buy anything at the station restaurant.* |
| Elle **ne** pense à **rien**. | *She's not thinking about anything.* |
| **Rien n**'est impossible. | *Nothing is impossible.* |
| **Personne n**'est prêt. | *Nobody is ready.* |

2. Like **jamais**, **rien** and **personne** may be used without **ne** when they answer a question.

---

[*]**Quelqu'un** is invariable in form: it can refer to both males and females.

—Qu'est-ce qu'il y a sur la voie? —*What's on the track?*
**—Rien.** —*Nothing.*
—Qui est au guichet? —*Who's at the ticket counter?*
**—Personne.** —*Nobody.*

## C. Negative Pronouns with Adjectives

When used with adjectives, the expressions **quelque chose**, **quelqu'un**, **ne... rien**, **ne... personne** are followed by **de** (**d'**) plus the masculine singular form of the adjective.

Y a-t-il **quelque chose de bon** au menu du wagon-restaurant? *Is there something good on the menu in the restaurant car?*
Il y a **quelqu'un d'intéressant** dans le compartiment d'à côté. *There is someone interesting in the next compartment.*
Il **n'**y a **rien d'amusant** dans ce journal. *There is nothing entertaining in this paper.*
Il **n'**y a **personne d'important** dans le wagon de première classe. *There is no one important in the first-class car.*

### *Vérifions!*

**A. À la gare.** Vous avez des ennuis avant de partir en voyage. Transformez les phrases suivantes.

**Suggestion**: Dictate affirmative statements to sts. with sts. either working at board or at seats. Then have them transform sentences to negative.

MODÈLE: Quelqu'un est prêt! → Personne n'est prêt!

1. Quelqu'un a acheté les billets.
2. Quelqu'un a apporté nos valises.
3. Tout est prêt.
4. Jean-Claude pense à quelque chose.
5. Eric a tout pris.
6. Claudine parle avec quelqu'un.

**B. Mais si!** Donnez une réponse affirmative pour chaque phrase négative.

**Suggestion**: Have sts. play roles of 2 people who don't agree on anything. One person is pessimistic and uses a complaining tone; the other is optimistic and answers with a positive, reassuring tone.

MODÈLE: —Il n'y a personne à la caisse (*cash register*).
—Mais si! Il y a quelqu'un à la caisse.

1. Il n'y a personne dans ce restaurant. Il n'y a rien de bon sur la carte.
2. Il n'y a rien dans ce magasin de sport. Il n'y a rien de joli ici.
3. Il n'y a personne dans cette agence de voyages. Il n'y a rien d'intéressant dans ces brochures.
4. Il n'y a rien de moderne dans ce quartier. Il n'y a rien d'intéressant dans les rues.

### Parlons-en!

**A. Vrai ou faux?** Regardez l'image à la page 234. Dites si les phrases suivantes sont vraies ou fausses. Corrigez celles qui sont fausses.

1. Le steward n'apporte rien aux voyageurs.
2. Il y a des voyageurs en première classe.
3. Il n'y a personne en classe affaires.
4. L'hôtesse de l'air en classe économique n'a rien sur son plateau (*tray*).
5. Personne n'attend pour monter dans l'avion.

**B. Qu'est-ce qui se passe** (*What's happening*)**?** Posez des questions à vos camarades pour apprendre ce qui se passe sur votre campus aujourd'hui.

**Suggestions:** Y a-t-il quelque chose d'intéressant dans la salle de conférences (*lecture hall*) cet après-midi? Y a-t-il quelqu'un d'intéressant au ciné-club ce soir? Y a-t-il quelque chose de délicieux au restau-u ____?

## Mise au point

**A. Tour du monde francophone.** Transformez les verbes du présent au passé composé.

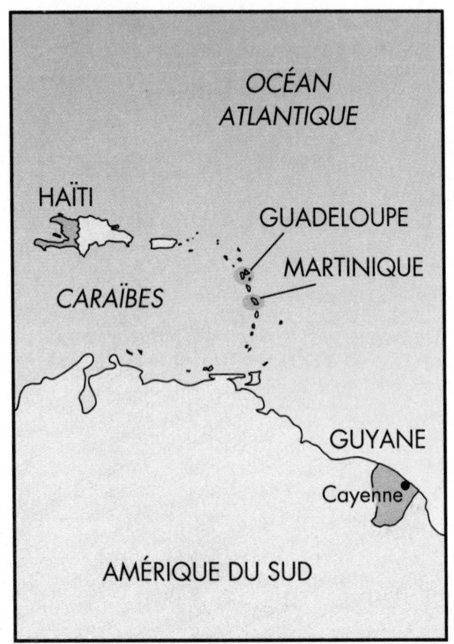


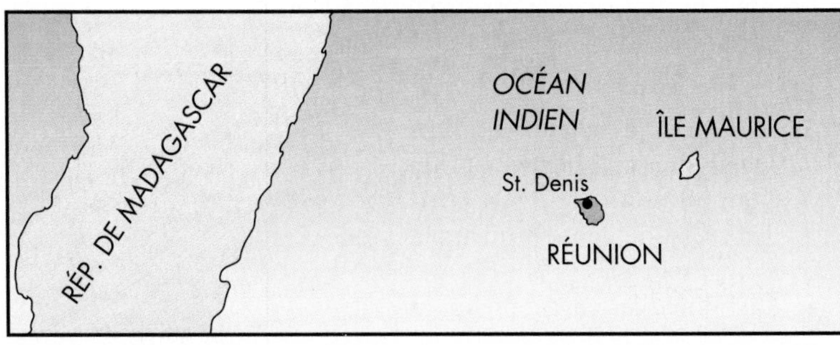


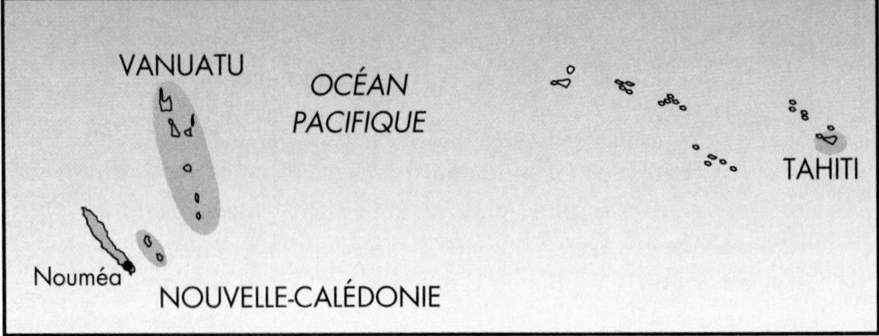

1. Nous partons de New York pour aller à la Guadeloupe.
2. Ensuite, nous allons à la Martinique.
3. Les plages de ces îles sont reposantes (*relaxing*).
4. Ensuite, nous partons pour la Réunion.
5. On arrive à Tahiti et on passe une semaine magnifique.
6. Nous avons envie de rester dans cette île à cause du temps magnifique.
7. Je visite aussi la Nouvelle-Calédonie.
8. Mes amis restent à Tahiti.
9. Nous passons aussi par la Guyane.
10. Nous retournons aux États-Unis très fatigués mais contents.

**B. Trouvez quelqu'un...** Circulez dans la classe et trouvez quelqu'un qui a fait les choses suivantes. Avec un(e) camarade, posez les questions et répondez. (Attention à la question qu'il faut poser!)

MODÈLE: regarder la télévision aujourd'hui (déjà) →
VOUS: As-tu déjà regardé la télévision aujourd'hui?
LE/LA CAMARADE: Oui, j'ai déjà regardé la télévision aujourd'hui. (Non, je n'ai pas encore regardé la télévision aujourd'hui).

**Suggestion**: Have sts. jot down numbers 1-6. Whenever they get an affirmative answer to a question, they jot down the speaker's name next to that number. The first st. to complete the list wins.

1. prendre sa voiture pour aller à l'université (souvent)
2. avoir quelque chose d'important à faire (ce soir)
3. voir quelqu'un d'intéressant (avant de venir en classe)
4. travailler jusqu'à une heure du matin (hier soir)
5. arriver en classe à 8 heures (ce matin)
6. finir tous les devoirs pour demain (déjà)

**C. Êtes-vous un grand voyageur?** Où allez-vous pour voir les choses suivantes?

MODÈLE: La fontaine de Trevi →
On va à Rome (en Italie) pour voir la fontaine de Trevi.

| | |
|---|---|
| 1. Carnac | a. la Bretagne (France) |
| 2. les Pyramides | b. l'Égypte |
| 3. Big Ben | c. Londres |
| 4. l'Amazone | d. l'Afrique |
| 5. le Sahara | e. l'Amérique du Sud |
| 6. la Grande Muraille (*wall*) | f. la Chine |

Faites le total des réponses correctes. Dans quelle catégorie êtes-vous?

4–6 Très bien! Vous êtes bien informé(e) et vous aimez les voyages.
1–3 Vous n'êtes pas un voyageur (une voyageuse) très passionné(e).

Maintenant, nommez d'autres choses à voir dans d'autres pays et mettez à l'épreuve (*test*) les connaissances (*knowledge*) géographiques de vos camarades de classe.

# Interactions

In Chapter 9, you practiced talking about traveling and transportation, discussing events in the past, and making negative comments. Act out the following situations, using the vocabulary and structures from this chapter.

1. **Un mauvais voyage.** You are in France. You are so angry with your travel agent that you call him or her to complain. Among other things, mention the following: the plane left late, your hotel room was not reserved (**réservé**), no one is friendly, there is nothing good to eat, there's so much traffic that it's impossible to drive, the phones don't work, etc.
2. **Devinez.** Describe a trip, telling where you went, when, and with whom. Mention some of your activities and the means of transportation. For each statement ask your partner to guess if you are telling the truth!

## LECTURE

### *Avant de lire*

**Anticipating content.** Reading often involves forming expectations and then confirming or changing them on the basis of what you learn as you read on. Suppose you find a press clipping that quotes the President of the United States, who is vividly describing his hatred of all foreigners. If you think it's an excerpt from a *New York Times* article, you may be concerned about the consequences for national security. If you read further and recognize it as a clipping from a political satire magazine, you may find it highly entertaining. What you expect has a profound influence on what you find in a text.

When reading in a foreign language it is especially useful to define your expectations about a text before reading it. Anticipating content enables you to predict some unfamiliar elements of the reading. Think of what you already know about the topic, and glance at the titles, opening lines, photos, and illustrations before you begin reading. In addition, it may be worthwhile to ask yourself what you know about the author and what you may be able to guess about other readers of the piece, based on its source.

Before reading the following text, try to answer these questions.

- What kind of text is this? How do you know?
- What means are used to draw your attention to the piece?
- For whom is the text written? How can you guess?

Now read the first two sentences of the text. What message do they convey?

As you read this ad, remember that your aim is not to understand every word. Try simply to guess the core meaning of most sentences, embodied in the subject-verb-object combinations. Read only to "get the gist" of the piece.

**Europcar, partenaire officiel d'Euro Disney Resort!** Lorsqu'Euro Disney choisit ses partenaires, c'est pour leur sérieux, leur dynamisme et la qualité de leurs services. Europcar est de ceux-là.[c] Et pour mieux[d] vous servir, nous avons créé une formule vraiment magique: 2 week-ends avec Europcar = 1 entrée gratuite à Euro Disney Resort. **Avec Europcar, les week-ends ont 4 jours.** Louez une voiture pour 2 jours et vous disposerez en permanence[e] de la possibilité de prolonger votre week-end, grâce à un forfait[f] très souple[g] et un tarif dégressif à partir du 2[e] jour... Quelle liberté! **En exclusivité pour vous, Europcar vous offre une entrée gratuite pour découvrir le monde merveilleux d'Euro Disney Resort.*** Partez 2 fois en week-end avec Europcar nous aurons[h] le plaisir de vous offrir une entrée gratuite pour Euro Disney Resort. Alors n'hésitez plus, soyez parmi[i] les premiers à ouvrir[j] les portes du Royaume Magique...

Renseignements Minitel 3614 Europcar -
Renseignements & réservations (1) 30 43 82 82

* Offre valable du 1er novembre 1991 au 31 janvier 1992, dans la limite des 400 places disponibles (utilisables à partir du 12 avril 1992) et pour 2 jours de location minimum.

## Compréhension

1. Selon la publicité, comment peut-on gagner une entrée gratuite à Euro Disney? 2. À quelle date commence cette offre? 3. Si une société (*company*) veut être un partenaire d'Euro Disney, quelles qualités doit-elle avoir? 4. Quelle marque de voiture a choisie Europcar? 5. Vous voulez réserver une voiture chez Europcar. Quel numéro de téléphone devez-vous composer? 6. Et vous, êtes-vous déjà allé(e) à Disneyland ou Disney World? Si oui, quand et avec qui?

[a] *rentals*
[b] *free*
[c] *de... one of those*
[d] *better*
[e] *en... permanently*
[f] *package*
[g] *flexible*
[h] *will have*
[i] *soyez... be among*
[j] *to open*

## PAR ÉCRIT

**Function:** Persuading
**Audience:** Students, staff, and faculty of your college or university
**Goal:** Write an article for the campus newspaper on the problems of transportation at your college or university. Use the following questions as a guide.

1. Quels sont les problèmes de transport sur le campus? Est-ce qu'il est difficile de garer (= stationner) sa voiture? Y a-t-il trop de voitures? assez de transports en commun? Est-il facile de sortir le soir sans voiture? Peut-on se déplacer à pied (*get around on foot*) sans ennuis (*problems*)?
2. Quel moyen de transport préfèrent la plupart (*majority*) des étudiants? Êtes-vous d'accord avec ces étudiants? Pourquoi ou pourquoi pas?
3. Proposez quelques réformes pour améliorer les problèmes de transport sur le campus.

**Steps**

1. Begin by jotting down some answers to the above questions. Make educated guesses and give your own opinions. This is a "freewriting stage"; do not attempt to edit what you have written at this point.
2. Then, reorganize your thoughts. Write a brief introduction, using the answer to the first question under number 1 as your topic sentence. (Your answers to the rest of the questions under number 1 will provide an overview of the transportation situation on your campus.)
3. Answer the set of questions under number 2 by presenting any facts you may know about the kinds of transportation preferred by students at your college.
4. Suggest some solutions to the problems, giving some examples of how they might work. Use some of the following expressions: **Il faut** + infinitive; **On doit**; **On dit que**; **Il est certain que**; **Il est probable que** (*It's likely that*); **J'espère que** (*I hope that*); **ne... plus**; **ne... jamais**; **Personne... ne**; **Rien... ne**.
   **Autres mots utiles:** les parkings (*parking lots*); les transports en commun; les parcomètres (*m., parking meters*); les navettes (*f., shuttles*).
5. Have a friend or classmate reread your first draft to see if what you've written is clear.
6. Make any necessary changes suggested by your classmate and check the draft for spelling, punctuation, and grammar errors. Focus especially on your use of the negative expressions and the past tense with **être**. Be prepared to read your composition to a small group of classmates.

## À L'ÉCOUTE!

**À l'écoute!** See scripts for listening passages and follow-up activities recorded on student cassette. Remind students that in the listening comprehension passages (as in real life) they will not understand every word they hear. They should focus globally on the general information in the passages and not be overly concerned about what they do not understand.

**I. Retour de voyage.** Alain is talking to Philippe about his vacation. First, look at the activities. Next, listen to the vocabulary and the conversation. Then, do the activities.

VOCABULAIRE UTILE

raconte *tell* (*a story*) (*imperative*)
partout *everywhere*
couscous *a North African grain dish*
du thé à la menthe *mint tea*

**A.** Circle the correct answer.

1. Alain a fait un voyage
   a. touristique  b. d'affaires  c. d'études
2. Alain est allé
   a. en Asie  b. en Afrique  c. en Amérique du Sud
3. Alain a visité
   a. Marrakech  b. Casablanca  c. Agadir
4. Le couscous est
   a. une boisson  b. un plat  c. un taxi
5. Il a bu
   a. du thé  b. du café  c. du vin
6. Alain est revenu avec
   a. deux valises  b. une valise seulement  c. trois valises.

**B. Vrai ou faux?**

1. _____ Philippe a voyagé en Amérique du Sud.
2. _____ Le Maroc est un pays bilingue.
3. _____ Au Maroc, on voit des femmes partout.
4. _____ Alain n'a pas aimé la cuisine marocaine.
5. _____ Il a rapporté beaucoup de souvenirs.

**II. Le pauvre Joseph.** Joseph is often absent-minded. You will hear a brief story about him. First, look at the activity. Next, listen to the vocabulary followed by the story. Then, do the activity.

VOCABULAIRE UTILE
tout d'un coup *all at once*
est tombée en panne *broke down*
a appelé *called*
le mécanicien *mechanic*
faire le plein d'essence *fill up (a car) with gas*

Number the events listed below in their chronological order, based on the story.

a. _____ La voiture est tombée en panne.
b. _____ Le mécanicien est arrivé.
c. _____ Joseph est parti de chez lui.
d. _____ Il est retourné jusqu'à sa voiture.
e. _____ Il a pris l'autoroute du nord.
f. _____ Il est descendu de sa voiture.
g. _____ Il a roulé pendant une heure.
h. _____ Il a attendu dix minutes.
i. _____ Il a appelé un garage.
j. _____ Il a vu un téléphone.

# Vocabulaire

## Verbes

**conduire** to drive
**construire** to construct
**descendre** to go down; to get off
**détruire** to destroy
**entrer** to enter
**faire le plein** to fill it up (*gas tank*)
**marcher** to work (*machine or object*)
**monter** to go up, climb
**mourir** to die
**naître** to be born
**passer** (**par**) to pass (by)
**rentrer** to return, go home
**retourner** to return; to go back
**rouler** to travel (*in a car*)
**tomber** to fall
**traduire** to translate
**traverser** to cross

À REVOIR: partir, voir, voyager

## Substantifs

**l'aéroport** (*m.*) airport
**l'arrivée** (*f.*) arrival
**l'autoroute** (*f.*) highway
**l'avion** (*m.*) airplane
**la carte d'embarquement** boarding pass
**la classe affaires** business class
**la classe économique** tourist class
**le compartiment** compartment
**le/la conducteur/trice** driver
**la couchette** berth
**le départ** departure
**l'ennui** (*m.*) problem, trouble
**la gare** train station
**le guichet** (ticket) window
**l'hôtesse de l'air** (*f.*) stewardess
**le métro** subway
**la motocyclette, la «moto»** motorcycle
**le/la passager/ère** passenger
**le/la pilote** pilot
**le quai** platform (train station)
**le steward** steward
**le train** train
**la valise** suitcase
**le vol** flight
**le wagon** train car
**la zone fumeur** smoking area
**la zone non-fumeur** non-smoking area

À REVOIR: l'endroit (*m.*), l'état (*m.*), la fois, le monde, le pays, la semaine, la voiture

## Expressions affirmatives et négatives

**déjà** already
**encore** still
**ne... jamais** never
**ne... pas du tout** not at all
**ne... pas encore** not yet
**ne... personne** no one, nobody
**ne... plus** no longer
**ne... rien** nothing
**parfois** sometimes
**quelque chose** something
**quelqu'un** someone
**seulement** only
**tout** everything
**tout le monde** everybody, everyone

## Mots et expressions divers

**à l'est/ouest** to the east/west
**à l'étranger** abroad, in a foreign country
**à l'heure** on time
**au nord/sud** to the north/south
**en retard** late, not on time
**si** yes (response to negative question)

# Intermède

## SITUATION

### En voiture!*

Situation: The *Situation* dialogues are recorded on the st. cassette packaged with the st. text.

**Contexte** *Geoffroy est venu faire des études d'optométrie à Nice. Il n'a pas encore eu le temps de visiter le Sud et a décidé de passer le week-end à Avignon pour voir le Palais des Papes° et le vieux pont.° Comme tout le monde, il prend le train.*

Palais... *Palace of the Popes* / *bridge*

**Objectif** *Geoffroy achète un billet° de train.*

*ticket*

GEOFFROY: (*au guichet*) À quelle heure est le prochain train pour Avignon, s'il vous plaît?

LE GUICHETIER: Vous avez un train dans vingt minutes et le suivant° est à vingt-deux heures.

le... *the next one*

GEOFFROY: Combien coûte le billet aller-retour° en deuxième classe?

*round-trip*

LE GUICHETIER: Deux cent quatre-vingt-quatorze francs.

GEOFFROY: Je veux un aller simple,° s'il vous plaît. Je peux régler° par chèques de voyage?

aller... *one-way ticket* / payer

LE GUICHETIER: Oui, s'ils sont en francs. Voilà votre billet. Vous avez une place° dans le compartiment 23, et vous partez du quai numéro 6.

*seat*

GEOFFROY: Merci.

LE GUICHETIER: Oh, n'oubliez pas de composter.°

*have your ticket punched*

## À propos

Suggestion: Ask several sts. to read the parts of the *Situation* first. Ask sts. to give French expression for following: 1. You want to know when the train leaves. 2. You want to know the price of a round-trip ticket. 3. You want to know the price of a second-class, one-way ticket. 4. You want to know if they accept traveler's checks. 5. You want to know what platform the train leaves from.

### Expressions utiles en voyage

EN VOITURE

Faites le plein (*Fill it up*), s'il vous plaît.
...de l'essence ordinaire ou du super?
Ma voiture est en panne (*broken down*).
Où y a-t-il une station-service (un garage), s'il vous plaît?

EN TAXI

C'est combien pour aller à Nation, s'il vous plaît?
(Emmenez-moi) à l'Hôtel du Centre, s'il vous plaît.

DANS LE MÉTRO (*SUBWAY*)

(Je voudrais) un ticket (de métro), s'il vous plaît.
(Je voudrais) un carnet (*book of tickets*), s'il vous plaît.

*En... *All aboard!*

EN AUTOBUS
Où est l'arrêt de bus (*bus stop*), s'il vous plaît?
(Je voudrais) un ticket (de bus), s'il vous plaît.
Quel bus faut-il prendre pour aller à...?

## Maintenant à vous!

**A. Questions personnelles.** Relisez le dialogue, puis répondez aux questions.

1. Pour faire un long voyage, quel moyen de transport préférez-vous? Pourquoi? Comment avez-vous voyagé la dernière fois que vous êtes parti(e)?
2. Prenez-vous parfois le train? Pourquoi (pas)? Quels sont les avantages de voyager en train? les inconvénients?
3. Avez-vous jamais fait un long voyage en voiture? Racontez où vous êtes allé(e), avec qui, et ce que vous avez fait en voyage.

**B. Jeux de rôles: En autobus.** Avec un(e) camarade, préparez une conversation entre un chauffeur de bus et un passager. Le passager ne sait pas (*doesn't know*) quel bus il faut prendre. Utilisez les expressions de l'*À Propos*. Puis jouez la scène devant la classe.

**Suggestion**: Ask sts. to form groups and choose one of the following variations on the dialogue. Have them write a short skit and present it to the class. The skits may be videotaped for viewing; tapes might be used in different classes. *Variations*: 1. *Vous prenez un billet aller-retour.* 2. *Vous allez à Paris et vous prenez une couchette (berth); le billet pour Paris coûte 750 F et le supplément couchette 100 F.*

### Jules Verne (1828–1905)

A pioneer of science fiction, Jules Verne is one of the most widely translated French writers. In his extremely popular novels, he anticipated a number of scientific and technical developments, including television. Several of his most famous novels have been made into films, including *Twenty Thousand Leagues Under the Sea* (*Vingt Mille Lieues sous les mers*, 1870), *From the Earth to the Moon* (*De la Terre à la Lune*, 1865), *A Journey to the Center of the Earth* (*Le Voyage au centre de la Terre*, 1864), and *Around the World in Eighty Days* (*Le Tour du monde en quatre-vingts jours*, 1873).

CHAPITRE **DIX**

# Bonnes nouvelles

**En avant**

—Est-ce que tu as déjà lu le journal ce matin?
—Oui, dans le métro.
—Alors, quoi de neuf?
—Oh, pas grand-chose. Tu sais, je ne lis que les grands titres et la page des sports.

**Communicative goals:** talking about communications, the media, and modern technology; describing and talking about the past; and speaking succinctly.

**En avant**: See scripts for follow-up questions recorded on student cassette.

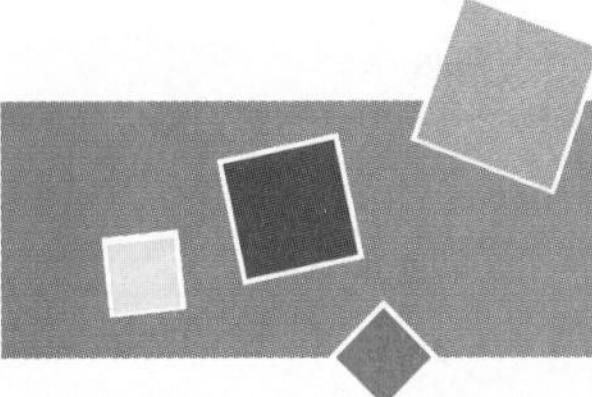

# Étude de vocabulaire

**Suggestions**: (1) Model pronunciation, with group and individual repetition. (2) *Devinettes.* Indicate objects with definitions or locations, such as: *Il est sur l'enveloppe* (*le timbre*). *Il est dans la cabine téléphonique* (*l'appareil, le téléphone*). *Ils sont dans le kiosque* (*les journaux, les magazines, les revues, etc.*). *C'est une des chaînes de la télévision française* (*TFI*).

## La communication et les médias

1. Nous écrivons et nous envoyons*...

Où est la dame sur le dessin? Qu'est-ce qu'il y a, en général, sur une enveloppe? Où trouve-t-on des boîtes aux lettres? Que fait-on quand on veut envoyer (*to send*) un message urgent?

**Additional vocab.**: *poster une lettre, envoyer une lettre aux États-Unis, un aérogramme, un colis, par avion, par voie de surface*

2. Nous lisons...

**Note**: It would be helpful to show slides of post offices (inside and outside), mail boxes, phone booths, phones in the *P et T*, and several kiosks. You may wish to bring in several types of French magazines for sts. to compare with American ones.

*For the complete conjugation of **envoyer**, **acheter**, and **appeler** (p. 265), see Appendix D: *Irregular Verbs* and *-er Verbs with Spelling Changes.*

Où va-t-on pour acheter des journaux? Quand est-ce qu'on regarde les petites annonces? Quels magazines achetez-vous régulièrement? quelles revues?* quels journaux?

**Additional activity**: *Conseils. Vous venez d'arriver en France et vous êtes un peu désorienté(e). Exposez votre problème et donnez des conseils.* MODÈLE: *Je voudrais trouver du travail.* → *Cherche un journal!* 1. *Je voudrais acheter un journal.* 2. *Je voudrais appeler un ami.* 3. *Je voudrais appeler une amie en Afrique.* 4. *Je voudrais acheter un timbre.* 5. *Je voudrais envoyer cette lettre.*

**Suggestion**: Teach sts. *en PCV* (*à percevoir* or *communication téléphonique payable par le destinataire*) in case they need to call collect from France.

3. Nous parlons...

D'après ce dessin, comment fait-on pour téléphoner en France?† Que doit-on chercher? Comment peut-on payer sa communication? Que dit la personne qui répond?

4. Nous écoutons et nous regardons...

**Quelques chaînes de la télévision française**

Télévision Française 1 (TF1) le journal

France 2 (F2) la publicité

France 3 (F3) une émission de musique

Canal Plus (Télévision privée par câble) une retransmission sportive

Voici, à la page suivante, un programme de la télévision française. Combien de chaînes y a-t-il? Comment s'appellent-elles? Quelles

---

*__Une revue__ is generally a monthly publication whose articles share a common theme and whose purpose is scholarly or informational. **Un magazine**, on the other hand, contains articles on a wide variety of topics and has many photographs and advertisements.

†Nearly all public phones require the **télécarte**, which can be purchased at the post office or a tobacco store (**bureau de tabac**). Many French collect the **télécartes** because they portray attractive scenes or famous people.

émissions vous sont familières? À première vue (*At first glance*) y a-t-il des différences entre les émissions françaises et américaines?

Maintenant imaginez que vous êtes en France et que vous voulez passer une partie de la journée à regarder la télé. Quelles émissions allez-vous choisir? Expliquez les raisons de votre choix.

**Suggestion**: Have sts. work in small groups to answer the questions and study the program.

**Additional activity**: *Une soirée de télévision française. Cherchez les émissions suivantes.* (*Donnez le nom de l'émission, la chaîne et l'heure de l'émission.*) 1. *une émission musicale* 2. *un film américain* 3. *un jeu*

**DU 22 MAI AU 28 MAI** **TOUTES VOS SOIRÉES**

| | SAMEDI | DIMANCHE | LUNDI |
|---|---|---|---|
| TF1 | 20.45 SÉRIE<br>COLUMBO<br>Avec Peter Falk (p. 59).<br>22.25 TÉLÉFILM<br>BRIGADE DE CHOC À LAS VEGAS 2<br>Avec Jeff Kaake, Craig Hurley (p. 60). | 20.45 CINÉMA<br>DOCTEUR POPAUL<br>Avec Jean-Paul Belmondo, Mia Farrow (p. 72).<br>22.45 CINÉMA<br>LA BARAKA<br>Avec Roger Hanin, Gérard Darmon (p. 73). | 20.45 MAGAZINE<br>TÉMOIN N°1<br>Par J. Pradel (p. 86).<br>22.45 MAGAZINE<br>À LA UNE<br>Par Catherine Nayl et Benoît Duquesne (p. 87). |
| France 2 | 20.50 HUMOUR<br>SURPRISE SUR PRISE<br>Par Marcel Béliveau et Georges Beller (p. 62).<br>22.25 VARIÉTÉS<br>TARATATA<br>Laurent Voulzy (p. 62). | 20.50 CINÉMA<br>RANDONNÉE POUR UN TUEUR<br>Avec S. Poitier (p. 75).<br>22.40 CINÉMA<br>LE DÉCLIN DE L'EMPIRE AMÉRICAIN<br>Avec D. Michel (p. 76). | 20.50 HOMMAGE<br>JOYEUX ANNIVERSAIRE MONSIEUR TRENET<br>(p. 89).<br>22.35 MAGAZINE<br>SAVOIR PLUS<br>**Sécurité : le marché de la peur** (p. 89). |
| France 3 | 20.45 TÉLÉFILM<br>NOTRE DAME DES ANGES<br>Avec J.-F. Perrier (p. 64).<br>22.45 MAGAZINE<br>VIS-À-VIS<br>**Idir et Johnny Clegg « a cappella »** (p. 64). | 20.45 JEU<br>SPÉCIAL QUESTIONS POUR UN CHAMPION<br>Finale des masters (p. 78).<br>23.15 CINÉMA<br>LA FIANCÉE DE FRANKENSTEIN<br>Avec Colin Clive (p. 78). | 20.45 CINÉMA<br>SUBWAY<br>De Luc Besson.<br>Avec I. Adjani (p. 91).<br>23.15 MAGAZINE<br>TOUT LE CINÉMA<br>Par Henry Chapier<br>En direct de Cannes (p. 91). |
| Canal+ | 20.30 TÉLÉFILM<br>PIÈGE DE FEU<br>Avec Lee Majors, Lisa Hartman (p. 66).<br>23.30 CINÉMA<br>RATMAN<br>Avec Nelson de La Rosa (p. 66). | 20.30 CINÉMA<br>LA SENTINELLE<br>D'Arnaud Desplechin.<br>Avec Emmanuel Salinger, Jean-Louis Richard, Bruno Todeschini, Marianne Denicourt (p. 80). | 20.35 CINÉMA<br>CONFESSIONS D'UN BARJO<br>Avec Hippolyte Girardot, Richard Bohringer (p. 92)<br>22.05 CINÉMA<br>LE SILENCE<br>Avec Ingrid Thulin (p. 93). |
| Arte | 20.40 DOCUMENT<br>L'ŒIL DU CAMERAMAN<br>De Jürgen Stumpfhaus (p. 68).<br>22.10 TÉLÉFILM<br>CAPPUCCINO MÉLANGE<br>Avec Josef Hader (p. 68). | 20.40 SPÉCIAL<br>SOIRÉE : MAX FRISCH<br>Avec à **20.45 Barbe-Bleue**<br>Téléfilm de K. Zanussi.<br>Avec Vadim Glowna, Karine Baal (p. 82). | 20.40 CINÉMA<br>ATLANTIC CITY<br>De Louis Malle.<br>Avec Susan Sarandon, Burt Lancaster (p. 95).<br>22.25 CINÉMA<br>LE PASSAGER<br>Avec Tony Curtis (p. 95). |
| M6 | 20.45 TÉLÉFILM<br>L'AMOUR DÉCHIRÉ<br>Avec Valerie Bertinelli, Michael Ontkean (p. 67).<br>23.25 TÉLÉFILM<br>LA PISTE DE L'HOMME MORT<br>Avec Peter Graves (p. 68). | 20.50 TÉLÉFILM<br>QUAND L'AMOUR S'EMMÊLE<br>Avec John Ritter (p. 81).<br>22.45 CINÉMA<br>BLACK EMANUELLE EN AMÉRIQUE<br>Avec Laura Gemser (p. 82). | 20.45 CINÉMA<br>LES CAVALIERS<br>Avec John Wayne, William Holden (p. 94).<br>22.50 TÉLÉFILM<br>TRAFICS À MIAMI<br>Avec Scott Feraco, Robert Sedgwick (p. 95). |

# Quelques verbes de communication

Dire bonjour

Lire le journal

Écrire une lettre

Mettre de l'argent

| | dire (*to say, to tell*) | lire (*to read*) | écrire (*to write*) | mettre (*to place, to put*) |
|---|---|---|---|---|
| je, j' | dis | lis | écris | mets |
| tu | dis | lis | écris | mets |
| il, elle, on | dit | lit | écrit | met |
| nous | disons | lisons | écrivons | mettons |
| vous | dites | lisez | écrivez | mettez |
| ils, elles | disent | lisent | écrivent | mettent |
| *Past participle:* | dit | lu | écrit | mis |

**Presentation**: Model pronunciation of verbs in short sentences, such as: *Je dis bonjour* (*tu, il,* etc.). *Je lis le journal. J'écris une lettre. Je mets la carte dans l'appareil.*

**Note**: Point out similarities in conjugations, then point out differences in second-person plural of *dire* and plural stem of *écrire*.

**Dire**, **lire**, and **écrire** have similar conjugations, except for the second-person plural of **dire** and the **v** in the plural stem of **écrire**. Another verb conjugated like **écrire** is **décrire** (*to describe*).

**A. Lettre aux parents**

1. Vous racontez à un(e) camarade ce que vous mettez dans la lettre que vous écrivez à vos parents. Complétez les phrases avec les verbes **décrire**, **dire**, **écrire**, **lire** et **mettre**, au présent. Faites tous les changements nécessaires.

Cet après-midi, je _____[1] une longue lettre à mes parents. Dans ma lettre, je _____[2] mes cours et ma vie à l'université. Je donne aussi beaucoup de détails sur mes camarades et mes professeurs parce que mes parents sont très curieux. Ils sont aussi très compréhensifs (*understanding*) et je leur _____[3] toujours la vérité quand j'ai des problèmes. Avant de fermer l'enveloppe, je _____[4] la lettre une dernière fois (*last time*). Puis je _____[5] la lettre à la boîte aux lettres.

2. Ensuite, mettez le passage au passé composé. Commencez par «Hier...»
3. Racontez la même histoire, mais cette fois commencez par «**mon** (**ma**) **camarade de chambre**», puis par «**Stéphanie et Albane**». Faites tous les changements nécessaires.

**B. Interview.** Posez les questions suivantes à un(e) de vos camarades, puis inversez les rôles.

1. Est-ce que tu écris souvent des lettres? des cartes postales? À qui écris-tu? D'habitude, pour donner de tes nouvelles à tes amis, préfères-tu écrire ou téléphoner?
2. Est-ce que tu aimes lire? Lis-tu le journal tous les jours? Si oui, lequel? As-tu déjà cherché du travail dans les petites annonces? Quel magazine achètes-tu régulièrement? As-tu lu un bon livre récemment? Lequel?
3. Est-ce que tu regardes la télévision tous les soirs? Quelles émissions préfères-tu? Que penses-tu de la télévision américaine? À ton avis, y a-t-il trop de publicité à la télévision?

D'après ses réponses, que pouvez-vous dire de votre camarade et de ses goûts?

**Follow-up**: Ask sts. to get information from each other: *Qu'est-ce que tu lis souvent? Quel le émission regardes-tu à la télévision? À qui écris-tu souvent?* Sts. can make a list of responses. They can share answers with whole class.

## Les nouvelles technologies

Le téléviseur

Le magnétoscope

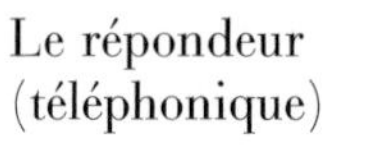

Le répondeur (téléphonique)

L'ordinateur

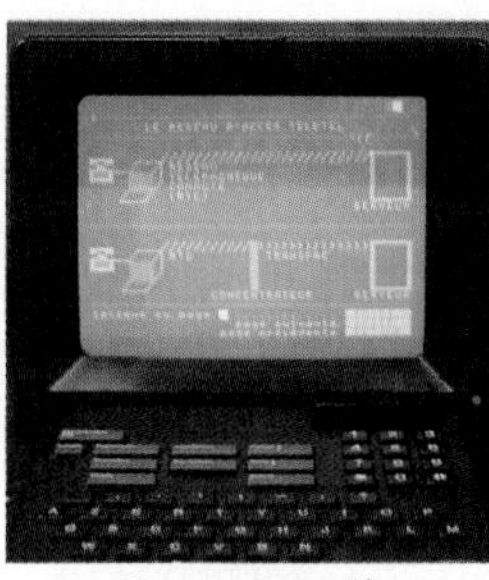

Le minitel*

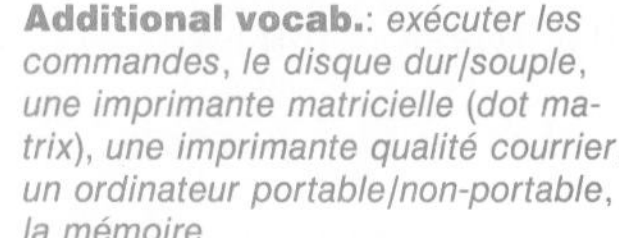

**Additional vocab.**: *exécuter les commandes, le disque dur/souple, une imprimante matricielle* (dot matrix), *une imprimante qualité courrier, un ordinateur portable/non-portable, la mémoire*

**A. Définitions.** Regardez les dessins et les photos et trouvez le mot qui correspond à chaque définition.

1. C'est une machine qui nous permet (*which allows us*) de faire les courses à la maison.
2. C'est une machine qui prend des messages.
3. C'est un appareil qui nous permet de regarder des films à la maison.
4. C'est une machine qui nous permet de préparer des textes écrits.
5. C'est un appareil qui nous aide à réserver des places dans le train.

**B. Les nouvelles technologies.** Posez les questions suivantes à un(e) ou plusieurs (*several*) camarades.

**Mots et expressions utiles:** le photocopieur, le répondeur téléphonique, le magnétophone (la cassette), le disque compact, le magnétoscope (la

**Suggestion**: Bring in pages advertising some of these items from a French or Francophone catalog. Use as an authentic reading document. Ask sts. to choose the item they prefer and discuss why they chose it.

---

*__Le minitel__ is a telecommunications terminal for the home that can be rented from the telephone company. It provides people in France with access to thousands of information sources and can be used to make plane reservations, buy theater tickets, pay bills, do shopping, and communicate with other subscribers.

vidéocassette), le caméscope, la base de données (*data*), le traitement de texte (*word processing*), programmer, faire des calculs, des recherches...

1. Avez-vous un ordinateur? Est-ce qu'il a changé votre façon de travailler? Expliquez.
2. Jouez-vous avec votre ordinateur? Quel est votre jeu préféré?
3. Quelles autres nouvelles technologies utilisez-vous? D'après vous, lesquelles sont indispensables? Expliquez pourquoi.
4. Préférez-vous regarder les films au magnétoscope ou au cinéma? Pourquoi?

## Un peu d'argot

| | |
|---|---|
| **passer un coup de fil** | téléphoner |
| **le canard** | le journal |
| **la télé / la téloche** | la télévision |
| **la pub** | la publicité |
| **le bouquin** | le livre |

EN CONTEXTE

SOPHIE: Dis donc, j'ai lu aujourd'hui dans **un canard** que le film *Indochine* passe à **la téloche** ce soir. Si tu veux, je te **passe un coup de fil** vers huit heures et on peut le voir ensemble.

JULIE: Non, merci, je dois finir **un bouquin** pour mon cours de littérature.

SOPHIE: Oh, mais tu peux le lire pendant **la pub**!

**Note**: In the expression *passer un coup de fil, fil* (wire) refers to the telephone wire. *Un canard* originally referred to rumors started by the media; now it means a newspaper. It is used humorously. *La télé* is short for *télévision* and *la pub* for *publicité*. They are part of everyday spoken language. *La téloche* is used only by youths. It is a very informal expression, not very elegant, but funny. *Le bouquin* comes from the Dutch word *boek*, meaning *book*. It is used by everyone informally.

**Follow-up**: Organize a debate on "*la télévision et les enfants—pour ou contre.*" Divide the class into small groups. Assign a position to each group and have sts. brainstorm about all the advantages and disadvantages of television. Ask each side to present its case; the other side responds. Several judges (3 or 4 sts. in the class) will determine the winner of the debate.

## France-culture

*La télévision en France.* Il y a quelques différences entre la télévision française et la télévision américaine. Aux États-Unis, les premières chaînes° (*networks*) étaient° (*were*) privées; la «télévision publique» est venue seulement plus tard. En France, au contraire, la télévision a été développée par le gouvernement pour diffuser° (*spread*) la culture, et l'importance des chaînes privées est un phénomène assez récent.

Aujourd'hui, il y six chaînes en France:

- **TF1** et **M6**, chaînes privées, retransmettent° (*broadcast*) des émissions très variées. Elles sont obligées aussi de diffuser un minimum d'émissions d'origine française ou européenne.

**Suggestion**: Show brief clips from a recorded French or *québécois* television program.

- **France 2** et **France 3**, chaînes sous le contrôle du gouvernement français, sont financées en partie par la publicité, en partie par une taxe (payée par toutes les personnes possédant° un poste de télévision). Toutes les deux° font des efforts pour passer des émissions culturelles. De plus, France 3 retransmet des émissions locales par ses émetteurs régionaux.
- **Canal Plus**, une autre chaîne privée, est codée: pour la regarder, il faut louer un appareil spécial, le «décodeur». Elle retransmet 24 heures surhr° 24 le vendredi et le samedi et passe° des films récents.
- **Arte**, la première chaîne européenne, est contrôlée par les gouvernements français et allemand. Elle retransmet des émissions culturelles européennes et des films européens en version originale.°

Dans les principales villes françaises on peut aussi s'abonner° aux chaînes par câbles. Et maintenant, avec l'emploi des satellites, un certain nombre de téléspectateurs français peuvent voir les émissions des chaînes des autres pays européens, des États-Unis et du monde entier.

*owning / Toutes... Both*

*out of*

*shows (films)*

*en... undubbed*

*subscribe*

**Follow-up**: Have sts. write a short description of a television program they have seen recently, and give their opinion of the program.

# Étude de grammaire

## 33. DESCRIBING THE PAST
## The *imparfait*

### Pauvre grand-mère!

MME CHABOT: Tu vois, quand **j'étais** petite, la télévision n'**existait** pas.
CLÉMENT: Mais alors, qu'est-ce que vous **faisiez** le soir?
MME CHABOT: Eh bien, nous **lisions**, nous **bavardions**; nos parents nous **racontaient** des histoires...
CLÉMENT: Pauvre grand-mère, ça **devait** être triste de ne pas pouvoir regarder «Santa Barbara» le soir...

Qui parle dans les phrases suivantes, Mme Chabot ou Clément?

1. La télévision n'existait pas quand j'étais petite.
2. Ça devait être triste de ne pas regarder «Santa Barbara».
3. Tu n'avais pas de télévision, mais avais-tu la radio?
4. La télévision existait-elle quand je suis né?
5. Nous n'avions que la radio et les journaux pour avoir les nouvelles.

The **passé composé** is used to relate events that began and ended in the past. In contrast, the **imparfait** (imperfect) is used to describe continuous, repeated, or habitual past actions or situations.* It is also used in descriptions.

The **imparfait** has several equivalents in English. For example, **je parlais** can mean *I talked, I was talking, I used to talk*, or *I would talk*.

## A. Formation of the *imparfait*

The formation of the **imparfait** is identical for all French verbs except **être**. To find the regular imperfect stem, drop the **-ons** ending from the present-tense **nous** form. Then add the imperfect endings.

nous parl~~ons~~ **parl-**
nous finiss~~ons~~ **finiss-**
nous vend~~ons~~ **vend-**
nous av~~ons~~ **av-**

| IMPARFAIT OF **parler** (*to speak, to talk*) | | | |
|---|---|---|---|
| je | parl**ais** | nous | parl**ions** |
| tu | parl**ais** | vous | parl**iez** |
| il, elle, on | parl**ait** | ils, elles | parl**aient** |

**Suggestion**: To practice listening comp., ask sts. to indicate whether they hear imperfect or present tense. 1. *Que faites-vous?* 2. *Nous visitons le musée.* 3. *Paul regardait la statue.* 4. *Vous allez à la banque?* 5. *Tu finis ton livre?* 6. *J'allais à la pharmacie.*

J'**allais** au bureau de poste tous les matins. — *I used to go to the post office every morning.*

Mon grand-père **disait** toujours: «L'excès en tout est un défaut». — *My grandfather always used to say, "Moderation in all things."*

Quand j'**habitais** avec les Huet, je **mettais** souvent la table. — *When I lived with the Huets, I would often set the table.*

Verbs with an imperfect stem that ends in **-i** (**étudier**: **étudi-**) have a double **i** in the first- and second-persons plural of the **imparfait**: **nous étud*ii*ons**, **vous étud*ii*ez**. The **ii** is pronounced as a long i sound [i:], to distinguish the **imparfait** from the present-tense forms **nous étudions** and **vous étudiez**.

Verbs with stems ending in **c** [s] or **g** [ʒ] have a spelling change when the **imparfait** endings start with **a**: **je mang*e*ais, nous mangions**; **elle commen*ç*ait, nous commencions**. In this way, the pronunciation of the stem is preserved.

**Note**: Point out that *changer*, *déranger*, *nager*, *juger*, and *voyager* are conjugated like *manger* in the imperfect.

*The differences between the **passé composé** and the **imparfait** are presented in detail in the next chapter.

## B. *Imparfait* of être

The verb **être** (*to be*) has an irregular stem in the **imparfait**: **ét-**.

| IMPARFAIT OF **être** (*to be*) | | | |
|---|---|---|---|
| j' | **étais** | nous | **étions** |
| tu | **étais** | vous | **étiez** |
| il, elle, on | **était** | ils, elles | **étaient** |

Quand tu **étais** petit, tu aimais bien lire les contes de la Mère l'oie. — *When you were little, you liked to read Mother Goose stories.*

J'**étais** très heureux quand j'habitais à Paris. — *I was very happy when I lived in Paris.*

Mes parents **étaient** à l'étranger à ce moment-là. — *My parents were abroad at that time.*

## C. Uses of the *imparfait*

In general, the **imparfait** is used to describe actions or situations that existed for an indefinite period of time in the past. There is usually no mention of the beginning or end of the event. The **imparfait** is used in the following situations.

1. In descriptions, to set a scene

   C'**était** une nuit tranquille à Paris. Il **pleuvait** et il **faisait** froid. M. Cartier **lisait** le journal. Mme Cartier **regardait** la télévision et Achille, leur chat, **dormait**. — *It was a quiet night in Paris. It was raining and (it was) cold. Mr. Cartier was reading the newspaper. Mrs. Cartier was watching television, and Achille, their cat, was sleeping.*

**Suggestion**: Model pronunciation of sentences. Point out the pronunciation of *faisait* [fəzɛ].

2. For habitual or repeated actions

   Quand j'étais jeune, j'**allais** chez mes grands-parents tous les dimanches. Nous **faisions** de belles promenades. — *When I was young, I went to my grandparents' home every Sunday. We would take (used to take) lovely walks.*

3. To describe feelings and mental or emotional states

   Claudine **était** très heureuse— elle **avait** envie de chanter. — *Claudine was very happy—she felt like singing.*

4. To tell the time of day or to express age in the past

| | |
|---|---|
| Il **était** cinq heures et demie du matin. | *It was 5:30* A.M. |
| C'était son anniversaire; il **avait** douze ans. | *It was his birthday; he was twelve years old.* |

5. To describe an action or situation that was happening when another event (usually in the **passé composé**) interrupted it

| | |
|---|---|
| Jean **lisait** le journal quand le téléphone a sonné. | *Jean was reading the paper when the phone rang.* |

## Mots-clés

*Talking about repeated past actions:* Use **tous les** (*m.*) or **toutes les** (*f.*) in the following expressions to indicate habitual actions.

| | |
|---|---|
| **tous les jours** | *every day* |
| **tous les après-midi (matins / soirs)** | *every afternoon (morning / evening)* |
| **toutes les semaines** | *every week* |

Other useful adverbs with the **imparfait** include the following.

| | |
|---|---|
| **d'habitude** | *as a rule, habitually* |
| **en général** | *generally* |
| **souvent** | *often* |

### Vérifions!

**A. Souvenirs d'enfance.** Qui dans votre famille faisait les choses suivantes quand vous étiez petit(e)?

**Suggestion**: May be done in small groups or as a writing ex.

**Expressions utiles**: mes parents, mon frère / ma sœur, mon meilleur ami (ma meilleure amie) et moi, je...

1. Qui lisait le journal tous les matins? 2. Qui regardait la télévision après le dîner? 3. Qui aimait écouter la radio le matin? 4. Qui faisait beaucoup de sport? 5. Qui étudiait tous les après-midi? 6. Qui lisait des bandes dessinées (*comics*)?

**B. Sorties.** L'an dernier, vous sortiez régulièrement avec vos amis. Faites des phrases complètes selon le modèle.

**Suggestion**: May be done with books closed.

MODÈLE: dîner ensemble → Nous dînions ensemble.

1. jouer aux cartes les jours de pluie 2. boire des cafés 3. faire des promenades l'après-midi 4. pique-niquer à la campagne 5. aller à la discothèque tous les week-ends 6. partir en vacances ensemble

## Parlons-en!

**A. C'était hier.** Regardez les tableaux et répondez aux questions.

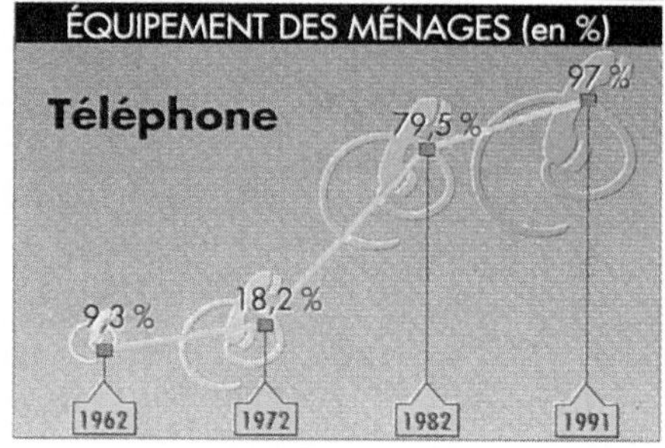


1. En 1972, combien de Français pouvaient téléphoner de chez eux (*from their homes*)?
2. En 1962, la télévision était en couleurs ou en noir et blanc?
3. En 1962, quel pourcentage de familles françaises avaient la télévision?
4. Combien de chaînes de télévision y avait-il en 1962?
5. Et vos grands-parents, qu'est-ce qu'ils faisaient en 1962? Est-ce qu'ils regardaient la télé? Est-ce qu'ils écoutaient la radio? Est-ce qu'ils lisaient le journal?

**B. Conversation.** Posez les questions suivantes à un(e) camarade. En 1985...

1. Quel âge avais-tu? 2. Habitais-tu à la campagne, dans une petite ville ou dans une grande ville? Avec qui habitais-tu? 3. Comment était ta maison ou ton appartement? 4. Étais-tu bon(ne) élève (*pupil*) à l'école (*school*)? Aimais-tu tes instituteurs (*teachers*)? 5. Étais-tu content(e)? Pourquoi ou pourquoi pas? 6. Où passais-tu tes vacances? 7. Faisais-tu du sport? 8. ?

**Suggestion**: Give sts. other information to find out: *lecture*, *frères et sœurs*, *animaux*, *loisirs*.

Maintenant décrivez au reste de la classe ce que votre camarade faisait en 1985.

# 34. SPEAKING SUCCINCTLY
## Direct Object Pronouns

**Les Cossec déménagent**

THIERRY: Qu'est-ce qu'on fait avec la télé?
MARYSE: On va **la** donner à ta sœur.
THIERRY: D'accord. Et avec tous nos livres?
MARYSE: On va **les** envoyer par la poste. Ils ont un tarif spécial pour les livres.
THIERRY: Tu as raison. Je n'ai pas envie de **les** jeter. Et le minitel, on va **le** vendre?
MARYSE: Mais non. Tu sais bien qu'on **le** loue aux P et T.* On doit **le** rendre avant la fin du mois.

Trouvez la réponse correcte et complétez la phrase.

1. Qu'est-ce qu'ils font avec la télé?
2. Et avec les livres?
3. Et avec le minitel?

a. Ils vont _____ envoyer par la poste.
b. Ils vont _____ donner à la sœur de Thierry.
c. Ils vont _____ rendre.

## A. Direct Object Nouns and Pronouns

Direct objects are nouns that receive the action of a verb. They usually answer the question *what?* or *whom?* For example, in the sentence *Robert dials the number*, the word *number* is the direct object of the verb *dials*.

Direct object pronouns (**les pronoms compléments d'objet direct**) replace direct object nouns: Robert dials *it*. In general, direct object pronouns replace nouns that refer to specific persons, places, objects, or situations.

| | |
|---|---|
| J'admire **la France**. Je **l'**admire. | *I admire France. I admire it.* |
| Je regarde **ma sœur**. Je **la** regarde. | *I look at my sister. I look at her.* |

**Presentation**: Some sts. have trouble recognizing direct or indirect objects in English. Giving English examples first may be best preparation for this grammar section. Ask students to find direct objects in these sentences: *Robert picks up the receiver. He sees the number in the phone book. He calls his friend on the phone. He gives him advice. His friend tells him some news. He wrote it in a letter*, etc.

**Suggestion**: Provide lots of examples so that sts. get used to hearing sentences with object pronouns. They may find it helpful to have one or two simple examples to call to mind as they do later exs. and activities: *Elle veut la pomme.* → *Elle la veut.* / *Il veut lire le livre.* → *Il veut le lire.*

*Mail and telephone services are run by the **Ministère des Postes et Télécommunications**, an important government agency. **P et T** (**postes et télécommunications**) was formerly called **PTT** (**poste, téléphone et télégraphe**).

# B. Forms and Position of Direct Object Pronouns

| DIRECT OBJECT PRONOUNS | | | |
|---|---|---|---|
| **me** (**m'**) | *me* | **nous** | *us* |
| **te** (**t'**) | *you* | **vous** | *you* |
| **le** (**l'**) | *him, it* | **les** | *them* |
| **la** (**l'**) | *her, it* | | |

Robert compose **le numéro**.

Robert **le** compose.

Robert composait **le numéro**.

Robert **le** composait.

**Note:** *Faire le numéro* is a common synonym of *composer le numéro*.

Robert a composé **le numéro**.

Robert **l'**a composé.

Usually, French direct object pronouns immediately precede the verb in the present and the imperfect tenses and the auxiliary verb in the **passé composé**. Third-person direct object pronouns agree in gender and in number with the nouns they replace: **le** replaces a masculine singular noun, **la** replaces a feminine singular noun, and **les** replaces plural nouns.

—Pierre lisait-il **le journal**? — *—Was Pierre reading the newspaper?*
—Oui, il **le** lisait. — *—Yes, he was reading it.*

—Veux-tu **ma revue**? — *—Do you want my magazine?*
—Oui, je **la** veux. — *—Yes, I want it.*

—Est-ce que vous postez **ces lettres**? — *—Are you mailing these letters?*
—Oui, je **les** poste. — *—Yes, I'm mailing them.*

—Anne a-t-elle lu **le journal**? — *—Did Anne read the newspaper?*
—Oui, elle **l'**a lu. — *—Yes, she read it.*

If the verb following the direct object pronoun begins with a vowel sound, the direct object pronouns **me**, **te**, **le**, and **la** become **m'**, **t'**, and **l'**.

J'achète la carte postale. Je **l'**achète. — *I'm buying the postcard. I'm buying it.*
Monique **t'**admirait. Elle ne **m'**admirait pas. — *Monique used to admire you. She didn't admire me.*
Nous avons lu le journal. Nous **l'**avons lu. — *We read the newspaper. We read it.*

If the direct object pronoun is the object of an infinitive, it is placed immediately before the infinitive.

| | |
|---|---|
| Annick va **chercher l'adresse**. Annick va **la chercher**. | *Annick is going to get the address. Annick is going to get it.* |
| Elle allait **la chercher**. Elle est allée **la chercher**. | *She was going to get it. She went to get it.* |

In a negative sentence, the direct object pronoun always immediately precedes the verb that refers to it.

| | |
|---|---|
| Nous ne regardons pas **la télé**. Nous ne **la** regardons pas. | *We don't watch TV. We don't watch it.* |
| Je ne vais pas acheter **les billets**. Je ne vais pas **les** acheter. | *I'm not going to buy the tickets. I'm not going to buy them.* |
| Elle n'est pas allée chercher **le journal**. Elle n'est pas allée **le** chercher. | *She did not go to get the newspaper. She did not go to get it.* |

The direct object pronouns also precede **voici** and **voilà**.

| | |
|---|---|
| **Le** voici! | *Here he (it) is!* |
| **Me** voilà! | *Here I am!* |

**Suggestion**: Have sts. pick out direct object pronouns in the following listening ex. and suggest noun(s) they might be replacing. You might give this as a partial dictation, with sts. writing only the pronoun, along with possible noun(s). 1. *Je ne les cherche pas.* 2. *Ils me cherchent.* 3. *Est-ce que tu la trouves?* 4. *Ils nous regardent.* 5. *Elle l'admire.* 6. *Nous les admirons aussi.* 7. *Tu vas la regarder?* 8. *Nous allons les acheter.* 9. *Ils t'appellent au téléphone.* 10. *Nous ne vous appelons pas.*

**Additional activity:** *Un coup de téléphone.* MODÈLE: *Je cherche la cabine téléphonique.* → *Je la cherche.* 1. *Je consulte l'annuaire.* 2. *Je décroche le combiné.* 3. *Je mets la carte.* 4. *Je compose le numéro.* 5. *J'écoute mes amis.*

## *Vérifions!*

**A. Eurêka!** Suivez le modèle.

MODÈLE: Je cherche le bureau de poste. → Le voilà. (*ou* Le voici.)

1. Où est l'annuaire?
2. Elle a perdu le numéro de téléphone.
3. Où est le téléphone?
4. Il cherche le kiosque.
5. Il a envie de lire *Le Monde* d'hier.
6. Avez-vous deux francs?
7. Où est l'adresse des Thibaudeau?
8. J'ai besoin de la grande enveloppe blanche.

**B. De quoi parlent-ils?** Vous êtes dans un café parisien et vous entendez les phrases suivantes. Trouvez dans la colonne de droite l'information qui correspond à chaque pronom.

| | |
|---|---|
| 1. Je vais les poster cet après-midi. | l'adresse |
| 2. Elle le consulte. | la télé |
| 3. Les étudiants l'écoutent. | les lettres |
| 4. Je l'écris sur l'enveloppe. | le numéro |
| 5. Nous venons de la lire. | l'annuaire |
| 6. Je les achète à la poste. | la revue |
| 7. Ma grand-mère la regarde souvent. | les timbres |
| 8. Je l'ai déjà composé. | le professeur |

**C. Projets de voyage.** Christian et Christiane font toujours la même chose. Avec un(e) camarade, parlez de leurs projets selon le modèle.

**Continuation:** *lire les annonces dans le journal*; *regarder la télévision*; *acheter la revue* Historia.

MODÈLE: étudier le français cette année →
—Est-ce qu'elle va étudier le français cette année?
—Oui, et il va l'étudier aussi.

1. apprendre le français très rapidement (*quickly*)
2. prendre l'avion pour Paris en juin
3. visiter la tour Eiffel
4. admirer la vue du haut de la tour Eiffel
5. prendre ses repas dans de bons restaurants
6. regarder les gens sur les Champs-Élysées
7. essayer de lire les romans (*novels*) de Flaubert

Maintenant imaginez que Christian est l'opposé de Christiane.

MODÈLE: —Est-ce qu'elle va étudier le français cette année?
—Oui, mais lui, il ne va pas l'étudier.

**Suggestions**: (1) Have sts. do interview and report answers as follows: *Doug, est-ce que Suzanne utilise souvent le téléphone?* Doug: *Oui, elle l'utilise souvent.* (etc.) (2) Dictate questions at board and have sts. write answers with object pronoun. Then compare individual responses. Example: *« Ah, Julia utilise souvent le téléphone, mais Mark ne l'utilise pas.»*

## *Parlons-en!*

**Interview.** Interviewez un(e) camarade de classe sur ses préférences. Votre camarade doit utiliser un pronom complément d'objet direct dans sa réponse.

1. Utilises-tu souvent le téléphone?
2. Appelles-tu souvent tes camarades de classe? tes professeurs? tes parents?
3. Est-ce que tes parents t'appellent souvent? et tes amis?
4. Regardes-tu souvent la télé?
5. Aimes-tu regarder la publicité?
6. Préfères-tu apprendre les nouvelles dans le journal ou à la radio? à la radio ou à la télé?
7. Lis-tu des revues internationales?

# 35. TALKING ABOUT THE PAST
## Agreement of the Past Participle

### L'opinion d'un téléspectateur américain en France

LE REPORTER: Avez-vous déjà regardé la télévision française?
L'AMÉRICAIN: Oui, je **l'ai regardée** hier soir.
LE REPORTER: Quelles **émissions** avez-vous **préférées**?
L'AMÉRICAIN: C'est difficile à dire...
LE REPORTER: Ne trouvez-vous pas qu'elle est très différente de la télévision américaine?
L'AMÉRICAIN: Eh bien... **les émissions** que j'ai **vues** sont plutôt semblables... «Santa Barbara», «Les Simpson»... Enfin oui, elles sont différentes—elles sont en français!

Et vous?

1. Est-ce que vous avez lu le journal ce matin?
2. Avez-vous regardé la télévision hier soir?
3. Quelles émissions avez-vous choisies? Les avez-vous aimées?

In the **passé composé**, the past participle is generally used in its basic form. However, when a direct object—noun or pronoun—precedes the auxiliary verb **avoir** plus the past participle, the participle agrees with the preceding direct object in gender and number.

| | |
|---|---|
| J'ai lu le **journal**. Je **l'ai lu**. | J'ai lu les **journaux**. Je **les** ai **lus**. |
| J'ai lu **la revue**. Je **l'ai lue**. | J'ai lu les **revues**. Je **les** ai **lues**. |
| Quels **amis** avez-vous **appelés**? | *Which friends did you call?* |
| Quelles **émissions** avez-vous **regardées**? | *Which programs did you watch?* |

### *Vérifions!*

**Suggestion**: May be done first with books closed for further practice of object pronouns. As an ex. on agreement of past participle, may be assigned as homework.

**Un nouveau travail.** Vous travaillez comme secrétaire. Votre patronne (*boss*) vous pose des questions. Répondez affirmativement ou négativement.

MODÈLE: Avez-vous regardé *le calendrier* ce matin? →
Oui, je l'ai regardé. (Non, je ne l'ai pas regardé.)

1. Est-ce que vous avez donné *notre numéro de téléphone* à Mme Milaud?
2. Est-ce que vous avez mis *le nouveau nom de la firme* sur les enveloppes?
3. Attendiez-vous *le facteur* à 5 heures hier soir?
4. Allez-vous finir *le courrier* (*mail*) avant midi?
5. Avez-vous appelé *Georges Dupic et Catherine Duriez*?
6. Avez-vous vu *Annick et Françoise* ce matin?
7. *M*'avez-vous comprise pendant la réunion (*meeting*) hier?
8. Est-ce que je *vous* dérange (*disturb*) si je téléphone à midi et demi?

**Additional activity:** *Conversation. Posez les questions suivantes à un(e) camarade. Il/Elle utilise, quand c'est possible, un pronom complément d'objet direct dans ses réponses. 1. Quand tu étais enfant, aimais-tu toujours l'école? les vacances? les voyages? l'aventure? Quelle sorte d'aventure aimais-tu? 2. L'année dernière, as-tu passé tes vacances à la montagne? à l'étranger? en famille? 3. As-tu déjà essayé le camping? l'alpinisme? le bateau? le ski? 4. As-tu lu le dernier numéro de* Time? *de* Newsweek? *de* Sports Illustrated? *de* l'Express? *5. As-tu lu les romans d'Albert Camus? les livres de Saint-Exupéry? 6. Quand as-tu appelé tes grands-parents? tes parents? ton professeur de français? Pourquoi?*

## Parlons-en!

**Conversation.**
Posez les questions suivantes à un(e) camarade. Il/Elle utilise, quand c'est possible, un pronom complément d'objet direct dans ses réponses.

1. Quand tu étais enfant, écoutais-tu quelquefois la radio? Préférais-tu regarder la télévision? Quels programmes-radio ou quelles émissions aimais-tu surtout?
2. Quels magazines ou quelles revues préférais-tu quand tu étais adolescent(e)? et maintenant?
3. As-tu lu des romans de Stephen King? de Toni Morrison? Aimes-tu les livres d'aventures? Aimes-tu mieux les romans d'amour? Quel est ton écrivain préféré?
4. Quelle est la meilleure (*best*) chaîne de télévision, à ton avis? Peux-tu nommer deux ou trois émissions que tu considères excellentes, et expliquer pourquoi?

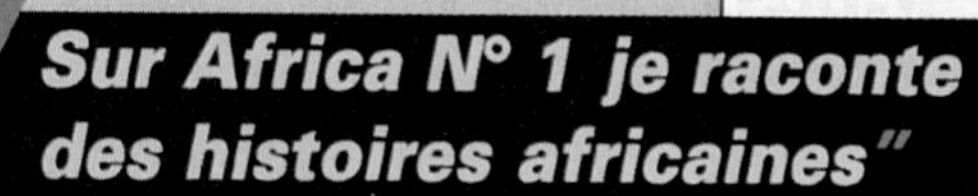

Hit-parade, concerts, interviews, derniers succès, nouveaux talents : la musique africaine, c'est le rythme d'Africa N° 1. Pourrait-il en être autrement quand l'ensemble de ses journalistes, animateurs et techniciens sont eux-mêmes africains.
Africa N° 1, c'est jour après jour l'information, la musique et le sport pour 20 millions d'auditeurs africains entre Dakar et Kinshasa.
Pour rester à la pointe de l'information à travers l'Afrique et dans le monde entier, branchez-vous sur l'Afrique en direct...
Branchez-vous sur Africa N° 1.

"HISTOIRES D'ENFANTS", "CARTE BLANCHE" : les émissions de Ghislaine sont la mémoire de l'Afrique.

AFRIQUE DE L'OUEST
de 07 h à 16 h : 17630 KHz
de 16 h à 21 h : 15475 KHz
ou de 05 h à 23 h : 9580 KHz
AFRIQUE CENTRALE
de 06 h à 24 h : 9580 KHz

BP 1 Libreville - GABON
Tél. : (241) 76 00 01
Fax : (241) 74 21 33
Télex : 5588 GO

L'AFRIQUE EN DIRECT

# 36. SPEAKING SUCCINCTLY Indirect Object Pronouns

**Journalistes pour le *Canard*?**

RÉGIS: Tu as écrit aux journalistes du *Canard Enchaîné*?*
NICOLE: Oui, je **leur** ai écrit.
RÉGIS: Ils **t'**ont répondu?
NICOLE: Oui, ils **nous** ont donné rendez-vous demain.
RÉGIS: Ils ont aimé nos caricatures politiques?
NICOLE: Ils ne **m'**ont encore rien dit: on va voir demain!

Retrouvez la phrase correcte dans le dialogue.

1. J'ai écrit aux journalistes.
2. Les journalistes ont donné rendez-vous à Nicole et à Régis.
3. Les journalistes n'ont encore rien dit à Nicole.

**Suggestion**: Bring in a copy of *Le Canard Enchaîné* for sts. to look over.

## A. Indirect Objects

As you know, direct object nouns and pronouns answer the questions *what?* or *whom?* Indirect object nouns and pronouns usually answer the questions *to whom?* or *for whom?* In English, the word *to* is frequently omitted: I gave the book *to Paul.* → I gave *Paul* the book. In French, the preposition **à** is *always* used before an indirect object noun.

**Presentation**: Point out that indirect object pronouns refer only to people or animals, never objects. Provide lots of oral examples so that sts. get used to hearing sentences with object pronouns.

| | |
|---|---|
| J'ai donné la caricature **à** Paul. | *I gave the cartoon to Paul.* |
| Elle a écrit une lettre **au** rédacteur. | *She wrote a letter to the editor.* |
| Nous montrons l'article **aux** amis. | *We show the article to (our) friends.* |
| Elle prête les photos **à** son frère. | *She lends the photos to her brother.* |

If a sentence has an indirect object, it usually has a direct object also. Some French verbs, however, can take only an indirect object. These include **téléphoner à**, **parler à**, and **répondre à**.

| | |
|---|---|
| Je téléphone (parle) souvent **à** mes amis. | *I often phone (speak) (to) my friends.* |
| Elle a répondu au professeur. | *She answered the professor.* |

*The *Canard Enchaîné* is a satirical weekly newspaper published in Paris.

## B. Indirect Object Pronouns

1. Indirect object pronouns replace indirect object nouns. They are identical in form to direct object pronouns, except for the third-person forms, **lui** and **leur**.

**Note**: Point out [ɥ] sound in *lui*.

| INDIRECT OBJECT PRONOUNS | | | |
|---|---|---|---|
| me, m' | (*to/for*) *me* | nous | (*to/for*) *us* |
| te, t' | (*to/for*) *you* | vous | (*to/for*) *you* |
| **lui** | (*to/for*) *him, her* | **leur** | (*to/for*) *them* |

2. The placement of indirect object pronouns is identical to that of direct object pronouns. However, the past participle does not agree with a preceding indirect object.

| | |
|---|---|
| Je **lui** ai montré la réception. | *I showed him (her) the (front) desk.* |
| On **m'**a demandé l'adresse de l'auberge de jeunesse. | *They asked me for the address of the youth hostel.* |
| Valérie **nous** a envoyé une carte postale. | *Valérie sent us a postcard.* |
| Nous n'allons pas **leur** téléphoner maintenant. | *We're not going to telephone them now.* |
| Je **leur** ai emprunté* la voiture. | *I borrowed the car from them.* |
| Ils **m'**ont prêté de l'argent. | *They loaned me some money.* |

3. In negative sentences, the object pronoun immediately precedes the conjugated verb.

| | |
|---|---|
| Je **ne** t'ai **pas** donné les billets. | *I didn't give you the tickets.* |
| Elle **ne** lui a **pas** téléphoné. | *She hasn't telephoned him.* |

### Vérifions!

**A. L'après-midi de Blondine.** Blondine va tous les vendredis après-midi chez sa grand-mère. Elle nous raconte ce qu'elle a fait vendredi dernier. Complétez son histoire avec les pronoms qui correspondent: **me**, **te**, **lui**, **nous**, **vous**, **leur**.

**Suggestion**: Give sts. a few minutes to work on this activity individually, before eliciting responses.

Après les cours, j'ai pris un café avec des amies. Je _____[1] ai montré mon nouveau walkman. Un peu plus tard, j'ai rendu visite à ma grand-mère. Je _____[2] ai apporté ses magazines préférés. Elle était très contente et elle _____[3] a dit: «Je vais _____[4] préparer un bon goûter». En fin d'après-midi, mon frère est arrivé. Il _____[5] a raconté ses aventures avec sa nouvelle moto.

---

***Emprunter** (*to borrow*) may take both a direct object (the thing borrowed) and an indirect object (the person from [**à**] whom it is borrowed).

Nous avons beaucoup ri. (*We laughed a lot.*) Au moment de partir, ma grand-mère _____[6] a demandé (à mon frère et à moi): «Je vous revois la semaine prochaine, les enfants?» «Bien sûr», nous _____[7] avons répondu, «à vendredi prochain!»

**B. N'oublie pas...** Au moment de dire au revoir, la grand-mère de Blondine se rappelle (*remembers*) plusieurs questions qu'elle voulait lui poser. Jouez le rôle de Blondine et répondez-lui, en utilisant des pronoms compléments d'objet indirect.

**Continuation**: *As-tu envoyé la carte postale à ta tante? Est-ce que tu as emprunté la voiture à ta mère? As-tu donné le cadeau au professeur?*

1. As-tu téléphoné à ton oncle? 2. Tu as écrit à ta tante Louise? 3. Tu as donné des timbres à ton frère pour sa collection? 4. As-tu répondu à M. et Mme Morin en Espagne? 5. Est-ce que tu as dit «bon anniversaire» à ton petit cousin? 6. Est-ce que tu as rendu à Jeannot et Janine le livre qu'ils nous ont prêté?

## Parlons-en!

**A. Au secours** (*Help*)! Qu'est-ce qu'on doit prêter ou offrir à ces personnes? (Vous pouvez utiliser les mots suivants dans vos réponses.)

**Suggestion**: Elicit several responses for each statement.

**Possibilités:** une lampe de poche (*flashlight*), un parasol, une paire de bottes, une robe du soir (*evening dress*), des lunettes de soleil, un parapluie, un sac de couchage, un collier (*necklace*) de perles, un *guide Michelin*, de la crème solaire, un chapeau, une tente, des chaises pliantes (*folding*), un anorak.

MODÈLE: Jean fait de l'alpinisme. Il fait très froid. (le guide) →
Le guide va lui prêter un chapeau et un anorak.

1. Marie est en ville. Il fait du vent, et il pleut aussi. (sa cousine)
2. Pierre et Marie sont à la plage. Il fait très chaud. (leurs amis)
3. Un vieux couple se promène à la campagne. Ils sont fatigués. (des passants [*passers-by*])
4. Marc et Christine font du camping. Ils ont oublié plusieurs choses essentielles. (un autre campeur)
5. Claudine va dîner dans un grand restaurant avec son fiancé et ses parents. (sa sœur)
6. Julie, une touriste américaine à Paris, ne veut voir que les monuments les plus renommés (*most famous*). (un ami français)

**Additional activity**: Prepare the following translation for sts. *En français, s'il vous plaît. Marc parle de ses vacances à la plage. Il écrit en anglais. Traduisez pour lui.* 1. *My French friends and I are spending our vacation at the beach.* 2. *I showed them the countryside.* 3. *I spoke to them about the region (région).* 4. *I sent postcards to my parents.* 5. *I explained (expliquer) the trip to them.* 6. *I telephoned a friend.* 7. *I talked to her about my vacation.* 8. *I sent her a telegram, too.* 9. *My friends needed money, so I lent them some francs.* 10. *They lent me some clothes.* 11. *I haven't yet had the time to go (le temps d'aller) to the beach!*

**B. Êtes-vous communicatif/ive** (*communicative*)? Posez les questions suivantes à un(e) camarade et créez de nouvelles questions sur le même sujet.

1. À qui as-tu écrit la semaine dernière? Qu'est-ce que tu lui as écrit? Pourquoi? En général, écris-tu souvent?
2. À qui as-tu téléphoné la semaine dernière? Qu'est-ce que tu lui as dit?
3. As-tu jamais envoyé un fax? À quelle occasion? À qui?

Ensuite, dites à la classe si votre camarade est très ou peu communicatif/ive. Pouvez-vous déterminer la personne la plus (*the most*) communicative de la classe?

# Nouvelles francophones

## TV5 en Louisiane

La chaîne de télévision francophone TV5 a été fondée° en 1984. Elle est basée sur des émissions tirées° de la télévision belge, suisse, québécoise et française (A2 et FR3). Depuis 1988, TV5 émet° en Europe, au Québec et au Canada.

*founded* *drawn* *broadcasts*

En octobre 1990, Lafayette en Louisiane est devenue la première ville aux États-Unis à proposer TV5 une fois par semaine. Depuis 1991, TV5 émet jour et nuit sur la chaîne câblée TV5 Louisiane. Beaucoup de villes et d'états américains ont demandé à cette chaîne le droit° de retransmettre les émissions de TV5.

*right*

# Mise au point

**A. Tourisme au Canada.** Loïc vient de rentrer du Canada et parle de son voyage avec son ami Vincent. Complétez le dialogue avec des pronoms d'objet direct ou indirect, selon le cas.

**Suggestion**: May be done in pairs with sts. playing roles.

VINCENT: Quand tu étais à Montréal, est-ce que tu écoutais la radio?
LOÏC: Oui, je ____[1] écoutais souvent.
VINCENT: Tu comprenais l'accent québécois?
LOÏC: Oui, je ____[2] comprenais, mais avec difficulté. Une fois, j'ai téléphoné à tes amis Jacques et Marie, et j'ai eu beaucoup de mal (*a lot of trouble*) à ____[3] comprendre.
VINCENT: De quoi ____[4] as-tu parlé?
LOÏC: D'une excursion que je voulais faire au lac Saint-Jean.
VINCENT: Est-ce que tu as pu ____[5] faire?
LOÏC: Oui, finalement nous ____[6] avons faite tous les trois. C'était formidable!
VINCENT: Est-ce que tu as envoyé beaucoup de cartes postales à Babette?
LOÏC: Oui, je ____[7] ai envoyé une carte postale tous les jours!
VINCENT: Et tu as pris beaucoup de photos?
LOÏC: Oh, oui. Tu veux ____[8] voir?
VINCENT: Avec plaisir. Tes photos sont toujours superbes!
LOÏC: Oh, j'oubliais, je ____[9] ai rapporté (*brought back*) un petit souvenir. C'est un livre d'Antonine Maillet, un écrivain québécois.
VINCENT: Merci beaucoup, ça ____[10] fait très plaisir (*gives pleasure; pleases*)!

**B. Mon enfance.** D'abord, posez les questions suivantes (et encore d'autres) à un(e) camarade. Ensuite, trouvez quelque chose que vous avez en commun avec ce (cette) camarade et une chose que vous n'avez pas en commun.

1. Quand tu étais petit(e), voyais-tu beaucoup de films? Quels films est-ce que tu aimais surtout (*especially*)? Avec qui allais-tu au cinéma?
2. Qu'est-ce que tu regardais à la télé? Quelles étaient tes émissions préférées? Jusqu'à quelle heure pouvais-tu regarder la télé?
3. Lisais-tu beaucoup? Quels livres est-ce que tu aimais? quelles bandes dessinées (*comic strips*)? Quand est-ce que tu lisais?

## Interactions

In this chapter, you practiced describing past events and referring to people or things succinctly. Act out the following situations, using the vocabulary and structures from the chapter.

1. **Au téléphone.** A friend (your partner) will soon be going to France. Describe how to use the phone and what expressions to use. She or he will ask questions for clarifications.
2. **La soirée.** Call a friend (your partner) to find out why she or he did not come to your party. Tell her or him who was there, what you talked about, and what you did. Describe how the party was. She or he will ask you questions to get a good description.

# Rencontres

## LECTURE

### Avant de lire

**Recognizing less obvious cognates.** An awareness of patterns of spelling variations will help you recognize less obvious cognates and guess the meanings of new words. Read the following hints and guess their definitions.

English words with the prefixes *dis-* and *un-* are often related in meaning to similar French words with the prefixes **dé-** or **dés-**.

| | | |
|---|---|---|
| **désordre** | **désastreux / euse** | **désagréable** |
| **défaire** | **dénouer** (**nouer** = *to tie*) | **découvrir** |

French words beginning with **es-** or **é-** often correspond to English words spelled with an initial *s-*.

**espace** **estomac** **état** **étrange** **étudier**

The circumflex accent in French frequently corresponds to an *s* that has not disappeared from the English cognate.

**honnête hôpital île tempête**

Many English nouns ending in *-or* or *-er* correspond to the masculine noun-ending in French of **-eur**.

**campeur serveur collaborateur professeur réacteur**

Notice these patterns in the following summaries from the film review *Première*, and watch for them in general as you read.

**DIMANCHE 16 MAI 20.35 ★ CANAL PLUS**

## LE RETOUR DE CASANOVA

FICHE. — Film français (Les Films Alain Sarde — Films A 2 — Canal Plus — CNC) d'Edouard Niermans. Scénario et dialogues : Jean-Claude Carrière et Edouard Niermans, d'après le roman « Casanovas Heimfahrt » (« Le retour de Casanova ») d'Arthur Schnitzler. Images : Jean Penzer. Musique : Michel Portal. 1992. Couleurs.

VIDEO. — Durée orig. : 1 h 38. TV : 1 h 30.

SUJET. — Après une vie d'aventures, de séductions, de fortunes et de voyages, Casanova désire rentrer chez lui, à Venise. Il a vieilli,[a] il est presque ruiné et ne vit plus que de sa légende et de son adresse aux cartes.[b] Hélas, les autorités de la Sérénissime République de Venise lui refusent pour l'instant[c] le visa d'entrée qu'il sollicite. En compagnie de son valet Camille, à qui il doit au moins un an de gages,[d] Casanova se voit contraint d'errer[e] dans le nord de l'Italie. Au cours de cette errance,[f] il rencontre Olivo, un homme à qui, autrefois, il rendit service[g] et qui ne l'a pas oublié. Riche et marié avec la belle Amélie, Olivo invite son bienfaiteur.[h]

**GENRE. — La dernière aventure amoureuse d'un séducteur de légende.**

INTERPRETES. — Alain Delon (Casanova), Fabrice Luchini (Camille), Elsa (Marcolina), Gilles Arbona (Olivo), Delia Boccardo (Amélie), Wadeck Stanczack (Lorenzi), Alain Cuny (marquis), Violetta Sanchez (marquise), Sandrine Blancke (Teresina), Rachel Bizet (Marie), Justine Leroux (Nanette), Sophie Bouilloux (Lise), Isabelle Gruault (Jeannette).

REDIF. — mardi 18 à 22.40 — jeudi 20 à 10.55 — lundi 24 — mardi 25 — vendredi 28 mai.

**LUNDI 17 MAI 22.35 ARTE**

## LA DESENCHANTEE

FICHE. — Film français (Production Cinéa — La Sept — CNC) de Benoît Jacquot. Scénario et dialogues : Benoît Jacquot. Images : Caroline Champetier. Musique : Jorge Arriacada. Musiques additionnelles : « Valse à quatre mains opus 39 » de Brahms, et « Wicked Game » de Chris Isaak. 1990. Couleurs.

VIDEO. — Durée orig. : 1 h 18. TV : 1 h 15.

SUJET. — Beth et « l'autre » ont 17 ans et sont amants. Un matin, il la défie[i] de coucher avec un homme laid[j] et vieux. Beth décide de le quitter. Chez elle, il y a Rémi, son frère de 8 ans, et sa mère malade. « L'oncle » subvient à leurs besoins[k] mais exige que Beth, qui le hait,[l] vienne chercher l'argent chez lui. En classe, sa révolte et son désenchantement s'expriment à travers un exposé sur Rimbaud. Son professeur lui reproche[m] son manque d'orthodoxie, tandis que son ami Chang la félicite.[n] L'après-midi, fuyant[o] « l'autre », Beth se rend dans une discothèque, où elle drague[p] Edouard. Une fois chez lui, elle s'enfuit pourtant au premier baiser.[q]

**GENRE. — Les maladresses et les désarrois de l'enfance dans ses conflits avec le monde des adultes.**

INTERPRETES. — Judith Godrèche (Beth), Marcel Bozonnet (Alphonse), Yvan Desny (l'oncle), Malcolm Conradt (l'autre), Thérèse Liotard (mère de Beth), Thomas Salsman (Rémi), Hai Truong Tu (Chang), Francis Mage (Edouard), Stéphane Auberghen (mère d'Edouard), Marion Ferry (prof), Caroline Bonmarchand (copine).

[a] *a... has gotten old*
[b] *ne... is living no more than in the legend of his past and on his skill at card-playing*
[c] *pour... for the time being*
[d] *wages*
[e] *contraint... compelled to wander*
[f] *wandering*
[g] *rendit... did a favor*
[h] *benefactor*
[i] *challenges*
[j] *ugly*
[k] *subvient... takes care of their needs*
[l] *hates*
[m] *lui... chides her for*
[n] *congratulates*
[o] *escaping*
[p] *picks up*
[q] *s'enfuit... flees, however, after the first kiss*

## *Compréhension*

Regardez bien le programme, puis répondez aux questions.

1. Avez-vous déjà vu un de ces films? Si oui, l'avez-vous aimé? Expliquez votre réponse.
2. Choisissez maintenant le film que vous préférez. Faites un court résumé de l'histoire en employant vos propres mots. Puis expliquez les raisons de votre choix.
3. Y a-t-il un film récent que vous ne voulez pas du tout voir? Pourquoi?
4. Quel film avez-vous vu dernièrement? L'avez-vous aimé? Qui étaient les acteurs?

## PAR ÉCRIT

**Function:** Writing letters
**Audience:** Someone you do not know
**Goal:** Write a letter to apply for a job. The situation is the following: The owner of a French restaurant, Madame Dupuy, has advertised in your campus newspaper. She would like to hire an American student waiter (waitress) because many of her clients are English-speaking tourists. Of course, the other staff members speak French. She is looking for someone with at least a few months of experience in restaurant work, who would benefit from the opportunity to work in France. Apply for the job. Say why you are interested, why you are qualified, and when you are available (**du 6 juin au 15 septembre**, for example). Mention your long-term goals (**le but à long terme**). Ask for more information. Useful opening line for job application: **J'aimerais me présenter pour le poste de serveur** (**serveuse**) **annoncé dans le** (***nom du journal***).

**Steps**

1. Use the letter on the following page and the suggestions below as guidelines for your letter. In French, a business letter begins with **Monsieur**, **Madame**, or **Mademoiselle**. If you do not know the gender of the recipient (**le destinataire**), use **Monsieur, Madame** together. Note the conventional closing sentence for the final paragraph of the letter; this sentence is loosely the equivalent of *Please accept my best wishes*. French business letters use the format you see on the following page.
2. Write a rough draft of the letter. It should contain all the information requested under **Goal** above.
3. Divide the letter into several paragraphs. Close with a strong statement about why you would be a well-qualified candidate for this position.
4. Reread your draft, checking for organization and details. Make sure you used the proper format and that you included your address and the date.

**Par écrit**: Call sts.' attention to the format of French letters.

New York, le 6 mai 1994
votre nom
votre adresse

nom du destinataire
adresse du destinataire

Monsieur, Madame,

J'ai l'intention de passer six mois en France pour perfectionner mon français. Pourriez-vous m'envoyer des renseignements sur vos cours de langues pour étudiants étrangers?

Je suis étudiant(e) en Sciences économiques à Columbia University; j'étudie le français depuis huit mois.

Je voudrais donc recevoir tous les renseignements nécessaires sur votre programme: description des cours, conditions d'admission, frais d'inscription, possibilités de logement, etc.

Veuillez agréer, Monsieur, Madame, l'expression de mes sentiments les meilleurs.

5. Have a classmate read your letter to see if what you have written is clear and interesting. Make any necessary changes.
6. Reread the composition again for spelling, punctuation, and grammar errors. Focus especially on your use of object pronouns and the imperfect tense. Be prepared to read your letter to a small group of classmates who will determine whether Madame Dupuy would consider you a strong candidate, based on the letter's information and presentation.

## À L'ÉCOUTE!

**À l'écoute!** See scripts for listening passages and follow-up activities recorded on student cassette. Remind students that in the listening comprehension passages (as in real life) they will not understand every word they hear. They should focus globally on the general information in the passages and not be overly concerned about what they do not understand.

**I. Où suis-je?** Vous allez entendre parler diverses personnes dans des situations variées. Lisez les activités ci-dessous avant d'écouter les séquences sonores qui leur correspondent.

**A.** Décidez où on peut entendre de telles bribes (*snatches*) de conversation.

1. La première séquence a lieu (*takes place*)
   a. dans une cabine téléphonique b. dans une boucherie c. dans un bureau de poste
2. La deuxième séquence a lieu
   a. dans une librairie b. dans un kiosque à journaux c. dans une boulangerie
3. La troisième séquence a lieu
   a. pendant un match de football b. à la radio c. au cinéma

## B. Vrai ou faux?

1. La première séquence:
   Cette personne
   _____ est en train d'acheter une télécarte.
   _____ veut envoyer une carte postale en Afrique.
2. La deuxième séquence:
   Cette personne
   _____ voudrait acheter un journal.
   _____ veut une revue sur le cinéma.
3. La troisième séquence:
   Cette personne dit que
   _____ le président de la République va aller aux États-Unis.
   _____ les deux présidents vont parler des produits agricoles.

**Suggestion**: Have sts. tell the story in the cartoon in the present tense.

**II. Les vacances chez grand-mère.** Viviane et Catherine se rappellent (*are remembering*) les vacances chez leur grand-mère quand elles étaient petites. Lisez l'activité ci-dessous avant d'écouter le vocabulaire et la conversation qui lui correspondent.

VOCABULAIRE UTILE
de bons goûters *afternoon snacks*
on ne s'ennuyait jamais *we never got bored*
grande *grown-up*

**Vrai ou faux?**

1. _____ Viviane adorait les histoires de sa grand-mère.
2. _____ La grand-mère n'avait pas de télévision.
3. _____ Les filles s'ennuyaient quelquefois.
4. _____ La grand-mère n'avait pas de jardin.
5. _____ Quand il pleuvait, la grand-mère jouait aux dominos avec les deux filles.
6. _____ La grand-mère avait un piano.

# Vocabulaire

## Verbes

**appeler** to call
**chanter** to sing
**commencer** to begin
**composer un numéro** to dial a number
**créer** to create
**décrire** to describe
**dire** to say, tell
**écrire (à)** to write (to)
**emprunter (à)** to borrow (from)
**envoyer** to send
**essayer** to try
**lire** to read
**prêter (à)** to lend (to)
**raconter** to tell, relate
**retransmettre** to broadcast

À REVOIR: écouter, entendre, jouer, regarder, rendre

## Substantifs

**l'adresse** (*f.*) address
**l'annuaire** (*m.*) telephone book
**l'appareil** (*m.*) apparatus; telephone
**la boîte aux lettres** mailbox
**le bureau de poste (la poste)** post office
**la cabine téléphonique** telephone booth
**la carte postale** postcard
**la chaîne** television channel; network
**l'école** (*f.*) school
**l'émission** (*f.*) program; broadcast
**l'enveloppe** (*f.*) envelope
**le journal (les journaux)** newspaper; news
**le kiosque** kiosk; newsstand
**la lettre** letter
**le magazine** (illustrated) magazine
**la monnaie** coins, change
**le numéro (de téléphone)** (telephone) number
**le paquet** package
**les petites annonces** (*f.*) classified ads
**la publicité** commercial; advertisement; advertising
**la revue** review, magazine
**la télécarte** telephone calling card
**le timbre** stamp

À REVOIR: le poste de télévision, la télévision

## Adjectifs

**content(e)** happy, pleased
**heureux/euse** happy, fortunate

## Les nouvelles technologies

**le magnétoscope** VCR
**le minitel** minitel
**l'ordinateur** (*m.*) computer
**le répondeur (téléphonique)** answering machine
**le téléviseur** television set

## Au téléphone

**Allô.** Hello.
**Qui est à l'appareil?** Who's calling?

## Mots et expressions divers

**d'habitude** habitually, usually
**surtout** especially
**tout, toute, tous, toutes** all; every
**tous les jours (matins**, etc.) every day (morning, etc.)
**toutes les semaines** every week

# Intermède

## SITUATION

### Coup de fil*

**Situation**: The *Situation* dialogues are recorded on the st. cassette packaged with the st. text.

**Note**: Point out to sts. telephone etiquette of saying *Bonjour, Madame/Monsieur.* Teach them the phrase *Je vous (te) dérange?* to use when calling friends or acquaintances.

**Note**: The *À propos* will provide sts. with other ways to react to news.

**Contexte** *Caroline Périllat rêve d'être hôtesse. Elle a terminé ses études à l'École Internationale d'Hôtesses de Paris et elle vient de trouver son premier job. Elle téléphone à sa sœur, Stéphanie, qui habite encore au Sénégal, pour lui annoncer la bonne nouvelle. Stéphanie est étudiante à l'Institut Supérieur de Tourisme de Dakar.*

**Objectif** *Caroline parle au téléphone.*

CAROLINE: Allô? Bonjour, Madame, c'est bien l'Institut de Tourisme?

LA STANDARDISTE°: Oui, c'est bien ça. — *operator, receptionist*

CAROLINE: Pourrais-je parler à Stéphanie Périllat, s'il vous plaît?

LA STANDARDISTE: C'est de la part de qui?° — C'est... *Who may I say is calling?*

CAROLINE: C'est de la part de Caroline Périllat, sa sœur.

LA STANDARDISTE: Ne quittez pas, je vous la passe.° — Ne... *Please hold, I'll transfer you to her.*

CAROLINE: Merci bien.

CAROLINE: Allô, Stéphanie? Devine! Je viens de décrocher° mon premier boulot.° — *to land (literally, to take down, detach, unhook)* / *job (familiar)*

STÉPHANIE: C'est génial°! Et c'est quoi comme boulot°? — *great* / c'est... *what kind of job is it?*

CAROLINE: Je suis chargée de l'accueil des vedettes° au Palais des Festivals de Cannes! — chargée... *responsible for welcoming stars*

STÉPHANIE: Ce n'est pas vrai! Tu rigoles°? — Tu... *Are you kidding?*

CAROLINE: Non je te jure,° c'est vrai. — je... *I swear*

STÉPHANIE: Eh bien, félicitations°! J'espère que tu es heureuse. — *congratulations*

CAROLINE: Évidemment,° je regrette seulement de ne pas pouvoir fêter ça avec toi... — *Of course*

STÉPHANIE: Écoute, je te quitte, tu vas avoir une facture° énorme. Mais je te rappelle demain soir, d'accord? — *(phone) bill*

CAROLINE: OK. Je t'embrasse.° À demain et dis bonjour aux parents de ma part.° — Je... *A big kiss* / dis... *tell the folks I said "hi"*

---

*Telephone call

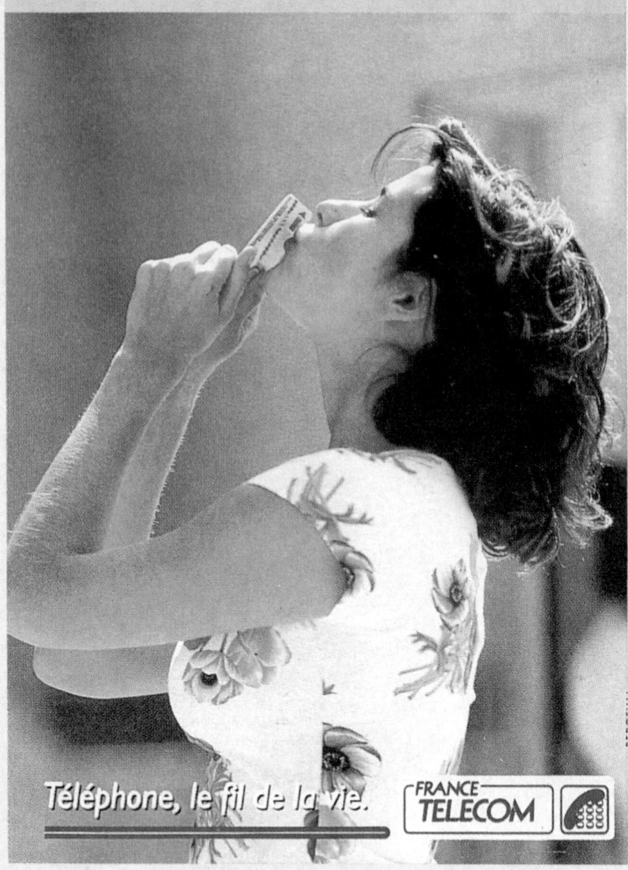

 **propos**

## Comment réagir à une nouvelle (*react to news*)

UNE BONNE NOUVELLE

C'est génial!
C'est formidable!
C'est super!
Je suis content(e) pour toi. (*I'm happy for you.*)

UNE MAUVAISE NOUVELLE

C'est dommage.
C'est horrible.
C'est dégoûtant (*disgusting*).
C'est un scandale!
Ça me rend malade. (*That makes me sick.*)

UNE NOUVELLE QUI VOUS LAISSE INDIFFÉRENT(E)

Ah bon!
Oh, ça m'est égal. (*That's all the same to me.*)
C'est pas grave. (*That's no big deal.*)
Je m'en fiche. (*I don't care.*)

## *Maintenant à vous!*

**A. Questions personnelles.** Relisez le dialogue, puis répondez aux questions.

1. Décrivez votre premier job. De quoi étiez-vous chargé(e)?
2. Avez-vous en général une facture téléphonique énorme? Pourquoi (pas)? À qui téléphonez-vous très souvent? Avez-vous tendance à parler longtemps? De quoi?
3. À votre avis, le téléphone est-il une technologie essentielle? Pourriez-vous vivre (*live*) sans téléphone? Commentez.

**B. Jeu de rôles: Quelle nouvelle!** Avec un(e) camarade, préparez la scène suivante. Utilisez les expressions de l'*À Propos*. Puis jouez la scène devant la classe.

Votre ami(e) vous téléphone pour vous raconter une très bonne (ou une très mauvaise) nouvelle. Réagissez de façon convenable (*appropriate*).

## PORTRAITS

### *Astérix le Gaulois*

Astérix le Gaulois est le héros comique de la bande dessinée° la plus populaire en France depuis 1959. Astérix, qui habite dans l'unique° village Gaulois° qui a pu résister à César, possède tous les attributs traditionnels du Français: individualisme, débrouillardise,° chauvinisme,° humour. Chaque aventure d'Astérix est une satire de la société d'aujourd'hui. Astérix est traduit en 40 langues et il est vendu dans le monde entier.

*bande... comic strip*
*one and only*
*in Gaul*
*resourcefulness (from the verb* **se débrouiller**, *which means to manage)*
*pride in one's heritage or country, often carried to excess*

CHAPITRE **ONZE**

# La vie urbaine

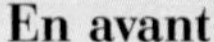

**En avant**

—Est-ce que tu habites en ville?
—Non, j'habite en banlieue.
—Tu dois passer beaucoup de temps dans les transports en commun!
—Oui, c'est le prix que l'on paie pour avoir une jolie maison avec un jardin.

**Communicative goals:** talking about city life, talking about Paris, describing past events, speaking succinctly, and saying what and whom you know.

**En avant**: See scripts for follow-up questions recorded on student cassette.

# Étude de vocabulaire

## Une petite ville

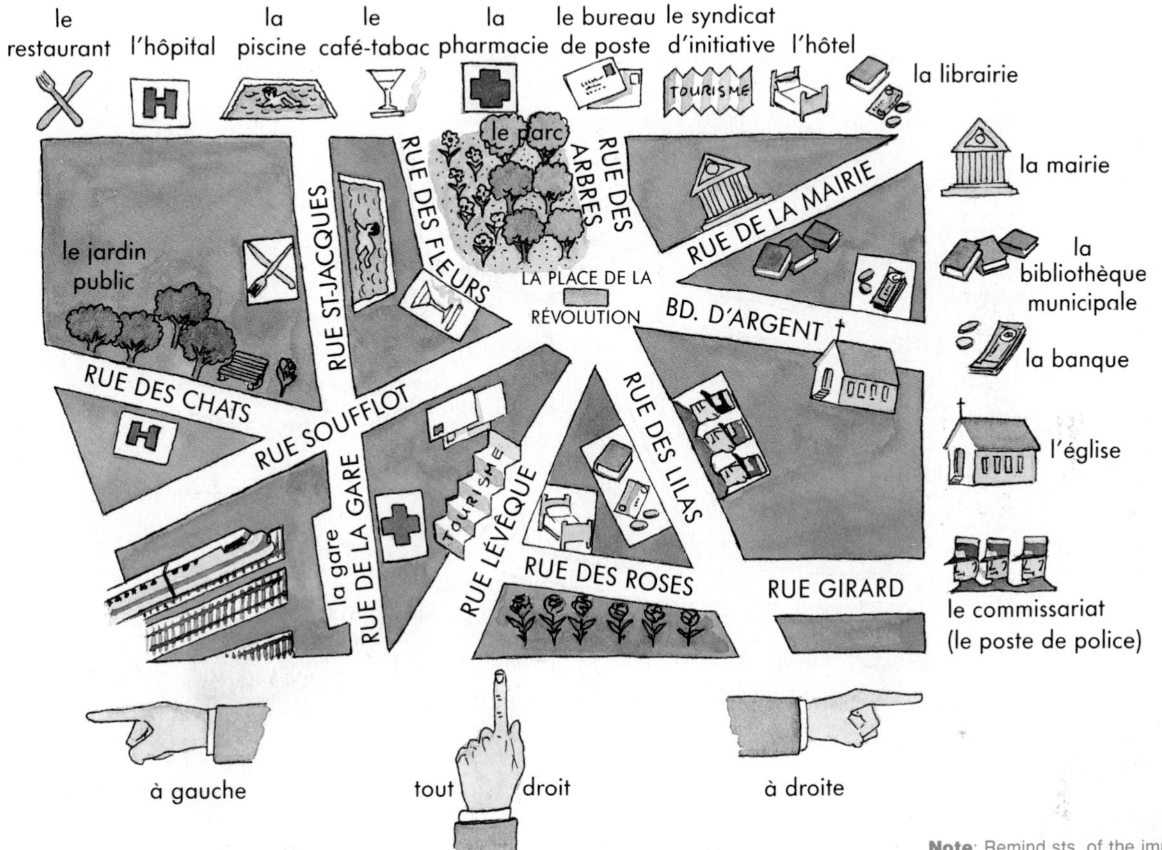

le restaurant
l'hôpital
la piscine
le café-tabac
la pharmacie
le bureau de poste
le syndicat d'initiative
l'hôtel
la librairie
la mairie
la bibliothèque municipale
la banque
l'église
le commissariat (le poste de police)
le jardin public
le parc
la gare
LA PLACE DE LA RÉVOLUTION
RUE ST-JACQUES
RUE DES FLEURS
RUE DES ARBRES
RUE DE LA MAIRIE
BD. D'ARGENT
RUE DES CHATS
RUE SOUFFLOT
RUE DE LA GARE
RUE LÉVÊQUE
RUE DES LILAS
RUE DES ROSES
RUE GIRARD
TOURISME

à gauche
tout droit
à droite

***Autres mots utiles:***

**le coin** corner
**jusqu'à** up to, as far as

Comment va-t-on de la banque à la pharmacie? On **prend** le boulevard d'Argent à droite et on va **jusqu'à** la place de la Révolution. On **traverse** la rue des Lilas et on **prend** la rue Lévêque à gauche. On **continue tout droit jusqu'au coin** et on **prend** la rue de la Gare **à droite**. La pharmacie est **en face de** la gare.

**Note**: Remind sts. of the importance of giving directions. Teach and review such expressions as *près de, en face de, à côté de, au coin de, devant, derrière, entre, tourner à droite, à gauche*. Teach *Où se trouve... ?* as a fixed expression. (See *À propos* at end of chapter for other useful expressions.)

**Suggestion**: Ask sts. to follow directions with a finger or trace route with a pencil. Have them give French equivalent of following expressions: *to the right; to the left; cross; continue straight ahead; across from; up to the corner.*

**A. Les endroits importants.** Où va-t-on...

1. pour toucher (*to cash*) un chèque de voyage? 2. pour acheter de l'aspirine? 3. pour parler avec le maire (*mayor*) de la ville? 4. pour obtenir des brochures touristiques? 5. pour nager? 6. pour admirer les plantes et les fleurs? 7. pour assister aux (*to attend*) services religieux? 8. pour acheter des timbres? 9. pour boire une bière?

**B. Où est-ce?** Précisez l'emplacement des endroits suivants.

MODÈLE: Où est l'hôtel? →
L'hôtel est en face du syndicat d'initiative dans la rue Lévêque.*

**Suggestion**: Have sts. describe locations in same manner using a map of campus or local town.

1. Où est le jardin public?
2. Où est le restaurant?
3. Où est la bibliothèque?
4. Où est l'église?
5. Où est la librairie?
6. Où est le syndicat d'initiative?

**C. Trouvez votre chemin** (*way*). Regardez le plan (*map*) de la ville. Imaginez que vous êtes à la gare. Un(e) touriste vous demande où est le bureau de poste; vous lui indiquez le chemin. Jouez les rôles avec un(e) camarade.

MODÈLE: LE/LA TOURISTE: Excusez-moi, pourriez-vous me dire où est le bureau de poste?
VOUS: Tournez à gauche. Prenez la rue Soufflot à droite et vous y êtes (*you're there*).
LE/LA TOURISTE: Je tourne à gauche, je prends la rue Soufflot à droite et j'y suis.

1. le café-tabac 2. le restaurant 3. l'hôtel 4. la banque 5. le poste de police 6. le parc 7. la mairie 8. la pharmacie 9. le jardin public 10. la place de la Révolution 11. la piscine 12. le syndicat d'initiative

Maintenant, avec un(e) autre camarade de classe, faites une liste de cinq ou six endroits sur votre campus ou dans votre ville. À tour de rôle (*Taking turns*), indiquez le chemin pour aller à ces endroits. Votre salle de classe est votre point de départ.

**Suggestions**: (1) Duplicate map and have sts. in pairs use it to follow the pathway as they describe how to get from place to place. (2) Describe route to your own house from the classroom. Have sts. try to describe their own routes.

**Additional activities**: **A.** Listening comp. practice. Tell sts. *Vous êtes devant la gare. Vous prenez la rue de la Gare jusqu'à la rue Soufflot, où vous tournez à droite. Continuez jusqu'à la place, et prenez la première rue à gauche. Où êtes-vous?* Continue giving directions to other places on the map.
**B.** *À pied. Expliquez comment on va de la banque aux endroits suivants. Indiquez le chemin.* 1. *à l'hôpital* 2. *à la piscine* 3. *à la bibliothèque* 4. *au syndicat d'initiative*

## Un peu d'argot

| | | | |
|---|---|---|---|
| **l'hosto** | l'hôpital | **un Parigot** (**une Parigote**) | un Parisien (une Parisienne) |
| **la bibli** | la bibliothèque | | |
| **le centre** | le centre-ville | | |

EN CONTEXTE
Mon cousin est un vrai **Parigot**. Il vit en plein **centre**, dans un vieil immeuble entre un **hosto** et une **bibli**.

**Note**: *L'hosto* is used by everyone informally. It is particularly popular with people in the medical field.
*Le centre* is part of everyday spoken language.
*La bibli* is used mostly by students.
*Parigot* is used to describe those people from Paris who believe they are different from the rest of the French. It must be used carefully, as it could be perceived as an insult.

*The French say **dans la rue**, but **sur le boulevard** and **sur l'avenue**.

# Paris et sa banlieue

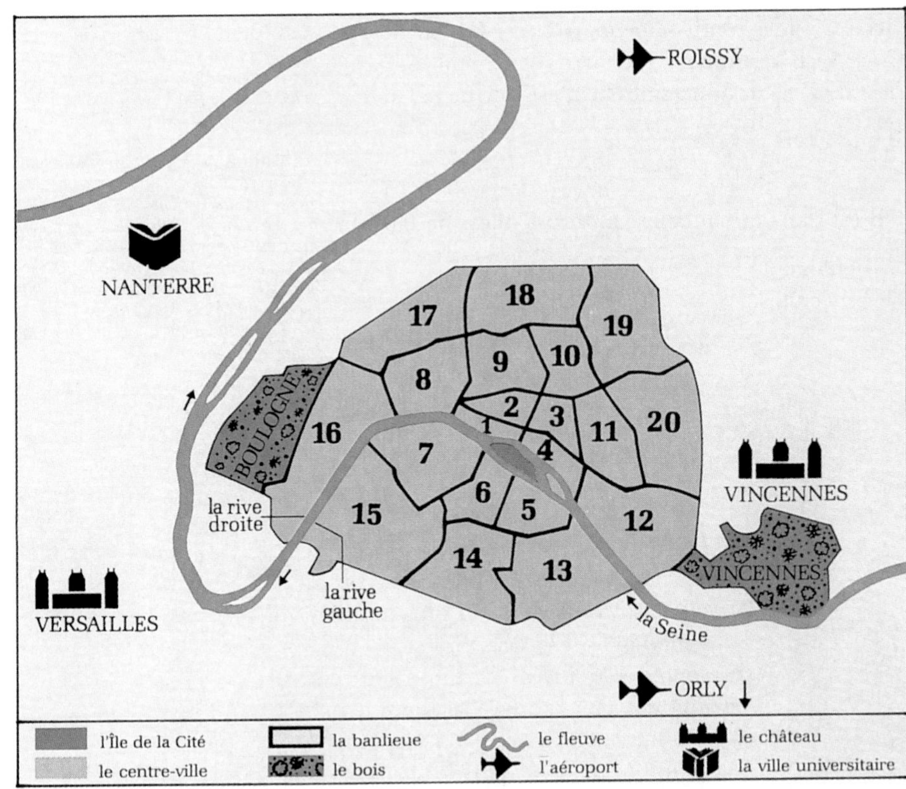


**Note**: Point out to students that a *ville universitaire* is a city with a university campus. Parts of the University of Paris have moved to new *villes universitaires* in suburbs, such as Nanterre. Point out that the *arrondissements* are numbered in a spiral pattern, whose center (*1er arr.*) is on the Right Bank near the *île de la Cité*.

***Autres mots utiles:***

**la carte** map (of a region, country)
**le plan** map (of a city)

Les vingt arrondissements (*wards*) de Paris:

| | |
|---|---|
| 1er le premier | 11e le onzième |
| 2e le deuxième | 12e le douzième |
| 3e le troisième | 13e le treizième |
| 4e le quatrième | 14e le quatorzième |
| 5e le cinquième | 15e le quinzième |
| 6e le sixième | 16e le seizième |
| 7e le septième | 17e le dix-septième |
| 8e le huitième | 18e le dix-huitième |
| 9e le neuvième | 19e le dix-neuvième |
| 10e le dixième | 20e le vingtième |

**Presentation**: Model pronunciation. Give other numbers in English and ask sts. to form ordinals: 22nd, 45th, 36th, 57th, 63rd, etc.

**Note**: Point out spelling and pronunciation of *vingt-et-unième*.

**Note**: Bring in slides or photos of Paris to show sts. the chief monuments and parks so that they can visualize the places they want to visit.

Ordinal numbers (*first, second,* and so on) are formed by adding **-ième** to cardinal numbers. Note the irregular form **premier** (**première**), and the spelling of **cinquième** and **neuvième**. **Le** and **la** do not elide before **huitième** and **onzième**: **le huitième**. The superscript abbreviation $^e$ indicates that a number should be read as an ordinal: 7 = **sept**; $7^e$ = **le/la septième**.

*Continuation: Quels arrondissements constituent le centre-ville? Quels arrondissements constituent les beaux quartiers résidentiels, Paris-Ouest? Quels arrondissements constituent le quartier des affaires sur la Rive droite, dans le centre-ville? Quels arrondissements constituent Paris-Est?*

**A. Les arrondissements de Paris.** Quels arrondissements trouve-t-on sur la Rive (*bank*) gauche de la Seine? sur la Rive droite? Quel arrondissement est situé au bord du Bois de Boulogne? du Bois de Vincennes? Où est l'île de la Cité?*

**B. Le plan de Paris.** Qu'est-ce que c'est?

MODÈLE: Versailles →
C'est un château. Il est dans la banlieue (*suburbs*) ouest de Paris.

1. Roissy
2. la Seine
3. Boulogne
4. Vincennes
5. Nanterre
6. Orly

*Additional activity: Imaginez que vous êtes à Paris avec un(e) camarade. Vous consultez un guide pour chercher ce que vous pouvez aller voir. Choisissez avec votre camarade 5 endroits différents. Votre camarade vous demande où ils se trouvent.* MODÈLE: CAMARADE: *Où est l'Opéra?* VOUS: *Il est sur la place de l'Opéra.* CAMARADE: *C'est dans quel arrondissement?* VOUS: *C'est dans le neuvième.*

## Nouvelles francophones

### Montréal

Fondée en 1642 par un Français, Paul de Chomedey, Montréal est la plus grande° ville francophone après Paris. Bilingue et cosmopolite, Montréal est un grand centre culturel qui vit° et bouge° à toute heure du jour et de la nuit. Après minuit il y a encore beaucoup de monde° dans les rues et dans les bars du côté de **la Place des Arts**. Il faut aussi se promener° dans **la rue Sainte-Catherine**. Ses boutiques élégantes, ses grands magasins font de Montréal une des capitales de la mode.°

Montréal est une ville contemporaine, qui sait aussi préserver son passé. De vieux édifices sont situés juste à côté de gratte-ciel° ultramodernes. **Le Palais des Congrès** à l'architecture futuriste sert de lien géographique° entre **le Vieux-Montréal** et le nouveau. Le Vieux-Montréal est d'ailleurs° l'un des plus remarquables ensembles architecturaux de l'Amérique du Nord avec une grande concentration d'édifices° des $17^e$, $18^e$ et $19^e$ siècles.°

*la... the largest*
*lives / moves*
*beaucoup... a lot of people*
*se... to walk*
*fashion*
*skyscrapers*
*sert... serves as a geographic link*
*besides*
*buildings*
*centuries*

*The **île de la Cité** is the historical center of Paris; it is one of the two islands on the Seine in Paris. The other is the **île St-Louis**.

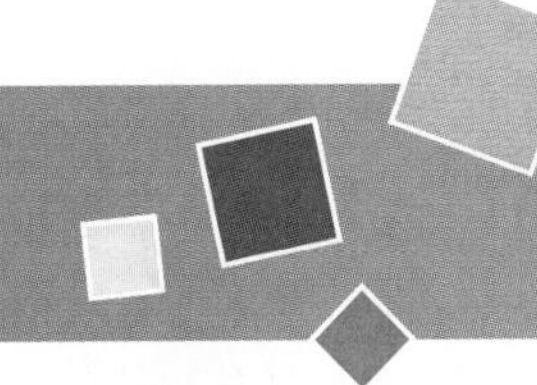

# Étude de grammaire

## 37. DESCRIBING PAST EVENTS
## The *passé composé* versus the *imparfait*

**Suggestion**: Ask sts. to read roles of minidialogue aloud while others follow in text. After reading, have sts. hypothesize about why verbs in italics are in given tense. From these hypotheses, go on to generalize and give explanations.

### Casablanca

ALAIN: Alors, tu nous racontes tes vacances au Maroc?

SYLVIE: Eh bien, je **suis partie** de Paris le 23 juillet. Il **faisait** un temps pourri, il **faisait** froid, il **pleuvait**, l'horreur! Mais quand je **suis arrivée** à Casablanca, le ciel **était** tout bleu, le soleil **brillait**, la mer **était** chaude...

RÉMI: Et tu **as aimé** la ville?

SYLVIE: Oui, beaucoup. Mais je **voulais** visiter une mosquée et je n'**ai** pas **pu** entrer.

ALAIN: Pourquoi?

SYLVIE: C'est de ma faute parce que je **portais** une mini-jupe.

Répondez aux questions.

1. Quel temps faisait-il à Paris le 23 juillet? et à Casablanca?
2. Que voulait faire Sylvie à Casablanca?
3. Pourquoi n'a-t-elle pas visité la mosquée?

When speaking about the past in English, you choose which past tense forms to use in a given context: *I visited Casablanca, I did visit Casablanca, I was visiting Casablanca, I used to visit Casablanca,* and so on. Usually only one of these options will convey exactly the meaning you want to express. Similarly in French, the choice between the **passé composé** and the **imparfait** depends on the kind of past action or condition that is being conveyed, and sometimes on the speaker's standpoint with respect to the past event.

The **passé composé** is used to indicate a single completed action, something that began and ended in the past, or a sequence of such actions.

The **imparfait** usually indicates an ongoing or habitual action in the past. It does not emphasize the end of that action.

| | |
|---|---|
| J'**écrivais** des lettres. | *I was writing letters.* (*ongoing action*) |
| J'**ai écrit** des lettres. | *I wrote* (*have written*) *letters.* (*completed action*) |
| Je **commençais** mes devoirs. | *I was starting on my homework.* (*ongoing*) |

J'**ai commencé** mes devoirs. — *I started (have started) my homework. (completed at a specific point in time)*

Elle **allait** au parc le dimanche.* — *She went (used to go) to the park on Sundays. (habitual)*

Elle **est allée** au parc dimanche. — *She went to the park on Sunday. (completed on a specific day)*

Contrast the two tenses by studying the sentences in this chart.

| IMPARFAIT | PASSÉ COMPOSÉ |
|---|---|
| 1. *Ongoing action with no emphasis on the completion or end of the action* | *Completed action, or a series of completed events or actions* |
| J'**allais** en France.<br>Je **visitais** des monuments. | Je **suis allé** en France.<br>J'**ai visité** des monuments. |
| 2. *Habitual or repeated action* | *A single event* |
| Je **voyageais** en France tous les ans.<br>Je **visitais** souvent le Centre Beaubourg. | J'**ai voyagé** en France l'année dernière.<br>J'**ai visité** Beaubourg un samedi matin. |
| 3. *Description or "background" information; how things were or what was happening when . . .* | *. . . an event or events occurred. ("foreground" information)* |
| Je **visitais** Beaubourg... | ...quand on **a annoncé** la projection d'un vieux film de Chaplin. |
| J'**étais** à Paris... | ...quand une lettre **est arrivée**. |
| 4. *Physical or mental states of being (general description)* | *Changes in an existing physical or mental state at a precise moment, or for a particular isolated cause* |
| Ma nièce **avait** peur des chiens. | Ma nièce **a eu** peur quand le chien a aboyé (*barked*). |

In summary, the **imparfait** is generally used for *descriptions* in the past, and the **passé composé** is generally used for the *narration* of specific events in the past. The **imparfait** also often sets the stage for an event expressed with the **passé composé**. The following passages illustrate the use of these two tenses.

*Remember the role of the definite article with days of the week: **le dimanche** (*on Sundays*); **dimanche** (*on Sunday*).

| IMPARFAIT | PASSÉ COMPOSÉ |
|---|---|
| Il **faisait** beau; le ciel (*sky*) **était** clair; les terrasses des cafés **étaient** pleines (*filled*) de gens; c'**était** un beau jour de printemps à Paris. | J'**ai continué** tout droit dans la rue Mouffetard, j'**ai traversé** le boulevard de Port-Royal et j'**ai descendu** l'avenue des Gobelins jusqu'à la place d'Italie. |

## ots-clés

**Suggestion**: Point out that these words can help determine whether to use the *passé composé* or the *imparfait* in an ex.

*Indicators of tense:* Here are some time expressions that often accompany the **imparfait** and the **passé composé**.

| IMPARFAIT | PASSÉ COMPOSÉ |
|---|---|
| d'habitude (*usually*) | une fois (*once*), deux fois... |
| de temps en temps | plusieurs fois |
| autrefois (*formerly*) | un week-end |
| le week-end | un jour |
| le lundi (le mardi...) | lundi (mardi...) |
| | soudain, tout d'un coup (*suddenly*) |
| **D'habitude,** nous **étudiions** à la bibliothèque. | **Un jour**, nous **avons étudié** au café. |
| Quand j'**étais** jeune, nous **allions** à la plage **le week-end**. | **Un week-end**, nous **sommes allés** à la montagne. |

### *Vérifions!*

**Suggestion**: Model a few sentences. Then have sts. do them in pairs for maximum oral practice. After 3 to 5 minutes, have whole group go over a few examples to make certain they have understood.

**A. Un dimanche pas comme les autres.** Votre voisin Marc Dufour était une personne routinière, mais un dimanche il a changé ses habitudes. Voici son histoire.

MODÈLE: le dimanche matin / dormir en général jusqu'à huit heures / mais ce dimanche-là / dormir jusqu'à midi →
Le dimanche matin, il dormait en général jusqu'à huit heures, mais ce dimanche-là, il a dormi jusqu'à midi.

1. normalement au petit déjeuner / prendre des céréales et une tasse de café / mais ce matin-là / manger un petit déjeuner copieux
2. après le petit déjeuner / faire toujours du jogging dans le parc / mais ce jour-là / rester longtemps au téléphone
3. souvent l'après-midi / regarder le match de football à la télé / mais cet après-midi-là / lire des poèmes dans le jardin

4. d'habitude le soir / sortir avec ses copains / mais ce soir-là / sortir avec une jeune fille
5. parfois / aller au cinéma ou / jouer aux cartes / mais ce soir-là / inviter son amie dans un restaurant élégant
6. normalement / rentrer chez lui assez tôt / mais ce dimanche-là / danser jusqu'au petit matin (*early morning*)

À votre avis, Marc est-il malade (*sick*)? amoureux (*in love*)? déprimé (*depressed*)?... Justifiez votre réponse. Et vous, est-ce qu'il y a des choses que vous faisiez autrefois que vous ne faites plus maintenant? Expliquez.

**B. Interruptions.** Annie était à la maison hier soir. Elle voulait faire plusieurs choses, mais il y a eu toutes sortes d'interruptions. Décrivez-les.

**Suggestion**: Have sts. write ex. out on paper while several sts. write sentences on board for verification. Ask sts. to clarify why each tense is used in both clauses.

MODÈLE: étudier... téléphone / sonner →
Annie étudiait quand le téléphone a sonné.

1. parler au téléphone / un ami... l'employé / couper la ligne (*to cut the line*)
2. écouter / disques... son voisin / commencer à faire / bruit (*noise*)
3. lire / journal... la propriétaire (*landlord*) / venir demander / argent
4. faire / devoirs... un ami / arriver
5. regarder / informations à la télé... son frère / changer de chaîne
6. dormir... téléphone / sonner de nouveau (*again*)

**C. Une année à l'université de Caen.** Marc a passé un an à Caen, une des grandes villes de Normandie. Il raconte son histoire. Choisissez l'imparfait ou le passé composé pour les verbes suivants.

**Suggestions**: (1) Use as dictation material, with verbs conjugated. Sts. write out story, their books closed, and underline verbs. Then they explain why a given tense was used in each instance. (2) Have sts. write out ex. for homework, with correction next day in class. (3) Have sts. do ex. orally, explaining use of appropriate tense for each item.

**Additional activity**: Make copies of the following translation. *Une nuit.* 1. *It was late and it was raining.* 2. *There was nobody on the streets.* 3. *We were going home, along* (*le long de*) *the Saint-Michel Boulevard.* 4. *Suddenly we heard a noise on our right.* 5. *Someone was coming* (*arriver*). 6. *We couldn't see anything.* 7. *I was scared.* 8. *Then I saw a friend from the office.* 9. *He was bringing my keys, forgotten on my desk.* 10. *We were so* (*si*) *happy that* (*que*) *we invited him to dinner.*

Mon année en Normandie était vraiment super, mais je devais passer beaucoup de temps à étudier. Je (*avoir*) cours le matin de 8 heures à 11 heures. L'après-midi, je (*étudier*), en général, à la bibliothèque. Le week-end, avec des amis, nous (*faire*) du tourisme. Le samedi, nous (*rester*) en ville et le dimanche, nous (*aller*) à la campagne. En octobre, nous (*faire*) une excursion à Rouen. Ce (*être*) très intéressant. Pour Noël, je (*rentrer*) chez mes parents. En février, je (*faire*) du ski dans les Alpes. Nous (*avoir*) de la chance car il (*faire*) très beau et je (*rentrer*) bien bronzé (*tanned*). De temps en temps, je (*manger*) chez les Levergeois, des amis français très sympathiques. Pendant ces dîners entre amis, je (*perfectionner*) mon français. Finalement, au début du mois de mai, je (*devoir*) quitter Caen. Je (*être*) triste (*sad*) de partir.

## Mots-clés

*Putting events in chronological order*

DÉPANNAGE (*emergency repair*)

| | | |
|---|---|---|
| **d'abord** | *first of all* | **D'abord**, j'ai garé (*parked*) la voiture. |

DÉPANNAGE (*emergency repair*)

| | | |
|---|---|---|
| **puis** | *next* | **Puis**, j'ai cherché une cabine téléphonique. |
| **ensuite** | *and then . . .* | **Ensuite**, j'ai tout expliqué au mécanicien. |
| **après** | *after that . . .* | **Après**, j'ai attendu dans la voiture. |
| **enfin** | *finally* | **Enfin**, il est arrivé. Maintenant, le carburateur fonctionne à merveille. |

**Puis** and **ensuite** can be used interchangeably.

**Suggestion**: Have sts. do items silently first. Then solicit completed sentences in correct order.

**D. Biographie de Marguerite Yourcenar.** Voici quelques faits (*facts*) importants de la vie de cette romancière (*novelist*) et historienne de langue française. Mettez-les dans l'ordre chronologique et utilisez des adverbes de temps.

1. Elle est allée aux États-Unis en 1958.
2. Elle a écrit son fameux livre *L'Œuvre au noir* en 1968.
3. Elle est née à Bruxelles en 1903.
4. Elle est morte en 1987 à l'âge de 84 ans dans le Maine, aux États-Unis.
5. Elle a été la première femme élue à l'Académie française, en 1980.

Maintenant, faites brièvement (*briefly*) votre propre autobiographie. Utilisez des adverbes de temps.

Marguerite Yourcenar

## *Parlons-en!*

**A. Conversation.** L'année dernière,...

1. Où étiez-vous? Où avez-vous étudié? Qu'est-ce que vous avez étudié?
2. Qu'est-ce que vous avez fait pendant vos vacances? Avez-vous fait un voyage? Où êtes-vous allé(e)? Comment était le voyage?
3. Et vos amis? Où étaient-ils l'année dernière? Qu'est-ce qu'ils ont fait pendant les vacances?

**Suggestions**: (1) Have sts. interview one another and take notes on answers. Ask them to write a *résumé* of responses. Collect potential listening comp. or dictation material. (2) Do as a whole-group activity, eliciting several oral responses for each question.

**B. Il était une fois...** (*Once upon a time . . .*). Racontez une histoire que vous avez vécue (*lived*) ou une histoire fantastique (inventez-la!) Utilisez les éléments suggérés pour organiser votre histoire et choisissez le temps convenable (**passé composé** ou **imparfait**).

**Suggestions:** l'heure, le temps, la description de la scène, la description des personnages, la description des sentiments...

**Expressions utiles:** soudain, tout à coup, d'habitude, en général, puis, ensuite, enfin, alors, autrefois, quand, souvent, parfois, toujours...

**Suggestions**: (1) Ask sts. to write out stories and read them to another group in class or to whole class. (2) Use stories as potential dictation or listening comp. material.

# 38. SPEAKING SUCCINCTLY The Pronouns *y* and *en*

**Paris: ville de l'amour**

MIREILLE: Tu es déjà allée au Parc Montsouris?
FABIENNE: Non, pas encore mais j'**y** vais samedi avec Vincent.
MIREILLE: Vincent? Dis-moi, tu as combien de petits amis?
FABIENNE: En ce moment, j'**en** ai deux. Mais je vais bientôt casser avec Jean-Marc.
MIREILLE: Et tu **en** as parlé à Jean-Marc?
FABIENNE: Non, pas encore. J'**y** pense mais j'ai un peu peur de sa réaction.

Trouvez la phrase équivalente dans le dialogue.

1. Je vais au Parc Montsouris samedi.
2. J'ai deux petits amis.
3. Tu as parlé à Jean-Marc de ta décision?
4. Je pense à lui parler.

## A. The Pronoun *y*

The pronoun **y** can refer to a place that has already been mentioned. It replaces a prepositional phrase, and its English equivalent is *there.*

**Presentation**: Model sentences in grammar sections and have sts. repeat sentences using *y*.

| | |
|---|---|
| —Fabienne est-elle déjà allée **au Parc Montsouris**? | *—Has Fabienne already gone to the Parc Montsouris?* |
| —Non, mais elle **y** va samedi. | *—No, but she is going there Saturday.* |
| —Mireille va-t-elle **au festival** avec elle? | *—Is Mireille going to the festival with her?* |
| —Non, elle n'**y** va pas avec elle. | *—No, she isn't going (there) with her.* |
| —Vont-ils **chez Fabienne** ce week-end? | *—Are they going to Fabienne's this weekend?* |
| —Oui, ils **y** vont ensemble. | *—Yes, they're going (there) together.* |

**Y** can replace the combination **à** + *noun* when the noun refers to a place or thing. This substitution is most often applied after certain verbs that are followed by **à**: **répondre à**, **réfléchir à**, **réussir à**, **penser à** (*to think about someone or something*), **jouer à**. (This substitution is not usually applied to the **à** + *noun* combination when the noun refers to a person; in these cases, a direct or indirect object pronoun is often used.)*

*In everyday French conversation, **y** is now used frequently to refer to people, in sentences such as: **Je pense *aux enfants*. J'*y* pense.**

| | |
|---|---|
| —As-tu répondu **à la lettre** de ta sœur? | —*Did you answer your sister's letter?* |
| —Oui, j'**y** ai répondu. | —*Yes, I answered it.* |
| —Elle pense déjà **au voyage** à Marseille? | —*Is she already thinking about the trip to Marseilles?* |
| —Non, elle n'**y** pense pas encore. | —*No, she's not thinking about it yet.* |

BUT

| | |
|---|---|
| —As-tu téléphoné **à ta mère?** | —*Did you call your mother?* |
| —Non, je ne **lui** ai pas téléphoné. | —*No, I didn't call her.* |

The placement of **y** is identical to that of object pronouns; it precedes a conjugated verb, an infinitive, or an auxiliary verb in the **passé composé**.

| | |
|---|---|
| La ville de Nice? Nous **y** cherchons une maison. | *The city of Nice? We're looking for a house there.* |
| Mon mari va **y** arriver jeudi. | *My husband will arrive there on Thursday.* |
| **Y** est-il allé en train ou en avion? | *Did he go there by train or by plane?* |

## B. The Pronoun *en*

**En** can replace a combination of a partitive article (**du**, **de la**, **de l'**, **des**) or indefinite article (**un**, **une**, **des**) plus a noun. **En** is then equivalent to English *some* or *any*. Like other object pronouns, **en** is placed directly before the verb which refers to it. In the **passé composé**, it is placed directly before the auxiliary verb.

| | |
|---|---|
| —Y a-t-il **des musées intéressants** à Avignon? | —*Are there interesting museums in Avignon?* |
| —Oui, il y **en** a. | —*Yes, there are (some).* |
| —Est-ce que vous avez visité **des sites touristiques** à Avignon? | —*Did you visit any tourist attractions in Avignon?* |
| —Oui, nous y **en** avons visité. | —*Yes, we visited some (there).* |
| —Avez-vous acheté **des souvenirs**? | —*Did you buy souvenirs?* |
| —Non, nous n'**en** avons pas acheté. | —*No, we didn't buy any.* |
| —Voici **du vin d'Avignon. En** veux-tu? | —*Here's some wine from Avignon. Do you want some?* |
| —Non merci. Je n'**en** veux pas. | —*No, thanks. I don't want any.* |

**En** can also replace a noun modified by a number or by an expression of quantity such as **beaucoup de**, **un kilo de**, **trop de**, **deux**, and so on. Only **en** (*of it*, *of them*) and the number or expression of quantity are used in place of the noun. Although *of it* (*them*) can be omitted in English, **en** must be used in French.

| | |
|---|---|
| —Avez-vous **une chambre**? | —*Do you have a room?* |
| —Oui, j'**en** ai **une**.* | —*Yes, I have one.* |
| —Y a-t-il **beaucoup de chambres** disponibles? | —*Are there a lot of rooms available?* |
| —Oui, il y **en** a **beaucoup**. | —*Yes, there are a lot.* |
| —**Combien de lits** voudriez-vous? | —*How many beds would you like?* |
| —J'**en** voudrais **deux**. | —*I'd like two.* |

**En** is also used to replace **de** plus a noun and its modifiers (unless the noun refers to people) in sentences with verbs or expressions that use **de**: **parler de**, **avoir envie de**, and so on.

| | |
|---|---|
| —Avez-vous besoin **de ce guide**? | —*Do you need this guide?* |
| —Oui, j'**en** ai besoin. | —*Yes, I need it.* |
| —Parliez-vous **des ruines romaines**? | —*Were you talking about the Roman ruins?* |
| —Non, nous n'**en** parlions pas. | —*No, we weren't talking about them.* |

## C. Y and en Together

**Y** precedes **en** when they are the objects of the same verb.

**Presentation**: Model sentences and have sts. repeat sentences with pronoun *en* or *y* and *en* together where appropriate to reinforce word order.

| | |
|---|---|
| —Est-ce qu'on trouve des ruines romaines à Avignon? | —*Can you find Roman ruins in Avignon?* |
| —Oui, on **y en** trouve. | —*Yes, you can find some* (*there*). |

The combination of **y en** is very common with the expression **il y a**.

| | |
|---|---|
| —Combien de terrains de camping y a-t-il? | —*How many campgrounds are there?* |
| —Il **y en** a sept. | —*There are seven* (*of them*). |
| —Combien de campeurs y avait-il? | —*How many campers were there?* |
| —Il **y en** avait à peu près cent cinquante. | —*There were about a hundred fifty* (*of them there*). |

### *Vérifions!*

**A. Roman policier.** Paul Marteau est détective. Il file (*trails*) une suspecte, Pauline Dutour. Doit-il aller partout (*everywhere*) où elle va?

**Suggestion**: Use for oral response, or have a few sts. at board and others at seats write response for each sentence read orally by instructor. Assign second part of ex. for homework.

*In a negative answer to a question containing **un**(**e**), the word **un**(**e**) is not repeated: **Je n'en ai pas.**

MODÈLE: Pauline Dutour va à Paris →
Marteau y va aussi. (*ou* Marteau n'y va pas.)

1. La suspecte entre dans un magasin de vêtements. 2. Elle va au cinéma. 3. Elle entre dans une cabine téléphonique. 4. Pauline reste longtemps dans un bistro. 5. La suspecte monte dans un taxi. 6. Elle va chez le coiffeur (*hairdresser*). 7. Elle entre dans un hôtel. 8. La suspecte va au bar de l'hôtel. 9. Maintenant elle va en prison.

Maintenant, racontez les aventures de Marteau au passé composé.

**Suggestion**: Could be done in groups of 3, with 2 sts. talking and a third taking notes to report back to the class.

**B. Un dîner chez Maxim.** Un(e) ami(e) vous interroge sur votre choix.

MODÈLE: pâté →
L'AMI(E): Tu as envie de manger du pâté? (Prends-tu du pâté?)
VOUS: Oui, j'en ai envie. (Oui, j'en prends.)
(*ou* Non, je n'en ai pas envie. / Non, je n'en prends pas.)

1. hors-d'œuvre 2. soupe 3. escargots 4. viande 5. légumes 6. vin 7. dessert 8. café

**Additional activity**: *Au café-tabac.* MODÈLE: *revues* (3) → *—Combien de revues voulez-vous? —J'en veux trois.* 1. *cartes postales* (2) 2. *timbres* (6) 3. *films* (2) 4. *tasses de café* (4) 5. *verres de vin* (3) 6. *glaces* (2) 7. *journaux* (1) 8. *cigares* (3)

**C. Correspondance.** Debbie va visiter la France. Elle pose des questions aux amis qui l'ont invitée. Donnez une réponse en utilisant **y** et **en**.

MODÈLE: Est-ce qu'on vend de la bonne moutarde à Dijon? →
Oui, on y en vend.

1. Est-ce qu'à Marseille on boit du pastis? 2. Est-ce qu'il y a beaucoup de fleurs à Nice? 3. Est-ce qu'on trouve des ruines romaines à Arles? 4. Est-ce qu'on trouve des châteaux dans la vallée de la Loire? 5. Est-ce que nous pouvons faire du bateau en Bretagne? 6. Est-ce qu'on fait du vin à Bordeaux?

**Suggestion**: If sts. need more practice, dictate stimulus sentences, with several sts. working at board. Have sts. replace noun phrases by erasing them and putting *y* and *en* in their appropriate place.

**Continuation**: *Est-ce qu'on boit de la bière à Strasbourg? Est-ce qu'on trouve des dolmens et des menhirs à Carnac? Est-ce qu'on entend des langues étrangères à Paris? Est-ce qu'on voit des bâtiments roses à Toulouse?*

## Parlons-en!

**A. Lettre à ma mère.** Lisez la lettre et répondez aux questions. Utilisez le pronom **en** dans vos réponses.

1. Est-ce que Marie a trouvé un appartement?
2. Combien de pièces y a-t-il?
3. Est-ce que Marie et ses copains parlent souvent de la vie parisienne?
4. Quand va-t-elle acheter un vélo?
5. Pourquoi ne veut-elle pas de voiture?

Paris le 3 septembre

Chère maman

Je suis à Paris depuis trois jours. J'ai déjà trouvé un appartement dans le 15ᵉ. J'ai une chambre, un salon et une petite cuisine. Ma copine me parle souvent de la vie parisienne. C'est une ville fascinante. Je vais acheter un vélo la semaine prochaine pour me promener sur les bords du canal St Martin. Je ne veux pas de voiture. C'est trop dangereux ici.

Je t'embrasse très fort. À bientôt.

Ta fille adorée

Marie

me... *ride along the banks*

**B. Votre ville.** Imaginez qu'un(e) touriste vous pose des questions sur votre ville. Jouez les rôles avec un(e) camarade. Utilisez dans vos réponses le pronom **en** et un nombre ou une expression de quantité. Donnez aussi le plus de détails possible.

MODÈLE: —Y a-t-il de grands magasins dans votre ville?
—Oui, il y en a beaucoup—Saks, Macy's, Nordstrom...
(Il y en a seulement deux, Macy's et Saks.)

1. Avez-vous une université dans votre ville?
2. Y a-t-il des musées intéressants à visiter?
3. Combien de cinémas et de théâtres avez-vous?
4. Est-ce qu'on peut faire beaucoup de sport?
5. Combien d'habitants y a-t-il dans votre ville?
6. Rencontre-t-on beaucoup d'étrangers?

Maintenant, votre camarade décrit votre ville à la classe. Il/Elle commence par «Mon/Ma camarade est de ______. Il y a beaucoup de grands magasins à ______...» Est-ce que tout le monde est d'accord avec cette description? Comparez les descriptions d'une même ville. Qui a donné le plus de détails? Qui a été le plus précis (la plus précise)?

## Mots-clés

*Asking someone's opinion*

| | |
|---|---|
| **Que pensez-vous de...*** | *What do you think of . . .* |
| **Qu'en penses-tu?** | *What do you think about that?* |
| **Est-ce que tu crois que...** | *Do you think that . . .* |
| **À votre (ton) avis,...** | *In your opinion . . .* |

**C. Échange d'opinions.** Avec un(e) camarade, donnez des opinions sur des sujets divers.

**Suggestions:** les musées, les touristes, les chauffeurs de taxi, les monuments, les grandes villes américaines, les transports en commun...

MODÈLE:
VOUS: Que penses-tu des voitures japonaises?
VOTRE CAMARADE: Elles sont jolies (trop petites, bon marché)... Et toi, qu'en penses-tu?
VOUS: Je (ne) les aime (pas). Elles (ne) sont (pas)...

**Suggestion**: Have sts. give an oral *résumé* of some of their partners' opinions.

**Continuation**: *la mode française, les films français, la classe de français*, etc.

*__Penser de__ is normally used to ask a person's opinion about something or someone; **penser à** means to be thinking about (to have on one's mind) something or someone.

## 39. SAYING WHAT AND WHOM YOU KNOW *savoir and connaître*

### Labyrinthe

**Note**: Mention that *l'île de la Cité* is where *Notre-Dame*, *la Sainte-Chapelle* and *le Palais de Justice* are located. Point out locations on map in this chapter.

MARCEL: Taxi! Vous **connaissez** la rue Vaucouleurs?
LE CHAUFFEUR: Mais bien sûr, je **sais** où elle est! Je **connais** Paris comme le fond de ma poche!
MARCEL: Je ne **sais** pas comment vous faites. Je me suis perdu hier dans l'Île de la Cité.
LE CHAUFFEUR: Je **connais** mon métier et puis, vous **savez**, avec un plan de Paris, ce n'est pas si difficile!

ALPHA TAXIS
JOUR ET NUIT
45.85.85.85
DES CHAUFFEURS A VOTRE SERVICE
RESERVATION – ABONNEMENT
PARIS – BANLIEUE
AEROPORT – PROVINCE
Renseignements Administratifs : Tél. : 45.85.60.45

Faites des phrases complètes pour décrire ce qui se passe (*what happens*) dans le dialogue.

| | | |
|---|---|---|
| Marcel | sait | la rue Vaucouleurs |
| le chauffeur | ne sait pas | où est la rue Vaucouleurs |
| | connaît | Paris |
| | ne connaît pas | comment le chauffeur fait son métier |

The verbs **savoir** and **connaître** both correspond to the English verb *to know*, but they are used differently.

| PRESENT TENSE OF **savoir** (*to know*) | | | |
|---|---|---|---|
| je | **sais** | nous | **savons** |
| tu | **sais** | vous | **savez** |
| il, elle, on | **sait** | ils, elles | **savent** |
| *Past participle:* su | | | |

| PRESENT TENSE OF **connaître** (*to know*) | | | |
|---|---|---|---|
| je | **connais** | nous | **connaissons** |
| tu | **connais** | vous | **connaissez** |
| il, elle, on | **connaît** | ils, elles | **connaissent** |
| *Past participle:* connu | | | |

**Note**: You may wish to point out that verbs like *connaître* are spelled with a circumflex on the letter *i* in each form where *i* precedes *t*: *elle connaît*, *il paraît*.

**Savoir** means *to know* or *to have knowledge of* a fact, *to know by heart*, or *to know how to* do something. It is frequently followed by an infinitive or by a subordinate clause introduced by **que**, **quand**, **pourquoi**, and so on.

| | |
|---|---|
| **Sais**-tu l'heure qu'il est? | *Do you know what time it is?* |
| **Savez**-vous où est le bureau de poste le plus proche d'ici? | *Do you know where the closest post office is?* |
| Je **sais** que le bureau de poste du boulevard Haussmann est fermé. | *I know that the post office on Boulevard Haussmann is closed.* |

In the **passé composé**, **savoir** means *to learn* or *to find out*.

| | |
|---|---|
| J'**ai su** hier que la mairie va être démolie. | *I learned yesterday that the city hall is going to be demolished.* |

**Connaître** means *to know* or *to be familiar* (*acquainted*) *with* someone or something. **Connaître**—never **savoir**—means *to know a person*. **Connaître** is always used with a direct object; it cannot be followed directly by an infinitive or by a subordinate clause.

| | |
|---|---|
| **Connais**-tu Marie-Françoise? | *Do you know Marie-Françoise?* |
| Non, je ne la **connais** pas. | *No, I don't know her.* |
| Ils **connaissent** très bien Dijon. | *They know Dijon very well.* |

In the **passé composé**, **connaître** means *to meet for the first time*. It is the equivalent of **faire la connaissance de**.

| | |
|---|---|
| **J'ai connu** Jean à l'université. | *I met Jean at the university.* |

## *Vérifions!*

**A. Dialogue.** Complétez les phrases avec **connaître** ou **savoir**.

**Suggestion**: Give sts. a short time to fill in blanks. Ask for volunteers to read each sentence. Ask another st. why answer is correct or incorrect.

É1: ____[1]-vous Paris, Monsieur?
É2: Je ____[2] seulement que c'est la capitale.
É1: ____[3]-vous quelle est la distance entre Paris et Marseille?
É2: Non, mais je ____[4] une agence de voyages où on doit le ____[5]. Ils ____[6] très bien le pays.
É1: ____[7]-vous s'il y a d'autres villes intéressantes à visiter?
É2: Comme je l'ai dit, je ne ____[8] pas bien ce pays, mais hier j'ai fait la connaissance d'un homme qui ____[9] où aller pour passer de bonnes vacances.
É1: Je voudrais bien ____[10] cet homme. ____[11]-vous où il travaille?

**B. Et vous?** Connaissez-vous Paris? Avec un(e) camarade, posez des questions et répondez-y.

MODÈLE: l'Opéra →
VOUS: Connaissez-vous l'Opéra?
VOTRE CAMARADE: Non, je ne le connais pas, mais je sais qu'on y va pour écouter de la musique.

La tour Eiffel et les fontaines du Trocadéro illuminées

| ENDROITS | DÉFINITIONS |
|---|---|
| l'Opéra | C'est le quartier des étudiants à Paris. |
| Notre-Dame de Paris | Le président y habite. |
| le Louvre | On y va pour écouter de la musique. |
| le Palais de l'Élysée | On y trouve une vaste collection de livres. |
| la tour Eiffel | C'est une église située dans l'île de la Cité. |
| la Bibliothèque nationale | C'est la structure en verre (*glass*) devant le Louvre. |
| le Quartier latin | On y trouve une riche collection d'art. |
| la Pyramide | Elle a 320 mètres de haut (*tall*) et elle est en fer. |

**Suggestion**: Slides or pictures of places mentioned would help make this more meaningful to sts.

**Continuation (A)**: 6. *Nomme deux villes que tu connais bien.* 7. *Nomme deux personnes que tu ne veux pas connaître et dis pourquoi.* 8. *Nomme deux personnes que tu veux connaître et dis pourquoi.* 9. *Nomme deux villes que tu veux connaître et dis pourquoi.*

## *Parlons-en!*

**A. Vos connaissances.** Utilisez ces phrases pour interviewer un ami (une amie). Dans les réponses, utilisez les verbes **savoir** ou **connaître**.

1. Nomme deux choses que tu sais faire.
2. Nomme deux choses que tu veux savoir faire un jour.
3. Nomme deux domaines (*fields*) où tu es plus ou moins (*more or less*) incompétent(e). (Je ne sais pas...)
4. Nomme une personne que tu as connue récemment.
5. Nomme quelqu'un que tu aimerais (*would like*) connaître.

**B. Une ville.** Donnez le nom d'une ville que vous connaissez bien. Ensuite, racontez ce que (*what*) vous savez sur cette ville.

MODÈLE: Je connais New York. Je sais qu'il y a d'immenses gratte-ciel (*skyscrapers*).

**Suggestions**: (1) Give sts. a moment to reflect. (2) Can be done as a game. St. gives hints: *Je sais qu'il y a d'énormes gratte-ciel dans cette ville. Je sais qu'elle est sur la côte est.* Others guess which city is described.

# France-culture

*Les villes françaises.* Les trois-quarts° des Français habitent dans des villes. Il y a Paris, bien sûr, et puis Lyon, Marseille, Toulouse, Bordeaux, Lille et Strasbourg parmi° les capitales régionales les plus importantes. Mais surtout, la France compte° de très nombreuses petites villes qui sont, en général, très anciennes et très différentes d'une région à l'autre.

*three quarters* / *among* / *includes*

La plupart des villes françaises ont été construites pendant le moyen âge.° L'église ou la cathédrale est située au centre de la ville. Les immeubles et les maisons du centre-ville sont souvent très anciens. Les rues étroites° sont réservées pour les piétons° et les voitures ne peuvent pas y rouler. Contrairement aux Américains qui ont abandonné le centre des villes pour aller habiter en banlieue,° beaucoup de Français vivent,° travaillent et font leurs courses dans le centre-ville. Le centre-ville est aussi le centre des loisirs: on y trouve des restaurants, cafés, discothèques, cinémas, théâtres et musées. Le vendredi soir et le samedi, les gens qui habitent en banlieue viennent faire un tour dans le centre et les rues sont très animées.°

*moyen... Middle Ages* / *narrow* / *pedestrians* / *the suburbs / live* / *lively*

Autour du° centre-ville, il y a de nombreux quartiers. Les bâtiments° y sont plus modernes. La vie dans ces quartiers ressemble à la vie dans les villages. Il y a des petits commerces (épiceries, boulangeries, boucheries, cafés...) et les gens connaissent leurs voisins.

*Autour... Around* / *buildings*

Vue d'ensemble du village de Montigny

# Mise au point

**A. La «grosse pomme».** Un(e) camarade vous pose des questions sur la ville de New York en utilisant le verbe **savoir** ou **connaître**. Dans vos réponses, utilisez un pronom complément d'objet direct. Suivez le modèle.

MODÈLE: UN(E) CAMARADE: Connais-tu le maire (*mayor*) de New York?
VOUS: Oui, je le connais. (*ou* Non, je ne le connais pas.)

1. utiliser le métro de New York 2. combien de théâtres il y a sur Broadway 3. Greenwich Village 4. que la France nous a donné la Statue de la Liberté 5. le musée Guggenheim 6. comment aller du centre-ville à l'aéroport JFK 7. le quartier Little Italy

**B. Les grandes villes.** Formez des phrases complètes et mettez les verbes de cette narration au passé composé ou à l'imparfait.

Suggestion: May be done as homework and checked in class, either with individuals working at board or with a transparency containing correct answers.

1. je / aimer / les grandes villes / quand / je / être / jeune
2. il y a / toujours / beaucoup / choses / à voir
3. les gens / être / intéressant / et / les bâtiments / être / beau
4. un jour / je / être / la banque / et je / voir / un hold-up
5. le voleur (*robber*) / avoir / un revolver
6. nous / avoir / peur
7. le voleur / prendre / l'argent / et il / partir
8. quelqu'un / téléphoner / la police
9. la police / le / trouver / en dix minutes / parce qu'il / avoir / difficultés / avec / voiture
10. voilà pourquoi / je / acheter / une maison / campagne

**C. Voyage imaginaire.** Pensez à une ville que vous aimez tout particulièrement (aux États-Unis ou à l'étranger). Décrivez-la au reste de la classe. Utilisez des pronoms d'objet direct ou indirect, **y** ou **en** dans votre description. Vos camarades doivent deviner le nom de la ville.

MODÈLE: VOUS: On y trouve des collines (*hills*). On la voit souvent dans des films. Beaucoup de touristes y vont pour admirer son célèbre pont (*bridge*) et pour visiter son célèbre quartier chinois.
VOS CAMARADES: C'est San Francisco!

**D. Interview.** Interviewez un(e) camarade au sujet de sa première visite d'une grande ville loin de chez lui/elle.

**Suggestions:** Où es-tu allé(e)? Quand? Combien de temps y es-tu resté(e)? Avec qui étais-tu? Qu'est-ce que tu y as fait? Qu'est-ce que tu y as vu? Étais-tu content(e) de ta visite? Pourquoi ou pourquoi pas?

Maintenant, résumez (*summarize*) pour la classe la visite de votre camarade. Utilisez les expressions **d'abord**, **puis**, **ensuite**, **après** et **enfin**.

Suggestion: *Résumé* can be done orally or in writing.

## Interactions

In this chapter, you learned how to tell stories in the past and to express the time of events. Act out the following situations, using the vocabulary and structures from this chapter.

1. **Journaliste.** You are interviewing a famous, rich person (your classmate) about his or her travels to France. Find out if she or he prefers the country or the cities. Ask what French city she or he prefers and why. Have him or her describe the city and a recent visit.
2. **Je suis perdu(e)!** Imagine that you are lost. Ask a stranger (your partner) the way to go downtown from where you are. She or he will give you directions, mentioning some landmarks. Ask questions if you are not sure where to go.

# Rencontres

## LECTURE

### Avant de lire

**Scanning paragraphs.** In Chapter 5 you studied topic sentences and the organization of paragraphs. Quickly scan each paragraph of this magazine article from the *Journal Français d'Amerique* about the mayor of a small village in Bretagne. As you scan, note the general function of each paragraph in the reading. Do not try to read every paragraph word for word, but look for keys to the major point made in each one. Indicate whether each paragraph presents a principal idea, an example, or an anecdote.

| PARAGRAPHE | IDÉE PRINCIPALE | EXEMPLE | ANECDOTE |
|---|---|---|---|
| premier | | | |
| deuxième | | | |
| troisième | | | |
| quatrième | | | |
| cinquième | | | |

PROFIL

## KOFI YAMGNANE

### MAIRE[a] BRETON ORIGINAIRE DU TOGO

**P**remier maire noir de France métropolitaine[b] et même[c] d'Europe, Kofi Yamgnane préside depuis plus de deux ans aux destinées[d] de Saint-Coulitz, un petit village breton (dans le Finistère) de 364 habitants. Mais M. Yamgnane n'est pas « que » maire. Il est aussi secrétaire d'Etat à l'Intégration du gouvernement Cresson.

Né au Togo (Afrique occidentale), Kofi Yamgnane est remarqué[e] dès 7 ans[f] par un Père jésuite, envoyé à l'école primaire puis au lycée de Lomé. En 1964, il débarque[g] à Brest avec le bac en poche[h] pour faire ses études. « A l'époque, se souvient-il,[i] j'étais le seul Noir de toute l'Université. Malgré[j] un accueil[k] souvent chaleureux[l] de la part des Bretons, je ne pouvais qu'éprouver[m] un fort sentiment d'isolement ».

Après un détour par l'Ecole des Mines de Nancy, il s'installe avec sa famille (sa femme est bretonne) à Saint-Coulitz en 1973. En 1983, un groupe d'agriculteurs le persuade de se présenter aux élections municipales. Il est élu.[n] Pendant son mandat,[o] il fera preuve[p] d'un esprit constructif et sera un modèle de dynamisme. En 1989, il enlèvera le siège[q] de maire.

Kofi Yamgnane

M. Yamgnane a eu l'idée, prise dans son village africain, de créer un Conseil des sages.[r] Il s'agit[s] d'un groupe de cinq femmes et de quatre hommes de plus de 60 ans, élus, qui se réunissent[t] une fois par mois pour donner leur avis sur les sujets appelés à être traités[u] ensuite par le Conseil municipal.

Monsieur le Maire fait décidément de sa commune une vitrine[v] de démocratie, que certains[w] d'ailleurs tentent[x] de copier.

[a]mayor [b]continental [c]even [d]aux... over the inhabitants [e]noticed [f]dès... from the age of seven

[g]disembarks [h]en... in hand (lit., in pocket) [i]À... At the time, he recalls, . . . [j]Despite [k]welcome [l]warm [m]experience

[n]elected [o]term [p]fera... shows [q]enlèvera... wins the seat [r]Conseil... Council of wise people [s]Il... It involves [t]se... meets

[u]appelés... meant to be tackled [v]"show-window," model [w]certains personnes [x]try

## Compréhension

Répondez aux questions suivantes.

1. Kofi Yamgnane n'est pas un maire comme les autres. Pourquoi?
2. En quelle année est-il venu en France? Pourquoi y est-il venu?
3. Dans quelle(s) ville(s) a-t-il fait ses études?
4. Où se trouve la ville de Saint-Coulitz? Combien d'habitants y a-t-il?
5. Qui a persuadé Kofi Yamgnane de faire de la politique?
6. Quelle idée africaine a-t-il appliquée dans le village de Saint-Coulitz?

# PAR ÉCRIT

**Function:** Narrating in the past
**Audience:** Instructor or classmates
**Goal:** Write a three-paragraph story in the past with a clear beginning and ending. Choose one of the following genres: **reportage ou fait divers** (*miscellaneous small news item*), **autobiographie**, or **biographie**.

### Steps

1. Begin by making an outline of your story. The introduction should set the scene in which you sketch the main characters, the setting, the time, and the circumstances. In the second paragraph, bring in a complication that affects or changes the state of affairs. Outline the occurrence and the reactions of the characters. In the third paragraph, describe briefly how the situation was resolved. End with a general conclusion which summarizes the outcome and explains what, if anything, was learned from the experience.
2. Write the rough draft, making sure it contains all the information mentioned above.
3. Review your draft, checking for inclusion of interesting details, description, and actions.
4. Have a classmate read your story to see if what you have written is interesting, clear, and organized. Make any necessary changes. Finally, reread the composition for spelling, punctuation, and grammar errors. Focus especially on your use of the past tenses. Be prepared to read your composition to a small group of classmates.

**À l'écoute!** See scripts for listening passages and follow-up activities recorded on student cassette. Remind students that in the listening comprehension passages (as in real life) they will not understand every word they hear. They should focus globally on the general information in the passages and not be overly concerned about what they do not understand.

# À L'ÉCOUTE!

**I. Pour aller au syndicat d'initiative.** Anne-Marie visite Blain, une petite ville dans le nord-ouest de la France. Elle demande à un passant où se trouve le syndicat d'initiative. Lisez les activités à la page suivante avant d'écouter le dialogue qui leur correspond.

**A.** Encerclez la bonne réponse d'après le dialogue.

1. Pour aller au syndicat d'initiative, Anne-Marie préfère
   a. marcher
   b. prendre le bus
2. Elle doit prendre la première rue
   a. à droite
   b. à gauche
3. Elle doit traverser
   a. la place de la Gare
   b. la rue Pasteur
4. À la rue Pasteur elle doit tourner à gauche dans la
   a. quatrième rue
   b. cinquième rue
5. Le syndicat d'initiative est en face
   a. d'une boulangerie
   b. du commissariat

**B.** Maintenant tracez le chemin sur la carte ci-dessous.

Encerclez le syndicat d'initiative. Y a-t-il un chemin plus court (*shorter route*) pour aller au syndicat d'initiative? Si oui, tracez-le aussi.

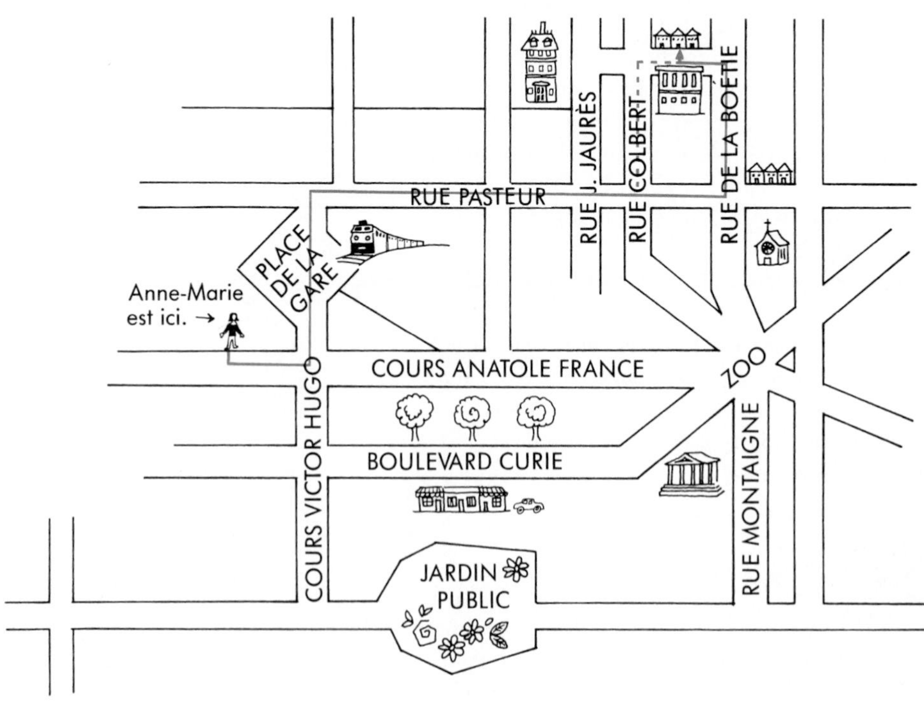

**II. Souvenirs de Marseille.** Lucien habitait Marseille il y a longtemps. Il en parle à Georges. Lisez l'activité ci-dessous avant d'écouter le vocabulaire et le dialogue qui lui correspondent.

VOCABULAIRE UTILE
un pastis *licorice-flavored alcoholic beverage*
ils riaient *they laughed*

Encerclez la bonne réponse d'après le dialogue.

1. Lucien est allé à Marseille ____.
   a. une fois
   b. deux fois
   c. trois fois
2. En 1965, il avait ____.
   a. 18 ans
   b. 28 ans
   c. 19 ans
3. En 1965, il ____ Marseille.
   a. détestait
   b. ne connaissait pas
   c. aimait
4. En 1965, tous les week-ends il ____.
   a. pêchait
   b. faisait du sport
   c. allait au cinéma
5. Il est retourné à Marseille en ____.
   a. 1982
   b. 1992
   c. 1972
6. Marseille ____.
   a. a changé
   b. n'a pas changé
   c. est devenue plus belle
7. Lucien ____ les petits magasins où il allait autrefois.
   a. a trouvé
   b. n'a pas trouvé
   c. a oublié
8. Il était ____.
   a. triste
   b. indifférent
   c. content
9. Il ____.
   a. est resté à Marseille
   b. a continué son voyage
   c. est retourné à Paris

Un quartier moderne à Grenoble

# Vocabulaire

## Verbes

**commencer** to begin
**connaître** to know; to be familiar with
**penser à** to think of, about
**penser de** to think of, about (to have an opinion about)
**savoir** to know (how)
**toucher** to cash (a check); to touch; to concern
**se trouver** to be located, situated

À REVOIR: écrire, prendre, réfléchir à, réussir à

## Substantifs

**l'arrondissement** (*m.*) ward, section (*of Paris*)
**la banlieue** suburbs
**le bâtiment** building
**le bois** forest, woods
**le boulevard** boulevard
**le café-tabac** bar-tobacconist
**la carte** map (*of a region, country*)
**le centre-ville** downtown
**le château** castle, château
**le chemin** way (road)
**le coin** corner
**le commissariat** (**le poste de police**) police station
**l'église** (*f.*) church
**l'île** (*f.*) island
**la mairie** town hall
**la piscine** swimming pool
**la place** square
**le plan** map (*of a city*)
**le poste de police** police station
**la Rive droite** the Right Bank (*in Paris*)
**la Rive gauche** the Left Bank (*in Paris*)
**le syndicat d'initiative** tourist information bureau
**la tour** tower

À REVOIR: la bibliothèque, le jardin, la librairie, la pièce, la rue

## Les nombres ordinaux

**le premier** (**la première**), **le/la deuxième,...** , **le/la cinquième,...** , **le/la huitième, le/la neuvième,...** , **le/la onzième,** etc.

## Les expressions temporelles

**autrefois** formerly
**d'abord** first, first of all, at first
**de temps en temps** from time to time
**enfin** finally
**puis** then, next
**soudain** suddenly
**tout d'un coup** suddenly; all at once
**une fois** once

## Mots et expressions divers

**à droite** (*prep.*) on (to) the right
**à gauche** (*prep.*) on (to) the left
**À votre** (**ton**) **avis,...** ? In your opinion, . . . ?
**de nouveau** (*adv.*) again
**en** (*pron.*) of them; of it; some
**en face de** (*prep.*) across from
**jusqu'à** up to, as far as
**là** (*adv.*) there
**partout** (*adv.*) everywhere
**Qu'en penses-tu?** What do you think of that?
**Que pensez-vous de... ?** What do you think about . . . ?
**tout droit** (*adv.*) straight ahead
**y** (*pron.*) there

## Mots apparentés

*Verbes:* **continuer, tourner**
*Substantifs:* **la banque, l'hôpital** (*m.*), **l'hôtel** (*m.*), **le monument, le musée, le parc, la pharmacie, la station** (**de métro**)
*Adjectifs:* **municipal**(**e**), **public/publique**

# Intermède

## SITUATION

### Aventure en métro

**Contexte** *Charles, un étudiant québécois, veut aller à l'École de Médecine, dans le Quartier latin, à Paris. Ses amis, Francis et Geneviève, lui expliquent comment y aller en métro.*

**Objectif** *Charles utilise le métro.*

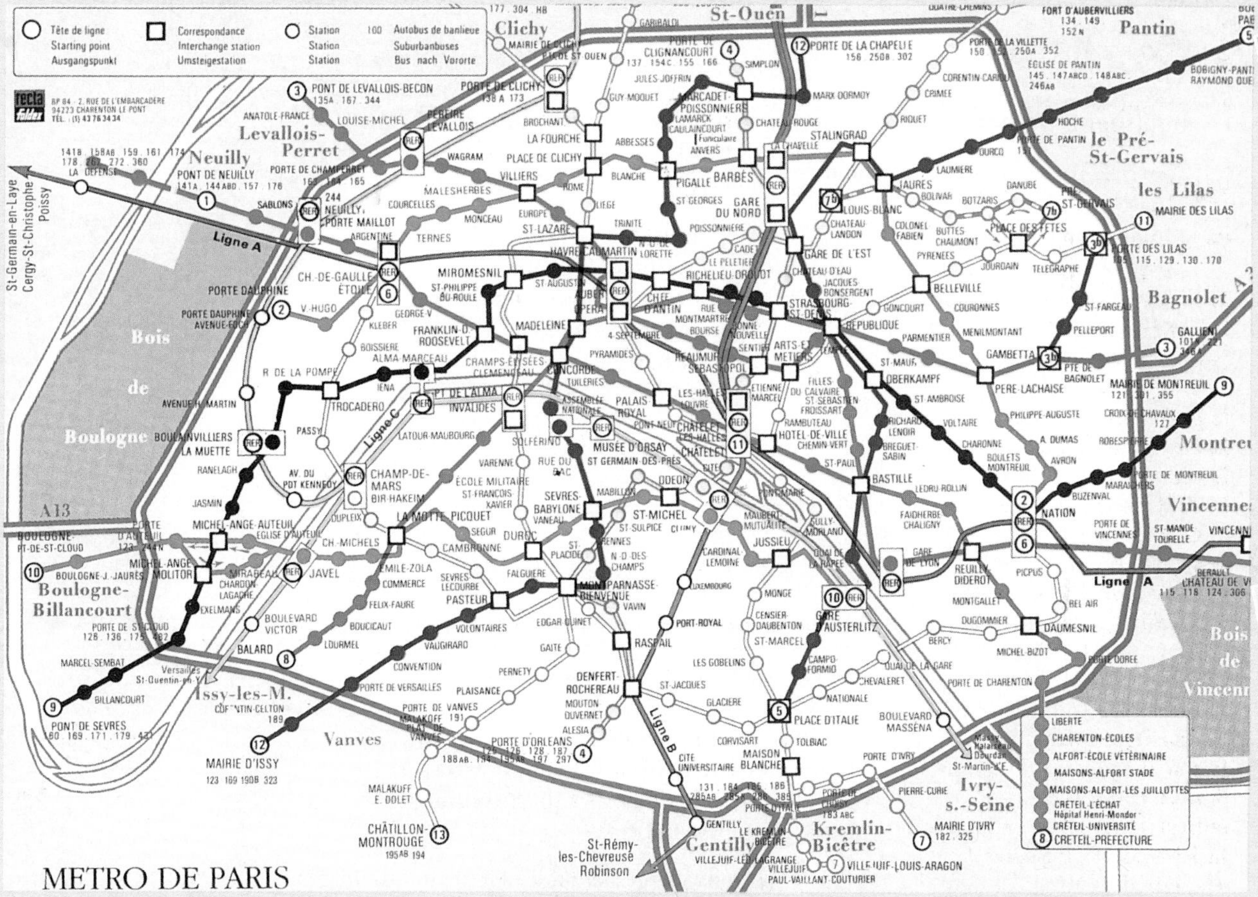

**Situation**: The *Situation* dialogues are recorded on the st. cassette packaged with the st. text.

METRO DE PARIS

GENEVIÈVE: Charles, tu peux y aller en métro, à l'École de Médecine.
CHARLES: Oui, mais comment fait-on pour y aller?
GENEVIÈVE: Viens, on va regarder la carte: quelle est la station près de l'École?
CHARLES: Odéon.

**Note**: This *Situation* allows sts. to practice function of giving and getting directions and to familiarize themselves with the Paris *métro*. See the *À propos* section for additional vocab.

FRANCIS: Bon, on est près d'Oberkampf.

GENEVIÈVE: Regarde la carte maintenant: comment fait-on pour aller d'Oberkampf à Odéon?

CHARLES: Heu... on va jusqu'à Strasbourg Saint-Denis, on change et on va jusqu'à Odéon.

GENEVIÈVE: Quand on va d'Oberkampf à Strasbourg Saint-Denis, on prend direction Pont de Sèvres et...

CHARLES: Attends, j'ai tout compris. Et quand on va de Strasbourg Saint-Denis à Odéon, on prend direction Porte d'Orléans. Super! Vous connaissez bien Paris maintenant.

GENEVIÈVE: Pas vraiment, mais on apprend vite!

**Suggestion**: Have sts. play roles of Charles, Geneviève, Francis and read dialogue aloud.

**Suggestion**: Bring in a metro map of Paris, if possible. Follow-up the *Situation* by playing the lost tourist in Paris who asks for directions to go to different monuments.

**Note**: Mention that the *SNCF* joined forces with the *RATP*, the Parisian transportation authority, to create the *RER* (*Réseau Express Régional*), a train system that serves Paris and has connections (*correspondances*) with the *Métro*. The *RER* permits a traveler to cover wide distances in the Paris region much faster than with the regular *Métro* lines alone, although these still seem amazingly efficient and pleasant to anyone used to American subway systems. The *RER* and *Métro* lines are always clearly marked with maps and directions in the various stations.

## À propos

### Comment demander son chemin

Pourriez-vous (Pourrais-tu) me dire...
- où est... ?
- dans quelle direction est... ?
- par où je dois passer pour... ?
- si... est loin d'ici / près d'ici?

### Comment indiquer le chemin

C'est...
- là-bas (*there*).
- derrière...
- devant...
- à côté de...
- de l'autre côté de...
- en face de...

Vous allez tout droit.

Vous tournez { à droite. / à gauche.

## *Maintenant à vous!*

**A. Questions personnelles.** Relisez le dialogue, puis répondez aux questions.

1. Quels transports en commun est-ce qu'il y a dans votre ville? Lesquels sont les plus importants dans votre vie?
2. Y a-t-il dans votre ville deux ou trois endroits où vous aimez passer beaucoup de temps (un parc ou un quartier, par exemple)? Décrivez-les.
3. Choisissez un endroit où vous allez régulièrement, et dites comment vous faites pour y arriver. (**D'abord, j'attends le bus...** )

**Suggestions (B)**: (1) Give sts. a few minutes to develop skit or dialogue. Dialogues can then be written down and handed in, or roles can be played for other class members. (2) Have sts. talk about impressions of American subway systems and write down major characteristics. Use lists to compare and contrast American and French systems.

**B. Jeu de rôles.** Un nouvel étudiant (Une nouvelle étudiante) vous demande le chemin pour aller dans divers endroits de votre campus. Jouez la scène avec un(e) camarade. Soyez précis(e) dans vos instructions. Le nouvel étudiant (La nouvelle étudiante) doit répéter les instructions pour vérifier qu'il/elle les a bien comprises. Utilisez les expressions de l'*À propos*.

# PORTRAITS

***Georges Eugène, Baron Haussmann (1809–1891)***

Préfet de la Seine (administrateur de la région parisienne) entre 1853 et 1870, le baron Haussmann a dirigé° les grands travaux° qui ont transformé Paris d'une ville médiévale en une ville moderne. Il a fait construire de grandes avenues rectilignes° (les «grands boulevards»), l'Opéra et les bois de Boulogne et de Vincennes (voir° le plan à la page 297). Cependant° son travail a provoqué beaucoup de controverses parce qu'il a déplacé° les habitants pauvres des vieux quartiers et a fait démolir° des bâtiments historiques.

*directed / grands... public works projects*

*long, straight*

*refer to / However*

*displaced*

*a... had demolished*

CHAPITRE **DOUZE**

# La France et les arts

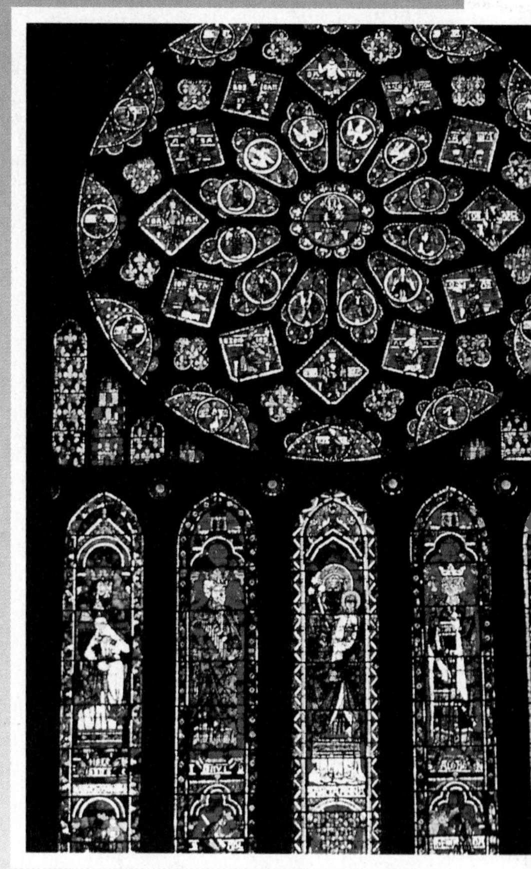

**En avant**

—Nous arrivons à Chartres. Oh, regarde la cathédrale, là-bas!

—Allons la visiter tout de suite.

—Tu as vu ces vitraux? Quelles couleurs!

—Ils sont du XIII$^{\text{ème}}$ siècle.

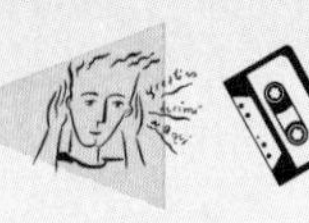

**En avant**: See scripts for follow-up questions recorded on student cassette.

**Communicative goals:** talking about France's historical and artistic heritage, talking about the arts, emphasizing and clarifying, expressing actions, speaking succinctly, and saying how to do something.

# Étude de vocabulaire

## Le patrimoine historique

La cathédrale d'Amiens, chef-d'œuvre (*masterpiece*) du moyen âge (l'époque médiévale: V$^{ème}$–XIV$^{ème}$ siècle [*century*])

Les arènes d'Arles, monument de l'époque romaine (59 av. J.C.*–V$^{ème}$ siècle)

**Presentation**: Model pronunciation of new vocab., reviewing use of ordinal numbers with *siècle*. Look at photos with sts. and encourage them to define main characteristics of each architectural style.

Chenonceaux, château de la Renaissance (XV$^{ème}$–XVI$^{ème}$ siècle)

*avant Jésus Christ

Versailles, château de l'époque classique (XVII$^{ème}$ siècle)

**Suggestion**: Throughout chapter, you will find appropriate occasions to bring in slides showing the arts and architecture of France. (See the slide sets available to adopters of *Rendez-vous*.)

**A. Définitions.** Regardez les quatre photos ci-dessus et complétez les phrases.

1. Une période historique, c'est une ____.
2. Une durée de cent ans, c'est un ____.
3. On a bâti (*built*) la cathédrale d'Amiens à l'époque ____.
4. L'époque historique qui se situe entre le V$^{ème}$ et le XIV$^{ème}$ siècles s'appelle (*is called*) le ____.
5. Le château de Chenonceaux a été bâti au ____.
6. Le château de Versailles date de l'époque ____.
7. Les arènes d'Arles datent de l'époque ____.

**Continuation**: 8. *La Renaissance a commencé au ____ siècle.* 9. *Le ____ a commencé au V$^{ème}$ siècle.* 10. *La Cathédrale de Chartres a été construite au ____ siècle.* 11. *La date du début de l'époque romaine, c'est ____ .*

**B. Leçon d'histoire.** Faites une phrase complète pour nommer le siècle et l'époque où les événements suivants se sont passés (*took place*). Remplacez les éléments en italique par des pronoms.

MODÈLE: *Christophe Colomb* est arrivé *au Nouveau Monde* en 1492. → Il y est arrivé au XV$^{ème}$ siècle, à l'époque de la Renaissance.

1. *Blaise Pascal* a inventé *la première machine à calculer* en 1642.
2. On a bâti *les arènes de Nîmes* au premier siècle.
3. *Guillaume, duc de Normandie*, a conquis (*conquered*) *l'Angleterre* en 1066.
4. *La ville de Paris* s'est appelée Lutèce du II$^{ème}$ siècle av. J.C. jusqu'au IV$^{ème}$ siècle après J.C.
5. *Jacques Cartier* a pris possession *du Canada* au nom de la France en 1534.
6. *Jeanne d'Arc* a essayé de prendre *la ville de Paris* en 1429.
7. *René Descartes* a écrit *sa «Géométrie»* en 1637.
8. *Charlemagne* est devenu roi (*king*) en 768.

**Suggestion (ex. B)**: Allow sts. a few minutes to work on answers, either individually or in pairs, before doing exercises orally.

**Additional activity**: *L'histoire plus récente. Répondez aux questions suivantes.* MODÈLE: *En quel siècle Thomas Edison a-t-il inventé l'ampoule électrique? → Il l'a inventée au dix-neuvième siècle.* 1. *En quel siècle a-t-on inventé la photographie?* 2. *En quel siècle Neil Armstrong a-t-il marché sur la lune?* 3. *En quel siècle a-t-on inventé la télévision?* 4. *En quel siècle a-t-on découvert de l'or en Californie?*

**C. À vous.** Imaginez que votre classe de français est en visite à Paris. Votre guide vous propose le choix de trois sites à visiter cet après-midi. Divisez-vous en groupes de trois ou quatre pour décider du site. Chaque groupe doit justifier son choix. Les autres peuvent poser des questions et faire des objections. Enfin, on vote. Voici les sites et les endroits à considérer:

**Suggestion (ex. C)**: Give sts. guidelines for justifying their choice of excursion. Example: *Pour justifier votre choix, dites* (a) *pourquoi vous voulez voir cet endroit;* (b) *ce qui rend cet endroit extraordinaire ou plus intéressant que les trois autres endroits;* (c) *les avantages d'y aller;* (d) *ce que vous espérez apprendre pendant la visite.*

**Les arènes de Lutèce**

**Histoire:** des arènes romaines de 15 000 places avec une arène séparée pour les combats des gladiateurs

**Aujourd'hui:** un jardin public très agréable où on peut flâner (*stroll*), pique-niquer ou rêver

**À proximité:** le Quartier latin

**Le palais du Louvre**

**Histoire:** ancienne résidence royale commencée au XIII$^{ème}$ siècle

**Aujourd'hui:** un magnifique musée d'art

**À proximité:** le quartier élégant de l'Opéra

**La cathédrale de Notre-Dame**

**Histoire:** Le grand chef-d'œuvre du moyen âge. Commencée en 1163 et finie en 1345. Son architecture de style gothique crée une atmosphère de mystère et de beauté.

**Aujourd'hui:** Toujours une église catholique. On peut monter les 387 marches (*steps*) jusqu'au sommet de sa tour et prendre de splendides photos de Paris.

**À proximité:** le Quartier latin, l'Île Saint-Louis, l'Hôtel de Ville (*City Hall*) de Paris

# Le patrimoine artistique

**Les œuvres d'art et de littérature**

La littérature

La sculpture

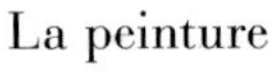
La peinture

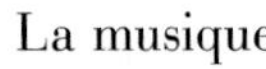
La musique

**A. Qui sont-ils?** Retrouvez la profession de ces artistes français. Si vous ne savez pas, devinez!

MODÈLE: Jean-Paul Sartre → C'est un écrivain.

1. Victor Hugo
2. Auguste Rodin
3. Pierre Auguste Renoir
4. Simone de Beauvoir
5. François Truffaut
6. Agnès Varda
7. Claude Debussy
8. Mary Cassatt*
9. Henri Matisse
10. Catherine Deneuve

peintre
sculpteur
musicien
cinéaste
écrivain
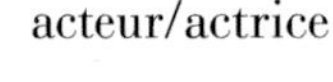
acteur/actrice

Le cinéma

*Mary Cassatt est née à Pittsburgh mais elle a vécu à Paris et a participé au mouvement impressionniste.

**B. Littérature.** Complétez les phrases avec les mots suivants: **poésie**, **acteur**, **roman**, **pièce de théâtre**, **écrivain**, **poème**.

1. *L'Étranger* est un ____ d'Albert Camus.
2. Molière était un ____ et un ____. Il a écrit des ____.
3. La vie de Verlaine et de Rimbaud était turbulente, mais leurs ____ sont parmi les chefs-d'œuvre de la ____ française.
4. Simone de Beauvoir a écrit des ____ et des essais sur la condition féminine.
5. *Les Fleurs du Mal* est un recueil (*collection*) de ____ de Charles Baudelaire.

**Additional activity:** Trivial Pursuit (*Remue-Méninges*). Give names of *expatriés* (*écrivains ou artistes étrangers qui ont vécu en France*) and see if sts. can name one of their works and country of origin. Examples: Chagall, Samuel Beckett, Picasso, F. Scott Fitzgerald, James Joyce, Oscar Wilde, Henry Miller, Gertrude Stein, Ernest Hemingway. Ask sts. to think up names to stump their classmates.

**C. Les goûts** (*tastes*) **artistiques.** Posez les questions à un(e) camarade.

1. Quel est ton roman préféré? C'est de qui?
2. Quel est ton peintre préféré? Pourquoi?
3. Connais-tu des artistes français? Lesquels?
4. Est-ce que tu écoutes de la musique classique? Quel est ton compositeur préféré (ta compositrice préférée)?
5. Aimes-tu la poésie? Quels poètes anglais ou américains aimes-tu? Connais-tu un poème par cœur (*by heart*)? Lequel?
6. Vas-tu quelquefois au théâtre? Quelle pièce as-tu vue récemment?
7. Aimes-tu aller au cinéma? Quel film as-tu vu récemment?

Maintenant, décrivez les goûts artistiques de votre camarade à la classe.

**Follow-up:** Use as a discussion question: *Pour quelles raisons les artistes vont-ils souvent habiter en France?*

# Deux verbes pour parler des arts

| **suivre** (*to follow*) | | | | **vivre** (*to live*) | | | |
|---|---|---|---|---|---|---|---|
| je | **suis** | nous | **suivons** | je | **vis** | nous | **vivons** |
| tu | **suis** | vous | **suivez** | tu | **vis** | vous | **vivez** |
| il, elle, on | **suit** | ils, elles | **suivent** | il, elle, on | **vit** | ils, elles | **vivent** |
| *Past participle:* suivi | | | | *Past participle:* vécu | | | |

**Suivre** and **vivre** are irregular verbs, and they have similar conjugations in the present tense. **Suivre un cours** means *to take a course.* **Poursuivre** (*to pursue*) is conjugated like **suivre**.

| | |
|---|---|
| L'impressionnisme a-t-il **suivi** le cubisme? | *Did Impressionism follow Cubism?* |
| Combien de cours d'art **suis**-tu? | *How many art courses are you taking?* |
| **Suivez** mes conseils! | *Follow my advice!* |
| A-t-il **poursuivi** ses études de musique? | *Did he pursue his musical studies?* |

**Suggestion**: Do as a preliminary activity: *Études ou vacances?* 1. *Qui suit le cours de sociologie? Jean le suit.* (*nous, Marie, vous, les Dupont*) 2. *Qui ne vit que pour les vacances? Chantal ne vit que pour les vacances.* (*je, Marie et François, tu*)

## Mots-clés

*Expressing* to live: vivre *or* habiter

Use **vivre** to express *to live, to be alive, to exist.* Use it also to express how one lives.

> Picasso **a vécu** jusqu'à 92 ans.
> Cette artiste ne **vit** pas dans le luxe (la misère).
> Ils **vivent** toujours dans cette région.

In general, use **habiter** to express *to reside.*

> Mary Cassatt **a habité** Paris pendant des années.
> Vous **habitez** rue de Rivoli?

**Vivre** is also used in certain idiomatic expressions.

| | |
|---|---|
| Elle est **difficile** (**facile**) **à vivre**. | *She's hard* (*easy*) *to live with.* |
| Il est parti sans raison apparente, «pour **vivre ma vie**», a-t-il dit. | *He left without apparent reason, to "live my own life," as he put it.* |

**A. Van Gogh.** Complétez l'histoire suivante par un des verbes: **suivre**, **poursuivre**, **vivre**, **habiter**. Mettez tous les verbes, excepté le numéro 7, au présent.

Vincent Van Gogh est né en 1853 à Groot-Zundert, aux Pays-Bas. En 1877, il _____[1] des cours pour devenir pasteur (*preacher*), mais malheureux ([*being*] *unhappy*), il change d'avis. Il _____[2] des études d'anatomie parce qu'il veut devenir artiste. Après des séjours en Belgique et aux Pays-Bas, où il peint *Les Mangeurs des pommes de terre*, il _____[3] à Paris, où il fait la connaissance des peintres impressionnistes. C'est Pissarro qui le convainc de peindre en couleurs vives (*bright*). À Paris, Van Gogh ne vend aucun* tableau; il _____[4] dans la misère (*poverty*). De 1888 jusqu'à sa mort, Van Gogh _____[5] le sud de la France où il _____[6] sa passion pour la peinture. De plus en plus tourmenté, il se suicide en 1890. Il _____[7] (passé composé) seulement jusqu'à l'âge de 37 ans, et n'a vendu qu'un tableau pendant sa vie.

**B. Conversation.** Répondez aux questions suivantes.

1. Quelle carrière voudriez-vous poursuivre? Suivez-vous déjà des cours qui mènent à (*lead to*) cette carrière?
2. Est-ce que la plupart (*majority*) des gens basent leur choix de carrière sur ce qui les intéresse? Si non, comment la choisissent-ils?

---

***ne... aucun**(**e**) is a negative expression used to mean *no, not one.*

3. Comment voulez-vous vivre dans dix ans? Dans le luxe en ville, par exemple, ou très simplement, à la campagne? Dans quelle sorte de logement voulez-vous habiter?
4. À votre avis, est-il plus important de suivre ses passions dans la vie ou de poursuivre la fortune? Expliquez.

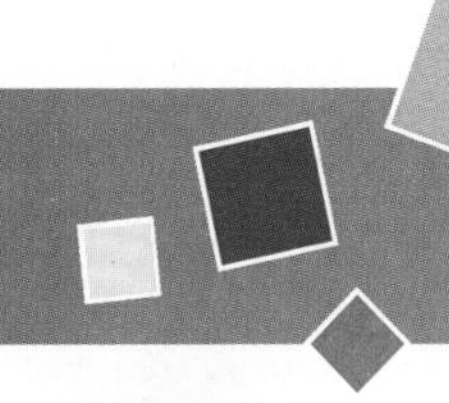

# Étude de grammaire

## 40. EMPHASIZING AND CLARIFYING Stressed Pronouns

**Presentation:** Make sure not to unduly stress pronouns in mini-dialogue with your voice. Instead, show how use of form itself creates emphasis in French.

**Note:** In many cases English uses intonation to obtain same effect of clarity or emphasis.

### Des visites artistiques

David est en visite à Paris avec ses parents et son frère. Il raconte leurs activités à Géraldine, une amie parisienne.

GERALDINE: Et **toi**, David, es-tu allé au Louvre?
DAVID: Non, il est trop grand pour **moi**. Je préfère le musée Picasso.
GERALDINE: **Moi** aussi! Mais tes parents, ils ont visité le Louvre?
DAVID: **Eux**? Oui, ils y sont allés plusieurs fois. Mais mon frère, **lui**, il préfère visiter les magasins et les discos!

Le musée Picasso à Paris

Les phrases suivantes sont des variantes des phrases du dialogue. Complétez ces phrases avec **moi**, **toi**, **lui** ou **eux**.

1. Tu es allé au Louvre, _____?
2. _____, j'aime mieux le musée Picasso.
3. Non, mais _____, ils l'ont visité.
4. _____, il n'aime pas les musées.

## A. Forms of Stressed Pronouns

Stressed pronouns (**les pronoms disjoints**) are used as objects of prepositions or for clarity or emphasis. The following chart shows their forms.

| | | | |
|---|---|---|---|
| **moi** | *I, me* | **nous** | *we, us* |
| **toi** | *you* | **vous** | *you* |
| **lui** | *he, him* | **eux** | *they, them* (*m.*) |
| **elle** | *she, her* | **elles** | *they, them* (*f.*) |
| **soi*** | *oneself* | | |

Note that several of the stressed pronouns (**elle**, **nous**, **vous**, **elles**) are identical in form to subject pronouns.

## B. Uses of Stressed Pronouns

Stressed pronouns are used in the following ways.

**Presentation:** Use pronouns in short sentences to illustrate their use. Have sts. repeat after your model. Examples: *Moi, j'aime le français. Robert, lui, le déteste. Et toi? Que penses-tu du français?* etc.

1. As objects of prepositions

| | |
|---|---|
| Nous allons travailler chez **toi** ce soir. | *We're going to work at your house tonight.* |
| Après **vous**! | *After you!* |
| Après le concert, tout le monde rentre chez **soi**. | *After the concert, everybody goes back to his/her (own) house.* |

2. As part of compound subjects

| | |
|---|---|
| **Martine et elle**† ont lu *À la recherche du temps perdu*‡ en entier. | *She and Martine read the entire* In Search of Lost Time. |
| **Michel et moi** avons joué ensemble une sonate de Debussy. | *Michel and I played a sonata of Debussy together.* |

3. With subject pronouns, to emphasize the subject

| | |
|---|---|
| Et **lui**, écrit-il un roman? | *What about him? Is he writing a novel?* |
| **Eux**, ils ont de la chance. | *As for them, they are lucky.* |
| Tu es brillant, **toi**. | *You're so brilliant*! |

When stressed pronouns emphasize the subject, they can be placed at the beginning or the end of the sentence.

4. After **ce** + **être**

| | |
|---|---|
| —C'est **vous**, Monsieur Lemaître? | *—Is it you, Mr. Lemaître?* |

---

*__Soi__ corresponds to the subjects **on**, **tout le monde**, and **chacun** (*each one*).

†In conversation, the plural subject is sometimes expressed in addition to the compound subject: **Martine et elle, elles ont lu le roman en entier**.

‡Long roman de Marcel Proust, en sept volumes. L'ancienne traduction anglaise du titre était *Remembrance of Things Past*.

| | |
|---|---|
| —Oui, c'est **moi**. | —*Yes, it's me* (it is I. |
| C'est **lui** qui faisait le cours sur Proust. | *He's the one who was teaching the course on Proust.* |

5. In sentences without verbs, such as one-word answers to questions and tag questions

| | |
|---|---|
| —Qui a visité le musée Delacroix? | —*Who has visited the Delacroix Museum?* |
| **—Toi!** | —*You!* |
| —As-tu pris mon livre d'art? | —*Did you take my art book?* |
| **—Moi?** | —*Me?* |
| Nous allons voir une bande vidéo sur la peinture moderne. **Et lui**? | *We're going to see a videotape on modern painting. What about him?* |

6. In combination with **même**(**s**) for emphasis

| | |
|---|---|
| Préparent-ils la bande vidéo **eux-mêmes**? | *Are they preparing the videotape themselves?* |
| Allez-vous choisir les images **vous-même**? | *Are you going to choose the pictures yourself?* |

## Vérifions!

**A. Au théâtre.** Vos amis et vous avez présenté une pièce de théâtre devant la classe. Décrivez vos sentiments pendant que vous attendiez le commencement de la pièce, à l'aide des pronoms disjoints.

MODÈLE: nous / fatigués → Nous, nous étions fatigués.

1. je / préoccupé(e)
2. Catherine / anxieuse
3. Louis / agité
4. Jessica et Christine / sérieuses
5. Marc et Angela / calmes
6. nous / heureux

**B. Pour monter la pièce** (*prepare the play*). D'autres étudiants vous ont aidé(e) à monter la pièce de l'exercice précédent. Dites ce qu'ils ont fait. Remplacez les mots en italique par des pronoms qui correspondent aux mots entre parenthèses. Faites attention à la conjugaison du verbe.

1. Qui a fait les costumes? C'est *moi* qui ai fait les costumes. (Suzanne, Georges, Pierre et Jean-Paul)
2. Vous avez écrit le scénario vous-même? Oui, *nous* l'avons écrit *nous*-mêmes. (je, une amie et moi, Richard et Jean-Claude, les acteurs)

**Additional activities:** (1) *Tempête de neige. Il neigeait hier soir et les étudiants suivants ont dû rester chez eux. Décrivez leurs activités selon le modèle.* MODÈLE: *vous → Vous avez fait vos devoirs chez vous. 1. nous 2. je 3. Marie et toi 4. Pierre et Marie 5. tu 6. mon ami Marc 7. les étudiantes en médecine 8. les étudiants de mon cours*
(2) *Quelle aventure! Tout d'un coup il n'y a plus d'électricité à la bibliothèque. On n'y voit plus rien. Chacun essaie de trouver ses camarades dans le noir. En français, s'il vous plaît.* T: *Nicole, is that you?* N: *Yes, it's me. Where are you?* T: *Me? I'm here, next to Jean-Michel.* VOICE: *I'm not Jean-Michel!* J-M: *I'm near the window. Where's Christophe?* N: *I don't know. Is that him next to the door?* T: *I think that's him. Claude is next to him, isn't he?* J-M: *No, that's not Claude. It's a coatrack (un portemanteau). He was studying with Marlène.* N: *With her? Why is he studying with her?* J-M: *You know why. She always passes the exams.*

## Parlons-en!

**Êtes-vous indépendant(e)?** Est-ce que vos camarades et vous faites régulièrement des choses intéressantes, utiles (*useful*) ou inhabituelles... ? Utilisez les pronoms disjoints + **même**(**s**) pour décrire ces activités.

**Verbes utiles:** acheter, aller, bâtir* (*to build*), devoir, faire, gagner, jouer, lire, pouvoir, préparer, réparer, travailler, vendre, venir, voir, vouloir, etc.

MODÈLES: Moi, je fais toujours le pain moi-même pour les repas à la maison.

J'ai une camarade qui, elle, répare elle-même sa voiture.

## 41. EXPRESSING ACTIONS Pronominal Verbs

### Une rencontre

**Suggestion:** Have sts. do the mini-dialogue, substituting their real names.

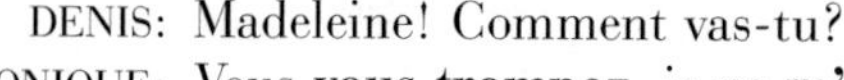

DENIS: Madeleine! Comment vas-tu?

VÉRONIQUE: Vous **vous trompez**, je ne **m'appelle** pas Madeleine.

DENIS: Je **m'excuse**, je **me demande** si je ne vous ai pas déjà rencontrée...

VÉRONIQUE: Je ne **me souviens** pas de vous avoir rencontré. Mais ça ne fait rien... Je **m'appelle** Véronique. Comment **vous appelez**-vous?

Retrouvez la phrase correcte dans le dialogue.

1. Vous avez tort, mon nom n'est pas Madeleine.
2. Pardon, je pense que je vous ai déjà rencontrée.
3. Mon nom est Véronique. Quel est votre nom?

Certain French verbs are always conjugated with two pronouns. Consequently, they are called pronominal verbs (**les verbes pronominaux**). The pronouns agree with the subject of the verb. **Se reposer** (*to rest*) and **s'amuser** (*to have fun*), for example, are pronominal verbs.

| **se reposer** (*to rest*) | | | | **s'amuser** (*to have fun*) | | | |
|---|---|---|---|---|---|---|---|
| je | **me** repose | nous | **nous** reposons | je | **m'**amuse | nous | **nous** amusons |
| tu | **te** reposes | vous | **vous** reposez | tu | **t'**amuses | vous | **vous** amusez |
| il, elle, on | **se** repose | ils, elles | **se** reposent | il, elle, on | **s'**amuse | ils, elles | **s'**amusent |

**Suggestion:** Model pronunciation of these verbs in full sentences: *Je m'amuse en classe. Tu t'amuses avec tes amis*, etc.

—Est-ce que tu **t'amuses** en général chez tes grands-parents? —*Do you usually have fun at your grandparents' house?*

—Oui, on **s'amuse** bien ensemble. —*Yes, we have a good time together.*

—Nous **nous entendons** bien. —*We get along well.*

---

*This verb is conjugated like the **-ir** verb **finir**.

Note that the reflexive pronouns **me**, **te**, and **se** become **m'**, **t'**, and **s'** before a vowel or a nonaspirate **h**.

Common reflexive pronominal verbs include the following.

| | |
|---|---|
| **s'appeler** | *to be named* |
| **s'arrêter** | *to stop* |
| **se demander** | *to wonder* |
| **se dépêcher** | *to hurry* |
| **se détendre** | *to relax* |
| **s'entendre** (**avec**) | *to get along* (*with*) |
| **s'excuser** | *to excuse oneself* |
| **s'installer** | *to settle down, settle in* |
| **se rappeler** | *to remember* |
| **se souvenir** (**de**) | *to remember* |
| **se tromper** | *to be wrong* |
| **se trouver** | *to be located* |

| | |
|---|---|
| L'autobus **s'arrête** devant le musée. | *The bus stops in front of the museum.* |
| Où **se trouve** l'arrêt? | *Where is the bus stop?* |
| Jean-Luc ne **se souvient** pas à quelle heure le musée ouvre. | *Jean-Luc doesn't remember what time the museum opens.* |
| Je vais **me dépêcher** pour arriver à l'heure. | *I'm going to hurry to arrive on time.* |

Note that word order in the negative and infinitive form follows the usual word order for pronouns: the reflexive pronoun precedes the verb.

**Presentation**: Use reflexive pronominal verbs in list in short, personalized questions, asking several sts. same question and having sts. remember responses of classmates. Do a quick transformation ex., having sts. change affirmative verbs to negative or vice versa. *Je me trompe.* → *Je ne me trompe pas.* etc.

**Note**: Point out that *de* is used with *se souvenir* but not with *se rappeler*.

## *Vérifions!*

**A. Question de logique.** Trouvez dans la colonne de droite la réponse logique aux phrases de la colonne de gauche.

1. Je dis que le Louvre est sur la rive gauche.
2. L'autobus part pour l'excursion dans cinq minutes et je ne suis pas encore prêt!
3. Tu as oublié d'apporter notre plan de la ville!
4. Quelle est la date de la construction du Louvre?
5. Toi et moi, nous aimons les mêmes musées!

a. Je ne me souviens pas de la date.
b. Tu te trompes!
c. Nous nous entendons bien.
d. Je me demande pour*qoui* tu n'y as pas pensé!
e. Il faut vous dépêcher.

**Suggestion**: Read the following sentences aloud. Have sts. react to them using the negative of one pronominal verb. *Je dis que 37 et 37 font 74. Je ne suis pas en retard pour mon cours de français. Martine et moi, nous nous disputons tout le temps. Tu t'appelles Hervé? La tour Eiffel est-elle à Strasbourg? J'ai beaucoup de choses à faire ce week-end.*

**B. Départ à la hâte.** Il est l'heure de partir pour Chartres mais vous avez un petit problème. Remplacez l'expression en italique par un des verbes pronominaux suivants: **se demander**, **se rappeler**, **se tromper**, **se trouver**, **se dépêcher**.

**Suggestion**: Ask sts. to work in pairs to complete the activity in writing and then to check answers with the whole class.

Où *est* mon sac à dos? Je ne *me souviens* plus où je l'ai mis. En plus, je dois *partir tout de suite*, je suis en retard. Mais je ne peux pas aller à Chartres sans mon appareil-photo. Je *veux savoir* si Jean-François l'a pris avec lui ce matin. Il peut facilement *faire une erreur* quand il est en retard.

## Parlons-en!

**A. Réflexions sur la personnalité.** Complétez les phrases suivantes. Puis comparez vos phrases avec celles de deux camarades de classe. Est-ce que vous vous ressemblez?

1. Je me dépêche quand...
2. Je ne m'entends pas du tout avec... parce que...
3. Quand je pense à mon enfance, je me rappelle surtout... (*nom*)
4. Je me demande souvent si...
5. Quand je me trompe, je...
6. Pour me détendre, j'aime...

**Suggestion**: Have sts. work individually to complete the answers and then compare their answers with those of 2 other sts.

**B. Trouvez quelqu'un qui...** Circulez dans la classe pour trouver quelqu'un qui fait une des activités suivantes. Faites-lui écrire son nom (*Have him/her write his/her name*) à côté de l'activité. Ensuite, trouvez quelqu'un qui fait l'activité suivante et continuez.

1. se dépêche toujours le matin
2. se souvient de son premier jour de classe à l'université
3. se trompe souvent en mathématiques
4. s'entend bien avec ses parents
5. ne s'entend pas bien avec ses frères ou ses sœurs
6. se repose en écoutant (*while listening*) de la musique classique
7. se détend en lisant un bon roman
8. se rappelle son meilleur ami (sa meilleure amie) à l'école primaire

Ensuite, comparez vos réponses.

# 42. SPEAKING SUCCINCTLY
## Using Double Object Pronouns

### Un tempérament artistique

Maryse veut une boîte de couleurs.

MARYSE: Allez maman, **achète-la-moi**!
MAMAN: **Écoute-moi** bien! Je ne peux pas **te l'offrir**. Je n'ai plus d'argent.
MARYSE: **Demandes-en** à papa!
MAMAN: D'accord, d'accord. Je vais **lui en parler**. Mais toi, ne **lui dis** rien. **Jure-le-moi**!
MARYSE: Je **te le jure**!

Trouvez la phrase correspondante dans le dialogue.

1. Tu m'achètes une boîte de couleurs!
2. Tu peux demander de l'argent à papa!
3. Ne parle pas de cela à papa!

## A. Order of Object Pronouns

When several object pronouns are used in a declarative sentence, they occur in a fixed sequence. If the sentence has both a direct object pronoun and an indirect object pronoun, the direct object pronoun is usually **le**, **la**, or **les**. The indirect object pronouns **me**, **te**, **nous**, and **vous** precede **le**, **la**, and **les**. **Lui** and **leur** follow them.* The pronouns **y** and **en**, in that order, come last.

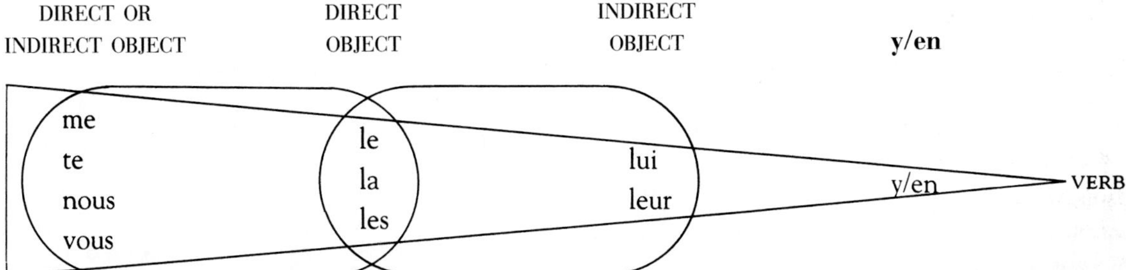


Presentation: Model sentences and have sts. repeat as a group. Sts. usually master pronoun placement by *hearing* many examples.

| | |
|---|---|
| —Le guide vous a-t-il expliqué la théorie des peintres impressionnistes? | —*Did the guide explain the theory of the Impressionist painters to you?* |
| —Oui, il **nous** l'a expliquée. | —*Yes, he explained it to us.* |
| —Avez-vous montré le tableau de Manet aux étudiants américains? | —*Did you show the Manet painting to the American students?* |
| —Oui, je **le leur** ai montré. | —*Yes, I showed it to them.* |
| —Est-ce que le guide a donné des livrets sur l'impressionnisme aux autres étudiants? | —*Did the guide give booklets on Impressionism to the other students?* |
| —Oui, il **leur en** a donné. | —*Yes, he gave them some.* |

In negative sentences with object pronouns, **ne** precedes the object pronouns; when the negative sentence is in the **passé composé**, **pas** follows the conjugated verb and precedes the past participle.

| | |
|---|---|
| —Ils nous ont envoyé les horaires des autres musées de Paris? | —*Did they send us the schedules of the other museums in Paris?* |
| —Non, ils **ne nous les ont pas** envoyés. | —*No, they didn't send them to us.* |

*It might help you to remember this formula: first and second person before third; direct object before indirect object. Apply the first part if it is relevant, then the second.

## B. Negative Commands with One or More Object Pronouns

The order of object pronouns in a negative command is the same as the order in declarative sentences. The pronouns precede the verb.

| | |
|---|---|
| N'**en** parlons pas! | *Let's not talk about it!* |
| N'**y** pense pas! | *Don't think about it!* |
| Ne **me** donnez pas de cadeau! | *Don't give me a present!* |
| Ne **me le** donnez pas! | *Don't give it to me!* |
| Ne **leur** dites pas que vous êtes venus! | *Don't tell them you came!* |
| Ne **le leur** dites pas! | *Don't tell them!* |

## C. Affirmative Commands with One Object Pronoun

In affirmative commands, object pronouns follow the verb and are attached with a hyphen. When **me** and **te** come at the end of the expression, they become **moi** and **toi**.

| | |
|---|---|
| La sonate? **Écrivez-la!** | *The sonata? Write it!* |
| Voici du papier. **Prenez-en!** | *Here's some paper. Take some!* |
| Tes amis? **Donne-leur** des billets! | *Your friends? Give them some tickets!* |
| **Parle-moi** des concerts! | *Tell me about the concerts!* |

As you know, the final **-s** is dropped from the **tu** form of regular **-er** verbs and of **aller** to form the **tu** imperative: **Parle! Va, tout de suite!** However, the **-s** is *not* dropped before **y** or **en** in the affirmative imperative: **Parles‿*en*!** [parl zɑ̃], **Vas‿*y*** [va zi]!

## D. Affirmative Commands with More Than One Object Pronoun

When there is more than one pronoun in an affirmative command, all direct object pronouns precede indirect object pronouns, followed by **y** and **en**, in that order. All pronouns follow the command form of the verb and are attached by hyphens. The forms **moi** and **toi** are used except before **y** and **en**, where **m'** and **t'** are used.

| | DIRECT OBJECT | INDIRECT OBJECT | | **y/en** |
|---|---|---|---|---|
| VERB | le<br>la<br>les | moi (m')<br>toi (t')<br>lui | nous<br>vous<br>leur | y/en |

—Voulez-vous ma carte d'entrée au musée?
—Oui, **donnez-la-moi**.

*—Do you want my museum entrance card?*
*—Yes, give it to me.*

—Je t'apporte du papier?
—Oui, **apporte-m'en**.

*—Shall I bring you some paper?*
*—Yes, bring me some.*

—Tu veux que je cherche l'horaire du musée?
—Oui, **cherche-le-moi**.

*—Do you want me to look for the museum schedule?*
*—Yes, look for it for me.*

—Est-ce que je dis aux autres que l'entrée est gratuite le mardi?
—Oui, **dites-le-leur**.

*—Shall I tell the others that admission is free on Tuesdays?*
*—Yes, tell them that* (*lit., tell it them*).

## Vérifions!

**A. Travail d'équipe** (*Teamwork*). Gisèle et ses camarades font un travail sur l'art du dix-neuvième siècle. Transformez les phrases selon le modèle.

MODÈLE: Gisèle donne ses notes à Christine. → Elle les lui donne.

1. Elle prête un livre sur Manet à Sylvie.
2. Christine décide d'emprunter (*borrow*) des diapositives (*slides*) à son professeur de français.
3. Le professeur offre aussi la vidéo «Vincent et Théo» aux trois filles.
4. Sylvie prend des notes sur Monet et les offre à Gisèle et à Christine.
5. Christine est chargée (*given the responsibility*) d'expliquer le pointillisme aux deux autres.
6. Les trois étudiantes présentent leur exposé aux autres étudiants du cours.

**B. Détails pratiques.** Vous faites une visite artistique de Paris. Répondez par **oui** ou **non** selon le modèle.

MODÈLE: —Achetez-vous vos guides (*guide books*) à la librairie?
—Oui, je les y achète. (Non, je ne les y achète pas.)

1. Prenez-vous vos repas dans les musées? 2. Achetez-vous vos cartes postales au musée? 3. Écoutez-vous de la musique classique dans les cathédrales? 4. Trouvez-vous des sculptures célèbres dans tous les musées? 5. Rencontrez-vous des cinéastes au ciné-club? 6. Prenez-vous des photos des tableaux importants dans les galeries d'art? 7. Obtenez-vous un billet d'entrée au secrétariat (*administration office*)? 8. Donnez-vous un pourboire aux guides des musées?

**C. Pour devenir un écrivain célèbre.** Dans les phrases suivantes remplacez les mots en italique par des pronoms.

1. N'oubliez jamais *vos cahiers à la maison*. 2. Prenez *des notes*. 3. Révisez *votre travail*. 4. Envoyez *votre roman à l'éditeur*. 5. Invitez *votre éditeur* à dîner. 6. Après la publication du roman, demandez *à vos amis* d'acheter un exemplaire.

**Additional activities:** (1) *Trouver du travail. Jean-Luc cherche du travail pour l'été. Demain il va rendre visite au directeur d'une agence de travail temporaire. Donnez-lui des conseils pour cette entrevue.* MODÈLE: *arriver à l'entrevue en avance Est-ce que je dois arriver à l'entrevue en avance? → Oui, arrives-y en avance.* (*Non, n'y arrive pas en avance.*) 1. *donner son curriculum vitæ au directeur* 2. *porter des vêtements bizarres* 3. *dire bonjour à tous les employés du bureau* 4. *apporter des fleurs pour la femme du directeur* 5. *inventer des histoires sur son expérience professionnelle* 6. *inviter la secrétaire de l'agence à dîner* 7. *donner des cigarettes au directeur* 8. *lui demander combien coûte sa cravate* 9. *lui parler de son expérience et de ses études* 10. *lui dire qu'il est très sympathique*
(2) Dictate the following sentences as board work, underline the appropriate words, and then have sts. transform the sentences using pronouns. *Pour devenir un étudiant modèle: Dans les phrases suivantes remplacez les mots soulignés par un pronom.* 1. *Ne parlez pas dans la bibliothèque.* 2. *Ne posez pas de questions inutiles.* 3. *N'oubliez pas vos notes.* 4. *Écrivez les mots français au tableau.* 5. *À la fin de l'année, invitez votre professeur à dîner.*

## Mots-clés

*Using pause fillers*

| | |
|---|---|
| **Eh bien,...** | *Well . . .* |
| **Voyons,...** | *Let's see, . . .* |
| **C'est-à-dire que...** | *That is / I mean . . .* |
| **Euh...** | *Uhmm . . .* |
| **Oui, mais...** | *Yes, but . . .* |
| **Alors,...** | *So, then . . .* |

**Suggestion**: Have sts. prepare this activity at home. Assign one French town or city to each st.; sts. look up basic information about famous places to visit or people from that city. In class sts. can work either in pairs or in groups; each st. is the "expert" on one place, and others ask him/her questions.

### *Parlons-en!*

**A. Interview.** Interrogez un(e) camarade sur une ville ou une région que vous pensez visiter. Suivez le modèle.

**Mots utiles:** un musée, une cathédrale, le cinéma, la musique, la sculpture, les tableaux, une pièce de théâtre, des acteurs/actrices célèbres, des compositeurs, des cinéastes, des écrivains, etc.

MODÈLE: —Est-ce qu'il y a une belle cathédrale à Strasbourg?
—Voyons... oui, il y en a une.

**B. Situations.** Vous entendez des fragments de conversation. Imaginez la situation.

MODÈLE: N'y touche pas! →
La mère de Jean vient de faire un gâteau.
Jean essaie d'en manger un morceau.

1. Vas-y! 2. N'y touche pas! 3. Ne m'en donne pas! 4. Ne les regardez pas! 5. Donne-la-lui! 6. Ne lui parle pas si fort! 7. Montre-les-moi! 8. Ne le lui dis pas!

**Suggestion**: Collect written situations created by individuals. Read some aloud to class and have sts. guess appropriate matching expression from 8 choices.

**Continuation**: *Ne me regardez pas! Ne le lui montrez pas!*

## 43. SAYING HOW TO DO SOMETHING
## Adverbs

**Presentation**: Have sts. find adjectives within appropriate adverbs and make a generalization about adverb formation.

### La Provence

ANNE-LAURE: **Demain**, je pars en Provence. Je vais visiter **rapidement** la maison de Renoir à Cagnes, puis le musée Matisse à Nice, le musée Picasso à Antibes...

SYLVAIN: Tu voyages **constamment**, toi?

ANNE-LAURE: Non, pas **vraiment**. Mais je veux **absolument** aller en Provence parce que beaucoup de peintres français y ont habité.

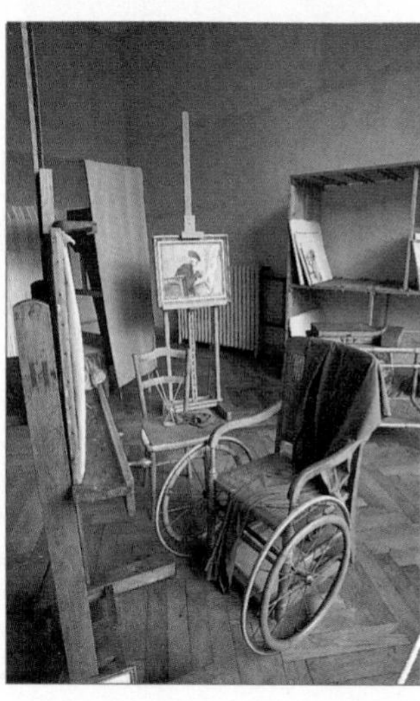

SYLVAIN: Et **maintenant**, qu'est-ce que tu fais?
ANNE-LAURE: Je vais voir la maison de Monet à Giverny, dans la banlieue parisienne.
SYLVAIN: **Franchement**, à part la peinture, qu'est-ce qui t'intéresse?
ANNE-LAURE: La musique classique... J'aime beaucoup Wagner.

Corrigez les phrases incorrectes.

1. Anne-Laure est partie en Provence hier.
2. Elle voyage très souvent.
3. Elle veut vraiment aller en Provence.
4. Demain, elle va visiter la maison de Monet.

Le studio de Renoir à Cagnes

# A. The Function and Formation of Adverbs

Adverbs (**les adverbes**, *m.*) modify a verb, an adjective, another adverb, or even a whole sentence: She learns *quickly*. He is *extremely* hardworking. They see each other *quite often*. *Afterward*, we'll go downtown. You have already learned a number of adverbs, such as **souvent**, **parfois**, **bien**, **mal**, **beaucoup**, **trop**, **peu**, **très**, **vite**, **d'abord**, **puis**, **ensuite**, **après**, and **enfin**. Many adverbs are formed from adjectives by adding the ending **-ment**, which often corresponds to *-ly* in English.

1. Most adverbs are formed by adding the ending **-ment** to the feminine form of an adjective.

**Note**: Mention irregular adverbs *précisément* and *énormément*.

| FEMININE ADJECTIVE | ADVERB | |
|---|---|---|
| lente | **lentement** | *slowly* |
| rapide | **rapidement** | *quickly* |
| franche | **franchement** | *frankly* |
| sérieuse | **sérieusement** | *seriously* |
| (mal)heureuse | **(mal)heureusement** | (*un*)*fortunately* |

2. If the masculine form of the adjective ends in a vowel, **-ment** is usually added directly to it.

| MASCULINE ADJECTIVE | ADVERB | |
|---|---|---|
| admirable (*m.* or *f.*) | **admirablement** | *admirably* |
| absolu | **absolument** | *absolutely* |
| poli | **poliment** | *politely* |
| vrai | **vraiment** | *truly, really* |

3. If the masculine form of the adjective ends in **-ent** or **-ant**, the corresponding adverbs have the endings **-emment** and **-amment**, respectively. The two endings have identical pronunciation: [a-mɑ̃].

| MASCULINE ADJECTIVE | ADVERB | |
|---|---|---|
| différent | **différemment** | *differently* |
| évident | **évidemment** | *evidently, obviously* |
| constant | **constamment** | *constantly* |
| courant | **couramment** | *fluently* |

## B. Position of Adverbs

1. When adverbs qualify adjectives or other adverbs, they usually precede them.

   Elle est **très** intelligente. — *She is very intelligent.*
   Il va **assez** souvent au cinéma. — *He goes to the movies pretty often.*

2. When a verb is in the present or imperfect tense, the qualifying adverb usually follows it. In negative constructions, the adverb comes after **pas**.

   Je travaille **lentement**. — *I work slowly.*
   Elle voulait **absolument** devenir écrivain. — *She wanted without fail (absolutely) to become a writer.*
   Vous ne l'expliquez pas **bien**. — *You aren't explaining it well.*

3. Short adverbs usually precede the past participle when the verb is in a compound form, following **pas** in a negative construction.

   J'ai **beaucoup** voyagé cette année. — *I've traveled a lot this year.*
   Il a **déjà** visité le Louvre. — *He has already visited the Louvre.*
   Elle n'est pas **souvent** allée en Normandie. — *She has not often been to Normandy.*
   Je n'ai pas **très** faim.* — *I'm not very hungry.*

4. Adverbs ending in **-ment** follow a verb in the present or imperfect tense, and usually follow the past participle when the verb is in the **passé composé**.

   Tu parles **couramment** le français. — *You speak French fluently.*
   Il était **vraiment** travailleur. — *He was really hardworking.*
   Paul n'a pas répondu **intelligemment**. — *Paul didn't respond intelligently.*

---

*Before the idiomatic expressions with **avoir**, one often uses an adverb: **J'ai très soif**; **Elle a très chaud**, etc.

## *Vérifions!*

**A. Ressemblances.** Donnez l'équivalent adverbial de chacun des adjectifs suivants.

Continuation: *lent, évident, franc, seul, indépendant.*

| | | | |
|---|---|---|---|
| 1. heureux | 4. vrai | 7. certain | 10. admirable |
| 2. actif | 5. différent | 8. constant | 11. poli |
| 3. long | 6. rapide | 9. absolu | 12. intelligent |

**B. Carrières.** Complétez les paragraphes suivants avec des adverbes logiques.

Suggestion: For homework or in-class activity. If done in class, give sts. a few minutes to work out answers individually. Then have them complete sentences orally, explaining choices.

1. Le linguiste

**Adverbes:** bien, ensuite, couramment, vite, bientôt, naturellement, évidemment, probablement.

Jean-Luc parle _____[1] l'anglais. Il a vécu aux États-Unis. Il est allé au lycée aux États-Unis et il a très _____[2] appris la langue pendant son séjour. _____[3], à l'université il a choisi la section langues étrangères. Il va _____[4] passer sa licence d'anglais. _____[5], il doit _____[6] choisir entre la traduction (*translation*) littéraire et l'enseignement. Ses parents sont professeurs et je pense qu'il va _____[7] choisir de devenir professeur.

2. L'actrice

**Adverbes:** exactement, beaucoup, absolument, fréquemment, seulement, constamment, souvent, bien, très.

Marie-Hélène veut _____[1] devenir actrice. Elle travaille _____[2] pour y arriver: en général, le matin, elle arrive sur la scène à six heures _____[3] et elle y reste _____[4] jusqu'à neuf heures du soir. Dans la journée, elle travaille _____[5] et prend _____[6] quinze minutes pour déjeuner. _____[7], elle est fatiguée le soir. Mais je pense qu'elle va réussir parce qu'elle est _____[8] travailleuse et ambitieuse.

## *Parlons-en!*

**A. Interview.** Interviewez un(e) camarade de classe sur ses préférences et ses habitudes. Votre camarade doit utiliser dans sa réponse un adverbe basé sur les mots entre parenthèses. Décidez ensuite quelle sorte de personne elle est (pratique, énergique, calme, patiente, travailleuse, etc.).

MODÈLE: Comment déjeunes-tu d'habitude? (rapide / lent) →
Je déjeune lentement pour me reposer. (Je déjeune rapidement parce que je suis toujours pressé[e].)

1. Quand fais-tu la sieste? (fréquent / rare)
2. Comment écoutes-tu les problèmes des autres? (patient / impatient)
3. Regardes-tu souvent ta montre? (constant / fréquent / rare / jamais)
4. Comment travailles-tu en général? (vigoureux / lent)

Maintenant décrivez le caractère de votre camarade.

**B. Opinions et habitudes.** Posez les questions à un(e) camarade. Dans sa réponse il/elle doit employer des adverbes.

1. À ton avis, doit-on beaucoup travailler pour réussir?
2. Comment doit-on choisir sa carrière future?
3. Est-ce que l'argent fait le bonheur (*happiness*)?
4. Est-ce que l'amitié est plus importante que la réussite (*success*)?
5. Quel est l'aspect le plus important de ta carrière future?

**Suggestion**: For whole-class or paired conversation practice. Tell sts. to think of as many responses as possible.

**Continuation**: *Sors-tu souvent avec tes amis? Comment doit-on étudier avant un examen de français?*

# France-culture

*La sauvegarde*° *du passé.* Les Français sont très fiers de leur passé et de leur patrimoine. Chaque été des groupes de volontaires aident à la restauration de châteaux, monuments ou sites historiques en ruine. Grâce aux° efforts d'organisations telles que° REMPART (Réhabilitation et Entretien des Monuments et du Patrimoine artistique), ces groupes travaillent sous la direction d'un architecte, d'un ingénieur ou d'un archéologue. Ces stages° sont très convoités,° surtout par les étudiants en architecture, car ils apprennent non seulement à retracer les plans d'un bâtiment historique à partir de vestiges° (portes, fenêtres, poutres°) mais aussi à le restaurer en utilisant des matériaux authentiques. Ainsi, par exemple, quand on a besoin de ciment° pour refaire le mur d'un château, on utilise les éléments naturels de la région (sable,° pierres°). Le ministère de la culture joue aussi un rôle important dans la sauvegarde des bâtiments en ruine. C'est lui qui classe° les monuments historiques et établit° les sites archéologiques.

*protection*
Grâce... *Thanks to*
telles... *such as*
*internships*
*sought after*
à... *starting with remains* / *beams*
*cement*
*sand* / *stones*
*classifies*
*establishes*

# Mise au point

**A. Une soirée studieuse.** Complétez l'histoire. Choisissez la réponse correcte parmi (*among*) les réponses suggérées.

Julien veut emprunter les *Mémoires d'une jeune fille rangée,** un livre de Simone de Beauvoir, à Valérie. Mais elle en a besoin. Donc elle ne (*la lui, le leur, le lui*) donne pas.

---

*Un récit autobiographique écrit en 1958 par Simone de Beauvoir (1908–1986), femme de lettres française. Elle était disciple et compagne de Jean-Paul Sartre et féministe ardente.

Valérie va lire chez Christine. Elle demande à Julien s'il veut étudier avec (*elles, eux, lui*). Valérie veut appeler Christine. Julien et elle cherchent son numéro dans l'annuaire. Enfin, ils (*le, lui en, le lui*) trouvent.

Quand Julien et Valérie arrivent chez Christine, elle (*eux, elles, leur*) prépare du café. Puis elle (*leur en, le lui, la leur*) offre.

Christine demande à Julien de lire un passage des *Mémoires* à Valérie et à (*lui, eux, elle*). Julien (*les leur, le lui, le leur*) lit. Enfin, ils essaient de répondre aux questions du professeur sur ce texte. Ils prennent leur cahier et ils (*y, lui, leur*) écrivent leurs réponses.

**B. Tête-à-tête.** Posez les questions suivantes à un(e) camarade. Ensuite, faites une observation intéressante sur votre camarade.

**Follow-up**: Ask sts. to share their observations with the entire class.

1. T'entends-tu bien avec tes amis? avec tes professeurs? avec tes parents? (Si votre camarade ne s'entend pas bien avec eux, demandez-lui pourquoi.)
2. Est-ce que tu te rappelles pourquoi tu as décidé d'aller à l'université? d'étudier le français? Est-ce que tes premières raisons sont toujours valables (*valid*)?
3. Connais-tu quelqu'un qui t'impressionne beaucoup? Comment s'appelle cette personne? De quels traits physiques (yeux, visage, cheveux, taille, etc.) te souviens-tu?
4. Veux-tu te marier (*to get married*) un jour? à quel âge? Où veux-tu t'installer avec ton mari (ta femme)?

**C. Qu'en pensez-vous?** Posez les questions suivantes à des camarades. Ils vont répondre en utilisant des adverbes.

**Suggestion**: Encourage sts. to use several different adverbs.

**Suggestions:** vite, tranquillement, admirablement, diligemment, heureusement, malheureusement, constamment, couramment, évidemment, franchement, poliment, absolument, lentement, souvent, intelligemment...

MODÈLE: Qu'est-ce qu'on doit faire pour avoir de bonnes notes? →
On doit étudier constamment.
On doit travailler intelligemment.

1. Qu'est-ce qu'on doit faire pour être bon professeur? 2. Qu'est-ce qu'on doit faire pour devenir président(e) des États-Unis? 3. Qu'est-ce qu'on doit faire pour courir dans un marathon? 4. Qu'est-ce qu'on doit faire pour devenir riche? 5. Qu'est-ce qu'on doit faire pour avoir de bons rapports (*a good relationship*) avec une autre personne?

## Interactions

In this chapter, you practiced how to specify the people and objects you are discussing and how to qualify actions. Act out the following situations, using the vocabulary and structures from this chapter.

1. **Une visite.** A friend is coming to visit you. He/She is interested in art, music, literature, and architecture. Talking on the phone with this friend, plan the itinerary of what museums, concert halls, galleries, and sites you might visit in your town or area. Your friend will ask you questions to get more information.
2. **Les vacances passées.** You and a friend are at a café. Talk about a real or imaginary cultural trip you took to a big city. Mention the places you remember visiting, the art, architecture you saw or the concerts and plays you may have seen. Discuss any people you may have met. Your friend will ask you questions to get more information.

*Le Petit Prince* est un conte (*tale*) très populaire en France. Il a été écrit par Antoine de Saint-Exupéry en 1943. Dans l'histoire, le Petit Prince habite sur une petite planète avec une rose pour seule compagnie. Un jour, il décide d'explorer d'autres planètes. Il arrive alors sur la terre où il découvre les hommes. Il trouve étrange leur façon (*way*) de voir les choses. Après de nombreuses aventures, il devient l'ami d'un aviateur à qui il fait ses confidences (*in whom he confides*). Dans l'extrait suivant, l'aviateur nous parle de la planète d'où vient le Petit Prince et donne son opinion sur les hommes.

**Suggestion**: Assign the passage for homework after previewing it with sts. It may be helpful for sts. to write out answers for the *Compréhension* questions.

## Avant de lire

**Awareness of audience.** One of the ways we decide what a text means is by inferring for whom it was written. Obviously, an article about rock music written for the alumni bulletin will make different points from an article written for the campus newspaper, since one is meant for alumni or families and the other for students. Inferring the intended audience is more difficult when you read fiction, yet it is crucial to understanding what the writer means. Look for subtle signs that suggest whom the writer is addressing. You can often deduce the assumed audience from the levels of ideas or language used. Are the ideas simple or sophisticated? Is the language straightforward and simple, or is it complex?

After you understand the general story line in this excerpt from *Le Petit Prince*, think about the implied audience for whom the story was written. Look for clues in the text, and discuss your conclusions with your classmates.

Note that *Le Petit Prince* contains some verb tenses that you may not recognize: the **passé simple** (a literary tense) and the **plus-que-parfait** (similar to the past perfect in English). Both are past tenses, as the context makes clear. You do not need to learn them; you need merely guess their meaning to understand the story. The most difficult and unfamiliar verbs are glossed in the margin.

# *Le Petit Prince (extrait)*[*]

J'ai de sérieuses raisons de croire que la planète d'où venait le petit prince est l'astéroïde B 612. Cet astéroïde n'a été aperçu° qu'une fois au télescope, en 1909, par un astronome turc.

Il avait fait alors une grande démonstration de sa découverte à un Congrès° International d'Astronomie.

Mais personne ne l'avait cru à cause de son costume. Les grandes personnes° sont comme ça.

Heureusement pour la réputation de l'astéroïde B 612 un dictateur turc imposa° à son peuple, sous peine de mort,° de s'habiller à l'Européenne.° L'astronome refit° sa démonstration en 1920, dans un habit très élégant. Et cette fois-ci tout le monde fut° de son avis.°

> aperçu: découvert
> Congrès: *convention*
> grandes personnes: grandes... adultes
> imposa: a imposé
> peine de mort: peine... *penalty of death* / de... *to dress European style*
> refit: a refait
> fut / avis: a été / opinion

Si je vous ai raconté ces détails sur l'astéroïde B 612 et si je vous ai confié° son numéro, c'est à cause des grandes personnes. Les grandes personnes aiment les chiffres.° Quand vous leur parlez d'un nouvel ami, elles ne vous questionnent jamais sur l'essentiel. Elles ne vous disent jamais: «Quel est le son de sa voix°? Quels sont les jeux qu'il préfère? Est-ce qu'il collectionne les papillons°?» Elles vous demandent: «Quel âge a-t-il? Combien a-t-il de frères? Combien pèse°-t-il? Combien gagne° son père?» Alors seulement elles croient le connaître. Si vous dites aux grandes personnes: «J'ai vu une belle maison en briques roses, avec des géraniums aux fenêtres et des colombes° sur le toit... » elles ne parviennent° pas à s'imaginer cette maison. Il faut° leur dire: «J'ai vu une maison de cent mille francs.» Alors elles s'écrient: «Comme c'est joli!»

> confié: *confided*
> chiffres: *numbers*
> voix: *voice*
> papillons: *butterflies*
> pèse / gagne: *weighs* / *earns*
> colombes / parviennent: *doves* / réussissent
> Il faut: Il... Il est nécessaire de

[*] Dessins réalisés par l'auteur, Antoine de Saint-Exupéry

## Compréhension

1. Comment s'appelle la planète d'où vient le petit prince?
2. C'est un astronome *français / turc / américain* qui a aperçu pour la première fois cet astéroïde au télescope en 1909.
3. Pourquoi est-ce que tout le monde a écouté cet astronome en 1920 et non en 1909? Qu'est-ce que l'astronome a changé?
4. Selon l'aviateur, qu'est-ce qui intéresse le plus les adultes? Qu'est-ce que les adultes ne voient pas quand ils font la connaissance de quelqu'un?
5. À votre avis, quelle affirmation exprime la pensée (*thought*) de l'auteur?
   a. Les hommes jugent les personnes et les choses d'après leur apparence, et non leur fond (*substance*).
   b. Les hommes sont curieux de détails.
   c. Les hommes sont obsédés (*obsessed*) par les chiffres.

   Êtes-vous d'accord avec l'opinion de l'auteur? Justifiez votre réponse avec des exemples de la vie réelle.
6. Trouvez dans le texte les phrases qui indiquent l'ironie de l'auteur.

## PAR ÉCRIT

**Function:** Describing (a cultural activity)
**Audience:** Classmates
**Goal:** To write an account of a cultural activity you enjoy and engage in fairly often, whether as a spectator (attending theater, concerts, films, etc.), a viewer of exhibits, reader, collector, browser, performer, or a creator (arts or crafts). Discuss how the activity fits into your everyday life: how often, where, with whom, your preferences, what you accomplish, why you enjoy it.

**Steps**

1. Make an outline. For each point, make a list of the vocabulary terms you will use. Arrange the points so that they fit together and the discussion flows smoothly.
2. Write a rough draft. Have a classmate read the draft and comment on its clarity and organization. Add new details and eliminate irrelevant ones if necessary.
3. Make any necessary changes. Finally, reread the composition for spelling, punctuation, and grammar errors. Focus especially on your use of adverbs and direct and indirect object pronouns. Be prepared to read your composition to a small group of classmates.

**À l'écoute!** See scripts for listening passages and follow-up activities recorded on student cassette. Remind students that in the listening comprehension passages (as in real life) they will not understand every word they hear. They should focus globally on the general information in the passages and not be overly concerned about what they do not understand.

## À L'ÉCOUTE!

**I. Les châteaux de la Loire.** Virginie parle de ses vacances avec Marc. Lisez les activités à la page suivante avant d'écouter le vocabulaire et le dialogue qui leur correspondent.

VOCABULAIRE UTILE
ses meubles d'époque *its antique furniture*
ses tapisseries *its tapestries*

**A. Vrai ou faux?**

1. _____ Virginie a voyagé avec un groupe de touristes allemands.
2. _____ Marc a déjà visité Blois.
3. _____ Virginie a mieux aimé Azay-le-Rideau.
4. _____ Elle n'aime pas les autres châteaux de la Loire.
5. _____ Elle a aussi visité le château de Chinon.
6. _____ Elle adore le moyen âge.

**B.** Encerclez la bonne réponse d'après le dialogue.

1. Virginie a visité les châteaux de la Loire
   a. en bus  b. en vélo  c. en voiture
2. Marc a visité le château de Blois en
   a. 1977  b. 1982  c. 1987
3. Le château de Blois date
   a. du moyen âge  b. de l'époque classique  c. de la Renaissance
4. Azay-le-Rideau se trouve sur
   a. une île  b. une montagne  c. un plateau
5. Le château de Chinon date
   a. de l'époque romaine  b. de la Renaissance  c. du moyen âge

**II. Arthur Rimbaud.** Jessica est en vacances en France. Elle aime beaucoup le poète Arthur Rimbaud et visite sa maison à Charleville. Le guide raconte la vie tourmentée (*tormented*) du poète. Lisez l'activité ci-dessous avant d'écouter le vocabulaire et la description qui lui correspondent.

VOCABULAIRE UTILE
s'est révolté *rebelled*
a renoncé à *renounced*
l'armée *army*
pourtant *nonetheless*

**Vrai ou faux?**

1. _____ Rimbaud a vécu au 19e siècle.
2. _____ C'était un écrivain catholique.
3. _____ Il admirait beaucoup Napoléon III (chiffres romains).
4. _____ Il a beaucoup voyagé pendant sa vie.
5. _____ Il a écrit des poèmes toute sa vie.
6. _____ Aujourd'hui Rimbaud est un mythe en France.

# Vocabulaire

## Verbes

**bâtir** to build
**dater (de)** to date from
**deviner** to guess
**emprunter (à)** to borrow (from)
**flâner** to stroll
**poursuivre** to pursue
**suivre** to follow; to take (*a course*)
**vivre** to live

## Verbes pronominaux

**s'amuser (à)** to have fun
**s'appeler** to be named
**s'arrêter** to stop
**se demander** to wonder
**se dépêcher** to hurry
**se détendre** to relax
**s'entendre (avec)** to get along (with)
**s'excuser** to excuse oneself
**s'installer** to settle down, settle in
**se rappeler** to remember
**se reposer** to rest
**se souvenir (de)** to remember
**se tromper** to be wrong
**se trouver** to be situated, found

## Substantifs

**l'acteur, l'actrice** actor
**les arènes** (*f.*) arena
**l'artiste** (*m., f.*) artist
**la cathédrale** cathedral
**le château** castle
**le chef-d'œuvre** (*pl.* **les chefs-d'œuvre**) masterpiece
**le/la cinéaste** filmmaker
**le/la compositeur, compositrice** composer
**la conférence** lecture
**l'écrivain** (*m.*), **la femme écrivain** writer
**l'époque** (*f.*) period (*of history*)
**l'événement** (*m.*) event
**l'horaire** (*m.*) schedule
**le moyen âge** Middle Ages
**le/la musicien(ne)** musician
**l'œuvre** (*f.*) **(d'art)** work (of art)
**le palais** palace
**le passé** past
**le patrimoine** legacy, patrimony
**le peintre, la femme peintre** painter
**la peinture** painting
**la pièce de théâtre** play
**la place** seat
**le poème** poem
**la poésie** poetry
**le poète** poet
**la reine** queen
**la Renaissance** Renaissance
**le roman** novel
**le sculpteur (la femme sculpteur)** sculptor
**la sculpture** sculpture
**le siècle** century
**le tableau** painting

**À REVOIR:** le cadeau, la carte postale, le cinéma

## Adjectifs

**classique** classical
**gothique** Gothic
**historique** historical
**magnifique** magnificent
**médiéval(e)** medieval
**romain(e)** Roman

## Adverbes

**constamment** constantly
**couramment** fluently
**poliment** politely
**vraiment** really

# Intermède

## SITUATION

**Situation:** The *Situation* dialogues are recorded on the st. cassette packaged with the st. text.

### Un village perché* en Provence

**Contexte** *Francine montre son pays natal à Karen, une jeune Américaine qui étudie avec elle à l'Université de Nice. Les deux étudiantes vont passer quelques jours dans la petite maison de campagne de la famille de Francine. Karen connaît les plages et les villes célèbres de la Côte d'Azur. Mais elle n'a jamais vu les collines° pittoresques de l'arrière-pays.° Le village perché de Saint-Paul-de-Vence est pour elle une véritable découverte.*

*hills / inland*

**Objectif** *Karen exprime son admiration pour le paysage vençois.°*

*de Vence*

Vue d'ensemble de Saint-Paul-de-Vence. De nos jours ce petit village provençal est un centre artistique important.

FRANCINE: Voilà, nous arrivons. Ce village fortifié, là-bas,° c'est Saint-Paul-de-Vence.

*over there*

KAREN: Mais il est absolument spectaculaire, ce village: il est bâti sur un rocher°!

*rock*

FRANCINE: C'est parce que les villageois° devaient se protéger contre les pirates maures,° au moyen âge. Tous les vieux villages par ici sont construits sur des hauteurs.°

*habitants d'un village* / *Moorish* / *heights*

KAREN: Je n'ai jamais rien vu d'aussi beau!

FRANCINE: Maintenant, regarde la vue du côté de la Méditerranée.

KAREN: Quel panorama splendide! Les couleurs sont si brillantes.

FRANCINE: Oui, c'est pourquoi tant de° peintres sont venus vivre ici.

*tant... so many*

KAREN: La plupart d'entre eux étaient des artistes du dix-neuvième et surtout du vingtième siècles, n'est-ce pas?

FRANCINE: Oui, demain nous allons voir la chapelle Matisse, ou le musée Picasso ou la maison de Renoir. Ils sont tous près d'ici.

---

**hillside (lit., perched)*

## À propos

### Comment exprimer l'admiration ou l'indignation

| | |
|---|---|
| VERBES | |
| J'aime (admire, adore)... | Je n'aime pas (Je déteste)... |
| CONSTRUCTIONS VERBALES | |
| Ça me plaît. | Ça ne me plaît pas du tout. |
| Ça me séduit (*appeals to me*). | Ça me dépasse. (*That's beyond me.*) |
| Ce qui me plaît, c'est que... | Ce qui me déplaît, c'est que... |
| CONSTRUCTIONS AVEC L'ADJECTIF | |
| C'est agréable. | C'est désagréable. |
| ... beau. | ... moche (*ugly*). |
| ... merveilleux. | ... scandaleux. |
| EXCLAMATIONS AVEC **quel** | |
| Quelle beauté! | Quelle horreur! |
| Quelle splendeur! | |

## Maintenant à vous!

**A. Questions personnelles.** Lisez encore une fois le dialogue, puis répondez aux questions.

1. À votre avis, quels sites aux États-Unis faut-il absolument voir? Décrivez un de ces sites en détail.
2. Quels aspects de la vie aux États-Unis préférez-vous que les touristes ne voient pas? Pourquoi?
3. Quand vous voyagez, aimez-vous visiter des endroits célèbres—des monuments, des musées, des bâtiments du gouvernement, etc.—ou préférez-vous plutôt flâner dans les rues et voir comment vivent les gens? Expliquez.

**B. Commentaire.** Quelle est votre réaction devant cette photo et la photo à la page suivante? Discutez-en avec des camarades. Utilisez les expressions de l'*À propos.*

**Suggestion**: For additional practice, bring in slides or magazine pictures to supplement those in the text.

La fontaine Stravinsky à Paris

Un ensemble d'immeubles modernes dans la banlieue nord parisienne

# PORTRAITS

## *Louise Labbé (1526–1566)*

Née à Lyon d'une famille bourgeoise, Louise Labbé est attachée à l'école poétique qui y fleurissait° au XVI^ème^ siècle. Elle a mené° une vie passionnée. Sa poésie, est caractérisée par une excellente maîtrise° technique, exprime la joie de vivre et le malheur d'aimer.

*flourished*
*led*
*mastery*

CHAPITRE **TREIZE**

# La vie de tous les jours

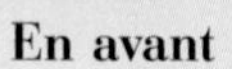

**En avant** — **En avant**: See scripts for follow-up questions recorded on student cassette.

—Alexandre et toi, vous pensez vous marier bientôt?
—Oui, l'été prochain.
—Ça fait longtemps que vous vous connaissez?
—Bientôt deux ans. Nous nous sommes rencontrés chez des amis et nous ne nous sommes plus quittés. Le vrai coup de foudre, quoi!

**Communicative goals:** talking about love, marriage, the human body, and daily life, reporting everyday events, expressing reciprocal actions, talking about the past, giving commands, and making comparisons.

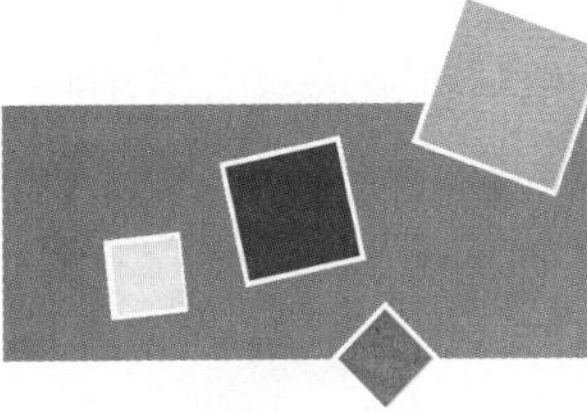

# Étude de vocabulaire

## L'amour et le mariage

Ils se rencontrent.
Ils tombent amoureux.

Les amoureux:
le coup de foudre*

Ils se fiancent.

Le couple:
les fiançailles

Ils se marient.

Le couple:
la cérémonie

Mais ils ne s'entendent pas toujours.

Les nouveaux mariés:
parfois, ils se disputent.

**A. Ressemblances.** Quels verbes de la colonne de droite correspondent aux différentes étapes (*stages*) d'un mariage?

| | |
|---|---|
| 1. la rencontre | a. Ils se marient. |
| 2. le coup de foudre | b. Ils sortent ensemble. |
| 3. les rendez-vous | c. Ils tombent amoureux. |
| 4. les fiançailles (*engagement*) | d. Ils se rencontrent. |
| 5. la cérémonie | e. Ils s'installent. |
| 6. l'installation (*setting up house*) | f. Ils se fiancent. |

**B. Seul ou ensemble?** D'après vous, quels sont les avantages et les inconvénients _____?

**Mots utiles:** être indépendant(e), solitaire, en sécurité, responsable, irresponsable, bourgeois(e), ennuyeux/se (*boring*), patient(e), libre...

1. des fiançailles 2. du mariage 3. du célibat (*single life*) 4. du divorce

**C. Conversation.** Posez les questions suivantes à un(e) camarade.

1. Sors-tu souvent seul(e)? avec un ami (une amie)? avec d'autres couples?
2. Es-tu déjà tombé(e) amoureux/euse? Tombes-tu souvent amoureux/euse?
3. Est-ce que le coup de foudre est une réalité? En as-tu fait l'expérience?
4. Est-ce que tout le monde doit se marier? Pourquoi? Pourquoi pas? À quel âge?

**Suggestion**: Do as a preview activity or as a whole-class activity to check understanding of these expressions.

**Follow-up (B)**: *Couples célèbres. Pouvez-vous nommer un couple...* 1. *tragique?* 2. *légendaire?* 3. *comique?* 4. *admirable?* 5. *détestable?* 6. *idéal?* 7. *aventureux?*

**Follow-up(C)**: Have sts. pretend they're at *une agence matrimoniale*. Directions: *Vous interviewez un jeune homme ou une jeune fille qui veut se marier. Quelles questions allez-vous lui poser pour pouvoir lui trouver le partenaire idéal?* MODÈLE: *Quels sont vos défauts? Quelles sont vos qualités?*

**Suggestion**: Ask sts. to describe their qualities, physical attributes, and likes/dislikes on a card. Collect cards to use as a source of candidates for the *agence matrimoniale*, above.

*Literally, *flash of lightning* = *love at first sight*.

# Le corps humain

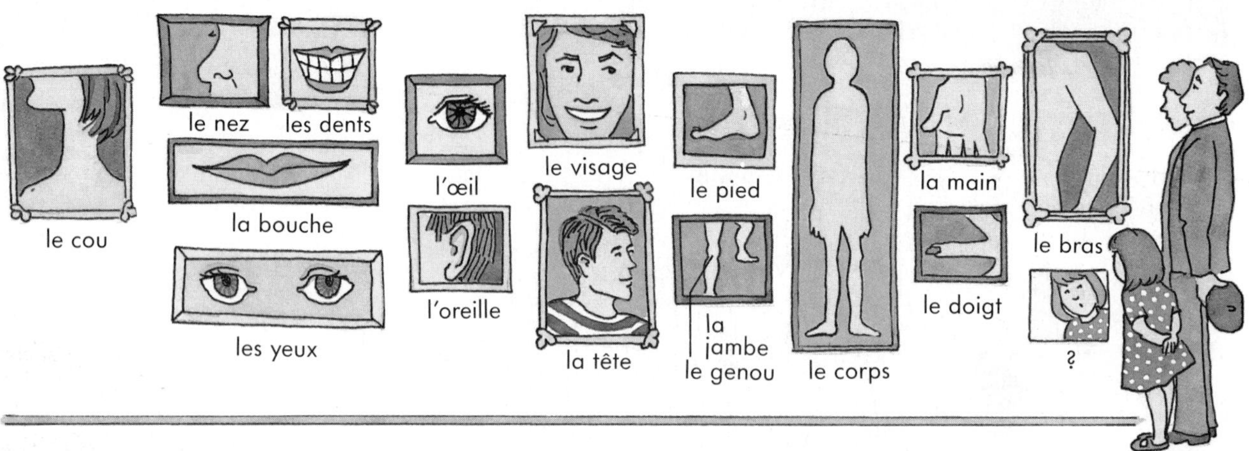


***Autres mots utiles:***

**avoir mal (à)** to hurt, to have a pain (in)

**J'ai mal à la tête.** My head hurts. (I have a headache.)

**la gorge** throat

**le ventre** abdomen

**Additional vocab.**: *le dos, la poitrine, l'épaule* (f.), *le poignet, la cuisse, la cheville, le doigt de pied*

**Presentation**: Model presentation for parts of body. Point to appropriate parts of body or use sketch or pictures from magazines as visual support.

**A. Exercice d'imagination.** Où ont-ils mal? Répondez d'après le modèle.

MODÈLE: Il y a beaucoup de bruit chez Martine. →
Elle a mal à la tête (aux oreilles).

1. Vous portez des paquets très lourds (*heavy*).
2. Les nouvelles chaussures d'Henri-Pierre sont trop petites.
3. J'ai mangé trop de chocolat.
4. Vous apprenez à jouer de la guitare.
5. Patricia a marché très longtemps.
6. La cravate de Patrice est trop serrée (*tight*).
7. Ils font du ski et il y a beaucoup de soleil.
8. Il fait extrêmement froid dehors (*outside*) et vous n'avez pas de gants.
9. Claudine va chez le dentiste.
10. Albert chante depuis deux heures.

**Continuation**: 11. *Martine a lu un livre pendant neuf heures.* 12. *Marc apprenait à faire du ski et il est tombé.* 13. *Vous êtes à un concert de rock et la musique est trop forte.*

**Additional activities**: (1) *Caractéristiques. Quelle est la caractéristique essentielle des personnages suivants?* MODÈLE: *un géant.* → *Il a un très grand corps.* 1. *un vampire* 2. *une girafe* 3. *un cyclope* 4. *un éléphant* 5. *Cléopâtre* 6. *le loup du Petit Chaperon rouge*
(2) *Énigme. Trouvez la partie ou les parties du corps définie(s) par chaque phrase.* 1. *Elle sert à parler.* 2. *Elles servent à écouter.* 3. *Ils servent à faire une promenade.* 4. *Ils servent à regarder.* 5. *Elles servent à toucher.* 6. *Elles servent à manger.* 7. *Il sert à sentir.* 8. *Ils servent à jouer du piano.*

**B. Devinettes.** Pensez à une partie du corps et donnez-en une définition au reste de la classe. Vos camarades vont deviner de quelle partie il s'agit.

MODÈLE: Vous en avez deux. C'est la partie du corps où on porte un pantalon. → les jambes

**Suggestion**: Play in groups of 4 or 5.

# La vie quotidienne*

Ils se réveillent et ils se lèvent.

Ils se brossent les dents.

Elle se maquille.

Ils se peignent.

Ils s'habillent.

Ils s'en vont.

Ils se couchent.

Ils s'endorment.

**A. Et votre journée?** Décrivez votre journée en employant le vocabulaire du dessin.

MODÈLE: À _____ heures, je me _____. → À sept heures, je me réveille.

**B. Habitudes quotidiennes.** Dites dans quelles circonstances on utilise les objets suivants.

1. un réveil 2. une brosse à dents 3. des vêtements 4. un fauteuil (*armchair*) confortable 5. un lit 6. un peigne 7. du rouge à lèvres (*lipstick*) 8. du dentifrice

**Suggestion**: Use transparency or magazine pictures to preview these verbs.

## Un peu d'argot

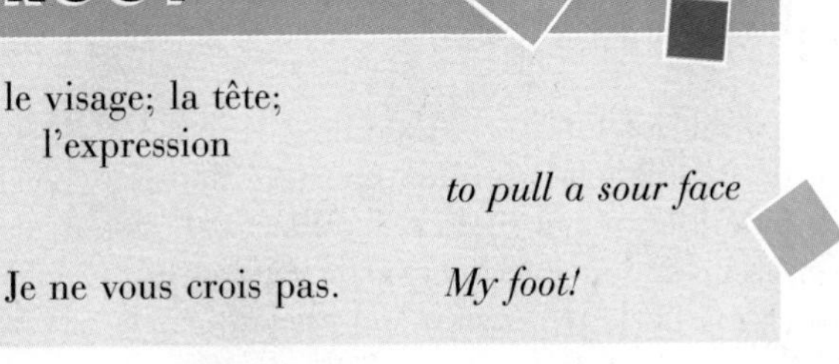

| | | |
|---|---|---|
| **la tronche** | le visage; la tête; l'expression | |
| **faire une drôle de tronche** | | *to pull a sour face* |
| **Mon œil!** | Je ne vous crois pas. | *My foot!* |

**Note**: *Tronche* comes from *tronc*, which means trunk or stump. It can be translated as *mug*. It is often used with *drôle* as in *avoir une drôle de tronche*, which means to have a weird looking face, or *faire une drôle de tronche*, which means to look peevish or to have a sour face. *Se tirer* and *s'engueuler* both have a vulgar edge. These expressions should only be used among peers. *Mon œil* can be used with virtually anyone. *Se marrer* is an informal way to say to have a good time.

*Everyday life

| | | |
|---|---|---|
| **On se tire?** | On s'en va? | *Shall we go?* |
| **Qu'est-ce qu'on s'est marré!** | Qu'est-ce qu'on s'est amusé! | *Boy, did we have a great time!* |
| **Ils se sont engueulés.** | Ils se sont disputés. | *They had a fight.* |

EN CONTEXTE

VALÉRIE: **Qu'est-ce qu'on s'est marré** au concert samedi soir!

LOUISE: **Mon œil!** Claude m'a dit que Sylvie **a fait une drôle de tronche** toute la soirée.

VALÉRIE: Oui, c'est vrai, Sylvie et François **se sont engueulés**, mais **je me suis tirée** et j'ai trouvé d'autres copains.

# France-culture

*La médecine en France.* Les Français font très attention à leur santé. C'est pour cela que le médecin de famille joue un rôle important dans leur vie. C'est lui que l'on appelle quand un membre de la famille tombe malade. En effet, en France les consultations à domicile font partie de° la routine quotidienne des médecins. Le prix de la consultation est fixé par la Sécurité Sociale, qui va rembourser° le patient entre 80 et 100% des frais° médicaux selon le cas.°

*les... home visits are part of*

*to reimburse / expenses*

*selon... depending on the case*

Le pharmacien aussi joue un rôle important.* Les Français demandent souvent conseil à leur pharmacien quand ils ont de petits problèmes de santé, comme par exemple un mal de gorge ou une indigestion. Le pharmacien leur recommande alors un médicament pour lequel on n'a pas besoin d'ordonnance.° Les médicaments qui sont prescrits par un docteur sont aussi remboursés, complètement ou en partie selon le cas, par la Sécurité Sociale.

*prescription*

Cette protection médicale est un choix qu'a fait la société française. Son coût° est très élevé. Le gouvernement français a dû augmenter les impôts° plusieurs fois pour la financer.

*cost / taxes*

# Étude de grammaire

## 44. REPORTING EVERYDAY EVENTS Pronominal Verbs (continued)

### Une rencontre

Suggestion: Have sts. do the mini-dialogue, substituting their real names.

LAURENT: Tu **t'en vas**?
PAULINE: Oui, il fait beau et je **m'ennuie** ici. Je vais **me promener** au bord du lac. Tu viens?
LAURENT: Non, je ne peux pas. J'ai beaucoup de travail.
PAULINE: Oh, tu exagères. Allez, on va **s'amuser** un peu!
LAURENT: Une autre fois. Si je **m'arrête** maintenant, je ne vais pas avoir le courage de finir plus tard.

1. Qui sort?
2. Est-ce que Pauline s'amuse?
3. Que va-t-elle faire?
4. Est-ce que Laurent se repose?
5. Est-ce qu'il veut s'arrêter de travailler?

*You will notice many pharmacies in French cities. Law requires that there be one pharmacy for every 3,000 inhabitants in cities of 30,000 or more; there is one pharmacy for every 2,500 inhabitants in towns of 5,000 to 30,000 people.

# A. Reflexive Pronominal Verbs

**Presentation**: Model forms of reflexive verbs using short sentences. Example: *Je m'habille vite le matin. Tu t'habilles à sept heures...* etc.

In reflexive constructions, the action of the verb "reflects or refers back" to the subject: *The child dressed* ***himself****. Did you hurt* ***yourself****? She talks to* ***herself****.* In these examples, the subject and the object are the same person. The reflexive pronouns in boldface can be either direct object pronouns (as in the first two example sentences) or indirect object pronouns (as in the last sentence). Common reflexive pronominal verbs include the following.

**se baigner** *to bathe; to swim*
**se brosser** *to brush*
**se coucher** *to go to bed*
**s'habiller** *to get dressed*
**se laver** *to wash oneself*
**se lever** *to get up*
**se maquiller** *to put on makeup*
**se peigner** *to comb one's hair*
**se raser** *to shave*
**se regarder** *to look at oneself*
**se réveiller** *to wake up*

**Note**: Remind sts. of spelling changes in *se lever*.

Toute la famille **se réveille** à six heures. — *The whole family wakes up at six o'clock.*
Pierre **se douche** et **se rase** pendant que Jacqueline **se maquille** et **se peigne**. — *Pierre showers and shaves while Jacqueline puts on makeup and combs her hair.*

Most reflexive pronominal verbs can also be used nonreflexively.

Aujourd'hui Pierre **lave** la voiture. — *Today Pierre is washing his car.*
Le bruit **réveille** tout le monde. — *The noise wakes up everyone.*

# B. Reflexive Pronominal Verbs with Two Objects

**Presentation**: Use reflexive pronominal verbs in short, personalized questions, asking several sts. same question and having sts. remember responses of classmates.

Some reflexive pronominal verbs can have two objects, one direct and one indirect. This frequently occurs with the verbs **se brosser** and **se laver** plus a part of the body. The definite article—not the possessive article, as in English—is used with the part of the body.

Chantal se brosse **les** dents. — *Chantal is brushing her teeth.*
Je me lave **les** mains. — *I'm washing my hands.*

# C. Idiomatic Pronominal Verbs

When certain verbs are used with reflexive pronouns, their meaning changes.

**aller** *to go* — **s'en aller** *to go away*
**appeler** *to call* — **s'appeler** *to be named*
**demander** *to ask* — **se demander** *to wonder*
**endormir** *to put to sleep*[*] — **s'endormir** *to fall asleep*

---

[*]Ce livre **endort** Paul.

| | |
|---|---|
| **entendre** *to hear* | **s'entendre** *to get along* |
| **ennuyer** *to bother* | **s'ennuyer** *to be bored* |
| **fâcher** *to make angry* | **se fâcher** *to get angry* |
| **installer** *to install* | **s'installer** *to settle in (to a new house)* |
| **mettre** *to place, to put* | **se mettre à** *to begin* |
| **perdre** *to lose* | **se perdre** *to get lost* |
| **promener** *to (take for a) walk** | **se promener** *to take a walk* |
| **tromper** *to deceive* | **se tromper** *to be mistaken* |
| **trouver** *to find* | **se trouver** *to be located* |

| | |
|---|---|
| Les jeunes mariés **s'en vont** en voyage de noces. | *The newlyweds are going away on their honeymoon trip.* |
| Après cela, Véronique va **se mettre à** chercher un appartement. | *Afterwards, Véronique is going to start looking for an apartment.* |
| Tu **te trompes**! Elle en a déjà trouvé un. | *You're wrong! She's already found one.* |
| Où **se trouve**-t-il? | *Where is it?* |

**Presentation**: Ask sts. brief questions using pronominal and nonpronominal verb forms alternately. Examples: *Vas-tu au laboratoire après ce cours? Tu t'en vas tout de suite après ce cours? Est-ce que tu appelles tes parents au téléphone? Comment s'appellent-ils?* etc.

**Suggestion**: For listening comp. practice, have sts. indicate whether they hear a pronominal or nonpronominal verb in each of these sentences. Have them write verb they hear: 1. *Les jeunes mariés s'en vont à la plage.* 2. *Ils la trouvent magnifique.* 3. *Ils s'entendent très bien.* 4. *Martine se met à nager.* 5. *Marc met son slip de bain.* 6. *Il se demande où est Martine.* 7. *Il entend sa voix.* 8. *Il la voit dans l'eau.* 9. *Il se lève pour aller se baigner avec elle.* This may also be used for full dictation.

## *Vérifions!*

**A. La routine.** Que font les membres de la famille Duteil?

MODÈLE: Annick se lave les mains.

Annick

**Suggestion**: May be done as homework and checked during class, at board, or on overhead transparency.

Le matin...

1. 

2. 

3. 

4. 

Plus tard...

5. 

6. 

7. 

8. 

Et vous, parmi ces activités, lesquelles faites-vous régulièrement?

*Jacques **promène** son chien tous les matins à six heures.

**B. Habitudes matinales.** Qui dans votre famille a les habitudes suivantes? Faites des phrases complètes. Puis comparez leurs habitudes aux vôtres (*to yours*). Commencez par «Moi aussi, je... » ou «Mais moi, je... »

| | |
|---|---|
| mon père | se regarder longtemps dans le miroir |
| ma mère | se lever souvent du pied gauche* |
| ma sœur | se réveiller toujours très tôt |
| mon frère | s'habiller rapidement / lentement |
| mes parents | se maquiller / se raser très vite |
| ? | se préparer à la dernière minute |
| | se brosser les cheveux pendant une heure |
| | s'en aller sans prendre de petit déjeuner |
| | se laver les cheveux tous les jours |
| | ne jamais se dépêcher |
| | se fâcher quand il/elle n'a pas de café |

**Suggestion**: May be assigned first as a written activity and then used for discussion.

**Additional activities**: (1) *La famille Martin. Tous les membres de la famille se couchent à une heure différente. À quelle heure se couchent-ils?* MODÈLE: *Sylvie Martin / 8h30 → Sylvie Martin se couche à huit heures et demie.* 1. *les grands-parents / 10h* 2. *vous / 9h30* 3. *tu / 10h45* 4. *je / 11h* 5. *nous / 11h15* 6. *Mme Martin / 11h30* 7. *M. Martin / minuit* 8. *Bernard / 1h du matin* (2) *Habitudes: Chacun a ses habitudes le matin. Faites des phrases complètes pour les décrire.* 1. *Sylvie / se regarder / longtemps / dans / le miroir* 2. *tu / se brosser / dents / avec / dentifrice* 3. *nous / se lever / du pied gauche* 4. *je / se réveiller / toujours / très tôt* 5. *Bernard et M. Martin / s'habiller / rapidement* 6. *vous / se préparer / tard / le matin*

**Suggestion**: For this activity, give sts. 5 minutes to circulate around the classroom.

## *Parlons-en!*

**A. Vos habitudes.** Comparez vos habitudes avec celles de vos camarades. Trouvez quelqu'un qui...

| | |
|---|---|
| se lève dix minutes avant de partir | se promène souvent le soir |
| s'en va sans prendre de petit déjeuner | se couche souvent après minuit |
| se réveille avant dix heures | a souvent du mal à† s'endormir |
| se lève souvent du pied gauche | |

**B. Interview.** Interrogez un(e) camarade sur une journée typique de sa vie à l'université. Posez-lui des questions avec les verbes **se réveiller**, **s'habiller**, **se dépêcher**, **s'en aller** (**en cours**), **s'amuser**, **s'ennuyer**, **se reposer**, **se promener** et **se coucher**. Ensuite, expliquez à la classe les différences et les ressemblances entre votre journée et celle de votre camarade.

**Suggestion**: Notes taken during interviews may be used in written composition describing daily routine of classmate, or activity can be used as stimulus for composition describing one's daily routine vs. a vacation schedule. If compositions are collected, use them for dictation or listening comp. material.

## 45. EXPRESSING RECIPROCAL ACTIONS
### Pronominal Verbs

### Le couple idéal

THIERRY: Tu vois, pour moi, le couple idéal c'est Jacquot et Patricia.
CHANTAL: Pourquoi est-ce que tu dis ça?
THIERRY: Parce qu'ils **s'adorent** tous les deux. Chaque fois que je les vois, ils **se regardent** amoureusement, ils **s'embrassent,** ils **se disent** des choses gentilles. Ils **se connaissent** depuis dix ans et je ne les ai jamais vus **se disputer**.

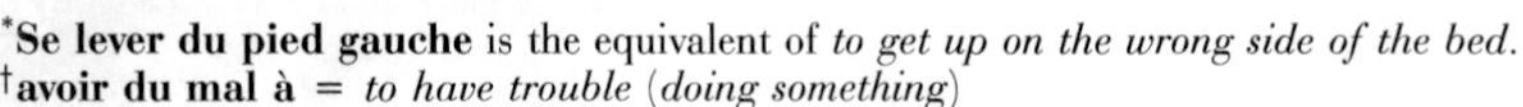

*__Se lever du pied gauche__ is the equivalent of *to get up on the wrong side of the bed.*
†**avoir du mal à** = *to have trouble* (*doing something*)

Vrai ou faux?

1. Patricia et Jacquot se disputent souvent.
2. Ils s'aiment.
3. Ils se connaissent depuis peu de temps.
4. Ils s'entendent bien.

The plural reflexive pronouns **nous**, **vous**, and **se** can be used to show that an action is reciprocal or mutual. Almost any verb that can take a direct or indirect object can be used reciprocally with **nous**, **vous**, and **se**.

| | |
|---|---|
| Ils **se** rencontrent par hasard. | *They meet by chance.* |
| Ils **s'**aiment. | *They love each other.* |
| Allons-nous **nous** téléphoner demain? | *Are we going to phone each other tomorrow?* |
| Vous ne **vous** quittez jamais. | *You are inseparable (never leave each other).* |

**Suggestion**: For listening comp. practice, ask sts. to indicate whether they hear a pronominal or nonpronominal verb in following sentences. Ask them to write verb they hear. 1. *Marie et Marc se parlent pendant les vacances à la mer.* 2. *Marie dit: Dépêche-toi, Marc.* 3. *Marc: Je me brosse les dents.* 4. *Il continue: Tu t'es déjà habillée?* 5. *Marie: Oui, je me prépare vite!* 6. *Marc: Je m'excuse. Je suis en retard.* 7. *Marie: Embrasse-moi.* 8. *Elle continue: Ne nous disputons pas.* 9. *Ils se sourient* (*smile*). This passage may also be used as a full dictation.

[a]Radio Télévision Luxembourg

## Vérifions!

**Une amitié sincère.** Mme Chabot raconte l'amitié qui unit sa famille à la famille Marnier. Complétez son histoire au présent.

Gisèle Marnier et moi, nous ____[1] depuis plus de quinze ans. Nous ____[2] tous les jours et nous parlons longtemps. Nous ____[3] souvent en ville. Quand nous partons en voyage, nous ____[4] des cartes postales.

s'écrire
se rencontrer
se téléphoner
se connaître

Nos maris ____[5] aussi très bien. Nos enfants ____[6] surtout pendant les vacances quand ils jouent ensemble. Parfois ils ____[7], mais comme ils ____[8] bien, ils oublient vite leurs différends (*disagreements*).

se disputer
se voir
s'entendre
s'aimer

**Suggestion**: Give sts. a few minutes to write out this activity before correcting it with the whole class.

**Additional activity**: *Une brève rencontre. Racontez au présent l'histoire un peu triste d'un jeune homme et d'une jeune fille qui ne forment pas le couple idéal. Dites quand et où chaque action a lieu.* 1. *se voir* 2. *se rencontrer* 3. *s'admirer* 4. *se donner rendez-vous* 5. *se téléphoner* 6. *s'écrire souvent* 7. *se revoir* 8. *se disputer* 9. (*ne plus*) *s'entendre* 10. *se détester* 11. *se quitter*

### Parlons-en!

**Rapports familiaux.** Posez les questions suivantes à un(e) camarade de classe.

1. Avec qui est-ce que tu t'entends bien dans ta famille?
2. Tes parents et toi, quand est-ce que vous vous téléphonez?
3. Tes frères et sœurs et toi, combien de fois par semaine, par mois, par an est-ce que vous vous voyez?
4. Est-ce que tu te disputes souvent avec tes frères et tes sœurs? Quand et pourquoi vous disputez-vous?
5. Tes cousins et toi, est-ce que vous vous connaissez bien? Pourquoi, ou pourquoi pas?

## 46. TALKING ABOUT THE PAST AND GIVING COMMANDS Pronominal Verbs

**Suggestion**: Have three sts. read roles aloud. Have others answer comprehension questions, using past-tense forms. For an inductive presentation, have sts. look at examples of past-tense formation and hypothesize about rules before going over grammar explanation.

**Un mariage d'amour**

MARTINE: Dis-moi Denis, **vous vous êtes rencontrés** comment?
DENIS: La première fois qu'**on s'est vu**, c'était à Concarneau.
VÉRONIQUE: **Souviens-toi**! Il pleuvait, tu es entré dans la boutique où je travaillais et...
DENIS: Et ça a été le coup de foudre! **Nous nous sommes mariés** cette année-là.

1. Véronique et Denis se sont-ils rencontrés par hasard?
2. Où se sont vus Véronique et Denis pour la première fois?
3. Quand se sont-ils mariés?

## A. Passé composé of Pronominal Verbs

All pronominal verbs are conjugated with **être** in the **passé composé**. The past participle agrees with the reflexive pronoun in number and gender when the pronoun is the *direct* object of the verb, but not when it is the *indirect* object.

**Suggestion**: Model verbs in short sentences. *Je me suis baigné(e) dans la mer.*

| PASSÉ COMPOSÉ OF **se baigner** (*to bathe; to swim*) | | | |
|---|---|---|---|
| je | me suis baigné(e) | nous | nous sommes baigné(e)s |
| tu | t'es baigné(e) | vous | vous êtes baigné(e)(s) |
| il | s'est baigné | ils | se sont baignés |
| elle | s'est baignée | elles | se sont baignées |
| on | s'est baigné | | |

| | |
|---|---|
| Nous **nous sommes mariés** en octobre. | *We got married in October.* |
| Vos parents **se sont**-ils **fâchés**? | *Did your parents get angry?* |
| Vous ne **vous êtes** pas **vus** depuis Noël? | *You haven't seen each other since Christmas?* |

**Note**: If you wish to, explain structure and rules of agreement for pronominal verbs in *passé composé*, where there is both a direct- and indirect-object pronoun. Example: *Elle s'est brossé les cheveux. Elle se les est brossés.*

Here are some of the more common pronominal verbs whose past participles do not agree with the pronoun: **se demander**, **se dire**, **s'écrire**, **s'envoyer**, **se parler**, **se téléphoner**. The reflexive pronoun of these verbs is indirect (**demander à**, **parler à**, etc.).

| | |
|---|---|
| Elles se sont **écrit** des cartes postales. | *They wrote postcards to each other.* |
| Ne se sont-ils pas **téléphoné** hier soir? | *Didn't they phone each other last night?* |
| Vous êtes-vous **dit** bonjour? | *Did you say hello to each other?* |

**Note:** you might mention word order of *s'en aller* conjugated in *passé composé: Je m'en suis allé*(e).

## B. Imperative of Pronominal Verbs

Reflexive pronouns follow the rules for the placement of object pronouns. In the affirmative imperative, they follow and are attached to the verb with a hyphen; **toi** is used instead of **te**. In the negative imperative, reflexive pronouns precede the verb.

| | |
|---|---|
| Habillez-**vous**. Ne **vous** habillez pas. | *Get dressed. Don't get dressed.* |
| Lève-**toi**. Ne **te** lève pas. | *Get up. Don't get up.* |

### Vérifions!

**A. Avant la soirée.** Hier, il y avait une soirée dansante à la Maison des Jeunes (*youth center*). Décrivez les activités de ces jeunes gens. Faites des phrases complètes au passé composé.

1. Roger / s'habiller / avec soin (*care*)
2. Christine et toi, vous / se reposer
3. Valérie et Gérard / s'amuser / à passer (*play*) des CD
4. Sylvie / s'endormir / sur le canapé
5. Christian et moi, nous / s'installer / devant la télévision
6. je / s'ennuyer / pendant trois heures

**Suggestion**: Give sts. a few minutes to write out this activity before correcting it with the whole class.

**Additional activity**: *Après la soirée. Chacun s'est couché à une heure différente.* MODÈLE: *Sylvie / 11h → Sylvie s'est couchée à onze heures. 1. vous / 11h30 2. nous / 11h45 3. tu / 12h 4. Christine / 12h35 5. je / 1h15 6. Roger et Christian / 1h20*

**B. Souvenirs.** Aline retrouve un vieil album de photos. Racontez son histoire au passé composé.

1. Elle s'installe pour regarder son album de photos. 2. Elle s'arrête à la première page. 3. Elle se souvient de son premier amour. 4. Elle ne se souvient pas de son nom. 5. Elle se trompe de personne. 6. Elle se demande où il est aujourd'hui. 7. Elle s'endort sur la page ouverte.

**Note**: Point out that *Elle s'est demandé...* does not show agreement of past participle.

## Mots-clés

*Telling someone to go away*

**Va-t'en!**
**Allez-vous-en!** } *Get going, go away!*

**C. Un rendez-vous difficile.** Un ami (Une amie) a rendez-vous avec quelqu'un qu'il/elle ne connaît pas. Il/Elle est très énervé(e) (*nervous*). Réagissez (*React*)! Utilisez l'impératif.

MODÈLE: Je ne *me suis* pas encore *préparé(e)*. (vite) → Prépare-toi vite!

1. À quelle heure est-ce que je dois *me réveiller*? (à 5h)
2. Je n'ai pas envie de *m'habiller*. (tout de suite)
3. Je ne *me souviens* pas de la rue. (rue Mirabeau)
4. J'ai peur de *me tromper*. (ne... pas)
5. Je dois *m'en aller* à 6h. (maintenant)

Maintenant, inversez les rôles. Mais cette fois votre camarade utilise *vous*.

MODÈLE: Je ne *me suis* pas encore *préparé(e)*. (vite) →
Préparez-vous vite!

### Parlons-en!

**Rapports.** Utilisez des verbes pronominaux au passé composé pour décrire les rapports entre les personnages historiques et fictifs suivants.

**Suggestion**: Give sts. a few minutes to write their commentaries. Elicit answers from several sts.

**Additional activity**: Have sts. recount where, when, and how a couple they know first met.

MODÈLE: Roosevelt, Churchill, de Gaulle →
Ils se sont vus, ils se sont parlé, ils se sont écrit des lettres et parfois ils se sont disputés.

1. Roméo et Juliette
2. Laurel et Hardy
3. Charlie Brown et Lucy
4. Sherlock Holmes et le Dr Watson
5. Antoine et Cléopâtre
6. Socrate et ses disciples
7. Caïn et Abel
8. Pierre et Marie Curie
9. Tarzan et Jane

## 47. MAKING COMPARISONS
## Comparative and Superlative of Adjectives

### Les courses

Laurence et Franck, nouveaux mariés, vont faire des courses ensemble pour la première fois.

LAURENCE: Nous allons où faire nos courses?

FRANCK: À Miniprix,* bien sûr! C'est **moins cher** et c'est **plus propre** que Trouvetout.

LAURENCE: Moi, j'ai horreur des grandes surfaces. Je préfère aller chez le petit épicier rue Leclerc. Les produits sont **plus chers**, d'accord, mais ils sont **plus frais**. Et puis, c'est **plus pratique** aussi: on n'a pas besoin de prendre la voiture. Et question accueil, cet épicier est **le meilleur** du quartier.

FRANCK: D'accord, ma chérie, mais en ce moment, la chose **la plus importante** est de faire des économies.

Vrai ou faux?

1. À Miniprix les produits sont plus chers que chez l'épicier.
2. Les produits sont moins frais à Miniprix.
3. C'est plus pratique d'aller chez l'épicier.
4. On trouve le meilleur accueil chez l'épicier.

## A. Comparison of Adjectives

In French, the following constructions can be used with adjectives to express a comparison. It is not always necessary to state the second term of the comparison.

**Presentation**: (1) Magazine pictures or drawings that can be easily compared are useful in presenting these notions. (2) Use names of famous people to further engage sts.' interest: *Les Rockefeller sont plus riches que moi. Sigourney Weaver a les cheveux plus longs que moi...*, etc.

1. **plus... que** (*more . . . than*)

| | |
|---|---|
| Chez l'épicier les produits sont **plus** chers (**qu'**à Miniprix). | *The products at the grocer's are more expensive (than at Miniprix).* |

2. **moins... que** (*less . . . than*)

| | |
|---|---|
| Franck pense que Miniprix est **moins** cher (**que** Trouvetout). | *Franck thinks Miniprix is less expensive (than Trouvetout).* |

3. **aussi... que** (*as . . . as*)

| | |
|---|---|
| Pour Laurence l'accueil est **aussi** important **que** la qualité des produits. | *For Laurence the friendly service is as important as the quality of the products.* |

Stressed pronouns are used after **que** when a pronoun is required.

| | |
|---|---|
| Elle est plus intelligente que **lui**. | *She is more intelligent than he is.* |

*Supermarché très populaire

## B. Superlative Form of Adjectives

To form the superlative of an adjective, use the appropriate definite article with the comparative adjective.

> Monique est frisée. → Solange est plus frisée que Monique. → Alice est **la** plus frisée des trois.
>
> OU
>
> Alice est frisée. → Solange est moins frisée qu'Alice. → Monique est **la** moins frisée des trois.

Superlative adjectives normally follow the nouns they modify, and the definite article is repeated.

| | |
|---|---|
| Alice est la jeune fille **la plus frisée** des trois. | *Alice is the girl with the curliest hair of the three.* |

Adjectives that usually precede the nouns they modify can either precede or follow the noun in the superlative construction. If the adjective follows the noun, the definite article must be repeated.

> les plus longues jambes
>
> OU
>
> les jambes les plus longues

The preposition **de** expresses *in* or *of* in a superlative construction.

| | |
|---|---|
| Alice et Grégoire habitent la plus belle maison **du** quartier. | *Alice and Grégoire live in the most beautiful house in the neighborhood.* |
| C'est le quartier le plus cher **de** la ville. | *It's the most expensive neighborhood in town.* |

**Note**: Stress the use of *de* in the superlative construction; sts. tend to use *dans*.

## C. Irregular Comparative and Superlative Forms

The adjective **bon**(**ne**) (*good*) has irregular comparative and superlative forms. **Mauvais**(**e**) has both a regular and an irregular form of the comparative and the superlative.

| | COMPARATIVE | SUPERLATIVE |
|---|---|---|
| bon(ne) | meilleur(e) | le/la meilleur(e) |
| mauvais(e) | plus mauvais(e)<br>pire | le/la plus mauvais(e)<br>le/la pire |

**Note**: Model pronunciation of *meilleur*.

La viande à Miniprix est bonne, mais la viande à Trouvetout est **meilleure**. — *The meat at Miniprix is good, but the meat at Trouvetout is better.*

Ce grand magasin est **le meilleur** de la ville. — *This department store is the best (one) in town.*

Ce détergent-ci est **plus mauvais** (**pire**) que ce détergent-là. — *This detergent is worse than that detergent.*

C'est **le plus mauvais** (**le pire**) des produits. — *It's the worst of products.*

## Vérifions!

**A. Comparaisons.** Regardez les deux dessins et répondez aux questions suivantes.

1. Qui est plus grand, le jeune homme ou la jeune fille? plus mince?
2. Est-ce que la jeune fille a l'air aussi dynamique que le jeune homme? aussi sympathique?
3. Qui est plus timide? plus bavard?
4. Est-ce que le jeune homme est aussi bon étudiant que la jeune fille?
5. Est-ce que le jeune homme est plus ou moins travailleur que la jeune fille?
6. Qui est le plus ambitieux des deux? le plus sportif des deux?

**B. Un couple de francophiles.** M. et Mme Smith adorent tout ce qui est français et ils ont tendance à exagérer. Donnez leur opinion en transformant les phrases selon le modèle.

MODÈLE: Le français est une très belle langue. →
Le français est la plus belle langue du monde.

1. La cuisine française est bonne.
2. Les vins de Bourgogne sont sophistiqués.
3. La civilisation française est très avancée.
4. Paris est une ville intéressante.
5. Les Français sont un peuple cultivé.
6. La France est un beau pays.

## Parlons-en!

**A. Mais ce n'est pas possible!** Vous aimez exagérer. Donnez votre opinion sur les sujets suivants. Pour chaque catégorie, proposez aussi d'autres exemples si possible.

**Follow-up**: Solicit responses from many sts. Ask them to react to each other's comments.

1. Le président _____ / bon ou mauvais / président / le XX$^{ème}$ siècle
2. Les Américains / les gens / généreux / le monde
3. Le manque (*lack*) d'éducation / le problème / sérieux / le monde actuel
4. _____ / le problème / grand / ma vie
5. _____ / la nouvelle / intéressant / l'année
6. _____ / l'athlète / bon / l'année

## Mots-clés

*Being emphatic*: Like **très**, the adverbs **bien** and **fort** are used to emphasize a point.

—Je crois que tout le monde est d'accord. Le célibat est **bien** plus facile que le mariage!
—Pas du tout! La vie des mariés peut être **fort** heureuse!
—Mais **bien** compliquée aussi!

**B. Opinions.** Changez les phrases suivantes, si nécessaire, pour indiquer votre opinion personnelle: **plus/moins/aussi... que**; **meilleur(e) / plus mauvais(e) que**. Regardez d'abord les expressions de Mots-clés. Utilisez ces mots, et justifiez vos opinions.

**Suggestion**: Ask sts. to work in pairs to compare their answers.

**Continuation**: *La famille est plus intéressante que la carrière. Les études sont moins importantes que les amis. Je suis moins heureux (heureuse) que mes parents.*

1. Les sports sont aussi importants que les études.
2. Les rapports humains sont aussi importants que les bonnes notes.
3. Grâce à la technologie, la vie des étudiants est meilleure qu'il y a vingt ans.
4. Les cours universitaires sont plus intéressants que les cours à l'école secondaire.
5. Comme étudiant(e), je suis plus sérieux/euse que la plupart de mes ami(e)s.

# Nouvelles francophones

## Mariages à l'algérienne

Le mariage est une institution et une tradition très importante en Algérie. Même s'il ne fait pas partie des cinq piliers° de l'Islam,* beaucoup d'Algériens le considèrent comme une obligation. On loue des Mercedes pour le cortège° et une salle dans un grand hôtel; on invite plusieurs centaines de personnes qui font la fête pendant trois jours. Un mariage peut coûter environ 70 000 dinars, ce qui est l'équivalent d'un an de salaire d'un cadre.° Les femmes portent des robes et des bijoux° magnifiques. Une dot° de 40 000 dinars ou plus est souvent donnée au marié.

*pillars*
*procession*
*executive*
*jewels* / *dowry*

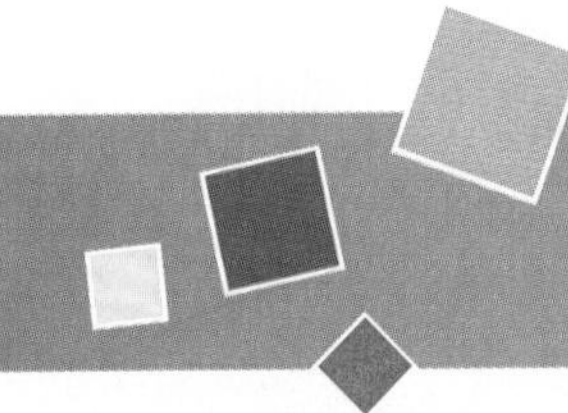

# Mise au point

**A. Vie quotidienne.** Faites des phrases complètes. Utilisez les verbes indiqués au temps convenable.

**Suggestion**: May be done as written work in class or as homework to be checked in class.

1. Le dimanche, nous / se réveiller / tard. Mais le week-end passé, nous / se lever / assez tôt / et nous / se promener / le parc.
2. Autrefois ma sœur / se coucher / avant minuit. Maintenant elle / se préparer / à passer / examen. Elle / se mettre / travailler / semaine passée / et maintenant / elle / travailler / tout le temps.
3. Tu / se brosser / les cheveux / ce matin? Préparer / toi / plus vite. Tu / s'habiller / trop lentement. Rappeler / toi / l'entrevue (*job interview*) / 9h.

---

*Les cinq obligations majeures ou piliers de l'Islam sont: 1. l'attestation de la foi; 2. la prière rituelle; 3. le jeûne (*fasting*) du Ramadan; 4. l'aumône légale (argent obligatoirement donné), et 5. le pèlerinage à La Mecque.

4. Je / se demander / si les voisins / s'amuser / hier chez nous. Ils / partir / vers 10h / soir. Ils / se regarder / plusieurs fois / avant de partir.

**B. Qui est-ce?** Regardez vos camarades de classe. Choisissez-en un(e) et décrivez-le/la. Aidez-vous des questions suivantes pour faire votre description. Vos camarades doivent deviner de qui il s'agit.

**Continuation**: Ask several sts. to make up questions and others to identify person in class. Example: *Qui est le plus sportif? la plus sportive? Qui est le/la plus âgé(e)?*

1. Qui a les cheveux les plus longs de la classe? Qui a les cheveux les plus roux? les plus noirs? les plus frisés?
2. Qui est la plus petite personne de la classe? la plus grande?
3. Qui a le nom le plus long? le plus court?
4. Qui est la personne la plus bavarde (*talkative*)? la plus calme?
5. Qui porte les vêtements les plus intéressants? les plus à la mode? les plus excentriques? Qui porte les chaussures les plus inhabituelles?
6. ?

Maintenant, trouvez d'autres camarades qui méritent une description au superlatif.

**C. Tête-à-tête.** Posez les questions suivantes à un(e) camarade. Ensuite, faites une observation intéressante sur votre camarade.

1. Est-ce que tu t'entends bien avec tes amis? avec tes professeurs? avec tes camarades de chambre? (Si votre camarade ne s'entend pas bien avec eux, demandez-lui pourquoi.)
2. As-tu déjà rencontré une personne qui t'a beaucoup impressionné(e)? Comment s'appelle cette personne? De quels traits physiques (yeux, visage, cheveux, taille, etc.) te souviens-tu?
3. Est-ce que tu te rappelles le moment où tu es tombé(e) amoureux/euse pour la première fois? C'était à quel âge, et avec qui? C'était le coup de foudre? C'était l'amour?
4. Veux-tu te marier un jour? À quel âge? Où veux-tu t'installer avec ton mari / ta femme?

## Interactions

In this chapter, you practiced talking about day-to-day activities and comparing people and things. Act out the following situations, using the vocabulary and structures from this chapter.

1. **Un cadeau.** You need to buy a gift for a relative. Tell the department store clerk (your partner) about this person. He/She will make several suggestions, describing and comparing the items. Choose the gift that you prefer, and thank the clerk.
2. **Un monstre.** Take a minute to draw an odd-looking monster that you saw roaming the streets near campus. Then, without showing your drawing to your partner, describe this strange being to him or her. Your partner will draw what you describe. Compare drawings to see how well your partner understood.

**Follow-up**: Have sts. show their classmates the monsters they have drawn and compare the drawings.

# Rencontres

## LECTURE

### *Avant de lire*

**Using the dictionary.** The following is an article from *Le Lundi*, a magazine from Quebec, about the marriage of Marithé (Marie-Thérèse Bellavance) and Tim Crack, two popular Canadian show business personalities. In this text, like any text in a foreign language, you will often encounter words that you do not understand. In these cases, always try to guess the word from context or other clues. If this does not help, use the dictionary.

When looking up unfamiliar words, do not accept the first meaning you see. Look for hints regarding the form of the word (verb, noun, gender, etc.) and its usage (commerce, music, medicine, etc.) Most good dictionaries provide examples of how words are used. When searching for the correct meaning of a word, consider the context in which it appears in the text you are reading.

Below is a list of words found in the reading. Look up the ones you do not know. Finally, match the French expressions with their definition.

| | |
|---|---|
| 1. a dépassé | a. jour qui précède |
| 2. veille | b. souhaits adressés à quelqu'un |
| 3. vœux | c. en plein (*full*) développement physique et intellectuel |
| 4. frôler | d. est allé plus loin que... |
| 5. mûr | e. toucher légèrement en passant |

**Note**: Some sts. may need background information about the cultural differences between Anglophone and Francophone Canadians to understand the reading. Point out that the friction between the two groups has developed because of the desire by Francophones to preserve their language and culture in a predominantly English-speaking country. Mention Quebec's recent attempts to secede from the union.

Coup de coeur

ANIMATRICE À CKOI

## MARITHÉ,

**ALIAS MARIE-THÉRÈSE BELLAVANCE**

**L'UNION D'UNE ANIMATRICE AVEC UN MAGICIEN**

**"Le mariage n'est pas une guarantie d'éternité. Mais nous avons le goût de vivre ensemble..."**

Par GÉO GIGÛERE

**La sympathique Marithé a pris mari! En effet, elle qui a dépassé la trentaine a trouvé l'amour entre deux continents! L'heureux élu?[a] Tim Crack, également dans le showbiz, qui s'est établi à Montréal parce qu'il trouvait que c'était "*une ville plus intéressante que Toronto!*" Imaginez la rencontre des deux familles le jour du mariage, le 10 août dernier! *Le Lundi* offre ses meilleurs voeux à ce charmant couple dont l'amour nous fait oublier les querelles qui opposent leurs provinces respectives!**

**♥ Comment vous êtes-vous rencontrés?**

**– C'était très romantique! L'an passé, ju suis allée passer un mois à Paris. La veille de mon départ pour Montréal, J'étais triste de revenir parce que je n'avais eu que des histoires d'amour pas très intéressantes dans la Ville Lumière,[b]**

[a] *chosen, elected*
[b] Ville... *City of light* (Paris)

que je ne rencontrais jamais de nouvelles personnes, etc. Le lendemain matin, dans l'avion Paris–Amsterdam–Montréal, je dis à ma copine de voyage, Loulou, qu'il me semblait bien connaître le gars assis à nos côtés.[c] Plus tard, dans l'avion Amsterdam–Montréal, je me suis encore trouvée[d] assise à ses côtés et nous avons passé les six heures de vol à bavarder.[e] Pendant la projection du film *Shirley Valentine*, je pense que quelque chose s'est passé.[f] Nous nous sommes un peu frôlés... Nous avons échangé nos numéros de téléphone et il m'a appelée deux jours plus tard... pour deux rendez-vouz. Le premier pour le lendemain et le second, pour to mardi suivant...

**♥ Que trouvez-vous de singulier[g] en Marithé?**

– Elle me fait rire et nous avons beaucoup de plaisir ensemble. Nous avons le même âge, ce qui est fort sympathique. Toute-fois, j'aime Elvis Presley, mais pas elle. Nous goûts musicaux sont très différents.

**♥ Quant à vous, Marithé, cela vous inquiète-t-il de prendre la responsabilité d'un mari?**

– Nullement.[h] Le mariage n'est pas une garantie d'éternité. Mais nous avons le goût de vivre ensemble et de faire fonctionner[i] cette relation. Tous les deux, nous avons eu une vie amoureuse bien remplie.[j] Nous sommes donc plus mûrs et avons réellement envie de partager[k] avec l'autre.

**♥ Vous allez désormais[l] vous appeler Marithé Crack?**

– Cela tombe bien[m] puisque tout le monde sait à quel point je suis craquée[n]! Non, je garde[o] mon nom comme cela se fait désormais. Nous, les femmes, avons travaillé assez fort pour conserver nos noms, n'est-ce pas?

**♥ Un Torontois qui épouse une Montréalaise francophone... pourriez-vous nous glisser un mot là-dessus[p]?**

– Tim s'est particulièrement bien intégré à Montréal. Il faut dire qu'il a une grande ouverture d'esprit.[q] Vous savez, son métier l'a amené de par le monde.[r] Et puis, il a choisi de vivre ici à cause d'affinités culturelles. Il s'est rapidement adapté. Cet été, par exemple, il a travaillé en français au Festival de jazz. Il est international. Comme moi, quoi!

[c]qu'il... *that I had a strong feeling I knew (recognized) the guy sitting next to us*
[d]je... *I found myself again*
[e]*chatting*
[f]s'est... *happened*
[g]*remarkable*
[h]*Not at all*
[i]*work*
[j]*busy*
[k]*share*
[l]*from now on*
[m]Cela... *It works out well*
[n]*crazy*
[o]*keep*
[p]nous... *say a word about that*
[q]une... *an open mind*
[r]l'a amené... *has taken him everywhere in the world*

## Compréhension

1. D'où est Marithé? et Tim? Quelle est leur profession?
2. Où se sont-ils rencontrés?
3. Quelles sont les qualités de Marithé que Tim apprécie?
4. Comment Marithé va-t-elle s'appeler après son mariage avec Tim?
5. Pourquoi leur mariage représente-t-il une combinaison culturelle originale?
6. Selon vous, est-ce que le mariage est une «garantie d'éternité»? Pourquoi ou pourquoi pas?
7. Selon vous, les femmes mariées doivent-elles prendre le nom de leur mari? garder leur nom? Pourquoi ou pourquoi pas?

## PAR ÉCRIT

**Function:** Writing about a memorable event
**Audience:** Your instructor and / or classmates
**Goal:** Write a description of an especially memorable day or occurrence from your childhood. If your memory is deficient, call on your imagination. This may be a unique opportunity to reinvent the past!

### Steps

1. Begin by free association or brainstorming. Devote 15 minutes to jotting down everything that comes to mind about the topic. Don't criticize your ideas at this stage; put them aside for a while when you have finished.
2. Go back and organize your notes. Some of them may seem irrelevant. Be sure to eliminate weak, uninteresting, or irrelevant ideas before you begin writing. Look for dominant points. The most interesting ones should be obvious to you; these will form the foundation of your essay. Then look for supporting details that make the main points clear and vivid. Try to be as specific and descriptive as possible.
3. Write the rough draft. Where appropriate, use comparisons and reflexive and pronominal verbs. Reread the draft for continuity and clarity.
4. Have a classmate read your composition to see if what you have written is interesting, clear, and well organized. Make any necessary changes.
5. Finally, read the composition again for spelling, punctuation, and grammar errors. When correcting, focus especially on your use of the reflexive and pronominal verbs and comparisons. Be prepared to read your composition to a small group of classmates.

## À L'ÉCOUTE!

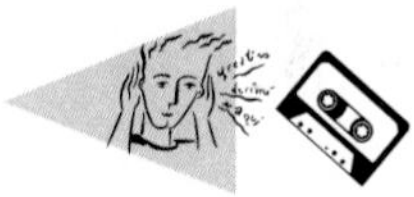

**À l'écoute!** See scripts for listening passages and follow-up activities recorded on student cassette. Remind students that in the listening comprehension passages (as in real life) they will not understand every word they hear. They should focus globally on the general information in the passages and not be overly concerned about what they do not understand.

**Un rêve bizarre.** Vincent raconte son rêve à Gilles. Lisez les activités ci-dessous avant d'écouter le vocabulaire et la conversation qui leur correspondent.

VOCABULAIRE UTILE
a disparu *disappeared*
dehors *outside*
m'emmènent *take me (away)*

**A.** Mettez les actions de Vincent dans l'ordre chronologique en les numérotant de 1 à 10.

_____ Il se rase.
_____ Personne ne lui dit bonjour.
__1__ Il se lève.
_____ Il s'en va au bureau.
_____ Il veut se peigner.
_____ Il crie «non»!
_____ Il se brosse les dents.
_____ Il se prépare le petit déjeuner.
_____ Il prend sa douche.
_____ Les policiers l'emmènent.

**B.** Vrai ou faux?

1. _____ Tous les matins, Vincent se lève à 7h30.
2. _____ Dans son rêve, il n'y a pas d'eau dans la douche.
3. _____ Dans son rêve, ses cheveux sont rouges.
4. _____ Dans son rêve, il se rase avec un couteau.
5. _____ Dehors, tout est bizarre.
6. _____ Il se réveille quand les policiers l'emmènent avec eux.

# Vocabulaire

## Verbes

**avoir mal (à)** to have pain; to hurt
**se baigner** to bathe; to swim
**se brosser (les cheveux, les dents)** to brush (one's hair, one's teeth)
**se coucher** to go to bed
**se disputer** to argue
**se doucher** to take a shower
**s'embrasser** to kiss
**s'en aller** to go away, go off (*to work*)
**s'endormir** to fall asleep
**s'ennuyer** to be bored
**se fâcher** to get angry
**se fiancer** to get engaged
**s'habiller** to get dressed
**se laver** to wash oneself
**se lever** to get up
**se maquiller** to put on makeup
**se marier (avec)** to get married
**se mettre à** (+ *inf.*) to begin to (*do something*)
**se peigner** to comb one's hair
**se perdre** to get lost
**se préparer** to get ready
**se promener** to take a walk
**se raser** to shave
**se regarder** to look at oneself, at each other
**se rencontrer** to meet
**se rendre à** to go to
**se réveiller** to awaken, wake up
**tomber amoureux/euse** to fall in love

À REVOIR: **connaître**; **rencontrer**; **sortir**; **s'amuser (à faire quelque chose)**; **s'arrêter (de)**; **se demander**; **se détendre**; **se dépêcher**; **s'entendre (avec)**; **s'excuser**; **s'installer**; **se rappeler**; **se reposer**; **se souvenir de**; **se tromper**; **se trouver**

## Substantifs

**l'amour** (*m.*) love
**l'amoureux/euse** lover, sweetheart
**la bouche** mouth
**le bras** arm
**le célibat** single life
**le corps** body
**le cou** neck
**le coup de foudre** flash of lightning; love at first sight
**la dent** tooth
**le doigt** finger
**les fiançailles** (*f. pl.*) engagement
**le genou** knee
**la gorge** throat
**la jambe** leg
**la main** hand
**le mariage** marriage
**le nez** nose
**les nouveaux mariés** newlyweds
**l'œil** (*m.*) (**les yeux**) eye
**l'oreille** (*f.*) ear
**le peigne** comb
**le pied** foot
**la rencontre** meeting, encounter
**la santé** health
**la tête** head
**le ventre** abdomen
**le visage** face

À REVOIR: **les cheveux** (*m., pl.*)

## Adjectifs

**amoureux/euse** loving, in love
**élevé(e)** high
**ennuyeux/euse** boring
**frisé(e)** curly
**lourd(e)** heavy
**meilleur(e)** better
**pire** worse
**pratique** practical
**propre** clean
**quotidien(ne)** daily, everyday

## Mots et expressions divers

**allez-vous-en!** go away!
**asseyez-vous (assieds-toi)** sit down
**aussi... que** as . . . as
**bien** (*adv.*) much
**dehors** outside
**fort** (*adv.*) very
**moins... que** less . . . than
**plus... que** more . . . than
**va-t'en!** get going, go away!

# Intermède

## SITUATION

### Visite à domicile

**Situation**: The *Situation* dialogues are recorded on the st. cassette packaged with the st. text.

**Contexte** *Mme Guirardi est un médecin généraliste.° Elle fait souvent ses visites à domicile le matin et voit ses autres patients dans son cabinet° l'après-midi.*

médecin... *general practitioner*
bureau

**Objectif** *Jérôme s'explique avec le médecin.*

JÉRÔME: Bonjour, docteur.
DR GUIRARDI: Bonjour, Jérôme. Asseyez-vous.* Alors, qu'est-ce qui ne va pas?
JÉRÔME: Docteur, j'ai très mal à la gorge, et j'ai un peu de fièvre.° — *fever*
DR GUIRARDI: Et cela dure° depuis combien de temps? — *persists*
JÉRÔME: Ça fait quatre ou cinq jours, déjà.
DR GUIRARDI: Bon, eh bien, laissez-moi vous ausculter°... Un peu de congestion, mais rien de grave. Ouvrez la bouche et dites *Aaaah*... — (avec un stéthoscope)
JÉRÔME: Aaaah...
DR GUIRARDI: Très bien. Vous avez des points° blancs dans la gorge, jeune homme. Je crois que c'est une angine.° — *spots* / inflammation de la gorge
JÉRÔME: Ça fait très mal quand j'avale.° — *swallow*
DR GUIRARDI: Nous allons vous prescrire un sirop qui va arranger° ça. Êtes-vous allergique à certains médicaments? — *make better*
JÉRÔME: Non, pas à ma connaissance.
DR GUIRARDI: Alors, voici votre ordonnance.° Prenez ces comprimés° trois fois par jour pendant cinq jours. — *prescription / tablets*
JÉRÔME: Merci bien, docteur.
DR GUIRARDI: Si votre fièvre monte, appelez-moi. Et je veux vous revoir si ça ne va pas mieux° dans quatre ou cinq jours. — *better*

## À propos

| Pour exprimer votre compassion à un(e) ami(e) malade | Pour exprimer votre manque (*lack*) de compassion à un(e) ami(e) malade |
|---|---|
| Oh, mon (ma) pauvre!<br>Je suis désolé(e). (*I'm very sorry.*) | C'est de ta faute, tu sais!<br>(*It's your fault, you know!*) |

---

**Sit down.* Consult the verb charts in the back of the text for the conjugation of the irregular verb **s'asseoir** (*to be seated, to sit down*). The form most useful to you now is the imperative: **Asseyez-vous**; **assieds-toi**.

| | |
|---|---|
| Je peux faire quelque chose?<br>Je peux t'apporter quelque chose?<br>Guéris vite! (*Get well soon!*) | Tu l'as cherché!<br>Tu as eu tort de... (te coucher si tard, manger tout cela, etc.) |

## *Maintenant à vous!*

**Suggestion**: Place following English expressions on 3 × 5 cards and have a few sts. draw cards at random. Sts. read expressions in English on card and other class members give French equivalent: *doctor's office / I have a sore throat. / What's wrong? / How long have you had this? / It really hurts! / I'm allergic to that medication. / Take these pills three times a day.*

**A. Questions personnelles.** Relisez le dialogue, puis répondez aux questions.

1. Êtes-vous déjà tombé(e) malade pendant un voyage? Comment vous sentiez-vous (*did you feel*)? Qu'est-ce que vous avez fait?
2. Avez-vous jamais eu un accident? (Où? Quand?) Vous êtes-vous cassé (*broken*) la jambe ou le bras?
3. Qu'est-ce qui se passe quand vous vous enrhumez (*get a cold*)? Où avez-vous mal? En général, avez-vous de la fièvre? Que faites-vous? Prenez-vous des médicaments? Consultez-vous un médecin?

**B. Jeu de rôles.** Jouez les scènes suivantes avec des camarades. Utilisez les expressions de l'*À propos*.

**Suggestion**: Have sts. review appropriate medical expressions from *Situation* in this chapter before doing role plays.

1. Vous voyagez en France avec un ami (une amie). Il/Elle tombe malade. Essayez de trouver pourquoi il/elle est tombé(e) malade. Qu'est-ce qu'il/elle a mangé? Quand s'est-il/elle couché(e)? Depuis quand a-t-il/elle mal au ventre, à la tête, etc.? Ayez de la compassion pour lui/elle.
2. La scène se passe (*takes place*) dans une résidence universitaire. Un(e) de vos ami(e)s est sorti(e) hier soir et il/elle a trop mangé et trop bu dans un restaurant très cher. Aujourd'hui il y a un examen, et votre ami(e) vient vous demander de l'aider à s'y préparer. Vous n'avez pas de compassion pour lui/elle.

## PORTRAITS

### *Louis Pasteur (1822–1895)*

Chimiste et biologiste français, Louis Pasteur est le fondateur de la microbiologie. Il a découvert une méthode de conservation des liquides: la pasteurisation. Il a aussi inventé les vaccins contre le choléra et la rage (*rabies*) (1885).

CHAPITRE **QUATORZE**

# Cherchons une profession

**En avant**

—Est-ce que tu as trouvé un job pour cet été?
—Oui, je vais travailler pour une petite société près de Nice.
—Je croyais que tu voulais faire un stage dans une société multinationale.
—Oui, mais j'ai changé d'avis. Tu comprends, travailler à dix minutes de la plage, c'est beaucoup plus agréable!

**Communicative goals:** talking about jobs and professions; talking about banking, finances, and money; talking about the future; and linking ideas.

**En avant**: See scripts for follow-up questions recorded on student cassette.

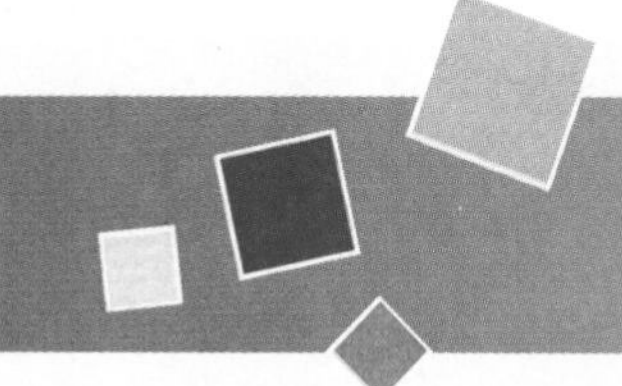

# Étude de vocabulaire

## Les Français au travail

1. **Les fonctionnaires:** ils travaillent pour l'État.

M. Durand, agent de police

Mlle Drouet, secrétaire de mairie

M. Martin, facteur

Mme Lambert, institutrice

Mme Guilloux, employée à la SNCF

2. **Les travailleurs salariés:** ils travaillent pour une entreprise.

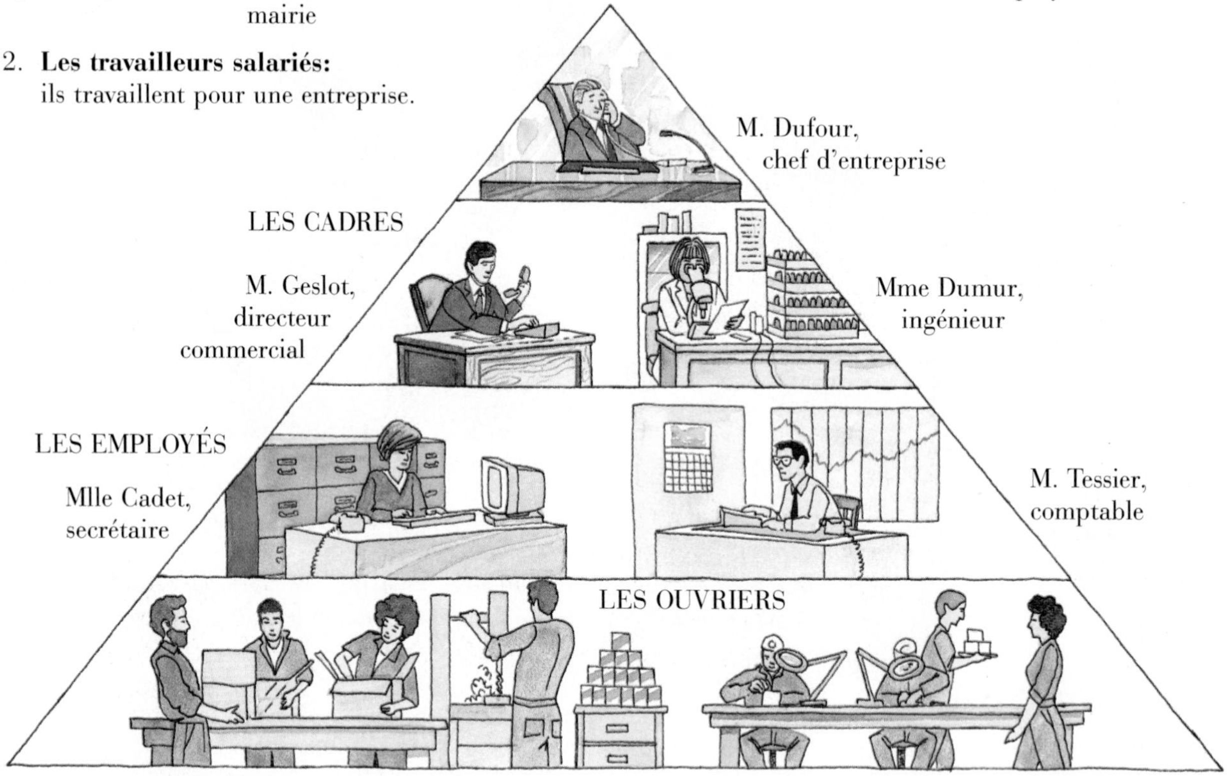

M. Dufour, chef d'entreprise

LES CADRES

M. Geslot, directeur commercial

Mme Dumur, ingénieur

LES EMPLOYÉS

Mlle Cadet, secrétaire

M. Tessier, comptable

LES OUVRIERS

3. **Les travailleurs indépendants:** ils travaillent pour leur compte.

**Presentation**: Model pronunciation of new vocab., with group repetition. Give names for other professions that sts. are interested in.

**Note**: Feminine forms of some of these professions include *une femme agent de police*; *une femme cadre*; *une femme médecin*; *une agricultrice*. Such forms are, however, rarely used.

- Les artisans

M. Lepape, plombier

Mme Simon, coiffeuse

- Les commerçants

M. Thétiot, boucher

M. Lefranc, marchand de vin

- Les professions de la santé

M. Morin, pharmacien

Mlle Duchamp, dentiste

Mme Duchesne, médecin

- Les autres professions libérales

Mme Aubry, avocate

M. Leconte, architecte

M. Colin, agriculteur

Mlle Cossec, artiste peintre

M. Kalubi, journaliste

**A. Définitions.** Quelle est la profession des personnes suivantes?

MODÈLE: Elle enseigne à l'école primaire. → C'est une institutrice.

1. Elle s'occupe (*takes care of*) des dents de ses patients.
2. Il travaille à la campagne.
3. Il règle la circulation automobile.
4. Elle vend des billets de train.
5. Elle s'occupe de la santé de ses patients.
6. Il distribue des lettres et des paquets.
7. Il vend de la viande aux clients.
8. Elle coupe (*cuts*) les cheveux des clients.
9. Elle tape des lettres sur un ordinateur.
10. Il vend des vins et des liqueurs.
11. Il prépare et vend des médicaments.
12. Elle fait des portraits et des paysages (*landscapes*).

**Suggestions**: (1) May be used for listening comp. (2) Encourage sts. to give definitions after practicing those in drill. You may want to put names of professions on 3 × 5 cards and have individuals choose cards, describing profession without naming it while others guess profession described.

**Additional activity**: *Études. Qu'ont-ils étudié?* MODÈLE: *les avocats → Les avocats ont étudié le droit.* 1. *les médecins* 2. *les architectes* 3. *les banquières* 4. *les ingénieurs* 5. *les artistes peintres* 6. *les interprètes* 7. *les magistrats* 8. *les publicitaires*

**Suggestion (ex. B)**: May be done in small groups.

**Follow-up (ex. B)**: Name other professions and have sts. describe stereotypes (e.g., clothes) of people in those professions.

**B. Stéréotypes.** Voici quelques dessins du caricaturiste français Jean-Pierre Adelbert. Choisissez la profession qui, selon vous, correspond le mieux à chaque dessin. Expliquez pourquoi.

**Professions:** chef d'entreprise, critique de cuisine, critique de cinéma, artiste peintre, journaliste de mode, plombier, coiffeur/euse, caricaturiste, instituteur/trice, vendeur/euse de CD et de vidéos rock, comptable, chômeur/euse (*unemployed person*),... ?

**C. L'embauche** (*Hiring*). Vous travaillez pour un cabinet de recrutement (*employment agency*) qui aide des employeurs à recruter leur personnel. Vos clients vous demandent votre opinion. Vos camarades de classe jouent les rôles des clients. Utilisez les mots du vocabulaire de ce chapitre (et des chapitres précédents, où nécessaire).

MODÈLE: ouvrir (*to open*) une banque →
LE/LA CAMARADE: Je veux ouvrir une banque. Quel genre de personnel est-ce que je dois embaucher?
VOUS: Vous avez besoin d'un directeur, de secrétaires, de comptables...

1. créer une entreprise
2. publier un journal
3. ouvrir un supermarché
4. ouvrir un salon de beauté
5. ouvrir une école

**Follow-up**: *Qui sont les collègues des personnes suivantes?* 1. *Jean-Pierre est serveur.* 2. *Julie est cadre.* 3. *Denise est comptable.* 4. *Francine est ouvrière agricole.* 5. *Claude est ouvrier.*

**D. Projets d'avenir.** Découvrez les futures professions de vos camarades de classe. Interviewez cinq étudiant(e)s pour découvrir quel métier ils/elles désirent faire après avoir terminé leurs études. Ensuite analysez les résultats. En général, avez-vous des ambitions différentes ou semblables (*similar*)?

MODÈLE: —Que veux-tu faire après tes études?
—Je veux (Je voudrais) devenir médecin dans une station de ski.

**Suggestion**: Give sts. 5 minutes to interview other students.

# À la banque

Rebecca Johnson est une architecte américaine.
Elle s'est installée en France, et elle va à la banque.

**Suggestion**: Use transparency, pictures, or realia to preview the vocab. as you model pronunciation.

1. Elle ouvre (*opens*) **un compte-chèques** (pour pouvoir **faire des chèques**) et **un compte d'épargne** (pour pouvoir **faire des économies**).

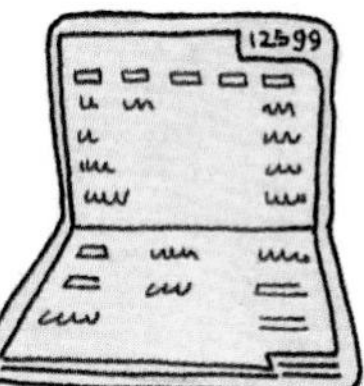

2. Elle prend aussi **une carte bancaire**.

3. Elle regarde **le cours du jour** et change ses dollars en francs.

| CHANGES | Monnaies | Cours du jour |
|---|---|---|
| États-Unis.... | 1 USD | 5,3529 |

4. Quelques jours plus tard, elle va au **distributeur automatique**. Avec sa carte bancaire, elle **retire** du **liquide** et **dépose** un chèque sur son compte-chèques.

***Autres mots utiles:***

**le carnet de chèques** checkbook
**déposer** to deposit
**l'emprunt** (*m.*) loan
**les frais** (*m. pl.*) expenses, costs
**le montant** sum
**le reçu** receipt
**toucher** to cash

**A. Un compte en banque en France.** D'après la brochure qui suit, indiquez si les déclarations suivantes sont vraies ou fausses. Si elles sont fausses, corrigez-les.

**Suggestion**: Do as a whole-class activity to check sts.' comprehension of vocab.

## Comment utiliser un Compte-Chèques. En deux mots.

Votre Compte-Chèques vous sert à régler vos dépenses[a] (ou à les faire régler directement par le Crédit Lyonnais), à recevoir votre argent et à mieux gérer[b] votre budget.

## Réglez vos dépenses courantes en toute sécurité.

Faites un chèque barré*: sans avoir d'argent liquide, vous payez vos achats dans les magasins, vos factures[c] vos frais de voyage...

Et si vous avez besoin d'argent liquide, vous pouvez en retirer facilement dans votre agence, comme dans toutes les agences du Crédit Lyonnais (jusqu'à 2.000 F par période de 7 jours).

Cependant, n'oubliez pas qu'avant d'émettre[d] un chèque, vous devez disposer sur votre compte d'une provision au moins égale au montant[e] du chèque.

## Comment verser de l'argent à votre compte.

Pour alimenter votre compte, vous pouvez déposer des sommes en espèces[f] ou sous forme de chèques bancaires ou postaux. Selon le cas, vous remplissez un formulaire de versement ou de[g] remise de chèques. Vous endossez (c'est-à-dire que vous signez au dos[h]) les chèques que vous remettez. Vous pouvez aussi envoyer les chèques endossés à votre agence, en précisant votre numéro de compte.

1. Il s'agit d'un compte d'épargne.
2. Vous pouvez vous servir de ce compte pour payer vos achats quand vous n'avez pas d'argent liquide sur vous.
3. Il n'y a aucune (*no*) limite à la somme d'argent qu'on peut retirer.
4. Avant de déposer un chèque sur votre compte, vous devez signer à côté de votre nom.
5. Vous êtes obligé(e) d'aller à la banque pour déposer de l'argent sur votre compte.
6. Ce compte-chèques ressemble à un compte courant typique aux États-Unis.

**Additional activities**: (1) *À la banque. Définitions. Complétez les phrases suivantes. 1. En général vous portez vos chèques dans un _______ de chèques. 2. N'oubliez pas de _______ les chèques que vous écrivez et d'_______ les chèques que vous déposez sur votre compte. 3. De temps en temps on reçoit de sa banque un relevé de compte où on a noté par écrit les sommes d'argent qu'on a _______ sur un compte et les sommes qu'on a _______. 4. L'argent déposé sur un compte d' _______ augmente automatiquement parce que la banque paie des intérêts.* (2) Ask personalized questions using the vocab. *Quelles sortes de comptes avez-vous? Touchez-vous souvent des chèques? À quelles occasions? Quelles cartes de crédit avez-vous? Quels en sont les avantages et les inconvénients? Combien de cartes bancaires avez-vous? Quels sont les avantages et les inconvénients des distributeurs automatiques?*

[a]vous... *allows you to make your payments (settle your accounts)*
[b]administrer *(manage)*
[c]*bills (statements, invoices)*
[d]qu'avant... *before writing (issuing)*
[e]vous... *your account must contain an amount at least equal to the amount of the check*
[f]*cash*
[g]remplissez... *fill out a deposit or remittance (deposit-by-mail) form*
[h]au... *on the back*

**B. Une globe-trotter.** Audrey vient d'arriver à Paris et veut changer de l'argent. Mettez les conseils suivants par ordre chronologique.

1. demander le cours du jour 2. prendre des chèques de voyage avec soi 3. prendre le reçu 4. compter l'argent 5. se présenter à un bureau de change (*money exchange office*) ou à une banque 6. vérifier le montant sur le reçu 7. montrer son passeport 8. dire combien d'argent on veut changer

**Suggestion**: Ask sts. to work in pairs to complete both parts of this activity.

Audrey suit vos conseils et entre dans un bureau de change. Elle veut changer en francs français des chèques de voyages en dollars ainsi que de l'argent liquide de divers pays qu'elle a visités. À l'aide des cours publiés dans le

**Follow-up**: Ask some sts. to play the roles in the *bureau de change*.

*A check with two parallel lines drawn across it, indicating "for deposit only." Note that the writer of the check, not the receiver, makes this indication.

journal, calculez approximativement combien de francs français elle va obtenir. Jouez la scène dans le bureau de change avec un(e) camarade.

Audrey a 350 dollars en chèques de voyage, 180 livres, 30 deutschemarks, 155 francs suisses et 75 yens.

**Note**: You may wish to find more up-to-date rates.

**MARCHÉ MONÉTAIRE**

| | |
|---|---|
| **Paris** (5 janv.) | **12 1/4-12 3/4 %** |
| **New-York** (4 janv.) | **3 1/2 %** |

**MARCHÉ INTERBANCAIRE DES DEVISES**

| | COURS COMPTANT | | COURS TERME TROIS MOIS | |
|---|---|---|---|---|
| | Demandé | Offert | Demandé | Offert |
| **$ E-U** | **5,5800** | **5,5820** | **5,7090** | **5,7160** |
| **Yen (100)** | **4,4550** | **4,4603** | **4,5543** | **4,5644** |
| **Ecu** | **6,6490** | **6,6543** | **6,6827** | **6,6957** |
| **Deutschemark** | **3,4120** | **3,4130** | **3,4459** | **3,4507** |
| **Franc suisse** | **3,7766** | **3,7806** | **3,8400** | **3,8484** |
| **Lire italienne (1000)** | **3,6291** | **3,6352** | **3,6239** | **3,6341** |
| **Livre sterling** | **8,4122** | **8,4209** | **8,5274** | **8,5448** |
| **Peseta (100)** | **4,7946** | **4,7985** | **4,7564** | **4,7684** |

**CHANGES**

**Dollar : 5,57 F ⬇**

Le dollar s'inscrivait en légère baisse, mardi 5 janvier, après sa forte progression des derniers jours. Il cotait à Paris 5,57 francs contre 5,5920 francs au cours indicatif de la Banque de France. Le mark repassait sous la barre de 3,41 francs après le communiqué commun des autorités monétaires françaises et allemandes.

| **FRANCFORT** | 4 janv. | 5 janv. |
|---|---|---|
| **Dollar** (en DM) | **1,6338** | **1,6360** |
| **TOKYO** | 4 janv. | 5 janv. |
| **Dollar** (en yens) | **124,90** | **125,25** |

**Note**: All of these expressions are very informal and should only be used among peers. *Fric* probably comes from *fricot*, a kind of stew.

| | | |
|---|---|---|
| **le fric** | l'argent | |
| **10, 100, 1 000 balles** | 10, 100, 1,100 francs | |
| **mettre du fric de côté** | faire des économies | |
| **être fauché(e)** | être sans argent | *to be broke* |
| **J'ai pas un rond!** | Je n'ai pas d'argent! | *I'm broke!* |

EN CONTEXTE

CLAUDINE: Je suis complètement **fauchée**. Peux-tu me prêter **300 balles**?

CLAIRE: Tu veux rire (*You must be kidding*)! **J'ai pas un rond** en ce moment. As-tu demandé à Marc?

CLAUDINE: Non, je crois qu'il **met du fric de côté** pour aller au Maroc cet été.

## Le budget de Marc Convert

Marc travaille dans une petite **société** (*company*) près de Marseille où il est responsable (*director*) commercial.

Il **gagne** 13 500 francs par mois.

Il **dépense** presque tout ce qu'il gagne pour vivre; le **coût de la vie** est très élevé dans les villes françaises. Mais il espère avoir une **augmentation de salaire** dans six mois. En ce moment, il **fait des économies** pour acheter une maison.

**A. Le budget d'un étudiant.** Un de vos amis a besoin de faire un emprunt à la banque pour continuer ses études. La banque lui demande de préparer un budget approximatif. Aidez-le à remplir le formulaire (*form*) en vous basant sur les dépenses d'un étudiant typique de votre université. (Donnez les chiffres en dollars USA.)

**Suggestion**: Ask sts. to work in pairs and then answer the questions as a whole class. Discuss ways to lower various expenses.

DÉPENSES (PAR MOIS)
Loyer (frais de logement) _____
Nourriture _____
Vêtements _____
Transports _____
Sorties/Loisirs _____
Fournitures (*supplies*) scolaires _____
Frais de scolarité _____
Autres _____
_____

Maintenant, comparez vos calculs avec ceux de vos camarades de classe. Essayez de vous mettre d'accord sur le budget d'un étudiant moyen (*average*) de votre université, puis répondez aux questions suivantes.

1. Combien doit gagner votre ami par mois?
2. S'il travaille quinze heures par semaine dans un restaurant près du campus, combien peut-il gagner?
3. Quelles autres sources de revenu a-t-il?
4. Combien doit-il emprunter alors pour continuer ses études ce semestre? (Il reste encore deux mois de classe.)

**B. Parlons d'argent!** Posez les questions suivantes à un(e) camarade.

1. Est-ce que tu travailles en ce moment? Si oui, qu'est-ce que tu fais comme travail?
2. Est-ce que tu as un compte-chèques? un compte d'épargne? une carte de crédit? Quelle carte?
3. Qu'est-ce que tu fais pour économiser de l'argent?
4. Est-ce que tu as un budget ou est-ce que tu vis au jour le jour (*from day to day*)? Pourquoi?

# Pour parler d'argent: Le verbe *ouvrir*

**Suggestion**: Model the verb in short sentences: *J'ouvre un compte d'épargne*, etc.

| PRESENT TENSE OF **ouvrir** (*to open*) | | | |
|---|---|---|---|
| j' | **ouvre** | nous | **ouvrons** |
| tu | **ouvres** | vous | **ouvrez** |
| il, elle, on | **ouvre** | ils, elles | **ouvrent** |
| *Past participle:* ouvert | | | |

The verb **ouvrir** (*to open*) is irregular. Verbs conjugated like **ouvrir** are **couvrir** (*to cover*), **découvrir** (*to discover*), **offrir** (*to offer*), and **souffrir** (*to suffer*). Note that these verbs are conjugated like **-er** verbs.

**Suggestion**: Use the following as a preliminary activity. *De l'argent.* 1. *Jean-Paul ouvre un compte d'épargne.* (*nous, je, tu*) 2. *Hier, Sylvie a ouvert un compte courant.* (*Paul et Henri, vous, elle*) 3. *Comment couvres-tu ces dépenses?* (*elles, on, vous*) 4. *Je vous offre mille francs.* (*nous, il, elles*) 5. *Il m'a offert de l'argent!* (*ils, Claudine et Marie*) 6. *Il souffre d'être trop riche.* (*je, ils, tu*) 7. *A-t-on beaucoup souffert pendant la crise de 29?* (*nos grands-parents, vous, elles*)

**A. Finances.** Ce mois-ci Jean-Paul a des problèmes d'argent. Racontez cette histoire en choisissant un des verbes suivants: **ouvrir**, **couvrir**, **découvrir**, **offrir**, **souffrir**. Utilisez le passé composé là où il est indiqué (*p.c.*).

> Le mois dernier Jean-Paul _____[1] (*p.c.*) un compte-chèques et un compte d'épargne. Sa grand-mère lui _____[2] (*p.c.*) de l'argent pour son anniversaire, mais il l'a utilisé pour les frais scolaires. Jean-Paul est très économe. Il _____[3] toujours ses dépenses (*expenses*). Mais ce mois-ci, il a acheté une nouvelle moto et il _____[4] parce qu'il ne peut pas sortir aussi souvent. Alors, il _____[5] les plaisirs de la lecture!

**B. Profil psychologique.** Demandez à un(e) camarade...

1. s'il (si elle) a un compte bancaire (si oui, dans quelle banque? pourquoi?)
2. s'il (si elle) couvre toujours ses dépenses
3. s'il (si elle) fait des économies et pourquoi
4. s'il (si elle) souffre quand il/elle est obligé(e) de faire des économies
5. combien de fois par semaine, ou par mois, il/elle retire de l'argent de son compte et combien de fois il/elle dépose de l'argent
6. si quelqu'un lui a récemment offert de l'argent et ce qu'il/elle en a fait

**Suggestion**: Ask several sts. to summarize profile of their neighbor.

Maintenant, dites ce que vous avez découvert et faites un petit portrait psychologique de votre camarade.

**Mots utiles:** avare (*stingy*), économe, impulsif/ive, généreux/euse, (im)prudent(e), négligent(e), un magnat des affaires (*tycoon*)

## France-culture

*Les Français et le travail.* La mentalité des Français vis-à-vis du travail a beaucoup changé depuis quelques années. Beaucoup d'entre eux considèrent la qualité de la vie plus importante que la réussite° matérielle. Ils préfèrent travailler moins même s'ils doivent gagner moins. La réussite matérielle et l'esprit carriériste° n'attirent plus qu'une minorité.°

De nombreuses réformes sociales ont été mises en place° pour répondre à ce changement de mentalité: les salariés français bénéficient de cinq semaines de vacances par an, et beaucoup ne travaillent que trente-cinq heures par semaine. De plus, le travail à mi-temps° et les horaires flexibles sont très populaires, surtout parmi les femmes qui peuvent ainsi consacrer plus de temps à leur famille.

*success*

*l'esprit... professional ambition / n'attirent... attract only a minority*

*mises... put into place*

*part-time*

Ce refus de l'aspect aliénant du travail révèle l'importance qu'on donne, en France, à la qualité de la vie. Le bonheur pour beaucoup de Français, c'est la réalisation de soi.° On aime prendre le temps de vivre. Mais cette nouvelle conception du travail n'est pas obligatoirement synonyme d'improductivité. Éliminer le stress, c'est améliorer° la qualité du travail. On retrouve alors un rythme plus naturel et efficace° qui permet d'avoir un meilleur équilibre personnel dans son travail. C'est le rejet de la routine. Ainsi le Français part à la reconquête du temps.°

*réalisation... self-realization*

*to improve*

*efficient*

*part... sets out to regain (lost) time*

| | |
|---|---|
| RFA | 1 697 |
| Belgique | 1 748 |
| FRANCE | 1 767 |
| Italie | 1 768 |
| Grande-Bretagne | 1 778 |
| Grèce | 1 840 |
| Espagne | 1 840 |
| Irlande | 1 864 |
| Etats-Unis | 1 912 |
| Portugal | 2 025 |
| Japon | 2 149 |

# Étude de grammaire

## 48. TALKING ABOUT THE FUTURE
### The Future Tense

**Suggestion**: Ask sts. to comment on the tenses of verbs in bold. Ask them to infer how the future is formed, using these examples.

**Son avenir**

LE PÈRE: Il **sera** écrivain, il **écrira** des romans et nous **serons** célèbres.

LA MÈRE: Il **sera** homme d'affaires, il **dirigera** une société et nous **serons** riches.

L'ENFANT: On **verra...** je **ferai** mon possible.

1. D'après son père, quelle sera la profession de l'enfant? Que fera-t-il?
2. D'après sa mère, quelle sera la profession de l'enfant? Que fera-t-il?
3. D'après l'enfant, que fera-t-il?

## A. The Future Tense

Presentation: (1) Remind sts. that they already know a type of future tense—the *futur proche* with *aller*. (2) Model pronunciation of verb forms for sts., using short sentences.

In French, the future is a simple tense, formed with the stem of the infinitive plus the endings **-ai**, **-as**, **-a**, **-ons**, **-ez**, **-ont**. The final **-e** of the infinitive of **-re** verbs is dropped.

| | **parler** (*to speak*) | **finir** (*to finish, to end*) | **vendre** (*to sell*) |
|---|---|---|---|
| je | parler**ai** | finir**ai** | vendr**ai** |
| tu | parler**as** | finir**as** | vendr**as** |
| il, elle, on | parler**a** | finir**a** | vendr**a** |
| nous | parler**ons** | finir**ons** | vendr**ons** |
| vous | parler**ez** | finir**ez** | vendr**ez** |
| ils, elles | parler**ont** | finir**ont** | vendr**ont** |

Demain nous **parlerons** avec le conseiller d'orientation. — *Tomorrow we will talk with the job counselor.*
Il te **donnera** des conseils. — *He will give you some advice.*
Ces conseils t'**aideront** peut-être à trouver du travail. — *Maybe this advice will help you to find a job.*

## B. Verbs with Irregular Future Stems

Note: Remind sts. that verbs like *venir* (*obtenir*, etc.) have the same type of future stem as *venir*.

Suggestion: Model future-tense stems by giving sts. short sentences to repeat in which verbs listed are used: *Nous irons en France l'année prochaine. Il fera si beau là-bas. Il ne pleuvra pas*, etc.

Suggestion: Mention the future stem of *mourir* (*je mourrai*) and *falloir* (*il faudra*).

Some verbs have irregular future stems.

| | | |
|---|---|---|
| aller: **ir-** | être: **ser-** | savoir: **saur-** |
| avoir: **aur-** | faire: **fer-** | venir: **viendr-** |
| devoir: **devr-** | pleuvoir: **pleuvr-** | voir: **verr-** |
| envoyer: **enverr-** | pouvoir: **pourr-** | vouloir: **voudr-** |

**J'irai** au travail la semaine prochaine. — *I'll go to work next week.*
Et toi, quand **enverras**-tu ta demande d'emploi? — *And you? When will you send in your job application?*
Pas de problème! **J'aurai** bientôt un poste. — *No problem! I will soon have a position.*
Alors, vous **devrez** tous les deux vous lever très tôt le matin. — *So both of you will have to get up very early in the morning.*
C'est vrai. Mais demain on **devra** célébrer cela! — *It's true. But tomorrow we should celebrate!*

Verbs with spelling irregularities in the present tense also have irregularities in the future tense. These include such verbs as **acheter**, **appeler**, and **payer**. See Appendix D: **-er** Verbs with Spelling Changes, at the end of the book.

## Mots-clés

*Saying when you will do something in the future*

demain; après-demain
ce week-end
dans trois jours (une demi-heure / un mois / deux semaines, etc.)
lundi (mardi, etc.) prochain; la semaine prochaine / le mois prochain / l'année prochaine
un jour (*someday*)
à l'avenir (*from now on*)

Ma chambre à Paris sera prête **lundi prochain.**
Nous partirons pour Paris **dans dix jours** (**la semaine prochaine**).
**Un jour**, vous aurez peut-être votre propre maison.
**À l'avenir**, nous ferons des économies, n'est-ce pas?

## C. Uses of the Future Tense

**Note**: If necessary, explain that *futur proche* cannot be used interchangeably in time clauses with simple future.

As you can see from the preceding examples, the use of the future tense parallels that of English. This is also true of the tense of verbs after an *if* clause in the present tense.

| | |
|---|---|
| Si je pose ma candidature pour ce poste, j'**aurai** peut-être des chances de l'obtenir. | *If I apply for this position, I may (will maybe) have some chance of getting it.* |
| Mais si tu ne te présentes pas, tu ne l'**auras** sûrement pas! | *But if you don't apply (present your candidacy), you surely will not get it!* |

However, in time clauses (dependent clauses following words like **quand**, **lorsque** [*when*], **dès que** [*as soon as*], or **aussitôt que** [*as soon as*]), the future tense is used in French if the action is expected to occur at a future time. English uses the present tense in this case.

| | |
|---|---|
| Je te **téléphonerai** *dès que* **j'arriverai.** | *I'll phone you as soon as I arrive.* |
| Nous **pourrons** en discuter *lorsque* l'avocat **sera** là. | *We'll be able to discuss it when the lawyer arrives.* |
| La discussion **commencera** *dès que* tout le monde **sera** prêt. | *The discussion will begin as soon as everyone is ready.* |

**Suggestion**: Use the following as preliminary activities. (1) *Notre avenir économique.* 1. *Qui gagnera beaucoup d'argent? Je gagnerai 4 580 F par mois.* (*elle / 4 800; ils / 9 870; tu / 6 750; vous / 3 520*) 2. *Qui économisera beaucoup d'argent? Tu économiseras 1 000 F par mois.* (*nous / 400; ils / 250; vous / 1 000; je / 100; elle / 500*) 3. *Qui vendra sa voiture? Vous vendrez votre voiture pour 45 000 F.* (*nous / 12 000; elle / 32 000*)
(2) *Stratégies: Mettez les verbes au futur.* 1. *Je cherche du travail.* 2. *Mon frère m'aide à chercher.* 3. *Il en parle à son directeur.* 4. *Mes parents m'offrent leur aide.* 5. *Nous mettons une petite annonce.* 6. *Tu m'aides à préparer une entrevue.* 7. *Je vais au rendez-vous.* 8. *L'entrevue se passe bien.* 9. *Je trouve un poste.* 10. *Nous fêtons ce succès ensemble.*

### Vérifions!

**A. Stratégies.** Votre meilleur ami (meilleure amie) cherche du travail pour cet été. Il/Elle doit se présenter demain à un entretien (*interview*). Dites ce qu'il/elle fera demain.

MODÈLE: se lever très tôt → Il/Elle se lèvera très tôt.

1. faire un peu de gymnastique pour se relaxer 2. s'habiller avec soin 3. prendre un petit déjeuner léger 4. mettre son curriculum vitæ dans sa serviette (*briefcase*) 5. aller au rendez-vous en métro pour éviter les embouteillages (*traffic jams*) 6. y arriver un peu en avance 7. se présenter brièvement 8. parler calmement 9. répondre avec précision aux questions de l'employeur 10. remercier l'employeur en partant (*when leaving*)

À votre avis, que devra-t-il/elle aussi faire d'autre pour être sûr(e) de réussir à son entretien?

**Suggestion**: For oral or written practice. Can be done as a rapid response ex., or sts. can write a short paragraph in future tense using sentences given.

**B. Jeu de société.** À une soirée vous jouez à la voyante (*fortune-teller*) et prédisez la carrière de chacun(e) de vos ami(e)s. Choisissez le verbe convenable pour décrire vos prédictions. Vous pouvez utiliser chaque verbe plusieurs fois.

**Verbes**: écrire, enseigner (*to teach*), vendre, jouer, devenir, participer, faire, s'occuper de (*to take care of, be concerned with*)

1. Vous _____ cosmonaute. 2. Vous _____ des bijoux à Alger. 3. Vous _____ le rôle de Hamlet à Londres. 4. Vous _____ à la construction d'un stade à Mexico. 5. Vous _____ des articles pour le *New York Times*. 6. Vous _____ des assurances-automobile à Québec. 7. Vous _____ de la publicité pour Toyota. 8. Vous _____ des malades à Dakar. 9. Vous _____ dans une école primaire à Seattle. 10. ?

**Follow-up**: Give additional practice with substitutions: *Les étudiants parlent de leur avenir. J'aurai une profession intéressante.* (*nous, tu, Thierry*); *Juliette sera avocate.* (*vous, Jean-Pierre et Francis, je*); *Tu iras travailler en France.* (*mes amies, Claudine, nous*); *Nous devrons beaucoup travailler.* (*vous, Sylvain, je, elles*)

## Parlons-en!

**A. Conversation.** Posez les questions suivantes à un(e) camarade de classe.

1. Qu'est-ce que tu feras quand l'année scolaire sera terminée? Continueras-tu tes études ou travailleras-tu? 2. Qu'est-ce que tu feras après tes études? Choisiras-tu une profession indépendante? salariée? Seras-tu fonctionnaire? commerçant(e)? artisan(e)? 3. Voyageras-tu souvent? Si oui, dans quels pays? pour quelles raisons? 4. Gagneras-tu beaucoup d'argent? Est-ce que cela sera important pour toi? 5. Où vivras-tu si tu en as le choix? Pourquoi?

**B. Interview.** Vous voulez savoir ce que votre camarade pense de l'avenir et vous lui posez les questions suivantes. Mais malheureusement il/elle ne vous prend pas au sérieux! L'interviewé(e) utilise toute son imagination et son humour pour répondre. À la fin, inversez les rôles.

MODÈLE: dès que tu auras ton diplôme →
—Que feras-tu dès que tu auras ton diplôme?
—Moi, plus tard, je vendrai des légumes biologiques (*organic*) à Athènes.

1. quand tu seras vieux (vieille) 2. si un jour tu es milliardaire 3. dans dix ans 4. lorsque tu te marieras 5. dès que tu pourras réaliser un de tes rêves 6. si tu n'obtiens pas tout ce que tu veux 7. lorsque tu auras des enfants 8. ?

**Suggestion**: Ask sts. to work in groups of 3: 2 will discuss; the third will listen to determine which answers are the most original, funny, and bizarre. This person will report back to the class.

À votre avis, parmi toutes les réponses, laquelle (*which one*) est la plus originale? la plus amusante? la plus bizarre?

## 49. LINKING IDEAS Relative Pronouns

**Suggestion**: Ask sts. to read the minidialogue and make hypotheses about the referent and meaning of the relative pronouns.

**Interview d'un chef d'entreprise**

LA JOURNALISTE: Et pourquoi dites-vous que vous avez fait trois ans d'études inutiles?

GENEVIÈVE: Eh bien, parce que pendant tout ce temps-là, c'était la création de bijoux **qui** m'intéressait.

LA JOURNALISTE: Les bijoux **que** vous créez sont fabriqués avec des matériaux naturels?

GENEVIÈVE: Oui. Je dessine aussi pour les magazines des bijoux fantaisie **qu**'on peut réaliser à la maison.

LA JOURNALISTE: Maintenant, votre entreprise fabrique des milliers de bijoux **dont** les trois-quarts partent au Japon?

GENEVIÈVE: Oui, et j'ai des tas de nouveaux projets!

1. Qu'est-ce qui intéressait Geneviève pendant ses études?
2. Qu'est-ce qu'on peut réaliser à la maison?
3. Les trois-quarts de quoi partent au Japon?

A relative pronoun (*who, that, which, whom, whose*) links a dependent (relative) clause to a main clause. A dependent clause is one that cannot stand by itself—for example, the italicized parts of the following sentences: The suitcase *that he is carrying* is mine; There is the store *in which we met.* In French, there are two sets of relative pronouns: those used as either the subject or direct object of a dependent clause and those used after a preposition.

### A. Relative Pronouns Used as Subject or Direct Object of a Dependent Clause

The relative pronoun used as the *subject* of a dependent clause is **qui** (*who, that, which*). The relative pronoun used as the *direct object* of a dependent clause is **que** (*whom, that, which*).* Both can refer to people and to things.

*You may recall that **qui** and **que** are used in asking questions as well (interrogative pronouns). See Chapter 4 for a review.

SUBJECT Je cherche l'artisane. **Elle** fabrique des bijoux.

↓

Je cherche l'artisane **qui** fabrique des bijoux.

OBJECT J'ai acheté des bijoux. Geneviève a fabriqué **ces bijoux**.

J'ai acheté les bijoux **que** Geneviève a fabriqués.*

**Qui** replaces the subject (**elle**) in the dependent clause in the first sentence. Since it is the subject of the clause, **qui** will always be followed by a conjugated verb (**qui fabrique**).

**Que** replaces the direct object (**ces bijoux**) in the second sentence. **Que** is followed by a subject plus a conjugated verb (**... que Geneviève a fabriqués**).

| QUI + CONJUGATED VERB | QUE + SUBJECT + VERB |
|---|---|
| Les architectes **qui ont organisé** la réunion sont français. | Les architectes **que j'ai vus** à la conférence viennent des États-Unis. |

Note in the sentence with **voir**, the past participle agrees with the preceding plural direct object **que** (**les architectes**).

**Qui** never elides with a following vowel sound: L'architecte **qui est** arrivé ce matin vient des États-Unis. **Que** does elide: L'architecte **qu'elle** a rencontré vient des États-Unis.

**Presentation**: Model sentences in each grammar section and have sts. repeat the transformations.

**Note**: Stress that relative pronouns are never omitted in French as they often are in English.

**Suggestion**: You may wish to present the relative pronouns using the following chart:

| | person | thing |
|---|---|---|
| **subject** | *qui* | *qui* |
| **object** | *que* | *que* |
| **with prep.** | *qui* | (*lequel* later) |
| **with *de*** | *dont* | *dont* |

**Suggestion**: Use the following as a grammatical sensitivity exercise. Have sts. number from 1 to 7. They write *S* for *sujet* when they hear relative pronoun *qui*, and *O* for *objet* when they hear relative pronoun *que* in following sentences: 1. *Voici les voyageurs qui arrivent.* 2. *Les valises qu'ils portent sont lourdes.* 3. *Le train qui les a amenés ici est déjà parti.* 4. *Le voyageur qui a cette valise verte est mon oncle.* 5. *C'est la valise que je lui ai donnée.* 6. *La femme qui l'accompagne est gentille.* 7. *C'est le premier voyage qu'ils font ensemble.* As follow-up activity, put sentences on board, underline and explain function of relative pronouns.

## B. Relative Pronouns Used as Objects of Prepositions

The relative pronoun **qui** can be used as the object of a preposition to refer to people.

| | |
|---|---|
| Le comptable **avec qui** je travaille est agréable. | *The accountant with whom I work is pleasant.* |
| L'ouvrier **à qui** M. Mesnard a donné du travail est travailleur. | *The worker to whom Mr. Mesnard gave some work is industrious.* |

## C. *Dont*

The pronoun *dont* is used to replace *de* (*du, de la, de l', des*) plus an object.

| | |
|---|---|
| Où est le reçu? J'ai besoin du reçu. | *Where is the receipt? I need the receipt.* |
| ↓ | ↓ |
| Où est le reçu **dont** j'ai besoin? | *Where is the receipt that I need?* |

*You may want to review the section on agreement of past participles in Chapter 9.

The pronoun **dont** is also used to express possession.

| | |
|---|---|
| C'est la passagère. Ses valises sont à la douane. | *That's the passenger. Her suitcases are at the customs office.* |
| ↓ | ↓ |
| C'est la passagère **dont** les* valises sont à la douane. | *That's the passenger whose suitcases are at the customs office.* |

## D. Où

*Où* is the relative pronoun of time and place. It can mean *where, when,*† or *which.*

| | |
|---|---|
| Le guichet **où** vous changez votre argent est là-bas. | *The window where you change your money is over there.* |
| Le 1er janvier, c'est le jour **où** je commence mon nouveau travail. | *The first of January, that's the day (when) I begin my new job.* |
| L'aéroport d'**où** vous êtes partis est maintenant fermé. | *The airport from which you departed is closed now.* |

### Vérifions!

**A. À la recherche d'un emploi.** Jean-Claude raconte comment il a passé sa semaine à chercher du travail. Reliez les phrases suivantes avec le pronom relatif **qui**.

1. Lundi, j'ai déjeuné avec un ami. Il connaît beaucoup de comptables.
2. Mardi, j'ai eu une interview à la Banque Nationale de Paris. Elle est près de la place de la Concorde.
3. Mercredi, j'ai parlé à un employé du Crédit Lyonnais. Il m'a beaucoup encouragé.
4. Jeudi, j'ai pris rendez-vous avec un membre de la Chambre de commerce. Il est expert-comptable.
5. Enfin samedi, j'ai reçu une lettre d'une société belge. Elle m'offre un poste de comptable à Bruxelles.
6. Et aujourd'hui je prends l'avion. Il me conduit vers ma nouvelle vie.

**B. Promenade sur la Seine.** Cet été, Marie-Claude travaille comme guide sur un bateau-mouche‡ à Paris. Complétez ses explications avec les pronoms relatifs **qui**, **que** ou **où**.

---

*When **dont** is used, there is no need for a possessive adjective. Note the use of the definite article (**les**).

†**Quand** is never used as a relative pronoun.

‡The **bateaux-mouches** are well-known tourist boats that travel up and down the Seine.

Ce bâtiment _____[1] vous voyez à présent dans l'Île de la Cité, c'est la Conciergerie. Autrefois une prison, c'est l'endroit _____[2] Marie-Antoinette a passé ses derniers jours. Et cette église _____[3] se trouve en face de nous, c'est Notre-Dame. Est-ce que vous voyez cette statue _____[4] ressemble à la Statue de la Liberté? Eh bien, c'est l'original de la statue _____[5] la France a donnée aux Américains. Voici le musée d'Orsay _____[6] vous pourrez admirer les peintres impressionnistes et _____[7] je vous recommande de visiter. Et un peu plus loin, le musée du Louvre _____[8] vous trouverez la Joconde et la Vénus de Milo. Et enfin, voici la tour Eiffel, _____[9] est le symbole de notre ville.

**C. Photos de vacances.** Jeannine a passé un mois dans un village d'artistes dans le Midi. Elle y a rencontré beaucoup de gens intéressants. Elle montre maintenant ses photos de vacances à ses amis.

**Suggestions**: (1) Have sts. write out new sentences first and then give orally. (2) Ask sts. to write 2 stimulus sentences as dictation at board and then link them, as in model.

MODÈLE: Voici un artisan. Ses poteries sont très chères. →
Voici un artisan dont **les** poteries sont très chères.

1. Michel est un jeune artiste. On peut admirer ses tableaux au musée de Marseille.
2. Voici Yan. Ses sculptures sont déjà célèbres dans le milieu artistique.
3. Et voilà Claire. On vend ses bijoux à Saint-Tropez.
4. Laurent est un jeune écrivain. Son premier roman vient d'être publié.

## Parlons-en!

**A. À la gare de Lyon.** Pendant les vacances d'hiver vous travaillez au Bureau des objets trouvés (*lost and found*) à la gare de Lyon. Avec des camarades, jouez les situations suivantes. Soyez imaginatif/ive et donnez beaucoup de détails.

MODÈLE: une valise / oublier sur le quai
LE/LA PASSAGER/ÈRE: Je cherche une valise que j'ai oubliée sur le quai hier matin.
VOUS: Comment est la valise que vous avez oubliée?
LE/LA PASSAGER/ÈRE: Elle est petite, en cuir rouge.

**Continuation**: 7. *passeport / laisser dans les toilettes* 8. *le plan de la ville / oublier sur un banc* (*bench*) 9. *mon imperméable / perdre dans le hall*

1. un parapluie / laisser au restaurant
2. des clés / perdre dans le hall
3. un livre / oublier dans le train
4. un billet de train / venir d'acheter
5. un carnet de chèques / laisser au bureau de change
6. un ami (une amie) / rencontrer dans le train

**B. Énigme.** Décrivez un objet, une personne ou un endroit à vos camarades. Utilisez des pronoms relatifs. Vos camarades vont essayer de trouver la chose dont vous parlez.

**Catégories suggérées:** une ville, un pays, un plat, un gâteau, une personne, une classe, un moyen de transport, une profession...

MODÈLE: VOUS: Je pense à un gâteau qui est français et dont le nom commence par un e.
UN(E) CAMARADE: Est-ce que c'est un éclair?

Maintenant, continuez ce jeu avec une différence. Vous ne donnez que la catégorie d'un objet ou d'une personne. Vos camarades vous demandent des précisions. Répondez-leur par **oui** ou **non**.

**Autres catégories suggérées:** un film, une émission de télévision, une pièce de théâtre, un acteur (une actrice), un chanteur (une chanteuse), un homme (une femme) politique (*politician*), un(e) athlète...

MODÈLE: VOUS: Je pense à un film.
VOS CAMARADES: C'est un film que tu as vu il y a longtemps?
C'est un film dont l'action se passe (*happens*) aux États-Unis?
C'est un film qui a gagné un *Oscar*?
C'est un film où Jody Foster a joué le rôle principal?
C'est *Silence of the Lambs*.

**Suggestion**: Give sts. a few minutes to create an *énigme* before soliciting individual responses. Or have sts. create one or two *énigmes* as homework to be presented orally during next class. May be done in groups of 5 sts.

# Mise au point

**A. Un poste au Canada.** Claudette rêve déjà de son voyage au Canada. Voici ce qu'elle fera. Choisissez le mot juste.

Claudette, (*qui / que / qu'*) est une jeune Parisienne, (*ira / sera / aura*) travailler au Canada l'an prochain. Elle habitera chez les Regimbault (*qui / que / qu'*) sont des amis de ses parents et chez (*dont / que / qui*) ses parents sont restés quand ils (*seront / ont / sont*) passés par Québec il y a assez longtemps. Le jour (*que / qui / où*) Claudette (*arrivera / arrive / arrivée*), la famille Regimbault (*viendront / viendra / verra*) la chercher à l'aéroport. Son avion, (*que / qui / où*) partira de l'aéroport Roissy-Charles de Gaulle, passera par New York. Ses bagages (*arrivaient / arriveront / arrivent*) plus tard. M. et Mme Regimbault, (*qui / que / dont*) le père de Claudette lui a beaucoup parlé, sont très gentils. Le bureau (*où / que / qui*) Claudette travaillera n'est pas loin de chez eux. C(e) (*sera / avait / a été*) un séjour (= une visite) très agréable.

**B. Travail et vacances.** Racontez les projets de Sabine. Reliez les deux phrases avec un pronom relatif. Le symbole ▲ indique le début (*beginning*) d'une proposition relative.

MODÈLE: Je travaille au tribunal (*court*). ▲ Je suis avocate au tribunal. → Je travaille au tribunal où je suis avocate.

1. Je prendrai bientôt des vacances. ▲ J'ai vraiment besoin de ces vacances.
2. Ma camarade de chambre ▲ viendra avec moi. Elle s'appelle Élise.
3. Elle travaille avec des comptables. ▲ Ces comptables sont très exigeants (*demanding*).
4. Nous irons à Neuchâtel. ▲ Les parents d'Élise ont une maison à Neuchâtel.
5. Hier Élise a téléphoné à son père. ▲ Le père d'Élise nous a invitées.
6. Élise a envie de voir sa mère. ▲ Elle pense souvent à sa mère.
7. J'ai acheté une nouvelle valise. ▲ Je mettrai tous mes vêtements de ski dans cette valise.
8. Nous resterons deux jours à Strasbourg. ▲ Nous visiterons le Palais de l'Europe à Strasbourg.
9. Nous rentrerons trois semaines plus tard, prêtes à reprendre le travail. ▲ Ce travail se sera accumulé (*piled up*).

Cherchez l'information demandée ci-dessous dans le récit de Sabine.

1. saison 2. durée des vacances 3. nationalité probable d'Élise 4. état d'esprit (= mental) de Sabine

**C. Conversation.** Posez les questions suivantes à un(e) camarade, qui vous les posera à son tour.

L'été prochain _____?

1. qu'est-ce que tu écriras? 2. qu'est-ce que tu liras? 3. qu'est-ce que tu achèteras?[*] 4. qui verras-tu? 5. où iras-tu? 6. que feras-tu? auras-tu un job?

# Interactions

In this chapter, you practiced talking about the future, and you learned to link sentences. Act out the following situations, using the vocabulary and grammar from this chapter.

1. **À la banque.** You need to cash some traveler's checks. Go to the teller (your partner) at the window. Tell him or her how much money you want to change. Unfortunately, you have forgotten your passport. Ask whether you can change the money anyway and whether you can establish a checking

[*]See Appendix D for the conjugation of **acheter**.

account, because you will be in France for a while. Thank the teller for the information.

2. **Un job.** You are being interviewed for a job as a bilingual teller in a bank. Greet the interviewer (your partner). Answer any questions the interviewer may have. Ask about salary (**le salaire**), advancement (**les possibilités d'avancement**), job security (**la sécurité de l'emploi**), and working conditions (**les conditions de travail**). Tell the interviewer why you would particularly like the job, and explain why you are qualified.

# Rencontres

## LECTURE

### *Avant de lire*

**More on skimming for the gist.** The following article is from *Télé Poche*, a French magazine about television programs and personalities. It may seem difficult at first because of the many unfamiliar words. Use your skills at contextual guessing and make use of all available clues.

Another skill to use is that of skimming. Before you begin, answer the questions below to get the gist of the article. Base your answers on the title, introduction, photo, and the topic sentences below.

PARAGRAPHE 1
*Je garde des souvenirs merveilleux lorsque j'étais reporter pour la chaîne américaine CBS, dans les années 70.*

PARAGRAPHE 2
*Trêve* (No more) *de nostalgie, Christine préfère se rappeler les moments intenses qu'elle a vécus au cours de ses nombreux reportages.*

PARAGRAPHE 3
*Christine avoue* (admits) *pourtant ne jamais regarder en arrière* (backwards).

**Questions**

- Who is the article about?
- What general topic is discussed?
- How old was she when she got started in her profession?

**LA PREMIÈRE FOIS**

# LES DÉBUTS AMÉRICAINS DE CHRISTINE OCKRENT

***« Seul l'avenir m'intéresse », assure Christine Ockrent. Néanmoins, pour Christophe Dechavanne et Philippe Bouvard,[a] elle a accepté d'évoquer ses tout premiers pas[b] de journaliste.***

***Lundi TF1, 20.45***

◀ *La vocation journalistique ? Pour Christine Ockrent, elle s'est révélée à l'âge de 20 ans.*

Blonde et mince dans son tailleur saumon, Christine Ockrent savoure une coupe de champagne dans sa loge.[c] Avant le coup d'envoi[d] de « La première fois »,[e] présentée par Christophe Dechavanne et Philippe Bouvard. L'occasion pour elle d'évoquer les prémices[f] de son parcours professionnel. « Je garde des souvenirs merveilleux lorsque j'étais reporter pour la chaîne américaine CBS, dans les années 70. Durant cette période d'apprentissage,[g] j'ai découvert mon métier. » Une vocation qui s'est révélée[h] à l'âge de 20 ans, avec la nouvelle de l'assassinat du Président Kennedy. « À partir de ce moment-là, j'ai eu envie de vivre de près[i] les événements de mon époque. » Pari tenu.[j] En 1981, elle présente la grand-messe[k] du 20 heures sur A 2.

Trêve de nostalgie, Christine préfère se rappeler les moments intenses qu'elle a vécus au cours de ses nombreux reportages. « Ceux qui m'ont le plus marquée[l] concernent des anonymes, dans des lieux perdus.[m] Beaucoup plus que Gorbatchev au Kremlin ou Reagan à la Maison Blanche. Par exemple, lorsque vous croisez le regard[n] de quelqu'un dans les décombres[o] yougoslaves ou au fin fond[p] de la Géorgie... » Difficile pour un reporter d'oublier les horreurs de la guerre[q]: « À Tel Aviv, la première attaque des Scuds irakiens m'a beaucoup frappée. Et se retrouver dans un abri[r] est tout aussi impressionnant. »

### Son meilleur souvenir ? ...« Le prochain ! »

Christine avoue pourtant ne jamais regarder en arrière. « Il n'y a que l'avenir qui m'intéresse. » Pour l'heure, c'est son émission « Direct » sur A2. « Il est possible que je continue, mais personne ne connaît précisément la grille[s] de rentrée. Et puis, j'ai de nouveaux projets en cours. » Sereine, Christine se dirige vers le plateau[t] pour raconter sa « Première fois ». À propos, quel est son meilleur souvenir ? « Le prochain, j'espère ! »

Florence MARTINELLI

[a] Christophe... *producers of the show on which Christine is a guest*
[b] *steps*
[c] *dressing room*
[d] le coup... *first broadcast*
[e] «La...» *television show where famous people are interviewed*
[f] *débuts*
[g] *apprenticeship*
[h] s'est... *was revealed to her*
[i] de... *close to*
[j] Pari... *A bargain she has kept*
[k] *news*
[l] *struck*
[m] lieux... *far-off places*
[n] croisez... *exchange glances*
[o] *ruins*
[p] au... *deep in the woods*
[q] *war*
[r] *bunker*
[s] *schedule*
[t] *stage*

## Compréhension

1. Quelle est la profession de Christine Ockrent?
2. Quand et pourquoi a-t-elle décidé de faire ce métier?
3. Que faisait-elle dans les années 70?
4. Quelles sortes d'événements et de personnes ont marqué Christine Ockrent?
5. Quels endroits Christine Ockrent a-t-elle visités au cours de sa carrière?
6. Et vous, est-ce que vous serez journaliste un jour? Pourquoi ou pourquoi pas?

# PAR ÉCRIT

**Function:** Narrating (a personal experience) in the past
**Audience:** Classmates and professor
**Goal:** The following brief passage is excerpted from the autobiography of Françoise Giroud (1916–),* *Si je mens* (1972). After reading it, use it as a model for your own paragraph answering the question **Quel genre d'enfance avez-vous eu?**

> —Quel genre d'enfance avez-vous eu?
> —Le genre bizarre.
> —Bizarre? Pourquoi?
> —Ce n'est pas facile à expliquer... Mon père a été essentiellement une absence, une légende. Une absence d'abord à cause de la guerre, puis d'une mission aux États-Unis dont il a été chargé par le gouvernement français, ensuite d'une maladie que l'on ne savait pas soigner à l'époque et dont il est mort. Cette maladie a duré des années pendant lesquelles je ne l'ai jamais vu. J'ai eu pour lui un amour fou. On parlait de lui, à la maison, comme d'un héros qui avait tout sacrifié à la France,...

**Steps**

1. Reread the passage above, paying special attention to the transitions between clauses within sentences. Note the following techniques, and use them as models to follow in setting up your own paragraph.
   a. Use of adverbs, such as **d'abord**, **et puis**, **enfin**, etc., to connect simple clauses within a sentence and provide a sense of chronological progression or movement.
   b. Use of relative pronouns, such as **qui**, **que**, **où**, and **dont**, to enchance movement and sophistication by connecting simple clauses into a complex whole.
2. Jot down a brief list of memories, events, or feelings that seem to characterize your childhood.
   a. Flesh out the list by adding a few relevant details to each item on the list.
   b. Find a word or short phrase that seems to summarize the list and offers a shorthand characterization of your childhood.
3. Write a rough draft, applying the principles under number 1 above.
4. Have a classmate read your story to see if what you have written is interesting, clear, and organized. Make any necessary changes. Finally, read the composition again, checking for spelling, punctuation, and grammar errors. Focus especially on your use of adverbs and relative pronouns. Be prepared to share your composition with your professor or classmates.

---

*Françoise Giroud was editor of the magazine *Elle* between 1945 and 1953, then helped found *L'Express*, where she became editor and then publisher. From 1974 to 1976 she served as French Secretary of State for the Status of Women and was Secretary of State for Culture in 1976–1977. She has also written several literary works.

# À L'ÉCOUTE!

**À l'écoute!** See scripts for listening passages and follow-up activities recorded on student cassette. Remind students that in the listening comprehension passages (as in real life) they will not understand every word they hear. They should focus globally on the general information in the passages and not be overly concerned about what they do not understand.

**Carrières.** Vous allez entendre trois offres d'emploi à la radio. Lisez les activités ci-dessous avant d'écouter le vocabulaire et les séquences sonores qui leur correspondent.

VOCABULAIRE UTILE
la comptabilité *accounting*
la rentrée prochaine *beginning of next academic year*

**A.** Déterminez de quel poste il s'agit dans chaque cas.

| | |
|---|---|
| Annonce 1 _____ | a. professeur |
| Annonce 2 _____ | b. ingénieur |
| Annonce 3 _____ | c. secrétaire |

**B.** Quels sont les points mentionnés dans ces offres d'emploi? Encerclez la bonne réponse.

PREMIÈRE OFFRE

1. La société recherche quelqu'un qui
   a. parle trois langues b. parle anglais c. parle espéranto
2. Cette personne devra avoir
   a. 15 ans d'expérience professionnelle b. entre 5 et 10 ans d'expérience professionnelle

DEUXIÈME OFFRE

3. Le responsable de gestion (*director of administration*) a besoin d'un assistant qui
   a. parle anglais et italien b. parle espagnol et anglais
4. Cette personne devra avoir
   a. 25 ans d'expérience professionnelle b. un bon sens de l'organisation

TROISIÈME OFFRE

5. L'université recherche un professeur de
   a. physique-chimie b. lettres c. sciences humaines
6. Cette université se trouve
   a. en Afrique du Sud b. en Amérique c. en Afrique de l'Ouest

**C.** Quelle annonce (numéro 1, 2 ou 3) convient à (*is appropriate for*) chacune des personnes suivantes? Encerclez le numéro.

1. Laurence Chassagne enseigne la physique et la chimie dans un lycée technique et rêve de partir à l'étranger.
   1 2 3
2. Carole Bernard parle trois langues couramment et est forte en calcul (*arithmetic*).
   1 2 3
3. Lionel Pelletier est spécialiste en informatique. Il voudrait trouver un travail avec plus de responsabilité.
   1 2 3

# Vocabulaire

## Verbes

**aider** to help
**couvrir** to cover
**découvrir** to discover
**dépenser** to spend (*money*)
**déposer** to deposit
**diriger** to direct
**embaucher** to hire
**faire des économies** to save (up) money
**faire un chèque** to write a check
**gagner** to earn, to win
**intéresser** to interest
**offrir** to offer
**ouvrir** to open
**remettre** to replace, to deliver
**retirer** to withdraw
**souffrir** to suffer
**toucher** to cash

## Substantifs

**l'argent liquide** (*m.*) cash
**l'augmentation** (*f.*) increase
**l'avenir** (*m.*) future
**le bijou** jewel
**le budget** budget
**le bureau de change** money exchange (office)
**le carnet de chèques** checkbook
**la carte bancaire** bank (ATM) card
**la carte de crédit** credit card
**le chèque** check
**le compte** account
  **le compte-chèques** checking account
  **le compte d'épargne** savings account
**le conseil** advice
**le cours** exchange rate
**le coût de la vie** cost of living
**la dépense** expense
**le distributeur automatique** automatic teller
**l'embauche** (*f.*) hiring
**l'emprunt** (*m.*) loan
**l'entreprise** (*f.*) company
**l'entretien** (*m.*) job interview
**les frais** (*m. pl.*) expenses, costs
**le montant** sum, amount
**le reçu** receipt
**le salaire** salary
**la société** company

À REVOIR: **l'horaire** (*m.*)

## Les professions

**l'agent** (*m.*) **de police** police officer
**l'agriculteur/trice** farmer
**l'architecte** (*m., f.*) architect
**l'artisan(e)** artisan, craftsperson
**l'artiste peintre** (*m., f.*) (artist) painter
**l'avocat(e)** lawyer
**le/la boucher/ère** butcher
**le cadre** middle or upper manager
**le chef d'entreprise** company head, top manager, boss
**le/la coiffeur/euse** hairdresser
**le/la commerçant(e)** shopkeeper
**le/la comptable** accountant
**le/la dentiste** dentist
**le/la directeur/trice** manager, head
**le/la directeur/trice commercial(e)** business manager
**l'employé(e) (de)** employee; someone employed (by); white-collar worker; (sales) clerk
**le facteur** letter carrier
**le/la fonctionnaire** civil servant
**l'ingénieur** (*m.*) engineer
**l'instituteur/trice** primary school teacher
**le/la journaliste** reporter
**le marchand de vin** wine merchant
**le médecin (la femme médecin)** doctor
**l'ouvrier/ière** (manual) worker
**le/la pharmacien(ne)** pharmacist
**le plombier** plumber
**le/la secrétaire** secretary
**le/la travailleur/euse** worker
  **le travailleur indépendant** self-employed worker
  **le travailleur salarié** salaried worker

À REVOIR: **l'acteur**, **l'actrice**; **l'artiste** (*m., f.*); **l'écrivain (la femme écrivain)**; **le/la peintre**; **le/la serveur/euse**

## Mots et expressions divers

**aussitôt que** as soon as
**à l'avenir** from now on
**dès que** as soon as
**dont** whose, of whom, of which
**un jour** someday
**lorsque** when
**où** where, when
**prochain(e)** next
**que** whom, that, which
**qui** who, that, which

# Intermède

## SITUATION

### Un travail temporaire

**Contexte** *Chaque année à la fin de l'été, les vendanges° sont un rendez-vous traditionnel des étudiants français et étrangers. Ils savent qu'ils gagneront peu d'argent, mais qu'ils vivront une expérience enrichissante: l'accueil° chez les viticulteurs° est chaleureux° et l'ambiance des vendanges toujours joyeuse.*

*grape harvests* · *welcome / winegrowers* · *warm*

**Objectif** *Jean-Marc cherche du travail.*

**Situation**: The *Situation* dialogues are recorded on the st. cassette packaged with the st. text.

**Note**: Tell sts. that they can work during the *vendanges* by applying with the various grape growers (*Bourgogne*, *Champagne*, *région de la Loire*).

JEAN-MARC: Bonjour, Monsieur, j'ai entendu dire que vous embauchez pour les vendanges.

M. MICHAUD: Oui, c'est exact. Vous avez déjà vendangé? Ce n'est pas toujours drôle, on travaille sous le soleil, sous la pluie...

JEAN-MARC: Oui, je sais, mais je travaille bien. Vous payez à l'heure?

M. MICHAUD: Oui, nous payons 35 francs de l'heure, et les journées sont de huit à dix heures.

JEAN-MARC: Et pour le logement et les repas?

M. MICHAUD: Je retiens° deux heures de travail par jour seulement. *withhold, charge*

JEAN-MARC: Je suppose que ça va durer° deux ou trois semaines au maximum? *last*

M. MICHAUD: Oh oui, sans doute, s'il ne fait pas trop mauvais temps.

JEAN-MARC: Eh bien, si vous voulez bien me prendre, ça m'intéresse.

M. MICHAUD: C'est d'accord. Mais n'oubliez pas: ici, on s'amuse bien, mais on travaille dur°! *hard*

## À propos

### Comment engager une conversation formelle au téléphone

| LA PERSONNE QUI TÉLÉPHONE | | LA PERSONNE QUI RÉPOND |
|---|---|---|
| [dring! dring!] | → | Transports Sud-Loire, j'écoute. |

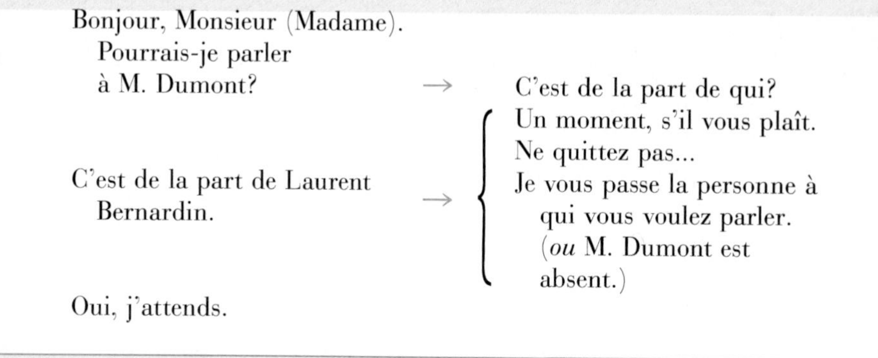

| | | |
|---|---|---|
| Bonjour, Monsieur (Madame). Pourrais-je parler à M. Dumont? | → | C'est de la part de qui? |
| C'est de la part de Laurent Bernardin. | → | Un moment, s'il vous plaît. Ne quittez pas... Je vous passe la personne à qui vous voulez parler. (*ou* M. Dumont est absent.) |
| Oui, j'attends. | | |

## *Maintenant à vous!*

**A. Questions personnelles.** Relisez le dialogue, puis répondez aux questions.

1. Avez-vous jamais eu un travail très dur? Racontez ce que vous avez fait. Qu'est-ce qui a rendu ce job difficile? Étiez-vous content(e) de ce travail, ou l'avez-vous détesté? Pourquoi?
2. Connaissez-vous des étudiant(e)s qui travaillent? À peu près combien sont-ils payés de l'heure? Que faut-il faire pour gagner davantage (*more*) d'argent?
3. Quel est, à votre avis, le job d'été idéal? Qu'est-ce que vous allez faire l'été prochain?

**B. Jeu de rôles.** Jouez la scène suivante avec un ou plusieurs camarades. Vous téléphonez à Mme Martin, responsable de gestion (*administration*) pour l'Europe à l'Agence France Presse. Elle a besoin d'un assistant dont la langue maternelle est l'anglais, mais avec une bonne connaissance du français. Vous avez vu l'offre d'emploi dans le journal *Le Monde*. Parlez d'abord à sa secrétaire, une personne peu aimable qui ne fait rien pour vous aider. La secrétaire est ferme et refuse de vous la passer. Essayez de la persuader de vous passer Mme Martin.

**Note**: Ask sts. to use expressions they learned in the *Situation* dialogue.

**Additional activity**: *Un poste pour l'été. Vous cherchez un poste pour l'été. Voilà une liste de postes possibles. Choisissez le poste que vous préférez (ou un autre qui vous intéresse) et imaginez la vie que vous aurez.* MODÈLE: *Je serai ______. Je travaillerai à/en/dans ______. Je gagnerai ______ par mois. Je serai content(e) parce que ______. Métiers et professions: serveur/serveuse, secrétaire, chauffeur de taxi,*

*caissier/caissière dans un supermarché, vendeur/vendeuse, moniteur/monitrice, donner des leçons particulières, charpentier*

## PORTRAITS

### *Marie Curie (1867–1934)*

Physicienne° d'origine polonaise,° Marie Curie a fait des recherches sur la radioactivité avec son mari, Pierre Curie. Elle a découvert le *polonium* et le *radium* (1898). Prix Nobel de physique en 1903 et de chimie en 1911, elle a été la première femme nommée professeur à la Sorbonne.

Physicist / Polish

CHAPITRE **QUINZE**

# Vive les loisirs!

**En avant**

—Qu'est-ce que tu fais ce week-end?

—Samedi je vais faire du tennis avec Christine et le soir, je vais voir Vanessa Paradis[*] en concert.

—Vanessa Paradis? Super! Et dimanche, tu veux venir au ciné avec moi? Je vais voir *Christophe Colomb*, un film de Depardieu.[*]

—OK!

**Communicative goals:** talking about leisure time activities, getting information, being polite, speculating, expressing actions, and making comparisons.

[*]Vanessa Paradis is a popular French singer. Gérard Depardieu is one of the leading stars of French movies.

**En avant**: See scripts for follow-up questions recorded on student cassette.

# Étude de vocabulaire

## Les loisirs préférés des Français

**Suggestion**: Model pronunciation of new vocab. Then ask sts. to describe in as much detail as possible actions depicted in drawings. Ask questions to expand on ideas presented. Examples: *Quelles chansons aimez-vous le mieux? Quel film avez-vous vu récemment? Quels sports aimez-vous jouer en plein air? Quels jeux de société préférez-vous?* etc.

**Les spectacles**
La chanson de variété*
Le cinéma

**Les activités de plein air**
La pêche
La pétanque
Le pique-nique
Le ski
La marche

**Les manifestations sportives**
Le football
Le cyclisme
Les matchs (de boxe, de football)

**Les jeux**
Les jeux de hasard
Les jeux de société

**Le bricolage**†
Le jardinage

**Les passe-temps**
Les collections
La lecture
La peinture

**A. Catégories.** La chanson de variété est un spectacle. Dans quelle(s) catégorie(s) de distractions classez-vous _____?

**Additional vocab.**: *la planche à voile, la planche à roulettes, le jogging, l'aérobic, les sorties, assister à.*

*__Une chanson de variété__ is a popular song, frequently associated with a particular singer and sung in a music hall or a small nightclub.

†**Le bricolage** is *puttering around, doing odd jobs around the house, building and repairing things oneself.* The verb form is **bricoler**.

1. un match de boxe
2. une collection de papillons (*butterflies*)
3. la fabrication de nouvelles étagères
4. la pêche
5. la roulette
6. la lecture
7. une partie (*game*) de frisbee
8. la réparation de votre bicyclette
9. un pique-nique
10. le poker
11. un concert de jazz
12. la pétanque
13. le cyclisme
14. la marche

**Suggestion**: May be done as a free-association activity or game, where sts. name first thing they think of. Word-association chains can be made from new words. Example: (1) *le base-ball*; *les hot-dogs*, *le stade*, *les Yankees*, etc.

**Continuation**: *le base-ball*? *l'opéra*? *la réparation d'une porte*? *la sculpture*? *une collection de timbres*?

**B. Le bricolage.** Le jardinage et la construction d'un barbecue sont deux formes de bricolage. Nommez deux formes de loisirs pour chaque catégorie.

1. les manifestations sportives 2. les jeux de société 3. les spectacles 4. les activités de plein air 5. les passe-temps

**Suggestion**: Ask sts. to work in small groups and report back to the class after doing the activity.

**C. Interview.** Posez les questions suivantes à un(e) camarade. D'après ses réponses, parlez brièvement à la classe du caractère ou de la personnalité de votre camarade.

**Expressions utiles:** sentimental(e), terre à terre (= pratique), actif/ive, créateur/trice, paresseux/euse, sportif/ive, énergique, (peu) doué(e) (*gifted*) pour les sports, audacieux/euse, (im)prudent(e), adroit(e), être un homme (une femme) à tout faire (*handy*), (n')avoir (pas) le goût du risque

**Suggestion**: Have sts. write a *résumé* of some of the answers of classmates and report to class, or hand *résumé* in as a written assignment.

Demandez-lui...

1. quelles sortes de chansons il/elle aime (les chansons d'amour? les chansons folkloriques? le rap?)
2. qui est son chanteur favori et sa chanteuse favorite, et pourquoi
3. à quelles sortes de spectacles il/elle assiste* souvent et à quel spectacle il/elle a assisté récemment
4. s'il (si elle) préfère faire du sport ou s'il (si elle) préfère assister à des manifestations sportives; à quelle manifestation sportive il/elle a assisté récemment
5. quel jeu de société il/elle préfère (le bridge? le Scrabble? le Monopoly?)
6. à quels jeux de hasard il/elle a joué, où il/elle y a joué et combien il/elle a gagné ou perdu
7. s'il (si elle) aime bricoler et quels objets il/elle a réparés ou fabriqués (= construits)
8. s'il (si elle) collectionne quelque chose

**D. Vive les loisirs!** Imaginez que vous êtes libre ce week-end et que vous ne savez pas quoi faire. Voici quelques suggestions.

D'après la publicité à la page suivante...

1. Quelles sont les différentes activités proposées?

---

*__Assister__ (__à__) is a **faux ami**, or false cognate, meaning *to attend*. To express *assisting or helping*, use **aider**.

2. Quelle activité vous semble la plus amusante? la moins intéressante? Expliquez pourquoi.
3. Imaginez que l'argent n'est pas un obstacle. Quel genre d'activité allez-vous choisir? Expliquez les raisons de votre choix.

## *Sélection spectacles*

### THÉÂTRE

**Fièvre romaine**, d'Edith Wharton. Mise en scène : Jean-Claude Buchard. Avec Suzanne Flon et Judith Magre. Théâtre du Rond-Point.
21 h du mardi au samedi ; 15 h le dimanche.
128 F (au lieu de 140 F). Code FIEVR.

**Good**, de C.P. Taylor.
Adaptation : Sam Karmann. Mise en scène : Jean-Pierre Bouvier. Avec Jean-Pierre Bouvier, Sam Karmann, Hélène Arie, Anne Jacquemin...
Théâtre de la Renaissance.
20 h 45 du mardi au samedi ; 15 h 30 le dimanche.
163, 123 F (au lieu de 180, 140 F). Code GOOD1.

**Père**, de Strindberg.
Mise en scène : Claude Yersin.
Théâtre de l'Est parisien.
Du 16 avril au 7 mai.
20 h 30 les mardi, mercredi, vendredi, samedi ; 19 h le jeudi ; 15 h le dimanche.
88 F (au lieu de 110 F). Code PERE1.

**Hors limite**, de Philippe Malignon. Mise en scène : Raymond Acquaviva. Avec Philippe Lelièvre et Jean-Pierre Malignon.
Théâtre Fontaine.
21 h du mardi au jeudi ; 18 h le samedi. 139 F (au lieu de 150 F). Code HLIMI.

### MUSIQUE-OPÉRA

**Ensemble orchestral de Paris**. Christian Ivaldi (piano), Christian Crenne (violon) : Brahms, Schubert. Salle Gaveau.
20 h 30 le 17 mai.
140, 115, 70, 36 F (au lieu de 160, 125, 75, 40 F). Code EOP34.

**L'enfant et les sortilèges**. Opéra en deux parties. Musique de Maurice Ravel. Livret de Colette. Direction musicale : Marc Soustrot. Orchestre philharmonique des Pays de la Loire. Théâtre des Champs-Elysées.
20 h 30 le mercredi 18 mai.
192 et 142 F (au lieu de 200 et 150 F). Code TCE27.

### DANSE

**Nous, les Tziganes**. Spectacle du Théâtre tzigane Romen de Moscou. Théâtre Mogador.
21 h les 5, 7, 10, 12 mai ; 16 h le 15 mai. 130, 98 F (au lieu de 150, 115 F). Code TZIGA.

### ROCK

**Pink Floyd**. Château de Versailles.
21 h 30 le 22 juin. 195 F. Code PINKF.

### SPORT

**Masters d'escrime**. Palais des Sports.
20 h 15 le 5 mai. 73 F (au lieu de 80 F). Code ESCRI.

*Prière de réserver vos spectacles 15 jours avant la date que vous avez choisie.*

| | |
|---|---|
| **se faire un resto / un ciné / un concert** | aller au restaurant / au cinéma / au concert |

| | |
|---|---|
| **faire la fête** | manger + boire + danser |
| **la boum** | la fête |
| **la boîte** | la discothèque |

EN CONTEXTE

LUC: Qu'est-ce qu'on (se) fait ce soir?
PATRICE: Moi, j'ai envie de **faire la fête**.
LUC: Moi, j'ai plutôt envie de **me faire un bon petit resto**.
MARC: Super! Et après **le resto** on **se fait un ciné**. D'accord?
PATRICE: Alors, je vais tout seul **en boîte**.

**Note**: *Boîte* literally means box. Note the expression: *aller en boîte*.

# Pour parler des loisirs: *courir* et *rire*

| PRESENT TENSE OF | **courir** (*to run*) | **rire** (*to laugh*) |
|---|---|---|
| je | cours | ris |
| tu | cours | ris |
| il, elle, on | court | rit |
| nous | cour**ons** | ri**ons** |
| vous | cour**ez** | ri**ez** |
| ils, elles | cour**ent** | ri**ent** |
| *Past participle:* | couru | ri |
| *Future stem:* | courr- | rir- |

**Suggestion**: Model pronunciation of verb forms in short sentences: *Je cours vite. Tu ris pendant le film.*

**A. Sondage sur le jogging.** Interviewez un(e) camarade pour savoir s'il (si elle) fait du jogging. Posez lui ces questions.

1. Combien de fois court-il/elle par semaine?
2. Pendant combien de temps court-il/elle?; ou Combien de kilomètres fait-il/elle? (1 mile = 1,6 kilomètres)
3. Depuis quand (*Since when*) fait-il/elle du jogging?

S'il (Si elle) a répondu non...

1. Pourquoi ne court-il/elle pas?
2. Pratique-t-il/elle un autre sport?
3. Que pense-t-il/elle des gens qui courent souvent?

Puis comparez les résultats des différents sondages.

**Suggestions**: (1) As a whole-class activity, sts. indicate answers to *Faites-vous du jogging?* by a show of hands. Call on a few sts. who answered yes and ask three questions of each st. as in a mini-conversation. Do same with sts. who answered no. (2) Use for pair work, with each st. asking the other questions associated with yes or no response given.

1. Dans votre classe y a-t-il plus d'étudiants qui courent ou plus d'étudiants qui ne courent pas?
2. Parmi les coureurs, qui court le plus par semaine? le moins?
3. Parmi les non-coureurs, qui a donné la raison la plus comique? la plus bizarre? Quels sont les sports les plus populaires?

**Follow-up**: After sts. have answered questions, have them organize a debate on joys and dangers of jogging, or of some other exercise activity, such as aerobics (*l'aérobic*) or bicycling. Give them help in forming arguments, either on board or on a handout: POUR: *bon pour la santé, un excellent exercice cardiovasculaire, bon pour la santé mentale, bon pour la circulation du sang, un bon moyen de perdre des kilos, un sport très bon marché*; CONTRE: *dangereux pour la santé, une vraie obsession, jugé dangereux pour les gens âgés, peut provoquer des accidents cardiaques, peut faire mal aux jambes et aux pieds.*

**B. Le rire.** Le rire est le passe-temps préféré de beaucoup de gens. Il nous aide aussi à surmonter les moments difficiles ou embarrassants de la vie. Avec un(e) camarade, choisissez dans la liste ci-dessous deux cas où le sens de l'humour nous aide, et expliquez pourquoi.

Le sens de l'humour nous aide dans les occasions où _____.

1. on a peur
2. on est embarrassé
3. on veut critiquer quelqu'un
4. il y a de la tension
5. on cache (*is hiding*) quelque chose
6. ?

**Suggestions**: (1) Have sts. do first part in small groups or in pairs, with second part for whole-class discussion, or vice versa. (2) Ask each st. to write down a short joke or riddle in French. It may be easiest if sts. have a model. For example, *Pourquoi l'éléphant s'est-il assis sur la table?* (*Parce que la chaise était trop petite.*) Collect the jokes and read a few at random.

**Et vous?** Aimez-vous rire? Avec un(e) camarade, répondez aux questions suivantes. Chaque fois que vous répondez **oui**, donnez un exemple.

1. Racontez-vous des blagues (*jokes*)? 2. Faites-vous souvent des jeux de mots (*puns*)? 3. Avez-vous un(e) comique préféré(e)? 4. Aimez-vous particulièrement un film amusant ou une pièce amusante? 5. Est-ce que vous riez quelquefois dans la classe de français? (Quand et pourquoi?)

**Follow-up**: To increase sts.' awareness of cultural aspects of humor, bring in several cartoons from French magazines and have sts. examine them and explain the humor.

# France-culture

**Suggestion**: You may wish to bring in magazines on sports and leisure: *Auto-Moto, Bateaux, France-Football, Mondial, La Voix des Sports, Tennis de France*, etc., and ask sts. to look them over.

*Les loisirs des Français.* Les loisirs occupent une place importante dans la vie des Français. Il existe actuellement un ministère du Temps libre pour les aider à organiser leurs activités. Mais que font-ils donc de leur temps libre?

L'un des passe-temps favoris du Français est le bricolage: dans sa maison ou dans son jardin, il trouve toujours quelque chose à réparer, à embellir° ou à remplacer. Cet amour du travail manuel montre l'importance que le Français accorde à son foyer.° Les Français sont aussi de grands collectionneurs: par exemple, de timbres, d'objets rares ou de bandes dessinées.° Ils passent souvent leurs week-ends à la recherche° d'objets rares, même si parfois ils doivent conduire très loin.

*decorate*
*household*
*bandes... comic strips / à... looking for*

Les Français aiment aussi beaucoup les sports, et ils sont de plus en plus nombreux à en faire régulièrement. Leur sport favori est le football, avec plus de vingt mille clubs et près de deux millions de membres dans tout le

**Suggestion**: Before discussing favorite leisure activities of the French, have sts. brainstorm about their favorite leisure activities, either together or in small groups, and rank in order the 5 most common ones. Then have them read and discuss *France-culture* in light of similarities and differences between the preferences of the French and their own.

Greg LeMond, vainqueur récent du Tour de France

pays. Le ski aussi est très populaire et beaucoup de familles profitent des vacances de Noël pour partir à la montagne. Le cyclisme connaît aussi un grand succès. Le Tour de France est peut-être l'événement sportif français le plus connu aux États-Unis. D'autres sports très pratiqués par les Français sont le tennis, la planche à voile, le jogging, l'aérobique et bien sûr la conversation qui, pour certains, reste encore le sport préféré!

# Étude de grammaire

## 50. GETTING INFORMATION Interrogative Pronouns

### Au match de rugby

BILL: **Qu'est-ce qu**'ils essaient de faire?
JEAN-PAUL: Eh bien, ils essaient de poser le ballon derrière la ligne de but de l'équipe adverse.
BILL: Oui, je sais, mais **que** font-ils en ce moment?
JEAN-PAUL: Ça s'appelle une mêlée.
BILL: Et c'est **quoi**, une mêlée?

JEAN-PAUL: C'est quand plusieurs joueurs de chaque équipe sont regroupés autour du ballon. Tu vois, un des joueurs l'a récupéré.
BILL: **Lequel?**
JEAN-PAUL: Philippot.
BILL: **Qu'est-ce qui** l'empêche de le passer vers le but?
JEAN-PAUL: Les règles du jeu, mon vieux! C'est du rugby, ce n'est pas du football américain.

Voici des réponses. Quelles en sont les questions?

1. Ils essaient de plaquer (*tackle*) le joueur qui court avec le ballon.
2. C'est Duval qui passe le ballon à Philippot.
3. Un essai, c'est l'avantage obtenu quand un joueur réussit à poser le ballon derrière la ligne de but.

## A. Forms of Interrogative Pronouns

**Suggestion**: Ask sts. to compare these to the relative pronouns so they do not become confused.

Interrogative pronouns—in English, *who? whom? which? what?*—can be used as the subject in a question, as the object of the verb, or as the object of a preposition. You have been using the French interrogative pronouns **qui** and **qu'est-ce que**. Following is a list of other French interrogative pronouns. Note that several have both a short form and a long form that is based on **est-ce que**.

**Note**: The long and short forms are presented. Sts. at this level should be encouraged to use the form they are most comfortable with, as long as they can recognize both.

| USE | PEOPLE | THINGS |
|---|---|---|
| *Subject of a question* | qui<br>qui est-ce qui | (*no short form*)<br>qu'est-ce qui |
| *Object of a question* | qui<br>qui est-ce que | que<br>qu'est-ce que |
| *Object of a preposition* | à qui | à quoi |

## B. Interrogative Pronouns as the Subject of a Question

As the *subject* of a question, the interrogative pronoun that refers to people has both a short and a long form. The pronoun that refers to things has only one form. Note that **qui** is always followed by a singular verb.

| PEOPLE | THINGS |
|---|---|
| **Qui** fait du jogging ce matin?<br>**Qui est-ce qui** fait du jogging ce matin? | **Qu'est-ce qui** se passe? (*What's happening?*) |

## C. Interrogative Pronouns as the Object of a Question

As the *object* of a question, the interrogative pronouns referring to people, as well as those referring to things, have both a long and a short form.

1. *Long forms*

PEOPLE: **Qui est-ce que**
THINGS: **Qu'est-ce que** + *subject* + *verb* + (*other elements*)?

| | |
|---|---|
| **Qui est-ce que** tu as vu sur le court de tennis ce matin? | *Whom did you see on the tennis court this morning?* |
| **Qu'est-ce que** Marie veut faire ce soir? | *What does Marie want to do this evening?* |

Suggestion: When sts. have reviewed forms and uses of interrogative pronouns, have them go back and analyze use of each pronoun in mini-dialogue (i.e., why a particular form is used in each case).

Remember that **qu'est-ce que** (**qu'est-ce que c'est que**) is a set phrase used to ask for a definition: *What is* ____? **Qu'est-ce que la pétanque?**

2. *The short form* **qui** is followed by an inverted subject and verb.

**Qui** (+ *noun subject*) + *verb-pronoun* + (*other elements*)?

| | |
|---|---|
| **Qui as-tu vu** à la salle de sports? | *Whom did you see at the gym?* |
| **Qui Marie a-t-elle vu** sur le court de tennis? | *Whom did Marie see on the tennis court?* |

Suggestion: As a listening comp. activity, ask sts. to indicate whether following questions are about people or things. It may help to have them imagine they are hearing only one side of a telephone conversation. 1. *Qui est arrivé?* 2. *De quoi avez-vous parlé?* 3. *Qu'est-ce qu'elle a dit?* 4. *Qu'est-ce qui s'est passé ce week-end?* 5. *Qui as-tu vu au match?* 6. *À qui as-tu parlé?* 7. *Que vas-tu faire ce soir?* 8. *Qui est-ce que tu as invité?* 9. *Qui est-ce qui va venir?* If this set of questions is used as dictation, ask sts. to act out conversation, giving answers to each question after they ask it.

3. *The short form* **que** is followed by an inverted subject and verb. This is true for both noun and pronoun subjects.

**Que** + *verb* + *subject* (*noun or pronoun*) + (*other elements*)?

| | |
|---|---|
| **Que cherches-tu?** | *What are you looking for?* |
| **Que cherche Jacqueline?** | *What is Jacqueline looking for?* |

## D. Use of *qui* and *quoi* After Prepositions

After a preposition or as a one-word question, **qui** is used to refer to people, and **quoi** is used to refer to things.

| | |
|---|---|
| **À qui** Michel parle-t-il? | *Who is Michel speaking to?* |
| **De qui** parles-tu? | *Who are you talking about?* |
| **À quoi** Corinne réfléchit-elle? | *What is Corinne thinking about?* |
| **De quoi** parlez-vous? | *What are you talking about?* |

## E. The Interrogative Pronoun *lequel*

Note: You may wish to introduce the forms of *lequel* for recognition only.

**Lequel**, **laquelle**, **lesquels**, and **lesquelles** (*which one*[*s*]?) are used to ask about a person or thing that has already been specified. These pronouns agree in gender and number with the nouns to which they refer.

| | |
|---|---|
| —Avez-vous vu cet opéra? | —*Have you seen this (that) opera?* |
| —**Lequel**? | —*Which one?* |
| —Vous rappelez-vous cette pièce de théâtre? | —*Do you remember this (that) play?* |
| —**Laquelle**? | —*Which one?* |

## *Vérifions!*

**A. À la Maison des jeunes et de la culture.*** Posez des questions sur les activités des jeunes à la MJC. Utilisez **qui** ou **qui est-ce qui**, en remplaçant les mots soulignés.

MODÈLE: Pierrot apprend à jouer du piano. →
Qui (Qui est-ce qui) apprend à jouer du piano?

1. Astrid va suivre un cours de poésie.
2. Paul apprend à faire un portrait dans le cours de peinture.
3. Jean-Loup écoute un concert de Debussy.
4. Le professeur choisit les meilleures œuvres à exposer.

Maintenant, posez des questions avec **que** ou **qu'est-ce que**.

MODÈLE: Sylvie regarde un film de François Truffaut au ciné-club. →
Que regarde Sylvie au ciné-club? (Qu'est-ce que Sylvie regarde au ciné-club?)

5. Les jeunes font des vases dans le cours de poterie.
6. On joue un air de Jacques Brel dans le cours de guitare.
7. Jean a fabriqué des étagères dans l'atelier de bricolage.
8. Marie a travaillé son service pendant son cours de tennis.

**Additional activity**: *Posons des questions. Remplacez le(s) mot(s) soulignés par un pronom interrogatif.* MODÈLE: *Claire invite le professeur. → Qui Claire invite-t-elle? (Qui est-ce que Claire invite?)* 1. *Marie court après le bus.* 2. *Jean court après Marie.* 3. *Marie court après sa sœur.* 4. *Mme Dulac fabrique des étagères.* 5. *M. Dulac fabrique une table.* 6. *M. Leroux a ouvert la bouteille.* 7. *Jean a ouvert la porte.* 8. *Gautier rit avec Jean.* 9. *Paulette a appris à faire de la poterie.* 10. *Jean-Paul a étudié la peinture.*

**B. Exposition à la MJC.** Vous êtes chargé(e) d'organiser une exposition à votre MJC, et vous donnez des instructions à un groupe de volontaires. Quelles questions vous posent-ils? Choisissez l'interrogatif correct.

MODÈLE: (qui / qu'est-ce que) William nous prêtera une... →
Qu'est-ce que William nous prêtera?

1. (qui / qu'est-ce qui) Le directeur a invité...
2. (qui / qu'est-ce que) Valérie va nous apporter une...
3. (qui / qui est-ce qui) Nous devons téléphoner à...
4. (à quoi / de quoi) Demain, vous voulez nous parler...

*The **MJC** (**Maison des jeunes et de la culture**) is a recreational center supported by the French government. There are **MJCs** all over France, offering work areas and courses in many hobbies and sports. They also sponsor cultural events, such as concerts, plays, art exhibits, and movies.

5. (qui est-ce qui / qui) Nadine viendra avec son...
6. (quoi / que) Vous pensez beaucoup à la...

**C. Une tranquille matinée de bricolage.** Ce matin il y a eu une grande confusion chez les Fontanet. La petite Emilie, rentrée de l'école maternelle (*kindergarten*), pose des questions sur tout ce qui s'est passé. Remplacez le(s) mot(s) souligné(s) par un pronom interrogatif.

**Suggestion**: Put correct answers on board or overhead as sts. give them.

MODÈLE: Papa a invité un ami. →
Qui papa a-t-il invité? (Qui est-ce que papa a invité?)

1. Maman fabriquait une petite table.
2. Jean-Louis faisait de la poterie.
3. Papa parlait avec son ami.
4. Jean-Louis a ouvert la porte.
5. Le chien a vu le facteur.
6. Maman a crié après le chien.
7. Le chien a couru après le facteur.
8. La poterie est tombée par terre (*to the ground*).
9. Papa a rattrapé (*caught*) le chien.
10. Le chien a cassé (*broke*) la petite table de maman.

## *Parlons-en!*

**A. Interview.** Avec un(e) camarade de classe, posez des questions et répondez-y à tour de rôle.

MODÈLE: acteurs comiques: Danny DeVito, Eddie Murphy →
VOUS: Lequel de ces acteurs comiques préfères-tu, Danny DeVito ou Eddie Murphy?
VOTRE AMI(E): Je préfère Eddie Murphy. Et toi, lequel préfères-tu?
VOUS: Je préfère ______.

**Suggestion**: Ask sts. to work in pairs or ask one st. to pose the question and call on someone else.

1. actrices: Sigourney Weaver, Whoopi Goldberg
2. peintres: le Français Degas, l'Espagnol Picasso
3. chanteuses: Madonna, Whitney Houston
4. loisirs: le bricolage, le jardinage
5. spectacles: les manifestations sportives, les chansons de variété
6. chansons: les chansons rock de Bruce Springsteen, de R.E.M.
7. ?

Que pouvez-vous dire des goûts de votre camarade?

**B. Le Grand-Duché de Luxembourg.** Ce petit pays est un endroit idéal pour les amoureux de la nature. Voici une description des montagnes dans le sud du pays et du paysage (*landscape*) de la région. Lisez-la rapidement, puis posez les questions suivantes à un(e) camarade de classe. Inversez les rôles au milieu de l'exercice.

**Suggestion**: Encourage sts. to guess the meaning of new words in context and to read mainly for the information requested in follow-up questions. Point out that *ardennais* is the adjective to indicate those living in the Ardennes. Give sts. a few minutes to read over the realia. Have pairs take turns asking each other questions. Give the second part as a writing assignment and have sts. report and answer questions the following day.

Le paysage montagneux, à la fois harmonieux et varié du Nord des Ardennes Luxembourgeoises, offre au visiteur le calme, le repos et la détente. De vastes hauts-plateaux ondulés où se développe une agriculture poussée, sont creusés par d'innombrables vallées étroites parfois aux rochers abrupts dont les flancs sont couverts de sapins et de chênes. La suite des saisons fait changer sans cesse le décor de ce paysage ardennais. Des sentiers

bien signalés parcourant les hauteurs et les pentes et permettant des vues magnifiques, invitent à de longues promenades bienfaisantes. Au terme de ces randonnées – l'appétit étant stimulé par l'air pur des hauteurs – le touriste saura apprécier les spécialités gastronomiques qu'une hostellerie traditionnaliste lui offre. En parcourant cette région, on découvre ses beautés.

BELGIQUE
LUXEMBOURG
FRANCE

1. Où se trouve le Luxembourg?
2. Comment s'appelle la chaîne de montagnes dans le sud du pays?
3. Qu'est-ce que ce paysage offre au visiteur?
4. De quoi sont couverts les flancs de la montagne?
5. Qu'est-ce qui fait changer sans cesse le paysage?
6. À quoi nous invitent les sentiers (*paths*)?
7. Qu'est-ce que le touriste appréciera après les randonnées (*walks in the country*)?
8. Que découvre-t-on quand on se promène dans la région?

Maintenant, décrivez un endroit de votre région ou un endroit que vous avez visité récemment (un parc national, une vallée, une ville, une forêt...) à vos camarades. Puis ils vous poseront ensuite des questions pour avoir plus de détails sur ce qu'on peut y voir et y faire.

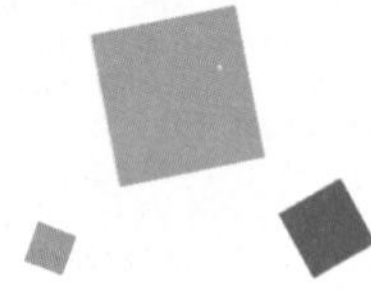

## 51. BEING POLITE; SPECULATING The Present Conditional

### Ah, si j'étais riche...

FRANÇOIS: Qu'est-ce que tu **ferais**, toi, si tu gagnais au loto*?

VINCENT: Moi, je crois que **j'achèterais** un vieux cinéma de quartier. Je **choisirais** tous les films que j'aime et tous mes copains **pourraient** entrer gratuitement.

*The French national lottery.

CHLOË: Moi, si je gagnais assez d'argent, je **m'installerais** dans le sud de la France et je **passerais** mon temps à faire de la peinture. J'**aurais** une grande maison et vous **pourriez** venir me voir tous les week-ends.

Et vous? Si vous gagniez au loto, qu'est-ce que vous feriez?

## A. Forms of the Conditional

In Chapter 9, you learned the forms of some verbs in the conditional. You may remember that in English, the conditional is a compound verb form consisting of *would* plus the infinitive: *he would travel, we would go*. In French, the **conditionnel** is a simple verb form. The imperfect tense endings **-ais**, **-ais**, **-ait**, **-ions**, **-iez**, **-aient** are added to the infinitive. The final **-e** of **-re** verbs is dropped before the endings are added.

**Note**: Point out the difference in pronunciation between the future ending (*-ai*) [e] and conditional endings (*-ais*) [ɛ].

**Presentation**: Model pronunciation in short sentences. Examples: *Je parlerais français. Nous finirions la leçon. Ils vendraient le livre.*

| | **parler** (*to speak*) | **finir** (*to finish, to end*) | **vendre** (*to sell*) |
|---|---|---|---|
| je | parler**ais** | finir**ais** | vendr**ais** |
| tu | parler**ais** | finir**ais** | vendr**ais** |
| il, elle, on | parler**ait** | finir**ait** | vendr**ait** |
| nous | parler**ions** | finir**ions** | vendr**ions** |
| vous | parler**iez** | finir**iez** | vendr**iez** |
| ils, elles | parler**aient** | finir**aient** | vendr**aient** |

Elle **passerait** son temps à faire de la peinture. — *She'd spend her time painting.*

Nous **pourrions** entrer gratuitement dans son cinéma. — *We'd be able to get into his movie theater for free.*

Elle **achèterait** une grande maison à la campagne. — *She'd buy a big house in the country.*

**Suggestion**: For listening comp. practice, ask sts. to indicate whether they hear verb in conditional or future. Ask them to imagine that conversation is with a travel agent. 1. *Pourriez-vous m'aider?* 2. *Nous serons à Québec au mois de juillet.* 3. *Mon ami Marc voudrait l'adresse d'une école de langues.* 4. *Monique préférerait visiter les musées.* 5. *Nous aurons tous envie de visiter la campagne.* 6. *Monique et Marc reviendront après un mois.* 7. *Mais moi, j'y passeral une semaine de plus si j'ai le temps.* Note: Passage can be used for partial or full dictation.

Verbs that have irregular stems in the future tense (Section 48) have the same irregular stems in the conditional.

S'il ne pleuvait pas, nous **irions** tous à la pêche. — *If it weren't raining, we would all go fishing.*

Elle **voudrait** venir avec nous. — *She would like to come with us.*

Est-ce que tu **aurais** le temps de m'aider à tout préparer? — *Would you have time to help me prepare everything?*

# B. Uses of the Conditional

1. As you learned in Chapter 9, the conditional is used to express wishes or requests. It lends a tone of deference or politeness that makes a request seem less abrupt. Compare these sentences.

| | |
|---|---|
| Je **veux** un billet. | *I want a ticket.* |
| Je **voudrais** un billet. | *I would like a ticket.* |
| **Pouvez**-vous m'indiquer ma place? | *Can you show me my seat?* |
| **Pourriez**-vous m'indiquer ma place? | *Could you show me my seat?* |

2. The conditional is used in the main clause of some sentences containing **si** (*if*) clauses. When the verb of an *if*-clause is in the imperfect, it expresses a condition, a conjecture, or a hypothetical situation. The conditional is used in the main clause to express what would happen if the hypothesis of the *if*-clause were true.

| | |
|---|---|
| Si j'**avais** le temps, je **jouerais** au tennis. | *If I had time, I would play tennis.* |
| Si nous **pouvions** pique-niquer tous les jours, nous **serions** contents. | *If we could go on a picnic every day, we would be happy.* |
| Elle **irait** avec vous au bord de la mer si elle **savait** nager. | *She would go to the seashore with you if she knew how to swim.* |

The **si** clause containing the condition is sometimes understood but not directly expressed.

| | |
|---|---|
| Je **viendrais** avec grand plaisir... (si tu m'invitais, si j'avais le temps, etc.). | *I would like to come . . .* (*if you invited me, if I had the time, etc.*). |

Remember that an *if*-clause in the present expresses a condition that, if fulfilled, will result in a certain action (stated in the future).

| | |
|---|---|
| Si j'**ai** le temps, je **jouerai** au tennis cet après-midi. | *If I have the time, I'll play tennis this afternoon.* |

Note that the future and the conditional are *never* used in the dependent clause (after **si**) of an *if*-clause sentence.

3. The present conditional of the verb **devoir** is used to give advice and corresponds to the English *should.*

| | |
|---|---|
| —J'aime bien les jeux de hasard. | *—I like games of chance.* |
| —Vous **devriez** aller à Monte Carlo. | *—You should go to Monte Carlo.* |
| —Elle a besoin d'exercice. | *—She needs some exercise.* |
| —Elle **devrait** faire du jogging. | *—She should go jogging.* |

## Mots-clés

*How to make requests and say thank you*: As you know, the conditional mode can be used to make requests politely. You might want to begin your request with a general question.

**Est-ce que je pourrais vous demander un petit service?** *May I ask you a favor?*

Don't forget to add **s'il vous plaît** (**s'il te plaît**) to the request and to say thank you.

**Merci, Monsieur.**
**Je ne sais pas comment vous remercier, Madame.**

Appropriate responses to **Merci**.

**Je vous en prie, Mademoiselle.** (*formal*)
**De rien.**
**Il n'y a pas de quoi.** (*more familiar*)

In polite conversation, the French use **Monsieur**, **Madame**, or **Mademoiselle** much more often than Americans use *ma'am* or *sir*.

### Vérifions!

**A. Préférences.** Qu'est-ce que ces amis voudraient faire ce soir?

1. je / vouloir / voir / pièce de théâtre
2. Robert / préférer / travailler / atelier
3. tu / choisir / d'assister à / match de boxe
4. nous / vouloir / parler / amis / café
5. Anne et Mireille / vouloir / nous / emmener (*to take*) / cinéma
6. vous / aimer / aller / piscine

**B. Après-midi de loisir.** Si vous pouviez choisir, laquelle de ces activités feriez-vous cet après-midi? Jouez la scène avec un(e) camarade.

MODÈLE: faire une promenade en ville ou à la campagne →
—Est-ce que tu ferais une promenade en ville ou à la campagne?
—Je ferais une promenade à la campagne.

1. jouer au tennis ou au squash 2. aller au cinéma ou au café 3. visiter un musée ou un parc 4. manger une pizza ou un sandwich 5. boire un café ou un Coca-Cola 6. parler anglais ou français 7. faire des courses ou la sieste 8. écouter de la musique classique ou du rock 9. acheter des vêtements ou des livres 10. lire des bandes dessinées ou un roman 11. rendre visite à un ami (une amie) ou à la famille 12. ?

## Parlons-en!

**A. Problèmes de loisir.** Donnez des conseils à un ami (une amie) qui a des difficultés à organiser son temps libre. Commencez par «À ta place, je ______.»

MODÈLE: VOTRE AMI(E): J'ai envie de danser!
VOUS: À ta place, j'irais dans une boîte de nuit (*nightclub*).

1. J'aime les sports. 2. J'aime les timbres rares. 3. J'ai envie de lire quelque chose d'intéressant. 4. J'aime fabriquer des meubles. 5. J'ai besoin de tranquillité. 6. J'admire les tableaux des impressionnistes français.

**Suggestion**: May be done in written form as in an advice column. Sts. can write their problem in brief paragraph to a campus newspaper advice columnist. Sts. then exchange problems with one another and write short answers, playing role of columnist. Sts. are encouraged to use conditional tenses as they give advice.

**B. De beaux rêves.** Imaginez ce que vous feriez dans les situations suivantes. Justifiez vos choix.

MODÈLE: si vous gagniez un voyage →
Si je gagnais un voyage, j'irais à Tahiti.

1. si vous receviez un chèque de 100 000 dollars
2. si vous deviez vivre dans une autre ville
3. si vous pouviez avoir la maison de vos rêves
4. si vous preniez de longues vacances
5. si vous veniez d'obtenir votre licence (*university degree*)

**C. L'été aux Arcs.** En France, beaucoup de stations de ski sont ouvertes l'été et offrent aux vacanciers de nombreux sports et loisirs. Voici ce qu'on peut faire aux Arcs, dans les Alpes.

**Suggestion**: Assign as homework for reading and writing practice. Ask sts. to decide whether they would like to vacation *aux Arcs*. (*Aimeriez-vous passer des vacances aux Arcs? Pourquoi ou pourquoi pas?*)

# Les Arcs, la station sports.

L'été aux Arcs, c'est la grande fête du sport. Golf, tennis, équitation, tir à l'arc, ski sur herbe, mountain-bike, rafting, canoë, delta-plane, alpinisme, escalade, randonnée, jogging, gymnastique, natation, arts martiaux... En tout, plus de 30 activités pour tous les goûts et tous les niveaux. Aux Arcs, on peut vraiment tout faire et toujours dans le cadre extraordinaire de l'un des plus beaux domaines de montagne d'Europe.

Mais aux Arcs, il n'y a pas que le sport et le soleil. Les Arcs, c'est autre chose. Aux Arcs, tout est conçu[a] pour rendre la vie plus agréable et plus riche, qu'il s'agisse de l'agencement des résidences,[b] du confort des appartements, des animations de la station ou de l'accueil des hôtels. Aux Arcs, les responsables forment une véritable équipe et travaillent tous en harmonie pour que chacun puisse vivre ses vacances comme il l'entend.[c] Aux Arcs, on est plus libre. Libre de vivre à 100 à l'heure ou de se faire simplement bronzer au soleil, libre de se dépenser[d] toute la journée ou de danser toutes les nuits, libre de s'éclater[e] entre copains ou de profiter de sa famille...

[a] *set up*
[b] qu'il... *whether it concerns the set-up of the condos*
[c] pour... *so that everybody can enjoy their vacation in their own way*
[d] se... *to wear oneself out*
[e] *to let one's hair down*

D'après cette brochure, si vous alliez aux Arcs cet été...:

1. Pourriez-vous faire du sport? Quel(s) sport(s) aimeriez-vous pratiquer?
2. Prendriez-vous beaucoup de photos? Pourquoi?
3. Auriez-vous le temps de prendre le soleil? de vous reposer?
4. Danseriez-vous tous les soirs?
5. Quelles autres activités aimeriez-vous faire?

# 52. EXPRESSING ACTIONS Prepositions After Verbs

**Sortie au cabaret**

CORINNE: Ce soir, nous avons **décidé de** t'emmener au cabaret de la Contrescarpe, à Montmartre.
CHUCK: Qu'est-ce que c'est qu'un cabaret?
JACQUES: Un cabaret, c'est une sorte de café où on **peut écouter** des chansons poétiques, ou satiriques...
CORINNE: Tu connais Georges Brassens, Jacques Brel, Barbara?
JACQUES: C'est grâce aux cabarets qu'ils **ont réussi à** percer.

1. Qu'est-ce que Corinne et Jacques ont décidé de faire?
2. Qu'est-ce qu'on peut faire dans un cabaret?
3. Qu'est-ce que Georges Brassens, Jacques Brel et Barbara ont réussi à faire grâce aux cabarets?

## A. Verbs Directly Followed by an Infinitive

Some verbs can be directly followed by an infinitive, without an intervening preposition. Among the most frequently used are the following.

| | | | |
|---|---|---|---|
| **aimer** | **détester** | **pouvoir** | **venir** |
| **aller** | **devoir** | **préférer** | **vouloir** |
| **désirer** | **espérer** | **savoir** | |

| | |
|---|---|
| Je **déteste chanter**. Mais je **sais** très bien **jouer** de la guitare. | *I hate singing but I can play the guitar very well.* |
| Sophie **ne peut pas aller** au ciné samedi soir. Elle **doit voir** sa grand-mère. | *Sophie cannot go to the movies on Saturday evening. She has to visit her grandmother.* |

## B. Verbs Followed by à Before an Infinitive

**Note**: Encourage sts. to memorize these verbs and prepositions. Inform them, however, of the difficulty of assimilating them all immediately.

Other verbs require the preposition **à** directly before the infinitive.

| | | | |
|---|---|---|---|
| **aider à** | **chercher à** | **continuer à** | **se mettre à** |
| **apprendre à** | **commencer à*** | **enseigner à** | |

J'**ai commencé à fumer** quand j'avais 16 ans. Caroline m'**a aidé à arrêter**. — *I started to smoke when I was 16. Caroline helped me quit.*

La semaine prochaine, je **me mets à faire** du tennis et je **continue à prendre** des cours de yoga deux fois par semaine. — *Next week I start playing tennis and I continue to take yoga classes twice a week.*

## C. Verbs Followed by de Before an Infinitive

Other verbs require the preposition **de** directly before the infinitive.

| | | | |
|---|---|---|---|
| **accepter de** | **décider de** | **finir de** | **rêver de** |
| **s'arrêter de** | **demander de** | **oublier de** | **venir de**† |
| **choisir de** | **empêcher de** | **permettre de** | |
| **conseiller de** | **essayer de** | **refuser de** | |

François **a décidé de prendre** des cours d'art dramatique. Il **rêve de devenir** acteur. Il **vient de jouer** un petit rôle dans *Le Cid* à l'université. L'année prochaine, il va **essayer d'entrer** au Conservatoire de Paris. — *François has decided to take drama classes. He dreams of becoming an actor. He just played a small role in* The Cid *at the university. Next year he is going to try to get into the Paris Conservatory.*

## D. *Penser* + Infinitive

When **penser** is followed by an infinitive, it means to count or plan on doing something.

Je **pense rester** chez moi ce week-end. — *I'm planning on staying home this weekend.*

---

***Commencer** is regularly followed by **à** plus an infinitive; **finir** is normally followed by **de** plus an infinitive. They can both be followed by **par**. **Commencer par** is used to talk about what you did first in a series of things; **finir par** means that you ended up by doing something.

Michel a **commencé par** jouer un petit rôle dans une comédie à l'université. Il a **fini par** devenir acteur à Hollywood.

†Note that the meaning of **venir** changes depending on whether it is directly followed by an infinitive or followed by **de** plus an infinitive. **Ils viennent dîner** means *They are coming to dinner.* **Ils viennent de dîner** means *They've just had dinner.*

## *Vérifions!*

**Au cabaret de la Contrescarpe.** Corinne, Chuck et Jacques arrivent à la Contrescarpe. Classez leurs activités par ordre chronologique.

**Suggestion**: Give sts. a minute to do the activity alone before eliciting responses. Correct order: 3, 2 (or 2, 3), 5, 1, 7, 4, 6

_____ Ils décident de commander du champagne.
_____ Ils se mettent à parler de poésie.
_____ Ils demandent au serveur de leur apporter l'addition.
_____ Ils choisissent de s'asseoir à une table près de la scène.
_____ Ils continuent à chanter en rentrant chez eux.
_____ Ils s'arrêtent de parler quand le spectacle commence.
_____ Ils n'oublient pas de laisser un pourboire au serveur.

## *Parlons-en!*

**A. Projets et activités.** Posez des questions à vos camarades pour vous informer de leurs projets et de leurs activités.

MODÈLE: aller / ce soir →
VOUS: Qu'est-ce que tu vas faire ce soir?
VOTRE CAMARADE: Je vais...

**Suggestion**: Solicit a variety of answers from several sts., or use in an interview format.

1. vouloir / ce week-end
2. aller / l'été prochain
3. devoir / demain
4. aimer / après les cours
5. penser / la semaine prochaine
6. détester / le soir
7. espérer / ce soir

**B. Résolutions de Nouvel An.** Racontez vos bonnes résolutions à vos camarades. Complétez les phrases suivantes avec un infinitif.

**Follow-up**: *Regardez de nouveau les résolutions que vous avez prises. Lesquelles allez-vous probablement réaliser?*

1. Cette année, je voudrais apprendre...
2. Je vais commencer...
3. J'ai aussi décidé...
4. Je vais essayer...
5. En plus, je vais m'arrêter...
6. Je vais chercher...
7. Enfin, je rêve...
8. Mais je refuse...

**C. Interview.** Posez les questions suivantes—en français, s'il vous plaît—à un(e) camarade de classe. Puis faites un résumé de ses réponses. Demandez à votre camarade...

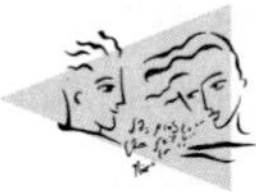

1. what he/she likes to do in the evening 2. what he/she hates to do in the house 3. if he/she is learning to do something interesting, and what it is 4. if he/she has decided to continue to study French 5. what he/she has to do after class 6. if he/she prefers going to a play or to a movie 7. if he/she has just read a good book, and what it was 8. what he/she knows how to do well 9. what he/she tries, but does not always succeed in doing well 10. if he/she forgot to do something this morning, and what it was 11. if he/she has stopped doing something recently, and what it was. 12. ?

**Suggestion**: Use corrected written *résumés* for dictation or listening practice.

# 53. MAKING COMPARISONS
## Adverbs and Nouns

### Le jazz

JENNIFER: Tu vas souvent en boîte le week-end?

BRUNO: Non, je vais **plus souvent** dans des bars de jazz **qu'**en boîte. Il n'y a pas **autant de** monde et j'aime **mieux** la musique.

JENNIFER: Moi aussi, j'adore le jazz. J'ai **plus de disques** de Duke Ellington **que de** Madonna. Mais le jazz, je l'écoute **le plus souvent** chez moi. Quand je vais en boîte, c'est pour danser et aussi parce qu'il y a **plus d'ambiance**.

Corrigez les phrases erronées.

1. Bruno va rarement dans des bars de jazz.
2. Il y a plus de gens dans les bars de jazz que dans les boîtes.
3. Jennifer a autant de disques de Madonna que de Duke Ellington.
4. Jennifer croit qu'il y a moins d'ambiance dans les bars de jazz.

## A. Comparative Forms of Adverbs

**Note**: This would be a good time to review formation of comparative and superlative of adjectives.

The same constructions you learned in Chapter 13 for the comparative forms of adjectives are used for the comparative forms of adverbs.

Soyez au meilleur de votre forme grâce à la Classe Affaires Canadien. Profitez d'un environnement reposant et confortable pour répéter ce texte, faire ces derniers ajustements ou tout simplement relaxer. On s'occupe du reste... La cabine Classe Affaires Canadien est agréable,

nos fauteuils sont des plus confortables et une attention toute particulière est portée aux repas.

Offerte vers 37 destinations canadiennes et internationales, la Classe Affaires Canadien va plus loin parce que, selon nous, tout voyage d'affaires doit avoir ses bons côtés.

Canadien *va plus loin*

1. **plus... que** (*more . . . than*)

Jeannine écoute les disques de Madonna **plus** volontiers (**que** moi). — *Jeannine listens to Madonna's records more willingly (than I).*

2. **moins... que** (*less . . . than*)

On écoute la musique **moins** attentivement dans les discos **que** dans les bars de jazz. — *People listen to the music less attentively at discos than at jazz bars.*

3. **aussi... que** (*as . . . as*)

Nous allons danser **aussi** souvent **que** possible. — *We go dancing as often as possible.*

## B. Superlative Forms of Adverbs

To form the superlative of an adverb, place **le** in front of the comparative form (**le plus...** or **le moins...** ). Since there is no direct comparison, **que** is not used.

Pierre s'en va tard. Louis s'en va plus tard. Michel s'en va **le plus tard**.

## C. The Comparative and Superlative Forms of *bien* and *mal*

Note the irregular comparative and superlative forms of **bien**. The comparative and superlative forms of **mal** are regular.*

**Note**: Review irregular forms for comparative and superlative of *bon* and *mauvais*, presented in Chapter 13.

| | COMPARATIVE | SUPERLATIVE |
|---|---|---|
| bien | mieux | le mieux |
| mal | plus mal | le plus mal |

*Irregular comparative and superlative forms of **mal** (**pis**, **le pis**) exist, but the regular forms are much more commonly used.

| | |
|---|---|
| Tu parles français **mieux** que moi. | *You speak French better than I.* |
| Mais c'est Jean-Claude qui le parle **le mieux**. | *But Jean-Claude speaks it best.* |
| Mais c'est moi qui étudie **le plus**! | *But I'm the one who studies the most!* |
| Roland joue **plus mal** au tennis que moi. | *Roland plays tennis worse than I.* |
| Mais c'est Marc qui y joue **le plus mal**. | *But Marc plays the worst.* |

## D. Comparisons with Nouns

**Presentation**: Magazine pictures or drawings that can be easily compared are useful in presenting these notions. Use names of famous people to further engage sts.' interest. Examples: *Les Getty ont plus d'argent que nous. J'ai moins de problèmes que le président des États-Unis.*

**Plus de...** (**que**), **moins de...** (**que**), and **autant de...** (**que**) express quantitative comparisons with nouns.

| | |
|---|---|
| Ils ont **plus d'**argent (**que** nous), mais nous avons **moins de** problèmes (**qu'**eux). | *They have more money* (*than we*), *but we have fewer problems* (*than they*). |
| Je suis **autant de** cours **que** toi ce semestre. | *I'm taking as many courses as you this semester.* |

### Vérifions!

**A. Les comparaisons.** Avec l'aide des signes, comparez ces personnes célèbres en utilisant des phrases complètes. Mettez les verbes au présent.

signes: + *more* = *as*
− *less*

1. Gene Siskel / aller au cinéma / = souvent / Roger Ebert
2. Mick Jagger / chanter / + mal / Paul McCartney
3. Jean-Michel Larqué* / jouer / + bien / au football / Jim Courier
4. Luciano Pavarotti / chanter / = bien / Placido Domingo
5. Ben Johnson / courir / − vite / Carl Lewis
6. Richard Dacoury† / jouer / − bien / au basket-ball / Charles Barkley

**B. Rivalités.** Voici deux familles, les Bayard et les Pascal. Comparez-les et imaginez leur vie d'après le dessin. Utilisez **plus de**, **moins de** et **autant de**.

**Suggestion**: Ask sts. to write out responses either in class or for homework. Have several sts. put sentences on board for correction, or have sts. check their work from a transparency.

MODÈLE: Les Bayard ont plus de maisons que les Pascal.

---

*Jean-Michel Larqué a été un célèbre footballeur français.
†Richard Dacoury joue au basket-ball en France.

les Pascal les Bayard

**Mots utiles:** argent, maisons, voitures, domestiques (*servant*), vêtements, enfants, problèmes, moments heureux, dépenses, scènes de ménage (*domestic arguments*), vacances, temps libre...

## Parlons-en!

**A. Les Français et le sport.** Regardez le tableau et faites au moins trois comparaisons entre les hommes et les femmes en ce qui concerne le sport.

MODÈLE: Les hommes font moins de natation que les femmes, mais ils font plus de ski que les femmes.

**Suggestion**: Ask sts. to write out 3 or more comparisons first before soliciting oral responses.

Ensuite, faites des comparaisons entre les hommes et les femmes en ce qui concerne le sport aux États-Unis.

Aux États-Unis, les femmes font-elles autant de sport que les hommes?
Aux États-Unis, quels sports les hommes font-ils plus que les femmes?

**Le ski d'abord**

Taux de pratique sportive pendant l'année écoulée (1988, en % de la population totale) :

| | Hommes | Femmes | Total |
|---|---|---|---|
| • Ski | 18,7 | 14,5 | 16,5 |
| • Gymnastique | 11,5 | 18,5 | 15,1 |
| • Cyclisme | 16,6 | 1,3 | 13,8 |
| • Natation | 12,2 | 13,7 | 13,0 |
| • Marche | 11,3 | 10,1 | 10,7 |
| • Gymnastique d'entretien | 6,3 | 11,4 | 8,9 |
| • Tennis | 11,2 | 5,6 | 8,3 |
| • Sports d'équipe | 10,9 | 1,8 | 6,2 |
| • Course à pied | 7,3 | 2,5 | 4,8 |
| • Football | 7,5 | 0,3 | 3,7 |
| • Ping-pong | 5,1 | 1,4 | 3,1 |
| • Musculation | 3,5 | 1,7 | 2,6 |
| • Planche à voile | 2,5 | 1,1 | 1,8 |
| • Sports de combat | 2,1 | 0,5 | 1,3 |
| **Total** | **53,4** | **42,5** | **47,7** |

**B. Habitudes** (*Habits*). Demandez à un(e) camarade combien de fois par semaine, par jour, par mois ou par an il/elle fait quelque chose, et puis comparez sa réponse avec vos propres habitudes.

**Autres possibilités:** lire le journal, faire du sport, regarder la télévision, partir en voyage...

MODÈLE:
VOUS: Combien de fois par semaine vas-tu au cinéma?
UN(E) CAMARADE: Une ou deux fois par semaine.
VOUS: J'y vais plus (moins, aussi) souvent que toi.

**Suggestions**: *prendre le bus / par semaine; faire du jogging / par semaine; aller au laboratoire de langues / par mois; téléphoner à ses parents / par mois; sortir avec des amis / par semaine; regarder la télévision / par semaine; écrire à ses parents / par mois; se regarder dans un miroir / par jour; se brosser les dents / par jour; se laver les cheveux / par semaine.*

# Nouvelles francophones

## Les Loisirs au Togo

La république du Togo est un petit état de l'Afrique occidentale situé entre le Ghana et le Bénin et bordé au sud par l'océan Atlantique. Le Togo est une ancienne° colonie française. Sa langue et sa culture ont été profondément influencées par la présence coloniale. Cependant, ce pays retient de nombreux aspects d'une société traditionnelle africaine.

*former*

Par exemple, les loisirs en général sont encore le domaine des hommes. Au Togo, comme dans la plupart des pays africains, les femmes restent au foyer en compagnie d'autres femmes de leur famille ou de leur village. Elles s'adonnent° à la broderie° des tapis, à la poterie, et parfois au tissage des pagnes° traditionnels appelés *kentés*.

*dedicate themselves / embroidery*
tissage... *weaving of loincloths*

Chez les hommes, le contact avec la culture occidentale et l'influence de l'héritage français ont contribué à la transformation des loisirs. En effet, beaucoup d'hommes passent leur temps libre à jouer ou à regarder des matchs de football. C'est sans doute le sport le plus populaire du pays. On l'appelle «la fièvre du dimanche soir». On en discute pendant des heures sous l'arbre du village ainsi qu'au restaurant dans les grandes villes.

Plus récemment, les amateurs de sensations fortes ont trouvé un nouveau passe-temps: le moto-cross. Les hommes peuvent passer toute une journée à regarder les champions du monde faire des acrobaties sur le circuit dangereux de Lomé, la capitale du Togo.

À Lomé, ainsi que dans les autres grandes villes, il y a maintenant des boîtes de nuit° où les hommes, comme les femmes, s'amusent et dansent au rythme d'une sorte de «world beat» local. Le disco, le rock et la congolaise sont populaires tandis que° les danses traditionnelles comme le Foyissi, le Simpa et l'Akpressé sont encore pratiquées dans les villages.

boîtes... *night clubs*
tandis... *while*

# Mise au point

**A. Le rêve: une vie sans travail.** Isabelle et Alain rêvent de s'arrêter de travailler. Isabelle nous raconte les activités qu'elle aimerait faire. Faites des phrases complètes en utilisant l'imparfait ou le conditionnel.

1. si / on / s'arrêter / travailler / on / pouvoir / dormir / toute la journée
2. on / apprendre / parler / allemand / espagnol
3. on / se mettre / voyager / autour / monde
4. je / essayer* / faire / peinture
5. et toi / tu / commencer / écrire / roman
6. nous / aider / mon père / finir / sa maison
7. et nous / continuer / bricoler / dans notre maison
8. on / prendre / enfin / temps de vivre

**B. Nommez trois choses...** Donnez par écrit votre réaction spontanée aux questions suivantes. Écrivez des phrases complètes. Puis, comparez vos réponses avec celles d'un(e) camarade de classe. Lesquelles sont identiques?

1. Nommez trois choses que vous feriez si vous étiez riche. 2. Donnez trois raisons pour lesquelles vous vous battriez (*you would fight*) si c'était nécessaire. 3. Nommez trois instruments de musique dont vous aimeriez jouer. 4. Nommez trois sports que vous aimeriez bien pratiquer. 5. Nommez trois personnes qui vous font souvent rire. 6. Nommez trois chanteurs (ou chanteuses) que vous admirez. 7. Nommez trois choses que vous feriez ce week-end si vous en aviez le temps.

**Suggestion**: Do as quickly as possible so that sts. name first 3 things that come to mind. Ask them to think of other categories to name in threes.

**C. Interview.** Posez les questions suivantes en français à un(e) camarade. Ensuite, résumez ses réponses.

1. Who in class has more leisure time than you? Why? 2. What sport would you like to be able to play better? 3. Which American plays tennis best? 4. What athlete (**athlète**, *m. et f.*) would you like to speak to the most? 5. Who in the class runs faster than you? How do you know? 6. Who in the class goes to the library as often as you? 7. Who in the class needs to study the least in order to (**pour**) have good grades (**notes**, *f.*)?

**Suggestion**: Type up correct form of these questions on 2 halves of a sheet, 3 or 4 questions on each half. Assign one st. in a group of 3 to ask first set of questions, one to ask the second set, and the third to act as group monitor, checking form of questions asked by 2 classmates. When a st. asks a question, the other should answer, as in an interview. The monitor can take notes on answers, if desired.

## Interactions

In this chapter, you practiced getting information, comparing and contrasting, and expressing wishes, requests, and conditions. Using the chapter vocabulary and structures, act out the following situations.

*See Appendix D for a conjugation of the verb **essayer**.

1. **Des conseils.** One of your acquaintances (your partner) needs to work harder in school. Compare your life with his/hers. You think that he/she has too many distractions. Find out more thoroughly what he/she does and with whom. Express your wishes and give advice on what to give up and how to get down to work.
2. **Un ancien ami (Une ancienne amie).** You run into an old friend (your partner) whom you have not seen for a few years. Stop and chat. Find out how your friend is getting along. Ask how his/her life has changed, whom he/she has seen lately, what his/her leisure activities are, what work he/she does. He/She will get the same information from you.

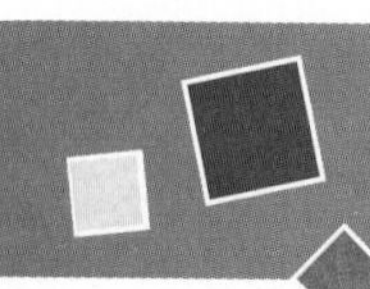

# Rencontres

## LECTURE

### *Avant de lire*

**What is it really about? Reading critically.** Newspapers and magazines use headlines to attract the readers' attention, but sometimes they are misleading: articles do not always "deliver" what the headlines promise. In the following article from the *Journal Français d'Amèrique*, note the headline and the photo. What does the article seem to be about? Then read the article. Does it meet your expectations? If you were the author, what title would you give it? What would you add or replace? Compare your responses to those of your classmates.

## *INDOCHINE*, Oscar du meilleur film étranger

Catherine Deneuve

Pour la première fois depuis 1978, la France obtient l'Oscar du meilleur film étranger.[a] *Indochine*, le film de Régis Wargnier, a en effet été primé[b] lors de[c] la grande soirée des Oscars d'Hollywood. Des millions de téléspectateurs ont pu ainsi voir Catherine Deneuve, superbe dans sa robe noire et rose Yves Saint-Laurent, recevoir la statuette dorée. Le film est une chronique de sang[d] et d'amour se déroulant[e] dans les années 1930, quand le colonialisme français touchait à sa fin.

La France a également obtenu l'Oscar du meilleur court métrage[f] pour *Omnibus*, de Sam Karmann; l'Oscar de la meilleure photographie revient à[g] Philippe Rousselot dans *A River Runs Through It*.

Rappelons qu'en 1990 *Cyrano de Bergerac* avait obtenu l'Oscar du meilleur costume, mais il faut remonter jusqu'en 1978 pour trouver un Oscar du meilleur film étranger remis[h] à la France. C'était pour le film *Sortez vos mouchoirs*[i] de Bertrand Blier, avec Gérard Depardieu, Patrick Dewaere et Carol Laure. Cette époque était sans doute heureuse car l'année précédente la France avait aussi obtenu cet Oscar, pour *Madame Rosa*, avec l'inoubliable Simone Signoret.

*Indochine*, qui a dépassé[j] les 600.000 entrées à Paris, avait obtenu en janvier le Golden Globe du meilleur film étranger et en mars cinq Césars, l'équivalent français des Oscars, dont celui de la meilleure actrice pour Catherine Deneuve.

[a] *foreign*
[b] *a... in fact received the prize*
[c] *lors... on the occasion*
[d] *blood*
[e] se... se passant
[f] court... *short film*
[g] revient... *goes to*
[h] donné
[i] Sortez... *Get out your handkerchiefs*
[j] *exceeded*

## Compréhension

1. Avant *Indochine*, quand la France a-t-elle obtenu son dernier Oscar du meilleur film étranger? Pour quel film?
2. Décrivez Catherine Deneuve le soir de la présentation des Oscars.
3. Donnez une brève description du film *Indochine*.
4. Quels autres Oscars les Français ont-ils reçus pour les films de 1992?
5. Le film *Indochine* a-t-il été un succès en France aussi? Comment le savez-vous?
6. Est-ce que vous auriez envie de voir ce film? Pourquoi ou pourquoi pas?
7. Aimez-vous les films étrangers? Pourquoi ou pourquoi pas?

# PAR ÉCRIT

**Function:** Writing a film review
**Audience:** Newspaper readers
**Goal:** To describe and evaluate a recent film in such a way that readers will be influenced to see it (or skip it).

**Steps**

1. Think about a film you have seen in the last few months. Jot down the important scenes you remember, some of the main aspects of the story, and your overall reaction to the work.
2. Consider the following expressions. (You can find other useful vocabulary terms in **À propos** and in the **Intermède** section of this chapter.)

   le metteur en scène / le cinéaste (*director*)
   tourner un film (*to make a film*)
   les personnages (*m.*) (*characters*)
   jouer le rôle principal
   la séquence (*scene*)
   l'action se déroule (*takes place*)

   l'intrigue (*f.*) (*plot*)
   vraisemblable (*believable, realistic*)
   invraisemblable (*unbelievable, unrealistic*)

3. Without telling the whole story, write a brief summary. Mention when and where the action takes place. Discuss the featured actor(s) or actress(es) and describe the main character(s). Give your subjective reaction to the film. End by persuading your readers to see (or not to see) the film.
4. Have a classmate read through the rough draft to see if your review is clear, interesting, and persuasive. Make any necessary changes.

5. Reread the composition, checking for spelling, punctuation, and grammar errors. Focus especially on your use of comparisons, verbs and prepositions, and questions.
6. Be prepared to have the instructor share your review with the class.

## À L'ÉCOUTE!

**À l'écoute!** See scripts for listening passages and follow-up activities recorded on st. cassette. Remind sts. that in the listening comprehension passages (as in real life) they will not understand every word they hear. They should focus globally on the general information in the passages and not be overly concerned about what they do not understand.

**Le Tour de France.** Vous allez entendre une retransmission à la radio de cette manifestation sportive. Lisez les activités avant d'écouter le vocabulaire et la retransmission qui leur correspond.

VOCABULAIRE UTILE
cette douzième étape *this twelfth lap* (*race*)
les coureurs *runners, racers*
se rapprochent *are getting closer*
le maillot jaune *yellow jersey* (*worn by current leader of the* **Tour**)

**A.** Encerclez la bonne réponse.

1. Cette étape du Tour de France se situe
   a. dans les Pyrénées   b. dans les Alpes   c. dans les Vosges
2. Le temps est
   a. gris   b. mauvais   c. beau
3. Pour voir les coureurs il y a
   a. beaucoup de gens   b. peu de gens
4. Alain Laville porte le numéro
   a. 62   b. 52   c. 42
5. Alain Laville est né
   a. à Paris   b. à Annecy   c. à Chamonix
6. Le coureur qui a gagné cette étape du Tour s'appelle
   a. Gilbert Monier   b. Alain Laville   c. Steve Johnson
7. Demain le Tour aura lieu
   a. à Annecy   b. à Chamonix   c. à Paris

**B.** Remplissez les tableaux en vous basant sur la retransmission.

1. De quelles nationalités sont les coureurs qui ont gagné la 12ème étape à Chamonix?

| CLASSEMENT DE L'ÉTAPE | | |
|---|---|---|
| | *n°* | *nationalité* |
| *1er* | 52 | Il est... français |
| *2ème* | 75 | |
| *3ème* | 142 | |

**2.** De quelles nationalité sont les coureurs qui sont les leaders du Tour en général?*

| CLASSEMENT DU TOUR | |
|---|---|
| | *nationalité* |
| *1*er<br>*2*ème<br>*3*ème | Il est... français |

# Vocabulaire

## Verbes

**accepter** (**de**) to accept
**assister à** to attend
**bricoler** to putter
**chercher à** to try to
**commencer par** begin by (doing something)
**conseiller** (**à, de**) to advise
**courir** to run
**décider** (**de**) to decide
**désirer** to desire, want
**emmener** to take (someone)
**empêcher** (**de**) to prevent (from)
**enseigner** (**à**) to teach
**espérer** to hope
**finir par** to end, finish by (doing something)
**indiquer** to show, point out
**se passer** to happen, take place
**penser** (+ *infinitive*) to plan on (doing something)
**permettre** (**de**) to permit, allow
**refuser** (**de**) to refuse
**remercier** to thank
**rire** to laugh

À REVOIR: **aider**; **faire du sport**; **gagner**; **jouer à**; **jouer de**; **perdre**

## Substantifs

**les activités de plein air** (*f.*) outdoor activities
**le bricolage** do-it-yourself work, puttering around
**la chanson de variété** popular song
**la collection** collection
**le cyclisme** cycling
**l'équipe** (*f.*) team
**le jardinage** gardening
**les jeux de hasard** (*m.*) games of chance
**les jeux de société** (*m.*) social games, group games
**la lecture** reading
**les loisirs** (*m.*) leisure activities
**la manifestation sportive** sporting event
**la marche** walking
**le passe-temps** hobby
**la pêche** fishing
**la pétanque** bocce ball, lawn bowling
**le pique-nique** picnic
**le service** favor
**le spectacle** show, performance

À REVOIR: **la chanson**; **le concert**

## Expressions interrogatives

**qui est-ce que**, **qu'est-ce qui**, **lequel**, **laquelle**, **lesquels**, **lesquelles**

## Mots et expressions divers

**autant** (**de**)**... que** as much (many) . . . as
**bien**, **mieux**, **le mieux** well, better, best
**demander un petit service** to ask a small favor
**être en train de** to be in the process of; to be in the middle of
**Je ne sais pas comment vous** (**te**) **remercier.** I don't know how to thank you.
**Je vous en prie. / Il n'y a pas de quoi. / De rien.** You're welcome.
**Qu'est-ce qui se passe?** What's happening? What's going on?

*Position in the **Tour** is calculated by adding up each racer's time in all **étapes** completed.

# Intermède

## SITUATION

### Séance de cinéma

**Situation**: The *Situation* dialogues are recorded on the st. cassette packaged with the st. text.

**Contexte** *Maureen, une Américaine, travaille au pair dans une famille française à Toulouse. Aujourd'hui elle va au cinéma avec une amie française, Gisèle.*

**Suggestion**: Have sts. read roles of *Maureen* and *Gisèle*. Then have sts. reread the roles in pairs before doing the *Jeu de roles*.

**Objectif** *Gisèle explique certaines différences culturelles.*

GISÈLE: Bonjour, je voudrais deux billets pour la séance° de deux heures, s'il vous plaît. Tiens, Maureen, tu peux donner les tickets à l'ouvreuse°?

MAUREEN: Oui, mais qu'est-ce que tu fais?

GISÈLE: Je cherche un peu de monnaie pour lui donner un pourboire.

MAUREEN: Ah, d'accord... C'est curieux, il n'y a pas de queue.°

GISÈLE: Oui, ici les cinémas ouvrent un peu avant la séance et on attend dans la salle.

MAUREEN: Et il n'y a rien à boire ou à manger?

GISÈLE: Si, une ouvreuse va passer pendant l'entracte.°

(*Maureen et Gisèle regardent l'annonce d'un film de Stephen Frears,* Les Liaisons dangereuses, *un vidéoclip° de Prince comme court métrage° et les publicités. Puis, c'est l'entracte.*)

MAUREEN: J'aimerais bien grignoter° quelque chose. Il y a du popcorn?

GISÈLE: Pas de popcorn, désolée°! Appelle l'ouvreuse!

MAUREEN: Écoute, Gisèle, c'est vraiment trop drôle.

GISÈLE: Qu'est-ce qui est drôle?

MAUREEN: C'est d'entendre Glenn Close parler français, avec cette drôle de voix.°

GISÈLE: C'est vrai, j'ai oublié. Les films étrangers sont généralement doublés° ici. Ça surprend°!

*séance: show*
*ouvreuse: usherette*
*queue: line*
*entracte: intermission*
*vidéoclip: music video*
*court métrage: film*
*grignoter... nibble, have a snack*
*désolée: sorry*
*voix: voice*
*doublés: dubbed*
*surprend: surprises (people)*

**Note**: Vocab. for expressing one's opinions about a film is given in the *À propos* section.

## À propos

### Comment critiquer un film

POUR EXPRIMER UNE OPINION FAVORABLE

Quel chef d'œuvre!
Je l'ai trouvé extraordinaire.
C'est un film remarquable.
Il est formidable.
Il est super.

POUR EXPRIMER UNE OPINION DÉFAVORABLE

Je ne le recommande à personne.
C'est un film vraiment minable (*shabby*)
Quel désastre!
Quel navet (*flop*)!

## *Maintenant à vous!*

**A. Questions personnelles.** Relisez le dialogue, puis répondez aux questions.

1. Aimez-vous aller au cinéma ou préférez-vous regarder des films à la maison? Quel genre de film aimez-vous le mieux? Quelle sorte de film refusez-vous de voir? Pourquoi?
2. Regardez-vous de temps en temps un film étranger—français, espagnol ou japonais, par exemple? En général, préférez-vous les films doublés ou en version originale, avec sous-titres? Pouvez-vous recommander un film étranger à vos camarades de classe?
3. Dans le dialogue, Gisèle explique des différences culturelles à Maureen. Racontez à un ami français (une amie française) ce qu'on fait d'habitude en entrant dans un spectacle typiquement américain, par exemple un match de base-ball ou de football, un «county fair» ou autre.

**B. Jeu de rôles.** Les expressions de l'*À propos* vous seront utiles dans les activités suivantes.

1. En groupes de trois ou quatre, créez des scènes où des amis sortent du cinéma en parlant (*while speaking*) du film qu'ils viennent de voir. Ils ne font pas mention du titre. Les autres étudiants essaient de deviner quel est le film en question.

   **Suggestions:** *Le Magicien d'Oz, Autant en emporte le vent, Terminator, Parfum de femme, Impardonnable, Le Garde du corps...*
2. Chaque membre de la classe nomme le dernier film qu'il/elle a vu et explique aux autres pourquoi ils devraient ou ne devraient pas aller le voir.
3. Chaque membre de la classe nomme son film, son acteur/actrice ou son cinéaste favori et explique brièvement pourquoi.

### *Marie-José Pérec (1968–)*

Barcelone 1992: Marie-José Pérec devient championne olympique du 400 mètres. Les Français l'appellent «la gazelle», mais elle ne veut pas consacrer° toute sa vie à l'athlétisme. Née à la Guadeloupe, arrivée à Paris à 16 ans, elle veut croquer la vie à pleines dents.° Elle mange chaque jour ses deux tablettes° de chocolat, se transforme en mannequin° pour Paco Rabanne* et fait les vitrines° des grands boulevards parisiens. À la fois° timide, impatiente, insouciante° et insolente, Marie-José Pérec attire l'attention des Français et du monde.

*to dedicate*
*croquer... to experience life to the fullest / bars (of candy)*
*model*
*fait... goes window shopping / À... At the same time, Simultaneously*
*carefree*

*A successful French designer especially noted for the line of men's colognes and accessories that bears his name.

CHAPITRE **SEIZE**

# Opinions et points de vue

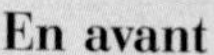

**En avant**

—À mon avis, il faut que le gouvernement prenne des mesures sévères contre les sociétés qui polluent l'environnement.

—Oui, mais ce n'est pas toujours facile.

—Tu sais, la pluie acide détruit nos forêts et les déchets industriels empoisonnent nos rivières. On finira par détruire la vie sur notre planète!

**Communicative goals:** talking about environmental and social problems, expressing attitudes, wishes, necessity, possibility, and emotion.

**En avant**: See scripts for follow-up questions recorded on student cassette.

# Étude de vocabulaire

## Les problèmes de l'environnement

[a]*wasting*
[b]*waste, refuse*

**Additional vocabulary**: *la marée noire, protéger les forêts, la déforestation tropicale, une explosion, une centrale nucléaire, une catastrophe nucléaire, une fuite de gaz, les pluies acides, la surpopulation, un nuage de gaz toxique, la disparition des espèces, les émissions de carbone, la couche d'ozone, des rayons ultraviolets, l'effet de serre, menacer la santé*

**Presentation**: (1) Have sts. repeat sentences. Ask them to find cognates and words of the same family. (2) Ask sts. to describe drawings using vocab. given. Encourage use of complete sentences. Have sts. write their descriptions first, then have a few of them presented to class.

**A. Association de mots.** Quels problèmes écologiques associez-vous avec les verbes suivants?

MODÈLE: gaspiller → le gaspillage des sources d'énergie

1. conserver 2. protéger 3. polluer 4. recycler 5. développer

**Suggestion**: Solicit from several sts. a variety of associations for each verb.

**B. Remèdes.** Expliquez quelles sont les actions nécessaires pour sauver (*to save*) notre planète. Utilisez **Il faut** ou **Il ne faut pas** suivi d'un infinitif.

MODÈLES: le contrôle des déchets industriels →
Il faut contrôler les déchets industriels.
le gaspillage de l'énergie →
Il ne faut pas gaspiller l'énergie.

1. la pollution de l'environnement
2. la protection de la nature
3. le développement de l'énergie solaire
4. la conservation des sources d'énergie
5. le gaspillage des ressources naturelles
6. le développement des transports en commun

## Les problèmes de la société moderne

### Le palmarès[a] de vos peurs en 1992*

| | | |
|---|---|---|
| 1 | Le chômage[b] | 79 |
| 2 | Les problèmes de la jeunesse[c] | 76 |
| 3 | Les catastrophes écologiques | 75 |
| 4 | La diminution[d] du montant des retraites[e] | 73 |
| 5 | La diminution des remboursements-maladie | 71 |
| 6 | Le cancer | 70 |
| 7 | La récession économique | 70 |
| 8 | La drogue | 69 |
| 9 | L'insécurité | 68 |
| 10 | Les troubles liés à l'immigration | 68 |
| 11 | L'augmentation[f] des impôts[g] | 67 |
| 12 | Les risques de guerre dans le monde | 66 |
| 13 | L'évolution de la situation dans l'ex-URSS | 64 |
| 14 | L'évolution de la situation en Algérie | 64 |
| 15 | Le SIDA[h] | 63 |
| 16 | Le développement de l'Islam en France | 63 |
| 17 | Les centrales nucléaires | 61 |
| 18 | La montée du Front National[i] | 60 |
| 19 | L'évolution de la situation en Yougoslavie | 59 |
| 20 | La baisse de vos revenus | 58 |
| 21 | La concurrence[j] économique du Japon | 52 |
| 22 | Les risques de guerre en Europe | 48 |
| 23 | La concurrence économique de l'Allemagne | 44 |
| 24 | La domination de l'Allemagne sur l'Europe | 41 |
| 25 | Le Marché unique européen | 32 |

*ont très peur ou assez peur

[a] *list*
[b] *unemployment*
[c] *youth, young people*
[d] *decrease*
[e] *montant... retirement benefits*
[f] *increase*
[g] *taxes*
[h] *AIDS*
[i] *right-wing anti-immigrant political party*
[j] *competition*

***Autres mots utiles:***

**le parti** political party
**la politique** politics; policy
**le politicien/la politicienne** politician
**élire** to elect
**s'engager (vers)** to get involved (in) (*a public issue, cause*)
**exiger** to necessitate, demand
**exprimer une opinion** to express an opinion
**faire grève** to strike
**manifester (pour/contre)** to demonstrate (*for/against*)
**soutenir** to support

**A. L'actualité.** Regardez au-dessus les résultats d'une enquête faite par *Le Figaro Magazine*. Lisez-les, puis répondez aux questions suivantes.

- Lesquels de ces thèmes sont évoqués (*brought up*) aux États-Unis?

**Suggestion**: Ask sts. to write notes on the topics in the list above. Ask them to read them to others in small groups. Sts. give short analysis of each others' political attitudes. Example: *Mark est assez conservateur. Il est contre l'ouverture des frontières aux immigrants. Il veut un budget militaire plus important.*

- Parmi ceux-là, lequel considérez-vous comme le plus important? le moins important? Comparez vos conclusions avec celles de vos camarades.
- Selon vous, que peut-on faire pour résoudre ces problèmes?
- Quels autres thèmes ajouteriez-vous à ce sondage? Choisissez deux thèmes qui vous intéressent particulièrement et commentez-les en commençant par **Il faut**.

## Mots-clés

*How to carry on a discussion*

To express a personal point of view:

| | |
|---|---|
| **Moi,...** | **Je pense que...** |
| **À mon avis,...** | **Je crois que...** |
| **Personnellement,...** | **J'estime que...** |
| **Pour ma part,...** | **Je trouve que...** |

Your point will often seem more convincing if you give examples or refer to other people's opinions. You can use the following expressions:

**Par exemple,...**
**On dit que...**
**J'ai entendu dire que...**

**B. À mon avis.** Choisissez une des expressions ci-dessus pour exprimer votre point de vue.

**Suggestion**: Assign for homework so sts. have time to prepare their thoughts.

MODÈLE: possible / contrôler le problème des déchets nucléaires →
À mon avis (Personnellement, Pour ma part), je crois (j'estime, je trouve) qu'il est (qu'il n'est pas) possible de contrôler le problème des déchets nucléaires, parce que...

1. essentiel / développer de nouvelles sources d'énergie
2. impossible / empêcher les accidents nucléaires
3. important / respecter la femme dans les publicités
4. indispensable / faire attention aux problèmes de la jeunesse
5. inutile / limiter l'immigration
6. essentiel / augmenter les impôts
7. dangereux / arrêter le développement des armes nucléaires

**C. Réagissez!** Donnez votre opinion personnelle sur les idées suivantes.

**Suggestion**: Have sts. use personal expressions from *Mots-clés* here.

1. protéger les personnes âgées contre la maladie 2. conserver les ressources naturelles d'un pays 3. combattre le racisme 4. réduire (*reduce*) le budget militaire 5. éliminer la faim dans le monde 6. soutenir les chômeurs (*unemployed*) 7. voter aux élections 8. dire «non» à la drogue

# Nouvelles francophones

## Immigration: la France divisée

Depuis quelques années, le problème de l'immigration est devenu un sujet brûlant° partout en Europe. En Allemagne le problème concerne surtout les Turcs, en Grande-Bretagne il concerne surtout les Jamaïcains, les Pakistanais et les Indiens, en France il concerne surtout les Maghrébins. Une conséquence de ce problème est la montée inquiétante° des partis politiques d'extrême-droite aux propos racistes.

*burning*
montée... *troubling rise*

Le Maghreb regroupe les pays de l'Afrique du Nord: l'Algérie, le Maroc et la Tunisie. Beaucoup de Maghrébins sont venus en France au début des années 70 quand la France avait besoin d'une main-d'œuvre° peu coûteuse° pour occuper des postes que les Français ne voulaient plus occuper. Plus tard ils ont fait venir leur famille en France et ils ont eu des enfants. Ces enfants sont français—ils parlent français, ils vont dans les écoles françaises—mais ils sont souvent perçus° comme des Arabes. Aujourd'hui il y a environ 1,5 million de Maghrébins en France plus 1,5 million de Français d'origine maghrébine (un total de 7% de la population française).

*labor force* / peu... *cheap*
*perceived*

Les Français sont très divisés sur la question de l'immigration. Il y en a qui souhaitent que la France ferme ses frontières pour empêcher l'arrivée de nouveaux immigrants. Une petite minorité veut que les immigrés retournent dans leur pays d'origine. Pourquoi existe-t-il de telles réactions en France, connue pour être le pays des droits de l'homme? Peur du chômage, de l'insécurité des villes et des banlieues, de la perte d'une certaine identité culturelle? Sans doute. Mais il y a aussi un grand nombre de Français qui soutiennent une politique de l'immigration qui garantit aux immigrants un respect de leur dignité et de leurs droits° humains.

*rights*

# Étude de grammaire

## 54. EXPRESSING ATTITUDES
## Regular Subjunctive Verbs

**Follow-up**: Ask sts. to play roles in groups of 3, substituting other groups for *le Conseil de l'université*.

### Votez pour Françoise!

FRANÇOISE: Alors, vous voulez que je **pose** ma candidature au Conseil de l'université!

SIMON: Oui, nous souhaitons que le Conseil **sorte** de son inertie et que ses délégués **prennent** conscience de leurs responsabilités politiques.

FRANÇOISE: Mais je me suis déjà présentée sans succès l'an dernier.

LUC: Cette année, Françoise, nous voulons que tu **réussisses**. Et nous te soutiendrons jusqu'au bout.

Retrouvez la phrase équivalente dans le dialogue.

1. Est-ce que je dois poser ma candidature au Conseil de l'université?
2. Nous espérons que le Conseil sortira de son inertie.
3. Nous espérons que ses délégués prendront conscience de leurs responsabilités.
4. Nous espérons que tu réussiras cette année.

## A. The Subjunctive Mood

All the verb tenses you have learned so far have been in the *indicative* mood (past, present, and future), in the *imperative* mood, which is used for direct commands or requests, or in the *conditional* mood, which is used to express hypothetical situations. In this chapter, you will begin to learn about the *subjunctive* mood.

The indicative is used to state facts. The subjunctive is used to express the opinions or attitudes of the speaker. It expresses such personal feelings as uncertainty, doubt, emotion, possibility, and desire, rather than fact.

The subjunctive is used infrequently in English. Compare the use of the indicative and the subjunctive in the following examples.

| INDICATIVE | SUBJUNCTIVE |
|---|---|
| He *goes* to Paris. | I insist that he *go* to Paris for the meeting. |
| We *are* on time. | They ask that we *be* on time. |
| She *is* the president. | She wishes that she *were* the president of the group. |

In French, the subjunctive is used more frequently than in English. It almost always occurs in a dependent clause beginning with **que** (*that*). The main clause contains a verb that expresses desire, emotion, uncertainty, or some other subjective view of the action to be performed. Here and in the next grammar section, where the forms of the subjunctive are presented, the examples and the exercises will illustrate the use of the subjunctive in dependent clauses introduced by **que** after verbs of volition, such as **désirer**, **souhaiter** (*to want, to wish*), **vouloir**, **aimer bien** (*to like*), and **préférer**.

Usually, the subjects of the main and dependent clauses are different.

| MAIN CLAUSE *Indicative* | DEPENDENT CLAUSE *Subjunctive* |
|---|---|
| Je veux | **que** vous **partiez**. |

## B. The Meaning of the Subjunctive

The French subjunctive has many possible English equivalents.

**que je parle** → *that I speak, that I'm speaking, that I do speak, that I may speak, that I will speak, me to speak*

| | |
|---|---|
| De quoi veux-tu **que je parle**? | *What do you want me to talk about?* |
| Il veut **que je** lui **parle** des élections. | *He wants me to speak to him about the elections.* |

## C. Forms of the Present Subjunctive

**Presentation**: Model pronunciation of verbs in short sentences. For example: *Il veut que je parle français, que je finisse la leçon, etc.*

For most verbs, the stem for the forms **je**, **tu**, **il**, **elle**, **on**, **ils**, **elles** of the subjunctive is found by dropping the **-ent** of the third-person plural (**ils/elles**) form of the present indicative. The endings are **-e**, **-es**, and **-ent**.

| INFINITIVE | **parler** | **vendre** | **finir** | **voir** |
|---|---|---|---|---|
| STEM | (ils) **parl**/ent | (ils) **vend**/ent | (ils) **finiss**/ent | (ils) **voi**/ent |
| ... que je | parl**e** | vend**e** | finiss**e** | voi**e** |
| ... que tu | parl**es** | vend**es** | finiss**es** | voi**es** |
| ... qu'il, elle, on | parl**e** | vend**e** | finiss**e** | voi**e** |
| ... qu'ils, elles | parl**ent** | vend**ent** | finiss**ent** | voi**ent** |

The stem for the **nous** and **vous** forms of the subjunctive is found by dropping the **-ons** from the first-person indicative plural (**nous**). The endings are **-ions** and **-iez**.

| INFINITIVE | **parler** | **vendre** | **finir** | **voir** |
|---|---|---|---|---|
| STEM | (nous) **parl**/ons | (nous) **vend**/ons | (nous) **finiss**/ons | (nous) **voy**/ons |
| ... que nous<br>... que vous | parl**ions**<br>parl**iez** | vend**ions**<br>vend**iez** | finiss**ions**<br>finiss**iez** | voy**ions**<br>voy**iez** |

Verbs that are regular in the indicative have the same stem for all persons in the subjunctive. Irregular verbs and verbs with spelling changes have two stems in the subjunctive.

> Marc veut que je **parl**e maintenant avec la journaliste.
> Mais elle préfère que nous nous **parl**ions plus tard.
>
> Voulez-vous que je la **rappell**e?
> Je veux bien que vous la **rappel**iez.
>
> J'aimerais bien qu'on **prenn**e rendez-vous plus tard.
> Mais Jacqueline préfère que vous **pren**iez rendez-vous tout de suite.

**Suggestion**: For listening comp. practice, ask sts. to listen for indicative or subjunctive in following sentences. They are to imagine that they are at a political rally where part of the candidates' speeches are made inaudible by cheers of the crowd. 1. *...que nous votons socialistes.* 2. *...que nous nous rappelions les problèmes des pauvres.* 3. *...que vous choisissiez les meilleurs candidats.* 4. *...que je suive vos conseils.* 5. *...que nous prenions le pouvoir.* 6. *...que vous parlez avec les candidats.*

## *Vérifions!*

**A. Stratégie électorale.** Françoise accepte de poser sa candidature au Conseil universitaire. Avec un groupe d'étudiants, elle prépare soigneusement sa campagne. Que veut Françoise?

MODÈLE: Elle veut que les étudiants / choisir / des délégués responsables. →
Elle veut que les étudiants choisissent des délégués responsables.

1. Elle veut que les étudiants / réfléchir / aux problèmes de l'université
2. Elle aimerait que nous / préparer / une stratégie électorale tout de suite
3. Elle préfère que vous / finir / les affiches aujourd'hui
4. Elle veut que Luc et Simon / organiser / un débat
5. Elle souhaite que la trésorière / établir / un budget
6. Elle insiste pour que je / convoquer / tous les volontaires ce soir

**B. Discours politique.** Ce soir, Françoise fait son premier discours de la campagne électorale. Voici ce qu'elle dit aux étudiants.

**Suggestion**: Do as a rapid response ex.

1. Je veux que le Conseil universitaire / agir / en faveur des étudiants
2. Je souhaite que vous / participer / aux décisions du Conseil
3. Je préfère que nous / discuter / librement des mesures à prendre
4. Je voudrais que nous / trouver / tous ensemble des solutions à vos problèmes

**Additional activities**: (1) *Stratégie. Un groupe d'étudiants prépare la campagne pour élire son candidat au Conseil de l'université. Que dit leur chef, Jean-Michel?* 1. *Jean-Michel veut que vous choisissiez un candidat.* (*les étudiants*, *nous*, *le secré-*

5. Je désire que l'université / prendre / en considération nos inquiétudes
6. Je voudrais que les professeurs / comprendre / nos positions
7. Je souhaite enfin que tous les candidats / se réunir / bientôt pour mieux exposer leurs idées
8. ?

taire) 2. *Il préfère que nous agissions tout de suite.* (tu, vous, je) 3. *Il voudrait que Michel finisse les affiches.* (Martine et Paulette, le secrétaire, vous) 4. *Il souhaite que tu réfléchisses à notre budget.* (la trésorière, je, elles) 5. *Il désire qu'elles réussissent à obtenir des votes.* (tu, nous, vous) (2) *Dictature. M. Lamoureux dirige son entreprise en véritable dictateur. Voici les ordres qu'il a donnés ce matin. Exprimez-les avec je veux que...* MODÈLE: *Vous devez écouter votre chef de service.* → *Je veux que vous écoutiez votre chef de service.* 1. *Vous devez mieux travailler.* 2. *Elle doit arriver à l'heure.* 3. *Ils doivent trouver une solution.* 4. *Nous devons envoyer ce télégramme.* 5. *Tu dois m'expliquer tes problèmes.* 6. *Il doit s'excuser de son erreur.* 7. *Nous devons convoquer les employés.* 8. *Ils doivent taper plus vite à la machine.* 9. *Vous devez appeler un inspecteur.* 10. *Tu dois te rappeler le nouvel horaire.*

## Parlons-en!

**Opinions.** Complétez les phrases suivantes et donnez vos opinions personnelles. Commencez avec **Je voudrais que...**

1. notre gouvernement (choisir de) _____
2. notre président (essayer de) _____
3. les étudiants (manifester plus/moins pour/contre) _____
4. nous (apprendre à) _____
5. nous (ne pas oublier que) _____
6. ?

**Suggestion**: Give sts. a few minutes to complete sentences, and elicit several answers for each question.

## 55. EXPRESSING ATTITUDES Irregular Subjunctive Verbs

Yvette Roudy, ancien ministre des droits de la femme

### Ancien ministre des droits de la femme

LA JOURNALISTE: On vous appelle «le ministre qui a fait des remous». Pourquoi?

YVETTE ROUDY: C'est parce que quand j'étais ministre j'ai lancé beaucoup de campagnes pour les droits de la femme.

- pour la contraception: Je voulais que les femmes **soient** convenablement informées.
- contre le sexisme: Nous ne voulions pas qu'on **puisse** exploiter le corps féminin dans les publicités.
- pour la féminisation des noms de profession: Nous ne voulions pas qu'il y **ait** des métiers féminins et des métiers masculins, mais des métiers pour tous!
- pour l'orientation et la formation professionnelle des femmes: Nous souhaitions que les femmes **sachent** s'engager vers des métiers d'avenir.

1. On est souvent mal informé sur la contraception. Mme Roudy voulait que les femmes _____ (être) convenablement informées.
2. De nos jours, les publicitaires exploitent souvent les femmes pour vendre des produits. Mme Roudy ne voulait pas qu'on _____ (pouvoir) exploiter le corps féminin.

3. Il y a des métiers masculins (*e.g.*, **le magistrat**) et des métiers féminins (*e.g.*, **l'ouvreuse**). Mme Roudy ne voulait pas qu'il y ____ (avoir) des métiers féminins et des métiers masculins, mais des métiers pour tous.
4. Souvent, les filles ne savent pas s'engager vers des métiers d'avenir. Mme Roudy voulait qu'elles le ____ (savoir).

Some verbs have irregular subjunctive stems. The endings themselves are all regular, except for some endings of **avoir** and **être**.

**Presentation**: Model pronunciation in short phrases. Example: *Le chef veut qu'il soit à l'heure... que nous sachions la vérité.*

| | **aller:** ***aill-/all-*** | **faire:** ***fass-*** | **pouvoir:** ***puiss-*** | **savoir:** ***sach-*** | **vouloir:** ***veuill-/voul-*** | **avoir:** ***ai-/ay-*** | **être:** ***soi-/soy-*** |
|---|---|---|---|---|---|---|---|
| ... que je/j' | aille | fasse | puisse | sache | veuille | aie | sois |
| que tu | ailles | fasses | puisses | saches | veuilles | aies | sois |
| qu'il, elle, on | aille | fasse | puisse | sache | veuille | ai**t** | soi**t** |
| que nous | allions | fassions | puissions | sachions | voulions | a**yons** | so**yons** |
| que vous | alliez | fassiez | puissiez | sachiez | vouliez | a**yez** | so**yez** |
| qu'ils, elles | aillent | fassent | puissent | sachent | veuillent | aient | soient |

Le prof veut que nous **allions** au débat. — *The professor wants us to go to the debate.*

Son parti veut que le gouvernement **fasse** des réformes. — *His (Her) party wants the government to make reforms.*

Le président préfère que les sénateurs **soient** présents. — *The President prefers the senators to be there.*

**Suggestion**: For listening comp. practice, ask sts. to listen for subjunctive or indicative form of irregular verbs. They are to imagine that they are talking long distance and that there is a lot of static. 1. *...que j'aille à la réunion.* 2. *...que Marc a le temps de faire cela.* 3. *...que tu sois présente.* 4. *...que nous pouvons poser des questions.* 5. *...que vous sachiez la vérité.* 6. *...que la candidate fasse le nécessaire.*

## Vérifions!

**A. Revendications.** Les délégués du Conseil universitaire donnent leurs directives aux étudiants. Recommencez leurs notes en remplaçant les sujets en italique par **vous**, puis par **les étudiants**.

**Suggestion**: Do as written transformation at board.

Nous ne voulons pas que *tu* ailles en cours aujourd'hui. Nous préférons que *tu* sois présent à la manifestation et que *tu* fasses grève. Nous désirons que *tu* aies une affiche lisible (*legible*). Naturellement, nous voudrions que *tu* puisses exprimer tes opinions librement.

**B. Engagement politique.** Les Legrand ont des opinions libérales. Quels conseils donnent-ils à leurs enfants? Suivez les modèles.

MODÈLES: Patrick—tu / être réactionnaire →
Patrick, nous ne voulons pas que tu sois réactionnaire.

Fabrice / être courageux →
Nous voulons que Fabrice soit courageux.

1. Jacques / être actif politiquement
2. Corinne et Jacques / avoir le courage de leurs opinions
3. Vous / avoir des amis racistes
4. Patrick / être bien informé
5. Sylvain—tu / être violent
6. Vous / être intolérant
7. Fabrice—tu / avoir de l'ambition politique
8. Patrick et Sylvain / avoir des idéaux pacifistes

### Parlons-en!

**Slogans.** Composez votre propre slogan politique selon les modèles des dessins. Utilisez **Vous voulez que** _____? et les verbes suivants: **avoir**, **être**, **faire**, **pouvoir**, **savoir**, **choisir**, **réformer**, **réussir à**, **servir à**, **vivre**, **perdre**, **comprendre**, **changer**, **préparer**, **s'unir** (*to unite*), **écouter**, **gagner**, **apporter**, **élire**, **voter**.

**Suggestion**: Give sts. a moment to write slogans. Ask some sts. to read slogans and have class choose most interesting ones.

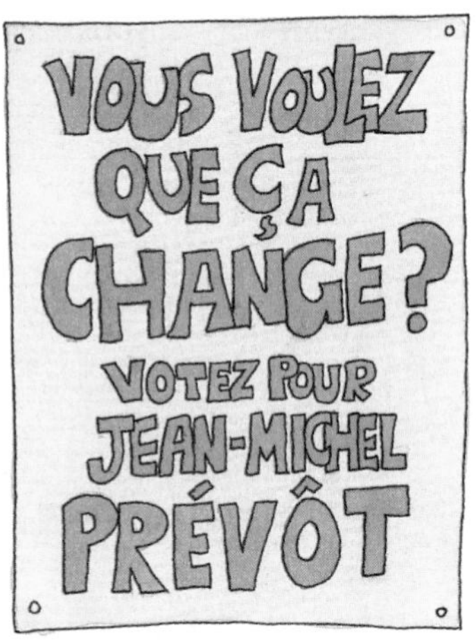


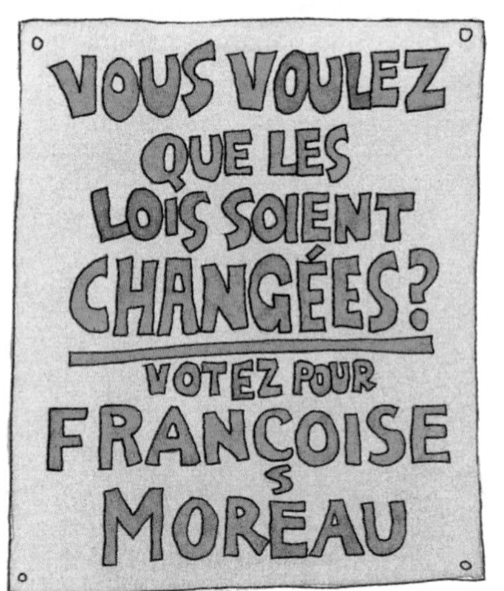

## 56. EXPRESSING WISHES, NECESSITY, AND POSSIBILITY
### The Subjunctive

**Service militaire obligatoire ou volontaire?**

PATRICK FAURE: (22 ANS) À mon avis, le service obligatoire, c'est un anachronisme à l'âge nucléaire.

GÉRARD BOURRELLY: (36 ANS) **Il est possible** que les jeunes s'intéressent plus au service si on leur donne une formation professionnelle.

FRANCIS CRÉPIN (25 ANS): **Il faut** qu'on abolisse le service obligatoire et qu'on établisse une armée de métier.
CHARLES PALLANCA (18 ANS): Mais si j'étais volontaire, **j'exigerais** que la solde soit au moins de 5 000 francs par mois!

Retrouvez la phrase correspondante selon le dialogue.

1. Il se peut que les jeunes s'intéressent plus à un service comprenant une formation professionnelle complémentaire.
2. Il faut abolir le service obligatoire et établir une armée de métier.
3. J'insisterais pour que la solde soit au moins de 5 000 francs par mois!

## A. Subjunctive with Verbs of Volition

When someone expresses a desire for someone else (or something) to behave in a certain way, the verb in the subordinate clause is usually in the subjunctive. The following construction is used.

| | |
|---|---|
| Mon père **veut que je fasse** mon service militaire. | *My father wants me to do my military service.* |
| Je **voudrais que le service militaire soit** aboli. | *I'd like compulsory military service to be abolished.* |

Note that an infinitive construction is used in English to express such a desire. The infinitive construction is possible in French only if the speaker is talking about a wish for him- or herself.

| | |
|---|---|
| **Je veux finir** mes études. | *I want to finish my studies.* |
| Et **ma mère veut** aussi **que** je les **finisse.** | *And my mother wants me to finish them too.* |

Verbs expressing desires (volition) include **aimer bien**, **désirer**, **exiger** (*to demand*), **préférer**, **souhaiter**, **vouloir**, and **vouloir bien**.

## B. The Subjunctive with Impersonal Expressions

An impersonal expression is one in which the subject does not refer to any particular person or thing. In English, the subject of an impersonal expression is usually *it: It is important that I go to class.* In French, many impersonal expressions—especially those that express will, necessity, judgment, possibility, or doubt—are followed by the subjunctive in the dependent clause.

**Presentation**: Go over expressions in chart, using short sentences to model each one. Have sts. repeat after your model.

**Suggestion**: Have sts. make up short completions for selected expressions from chart.

| IMPERSONAL EXPRESSIONS USED WITH THE SUBJUNCTIVE* | |
|---|---|
| *Will or necessity* | *Possibility, judgment, or doubt* |
| il est essentiel que | il est normal que |
| il est important que | il est peu probable que |
| il est indispensable que | il est possible/impossible que |
| il est nécessaire que | il se peut que (*it's possible that*) |
| il est préférable que | il semble que (*it seems that*) |
| il faut que† (*it's necessary that*) | |
| il vaut mieux que† (*it's better that*) | |

**Il est important que** le racisme **disparaisse**. — *It's important that racism disappear.*
**Il faut que** vous **soyez** au courant de la politique. — *You must (It's necessary that you) keep up with politics.*
**Il est peu probable que** le sexisme **soit** tout à fait éliminé. — *It's not likely that sexism will be (is) totally eliminated.*
**Il se peut que** d'autres pays **possèdent** des armes nucléaires. — *It's possible that other countries possess nuclear weapons.*

## C. The Infinitive with Impersonal Expressions

When no specific subject is mentioned, impersonal expressions are followed by the infinitive instead of the subjunctive. Compare the following sentences.

Il vaut mieux **attendre**. — *It's better to wait.*
Il vaut mieux **que nous attendions**. — *It's better that we wait.*

Il est important **de voter**. — *It's important to vote.*
Il est important **que vous votiez**. — *It's important that you vote.*

Note that the preposition **de** is used before the infinitive after impersonal expressions that contain **être**.

*Except for **il faut que**, **il vaut mieux que**, and **il semble que** these impersonal expressions are usually limited to writing and formal discourse.
†The infinitive of the verb conjugated in the expression **il faut que** is **falloir** (*to be necessary*). The infinitive of the verb in **il vaut mieux que** is **valoir** (*to be worth*).

## Vérifions!

**A. Comment gagner?** Donnez des conseils à Jeanne Laviolette, candidate à la mairie de Dijon, en suivant le modèle.

MODÈLE: Il est important de savoir écouter les gens. →
Il est important que vous sachiez écouter les gens.

1. Pour être maire, il faut être dynamique et responsable.
2. Il est essentiel de ne pas avoir peur d'agir (*to act*).
3. Il est nécessaire de rester calme en toutes circonstances.
4. Il est préférable de parler souvent aux électeurs.
5. Il faut faire attention aux problèmes des jeunes.
6. Il est indispensable de gagner la confiance des commerçants.
7. ?

**Continuation**: Have sts. think of a few more *conseils*.

**Follow-up**: Using expressions in Ex. A, have sts. give advice to following statements: *Je veux vivre longtemps. Je veux perfectionner mon français. Je veux être riche. Je veux m'amuser ce week-end.*

**B. La routine de tous les jours.** Posez des questions à un(e) camarade de classe. Suivez le modèle.

MODÈLE: nécessaire / faire la cuisine chaque soir?
VOUS: Est-il nécessaire que tu fasses la cuisine chaque soir?
VOTRE CAMARADE: Oui, il est nécessaire que je fasse la cuisine chaque soir. (Non, il n'est pas nécessaire que je fasse la cuisine chaque soir.)

1. vaut mieux / aller au cours de français tous les jours
2. préférable / faire ton lit chaque matin
3. faut / nettoyer ta chambre tous les jours
4. normal / pouvoir dormir tard le matin
5. indispensable / étudier chaque soir
6. important / lire le journal chaque jour
7. ?

## Parlons-en!

**A. Problèmes contemporains.** Discutez des problèmes suivants avec un(e) camarade. Offrez des solutions. Utilisez une des expressions suivantes: **il est important que**, **il faut que**, **il est nécessaire que**, **il est indispensable que**, **il est essentiel que**, **il est préférable que**.

1. l'immigration clandestine aux États-Unis
2. le stress chez les jeunes
3. la pollution
4. le chômage
5. le gaspillage des sources d'énergie
6. la violence dans les villes
7. l'effet de serre (*greenhouse*)

**Suggestion**: With whole class, solicit several individual reactions to statements. For second part, where sts. propose solutions to problems, have sts. brainstorm in pairs or in small groups. Compare group contributions.

**Continuation**: *Le terrorisme, les pirates de l'air, la pauvreté.*

**B. Et vous?** Y a-t-il quelqu'un qui essaie d'influencer vos choix?

Suggestion: Give sts. a minute to reflect before writing sentences. Ask several sts. to write sentences at board.

MODÈLE: Oui. Mes amis veulent que j'arrête de fumer. (*ou* Oui. Mon ami Philippe me dit qu'il est essentiel que j'arrête de fumer.)

**C. Nécessités et probabilités.** Quelle sera votre vie? Répondez aux questions suivantes. Dans chaque réponse, utilisez une de ces expressions: **il se peut que, il est peu probable que, il est impossible que, il est possible que, il est essentiel, il faut que, il est nécessaire que**.

MODÈLE: Ferez-vous une découverte (*discovery*) importante? →
Il est peu probable que je fasse une découverte importante.

1. Vous marierez-vous? 2. Apprendrez-vous une langue étrangère? 3. Voyagerez-vous beaucoup? 4. Deviendrez-vous célèbre? 5. Serez-vous riche? 6. Saurez-vous jouer du piano? 7. Écrirez-vous un roman? 8. Ferez-vous la connaissance d'un président des États-Unis? 9. Irez-vous en Chine? 10. Vivrez-vous jusqu'à l'âge de cent ans?

Maintenant, utilisez ces questions pour interviewer un(e) camarade de classe.

MODÈLE: VOUS: Feras-tu une découverte importante?
VOTRE AMI(E): Oui, il est important que je fasse une découverte importante. (Non, il est peu probable que je fasse une découverte importante.)

## 57. EXPRESSING EMOTION
## The Subjunctive

Suggestion: Ask sts. to comment on the highlighted expressions and say why they might require the subjunctive.

### L'Europe unie

Plusieurs Français donnent leur opinion sur l'unification politique et économique de l'Europe.

JEAN-PIERRE (35 ANS): Je suis **content** que la France **dise** «oui» à l'Europe.

ISABELLE (24 ANS): Nous, nous avons **peur** que les nationalistes **deviennent** violents comme en Bosnie-Herzégovine.

CLAUDE (40 ANS): Je **regrette** que les Suisses ne **veuillent** pas faire partie de l'Europe.

NICOLE (30 ANS): Je **doute** que l'Europe **puisse** régler le problème du chômage.

MONIQUE (52 ANS): Je suis **furieuse** que les Américains **imposent** des taxes sur les produits agricoles européens.

Le drapeau européen

Complétez les phrases selon le dialogue.

1. Claude ____ que les Suisses ne ____ pas faire partie de l'Europe.
2. Monique est ____ que les Américains ____ des taxes sur les produits agricoles européens.
3. Nicole ____ que l'Europe ____ régler le problème du chômage.
4. Jean-Pierre est ____ que la France ____ «oui» à l'Europe.
5. Isabelle a ____ que les nationalistes ____ violents comme en Bosnie-Herzégovine.

## A. Expressions of Emotion

The subjunctive is frequently used after expressions of emotion.

| EXPRESSIONS OF EMOTION |
|---|
| *happiness*: être content(e), être heureux/euse<br>*regret*: être désolé(e), être triste, regretter (*to be sorry*)<br>*surprise*: être surpris(e), être étonné(e)<br>*fear*: avoir peur<br>*relief*: être soulagé(e)<br>*anger*: être furieux/euse |

| | |
|---|---|
| Le président **est content** que les électeurs **aient** confiance en lui. | *The President is pleased that the voters have confidence in him.* |
| Les électeurs **ont peur** que l'inflation **soit** un problème insoluble. | *The voters are afraid that inflation is an insurmountable problem.* |
| Les écologistes **sont furieux** que les lois contre la pollution des forêts et des rivières **soient** tellement faibles. | *The ecologists are angry that the laws against polluting the forests and rivers are so weak.* |

As with verbs of volition, there must be different subjects in the main and dependent clauses. Otherwise, an infinitive is used.

| | |
|---|---|
| **Le président est content de rencontrer** le Premier ministre du Canada. | *The President is happy to meet the Prime Minister of Canada.* |

## B. Impersonal Expressions of Emotion

The subjunctive is also used following impersonal expressions of emotion.

il est stupide que*
il est bizarre que
il est bon que*
il est dommage que (*it's too bad that*)
il est juste/injuste que
il est utile/inutile que

**Il est dommage que** la guerre y **continue**. — *It's too bad that war is continuing there.*
**Est-il bon que** les enfants aussi **expriment** leurs opinions? — *Is it good that children also express their opinions?*
**Il est stupide que** tant de citoyens ne **votent** pas. — *It is stupid that so many citizens do not vote.*

**Additional activities**: (1) *La réunion du Club de Ski ou le film? Chantal et son amie Annick parlent de ce qu'elles vont faire ce soir. En français, s'il vous plaît.* C: *I'm happy that we have that meeting this evening!* A: *I think there will be a lot of people* (beaucoup de monde) *there.* C: *Yes. Is your friend Michel coming with us?* A: *I doubt that he's coming this evening. He wants Paul to go with him to the movies.* C: *Do you think we can go with them?* A: *What? I thought that you wanted to go to the meeting! Do you want me to call him?* C: *Let's call him! I hope we can find his number!* (2) *Problèmes sociaux. Donnez votre réaction aux idées suivantes. Utilisez des expressions que vous avez apprises dans ce chapitre.* (Suggestion: After a st. reads a sentence, ask *Êtes-vous d'accord*? and have students change sentence to conform with their beliefs.) MODÈLE: *La technologie change la vie.* → *À mon avis, il est évident que la technologie change la vie.* 1. *On gaspille très peu d'énergie aujourd'hui.* 2. *L'atmosphère est moins polluée maintenant qu'il y a dix ans.* 3. *Le gouvernement est en train de développer l'énergie solaire.* 4. *Il n'est pas nécessaire de conserver l'énergie.* 5. *Les déchets industriels ne posent plus de problèmes.* 6. *On n'a plus besoin d'économiser l'essence.* 7. *Les femmes sont toujours respectées dans les publicités.* 8. *Les médias ont trop de liberté.* 9. *La guerre existera toujours.* 10. *La faim n'existe plus dans le monde.*

### *Vérifions!*

**A. Sentiments.** Complétez les phrases de façon logique en choisissant une des expressions en italique.

MODÈLE: Nous sommes furieux / *les leaders politiques sont très responsables face aux électeurs / la télévision n'analyse pas les problèmes actuels* →
Nous sommes furieux que la télévision n'analyse pas les problèmes actuels.

1. Je suis désolé(e) / *tu es malade aujourd'hui / tu réussis à l'examen.*
2. Mes parents ont peur / *je finis mes études très rapidement / je ne finis pas mes études.*
3. Je regrette / *mon frère et moi ne sommes jamais d'accord / mon frère et moi nous amusons souvent ensemble.*
4. Mon amie Catherine est soulagée / *il y a enfin deux femmes à la Cour suprême / le taux* (rate) *de chômage est élevé cette année.*
5. Les sénateurs sont étonnés / *le public ne veut pas payer plus d'impôts / le public veut payer plus d'impôts.*

**B. Le journal.** Voici des titres (*headlines*) adaptés de divers journaux français. Donnez votre réaction à chaque situation. Utilisez les expressions suivantes: **être content(e)**, **heureux/euse**, **désolé(e)**, **triste**, **surpris(e)**, **étonné(e)**, **soulagé(e)**, **fâché(e)**, **furieux/euse**, **regretter**, **avoir peur**, **il est stupide (bizarre**, **bon**, **dommage**, **juste/injuste**, **utile/inutile) que**.

**Suggestion**: Give sts. a few minutes to prepare.

*The French often say **c'est stupide que**, **c'est bon que**, etc. in everyday conversation.

MODÈLE: **Les femmes et les chômeurs fument davantage** (*more*) →
Il est dommage que les femmes et les chômeurs fument davantage.

1. **Le Club Méditerranée ouvre son premier village en Chine**
2. **L'Europe aime la France** (La majorité des Européens choisiraient la France comme terre d'accueil [*country where they would settle*].)
3. **Le froid tue** (*kills*) **5 sans-abri** (*homeless*) (Des centres d'hébergement [*shelters*] exceptionnels ont ouvert leurs portes aux victimes du froid.)
4. **Les Français disent «non» à la drogue** (68% des Français sont favorables au maintien de l'interdiction totale des ventes et de la consommation de drogues, selon un sondage.)
5. **Perrier va supprimer** (*eliminate*) **un emploi sur sept** (Le groupe Perrier [eaux minérales] a annoncé qu'il comptait supprimer 750 emplois.)

## *Parlons-en!*

**A. Émotions.** Donnez votre opinion personnelle sur les problèmes de la société américaine.

**Suggestion**: To prepare ex., ask sts. to make a list of 5 current events to bring to class.

MODÈLE: Je suis heureux/euse que... les États-Unis aident plusieurs pays du tiers-monde (*third world*).

1. Je suis heureux/euse que...
2. Je regrette que...
3. Il est injuste que...
4. Il est bon que...
5. Il est bizarre que...

**B. Encore des émotions.** Reprenez les *trois premières* phrases de l'exercice A. Maintenant demandez à cinq autres étudiants comment ils ont complété ces phrases. Pouvez-vous trouver quelqu'un qui a les mêmes opinions que vous?

MODÈLE: É1: Qu'est-ce qui te rend heureux/euse?
É2: Je suis heureux/euse que le maire fasse quelque chose pour aider les sans-abri (*homeless*).

**Suggestion**: Have several sts. read their answers.

# France-culture

*L'Europe et les Européens.* En décembre 1992, le traité de Maastricht a été ratifié par dix pays de la CEE (Communauté économique européenne): Allemagne, Italie, Espagne, France, Portugal, Hollande, Grèce, Irlande, Belgique et Luxembourg. Les Anglais et les Danois ont exprimé leur refus. Depuis ce temps-là, les Anglais et les Danois ont aussi ratifié le traité. Pourtant les Européens sont divisés sur la question de l'Europe: seulement 51% des Français ont voté «oui» aux élections sur le traité de Maastricht.

Quelles sont les principales mesures du traité de Maastricht?

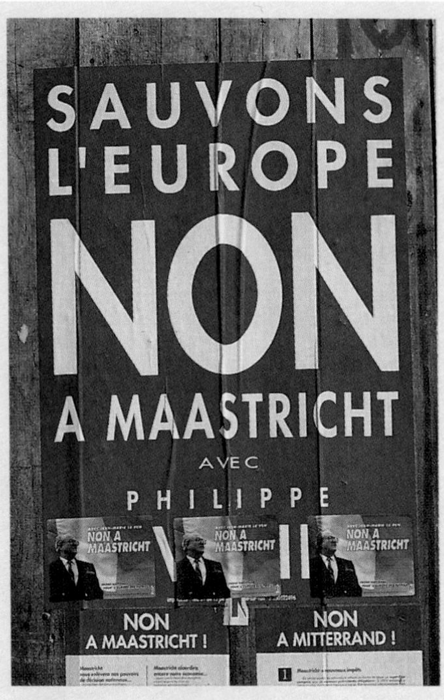


Le traité de Maastricht n'a pas été voté à l'unanimité en France.

1. La libre° circulation des biens° et des services. Cela veut dire, par exemple, qu'un Français pourra aller acheter sa voiture en Allemagne ou en Italie sans payer de taxes à l'importation. Cela veut dire aussi qu'un Français pourra aller travailler ou étudier librement dans n'importe quel° pays de la CEE.
2. L'harmonisation des taxes sur les produits (taxe à valeur ajoutée)° entre les pays de la CEE qui auparavant° variaient selon les pays (par exemple entre 0 et 30% de taxes sur une voiture).
3. Une monnaie commune: l'ECU (*European currency unit*). Il n'y aura donc plus de francs français ou de Deutsch Marks.
4. Enfin, une politique de défense commune pour tous les pays de la CEE à partir de° 1995.

*free / goods*

n'importe... *any*

taxe... *value added tax*

*before*

à... *from*

Alors, de quoi les Européens ont-ils peur? L'Europe est un vieux continent composé de petits pays qui ont chacun une très vieille identité culturelle et des traditions très anciennes. En disant «oui» à l'Europe, ils ont peur de perdre cette identité et ces traditions. Ils ont peur d'être noyés° dans cette immense Europe et d'être dirigés par des bureaucrates qu'ils ne connaissent pas. Les Français ont peur que la France ne soit plus la France; les Anglais ont peur que l'Angleterre ne soit plus l'Angleterre. En fait, une majorité d'Européens veulent une Europe unie économiquement pour faire face au défi° contre les États-Unis et le Japon mais beaucoup se méfient° d'une Europe unie politiquement.

*drowned*

faire... *to take on the challenge* / se... *are distrustful*

# Mise au point

**A. Émotions.** Complétez les phrases qui se trouvent au-dessous de chaque dessin. Puis, un étudiant (une étudiante) fait sa propre (*own*) phrase pour commenter le dessin. Enfin, les autres étudiants choisissent la phrase qu'ils préfèrent comme légende (*caption*).

**Follow-up (ex. B)**: Ask sts. to work in groups to write a brochure such as the one presented on how to react to (a) *un tremblement de terre* (b) *un accident de voiture* (c) *le danger d'une bombe*. See realia page 453.

1. Pierre est content que ____.
   a. sa sœur / s'en aller / bientôt / université
   b. son père / venir de / lui / acheter / voiture
   c. ?

2. Chantal est triste que ____.
   a. Jean-Pierre / (ne... pas) vouloir / sortir / soir
   b. personne / (ne... ) comprendre / ses idées
   c. ?

3. Jacques est furieux que ____.
   a. Barbara / (ne... pas) le prendre / au sérieux
   b. Chantal / lui / (ne... pas) écrire / plus souvent
   c. ?

4. Mme Hugo a peur que ____.
   a. sa fille / (ne... pas) être / à l'heure / soir
   b. ses enfants / (ne... pas) faire attention
   c. ?

**B. Le feu: un danger écologique.** Voici quelques conseils pour vous protéger du feu (*fire*), publiés par le Conservatoire de la forêt méditerranéenne.

Imaginez que vous expliquez à un(e) camarade ce qu'il/elle doit faire en cas d'incendie (*fire*). Reprenez les conseils et faites des phrases avec des expressions impersonnelles.

MODÈLE: Il faut (Il est indispensable, essentiel) que tu téléphones au 18 immédiatement.

**les 10 Gestes qui sauvent du feu !**

**Ce n'est pas chez vous :**

**1 UNE FUMEE : TELEPHONEZ AU 18** (appel gratuit - intervention gratuite 24 h / 24 h)... Même si vous pensez que quelqu'un peut l'avoir déjà fait.

**2 N'ALLEZ PAS VOIR EN BADAUD[a] : VOUS GENERIEZ[b] LES SECOURS.**

**3 SUIVEZ LES CONSEILS DES POMPIERS.**

**C'est chez vous :**

**4 TELEPHONEZ AU 18** (appel gratuit - intervention gratuite 24 h/ 24 h). Ce doit être votre premier geste.

**5 RESTEZ SUR PLACE DANS LA MAISON.** Ne cédez pas à la tentation de fuir sur la route.

**RESTEZ ACTIF** en attendant les pompiers... comme après leur arrivée

**6 FERMEZ TOUS LES VOLETS[c] ET PORTES** (le plus hermétiquement possible, en colmatant avec des linges mouillés).

**7 ARROSEZ[d] PORTES ET VOLETS EN BOIS.**

**8 COUPEZ LE GAZ.** Sachez que vos bouteilles de gaz sont moins dangereuses à l'intérieur, à l'abri dans la maison.

**9 FAITES QUELQUES RESERVES D'EAU** sans toutefois la gaspiller.

**10 COUCHEZ VOUS EN CAS DE PENETRATION DES FUMEES[e] :** C'est au ras du sol qu'il y a le plus d'oxygène... Gardez votre sang-froid sur une maison ainsi défendue, le feu passe très vite : en moyenne 5 minutes par vent de 50 km/h.

Pour toutes précisions, pour tout renseignement complémentaire, n'hésitez pas à nous appeler. Nous sommes à votre disposition. Gratuitement.

**05.06.18.18**

de 8h à 20h tous les jours du 1.07 au 15.09.87

[a]voir... rubbernecking
[b]would get in the way of
[c]shutters
[d]Wet down
[e]smoke

Les journaux présentent différents points de vue et perspectives sur la société contemporaine.

Puis, par petits groupes, imaginez quels conseils on pourrait donner dans les situations suivantes:

1. En cas d'inondation
2. En cas de tremblement de terre

**C. Un monde meilleur.** À votre avis, que faudrait-il faire pour changer le monde? Faites cinq propositions en utilisant **il faudrait que**, **je voudrais que**, **j'aimerais que...**

MODÈLE: Je voudrais qu'une femme soit présidente des États-Unis.

## Interactions

In this chapter, you practiced expressing opinions, attitudes, and emotions in French. Use the vocabulary and structures from the chapter to debate a topic.

**Débat.** Working with four classmates, pick one of the following topics and conduct a brief debate. Be sure that everyone has a chance to talk. Agree upon a conclusion, and compare it to the conclusions reached by the other debating groups in the class.

1. Les lois devraient punir, en les imposant fortement, les sociétés qui polluent l'environnement.
2. Pour mieux protéger l'environnement, le gouvernement devrait augmenter les impôts sur l'essence des voitures.

# Rencontres

## LECTURE

Boris Vian (1920–1959) was an important poet and composer who wrote both the music and lyrics of his songs. This reading, *Le Déserteur*, is a protest song written in the 1950s. One of Boris Vian's most popular compositions, *Le Déserteur* became the "national anthem" of the antiwar protest in France.

### Avant de lire

**Understanding poetry and songs.** In French, poetry and song differ from ordinary speech, not only in the tendency to use figurative language (comparisons, metaphors, etc.), but also in pronunciation. Unlike speech, where the accent tends to fall on the last syllable of a phrase, poetry and songs tend to have regularly accented rhythms. In traditional verse, the "silent e" of speech is pronounced (or sung) and forms part of the rhythmic pattern. Furthermore, French verse traditionally follows strict and complicated rules for rhyme. To fit these patterns, sentence structures may be rearranged.

Although "Le Déserteur" generally uses the vocabulary of everyday speech, its rhythms and rhymes are typical of French poetry. Read the text aloud and listen for the rhythm and the rhymes. Then read the text again for sense, and note how the units of meaning (phrases, sentences) follow the rhythmic structure.

Finally, note where the literal meaning of the text departs from ordinary reality and how these departures contribute to the impact of the message.

# Le Déserteur

Monsieur le Président,
Je vous fais une lettre
Que vous lirez peut-être
Si vous avez le temps.
Je viens de recevoir
Mes papiers militaires
Pour partir à la guerre
Avant mercredi soir.
Monsieur le Président,
Je ne veux pas la faire,
Je ne suis pas sur terre
Pour tuer[a] de pauvres gens.
C'est pas pour vous fâcher,[b]
Il faut que je vous dise,
Ma décision est prise,
Je m'en vais déserter.

Depuis que je suis né,
J'ai vu mourir mon père,
J'ai vu partir mes frères
Et pleurer mes enfants.
Ma mère a tant souffert
Qu'elle est dedans sa tombe
Et se moque des[c] bombes
Et se moque des vers.[d]
Quand j'étais prisonnier,
On m'a volé[e] ma femme,
On m'a volé mon âme[f]
Et tout mon cher passé.
Demain de bon matin,
Je fermerai ma porte
Au nez[g] des années mortes
J'irai sur les chemins.[h]

Je mendierai[i] ma vie
Sur les routes de France,
De Bretagne en Provence,
Et je crierai[j] aux gens
Refusez d'obéir,
Refusez de la faire,
N'allez pas à la guerre,
Refusez de partir.
S'il faut donner son sang,[k]
Allez donner le vôtre,
Vous êtes bon apôtre,[l]
Monsieur le Président.
Si vous me poursuivez,[m]
Prévenez[n] vos gendarmes[o]
Que je n'aurai pas d'armes
Et qu'ils pourront tirer.[p]

[a] *kill*
[b] *pour... to make you angry*
[c] *se... does not care about*
[d] *worms*
[e] *stole*
[f] *soul*
[g] *Au... In the face*
[h] *J'... I'll hit the road*
[i] *Je... I'll beg*
[j] *je... I'll shout*
[k] *blood*
[l] *Vous... You play the saint*
[m] *chase*
[n] *Inform*
[o] *French military police*
[p] *fire*

Paroles: Boris Vian. Musique : Boris Vian et Harold Berg.

Interprètes : Boris Vian, Mouloudji, Richard Anthony, les Sunlight.

La chanson date en réalité de 1955.
Quand Europe n° 1 diffuse pour la première fois *Le Déserteur*, le scandale éclate.
Les instances politiques n'apprécient guère la chanson et la censure l'interdit. La guerre d'Algérie vient de commencer.
Il faudra attendre 1966, avec la vogue du protest song, et que Peter, Paul and Mary l'enregistrent pour que la chanson ressuscite.

## Compréhension

1. En quelle année Boris Vian a-t-il écrit cette chanson? À cause de quel événement historique l'a-t-il écrite?
2. Selon la chanson, pourquoi veut-il déserter?
3. Quel conseil donne-t-il aux Français?
4. Quel conseil donne-t-il au président de la République?
5. Cette chanson a été censurée (*was censured*) pendant 11 ans. Êtes-vous d'accord avec cette action? Pourquoi, ou pourquoi pas?
6. Connaissez-vous des chansons américaines semblables ou comparables au *Déserteur*? Lesquelles? Quand et pourquoi ont-elles été composées?

## PAR ÉCRIT

**Function:** Writing to persuade
**Audience:** Readers of an editorial page
**Goal:** Write your opinion (in the form of a guest editorial or an "op-ed" piece) on one of the topics treated in the chapter, or on a recent, controversial event. You will attempt to persuade the readers to accept your point of view.

**Steps**

1. Begin by choosing a topic which interests you. Take about five minutes to jot down the issues or facts that come to mind while thinking about the topic.
2. Prepare your first draft following these guidelines:
   a. Present the subject. Explain to your reader why you are writing. Describe the event or issue briefly but clearly.
   b. Present your argument against opposing opinions. Summarize two or three of your opponents' main arguments, and refute them. Provide a clear justification for your own views.
   c. If appropriate, present several possible solutions to the problem.
   d. Write a general conclusion.
3. Refine the rough draft. Use expressions such as **Il faut se rappeler que**, **Il ne faut pas oublier que**, **À mon avis**, **Contrairement à ce que** (*what*) **l'on croit généralement**, **de plus**, **en premier** (**second**, **troisième**, etc.), **Il**

**est bizarre que**, **Il est nécessaire que**, **Il faut que**, **d'autre part** (*on the other hand*), **Il en résulte que** (*As a result*), etc.

4. Bring your draft to class and ask for "feedback" from a classmate.
5. Write a second draft incorporating suggestions, as warranted. Check your draft for spelling and grammar. Pay particular attention to your use of the subjunctive mood.
6. Complete the final version and be prepared to share it with classmates and/or your instructor.

## À L'ÉCOUTE!

**À l'écoute!** See scripts for listening passages and follow-up activities recorded on student cassette. Remind students that in the listening comprehension passages (as in real life) they will not understand every word they hear. They should focus globally on the general information in the passages and not be overly concerned about what they do not understand.

**I. Le candidat.** Vous allez entendre une interview avec un politicien, M. Maurice Deschamps. Lisez les activités ci-dessous avant d'écouter le vocabulaire et le dialogue qui leur correspondent.

VOCABULAIRE UTILE
honnête *honest*
agir *to act*

**A.** Encerclez la bonne réponse, selon le dialogue. (Il y a quelquefois plusieurs réponses possibles.)

1. M. Deschamps espère devenir
   a. député à Dijon
   b. maire de Lyon
   c. premier ministre
2. Selon lui, un chef du gouvernement doit être
   a. ambitieux
   b. travailleur
   c. honnête
   d. dynamique
   e. responsable
3. Il doit aussi
   a. savoir écouter
   b. avoir des contacts à Paris
   c. ne pas avoir peur d'agir
4. M. Deschamps constate qu'il est indispensable
   a. que les électeurs aient confiance en leur maire
   b. que les électeurs participent eux-mêmes au gouvernement
5. Pour gagner la confiance des électeurs, selon Deschamps, il faut
   a. protéger les intérêts de la ville
   b. développer de nouveaux programmes sociaux
   c. réduire les impôts

6. Selon lui, les problèmes de la ville qui exigent une attention immédiate sont
   a. la sécurité sociale
   b. le chômage
   c. la pollution
   d. l'éducation
   e. l'immigration

**B.** Cochez les opinions exprimées par M. Deschamps pendant l'interview.

1. _____ Pour être le maire d'une grande ville, il faut savoir écouter.
2. _____ Un maire doit être ouvert à toutes les suggestions.
3. _____ Un maire doit développer de nouveaux programmes d'enseignement technique.
4. _____ La hausse de la criminalité dans la région est le problème qui m'inquiète le plus.
5. _____ Pour être élus, la plupart des candidats promettent l'impossible.
6. _____ Nous devons protéger nos rivières et nos forêts contre les déchets industriels.

**II. Les informations.** Vous allez entendre un flash d'informations à la radio. Lisez les activités ci-dessous avant d'écouter le vocabulaire et le flash d'informations qui leur correspondent.

VOCABULAIRE UTILE
en hommage à *in recognition of*
une balle *a bullet*
un chiffre record *a record number*
ne jetez plus *don't throw away any more*
la coupe d'Europe *European Cup*

**A.** Encerclez les thèmes qui sont traités dans ce flash d'informations.

1. le SIDA
2. l'éducation
3. le racisme
4. la drogue
5. la Bosnie-Herzégovine
6. le chômage
7. le logement
8. la politique
9. l'écologie
10. la sécurité sociale
11. le recyclage
12. le sport
13. l'agriculture

**B.** Associez les éléments de chaque colonne.

1. recyclage
2. séparation
3. chiffre record
4. coupe d'Europe
5. manifestation

a. 3 millions de chômeurs
b. Limoges
c. Rachid Bencherif
d. «La Journée de la terre»
e. les «Verts» et «Génération écologie»

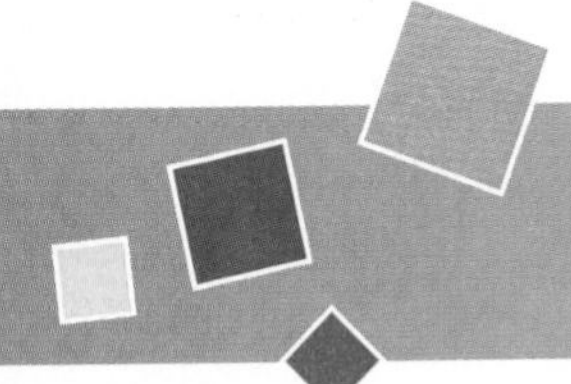

# Vocabulaire

## Verbes

**abolir** to abolish
**conserver** to conserve
**contrôler** to inspect, monitor
**développer** to develop
**douter** to doubt
**élire** to elect
**s'engager** (**vers**) to get involved (*in a public issue, cause*)
**estimer** to consider; to believe; to estimate
**exiger** to require; to demand
**exprimer une opinion** to express an opinion
**faire grève** to strike
**falloir** to be necessary
**gaspiller** to waste
**manifester** (**pour/contre**) to demonstrate (for/against)
**polluer** to pollute
**protéger** to protect
**reconnaître** to recognize
**recycler** to recycle
**regretter** to regret, be sorry
**sauver** to save, rescue
**souhaiter** to wish, desire
**soutenir** to support
**valoir** to be worth

À REVOIR: **conduire**, **empêcher**, **perdre**, **vivre**

## Substantifs

**l'augmentation** (*f.*) increase
**la baisse** lowering
**le chômage** unemployment
**le/la citoyen**(**ne**) citizen
**le contrôle** control, overseeing
**le déchet** waste (material)
**la diminution** decrease
**l'électeur/trice** voter
**le gaspillage** wasting
**la guerre** war
**les impôts** (*m. pl.*) taxes
**la jeunesse** youth, young people
**la montée** rise
**le parti** political party
**la politique** politics; policy
**le politicien/la politicienne** politician
**le problème** problem
**la réussite** success, accomplishment

À REVOIR: **les transports**, **la vie**

## Substantifs apparentés

**l'accident** (*m.*), **l'atmosphère** (*f.*), **le budget** (**militaire**), **le conflit**, **la conservation**, **le développement**, **l'énergie** (*f.*) **nucléaire/solaire**, **l'environnement** (*m.*), **le gouvernement**, **l'inflation** (*f.*), **la légalisation**, **la liberté d'expression**, **les médias** (*m.*), **la nature**, **l'opinion publique** (*f.*), **la pollution**, **la prolifération**, **la protection**, **le recyclage**, **la réforme**, **les ressources naturelles**, **le sexisme**, **la source**

## Adjectifs

**désolé**(**e**) sorry
**écologiste** ecological
**étonné**(**e**) surprised
**fâché**(**e**) angry
**furieux/euse** furious
**industriel**(**le**) industrial
**soulagé**(**e**) relieved
**sûr**(**e**) sure, certain
**surpris**(**e**) surprised

## Expressions impersonnelles

**il est...** it is . . .
**dommage** too bad
**étrange** strange
**fâcheux** unfortunate
(**in**)**utile** useless/useful
**il se peut que...** it is possible that . . .
**il semble que...** it seems that . . .
**il vaut mieux** (**que**)**...** it is better (that . . . )

## Expressions impersonnelles apparentées

**il est... clair**, **essentiel**, **évident**, **important**, (**im**)**possible**, **indispensable**, (**in**)**juste**, **nécessaire**, **normal**, **peu probable**, **préférable**, **probable**, **stupide**, **urgent**

## Mots et expressions divers

**par exemple** for example
**personnellement** personally
**la plupart** (**de**) most (of)
**pour ma part** in my opinion, as for me

# Intermède

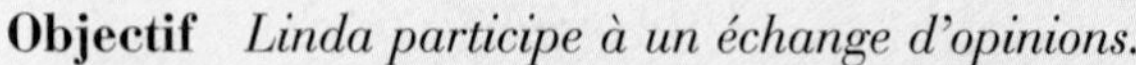

## L'Amérique en question

**Situation**: The *Situation* dialogues are recorded on the st. cassette packaged with the st. text.

**Contexte** *Linda est une étudiante américaine en première année de faculté à Montpellier. Ses amis, tous étudiants français ou francophones, aiment discuter avec elle des États-Unis.*

**Objectif** *Linda participe à un échange d'opinions.*

LINDA: Il y a des stéréotypes sur les Américains ici?

NADINE: Oui, on dit souvent que les Américains sont naïfs, qu'ils ne pensent qu'à l'argent...

LOUIS: Mais on est aussi fasciné par certains aspects des États-Unis: Hollywood, les rappeurs, la conquête de l'espace, Silicon Valley...

LINDA: C'est un sentiment un peu ambivalent, quand même,° non?

VIVIANE: Oui. Et en politique, par exemple, ça a été très difficile pour les Français de voir des présidents américains qui n'étaient pas des «spécialistes», tu sais... des membres d'une élite intellectuelle.

LINDA: Je crois que c'est particulièrement vrai des Parisiens. En province, on admire l'Amérique, non?

NADINE: Oui, mais je crois que l'Amérique a connu avant nous des problèmes sociaux très graves: le racisme, la drogue, la violence...

DANIEL: Maintenant que nous nous débattons° aussi avec ces problèmes, il est difficile d'être aussi critique envers les U.S.A.

LINDA: Mais est-ce que vous connaissez l'Amérique seulement par les films et les journaux?

LOUIS: Eh bien moi, j'ai vécu aux États-Unis, et j'ai trouvé qu'il faut beaucoup se battre° pour y survivre.° On n'est pas protégé contre la maladie ou le chômage. Finalement, j'ai trouvé que l'individu est très isolé.

VIVIANE: Oui, mais malgré tout, beaucoup de jeunes voudraient partir vivre aux États-Unis. Ils veulent tenter° l'aventure américaine.

quand... *all the same*

nous... *we're struggling*

se... *fight, struggle* / *survive*

essayer

## À propos

### Comment donner des conseils

Je vous (te) conseille de (+ *infinitif*)...
À votre (ta) place, je (+ *verbe au conditionnel*)...
Je suis convaincu(e) / persuadé(e) que (+ *sujet* + *verbe à l'indicatif*)...

Savez-vous (Sais-tu) que (+ *sujet* + *verbe à l'indicatif*)...
Je recommande que vous (tu) (+ *verbe au subjonctif*)...
Vous devriez (Tu devrais) (+ *infinitif*)...
N'oubliez pas (N'oublie pas) que (+ *sujet* + *verbe à l'indicatif*)...

## *Maintenant à vous!*

**A. Questions personnelles.** Relisez le dialogue, puis répondez aux questions.

1. Donnez vos opinions personnelles sur les observations suivantes.
   - Les Américains sont naïfs.
   - L'argent est la préoccupation essentielle aux États-Unis.
   - Les présidents américains n'appartiennent (*belong*) pas à une élite intellectuelle.
   - Aux États-Unis, l'individu est isolé et mal protégé.
2. Quels sont les stéréotypes que les Américains expriment en décrivant les Français?
3. Vos amis et vous, parlez-vous de temps en temps des problèmes sociaux mentionnés par Nadine: le racisme, la drogue, la violence, l'isolement de l'individu? Si oui, qu'en dites-vous?

**B. Jeu de rôles.** Avec plusieurs camarades, jouez une scène dans laquelle une personne doit prendre une décision de grande importance. Les autres étudiants donnent des conseils à cette personne et discutent avec elle de son problème. Utilisez les expressions de l'*À propos*.

**Suggestions**: Quelqu'un va...

- refuser de s'inscrire (*register*) au service militaire
- manifester contre les centrales nucléaires
- se marier avec quelqu'un dont il vient de faire connaissance
- quitter l'université sans obtenir son diplôme

## PORTRAITS

### *Eugène Delacroix (1798–1863)*

Grand peintre romantique, Eugène Delacroix a, dans ses tableaux dynamiques (et quelquefois violents), exprimé de vives émotions avec les couleurs. Il a représenté des sujets mythologiques, des événements historiques et, après une visite en Algérie, «l'exotisme oriental». Parmi ses tableaux les plus connus sont *Les Massacres de Scio* (1824), *La Grèce expirant à Missolonghi* (1827) et *La Mort de Sardanaple* (1828). Son tableau le plus célèbre, *La Liberté guidant le peuple*, censuré en 1830, n'a été montré au public qu'en 1861.

CHAPITRE **DIX-SEPT**

# Le monde francophone

**En avant**

—Je me crois au paradis.

—Moi aussi. Je n'ai jamais vu de coucher de soleil aussi beau.

—C'était une excellente idée de venir à Raiatea.

—C'est vrai, c'est moins connu que Tahiti ou Bora Bora et beaucoup plus tranquille.

**Communicative goals:** talking about the French-speaking world, talking about quantity, expressing doubt and uncertainty, and expressing subjective viewpoints.

**En avant**: See scripts for follow-up questions recorded on student cassette.

# Étude de vocabulaire

## Histoire de la francophonie

**Note**: As introduction to this chapter, have sts. name as many French-speaking countries/areas outside of France as they can. Ask whether some sts. have visited these countries.

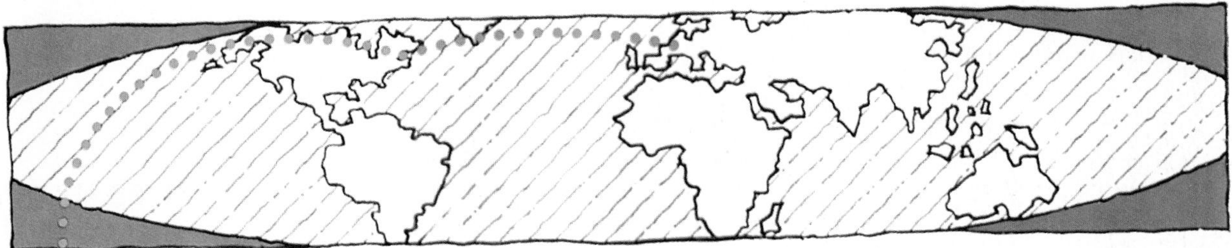

**XVI^e siècle:** Arrivée de Jacques Cartier au Canada; expansion française dans la région des Alpes et de la Côte d'Azur.

**XVII^e siècle:** Champlain fonde Québec; établissements des Antilles (Haïti, Martinique, Guadeloupe). Fondation de Montréal; la Nouvelle-France s'étend (*stretches*) vers l'Ouest jusqu'aux Rocheuses et le long du Mississippi jusqu'en Louisiane. En Inde, établissements français de Chandernagor et de Pondichéry.

**XIX^e siècle:** Implantation française en Algérie (1830), en Indochine (1859), au Sénégal (1854), en Tunisie (1881), à Madagascar (1883). Établissements de «l'Afrique équatoriale française» et de «l'Afrique occidentale française». Indépendance d'Haïti.

**XX^e siècle:** De 1954 à 1962, indépendance de l'Indochine, du Maroc, de la Tunisie, de l'Algérie et de seize pays de l'Afrique noire.

1961 – Établissement de la Maison du Québec à Paris. Creation de l'Association des universités partiellement ou entièrement de langue française (AUPELF).

1962 – Début de l'implantation d'ambassades canadiennes en Afrique francophone.

1965 – Premiers accords de coopération entre la France et le Québec

1967 – Création de l'Association internationale des parlementaires de langue française (AIPLF).

1968 – Le Parti Québécois prend le pouvoir au Québec. L'Acte 101 (une loi qui exige l'utilisation de la langue française dans l'éducation, le commerce, et la vie publique) est voté. Beaucoup d'entreprises anglophones quittent Montréal pour s'installer à Toronto.

1986 – Premier Sommet de la francophonie à Paris.

1987 – Deuxième Sommet de la francophonie à Quebec. Les pays francophones se réunissent tous les deux ans depuis 1987.

1993 – La destinée du Québec n'est pas encore décidée. Certains Québécois veulent que le Québec soit une société distincte et libre; d'autres ne veulent pas se séparer du Canada.

**Suggestion**: *Voyage dans le monde francophone.* Trace an imaginary voyage on a map of the world, with students describing the itinerary. Example: *Phileas Fogg est allé à Québec, et puis à Montréal. Ensuite, il est descendu à Haïti.*

**A. Un peu d'histoire et de géographie.** Répondez aux questions suivantes.

1. En quel siècle Jacques Cartier est-il arrivé au Nouveau Monde?
2. Qui a fondé Québec?
3. Dans quelles régions d'Amérique s'étend la Nouvelle-France?
4. Nommez trois colonies françaises au XIX$^{\text{ème}}$ siècle. Quel pays devient indépendant à cette époque?
5. Où et quand a eu lieu le premier Sommet de la francophonie?
6. Avez-vous déjà visité un pays francophone? Si oui, lequel? Si non, lequel aimeriez-vous visiter? Expliquez votre réponse.
7. Maintenant, consultez la carte au début du livre et nommez cinq pays francophones d'Afrique occidentale. Où est-ce qu'on parle français en Afrique orientale? Nommez trois îles francophones. Que savez-vous de ces différents pays ou régions? Avec quels pays associez-vous les expressions suivantes: le tourisme? le Maghreb? la décolonisation? les territoires d'outre-mer? le bilinguisme? les Cajuns?

**Answers**: 1. d 2. e 3. b 4. f 5. a 6. c

**B. Le Nouveau Monde francophone.** Voici des faits qui ont marqué l'histoire du Nouveau Monde. Trouvez dans la colonne de droite le nom qui correspond à chaque définition. Puis, avec un(e) camarade, essayez de mettre ces événements par ordre chronologique.

1. Il a exploré le Canada au XVI$^{\text{ème}}$ siècle et a pris possession de ces territoires au nom de la France.
2. Il a descendu le Mississippi jusqu'au golfe du Mexique en 1682.
3. Il a exploré la mer des Caraïbes et a découvert l'île d'Haïti en 1492.
4. Il a fondé la ville de Québec en 1608.
5. Un état américain doit son nom à ce roi de France.
6. Bienville a fondé cette ville en 1718 et l'a nommée en l'honneur du régent, le duc d'Orléans.

a. Louis XIV
b. Christophe Colomb
c. La Nouvelle-Orléans
d. Jacques Cartier
e. Cavelier de La Salle
f. Samuel de Champlain

**C. La francophonie aux États-Unis.** Regardez la carte des États-Unis. Qu'est-ce que ces villes ont de particulier? Savez-vous ce que ces noms veulent dire?

**Suggestion**: Ask sts. to think of other names of cities. Examples: Louisville, Ky.; Mascotte, Fla.; Macon, Ga.; La Perouse, Hawaii; Des Moines, Iowa; Lafayette, Indiana; Corinne, Utah; Claudeville, Va.; Gros Ventre, Wy.; Raton, New Mexico; Racine, Wi.

Territoire français avant 1763

Beaux Arts, Wash.
Coeur d'Alene, Idaho
Malheur, Ore.
La Porte, Ca.
Lac qui Parle, Minn.
Pierre, S. Dak.
Fond du Lac, Wis.
Detroit, Mich.
Joliet, Ill.
Notre Dame, Ind.
Chagrin Falls, Ohio
Normandy Beach, N.J.
Paris, Me.
Orleans, Vt.
St. Louis, Mo.
Marquette, Kans.
Versailles, Ky.
Fayetteville, Ark.
Bourbon, Miss.
Louisville, Ala.
Baton Rouge, La.
La Salle, Tex.
"Territoire français avant 1763"

**Continuation**: Ask additional questions: 1. *Comment est-ce qu'on prononcerait votre* (*continued below*) nom en France? 2. *Combien de francophones connaissez-vous? Où habitent-ils?* 3. *Connaissez-vous quelqu'un qui habite une ville portant un nom français?*

**D. Interview.** Bien sûr, il n'y a pas que des personnes d'origine française en Amérique! Interrogez votre camarade sur l'origine de sa famille et ensuite, présentez à la classe un résumé de ce que vous avez appris. Demandez à votre camarade...

**Suggestion**: Use for whole-class or small-group discussion. Have sts. recall responses of classmates when appropriate.

1. de quelle nationalité il/elle est
2. d'où viennent ses parents, ses grands-parents et ses arrière-grands-parents
3. quand ses ancêtres sont venus en Amérique
4. quelle a été, à son avis, la réaction de ses ancêtres quand ils sont arrivés aux États-Unis
5. s'il (si elle) a visité (ou visitera) le pays de ses ancêtres
6. s'il (si elle) parle la langue de ses ancêtres
7. si on conserve, chez lui (chez elle), certaines traditions ethniques
8. s'il (si elle) trouve qu'il est important de connaître ses origines

## Le Carnaval

Le défilé de chars — Les costumes d'Haïti — Le grand bal masqué à la French Opera House de la Nouvelle-Orléans — Le bonhomme de neige, roi du Carnaval à Québec

Un défilé de chars à Québec

**Le Carnaval.** Cette fête populaire est célébrée dans plusieurs pays francophones. Répondez aux questions suivantes.

1. Qui est le roi du Carnaval à Québec?
2. Quel est l'événement du Mardi Gras le plus important à La Nouvelle-Orléans?
3. Que portent les gens à Haïti pour fêter (*celebrate*) le Mardi Gras?
4. Comment s'appelle une procession de gens déguisés et de musiciens?
5. Comment s'appelle le véhicule décoré qui fait partie d'un défilé?
6. Connaissez-vous d'autres pays, régions ou villes où on fête le Carnaval? Avez-vous déjà participé à un Carnaval? Où et quand?
7. À quelle occasion y a-t-il un grand défilé à New York? Y en a-t-il aussi un dans votre ville ou votre région? De quoi se compose généralement ce défilé?
8. Pour quelle fête américaine se déguise-t-on généralement? Quels costumes avez-vous portés dans le passé? Quel costume avez-vous l'intention de porter la prochaine fois? Avez-vous jamais eu de grandes aventures lorsque vous étiez déguisé(e)? Racontez-les à la classe.

**Suggestion**: Give sts. a minute to answer before doing together.

**Follow-up**: Use this activity for listening comp. practice. *Où sont-ils? 1. Marc et Marie ont vu un grand défilé et ils ont entendu de la musique acadienne. 2. Jean et Martine ont beaucoup aimé le bonhomme de neige du Carnaval. 3. On est dans la deuxième ville francophone du monde. C'est une ville très moderne où les jeux olympiques ont eu lieu il y a plusieurs années.*

## Splendeurs africaines

La beauté et la variété culturelle des pays africains attirent (*attract*) des visiteurs du monde entier. Voici quelques brochures pour vous faire rêver.

**Suggestion**: Ask sts. to find *le Maroc* and *la Guinée* on map, then work in groups to answer the questions.

**Follow-up**: You may wish to ask sts. to research other francophone countries to get similar information (languages, religion, climate, cultural attractions) presented in the realia.

### Le Maroc

**Un Royaume aux mille facettes : villes impériales, grands souks de Marrakech, étroite Médina de Fèz, route des Kasbahs du Sud, déserts, longues plages de sable blanc d'Agadir...**

**Le Maroc, c'est tout cela et bien plus... Un pays de soleil chaleureux et accueillant.**

**Climat** : A Marrakech, les températures varient de 5° le soir à 20° en janvier jusqu'à 37/38° en août et même plus lorsque souffle l'hamattan. A Agadir, il ne fait jamais moins de 7° le soir et 20/21° à midi jusqu'à 27° en été, mais temps couvert le matin et toujours du vent pour rafraîchir. Attention! Dans le grand Sud, l'hiver, les nuits sont très froides.

**Formalités** : Carte d'identité valide si l'on voyage avec un groupe. Un passeport valide est plutôt conseillé.

**Monnaie. Change** : L'unité monétaire est le Dirham qui vaut 0,75 FF environ.

### La Guinée

**Vue d'avion, la Guinée se présente sous la forme d'une banane, au sud du Sénégal et s'étend de l'océan à la forêt vierge.**

**Climat** : Le climat tropical du pays est caractérisé par l'alternance de deux saisons qui varient suivant les régions et l'altitude. En général: juillet à octobre saison des pluies, décembre à avril saison sèche.

**Formalités** : Passeport valide + visa

**Monnaie** : Franc guinéen; 1FF = 45FG

**Splendeurs africaines.** Répondez aux questions suivantes.

- Où se trouve chaque pays? Consultez la carte au début de votre livre.
- Quelle est l'unité monétaire du Maroc? Et de la Guinée?
- Décrivez le climat des deux pays.
- Quels paysages sont typiques de chaque pays?
- Quels attraits culturels trouve-t-on au Maroc?
- Si vous pouviez visiter un de ces deux pays, lequel choisiriez-vous? Justifiez votre choix.

Le Maroc

# Nouvelles francophones

## Le français en Amérique du Nord

On retrouve les traces de l'influence française un peu partout aux États-Unis et au Canada. De nombreuses villes américaines portent des noms d'origine française, tels que° Baton Rouge, Des Moines, Montpelier ou Detroit. D'autres portent le nom d'explorateurs français comme Marquette, Joliet, La Salle ou Champlain.

tels... *such as*

**Presentation**: Discuss pronunciation differences in *québécois*—nasals and rolling of the **r**. If possible, bring a song (lyrics plus record or tape) to demonstrate vocabulary and pronunciation.

C'est en Louisiane que cette influence est la plus visible. En 1682 l'explorateur français Cavelier de La Salle a pris possession d'un immense territoire de chaque côté du Mississippi au nom de Louis XIV. Il l'a baptisé, en son honneur, Louisiane. Le nombre des colons° français a rapidement augmenté avec l'arrivée des Acadiens. Les Acadiens étaient les Canadiens français qui vivaient en Acadie (Nouvelle-Écosse) et qui ont été chassés° par les Anglais quand la France leur a cédé le territoire en 1713. C'est alors que beaucoup d'entre eux sont venus s'installer aux États-Unis, en Nouvelle-Angleterre et surtout dans les bayous en Louisiane. Avec le temps la prononciation du mot «Acadien» est devenue «Cajun», mot que l'on utilise toujours pour nommer leurs descendants. Les Cajuns ont préservé leur langue et leurs coutumes, et la musique cadjine est devenue célèbre de nos jours.

*colonists*

ont... *were driven out*

Le français est la deuxième langue étrangère parlée aux États-Unis, après l'espagnol. En 1990, il y avait 1,7 million de Francophones aux États-Unis. Ils habitent surtout les états du New Hamphire, du Maine, de la Louisiane et du Vermont.

Au Canada, 28 pour cent de la population parle français. La majorité des Francophones vivent dans la province de Québec. Montréal est la deuxième ville francophone du monde après Paris, et son université est la plus importante université de langue française en dehors du territoire français. De nos jours, l'anglais et le français sont les deux langues officielles du pays.

Une rue du Vieux Carré à La Nouvelle-Orléans

# 58. TALKING ABOUT QUANTITY
## Indefinite Adjectives and Pronouns

**Des vacances à la Martinique**

JULIEN: Alors, vos vacances à la Martinique?

LAURENCE: **Tout** s'est très bien passé. Nous sommes restés **quelques** jours à Fort-de-France, la capitale, puis nous nous sommes détendus à la plage. Tu sais, les gens sont très sympa, mais ils ont **tous** un accent que nous avions du mal à comprendre. On avait parfois l'impression qu'il y en avait **quelques-uns** qui ne nous comprenaient pas non plus.

FRANCK: Et **chaque** fois qu'ils disaient **quelque chose**, on devait leur demander de répéter. C'est marrant. **Certains** mots sont les **mêmes** que chez nous mais **d'autres** sont complètement différents.

Vrai ou faux? Corrigez les phrases fausses.

1. Tout s'est mal passé.
2. Ils sont restés plusieurs jours à Fort-de-France.
3. Quelques personnes ont un accent que Franck et Laurence ne comprenaient pas.
4. Les Martiniquais et les Français utilisent exactement les mêmes termes (les mêmes mots).

## A. Forms and Uses of *tout*

1. The adjective **tout** (**toute**, **tous**, **toutes**)

   As an adjective, **tout** can be followed by an article, a possessive adjective, or a demonstrative adjective.

| | |
|---|---|
| Nous avons marché **toute la journée** pour arriver au sommet du volcan. | *We hiked all day to reach the summit of the volcano.* |
| Nous étions là-haut avec **tous nos amis**. | *We were up there with all our friends.* |
| As-tu apporté **toutes ces provisions**? | *Did you bring all those supplies?* |

2. The pronoun **tout**

As a pronoun (masculine singular), the form **tout** means *all, everything.*

| | |
|---|---|
| **Tout** va bien! | *Everything is fine!* |
| **Tout** est possible dans ce pays. | *Everything is possible in this country.* |

**Tous** and **toutes** mean *everyone, every one* (*of them*), *all of them.* When **tous** is used as a pronoun, the final **s** is pronounced: **tous** [tus].

| | |
|---|---|
| Tu vois ces jeunes gens? Ils veulent **tous** faire une danse traditionnelle. | *Do you see those young people? They all want to do a traditional dance.* |
| Ces photos sont arrivées hier. Sur **toutes**, on voit des costumes traditionnels. | *These photos arrived yesterday. In all of them, you see traditional costumes.* |

## B. Other Indefinite Adjectives and Pronouns

Indefinite adjectives and pronouns refer to unspecified things, persons, or qualities. They are also used to express sameness (the same one) and difference (another). Here is a list of the most frequently used indefinite adjectives and pronouns in French.

**Presentation**: After charts have been studied and discussed, have sts. go back to minidialogue to classify indefinite adjectives and pronouns according to type.

| ADJECTIVES | | PRONOUNS | |
|---|---|---|---|
| **quelques** (+ *noun*) | *some* | **quelqu'un** (*invariable*) | *someone, anyone* |
| | | **quelqu'un de** (+ *masc. adj.*) | *someone, anyone* (+ *adj.*) |
| | | **quelque chose** | *something, anything* |
| | | **quelque chose de** (+ *masc. adj.*) | *something, anything* (+ *adj.*) |
| | | **quelques-uns/quelques-unes** (*pl.*) | *some, a few* |
| **chaque** (+ *noun*) | *each, every* | **chacun/chacune** | *each* (*one*) |

| EXPRESSIONS USED AS ADJECTIVES AND PRONOUNS | |
|---|---|
| **un**(**e**) **autre** (*another*) | **certain**(**e**)**s** (*certain*) |
| **d'autres*** (*others*) | **le/la même; les mêmes** (*the same*) |
| **l'autre/les autres** (*the other*[*s*]) | **plusieurs** (**de**) (*several* [*of*]) |

*Note that **de** is used without an article before **autres** whether **autres** modifies a noun or stands alone as a pronoun.

| ADJECTIVES | | PRONOUNS |
|---|---|---|
| J'ai **quelques** amis à Tahiti. | { | **Quelques-uns** sont agriculteurs. **Quelqu'un** m'a envoyé un livre sur Tahiti. |
| Nous avons **plusieurs** choix. | → | **Plusieurs** de ces choix sont extrêmement difficiles. |
| **Chaque** voyageur voudrait visiter une île différente. | → | **Chacun** des voyageurs fera un circuit différent. |
| Veux-tu **une autre** tasse de thé? | → | Non, si j'en prenais **une autre**, je ne pourrais pas dormir. |
| Où est **l'autre** autocar? | → | **L'autre** est parti. |
| **Les autres** passagers sont partis. | → | **Les autres** sont partis. |
| J'ai **d'autres** problèmes. | → | J'en ai **d'autres**. |
| Ce sont **les mêmes** voyageurs. | → | **Les mêmes** sont en retard. |

**Follow-up**: For a synthesis of this section, use the following dictation as a full or partial dictation, with only underlined words left out. *Je connais plusieurs personnes qui ont la même passion que moi pour la nature. Quelques-uns préfèrent la plage; d'autres passent leur temps libre à faire du camping dans les montagnes. Certains de mes amis aiment faire quelque chose de différent chaque week-end. Moi, j'aime faire du camping. J'ai tout l'équipement nécessaire pour toutes les conditions: la pluie, les tempêtes, la neige, la chaleur! J'ai quelques amis qui ont le même enthousiasme que moi pour la vie en plein air, mais ils ont d'autres idées sur le confort: chaque fois qu'ils font une randonnée, ils la font en voiture! À chacun son goût!*

The indefinite pronouns **quelqu'un** and **quelque chose** are singular and masculine. Remember that adjectives that modify these pronouns follow them and are introduced by **de**.

| | |
|---|---|
| Je connais **quelqu'un d'intéressant** dans la capitale. | *I know someone interesting in the capital.* |
| Il a toujours **quelque chose de drôle** à dire. | *He always has something amusing to say.* |

## *Vérifions!*

**A. À Dakar.** Jeanne-Marie a passé quelque temps à Dakar, capitale du Sénégal. Jouez le rôle de Jeanne-Marie et répondez aux questions posées avec **tout**, **toute**, **tous** ou **toutes**.

MODÈLE: As-tu visité les marchés? → Oui, j'ai visité tous les marchés.

1. As-tu vu le musée anthropologique?
2. As-tu photographié les églises de la ville?
3. Est-ce que tu as visité les bâtiments de l'université?
4. As-tu vu la vieille ville?
5. Tu as lu l'histoire du Sénégal?
6. Est-ce que tu as fait le tour des plantations?

**Additional activity**: *Excursion. Faites les substitutions indiquées.* 1. *Jean-Paul a vu tout le paysage.* (*fermes, champs, vignobles*) 2. *Tous mes camarades ont pris des photos.* (*amis, professeurs, amies*) 3. *Nous avons apporté tous les appareils-photo.* (*provisions, tentes, vêtements*)

**B. L'île de la Martinique.** Estelle a passé de nombreuses années à la Martinique. Elle y pense toujours avec nostalgie. Complétez les phrases.

**Suggestion**: Remind sts. to look for clues other than meaning, such as gender and number of pronouns.

«J'aime la Martinique. On y trouve encore (quelques-unes / d'autres)[1] des belles maisons coloniales bâties par les planteurs français. (Chacun / Certains)[2] jours, à Fort-de-France, je me promenais dans les marchés en plein air, près du port. (Certaines / D'autres)[3] fois, je restais sur la place de la Savane pendant de longues heures. Il y a, tout près de la place, (quelques / quelques-unes)[4] maisons décorées avec du fer forgé (*wrought iron*) qui me rappellent La Nouvelle-Orléans.

(Certaines / Quelque)[5] choses ont changé, il est vrai, mais on trouve encore les (plusieurs / mêmes)[6] gommiers (*gum-trees*) et ces bateaux pittoresques aux couleurs vives, que Gauguin* aimait tant.»

### Parlons-en!

**La première chose qui vient à l'esprit** (*mind*). Avec un(e) camarade de classe, posez des questions—en français, s'il vous plaît—à partir des indications suivantes. Votre camarade doit donner la première réponse qui lui vient à l'esprit.

**Suggestion**: Give sts. a few minutes to prepare questions. Ask sts. to circulate, posing their questions to 5 or 6 people. Afterward, ask sts. to report their findings, using the following expressions: *Certains étudiants disent... Quelqu'un pense... La même personne ajoute... Les autres trouvent que...*

MODÈLE: someone *important* →
VOUS: Est-ce que tu as jamais rencontré quelqu'un d'important?
VOTRE CAMARADE: Non, mais une fois mon frère a rencontré Jay Leno.

1. something important 2. something stupid 3. something funny 4. someone funny 5. all the large cities in Quebec 6. a few of the Francophone countries (*pays*) in Africa 7. several French cities 8. other French cities 9. another Canadian city

## 59. EXPRESSING DOUBT AND UNCERTAINTY
## The Subjunctive

### La France et l'Afrique

KOFI: **Crois-tu** que la France **doive** intervenir militairement dans les pays africains où il y a des difficultés politiques?
KARIM: Je **ne suis pas sûr** que ce **soit** une bonne solution.
KOFI: Pourquoi?
KARIM: Parce que **je ne pense pas** que cela **puisse** changer la situation politique.

Complétez les phrases selon le dialogue.

1. Karim ne croit pas que la France ____ intervenir militairement dans les pays africains.
2. Il n'est pas sûr que ce ____ une bonne solution.
3. Il ne pense pas que cette intervention ____ changer la situation politique.

*Le peintre français Paul Gauguin a vécu à la Martinique et aussi à Tahiti. (Voir la page 232.)

## A. Expressions of Doubt and Uncertainty

The subjunctive is used—with a change of subject—after expressions of doubt and uncertainty, such as **je doute**, **je ne suis pas sûr**, and **je ne suis pas certain**.

| | |
|---|---|
| Beaucoup de femmes **ne sont pas sûres** que leur statut **soit** égal au statut des hommes. | *Many women aren't sure that their status is equal to the status of men.* |
| Les jeunes **doutent** souvent que les hommes et les femmes politiques **soient** honnêtes. | *Young people often doubt that politicians are honest.* |

## B. *Penser* and *croire*

In the affirmative, such verbs as **penser** and **croire** are followed by the indicative. In the negative and interrogative, they express a degree of doubt and uncertainty and can then be followed by the subjunctive. In spoken French, however, the indicative is more commonly used.

| | |
|---|---|
| Je **pense** que la presse **est** libre. | *I think the press is free.* |
| **Pensez**-vous que la presse **soit** libre?<br>**Pensez**-vous que la presse **est** libre? | *Do you think the press is free?* |
| Je **ne crois pas** que la démocratie **soit** en danger.<br>Je **ne crois pas** que la démocratie **est** en danger. | *I don't think that democracy is in danger.* |

## C. The Indicative with Expressions of Certainty or Probability

The following impersonal expressions are followed by the *indicative* because they imply certainty or probability.*

| IMPERSONAL EXPRESSIONS USED WITH THE INDICATIVE | |
|---|---|
| il est certain que | il est probable que |
| il est clair que | il est sûr que |
| il est évident que | il est vrai que |

*French speakers often use **c'est** with these impersonal expressions, rather than **il est**, in everyday conversation.

| | |
|---|---|
| **Il est probable que** la France et le Zaïre **feront** plus d'échanges culturels et commerciaux pendant les années 90. | *It's probable that France and Zaire will engage in more cultural and commercial exchanges during the nineties.* |
| **Il est clair que** la langue française **restera** importante au Zaïre. | *It's clear that the French language will continue to be important in Zaire.* |
| **Il est vrai que** les Zaïrois **veulent** préserver leur propre identité. | *It's true that the Zaireans want to preserve their own identity.* |

## Vérifions!

**A. Réflexions sur l'Afrique francophone.** Complétez les phrases avec le subjonctif ou l'indicatif des verbes, selon le cas.

1. Il est sûr que le Burkina-Faso _____ (*aller*) bientôt changer de régime politique.
2. Pensez-vous que le Sénégal _____ (*être*) un pays en voie de développement (*developing*) ou un pays industrialisé?
3. Les observateurs diplomatiques ne croient pas que l'assistance étrangère _____ (*pouvoir*) améliorer la crise économique et sociale de l'Afrique centrale.
4. On doute que les Sénégalais _____ (*vouloir*) un changement radical de régime.
5. D'autre part, il est évident que, au Zaïre, le peuple _____ (*avoir*) très soif de démocratie.
6. Je ne crois pas que le régime militaire _____ (*devoir*) être soutenu pour empêcher une révolution populaire.

**B. Discussion.** Avec un(e) camarade, discutez des idées ci-dessous. Choisissez une phrase et posez une question. Votre camarade répond selon sa conviction.

**Réponses possibles:** Je crois... Je ne crois pas... Je pense... Je ne pense pas... Je suis sûr(e)... Je doute... Je suis certain(e)... Je ne suis pas certain(e)... J'espère...

**Suggestion**: May be done as whole-class discussion. One st. makes up a sentence and several others react.

MODÈLE: Le président est honnête. →
VOUS: Crois-tu que le président soit honnête?
VOTRE AMI(E): Oui, je crois qu'il est honnête. (Non, je ne crois pas qu'il soit honnête.)

IDÉES À DISCUTER

1. Nous avons besoin d'une armée plus moderne.
2. Le peuple* américain sait voter intelligemment.
3. Le gouverneur de votre état a de bonnes idées.
4. Le pouvoir (*power*) doit être dans les mains du peuple.

**Follow-up**: Ask sts. working in pairs to make a brief statement about their political ideas, using sentences as guides. They may also wish to add political slogans.

---

*__Le peuple__ is generally used to refer to the population of a nation: **Le peuple français a perdu un grand chef quand de Gaulle est mort**. Use **les gens** to express *people* in the sense of "many persons."

5. On doit limiter l'immigration aux États-Unis.
6. Les États-Unis peuvent assumer la croissance (*absorb the growth*) de l'immigration.
7. Les pays développés doivent aider les pays en voie de développement.
8. L'enseignement bilingue est une bonne idée.

### Parlons-en!

**Opinions et croyances.** Complétez les phrases de façon logique. Exprimez une opinion personnelle.

1. C'est vrai que... 2. Personne ne croit que... 3. Je ne suis pas sûr(e) que... 4. Il est probable que... 5. Beaucoup d'étudiants trouvent que...

## 60. EXPRESSING SUBJECTIVE VIEWPOINTS Alternatives to the Subjunctive

### Les Antilles, mythe et réalité

FRANCINE: Les Antilles, pour moi, ce sont les récifs coraliens, les sites archéologiques précolombiens, les plages de sable blanc...

SYLVAIN: **Il faut** tout de même **savoir** que nous n'avons pas que du soleil à vendre!

VINCENT: **Avant de partir**, tu devrais visiter une bananeraie, une distillerie de rhum et notre port très moderne.

SYLVAIN: **J'espère** que **tu sais** que notre niveau de vie, ici en Martinique,* est le plus élevé des Caraïbes...

FRANCINE: C'est vrai, **il est important** de **se moderniser**. Mais **j'espère**, moi, que **vous saurez** protéger la beauté de votre pays.

Trouvez la phrase équivalente selon le dialogue.

1. Il faut qu'on sache que nous n'avons pas que du soleil à vendre.
2. Avant que tu partes, tu devrais visiter une bananeraie, une distillerie de rhum et notre port très moderne.
3. Je souhaite que tu saches que notre niveau de vie, ici en Martinique, est le plus élevé des Caraïbes.
4. C'est vrai, il est important que les pays se modernisent.
5. Mais je veux, moi, que vous sachiez protéger la beauté de votre pays!

**Suggestion**: Ask sts. to read the minidialogue in small groups. Afterward, ask them to speculate on why the expressions in bold do not require the subjunctive mood.

*The French generally say **à la Martinique** and **à la Guadeloupe**, but the inhabitants of those islands tend to say **en Martinique** and **en Guadeloupe**.

It is sometimes possible, and even preferable, to avoid using the subjunctive. Several alternatives are presented here.

## A. Infinitive as Alternative to the Subjunctive

An infinitive is generally used instead of the subjunctive if the subject of the dependent clause is the same as that of the main clause, or if the subject is not specified.

| CONJUGATED VERB + INFINITIVE | CONJUGATED VERB + **que** + SUBJUNCTIVE |
|---|---|
| Je **veux** le **savoir**. (*I want to know it.*) | Je **veux que** tu le **saches**. (*I want you to know it.*) |

| IMPERSONAL EXPRESSION + INFINITIVE | IMPERSONAL EXPRESSION + **que** + SUBJECT + CONJUNCTION |
|---|---|
| **Il est bon de faire** ce voyage. (*It's a good idea to take this trip.*) | Il est bon **que vous fassiez** ce voyage. (*It's good for you to take this trip. / It's good that you're taking this trip.*) |

## B. *Espérer* plus Indicative

The verb **espérer**, followed by the indicative, can be used instead of the verb **souhaiter** or other constructions that express a wish or desire. When **espérer** is in the main clause, the verb in the dependent clause is in the future tense if the action is expected to occur in the future.

| | |
|---|---|
| Je **souhaite** que ton voyage aux Antilles **soit** intéressant. | *I hope that your trip to the Antilles is (will be) interesting.* |
| J'**espère** que ton voyage aux Antilles **sera** intéressant. | *I hope that your trip to the Antilles will be interesting.* |

## C. *Devoir* plus Infinitive

The verb **devoir**, followed by an infinitive, can sometimes be used instead of **il faut que** or **il est nécessaire que**. There is a slight difference in meaning, however, since **devoir** does not convey as strong a sense of obligation as **il faut que** and **il est nécessaire que**.

| | |
|---|---|
| Je **dois aller** au Québec. | *I must (should) go to Quebec.* |
| Il **faut que** j'**aille** au Québec. | *I have to go to Quebec.* |
| Il **est nécessaire que** j'**aille** au Québec. | *It's necessary for me to go to Quebec.* |

## Vérifions!

**A. Cours d'été à Montréal.** La classe de Thierry va suivre des cours d'été dans une université canadienne. Exprimez leurs espoirs (*hopes*). Employez **espérer** au lieu de **souhaiter**.

**Suggestion**: May be done as dictation, followed by transformation at board or at seats.

**Continuation**: 6. *Vous souhaitez que nous perfectionnions notre français.* 7. *Thierry souhaite que le professeur parle lentement.* 8. *Il souhaite aussi que le professeur soit sympa.*

MODÈLE: Je souhaite que mes amis puissent me rendre visite! →
J'espère que mes amis pourront me rendre visite!

1. Nous souhaitons que le campus soit agréable.
2. Je souhaite que les cours soient intéressants.
3. Mes camarades souhaitent qu'on aille danser tous les soirs.
4. Tu souhaites qu'il y ait un bon restaurant à la faculté.
5. Notre professeur souhaite que nous apprenions beaucoup.

**B. Vie européenne.** Il faut que les Canadiens francophones et anglophones apprennent à vivre ensemble. En Europe, la diversité linguistique et culturelle est encore plus prononcée. Qu'est-ce qui est important pour les Européens? Donnez l'équivalent de chacune des phrases suivantes. Utilisez **devoir** + *infinitif* au lieu de l'expression **il faut que**.

**Suggestion**: For oral work, or as dictation, with transformations done in writing at board or at seats.

**Continuation**: *Il faut que les Suisses passent leurs vacances en Espagne. Il faut que les Allemands achètent leur vin en France. Il faut que tu achètes ta bière en Allemagne.*

MODÈLE: Il faut que nous nous respections mutuellement. →
Nous devons nous respecter mutuellement.

1. Il faut que les Européens affirment leur unité politique et économique.
2. Il faut que nous développions nos échanges culturels.
3. Il faut que les nations européennes travaillent ensemble.
4. Il faut que les Anglais achètent des Renault.
5. Il faut que les Français achètent des Rolls-Royce!

## Parlons-en!

**Des conseils.** Donnez des conseils à vos amis qui vous expliquent leurs souhaits. Utilisez des expressions comme **il faut**, **il est nécessaire de**, **vous devez**, **j'espère que**.

**Suggestion**: Solicit as many variations on answers as possible. As an alternative format, use as brainstorming activity in groups.

1. Je veux vivre longtemps (*a long time*). Qu'est-ce que je dois faire?
2. Je veux perfectionner mon français. Qu'est-ce que je dois faire?
3. Je veux être riche un jour. Qu'est-ce que je dois étudier?
4. Je veux beaucoup m'amuser cet été. Où est-ce que je dois voyager?
5. Je veux rencontrer beaucoup de francophones. Qu'est-ce que je peux faire aux États-Unis pour en rencontrer? et à l'étranger?

# Nouvelles francophones

## Le français en Afrique

L'héritage français le plus frappant° en Afrique est peut-être tout simplement le français. En effet, le français est la langue officielle de dix-huit pays d'Afrique noire et il est aussi parlé couramment dans bien d'autres, comme ceux du Maghreb (la Tunisie, l'Algérie, le Maroc). Mais pourquoi parle-t-on français en Afrique?

*striking*

On le parle pour des raisons historiques. Déjà au XVII$^{ème}$ siècle, les Français faisaient du commerce avec certains pays africains, tels que° le Sénégal, où ils ont fondé° le port de Saint-Louis en 1659. Mais l'histoire de la francophonie commence avec la colonisation de l'Afrique par les Français et les Belges au XIX$^{ème}$ siècle.

*tels... such as*

*founded*

À la veille° de la Deuxième Guerre mondiale la France était la seconde puissance coloniale du monde. Cet empire colonial se composait de presque toute l'Afrique du Nord, de l'Afrique occidentale et équatoriale, ainsi que° de l'île de Madagascar. Les Français ont imposé leur langue dans tous ces pays. Ils ont fait venir de France des instituteurs qui l'ont enseignée dans les écoles. Beaucoup d'Africains sont aussi allés faire leurs études en France.

*À... Just before (literally, the day before)*

*ainsi... as well as*

Pendant les années 50 et 60, les pays africains ont l'un après l'autre proclamé leur indépendance. Ils ont dû alors faire face à de nombreuses difficultés politiques et économiques. Ils ont aussi essayé de retrouver leur propre identité. Alors pourquoi ont-ils gardé la langue de leurs colonisateurs?

Tout d'abord, le découpage° artificiel des frontières par les colons a souvent rassemblé des populations d'origines ethniques différentes; ensuite, à cause de la diversité des langues locales, le français s'est trouvé être la seule langue commune; enfin, le besoin de maintenir une ouverture avec le reste du monde a poussé de nombreux pays africains à conserver le français, langue internationale, comme langue officielle ou comme seconde langue.

*carving up*

De nos jours, le français est aussi la langue littéraire des pays africains. Le nombre d'écrivains et de poètes francophones y augmente de jour en jour. Parmi les plus célèbres, il y a Yambo Ouologuem du Mali, premier écrivain africain à gagner un prix littéraire français important, et Ahmadou Kourouma, de Côte-d'Ivoire, auteur de romans prépondérants en langue française.

Yambo Ouologuem

Ahmadou Kourouma

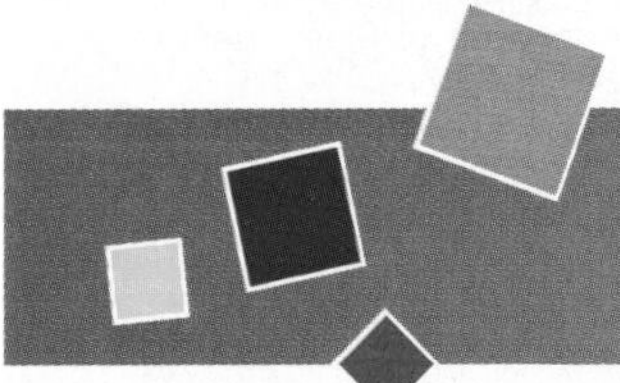

# Mise au point

**A. L'avenir.** Comment sera la société de l'avenir? Exprimez vos opinions. Commencez chaque phrase par une des expressions de la colonne de droite.

1. Il y aura des colons (*settlers*) sur la lune (*moon*).
2. Il n'y aura qu'une seule nation.
3. L'anglais sera la langue universelle.
4. Les robots remplaceront les gens dans beaucoup de domaines.
5. Tous les robots parleront anglais.
6. On fera tout par ordinateur.
7. Les villes seront sous terre (*underground*).
8. La vie deviendra beaucoup plus agréable.
9. ?

Il est possible que
Il se peut que
Il est peu probable que
Il est sûr que
J'espère que
Il est préférable que
Il est probable que

**B. Projets de vacances.** Complétez le dialogue suivant avec un des adjectifs ou des pronoms indéfinis à droite.

JULIEN: _____[1] les ans, c'est la _____[2] chose. _____[3] fois que je propose un voyage au Sénégal, tu as d'_____[4] suggestions.

BÉNÉDICTE: Mais j'ai rencontré _____[5] qui m'a dit que _____[6] touristes ont eu des problèmes de santé au Sénégal. D'ailleurs, cette année je voudrais faire _____[7] de différent. J'aimerais faire de l'alpinisme en Suisse.

JULIEN: De l'alpinisme! Mais c'est très dangereux! Bon, eh bien, cette année _____[8] fera ce qu'il voudra. Moi, je pars au Sénégal.

autres
chaque
même
tous
chacun
plusieurs
quelque chose
quelqu'un

**C. Interview.** Interrogez un(e) camarade sur les sujets suivants. Vous allez utiliser le subjonctif dans vos questions, mais votre camarade va éviter (*avoid*) l'emploi du subjonctif dans ses réponses.

MODÈLE: connaître d'autres cultures (nécessaire) →
—Est-il important qu'on connaisse d'autres cultures?
—Oui, il est important de connaître d'autres cultures parce que...

Demandez à votre camarade...

1. apprendre une langue étrangère (nécessaire)
2. voyager dans les pays du tiers-monde (*third-world*) (utile)
3. enseigner les langues étrangères à l'école primaire (bon)
4. s'informer sur les cultures étrangères sans jamais voyager (possible)

# Interactions

In this chapter, you practiced talking about quantities, expressing doubt, uncertainty, and subjective viewpoints. Use the vocabulary and structures from the chapter to act out the following situations.

**1. La Coopération** (*overseas volunteer service*). A friend of yours has been accepted as a Peace Corps volunteer and assigned to work in a village in Gabon. You ask what he/she thinks the experience will be like, what clothing or equipment will be needed, what kind of work he/she plans to do, etc. Your friend responds by expressing his/her wishes, beliefs, hopes, and preferences.

**2. Mon avenir.** You have been a very successful student. Everyone agrees that you will go far in your field. You are being interviewed by the college newspaper about what you will be doing in ten years. Describe what you think, hope, wish, or believe your future will be like.

# Rencontres

## LECTURE

### *Avant de lire*

**More on guessing from context: Deciding what is important.** The following profile of a popular *Québécois* entertainer, from the Canadian magazine *Le Lundi*, appears to give "complete" information about him, using forty different categories, but how much does it really tell us? Before reading it, look at the main head, the photo, and the boldfaced category that follows each number. How much can you learn from this information alone? Of the boldfaced categories, which imply that the following section contains information important to understanding the career and personality of the subject, and which deal with issues that are secondary or frivolous?

While reading, jot down a list of the items you find most interesting or most important about Léandre Éthier, then compare your list with those of your classmates. Do you agree with them about what is important to know about someone?

In this reading there are no glosses. Do your best to guess (from context or by noting cognates) the words and expressions you do not know.

# les 40 secrets de LÉANDRE

**1. Nom:** Léandre Éthier.
**2. Date de naissance:** Le 23 juin 1956.
**3. Lieu de naissance:** Montréal.
**4. Taille:** 1,85 m.
**5. Poids:** 75 kg.
**6. Couleur des cheveux:** Châtains.
**7. Couleur des yeux:** Bruns.
**8. Ce qu'il fait dans la vie:** Auteur-compositeur-interprète. Il écrit aussi pour les autres, dont les frères Groulx *(Tout seul au monde)* et Motion.
**9. État civil:** Célibataire.
**10. Enfants:** Aucun.
**11. Parents:** Sa mère se prénomme Janine. Son père, Hervé, a été typographe; avant tout, c'était un artiste (peintre, dessinateur ainsi que musicien), mais il a dû délaisser ces passions pour un emploi stable et rémunérateur à cause de l'importance de sa famille.
**12. Frères et soeurs:** Ils sont sept enfants. De l'aînée au cadet: Marguerite, Chantal, Jacinthe, Martial, Léandre, Jasmin et Carl.
**13. Enfance:** Il a eu une enfance heureuse et sans problèmes, sauf qu'il était le mouton noir de la famille.
**14. Premiers métiers:** Il a été enfant de choeur, livreur de journaux, vendeur itinérant, fossoyeur, chauffeur, D.-J. et a fait tous les métiers liés à l'hôtellerie. Il a aussi fait de la démolition et de la rénovation. 36 métiers, 36 misères!
**15. Expériences dans le milieu:** Il considère qu'il est un peu retardataire, car il n'était pas un défonceur de portes. Voilà pourquoi il n'évolue professionnellement que depuis trois ans. La musique a toujours occupé une place importante dans sa vie, et de seize à 22 ans, il a donné de nombreux spectacles dans des salles d'importance secondaire. Il s'est donné à ses 36 métiers et, il y a trois ans, il a décidé d'écrire en français, lui qui a tant de facilité en anglais. Puis a débuté le conte de fées. Il avait proposé une chanson à des compagnies de disques; au retour d'une excursion de pêche avec ses frères et son père, un message l'attendait: Audiogram désirait endisquer sa chanson!
**16. Récompenses professionnelles:** Il y a dix ans, il a été l'un des dix finalistes du concours *L'Esprit de Chom.*

## IL ÉTAIT LE MOUTON NOIR DE SA FAMILLE

PAR MARIE-CLAIRE BISSONNETTE

**17. Rêve d'enfance:** Être explorateur.
**18. Principales qualités:** Il est sympathique, tendre, amoureux de la vie, généreux et toujours à l'écoute des autres.
**19. Principaux défauts:** Il est trop perfectionniste et excessif.
**20. Arbre, fleur et pierre (précieuse) préférés:** Sa préférence va au saule pleureur et au chêne. Il aime beaucoup les tulipes et les nénuphars. Sa pierre précieuse préférée est le lapis-lazuli.
**21. Animal préféré:** Le lama qui, à ses yeux, a un côté très digne.
**22. Couleurs préférées:** Le lavande et le bleu.
**23. Vêtement préféré:** Les jeans.
**24. Sports préférés:** Le patinage, le ski, la natation, la voile et surtout la marche.
**25. Boissons préférées:** Le dry martini, très sec et avec beaucoup d'olives!
**26. Mets préférés:** Les plats italiens, indiens et séchuanais ainsi que les sushis.
**27. Superstition:** Aucune, quoique son intuition soit si forte que parfois, elle l'empêche d'agir.
**28. Voiture préférée:** Une MG 1958.
**29. Jour de la semaine préféré:** Le vendredi. C'est le dernier coup de coeur à donner et c'est l'annonce du plaisir.
**30. Chanteuses et chanteurs préférés:** Reggiani, Cocciante, Gold, Suchon, les Beatles, Sting, Joni Mitchel, Van Morrison, Rickie Lee John.
**31. Actrices et acteurs préférés:** Il aime bien Robert De Niro et Woody Allen, mais il n'a pas vraiment d'idoles au cinéma.
**32. Genre de films préféré:** Surtout les films italiens, ensuite les films d'action comme *Fatal Attraction* ou *Silence of the lambs.*
**33. Parfums préférés:** Gucci et Antheus.
**34. Lieu de résidence:** Montréal.
**35. Ville de prédilection:** Venise, même s'il n'y est jamais allé.
**36. Plus agréable souvenir:** La première fois qu'il a pris l'avion. Il voyageait seul et a séjourné au Mexique pendant trois mois.
**37. Plus désagréables souvenirs:** Les déchirures sentimentales.
**38. Causes sociales:** L'écologie et l'Association des grands frères.
**39. Projets:** Il travaille en ce moment à la promotion de sa nouvelle chanson, *Goodbye my love.*
**40. Philosophie:** Prendre le temps de bien faire les choses, de bien manger, de bien vivre, de bien aimer, de bien écouter les autres. Le titre de son album est d'ailleurs *Prendre le temps.*

## Compréhension

1. Quelle est la profession de Léandre? Quels autres métiers a-t-il exercés?
2. Comment s'appellent les frères de Léandre?
3. Comme enfant, est-ce qu'il était un prodige? Expliquez.
4. Est-ce qu'il a des goûts exotiques?
5. Quel semble être le pays préféré de Léandre?
6. À votre avis, pourquoi se considère-t-il le mouton noir de sa famille?
7. Est-ce que Léandre Éthier est un nationaliste québécois? Comment le savez-vous?
8. Que voulez-vous savoir de plus sur la vie de Léandre Éthier?

# PAR ÉCRIT

**Function:** Describing and hypothesizing
**Audience:** Anonymous readers of a gossip column
**Goals:** Discuss the personal and professional life of a celebrity (either a real person, or someone of your own invention)

**Steps**

1. Choose a celebrity. Jot down information for a general description: his/her primary activity, the achievements that have made him/her famous.
2. Speculate about some aspects of the celebrity's life or career that may not be known to the public. Use such expressions as **je crois que**, **je ne crois pas que**, **il est sûr que**, **il n'est pas certain que**, **on doit**, **il se peut que**, **il est possible** (**impossible**) **que**, **il est probable que**.
3. Make some hypotheses about how your subject's career can be expected to develop in the near future, and what he/she will probably accomplish over the next few years.
4. Write three paragraphs that correspond with the information from steps 1–3.
5. Bring your draft to class and ask a classmate to comment on whether your column is clear and interesting.
6. Incorporate your classmate's suggestions, if warranted, into the second draft of your column. Examine it for spelling and grammar errors. Pay particular attention to the use of the subjunctive.
7. Be prepared to share your composition with other classmates or your instructor.

**À l'écoute!** See scripts for listening passages and follow-up activities recorded on student cassette. Remind students that in the listening comprehension passages (as in real life) they will not understand every word they hear. They should focus globally on the general information in the passages and not be overly concerned about what they do not understand.

# À L'ÉCOUTE!

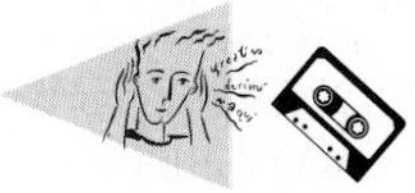

**I. Héritage français.** Jim Bonnet et Louis Lafleur ont de lointaines origines françaises. Ils racontent l'histoire de leur famille. Lisez les activités ci-dessous avant d'écouter le vocabulaire et les histoires qui leur correspondent.

VOCABULAIRE UTILE

| | |
|---|---|
| les bayous | *bayous, swamps* |
| leurs coutumes | *their customs, traditions* |
| semblable | *similar* |
| s'établir | *to settle* |

**A.** Donnez les renseignements suivants.

| | JIM | LOUIS |
|---|---|---|
| Nationalité | 1 ________ | 6 ________ |
| La région d'origine des ancêtres (en France) | 2 ________ | 7 ________ |
| Pays où les ancêtres sont allés | 3 ________ | 8 ________ |
| Lieu où ils se sont exilés après l'arrivée des Anglais | 4 ________ | 9 ________ |
| Résidence actuelle (*current*) | 5 ________ | 10 ________ |

**B. Vrai ou faux?** Corrigez les phrases fausses.

JIM
1. _____ Ses ancêtres étaient des Acadiens.
2. _____ Beaucoup d'Acadiens ont émigré en Louisiane.
3. _____ La famille de Jim parle français à la maison.
4. _____ Les Cajuns sont les descendants des Canadiens-Anglais.
5. _____ Jim va souvent en France.

LOUIS
6. _____ Ses ancêtres étaient des Français.
7. _____ Le territoire français au Canada est devenu anglais en 1713.
8. _____ Les Acadiens de Nouvelle-Angleterre sont retournés au Canada au XIXème siècle.
9. _____ Chez Louis, personne ne parle français.
10. _____ Louis a fait ses études en France.

**II. Étudiants francophones.** Rangira, Kai et Farah viennent de pays qui ont connu une influence française. Ils sont étudiants en France dans la même université. Lisez les activités ci-dessous avant d'écouter le dialogue qui leur correspond.

**A.** Associez les trois pays avec les phrases suivantes.

Algérie = A  Viêt-Nam = V  Zaïre = Z

1. _____ Ce pays en Afrique était une colonie belge.
2. _____ Ce pays en Indochine était une colonie française.
3. _____ Ce pays en Afrique du Nord était une colonie française.
4. _____ On a besoin de parler français pour y travailler.
5. _____ Le français est parlé dans la rue; il y a une élite qui est vraiment bilingue.
6. _____ On y parle peu français maintenant.

**B. Vrai ou faux?**

1. _____ Au Viêt-Nam, on enseigne le français comme deuxième langue à l'école.
2. _____ Les jeunes Vietnamiens sont très influencés par la culture française.
3. _____ Beaucoup de Zaïrois parlent français à la maison.
4. _____ Beaucoup de jeunes Zaïrois finissent leurs études en France.
5. _____ Les rapports entre les Algériens et les Français ne sont pas très bons.

## Verbes

**amener** to bring (*a person somewhere*)
**avoir du mal (à)** to have trouble, difficulty
**coloniser** to colonize
**découvrir** to discover
**se déguiser** to disguise oneself (to dress up in disguise)
**douter** to doubt
**fêter** to celebrate
**perfectionner** to perfect

À REVOIR: **s'amuser**, **augmenter**, **connaître**, **s'installer**, **se promener**, **rencontrer**, **voyager**

## Substantifs

**l'ancêtre** (*m., f.*) ancestor
**le bal masqué** masked ball
**le bonhomme de neige** snowman
**le Carnaval** Carnival
**le char** float (*parade*)
**le costume** costume
**le défilé** parade
**l'écrevisse** (*f.*) crayfish
**l'établissement** (*m.*) settlement
**la francophonie** French-speaking world
**le Mardi Gras** Mardi Gras, Shrove Tuesday
**le mélange** mixture
**le québécois** Quebecois (*language*)

À REVOIR: **les arrière-grands-parents, la campagne**

## Noms géographiques

**l'Acadie** (*f.*) Acadia
**les Antilles** (*f.*) Antilles (Islands) (Caribbean Islands)
**la Guadeloupe** Guadeloupe
**Haïti** (*m.*) Haiti
**la Martinique** Martinique
**la mer des Caraïbes** (**la mer des Antilles**) Caribbean Sea
**Montréal** Montreal
**la Nouvelle-Écosse** Nova Scotia
**La Nouvelle-Orléans** New Orleans
**le Québec** Quebec (province)
**Québec** Quebec (city)
**les Rocheuses** the Rockies (Rocky Mountains)
**Terre-Neuve** (*f.*) Newfoundland

## Adjectifs

**acadien(ne)** Acadian, Cajun
**accueillant(e)** hospitable
**anglophone** English-speaking
**francophone** French-speaking
**marrant(e)** funny
**québécois(e)** of Quebec

## Adjectifs et pronoms indéfinis

**un(e) autre** another
**d'autres** others
**l'autre/les autres** the others
**certain(e)** certain
**chacun(e)** each (one)
**chaque** each
**le/la même; les mêmes** the same one(s)
**plusieurs (de)** several
**quelques** (*adj.*) some, a few
**quelques-uns/unes** (*pron.*) some, a few

## Mots et expressions divers

**suivant** according to

# Intermède

## SITUATION

### Promenade à La Nouvelle-Orléans

**Situation**: The *Situation* dialogues are recorded on the st. cassette packaged with the st. text.

**Contexte** *Corinne Legrand et ses cousins français, Thierry et Fabrice, font le tour de La Nouvelle-Orléans, où Corinne est née. Partout en ville, ses cousins retrouvent les traces de l'héritage français, mais ils découvrent aussi une culture locale, résultat d'une histoire mouvementée° qui a rassemblé ° avec les Créoles,° des populations d'origines et de cultures très diverses.*

avec beaucoup d'événements différents / a... a groupé / *descendants of French settlers in Louisiana and the Antilles*

**Objectif** *Corinne raconte à ses cousins l'origine du vaudou à La Nouvelle-Orléans.*

THIERRY: Dis-moi ce que ça représente, ce culte vaudou de La Nouvelle-Orléans.

CORINNE: C'est un mélange de croyances° locales et de catholicisme dont le but° est de libérer l'homme du démon.°

*beliefs* / objectif
*Satan*

FABRICE: Mais quelle est l'origine du vaudou?

CORINNE: Eh bien, son développement est lié° à l'histoire des Antilles, que les Français ont colonisées. Ces colons° ont créé d'immenses plantations de canne à sucre, de café et de coton. Pour subvenir à leur besoin° abondant de main-d'œuvre,° ces Français ont utilisé des esclaves africains qui ont alors introduit leurs croyances religieuses dans les Caraïbes.

attaché
les pionniers qui colonisent
subvenir... *meet their needs*
main... des groupes de travailleurs

THIERRY: Mais, quel rapport avec la Louisiane?

CORINNE: Eh bien, voilà: d'abord, beaucoup d'esclaves antillais sont venus en Louisiane lorsque la Révolution française a aboli l'esclavage en 1794. Ensuite, un très grand nombre de planteurs blancs ont abandonné Haïti quand ce pays est devenu une république indépendante en 1804.

FABRICE: Et ils ont emmené leurs esclaves avec eux?

CORINNE: C'est exact. Et c'est comme ça que La Nouvelle-Orléans est devenue une capitale du vaudou.

FABRICE: Et ce culte, est-ce qu'il existe toujours?

CORINNE: Ça, c'est une autre histoire...

## À propos

### Comment hésiter en français

L'hésitation, dans la conversation, joue un rôle important dans toutes les langues. Voici des expressions qui marquent l'hésitation en français.

| | |
|---|---|
| Euh,... ou Heu (*alternate spelling*) [ø] | ... vous savez... |
| Voyons,... | ... tu sais... |
| Écoutez... | ... comment dirais-je... |
| Eh bien... | |

**Suggestion**: Ask sts. what sounds or words (such as *um* and *"You know . . ."*) serve for hesitation in English. Point out that *um* should not be "transferred" to French.

## Maintenant à vous!

Relisez le dialogue, puis répondez aux questions.

**Suggestion**: Encourage sts. to use the expressions for hesitation presented in *À propos*.

1. Quels groupes ethniques ont influencé la région où vous habitez? Quelles traditions montrent cette influence?
2. Connaissez-vous l'histoire d'un des peuples immigrés tels que les Irlandais, les Japonais ou autres? Racontez brièvement pourquoi ils sont venus aux États-Unis et ce qui leur est arrivé.
3. Quelles régions du monde les Anglais ont-ils colonisées au XVIIIème et au XIXème siècles? Est-ce qu'on y voit encore une influence anglaise? Commentez.

## PORTRAITS

### Aimé Césaire (1913–)

Né à la Martinique, descendant d'anciens esclaves africains, Aimé Césaire a fait ses études à l'École Normale Supérieure à Paris. Il est devenu professeur à la Martinique et puis député communiste et maire° de Fort-de-France, la capitale de la Martinique. Mais Aimé Césaire est avant tout un grand écrivain. Il exprime dans ses poèmes son mépris et sa haine° pour le colonisateur européen: «Je pousserai d'une telle raideur° le grand cri nègre que les assises° du monde en seront ébranlées.°» Parmi ses œuvres on trouve *Cahiers d'un retour au pays natal* (1939), *Les Armes miraculeuses* (1946) et *La Tragédie du roi Christophe* (1964).

*mayor*

son... *his scorn and hatred*

Je... *I will utter so forcefully* / *foundations*

*shaken*

Aimé Césaire avec François Mitterrand

CHAPITRE **DIX-HUIT**

# La société contemporaine: lectures et activités

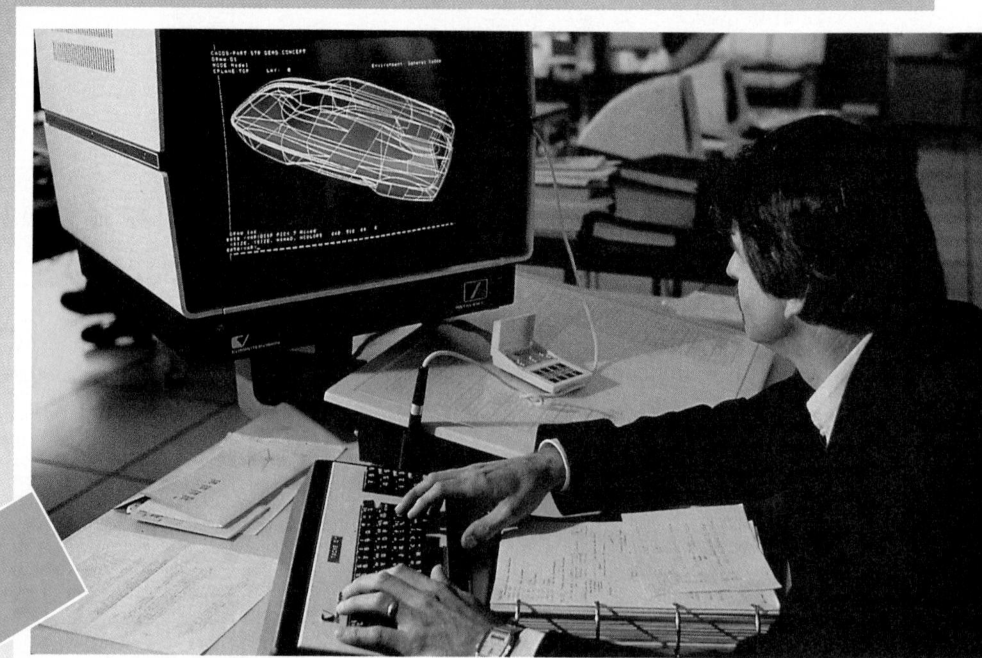

Qu'est-ce qui nous attend en l'an 2000?

**Communicative goals:** expressing opinions, describing, comparing, and narrating.

**Note**: The theme of this chapter is contemporary life in society. The purpose is to practice reading, speaking, listening, and writing at the Intermediate Level of the ACTFL proficiency guidelines. This chapter reviews important grammar and vocab. from Chapters 1–17. Activities review functions such as describing, narrating, hypothesizing, etc.

# La France qui change

La société française, comme la société américaine, est en pleine évolution. La France est un pays attaché à ses traditions mais qui sait aussi vivre à la pointe° du progrès. C'est toujours le pays de la bonne cuisine et de la haute couture, mais aussi des trains les plus rapides du monde. La majorité de familles françaises possède des micro-ordinateurs. La technologie a révolutionné le style de vie des Français. Des robots construisent leurs voitures et des ordinateurs font leurs traductions. Les Français peuvent traverser l'Atlantique en quatre heures avec le Concorde.

*à... on the cutting edge*

Cependant, sur le plan social, on constate° une baisse du niveau de vie. Les gens sans domicile fixe, les chômeurs et les personnes atteintes du SIDA ou du cancer sont de plus en plus nombreux. Les divorces sont plus fréquents, l'air et l'eau plus pollués. Le racisme est souvent une cause de violence. Cette contradiction apparente entre la révolution technologique et l'augmentation des problèmes sociaux fait peur aux Français. On peut se demander ce qui caractérisera le troisième millénaire pour eux.

*notes*

# LA FRANCE DE 1993 : CE QUI A CHANGÉ

**Davantage d'unions libres,[a] de femmes au travail, de jeunes dans l'enseignement supérieur, de personnes âgées ou assistées, de cancer et de sida. A cela ajoutez, moins de villages ruraux et d'agriculteurs, d'emplois stables, d'ouvriers d'usine. En une génération, les Français ont connu des mutations sans précédent.**

*Par Sévérine Gamazic de l'Agence France-Presse*

En premier lieu, figure l'éclatement,[b] en 20 ans, du modèle familial traditionnel. Le nombre de mariages, en baisse continue depuis 1972, va de pair avec la progression du divorce (un mariage sur trois) et l'union libre. Un million de femmes élèvent seules leurs enfants, deux foix plus qu'en 1968.

Autre tendance forte depuis 30 ans : la montée du travail des femmes. Les trois-quarts des femmes d'âge actif travaillent, alors qu'en 1962, seulement la moitié d'entre elles avaient un emploi hors du foyer. Cette poussée[c] provoque l'essor[d] des gardes d'enfants à l'extérieur : chaque jour 2,3 millions d'enfants de moins de trois ans sont confiés à une crèche, une nourrice[e] ou une gardienne.

## EMPLOIS PLUS PRÉCAIRES

Le marché de l'emploi a subi de profonds changements. A la suite des deux chocs pétroliers, le chômage a connu une forte progression entre 1979 et 1992, passant de 6 % à plus de 10 %.

Depuis 1985, on constate[f] une montée de l'emploi précaire. Le nombre de contrats temporaires a doublé au cours des dernières années.

L'insertion des jeunes dans le monde du travail est un problème crucial. Au sortir des études, il devient difficile de trouver un emploi stable. Dans le recrutement, les différences de formation, de sexe et d'origine sociale ont pris de l'importance : em-

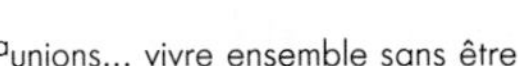

[a]unions... vivre ensemble sans être mariés
[b]*blow-up; dispersal*
[c]*growth*
[d]*expansion*
[e]*nurse, nanny*
[f]*notes*

plois moins qualifiés plus fréquents pour les garçons, emplois précaires pour les filles.

Selon l'INSEE, la France devra aussi relever le « défi » que constituent l'augmentation des effectifs des lycées et la tendance vers un enseignement supérieur de masse. En effet, où trouver les emplois pour ces jeunes, de plus en plus instruits?

Comme dans les autres pays industrialisés, le paysage salarial s'est transformé en France. L'emploi ouvrier a fortement diminué dans les usines, tandis que le secteur tertiaire a gagné de nombreux emplois.

Les conditions de travail ont également changé: 60 % des cadres utilisent l'informatique, contre 36 % des employés. Depuis 1982, le nombre d'ingénieurs et cadres informatiques a triplé.

Nombreux sont les Français persuadés qu'une retraite active est un gage de longévité.

## LA FRANCE RURALE S'EFFACE

La France rurale s'efface devant une civilisation « périurbaine » dévorante. Les 8.000 derniers villages de France tiendraient à l'intérieur du boulevard périphérique parisien.

Dans le domaine quotidien, les ménages français tentent d'améliorer leur confort: 76 % possèdent douche, WC et chauffage central, 37 % un magnétoscope, 31 % un lave-vaisselle.

Enfin, les Français vieillissent. Avec une fécondité qui n'assure pas le renouvellement des générations (taux 1,78 enfant par femme) même si on assiste à une émergence des maternités après 30 ans, le nombre de personnes âgées progresse. En 2050, les plus de 60 ans représenteront 34 % de la population.

Ce vieillissement est accentué par l'allongement continu de l'espérance de vie. Si en 1800, une Française pouvait espérer vivre 30 ans, elle peut vivre aujourd'hui 81 ans. Les Françaises détiennent d'ailleurs le record de longévité en Europe.

Ce plus récent rapport de l'INSEE traite aussi pour la première fois de deux maladies actuelles: le cancer qui ne cesse de progresser, notamment chez les fumeurs, et le sida, qui est en train de faire remonter les courbes épidémiologiques qu'avaient infléchies l'apparition des antibiotiques.

## Compréhension

1. Nommez trois ou quatre choses qui ont changé en une génération en France.
2. Quel est le taux de divorce en France?
3. Combien de femmes élèvent seules leurs enfants?
4. Comparez le pourcentage de femmes qui travaillent hors du foyer aujourd'hui avec celui de 1962.
5. Quel est le taux de chômage en France?
6. Est-ce que les jeunes sont en général plus ou moins instruits qu'avant? Pourquoi est-ce que c'est un problème?
7. Comment les conditions de travail ont-elles changé?
8. Donnez des exemples d'amélioration du confort dans les maisons françaises.

9. De nos jours, quelle est l'espérance de vie des Françaises? Qu'en était-il en 1800?
10. Quelles sont les deux maladies les plus fréquentes en France?

## Maintenant à vous!

**A. Comparaisons**

1. En quoi les États-Unis ressemblent-ils à la France? Cherchez les statistiques suivantes sur les États-Unis et comparez-les à celles sur la France. En quoi les deux pays sont-ils semblables?

   le taux de divorce
   le taux de chômage
   le taux de natalité (naissance)
   le pourcentage d'Américains qui ont une douche, le chauffage central, un magnétoscope, un lave-vaisselle
   l'espérance de vie d'une Américaine

2. Ensuite comparez les faits suivants. À partir de ces faits, tirez des conclusions sur la vie en France et la vie aux États-Unis.

| | La France | Les Etats-Unis |
|---|---|---|
| Nombre de meurtres pour 100 000 habitants | 4,6 | 9,4 |
| Nombre de condamnés pour trafic ou usage de drogues pour 100 000 habitants | 87 | 346 |
| Nombre de personnes en prisons pour 100 000 habitants | 81 | 426 |
| Nombre d'avocats pour 100 000 habitants | 32 | 310 |

**B. De quoi avez-vous peur?** Choisissez dans la liste suivante les deux choses qui menacent le plus notre vie de tous les jours et expliquez pourquoi.

1. le chômage
2. la crise du logement
3. la drogue
4. la violence
5. la destruction de l'environnement

**C. La famille et les valeurs en société.** Discutez des questions suivantes avec des camarades de classe.

1. Pensez-vous que vos grands-parents passaient plus de temps avec leurs enfants que les parents d'aujourd'hui? Pourquoi, ou pourquoi pas?
2. De plus en plus, les enfants de moins de trois ans sont confiés à une crèche ou une gardienne pendant que leurs parents travaillent. Quelle est la cause de ce phénomène? Quelles en sont les conséquences pour les enfants?
3. Que comptez-vous faire quand vous aurez votre diplôme? À quelles difficultés devrez-vous probablement faire face?

4. Pour quelles raisons est-ce que beaucoup de jeunes d'aujourd'hui retournent vivre chez leurs parents? Quelles difficultés cette situation crée-t-elle pour les jeunes? Et pour leurs parents?
5. Que signifie pour vous «la réussite dans la vie»? Gagner de l'argent? Poursuivre une aventure? Élever les enfants? Aider les autres?
6. En quel sens est-ce que la vie est meilleure aujourd'hui qu'il y a 50 ans? En quel sens est-elle devenue plus difficile?

**D. Par écrit**

1. **Dormir pendant 50 ans.** Imaginez que quelqu'un s'est endormi il y a 50 ans et s'est réveillé aujourd'hui. Décrivez les réactions de cette personne. Que remarque-t-elle? Que pense-t-elle de la technologie, de la vie sociale et du système éducatif?
2. **Comment sera la vie?** Imaginez comment sera votre vie dans 15 ans. Où serez-vous et que ferez-vous? Comment sera la vie de tous les jours? Comment la vie professionnelle évoluera-t-elle? Et les loisirs? À votre avis, la société sera-t-elle meilleure ou pire? Expliquez votre réponse.

# La planète en péril

Jacques Prévert (1900–1977) est un poète français qui décrit dans ses poèmes les problèmes de la vie quotidienne. Dans «Soyez polis», il présente les difficultés de la vie en société, vis-à-vis des autres et de notre environnement. Avant de lire ce poème, parcourez-le et cherchez les verbes pour en comprendre le sens général.

## Soyez polis*

Soyez polis
Crie l'homme
Soyez polis avec les aliments
Soyez polis
Avec les éléments avec les éléphants
Soyez polis avec les femmes
Et avec les enfants

**Suggestion**: Have sts. write a brief poem modelled on *Soyez polis*.
Soyez...
Crie(nt)...
Soyez... avec...
Avec... avec...
Soyez... avec...
Et avec...

*The version offered here is an excerpt.

Soyez polis
Avec les gars du bâtiment°
Soyez polis
Avec le monde vivant.

gars... ouvriers qui travaillent dans la construction

© S. WEISS / PHOTO RESEARCHERS, INC.

Un paysage fleuri, en Provence

. . .

Il faut aussi être très poli avec la terre
Et avec le soleil
Il faut les remercier le matin en se réveillant
Il faut les remercier
Pour la chaleur
Pour les arbres
Pour les fruits
Pour tout ce qui est bon à manger
Pour tout ce qui est beau à regarder
À toucher
Il faut les remercier
Il ne faut pas les embêter°... les critiquer
Ils savent ce qu'ils ont à faire
Le soleil et la terre
Alors il faut les laisser faire°
Ou bien ils sont capables de se fâcher
Et puis après
On est changé
En courge°
En melon d'eau
Ou en pierre à briquet°
Et on est bien avancé°...

ennuyer

les... les laisser libres

gourde (légume)

pierre... pierre pour faire du feu

on... on n'a pas fait de progrès

. . .

En somme pour résumer
Deux points° ouvrez les guillemets:°
«Il faut que tout le monde soit poli avec
le monde ou alors il y a des
guerres... des épidémies des tremblements
de terre des paquets de mer° des
coups de fusil°...
Et de grosses méchantes° fourmis° rouges
qui viennent vous dévorer les pieds
pendant qu'on dort la nuit.»

: (deux points) / « » (guillemets)

paquets... tempêtes en mer

coups... décharges d'une arme à feu

cruelles/insectes qui aiment les pique-niques

## Compréhension

1. D'après ce poème, avec qui et avec quoi faut-il être poli? De quelle façon doit-on manifester la politesse?

2. Quelles sont les conséquences quand on n'est pas poli avec la terre?
3. D'après vous, quel message veut communiquer le poète?
4. En quoi est-il poétique de parler de politesse envers la nature?

## Maintenant à vous!

**A. Opinions personnelles.** Avec un(e) camarade, discutez des questions suivantes. Utilisez dans vos réponses **je pense**, **je ne pense pas**, **je crois**, **je ne crois pas**, **je doute**, **je suis certain(e)**, **je ne suis pas certain(e)**, **j'espère...**

1. Pensez-vous que Jacques Prévert utilise des images exagérées pour établir son point de vue? Quelles images considérez-vous les plus drôles? les plus bizarres? Pensez-vous qu'elles soient enfantines? À votre avis, quel adjectif décrirait le mieux ce poème?
2. Est-ce que les gens sont, en général, polis ou impolis entre eux? avec la nature? Et vous, quel est votre comportement envers les autres? envers la nature?

**B. Que pouvons-nous faire?** Lisez les propos à droite, puis discutez des questions suivantes entre vous.

**2 FRANÇAIS SUR 5** sont écologistes ou du moins ont déjà voté (14%) ou envisagent de voter pour les écologistes à l'avenir (28%). 41% qualifient la défense de l'environnement d'objectif «prioritaire» contre 53% qui la jugent «très importante mais pas prioritaire» et 4% «pas très» ou (1%) «pas du tout» importante.

1. Est-ce que les Américains que vous connaissez se considèrent écologistes? Ont-ils raison, d'après vous?
2. Y a-t-il un parti politique «vert» ou écologiste aux États-Unis?
3. Quelles organisations aux États-Unis correspondraient aux partis écologistes européens? Êtes-vous membre d'une de ces organisations?
4. Comment peut-on soutenir (*support*) le mouvement écologiste ici?

Maintenant, faites un sondage parmi vos camarades pour déterminer quelles questions les préoccupent le plus parmi les suivantes.

_____ les sources d'énergie
_____ la pollution
_____ l'élimination des déchets industriels et ménagers
_____ le réchauffement de la planète
_____ la surpopulation
_____ le trou dans l'ozone
_____ la disparition des espèces de plantes et d'animaux

Demandez-leur aussi de proposer une ou plusieurs solutions à «leur» problème, et analysez les réponses obtenues.

**C. Par écrit...** Écrivez un article pour le journal de votre université. Donnez des conseils aux étudiants pour les aider à se préparer pour l'avenir. Répondez, par exemple, aux questions suivantes: Qu'adviendra-t-il (*What will become*) de la terre dans 25 ans? Quels seront les principaux changements technologiques (par exemple: dans le domaine des communications, des ordinateurs, des moyens de transport)? Comment sera l'environnement?

# La coopération internationale

La coopération avec les pays du Tiers Monde (les pays en voie de développement) est une des priorités de la politique extérieure française. Par exemple, un jeune Français peut faire son service militaire (10 mois) dans le service d'aide technique pour les DOM-TOM (Départements-Territoires français d'outre-mer). Le ministère de la Coopération organise la plupart de ces programmes, qui soutiennent les coopérants enseignants et techniciens. Actuellement, il y a 16 000 coopérants. L'article à droite décrit leur mission et l'évolution de leur fonction.

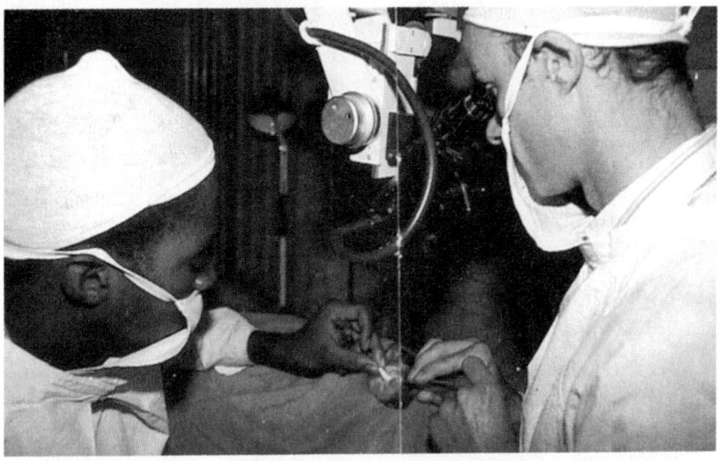

## Les Coopérants

*Un important réseau d'hommes et de femmes sur le terrain*

*Qui sont-ils ?*
Ils sont 16 000 civils français à travers le monde à coopérer, auxquels il convient d'ajouter les quelque 5 500 volontaires du Service National, techniciens et enseignants, partis pour 16 mois.

*Où sont-ils ?*
La France est ainsi le pays qui envoie proportionnellement à sa population le plus d'assistants techniques outre-mer. Les trois quarts d'entre eux assument des tâches d'enseignement. 85 % résident en Afrique, dont 55 % en Afrique subsaharienne et 30 % en Afrique septentrionale.

*Que font-ils ?*
Exerçant aussi dans des domaines aussi variés que la formation et la recherche agricoles, l'industrie et les travaux publics, les services culturels, les assistants techniques représentent la force humaine indispensable à la réussite de la coopération. L'aide au développement ne pourrait se faire sans leur capacité d'intégration, leur faculté d'apprécier sur place une situation donnée, leur habitude d'œuvrer avec les partenaires locaux à la réalisation d'objectifs arrêtés en commun.

## Compréhension

1. À votre avis, que veut dire le terme «coopérer»?
2. Quels sont les deux types de coopérants? Qu'est-ce que le Service National?
3. Où vont les coopérants, en général?
4. Dans quels domaines les coopérants travaillent-ils? Donnez un exemple de métier dans chaque domaine.
5. Pensez-vous que leur travail soit important? Justifiez votre réponse.
6. Aimeriez-vous être coopérant? Pourquoi, ou pourquoi pas?

## Maintenant à vous!

**A. Profil d'un coopérant.** Connaissez-vous des Américain(e)s qui font de la «coopération», en travaillant, par exemple, pour le Peace Corps, Vista ou d'autres organisations semblables? Par petits groupes, essayez de définir ce qui pousse les coopérants à partir.

**Note**: These activities can serve as culmination activities for the class. They are final activities for a classroom where interaction and communication have been the focus.

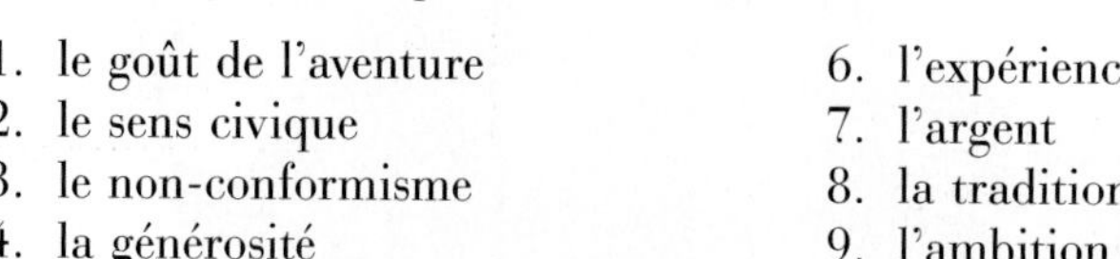

1. le goût de l'aventure
2. le sens civique
3. le non-conformisme
4. la générosité
5. l'esprit d'indépendance
6. l'expérience
7. l'argent
8. la tradition
9. l'ambition
10. ?

D'après les résultats obtenus, choisissez trois adjectifs qui définissent le mieux la personnalité du coopérant. Puis faites son portrait psychologique: goûts, passe-temps, sports.

**Fiche signalétique**

Nom de famille ____________________

Prénom ____________________

Né(e) ____________________

Domicile ____________________

Nationalité ____________________

Profession ____________________

Diplômes ____________________

Personnalité ____________________

Préférences ____________________

Enfin, comparez vos résultats avec ceux des autres groupes et commentez-les. Y aurait-il un profil typique? Lequel?

**B. Jeu géographique.** Familiarisez-vous avec les pays francophones d'Afrique en étudiant la carte d'Afrique au début du livre. Notez aussi les villes principales. Ensuite, en utilisant le tableau ci-contre, faites deviner à un(e) partenaire l'emplacement géographique de dix pays sur le tableau. En prime: nommez une des villes principales. Celui/Celle qui réussit à situer le plus de pays est le gagnant (la gagnante).

MODÈLE: —Où se trouve l'Algérie?
—L'Algérie se trouve en Afrique du Nord, entre le Maroc et la Tunisie. Alger est une des villes principales.

**Assistance technique civile***

PRINCIPAUX PAYS

|  | |
|---|---|
| Côte-d'Ivoire | 3092 |
| Maroc | 2633 |
| Algérie | 1444 |
| Sénégal | 1014 |
| Cameroun | 611 |
| Gabon | 598 |
| Tunisie | 594 |
| Madagascar | 466 |
| Djibouti | 429 |
| Congo | 353 |
| Niger | 345 |
| Centrafrique | 338 |
| Burkina-Faso | 316 |
| Mauritanie | 281 |
| Mali | 259 |
| Togo | 185 |
| Zaïre | 129 |

**C. Offre d'emploi.** Vous travaillez pour une agence qui place des coopérants à l'étranger. Vous avez un poste d'enseignant à pourvoir (*fill*).

1. Définissez le poste en donnant le plus de détails possible. Inventez les renseignements mais soyez logique.
   a. en quoi consiste le travail
   b. le lieu de travail
   c. le salaire
   d. la durée du travail
   e. les conditions de logement
   f. les conditions du voyage
   g. les loisirs sur place
   h. le genre de personne recherchée
2. Un(e) candidat(e) se présente pour le poste. Préparez une liste de questions, puis interviewez-le/la. Il/Elle vous pose beaucoup de questions sur le travail, les conditions et le pays. À votre tour, vous lui posez des questions sur son éducation, ses goûts et les raisons qui le/la poussent à partir à l'étranger. Jouez les rôles avec un(e) camarade.
3. Allez-vous l'embaucher? Va-t-il/elle accepter l'offre? Justifiez vos réponses.

**D. En route!** Imaginez que vous avez la possibilité de partir à l'étranger pour travailler pendant un an grâce à un programme d'échange. Où iriez-vous? Qu'aimeriez-vous faire? Faites d'abord une liste détaillée de vos projets, du choix du pays, du type de travail, de ce que vous vous attendez (*expect*) à trouver là-bas et de ce que vous pensez pouvoir y faire. À quels problèmes vous faudra-t-il sans doute faire face? Ensuite, faites une courte présentation à la classe en utilisant le futur et le conditionnel.

**E. Par écrit.** Vous aimeriez partir pour la coopération. Écrivez une demande d'emploi à Mme Péguy, responsable du recrutement. Dans votre lettre, définissez le poste que vous désirez. Puis expliquez en détail vos qualifications professionnelles et parlez aussi de vos goûts. Donnez votre adresse et votre numéro de téléphone. Soyez convaincant(e) pour persuader Mme Péguy de vous embaucher.

**Expressions utiles:** assistant(e) technique, médical(e); enseignant(e) (anglais, maths, sciences naturelles, informatique... ); ingénieur agricole...

## Interactions

In this chapter, you reviewed some of the most important grammar and vocabulary from Chapters 1 to 17. Use the following situations to bring your academic year to a close.

**1. Dire au revoir.** Circulate in class, and say good-bye to several classmates. Tell them about what you will be doing in the near and distant future. When you have finished, be prepared to summarize for the whole class what at least five class members will be doing.

**2. Joies et regrets.** Now that the academic year is ending, explain your feelings to a partner. Talk about what you liked and disliked. Mention what you thought of your instructors and fellow students. Describe your hopes for the coming year. Your partner will react and describe his or her own feelings to you.

## À L'ÉCOUTE!

**Débat sur la publicité.** Deux étudiants en philosophie, Bernard et Florence, ont organisé un débat sur le rôle de la publicité dans la société actuelle. Voici leurs opinions. Lisez l'activité ci-dessous avant d'écouter le vocabulaire et le dialogue qui lui correspondent.

VOCABULAIRE UTILE
le seul but *the only goal*
font appel à *appeal to*
la pub *advertising*
la marque *brand* (*label*)
pas à pas *step by step*
le fabricant *manufacturer*
il te racontera n'importe quoi *he will tell you just anything*
tu sous-estimes *you underestimate*

Encerclez la bonne réponse selon le dialogue.

1. Florence
   a. approuve la publicité
   b. critique la publicité
2. Bernard
   a. approuve la publicité
   b. critique la publicité
3. Dans un exemple cité au cours du débat, quel produit est présenté au moyen d'un bel homme élégant?
   a. les gâteaux
   b. les cigarettes
   c. les ordinateurs

4. Dans un autre exemple, quelle annonce publicitaire explique clairement comment le produit fonctionne? L'annonce pour
   a. un minitel
   b. une chaîne stéréo
   c. un ordinateur
5. Selon Bernard, les publicités servent à
   a. influencer les gens qui n'ont pas beaucoup de personnalité
   b. informer le public des nouveaux produits sur le marché
   c. exercer une influence subliminale sur le consommateur
6. Selon Florence, les publicités
   a. créent des besoins artificiels
   b. informent le public des nouveaux produits sur le marché
   c. associent les produits à une image de la perfection
7. Florence semble avoir une opinion
   a. très positive
   b. assez cynique
   c. assez ambiguë
8. À la fin, Bernard accuse Florence de faire exactement ce qu'elle reproche aux publicités, c'est-à-dire
   a. de faire appel aux impulsions les plus basses
   b. de raconter n'importe quoi pour convaincre les autres
   c. de se servir d'un stéréotype négatif pour défendre son point de vue

# Appendices

# Appendix A

## The *passé simple*

1. The **passé simple** is a past tense often used in printed narrative material. It is not a conversational tense. Verbs that would be used in the **passé composé** in informal speech or writing are in the **passé simple** in formal writing. You may want to learn to recognize the forms of the **passé simple** for reading purposes. The **passé simple** of regular **-er** verbs is formed by adding the endings **-ai**, **-as**, **-a**, **-âmes**, **-âtes**, and **-èrent** to the verb stem. The endings for **-ir** and **-re** verbs are: **-is**, **-is**, **-it**, **-îmes**, **-îtes**, and **-irent**.

| | parler | finir | perdre |
|---|---|---|---|
| je | parlai | finis | perdis |
| tu | parlas | finis | perdis |
| il, elle, on | parla | finit | perdit |
| nous | parlâmes | finîmes | perdîmes |
| vous | parlâtes | finîtes | perdîtes |
| ils, elles | parlèrent | finirent | perdirent |

2. Here are the third-person forms (**il**, **elle**, **on**; **ils**, **elles**) of some verbs that are irregular in the **passé simple**. The rest can be found in Appendix D.

| INFINITIVE | PASSÉ SIMPLE |
|---|---|
| avoir | il eut, ils eurent |
| dire | il dit, ils dirent |
| être | il fut, ils furent |
| faire | il fit, ils firent |

# Appendix B

## Other Perfect Verb Constructions

In addition to the **passé composé**, French has several other perfect verb forms (conjugated forms of **avoir** or **être** + the past participle of a verb). Following are the most common perfect constructions.

## The Pluperfect

The pluperfect tense (also called the past perfect) is formed with the imperfect of the auxiliary verb (**avoir** or **être**) + the past participle of the main verb.

| | parler | sortir | se réveiller |
|---|---|---|---|
| je/j' | avais parlé | étais sorti(e) | m'étais réveillé(e) |
| tu | avais parlé | étais sorti(e) | t'étais réveillé(e) |
| il, elle, on | avait parlé | était sorti(e) | s'était réveillé(e) |
| nous | avions parlé | étions sorti(e)s | nous étions réveillé(e)s |
| vous | aviez parlé | étiez sorti(e)(s) | vous étiez réveillé(e)(s) |
| ils, elles | avaient parlé | étaient sorti(e)s | s'étaient réveillé(e)s |

The pluperfect is used to indicate an action or event that occurred before another past action or event, either stated or implied: *I had already left for the country (when my friends arrived in Paris).*

Quand j'ai téléphoné aux Dupont, ils **avaient** déjà **décidé** d'acheter la ferme. — *When I phoned the Duponts, they had already decided to buy the farm.*

Marie s'**était réveillée** avant moi. Elle **était** déjà **sortie** à sept heures. — *Marie had awakened before me. She had already left by seven o'clock.*

## The Future Perfect

The future perfect is formed with the future of the auxiliary verb (**avoir** or **être**) + the past participle of the main verb.

| | parler | sortir | se réveiller |
|---|---|---|---|
| je/j' | aurai parlé | serai sorti(e) | me serai réveillé(e) |
| tu | auras parlé | seras sorti(e) | te seras réveillé(e) |
| il, elle, on | aura parlé | sera sorti(e) | se sera réveillé(e) |
| nous | aurons parlé | serons sorti(e)s | nous serons réveillé(e)s |
| vous | aurez parlé | serez sorti(e)(s) | vous serez réveillé(e)(s) |
| ils, elles | auront parlé | seront sorti(e)s | se seront réveillé(e)s |

The future perfect can be used to express a future action that will already have taken place when another future action occurs. The subsequent action is always expressed by the simple future.

Je publierai mes résultats quand j'**aurai terminé** cette expérience. — *I'll publish the results when I've finished this experiment.*

Aussitôt que mes collègues **seront revenus**, ils liront mon rapport. — *As soon as my colleagues have returned, they'll read my report.*

## The Past Conditional

The past conditional (or conditional perfect) is formed with the conditional of the auxiliary verb (**avoir** or **être**) + the past participle of the main verb.

| | parler | sortir | se réveiller |
|---|---|---|---|
| je/j' | aurais parlé | serais sorti(e) | me serais réveillé(e) |
| tu | aurais parlé | serais sorti(e) | te serais réveillé(e) |
| il, elle, on | aurait parlé | serait sorti(e) | se serait réveillé(e) |
| nous | aurions parlé | serions sorti(e)s | nous serions réveillé(e)s |
| vous | auriez parlé | seriez sorti(e)(s) | vous seriez réveillé(e)(s) |
| ils, elles | auraient parlé | seraient sorti(e)s | se seraient réveillé(e)s |

The past conditional is used to express an action or event that would have occurred if some set of conditions (stated or implied) had been present: *We would have worried* (*if we had known*).

### Uses of the Past Conditional

The past conditional is used in the main clause of an *if*-clause sentence when the verb of the *if*-clause is in the pluperfect.

Si j'**avais eu** le temps, j'**aurais visité** Nîmes. — *If I had had the time, I would have visited Nîmes.*

Si les Normands n'**avaient** pas **conquis** l'Angleterre en 1066, l'anglais **aurait été** une langue très différente. — *If the Normans had not conquered England in 1066, English would have been a very different language.*

The underlying set of conditions (the *if*-clause) is sometimes not stated.

À ta place, j'**aurais parlé** au guide. — *In your place, I would have spoken to the guide.*
Nous **serions allés** au lac. — *We would have gone to the lake.*

### The Past Conditional of *devoir*

The past conditional of **devoir** means *should have* or *ought to have*. It expresses regret about something that did not take place in the past.

J'**aurais dû prendre** l'autre chemin. — *I should have taken the other road.*
Nous **aurions dû acheter** un plan. — *We should have bought a map.*

## The Past Subjunctive

The past subjunctive is formed with the present subjunctive of the auxiliary verb (**avoir** or **être**) + the past participle of the main verb.

| | PAST SUBJUNCTIVE OF **parler** | PAST SUBJUNCTIVE OF **venir** |
|---|---|---|
| que je/j' | **aie parlé** | **sois venu(e)** |
| que tu | **aies parlé** | **sois venu(e)** |
| qu'il, elle, on | **ait parlé** | **soit venu(e)** |
| que nous | **ayons parlé** | **soyons venu(e)s** |
| que vous | **ayez parlé** | **soyez venu(e)(s)** |
| qu'ils, elles | **aient parlé** | **soient venu(e)s** |

Je suis content que tu **aies parlé** avec Claudette. — *I'm glad you've spoken with Claudette.*

Il est dommage qu'elle ne **soit** pas encore **venue**. — *It's too bad that she hasn't come yet.*

The past subjunctive is used under the same circumstances as the present subjunctive except that it indicates that the action or situation described in the dependent clause occurred *before* the action or situation described in the main clause. Compare these sentences:

Je suis content que tu **viennes**. — *I'm happy that you are coming.*
Je suis content que tu **sois venu(e)**. — *I'm happy that you came.*

Je doute qu'ils le **comprennent**. — *I doubt that they understand it.*
Je doute qu'ils l'**aient compris**. — *I doubt that they have understood it.*

# Appendix C

## Pronouns

### Demonstrative Pronouns

Demonstrative pronouns such as *this one, that one,* refer to a person, thing, or idea that has been mentioned previously. In French, they agree in gender and number with the nouns they replace.

| | SINGULAR | | PLURAL | |
|---|---|---|---|---|
| *Masculine* | **celui** | *this one, that one, the one* | **ceux** | *these, those, the ones* |
| *Feminine* | **celle** | *this one, that one, the one* | **celles** | *these, those, the ones* |

French demonstrative pronouns cannot stand alone. They must be used in one of the following ways:

1. with the suffix **-ci** (to indicate someone or something located close to the speaker) or **-là** (for someone or something more distant from the speaker)

| | |
|---|---|
| Voici deux affiches. Préférez-vous **celle-ci** ou **celle-là**? | *Here are two posters. Do you prefer this one or that one?* |

2. followed by a prepositional phrase (often a construction with **de**)

| | |
|---|---|
| Quelle époque t'intéresse? **Celle** du moyen âge ou **celle** de la Renaissance? | *Which period interests you? That of the Middle Ages or that of the Renaissance?* |

3. followed by a dependent clause introduced by a relative pronoun

| | |
|---|---|
| On trouve des villages anciens dans plusieurs parcs: **ceux** qui sont dans le Parc de la Brière sont en ruine; **ceux** qui sont dans les parcs de la Lorraine et du Morvan ont été restaurés. | *One finds very old villages in several parks: those that are in Brière Park are in ruins; those that are in the Lorraine and Morvan parks have been restored.* |

### Indefinite Demonstrative Pronouns

**Ceci** (*this*), **cela** (*that*), and **ça** (*that*, informal) are indefinite demonstrative pronouns; they refer to an idea or thing with no definite antecedent. They do not show gender or number.

| | |
|---|---|
| Cela (**Ça**) n'est pas important. | *That's not important.* |
| Regarde **ceci** de près. | *Look at this closely.* |
| Qu'est-ce que c'est que **ça**? | *What's that?* |

## Relative Pronouns

### A. Ce *qui* and ce *que*

**Ce qui** and **ce que** are indefinite relative pronouns similar in meaning to **la chose qui** (**que**) or **les choses qui** (**que**). They refer to an idea or a subject that is unspecified and has neither gender nor number, often expressed as *what.*

| | |
|---|---|
| —Dites-moi **ce qui** est arrivé au touriste américain. | *—Tell me what happened to the American tourist.* |
| —Je ne sais pas **ce qui** lui est arrivé. | *—I don't know what happened to him.* |
| —Dites-moi **ce que** vous avez fait à Pointe-à-Pitre. | *—Tell me what you did in Point-à-Pitre.* |
| —Je n'ai pas le temps de vous dire tout **ce qu'**on a fait. | *—I don't have time to tell you everything we did.* |

### B. *Lequel*

**Lequel** (**laquelle**, **lesquels**, **lesquelles**) is the relative pronoun used as an object of a preposition to refer to things and people. **Lequel** and its forms contract with **à** and **de**.

Où est l'agence de voyage **devant laquelle** il attend? — *Where is the travel agency in front of which he's waiting?*

L'hôtel **auquel** j'écris est à la Guadeloupe. — *The hotel to which I am writing is in Guadeloupe.*

Ce sont des gens **parmi lesquels** je me sens bien. — *They're people among whom I feel comfortable.*

## Possessive Pronouns

Possessive pronouns replace nouns that are modified by a possessive adjective or other possessive construction. In English, the possessive pronouns are *mine*, *yours*, *his*, *hers*, *its*, *ours*, and *theirs*. In French, the appropriate definite article is always used with the possessive pronoun.

| | SINGULAR | | PLURAL | |
|---|---|---|---|---|
| | *Masculine* | *Feminine* | *Masculine* | *Feminine* |
| *mine* | le mien | la mienne | les miens | les miennes |
| *yours* | le tien | la tienne | les tiens | les tiennes |
| *his/hers/its* | le sien | la sienne | les siens | les siennes |
| *ours* | le nôtre | la nôtre | les nôtres | |
| *yours* | le vôtre | la vôtre | les vôtres | |
| *theirs* | le leur | la leur | les leurs | |

| POSSESSIVE CONSTRUCTION + *NOUN* | | POSSESSIVE PRONOUN |
|---|---|---|
| Où sont **leurs bagages**? | → | **Les leurs** sont ici. |
| C'est **mon frère** là-bas. | → | Ah oui? C'est **le mien** à côté de lui. |
| La **voiture de Frédérique** est plus rapide que **ma voiture**. | | Ah oui? **La sienne** est aussi plus rapide que **la mienne**. |

# Appendix D

## Verb Charts

| VERB | INDICATIVE | | | |
|---|---|---|---|---|
| | PRESENT | PASSÉ COMPOSÉ | IMPERFECT | PLUPERFECT |
| **1. Auxiliary verbs** | | | | |
| **avoir**[1] | ai | ai eu | avais | avais eu |
| (*to have*) | as | as eu | avais | avais eu |
| ayant | a | a eu | avait | avait eu |
| eu | avons | avons eu | avions | avions eu |
| | avez | avez eu | aviez | aviez eu |
| | ont | ont eu | avaient | avaient eu |
| **être** | suis | ai été | étais | avais été |
| (*to be*) | es | as été | étais | avais été |
| étant | est | a été | était | avait été |
| été | sommes | avons été | étions | avions été |
| | êtes | avez été | étiez | aviez été |
| | sont | ont été | étaient | avaient été |
| **2. Regular verbs** | | | | |
| **-er** verbs | parle | ai parlé | parlais | avais parlé |
| **parler** | parles | as parlé | parlais | avais parlé |
| (*to speak*) | parle | a parlé | parlait | avait parlé |
| parlant | parlons | avons parlé | parlions | avions parlé |
| parlé | parlez | avez parlé | parliez | aviez parlé |
| | parlent | ont parlé | parlaient | avaient parlé |
| **-ir** verbs | finis | ai fini | finissais | avais fini |
| **finir** | finis | as fini | finissais | avais fini |
| (*to finish*) | finit | a fini | finissait | avait fini |
| finissant | finissons | avons fini | finissions | avions fini |
| fini | finissez | avez fini | finissiez | aviez fini |
| | finissent | ont fini | finissaient | avaient fini |

[1]The left-hand column of each chart contains the infinitive, the present participle, and the past participle of each verb. Conjugated verbs are shown without subject pronouns.

| | | CONDITIONAL | | SUBJUNCTIVE | IMPERATIVE |
|---|---|---|---|---|---|
| PASSÉ SIMPLE | FUTURE | PRESENT | PAST | PRESENT | |
| eus | aurai | aurais | aurais eu | aie | |
| eus | auras | aurais | aurais eu | aies | aie |
| eut | aura | aurait | aurait eu | ait | |
| eûmes | aurons | aurions | aurions eu | ayons | ayons |
| eûtes | aurez | auriez | auriez eu | ayez | ayez |
| eurent | auront | auraient | auraient eu | aient | |
| fus | serai | serais | aurais été | sois | |
| fus | seras | serais | aurais été | sois | sois |
| fut | sera | serait | aurait été | soit | |
| fûmes | serons | serions | aurions été | soyons | soyons |
| fûtes | serez | seriez | auriez été | soyez | soyez |
| furent | seront | seraient | auraient été | soient | |
| parlai | parlerai | parlerais | aurais parlé | parle | |
| parlas | parleras | parlerais | aurais parlé | parles | parle |
| parla | parlera | parlerait | aurait parlé | parle | |
| parlâmes | parlerons | parlerions | aurions parlé | parlions | parlons |
| parlâtes | parlerez | parleriez | auriez parlé | parliez | parlez |
| parlèrent | parleront | parleraient | auraient parlé | parlent | |
| finis | finirai | finirais | aurais fini | finisse | |
| finis | finiras | finirais | aurais fini | finisses | finis |
| finit | finira | finirait | aurait fini | finisse | |
| finîmes | finirons | finirions | aurions fini | finissions | finissons |
| finîtes | finirez | finiriez | auriez fini | finissiez | finissez |
| finirent | finiront | finiraient | auraient fini | finissent | |

| VERB | INDICATIVE PRESENT | PASSÉ COMPOSÉ | IMPERFECT | PLUPERFECT |
|---|---|---|---|---|
| **-re** verbs | perds | ai perdu | perdais | avais perdu |
| **perdre** | perds | as perdu | perdais | avais perdu |
| (*to lose*) | perd | a perdu | perdait | avait perdu |
| perdant | perdons | avons perdu | perdions | avions perdu |
| perdu | perdez | avez perdu | perdiez | aviez perdu |
| | perdent | ont perdu | perdaient | avaient perdu |
| **3. Intransitive verbs conjugated with *être*[2]** | | | | |
| **entrer** | entre | suis entré(e) | entrais | étais entré(e) |
| (*to enter*) | entres | es entré(e) | entrais | étais entré(e) |
| entrant | entre | est entré(e) | entrait | était entré(e) |
| entré | entrons | sommes entré(e)s | entrions | étions entré(e)s |
| | entrez | êtes entré(e)(s) | entriez | étiez entré(e)(s) |
| | entrent | sont entré(e)s | entraient | étaient entré(e)s |
| **4. Pronominal verbs** | | | | |
| **se laver** | me lave | me suis lavé(e) | me lavais | m'étais lavé(e) |
| (*to wash* | te laves | t'es lavé(e) | te lavais | t'étais lavé(e) |
| *oneself*) | se lave | s'est lavé(e) | se lavait | s'était lavé(e) |
| se lavant | nous lavons | nous sommes lavé(e)s | nous lavions | nous étions lavé(e)s |
| lavé | vous lavez | vous êtes lavé(e)(s) | vous laviez | vous étiez lavé(e)(s) |
| | se lavent | se sont lavé(e)s | se lavaient | s'étaient lavé(e)s |
| **5. Irregular verbs[3]** | | | | |
| **aller** | vais | suis allé(e) | allais | |
| (*to go*) | vas | es allé(e) | allais | |
| allant | va | est allé(e) | allait | |
| allé | allons | sommes allé(e)s | allions | |
| | allez | êtes allé(e)(s) | alliez | |
| | vont | sont allé(e)s | allaient | |

[2]Other intransitive verbs conjugated with **être** in compound tenses are **aller**, **arriver**, **descendre**, **devenir**, **monter**, **mourir**, **naître**, **partir** (**repartir**), **passer**, **rentrer**, **rester**, **retourner**, **revenir**, **sortir**, **tomber**, and **venir**. Note that **descendre**, **monter**, **passer**, **retourner**, and **sortir** may sometimes be used as transitive verbs (i.e., with a direct object), in which case they are conjugated with **avoir** in compound tenses.

[3]Note that the pluperfect and past conditional forms are not listed in this appendix for irregular verbs.

| | | CONDITIONAL | | SUBJUNCTIVE | IMPERATIVE |
|---|---|---|---|---|---|
| PASSÉ SIMPLE | FUTURE | PRESENT | PAST | PRESENT | |
| perdis | perdrai | perdrais | aurais perdu | perde | |
| perdis | perdras | perdrais | aurais perdu | perdes | perds |
| perdit | perdra | perdrait | aurait perdu | perde | |
| perdîmes | perdrons | perdrions | aurions perdu | perdions | perdons |
| perdîtes | perdrez | perdriez | auriez perdu | perdiez | perdez |
| perdirent | perdront | perdraient | auraient perdu | perdent | |
| | | | | | |
| entrai | entrerai | entrerais | serais entré(e) | entre | |
| entras | entreras | entrerais | serais entré(e) | entres | entre |
| entra | entrera | entrerait | serait entré(e) | entre | |
| entrâmes | entrerons | entrerions | serions entré(e)s | entrions | entrons |
| entrâtes | entrerez | entreriez | seriez entré(e)(s) | entriez | entrez |
| entrèrent | entreront | entreraient | seraient entré(e)s | entrent | |
| | | | | | |
| me lavai | me laverai | me laverais | me serais lavé(e) | me lave | |
| te lavas | te laveras | te laverais | te serais lavé(e) | te laves | lave-toi |
| se lava | se lavera | se laverait | se serait lavé(e) | se lave | |
| nous lavâmes | nous laverons | nous laverions | nous serions lavé(e)s | nous lavions | lavons-nous |
| vous lavâtes | vous laverez | vous laveriez | vous seriez lavé(e)(s) | vous laviez | lavez-vous |
| se lavèrent | se laveront | se laveraient | se seraient lavé(e)s | se lavent | |
| | | | | | |
| allai | irai | irais | | aille | |
| allas | iras | irais | | ailles | va |
| alla | ira | irait | | aille | |
| allâmes | irons | irions | | allions | allons |
| allâtes | irez | iriez | | alliez | allez |
| allèrent | iront | iraient | | aillent | |

| VERB | INDICATIVE | | |
|---|---|---|---|
| | PRESENT | PASSÉ COMPOSÉ | IMPERFECT |
| **asseoir**[4]<br>(*to seat*)<br>asseyant<br>assis | assieds<br>assieds<br>assied<br>asseyons<br>asseyez<br>asseyent | ai assis<br>as assis<br>a assis<br>avons assis<br>avez assis<br>ont assis | asseyais<br>asseyais<br>asseyait<br>asseyions<br>asseyiez<br>asseyaient |
| **battre**<br>(*to beat*)<br>battant<br>battu | bats<br>bats<br>bat<br>battons<br>battez<br>battent | ai battu<br>as battu<br>a battu<br>avons battu<br>avez battu<br>ont battu | battais<br>battais<br>battait<br>battions<br>battiez<br>battaient |
| **boire**<br>(*to drink*)<br>buvant<br>bu | bois<br>bois<br>boit<br>buvons<br>buvez<br>boivent | ai bu<br>as bu<br>a bu<br>avons bu<br>avez bu<br>ont bu | buvais<br>buvais<br>buvait<br>buvions<br>buviez<br>buvaient |
| **conduire**<br>(*to lead,*<br>*to drive*)<br>conduisant<br>conduit | conduis<br>conduis<br>conduit<br>conduisons<br>conduisez<br>conduisent | ai conduit<br>as conduit<br>a conduit<br>avons conduit<br>avez conduit<br>ont conduit | conduisais<br>conduisais<br>conduisait<br>conduisions<br>conduisiez<br>conduisaient |
| **connaître**<br>(*to be*<br>*acquainted*)<br>connaissant<br>connu | connais<br>connais<br>connaît<br>connaissons<br>connaissez<br>connaissent | ai connu<br>as connu<br>a connu<br>avons connu<br>avez connu<br>ont connu | connaissais<br>connaissais<br>connaissait<br>connaissions<br>connaissiez<br>connaissaient |
| **courir**<br>(*to run*)<br>courant<br>couru | cours<br>cours<br>court<br>courons<br>courez<br>courent | ai couru<br>as couru<br>a couru<br>avons couru<br>avez couru<br>ont couru | courais<br>courais<br>courait<br>courions<br>couriez<br>couraient |

[4]**S'asseoir** (pronominal form of **asseoir**) means *to be seated* or *to take a seat.* The imperative forms of **s'asseoir** are **assieds-toi**, **asseyons-nous**, and **asseyez-vous**.

| PASSÉ SIMPLE | FUTURE | CONDITIONAL PRESENT | SUBJUNCTIVE PRESENT | IMPERATIVE |
|---|---|---|---|---|
| assis | assiérai | assiérais | asseye | |
| assis | assiéras | assiérais | asseyes | assieds |
| assit | assiéra | assiérait | asseye | |
| assîmes | assiérons | assiérions | asseyions | asseyons |
| assîtes | assiérez | assiériez | asseyiez | asseyez |
| assirent | assiéront | assiéraient | asseyent | |
| battis | battrai | battrais | batte | |
| battis | battras | battrais | battes | bats |
| battit | battra | battrait | batte | |
| battîmes | battrons | battrions | battions | battons |
| battîtes | battrez | battriez | battiez | battez |
| battirent | battront | battraient | battent | |
| bus | boirai | boirais | boive | |
| bus | boiras | boirais | boives | bois |
| but | boira | boirait | boive | |
| bûmes | boirons | boirions | buvions | buvons |
| bûtes | boirez | boiriez | buviez | buvez |
| burent | boiront | boiraient | boivent | |
| conduisis | conduirai | conduirais | conduise | |
| conduisis | conduiras | conduirais | conduises | conduis |
| conduisit | conduira | conduirait | conduise | |
| conduisîmes | conduirons | conduirions | conduisions | conduisons |
| conduisîtes | conduirez | conduiriez | conduisiez | conduisez |
| conduisirent | conduiront | conduiraient | conduisent | |
| connus | connaîtrai | connaîtrais | connaisse | |
| connus | connaîtras | connaîtrais | connaisses | connais |
| connut | connaîtra | connaîtrait | connaisse | |
| connûmes | connaîtrons | connaîtrions | connaissions | connaissons |
| connûtes | connaîtrez | connaîtriez | connaissiez | connaissez |
| connurent | connaîtront | connaîtraient | connaissent | |
| courus | courrai | courrais | coure | |
| courus | courras | courrais | coures | cours |
| courut | courra | courrait | coure | |
| courûmes | courrons | courrions | courions | courons |
| courûtes | courrez | courriez | couriez | courez |
| coururent | courront | courraient | courent | |

| VERB | INDICATIVE | | |
|---|---|---|---|
| | PRESENT | PASSÉ COMPOSÉ | IMPERFECT |
| **craindre** | crains | ai craint | craignais |
| (*to fear*) | crains | as craint | craignais |
| craignant | craint | a craint | craignait |
| craint | craignons | avons craint | craignions |
| | craignez | avez craint | craigniez |
| | craignent | ont craint | craignaient |
| **croire** | crois | ai cru | croyais |
| (*to believe*) | crois | as cru | croyais |
| croyant | croit | a cru | croyait |
| cru | croyons | avons cru | croyions |
| | croyez | avez cru | croyiez |
| | croient | ont cru | croyaient |
| **devoir** | dois | ai dû | devais |
| (*to have to,* | dois | as dû | devais |
| *to owe*) | doit | a dû | devait |
| devant | devons | avons dû | devions |
| dû | devez | avez dû | deviez |
| | doivent | ont dû | devaient |
| **dire**[5] | dis | ai dit | disais |
| (*to say,* | dis | as dit | disais |
| *to tell*) | dit | a dit | disait |
| disant | disons | avons dit | disions |
| dit | dites | avez dit | disiez |
| | disent | ont dit | disaient |
| **dormir**[6] | dors | ai dormi | dormais |
| (*to sleep*) | dors | as dormi | dormais |
| dormant | dort | a dormi | dormait |
| dormi | dormons | avons dormi | dormions |
| | dormez | avez dormi | dormiez |
| | dorment | ont dormi | dormaient |
| **écrire**[7] | écris | ai écrit | écrivais |
| (*to write*) | écris | as écrit | écrivais |
| écrivant | écrit | a écrit | écrivait |
| écrit | écrivons | avons écrit | écrivions |
| | écrivez | avez écrit | écriviez |
| | écrivent | ont écrit | écrivaient |

[5]Verbs like **dire**: **contredire** (**vous contredisez**), **interdire** (**vous interdisez**), **prédire** (**vous prédisez**)
[6]Verbs like **dormir**: **mentir**, **partir**, **repartir**, **sentir**, **servir**, **sortir**. (**Partir**, **repartir**, and **sortir** are conjugated with **être**.)
[7]Verbs like **écrire**: **décrire**

| PASSÉ SIMPLE | FUTURE | CONDITIONAL PRESENT | SUBJUNCTIVE PRESENT | IMPERATIVE |
|---|---|---|---|---|
| craignis | craindrai | craindrais | craigne | |
| craignis | craindras | craindrais | craignes | crains |
| craignit | craindra | craindrait | craigne | |
| craignîmes | craindrons | craindrions | craignions | craignons |
| craignîtes | craindrez | craindriez | craigniez | craignez |
| craignirent | craindront | craindraient | craignent | |
| crus | croirai | croirais | croie | |
| crus | croiras | croirais | croies | crois |
| crut | croira | croirait | croie | |
| crûmes | croirons | croirions | croyions | croyons |
| crûtes | croirez | croiriez | croyiez | croyez |
| crurent | croiront | croiraient | croient | |
| dus | devrai | devrais | doive | |
| dus | devras | devrais | doives | dois |
| dut | devra | devrait | doive | |
| dûmes | devrons | devrions | devions | devons |
| dûtes | devrez | devriez | deviez | devez |
| durent | devront | devraient | doivent | |
| dis | dirai | dirais | dise | |
| dis | diras | dirais | dises | dis |
| dit | dira | dirait | dise | |
| dîmes | dirons | dirions | disions | disons |
| dîtes | direz | diriez | disiez | dites |
| dirent | diront | diraient | disent | |
| dormis | dormirai | dormirais | dorme | |
| dormis | dormiras | dormirais | dormes | dors |
| dormit | dormira | dormirait | dorme | |
| dormîmes | dormirons | dormirions | dormions | dormons |
| dormîtes | dormirez | dormiriez | dormiez | dormez |
| dormirent | dormiront | dormiraient | dorment | |
| écrivis | écrirai | écrirais | écrive | |
| écrivis | écriras | écrirais | écrives | écris |
| écrivit | écrira | écrirait | écrive | |
| écrivîmes | écrirons | écririons | écrivions | écrivons |
| écrivîtes | écrirez | écririez | écriviez | écrivez |
| écrivirent | écriront | écriraient | écrivent | |

| VERB | INDICATIVE | | |
|---|---|---|---|
| | PRESENT | PASSÉ COMPOSÉ | IMPERFECT |
| **envoyer**<br>(*to send*)<br>envoyant<br>envoyé | envoie<br>envoies<br>envoie<br>envoyons<br>envoyez<br>envoient | ai envoyé<br>as envoyé<br>a envoyé<br>avons envoyé<br>avez envoyé<br>ont envoyé | envoyais<br>envoyais<br>envoyait<br>envoyions<br>envoyiez<br>envoyaient |
| **faire**<br>(*to do,*<br>*to make*)<br>faisant<br>fait | fais<br>fais<br>fait<br>faisons<br>faites<br>font | ai fait<br>as fait<br>a fait<br>avons fait<br>avez fait<br>ont fait | faisais<br>faisais<br>faisait<br>faisions<br>faisiez<br>faisaient |
| **falloir**<br>(*to be*<br>*necessary*)<br>fallu | il faut | il a fallu | il fallait |
| **lire**[8]<br>(*to read*)<br>lisant<br>lu | lis<br>lis<br>lit<br>lisons<br>lisez<br>lisent | ai lu<br>as lu<br>a lu<br>avons lu<br>avez lu<br>ont lu | lisais<br>lisais<br>lisait<br>lisions<br>lisiez<br>lisaient |
| **mettre**[9]<br>(*to put*)<br>mettant<br>mis | mets<br>mets<br>met<br>mettons<br>mettez<br>mettent | ai mis<br>as mis<br>a mis<br>avons mis<br>avez mis<br>ont mis | mettais<br>mettais<br>mettait<br>mettions<br>mettiez<br>mettaient |
| **mourir**<br>(*to die*)<br>mourant<br>mort | meurs<br>meurs<br>meurt<br>mourons<br>mourez<br>meurent | suis mort(e)<br>es mort(e)<br>est mort(e)<br>sommes mort(e)s<br>êtes mort(e)(s)<br>sont mort(e)s | mourais<br>mourais<br>mourait<br>mourions<br>mouriez<br>mouraient |

[8]Verbs like **lire**: **élire**, **relire**
[9]Verbs like **mettre**: **permettre**, **promettre**, **remettre**

| PASSÉ SIMPLE | FUTURE | CONDITIONAL PRESENT | SUBJUNCTIVE PRESENT | IMPERATIVE |
|---|---|---|---|---|
| envoyai | enverrai | enverrais | envoie | |
| envoyas | enverras | enverrais | envoies | envoie |
| envoya | enverra | enverrait | envoie | |
| envoyâmes | enverrons | enverrions | envoyions | envoyons |
| envoyâtes | enverrez | enverriez | envoyiez | envoyez |
| envoyèrent | enverront | enverraient | envoient | |
| fis | ferai | ferais | fasse | |
| fis | feras | ferais | fasses | fais |
| fit | fera | ferait | fasse | |
| fîmes | ferons | ferions | fassions | faisons |
| fîtes | ferez | feriez | fassiez | faites |
| firent | feront | feraient | fassent | |
| il fallut | il faudra | il faudrait | il faille | |
| lus | lirai | lirais | lise | |
| lus | liras | lirais | lises | lis |
| lut | lira | lirait | lise | |
| lûmes | lirons | lirions | lisions | lisons |
| lûtes | lirez | liriez | lisiez | lisez |
| lurent | liront | liraient | lisent | |
| mis | mettrai | mettrais | mette | |
| mis | mettras | mettrais | mettes | mets |
| mit | mettra | mettrait | mette | |
| mîmes | mettrons | mettrions | mettions | mettons |
| mîtes | mettrez | mettriez | mettiez | mettez |
| mirent | mettront | mettraient | mettent | |
| mourus | mourrai | mourrais | meure | |
| mourus | mourras | mourrais | meures | meurs |
| mourut | mourra | mourrait | meure | |
| mourûmes | mourrons | mourrions | mourions | mourons |
| mourûtes | mourrez | mourriez | mouriez | mourez |
| moururent | mourront | mourraient | meurent | |

| VERB | INDICATIVE | | |
|---|---|---|---|
| | PRESENT | PASSÉ COMPOSÉ | IMPERFECT |
| **naître** | nais | suis né(e) | naissais |
| (*to be born*) | nais | es né(e) | naissais |
| naissant | naît | est né(e) | naissait |
| né | naissons | sommes né(e)s | naissions |
| | naissez | êtes né(e)(s) | naissiez |
| | naissent | sont né(e)s | naissaient |
| **ouvrir**[10] | ouvre | ai ouvert | ouvrais |
| (*to open*) | ouvres | as ouvert | ouvrais |
| ouvrant | ouvre | a ouvert | ouvrait |
| ouvert | ouvrons | avons ouvert | ouvrions |
| | ouvrez | avez ouvert | ouvriez |
| | ouvrent | ont ouvert | ouvraient |
| **plaire** | plais | ai plu | plaisais |
| (*to please*) | plais | as plu | plaisais |
| plaisant | plaît | a plu | plaisait |
| plu | plaisons | avons plu | plaisions |
| | plaisez | avez plu | plaisiez |
| | plaisent | ont plu | plaisaient |
| **pleuvoir** | il pleut | il a plu | il pleuvait |
| (*to rain*) | | | |
| pleuvant | | | |
| plu | | | |
| **pouvoir** | peux, puis | ai pu | pouvais |
| (*to be able*) | peux | as pu | pouvais |
| pouvant | peut | a pu | pouvait |
| pu | pouvons | avons pu | pouvions |
| | pouvez | avez pu | pouviez |
| | peuvent | ont pu | pouvaient |
| **prendre**[11] | prends | ai pris | prenais |
| (*to take*) | prends | as pris | prenais |
| prenant | prend | a pris | prenait |
| pris | prenons | avons pris | prenions |
| | prenez | avez pris | preniez |
| | prennent | ont pris | prenaient |

[10]Verbs like **ouvrir**: **couvrir**, **découvrir**, **offrir**, **souffrir**
[11]Verbs like **prendre**: **apprendre**, **comprendre**, **surprendre**

| PASSÉ SIMPLE | FUTURE | CONDITIONAL PRESENT | SUBJUNCTIVE PRESENT | IMPERATIVE |
|---|---|---|---|---|
| naquis | naîtrai | naîtrais | naisse | |
| naquis | naîtras | naîtrais | naisses | nais |
| naquit | naîtra | naîtrait | naisse | |
| naquîmes | naîtrons | naîtrions | naissions | naissons |
| naquîtes | naîtrez | naîtriez | naissiez | naissez |
| naquirent | naîtront | naîtraient | naissent | |
| ouvris | ouvrirai | ouvrirais | ouvre | |
| ouvris | ouvriras | ouvrirais | ouvres | ouvre |
| ouvrit | ouvrira | ouvrirait | ouvre | |
| ouvrîmes | ouvrirons | ouvririons | ouvrions | ouvrons |
| ouvrîtes | ouvrirez | ouvririez | ouvriez | ouvrez |
| ouvrirent | ouvriront | ouvriraient | ouvrent | |
| plus | plairai | plairais | plaise | |
| plus | plairas | plairais | plaises | plais |
| plut | plaira | plairait | plaise | |
| plûmes | plairons | plairions | plaisions | plaisons |
| plûtes | plairez | plairiez | plaisiez | plaisez |
| plurent | plairont | plairaient | plaisent | |
| il plut | il pleuvra | il pleuvrait | il pleuve | |
| pus | pourrai | pourrais | puisse | |
| pus | pourras | pourrais | puisses | |
| put | pourra | pourrait | puisse | |
| pûmes | pourrons | pourrions | puissions | |
| pûtes | pourrez | pourriez | puissiez | |
| purent | pourront | pourraient | puissent | |
| pris | prendrai | prendrais | prenne | |
| pris | prendras | prendrais | prennes | prends |
| prit | prendra | prendrait | prenne | |
| prîmes | prendrons | prendrions | prenions | prenons |
| prîtes | prendrez | prendriez | preniez | prenez |
| prirent | prendront | prendraient | prennent | |

| VERB | INDICATIVE | | |
|---|---|---|---|
| | PRESENT | PASSÉ COMPOSÉ | IMPERFECT |
| **recevoir**[12] | reçois | ai reçu | recevais |
| (*to receive*) | reçois | as reçu | recevais |
| recevant | reçoit | a reçu | recevait |
| reçu | recevons | avons reçu | recevions |
| | recevez | avez reçu | receviez |
| | reçoivent | ont reçu | recevaient |
| **rire** | ris | ai ri | riais |
| (*to laugh*) | ris | as ri | riais |
| riant | rit | a ri | riait |
| ri | rions | avons ri | riions |
| | riez | avez ri | riiez |
| | rient | ont ri | riaient |
| **savoir** | sais | ai su | savais |
| (*to know*) | sais | as su | savais |
| sachant | sait | a su | savait |
| su | savons | avons su | savions |
| | savez | avez su | saviez |
| | savent | ont su | savaient |
| **suivre** | suis | ai suivi | suivais |
| (*to follow*) | suis | as suivi | suivais |
| suivant | suit | a suivi | suivait |
| suivi | suivons | avons suivi | suivions |
| | suivez | avez suivi | suiviez |
| | suivent | ont suivi | suivaient |
| **tenir** | tiens | ai tenu | tenais |
| (*to hold,* | tiens | as tenu | tenais |
| *to keep*) | tient | a tenu | tenait |
| tenant | tenons | avons tenu | tenions |
| tenu | tenez | avez tenu | teniez |
| | tiennent | ont tenu | tenaient |
| **valoir** | vaux | ai valu | valais |
| (*to be* | vaux | as valu | valais |
| *worth*) | vaut | a valu | valait |
| valant | valons | avons valu | valions |
| valu | valez | avez valu | valiez |
| | valent | ont valu | valaient |

[12]Verbs like **recevoir**: **apercevoir**, **s'apercevoir de**, **décevoir**

| PASSÉ SIMPLE | FUTURE | CONDITIONAL PRESENT | SUBJUNCTIVE PRESENT | IMPERATIVE |
|---|---|---|---|---|
| reçus | recevrai | recevrais | reçoive | |
| reçus | recevras | recevrais | reçoives | reçois |
| reçut | recevra | recevrait | reçoive | |
| reçûmes | recevrons | recevrions | recevions | recevons |
| reçûtes | recevrez | recevriez | receviez | recevez |
| reçurent | recevront | recevraient | reçoivent | |
| ris | rirai | rirais | rie | |
| ris | riras | rirais | ries | ris |
| rit | rira | rirait | rie | |
| rîmes | rirons | ririons | riions | rions |
| rîtes | rirez | ririez | riiez | riez |
| rirent | riront | riraient | rient | |
| sus | saurai | saurais | sache | |
| sus | sauras | saurais | saches | sache |
| sut | saura | saurait | sache | |
| sûmes | saurons | saurions | sachions | sachons |
| sûtes | saurez | sauriez | sachiez | sachez |
| surent | sauront | sauraient | sachent | |
| suivis | suivrai | suivrais | suive | |
| suivis | suivras | suivrais | suives | suis |
| suivit | suivra | suivrait | suive | |
| suivîmes | suivrons | suivrions | suivions | suivons |
| suivîtes | suivrez | suivriez | suiviez | suivez |
| suivirent | suivront | suivraient | suivent | |
| tins | tiendrai | tiendrais | tienne | |
| tins | tiendras | tiendrais | tiennes | tiens |
| tint | tiendra | tiendrait | tienne | |
| tînmes | tiendrons | tiendrions | tenions | tenons |
| tîntes | tiendrez | tiendriez | teniez | tenez |
| tinrent | tiendront | tiendraient | tiennent | |
| valus | vaudrai | vaudrais | vaille | |
| valus | vaudras | vaudrais | vailles | vaux |
| valut | vaudra | vaudrait | vaille | |
| valûmes | vaudrons | vaudrions | valions | valons |
| valûtes | vaudrez | vaudriez | valiez | valez |
| valurent | vaudront | vaudraient | vaillent | |

| VERB | INDICATIVE PRESENT | PASSÉ COMPOSÉ | IMPERFECT |
|---|---|---|---|
| **venir**[13] | viens | suis venu(e) | venais |
| (*to come*) | viens | es venu(e) | venais |
| venant | vient | est venu(e) | venait |
| venu | venons | sommes venu(e)s | venions |
| | venez | êtes venu(e)(s) | veniez |
| | viennent | sont venu(e)s | venaient |
| **vivre** | vis | ai vécu | vivais |
| (*to live*) | vis | as vécu | vivais |
| vivant | vit | a vécu | vivait |
| vécu | vivons | avons vécu | vivions |
| | vivez | avez vécu | viviez |
| | vivent | ont vécu | vivaient |
| **voir** | vois | ai vu | voyais |
| (*to see*) | vois | as vu | voyais |
| voyant | voit | a vu | voyait |
| vu | voyons | avons vu | voyions |
| | voyez | avez vu | voyiez |
| | voient | ont vu | voyaient |
| **vouloir** | veux | ai voulu | voulais |
| (*to wish,* | veux | as voulu | voulais |
| *to want*) | veut | a voulu | voulait |
| voulant | voulons | avons voulu | voulions |
| voulu | voulez | avez voulu | vouliez |
| | veulent | ont voulu | voulaient |

## 6. *-er* Verbs with Spelling Changes

Certain verbs ending in **-er** require spelling changes. Models for each kind of change are listed here. Stem changes are in boldface type.

| VERB | PRESENT | PASSÉ COMPOSÉ | IMPERFECT |
|---|---|---|---|
| **commencer**[14] | commence | ai commencé | **commençais** |
| (*to begin*) | commences | as commencé | **commençais** |
| **commençant** | commence | a commencé | **commençait** |
| commencé | **commençons** | avons commencé | commencions |
| | commencez | avez commencé | commenciez |
| | commencent | ont commencé | **commençaient** |

[13]Verbs like **venir**: **devenir** (**elle est devenue**), **revenir** (**elle est revenue**), **maintenir** (**elle a maintenu**), **obtenir** (**elle a obtenu**), **se souvenir de** (**elle s'est souvenue de...**)
[14]Verbs like **commencer**: **dénoncer**, **divorcer**, **menacer**, **placer**, **prononcer**, **remplacer**, **tracer**

| PASSÉ SIMPLE | FUTURE | CONDITIONAL PRESENT | SUBJUNCTIVE PRESENT | IMPERATIVE |
|---|---|---|---|---|
| vins | viendrai | viendrais | vienne | |
| vins | viendras | viendrais | viennes | viens |
| vint | viendra | viendrait | vienne | |
| vînmes | viendrons | viendrions | venions | venons |
| vîntes | viendrez | viendriez | veniez | venez |
| vinrent | viendront | viendraient | viennent | |
| vécus | vivrai | vivrais | vive | |
| vécus | vivras | vivrais | vives | vis |
| vécut | vivra | vivrait | vive | |
| vécûmes | vivrons | vivrions | vivions | vivons |
| vécûtes | vivrez | vivriez | viviez | vivez |
| vécurent | vivront | vivraient | vivent | |
| vis | verrai | verrais | voie | |
| vis | verras | verrais | voies | vois |
| vit | verra | verrait | voie | |
| vîmes | verrons | verrions | voyions | voyons |
| vîtes | verrez | verriez | voyiez | voyez |
| virent | verront | verraient | voient | |
| voulus | voudrai | voudrais | veuille | |
| voulus | voudras | voudrais | veuilles | veuille |
| voulut | voudra | voudrait | veuille | |
| voulûmes | voudrons | voudrions | voulions | veuillons |
| voulûtes | voudrez | voudriez | vouliez | veuillez |
| voulurent | voudront | voudraient | veuillent | |

| PASSÉ SIMPLE | FUTURE | CONDITIONAL PRESENT | SUBJUNCTIVE PRESENT | IMPERATIVE |
|---|---|---|---|---|
| **commençai** | commencerai | commencerais | commence | |
| **commenças** | commenceras | commencerais | commences | commence |
| **commença** | commencera | commencerait | commence | |
| **commençâmes** | commencerons | commencerions | commencions | **commençons** |
| **commençâtes** | commencerez | commenceriez | commenciez | commencez |
| commencèrent | commenceront | commenceraient | commencent | |

| VERB | INDICATIVE | | |
|---|---|---|---|
| | PRESENT | PASSÉ COMPOSÉ | IMPERFECT |
| **manger**[15] | mange | ai mangé | **mangeais** |
| (*to eat*) | manges | as mangé | **mangeais** |
| **mangeant** | mange | a mangé | **mangeait** |
| mangé | **mangeons** | avons mangé | mangions |
| | mangez | avez mangé | mangiez |
| | mangent | ont mangé | **mangeaient** |
| **appeler**[16] | **appelle** | ai appelé | appelais |
| (*to call*) | **appelles** | as appelé | appelais |
| appelant | **appelle** | a appelé | appelait |
| appelé | appelons | avons appelé | appelions |
| | appelez | avez appelé | appeliez |
| | **appellent** | ont appelé | appelaient |
| **essayer**[17] | **essaie** | ai essayé | essayais |
| (*to try*) | **essaies** | as essayé | essayais |
| essayant | **essaie** | a essayé | essayait |
| essayé | essayons | avons essayé | essayions |
| | essayez | avez essayé | essayiez |
| | **essaient** | ont essayé | essayaient |
| **acheter**[18] | **achète** | ai acheté | achetais |
| (*to buy*) | **achètes** | as acheté | achetais |
| achetant | **achète** | a acheté | achetait |
| acheté | achetons | avons acheté | achetions |
| | achetez | avez acheté | achetiez |
| | achètent | ont acheté | achetaient |
| **préférer**[19] | **préfère** | ai préféré | préférais |
| (*to prefer*) | **préfères** | as préféré | préférais |
| préférant | **préfère** | a préféré | préférait |
| préféré | préférons | avons préféré | préférions |
| | préférez | avez préféré | préfériez |
| | **préfèrent** | ont préféré | préféraient |

[15]Verbs like **manger**: **bouger**, **changer**, **dégager**, **engager**, **exiger**, **juger**, **loger**, **mélanger**, **nager**, **obliger**, **partager**, **voyager**
[16]Verbs like **appeler**: **épeler**, **jeter**, **projeter**, (**se**) **rappeler**
[17]Verbs like **essayer**: **employer**, (**s'**) **ennuyer**, **nettoyer**, **payer**
[18]Verbs like **acheter**: **achever**, **amener**, **emmener**, (**se**) **lever**, (**se**) **promener**
[19]Verbs like **préférer**: **célébrer**, **considérer**, **espérer**, (**s'**) **inquiéter**, **pénétrer**, **posséder**, **répéter**, **révéler**, **suggérer**

| PASSÉ SIMPLE | FUTURE | CONDITIONAL PRESENT | SUBJUNCTIVE PRESENT | IMPERATIVE |
|---|---|---|---|---|
| **mangeai** | mangerai | mangerais | mange | |
| **mangeas** | mangeras | mangerais | manges | mange |
| **mangea** | mangera | mangerait | mange | |
| **mangeâmes** | mangerons | mangerions | mangions | **mangeons** |
| **mangeâtes** | mangerez | mangeriez | mangiez | mangez |
| mangèrent | mangeront | mangeraient | mangent | |
| appelai | **appellerai** | **appellerais** | **appelle** | |
| appelas | **appelleras** | **appellerais** | **appelles** | **appelle** |
| appela | **appellera** | **appellerait** | **appelle** | |
| appelâmes | **appellerons** | **appellerions** | appelions | appelons |
| appelâtes | **appellerez** | **appelleriez** | appeliez | appelez |
| appelèrent | **appelleront** | **appelleraient** | **appellent** | |
| essayai | **essaierai** | **essaierais** | **essaie** | |
| essayas | **essaieras** | **essaierais** | **essaies** | **essaie** |
| essaya | **essaiera** | **essaierait** | **essaie** | |
| essayâmes | **essaierons** | **essaierions** | essayions | essayons |
| essayâtes | **essaierez** | **essaieriez** | essayiez | essayez |
| essayèrent | **essaieront** | **essaieraient** | **essaient** | |
| achetai | **achèterai** | **achèterais** | **achète** | |
| achetas | **achèteras** | **achèterais** | **achètes** | **achète** |
| acheta | **achètera** | **achèterait** | **achète** | |
| achetâmes | **achèterons** | **achèterions** | achetions | achetons |
| achetâtes | **achèterez** | **achèteriez** | achetiez | achetez |
| achetèrent | **achèteront** | **achèteraient** | **achètent** | |
| préférai | préférerai | préférerais | **préfère** | |
| préféras | préféreras | préférerais | **préfères** | **préfère** |
| préféra | préférera | préférerait | **préfère** | |
| préférâmes | préférerons | préférerions | préférions | préférons |
| préférâtes | préférerez | préféreriez | préfériez | préférez |
| préférèrent | préféreront | préféreraient | **préfèrent** | |

# Appendix E

## Translations of Functional Mini-dialogues

### 1. Identifying People and Things: Articles and Nouns

*In the University District*

*Alex, an American student, is visiting the university with Mireille, a French student.* MIREILLE: There are the library, the bookstore, and the student cafeteria. ALEX: Is there also a café? MIREILLE: Yes, of course; here's the café. It's the center of university life! ALEX: Is it ever! There are twenty or thirty people here, and only one student in the library!

### 2. Expressing Quantity: Plural Articles and Nouns

*An Eccentric Professor*

THE PROFESSOR: Here is the grading system: zero [points] for imbeciles, four for mediocre students, eight for geniuses, and ten for the professor. Are there any questions?

### 3. Expressing Actions: -er Verbs

*Meeting of Friends at the Sorbonne*

XAVIER: Hi, Françoise! Are you visiting the university? FRANÇOISE: Yes, we're admiring the library right now. This is Paul, from New York, and Mireille, a friend [of mine]. XAVIER: Hello, Paul. Do you speak French? PAUL: Yes, a little bit. XAVIER: Hello, Mireille. Are you a student here? MIREILLE: Oh, no. I work in the library.

### 4. Expressing Disagreement: Negation Using *ne...pas*

*The End of a Friendship?*

BERNARD: Things aren't great with Martine [and me]. She likes to dance, I don't like dancing. I like to go skiing, and she doesn't like sports. She's studying biology, and I don't like science . . .

MARTINE: Things aren't great with Bernard [and me]. He doesn't like to dance, I like dancing. I don't like skiing, and he likes sports. He's a humanities student, and I don't like literature . . .

### 5. Identifying People and Things: *The Verb être*

*Fabrice's Genius*

FABRICE: Well, I'm ready to work! MARTINE: Me too, but where are the books and the dictionary? FABRICE: Um . . . oh yeah, look, there they are. The dictionary is under the hat and the notebooks are on top of the jacket. Now we're ready. MARTINE: You know, Fabrice, you do very well in literature, but as far as organization is concerned, you're a zero! FABRICE: Maybe, but chaos is a sign of genius!

### 6. Describing People and Things: Descriptive Adjectives

*Computerized Dating Services*

He is [should be] sociable, charming, serious, good-looking, idealistic, athletic . . . She is [should be] sociable, charming, serious, good-looking, idealistic, athletic . . . [COMPUTER]: They're hard to please!

### 7. Getting Information: *Yes/No* Questions

*A Discussion Between Friends*

TOURIST: Is this an accident? POLICE OFFICER: No, it's not an accident. TOURIST: Is it a demonstration? POLICE OFFICER: Of course not! TOURIST: So it's a fight? POLICE OFFICER: Not really. It's an animated discussion between friends.

### 8. Mentioning a Specific Place or Person: The Prepositions *à* and *de*

*Arnaud and Delphine, Two Typical French Students*

They live in the dormitory. They eat in the cafeteria. They play volleyball in the gym. On the weekend, they play cards with friends. They like talking about professors, the English exam, French literature class, and university life.

## 9. Expressing Actions: *-ir* Verbs

### *Down with Term Papers!*

*Khaled and Naima have term papers in history.* KHALED: Which topic are you choosing? NAIMA: I don't know, I'm thinking it over. OK, I'm choosing the first topic—Napoleon's empire. (*Two days later.*) KHALED: Well, are you ready? NAIMA: Wait, I'm finishing up my conclusion, and then I'm coming. And if I manage to get 15 out of 20, we'll have a party!

## 10. Expressing Possession and Sensations: The Verb *avoir*

### *Roommates*

JEAN-PIERRE: You have a very pleasant room, and it seems quiet . . . FLORENCE: Yes. I need lots of quiet in order to work. JEAN-PIERRE: Do you have a nice roommate? FLORENCE: Yes, we're lucky: we both like tennis, quiet . . . and messiness!

## 11. Expressing the Absence of Something: Indefinite Articles in Negative Sentences

### *Student Comfort*

NATHALIE: Where is the toilet? ANNE: Sorry, I don't have a toilet in my room. It's in the hallway. NATHALIE: But do you have a shower? ANNE: No; no toilet, no shower, but I do have a little kitchenette and . . . NATHALIE: And a TV? ANNE: No, there's no TV, but I do have a stereo.

## 12. Getting Information: *où, quand, comment, pourquoi,* etc.

### *Room for Rent*

MME GÉRARD: Hello, miss. What's your name? AUDREY: Audrey Delorme. MME GÉRARD: Are you a student? AUDREY: Yes. MME GÉRARD: Where do you go to school? AUDREY: At the Sorbonne. MME GÉRARD: That's very good. And what are you studying? AUDREY: Philosophy. MME GÉRARD: Oh, that's serious. How many hours of class do you have? AUDREY: 21 hours per week. MME GÉRARD: So you need an inexpensive room? AUDREY: Yes, that's right. When will the room be available? MME GÉRARD: Today. It's yours.

## 13. Expressing Possession: *mon, ton,* etc.

### *The House as a Reflection of Social Standing*

*Marc, a student at the Sorbonne, is taking a brief tour of Paris and the suburbs with his Vietnamese friend Thuy. While driving, he points out the different kinds of housing to Thuy.* My brother-in-law has a lot of money. There's his villa; it's great, isn't it? Our house is small, but comfortable; my family is pretty happy. Out here in the suburbs you see the big housing projects where families of workers and immigrants mostly live. Their buildings are called HLMs.

## 14. Talking About Your Plans and Destinations: The Verb *aller*

### *A Model Father*

SIMON: Are we playing tennis this afternoon? STÉPHANE: No, I'm going to the zoo with Céline. SIMON: So [how about] tomorrow? STÉPHANE: I'm sorry, but tomorrow I'm going to take Sébastien to the dentist. SIMON: What a model father [you are]!

## 15. Expressing What You Are Doing or Making: The Verb *faire*

### *A Question of Organization*

SANDRINE: Do you and your roommate eat in the cafeteria? MARION: No, Candice and I are very organized. She does the shopping and I cook. SANDRINE: And who does the dishes? MARION: The dishwasher, of course!

## 16. Expressing Actions: *-re* Verbs

### *Beauregard at the Restaurant*

JILL: Do you hear that? GÉRARD: No. What's the matter? JILL: I hear a noise under the table. GENEVIÉVE: Oh, that! That's Beauregard . . . He's waiting for the chicken . . . and he doesn't like waiting . . .

## 17. Talking About Food and Drink: *-re* Verbs: *prendre* and *boire*

### *At the Restaurant*

WAITER: What will you have, sir? Ma'am? JEAN-MICHEL: We'll have the chicken with cream and the vegetables. WAITER: And what will you have to drink? JEAN-MICHEL: I'll have a beer, and for the lady, a bottle of mineral water, please.

## 18. Expressing Quantity: Partitive Articles

*No Dessert*

JULIEN: What are we having to eat today, mommy? MME TESSIER: There's chicken with potatoes. JULIEN: And the chocolate mousse in the fridge, is it for lunch today? MME TESSIER: No, no; the mousse is for this evening. For lunch, there is fruit or coffee ice cream. JULIEN: I don't like ice cream and I don't like fruit! But I love mousse! MME TESSIER: The answer is no!

## 19. Giving Commands: The Imperative

*The Enemy of a Good Meal*

FRANÇOIS: Martine, pass me the salt, please . . . [*Martine passes the salad to François.*] FRANÇOIS: No, come on! Use your ears a little . . . I asked you for the salt! MARTINE: François, be a dear—don't talk so loud. I can't hear the television . . .

## 20. Pointing Out People and Things: Demonstrative Adjectives

*A Dinner with Friends*

BRUNO: This roast beef is really delicious! ANNE: Thank you. BRUNO: Can I try a little more of that sauce? ANNE: But of course. MARIE: These green beans, mmm! Where do you do your shopping? ANNE: Rue Contrescarpe. MARIE: Me too. I just love that street, that village-like feeling, those little shops . . .

## 21. Expressing Desire, Ability, and Obligation: The Verbs *vouloir*, *pouvoir*, and *devoir*

*Le Procope*

MARIE-FRANCE: Would you like some coffee? CAROLE: No, thanks, I can't drink coffee. I have to be careful. I have an exam today. If I drink coffee, I'll be too nervous. PATRICK: I only drink coffee on the days when I have exams. It inspires me, the way it inspired Voltaire!

## 22. Asking About Choices: The Interrogative Adjective *quel*

*Henri Lefèvre, Restaurant Owner in Albertville*

*Dan Bartell, an American journalist, asks Henri Lefèvre some questions.* DAN BARTELL: What is the main difference between traditional cooking and the *nouvelle cuisine*? HENRI LEFÈVRE: The sauces, my friend, the sauces. DAN BARTELL: And which sauces do you make? HENRI LEFÈVRE: I really like to make the traditional sauces like *bordelaise* and *beurre blanc* [white butter]. DAN BARTELL: Which wines do you buy for your restaurant? HENRI LEFÈVRE: I buy mostly red wines from Burgundy and white wines from Anjou.

## 23. Describing People and Things: The Placement of Adjectives

*A New Restaurant*

CHLOË: There's a new restaurant in the neighborhood. VINCENT: Great! Where? CHLOË: Next to the little grocery store. It's called "The Good Old Days." VINCENT: That's a nice name. Let's go there Saturday night. CHLOË: Good idea!

## 24. Expressing Actions: *dormir* and Similar Verbs; *venir*

*The Joy of Nature*

STÉPHANE: Where are you going on vacation this summer? ANNE-LAURE: This year we're going to Martinique. We're going to camp in a little village 30 kilometers from Fort-de-France. We'll drink *ti'punch*, go out every night, and sunbathe by the coconut trees. A dream, huh? Come with us. We're leaving August 2. STÉPHANE: No thanks, the sea is not for me. Smelling fish, sleeping with mosquitoes, no way! ROMAIN: You never change, that's for sure. The gentleman needs his creature comforts! Too bad for you! We just love sleeping in the open, feeling the sea breeze, and admiring the stars.

## 25. Talking About the Past: The *passé composé* with *avoir*

*At the Hotel*

GUEST: Good morning, ma'am. I made a reservation for a room for two people. EMPLOYÉE: Your name, please? GUEST: Bernard Meunier. EMPLOYÉE: Hmm . . . yes, Room 12, on the ground floor. You asked for a room with a view of the sea, is that right? GUEST: Yes, that's right. EMPLOYÉE: All right, then, please fill out this card.

## 26. Expressing How Long: *depuis, pendant, il y a*

### *A Question of Practice*

MONIQUE: How long have you been entering competitions? FRANÇOISE: Since 1985. How about you: how long have you been windsurfing? MONIQUE: Only for the last two weeks! FRANÇOISE: I started eight years ago. Ever since I started windsurfing, I've been spending my vacations at the beach. MONIQUE: It's hard, but it's fabulous. Yesterday I was able to stay on the board for four minutes.

## 27. Expressing Location: Using Prepositions with Geographical Names

### *Bruno in the Congo*

*Bruno is on vacation in the Congo. He has met Kofi.* KOFI: Where in France do you come from? BRUNO: From Marseille. KOFI: It must be beautiful there! Tell me, do you have plans for future vacations? BRUNO: Yeah, lots. First, I'm going to Mexico next year with my girlfriend. And in the future I want to go to Russia, Quebec, Senegal, and also Asia. KOFI: Which town would you like to live in? BRUNO: Verona, in Italy, so I could find my Juliet.

## 28. Expressing Observations and Beliefs: *voir* and *croire*

### *Where Are the Keys?*

MICHAËL: I think I've lost the car keys. VIRGINIE: What? They must be at the restaurant. MICHAËL: You think so? VIRGINIE: I'm not sure, but we can go check. (*At the restaurant.*) MICHAËL: You're right. They're over there on the table. I see them. VIRGINIE: Whew! Well, what do you want to do now? MICHAËL: Let's go see the pyramid at the Louvre.

## 29. Talking About the Past: The *passé composé* with *être*

### *Sunday Morning Explanations*

MME FERRY: I would really like to know where you went last night! And what time did you get home? STEPHANIE: Not late, mom. I went out with some friends. We went to have a drink at Laurent's, we stayed there about an hour, then we left to go to the movies. I got back to the house right after the movie. MME FERRY: Are you sure? Because your father got back from the soccer game at 11 and didn't see the car in the garage . . .

## 30. Expressing Wishes and Polite Requests: The Present Conditional

### *A Weekend in London*

JULIE: Would you have some good fares to London right now? AGENT: You're in luck! We have a flight with a promotional fare of 550 francs round-trip. JULIE: Great! And could you reserve a hotel room for me from September 3 to September 7? AGENT: No problem! In what part of London would you like to be? JULIE: I'd like to find a hotel, not too expensive, near Hyde Park.

## 31. Expressing Negation: Affirmative and Negative Adverbs

### *The Super-train (TGV)*

PATRICIA: Have you taken the TGV yet? FRÉDÉRIC: No, not yet, but I've reserved a seat for next Saturday. I'm going to see my parents in Brittany. PATRICIA: Do you always have to make an advance reservation for the TGV? FRÉDÉRIC: Yes, it's required. I don't like that system at all, because I hate to look ahead; I like to leave at the last minute, I never make plans, and I've never kept an appointment book.

## 32. Expressing Negation: Affirmative and Negative Pronouns

### *Coin-operated Luggage Lockers*

SERGE: Is there something wrong? JEAN-PIERRE: Yes, I'm having trouble with the locker. It doesn't work. SERGE: Oh, that! There's nothing more annoying [than that]! JEAN-PIERRE: Everyone always seems to find a locker that works, except me. SERGE: Look, someone is taking their luggage out of one of the lockers. There, you can be sure that one works. JEAN-PIERRE: Excellent idea!

## 33. Describing the Past: The *imparfait*

### *Poor Grandmother!*

MME CHABOT: You see, when I was little, television didn't exist. CLÉMENT: So what did you do in the evenings? MME CHABOT: Well, we read, we chatted; our parents told us stories . . . CLÉMENT: Poor Grandmother, it must have been sad not to be able to watch *Santa Barbara* at night . . .

## 34. Speaking Succinctly: Direct Object Pronouns

*The Cossecs Are Moving*

THIERRY: What should we do with the TV? MARYSE: We're going to give it to your sister. THIERRY: Okay. And all our books? MARYSE: We're going to send them by mail. They have a special book rate. THIERRY: You're right. I didn't want to throw them away. And are we going to sell the minitel? MARYSE: Of course not! You *know* that we rent it from the phone company. We have to return it before the end of the month.

## 35. Talking About the Past: Agreement of the Past Participle

*Opinion of an American TV Viewer in France*

REPORTER: Have you watched French television yet? AMERICAN: Yes, I watched it last night. REPORTER: Which shows did you like best? AMERICAN: That's hard to say . . . REPORTER: Don't you think it's very different from American TV? AMERICAN: Well . . . the programs I saw are rather similar . . . *Santa Barbara*, *The Simpsons* . . . That is, sure, they're different: they're in French!

## 36. Speaking Succinctly: Indirect Object Pronouns

*Journalists for the* Canard*?*

RÉGIS: Did you write to the journalists at the *Canard Enchaîné*? NICOLE: Yes, I wrote to them. RÉGIS: Have they answered you? NICOLE: Yes, they made an appointment with us for tomorrow. RÉGIS: Did they like our political cartoons? NICOLE: They haven't said anything to me [about that] yet: we'll see tomorrow!

## 37. Describing Past Events: The *passé composé* versus the *imparfait*

*Casablanca*

ALAIN: So, are you going to tell us about your vacation in Morocco? SYLVIE: Well, I left Paris July 23. The weather was terrible: it was cold and raining. Awful! But when I arrived in Casablanca, the sky was bright blue, the sun was shining, the sea was warm . . . REMI: Did you like the city? SYLVIE: Yes, a lot. But I wanted to visit a mosque and I couldn't get in. ALAIN: Why? SYLVIE: It was my fault, because I was wearing a miniskirt.

## 38. Speaking Succinctly: The Pronouns *y* and *en*

*Paris, City of Love*

MIREILLE: Have you gone to the Parc Montsouris yet? FABIENNE: No, not yet, but I'm going there Saturday with Vincent. MIREILLE: Vincent? Tell me, how many boyfriends do you have? FABIENNE: Right now I have two. But I'm going to break up with Jean-Marc soon. MIREILLE: Have you talked to Jean-Marc about it? FABIENNE: No, not yet. I'm thinking about it, but I'm a bit afraid of how he'll react.

## 39. Saying What and Whom You Know: *savoir* and *connaître*

*Labyrinth*

MARCEL: Taxi! Are you familiar with Vaucouleurs Street? TAXI DRIVER: Of course I know where it is! I know Paris like the back of my hand [literally, pocket]! MARCEL: I don't know how you do it. I got lost yesterday in the Île de la Cité. TAXI DRIVER: I know my job; and besides, you know, with a map of Paris it's not that hard!

## 40. Emphasizing and Clarifying: Stressed Pronouns

*Artistic Visits*

*David is visiting Paris with his parents and his brother. He's telling Geraldine, a Parisian friend, about their activities.* GERALDINE: David, did you go to the Louvre? DAVID: No, it's too big for me. I prefer the Picasso Museum. GERALDINE: Me, too! But did your parents visit the Louvre? DAVID: Them? Yes, they went there several times. But my brother prefers visiting the shops and discos.

## 41. Expressing Actions: Pronominal Verbs

*A Meeting*

DENIS: Madeleine! How are you? VÉRONIQUE: You're making a mistake. My name is not Madeleine. DENIS: I'm sorry. I wonder . . . haven't I met you before . . . ? VÉRONIQUE: I don't remember having met you. But that doesn't matter . . . my name is Véronique. What's your name?

## 42. Speaking Succinctly: Using Double Object Pronouns

### An Artistic Temperament

*Maryse wants a box of paints.* MARYSE: Go on, Mommy, buy it for me! MOTHER: Listen to me carefully! I can't give it to you. I don't have any more money. MARYSE: Ask Daddy for some! MOTHER: All right, all right. I'll go talk to him about it. But don't *you* say anything to him, swear it! MARYSE: I swear it!

## 43. Saying How to Do Something: Adverbs

### Provence

ANNE-LAURE: Tomorrow I'm leaving for Provence. I'm going to make a quick visit to Renoir's house at Cagnes, then to the Matisse Museum at Nice, to the Picasso Museum at Antibes . . . SYLVAIN: Do you travel constantly? ANNE-LAURE: No, not really, but I absolutely want to go to Provence because many French painters lived there. SYLVAIN: And now, what are you doing? ANNE-LAURE: I'm going to see Monet's house at Giverny, in the suburbs of Paris. SYLVAIN: Tell me frankly: aside from painting, what interests you? ANNE-LAURE: Classical music . . . I like Wagner a lot.

## 44. Reporting Everyday Events: Pronominal Verbs (*continued*)

### An Encounter

LAURENT: Are you leaving? PAULINE: Yes, it's nice out and I'm bored here. I'm going to take a walk along the lake. Will you come along? LAURENT: No, I can't, I have a lot of work. PAULINE: Oh, you're making too much of it. Come on, we'll go have some fun! LAURENT: Some other time. If I stop now, I won't have the courage to finish up later.

## 45. Expressing Reciprocal Actions: Pronominal Verbs

### The Ideal Couple

THIERRY: You see, for me the ideal couple is Jacquot and Patricia. CHANTAL: Why do you say that? THIERRY: Because they both love each other. Every time I see them they gaze at each other lovingly, they kiss, and they say sweet things to each other. They have known each other for ten years and I've never seen them argue.

## 46. Talking About the Past and Giving Commands: Pronominal Verbs

### A Love Match

MARTINE: Tell me, Denis, how did you meet each other? DENIS: We saw each other for the first time in Concarneau. VÉRONIQUE: Remember? It was raining, you came into the boutique where I worked and . . . DENIS: And it was love at first sight! We got married that same year.

## 47. Making Comparisons: Comparative and Superlative of Adjectives

### Shopping

*Laurence and Franck, newlyweds, are going shopping together for the first time.* LAURENCE: Where are we going to shop? FRANCK: At the Miniprix, of course! It's less expensive and cleaner than Trouvetout. LAURENCE: I hate big discount chains. I prefer to go to the little grocer on Rue Leclerc. The products are more expensive, I agree, but they're fresher. And then it's also more practical: you don't need to take the car. As for friendly service, this grocer is the best in the neighborhood. FRANCK: I agree, sweetheart, but right now the most important thing is to save money.

## 48. Talking About the Future: The Future Tense

### His Future

FATHER: He'll be a writer, he'll write novels, and we'll be famous. MOTHER: He'll be a businessman, he'll be the head of a company, and we'll be rich. CHILD: We'll see . . . I'll do what I can.

## 49. Linking Ideas: Relative Pronouns

### Interviewing the Head of a Business

JOURNALIST: And why do you say that you studied for three years in vain? GENEVIÉVE: Well, because all that time, it was making jewelry that interested me. JOURNALIST: The jewelry you create is made out of natural materials? GENEVIÉVE: Yes. I also design costume jewelry, for magazines, that people can make at home. JOURNALIST: Now, your business makes thousands of pieces of jewelry, three quarters of which go to Japan? GENEVIÉVE: Yes, and I have loads of new projects!

## 50. Getting Information: Interrogative Pronouns

### *At the Rugby Game*

BILL: What are they trying to do? JEAN-PAUL: Well, they're trying to get the ball behind the goal line of the other team. BILL: Yes, I know, but what are they doing right now? JEAN-PAUL: This is called a scrummage. BILL: And what's a scrummage? JEAN-PAUL: That's when several players from each team are clustered around the ball. You see, one of the players got it. BILL: Which one? JEAN-PAUL: Philippot. BILL: What's keeping him from throwing it toward the goal? JEAN-PAUL: The rules of the game, pal! This is rugby; it's not American football.

## 51. Being Polite; Speculating: The Present Conditional

### *Oh, if I Were Rich . . .*

FRANÇOIS: What would you do if you won the lottery? VINCENT: Me? I'd buy an old neighborhood movie theater. I would choose all the films I like and all my friends could get in for free. CHLOË: If I had enough money, I'd settle in the south of France and would spend the rest of my days painting. I'd have a big house, and you could both come and see me every weekend.

## 52. Expressing Actions: Prepositions After Verbs

### *Going out to the Cabaret*

CORINNE: Tonight we've decided to take you to the Contrescarpe cabaret in Montmartre. CHUCK: What is a cabaret? JACQUES: A cabaret is a kind of café where you can listen to ballads and satirical songs . . . CORINNE: Do you know Georges Brassens, Jacques Brel, Barbara? JACQUES: It's because of the cabarets that they were able to make a name for themselves.

## 53. Making Comparisons: Adverbs and Nouns

### *Jazz*

JENNIFER: Do you often go to night clubs on the weekends? BRUNO: No, I go to jazz bars more often than night clubs. There aren't as many people and I like the music better. JENNIFER: I love jazz, too. I have more records of Duke Ellington than of Madonna. But jazz . . . I listen to it more often at my place. When I go to a night club, it's to dance, and also because there's more atmosphere.

## 54. Expressing Attitudes: Regular Subjunctive Verbs

### *Vote for Françoise!*

FRANÇOISE: So, you want me to run for the university council! SIMON: Yes, we wish the council would get over its inertia and that the delegates would realize what their political responsibilities are. FRANÇOISE: But I already ran without any luck last year. LUC: This year, Françoise, we want you to win. And we'll support you to the end.

## 55. Expressing Attitudes: Irregular Subjunctive Verbs

### *Former Minister of Women's Rights*

JOURNALIST: They call you "the minister who made waves." Why is that? YVETTE ROUDY: That's because, when I was minister, I initiated a lot of campaigns for women's rights: ■ for birth control: I wanted women to be properly informed ■ against sexism: We didn't want advertising to be able to exploit the female body ■ for the feminization of professional titles: We didn't want there to be female careers and male careers, but careers for everyone! ■ for career counseling and training for women: We wanted women to know how to prepare for the careers of the future.

## 56. Expressing Wishes, Necessity, and Possibility: The Subjunctive

### *The Draft or Voluntary Military Service?*

PATRICK FAURE (22): In my opinion, the draft is an anachronism in the nuclear age. GÉRARD BOURRELLY (36): It's possible that young people will become more interested in military service if it gives them professional training. FRANCIS CRÉPIN (25): We have to do away with the draft and set up a career army. CHARLES PALLANCA (18): But if I were a volunteer, I would insist that the salary be at least 5,000 francs a month!

## 57. Expressing Emotion: The Subjunctive

### *A United Europe*

*Several French people are expressing their opinions about the political and economic unification of Europe.* JEAN-PIERRE (35): I'm glad that France is saying "yes" to Europe. ISABELLE (24): *We're* afraid the nationalists will become violent, like in Bosnia-Herzogovina. CLAUDE (40):

I'm sorry the Swiss don't want to be part of Europe. NICOLE (30): I doubt whether Europe can settle the problem of unemployment. MONIQUE (52): I'm furious that the Americans put taxes on European agricultural products.

## 58. Talking About Quantity: Indefinite Adjectives and Pronouns

### *A Vacation in Martinique*

JULIEN: So, your vacation in Martinique? LAURENCE: Everything went really well. We stayed for a few days in the capital, Fort-de-France, then we relaxed on the beach. You know, the people are very nice, but they all have an accent that we had trouble understanding. We sometimes had the impression that some of them didn't understand us, either. FRANCK: And every time they said something, we had to ask them to repeat it. It's funny: some words are the same as ours, but others are completely different.

## 59. Expressing Doubt and Uncertainty: The Subjunctive

### *France and Africa*

KOFI: Do you believe France should intervene militarily in African countries where there are military problems? KARIM: I'm not so sure that's a good solution. KOFI: Why? KARIM: Because I don't think it can change the political situation.

## 60. Expressing Subjective Viewpoints: Alternatives to the Subjunctive

### *The Antilles, Myth and Reality*

FRANCINE: For me, the Antilles are coral reefs, pre-Columbian archaeological sites, beaches of white sand . . . SYLVAIN: Still, you have to know that we don't just have sun to offer! VINCENT: Before you leave, you should visit a banana plantation, a rum distillery, and our very modern port. SYLVAIN: I hope you know that our standard of living here in Martinique is the highest in the Caribbean . . . FRANCINE: It's true, it's important to modernize. But I hope you'll be able to safeguard the beauty of your country.

## Answers to *À l'écoute!* Listening Comprehension Activities

### Chapitre 1

1. c 2. a 3. d 4. b 5. e

### Chapitre 2

Fatima—Tunisie—espagnol—cinéma
François—Canada (Québec)—philosophie—sport
Scott—Angleterre—sociologie—café

### Chapitre 3

A. Patrice is the person on the right.
B. 1. b 2. a 3. b 4. b 5. a 6. a

### Chapitre 4

1. b, e, f
2. b, c, g, h

### Chapitre 5

1. Gérard 2. Géraldine 3. Marie 4. Juliette
5. Laurence 6. Franck 7. Léa

### Chapitre 6

A. See map below. B. Answers will vary.

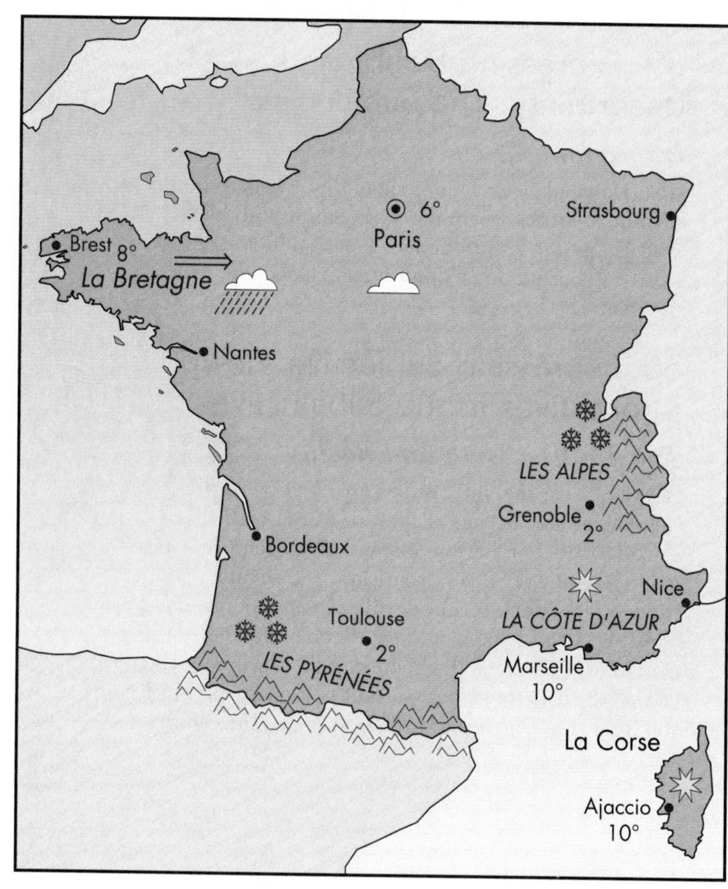

**Chapitre 7**

Partie I: A. 1. d 2. b 3. a 4. c

B. 3

Partie II: 1. a 2. b 3. b 4. a 5. a 6. a

**Chapitre 8**

Partie I: A. 1. V 2. F 3. V 4. F 5. F 6. V

B. 1. J-Y 2. J-Y 3. J-Y 4. S 5. S 6. S

Partie II: 1. c 2. a 3. b 4. a

**Chapitre 9**

Partie I: 1. a 2. b 3. a 4. b 5. a 6. c

Partie II: A. a. 4 b. 10 c. 1 d. 8 e. 2 f. 5 g. 3 h. 9 i. 7 j. 6

B. Il a oublié de faire le plein.

**Chapitre 10**

Partie I: A. 1. c 2. b 3. b

B. 1. F / F 2. F / V 3. F / V

Partie II: 1. V 2. V 3. F 4. F 5. F 6. V

**Chapitre 11**

Partie I: A. 1. a 2. b 3. a 4. b 5. b

B.

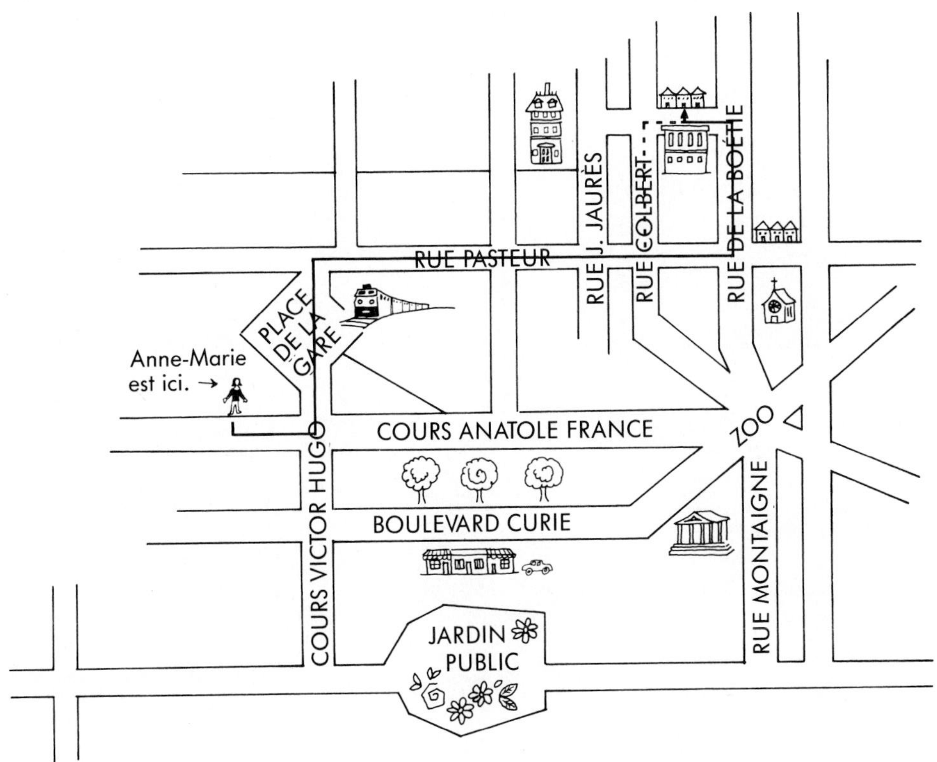


Partie II: 1. b 2. a 3. c 4. a 5. b 6. a 7. b 8. a 9. c

**Chapitre 12**

Partie I: A. 1. F 2. V 3. V 4. F 5. F 6. V

B. 1. c 2. b 3. c 4. a 5. c

Partie II: 1. V 2. F 3. F 4. V 5. F 6. V

**Chapitre 13**

A. 5 8 1 7 4 10 3 6 2 9

B. 1. V 2. F 3. F 4. V 5. F 6. V

**Chapitre 14**

A. 1. b 2. c 3. a

B. 1. b 2. b 3. b 4. b 5. a 6. c

C. 1. Annonce numéro 3 2. Annonce numéro 2 3. Annonce numéro 1

**Chapitre 15**

A. 1. b 2. c 3. a 4. b 5. c 6. b 7. a

B. 1. 1ère: français; 2ème: français; 3ème: américain 2. 1ère: français; 2ème: espagnol; 3ème: italien

## Chapitre 16

Partie I: A. 1. b 2. c,d,e 3. a,c 4. a 5. a 6. b,c

B. 1, 2, 5

Partie II: A. 3, 6, 8, 9, 11, 12

B. 1. d 2. e 3. a 4. b 5. c

## Chapitre 17

Partie I: A. 1. américain 2. la Normandie 3. le Canada 4. la Louisiane 5. La Nouvelle-Orléans 6. canadien (*ou* québécois) 7. la Bretagne 8. le Canada (*ou* l'Acadie) 9. l'état de Maine 10. Québec

B. 1. V 2. V 3. F Ils parlent anglais. 4. F Ils sont les descendants des Canadiens-Français. 5. V 6. V 7. V 8. V 9. F Tout le monde parle français chez lui. 10. F Il n'a pas encore visité la France.

Partie II: A. 1. Z 2. V 3. A 4. Z 5. A 6. V

B. 1. V 2. F 3. F 4. V 5. F

## Chapitre 18

1. b 2. a 3. b 4. c 5. b 6. c 7. b 8. c

# Lexiques

# Lexique français-anglais

This end vocabulary provides contextual meanings of French words used in this text. It does *not* include proper nouns (unless presented as active vocabulary), abbreviations, exact cognates, most near cognates, past participles used as adjectives if the infinitive is listed, or regular adverbs formed from adjectives listed. Adjectives are listed in the masculine singular form; feminine endings or forms are included when irregular. An asterisk (*) indicates words beginning with an aspirate *h*. Active vocabulary is indicated by the number of the chapter in which it first appears.

**Abbreviations**

*A.* archaic
*ab.* abbreviation
*adj.* adjective
*adv.* adverb
*art.* article
*conj.* conjunction
*fam.* familiar or colloquial
*f.* feminine noun
*Gram.* grammatical term
*indic.* indicative (mood)
*inf.* infinitive
*interj.* interjection
*interr.* interrogative
*inv.* invariable
*irreg.* irregular
*m.* masculine noun
*n.* noun
*neu.* neuter
*pl.* plural
*p.p.* past participle
*prep.* preposition
*pron.* pronoun
*Q.* Quebec usage
*s.* singular
*s.o.* someone
*s.th.* something
*subj.* subjunctive
*tr. fam.* very colloquial, argot
*v.* verb

**à** *prep.* to; at; in (2)
**abandonner** to give up; to abandon; to desert
**abats** *m. pl.* giblets, offal
**abolir** to abolish (16)
**abondant** *adj.* abundant
**s'abonner (à)** to subscribe (to)
**aboyer (il aboie)** to bark (*dog*)
**abri** *m.* shelter; **à l'abri de** sheltered from; **les sans-abri** *m. pl.* the homeless
**abricot** *m.* apricot
**abrupt** *adj.* steep
**absolu** *adj.* absolute
**Acadie** *f.* Acadia (*Nova Scotia*) (17)
**acadien(ne)** *adj.* Acadian; **Acadien(ne)** *m., f.* Acadian (*person*) (17)
**accéder (j'accède)** to accede; to gain access
**accent** *m.* accent; **accent aigu (grave, circonflexe)** acute (grave, circumflex) accent
**accentuer** to accentuate, emphasize, stress
**accepter (de)** to accept; to agree to (15)
**accès** *m.* access
**accident** *m.* accident (16)
**accompagner** to accompany, go along with
**accord** *m.* agreement; **d'accord** all right, O.K.; agreed; **être d'accord** to agree, be in agreement; **se mettre d'accord** to reconcile, come to an agreement
**accorder** to grant, bestow, confer; **s'accorder** to be in agreement
**accroissement** *m.* growth
**accroître** (*like* **croître**) *irreg.* to increase, add to
**accueil** *m.* greeting, welcome
**accueillant** *adj.* hospitable, welcoming; appealing (17)
**s'accumuler** to accumulate, gather
**accuser (de)** to accuse (of)
**achat** *m.* purchase (8)
**acheminement** *m.* sending, forwarding, delivery
**acheter (j'achète)** to buy (6)
**acquérir** (*p.p.* **acquis**) *irreg.* to acquire, obtain
**acrobatie** *f.* acrobatics; **faire des acrobaties** to do stunts, acrobatics
**acte** *m.* act; law; certificate
**acteur (actrice)** *m., f.* actor (actress) (12)
**actif/ive** *adj.* active; working
**action** *f.* action; gesture; **jour** (*m.*) **de l'Action de Grâce** Thanksgiving Day (*U.S., Canada*)
**actualité** *f.* piece of news; present-day event
**actuel(le)** *adj.* present, current
**actuellement** *adv.* now, at the present time
**adapter** to adapt; **s'adapter à** to adapt oneself, get accustomed to
**addition** *f.* bill, check (*in a restaurant*) (7); addition
**adieu** *interj.* good-bye
**adjectif** *m., Gram.* adjective
**admettre** (*like* **mettre**) *irreg.* to admit, accept
**administrateur/trice** *m., f.* administrator
**admirer** to admire
**adolescent(e)** *m., f., adj.* adolescent, teenager
**adorer** to love, adore (2)
**adresse** *f.* address (10)
**adroit** *adj.* clever; dexterous
**adulte** *m., f.* adult; *adj.* adult
**adversaire** *m., f.* opponent, adversary

**adverse** *adj.* opposing; opposite
**aéré** *adj.* ventilated; light
**aérien(ne)** *adj.* aerial; by air; airline; **compagnie** (*f.*) **aérienne** airline
**aérobic, aérobique** *f.* aerobics (5); **faire de l'aérobic** to do aerobics (5)
**aéroport** *m.* airport (9)
**affaire** *f.* affair; business matter; *pl.* belongings; business (9); **avoir affaire à** to deal with; **classe** (*f.*) **affaires** business class (9); **homme (femme) d'affaires** *m., f.* businessman (woman)
**affamé(e)** *m., f.* starving person; *adj.* starving
**affichage** *m.* display; advertisement; **tableau** (*m.*) **d'affichage** schedule display board
**affiche** *f.* poster (4); billboard
**affirmatif/ive** *adj.* affirmative
**affreux/euse** *adj.* horrible, frightful (5)
**afin de** *prep.* to, in order to
**âge** *m.* age; years; epoch; **moyen âge** *m. s.* Middle Ages (12); **quel âge avez-vous?** how old are you?
**âgé** *adj.* aged; old; elderly
**agence** *f.* agency; **agence de voyages** travel agency
**agencement** *m.* arrangement; fitting out
**agenda** *m.* engagement book, pocket calendar
**agent** *m.* agent; **agent de police** police officer, policeman (woman) (14)
**agglomération** *f.* agglomeration, urban center
**agir** to act (4); **il s'agit de** it's about, it's a question of
**agité** *adj.* agitated, restless
**agneau** *m.* lamb; **côte** (*f.*) **d'agneau** lamb chop
**agréable** *adj.* agreeable, pleasant, nice (3)
**agréer** to accept, recognize; **veuillez agréer... l'expression de mes sentiments les meilleurs** very truly yours
**agressif/ive** *adj.* aggressive
**agressivité** *f.* aggressiveness
**agricole** *adj.* agricultural
**agriculteur/trice** *m., f.* farmer (14)
**agrumes** *m. pl.* citrus fruits
**ah bon? ah oui?** *interj.* really? (6)
**aide** *f.* help, assistance; **à l'aide de** with the help of
**aider** to help (14)
**aigu** *adj.* sharp, acute; **accent** (*m.*) **aigu** acute accent (**é**)
**ailleurs** *adv.* elsewhere; **d'ailleurs** *adv.* moreover; anyway; **nulle part ailleurs** nowhere else
**aimable** *adj.* likable, friendly
**aimer** to like; to love (2); **aimer bien** to like; **aimer mieux** to prefer (2); **j'aimerais** + *inf.* I would like (7); **je n'aime... pas du tout** I don't like . . . at all (6)
**aîné(e)** *m., f.* oldest sibling
**ainsi** *conj.* thus, so, such as; **ainsi que** *conj.* as well as, in the same way as; **et ainsi de suite** and so on
**air** *m.* air; look; tune; **avoir l'air (de)** to seem, look (like) (4); **de plein air** outdoor (15); **en plein air** outdoors, in the open air; **hôtesse** (*f.*) **de l'air** flight attendant, stewardess (9)
**ajouté** *adj.* added; **taxe** (*f.*) **à valeur ajoutée** value-added tax
**ajouter** to add
**album** *m.* (photo) album; picture book
**alcoolisé** *adj.* alcoholic
**algèbre** *f.* algebra
**Algérie** *f.* Algeria (8)
**aliénant** *adj.* alienating
**aliment(s)** *m.* food, nourishment
**alimentaire** *adj.* alimentary, pertaining to food
**alimentation** *f.* food, feeding, nourishment; **magasin** (*m.*) **d'alimentation** food store
**alimenter** to feed; to supply
**Allemagne** *f.* Germany (8)
**allemand** *adj.* German; *m.* German (*language*); **Allemand(e)** *m., f.* German (*person*) (2)
**aller** *irreg.* to go (5); **aller** + *inf.* to be going (*to do s.th.*) (5); **aller mal** to feel bad (5); **allez-vous-en!** go away! (13); **billet** (*m.*) **aller-retour** round-trip ticket; **ça va?** how's it going? (1); **ça va bien (mal)** fine (bad[ly]) (things are going well [badly]) (1); **comment allez-vous?** how are you? (1); **s'en aller** to go off, leave (13)
**allô** *interj.* hello (*phone greeting*) (10)
**allocation** *f.* allotment; pension; **allocations familiales** family subsidies
**allongement** *m.* lengthening, extension
**allumette** *f.* match, matchstick; **pommes** (*f. pl.*) **allumettes** shoestring potatoes
**alors** *adv.* so (3); then, in that case (5)
**alpinisme** *m.* mountaineering (8), mountain climbing; **faire de l'alpinisme** to go mountain climbing
**alternance** *f.* alternance; alternation
**alternatif/ive** *adj.* alternative; *f.* alternative
**altruiste** *adj.* altruistic
**amande** *f.* almond
**amateur** *m.* amateur; connoisseur; *adj.* amateur, nonprofessional
**ambassade** *f.* embassy
**ambiance** *f.* atmosphere, surroundings
**ambitieux/ieuse** *adj.* ambitious
**âme** *f.* soul; spirit
**amélioration** *f.* improvement
**améliorer** to improve, better
**aménageable** *adj.* suitable for improvement or conversion
**aménagé** *adj.* equipped, set up
**amener (j'amène)** to bring (*s.o. somewhere*) (17); to take
**américain** *adj.* American; **Américain(e)** *m., f.* American (*person*) (2)
**américanophile** *adj.* lover, partisan of the U.S.
**ami(e)** *m., f.* friend (2); **petit(e) ami(e)** *m., f.* boyfriend (girlfriend)
**amical** *adj.* friendly
**amitié** *f.* friendship
**amour** *m.* love (13)
**amoureux/euse** *adj.* loving, in love (13); *m., f.* lover, sweetheart (13), person in love; **tomber amoureux/euse (de)** to fall in love (with) (13); **vie** (*f.*) **amoureuse** love life
**amphithéâtre** (*fam.* **amphi**) *m.* lecture hall (2), amphitheater
**amusant** *adj.* amusing, fun (2)
**amuser** to entertain, amuse; **s'amuser (à)** to have fun, have a good time (12)
**an** *m.* year (8); **avoir (vingt) ans** to be (twenty) years old (4); **l'an dernier (passé)** last year; **par an** per year, each year
**analyser** to analyze
**ananas** *m.* pineapple
**anarchiste** *adj.* anarchistic
**ancêtre** *m., f.* ancestor (17)
**ancien(ne)** *adj.* old, antique (7); former; ancient; **ancien combattant** *m.* war veteran
**angine** *f.* sore throat, strep throat
**anglais** *adj.* English; *m.* English (*language*); **Anglais(e)** *m., f.* Englishman(woman) (2)
**Angleterre** *f.* England (8)
**anglophone** *adj.* English-speaking (17)
**animateur/trice** *m., f.* host (hostess) (*radio, T.V.*); motivator (*in marketing*)

**animation** *f.* social, cultural events
**animer** to animate; to motivate, organize; to host (*show*)
**année** *f.* year (8); **l'année prochaine (dernière, passée)** next (last) year; **année scolaire** academic, school year; **les années (cinquante)** the decade (era) of the (fifties) (8)
**anniversaire** *m.* anniversary; birthday; **bon anniversaire** happy birthday
**annonce** *f.* announcement, ad; **petites annonces** *pl.* (classified) ads (10)
**annoncer (nous annonçons)** to announce, declare
**annuaire** *m.* telephone book (10)
**annuel(le)** *adj.* annual, yearly
**anonyme** *m., f.* anonymous person
**anorak** *m.* (ski) jacket (8), windbreaker
**antenne** *f.* antenna
**anthropologique** *adj.* anthropological
**Antilles** *f. pl.* Antilles (*islands*), Caribbean Islands (17); **mer** (*f.*) **des Antilles** Caribbean (17)
**antinucléaire** *adj.* anti-nuclear
**antipathique** *adj.* unlikable
**anxieux/ieuse** *adj.* anxious
**août** August (4)
**apercevoir** (like **recevoir**) *irreg.* to perceive, notice
**aperçu** *adj.* noticed
**apôtre** *m.* apostle
**appareil** *m.* apparatus; device; appliance; (*still*) camera; **appareil-photo** *m.* (*still*) camera; **qui est à l'appareil?** who's speaking? (10)
**apparence** *f.* appearance
**apparenté** *adj.* related; cognate (*word*)
**apparition** *f.* (first) appearance
**appartement** (*fam.* **appart**) *m.* apartment (5)
**appartenir** (*like* **tenir**) **à** *irreg.* to belong to
**appel** *m.* call; **faire appel à** to call on, appeal to
**appelé** *adj.* called; named (9)
**appeler (j'appelle)** to call (10); to name; **comment s'appelle... ?** what's . . .'s name?; **comment vous appelez-vous?** what's your name? (1); **je m'appelle...** my name is . . . (1); **s'appeler** to be named, called (12)
**appétit** *m.* appetite; **bon appétit!** enjoy your meal!
**appliquer** to apply
**apporter** to bring, carry (7); to furnish
**apposé** *adj.* (af)fixed, attached
**apprécier** to appreciate, value
**apprendre** (*like* **prendre**) *irreg.* to learn (6); to teach; **apprendre à** to learn (how) to
**apprentissage** *m.* apprenticeship; learning
**approuver** to approve
**approximatif/ive** *adj.* approximate
**après** *prep.* after (2); afterward (5); **après avoir (être)...** after having . . .; **d'après** *prep.* according to
**après-midi** *m.* or *f.* afternoon (5); **cet(te) après-midi** this afternoon (5); **de l'après-midi** in the afternoon (6)
**arachide** *f.* peanut
**arbre** *m.* tree (5)
**arc** *m.* bow (*weapon*); arch; **tir** (*m.*) **à l'arc** archery
**archéologique** *adj.* archeological
**archéologue** *m., f.* archeologist
**architecte** *m., f.* architect (14)
**ardent** *adj.* burning; ardent
**arène(s)** *f.* arena (12); bullring
**argent** *m.* money (7); silver; **argent liquide** cash (14)
**argot** *m.* slang, argot
**arme** *f.* weapon, arm
**armée** *f.* army (12); **armée de métier** professional army
**armoire** *f.* wardrobe; closet
**armoiries** *f. pl.* coat of arms
**arranger (nous arrangeons)** to arrange; to fix; to accommodate
**arrêt** *m.* stop; **arrêt d'autobus** bus stop
**arrêter (de)** to stop; to arrest; **s'arrêter** to stop (*oneself*) (12)
**arrière** *adv.* back; **arrière-grand-parent** *m.* great-grandparent (5); **en arrière** in back
**arrivée** *f.* arrival (9)
**arriver** to arrive, come (3); to happen
**arrondissement** *m.* ward, section (*of Paris*) (11)
**arrosé** *adj.* laced (*with liquor*)
**arroser** to water; to sprinkle; to wash down
**art** *m.* art; **beaux-arts** *m. pl.* fine arts; **œuvre** (*f.*) **d'art** work of art (12)
**artichaut** *m.* artichoke
**artificiel(le)** *adj.* artificial
**artisan(e)** *m., f.* artisan, craftsperson (14)
**artiste** *m., f.* artist (12); **artiste-peintre** *m., f.* (artist) painter (14)
**aspirer à** to aim at, yearn for
**assaisonnement** *m.* seasoning
**assassinat** *m.* murder
**assassiner** to murder, assassinate
**asseoir** (*p.p.* **assis**) *irreg.* to seat; **asseyez-vous (assieds-toi)** sit down (13); **s'asseoir** to sit down (13)
**assez** *adv.* somewhat (3); rather, quite; **assez de** *adv.* enough (6)
**assiette** *f.* plate (6)
**assis** *adj.* seated; **les assises** (*f. pl.*) **du monde** the foundations of society
**assistance** *f.* assistance, help; social welfare
**assister** to help, assist; **assister à** to attend (15), go to (*concert, etc.*)
**associer** to associate; **s'associer avec** to be associated with
**assortiment** *m.* assortment
**assumer** to assume; to take on
**assurance** *f.* assurance; insurance; **assurances-auto(mobile)** *pl.* car insurance
**assurer** to insure; to assure
**astéroïde** *m.* asteroid
**astronome** *m., f.* astronomer
**atelier** *m.* workshop; (*art*) studio
**athlétisme** *m.* athletics; track and field
**atmosphère** *f.* atmosphere (16)
**attaché** *adj.* attached; buckled
**attaque** *f.* attack
**atteindre** (*like* **craindre**) *irreg.* to reach; to affect
**atteint** *adj.* stricken; affected
**attendre** to wait for (5)
**attention** *f.* attention; **faire attention à** to pay attention to (5)
**attentivement** *adv.* attentively
**attirer** to attract; to draw
**attrait** *m.* attraction, lure; attractiveness; charm
**attraper** to catch
**attribuer** to attribute; to grant, give
**auberge** *f.* inn; **auberge de jeunesse** youth hostel
**aucun(e) (ne... aucun[e])** *adj., pron.* none; no one, not one, not any; anyone; any (8)
**audacieux/euse** *adj.* bold, audacious
**audio-visuel(le)** *adj.* audiovisual; *m.* audiovisual, broadcast media
**auditeur/trice** *m., f.* auditor, listener
**augmentation** *f.* increase, raise (14); **augmentation de salaire** raise
**augmenter** to increase
**aujourd'hui** *adv.* today; nowadays (1)
**auparavant** *adv.* previously
**auprès de** *prep.* close to; with; for
**ausculter** to listen with a stethoscope

**aussi** *adv.* also (3); so; as; consequently; **aussi... que** as . . . as (13)
**aussitôt** *conj.* immediately, at once, right then; **aussitôt que** as soon as (14)
**autant** *adv.* as much, so much, as many, so many; just as soon; **autant (de)... que** as many (much) . . . as (15); **pour autant** for all that
**auteur** *m.* author
**auto** *f., fam.* car, auto
**autobiographique** *adj.* autobiographical
**autobus** (*fam.* **bus**) *m.* bus (5)
**autocar** *m.* (*interurban*) bus
**automatique** *adj.* automatic; **distributeur** (*m.*) **automatique** automatic teller (14)
**automne** *m.* autumn, fall (6); **en automne** in the autumn (6)
**automobile** (*fam.* **auto**) *f., adj.* automobile, car; **assurances-automobile** *f. pl.* car insurance
**autorisé** *adj.* authorized
**autoroute** *f.* highway (9), freeway
**auto-stop** *m.* hitchhiking
**autour de** *prep.* around
**autre** *adj., pron.* other (4); another (4); *m., f.* the other (17); *pl.* the others, the rest (17); **d'autre part** on the other hand; **de l'autre côté** on the other side; **de part et d'autre** on both sides, here and there; **quoi d'autre** what else
**autrefois** *adv.* formerly (11), in the past
**auxiliaire** *m., Gram.* auxiliary (verb)
**avaler** to swallow
**avance** *f.* advance; **à l'avance** beforehand; **d'avance** in advance, earlier, ahead of time; **en avance** early
**avancé** *adj.* advanced
**avancement** *m.* promotion; advancement
**avant** *adv.* before (*in time*); *prep.* before, in advance of; *m.* front; **avant de** + *inf.* (*prep.*) before; **avant que** + *subj.* (*conj.*) before
**avant-hier** *adv.* the day before yesterday (8)
**avantage** *m.* advantage, benefit
**avantageux/euse** *adj.* advantageous
**avare** *adj.* miserly, stingy
**avec** *prep.* with (2)
**avenir** *m.* future (14); **à l'avenir** in the future, henceforth (14)
**aventure** *f.* adventure
**aventureux/euse** *adj.* adventurous
**aventurier/ière** *m., f.* adventurer
**aviateur/trice** *m., f.* aviator
**avion** *m.* airplane (9); **en avion** by plane
**avis** *m.* opinion; **à votre (ton) avis** in your opinion (11); **changer d'avis** to change one's mind
**avocat(e)** *m., f.* lawyer (14)
**avoir** (*p.p.* **eu**) *irreg.* to have (4); **avoir affaire à** to deal with; **avoir (20) ans** to be (20) years old (4); **avoir besoin de** to need (4); **avoir chaud** to be hot, warm (4); **avoir confiance en** to have confidence in; **avoir de la chance** to be lucky (4); **avoir du mal à** to have trouble, difficulty (17); **avoir envie de** to feel like; to want to (4); **avoir faim** to be hungry (4); **avoir froid** to be, feel cold (4); **avoir honte (de)** to be ashamed (of) (4); **avoir horreur de** to hate (6); **avoir l'air (de)** to look (like) (4); **avoir la trouille** to have stage fright; to be terrified; **avoir le temps (de)** to have the time (to); **avoir mal (à)** to have pain; to hurt (13); **avoir peur (de)** to be afraid (of) (4); **avoir raison** to be right (4); **avoir rendez-vous** to have a date, an appointment (4); **avoir soif** to be thirsty (4); **avoir sommeil** to be sleepy (4); **avoir tort** to be wrong (4); **en avoir assez** *fam.* to be fed up with, sick of; **en avoir marre** *fam.* to be fed up with, sick of; **il y a** there is, there are; ago
**avouer** to confess, admit
**avril** April (4)

**baccalauréat** (*fam.* **bac**) *m.* baccalaureate (*French secondary school degree*)
**badaud(e)** *m., f.* idler, rubberneck
**bagagerie** *f.* luggage store
**bagages** *m. pl.* luggage
**bagnole** *f., fam.* car; jalopy
**bague** *f.* ring (*jewelry*); **bague de fiançailles** engagement ring (13)
**baguette (de pain)** *f.* French bread, baguette (7)
**baie** *f.* bay
**baignade** *f.* swim, swimming
**baigner** to bathe; **se baigner** to bathe (*oneself*); to swim (13)
**bain** *m.* bath; swim; **maillot** (*m.*) **de bain** swimsuit, bathing suit (3); **salle** (*f.*) **de bains** bathroom (5); **slip** (*m.*) **de bain** men's swimsuit
**baisse** *f.* lowering, reduction (16)
**bal** *m.* dance, ball; **bal masqué** masked ball, costume party (17)
**balcon** *m.* balcony (5)
**balle** *f.* (*small*) ball; tennis ball; bullet (16); *pl., tr. fam.* French francs, money
**ballon** *m.* (*soccer, basket*) ball; balloon; **ballon à air chaud** hot-air balloon
**banane** *f.* banana
**bananeraie** *f.* banana plantation
**banc** *m.* bench
**bancaire** *adj.* banking, bank; **carte** (*f.*) **bancaire** bank (ATM) card (14); **compte** (*m.*) **bancaire** bank account
**bande** *f.* band; group; gang; (*cassette, video*) tape; **bande dessinée** comic strip; *pl.* comics
**banlieue** *f.* suburbs (11); **en banlieue** in the suburbs
**banque** *f.* bank (11); **compte** (*m.*) **en banque** bank account
**baptiser** to baptize; to name
**bar** *m.* bar; snack bar; pub
**barde** *f.* bard (*layer of bacon on a roast*)
**barré** *adj.* crossed; crossed out; **chèque** (*m.*) **barré** check payable to bank only
**bas(se)** *adj.* low; bottom; *adv.* low, softly; **à bas...** down with . . . ; **en bas** at the bottom; downstairs; **là-bas** *adv.* over there
**baser** to base; **se baser sur** to be based on
**basket-ball** (*fam.* **basket**) *m.* basketball; **jouer au basket** to play basketball
**bassin** *m.* basin; pond; wading pool
**bateau** *m.* boat; **bateau à voile** sailboat (8); **bateau-mouche** *m.* tourist boat on the Seine; **en (par) bateau** by boat, in a boat; **faire du bateau** to go boating
**bâtiment** *m.* building (11)
**bâtir** to build (12)
**battre** (*p.p.* **battu**) *irreg.* to beat; **se battre** to fight
**bavard** *adj.* talkative
**bavarder** to chat; to talk
**bavette: bifteck** (*m.*) **bavette** sirloin of beef
**bayou** *m.* bayou, Louisiana swamp (17)
**BCBG** *ab.* **(bécébégé): bon chic bon genre** "preppy" fad
**beau (bel, belle [beaux, belles])** *adj.* handsome; beautiful (3); **il fait beau** it's nice (weather) out (6)
**beaucoup (de)** *adv.* very much, a lot (1); much, many
**beau-frère** *m.* brother-in-law; stepbrother (5)
**beau-père** *m.* father-in-law; stepfather (5)
**beaux-arts** *m. pl.* fine arts

**bébé** *m.*. *fam.* baby
**bécane** *f.*, *tr. fam.* motorcycle
**Belgique** *f.* Belgium (8)
**belle-mère** *f.* mother-in-law; stepmother (5)
**belle-sœur** *f.* sister-in-law; stepsister (5)
**ben** *interj.*, *fam.* well!
**bénéficier (de)** to profit, benefit (from)
**besoin** *m.* need; **avoir besoin de** to need (4)
**beurre** *m.* butter (6)
**bibliothèque** (*fam.* **bibli**) *f.* library (2)
**biche** *f.* doe, hind
**bicyclette** *f.* bicycle (8); **faire de la bicyclette** to cycle, go biking
**bidoche** *f.*, *tr. fam.* meat
**bidon** *m.* can; large drum (*container*)
**bien** *adv.* well, good (5), quite; much (13); comfortable; *m.* good; *pl.* goods, belongings; **aimer bien** to like; **aussi bien que** as well as; **bien (mieux, le mieux)** *adv.* well (better, best) (15); **bien cuit** well-done (*meat*); **bien des** many (7); **bien que** + *subj.* (*conj.*) although (17); **bien sûr** *interj.* of course (6); **bien sûr que oui (non)** of course (not) (6); **ça va bien** fine (things are going well) (1); **eh bien** *interj.* well! (3); **je vais bien** I'm fine; **merci bien** thanks a lot; **ou bien** or else; **s'amuser bien** to have a good time; **s'entendre bien** to get along (well); **très bien, merci** very well, thank you (1); **vouloir bien** to be willing (to) (7)
**bien-être** *m.* well-being; welfare
**bienfaisant** *adj.* beneficial
**bientôt** *adv.* soon (5); **à bientôt!** *interj.* see you soon! (1)
**bienvenu(e)** *m.*, *f.* welcome
**bière** *f.* beer (6)
**bifteck** *m.* steak (6)
**biguine** *f.* beguine (*South American dance*)
**bijou** *m.* jewel (14); piece of jewelry
**bilingue** *adj.* bilingual
**bilinguisme** *m.* bilingualism
**billet** *m.* bill (*currency*) (7); ticket; **billet aller-retour** round-trip ticket
**biologie** *f.* biology (2)
**biscuit (sec)** *m.* cookie
**bise** *f.*, *fam.* kiss, smack; **faire la bise** to kiss on both cheeks (*in greeting*); **grosses bises** love and kisses
**bistro(t)** *m.* bar, pub
**blague** *f.* joke
**blanc(he)** *adj.* white (3)
**blasé** *adj.* indifferent, blasé
**blé** *m.* wheat; *tr. fam.* money, cash
**bleu** *adj.* blue (3); *m.* blue cheese
**bloc** *m.* block
**blond(e)** *m.*, *f.*, *adj.* blond (4)
**blouson** *m.* windbreaker (3); jacket
**bœuf** *m.* beef; ox; **bœuf bourguignon** beef stew (*with red wine and onions*); **consommé** (*m.*) **de bœuf** beef consommé; **rôti (filet)** (*m.*) **de bœuf** roast beef; filet
**bof!** *interj. and gesture of skepticism*
**boire** (*p.p.* **bu**) *irreg.* to drink (6)
**bois** *m.* forest, wood(s) (11)
**boisson** *f.* drink, beverage (6)
**boîte** *f.* box; can (7); nightclub; *fam.* workplace; **boîte (de conserve)** can (of food) (7); **boîte aux lettres** mailbox (10); **boîte de couleurs** box of colored pencils
**bol** *m.* wide cup (6); bowl
**bon(ne)** *adj.* good (7); right, correct; *f.* maid, chambermaid; **ah bon? ah oui?** really? (6); **bon anniversaire** happy birthday; **bon appétit** enjoy your meal; **bon chic bon genre (BCBG)** "preppie"; **bon marché** *adj. inv.* cheap, inexpensive; **bonne chance** good luck; **bonne route** have a good trip; **de bonne heure** early (6); **le bon vieux temps** the good old days; **sentir bon** to smell good
**bonbon** *m.* (piece of) candy
**bonheur** *m.* happiness
**bonhomme** *m.* (little) fellow; **bonhomme de neige** snowman (17)
**bonjour** *interj.* hello, good day (1)
**bonsoir** *interj.* good evening (1)
**bord** *m.* board; edge, bank, shore; **à bord** on board; **au bord de** on the banks (shore) of
**bordure** *f.* border, edge; curb; **en bordure de** running along, bordering
**bosseur/euse** *m.*, *f.*, *fam.* hard-worker
**botte(s)** *f.* boot(s) (3)
**boucanier** *m.* pirate, buccaneer
**bouche** *f.* mouth (13)
**boucher/ère** *m.*, *f.* butcher (14)
**boucherie** *f.* butcher shop (7); **boucherie-charcuterie** *f.* combination butcher and deli
**bouffe** *f.*, *fam.* large, copious meal (*with friends*)
**bouffer** *fam.* to gobble; to eat
**bouger (nous bougeons)** to move
**boulangerie** *f.* bakery (7); **boulangerie-pâtisserie** *f.* bakery-pastry shop
**boulot** *m.*, *fam.* job; work
**boum** *f.*, *fam.* party
**bouquin** *m.*, *fam.* book
**bourgeois** *adj.* bourgeois; middle-class
**bourse** *f.* scholarship; grant
**bout** *m.* end; bit; morsel; **au bout (de)** at the end (of); **jusqu'au bout** until the very end
**bouteille** *f.* bottle (6)
**boutique** *f.* shop, store
**boxe** *f.* boxing; **match** (*m.*) **de boxe** boxing match (15)
**branché** *m.*, *f.*, *adj.*, *fam.* "with it," cool (*person*)
**bras** *m.* arm (13)
**bref (brève)** *adj.* short, brief
**Brésil** *m.* Brazil (8)
**brevet** *m.* diploma; certificate; **brevet d'études** lower school diploma in France
**bribes** *f. pl.* scraps, snippets
**bricolage** *m.* do-it-yourself, home projects
**bricoler** to putter (*around the house*) (15)
**brièvement** *adv.* briefly
**brillant** *adj.* brilliant; shining
**briller** to shine, gleam
**brique** *f.* brick
**briquet** *m.* cigarette lighter
**broder** to embroider
**bronzer** to get a suntan (8)
**brosse** *f.* brush; chalkboard eraser; **brosse à dents** toothbrush
**brosser** to brush; **se brosser les cheveux (les dents)** to brush one's hair (teeth) (13)
**brouillard** *m.* fog
**brousse** *f.* bush, wilderness
**bruit** *m.* noise (5)
**brûlant** *m.* burning; urgent
**brumeux/euse** *adj.* foggy, misty
**brun** *adj.* brown; dark-haired, brunette
**brutalement** *adv.* brutally; abruptly
**bruyant** *adj.* noisy
**bûche** *f.* log; **bûche de Noël** yule-log (*pastry*)
**bûcheron** *m.* woodcutter
**budget** *m.* budget (14); **budget militaire** military budget (16)
**bureau** *m.* desk (1); office (5); **bureau de change** money exchange (office) (14); **bureau de poste** post office (10); **bureau de tabac** (*government-licensed*) tobacconist

**bureaucrate** *m., f.* bureaucrat
**but** *m.* goal; objective; **but à long terme** long-term goal

**ça** *pron.* this, that; it; **ça m'est égal** it's all the same to me; **ça peut aller** it's going o.k.; **ça va?** how's it going? (1); **ça va** fine (things are going well) (1); **ça va bien (mal)** things are going well (badly); **comme ci, comme ça** so-so (1)
**cabine** *f.* cabin; booth; **cabine téléphonique** telephone booth (10)
**cabinet** *m.* office; study; closet
**câblé** *adj.* cabled, wired
**cacao** *m.* cocoa
**cacher** to hide; **se cacher** to hide (*oneself*)
**cadeau** *m.* present, gift
**cadet(te)** *m., f.* youngest brother or sister
**cadre** *m.* frame; setting; middle or upper manager (14)
**café** *m.* café; (cup of) coffee (2); **café au lait** coffee with milk; **café-tabac** *m.* bar-tobacconist (11)
**cahier** *m.* notebook (1); workbook
**caisse** *f.* cash register; box, crate; *tr. fam.* car
**caissier/ière** *m., f.* cashier
**calcul** *m.* calculation; arithmetic; calculus; **faire des calculs** to do calculations
**calculé** *adj.* calculated, deliberate
**calculer** to calculate, figure; **machine** (*f.*) **à calculer** adding machine
**calendrier** *m.* calendar
**calme** *m., adj.* calm (3)
**calmer** to calm (down)
**camarade** *m., f.* friend, companion (4); **camarade de chambre** roommate (4); **camarade de classe** classmate, schoolmate
**caméra** *f.* movie camera; **caméra vidéo** video camera
**caméscope** *m.* camcorder, video camera
**camion** *m.* truck
**campagne** *f.* country(side) (8); campaign; **à la campagne** in the country; **pain** (*m.*) **de campagne** country-style, wheat bread; **pâté** (*m.*) **de campagne** terrine; (country-style) pâté (7)
**campement** *m.* camp, encampment
**camper** to camp
**campeur/euse** *m., f.* camper
**camping** *m.* camping (8); campground; **faire du camping** to go camping; **terrain** (*m.*) **de camping** campground
**Canada** *m.* Canada (8)
**canal** *m.* channel; canal
**canapé** *m.* sofa, couch (4)
**canard** *m.* duck; *tr. fam.* newspaper; **canard laqué** Peking duck
**cancéreux/euse** *adj.* cancerous
**candidat(e)** *m., f.* candidate; applicant
**candidature** *f.* candidacy
**canne** *f.* cane, walking stick; **canne à sucre** sugar cane
**canoë** *m.* canoe; **faire du canoë** to canoe, go canoeing
**capacité** *f.* ability; capacity
**capital** *adj.* capital, chief
**capitale** *f.* capital (*city*)
**car** *conj.* for, because
**caractère** *m.* character
**caractérisé** *adj.* characterized
**caractéristique** *f.* characteristic, trait
**carafe** *f.* pitcher; decanter (6)
**Caraïbes** *f. pl.* Caribbean (*islands*) (17); **mer** (*f.*) **des Caraïbes** Caribbean (*sea*) (17)
**caravane** *f.* (camping) trailer
**carburateur** *m.* carburetor
**cardiaque** *adj.* cardiac; **crise** (*f.*) **cardiaque** heart attack
**caricature** *f.* caricature; political cartoon
**caricaturiste** *m., f.* caricaturist, cartoonist
**carlingue** *f.* cockpit, cabin (*plane*)
**carnaval** *m.* carnival (17)
**carnet** *m.* notebook; booklet; book of tickets; **carnet de chèques** checkbook (14)
**carotte** *f.* carrot (6)
**carré** *adj.* square; **mètre** (*m.*) **carré** square meter
**carrière** *f.* career
**carriériste** *adj.* career-oriented
**carte** *f.* card (3); menu (7); map (*of region, country*) (11); **à la carte** à la carte, from the menu; **carte bancaire** bank (ATM) card (14); **carte de crédit** credit card (14); **carte d'embarquement** boarding pass (9); **carte d'étudiant** student ID card; **carte d'identité** identification card; **carte postale** postcard (10); **jouer aux cartes** to play cards
**cartouche** *m.* cartouche, tablet (*architectural*)
**cas** *m.* case; **en cas de** in case of, in the event of; **selon le cas** as the case may be
**casier** *m.* locker
**casquette** *f.* cap
**casse-croûte** *m.* snack, light lunch
**casser** to break; **casser avec** to break off relations with; **se casser le bras** to break one's arm
**casse-tête** *m.* puzzle, riddle game
**cassette** *f.* cassette tape (*video or audio*) (4); **lecteur** (*m.*) **de cassettes** video player; cassette player (4)
**cassis** *m.* blackcurrant (*liquor*)
**catégorie** *f.* category, class
**cathédrale** *f.* cathedral (12)
**cause** *f.* cause; **à cause de** because of
**CD: lecteur-CD** *m.* compact disk player
**ce (cet, cette, ces)** *pron., adj.* this, that (5); **c'est un (une)...** it's a . . . (1); **ce week-end** this weekend (5); **cet après-midi (ce matin, ce soir)** this afternoon (morning, evening) (5)
**ceci** *pron.* this, that
**céder (je cède)** to give in; to give up; to give away
**cédille** *f.* cedilla
**cela (ça)** *pron.* this, that (7)
**célèbre** *adj.* famous
**célébrer (je célèbre)** to celebrate
**célibat** *m.* single life (13)
**célibataire** *m., f., adj.* single (*person*) (5)
**celui (ceux, celle, celles)** *pron.* the one, the ones, this one, that one, these, those
**censure** *f.* censorship
**censurer** to censor
**cent** *adj.* one hundred
**centaine** *f.* about one hundred
**centime** *m.* centime, 1/100th of a franc (7)
**centrale** *f.* power station; **centrale nucléaire** nuclear power plant
**centre** *m.* center; **centre-ville** *m.* downtown (11)
**cependant** *adv.* in the meantime; meanwhile; *conj.* yet, still, however, nevertheless
**céréales** *f. pl.* cereal; grains
**cérémonie** *f.* ceremony
**certain** *adj.* sure; particular; certain (17); *pl., pron.* certain ones, some people (17); **il est certain que** + *indic.* it's certain that
**cerveau** *m.* brain
**cesse** *f.* ceasing; **sans cesse** ceaselessly
**cesser (de)** to stop, cease
**c'est-à-dire** *conj.* that is to say
**chacun(e)** *m., f., pron.* each, everyone (9); each (one) (17)

**chagrin** *m.* sorrow, sadness
**chaîne** *f.* television channel; network (10); chain; range (*mountain*); **chaîne câblée** cable channel; **chaîne stéréo** stereo (system) (4)
**chaise** *f.* chair (1)
**chaleur** *f.* heat; warmth
**chaleureux/euse** *adj.* warm; friendly
**chambre** *f.* (bed)room (4); hotel room; **camarade** (*m., f.*) **de chambre** roommate (4)
**champignon** *m.* mushroom
**champion(ne)** *m., f.* champion
**chance** *f.* luck; possibility; opportunity; **avoir de la chance** to be lucky (4); **bonne chance** good luck
**change** *m.* currency exchange; **bureau** (*m.*) **de change** money exchange (office) (14)
**changement** *m.* change
**changer (nous changeons)** to change; to exchange (*currency*); **changer d'avis** to change one's mind; **changer de l'argent** to exchange currency
**chanson** *f.* song; **chanson de variété** popular song (15)
**chanter** to sing (10)
**chanteur/euse** *m., f.* singer (10)
**chantilly: crème** (*f.*) **chantilly** whipped cream
**chapeau** *m.* hat (3)
**chapelle** *f.* chapel
**chapitre** *m.* chapter
**chaque** *adj.* each, every (17)
**char** *m.* wagon; parade float (17)
**charbon** *m.* coal
**charcuterie** *f.* deli; cold cuts; pork butcher (7)
**chargé (de)** *adj.* in charge of, responsible for; heavy, loaded; busy
**chargement** *m.* loading; shipping
**charlotte** *f.* cake with whipped cream and fruit
**charmant** *adj.* charming
**chasse** *f.* hunting
**chassé** *adj.* chased, pursued
**chat(te)** *m., f.* cat
**châtain** *adj.* brown, chestnut-colored (*hair*) (4)
**château** *m.* castle, chateau (11)
**châtelaine** *f.* chatelaine, lady of the manor
**chaud** *adj.* warm; hot (6); **avoir chaud** to feel warm, hot (4); **il fait chaud** it (the weather) is warm, hot (6)
**chauffage** *m.* heat; heating system
**chauffé** *adj.* heated; **piscine** (*f.*) **chauffée** heated swimming pool
**chauffeur/euse** *m., f.* chauffeur; driver
**chaussée** *f.* pavement; **rez-de-chaussée** *m.* ground-level (*apartment*) (5)
**chaussettes** *f. pl.* socks (3)
**chaussures** *f. pl.* shoes (3); **chaussures de ski (de montagne)** ski (hiking) boots (8)
**chef** *m.* leader; head; chef, head cook; **chef de cuisine** head cook, chef; **chef d'entreprise** company head, top manager, boss (14); **terrine** (*f.*) **du chef** chef's special pâté
**chef-d'œuvre** *m.* (*pl.* **chefs-d'œuvre**) masterpiece (12)
**chemin** *m.* way (11); road; path; **chemin de fer** railroad; **demander son chemin** to ask directions
**cheminée** *f.* fireplace; hearth
**chemise** *f.* shirt (3)
**chemisier** *m.* (*woman's*) shirt, blouse (3)
**chêne** *m.* oak (*tree*)
**chèque** *m.* check (14); **carnet** (*m.*) **de chèques** checkbook (14); **chèque barré** check payable only to bank; **chèque de voyage** traveler's check; **chèque postal** postal money order; **compte-chèques** *m.* checking account; **déposer un chèque** to deposit a check; **endosser un chèque** to endorse a check; **faire un chèque** to write a check (14); **remise** (*f.*) **de chèques** remittance by check; **toucher un chèque** to cash a check (11)
**cher (chère)** *adj.* expensive (7); dear (2); **coûter cher** to be expensive
**chercher** to look for (2); to pick up; **chercher à** to try to (15)
**cheval** *m.* horse (8); **faire du cheval** to ride horseback (8)
**cheveux** *m. pl.* hair (4); **se brosser (se laver) les cheveux** to brush (wash) one's hair
**chez** at the home (establishment) of (5); **chez moi** at my place
**chic** *m.* chic; style; *adj. inv.* chic, stylish; **bon chic bon genre (BCBG)** "preppie"
**chien(ne)** *m., f.* dog (4)
**chiffre** *m.* number, digit; **chiffre record** record number (16)
**chimie** *f.* chemistry (2)
**chimique** *adj.* chemical
**chimiste** *m., f.* chemist
**Chine** *f.* China (8)
**chinois** *adj.* Chinese; *m.* Chinese (*language*); **Chinois(e)** *m., f.* Chinese (*person*) (2)
**chirurgien(ne)** *m., f.* surgeon
**choc** *m.* shock
**chocolat** *m.* chocolate (6); hot chocolate; **éclair** (*m.*) **au chocolat** chocolate eclair; **mousse** (*f.*) **au chocolat** chocolate mousse; **pain** (*m.*) **au chocolat** chocolate croissant
**chœur** *m.* chorus; **enfant** (*m.*) **de chœur** choirboy
**choisir (de)** to choose (to) (4)
**choix** *m.* choice (2); **au choix** of your choosing
**chômage** *m.* unemployment (16)
**chômeur/euse** *m., f.* unemployed person
**chose** *f.* thing; **autre chose** something else; **pas grand-chose** not much; **quelque chose** something (9); **quelque chose d'important** something important
**chou** *m.* cabbage
**chouette** *adj. inv., fam.* cute (5); super, neat
**chou-fleur** (*pl.* **choux-fleurs**) *m.* cauliflower
**chronique** *f.* chronicle; news
**chronologique** *adj.* chronological
**chute** *f.* fall, descent; waterfall
**ci: comme ci, comme ça** so-so (1)
**ci-dessous** *adv.* below
**ci-dessus** *adv.* above, previously
**ciel** *m.* sky, heaven; **gratte-ciel** *m. inv.* skyscraper
**ciment** *m.* cement
**cinéaste** *m., f.* filmmaker (12)
**ciné-club** *m.* film club
**cinéma** (*fam.* **ciné**) *m.* movies; movie theater (2)
**cinq** *adj.* five (1)
**cinquante** *adj.* fifty (1); **les années** (*f. pl.*) **cinquante** the fifties
**cinquième** *adj.* fifth (11)
**circonflexe** *m.* circumflex (*accent*)
**circonstance** *f.* circumstance; occurrence
**circuit** *m.* circuit; organized tour
**circulation** *f.* traffic; circulation
**circuler** to circulate; to travel
**citadin(e)** *m., f.* city dweller
**cité** *f.* area in a city; **cité universitaire** (*fam.* **cité-u**) university residence complex (2)
**citoyen(ne)** *m., f.* citizen (16)
**citron** *m.* lemon
**civil** *adj.* civil; **état** (*m.*) **civil** civil, marital status

**clafoutis** *m.* fruit cobbler (*dessert*)
**clair** *adj.* light, bright; light-colored; clear; evident (16)
**clandestin(e)** *m., f.* clandestine, underground person; *adj.* clandestine, secret
**clarinette** *f.* clarinet
**classe** *f.* class; classroom; **camarade** (*m., f.*) **de classe** classmate; **classe affaires (économique)** business (tourist) class (9); **livre** (*m.*) **de classe** textbook; **première (deuxième) classe** first (second) class; **salle** (*f.*) **de classe** classroom (1)
**classement** *m.* classification
**classer** to classify; to sort
**classique** *adj.* classical (12); classic; **musique** (*f.*) **classique** classical music
**clé, clef** *f.* key (8); **clé de voûte** keystone (*architecture*); **mot-clé** *m.* key word
**client(e)** *m., f.* customer, client
**climat** *m.* climate
**climatisation** *f.* air-conditioning
**climatisé** *adj.* air-conditioned
**cloche** *f.* bell
**club** *m.* club (*social, athletic*); **ciné-club** *m.* film club
**coca** *m., fam.* cola drink
**cocher** to check off (*list*)
**coco: lait** (*m.*) **de coco** coconut milk; **noix** (*f.*) **de coco** coconut
**cocoteraie** *f.* coconut plantation
**cocotier** *m.* coconut tree
**cocotte** *f.* stew-pan
**code** *m.* code; **code postal** postal, zip code
**codé** *adj.* coded
**cœur** *m.* heart; **au cœur de** at the heart, center of
**coffre** *m.* chest; trunk (*of car*)
**coiffeur/euse** *m., f.* hairdresser (14); barber
**coin** *m.* corner (11)
**collection** *f.* collection (15)
**collectionner** to collect
**collectionneur/euse** *m., f.* collector
**collier** *m.* necklace
**colline** *f.* hill
**colmater** to fill in; to clog up
**colon** *m.* colonist
**colonie** *f.* colony; **colonie de vacances** summer camp
**colonisateur/trice** *m., f.* colonizer
**coloniser** to colonize (17)
**colonne** *f.* column
**combattant** *m.* fighter, combatant; **ancien combattant** war veteran
**combattre** (*like* **battre**) *irreg.* to fight
**combien (de)?** *adv.* how much? how many? (1)
**combinaison** *f.* combination
**combustible** *m.* fuel
**comédie** *f.* comedy; theater
**comique** *m., f.* comedian, comic; *adj.* funny, comical, comic
**commander** to order (*in a restaurant*) (6); to give orders
**comme** *adv.* as, like, how; **comme ci, comme ça** so-so (1)
**commencement** *m.* beginning
**commencer (nous commençons) (à)** to begin (to) (11); **commencer par** to begin by (*doing s.th.*) (15)
**comment** *adv.* how (1); **comment?** what? how? (1); **comment allez-vous?** how are you? (1); **comment ça va?** how are you? how's it going? **comment dit-on?** how do you say?; **comment est-il/elle?** what's he (she, it) like?; **comment s'appelle-t-il/elle?** what's his (her) name?; **comment vous appelez-vous?** what's your name? (1); **je ne sais pas comment vous (te) remercier** I don't know how to thank you (15)
**commentaire** *m.* commentary, remark
**commenter** to comment
**commerçant(e)** *m., f.* shopkeeper (14)
**commerce** *m.* business
**commissariat (de police)** *m.* police station (11)
**commission** *f.* commission; errand; **commission de vente** sales commission
**commode** *f.* chest of drawers (4); *adj.* convenient; comfortable
**commun** *adj.* ordinary, common, shared, usual; popular; **en commun** in common; **transports** (*m. pl.*) **en commun** public transportation
**communauté** *f.* community
**communicatif/ive** *adj.* communicative
**communication** *f.* communication; phone call
**communiquer** to communicate; to adjoin
**compact disc** *m.* compact disk player
**compagnie** *f.* company; **compagnie aérienne** airline
**compagnon (compagne)** *m., f.* companion
**comparaison** *f.* comparison
**comparatif/ive** *adj.* comparative; *m., Gram.* comparative
**comparer** to compare
**compartiment** *m.* compartment (9)
**complément** *m.* complement; **pronom** (*m.*) **complément d'objet direct** *Gram.* direct object pronoun
**complémentaire** *adj.* complementary
**complet/ète** *adj.* complete; whole; filled; **pension** (*f.*) **complète** full board
**compléter (je complète)** to complete, finish
**compliqué** *adj.* complicated
**comportement** *m.* behavior
**composé** *adj.* composed; **passé** (*m.*) **composé** *Gram.* present perfect
**composer** to compose; to make up; **composer un numéro** to dial a (phone) number (10); **se composer de** to be composed of
**compositeur/trice** *m., f.* composer (12)
**composter** to stamp (*date*); to punch (*ticket*)
**compréhensif/ive** *adj.* understanding
**compréhension** *f.* understanding
**comprendre** (*like* **prendre**) *irreg.* to understand (6); to comprise, include; **je ne comprends pas** I don't understand (1)
**comprimé** *m.* tablet, pill
**compris** *adj.* included; **tout compris** all inclusive
**comptabilité** *f.* accounting (14)
**comptable** *m., f.* accountant (14); **expert(e)-comptable** *m., f.* certified public accountant
**compte** *m.* account (14); **compte bancaire** bank account; **compte-chèques** *m.* checking account (14); **compte courant** checking account; **compte d'épargne** savings account (14)
**compter (sur)** to plan (on); to intend; to count
**comté** *m.* county
**conception** *f.* conception; idea, notion
**concerner** to concern
**concorde** *f.* agreement, concord; *m.* Concord, supersonic plane
**concours** *m.* competition; competitive exam
**conçu** *adj.* conceived, designed
**concurrence** *f.* competition
**condamnable** *adj.* condemnable, blamable

**condamnation** *f.* condemnation
**condamné(e)** *m., f.* convicted (*person*)
**condition** *f.* condition; situation; **conditions d'admission** admission requirements
**conditionné** *adj.* conditioned
**conditionnel** *m., Gram.* conditional
**conducteur/trice** *m., f.* driver (9)
**conduire** (*p.p.* **conduit**) *irreg.* to drive (9); to take; to conduct; **permis** (*m.*) **de conduire** driver's license
**conduite** *f.* behavior; driving; guidance
**confectionné** *adj.* created, concocted
**conférence** *f.* lecture (12); conference; **salle** (*f.*) **de conférence** meeting room
**confiance** *f.* confidence; **avoir confiance en** to have confidence in; to trust; **faire confiance à** to trust
**confidence** *f.* confidence, secret; **faire une confidence à** to tell a secret to
**confier** to confide; to give
**confiture** *f.* jam, preserves
**conflit** *m.* conflict (16)
**conformiste** *m., f., adj.* conformist (3)
**confort** *m.* comfort; amenities
**confortable** *adj.* comfortable
**congé** *m.* leave (*from work*), vacation
**Congo** *m.* Congo (8)
**congrès** *m.* congress; meeting, convention
**conjugaison** *f., Gram.* (verb) conjugation
**conjuguer** *Gram.* to conjugate
**connaissance** *f.* knowledge; acquaintance; consciousness; **à ma connaissance** to my knowledge; **enchanté(e) de faire votre connaissance** delighted to meet you; **faire connaissance** to get acquainted; **faire la connaissance de** to meet (*for the first time*) (5)
**connaître** (*p.p.* **connu**) *irreg.* to know; to be familiar with (11)
**connu** *adj.* known; famous
**conquérir** (*p.p.* **conquis**) *irreg.* to conquer
**conquête** *f.* conquest
**consacrer** to consecrate; to devote
**conscience** *f.* conscience; consciousness; **prendre conscience de** to become aware of
**conseil** *m.* (piece of) advice (14); council; **donner conseil à** to give advice to
**conseiller (de)** to advise (to) (15)
**conseiller/ère** *m., f.* advisor; counselor; **conseiller/ère d'orientation** guidance counselor
**conservation** *f.* conserving; preservation (16)
**conservatoire** *m.* conservatory
**conserve** *f.* preserve(s), canned food; **boîte** (*f.*) **de conserve** can of food (7)
**conserver** to conserve, preserve (16)
**considération** *f.* consideration; **prendre en considération** to take into consideration
**considérer (je considère)** to consider; **se considérer** to consider oneself, each other
**consigne** *f.* order(s), rule(s); baggage room, check room; **consigne automatique** coin locker
**consister (à, en)** to consist (in, of)
**consommateur/trice** *m., f.* consumer
**consommation** *f.* consumption; consumerism
**consommé** *m.* clear soup, consommé; *adj.* consumed
**constamment** *adv.* constantly (12)
**constater** to notice; to remark
**constituer** to constitute
**construire** (*like* **conduire**) *irreg.* to construct, build (9)
**consultation** *f.* consulting; consultation; doctor's visit
**consulter** to consult
**conte** *m.* tale, story; **conte de fée(s)** fairy tale
**contempler** to contemplate, meditate upon
**contemporain** *adj.* contemporary
**contenir** (*like* **tenir**) *irreg.* to contain
**content** *adj.* happy, pleased (10); **être content(e) de** + *inf.* to be happy about; **être content(e) que** + *subj.* to be happy that
**contenter** to please, make happy; **se contenter de** to be content with, satisfied with
**continuer (à, de)** to continue (to) (11)
**contrainte** *f.* constraint; **sans contrainte** free, unconstrained
**contraire** *adj.* opposite; *m.* opposite; **au contraire** on the contrary (6)
**contrairement (à)** *adv.* contrarily, contrary (to)
**contrat** *m.* contract
**contre** *prep.* against; contrasted with
**contrôle** *m.* control, overseeing (16)
**contrôler** to inspect, monitor (16)
**contrôleur/euse** *m., f.* ticket collector; conductor
**controverse** *f.* controversy
**convaincre** (*like* **vaincre**) *irreg.* to convince
**convaincu** *adj.* sincere, earnest; convinced
**convenable** *adj.* proper; appropriate
**convenir** (*like* **venir**) *irreg.* to fit; to be suitable
**convention** *f.* convention; agreement
**convoité** *adj.* desired, coveted
**convoquer** to summon, invite, convene
**coopérant(e)** *m., f.* member of **la Coopération** (*French national service corps*)
**coopérer (je coopère)** to cooperate
**copain (copine)** *m., f., fam.* friend, pal
**copieux/euse** *adj.* copious, abundant
**coq** *m.* rooster; **coq au vin** chicken prepared with red wine
**coquette** *f.* flirt, coquette
**coralien(ne)** *adj.* coral
**corps** *m.* body (13)
**correspondance** *f.* correspondence; transfer, change (*of trains*)
**correspondant(e)** *m., f.* correspondent; pen pal; *adj.* corresponding
**correspondre** to correspond
**corriger (nous corrigeons)** to correct
**cortège** *m.* procession
**cosmopolite** *adj.* cosmopolitan
**costume** *m.* (*man's*) suit (3); costume (17)
**côte** *f.* coast; rib; rib steak; side; **côte d'agneau (de porc)** lamb (pork) chop (7)
**côté** *m.* side; **à côté (de)** *prep.* by, near, next to; at one's side (3); **(d')à côté** (from) next door; **de côté** aside; **de l'autre côté (de)** from, on the other side (of)
**Côte-d'Ivoire** *f.* Ivory Coast (8)
**côtelette** *f.* cutlet, (*lamb, pork*) chop
**coton** *m.* cotton; **en coton** (*made of*) cotton
**cou** *m.* neck (13)
**couchage: sac** (*m.*) **de couchage** sleeping bag (8)
**couche** *f.* layer; stratum; *pl.* (*baby's*) diapers; *pl.* childbirth; **couche d'ozone** ozone layer
**coucher** to put to bed; **coucher** (*m.*) **de soleil** sunset; **se coucher** to go to bed; to set (*sun*) (13)

**couchette** *f.* couchette; berth (*train*) (9)
**coudre** (*p.p.* **cousu**) *irreg.* to sew
**couleur** *f.* color; **boîte** (*f.*) **de couleurs** box of colored pencils, paints; **de quelle couleur est... ?** what color is . . . ?; **en couleur(s)** color; colored
**couloir** *m.* hall(way) (5)
**coup** *m.* blow; coup; (gun)shot; influence; **coup de fil** *fam.* phone call; **coup de foudre** flash of lightning; love at first sight (13); **coup d'état** government overthrow, coup d'état; **coup de téléphone** telephone call; **tout à coup** *adv.* suddenly; **tout d'un coup** *adv.* at once, all at once (11)
**coupe** *f.* trophy, cup (16); champagne glass; **coupe** (*f.*) **d'Europe** European Cup (*soccer*) (16)
**couper** to cut; to divide; to censor
**courageux/euse** *adj.* courageous (3)
**couramment** *adv.* fluently; commonly (12)
**courant** *adj.* frequent; general, everyday; *m.* current; **compte** (*m.*) **courant** checking account; **être au courant** to be up (to date) with
**courbe** *f.* curve
**coureur/euse** *m., f.* runner
**courge** *f.* squash, gourd
**courir** (*p.p.* **couru**) *irreg.* to run (15)
**couronné** *adj.* crowned
**courrier** *m.* mail
**cours** *m.* course (2); exchange rate (14); price; **au cours de** *prep.* during; **cours du jour** today's exchange rate; **en cours** current, present; **suivre un cours** to take a course
**course** *f.* race; errand; **faire les courses** to do errands (5); to shop
**court** *adj.* short (*not used for people*) (4); *m.* (tennis) court
**court-métrage** *m.* short subject, documentary
**couscous** *m.* couscous (*North African cracked-wheat dish*) (9)
**couscoussier** *m.* couscous pan (*with steamer*)
**cousin(e)** *m., f.* cousin (5)
**coût** *m.* cost; **coût de la vie** cost of living (14)
**couteau** *m.* knife (6)
**coûter** to cost; **coûter cher** to be expensive
**coûteux/euse** *adj.* costly, expensive
**coutume** *f.* custom (17)
**couture** *f.* sewing; clothes design; ***haute couture** high fashion
**couturier/ière** *m., f.* fashion designer; dressmaker
**couvert** *adj.* covered; cloudy; *m.* table setting; **mettre le couvert** to set the table
**couverture** *f.* blanket
**couvrir** (*like* **ouvrir**) *irreg.* to cover (14)
**craie** *f.* chalk (1)
**craqué** *adj., tr. fam.* cracked up
**cravate** *f.* tie (3)
**crayon** *m.* pencil (1)
**créateur/trice** *m., f.* creator; *adj.* creative
**créatif/ive** *adj.* creative
**crèche** *f.* child-care center
**crédit** *m.* credit; *pl.* funds, investments; **carte** (*f.*) **de crédit** credit card (14)
**créer** to create (10)
**crème** *f.* cream (6); **crème de cassis** blackcurrant liquor; **crème de marrons** chestnut purée; **crème glacée** ice cream; **crème solaire** sunscreen
**crêpe** *f.* crepe, French pancake
**crêperie** *f.* creperie, restaurant featuring **crêpes**
**crête** *f.* crest; spiked hair
**creusé** *adj.* hollowed out; furrowed
**crevette** *f.* shrimp
**cri** *m.* shout
**crier** to cry out; to shout
**criminaliser** to refer to criminal court
**crise** *f.* crisis; recession; depression; **crise cardiaque** heart attack; **crise économique** recession; depression
**cristallisé** *adj.* crystalized
**critère** *m.* criterion
**critique** *f.* criticism; critique; *m., f.* critic; *adj.* critical; **faire la critique** to review, criticize
**critiquer** to criticize
**croire** (*p.p.* **cru**) **(à)** *irreg.* to believe (in) (8); **croire que** to believe that (8)
**croisé** *adj.* crossed; **mots** (*m. pl.*) **croisés** crossword puzzle
**croiser** to cross; to run across
**croisière** *f.* cruise
**croissance** *f.* growth, development; **taux** (*m.*) **de croissance** growth rate
**croissant** *m.* croissant (*roll*) (6)
**croissanterie** *f.* snack bar featuring croissant sandwiches
**croque-monsieur** *m.* grilled cheese and ham sandwich
**croquer** to munch; to crunch
**croûte** *f.* crust; **casse-croûte** *m.* snack
**croyance** *f.* belief
**crudité** *f.* raw vegetable; *pl.* plate of raw vegetables
**cruel(le)** *adj.* cruel
**crustacé** *m.* crustacea, shellfish
**cuillère** *f.* spoon (6); **cuillère à soupe** soup spoon, tablespoon (6); **petite cuillère** teaspoon
**cuillerée** *f.* spoonful
**cuir** *m.* leather; **en cuir** (*made of*) leather
**cuisine** *f.* cooking; food, cuisine (6); kitchen (5); **chef** (*m.*) **de cuisine** head cook, chef; **faire la cuisine** to cook (5); **livre** (*m.*) **de cuisine** cookbook; **nouvelle cuisine** light, low-fat cuisine
**cuisiner** to cook
**cuisinette** *f.* kitchenette
**cuisson** *f.* cooking (*process*)
**cuit** *adj.* cooked; **bien cuit** well done (*meat*)
**cuivre** *m.* copper; brass
**culinaire** *adj.* culinary, cooking
**culte** *m.* cult; religion
**cultivé** *adj.* educated; cultured
**culture** *f.* education; culture
**culturel(le)** *adj.* cultural
**curieux/euse** *adj.* curious
**cyclisme** *m.* cycling (15)
**cycliste** *m., f.* bicycle rider, cyclist
**cynique** *adj.* cynical

**d'abord** *adv.* first, first of all, at first (11)
**d'accord** *interj.* O.K., agreed (2)
**d'ailleurs** *adv.* besides, moreover
**dalle: avoir la dalle** *tr. fam.* to be very hungry, starving
**dame** *f.* lady, woman; **messieurs-dames** ladies and gentlemen
**dangereux/euse** *adj.* dangerous
**dans** *prep.* within, in (2); **dans quatre jours** in four days (5)
**dansant** *adj.* dancing; **soirée** (*f.*) **dansante** dance
**danse** *f.* dance; dancing
**danser** to dance (2)
**date** *f.* date (*time*); **date de naissance** date of birth
**dater de** to date from (12)
**d'autres** *pron.* others (17)
**davantage** *adv.* more
**de** *prep.* of, from, about (2)
**débarquement** *m.* debarkation, landing
**débat** *m.* debate
**se débattre** (*like* **battre**) *irreg.* to fight; to struggle

**débrouillardise** *f., fam.* resourcefulness
**se débrouiller** to manage, get along
**début** *m.* beginning; **au début (de)** in, at the beginning (of)
**débutant(e)** *m., f.* beginner
**débuter** to begin
**décembre** December (4)
**décès** *m.* demise, death
**décevant** *adj.* disappointing
**décharge** *f.* (*electrical*) discharge; unloading
**déchets** *m. pl.* (*industrial*) waste (16); debris; **déchets nucléaires** nuclear waste
**déchirure** *f.* tear, rent, split
**décidément** *adv.* decidedly; definitely
**décider (de)** to decide (to) (15)
**décision** *f.* decision; **prendre une décision** to make a decision
**se déclarer** to declare oneself
**déclin** *m.* decline
**décodeur** *m.* decoder
**décollage** *m.* take off (*airplane*)
**décoloré** *adj.* bleached; colorless; faded
**décombres** *m. pl.* rubble, debris
**décontracté** *adj.* relaxed
**décor** *m.* decor; scenery
**décorer (de)** to decorate (with)
**découpage** *m.* cutting up, carving up
**découverte** *f.* discovery
**découvrir** (*like* **ouvrir**) *irreg.* to discover, learn (14)
**décrire** (*like* **écrire**) *irreg.* to describe (10)
**décrit** *adj.* described
**décrocher** *fam.* to get, receive
**dedans** *prep., adv.* within, inside
**dédoublé** *adj.* divided into two (*parts*)
**défaut** *m.* defect, fault
**défavorable** *adj.* unfavorable
**défendre** to defend; **défendre de** to forbid
**défi** *m.* challenge
**défilé** *m.* parade (17); procession
**défini** *adj.* defined; definite; **article** (*m.*) **défini** *Gram.* definite article
**définir** to define
**défonceur/euse** *m., f.* smasher, destroyer
**dégoûtant** *adj.* disgusting
**degré** *m.* degree
**se déguiser** to disguise oneself, wear a costume (17)
**déguster** to taste; to relish; to eat, drink
**dehors** *adv.* outdoors; outside (13); **en dehors de** outside of, besides
**déjà** *adv.* already (9)
**déjeuner** to have lunch; *m.* lunch (6); **petit déjeuner** breakfast (6)
**délaisser** to forsake, abandon
**délégué(e)** *m., f.* delegate
**délicieux/euse** *adj.* delicious
**deltaplane** *m.* hang glider
**déluge** *m.* deluge, flood
**demain** *adv.* tomorrow (5); **à demain** see you tomorrow
**demande** *f.* request; application; **demande d'emploi** job application
**demander** to ask (for), request (4); **se demander** to wonder (12)
**démarche** *f.* (*necessary*) step
**déménagement** *m.* moving (*out of a house*)
**déménager (nous déménageons)** to move (*house*)
**demi** *adj.* half; **il est minuit et demi** it's twelve-thirty A.M. (6)
**demi-frère** *m.* half brother; stepbrother (5)
**demi-heure** *f.* half hour
**demi-pension** *f.* partial board (*with room*)
**demi-sœur** *f.* half sister; stepsister (5)
**démocratie** *f.* democracy
**démolir** to demolish, destroy
**démonstratif/ive** *adj.* demonstrative; **adjectif** (*m.*) **démonstratif** *Gram.* demonstrative adjective
**dent** *f.* tooth (13); **à pleines dents** fully, completely; **brosse** (*f.*) **à dents** toothbrush; **se brosser les dents** to brush one's teeth
**dentifrice** *m.* toothpaste
**dentiste** *m., f.* dentist (14)
**départ** *m.* departure (9); **point** (*m.*) **de départ** starting point
**département** *m.* department; district
**dépasser** to go beyond; to pass, surpass
**se dépêcher (de)** to hurry (to) (12)
**dépendance** *f.* dependency; outbuilding
**dépense** *f.* expense (14); spending
**dépenser** to spend (*money*) (14); **se dépenser** to waste, spend one's time
**dépit** *m.* spite; **en dépit de** in spite of
**déplacement** *m.* moving, change of place; travel
**déplacer (nous déplaçons)** to displace; to shift; to remove; **se déplacer** to move around, go somewhere
**déplaire** (*like* **plaire**) *irreg.* to displease
**déporté** *adj.* deported
**déposer** to deposit (14); **déposer de l'argent** to deposit money
**déprimé** *adj.* depressed
**depuis (que)** *prep.* since, for (8); **depuis combien de temps** how long
**député** *m.* delegate, deputy
**déranger (nous dérangeons)** to disturb, bother
**dériveur** *m.* sailboat; drifter
**dernier/ière** *adj.* last (8); most recent; past; **la dernière fois** the last time; **l'an dernier (l'année dernière)** last year
**dernièrement** *adv.* lately, recently
**se dérouler** to unfold; to develop
**derrière** *prep.* behind (3); *m.* back, rear
**dès** *prep.* from (*then on*); **dès que** *conj.* as soon as (14)
**désagréable** *adj.* disagreeable, unpleasant (3)
**désastre** *m.* disaster
**désastreux/euse** *adj.* disastrous
**descendre** to go down; to get off (9); to take down; to go down (*street, river*); **descendre à** to go down (*south*) to (5); **descendre de** to get down (from), get off (5)
**désert** *m.* desert; wilderness
**déserter** to desert; to run away
**déserteur** *m.* deserter; defector
**désir** *m.* desire
**désirer** to desire, want (15)
**désolé** *adj.* sorry (16); **(je suis) désolé(e)** I'm sorry (8)
**désordre** *m.* disorder, confusion; **en désordre** disorderly, untidy (4)
**désormais** *adv.* henceforth
**dessert** *m.* dessert (6)
**dessin** *m.* drawing
**dessinateur/trice** *m., f.* designer; sketcher
**dessiné** *adj.* drawn, sketched; **bande** (*f.*) **dessinée** comic strip; *pl.* comics
**dessiner** to draw
**dessous** *adv.* under, underneath; **ci-dessous** *adv.* below
**dessus** *adv.* above; over; on; **ci-dessus** *adv.* above, previously; **là-dessus** on that subject
**destinataire** *m., f.* recipient
**destination** *f.* destination; **à destination de** in the direction of; heading for
**destiné (à)** *adj.* designed (for), aimed (at)
**destinée** *f.* destiny, future
**détail** *m.* detail; **en détail** in detail
**détaillé** *adj.* detailed

**se détendre** to relax (12)
**détenir** (*like* **tenir**) *irreg.* to be in possession of
**détente** *f.* relaxation; detente
**déterminer** to determine
**détester** to detest; to hate (2)
**détruire** (*like* **conduire**) *irreg.* to destroy (9)
**deux** *adj.* two (1); **tous (toutes) les deux** both (of them)
**deuxième** *adj.* second (5); **deuxième classe** second-class (*travel*); **Deuxième Guerre** (*f.*) **mondiale** Second World War
**devant** *prep.* before, in front of (2)
**développé** *adj.* developed; industrialized
**développement** *m.* development (16); developing (*photo*); **pays** (*m.*) **en voie de développement** developing country
**développer** to spread out; to develop (16); **se développer** to expand; to develop
**devenir** (*like* **venir**) *irreg.* to become (8); *m.* evolution, change
**devenu** *adj.* became
**deviner** to guess (12)
**devinette** *f.* riddle, conundrum
**dévoiler** to reveal, disclose
**devoir** (*p.p.* **dû**) *irreg.* to owe; to have to, be obliged to (7); *m.* duty; *m. pl.* homework (5); **faire ses devoirs** to do one's homework (5)
**dévorant** *adj.* ravenous; devouring
**dévorer** to devour
**d'habitude** *adv.* habitually, usually (10)
**diamant** *m.* diamond
**diapositive** *f.* (*photographic*) slide
**dictateur/trice** *m., f.* dictator
**dictionnaire** *m.* dictionary (2)
**diététique** *f.* dietetics, nutrition; *adj.* dietetic
**dieu** *m.* god
**différemment** *adv.* differently
**différend** *m.* disagreement, difference
**différent** *adj.* different (3)
**difficile** *adj.* difficult (3)
**diffuser** to broadcast; to disseminate
**diffusion** *f.* broadcasting
**digestif** *m.* brandy, liqueur
**digne** *adj.* worthy
**diligemment** *adv.* diligently
**dimanche** *m.* Sunday (1)
**diminuer** to lessen, diminish
**diminution** *f.* decrease, reduction (16)
**dinde** *f.* turkey
**dîner** to dine, have dinner (6); *m.* dinner (6)
**diplomate** *m., f.* diplomat; *adj.* diplomatic, tactful
**diplomatique** *adj.* diplomatic (*of the diplomatic corps*)
**diplôme** *m.* diploma
**diplômé(e)** *m., f.* graduate; holder of a diploma; *adj.* graduated
**dire** (*p.p.* **dit**) *irreg.* to say, tell (10); **c'est-à-dire** that is to say, namely; **dis donc** *interj.* say, listen; **que veut dire... ?** what does . . . mean? (7); **se dire** to say to one another; **vouloir dire** to mean (7)
**direct** *adj.* direct, straight; live (*broadcast*); through, fast (*train*); **en direct** live (*broadcasting*); **pronom** (*m.*) **(complément) d'objet direct** *Gram.* direct object pronoun
**directeur/trice** *m., f.* manager, head (14)
**direction** *f.* direction; management; leadership
**directives** *f. pl.* rules of conduct, directives
**diriger** (**nous dirigeons**) to direct (14); to govern, control; **se diriger vers** to go, make one's way, toward
**disc: compact disc** *m.* CD player
**disco** *m.* disco music
**discothèque** (*fam.* **disco**) *f.* discothèque
**discours** *m.* discourse; speech
**discuter (de)** to discuss
**disjoint: pronom** (*m.*) **disjoint** *Gram.* disjunctive, stressed pronoun
**disparaître** (*like* **connaître**) *irreg.* to disappear (13)
**disparition** *f.* disappearance
**disponible** *adj.* available
**disposer de** to have (available); to dispose, make use of
**disposition** *f.* disposition; ordering; **à votre disposition** at your disposal
**dispute** *f.* quarrel
**se disputer (avec)** to quarrel (with) (13)
**disque** *m.* record (4), recording
**dissertation** *f.* essay, term paper
**distraction** *f.* recreation; entertainment; distraction
**se distraire** (*like* **traire**) *irreg.* to have fun, amuse oneself
**distrait** *adj.* distracted, absentminded (9)
**distribuer** to distribute
**distributeur/trice** *m., f.* distributor; *m.* vending machine; **distributeur automatique** automatic teller (ATM) (14)
**divers** *adj.* changing; varied, diverse; **fait** (*m.*) **divers** news item, incident
**se divertir** to enjoy oneself, have a good time
**divertissement** *m.* amusement, pastime
**se diviser** to divide up
**divorcé(e)** *adj.* divorced; *m., f.* divorced person (5)
**dix** *adj.* ten (1); **dix-sept (-huit, -neuf)** *adj.* seventeen (eighteen, nineteen) (1)
**dixième** *adj.* tenth
**docteur** *m.* doctor
**doigt** *m.* finger (13)
**domaine** *m.* domain; specialty
**domestique** *m., f.* servant; *adj.* domestic
**domicile** *m.* domicile, place of residence, home; **à domicile** at home; **visite** (*f.*) **à domicile** house call
**dominante** *f.* prevailing, dominant note
**dominical** *adj.* pertaining to Sunday(s)
**dommage** *m.* damage; pity; too bad (8); **c'est dommage** it's too bad, what a pity; **il est dommage que** + *subj.* it's too bad that (16)
**donc** *conj.* then; therefore (3); **dis donc** *interj.* say, listen
**données** *f. pl.* data; **base** (*f.*) **de données** data base
**donner** to give (2); **donner des conseils** to give advice; **donner sur** to open out onto, overlook (4)
**dont** whose, of whom, of which (14)
**doré** *adj.* gold; golden; gilt
**dormir** *irreg.* to sleep (8)
**dortoir** *m.* dormitory
**dos** *m.* back; **sac** (*m.*) **à dos** backpack (2)
**dot** *f.* dowry
**douane** *f.* customs (*at the border*)
**doublé** *adj.* dubbed (*film*); doubled
**doubler** to pass (*a car*); to double; to dub
**douceur** *f.* softness; gentleness; sweetness
**douche** *f.* shower (*bath*) (4); **prendre une douche** to take a shower
**se doucher** to take a shower (13)
**doué** *adj.* talented, gifted; bright; **être doué(e) pour** to be talented in
**douloureuse** *f., tr. fam.* bill (*in restaurant*)
**doute** *m.* doubt; **sans doute** probably, no doubt

**douter** to doubt (16)
**douteux/euse** *adj.* doubtful, uncertain, dubious
**doux (douce)** *adj.* sweet, kindly, pleasant; soft, gentle; **à feu doux** on low heat
**douzaine** *f.* dozen; about twelve
**douze** *adj.* twelve (1)
**douzième** *adj.* twelfth
**dramatique** *adj.* dramatic; **arts** (*m. pl.*) **dramatiques** theater, theater arts
**drap** *m.* (*bed*) sheet
**drapeau** *m.* flag
**drogue** *f.* drug
**droit** *m.* law (2); right; fee, royalty; **faculté** (*f.*) **de droit** law school; **les droits de l'homme** the rights of man
**droit** *adj.* right; straight; *adv.* straight on; *f.* right; right hand; **à droite (de)** *prep.* on the right (of) (11); **aller tout droit** to go straight ahead (11); **extrême-droite** *f.* far right (*political*); **Rive** (*f.*) **droite** Right Bank (*of the Seine*) (11)
**drôle** *adj.* funny, odd (3); **un(e) drôle de...** a funny, odd . . .
**duc** *m.* duke
**dur** *adj.* hard; difficult; **en dur** concrete, stone; **travailler dur** to work hard
**durant** *prep.* during
**durée** *f.* duration, length
**durer** to last, continue; to endure; to last a long time
**dynamique** *adj.* dynamic (3)

**eau** *f.* water (6); **eau minérale** mineral water (6); **salle** (*f.*) **d'eau** half-bath (*toilet and sink*)
**ébranlé** *adj.* shaken, upset
**échange** *m.* exchange (17)
**échanger (nous échangeons)** to exchange
**échec** *m.* failure; checkmate; *pl.* chess (2); **jouer aux échecs** to play chess
**échelle** *f.* scale; ladder
**éclair** *m.* éclair (*custard pastry with chocolate*) (7)
**éclaircie** *f.* clearing (*in weather*)
**éclairé** *adj.* lit, lighted
**éclatement** *m.* bursting, rupture
**éclater** to break out; to burst; **s'éclater** *fam.* to enjoy oneself intensely
**école** *f.* school (10); **école maternelle** preschool, kindergarten; **école primaire (secondaire)** primary (secondary) school; **grandes écoles** (*French state-run*) graduate schools
**écologie** *f.* ecology
**écologique** *adj.* ecological
**écologiste** *m., f.* ecologist (*politics*); *adj.* ecological (16)
**économe** *adj.* thrifty, economical
**économie** (*fam.* **éco**) *f.* economics; economy; *pl.* savings; **faire des économies** to save (*money*) (14)
**économique** *adj.* economic; financial; economical; **classe** (*f.*) **économique** tourist class (9); **sciences** (*f. pl.*) **économiques** economics
**économiser** to save (*money*)
**écoulé** *adj.* of last (*month, year*)
**écoute: à l'écoute** *adv.* listening (in)
**écouter** to listen to (2)
**écrevisse** *f.* crayfish (17)
**s'écrier** to cry out, exclaim
**écrire** (*p.p.* **écrit**) **(à)** *irreg.* to write (to) (10)
**écrit** *adj.* written; **par écrit** in writing
**écrivain (femme-écrivain)** *m., f.* writer (12)
**édifice** *m.* building, edifice
**éditeur/trice** *m., f.* editor; publisher
**édition** *f.* publishing; edition
**éducatif/ive** *adj.* educational
**éducation** *f.* upbringing; breeding; education
**effacer (nous effaçons)** to erase
**effectif** *m.* manpower; size (*of working group*)
**effectivement** *adv.* effectively; actually, in reality
**effet** *m.* effect; **effet de serre** greenhouse effect; **en effet** as a matter of fact, indeed
**efficace** *adj.* efficient, useful
**effort** *m.* effort, attempt; **faire un (des) effort(s) pour** to try, make an effort to
**égal** *adj.* equal; all the same; **cela (ça) m'est égal** I don't care, it's all the same to me
**également** *adv.* equally; likewise, also
**égalité** *f.* equality
**église** *f.* church (11)
**égoïste** *m., f., adj.* selfish (*person*)
**eh bien!** *interj.* well! well then! (3)
**électeur/trice** *m., f.* voter (16)
**électricité** *f.* electricity
**électronique** *f.* electronics; *adj.* electronic
**électronucléaire** *adj.* electro-nuclear
**élève** *m., f.* pupil, student
**élevé** *adj.* high (13); raised; brought up
**élever (j'élève)** to raise; to lift up
**éliminer** to eliminate
**élire** (*like* **lire**) *irreg.* to elect (16)
**elle** *pron., f. s.* she; her; **elle-même** *pron., f. s.* herself; **elles** *pron., f. pl.* they; them
**élu(e)** *m., f., adj.* elected, chosen (*person*)
**embarquement** *m.* embarkation; **carte** (*f.*) **d'embarquement** boarding pass (9)
**embarrassant** *adj.* embarrassing
**embarrassé** *adj.* embarrassed
**embauche** *f.* hiring (14)
**embaucher** to hire (14)
**embellir** to beautify; to embellish
**embêter** to annoy; to bore
**embouteillage** *m.* traffic jam
**embrasser** to kiss; to embrace; **je t'embrasse** love (*closing of letter*); **s'embrasser** to embrace or kiss each other (13)
**émetteur** *m.* transmitter
**émettre** (*like* **mettre**) *irreg.* to emit, broadcast; to issue
**émigrer** to emigrate
**émission** *f.* program; broadcast (10)
**emmener (j'emmène)** to take (*s.o. somewhere*) (15); to take along
**empêcher (de)** to prevent (from) (15); to preclude
**empereur** *m.* emperor
**emplacement** *m.* location
**emploi** *m.* use; job, position; **demande** (*f.*) **d'emploi** job application; **offre** (*f.*) **d'emploi** job offer
**employé(e)** *m., f.* employee; white-collar worker (14); **employé(e) de** s.o. employed by (14)
**employer (j'emploie)** to use; to employ
**employeur/euse** *m., f.* employer
**empoisonner** to poison
**emporter** to take (*s.th. somewhere*); to take out (*food*)
**emprunt** *m.* loan (14); **faire un emprunt** to take out a loan
**emprunter (à)** to borrow (from) (12)
**en** *prep.* in; to (2); like; in the form of; *pron.* of them; of it; some; any (11)
**encercler** to circle, encircle
**enchaîné** *adj.* chained, fettered
**enchanté** *adj.* enchanted; pleased; **enchanté(e) de faire votre connaissance** delighted to meet you

**encore** *adv.* still (9); again; yet; even; more; **encore une fois** once more; **ne... pas encore** not yet
**encourager (nous encourageons) (à)** to encourage (to)
**encyclopédie** *f.* encyclopedia
**endisquer** to record (*an album*)
**s'endormir** to fall asleep (13)
**endosser** to endorse (*check*)
**endroit** *m.* place, spot (8)
**énergétique** *adj.* pertaining to energy
**énergie** *f.* energy; **énergie nucléaire (solaire)** nuclear (solar) energy (16)
**énergique** *adj.* energetic
**énervant** *adj.* aggravating, irritating
**énervé** *adj.* irritated, upset
**enfance** *f.* childhood
**enfant** *m., f.* child (5); **petit-enfant** *m.* grandchild (5)
**enfantin** *adj.* childish; juvenile
**enfin** *adv.* finally, at last (11)
**engagement** *m.* (*political*) commitment
**engager (nous engageons)** to open; to begin, start; **s'engager vers** to commit oneself to (16)
**s'engueuler** *fam.* to quarrel, scold each other
**énigme** *f.* riddle, enigma
**enlever (j'enlève)** to remove, take off
**ennemi(e)** *m., f.* enemy
**ennui** *m.* trouble (9); problem; worry; boredom
**ennuyer (j'ennuie)** to bother; to bore; **s'ennuyer** to be bored, get bored (13)
**ennuyeux/euse** *adj.* boring (13); annoying
**énorme** *adj.* huge, enormous
**enquête** *f.* inquiry; investigation
**enquêteur/euse** *m., f.* investigator; reporter
**enregistrer** to record; to check in
**s'enrhumer** to catch cold
**enrichissant** *adj.* enriching
**enseignant(e)** *m., f.* teacher, instructor
**enseignement** *m.* teaching; education (15)
**enseigner (à)** to teach (to) (15)
**ensemble** *adv.* together; *m.* ensemble; whole
**ensoleillé** *adj.* sunny
**ensuite** *adv.* then, next (7)
**entendre** to hear (5); **s'entendre (bien, mal) avec** to get along (well, badly) with (12)
**enthousiasme** *m.* enthusiasm
**enthousiaste** *adj.* enthusiastic (3)
**entier/ière** *adj.* entire, whole, complete; **en entier** entirely
**entourer (de)** to surround (with)
**entracte** *m.* intermission
**entraînement** *m.* (*athletic*) training, coaching
**entre** *prep.* between, among (4)
**entrecôte** *f.* rib steak
**entrée** *f.* entrance, entry; admission; first course (*meal*) (7)
**entreprise** *f.* business, company (14); **chef** (*m.*) **d'entreprise** company head, top manager, boss (14)
**entrer (dans)** to enter (9)
**entretien** *m.* maintenance; conversation; job interview (14)
**entrevue** *f.* (*job*) interview
**enveloppe** *f.* envelope (10)
**envers** *prep.* to; toward; in respect to; **à l'envers** upside down; inside out
**envie** *f.* desire; **avoir envie de** to want; to feel like (4)
**environ** *adv.* about, approximately (4)
**environnement** *m.* environment (16); milieu
**envisager (nous envisageons)** to envision
**envoi: coup** (*m.*) **d'envoi** kickoff, free kick (*soccer*)
**envoyer (j'envoie)** to send (10)
**épais(se)** *adj.* thick
**épargne** *f.* saving, thrift; **compte** (*m.*) **d'épargne** savings account (14)
**épaule** *f.* shoulder
**épice** *f.* spice
**épicé** *adj.* spicy
**épicerie** *f.* grocery store (7)
**épicier/ière** *m., f.* grocer
**épidémie** *f.* epidemic
**épidémiologique** *adj.* epidemiological
**épinards** *m. pl.* spinach
**époque** *f.* period (*of history*) (12); **à l'époque de** at the time of; **meubles** (*m. pl.*) **d'époque** antique furniture
**épouser** to marry
**époux (épouse)** *m., f.* spouse; husband (wife)
**épreuve** *f.* test; trial; examination; **mettre à l'épreuve** to test
**éprouver** to feel; to experience
**équilibre** *m.* equilibrium, balance
**équilibré** *adj.* balanced, well-balanced
**équipe** *f.* team (15); working group; **sports** (*m. pl.*) **d'équipe** team sports; **travail** (*m.*) **d'équipe** teamwork
**équipé** *adj.* equipped
**équipement** *m.* equipment; gear
**équitation** *f.* horseback riding
**érable** *m.* maple; **sirop** (*m.*) **d'érable** maple syrup
**erreur** *f.* error; mistake
**erroné** *adj.* wrong, erroneous
**éruption** *f.* eruption; rash (*skin*)
**escalade** *f.* climbing; **faire de l'escalade** to go rock climbing, mountain climbing
**escalier** *m.* stairs, stairway (5)
**escalope** *f.* (*veal*) scallop
**escargot** *m.* snail; escargot
**esclavage** *m.* slavery
**esclave** *m., f.* slave
**escrime** *f.* fencing (*sport*)
**espace** *m.* space
**Espagne** *f.* Spain (8)
**espagnol** *adj.* Spanish; *m.* Spanish (*language*); **Espagnol(e)** *m., f.* Spanish (*person*) (2)
**espèce** *f.* species; cash; **en espèces** in cash
**espérance** *f.* hope; expectancy; **espérance de vie** life expectancy
**espérer (j'espère)** to hope (15)
**espoir** *m.* hope
**esprit** *m.* mind; spirit; wit
**essai** *m.* trial; experiment; attempt
**essayer (j'essaie) (de)** to try (to) (10)
**essence** *f.* gasoline, gas; essence; **faire le plein d'essence** to fill the tank
**essentiel(le)** *adj.* essential; **il est essentiel que** + *subj.* it's essential that (16)
**essor** *m.* flight, rise
**est** *m.* east (9); **à l'est** to the east (9)
**estimer** to consider; to believe; to estimate (16); **s'estimer** to think oneself
**et** *conj.* and (2); **et puis?** and (then) next? (7); **et quart** quarter past (*the hour*) (6); **et toi (vous)?** and you? (1)
**établir** to establish, set up; **s'établir** to settle; to set up
**établissement** *m.* settlement; establishment
**étage** *m.* floor (*of building*); **premier étage** second floor (*in France*) (5)
**étagère** *f.* shelf (4); étagère
**étape** *f.* stage; stopping place
**état** *m.* state (8); shape; **coup** (*m.*) **d'état** coup, government overthrow; **en bon (mauvais) état** in good (bad) condition; **secrétaire** (*m., f.*) **d'état** secretary of state
**États-Unis** *m. pl.* United States (of America) (8)

**été** *m.* summer (6); **en été** in summer (6); **job** (*m.*) **d'été** summer job
**s'étendre** to spread (out), extend
**éternel(le)** *adj.* eternal
**éternité** *f.* eternity
**étoile** *f.* star; **à la belle étoile** in the open air
**étonnant** *adj.* astonishing, surprising
**étonné** *adj.* surprised (16); astonished
**étrange** *adj.* strange (16)
**étranger/ère** *adj.* foreign; *m., f.* stranger; foreigner; **à l'étranger** abroad, in a foreign country (9); **langue** (*f.*) **étrangère** foreign language (2)
**être** (*p.p.* **été**) *irreg.* to be (3); *m.* being; **c'est (ce n'est pas)** it's (it isn't); **comment est-il/elle?** what's he/she like?; **être en train de** to be in the process of, in the middle of (15); **être fauché(e)** *fam.* to be broke, without money; **être raide** *tr. fam.* to be broke, without money; **nous sommes lundi (mardi...** ) it's Monday (Tuesday . . . ) (1); **peut-être** *adv.* perhaps, maybe (5)
**étroit** *adj.* narrow, small
**étude** *f.* study; *pl.* studies; **faire des études** to study
**étudiant(e)** *m., f., adj.* student (1); **carte** (*f.*) **d'étudiant** student ID card
**étudier** to study (2)
**euh...** *interj.* uh . . .
**eux** *pron., m. pl.* them; **eux-mêmes** *pron., m., pl.* themselves
**évalué** *adj.* appraised; evaluated
**évasion** *f.* escape
**événement** *m.* event (12)
**éventuellement** *adv.* possibly
**évidemment** *adv.* evidently, obviously
**évident** *adj.* obvious, clear; **il est évident que** + *indic.* it is clear that (16)
**évier** *m.* (kitchen) sink
**éviter** to avoid
**évoluer** to evolve, advance
**évolutif/ive** *adj.* evolutive; with potential
**évoquer** to evoke, call to mind
**exagérer (j'exagère)** to exaggerate
**examen** (*fam.* **exam**) *m.* test, exam (2); examination; **passer un examen** to take an exam (4); **réussir à un examen** to pass a test
**excentrique** *adj.* eccentric (3)
**excepté** *prep.* except
**exceptionnel(le)** *adj.* exceptional
**excès** *m.* excess
**excessif/ive** *adj.* excessive
**exclusif/ive** *adj.* exclusive
**excursion** *f.* excursion, outing; **faire une excursion** to go on an outing
**s'excuser (de)** to excuse oneself (for) (12); **excusez-moi** excuse me, pardon me (1)
**exécution** *f.* carrying out; execution
**exemplaire** *adj.* exemplary
**exemple** *m.* example; **par exemple** for example (16)
**exercer (nous exerçons)** to exercise; to practice
**exercice** *m.* exercise; **faire de l'exercice** to do exercise(s)
**exigeant** *adj.* demanding; difficult
**exiger (nous exigeons)** to require, demand (16)
**s'exiler** to exile oneself, leave one's country
**exister** to exist
**expédition** *f.* shipping
**expérience** *f.* experience; experiment; **faire l'expérience de** to experience
**expert(e)** *m., f.* expert; **expert(e)-comptable** *m., f.* certified public accountant
**expirer** to breathe out; to expire
**explication** *f.* explanation
**expliquer** to explain; **s'expliquer avec** to explain oneself; to have it out with
**exploiter** to exploit
**explorateur/trice** *m., f.* explorer
**explorer** to explore
**exposé** *m.* presentation, exposé
**exposer** to expose, show; to display
**exposition** *f.* exhibition; show
**expression** *f.* expression; term; **liberté** (*f.*) **d'expression** freedom of expression (16)
**exprimer** to express; **exprimer une opinion** to express an opinion (16)
**extérieur** *m., adj.* exterior; outside; **à l'extérieur** (on the) outside, out-of-doors
**extrait** *m.* excerpt; extract
**extraordinaire** *adj.* extraordinary
**extrême** *adj.* extreme; **extrême-droite** *f.* extreme right (*political*)

**fabricant(e)** *m., f.* manufacturer
**fabrication** *f.* manufacture
**fabriquer** to manufacture, make
**fac** *f., fam.* (**faculté**) university department or school
**face** *f.* face; façade; **en face (de)** *prep.* opposite, facing, across from (11); **faire face à** to confront
**facette** *f.* facet
**fâché** *adj.* angry (16); annoyed
**fâcher** to anger; to annoy; **se fâcher** to get angry (13)
**fâcheux/euse** *adj.* unfortunate (16); troublesome
**facile** *adj.* easy (3)
**facilité** *f.* aptitude, talent; easiness
**façon** *f.* way, manner, fashion; **de façon (logique)** in a (logical) way
**facteur** *m.* factor; letter carrier (14)
**facture** *f.* bill (*to pay*)
**faculté** *f* ability; (*fam.* **fac**) division (*university*) (2); **faculté de droit (de médecine)** law (medical) school; **faculté des lettres** School of Arts and Letters; **faculté des sciences naturelles** School of Natural Science
**faible** *adj.* weak; small
**faim** *f.* hunger; **avoir faim** to be hungry (4)
**faire** to do (5); to make; to form; to be; **faire appel à** to appeal to, call upon; **faire attention (à)** to be careful (of); to watch out (for) (5); **faire beau (il fait beau)** to be good weather (it's nice out) (6); **faire chaud (il fait chaud)** to be warm, hot (out) (it's warm, hot) (6); **faire de la bicyclette** to cycle, go biking; **faire de la chasse sportive** to do sport hunting; **faire de l'aérobic** to do aerobics (5); **faire de la gymnastique** (*fam.* **gym**) to do gymnastics; to exercise; **faire de l'alpinisme** to go mountain climbing; **faire de la peinture** to paint; **faire de la planche à voile** to go windsurfing; **faire de la politique** to go in for politics; **faire de la voile** to go sailing (5); **faire de l'exercice** to do exercises; to exercise; **faire des acrobaties** to do acrobatics, stunts; **faire des calculs** to do calculations; **faire des courses** to do errands (5); **faire des économies** to save (up) money (14); **faire des études** to study; **faire des préparatifs** to prepare, make preparations; **faire du bateau** to go boating; **faire du bruit** to make noise; **faire du camping** to camp, go camping; **faire du canoë** to go canoeing; **faire du cheval** to go horseback riding; **faire du commerce** to trade, do business; **faire du jardinage** to garden (15); **faire du jogging** to run, jog (5); **faire du ski** to ski (5); **faire du ski de fond** to go

cross-country skiing (8); **faire du ski nautique** to go waterskiing; **faire du soleil (il fait du soleil)** to be sunny (it's sunny) (6); **faire du sport** to do sports (5); **faire du tennis** to play tennis; **faire du tourisme** to go sightseeing; **faire du vélo** to go cycling (5); **faire du vent (il fait du vent)** to be windy (it's windy) (6); **faire face à** to face, confront; **faire faire** to have done, make s.o. do s.th.; **faire frais (il fait frais)** to be cool (out) (it's cool) (6); **faire froid (il fait froid)** to be cold (out) (it's cold) (6); **faire (la) grève** to strike, go on strike (16); **faire la bise** to kiss on both cheeks (*in greeting*); **faire la connaissance de** to meet (*for the first time*) (5); **faire la cuisine** to cook (5); **faire la fête** to party; **faire la lessive** to do the laundry (5); **faire la sieste** to take a nap; **faire la vaisselle** to do the dishes (5); **faire le lit** to make the bed; **faire le marché** to do the shopping, go to the market (5); **faire le ménage** to do the housework (5); **faire le plein (d'essence)** to fill it up (with gas) (9); **faire les courses** to do errands (5); **faire les valises** to pack one's bags; **faire le tour de** to go around; to tour; **faire mauvais (il fait mauvais)** to be bad weather (out) (it's bad out) (6); **faire partie de** to belong to; **faire ses devoirs** to do one's homework (5); **faire sombre** to be dark; **faire son possible** to do one's best; **faire un chèque** to write a check (14); **faire un cours** to give, teach a course; **faire une drôle de tête (de tronche)** *fam.* to act strangely; **faire une erreur** to make a mistake; **faire une excursion** to go on an outing; **faire un emprunt** to take out a loan; **faire une promenade** to take a walk (5); **faire un petit service** to do a favor (15); **faire un pique-nique** to go on a picnic; **faire un safari-photos** to go on a photo-safari; **faire un stage** to do an internship; **faire un temps pourri** *fam.* to be rotten weather; **faire un tour** to take a walk, ride (5); **faire un voyage** to take a trip (5); **se faire un resto (un ciné)** *tr. fam.* to go to a restaurant (to the movies)

**fait** *m.* fact; *adj.* made; **tout à fait** *adv.* completely, entirely

**falloir** (*p.p.* **fallu**) *irreg.* to be necessary (16); to be lacking; **il faut** + *inf.* it is necessary to; one needs (7)

**fameux/euse** *adj.* famous

**familial** *adj.* family

**familiariser** to familiarize

**familier/ière** *adj.* familiar

**famille** *f.* family (5); **en famille** with one's family; **pension** (*f.*) **de famille** family boarding house

**fanatisme** *m.* fanaticism

**fantaisie** *f.* fantasy; novelty; **bijoux** (*m. pl.*) **fantaisie** costume jewelry

**farine** *f.* flour

**fascinant** *adj.* fascinating

**fasciné** *adj.* fascinated

**fatigant** *adj.* tiring

**fatigue** *f.* tiredness, fatigue

**fatigué** *adj.* tired

**fauché** *adj., fam.* broke, without money

**faut (il)** it is necessary to; one needs (7)

**faute** *f.* fault, mistake

**fauteuil** *m.* armchair, easy chair

**faux (fausse)** *adj.* false (7)

**faveur** *f.* favor; **en faveur de** supporting, backing

**favori(te)** *adj.* favorite (8)

**fécondité** *f.* fertility

**fédératif/ive** *adj.* federal (*constitution*)

**fédéré** *adj.* federated

**fée** *f.* fairy; **conte** (*m.*) **de fée(s)** fairy tale

**félicitations** *f. pl.* congratulations

**féminin** *adj.* feminine

**femme** *f.* woman (2); wife (5); **femme d'affaires** businesswoman; **femme de ménage** cleaning woman, housekeeper; **femme politique** politician (16)

**fenêtre** *f.* window (1)

**fer** *m.* iron; **chemin** (*m.*) **de fer** railroad; **fer forgé** wrought iron

**ferme** *adj.* firm; **tenir ferme** to stand firm

**fermer** to close (8)

**fête** *f.* holiday (4); celebration, party; saint's day, name day (4); *pl.* Christmas season; **faire la fête** to party; **fête des Anciens Combattants** Armistice Day, Veterans Day; **fête des Rois** Feast of the Magi, Epiphany; **fête du travail** labor day; **jour** (*m.*) **de fête** holiday

**fêter** to celebrate (17); to observe a holiday

**feu** *m.* fire; traffic light; **à feu doux** on low heat

**feuilleté** *adj.* flaky (*pastry*)

**fève** *f.* bean

**février** February (4)

**fiançailles** *f. pl.* engagement (13); **bague** (*f.*) **de fiançailles** engagement ring (13)

**fiancé(e)** *m., f., adj.* fiancé(e), betrothed

**se fiancer (nous nous fiançons)** to become engaged

**fibre** *f.* fiber, filament

**fiche** *f.* index card; form (*to fill out*); deposit slip; **fiche d'identité** identity card

**fictif/ive** *adj.* fictitious

**fidèle** *adj.* faithful

**fier (fière)** *adj.* proud (3); **être fier (fière) de** to be proud of

**fièvre** *f.* fever

**figure** *f.* face; figure

**figurer** to appear

**fil** *m.* thread; cord; **coup** (*m.*) **de fil** *fam.* phone call

**filer** to trail, follow

**filet** *m.* fillet (*fish, meat*) (7); **faux filet** sirloin (*of beef*); **filet de porc (de bœuf)** pork (beef) filet

**filiale** *f.* subsidiary

**fille** *f.* girl; daughter (5); **jeune fille** girl, young woman (3); **petite-fille** granddaughter (5)

**film** *m.* movie, film (2); **un film doublé** a dubbed movie

**fils** *m.* son (5); **petit-fils** grandson (5)

**fin** *f.* end; purpose; *adj.* fine, thin; **à la fin de** at the end of; **au fin fond de** in the heart of; **en fin d'après-midi** in the late afternoon; **extra-fin** *adj.* superfine; **mi-fin** *adj.* medium-cut (*vegetables*); **toucher à sa fin** to draw to a close

**finalement** *adv.* finally

**finaliste** *m., f.* finalist

**finance** *f.* finance; *pl.* finances

**financer (nous finançons)** to finance

**financier/ière** *adj.* financial

**finir (de)** to finish (4); **finir par** to end, finish by (*doing s.th.*) (15)

**firme** *f.* firm, company

**fixe** *adj.* fixed

**fixer** to fix; to make firm

**flanc** *m.* (*mountain*) side

**flâner** to stroll (12)

**flash (d'informations)** *m.* newsbrief

**fleur** *f.* flower (4); **fleur de lis** fleur de lys, trefoil

**fleurette** *f.* floweret

**fleurir** to flower; to flourish
**fleuve** *m.* river (*flowing into the sea*) (8)
**flotte** *f., tr. fam.* water
**flûte** *f.* flute
**foie** *m.* liver; **pâté** (*m.*) **de foie gras** goose liver pâté
**fois** *f.* time, occasion; times (*arithmetic*); **encore une fois** again; **il était une fois** once upon a time; **la première (dernière) fois** the first (last) time; **une fois** once (11); **une fois par (semaine)** once a (week) (5)
**folklorique** *adj.* traditional; folk (*music, etc.*)
**fonction** *f.* function; use, office; **en fonction de** as a function of; according to
**fonctionnaire** *m., f.* civil servant (14)
**fonctionnement** *m.* working order, functioning
**fonctionner** to function, work
**fond** *m.* bottom; back, background; *pl.* funds, funding; **au fin fond de** in the heart of; **ski** (*m.*) **de fond** cross-country skiing (8)
**fondateur/trice** *m., f.* founder
**fondation** *f.* founding, settlement
**fonder** to found
**fondre** to melt
**fondue** *f.* fondue (*Swiss melted cheese dish*)
**fontaine** *f.* fountain
**football** (*fam.* **foot**) *m.* soccer; **football américain** football; **match** (*m.*) **de foot** soccer game
**footballeur** *m.* soccer player
**force** *f.* strength; **force de vente** sales force
**forcer (nous forçons)** to force, compel; **forcer sur** to stress, emphasize; to overdo
**forêt** *f.* forest (8)
**formation** *f.* education, training
**forme** *f.* form; shape; figure; **en (bonne, pleine) forme** physically fit; **en (sous) forme de** in the form of; **salle** (*f.*) **de mise en forme** fitness, conditioning room; **tenir la forme** to stay in shape
**formel(le)** *adj.* formal
**former** to form, shape; to train
**formidable** *adj.* great, wonderful (5)
**formulaire** *m.* form (*to fill out*); **remplir un formulaire** to fill out a form
**formuler** to formulate
**fort** *adj.* strong; heavy; *adv.* strongly; loudly, loud; very (13); often; a lot; **parler fort** to speak loudly; **travailler fort** to work hard
**fortifié** *adj.* fortified
**fossoyeur/euse** *m., f.* gravedigger
**fou (fol, folle)** *adj.* crazy, mad; **amour** (*m.*) **fou** mad passion
**foudre** *f.* lightning; **coup** (*m.*) **de foudre** thunderbolt; love at first sight (13)
**foulard** *m.* scarf
**foule** *f.* crowd
**fourchette** *f.* fork (6)
**fourmi** *f.* ant
**fournir** to furnish, supply, provide
**fournitures** *f. pl.* supplies, equipment; **fournitures scolaires** school supplies
**foyer** *m.* hearth; home (5); student residence
**frais** *m. pl.* fees; expense(s) (14); **frais d'inscription (de scolarité)** school, university (tuition) fees
**frais (fraîche)** *adj.* cool (6); fresh (7); **faire frais (il fait frais)** to be cool (out) (it's cool) (6)
**fraise** *f.* strawberry (6)
**framboise** *f.* raspberry
**franc** *m.* franc (*French, Swiss currency*) (7)
**franc(he)** *adj.* frank; truthful; honest
**français** *adj.* French; *m.* French (*language*); **Français(e)** *m., f.* Frenchman (woman) (2)
**France** *f.* France (8)
**francophone** *adj.* French-speaking (17)
**francophonie** *f.* French-speaking world
**frangin(e)** *m., f., tr. fam.* brother (sister)
**franglais** *m.* English or American terms used in French
**frappant** *adj.* striking
**frappé** *m.* iced drink
**frapper** to strike; to knock; to levy (*tax*)
**fréquemment** *adv.* frequently, often
**fréquenté** *adj.* much visited, popular
**frère** *m.* brother (5); **beau-frère** brother-in-law (5); **demi-frère** half brother; step brother (5)
**fric** *m., fam.* money, cash; **mettre du fric de côté** *fam.* to put some cash aside
**frigo** *m., fam.* fridge, refrigerator
**friperie** *f., fam.* secondhand clothes shop
**frisé** *adj.* curly (13)
**frit** *adj.* fried; **frites** *f. pl.* French fries (6)
**froid** *adj.* cold; *m.* cold (6); **avoir froid** to be cold (4); **faire froid (il fait froid)** to be cold (out) (it's cold) (6); **garder son sang-froid** to keep one's cool
**frôler** to touch lightly, brush
**fromage** *m.* cheese (6)
**frometon** *m., tr. fam.* cheese
**frontière** *f.* frontier; border
**fruit** *m.* fruit (6); **jus** (*m.*) **de fruit** fruit juice (7)
**fuir** (*p.p.* **fui**) *irreg.* to flee, run away; to shun
**fumée** *f.* smoke
**fumer** to smoke (8)
**fumeur/euse** *m., f.* smoker (9); **section (zone)** (*f.*) **fumeurs (non-fumeurs)** smoking (non-smoking) section (9)
**funky** *m.* funk rock (*music*)
**furieux/euse** *adj.* furious (16)
**fusil** *m.* gun; rifle
**futé** *adj.* sharp, smart, crafty
**futur** *m., Gram.* future (tense); *adj.* future
**futuriste** *adj.* futuristic

**gâcher** to spoil, bungle
**gagnant(e)** *m., f.* winner
**gagner** to win; to earn (14)
**galerie** *f.* gallery; roof rack (*car*)
**galette** *f.* pancake; tart, pie; **galette des rois** Twelfth Night cake
**gamme** *f.* range, gamut; ***haut de gamme** *adj.* high-level, top-flight
**gant** *m.* glove; **gants de ski** ski gloves (8)
**garantie** *f.* guarantee; safeguard
**garantir** to guarantee
**garçon** *m.* boy; café waiter
**garde** *f.* watch; *m., f.* guard
**garder** to keep, retain; to take care of; **garder son sang-froid** to keep one's cool
**gardien(ne)** *m., f.* caretaker; babysitter
**gare** *f.* station; train station (9); **gare de chargement** loading dock
**garer** to park
**gars** *m., fam.* guy, fellow
**gaspillage** *m.* waste (16)
**gaspiller** to waste
**gastronomique** *adj.* gastronomical
**gâteau** *m.* cake (6)
**gauche** *adj.* left; *f.* left; **à gauche** on the, to the left (11); **Rive** (*f.*) **gauche** Paris Left Bank (11); **se lever du pied gauche** to get up on the wrong side of the bed
**gaz** *m.* gas; **couper le gaz** to shut off the gas

**géant** *adj.* giant
**gendarme** *m.* gendarme (*French state police officer*)
**généalogique** *adj.* genealogical; family
**gêner** to annoy, bother
**général** *adj.* general; **en général** in general (2)
**généraliste** *m., f.* general practitioner (M.D.)
**généreux/euse** *adj.* generous
**générosité** *f.* generosity
**génial** *adj.* brilliant, inspired; *fam.* neat, delightful (5)
**génie** *m.* genius
**genou** (*pl.* **genoux**) *m.* knee (13)
**genre** *m.* gender; kind, type; **bon chic bon genre (BCBG)** "preppie"
**gens** *m. pl.* people; **jeunes gens** young men; young people
**gentil(le)** *adj.* nice, pleasant (3); kind
**gentillesse** *f.* kindness, niceness
**gentiment** *adv.* nicely, prettily
**géographie** (*fam.* **géo**) *f.* geography (2)
**géologie** *f.* geology (2)
**géométrie** *f.* geometry
**géothermie** *f.* geothermics
**gérer (je gère)** to manage, administer
**geste** *m.* gesture; movement
**gestion** *f.* management
**gigot (d'agneau)** *m.* leg of lamb
**glace** *f.* ice cream (7); ice; mirror; ***hockey** (*m.*) **sur glace** ice hockey; **patin** (*m.*) **à glace** ice-skating
**glacé** *adj.* iced; frozen; **crème** (*f.*) **glacée** ice cream; **marrons** (*m. pl.*) **glacés** candied chestnuts
**glauque** *adj.* sea-green
**glisser** to slide; to slip
**golfe** *m.* gulf
**gommier** *m.* gum tree, eucalyptus
**gorge** *f.* throat (13); gorge; **avoir mal à la gorge** to have a sore throat
**gothique** *adj.* gothic (12)
**gourde** *f.* gourd, winter squash
**gourmand(e)** *adj.* gluttonous, greedy; *m., f.* glutton, gourmand; **je suis gourmand(e)** I like to eat (6)
**gourmet** *m.* gourmet, lover of fine food
**goût** *m.* taste; **avoir le goût de** to have a taste for
**goûter** *m.* afternoon snack (6); **goûter à** to taste (7)
**goûteux/euse** *adj.* tasty, flavorful
**gouvernement** *m.* government (16)
**gouverneur** *m.* governor
**grâce** *f.* grace; pardon; **grâce à** *prep.* thanks to; **jour** (*m.*) **de l'Action de Grâce** Thanksgiving Day (*U.S., Canada*)
**grammaire** *f.* grammar
**gramme** *m.* gram
**grand** *adj.* great; large, tall; big (4); **grande surface** *f.* mall; superstore; **grand magasin** *m.* department store; **grande personne** *f.* adult, grown-up (10); **grandes écoles** *f. pl.* state-run graduate schools; **Train** (*m.*) **à Grande Vitesse (TGV)** (*French high-speed*) bullet train
**grand-chose: pas grand-chose** *pron. m.* not much
**grandiose** *adj.* grand, imposing
**grand-mère** *f.* grandmother (5)
**grand-messe** *f.* high mass
**grand-père** *m.* grandfather (5)
**grands-parents** *m. pl.* grandparents (5); **arrière-grand-parent** *m.* great-grandparent (5)
**gras(se)** *adj.* fat; oily; rich; **Mardi** (*m.*) **Gras** Mardi Gras, Shrove Tuesday (17); **pâté** (*m.*) **de foie gras** goose liver pâté
**gratte-ciel** (*pl.* **les gratte-ciel**) *m., inv.* skyscraper
**gratuit** *adj.* free (*of charge*)
**grave** *adj.* grave, serious; **accent** (*m.*) **grave** grave accent (è)
**Grèce** *f.* Greece (8)
**grève** *f.* strike, walkout; **faire (la) grève** to (go on) strike (16)
**grignotage** *m.* nibbling
**grignoter** to nibble; to snack
**grillade** *f.* grilled meat
**grille** *f.* schedule, programming
**grillé** *adj.* toasted; grilled; broiled
**gris** *adj.* gray (3)
**gros(se)** *adj.* big; fat; stout; loud; **grosses bises** *fam.* hugs and kisses (*closing of letter*)
**grossir** to gain weight
**grotte** *f.* cave, grotto
**Guadeloupe** *f.* Guadeloupe (17)
**guère** *adv.* but little; **ne... guère** scarcely, hardly
**guérir** to cure
**guerre** *f.* war (16); **Première (Deuxième) Guerre mondiale** First (Second) World War
**guichet** *m.* (ticket) window (9), counter, booth
**guichetier/ière** *m., f.* bank teller; ticket-seller
**guide** *m.* guide; guidebook; instructions
**guider** to guide
**guillemets** *m. pl.* French quotation marks (« »)
**guitare** *f.* guitar; **jouer de la guitare** to play the guitar
**guitariste** *m., f.* guitarist
**gymnase** *m.* gymnasium
**gymnastique** (*fam.* **gym**) *f.* gymnastics; exercise; **faire de la gymnastique** to do gymnastics, exercises

**s'habiller** to get dressed (13)
**habit** *m.* clothing, dress
**habitant(e)** *m., f.* inhabitant; resident
**habitation** *f.* lodging, housing; **Habitation à Loyer Modéré (H.L.M.)** French public housing
**habiter** to live (2)
**habitude** *f.* habit; **comme d'habitude** as usual; **d'habitude** *adv.* usually, habitually (10)
**habituellement** *adv.* habitually
***haché** *adj.* ground; chopped up (*meat*)
***haine** *f.* hatred
***haïr** *irreg.* to hate, detest
**Haïti** *m.* Haiti (8)
***hall** *m.* entrance hall; lounge (*hotel*)
***haricot** *m.* bean; ***haricots** (*pl.*) **mange-tout** string beans; sugar peas; ***haricots verts** green beans (6)
**harmonieux/euse** *adj.* harmonious
**harmonisation** *f.* harmonizing, bringing into line
***hasard** *m.* chance, luck; **jeux** (*m.*) **de *hasard** games of chance (15); **par *hasard** by accident, by chance
***hâte** *f.* haste; **partir à la *hâte** to leave in a hurry
***hausse** *f.* rise; **en *hausse** rising, on the rise
***haut** *adj.* high; higher; tall; upper; *m.* top; height; **de *haut** high (*in measuring*); **du *haut de** from the top of; ***haut de gamme** *adj.* high-level, top-flight; ***haute couture** *f.* high fashion
***hauteur** *f.* height
**hebdomadaire** *m., adj.* weekly
**hébergement** *m.* lodging, accommodations
***hélas!** *interj.* alas!
**hélicoptère** *m.* helicopter

**herbe** *f.* grass
**héritage** *m.* inheritance; heritage
***héros** *m.* hero
**hésiter (à)** to hesitate (to)
***heu!** *interj.* ah! hm!
**heure** *f.* hour; time (6); **à l'heure** on time (9); per hour; **à quelle heure** what time; **à tout à l'heure** see you later (4); **de bonne heure** early (6); **de l'heure** an hour, per hour; **demi-heure** *f.* half-hour; **il est une heure et demie** it's one-thirty (6); **quelle heure est-il?** what time is it? (6); **tout à l'heure** in a short while; a short while ago (5)
**heureusement** *adv.* fortunately, luckily
**heureux/euse** *adj.* happy; fortunate (10)
**hier** *adv.* yesterday (8); **avant-hier** day before yesterday; **hier matin (soir)** yesterday morning (evening)
**histoire** *f.* history (2); story
**historien(ne)** *m., f.* historian
**historique** *adj.* historical (12)
**hiver** *m.* winter (6); **en hiver** in the winter (6)
***hockey (sur glace)** *m.* ice hockey
**hommage** *m.* homage, respects; **en hommage à** in recognition of (16)
**homme** *m.* man (2); **homme d'affaires** businessman; **homme politique** politician (16); **jeune homme** young man (3)
**honnête** *adj.* honest
**honnêteté** *f.* honesty
**honneur** *m.* honor; **en l'honneur de** in honor of
***honte** *f.* shame; **avoir *honte de** to be ashamed of (4)
**hôpital** (*fam.* **hosto**) *m.* hospital (11)
**horaire** *m.* schedule (12)
**horlogerie** *f.* watchmaking
**horreur** *f.* horror; **avoir horreur de** to hate, detest (6); **quelle horreur!** how awful!
***hors de** *prep.* out of, outside of
***hors-d'œuvre** (*pl.* **les hors d'œuvre**) *m.* appetizer (7)
**hospitalier/ière** *adj.* hospitable
**hostellerie** *f.* high-quality country inn
**hosto** *m., tr. fam.* hospital
**hôtel** *m.* hotel (11); **hôtel de ville** town hall, city hall
**hôtelier/ière** *m., f.* hotel-keeper
**hôtellerie** *f.* inn; hotel trade
**hôtesse** *f.* hostess; **hôtesse de l'air** flight attendant, stewardess (9)
**huile** *f.* oil (7); **sardines** (*f. pl.*) **à l'huile** sardines; (packed) in oil (7)
***huit** *adj.* eight (1)
***huitième** *m.* one-eighth; *adj.* eighth
**huître** *f.* oyster (7)
**humain** *adj.* human; *m.* human being
**humeur** *f.* temperament, disposition; mood
**humidité** *f.* humidity, dampness
**humour** *m.* humor; **avoir le sens de l'humour** to have a sense of humor
**hypocrite** *m., f.* hypocrite; *adj.* hypocritical
**hypothèse** *f.* hypothesis

**ici** *adv.* here (1); **par ici** this way, in this direction
**idéal** *m.* ideal; *adj.* ideal
**idéaliste** *m., f.* idealist; *adj.* idealistic
**idée** *f.* idea
**identifier** to identify
**identique** *adj.* identical
**identité** *f.* identity; identification; **fiche** (*f.*) **d'identité** ID card
**il** *pron., m. s.* he; it; there; **il y a** there is/are (1); ago (8); **il y a... ?** is/are there . . . ?; **il y a... que** for (*period of time*); it's been . . . since; **il n'y a pas de quoi** you're welcome (15)
**île** *f.* island (11)
**illuminé** *adj.* lit, illuminated
**ils** *pron., m. pl.* they
**image** *f.* picture; image
**imaginaire** *adj.* imaginary
**imaginatif/ive** *adj.* imaginative
**imaginer** to imagine
**imiter** to imitate
**immédiat** *adj.* immediate
**immeuble** *m.* (apartment, office) building (4)
**immigré(e)** *m., f.* immigrant
**immigrer** to immigrate
**imparfait** *m., Gram.* imperfect (*verb tense*)
**impatient** *adj.* impatient (3)
**impératif** *m., Gram.* imperative, command
**imperméable** *m.* raincoat (3)
**impersonnel(le)** *adj.* impersonal
**implantation** *f.* establishment; site
**important** *adj.* important; large, sizeable; **il est important que** + *subj.* it's important that (16)
**importer** to import; to matter; **n'importe quel(le)** any, no matter which; **n'importe quoi** anything (at all)
**imposer** to impose
**impossible** *adj.* impossible; *m.* the impossible; **il est impossible que** + *subj.* it's impossible that (16)
**impôts** *m. pl.* (*direct*) taxes (16)
**impressionnant** *adj.* impressive
**impressionner** to impress
**improductivité** *f.* nonproductiveness
**improviser** to improvise
**impulsif/ive** *m., f.* impulsive person; *adj.* impulsive
**impulsion** *f.* impulse
**inactif/ive** *adj.* inactive; *m., f.* unemployed
**inclus** *adj.* included
**inconnu(e)** *m., f.* stranger; *adj.* unknown
**inconvénient** *m.* disadvantage
**incroyable** *adj.* unbelievable, incredible (7)
**Inde** *f.* India (8)
**indéfini** *adj.* indefinite; **article** (*m.*) **indéfini** *Gram.* indefinite article; **pronom** (*m.*) **indéfini** *Gram.* indefinite pronoun
**indépendance** *f.* independence; **fête** (*f.*) **de l'indépendance** Independence Day
**indépendant** *adj.* independent; **travailleur/euse** (*m., f.*) **indépendant(e)** self-employed worker (14)
**indicatif** *m., Gram.* indicative
**indication** *f.* instructions; information sign
**indifféremment** *adv.* indifferently; equally (well)
**indiquer** to show, point out (15)
**indispensable** *adj.* indispensable; **il est indispensable que** + *subj.* it's indispensable that (16)
**individu** *m.* individual, person
**individualiste** *adj.* individualistic, nonconformist (3)
**individuel(le)** *adj.* individual; private
**industrialisé** *adj.* industrialized
**industriel(le)** *adj.* industrial (16); **déchets** (*m. pl.*) **industriels** toxic waste
**inertie** *f.* inertia
**inexistant** *adj.* nonexistent
**inférieur** *adj.* inferior; lower
**infinitif** *m., Gram.* infinitive
**inflation** *f.* inflation (16)

**infléchi** *adj.* bent; inflected
**influençable** *adj.* susceptible (*to influence*)
**influencer (nous influençons)** to influence
**information** *f.* information, data; *pl.* news (broadcast); **flash** (*m.*) **d'informations** newsbrief
**informatique** *f., adj.* computer science (2)
**informé** *adj.* informed; **bien (mal) informé** well- (badly) informed
**informel(le)** *adj.* informal
**informer** to inform
**ingénieur** *m.* engineer (14)
**inhabituel(le)** *adj.* unusual
**initiative** *f.* initiative; **syndicat** (*m.*) **d'initiative** (local) chamber of commerce; tourist bureau
**injuste** *adj.* unjust, unfair; **il est injuste que** + *subj.* it's unfair that (16)
**innombrable** *adj.* innumerable
**inondation** *f.* flood, inundation
**inoubliable** *adj.* unforgettable
**inquiétant** *adj.* disturbing, worrisome
**inquiéter (j'inquiète)** to worry
**inquiétude** *f.* worry
**inscription** *f.* matriculation; registration; **frais** (*m. pl.*) **d'inscription** university fees, tuition
**inscrire** (*like* **écrire**) *irreg.* to register, enroll; to check in; **s'inscrire (à)** to join; to enroll; to register
**insister** to insist
**insociable** *adj.* unsociable (3)
**insolent** *adj.* extraordinary; insolent
**insolite** *adj.* unusual
**insoluble** *adj.* unsolvable
**insouciant** *adj.* carefree
**inspecteur/trice** *m., f.* inspector
**installation** *f.* moving in; installation
**installer** to install; to set up; **s'installer (dans)** to settle down, settle in (12)
**instances** *f. pl.* authorities
**institut** *m.* institute; trade school
**instituteur/trice** *m., f.* elementary, primary school teacher (14)
**instruit** *adj.* learned, instructed
**instrument** *m.* instrument; **jouer d'un instrument** to play a musical instrument
**s'intégrer (je m'intègre) (à)** to integrate oneself, get assimilated (into)
**intellectuel(le)** *adj.* intellectual (3); *m., f.* intellectual (*person*)
**intelligemment** *adv.* intelligently
**intensif/ive** *adj.* intensive
**intention** *f.* intention; meaning; **avoir l'intention de** to intend to
**interdiction** *f.* prohibition
**interdire** (*like* **dire, vous interdisez**) **(de)** *irreg.* to forbid (to)
**intéressant** *adj.* interesting (3)
**intéresser** to interest (14); **s'intéresser à** to be interested in
**intérêt** *m.* interest, concern
**intérieur** *m.* interior; *adj.* interior; **à l'intérieur** inside
**intermède** *m.* interlude
**interprète** *m., f.* interpreter; actor; player
**interpréter (j'interprète)** to interpret
**interrogatif/ive** *adj., Gram.* interrogative
**interrogatoire** *m.* interrogation, examination
**interroger (nous interrogeons)** to question
**intervenir** (*like* **venir**) *irreg.* to intervene
**intervention** *f.* intervention; speech; operation
**interviewé(e)** *m., f.* interviewee
**interviewer** to interview
**intime** *adj.* intimate; private
**intrigue** *f.* plot; intrigue
**introduire** (*like* **conduire**) *irreg.* to introduce
**intrus(e)** *m., f.* intruder
**inutile** *adj.* useless (16)
**inventer** to invent
**inverser** to reverse; to invert
**invité(e)** *m., f.* guest; *adj.* invited
**inviter** to invite
**invraisemblable** *adj.* unlikely, improbable
**irréconciliable** *adj.* irreconcilable
**irresponsable** *adj.* irresponsible
**isolé** *adj.* isolated; detached
**isolement** *m.* isolation, loneliness
**Italie** *f.* Italy (8)
**italien(ne)** *adj.* Italian; *m.* Italian (*language*); **Italien(ne)** *m., f.* Italian (*person*) (2)
**italique** *m.* italic; **en italique** in italics
**itinéraire** *m.* itinerary
**ivoire** *m.* ivory; **Côte-d'Ivoire** *f.* Ivory Coast (8)

**jamais (ne... jamais)** *adv.* never, ever (9)
**jambe** *f.* leg (13)
**jambon** *m.* ham (6)
**janvier** January (4)
**Japon** *m.* Japan (8)
**japonais** *adj.* Japanese; *m.* Japanese (*language*); **Japonais(e)** *m., f.* Japanese (*person*) (2)
**jardin** *m.* garden (5)
**jardinage** *m.* gardening; **faire du jardinage** to garden (15)
**jardiner** to garden
**jardinier/ière** *m., f.* gardener; **assiette** (*f.*) **du jardinier** vegetable plate
**jaune** *adj.* yellow (3)
**je** *pron., s.* I
**jean(s)** *m.* (*blue*) jeans (3)
**jeter (je jette)** to throw; to throw away; **ne jetez plus** don't throw away any more (16)
**jeu** (*pl.* **jeux**) *m.* game; game show; **jeu de mots** play on words; **jeu de rôles** role-playing game; **jeux de *hasard** games of chance (15); **jeux de société** social games; group games (15)
**jeudi** *m.* Thursday (1)
**jeune** *adj.* young (7); *m. pl.* young people, youth; **jeune fille** *f.* girl, young woman (3); **jeune homme** *m.* young man (3); **jeunes gens** *m. pl.* young men; young people; **jeunes mariés** *m. pl.* newlyweds
**jeunesse** *f.* youth; **auberge** (*f.*) **de jeunesse** youth hostel
**jogging** *m.* jogging; **faire du jogging** to go jogging (5)
**joie** *f.* joy
**joli** *adj.* pretty (7)
**jouer** to play; **jouer à** to play (*a sport or game*) (3); to play at (*being*); **jouer au tennis** to play tennis; **jouer aux cartes** to play cards; **jouer de** to play (*a musical instrument*) (3); **jouer du piano** to play the piano
**jouet** *m.* toy
**joueur/euse** *m., f.* player
**jour** *m.* day; **dans quatre jours** in four days (5); **de nos jours** these days, currently; **du jour** today's (*menu, exchange rate*); **par jour** per day, each day; **plat** (*m.*) **du jour** today's special (*restaurant*); **quel jour sommes-nous?** what day is it? (1); **quinze jours** two weeks (8); **tous les jours** every day (5); **un jour** someday (14)
**journal** (*pl.* **journaux**) *m.* newspaper, news (10); journal, diary
**journaliste** *m., f.* reporter (14)

**journée** *f.* (*whole*) day (6); **pendant la journée** during the day; **toute la journée** all day long
**joyeux/euse** *adj.* joyous; happy, joyful
**juger (nous jugeons)** to judge
**juillet** July (4)
**juin** June (4)
**jupe** *f.* skirt (3); **mini-jupe** *f.* miniskirt
**jurer** to swear
**jus** *m.* juice; **jus de fruit** fruit juice (7); **jus d'orange** orange juice
**jusqu'à (jusqu'en)** *prep.* until, up to (11); **jusque-là** until then
**juste** *adj.* just; right, exact; *adv.* just, precisely; accurately; **il est juste que** + *subj.* it's fair, equitable that (16); **mot** (*m.*) **juste** the right word
**justifier** to justify

**kilo(gramme) (kg.)** *m.* kilogram (7)
**kilomètre (km.)** *m.* kilometer
**kiosque** *m.* kiosk; newsstand (10)

**la** *art., f. s.* the; *pron., f. s.* it, her
**là** *adv.* there (11); **là-bas** *adv.* over there; **oh, là, là!** *interj.* good heavens! my goodness!
**laboratoire** (*fam.* **labo**) *m.* laboratory
**lac** *m.* lake (8); **au bord du lac** on the lake shore
**lagune** *f.* laguna
**laid** *adj.* ugly (4)
**laideur** *f.* ugliness
**laine** *f.* wool
**laisser** to let, allow; to leave (*behind*) (7)
**lait** *m.* milk (6); **café** (*m.*) **au lait** coffee with hot milk
**laitier/ière** *adj.* dairy, milk; **produits** (*m. pl.*) **laitiers** dairy products
**lampe** *f.* lamp; light fixture (4); **lampe de poche** flashlight
**lancer (nous lançons)** to launch; to throw (at); to drop
**langage** *m.* language; jargon
**langouste** *f.* lobster
**langue** *f.* language; tongue; **langue étrangère** foreign language (2); **langue maternelle** native language
**lapin** *m.* rabbit
**laqué** *adj.* lacquered, glazed; **canard** (*m.*) **laqué** Peking duck
**lard** *m.* bacon
**large** *adj.* wide
**laser** *m.* laser; **lecteur** (*m.*) **laser** CD player; **platine** (*f.*) **laser** laser-disk player
**lavabo** *m.* bathroom sink (4)
**lavande** *m.* lavender (*color*); *f.* lavender (*plant*)
**lave-vaisselle** *m.* (*automatic*) dishwasher
**laver** to wash; **se laver** to wash (*oneself*) (13); **se laver les mains** to wash one's hands
**laveuse** *f.* washing machine
**le** *art., m. s.* the; *pron., m. s.* it, him
**leçon** *f.* lesson
**lecteur/trice** *m., f.* reader; *m.* disk drive; **lecteur** (*m.*) **de cassettes (de CD)** cassette (CD) player (4)
**lecture** *f.* reading (15)
**légalisation** *f.* legalization (16)
**légende** *f.* legend; caption
**léger (légère)** *adj.* light; lightweight; slight; mild
**législatif/ive** *adj.* legislative
**légume** *m.* vegetable (6)
**lendemain (le)** *m.* the next day, following day
**lent** *adj.* slow
**lequel (laquelle, lesquels, lesquelles)** *pron.* which one, who, whom, which (15)
**les** *art., pl., m., f.* the; *pron., pl., m., f.* them
**lessive** *f.* laundry; **faire la lessive** to do the laundry (5)
**lettre** *f.* letter (10); *pl.* literature; humanities; **boîte** (*f.*) **aux lettres** mailbox (10); **faculté** (*f.*) **des lettres** School of Arts and Letters; **homme** (*m.*) (**femme** [*f.*]) **de lettres** writer, literary figure; **poster une lettre** to mail a letter
**leur** *adj., m., f.* their; *pron., m., f.* to them; **le/la/les leur(s)** *pron.* theirs
**lever (je lève)** to raise, lift; **se lever** to get up; to get out of bed (13)
**lèvres** *f. pl.* lips; **rouge** (*m.*) **à lèvres** lipstick
**lexique** *m.* lexicon, glossary
**liaison** *f.* liaison; love affair
**libérer (je libère)** to free
**liberté** *f.* freedom; **liberté d'expression** freedom of expression (16)
**librairie** *f.* bookstore (2)
**libre** *adj.* free; available; vacant; **être libre de** to be free to; **plongée** (*f.*) **libre** free fall, diving; **temps** (*m.*) **libre** leisure time
**licence** *f.* French university degree (= *U.S. bachelor's degree*)
**lié** *adj.* linked, tied
**lien** *m.* tie, bond
**lieu** *m.* place (2); **au lieu de** *prep.* instead of, in the place of; **avoir lieu** to take place
**lieue** *f., A.* league (*approx. 2.5 miles*)
**lièvre** *m.* hare
**ligne** *f.* line; bus line; figure; **couper la ligne** to cut off (*phone call*)
**limite** *f.* limit; boundary
**limiter** to limit
**limonade** *f.* lemonade; soft drink
**linge** *m.* (*household*) linen; cloth
**linguiste** *m., f.* linguist
**linguistique** *f.* linguistics (2); *adj.* language; linguistic
**liqueur** *f.* liquor
**liquide** *m., adj.* liquid; **argent** (*m.*) **liquide** cash (14)
**lire** (*p.p.* **lu**) *irreg.* to read (10)
**lisible** *adj.* legible
**liste** *f.* list
**lit** *m.* bed (4); **wagon-lit** *m.* sleeping car
**litre** *m.* liter
**littéraire** *adj.* literary
**littérature** *f.* literature (2)
**livre** *m.* book (1)
**livret** *m.* booklet; libretto, book (*opera*)
**livreur/euse** *m., f.* delivery person
**locataire** *m., f.* renter, tenant
**location** *f.* rental
**loge** *f.* concierge's apartment; box (*theater*)
**logement** *m.* lodging(s), place of residence (4)
**loger (nous logeons)** to house; to dwell, live
**logique** *adj.* logical
**loi** *f.* law
**loin (de)** *adv., prep.* far from (5)
**lointain** *adj.* distant
**loisirs** *m. pl.* leisure activities (15)
**long(ue)** *adj.* long (4); slow; **à long terme** long term; **le long de** *prep.* along, alongside
**longer (nous longeons)** to run along, go along
**longévité** *f.* longevity
**longtemps** *adv.* long; (for) a long time; **il y a longtemps** a long time ago
**lors de** *prep.* at the time of

**lorsque** *conj.* when (14)
**loto** *m.* lottery
**louer** to rent (4); to reserve
**lourd** *adj.* heavy (13)
**loyer** *m.* rent (*payment*); **Habitation** (*f.*) **à Loyer Modéré (H.L.M.)** French public housing
**lui** *pron., m., f.* he; it; to him; to her; to it; **lui-même** *pron., m. s.* himself
**lumière** *f.* light
**lundi** *m.* Monday (1)
**lune** *f.* moon
**lunettes** *f. pl.* (eye)glasses (8); **lunettes de ski** ski goggles (8); **lunettes de soleil** sunglasses (8); **lunettes noires** dark glasses
**lutte** *f.* struggle, battle; wrestling
**lutter** to fight; to struggle
**luxe** *m.* luxury; **de luxe** luxury; first-class
**luxueux/euse** *adj.* luxurious
**lycée** *m.* French secondary school

**ma** *adj., f. s.* my
**machine** *f.* machine; **machine à calculer** calculator
**Madame (Mme)** (*pl.* **Mesdames**) *f.* Madam, Mrs. (1)
**Mademoiselle (Mlle)** (*pl.* **Mesdemoiselles**) *f.* Miss (1)
**magasin** *m.* store, shop (7); **grand magasin** department store; **magasin d'alimentation** food store
**magazine** *m.* (*illustrated*) magazine (10)
**magicien(ne)** *m., f.* magician
**magistrat** *m.* judge, magistrate
**magnat** *m.* magnate, tycoon
**magnétophone** *m.* tape recorder
**magnétoscope** *m.* videocassette recorder (VCR) (10)
**magnifique** *adj.* magnificent (12)
**mai** May (4)
**maigre** *adj.* thin
**maillot** *m.* jersey, T-shirt; **maillot de bain** swimsuit (3)
**main** *f.* hand (13); **sac** (*m.*) **à main** handbag, purse (2); **se laver les mains** to wash one's hands
**main-d'œuvre** *f.* labor, manpower
**maintenant** *adv.* now (2)
**maintenir** (*like* **tenir**) *irreg.* to maintain; to keep up
**maintien** *m.* keeping, upholding
**maire** *m.* mayor
**mairie** *f.* town (city) hall (11)
**mais** *conj.* but (2); *interj.* why
**maison** *f.* house, home (4); company, firm; **à la maison** at home
**maître (maîtresse)** *m., f.* master (mistress); **maître d'hôtel** maître d'; head waiter
**maîtrise** *f.* master's degree; mastery; control
**mal** *adv.* badly (5); *m.* evil; pain (*pl.* **maux**); **aller mal** to feel bad, ill (5); **avoir du mal à** to have trouble, difficulty (17); **avoir mal (à)** to hurt, have a pain (13); **avoir mal à la tête (aux oreilles)** to have a headache (earache); **ça va mal** bad(ly) (things are going badly) (1); **pas mal** not bad (1)
**malade** *m., f.* sick person; *adj.* sick **tomber malade** to get sick
**maladie** *f.* illness, disease
**malgré** *prep.* in spite of
**malheur** *m.* misfortune, calamity
**malheureusement** *adv.* unfortunately; sadly
**malheureux/euse** *adj.* unhappy; miserable
**maman** *f., fam.* mom, mommy
**mamie** *f., fam.* grandma
**mange-tout: *haricots** (*m. pl.*) **mange-tout** string beans; sugar peas
**manger (nous mangeons)** to eat (2)
**manière** *f.* manner, way; **bonnes manières** *f. pl.* good manners
**manifestation** *f.* (*political*) demonstration; **manifestation sportive** sports event (15)
**manifesté** *adj.* shown, demonstrated
**manifester (pour, contre)** to demonstrate (for, against) (16)
**mannequin** *m.* model (*fashion*); mannequin
**manque** *m.* lack, shortage
**manteau** *m.* coat, overcoat (3)
**manuel(le)** *adj.* manual
**manufacture** *f.* making, fabrication
**manuscrit** *adj.* handwritten
**se maquiller** to put on makeup (13)
**marchand(e)** *m., f.* merchant, shopkeeper; **marchand(e) de vin** wine merchant (14)
**marche** *f.* walking (15); step (*stair*)
**marché** *m.* market (5); **bon marché** *adj. inv.* cheap, inexpensive; **faire le marché** to do the shopping, go to the market (5); **le Marché commun** the Common Market
**marcher** to walk; to work, go (*device*) (9)
**mardi** *m.* Tuesday (1); **Mardi Gras** Mardi Gras, Shrove Tuesday (17)
**mari** *m.* husband (5)
**mariage** *m.* marriage; wedding (13)
**marié(e)** *m., f.* groom (bride); *adj.* married (5); **jeunes (nouveaux) mariés** *m. pl.* newlyweds, newly married couple; **robe** (*f.*) **de mariée** wedding gown
**marier** to link, join; **se marier (avec)** to get married; to marry s.o. (13)
**marin** *adj.* maritime, of the sea; **plongée** (*f.*) **sous-marine** skin diving (8)
**Maroc** *m.* Morocco (8)
**marque** *f.* mark; trade name, brand
**marquer** to mark; to indicate
**marrant** *adj., fam.* funny, hilarious (17)
**marre: en avoir marre (de)** *fam.* to be fed up with
**se marrer** *fam.* to have a good time
**marron** *adj. inv.* brown (3); maroon; *m.* chestnut; **crème** (*f.*) **de marrons** chestnut purée; **marrons glacés** candied chestnuts
**mars** March (4)
**martial** *adj.* martial; warlike; **arts** (*m.*) **martiaux** martial arts
**Martinique** *f.* Martinique (17)
**masculin** *adj.* masculine
**masque** *m.* mask
**masqué** *adj.* masked; **bal** (*m.*) **masqué** masked ball, costume party (17)
**massacré(e)** *m., f.* massacred (*person*)
**masse** *f.* mass, quantity
**match** *m.* game; **match de foot (de boxe)** soccer game (boxing match)
**matérialiste** *adj.* materialistic
**matériau** (*pl.* **matériaux**) *m.* material; building material
**matériel(le)** *adj.* material
**maternel(le)** *adj.* maternal; **école** (*f.*) **maternelle** nursery school, preschool; **langue** (*f.*) **maternelle** native language
**maternité** *f.* maternity, child-bearing
**mathématicien(ne)** *m., f.* mathematician
**mathématiques** (*fam.* **maths**) *f. pl.* mathematics (2)
**matière** *f.* academic subject; matter; material
**matin** *m.* morning (5); **dix heures du matin** ten A.M. (6); **tous les matins** every morning (10)
**matinal** *adj.* morning
**matinée** *f.* morning (*duration*) (8)

**mauvais** *adj.* bad (7); wrong; **en mauvais état** in bad condition; **être de mauvaise humeur** to be in a bad mood; **il fait mauvais** it's bad (weather) out (6); **le/la plus mauvais(e)** the worst; **plus mauvais** worse
**mécanicien(ne)** *m., f.* mechanic (9); technician
**méchanceté** *f.* spitefulness
**méchant** *adj.* naughty, bad; wicked
**médecin (femme médecin)** *m., f.* doctor, physician (14)
**médecine** *f.* medicine (*study, profession*)
**médias** *m. pl.* media (16)
**médicament** *m.* medication; drug
**médiéval** *adj.* medieval (12)
**médiocre** *m., f.* mediocre person; *adj.* mediocre
**meilleur** *adj.* better (13); **le/la meilleur(e)** the best; **meilleurs vœux** best wishes
**mélange** *m.* mixture, blend (17)
**mélangé** *adj.* mixed
**mêlée** *f.* scrum (*rugby*)
**melon** *m.* melon; **melon d'eau** watermelon
**membre** *m.* member
**même** *adj.* same; itself; very same; *adv.* even (7); **le/la/les même(s)** the same one(s) (17); **quand même** anyway; even though; **tout de même** all the same, for all that
**menacer (nous menaçons) (de)** to threaten (to)
**ménage** *m.* housekeeping; household; **faire le ménage** to clean house (5); **femme** (*f.*) **de ménage** cleaning woman, housekeeper
**ménager/ère** *m., f.* homemaker; *adj.* household
**mendier** to beg
**mener (je mène)** to take; to lead
**mensonge** *m.* lie
**menthe** *f.* mint; **thé** (*m.*) **à la menthe** mint tea (9)
**mention** *f.* announcement; **faire mention de** to mention
**mentionner** to mention
**menu** *m.* menu; fixed-price menu (7)
**mépris** *m.* scorn
**mer** *f.* sea, ocean (8); **au bord de la mer** at the seashore; **fruits** (*m. pl.*) **de mer** seafood; **mer des Caraïbes (des Antilles)** Carribean (*sea*) (17)
**merci** *interj.* thank you (1); **merci bien** thanks a lot
**mercredi** *m.* Wednesday (1)
**mère** *f.* mother (5); **belle-mère** mother-in-law; stepmother (5); **grand-mère** grandmother (5)
**mériter** to deserve
**merveille** *f.* marvel; **à merveille** *adv.* marvelously
**merveilleux/euse** *adj.* marvelous
**mes** *adj., m., f., pl.* my
**messe** *f.* (*Catholic*) Mass; **grand-messe** *f.* high mass
**messieurs-dames** ladies and gentlemen
**mesure** *f.* measure; extent; **prendre des mesures** to take measures
**mesurer** to measure
**métallurgie** *f.* metallurgy
**météo** *f., fam.* weather forecast
**méthode** *f.* method
**métier** *m.* trade, profession; **armée** (*f.*) **de métier** professional army
**métrage** *m.* footage, length; **court-métrage** *m.* short subject (*film*)
**mètre** *m.* meter
**métro** *m.* subway (*train, system*) (9); **station** (*f.*) **de métro** metro station (11)
**métropolitain** *adj.* metropolitan; from, of mainland France
**mets** *m. s.* food, dish
**metteur/euse en scène** *m., f.* producer; film director
**mettre** (*p.p.* **mis**) *irreg.* to place; to put on (8); to turn on; to take (*time*); to admit, grant; **mettre à l'épreuve** to test, put to the test; **mettre de l'argent de côté** to put (some) money aside; **mettre des vêtements** to put on clothes; **mettre en œuvre** to put into practice; **mettre en place** to install, put in place; **mettre la table (le couvert)** to set the table; **se mettre à** to begin to (13); **se mettre d'accord** to reach an agreement
**meuble** *m.* piece of furniture (5); **meubles d'époque** antique furniture
**meublé** *adj.* furnished (4)
**meurtre** *m.* murder
**Mexique** *m.* Mexico (8)
**mi: à mi-temps** half-time, part-time (*work*)
**micro-ordinateur** (*fam.* **micro**) *m.* personal computer
**midi** noon (6); *m.* south-central region of France; **après-midi** *m.* afternoon (4); **de l'après-midi** in the afternoon (6); **il est midi** it's noon (6)
**miel** *m.* honey
**mien(ne)(s) (le/la/les)** *pron., m., f.,* mine
**mieux** *adv.* better; **aimer mieux** to prefer (2); **aller mieux** to be better, go better; **bien, mieux, le mieux** good, better, the best (15); **il vaut mieux que** + *subj.* it's better that (16); **tant mieux** so much the better
**mignon(ne)** *adj., fam.* cute
**mijoter** to simmer; *fam.* to cook
**mil** *m.* thousand (*for years*)
**milieu** *m.* environment; milieu; middle; **au milieu de** in the middle of
**militaire** *m.* soldier; *adj.* military; **budget militaire** military budget (16)
**mille** *adj.* thousand
**millénaire** *m.* one thousand; *adj.* millennial
**milliardaire** *m., f.* billionnaire
**millier** *m.* (around) a thousand
**minable** *adj., fam.* sorry, shabby; disappointing
**mince** *adj.* thin; slender
**mincir** to grow thin
**minéral** *adj.* mineral; **eau** (*f.*) **minérale** mineral water (6)
**minet(te)** *m., f.* trendy young man (woman)
**mini-jupe** *f.* miniskirt
**ministère** *m.* ministry
**ministre** *m.* minister; **premier ministre** prime minister
**minitel** *m.* French personal communications terminal (10)
**minuit** midnight (6); **il est minuit** it's midnight (6)
**minute** *f.* minute; **en dix minutes** within, in ten minutes
**mirabelle** *f.* mirabelle plum
**miraculeux/euse** *adj.* miraculous
**miroir** *m.* mirror (4)
**mise** *f.* putting; **mise au point** restatement; **mise en forme** fitness training; **mise en scène** production, staging, setting; direction
**misérable** *adj.* poor, wretched
**misère** *f.* misery, poverty
**mobylette** (*fam.* **mob**) *f.* moped, scooter
**mocassins** *m. pl.* loafers
**moche** *adj., fam.* ugly; rotten
**mode** *f.* fashion, style; **à la mode** in style
**modèle** *m.* model; pattern
**modéré** *adj.* moderate

**moderniser** to modernize
**moderniste** *adj.* modernistic
**modeste** *adj.* modest, humble
**modifier** to modify, transform
**moi** *pron. s.* I, me; **à moi** mine; **chez moi** at my place; **excusez-moi** excuse me (1); **moi aussi (moi non plus)** me too (me neither)
**moins** *adv.* less; minus; **au moins** at least; **le moins** the least; **moins le quart** quarter to (*the hour*) (6); **moins (de)... que** less . . . than (13); **plus ou moins** more or less
**mois** *m.* month (8); **par mois** per month
**moitié** *f.* half
**moment** *m.* moment; **à ce moment-là** then, at that moment; **en ce moment** now, currently
**mon** *adj., m. s.* my
**monde** *m.* world (8); people; society; **tiers monde** Third World, developing nations; **tour** (*m.*) **du monde** trip around the world; **tout le monde** everybody, everyone (9)
**mondial** *adj.* world; worldwide; **Première (Deuxieme) Guerre** (*f.*) **mondiale** First (Second) World War
**monétaire** *adj.* monetary
**monnaie** *f.* coins; change (10); currency (*units*)
**monotone** *adj.* monotonous
**Monsieur (M.)** (*pl.* **Messieurs**) *m.* Mister; gentleman; Sir (1); **croque-monsieur** *m.* grilled cheese and ham sandwich
**monstre** *m.* monster
**mont** *m.* hill; mountain
**montagne** *f.* mountain (8); **à la montagne** in the mountains
**montagneux/euse** *adj.* mountainous
**montant** *m.* sum, amount (14); total
**montée** *f.* rise (16), ascent; going up
**monter (dans)** to set up, organize; to put on; to carry up; to go up; to climb (into) (9)
**montre** *f.* watch; wristwatch
**Montréal** Montreal (17)
**montrer** to show (10)
**monument** *m.* (*historical*) monument (11)
**se moquer de** to make fun of; to mock
**moquette** *f.* wall-to-wall carpeting
**moral** *m.* state of mind, spirits; *adj.* moral; psychological
**morceau** *m.* piece (7); **morceau de gâteau** piece of cake
**mort(e)** *m., f.* dead person; *adj.* dead; **mort de fatigue** dead-tired
**mortel(le)** *adj.* mortal; fatal; *fam.* deadly dull
**mosquée** *f.* mosque
**mot** *m.* word (4); note; **faire des mots croisés** to do crossword puzzles; **le mot juste** the right, exact word; **mot apparenté** related word, cognate; **mot-clé** *m.* key word
**moteur** *m.* motor; engine
**motion** *f.* motion; proposal
**motivé** *adj.* motivated
**motocyclette** (*fam.* **moto**) *f.* motorcycle, motorbike (9)
**mouche** *f.* fly; housefly; **bateau-mouche** (*pl.* **bateaux-mouches**) *m.* tourist boat on the Seine
**mouchoir** *m.* handkerchief; kleenex
**mouillé** *adj.* wet, damp
**mourir** (*p.p.* **mort**) *irreg.* to die (9)
**mousquetaire** *m.* musketeer
**mousse** *f.* moss; foam; **mousse au chocolat** chocolate mousse
**moustique** *m.* mosquito
**moutarde** *f.* mustard
**mouton** *m.* mutton; sheep
**mouvement** *m.* movement
**mouvementé** *adj.* animated, eventful
**moyen(ne)** *adj.* average; *m.* mean(s); way; *f.* average; **de taille moyenne** of medium height (4); **en moyenne** on average; **moyen âge** *m. s.* Middle Ages (12)
**multipartisme** *m.* multi-party system
**municipal** *adj.* municipal (11)
**mur** *m.* wall (4); **tapis** (*m.*) **mur à mur** *Q.* wall-to-wall carpet
**muraille** *f.* wall, fence
**musculation** *f.* muscle development
**musée** *m.* museum (11)
**musicien(ne)** *m., f.* musician (12)
**musique** *f.* music (2); **musique classique** classical music
**mutation** *f.* change, alteration
**mutuellement** *adv.* mutually
**myrtille** *f.* huckleberry; blueberry
**mystère** *m.* mystery
**mystérieux/euse** *adj.* mysterious
**mythologique** *adj.* mythological

**nager (nous nageons)** to swim (8)
**nageur/euse** *m., f.* swimmer
**naïf (naïve)** *adj.* naïve; simple (3)
**naissance** *f.* birth; **date** (*f.*) **de naissance** date of birth
**naître** (*p.p.* **né**) *irreg.* to be born (9)
**natal** *adj.* native
**natation** *f.* swimming
**national** *adj.* national; **fête** (*f.*) **nationale** French national holiday, Bastille Day (*July 14*)
**nationaliste** *m., f., adj.* nationalist; nationalistic
**nature** *f.* nature (16); *adj.* plain (*food*)
**naturel(le)** *adj.* natural; **ressources** (*f. pl.*) **naturelles** natural resources (16); **sciences** (*f. pl.*) **naturelles** natural sciences
**nautique** *adj.* nautical; **faire du ski nautique** to go waterskiing (8)
**navarin** *m.* stew; lamb stew
**navet** *m.* turnip; *fam.* dud, flop (*show*)
**navette** *f.* shuttle bus
**ne** *adv.* no; not; **ne... aucun(e)** none, not one; **ne... jamais** never, not ever (9); **ne... ni... ni** neither . . . nor; **ne... pas** no; not; **ne... pas du tout** not at all (9); **ne... pas encore** not yet (9); **ne... personne** no one (9); **ne... plus** no more (6), no longer (9); **ne... que** only (9); **ne... rien** nothing (9); **n'est-ce pas?** isn't it (so)? isn't that right?
**né** *adj.* born
**néanmoins** *adv.* nevertheless
**nécessaire** *m.* necessaries, the indispensable; *adj.* necessary; **il est nécessaire que** + *subj.* it's necessary that (16)
**nécessité** *f.* need
**négatif/ive** *adj.* negative
**nègre (négresse)** *m., f.* Negro (Negress)
**négritude** *f.* Negritude, Negro condition
**neige** *f.* snow (6); **bonhomme** (*m.*) **de neige** snowman (17)
**neiger (il neigeait)** to snow (6); **il neige** it's snowing (6)
**nénuphar** *m.* water lily
**nerveux/euse** *adj.* nervous (3)
**net(te)** *adj.* neat, clear; net (*weight*)
**neuf** *adj.* nine (1)
**neuf (neuve)** *adj.* new, brand-new; **quoi de neuf?** what's new?
**neuvième** *adj.* ninth
**neveu** *m.* nephew (5)
**nez** *m.* nose (13)
**ni** neither; nor; **ne... ni... ni** neither . . . nor
**nicher** *fam.* to live; to build a nest

**nièce** *f.* niece (5)
**nihiliste** *adj.* nihilistic
**niveau** *m.* level; **niveau de vie** standard of living
**noces** *f. pl.* wedding; **voyage** (*m.*) **de noces** honeymoon trip
**Noël** *m.* Christmas; **bûche** (*f.*) **de Noël** yule-log (*pastry*); **père** (*m.*) **Noël** Santa Claus; **réveillon** (*m.*) **de Noël** midnight Christmas dinner
**noir** *adj.* black (3); **lunettes** (*f. pl.*) **noires** dark glasses
**noisette** *f.* hazelnut
**noix** *f.* nut; **noix de coco** coconut
**nom** *m.* noun; name
**nombre** *m.* number; quantity; **nombres** (*pl.*) **ordinaux** ordinal numbers (11)
**nombreux/euse** *adj.* numerous
**nommer** to name; to appoint
**non** *interj.* no; not (1); **moi non plus** me neither; **non plus** neither, not . . . either
**nord** *m.* north (9); **au nord** to the north (9); **nord-est** *m.* northeast; **nord-ouest** *m.* northwest
**normal** *adj.* normal; **il est normal que** + *subj.* it's normal that (16)
**Norvège** *f.* Norway (8)
**nos** *adj., m., f., pl.* our; **de nos jours** these days, currently
**nostalgie** *f.* nostalgia
**notamment** *adv.* notably; especially
**notation** *f.* grading; notation
**note** *f.* note; grade (*in school*); bill; **prendre des notes** to take notes
**noter** to notice
**notion** *f.* notion, idea, knowledge
**notre** *adj., m., f., s.* our
**nôtre(s)** **(le/la/les)** *pron., m., f.* ours; our own (*people*)
**nourrice** *f.* nurse; nanny
**nourrissant** *adj.* nourishing
**nourriture** *f.* food
**nous** *pron., pl.* we; us; **nous sommes lundi (mardi...** ) it's Monday (Tuesday . . . ) (1)
**nouveau (nouvel, nouvelle [nouveaux, nouvelles])** *adj.* new (7); **à nouveau** once more; **de nouveau** again (11); **nouveaux-mariés** *m. pl.* newlyweds
**nouvelle** *f.* piece of news; short story; *pl.* news, current events (13); **bonne (mauvaise) nouvelle** good (bad) news
**Nouvelle-Écosse** *f.* Nova Scotia (17)
**Nouvelle-Orléans (La)** *f.* New Orleans (17)
**novembre** November (4)
**noyé** *adj.* drowned
**nuage** *m.* cloud
**nuageux/euse** *adj.* cloudy
**nucléaire** *adj.* nuclear; **centrale** (*f.*) **nucléaire** nuclear power plant; **déchets** (*m. pl.*) **nucléaires** nuclear waste; **énergie** (*f.*) **nucléaire** nuclear power (16)
**nuit** *f.* night (8); **boîte** (*f.*) **de nuit** nightclub; **de nuit** at night
**nul(le)** *adj., pron.* no, not any; null; **ne... nulle part** *adv.* nowhere
**nullement** *adv.* not at all, by no means
**numéro** *m.* number; **composer le numéro** to dial (*phone number*) (10); **numéro de téléphone** telephone number (10)
**numéroter** to number
**nutritif/ive** *adj.* nutritive, nourishing

**obéir (à)** to obey
**objectif** *m.* goal, objective
**objet** *m.* objective; object; **bureau** (*m.*) **des objets perdus** lost and found office; **pronom** (*m.*) **complément d'objet direct (indirect)** *Gram.* direct (indirect) object pronoun
**obligatoire** *adj.* obligatory; mandatory; **service** (*m.*) **obligatoire** mandatory military service
**obligé** *adj.* obliged, required; **être obligé de** to be obliged to
**obsédé** *adj.* obsessed
**observateur/trice** *m., f.* observer
**observer** to observe
**obtenir** (*like* **tenir**) *irreg.* to obtain, get (8)
**occasion** *f.* opportunity; occasion; bargain; **avoir l'occasion de** to have the chance to
**occident** *m.* the west
**occidental** *adj.* western, occidental
**occupé** *adj.* occupied; held; busy
**occuper** to occupy; **s'occuper de** to look after, be interested in
**octobre** October (4)
**odeur** *f.* odor, smell
**œil** (*pl.* **yeux**) *m.* eye; look (13); **mon œil!** *interj.* my eye!
**œuf** *m.* egg (6)
**œuvre** *f.* work; artistic work (12); **chef-d'œuvre** (*pl.* **chefs-d'œuvre**) *m.* masterpiece (12); ***hors-d'œuvre** (*pl.* **les *hors-d'œuvre**) *m.* hors-d'œuvre, appetizer (7); **main** (*f.*) **d'œuvre** manpower; **œuvre d'art** work of art (12)
**œuvrer** to work (*towards*)
**offert** *adj.* offered
**office** *m.* bureau; **office du tourisme** tourist bureau
**officiel(le)** *adj.* official
**offre** *f.* offer; **offre d'emploi** job offer
**offrir** (*like* **ouvrir**) *irreg.* to offer (14)
**oie** *f.* goose
**oignon** *m.* onion
**ombre** *f.* shadow
**omelette** *f.* omelet
**oncle** *m.* uncle (5)
**ondulé** *adj.* wavy, undulating
**onze** *adj.* eleven (1)
**onzième** *adj.* eleventh
**opinion** *f.* opinion; **exprimer une opinion** to express an opinion (16); **opinion publique** public opinion
**opposé** *m.* the opposite; *adj.* opposing, opposite
**opposer** to oppose
**optimiste** *m., f.* optimist (3); *adj.* optimistic
**option** *f.* choice, option; **en option** possibility of
**optométrie** *f.* optometry
**or** *m.* gold; *conj.* now; well
**orage** *m.* storm
**orageux/euse** *adj.* stormy
**orange** *adj. inv.* orange; *m.* orange (*color*) (3); *f.* orange (*fruit*); **jus** (*m.*) **d'orange** orange juice
**orchestre** *m.* orchestra
**ordinaire** *adj.* ordinary, regular
**ordinal** *adj.* ordinal; **nombres** (*m. pl.*) **ordinaux** ordinal numbers (11)
**ordinateur** *m.* computer (4); **micro-ordinateur** *m.* personal computer
**ordonnance** *f.* prescription
**ordonné** *adj.* orderly, tidy
**ordre** *m.* order; command; **en ordre** orderly, neat (4)
**oreille** *f.* ear (13)
**organiser** to organize
**orientation** *f.* orientation; **conseiller/ère** (*m., f.*) **d'orientation** guidance counselor
**original** *adj.* eccentric; original
**origine** *f.* origin; **d'origine française** of French extraction
**orphelin(e)** *m., f.* orphan

**orthographe** *f.* spelling
**os** *m.* bone
**otage** *m.* hostage
**ou** *conj.* or; either (2); **ou bien** or else
**où** *adv.* where (3); *pron.* where, in which, when (14); **où est... ?** where is . . . ?
**ouais** *interj., fam.* yes (**oui**)
**oublier (de)** to forget (to) (8)
**ouest** *m.* west (9); **à l'ouest** to the west (9); **nord-ouest** *m.* northwest; **sud-ouest** *m.* southwest
**oui** *interj.* yes (1)
**outre** *prep.* beyond, in addition to; **outre-mer** *adv.* overseas
**ouvert** *adj.* open (7); frank
**ouverture** *f.* opening
**ouvreuse** *f.* usher (*movies*)
**ouvrier/ière** *m., f.* (*manual*) worker (14)
**ouvrir** (*p.p.* **ouvert**) *irreg.* to open (14)
**oxygène** *m.* oxygen
**ozone** *m.* ozone; **couche** (*f.*) **d'ozone** ozone layer

**paiement** *m.* payment
**pain** *m.* bread (6); **baguette** (*f.*) **de pain** (French) bread, baguette (7); **pain au chocolat** chocolate-filled roll; **pain de campagne** country-style, wheat bread
**pair** *adj.* even; **au pair** au pair (*child-care by foreign student*)
**paire** *f.* pair
**paisible** *adj.* peaceful, tranquil
**paix** *f.* peace
**palais** *m.* palace (12); palate (*in mouth*)
**palier** *m.* (*stair*) landing, floor
**palmarès** *m. s.* prize, honors list
**panaché** *m.* mixed dish, salad
**panne** *f.* (*mechanical*) breakdown; **être en panne** to have a breakdown; **tomber en panne** to have a (*mechanical*) breakdown (9)
**panorama** *m.* view; panorama
**pantalon** *m.* (pair of) pants (3)
**papa** *m., fam.* dad, daddy
**pape** *m.* pope
**papeterie** *f.* stationery store, stationers'
**papier** *m.* paper
**papillon** *m.* butterfly
**papy** *m., fam.* grandpa
**Pâques** *f. pl.* Easter
**paquet** *m.* package (10); **paquet de mer** stormy sea
**par** *prep.* by, through; **par bateau** by boat; **par écrit** in writing; **par exemple** for example (16); **par *hasard** by chance; **par jour (semaine, etc.)** per day (week, etc.); **par ordre (de)** in order (of); **par terre** on the ground (3)
**parachutisme** *m.* parachuting
**paradis** *m.* paradise
**paralysé** *adj.* paralyzed
**parapluie** *m.* umbrella (8)
**parc** *m.* park (11)
**parce que** *conj.* because (3)
**parcomètre** *m.* parking meter
**parcourir** (*like* **courir**) *irreg.* to travel through, traverse
**parcours** *m. s.* route, course, distance to cover
**pardon** *interj.* pardon me (1)
**parent(e)** *m., f.* parent; relative; **arrière-grand-parent** *m.* great-grandparent (5); **grand-parent** grandparent (5)
**parenthèse** *f.* parenthesis
**paresseux/euse** *adj.* lazy (3)
**parfait** *adj.* perfect
**parfois** *adv.* sometimes (9)
**parfum** *m.* perfume; flavor
**pari** *m.* bet (*gambling*)
**parigot(e)** *m., f., tr. fam.* Parisian
**parisien(ne)** *adj.* Parisian; **Parisien(ne)** *m., f.* Parisian (*person*) (3)
**parking** *m.* parking lot
**parlement** *m.* parliament
**parlementaire** *adj.* parliamentary
**parler (à, de)** to speak (to, of) (2); to talk; *m.* speech
**parmi** *prep.* among
**parole** *f.* word
**part** *f.* share, portion; role; **à part** besides; separately; **c'est de la part de X** X is calling; **d'autre part** on the other hand; **de ma (votre) part** from me (you); **de part et d'autre** on both sides, here and there; **ne... nulle part** nowhere; **pour ma part** in my opinion, as for me (16); **quelque part** somewhere
**partager (nous partageons)** to share
**partenaire** *m., f.* partner
**parti** *m.* (*political*) party (16)
**participe** *m., Gram.* participle
**participer à** to participate in
**particulier/ière** *adj.* particular, special; **en particulier** *adv.* particularly
**partie** *f.* part; game, match; outing; **en partie** in part; **faire partie de** to be part of
**partiellement** *adv.* partially
**partir** (*like* **dormir**) **(à, de)** *irreg.* to leave (for, from) (8); **à partir de** *prep.* starting from
**partitif/ive** *adj., Gram.* partitive
**partout** *adv.* everywhere (11)
**parvenir** (*like* **venir**) **à** *irreg.* to attain; to succeed in
**pas (ne... pas)** not; **ne... pas du tout** not at all (9); **ne... pas encore** not yet (9); **pas à pas** step-by-step; **pas du tout** not at all (5); **pas grand-chose** not much; **pas mal** not bad(ly) (1)
**passage** *m.* passage; passing
**passager/ère** *m., f.* passenger (9)
**passant(e)** *m., f.* passerby
**passé** *m.* past (12); *adj.* past, gone, last (8)
**passeport** *m.* passport
**passer** to pass, spend (*time*) (6); **passer par** to pass by, through (9); **passer un coup de fil** *fam.* to make a phone call; **passer un examen** to take an exam (4); **qu'est-ce qui se passe?** what's happening? (15); **se passer** to happen, take place; to go (15)
**passe-temps** *m.* pastime, hobby (15)
**passionnant** *adj.* exciting, thrilling
**passionné** *adj.* passionate, intense
**pasteur** *m.* (*Protestant*) minister
**pastis** *m.* pastis (*aniseed aperitif*)
**patate** *f., tr. fam.* potato
**pâtes** *f. pl.* pasta, noodles
**pâté** *m.* liver paste, pâté; **pâté de campagne** (country-style) pâté (7); **pâté de foie gras** goose liver pâté
**patent** *adj.* obvious
**patience** *f.* patience; **perdre patience** to lose patience
**patient** *m., f.* (*hospital*) patient; *adj.* patient (3)
**patienter** to wait
**patin** *m.* skate, ice skate; **faire du patin à glace** to go ice-skating
**patinage** *m.* skating
**pâtisserie** *f.* pastry; pastry shop (7)
**pâtissier/ière** *m., f.* pastry shop owner; pastry chef
**patrimoine** *m.* legacy, patrimony (12)
**patron(ne)** *m., f.* boss, employer
**pauvre** *adj.* poor; unfortunate (7)
**pauvreté** *f.* poverty
**payant** *adj.* paying, charged for
**payer (je paie)** to pay, pay for
**pays** *m.* country (*nation*) (8); **pays en voie de développement** developing nation

**paysage** *m.* landscape, scenery
**paysan(ne)** *m., f., adj.* peasant
**pêche** *f.* fishing (15); peach
**pêcher** to fish (8)
**pêcheur/euse** *m., f.* fisherman (woman)
**pédagogie** *f.* pedagogy
**peigne** *m.* comb (13)
**se peigner** to comb one's hair (13)
**peindre** (*like* **craindre**) *irreg.* to paint
**peine** *f.* punishment, sentence; **peine de mort** death penalty
**peintre** *m.* painter (12); **artiste-peintre** *m.*, f. painter (*artist*) (14)
**peinture** *f.* paint; painting (12)
**pendant** *prep.* during (5); **pendant les vacances** during vacation (5)
**penser** to think; to reflect; to expect, intend; **penser** + *inf.* to plan on (*doing s.th.*) (15); **penser à** to think of, about (11); **penser de** to think of, have an opinion about (11); **que pensez-vous de... ? qu'en pensez-vous?** what do you think of . . . ? what do you think about it? (11)
**pensif/ive** *adj.* pensive, thoughtful
**pension** *f.* board, meals; boardinghouse; **pension complète** full board
**pente** *f.* slope
**Pentecôte** *f.* Pentecost
**pépé** *m., fam.* grandpa
**percer (nous perçons)** to make a name, become popular
**perché** *adj.* perched
**perçu** *adj.* perceived
**perdre** to lose (5); to waste; **perdre patience** to exhaust one's patience; **se perdre** to get lost (13)
**perdu** *adj.* lost; wasted; anonymous
**père** *m.* father (5); **beau-père** father-in-law; stepfather (5); **grand-père** grandfather (5)
**perfectionnement** *m.* perfecting
**perfectionner** to perfect (17)
**performant** *adj.* performing (well)
**péril** *m.* danger, peril
**période** *f.* period (*of time*)
**périphérique** *adj.* peripheral
**périple** *m.* long journey, odyssey
**périr** to perish
**perle** *f.* pearl; bead
**permettre** (*like* **mettre**) **(à)** *irreg.* to permit, allow, let (15)
**permis** *m.* license
**persévérant** *adj.* persevering, dogged
**persister** to persist, last
**personnage** *m.* (*fictional*) character
**personnalité** *f.* personality
**personne** *f.* person (3); **grande personne** adult, grown-up; **ne... personne** nobody, no one (9)
**personnel(le)** *m.* personnel; *adj.* personal
**personnellement** *adv.* personally (16)
**perspective** *f.* view; perspective
**persuader** to persuade, convince
**perte** *f.* loss
**peser (je pèse)** to weigh
**pessimiste** *adj.* pessimistic (3)
**pétanque** *f.* bocce ball, lawn bowling (*So. France*) (15)
**petit** *adj.* little; short (4); very young; *m. pl.* young ones; little ones; **petit déjeuner** *m.* breakfast (6); **petite cuillère** *f.* teaspoon; **petit-enfant** *m.* grandchild (5); **petite-fille** *f.* granddaughter (5); **petites annonces** *f. pl.* classified ads (10); **petit-fils** *m.* grandson (5); **petits gâteaux** *m. pl.* cookies
**pétrole** *m.* oil, petroleum
**pétrolier/ière** *adj.* petroleum
**peu** *adv.* little; few; not very; hardly (3); **à peu près** *adv.* nearly; **il est peu probable que** + *subj.* it's doubtful that (16); **un peu** a little (3)
**peuple** *m.* nation; people of a country
**peur** *f.* fear; **avoir peur (de)** to be afraid (of) (4)
**peut-être** *adv.* perhaps, maybe (5)
**pharmaceutique** *adj.* pharmaceutical
**pharmacie** *f.* pharmacy, drugstore (11)
**pharmacien(ne)** *m., f.* pharmacist (14)
**phénomène** *m.* phenomenon
**philosophe** *m., f.* philosopher
**philosophie** (*fam.* **philo**) *f.* philosophy (2)
**photo** *f.* picture, photograph; **appareil-photo** *m.* (*still*) camera; **prendre des photos** to take photos
**photocopieur** *m.* photocopy machine
**photographe** *m., f.* photographer
**photographie** (*fam.* **photo**) *f.* photo(graph); photography
**photographier** to photograph
**phrase** *f.* sentence
**physicien(ne)** *m., f.* physicist
**physique** *m.* physical appearance; *f.* physics (2); *adj.* physical
**pianiste** *m., f.* pianist
**piano** *m.* piano; **jouer du piano** to play the piano
**piaule** *f., tr. fam.* room, bedroom
**pichet** *m.* pitcher, small carafe
**pièce** *f.* piece; room (*of a house*) (5); coin (7); each; **pièce de théâtre** (*theatrical*) play (12)
**pied** *m.* foot (13); **à pied** on foot; **au pied de** at the foot of; **de plain-pied** on one floor; at a level (with); **se lever du pied gauche** to get up on the wrong side of the bed
**pierre** *f.* stone
**piéton(ne)** *m., f., adj.* pedestrian
**pieu** *m., tr. fam.* bed
**pif** *m., tr. fam.* nose
**pilier** *m.* pillar
**pilote** *m., f.* pilot (9)
**pilule** *f.* pill
**pinard** *m., tr. fam.* wine
**pionnier/ière** *m., f.* pioneer
**pique-nique** *m.* picnic (15); **faire un pique-nique** to go on a picnic
**pique-niquer** to have a picnic
**pire** *adj.* worse (13); **le/la pire** the worst
**pirogue** *f.* (dugout) canoe
**pis** *adv.* worse; **le pis** the worst; **tant pis** too bad
**piscine** *f.* swimming pool (11); **piscine chauffée** heated swimming pool
**piste** *f.* path, trail; course; slope; **ski** (*m.*) **de piste** downhill skiing (8)
**pittoresque** *adj.* picturesque
**place** *f.* place; position; (public) square (11); seat (12); **à votre (ta) place** in your place, if I were you; **mettre en place** to put into place
**plage** *f.* beach (8); **serviette** (*f.*) **de plage** beach towel (8)
**plain: de plain-pied** on one floor, on a level with
**plaire** (*p.p.* **plu**) **à** *irreg.* to please; **s'il te (vous) plaît** *interj.* please (2)
**plaisir** *m.* pleasure
**plan** *m.* plan; diagram; (*city*) map (11)
**planche** *f.* board; **faire de la planche à voile** to go windsurfing (8)
**planète** *f.* planet
**plaque** *f.* package (*of frozen food*)
**plaquer** *fam.* to abandon, ditch
**plat** *adj.* flat; *m.* dish; course (*meal*) (7); **plat de résistance** main course, dish; **plat du jour** today's special (*restaurant*); **plat principal** main course
**plateau** *m.* tray; plateau
**platine** *f.* turntable; **platine** (*f.*) **laser** laser disk player

**plein (de)** *adj.* full (of); **à pleines dents** *fam.* fully; **de, en plein air** (in the) open air, outdoor(s) (15); **en plein centre** right in the middle; **faire le plein (d'essence)** to fill up (with gasoline) (9)
**pleurer** to cry, weep
**pleureur: saule** (*m.*) **pleureur** weeping willow
**pleuvoir** (*p.p.* **plu**) *irreg.* to rain (8); **il pleut** it's raining (6)
**pliant** *adj.* folding
**plombier** *m.* plumber (14)
**plongée** *f.* diving; **faire de la plongée sous-marine** to go skin diving, scuba diving (8)
**pluie** *f.* rain
**plupart: la plupart (de)** most, the majority (of) (16)
**pluridisciplinaire** *adj.* multidisciplinary
**pluriel** *m. Gram.* plural
**plus (de)** *adv.* more; more . . . than . . . (-er) (13); plus; **de plus en plus** more and more; **de plus, en plus** in addition; **le/la/les plus** + *adj.* most; **le plus** + *adv.* most; **ne... plus** no longer, not anymore (9); **plus tard** later
**plusieurs (de)** *adj., pron.* several (of) (17)
**plutôt** *adv.* instead; rather (7)
**poche** *f.* pocket; **lampe** (*f.*) **de poche** flashlight
**poème** *m.* poem (12)
**poésie** *f.* poetry (12)
**poète** *m.* poet (12)
**poétique** *adj.* poetic, poetry
**poids** *m.* weight
**point** *m.* point; dot; period (*punctuation*); **mise** (*f.*) **au point** restatement; focusing; **ne... point** not at all; **point de départ** starting point; **point de vue** point of view
**poire** *f.* pear (6)
**pois** *m.* pea; **petits pois** green peas
**poisson** *m.* fish (6)
**poissonnerie** *f.* fish store (7)
**poivrade: sauce** (*f.*) **poivrade** vinaigrette dressing
**poivre** *m.* pepper (6); **steak** (*m.*) **au poivre** pepper steak
**poivrière** *f.* pepper shaker
**poivron** *m.* green pepper
**poli** *adj.* polite; polished
**police** *f.* police; **agent** (*m.*) **de police** police officer (14); **poste** (*m.*) **de police** police station (11)
**policier/ière** *adj.* pertaining to the police; *m.* police officer; **roman** (*m.*) **policier** detective novel
**poliment** *adv.* politely (12)
**politesse** *f.* politeness; good breeding
**politique** *f.* politics; policy (16); *adj.* political; **homme (femme) politique** *m., f.* politician (16)
**polluant** *adj.* polluting
**polluer** to pollute (16)
**pollution** *f.* pollution (16)
**polytechnique** *adj.* polytechnical (*school*)
**pomme** *f.* apple (6); **pomme de terre** potato (6); **pommes allumettes** shoestring, matchstick potatoes; **tarte** (*f.*) **aux pommes** apple tart
**pompier** *m.* firefighter
**ponctuel(le)** *adj.* punctual
**pont** *m.* bridge
**populaire** *adj.* popular; common; of the people
**porc** *m.* pork (7)
**porte** *f.* door (1)
**porter** to wear; to carry (3)
**porto** *m.* port (*wine*)
**Portugal** *m.* Portugal (8)
**poser** to put (down); to state; to pose; to ask; **poser sa candidature** to apply; to run (*for office*); **poser une question** to ask a question
**positif/ive** *adj.* positive
**posséder (je possède)** to possess
**possessif/ive** *adj.* possessive
**possession** *f.* possession; **prendre possession de** to take possession of
**possible** *adj.* possible; **aussi souvent que possible** as often as possible; **faire son possible** to do one's best; **il est possible que** + *subj.* it's possible that (16)
**postal** *adj.* postal, post; **carte** (*f.*) **postale** postcard (10); **code** (*m.*) **postal** postal, zip code
**poste** *m.* position; employment; *f.* post office; postal service; **bureau** (*m.*) **de poste** post office (10); **poste** (*m.*) **de police** police station (11); **poste** (*m.*) **de télévision** TV set (5)
**poster** to mail (*a letter*)
**pot: avoir du pot** *m., tr. fam.* to be lucky
**poterie** *f.* pottery
**pouce** *m.* thumb; inch; **déjeuner sur le pouce** to have a quick lunch
**poule** *f.* hen
**poulet** *m.* chicken (6)
**pour** *prep.* for; in order to (2); **pour autant** for all that; **pour ma part** in my opinion, as for me (16)
**pourboire** *m.* tip, gratuity (7)
**pourcentage** *m.* percentage
**pourquoi** *adv., conj.* why (4)
**poursuivre** (*like* **suivre**) *irreg.* to pursue (12)
**pourtant** *adv.* however, yet, still, nevertheless (12)
**pourvoir (à)** *irreg.* to fill (*vacancy*)
**poussé** *adj.* elaborate, advanced; exhaustive
**poussée** *f.* growth; thrust
**pousser** to push; to encourage; to emit; to grow; **pousser un cri** to utter a cry
**poutre** *f.* beam (*roof*)
**pouvoir** (*p.p.* **pu**) *irreg.* to be able (7); *m.* power, strength; **il se peut que** + *subj.* it's possible that (16)
**pratique** *adj.* practical (13); *f.* practice
**pratiquement** *adv.* practically, almost
**pratiquer** to practice, exercise (*sport*)
**précaire** *adj.* precarious
**précédent** *adj.* preceding
**précéder (je précède)** to precede
**précieux/euse** *adj.* precious
**précis** *adj.* precise, fixed, exact
**précisément** *adv.* precisely, exactly
**préciser** to state precisely; to specify
**prédire** (*like* **dire, vous prédisez**) *irreg.* to predict, foretell
**préférable** *adj.* preferable, more advisable; **il est préférable que** + *subj.* it's preferable that (16)
**préféré** *adj.* favorite, preferred (5)
**préférer (je préfère)** to prefer, like better (6)
**préfet** *m.* prefect, commissioner
**préfrit** *adj.* pre-fried
**prémices** *f. pl.* first fruits, beginnings
**premier/ière** *adj.* first (11); **premier (deuxième) étage** second (third) floor (*in France*) (5); **premier ministre** *m.* prime minister
**prendre** (*p.p.* **pris**) *irreg.* to take; to have (to eat) (6); **prendre au sérieux** to take seriously; **prendre conscience de** to realize, become aware of; **prendre l'avion** to take a plane; **prendre le soleil** to sit in the sun; **prendre possession de** to take possession of; **prendre rendez-vous** to make an appointment, a date; **prendre son temps** to take one's time; **prendre une décision** to make a decision; **prendre**

une douche to take a shower; **prendre une photo** to take a photo; **prendre un verre** *fam.* to have a drink
**prénom** *m.* first, Christian name
**se prénommer** to have as a first name
**préoccuper** to preoccupy, concern; **se préoccuper de** to concern, preoccupy oneself with
**préparatifs** *m. pl.* preparations
**préparatoire** *adj.* preparatory
**préparer** to prepare (5); **se préparer (à)** to prepare oneself, get ready (for) (13)
**près (de)** *adv.* near, close to (4)
**prescrire** (*like* **écrire**) *irreg.* to prescribe
**présent** *m.* present; *adj.* present
**présenter** to present; to introduce; to put on (*a performance*); **je vous (te) présente...** I want you to meet . . .
**présidence** *f.* presidency
**président(e)** *m., f.* president
**présidentiel(le)** *adj.* presidential
**presque** *adv.* almost, nearly (6)
**presse** *f.* press (*media*)
**pressé** *adj.* in a hurry, rushed
**prêt** *adj.* ready (3); *m.* loan
**prêter (à)** to lend to (10)
**prévenir** (*like* **venir**) *irreg.* to warn, inform; to prevent, avert
**préventif/ive** *adj.* preventive
**prévoir** (*like* **voir**) *irreg.* to foresee, anticipate
**prévu** *adj.* expected, anticipated; **quelque chose de prévu** something planned
**prier** to pray; to beg, entreat; to ask (*s.o.*); **je vous (t')en prie** please; you're welcome (15)
**prière de** please, be so kind as to
**primaire** *adj.* primary; **école** (*f.*) **primaire** primary school
**prime** *f.* premium; **en prime** as a bonus
**primé** *adj.* awarded a prize
**principal** *adj.* principal, most important; **plat** (*m.*) **principal** main course
**printanier/ière** *adj.* spring (like)
**printemps** *m.* spring (6); **au printemps** in the spring (6)
**prioritaire** *adj.* priority
**priorité** *f.* right of way; priority
**pris** *adj.* occupied; **prise** *f.* taking
**prisonnier/ière** *m., f.* prisoner
**privé** *adj.* private
**privilégier** to favor
**prix** *m.* price (7); prize
**probable** *adj.* probable; **il est peu probable que** + *subj.* it's doubtful that (16); **il est probable que** + *indic.* it's probable that (16)
**problème** *m.* problem (16)
**procédé** *m.* process, method
**prochain** *adj.* next (14); **la semaine prochaine** next week (5)
**proche (de)** *adj., adv.* near, close; *m. pl.* close relatives; **futur** (*m.*) **proche** *Gram.* immediate, near future
**proclamer** to proclaim
**prodige** *m.* prodigy
**producteur/trice** *m., f.* producer
**produire** (*like* **conduire**) *irreg.* to produce
**produit** *m.* product (7); **produits laitiers** dairy products
**professeur** (*fam.* **prof**) *m.* professor; teacher (1)
**professionnel(le)** *m., f.* professional; *adj.* professional
**profil** *m.* profile; outline; cross section
**profiter de** to take advantage of, profit from
**profond** *adj.* deep
**programme** *m.* program; design, plan; agenda
**programmer** to program
**programmeur/euse** *m., f.* programmer
**progrès** *m.* progress
**progresser** to progress
**progression** *f.* progress, advancement
**progressiste** *adj.* progressive
**projet** *m.* project; plan (5)
**prolifération** *f.* proliferation (16)
**promenade** *f.* walk; ride (5); **faire une promenade (en voiture)** to go on an outing (*car ride*) (5)
**promener (je promène)** to take out walking; **se promener** to go for a walk, drive, ride (13)
**promettre** (*like* **mettre**) **(de)** *irreg.* to promise (to)
**promotion** *f.* promotion; sale, store special; **en promotion** on special
**promotionnel(le)** *adj.* special, bargain
**pronom** *m., Gram.* pronoun; **pronom complément d'objet direct (indirect)** *Gram.* direct (indirect) object pronoun; **pronom interrogatif (relatif, tonique)** *Gram.* interrogative (relative, stressed) pronoun
**pronominal** *adj., Gram.* pronominal; **verbe** (*m.*) **pronominal** *Gram.* pronominal, reflexive verb
**prononcer (nous prononçons)** to pronounce; **se prononcer** to declare one's opinion
**pronostic** *m.* forecast
**proportionnellement** *adv.* proportionally
**propos** *m.* talk; utterance; **à propos de** *prep.* with respect to
**proposer** to propose
**propre** *adj.* own; proper; clean (13)
**propriétaire** *m., f.* owner; landlord
**propriété** *f.* property
**protection** *f.* protection (16)
**protéger (je protège, nous protégeons)** to protect (16)
**protestation** *f.* protest; objection
**provision** *f.* supply; *pl.* groceries
**provoquer** to provoke
**proximité** *f.* proximity, closeness; **à proximité de** near
**psychologie** (*fam.* **psycho**) *f.* psychology (2)
**psychologique** *adj.* psychological
**psychologue** *m., f.* psychologist
**public (publique)** *adj.* public (11); *m.* public; audience; **opinion** (*f.*) **publique** public opinion (16); **transports** (*m. pl.*) **publics** public transportation
**publicitaire** *m., f.* advertising person; *adj.* pertaining to advertising
**publicité** (*fam.* **pub**) *f.* commercial; advertisement; advertising (10)
**publier** to publish
**puis** *adv.* then, next (11); besides; **et puis** and then; and besides
**puisque** *conj.* since, as, seeing that
**puissance** *f.* power
**pull-over** (*fam.* **pull**) *m.* pullover (*sweater*) (3)
**punir** to punish
**pur** *adj.* pure
**purée** *f.* purée, mashed (*vegetables*)

**quai** *m.* quai; platform (*station*) (9)
**qualificatif/ive** *adj.* qualifying, qualificative
**qualifier** to qualify
**qualité** *f.* quality; characteristic
**quand** *adv., conj.* when (3); **depuis quand?** since when?; **quand même** even though; anyway
**quarante** *adj.* forty (1)
**quart** *m.* quarter; fourth (6); quarter of an hour; **et quart** quarter past (*the hour*) (6); **moins le quart** a quarter to (*before the hour*) (6)

**quartier** *m.* quarter, neighborhood (2)
**quatorze** *adj.* fourteen (1)
**quatorzième** *adj.* fourteenth
**quatre** *adj.* four (1)
**quatrième** *adj.* fourth
**que** what (4); whom, that which (14); **ne... que** *adv.* only (9); **qu'en penses-tu?** what do you think of that? (11); **qu'est-ce que** what? (*object*) (4); **qu'est-ce que c'est?** what is it? (1); **qu'est-ce qui** what? (*subject*) (15); **qu'est-ce qui se passe?** what's happening? what's going on? (15); **que pensez-vous de... ?** what do you think about . . . ? (11); **que veut dire... ?** what does . . . mean? (7)
**Québec** *m.* Quebec (*province*) (8); Quebec (*City*) (17)
**québécois** *m.* Quebecois (*language*); *adj.* from, of Quebec (17); **Québécois(e)** *m., f.* Quebecer
**quel(le)(s)** *interr. adj.* what, which (7); what a; **quel âge avez-vous?** how old are you?; **quel jour sommes-nous?** what day is it? (1); **quel temps fait-il?** how's the weather? (6); **quelle heure est-il?** what time is it? (6)
**quelque(s)** *adj.* some, any; a few; somewhat; **quelque chose** *pron.* something (9); **quelque part** *adv.* somewhere
**quelquefois** *adv.* sometimes (2)
**quelques** *adj.* some, a few (17); **quelques-uns/unes** *pron.* some, a few (17)
**quelqu'un** *pron., neu.* someone, somebody (9)
**quenelle** *f.* fish dumpling, quenelle
**querelle** *f.* quarrel
**question** *f.* question; **poser des questions** to ask questions
**questionner** to question, ask questions
**queue** *f.* line (*of people*)
**qui** *pron.* who, whom (3); **qu'est-ce qui** what? (*subject*) (15); **qui est à l'appareil?** who's calling? (10); **qui est-ce que** whom? (*object*) (15); **qui est-ce qui** who? (*subject*) (15)
**quiche** *f.* quiche (*egg custard pie*); **quiche lorraine** *egg custard pie with bacon*
**quinze** *adj.* fifteen (1); **quinze jours** two weeks
**quinzième** *adj.* fifteenth
**quitter** to leave (*s.o. or someplace*) (8); **se quitter** to separate
**quoi (à quoi, de quoi)** *pron.* which; what (4); **il n'y a pas de quoi** you're welcome (15); **n'importe quoi** anything; no matter what; **quoi d'autre** what else
**quoique** *conj.* although
**quotidien(ne)** *adj.* daily, everyday (13)

**raconter** to tell, relate (10)
**radio** *f.* radio (2); x-ray
**radioactif/ive** *adj.* radioactive
**rafraîchir** to refresh
**rage** *f.* rabies
**ragoût** *m.* meat stew, ragout
**raide** *adj.* stiff; straight (*hair*) (4)
**raideur** *f.* stiffness
**raisin** *m.* grape(s); raisin
**raison** *f.* reason; **avoir raison** to be right (4)
**raisonnable** *adj.* reasonable; rational (3)
**ramener (je ramène)** to bring back
**randonnée** *f.* tour, trip; ride; hike (8); **faire une randonnée (à pied)** to go on a hike
**rangé** *adj.* tidy; dutiful
**ranger (nous rangeons)** to put in order; to arrange, categorize
**rapide** *adj.* rapid, fast
**rappeler (je rappelle)** to remind; to recall; to call again; **se rappeler** to recall, remember (12)
**rappeur/euse** *m., f.* rap singer
**rapport** *m.* connection, relation; report; *pl.* relations
**rapporter** to bring back; to return; to report
**se rapprocher (à)** to draw nearer (to)
**raquette** *f.* racket
**rarement** *adv.* rarely (2)
**ras: au ras de** at the level of
**se raser** to shave (13)
**rasoir** *m.* razor
**rassembler** to gather
**rassurer** to reassure
**raté** *adj.* missed; failed
**ratifier** to ratify
**réactionnaire** *adj.* reactionary
**réagir** to react
**réaliser** to carry out, fulfill, create
**réaliste** *m., f., adj.* realist; realistic (3)
**réalité** *f.* reality; **en réalité** in reality
**récemment** *adv.* recently, lately
**récent** *adj.* recent, new, late
**réception** *f.* hotel, lobby desk
**réceptionniste** *m., f.* receptionist
**recette** *f.* recipe
**recevoir** (*p.p.* **reçu**) *irreg.* to receive; to entertain (*guests*)
**réchauffement** *m.* reheating; warming
**recherche** *f.* (*piece of*) research; search; **à la recherche de** in search of; **faire des recherches** to do research
**recherché** *adj.* sought after; studied, affected
**rechercher** to seek; to search for
**récif** *m.* (coral) reef
**récit** *m.* account, story
**recommandation** *f.* recommendation
**recommander** to recommend
**recommencer (nous recommençons)** to start again
**récompense** *f.* reward, recompense
**reconnaître** (*like* **connaître**) *irreg.* to recognize (16)
**reconquête** *f.* reconquest
**recourir à** to have recourse to
**recours** *m.* recourse; **avoir recours à** to have recourse to
**récréation** (*fam.* **récré**) *f.* recreation
**recrutement** *m.* recruiting, recruitment
**recruter** to recrute
**recteur** *m.* university president, chancellor
**rectifier** to rectify
**rectiligne** *adj.* rectilinear
**reçu** *adj.* received; entertained; *m.* receipt (14)
**récupérer (je récupère)** to recover, get back
**recyclage** *m.* recycling (16)
**recycler** to recycle (16)
**rédacteur/trice** *m., f.* writer; editor
**rédaction** *f.* editorial staff
**réduire** (*like* **conduire**) *irreg.* to reduce
**réécouter** to listen to again
**réel(le)** *adj.* real, actual
**refaire** to make again; to redo
**référence** *f.* reference; **sous référence** with a reference number
**se référer (je me réfère)** to refer
**réfléchir (à)** to reflect; to think (about) (4)
**reflet** *m.* reflection
**réflexe** *m.* reflex
**réflexion** *f.* reflection, thought
**réforme** *f.* reform (16)
**réformer** to reform
**réfrigérateur** *m.* refrigerator
**refus** *m.* refusal
**refuser (de)** to refuse (to) (15)
**se régaler** to feast on, treat oneself
**regard** *m.* glance; gaze, look

**regarder** to look at; to watch (2); **se regarder** to look at oneself, each other (13)
**régime** *m.* diet; régime; **être au régime** to be on a diet
**régional** *adj.* local, of the district
**règle** *f.* rule
**régler (je règle)** to regulate, adjust; to settle
**regretter** to regret, be sorry (16); to miss
**regrouper** to regroup; to contain
**reine** *f.* queen (12)
**rejet** *m.* rejection
**rejeter (je rejette)** to reject
**rejoindre** (*like* **craindre**) *irreg.* to (re)join
**rejouer** to play again
**relâché** *adj.* relaxed
**relais** *m.* stop, coach stop
**relatif/ive** *adj.* relative; **pronom** (*m.*) **relatif** *Gram.* relative pronoun
**relation** *f.* relation; relationship
**se relaxer** to relax
**relever (je relève)** to raise; to bring up; to point out
**relier** to tie, link
**religieux/euse** *adj.* religious
**relire** (*like* **lire**) *irreg.* to reread
**remarquable** *adj.* remarkable
**remarque** *f.* remark
**remboursement** *m.* reimbursement
**rembourser** to reimburse
**remède** *m.* remedy; treatment
**remercier (de)** to thank (for) (15); **je ne sais pas comment vous (te) remercier** I don't know how to thank you (15)
**remettre** (*like* **mettre**) *irreg.* to hand in; to replace; to deliver (14)
**remis** *adj.* awarded, given
**remise** *f.* remittance
**remonter** to go back (up); to revive
**remous** *m.* stir
**remplacer (nous remplaçons)** to replace
**remplir** to fill (in, out, up)
**rémunérateur/trice** *adj.* remunerative
**rémunéré** *adj.* compensated, paid
**renaissance** *f.* Renaissance (12)
**rencontre** *f.* meeting, encounter (13)
**rencontrer** to meet, encounter; **se rencontrer** to meet each other; to get together (13)
**rendez-vous** *m.* meeting, appointment; date; meeting place; **avoir rendez-vous avec** to have an appointment with (4); **faire (prendre) rendez-vous** to make an appointment
**rendre** to give (back) (5); **rendre malade** to make (*s.o.*) sick; **rendre visite à** to visit (*s.o.*) (5); **se rendre (à, dans)** to go to (13)
**renforcer (nous renforçons)** to reinforce
**renommé** *adj.* renowned
**renoncer (nous renonçons) à** to give up, renounce (12)
**renouvelable** *adj.* renewable
**renouvellement** *m.* renewal
**rénover** to renovate, restore
**renseignement** *m.* (*piece of*) information
**rentrée (des classes)** *f.* beginning of the school year (14)
**rentrer** to return; to go home (9)
**réparation** *f.* repair
**réparer** to repair
**repartir** (*like* **partir**) *irreg.* to leave (again)
**repas** *m.* meal, repast (6)
**répertoire** *m.* repertory
**répéter (je répète)** to repeat (1)
**répondeur (téléphonique)** *m.* answering machine (10)
**répondre (à)** to answer, respond (5)
**réponse** *f.* answer, response
**reportage** *m.* reporting; commentary
**repos** *m.* rest, relaxation
**reposant** *adj.* restful
**reposer (sur)** to put down again; to rest, refresh; to be based (on); **se reposer** to rest (12)
**reprendre** (*like* **prendre**) *irreg.* to take (up) again; to continue
**représentant(e)** *m., f.* representative
**représentatif/ive** *adj.* representative
**représentation** *f.* performance (*show*)
**représenter** to represent
**repris** *adj.* continued; revived
**reproche** *m.* reproach
**république** *f.* republic
**requin** *m.* shark
**réseau** *m.* net; network
**réserve** *f.* reservation; preserve; reserve
**réservé** *adj.* reserved; shy
**réserver** to reserve; to keep in store
**réservoir** *m.* reservoir; gas tank
**résidence** *f.* residence; apartment building
**résider** to reside
**résistance: plat** (*m.*) **de résistance** main dish, course
**résister (à)** to resist
**résoudre** (*p.p.* **résolu**) *irreg.* to solve, resolve
**respecter** to respect, have regard for; **se respecter** to respect one another
**respectif/ive** *adj.* respective
**responsabilité** *f.* responsibility
**responsable** *m., f.* supervisor; staff member; *adj.* responsible
**ressemblance** *f.* resemblance
**ressembler à** to resemble; **se ressembler** to look alike, be similar
**ressources** *f. pl.* resources; funds; **ressources naturelles** natural resources (16)
**ressusciter** to revive, resuscitate
**restaurant** *m.* restaurant (2); **restau-u** *m., fam.* university restaurant
**restaurateur/trice** *m., f.* restaurant owner
**restauration** *f.* restoration; restaurant business
**restaurer** to restore
**reste** *m.* rest, remainder
**rester** to stay, remain (5); to be remaining
**resto: se faire un resto** *tr. fam.* to go to a restaurant
**résultat** *m.* result
**résulter** to result, follow
**résumer** to summarize
**retard** *m.* delay; **en retard** late (9)
**retardataire** *adj.* late, backward
**retenir** (*like* **tenir**) *irreg.* to retain; to keep, hold
**retirer** to withdraw (14)
**retour** *m.* return; **au retour** upon returning; **billet** (*m.*) **aller-retour** round-trip ticket
**retourner** to return; to go back (9)
**retracer (nous retraçons)** to retrace
**retrait** *m.* withdrawal; suspension
**retraite** *f.* retreat; retirement; pension; **en retraite** retired
**retraité(e)** *m., f.* retired person; *adj.* retired
**retransmettre** (*like* **mettre**) *irreg.* to broadcast (10)
**retransmission** *f.* broadcast
**retrouver** to find (again); to regain; **se retrouver** to meet (again)
**réunion** *f.* meeting; reunion
**réunir** to unite, reunite; **se réunir** to get together; to hold a meeting
**réussi** *adj.* successful
**réussir (à)** to succeed, be successful (in); to pass (*a test*) (4)
**réussite** *f.* success, accomplishment (16)
**rêve** *m.* dream; **faire un rêve** to have a dream
**réveil** *m.* alarm clock (4)

**réveiller** to wake, awaken (*s.o.*); **se réveiller** to wake up (13)
**réveillon** *m.* Christmas Eve or New Year's Eve dinner
**révéler (je révèle)** to reveal
**revendication** *f.* demand; claim
**revenir** (*like* **venir**) *irreg.* to return (8); to come back (*someplace*) (9)
**revenus** *m. pl.* personal income
**rêver (de, à)** to dream (about, of) (2)
**réviser** to review, revise
**revoir** (*like* **voir**) *irreg.* to see (again) (8); **au revoir** goodbye, see you soon (1)
**se révolter** to revolt, rebel (12)
**revue** *f.* magazine (4); review (10); journal
**rez-de-chaussée** *m.* ground floor, first floor (5)
**rhum** *m.* rum
**rideaux** *m. pl.* curtains (4)
**rien (ne... rien)** *pron.* nothing (9); **de rien** you're welcome (15)
**rigoler** *fam.* to laugh; to have fun
**rigolo(te)** *adj., fam.* funny
**rire** (*p.p.* **ri**) *irreg.* to laugh (15); *m.* laughter
**risque** *m.* risk
**rissoler** to brown (*cooking*)
**rivalité** *f.* rivalry
**rive** *f.* (river)bank; **Rive gauche (droite)** the Left (Right) Bank (*in Paris*) (11)
**rivière** *f.* river, tributary
**riz** *m.* rice
**robe** *f.* dress (3)
**rocher** *m.* rock, crag
**rocker/euse** *m., f., fam.* rocker, rock fan
**roi** *m.* king; **fête** (*f.*) **des Rois** Feast of the Magi, Epiphany
**rôle** *m.* part, character, role; **à tour de rôle** in turn, by turns; **jouer le rôle de** to play the part of
**romain** *adj.* Roman (12)
**roman** *m.* novel (12); **roman policier** detective novel
**romancier/ière** *m., f.* novelist
**rose** *adj.* pink (3); *f.* rose
**rôti** *adj.* roast(ed); *m.* roast (7)
**rouge** *adj.* red (3); **rouge** (*m.*) **à lèvres** lipstick
**roulé** *adj.* rolled (up)
**rouler** to travel (*by car, train*) (9)
**route** *f.* road, highway (8); **en route** on the way, en route
**routinier/ière** *adj.* routine, following a routine
**roux (rousse)** *m., f.* redhead; *adj.* redheaded (4)
**royaume** *m.* realm, kingdom
**rue** *f.* street (4)
**ruine** *f.* ruin; decay; collapse; **en ruine(s)** in ruins
**russe** *adj.* Russian; *m.* Russian (*language*); **Russe** *m., f.* Russian (*person*) (2)
**Russie** *f.* Russia (8)
**rythme** *m.* rhythm

**sable** *m.* sand
**sac** *m.* sack; bag; handbag; **sac à dos** backpack (3); **sac à main** handbag (3); **sac de couchage** sleeping bag (8)
**sachet** *m.* packet
**sacrifier** to sacrifice
**safari-photo** *m.* photo safari
**sage** *adj.* good, well-behaved; wise
**saignant** *adj.* rare (*meat*); bloody
**saint(e)** *m., f.* saint; *adj.* holy; **Saint-Valentin** *f.* Valentine's Day; **vendredi** (*m.*) **saint** Good Friday
**saison** *f.* season
**salade** *f.* salad; lettuce (6)
**salaire** *m.* salary (14); paycheck
**salarial** *adj.* pertaining to wages
**salarié(e)** *m., f.* wage earner; *adj.* salaried; **travailleur/euse** (*m., f.*) **salarié(e)** salaried worker (14)
**salière** *f.* salt shaker
**salle** *f.* room; auditorium; **salle à manger** *f.* dining room (5); **salle d'eau** half-bath (*toilet and sink*); **salle de bains** bathroom (5); **salle de classe** classroom (1); **salle de conférence** meeting room; **salle de gymnastique** gym, gymnasium; **salle de musculation** weight, training room; **salle de récréation** game room, rec room; **salle de (re)mise en forme** exercise, fitness room; **salle de séjour** living room (5); **salle de sports** gymnasium
**salon** *m.* salon; living room
**saluer** to greet; to salute
**salut!** *interj.* hi! bye! (1)
**salutation** *f.* greeting; closing (*letter*)
**samedi** *m.* Saturday (1)
**sandales** *f. pl.* sandals (3)
**sang** *m.* blood
**sang-froid** *m.* coolness, self-control; **garder son sang-froid** to keep one's cool
**sanglier** *m.* boar
**sans** *prep.* without; **sans cesse** ceaselessly; **sans doute** doubtless, for sure
**sans-abri** *m. pl.* homeless (*persons*)
**santé** *f.* health (13); **à votre (ta) santé!** cheers! to your health!
**sapin** *m.* fir tree
**sardines** (*f. pl.*) **à l'huile** sardines (packed) in oil (7)
**satirique** *adj.* satirical
**satisfait** *adj.* satisfied; pleased
**sauce** *f.* sauce; gravy; salad dressing
**saucisse** *f.* sausage (7)
**saucisson** *m.* hard salami
**sauf** *prep.* except; **sauf que** except that
**saule** *m.* willow (*tree*); **saule pleureur** weeping willow
**saumon** *m.* salmon; *adj.* salmon-colored
**sauté** *adj.* pan-fried, sautéed
**sauter** to jump; to skip; to sauté
**sauvage** *adj.* rough; undeveloped
**sauvegarde** *f.* safeguard
**sauver** to save, rescue (16)
**savane** *f.* savanna
**savoir** (*p.p.* **su**) *irreg.* to know (how) (11); **en savoir plus** to know more about it
**savoir-faire** *m.* ability, know-how; tact
**savourer** to savor; to relish
**savoureux/euse** *adj.* tasty, delicious
**scandaleux/euse** *adj.* scandalous
**scène** *f.* stage; scenery; scene; **metteur/euse** (*m., f.*) **en scène** stage director; **mise** (*f.*) **en scène** (*stage*) direction, staging
**sceptique** *adj.* skeptical
**science** *f.* science; **sciences économiques** economics; **sciences humaines** humanities; **sciences naturelles** natural sciences; **sciences sociales** social sciences
**scolaire** *adj.* pertaining to schools, school, academic; **année** (*f.*) **scolaire** school year; **fournitures** (*f. pl.*) **scolaires** school supplies; **frais** (*m. pl.*) **scolaires (de scolarité)** tuition, fees
**sculpteur (femme sculpteur)** *m., f.* sculptor (12)
**sculpture** *f.* sculpture (12)
**se (s')** *pron.* oneself; himself; herself; itself; themselves; to oneself, etc.; each other
**séance** *f.* session, meeting; performance

**sec (sèche)** *adj.* dry; **biscuit** (*m.*) **sec** cookie, wafer
**sécheuse** *f.* clothes dryer
**second(e)** *adj.* second; *f.* second (*unit of time*)
**secondaire** *adj.* secondary
**secours** *m.* help; rescue service; **au secours!** help!
**secret/ète** *adj.* secret, private; *m.* secret
**secrétaire** *m., f.* secretary (14)
**secrétariat** *m.* administrative office(s)
**secteur** *m.* sector
**section** *f.* section; division; **la section d'anglais** the English department; **section fumeurs (non-fumeurs)** smoking (nonsmoking) section (9)
**sécurité** *f.* security; safety
**séduire** (*like* **conduire**) *irreg.* to charm, win over; to seduce
**seigneur** *m.* lord
**seize** *adj.* sixteen (1)
**seizième** *adj.* sixteenth
**séjour** *m.* stay, sojourn; **salle** (*f.*) **de séjour** living room (5)
**séjourner** to spend some time, stay
**sel** *m.* salt (6)
**selon** *prep.* according to
**semaine** *f.* week (8); **la semaine prochaine** next week (5); **toutes les semaines** every week (10); **une fois par semaine** once a week (5)
**semblable (à)** *adj.* like, similar, such (17); **semblables** *m. pl.* fellow men, fellow beings
**sembler** to seem; to appear; **il semble que** + *subj.* it seems that (16)
**semestre** *m.* semester
**séminaire** *m.* seminar
**sénateur** *m.* senator
**Sénégal** *m.* Senegal (8)
**sens** *m.* meaning; sense; way, direction; **avoir le sens de l'humour** to have a sense of humor
**sensationnel(le)** *adj.* sensational, marvelous
**sensibilisé** *adj.* sensitized
**sensiblement** *adv.* perceptibly, noticeably
**sensoriel(le)** *adj.* sensory
**sentier** *m.* path
**sentiment** *m.* feeling
**sentir** (*like* **partir**) *irreg.* to feel; to sense; to smell (of) (8)
**se séparer** to separate (from)
**sept** *adj.* seven (1)
**septembre** September (4)
**septentrional** *adj.* northern
**septième** *adj.* seventh
**serein** *adj.* serene, calm
**sérieux/euse** *adj.* serious (3); **prendre au sérieux** to take seriously
**serre** *f.* greenhouse; **effet** (*m.*) **de serre** greenhouse effect
**serré** *adj.* tight, snug
**serveur/euse** *m., f.* bartender; waiter (waitress) (7)
**service** *m.* favor (15); service; military service; **faire un petit service** to do a favor (15)
**serviette** *f.* napkin (6); towel; briefcase; **serviette de plage** beach towel (8)
**servir** (*like* **partir**) *irreg.* to serve (8); to wait on; to be useful; **servir à** to be of use in, be used for; **servir de** to serve as, take the place of; **se servir** to help oneself; **se servir de** to use
**ses** *adj. m., f., pl.* his; her; its; one's
**seul** *adj.* alone; single; only; **tout(e) seul(e)** all alone
**seulement** *adv.* only (9)
**sévère** *adj.* severe; stern, harsh
**sexisme** *m.* sexism (16)
**short** *m.* (*pair of*) shorts (3)
**si** *adv.* so; so much; yes (*response to negative*) (9); *conj.* if; whether (3); **même si** even if; **s'il vous (te) plaît** please (2)
**sida (SIDA)** *m.* AIDS
**siècle** *m.* century (12)
**siège** *m.* seat; place; headquarters
**sien(ne)(s) (le/la/les)** *pron., m., f.* his/hers
**sieste** *f.* nap; **faire la sieste** to take a nap
**signalé** *adj.* marked, indicated
**signalétique** *adj.* descriptive
**signe** *m.* sign, gesture
**signer** to sign
**signification** *f.* meaning
**signifier** to mean
**silencieux/euse** *adj.* silent
**similaire** *adj.* similar
**simple** *adj.* simple; **aller** (*m.*) **simple** one-way ticket
**simplifié** *adj.* simplified
**sincère** *adj.* sincere (3)
**singulier/ière** *adj.* singular; *m. Gram.* singular (*form*)
**sirop** *m.* syrup; **sirop d'érable** maple syrup
**situation** *f.* situation; job
**se situer** to be situated, located
**six** *adj.* six (1)
**sixième** *adj.* sixth
**ski** *m.* skiing (5); *pl.* skis (8); **chaussures** (*f. pl.*) **de ski** ski boots (8); **faire du ski** to ski (5); **gants** (*m. pl.*) **de ski** ski gloves (8); **lunettes** (*f. pl.*) **de ski** sunglasses (8); **ski de fond** cross-country skiing (8); **ski de piste** downhill skiing (8); **ski nautique** waterskiing (8)
**skier** to ski (2)
**skieur/euse** *m., f.* skier
**slip (de bain)** *m.* men's bathing suit
**snob** *adj. inv.* snobbish (3)
**sobre** *adj.* sober
**sociable** *adj.* sociable (3)
**social** *adj.* social; **sciences** (*f. pl.*) **sociales** social sciences
**société** *f.* society; organization; company (14); **jeux** (*m. pl.*) **de société** social games, group games (15)
**sociologie** (*fam.* **socio**) *f.* sociology (2)
**sœur** *f.* sister (5); **belle-sœur** sister-in-law (5); **demi-sœur** half sister; stepsister (5)
**soi (soi-même)** *pron., neu.* oneself
**soif** *f.* thirst; **avoir soif** to be thirsty (4)
**soigner** to take care of; to treat
**soigneusement** *adv.* carefully
**soin** *m.* care
**soir** *m.* evening (5); **ce soir-là** that evening; **demain (hier) soir** tomorrow (yesterday) evening; **du soir** in the evening (6); **le lundi (le vendredi) soir** Monday (Friday) evenings (5); **lundi soir** Monday evening (5)
**soirée** *f.* party (2); evening (8)
**soixante** *adj.* sixty (1)
**sol** *m.* soil; ground; floor; **au ras du sol** at ground level; **sous-sol** *m.* basement, cellar
**solaire** *adj.* solar; **énergie** (*f.*) **solaire** solar energy; **huile (crème)** (*f.*) **solaire** sunscreen; tanning lotion
**solde** *f.* (*soldier's*) pay, wages
**sole** *f.* sole (*fish*) (7)
**soleil** *m.* sun (6); **coucher** (*m.*) **de soleil** sunset; **faire du soleil (il fait du soleil)** to be sunny (out) (it's sunny) (6); **lunettes** (*f. pl.*) **de soleil** sunglasses (8); **prendre le soleil** to sit in the sun
**solitaire** *adj.* solitary; single; alone
**sombre** *adj.* dark; gloomy
**somme** *f.* sum, total; amount

**sommeil** *m.* sleep; **avoir sommeil** to be sleepy (4)
**sommet** *m.* summit, top
**sonate** *f.* sonata
**sondage** *m.* opinion poll; **faire un sondage** to conduct a survey
**songer (nous songeons) (à)** to think, imagine
**sonner** to ring (*bell*)
**sonnette** *f.* bell; doorbell
**sophistiqué** *adj.* sophisticated
**sorbet** *m.* sorbet, sherbet
**sorte** *f.* sort, kind; manner
**sortie** *f.* exit; going out; evening out
**sortilège** *m.* witchcraft, spell
**sortir** to leave; to take out; to go out (8)
**sou** *m.* sou (*copper coin*); cent; *pl. fam.* money
**souci** *m.* care, worry
**soudain** *adj.* sudden; *adv.* suddenly (11)
**souffler** to blow (*wind*)
**souffrir** (*like* **ouvrir**) **(de)** *irreg.* to suffer (from) (14)
**souhait** *m.* wish
**souhaiter** to wish, desire (16)
**soulagé** *adj.* relieved (16)
**soupe** *f.* soup; **cuillère** (*f.*) **à soupe** tablespoon, soupspoon (6)
**source** *f.* source (16)
**sous** *prep.* under, beneath (3); **sous forme de** in the form of
**sous-estimer** to underestimate
**sous-marin** *adj.* underwater; *m.* submarine; **plongée** (*f.*) **sous-marine** skin diving (8)
**sous-sol** *m.* basement, cellar
**sous-titre** *m.* subtitle (*movies*)
**soutenir** (*like* **tenir**) *irreg.* to support (16); to assert
**soutien** *m.* support
**souvenir** *m.* memory, recollection; souvenir; **jour** (*m.*) **du souvenir** Memorial, Remembrance Day; **se souvenir** (*like* **venir**) **de** *irreg.* to remember (12)
**souvent** *adv.* often (2)
**spacieux/euse** *adj.* spacious
**speaker (speakerine)** *m., f.* radio, TV announcer
**spécialement** *adv.* especially
**spécialisation** *f.* specialization; (*academic*) major
**se spécialiser (en)** to specialize (in)
**spécialiste** *m., f.* specialist
**spécialité** *f.* speciality (*in cooking*)
**spectacle** *m.* show, performance (15)
**spectaculaire** *adj.* spectacular
**splendeur** *f.* splendor
**spontané** *adj.* spontaneous
**sport** *m.* sport(s) (2); **faire du sport** to do, participate in sports (5)
**sportif/ive** *adj.* athletic; sports-minded (3); **manifestation** (*f.*) **sportive** sports event (15)
**stade** *m.* stadium
**stage** *m.* training course; practicum, internship
**standardiste** *m., f.* switchboard operator
**station** *f.* resort (*vacation*); station; **station de métro** subway station (11); **station de ski** ski resort
**stationner** to park
**statistique** *f.* statistic(s)
**statut** *m.* status
**stéréo** *adj. m., f.* stereo(phonic); **chaîne** (*f.*) **stéréo** stereo system (4)
**steward** *m.* flight attendant, steward (9)
**stimulé** *adj.* stimulated
**stratégie** *f.* strategy
**studieux/euse** *adj.* studious
**studio** *m.* studio apartment
**stupéfiant** *adj.* astounding, amazing
**stupide** *adj.* stupid; foolish; **il est stupide que** + *subj.* it's idiotic that (16)
**style** *m.* style; **style de vie** lifestyle
**stylo** *m.* pen (1)
**styrène** *m.* polystyrene
**subir** to undergo; to endure
**subjonctif** *m., Gram.* subjunctive (*mood*)
**substantif** *m., Gram.* noun, substantive
**substituer** to substitute
**se succéder (ils se succèdent)** to follow one another
**succès** *m.* success
**sucre** *m.* sugar (6); **canne** (*f.*) **à sucre** sugar cane
**sud** *m.* south (9); **au sud** to the south (9)
**Suède** *f.* Sweden (8)
**suffire** (*like* **conduire**) *irreg.* to suffice
**suffisant** *adj.* sufficient
**suggéré** *adj.* suggested
**se suicider** to commit suicide
**Suisse** *f.* Switzerland (8); *m., f.* Swiss (*person*); **suisse** *adj.* Swiss
**suite** *f.* continuation; series; result; **et ainsi de suite** and so on; **tout de suite** immediately (5)
**suivant** *adj.* following; *prep.* according to (17)
**suivi (de)** *adj.* followed (by)
**suivre** (*p.p.* **suivi**) *irreg.* to follow; **suivre un cours** to take a class, a course (12)
**sujet** *m.* subject; topic
**super** *adj. inv., fam.* super, fantastic
**superbe** *adj.* superb, magnificent (5)
**superficie** *f.* surface, area
**supérieur** *adj.* superior; upper; **études** (*f. pl.*) **supérieures** higher education
**superlatif/ive** *adj.* superlative; *m., Gram.* superlative
**supermarché** *m.* supermarket
**superstitieux/euse** *adj.* superstitious
**supplément** *m.* supplement, addition; supplementary charge
**supplémentaire** *adj.* supplementary, additional
**supportable** *adj.* bearable, tolerable
**supporter** to tolerate, put up with; to sustain
**supposer** to suppose
**supprimer** to abolish, suppress; to delete
**sur** *prep.* on; on top; out of (3); about; **donner sur** to overlook (4)
**sûr** *adj.* sure, certain (16); safe; **bien sûr** of course; **bien sûr que oui (non)** of course (not) (6)
**sûrement** *adv.* certainly, surely
**surface** *f.* surface; **grande surface** shopping mall, superstore
**surgelé** *adj.* frozen
**surmonter** to overcome, get over
**surpopulation** *f.* overpopulation
**surprenant** *adj.* surprising
**surprendre** (*like* **prendre**) *irreg.* to surprise
**surpris** *adj.* surprised (16)
**surtout** *adv.* especially (10); above all
**survivre** (*like* **vivre**) *irreg.* to survive
**suspect(e)** *m., f.* suspect; *adj.* suspicious, doubtful
**syllabe** *f.* syllable
**sympathique** (*fam.* **sympa**) *adj.* nice, likable (3)
**syndicat** *m.* labor union; **syndicat d'initative** (local) tourist information bureau (11)
**synonyme** *m.* synonym; *adj.* synonymous
**synthèse** *f.* synthesis
**système** *m.* system

**ta** *adj., f. s., fam.* your
**tabac** *m.* tobacco; **café-tabac** *m.* café-tobacconist (*government-licensed*) (11)

**tableau** *m.* painting (12); chart; **tableau (noir)** blackboard, chalkboard (1); **tableau d'affichage** schedule display board
**tablette** *f.* cake, tablet; bar (*of chocolate*)
**tâche** *f.* task
**taille** *f.* waist; build; size; **de taille moyenne** average height (4)
**tailleur** *m.* (*woman's*) suit (3); tailor
**tandis que** *conj.* while; whereas
**tant** *adv.* so much; so many; **tant de** so many, so much; **tant mieux** so much the better; **tant pis** too bad
**tante** *f.* aunt (5)
**taper** to hit; to type
**tapis** *m.* rug (4)
**tapisserie** *f.* tapestry (12)
**tard** *adv.* late (6); **il est tard** it's late (6); **plus tard** later
**tarif** *m.* tariff; fare, price
**tarte** *f.* tart; pie (6); **tarte aux pommes** apple tart
**tartine** *f.* bread and butter sandwich
**tas** *m.* lot, pile
**tasse** *f.* cup (6)
**tata, tatie** *f., tr. fam.* aunt
**taux** *m.* rate; **taux de chômage (de croissance)** unemployment (growth) rate
**taxes** *f. pl.* indirect taxes
**taxi** *m.* taxi; **chauffeur** (*m.*) **de taxi** cab driver
**te (t')** *pron.* you; to you
**technicien(ne)** *m., f.* technician
**technique** *f.* technique; *adj.* technical
**technologique** *adj.* technological
**tee-shirt** (*pl.* **tee-shirts**) *m.* T-shirt (3)
**teinte** *f.* tint, shade, hue
**teinté** *adj.* tinged, colored
**tel(le)** *adj.* such; **tel(le) que** such as, like
**télécarte** *f.* telephone calling card (10)
**télégramme** *m.* telegram
**téléphone** *m.* telephone (4); **numéro** (*m.*) **de téléphone** telephone number (10)
**téléphoner (à)** to phone, telephone (3); **se téléphoner** to call one another
**téléphonique** *adj.* telephonic, by phone; **cabine** (*f.*) **téléphonique** phone booth (10); **répondeur** (*m.*) **téléphonique** telephone answering machine
**téléspectateur/trice** *m., f.* television viewer
**télévision** (*fam.* **télé**) *f.* television (2); **poste** (*m.*) **de télévision** TV set (5)
**tellement** *adv.* so; so much
**téloche** *f., tr. fam.* television
**tempête** *f.* tempest, storm
**temporaire** *adj.* temporary
**temporel(le)** *adj.* temporal, pertaining to time
**temps** *m., Gram.* tense; time (5); weather (6); **à mi-temps** half-time, part-time; **avoir le temps de** to have time to; **depuis combien de temps** since when, how long; **de temps en temps** from time to time (11); **le bon vieux temps** the good old days; **prendre le temps (de)** to take the time (to); **quel temps fait-il?** what's the weather like? (6); **temps libre** leisure time; **tout le temps** always, the whole time
**tendance** *f.* tendency; trend; **avoir tendance à** to have a tendency to
**tendre** *adj.* tender, sensitive; soft
**teneur** *f.* content(s)
**tenir** (*p.p.* **tenu**) *irreg.* to hold; to keep; **tenir à** to cherish; to be anxious to; **tenir ferme** to be stubborn, hold one's ground; **tenir la forme** to stay in shape, stay fit
**tennis** *m.* tennis; *pl.* tennis shoes (3); **court** (*m.*) **de tennis** tennis court; **jouer au tennis** to play tennis
**tentation** *f.* temptation
**tente** *f.* tent (8)
**tenter (de)** to tempt; to try, attempt (to)
**tenue** *f.* (*manner of*) dress, costume
**terme** *m.* term; **au terme de** at the end of; **but** (*m.*) **à long terme** long-term goal
**terminer** to end; to finish
**terrain** *m.* ground; land; **terrain de camping** campground
**terrasse** *f.* terrace, patio (5)
**terre** *f.* land; earth; the planet Earth; **par terre** on the ground (3); **pomme** (*f.*) **de terre** potato (6); **terre à terre** practical, down-to-earth; **tremblement** (*m.*) **de terre** earthquake
**Terre-Neuve** *f.* Newfoundland (17)
**terrible** *adj.* terrible; great; **pas terrible** not bad, not terrible
**terrine** *f.* (*type of*) pâté
**territoire** *m.* territory
**tertiaire** *adj.* tertiary
**tes** *adj. m., f., pl.* your
**tester** to test
**tête** *f.* head (13); mind; *fam.* face; **avoir mal à la tête** to have a headache; **tête-à-tête** *m.* intimate conversation, tête à tête
**texte** *m.* text; passage; **traitement** (*m.*) **de texte** word processing
**thé** *m.* tea (6); **thé à la menthe** mint tea
**théâtre** *m.* theater; **pièce** (*f.*) **de théâtre** (*theatrical*) play (12)
**théorie** *f.* theory
**thèse** *f.* thesis
**thon** *m.* tuna
**ticket** *m.* ticket (*subway, movie*)
**tiens!** *interj.* well, well! (*expresses surprise*)
**tiers** *m.* one-third; *adj.* third; **Tiers Monde** Third World
**tigre** *m.* tiger
**timbre** *m.* stamp (10)
**timide** *adj.* shy; timid
**tinque** *Q., m.* tank
**tir** (*m.*) **à l'arc** archery
**tiré (de)** *adj.* drawn, adapted (from)
**tirer** to draw (out); to shoot, fire at; to pull; **se tirer** *fam.* to leave, depart
**tiroir** *m.* drawer
**titre** *m.* title; degree; **sous-titre** *m.* subtitle (*movies*)
**toi** *pron., s., fam.* you; **toi-même** yourself
**toilette** *f.* grooming; *pl.* bathroom, toilet; **faire sa toilette** to wash up; to get ready
**toit** *m.* roof
**tomate** *f.* tomato (6)
**tombe** *f.* tomb, grave
**tomber** to fall (9); **tomber amoureux/euse (de)** to fall in love (with) (13); **tomber bien** to be lucky, a lucky coincidence; **tomber en panne** to have a (*mechanical*) breakdown (9); **tomber malade** to become ill
**ton** *adj. m. s., fam.* your
**tonton** *m., tr. fam.* uncle
**tonus** *m.* muscle tone
**tort** *m.* wrong; **avoir tort** to be wrong (4)
**tôt** *adv.* early (6); **il est tôt** it's early
**toucher (à)** to touch; to concern (11); **toucher à sa fin** to near its end; **toucher un chèque** to cash a check (11)
**toujours** *adv.* always (2); still
**tour** *f.* tower (11); *m.* walk, ride (5); turn; tour; trick; **à son (votre) tour** in his/her (your) turn; **à tour de rôle** in turn, by turns; **faire le tour de** to go around, take a tour of; **faire un tour** to take a walk, ride (5)

**tourisme** *m.* tourism; **faire du tourisme** to go sightseeing
**touriste** *m., f.* tourist
**touristique** *adj.* tourist
**tourmenté** *adj.* uneasy; tortured
**tourner (à)** to turn, turn into (11); **tourner un film** to make, shoot a movie
**Toussaint** *f.* All Saints' Day (*November 1*)
**tout(e)** (*pl.* **tous, toutes**) *adj., pron.* all; every (10); everything (9); each; any; **tout** *adv.* wholly, entirely, quite, very, all; **à tout à l'heure** bye, see you later (4); **à tout moment** at any time, moment; **en tout** altogether; **(ne...) pas du tout** not at all (5); **tous (toutes) les deux** both (of them); **tous les jours** every day (5); **tous les matins** every morning (10); **tout à coup** suddenly; **tout à l'heure** in a while; a while ago (5); **tout de suite** immediately (5); **tout droit** *adv.* straight ahead (11); **tout d'un coup** at once, all at once (11); **toutes les semaines** every week (10); **tout le monde** everybody, everyone (9); **tout le temps** all the time; **tout(e) seul(e)** all alone; **tout va bien** everything is going well
**toutefois** *adv.* however, nevertheless
**trace** *f.* trace; impression; footprint
**tracer (nous traçons)** to draw; to trace out
**traditionaliste** *adj.* traditionalistic
**traditionnel(le)** *adj.* traditional
**traduction** *f.* translation
**traduire** (*like* **conduire**) *irreg.* to translate (9)
**trafic** *m.* traffic; trade
**tragédie** *f.* tragedy
**train** *m.* train (9); **billet** (*m.*) **de train** train ticket; **en train** by train; **être en train de** to be in the process of (15)
**trait** *m.* trait, characteristic
**traité** *m.* treaty; *adj.* treated
**traitement** *m.* treatment; **traitement de texte** word processing
**traiter** to treat
**traiteur** *m.* caterer, deli owner
**tranche** *f.* slice (7); block, slab
**tranché** *adj.* sliced, cut out
**tranquille** *adj.* quiet, calm (4)
**tranquillité** *f.* tranquility; calm
**transformer** to transform; to change
**transmettre** (*like* **mettre**) *irreg.* to transmit, pass on
**transport(s)** *m.* transportation (16); **moyen** (*m.*) **de transport** means of transportation; **transports** (*m. pl.*) **en commun, publics** public transportation
**transporter** to carry, transport
**travail** (*pl.* **travaux**) *m.* work (2); project; job; employment; *pl.* public works
**travailler** to work (2); **travailler dur** to work hard
**travailleur/euse** *m., f.* worker (14); *adj.* hardworking (3); **travailleur/euse indépendant(e)** self-employed worker (14); **travailleur/euse salarié(e)** salaried worker (14)
**travers: à travers** *prep.* through
**traverser** to cross (9)
**treize** *adj.* thirteen (1)
**treizième** *adj.* thirteenth
**tréma** *m.* diæresis, umlaut (**ë**)
**tremblement** *m.* shaking, trembling; **tremblement de terre** earthquake
**trentaine** *f.* around thirty
**trente** *adj.* thirty (1)
**très** *adv.* very (3); most; very much; **très bien** very well (good) (1); **très bien, merci** very well, thank you
**trésorier/ière** *m., f.* treasurer
**trêve** *f.* respite, intermission; truce
**tribunal** *m.* tribunal; court of justice
**tricoter** to knit
**trilingue** *adj.* trilingual
**tripler** to triple
**triste** *adj.* sad
**trois** *adj.* three (1)
**troisième** *adj.* third
**tromper** to deceive; **se tromper (de)** to be mistaken, make a mistake (12)
**trompette** *f.* trumpet
**tronche** *f., tr. fam.* head; **faire une drôle de tronche** to act funny, odd
**trop (de)** *adv.* too much (of) (6); too many (of); **beaucoup trop** much too much
**trottoir** *m.* sidewalk
**trou** *m.* hole
**trouble** *m.* disturbance; trouble
**trouille** *f., fam.* stage fright
**trouver** to find (2); to deem; to like; **se trouver** to be; to be located (11)
**truite** *f.* trout
**tu** *pron., s., fam.* you
**tuer** to kill
**tune** *f., tr. fam.* money
**Tunisie** *f.* Tunisia (8)
**type** *m.* type; *fam.* guy
**typique** *adj.* typical
**typographe** *m., f.* typographer
**tzigane** *m., f., adj.* gypsy

**un(e)** *art., adj., pron.* one (1); **un(e) autre** another (17); **un jour** some day (14); **un peu** a little (3); **une fois** once (11); **une fois par semaine** once a week (5)
**uni** *adj.* plain (*material*); united; close; **États-Unis** *m. pl.* United States
**unifié** *adj.* unified, in agreement
**union** *f.* union; marriage; **union libre** living together, common-law marriage
**unique** *adj.* only, sole; **enfant** (*m.*) **unique** only child
**unir** to unite
**unité** *f.* unity; unit; department
**universel(le)** *adj.* universal
**universitaire** *adj.* (*of or belonging to the*) university; **cité** (*f.*) **universitaire** (*fam.* **cité-u**) student residence complex (2)
**université** *f.* university (2)
**urbain** *adj.* urban, city
**urgent** *adj.* urgent; **il est urgent que** + *subj.* it's urgent that (16)
**usage** *m.* use; usage
**user** to use (up); **user de** to use
**usine** *f.* factory
**utile** *adj.* useful (16)
**utilisation** *f.* utilization, use
**utiliser** to use, utilize

**vacances** *f. pl.* vacation (5); **partir (aller) en vacances** to leave on vacation; **pendant les vacances** during vacation (5)
**vacancier/ière** *m., f.* vacationer
**vaccin** *m.* vaccine
**vachement** *adv., fam.* very, tremendously
**vagabonder** to wander, roam
**vainqueur** *m.* winner
**vaisselle** *f.* dishes (5); **faire la vaisselle** to wash, do the dishes (5)
**val** *m.* valley
**valable** *adj.* valid, good
**Valentin: Saint-Valentin** *f.* Valentine's Day
**valeur** *f.* value; worth; **taxe** (*f.*) **à valeur ajoutée** value-added tax
**valise** *f.* suitcase (9); **faire les valises** to pack one's bags
**vallée** *f.* valley

**valoir** (*p.p.* **valu**) *irreg.* to be worth (16); **il vaut mieux que** + *subj.* it is better that (16)
**vanille** *f.* vanilla
**vaniteux/euse** *m., f.* vain, haughty person
**varier** to vary; to change
**variété** *f.* variety; *pl.* variety show; **chanson** (*f.*) **de variété** popular song (15)
**vaste** *adj.* vast; wide, broad
**va-t-en!** *fam.* get going, go away! (13)
**vaudou** *m.* voodoo (17)
**veau** *m.* veal; calf
**vécu** *adj.* lived; real-life
**vedette** *f.* star, celebrity (*m.* or *f.*)
**végétarien(ne)** *m., f., adj.* vegetarian
**véhicule** *m.* vehicle
**veille** *f.* the day (evening) before; eve
**vélo** *m., fam.* bike; **en vélo** by bike; **faire du vélo** to go cycling (5)
**vendange** *f.* grape harvest
**vendanger (nous vendangeons)** to harvest grapes
**vendeur/euse** *m., f.* salesperson
**vendre** to sell (5)
**vendredi** *m.* Friday (1)
**venir** (*p.p.* **venu**) *irreg.* to come (8); **venir de** + *inf.* to have just (*done s.th.*) (8)
**vent** *m.* wind (6); **faire du vent (il fait du vent)** to be windy (it's windy) (6)
**vente** *f.* sale; selling; **en vente** for sale
**ventre** *m.* abdomen, belly (13)
**venu(e)** *m., f.* comer, arrival; *adj.* arrived
**ver** *m.* worm, earthworm
**verbe** *m.* verb; language
**verdure** *f.* greenery, foliage
**vérifier** to verify
**véritable** *adj.* true; real
**vérité** *f.* truth
**verlan** *m.* *type of French student slang*
**verre** *m.* glass (6); **prendre un verre** *fam.* to have a drink; **un verre de** a glass of
**vers** *prep.* around, about (*with time expressions*) (6); toward(s), to; about; *m.* line (*of poetry*)
**versement** *m.* (*bank*) deposit, payment
**verser** to pour (in); to deposit
**version** *f.* version; **en version originale** original version, not dubbed (*movie*)
**vert** *adj.* green (3); (*politically*) "green"; ***haricots** (*m. pl.*) **verts** green beans (6)
**veste** *f.* sports coat, blazer (3)
**veston** *m.* suit jacket (3)
**vêtement** *m.* garment; *pl.* clothes, clothing
**vétérinaire** *m., f.* veterinary, veterinarian
**viande** *f.* meat (6)
**victime** *f.* victim (*m.* or *f.*)
**vide** *adj.* empty
**vidéo** *f., fam.* video (cassette); *adj.* video; **caméra** (*f.*) **vidéo** videocamera
**vie** *f.* life (2); **coût** (*m.*) **de la vie** cost of living (14)
**vieillir** to grow old
**vieillissement** *m.* aging
**vierge** *adj.* virgin; **forêt** (*f.*) **vierge** virgin forest
**vieux (vieil, vieille)** *adj.* old (7); **le bon vieux temps** the good old days
**vigoureux/euse** *adj.* vigorous, strong
**villa** *f.* bungalow; single-family house; villa
**villageois(e)** *m., f., adj.* villager
**ville** *f.* city (2); **centre-ville** *m.* downtown (11); **en ville** in town, downtown
**vin** *m.* wine (6); **marchand(e)** (*m., f.*) **de vin** wine seller (14)
**vingt** *adj.* twenty (1); **vingt et un (vingt-deux...** ) *adj.* twenty-one (twenty-two . . . ) (1)
**vingtaine** *f.* about twenty
**vingtième** *adj.* twentieth
**violet(te)** *adj.* purple, violet (3); *m.* violet (*color*); *f.* violet (*flower*)
**violon** *m.* violin
**vis-à-vis (de)** *adv.* opposite, facing; towards
**visa** *m.* visa; signature
**visage** *m.* face (13)
**viser** to aim at
**visite** *f.* visit (2); **rendre visite à** to visit (*people*) (5)
**visiter** to visit (*a place*) (2)
**visiteur/euse** *m., f.* visitor
**vite** *adv.* quickly, fast, rapidly
**vitesse** *f.* speed; **Train** (*m.*) **à Grande Vitesse (TGV)** (*French high-speed*) bullet train
**viticulteur/trice** *m., f.* grape grower
**vitrail** (*pl.* **vitraux**) *m.* stained-glass window
**vitrine** *f.* display window, store window
**vivant** *adj.* living; alive
**vivre** (*p.p.* **vécu**) *irreg.* to live (12); **vive... !** hurrah for . . . !
**vocabulaire** *m.* vocabulary
**vœux** *m. pl.* wishes, good wishes
**vogue** *f.* fashion, vogue
**voici** *prep.* here is/are (1)
**voie** *f.* way, road; course; lane; railroad track; **pays** (*m.*) **en voie de développement** developing nation
**voilà** *prep.* there is/are (1)
**voile** *f.* sail (5); **bateau** (*m.*) **à voile** sailboat (8); **faire de la voile** to sail (5); **planche** (*f.*) **à voile** windsurfing (8)
**voir** (*p.p.* **vu**) *irreg.* to see (8)
**voisin(e)** *m., f.* neighbor (8)
**voiture** *f.* car (3)
**voix** *f.* voice; vote
**vol** *m.* flight (9); burglary, theft
**volaille** *f.* poultry, fowl
**volcan** *m.* volcano
**voler** to fly; to steal
**volet** *m.* shutter (*window*)
**voleur/euse** *m., f.* thief
**volley-ball** (*fam.* **volley**) *m.* volleyball; **jouer au volley** to play volleyball
**volontaire** *m., f., adj.* volunteer
**volonté** *f.* will, willingness
**volontiers** *adv.* willingly, gladly
**voter** to vote
**votre** *adj., m., f.* your
**vôtre(s) (le/la/les)** *pron., m., f.* yours; *pl.* your close friends, relatives
**vouloir** (*p.p.* **voulu**) *irreg.* to wish, want (7); **que veut dire... ?** what does . . . mean? (7); **vouloir bien** to be willing (7); **vouloir dire** to mean (7)
**vous** *pron.* you; yourself; to you; **chez vous** where you live; **et vous?** and you? (1); **s'il vous plaît** please; **vous-même** *pron.* yourself
**voûte** *f.* vault, arch; **clé** (*f.*) **de voûte** keystone (*architecture*)
**voyage** *m.* trip (5); **agence** (*f.*) **de voyages** travel agency; **chèque** (*m.*) **de voyage** traveler's check; **faire un voyage** to take a trip (5)
**voyager (nous voyageons)** to travel (8)
**voyageur/euse** *m., f.* traveler
**voyant(e)** *m., f.* fortune teller, medium
**vrai** *adj.* true, real (7)
**vraiment** *adv.* truly, really (12)
**vraisemblable** *adj.* plausible, believable
**vue** *f.* view; panorama; sight; **à première vue** at first glance; **point** (*m.*) **de vue** point of view

**wagon** *m.* train car (9); **wagon-lit** *m.* sleeping car; **wagon-restaurant** *m.* dining car

**week-end** *m.* weekend (5); **ce week-end** this weekend (5); **le week-end** on weekends (5)

**y** *pron.* there (11); **il y a** there is (are) (1); ago (8); **il n'y a pas de...** there isn't (aren't) . . . ; **qu'est-ce qu'il y a dans... ?** what's in . . . ?; **y a-t-il... ?** is (are) there . . .?

**yaourt** *m.* yoghurt
**yeux** (*m. pl.* of **œil**) eyes (4)

**Zaïre** *m.* Zaire (8)
**zèbre** *m.* zebra
**zodiac** *m.* rubber raft
**zone** *f.* zone, area; **zone fumeurs (non-fumeurs)** smoking, nonsmoking area (9)
**zoologique** *adj.* zoological; **jardin** (*m.*) **zoologique** zoological gardens, zoo
**zut!** *interj.* darn! drat!
**zydéco: musique** (*f.*) **zydéco** Cajun country music (*name derived from* **les haricots**)

# Lexique anglais-français

This English-French end vocabulary includes the words in the active vocabulary lists of all chapters. See the introduction to the *Lexique français-anglais* for a list of abbreviations used.

**abdomen** ventre *m.*
**able: to be able** pouvoir
**abolish** abolir
**about** (*with time*) vers
**abroad** à l'étranger
**Acadia** Acadie *f.*
**Acadian** acadien(ne)
**accept** accepter (de)
**accident** accident *m.*
**accomplishment** réussite *f.*
**according to** suivant
**account** compte *m.*; **checking account** compte-chèques *m.*; **savings account** compte d'épargne
**accountant** comptable *m., f.*
**across from** en face de
**act** agir
**activities (leisure)** loisirs *m. pl.*
**actor, actress** acteur *m.*, actrice *f.*
**address** adresse *f.*
**adore** adorer
**ads (classified)** petites annonces *f. pl.*
**advertisement, advertising** publicité *f.*
**advice** conseil *m.*
**advise (to)** conseiller (à)
**aerobics** aérobic *f.*; **to do aerobics** faire de l'aérobic
**afraid: to be afraid of** avoir peur de
**after** après
**afternoon** après-midi *m.*; **afternoon snack** goûter *m.*; **in the afternoon** de l'après-midi; **this afternoon** cet après-midi
**afterward** après
**again** de nouveau
**age: Middle Ages** moyen âge *m.*
**ago** il y a
**agreeable** agréable
**agreed** d'accord
**ahead: straight ahead** tout droit
**airplane** avion *m.*
**airport** aéroport *m.*
**alarm clock** réveil *m.*
**Algeria** Algérie *f.*
**all** tout, toute, tous, toutes; **not at all** ne... pas du tout
**allow (to)** permettre (de)
**almost** presque
**already** déjà
**also** aussi
**always** toujours
**American** (*person*) Américain(e) *m., f.*
**amount** montant *m.*
**amusing** amusant(e)
**ancestor** ancêtre *m., f.*
**and** et; **and you?** et vous? (et toi?)
**angry** fâché(e); **to get angry** se fâcher
**another** un(e) autre
**answer** répondre à; **answering machine** répondeur (*m.*) téléphonique
**Antilles** (*islands*) Antilles *f. pl.*
**antique** ancien(ne)
**apartment** appartement *m.*
**appetizer** *hors-d'œuvre *m.*
**apple** pomme *f.*
**appointment: to have an appointment** avoir rendez-vous
**approximately** environ
**April** avril
**architect** architecte *m., f.*
**area: smoking, nonsmoking area** zone (*f.*) (non-)fumeurs
**arena** arènes *f. pl.*
**argue** se disputer
**arm** bras *m.*
**around** (*with time*) vers
**arrival** arrivée *f.*
**arrive** arriver
**art (work of)** œuvre (*f.*) (d'art)
**artisan** artisan(e) *m., f.*
**artist** artiste *m., f.*
**as . . . as** aussi... que; **as much/many . . . as** autant (de)... que; **as soon as** dès que, aussitôt que
**ashamed: to be ashamed** avoir honte
**ask (for)** demander
**asleep: to fall asleep** s'endormir
**at** à
**athletic** sportif/ive
**atmosphere** atmosphère *f.*
**attend** assister à
**attendant (flight)** hôtesse (*f.*) de l'air; steward *m.*
**August** août
**aunt** tante *f.*
**automatic teller** distributeur (*m.*) automatique
**autumn** automne *m.*; **in autumn** en automne
**average** moyen(ne); **average height** de taille moyenne
**awaken** se réveiller
**awful** affreux/euse

**backpack** sac (*m.*) à dos
**bad** mauvais(e) *adj.*; **bad(ly)** mal *adv.*; **it's bad (out)** il fait mauvais; **not bad(ly)** pas mal; **things are going badly** ça va mal; **to feel bad** aller mal; **too bad** dommage *interj.*
**bag: sleeping bag** sac (*m.*) de couchage
**bakery** boulangerie *f.*
**balcony** balcon *m.*
**ball: bocce ball** pétanque *f.*; **masked ball** bal (*m.*) masqué
**bank** banque *f.*; **bank (ATM) card** carte (*f.*) bancaire; **the Left Bank** (*in Paris*) Rive (*f.*) gauche; **the Right Bank** (*in Paris*) Rive (*f.*) droite
**bar-tobacconist** café-tabac *m.*
**bathe** se baigner
**bathroom** salle (*f.*) de bains; **bathroom sink** lavabo *m.*
**be** être; **here is/are** voici; **how are you?** comment allez-vous?; **is/are there . . . ?** il y a... ?; **there is/are** il y a; voilà;

**to be in the middle (the process) of** être en train de
**beach** plage *f.*; **beach towel** serviette (*f.*) de plage
**beans: green beans** *haricots (*m. pl.*) verts
**beautiful** beau, bel, belle (beaux, belles)
**because** parce que
**become** devenir
**bed** lit *m.*; **to go to bed** se coucher
**beer** bière *f.*
**begin** commencer; **to begin by** (*doing s. th.*) commencer par; **to begin to** (*do s. th.*) se mettre à + *inf.*
**behind** derrière
**Belgium** Belgique *f.*
**believe** croire; estimer; **to believe in** croire à; **to believe that** croire que
**berth** couchette *f.*
**beside** à côté de
**best** le mieux (*adv*); le/la/les meilleur(e)(s) (*adj.*)
**better** meilleur(e) *adj.*; mieux *adv.*; **it is better that** il vaut mieux que + *subj.*
**between** entre
**beverage** boisson *f.*
**bicycle** bicyclette *f.*
**big** grand(e)
**bill** addition (*restaurant*) *f.*; billet (*currency*) *m.*
**biology** biologie *f.*
**black** noir(e)
**blackboard** tableau (noir) *m.*
**blazer** veste *f.*
**blond(e)** blond(e)
**blouse** chemisier *m.*
**blue** bleu(e)
**boarding pass** carte (*f.*) d'embarquement
**bocce ball** pétanque *f.*
**body** corps *m.*
**book** livre *m.*; **telephone book** annuaire *m.*
**bookshelf** étagère *f.*
**bookstore** librairie *f.*
**booth (telephone)** cabine (*f.*) téléphonique
**boots** bottes *f. pl.*; **hiking boots** chaussures (*f. pl.*) de montagne; **ski boots** chaussures (*f. pl.*) de ski
**bore: to be bored** s'ennuyer
**boring** ennuyeux/euse
**born: to be born** naître
**borrow (from)** emprunter (à)
**boss** chef (*m.*) d'entreprise
**bottle** bouteille *f.*
**boulevard** boulevard *m.*
**bowling (lawn)** pétanque *f.*
**brave** courageux/euse
**Brazil** Brésil *m.*
**bread** pain *m.*; **loaf of bread** baguette (*f.*) de pain
**breakfast** petit déjeuner *m.*
**bring** apporter; **to bring** (*a person somewhere*) amener
**broadcast** émission *f.*; retransmettre *v.*
**brother-in-law** beau-frère *m.*
**brown** châtain(s) (*hair*); marron
**brush (hair, teeth)** se brosser (les cheveux, les dents)
**budget** budget *m.*
**build** bâtir
**building** bâtiment *m.*; immeuble (*office, apartment*) *m.*
**bus** autobus *m.*
**business class** classe (*f.*) affaires
**but** mais
**butcher** boucher/ère *m., f.*; **butcher shop** boucherie *f.*; **pork butcher** charcuterie *f.*
**buy** acheter

**café** café *m.*
**Cajun** acadien(ne)
**cake** gâteau *m.*
**call** appeler; **telephone calling card** télécarte *f.*; **who's calling?** qui est à l'appareil?
**calm** calme; tranquille
**camping** camping *m.*
**can** (*to be able*) pouvoir; **can (of food)** boîte (*f.*) (de conserve)
**Canada** Canada *m.*
**car** voiture *f.*; **train car** wagon *m.*
**carafe** carafe *f.*
**cards** cartes *f. pl.*; **bank (ATM) card** carte bancaire; **credit card** carte de crédit
**careful: to be careful** faire attention
**Caribbean Islands** Antilles *f. pl.*
**Caribbean Sea** mer (*f.*) des Caraïbes (des Antilles)
**Carnival** Carnaval *m.*
**carrier (letter)** facteur *m.*
**carrot** carotte *f.*
**carry** apporter; porter
**case: in that case** alors
**cash** argent (*m.*) liquide; **to cash (a check)** toucher (un chèque)
**cassette player** lecteur (*m.*) de cassettes; **cassette tape** cassette *f.*
**castle** château *m.*
**cathedral** cathédrale *f.*
**CD player** lecteur (*m.*) de CD
**celebrate** fêter
**cent** (*1/100th of a franc*) centime *m.*
**century** siècle *m.*
**certain** certain(e); sûr(e)
**chair** chaise *f.*
**chance: games of chance** jeux (*m. pl.*) de hasard
**change** monnaie *f.*
**channel** (*television*) chaîne *f.*
**chateau** château *m.*
**check** addition (*restaurant*) *f.*; chèque (*bank*) *m.*; **checkbook** carnet (*m.*) de chèques; **checking account** compte-chèques *m.*; **to write a check** faire un chèque
**cheese** fromage *m.*
**chemistry** chimie *f.*
**chess** échecs *m. pl.*
**chest (of drawers)** commode *f.*
**chicken** poulet *m.*
**child** enfant *m., f.*
**China** Chine *f.*
**Chinese** (*person*) Chinois(e) *m., f.*
**chocolate** chocolat *m.*
**choice** choix *m.*
**choose** choisir
**chop** côte *f.*
**church** (*Catholic*) église *f.*
**citizen** citoyen(ne) *m., f.*
**city** ville *f.*
**civil servant** fonctionnaire *m., f.*
**class (business)** classe (*f.*) affaires; **tourist class** classe économique
**classical** classique
**classified ads** petites annonces *f. pl.*
**classroom** salle (*f.*) de classe
**clean** propre
**clear** clair(e)
**climb** monter
**clock (alarm)** réveil *m.*
**close** fermer
**close to** près de
**coat** manteau *m.*; **sports coat** veste *f.*
**coffee (cup of)** un café *m.*
**coin** pièce *f.*; **coins** monnaie *f.*
**cold** froid *m.*; **it's cold** il fait froid; **to be cold** avoir froid
**collection** collection *f.*
**colonize** coloniser
**comb** peigne *m.*; **to comb one's hair** se peigner
**come** venir; **to come back** (*someplace*) revenir

**commercial** publicité *f.*
**company** entreprise *f.*; société *f.*; **company head** chef (*m.*) d'entreprise
**compartment** (*train*) compartiment *m.*
**composer** compositeur/trice *m., f.*
**computer** ordinateur *m.*; **computer science** informatique *f.*
**concern** toucher
**conflict** conflit *m.*
**conformist** conformiste
**Congo** Congo *m.*
**conservation** conservation *f.*
**conserve** conserver
**consider** estimer
**constantly** constamment
**construct** construire
**continue** continuer
**contrary: on the contrary** au contraire
**control** contrôle *m.*
**cooking** cuisine *f.*; **to cook** faire la cuisine
**cool** frais (fraîche); **it's cool** il fait frais
**corner** coin *m.*
**cost of living** coût (*m.*) de la vie
**costume** costume *m.*; **costume party** bal (*m.*) masqué
**country** (*nation*) pays *m.*; **country(side)** campagne *f.*
**courageous** courageux/euse
**course** (*academic*) cours *m.*; **course** (*meal*) plat *m.*; **first course** entrée *f.*; **of course (not)** bien sûr que oui (non)
**cousin** cousin(e) *m., f.*
**cover** couvrir
**craftsperson** artisan(e) *m., f.*
**crayfish** écrevisse *f.*
**cream** crème *f.*; **ice cream** glace *f.*
**create** créer
**credit card** carte (*f.*) de crédit
**croissant** croissant *m.*
**cross** traverser; **cross-country skiing** ski (*m.*) de randonnée; ski de fond
**cup** tasse *f.*; **cup of coffee** un café *m.*; **wide cup** bol *m.*
**curly** frisé(e)
**curtains** rideaux *m. pl.*
**cute** chouette
**cycling** cyclisme *m.*; vélo *m.*; **to go cycling** faire du vélo

**daily** quotidien(ne)
**dance** danser
**date (from)** dater (de)
**daughter** fille *f.*
**day** jour *m.*; **entire day** journée *f.*; **every day** tous les jours; **the day before yesterday** avant-hier; **what day is it?** quel jour sommes-nous?
**dear** cher (chère)
**decade: the decade of (the fifties)** les années (cinquante) *f. pl.*
**December** décembre
**decide (to)** décider (de)
**decrease** diminution *f.*
**delay** retard *m.*
**deli** charcuterie *f.*
**delightful** génial(e)
**deliver** remettre
**demand** exiger
**demonstrate (for, against)** manifester (pour, contre)
**dentist** dentiste *m., f.*
**departure** départ *m.*
**deposit** déposer
**describe** décrire
**desire** désirer
**desk** bureau *m.*
**dessert** dessert *m.*
**destroy** détruire
**detest** détester
**develop** développer
**development** développement *m.*
**dial (a number)** composer (un numéro)
**dictionary** dictionnaire *m.*
**die** mourir
**different** différent(e)
**difficult** difficile
**difficulty: to have difficulty (in)** avoir du mal (à)
**dine** dîner
**dining room** salle (*f.*) à manger
**dinner** dîner *m.*; **to have dinner** dîner
**direct** diriger
**disagreeable** désagréable
**discover** découvrir
**disguise oneself** se déguiser
**dishes** vaisselle *f.*; **to do the dishes** faire la vaisselle
**district** quartier *m.*; arrondissement *m.*
**division** (*academic*) faculté *f.*
**divorced** divorcé(e)
**do** faire
**doctor** médecin (femme médecin) *m., f.*
**dog** chien(ne) *m., f.*
**door** porte *f.*
**doubt** douter
**downhill skiing** ski (*m.*) de piste
**downtown** centre-ville *m.*
**drawers (chest of)** commode *f.*
**dream** rêver
**dress** robe *f.*; **to dress up in disguise** se déguiser; **to get dressed** s'habiller
**drink** boisson *f.*; **to drink** boire
**drive** conduire
**driver** conducteur/trice *m., f.*
**drugstore** pharmacie *f.*
**during** pendant
**dynamic** dynamique

**each (one)** chacun(e) *pron.*; chaque *adj.*
**ear** oreille *f.*
**early** de bonne heure; tôt
**earn** gagner
**east** est *m.*; **to the east** à l'est
**easy** facile
**eat** manger; **I like to eat** je suis gourmand(e)
**eccentric** excentrique
**eclair** éclair (*pastry*) *m.*
**ecological** écologique
**egg** œuf *m.*
**eight** *huit
**eighteen** dix-huit
**elect** élire
**eleven** onze
**employee** employé(e) *m., f.*; **s.o. employed (by)** employé(e) (de)
**encounter** rencontre *f.*
**end by** (*doing s.th.*) finir par
**energy** énergie *f.*; **nuclear energy** énergie nucléaire; **solar energy** énergie solaire
**engagement** fiançailles *f. pl.*
**engineer** ingénieur *m.*
**England** Angleterre *f.*
**English** (*person*) Anglais(e) *m., f.*; **English-speaking** anglophone
**enough** assez de
**enter** entrer
**enthusiastic** enthousiaste
**envelope** enveloppe *f.*
**environment** environnement *m.*
**era: the era of (the fifties)** les années (cinquante) *f. pl.*
**errands** courses *f. pl.*; **to do errands** faire les courses
**especially** surtout
**essential** essentiel(le)
**establishment: at the establishment of** chez
**estimate** estimer
**even** même
**evening** soir *m.*; **entire evening** soirée *f.*; **good evening** bonsoir; **in the evening** du soir; **Monday/Friday evenings** le lundi/le vendredi soir; **this evening** ce soir *m.*

**event** événement *m.*; **sports event** manifestation (*f.*) sportive
**every** tout, toute, tous, toutes; **every day** tous les jours; **every one** chacun(e) *pron.*; **every week** toutes les semaines
**everyday** quotidien(ne)
**everyone** tout le monde
**everything** tout
**everywhere** partout
**evident** évident(e)
**exam** examen *m.*; **to take an exam** passer un examen
**example: for example** par exemple
**exchange rate** cours *m.*; **money exchange (office)** bureau (*m.*) de change
**excuse (oneself)** s'excuser; **excuse me** excusez-moi
**expense** dépense *f.*; frais *m. pl.*
**expensive** cher (chère)
**express (an opinion)** exprimer (une opinion)
**expression: freedom of expression** liberté (*f.*) d'expression
**eye** œil *m.* (*pl.* yeux)

**face** visage *m.*
**fair** juste
**fall** automne *m.*; tomber
**false** faux (fausse)
**familiar: to be familiar with** connaître
**family** famille *f.*
**far from** loin de
**farmer** agriculteur/trice *m., f.*
**father-in-law** beau-père *m.*
**favor** service *m.*; **to do a favor** faire un petit service
**favorite** préféré(e)
**February** février
**feel** sentir; **to feel bad** aller mal
**few: a few** quelques
**fifteen** quinze
**fifth** cinquième
**fifty** cinquante
**fill it up** faire le plein
**fillet** (*beef, fish*) filet *m.*
**film** film *m.*
**filmmaker** cinéaste *m., f.*
**finally** enfin
**find** trouver
**fine** bien; ça va bien
**finger** doigt *m.*
**finish** finir (de); **to finish by** (*doing s.th.*) finir par
**first** d'abord *adv.*; premier/ière *adj.*; **first of all** d'abord
**fish** poisson *m.*; **fish store** poissonnerie *f.*; **fishing** pêche *f.*; **to fish** pêcher
**five** cinq
**fixed price menu** menu *m.*
**flash of lightning** coup (*m.*) de foudre
**flight** vol *m.*; **flight attendant** hôtesse (*f.*) de l'air; steward *m.*
**float** (*parade*) char *m.*
**floor (ground)** rez-de-chaussée *m.*; **second floor** premier étage *m.*; **third floor** deuxième étage *m.*
**flower** fleur *f.*
**fluently** couramment
**follow** suivre
**food** cuisine *f.*
**foot** pied *m.*
**for** depuis; pour; **for example** par exemple
**foreign: in a foreign country** à l'étranger; **foreign language** langue (*f.*) étrangère
**foreigner** étranger/ère *m., f.*
**forest** bois *m.*; forêt *f.*
**forget (to)** oublier (de)
**fork** fourchette *f.*
**formerly** autrefois
**fortunate** heureux/euse
**forty** quarante
**found: to be found** se trouver
**four** quatre
**fourteen** quatorze
**fourth** quart *m.*
**franc** franc (*currency*) *m.*
**France** France *f.*
**freedom (of expression)** liberté (*f.*) (d'expression)
**French** (*person*) Français(e) *m., f.*; **french fries** frites *f. pl.*; **French-speaking** francophone
**fresh** frais (fraîche)
**Friday** vendredi *m.*
**friend** ami(e) *m., f.*
**fries** frites *f. pl.*
**from** de
**front: in front of** devant
**fruit** fruit *m.*; **fruit juice** jus (*m.*) de fruit
**fun** amusant(e); **to have fun** s'amuser (à)
**funny** drôle
**furious** furieux/euse
**furniture (piece of)** meuble *m.*
**future** avenir *m.*; **in the future** à l'avenir

**game (of chance)** jeu (*m.*) (de hasard); **group, social games** jeux (*pl.*) de société
**garden** jardin *m.*
**gardening** jardinage *m.*
**generally** en général
**geography** géographie *f.*
**geology** géologie *f.*
**German** (*person*) Allemand(e) *m., f.*
**Germany** Allemagne *f.*
**get** obtenir; **get going!** va-t-en!; **to get along (with)** s'entendre (avec); **to get off of, down from** descendre (de); **to get up** se lever
**girl** jeune fille *f.*
**give** donner; **to give back** rendre
**glass** verre *m.*; **(eye)glasses** lunettes *f. pl.*
**gloves (ski)** gants (*m. pl.*) (de ski)
**go: to go** aller; **go away! get going!** allez-vous-en! (va-t-en!); **how's it going?** ça va?; **to be going** (*to do s.th.*) aller + *inf.*; **to go back** retourner; **to go down** descendre; **to go home** rentrer; **to go off** s'en aller; **to go out** sortir (de); **to go to** se rendre à; **to go up** monter; **what's going on?** qu'est-ce qui se passe?
**goggles: ski goggles** lunettes (*f. pl.*) de ski
**good** bien *adv.*; bon(ne) *adj.*; **good-bye** au revoir; **good-day** bonjour; **good evening** bonsoir
**Gothic** gothique
**government** gouvernement *m.*
**grandchild** petit-enfant *m.*
**granddaughter** petite-fille *f.*
**grandfather** grand-père *m.*
**grandmother** grand-mère *f.*
**grandparents** grands-parents *m. pl.*
**grandson** petit-fils *m.*
**gray** gris(e)
**great** formidable
**great-grandparent** arrière-grand-parent *m.*
**Greece** Grèce *f.*
**green** vert(e); **green beans** *haricots (*m. pl.*) verts
**grocery store** épicerie *f.*
**ground: on the ground** par terre; **ground floor** rez-de-chaussée *m.*
**group games** jeux (*m. pl.*) de société
**Guadeloupe** Guadeloupe *f.*

**habitually** d'habitude
**hair** cheveux *m. pl.*
**hairdresser** coiffeur/euse *m., f.*
**Haiti** Haïti *m.*
**half** demi(e); **half brother** demi-frère *m.*; **half past** (*the hour*) et demi(e); **half sister** demi-sœur *f.*

**hall** couloir *m.*; **lecture hall** amphithéâtre *m.*; **town hall** mairie *f.*
**ham** jambon *m.*
**hand** main *f.*
**handbag** sac (*m.*) à main
**handsome** beau, bel, belle (beaux, belles)
**happen** se passer; **what's happening?** qu'est-ce qui se passe?
**happy** content(e); heureux/euse
**hardly** peu
**hardworking** travailleur/euse
**hat** chapeau *m.*
**have** avoir; **to have** (to eat) prendre; **to have to** devoir
**head** directeur/trice *m., f.*; tête *f.*; **company head** chef (*m.*) d'entreprise
**health** santé *f.*
**hear** entendre
**heavy** lourd(e)
**height: average height** de taille moyenne
**hello** bonjour; **hello** (*telephone*) allô
**help** aider
**here** ici; **here is/are** voici
**hi!** salut!
**high** élevé(e)
**highway** autoroute *f.*
**hike** randonnée *f.*; **hiking boots** chaussures (*f. pl.*) de montagne
**hilarious** marrant(e)
**hire** embaucher; **hiring** embauche *f.*
**historical** historique
**history** histoire *f.*
**hobby** passe-temps *m.*
**holiday** fête *f.*
**home** foyer *m.*; maison *f.*; **at the home of** chez; **to go home** rentrer
**homework** devoirs *m. pl.*; **to do homework** faire ses devoirs
**hope** espérer
**horse** cheval *m.*
**hospitable** accueillant(e)
**hospital** hôpital *m.*
**hot** chaud; **it's hot** il fait chaud; **to be hot** avoir chaud
**hotel** hôtel *m.*
**hour** heure *f.*; **quarter before the hour** moins le quart
**house** maison *f.*
**housework: to do the housework** faire le ménage
**how** comment; **how are you?** comment allez-vous?; **how many . . . ?** combien (de)... ?; **how's it going?** ça va?
**hungry: to be hungry** avoir faim
**hurry** se dépêcher
**hurt** avoir mal
**husband** mari *m.*

**ice cream** glace *f.*
**idealistic** idéaliste
**if** si
**immediately** tout de suite
**impatient** impatient(e)
**important** important(e)
**impossible** impossible
**in** à; en; dans; **in four days** dans quatre jours; **in the afternoon** de l'après-midi
**increase** augmentation *f.*
**indispensable** indispensable
**individualistic** individualiste
**industrial** industriel(le)
**inflation** inflation *f.*
**information: tourist information bureau** syndicat (*m.*) d'initiative
**inspect** contrôler
**instead** plutôt
**intellectual** intellectuel(le)
**intelligent** intelligent(e)
**interest** intéresser
**interesting** intéressant(e)
**interview (job)** entretien *m.*
**involve: to get involved (in)** s'engager (vers)
**island** île *f.*
**it's a . . .** c'est un(e)...
**Italian** (*person*) Italien(ne) *m., f.*
**Italy** Italie *f.*
**Ivory Coast** Côte-d'Ivoire *f.*

**jacket (ski)** anorak *m.*; **suit jacket** veston *m.*
**January** janvier
**Japan** Japon *m.*
**Japanese** (*person*) Japonais(e) *m., f.*
**jeans** jean *m.*
**jewel** bijou *m.*
**jog** faire du jogging
**juice (fruit)** jus (*m.*) de fruit
**July** juillet
**June** juin
**just** juste; **to have just done s.th.** venir de + *inf.*

**key** clé, clef *f.*
**kilo** kilogramme *m.*
**kiosk** kiosque *m.*
**kiss** s'embrasser
**kitchen** cuisine *f.*
**knee** genou *m.* (*pl.* genoux)
**knife** couteau *m.*
**know** connaître; **to know (how)** savoir

**lake** lac *m.*
**lamp** lampe *f.*
**language (foreign)** langue (*f.*) (étrangère)
**last** dernier/ière; passé(e)
**late** en retard; tard
**laugh** rire
**law** droit *m.*
**lawn bowling** pétanque *f.*
**lawyer** avocat(e) *m., f.*
**lazy** paresseux/euse
**learn** apprendre (à)
**leave (for, from)** partir (à, de); **to leave** (*behind*) laisser; **to leave** (*go out*) sortir; **to leave** (*s.o. or someplace*) quitter
**lecture** conférence *f.*; **lecture hall** amphithéâtre *m.*
**left: on the left** à gauche; **the Left Bank** (*in Paris*) Rive (*f.*) gauche
**leg** jambe *f.*
**legacy** patrimoine *m.*
**legalization** légalisation *f.*
**leisure (activities)** loisirs *m. pl.*
**lend (to)** prêter (à)
**less . . . than** moins... que
**letter** lettre *f.*; **letter carrier** facteur *m.*
**lettuce** salade *f.*
**library** bibliothèque *f.*
**life** vie *f.*
**lightning: flash of lightning** coup (*m.*) de foudre
**like** aimer; **I don't like . . . at all** je n'aime pas du tout...; **I would like** j'aimerais
**likely** probable
**linguistics** linguistique *f.*
**listen** écouter
**literature** littérature *f.*
**little: a little** un peu
**live** habiter; vivre
**living: cost of living** coût (*m.*) de la vie; **living room** salle (*f.*) de séjour
**loaf (of bread)** baguette (*f.*) (de pain)
**loan** emprunt *m.*
**locate: to be located** se trouver
**lodging** logement *m.*
**long** long(ue)
**longer: no longer** ne... plus
**look (at)** regarder; **to look (like)** avoir l'air (de); **to look at each other, at oneself** se regarder; **to look for** chercher

**lose** perdre; **to get lost** se perdre
**lot: a lot** beaucoup
**love** adorer; aimer; amour *m.*; **love at first sight** coup (*m.*) de foudre; **lover; loving** amoureux/euse *m., f.*; **to fall in love** tomber amoureux/euse
**lowering** baisse *f.*
**lucky: to be lucky** avoir de la chance
**lunch** déjeuner *m.*; **to have lunch** déjeuner

**ma'am** Madame (Mme)
**machine (answering)** répondeur (*m.*) téléphonique
**magazine** (*illustrated*) magazine *m.*
**magazine** (*journal*) revue *f.*
**magnificent** magnifique
**mailbox** boîte (*f.*) aux lettres
**makeup: to put on makeup** se maquiller
**man** homme *m.*; **young man** jeune homme *m.*
**manager** directeur/trice *m., f.*; **middle/upper manager** cadre *m.*; **top manager** chef (*m.*) d'entreprise
**many: how many . . . ?** combien (de)... ?
**map** plan (*city*) *m.*; carte (*region, country*) *f.*
**March** mars
**Mardi Gras** Mardi Gras
**market** marché *m.*; **to go to the market** faire le marché
**marriage** mariage *m.*
**married** marié(e); **to get married** se marier (avec)
**Martinique** Martinique *f.*
**masked ball** bal (*m.*) masqué
**masterpiece** chef-d'œuvre *m.*
**mathematics (math)** mathématiques (maths) *f. pl.*
**May** mai
**maybe** peut-être
**me: as for me** pour ma part
**meal** repas *m.*
**mean** vouloir dire; **what does . . . mean?** que veut dire... ?
**meat** viande *f.*
**media** médias *m. pl.*
**medieval** médiéval(e)
**meet** se rencontrer; **to meet (for the first time)** faire la connaissance de
**meeting** rencontre *f.*; **to have a meeting** avoir rendez-vous
**menu** carte *f.*; **fixed price menu** menu *m.*
**merchant (wine)** marchand(e) (*m., f.*) (de vin)
**messy** en désordre
**metro station** station (*f.*) de métro
**Mexico** Mexique *m.*
**middle: Middle Ages** moyen âge *m.* s.; **to be in the middle of** être en train de
**midnight** minuit
**military budget** budget (*m.*) militaire
**milk** lait *m.*
**minitel** minitel *m.*
**mirror** miroir *m.*
**Miss** Mademoiselle (Mlle)
**mixture** mélange *m.*
**Monday** lundi *m.*; **it's Monday (Tuesday . . . )** nous sommes lundi (mardi...)
**money** argent *m.*; **money exchange (office)** bureau (*m.*) de change
**monitor** contrôler
**month** mois *m.*
**Montreal** Montréal
**monument** monument *m.*
**more . . . than** plus... que; **no more** ne... plus
**morning** matin *m.*; **entire morning** matinée *f.*; **in the morning** du matin; **this morning** ce matin
**Morocco** Maroc *m.*
**most (of)** la plupart (de) *f.*
**mother-in-law** belle-mère *f.*
**motorcycle** motocyclette *f.*
**mountain** montagne *f.*
**mountaineering** alpinisme *m.*
**mouth** bouche *f.*
**movie** film *m.*; **movie theater; movies** cinéma *m.*
**Mr.** Monsieur (M.)
**Mrs.** Madame (Mme)
**much** bien *adv.*; **as much/many . . . as** autant (de)... que; **too much** trop (de); **very much** beaucoup
**municipal** municipal(e)
**museum** musée *m.*
**music** musique *f.*
**musician** musicien(ne) *m., f.*

**naive** naïf (naïve)
**named: to be named** s'appeler; **my name is . . .** je m'appelle... ; **what's your name?** comment vous appelez-vous?
**napkin** serviette *f.*
**natural** naturel(le); **natural resources** ressources (*f. pl.*) naturelles
**nature** nature *f.*
**necessary** nécessaire; **it is necessary to** il est nécessaire de + *inf.*; il faut...; **to be necessary** falloir
**neck** cou *m.*
**necktie** cravate *f.*
**need** avoir besoin de; **one needs** il est nécessaire de; on a besoin de + *inf.*
**neighbor** voisin(e) *m., f.*
**nephew** neveu *m.*
**nervous** nerveux/euse
**network** chaîne *f.*
**never** ne... jamais
**new** nouveau, nouvel, nouvelle
**New Orleans** La Nouvelle-Orléans
**Newfoundland** Terre-Neuve *f.*
**newspaper** journal *m.*
**newsstand** kiosque *m.*
**next** ensuite, puis *adv.*; prochain(e) *adj.*; **next to** à côté de; **next week** la semaine prochaine
**nice** beau (*weather*); gentil(le); sympathique (sympa); **it's nice (out)** il fait beau
**niece** nièce *f.*
**night** nuit *f.*; **at night** du soir
**nine** neuf
**nineteen** dix-neuf
**no** non; **no longer, no more** ne... plus; **no one, nobody** ne... personne
**noise** bruit *m.*
**nonsmoking area** zone (*f.*) non-fumeurs
**noon** midi
**normal** normal(e)
**north** nord *m.*; **to the north** au nord
**nose** nez *m.*
**not (at all)** ne... pas (du tout); **not bad(ly)** pas mal; **not very** peu; **not yet** ne... pas encore
**notebook** cahier *m.*
**nothing** ne... rien
**Nova Scotia** Nouvelle-Écosse *f.*
**novel** roman *m.*
**November** novembre
**now** maintenant; **from now on** à l'avenir
**nuclear energy** énergie (*f.*) nucléaire
**number** numéro *m.*; **to dial a number** composer un numéro

**obliged: to be obliged to** devoir
**obtain** obtenir
**ocean** mer *f.*
**o'clock: the time is . . . o'clock** il est... heures
**October** octobre
**odd** drôle
**of** de; **of course (not)** bien sûr que oui (non); **of it (of them)** en
**offer** offrir
**office** bureau *m.*

**officer** (**police**) agent (*m.*) de police
**often** souvent
**okay** d'accord
**old** ancien(ne); vieux, vieil, vieille
**on** (**top**) sur; **on the ground** par terre
**once** une fois; **all at once** tout d'un coup; **once a week** une fois par semaine
**one** un(e)
**only** ne... que; seulement
**open** ouvrir
**opinion: in my opinion** pour ma part; à mon avis; **in your opinion** à votre (ton) avis; **public opinion** opinion (*f.*) publique; **to express an opinion** exprimer une opinion; **to have an opinion about** penser de
**optimistic** optimiste
**or** ou
**orange** orange
**order: in order** en ordre; **in order to** pour; **to order** commander (*restaurant*)
**other** autre; **others** d'autres; **the other(s)** le/la/les autre(s)
**outdoors** de plein air
**outside** dehors
**overseeing** contrôle *m.*
**owe** devoir
**oyster** huître *f.*

**package** paquet *m.*
**pain: to have pain** avoir mal (à)
**painter** artiste-peintre *m., f.*; peintre *m.*
**painting** peinture *f.*; tableau *m.*
**palace** palais *m.*
**pants** pantalon *m.*
**parade** défilé *m.*; **parade float** char *m.*
**pardon** (**me**) pardon
**Parisian** parisien(ne)
**park** parc *m.*
**party** soirée *f.*; **costume party** bal (*m.*) masqué; **political party** parti *m.*
**pass** (*time*) passer; **boarding pass** carte (*f.*) d'embarquement; **to pass** (*a test*) réussir à; **to pass by** passer par
**passenger** passager/ère *m., f.*
**past** passé *m.*
**pastry, pastry shop** pâtisserie *f.*
**pâté** (**country-style**) pâté (*m.*) (de campagne)
**patient** patient(e)
**patrimony** patrimoine *m.*
**pear** poire *f.*
**pen** stylo *m.*
**pencil** crayon *m.*
**pepper** poivre *m.*
**perfect** perfectionner
**performance** spectacle *m.*
**period** (*of history*) époque *f.*
**permit** (**to**) permettre (de)
**person** personne *f.*
**personally** personnellement
**pessimistic** pessimiste
**pharmacist** pharmacien(ne) *m., f.*
**pharmacy** pharmacie *f.*
**philosophy** philosophie *f.*
**phone** téléphoner (à)
**physics** physique *f.*
**picnic** pique-nique *m.*
**pie** tarte *f.*
**piece** morceau *m.*; **piece of furniture** meuble *m.*
**pilot** pilote *m., f.*
**pink** rose
**place** endroit *m.*; lieu *m.*; **to place** (put) mettre
**plan on** (*doing s.th.*) penser + *inf.*; **plans** projets *m. pl.*
**plate** assiette *f.*
**platform** (*train*) quai *m.*
**play** (*theater*) pièce (*f.*) de théâtre; **to play** (*a musical instrument*) jouer de; **to play** (*a sport or game*) jouer à
**player** (**cassette, CD**) lecteur (*m.*) (de cassettes, de CD)
**pleasant** gentil(le)
**please** s'il vous (te) plaît; **pleased** content(e)
**plumber** plombier *m.*
**poem** poème *m.*
**poet** poète *m.*
**poetry** poésie *f.*
**point out** indiquer
**police officer, policeman** (**woman**) agent (*m.*) de police; **police station** commissariat *m.*; poste (*m.*) de police
**policy** politique *f.*
**politely** poliment
**political party** parti *m.*
**politician** homme (femme) politique *m., f.*
**politics** politique *f.*
**pollute** polluer
**pollution** pollution *f.*
**pool** (**swimming**) piscine *f.*
**poor** pauvre
**popular song** chanson (*f.*) de variété
**pork** porc *m.*; **pork butcher** charcuterie *f.*
**Portugal** Portugal *m.*
**possible** possible; **it is possible that** il est possible que + *subj.*
**post office** bureau (*m.*) de poste
**postcard** carte (*f.*) postale
**poster** affiche *f.*
**potato** pomme (*f.*) de terre
**practical** pratique
**prefer** aimer mieux; préférer
**preferable** préférable
**preferred** préféré(e)
**prepare** préparer
**pretty** joli(e)
**prevent** (**from**) empêcher (de)
**price** prix *m.*; **fixed price menu** menu *m.*
**primary school teacher** instituteur/trice *m., f.*
**probable** probable
**problem** problème *m.*
**process: to be in the process of** être en train de
**professor** professeur *m.*
**program** (*TV, radio*) émission *f.*
**proliferation** prolifération *f.*
**protect** protéger
**protection** protection *f.*
**proud** fier (fière)
**psychology** psychologie *f.*
**public** public (publique); **public opinion** opinion (*f.*) publique
**purchase** achat *m.*
**pursue** poursuivre
**put on** mettre
**putter** (**around**) bricoler

**quarter** (*one-fourth*) quart *m.*; **quarter before** (*the hour*) moins le quart; **quarter past** (*the hour*) et quart; **quarter** (*district*) quartier *m.*
**Quebec** (*city*) Québec; **of, from Quebec** québécois(e); **Quebec** (*province*) Québec *m.*; **Quebecois** (*language*) québécois *m.*
**queen** reine *f.*
**quiet** tranquille

**radio** radio *f.*
**rain** pleuvoir; **it's raining** il pleut
**raincoat** imperméable *m.*
**rarely** rarement
**rate** (**of exchange**) cours (*m.*) (du change)
**rather** plutôt
**read** lire; **reading** lecture *f.*
**ready** prêt(e); **to get ready** se préparer
**realistic** réaliste
**really** vraiment; **oh, really?** ah, bon?
**reasonable** raisonnable

**receipt** reçu *m.*
**recognize** reconnaître
**record(ing)** disque *m.*
**recycle** recycler
**recycling** recyclage *m.*
**red** rouge
**redheaded** roux (rousse)
**reform** réforme *f.*
**refuse (to)** refuser (de)
**regret** regretter
**relate** (*tell*) raconter
**relax** se détendre
**relieved** soulagé(e)
**remain** rester
**remember** se rappeler; se souvenir (de)
**Renaissance** Renaissance *f.*
**rent** louer
**repeat** répéter
**replace** (*put back*) remettre
**reporter** journaliste *m., f.*
**require** exiger
**rescue** sauver
**residence: university residence complex** cité-universitaire (cité-u) *f.*
**resource: natural resources** ressources (*f. pl.*) naturelles
**rest** se reposer
**restaurant** restaurant *m.*
**return** retourner; (*go home*) rentrer; (*come back*) revenir
**review** revue *f.*
**ride (car)** tour *m.*; promenade *f.*; **to take a ride** faire un tour
**right: on (to) the right** à droite; **the Right Bank** (*in Paris*) Rive (*f.*) droite; **to be right** avoir raison
**rise** montée *f.*
**river** fleuve *m.*
**road** route *f.*
**roast** rôti *m.*
**Roman** romain(e)
**room** pièce *f.*; chambre (*bedroom*) *f.*
**roommate** camarade (*m., f.*) de chambre
**rug** tapis *m.*
**run** courir; faire du jogging
**Russia** Russie *f.*
**Russian** (*person*) Russe *m., f.*

**sailboat** bateau (*m.*) à voile
**sailing** voile *f.*; **to go sailing** faire de la voile
**salad** salade *f.*
**salaried worker** travailleur/euse (*m., f.*) salarié(e)
**salary** salaire *m.*
**salt** sel *m.*
**same** même; **the same one(s)** le/la/les même(s)
**sandals** sandales *f. pl.*
**sardines (in oil)** sardines (*f. pl.*) (à l'huile)
**Saturday** samedi *m.*
**sausage** saucisse *f.*
**save** (*rescue*) sauver; **savings account** compte (*m.*) d'épargne; **to save (up) money** faire des économies
**say** dire
**schedule** horaire *m.*
**school** école *f.*; **primary school teacher** instituteur/trice *m., f.*
**sculptor** sculpteur (femme-sculpteur) *m., f.*
**sculpture** sculpture *f.*
**sea** mer *f.*
**seat** (*theater*) place *f.*
**second** deuxième; **second floor** premier étage *m.*
**secretary** secrétaire *m., f.*
**section** (*of Paris*) arrondissement *m.*
**see** voir; **see you soon** à bientôt; **to see again** revoir
**seems: it seems that** il semble que + *subj.*
**self-employed worker** travailleur/euse (*m., f.*) indépendant(e)
**sell** vendre
**send** envoyer
**Senegal** Sénégal *m.*
**sense** sentir *v.*
**September** septembre
**serious** sérieux/euse
**serve** servir
**set** (*TV*) poste (*m.*) de télévision
**settle (down, in)** s'installer
**seven** sept
**seventeen** dix-sept
**several** plusieurs
**sexism** sexisme *m.*
**shave** se raser
**shirt** chemise *f.*
**shoes** chaussures *f. pl.*; **tennis shoes** tennis *m. pl.*
**shop** (*store*) magasin *m.*; **pastry shop** pâtisserie *f.*
**shopkeeper** commerçant(e) *m., f.*
**shopping: to do the shopping** faire le marché
**short** court(e) (*hair*); petit(e) (*person*)
**shorts** short *m.*
**show** spectacle *m.*; **to show** indiquer; montrer
**shower** douche *f.*; **to take a shower** se doucher
**Shrove Tuesday** Mardi Gras
**since** depuis
**sincere** sincère
**sing** chanter
**single** (*person*) célibataire *m., f.*; **single life** célibat *m.*
**sir** Monsieur (M.)
**sister** sœur *f.*; **sister-in-law** belle-sœur *f.*
**sit down** asseyez-vous (assieds-toi)
**situate: to be situated** se trouver
**six** six
**sixteen** seize
**sixty** soixante
**ski** ski *m.*; **ski boots** chaussures (*f. pl.*) de ski; **ski gloves** gants (*m. pl.*) de ski; **ski goggles** lunettes (*f. pl.*) de ski; **ski jacket** anorak *m.*; **to ski** faire du ski; skier
**skiing** ski *m.*; **cross-country skiing** ski de fond; **downhill skiing** ski de piste; **to go skiing** faire du ski; **waterskiing** ski nautique
**skin diving** plongée (*f.*) sous-marine
**skirt** jupe *f.*
**sleep** dormir
**sleeping bag** sac (*m.*) de couchage
**sleepy: to be sleepy** avoir sommeil
**slice** tranche *f.*
**smell** sentir
**smoke** fumer
**smoker** fumeur/euse *m., f.*
**smoking area** zone (*f.*) fumeurs
**snack: afternoon snack** goûter *m.*
**snob** snob
**snow** neige *f.*; neiger; **it's snowing** il neige
**snowman** bonhomme (*m.*) de neige
**so** alors; **so-so** comme ci, comme ça
**sociable** sociable
**social games** jeux (*m. pl.*) de société
**sociology** sociologie *f.*
**socks** chaussettes *f. pl.*
**sofa** canapé *m.*
**solar energy** énergie (*f.*) solaire
**sole** (*fish*) sole *f.*
**some** en *pron.*; quelques *adj.*
**someday** un jour
**someone** quelqu'un
**something** quelque chose
**sometimes** parfois; quelquefois
**somewhat** assez

**son** fils *m.*
**song (popular)** chanson (*f.*) de variété
**soon** bientôt; **as soon as** aussitôt que; dès que; **see you soon** à bientôt
**sorry** désolé(e); **to be sorry** regretter
**soupspoon** cuillère (*f.*) à soupe
**source** source *f.*
**south** sud *m.*; **to the south** au sud
**Spain** Espagne *f.*
**Spanish** (*person*) Espagnol(e) *m., f.*
**speak** parler
**spend** (*money*) dépenser; (*time*) passer
**sport(s)** sport *m.*; **sports coat** veste *f.*; **sports event** manifestation (*f.*) sportive; **sports-minded** sportif/ive; **to do sports** faire du sport
**spring** printemps *m.*; **in the spring** au printemps
**square** (*in city*) place *f.*
**stairway** escalier *m.*
**stamp (postage)** timbre *m.*
**stand: I can't stand . . .** j'ai horreur de...
**state** état *m.*; **United States** États-Unis *m., pl.*
**station (subway)** station (*f.*) de métro; **police station** commissariat *m.*; poste (*m.*) de police; **train station** gare *f.*
**stay** rester
**steak** bifteck *m.*
**stepbrother** beau-frère *m.*
**stepfather** beau-père *m.*
**stepmother** belle-mère *f.*
**stepsister** belle-sœur *f.*
**stereo** chaîne (*f.*) stéréo
**steward, stewardess** steward *m.*, hôtesse (*f.*) de l'air
**still** encore
**stop** s'arrêter
**store** magasin *m.*; **fish store** poissonnerie *f.*; **grocery store** épicerie *f.*
**straight** (*hair*) raide
**straight ahead** tout droit
**strange** étrange
**stranger** étranger/ère *m., f.*
**strawberry** fraise *f.*
**street** rue *f.*
**strike: to (go on) strike** faire (la) grève
**stroll** flâner
**student** étudiant(e) *m., f.*
**study** étudier
**stupid** stupide
**suburbs** banlieue *f.*
**subway** métro *m.*; **subway station** station (*f.*) de métro
**succeed (at)** réussir (à)
**success** réussite *f.*
**suddenly** soudain; tout à coup
**suffer** souffrir
**sugar** sucre *m.*
**suit** (*man's*) costume *m.*; (*woman's*) tailleur *m.*; **suit jacket** veston *m.*
**suitcase** valise *f.*
**sum** montant *m.*
**summer** été *m.*; **in summer** en été
**sun** soleil *m.*; **it's sunny** il fait du soleil
**Sunday** dimanche *m.*
**sunglasses** lunettes (*f. pl.*) de soleil
**suntan: to get a suntan** bronzer
**superb** superbe
**support** soutenir
**sure** sûr(e)
**surprised** étonné(e); surpris(e)
**sweater** pull-over *m.*
**sweetheart** amoureux/euse *m., f.*
**swim** nager; se baigner
**swimming pool** piscine *f.*
**swimsuit** maillot (*m.*) de bain
**Switzerland** Suisse *f.*

**table** table *f.*
**take** prendre; **to take** (*a course*) suivre; **to take** (*s.o.*) emmener; **to take a ride** faire un tour; **to take a trip** faire un voyage; **to take a walk** faire un tour; se promener; **to take an exam** passer un examen; **to take out** sortir; **to take place** se passer
**tall** grand(e)
**tape (cassette)** cassette *f.*
**taste** goûter *v.*
**taxes** impôts *m. pl.*
**tea** thé *m.*
**teach** enseigner (à); apprendre (à)
**teacher** professeur *m.*; **primary school teacher** instituteur/trice *m., f.*
**team** équipe *f.*
**telephone** téléphone *m.*; **telephone book** annuaire *m.*; **telephone booth** cabine (*f.*) téléphonique; **telephone calling card** télécarte *f.*; **telephone number** numéro (*m.*) de téléphone
**television** télévision *f.*; **T.V. set** poste (*m.*) de télé; **television channel** chaîne *f.*
**tell** dire; raconter
**teller: automatic teller** distributeur (*m.*) automatique
**ten** dix
**tennis shoes** tennis *m. pl.*
**tent** tente *f.*
**terrace** terrasse *f.*
**test** examen *m.*; **to pass a test** réussir à un examen
**thank you** merci; **I don't know how to thank you** je ne sais pas comment vous (te) remercier; **to thank** remercier
**that** cela (ça); que; qui *rel. pron.*
**theater** (*movie*) cinéma *m.*
**then** alors; ensuite; puis; **well then** eh bien...
**there** là *adv.*; y *pron.*; **is/are there . . . ?** il y a... ?; **there is/are** voilà; il y a
**therefore** alors; donc
**think (of, about)** réfléchir (à); penser (à); **to think (have an opinion) about** penser de; **what do you think about . . . ?** que pensez-vous (penses-tu) de... ?; **what do you think of that?** qu'en pensez-vous (penses-tu)?
**third floor** deuxième étage *m.*
**thirsty: to be thirsty** avoir soif
**thirteen** treize
**thirty** trente
**this** cela (ça); ce, cet, cette, ces
**three** trois
**throat** gorge *f.*
**Thursday** jeudi *m.*
**ticket window** guichet *m.*
**tidy** en ordre
**tie** (*necktie*) cravate *f.*
**time** heure *f.*; temps *m.*; **from time to time** de temps en temps; **not on time** en retard; **on time** à l'heure; **to pass, spend (time)** passer (du temps); **what time is it?** quelle heure est-il?; **the time is . . . o'clock** il est... heures
**tip** (*gratuity*) pourboire *m.*
**today** aujourd'hui
**tomorrow** demain
**too: too bad** dommage *interj.*; **too much** trop (de)
**tooth** dent *f.*
**top: on top** sur
**touch** toucher
**tourist class** classe (*f.*) économique; **tourist information bureau** syndicat (*m.*) d'initiative
**towel: beach towel** serviette (*f.*) de plage
**tower** tour *f.*
**town hall** mairie *f.*
**train** train *m.*; **train car** wagon *m.*; **train station** gare *f.*
**translate** traduire
**transportation** transports *m. pl.*
**travel** voyager; (*in a car*) rouler
**tree** arbre *m.*

**trip** voyage *m.*; **to take a trip** faire un voyage
**trouble** ennui *m.*; **to have trouble (in)** avoir du mal (à)
**true** vrai(e)
**try (to)** essayer (de); chercher (à)
**T-shirt** tee-shirt *m.*
**Tuesday** mardi *m.*; **Shrove Tuesday** Mardi Gras
**Tunisia** Tunisie *f.*
**turn** tourner
**TV (set)** poste (*m.*) de télévision
**twelve** douze
**twenty** vingt; **twenty-one** vingt et un; **twenty-two** vingt-deux
**two** deux

**ugly** laid(e)
**umbrella** parapluie *m.*
**uncle** oncle *m.*
**under** sous
**understand** comprendre; **I don't understand** je ne comprends pas
**unemployment** chômage *m.*
**unfair** injuste
**unfortunate** fâcheux/euse; pauvre
**United States** États-Unis *m. pl.*
**university** université *f.*; **university residence complex** cité-universitaire (cité-u) *f.*
**unjust** injuste
**unlikely** peu probable
**unsociable** insociable
**until** jusqu'à
**urgent** urgent(e)
**useful** utile
**useless** inutile
**usually** d'habitude

**vacation** vacances *f. pl.*; **during vacation** pendant les vacances
**VCR** magnétoscope *m.*
**vegetable** légume *m.*
**very** très; fort *adv.*; **not very** peu; **very much** beaucoup; **very well, good** très bien
**violet** violet(te)
**visit** visite *f.*; **to visit** (*a place*) visiter; **to visit** (*s.o.*) rendre visite à
**voodoo** vaudou *m.*
**voter** électeur/trice *m., f.*

**wait (for)** attendre
**waiter, waitress** serveur *m.*, serveuse *f.*
**wake up** se réveiller
**walk** promenade *f.*; tour *m.*; **to take a walk** se promener; faire un tour; **walking** marche *f.*
**wall** mur *m.*
**want** avoir envie de; désirer; vouloir
**war** guerre *f.*
**ward** (*of Paris*) arrondissement *m.*
**warm: to be warm** avoir chaud
**wash (*oneself*)** se laver
**waste** gaspillage *m.*; (*material*) déchet *m.*
**watch** regarder; **to watch out** faire attention
**water** eau *f.*; **waterskiing** ski (*m.*) nautique
**way** (*road*) chemin *m.*
**wear** porter
**weather** temps *m.*; **how's the weather?** quel temps fait-il?; **it's bad (good) weather** il fait mauvais (beau)
**Wednesday** mercredi *m.*
**week** semaine *f.*; **every week** toutes les semaines; **next week** la semaine prochaine; **once a week** une fois par semaine
**weekend: this weekend** ce week-end; **on weekends** le week-end
**welcome: you're welcome** de rien; il n'y a pas de quoi; je vous en prie
**well** bien *adv.*; **things are going well** ça va bien; **very well, good** très bien; **well then** eh bien...
**west** ouest *m.*; **to the west** à l'ouest
**what** que; qu'est-ce qui; **to what** à quoi; **what?** comment?; **what is it?** qu'est-ce que c'est?
**when** quand; lorsque; où *relative pron.*
**where** où
**which** lequel, laquelle, lesquels, lesquelles; que, qui *relative pron.*; quel, quelle, quels, quelles *interr. adj.*; **of which** dont
**while: in a while** tout à l'heure
**white** blanc(he); **white-collar worker** employé(e) *m., f.*
**who** qui; qui est-ce qui
**whom** qui est-ce que; **of whom** dont; **to whom** à qui

**whose** dont
**why** pourquoi
**wife** femme *f.*
**willing: to be willing** vouloir bien
**win** gagner
**wind** vent *m.*; **it's windy** il fait du vent
**windbreaker** blouson *m.*
**window** fenêtre *f.*; **ticket window** guichet *m.*
**windsurfer** planche (*f.*) à voile
**wine** vin *m.*; **wine merchant** marchand(e) (*m., f.*) de vin
**winter** hiver *m.*; **in winter** en hiver
**wish** avoir envie de; souhaiter
**with** avec
**withdraw** retirer
**woman** femme *f.*; **young woman** jeune fille *f.*
**wonder** se demander
**wood(s)** bois *m.*; forêt *f.*
**word** mot *m.*
**work** travail *m.*; **to work** travailler; (*device*) marcher; **work (of art)** œuvre (*f.*) (d'art)
**worker** travailleur/euse *m., f.*; (*manual*) ouvrier/ière *m., f.*; **salaried worker** travailleur/euse salarié(e); **self-employed worker** travailleur/euse indépendant(e); **white-collar worker** employé(e) *m., f.*
**world** monde *m.*
**worse** pire
**worth: to be worth** valoir
**write (to)** écrire (à)
**writer** écrivain (femme-écrivain) *m., f.*
**wrong: to be wrong** avoir tort; se tromper

**year** an *m.*; **entire year** année *f.*; **to be (20) years old** avoir (20) ans
**yellow** jaune
**yes** oui; si (*affirmative answer to negative question*)
**yesterday** hier; **the day before yesterday** avant-hier
**yet: not yet** ne... pas encore
**you: and you?** et vous? (et toi?)
**young** jeune; **young man** jeune homme *m.*; **young woman** jeune fille *f.*

**Zaire** Zaïre *m.*

# Index

# Index

This index is divided into two parts: Part I (Grammar) covers topics in grammar, structure, and usage; Part II (Topics) lists cultural, functional (**À propos**), and vocabulary topics treated in the text. Topics in Part II appear as groups; they are not cross-referenced.

## Part I: Grammar

# Part II: Topics

**Text and Art Credits**

**Photos** *page 1* © Beryl Goldberg; *3* © Spencer Grant/The Picture Cube; *6* (*top left*) © Henebry Photography; (*top center*) © Richard Lucas/The Image Works; (*top right*) © D. H. Hessell/Stock, Boston; (*bottom*) © Jean du Boisberranger/Agence Ernoult Features; *14* © Greg Meadors/Stock, Boston; *15* (*clockwise from top left*) © Bruno Maso/PhotoEdit; © Matt Jacob/The Image Works; © Owen Franken/Stock, Boston; © Ulrike Welsch; *16* (*top*) © Ulrike Welsch; (*bottom*) © Ulrike Welsch; *22* Courtesy Alliance Française de la Jamaique, photo © Althea Bartley; *31* © Beryl Goldberg; *38* © Bruno Maso/PhotoEdit; *47* Collection Roger-Viollet, Paris; *48* © Chip and Rosa Maria de la Cueva Peterson; *67* © Greg Meadors/Stock, Boston; *74* (*top*) © Alan Carey/The Image Works; (*center*) © Chip and Rosa Maria de la Cueva Peterson; (*bottom*) © Peter Menzel/Stock, Boston; *79* © UPI/Bettmann Newsphotos; *80* © Beryl Goldberg; *82* © Beryl Goldberg; *86* © Stuart Cohen/Comstock; *98* © Andrew Brilliant; *103* © Andrew Brilliant; *104* (*top left*) © Hugh Rogers/Monkmeyer Press Photos; (*top right*) © Yannick Le Gal/Agence Ernoult Features; (*bottom*) © Stuart Cohen/Comstock; *108* © Gastaud/Sipa Press; *109* © Charles Gupton/Stock, Boston; *111* © Carol Palmer & Andrew Brilliant; *114* © Tony Stone Images; *119* © Ulrike Welsch; *128* © Greg Meadors/Stock, Boston; *132* © Mark Antman/The Image Works; *137* (*left*) © I.P.A./The Image Works; (*right*) © Werner Wolff/Black Star; *138* © Nathan Benn/Woodfin Camp & Associates; *146* (*left to right*) © J. Messerschmidt/Tony Stone Images; © Jean-Daniel Sudres/Scope; © George Hunter/Tony Stone Images; © Mary Ann Brockman; *148* © Ulrike Welsch; *149* © Chip and Rosa Maria de la Cueva Peterson; *163* (*top*) © Mark Antman/The Image Works; (*bottom*) © Mark Antman/The Image Works; *167* © Robert Bretzfelder/PhotoEdit; *168* © Scala/Art Resource; *169* © Henebry Photography; *177* © Owen Franken/Stock, Boston; *178* © Jean Abbott/The Picture Cube; *186* © Sabine Weiss/Photo Researchers; *199* (*top*) © Henebry Photography; (*bottom*) © Michel Ginies/Sipa Press; *200* © Chip and Rosa Maria de la Cueva Peterson; *203* © Jacques Sierpinski/Scope; *204* (*top left*) Courtesy of IBM Archives; (*top right*) Collection Roger-Viollet, Paris; (*bottom left*) © The Bettmann Archive; (*bottom right*) © The Bettmann Archive; *206* © Burt Glinn/Magnum; *210* © Didier Givois/Agence Vandystadt; *214* ©Photo Edit; *225* © Francis de Richemond/The Image Works; *227* © Craig Aurness/Woodfin Camp & Associates; *232* (*left*) Giraudon/Art Resource; (*right*)

# About the Authors

**Judith A. Muyskens** is Professor of French at the University of Cincinnati where she teaches courses in methodology and French language, supervises teaching assistants, and is department head. She received her doctoral degree from Ohio State University in Foreign Language Education with a minor in twentieth-century French literature. She has contributed to various professional publications, including *Modern Language Journal, Foreign Language Annals*, and the *ACTFL Foreign Language Education Series*. She is also coauthor of several other French textbooks, including *Bonjour, ça va?*

**Alice C. Omaggio Hadley,** Ph.D., Ohio State University, is Associate Professor of French at the University of Illinois at Urbana-Champaign, where she is Director of Basic Language Instruction. She supervises teaching assistants and is responsible for the curriculum development, testing, and administration of the elementary and intermediate language program. She is coauthor of the college French texts *Bonjour, ça va?* and *Kaléidoscope* and is author of a language teaching methods text, *Teaching Language in Context*, now in its second edition. Her publications have appeared in various professional journals and she has given numerous workshops throughout the country.

**Thierry Duchesne** has his **CAPES** from France. He holds a **licence** from the University of Angers in English literature with a specialization in French as a foreign language. He has lived in the U.S. and taught French at the University of Cincinnati.

**Claudine Convert-Chalmers** is an **agrégée** from France who has taught all levels of French at the College of Marin in California. She holds degrees in French and English literature and a doctoral degree in Franco-American Civilization from the University of Nice, where she completed her **CAPES** and **Agrégation** training. The title of her dissertation is *L'aventure française à San Francisco durant la ruée vers l'or.* She has lived and taught in Marin County, California since 1977 and is coauthor of several texts, including *Bonjour, ça va?* and *Entrée en scène.*

Giraudon/Art Resource; *233* © Hugh Rogers/Monkmeyer Press Photos; *245* © Steve Vidler/Leo de Wys, Inc.; *247* © Hartman-De Witt/Comstock; *262* (*top*) © Owen Franken/Stock, Boston; (*bottom left*) Collection Roger-Viollet, Paris; *263* © Andrew Brilliant; *268* (*left*) Courtesy Apple Computers; (*right*) © Philippe Imbault/Tony Stone Images; *294* © Stuart Cohen/Comstock; *298* (*top*) © Beryl Goldberg; (*bottom*) © Jeffrey Greenberg/Photo Researchers; *303* © Gamma-Liaison; *311* © Henebry Photography; *312* © Ulrike Welsch; *317* © H. Silvester/Photo Researchers, Inc.; *321* (*left*) Collection Roger-Viollet, Paris; (*right*) © Rolf Adlercreutz/Gamma-Liaison; *322* © Fay Torresyap/Stock, Boston; *323* (*left*) © Canbazard/Explorer; (*top right*) © Peter Gonzalez; (*bottom right*) © Hugh Rogers/Monkmeyer Press Photos; *324* © Thomas Wear/Comstock; *325* (*left*) © Comstock; (*top right*) © Mark Antman/The Image Works; (*bottom right*) © Alan Padley; *329* © Stephen Brown/Gamma-Liaison; *339* © Joseph Nettis/Photo Researchers; *349* © Owen Franken/Stock, Boston; *350* © Dawn Woods; *351* (*top*) © Owen Franken/Stock, Boston; (*bottom*) Collection Roger-Viollet, Paris; *352* © Henebry Photography; *356* © Beryl Goldberg; *369* © G. Spengler/Sygma; *376* © The Bettmann Archive; *377* © Thomas Craig/The Picture Cube; *383* © Carol Palmer & Andrew Brilliant; *401* © Veiller/Photo Researchers; *402* Collection Roger-Viollet, Paris; *403* © Jean-Luc Tabuteau/The Image Works; *409* © Gamma-Liaison; *410* © Jean-Marc Loubat/Agence Vandystadt; *426* (*left*) © Alain Denize/Gamma-Liaison; (*right*) © Betty Press/Picture Group; *433* © Pool J. O. Barcelone/Gamma-Liaison; *434* © Charles

Gupton/Stock, Boston; *438* © Job/Sipa Press; *442* © Elizabeth Marshall/Gamma-Liaison; *445* © Chris Steele-Perkins/Magnum; *449* © Comstock; *452* © Eric Brissaud/Gamma-Liaison; *453* (*bottom left*) © J. M. Truchet/Tony Stone Images; *461* Collection Roger-Viollet, Paris; *462* © Joel Simon; *465* © Stuart Cohen/Comstock; *467* (*top*) © R. Everts/Tony Stone Images; (*bottom*) © Carle/Stock, Boston; *468* © Dourdin/Photo Researchers; *477* (*left*) Courtesy Editions du Seuil, Paris; (*right*) © Ulf Anderson/Gamma-Liaison; *485* © Zihnioglu/Sipa Press; *486* © Peter Menzel; *491* © S. Weiss/Photo Researchers

**Realia and Cartoons** *page 4 L'Humanité; 19* Interarts; *22* Courtesy *France Magazine; 30 Guide Pratique d'Angers; 52* Agfa Gevaert, S.A.; *102* Copyright © Christiane Charillon — Paris; *113 Paris Match; 118 Madame Figaro; 147 Les Dernières Nouvelles d'Alsace; 155* From *Le Nouvel Observateur; 188 GaultMillau Magazine; 224* © Club Med; *227* © Claude Verrier, Intermonde-Presse; *266 Télépoche; 274* NYTSS/*L'Express; 278 Paris Match; 293* © 1993 Les éditions Albert René/Goscinny/Uderzo; *336* cartoon by Laville; *361* RTL; *367 Printemps*, Grands Magazins; *386* From *Francoscopie 91* by Gérard Mermet (Paris: Larousse); *383 Le Monde; 406 Le Point; 422* BCP Strategie Creativité, Inc.; *425* From *Francoscopie 91* by Gérard Mermet (Paris: Larousse); *436 Figaro-Magazine; 489* Information from *We're Number One: Where America Stands and Falls in the New World Order* by A. Shapiro (New York: Vintage, 1992); *492 Journal Français d'Amérique; 495* From *Quid 92* by Dominique and Michèle Frémy

**Readings** *page 131* From *Francoscopie 91* by Gérard Mermet (Paris: Larousse); *194 Bon Sens Magazine; 226* © *Vital; 257* © The Walt Disney Company; *286 Ciné-Télévision Revue; 314 Journal Français d'Amérique; 345* Excerpt and illustrations from *Le Petit Prince* by Antoine de Saint-Exupéry, copyright © 1943, by Harcourt Brace Jovanovich, Inc., and renewed 1971 by Consuelo de Saint-Exupéry—reprinted by permission of the publisher; *371 Le Lundi; 397 Télépoche; 428 Journal Français d'Amérique; 455* From *La Chanson Française à travers ses succes* (Paris: Larousse); *480 Le Lundi; 487 Journal Français d'Amérique; 490* From "Soyez Polis" by Jacques Prévert, © Éditions Gallimard

# Scripts for the Instructor

The scripts in this section correspond to the material that is recorded on the listening comprehension cassette packaged with the student textbook.

The cassette contains the following material for each chapter:

**En avant.** A very brief chapter opening dialogue sets the theme and context of each chapter. Students listen to the dialogue, then answer a short set of questions on its content. As the theme and vocabulary are new to students, the follow-up questions (true/false and either/or) are in English and do not require any active production. Answers to the *En avant* questions are given on the cassette and appear also here in these scripts.

**À l'écoute!** This section contains simulated-authentic listening comprehension passages tied to activities in the text. Students do not see the passages but only hear them. The corresponding activities in the text are in French and check that students have understood the main points of the passage. Passages include conversations, radio announcements, sportscasting, descriptions, stories, game shows, and so on. Answers to the *À l'écoute!* activities are found in Appendix F of the text.

**Situation.** The *Situation* dialogue in the *Intermède* section at the end of each chapter integrates the vocabulary and grammar from the chapter in a functional context. This dialogue is included on the cassette to give students additional listening practice. The text includes comprehension questions, personalized questions, and role-plays that spin off the content of the dialogue.

Only the recorded material that does not already appear in the text is printed in these scripts. These scripts, therefore, contain the following: the *En avant* direction line, follow-up questions, and answers; and the *À l'écoute!* listening comprehension passages. Please look at the actual chapters for the corresponding *En avant* dialogues, *À l'écoute!* activities, and *Situation* dialogues.

All recorded material is indicated in the text with a listening icon and a cassette symbol.

## Chapitre 1: Premier rendez-vous

### En avant

Look at the opening photo in Chapter 1 of your textbook as you listen to this recorded version of the photo caption.

...

Now answer true or false to the following statements. You will hear the correct answer immediately after each item.

1. Marc is talking to one of his teachers. / false
2. The other person says things are going well. / true
3. Marc isn't feeling well today. / false

### À l'écoute!

*Les bonnes manières*

a. —Salut, ça va?
—Ça peut aller. Et toi?
—Pas mal, merci.

b. —Bonsoir, monsieur. Comment allez-vous?
—Bien, merci. Et vous?
—Pas mal, merci.

c. —Bonjour, Anne. Comment vas-tu?
—Très bien. Et vous, mademoiselle?
—Très bien aussi, merci.

d. —Salut! Voilà ton livre de français.
—Merci beaucoup.
—De rien.

e. Bonjour. Je m'appelle Anne Dubois. Et vous, comment vous appelez-vous?

## Chapitre 2: La vie universitaire

### En avant

Look at the opening photo in Chapter 2 of your textbook as you listen to this conversation between Catherine and Luc.

...

Now answer true or false to the following statements. You will hear the correct answer immediately after each item.

1. Catherine has a physics class today. / true
2. Luc likes chemistry very much. / false

### À l'écoute!

*Les étudiants étrangers*

—Moi, je m'appelle François et je suis québécois. À Paris, j'étudie la philosophie et j'habite à la cité-u. J'aime le football et j'adore Paris.

—Bonjour, je suis tunisienne et je m'appelle Fatima. Je parle anglais, français et arabe, et j'étudie l'espagnol. J'adore le cinéma et à Paris, il y a des cinémas partout!

—Salut, je m'appelle Scott et je suis anglais. J'étudie la sociologie, mais je ne travaille pas souvent. J'aime mieux aller au café. Paris, c'est super!

## Chapitre 3: Descriptions

### En avant

Look at the opening photo in Chapter 3 of your textbook as you listen to this conversation between Madame Martin and Madame Dupont.

...

Now answer true or false to the following statements. You will hear the correct answer immediately after each item.

1. The two women are admiring several skirts. / false
2. The second woman says her favorite color is green. / true

### À l'écoute!

*Mon meilleur copain*

Patrice, c'est mon meilleur copain. Il habite à Nice et il étudie l'anglais. Il est vachement drôle et très sympa. Il adore la musique. Il joue de la guitare électrique et son guitariste préféré, c'est Jimmy Hendrix. Patrice, ce n'est pas un intellectuel. Il est intelligent, mais il n'aime pas travailler. Il a un look un peu rocker: il porte toujours un jean, un tee-shirt, un blouson de cuir noir et des bottes.

## Chapitre 4: Le logement

### En avant

Look at the opening photo in Chapter 4 of your textbook as you listen to this conversation between Catherine and Luc.

...

Now answer true or false to the following statements. You will hear the correct answer immediately after each item.

1. Luc doesn't like Catherine's studio apartment. / false

2. Catherine finds the studio small. / true
3. Catherine shares the studio with her sister. / false

**À l'écoute!**

*Chambre à louer*

LAURENCE: Allô! Madame Boussard?
MME BOUSSARD: Oui. Bonjour!
LAURENCE: Bonjour, madame! Avez-vous une chambre à louer?
MME BOUSSARD: Oui, en effet.
LAURENCE: Et comment est la chambre?
MME BOUSSARD: Elle est très grande et très confortable. Elle est très calme aussi. Et il y a deux grandes fenêtres qui donnent sur un parc.
LAURENCE: Est-ce qu'elle est meublée?
MME BOUSSARD: Oui. Il y a un lit, un canapé, une table et deux chaises... ah, il y a une commode aussi.
LAURENCE: Parfait. Est-ce que je peux la visiter cet après-midi?
MME BOUSSARD: Oui, bien sûr!
LAURENCE: Bien, au revoir, madame. À tout à l'heure!
MME BOUSSARD: Au revoir.

## **Chapitre 5:** Famille et foyer

**En avant**

Look at the opening photo in Chapter 5 of your textbook as you listen to this brief conversation.

...

Now answer true or false to the following statements. You will hear the correct answer immediately after each item.

1. The little boy wants his father to read another story. / true
2. The children's father wants them to go to bed. / true

**À l'écoute!**

*Une grande famille*

Moi, j'ai une famille super. Ils sont tous très gentils. Les parents de mon père s'appellent Henri et Virginie. Henri a soixante-dix-huit ans, et Virginie a soixante-douze ans. Ils ont trois enfants: mon papa qui s'appelle Georges, mon oncle qui s'appelle Gérard et ma tante qui s'appelle Nicole. Gérard habite ici à Nantes, comme nous, mais Tante Nicole habite à Tours.

Mon oncle Gérard, c'est le mari de Josiane. Il est professeur au lycée de Nantes. Josiane travaille dans une banque. Ils ont deux enfants: mon cousin Raphael et ma cousine Géraldine. Ils sont très sympa tous les deux. Raphael a douze ans et il est très drôle. C'est un garçon aux cheveux noirs, toujours en désordre, et aux yeux gris. Géraldine, qui a cinq ans, est adorable. Elle a les cheveux châtains et les yeux verts.

Les parents de ma mère s'appellent Charles et Marie. Ils habitent à Tours, pas loin de ma tante Nicole. Ma mère est fille unique; elle s'appelle Juliette. Elle est artiste, et elle travaille dans son atelier ici à la maison.

J'ai une petite sœur de neuf ans: Laurence. Elle est très chouette. Et puis j'ai aussi un grand frère de vingt-sept ans qui habite à Paris. Il s'appelle Franck. Sa femme, Caroline, est belle et intelligente. Ils ont un petit bébé de six mois, une fille. Elle s'appelle Léa et je l'adore!

## **Chapitre 6:** Les Français à table

**En avant**

Look at the opening photo in Chapter 6 of your textbook as you listen to the following conversation.

...

Now answer true or false to the following statements. You will hear the correct answer immediately after each item.

1. The two people are talking about an apple tart. / false
2. The man ordered the dessert from a local restaurant. / false
3. He offers to share the recipe with his friend. / true

**À l'écoute!**

*La météo*

Bonjour! Eh bien, aujourd'hui, il pleut en Bretagne et il y a beaucoup de vent. À Paris, il fait mauvais, il y a de gros nuages mais il ne pleut pas. Sur les Alpes et les Pyrénées, il neige beaucoup; mais il fait du soleil sur la Côte d'Azur et la Corse.

Quelques températures relevées aujourd'hui à midi:

- À Brest, 8 degrés
- À Paris, 6
- À Grenoble et Toulouse, 2
- À Marseille et Ajaccio, 10

**Exercice B.** Vrai ou faux? Listen to the following statements and decide whether they are true or false, according to the weather conditions *in your area.*

1. Nous sommes au printemps.
2. Nous sommes en hiver.
3. Nous sommes en été.
4. Nous sommes en automne.
5. Il fait beau.
6. Il pleut.
7. Il fait chaud.
8. Il fait froid.
9. Il fait du vent.
10. Le temps est nuageux.

II. *Un repas inoubliable*

SERVEUR: Bonsoir, messieurs-dames.
THOMAS: Bonsoir. Nous avons une réservation pour huit heures.
SERVEUR: Oui, et à quel nom, s'il vous plaît?
THOMAS: Blanchard.
SERVEUR: Oui, par ici, s'il vous plaît. Voici la carte.
THOMAS: Merci.
(Pause)
SERVEUR: Avez-vous choisi?
MARISE: Oui. Pour commencer je vais prendre des huîtres, et ensuite le filet de bœuf.
SERVEUR: Bien, madame. Et vous, monsieur?
THOMAS: Pour moi le steak au poivre.
SERVEUR: Et comme boisson?
THOMAS: Apportez-nous du champagne, s'il vous plaît.
MARISE: Du champagne!
THOMAS: Et pourquoi pas? C'est la fête aujourd'hui!

## Chapitre 7: On mange bien en France!

### En avant

Look at the opening photo in Chapter 7 of your textbook as you listen to the following conversation.

...

Now answer the following questions. You will hear the correct answer immediately after each item.

1. What kind of fish is the customer buying, salmon or tuna? / salmon
2. Did she buy anything else from the fish vendor? / no

### À l'écoute!

I. *Les supermarchés Traffic*

C'est le mois des promotions chez Traffic! Des prix incroyables! Cinq francs le kilo d'oranges ou de bananes! Grande sélection de fromages, de saussices, de porc et de jambon à quarante francs le kilo! Trois francs le litre de jus de pomme! Trois francs la boîte de petits pois, deux francs cinquante la baguette! Et bien d'autres produits à des prix incroyables! Les supermarchés Traffic sont ouverts tous les jours de neuf heures à 21 heures. Venez vite! Nous attendons votre visite!

## Chapitre 8: Vive les vacances!

### En avant

Look at the opening photo in Chapter 8 of your textbook as you listen to the following conversation between Georges and Janine.

...

Now answer the following questions. You will hear the correct answer immediately after each item.

1. Who seems to be more athletic, Georges or Janine? / Janine
2. Which sport does Janine like, swimming or sailing? / sailing
3. What does Georges like to do on vacation mornings, go jogging or sleep in? / sleep in

### À l'écoute!

I. *Souvenirs de vacances*

SANDRINE: Salut, Jean-Yves. Tu as passé de bonnes vacances?
JEAN-YVES: Excellentes. Et toi?
SANDRINE: Moi aussi. Qu'est-ce que tu as fait?

JEAN-YVES: J'ai passé quinze jours à la campagne, chez ma grand-mère.

SANDRINE: Tu aimes passer les vacances à la campagne?

JEAN-YVES: Oui, c'est agréable. Les gens sont très gentils, ils prennent le temps de vivre et ne sont pas toujours nerveux comme en ville.

SANDRINE: Tu as fait du sport?

JEAN-YVES: Oui, j'ai joué au tennis presque tous les jours et j'ai fait mon sport favori en vacances: dormir! Et toi, qu'est-ce que tu as fait cet été?

SANDRINE: Moi, j'ai profité du soleil. J'ai passé tout le mois de juillet à la mer avec ma famille.

JEAN-YVES: Tu as fait de la planche à voile?

SANDRINE: Non, j'ai eu peur d'essayer. Mais j'ai fait beaucoup de bateau. J'ai aussi rencontré sur la plage un groupe de jeunes très sympa. On a joué au volley-ball et le soir on a beaucoup dansé.

II. *Géopari*

L'ANIMATEUR: Bonjour, monsieur! Comment vous appelez-vous?

GILLES: Gilles Goulu.

L'ANIMATEUR: Et bien, Gilles, vous êtes prêt? Première question: dans quel pays se trouve la ville d'Oslo?

GILLES: Euh... Oslo... euh... en Suède.

L'ANIMATEUR: Désolé, mon cher Gilles. C'est en Norvège. Deuxième question: Dans quelle ville se trouve la Maison Blanche?

GILLES: Euh... attendez c'est euh... aux États-Unis à Washington.

L'ANIMATEUR: Excellent! Troisième question: où se trouve le Taj Mahal?

GILLES: Le Taj Mahal?... aucune idée, désolé, je ne sais pas.

L'ANIMATEUR: Et bien, mon cher ami, c'est en Inde. Enfin dernière question, c'est facile: où se trouve la plage d'Ipanéma?

GILLES: Euh... ah oui! C'est au Brésil.

L'ANIMATEUR: Oui, c'est ça, mais je veux la ville, quelle ville?

GILLES: Euh... attendez... à Sao Paulo.

L'ANIMATEUR: Et non, dommage! C'est Rio de Janeiro. Et bien, mon cher Gilles, vous avez une bonne réponse. Vous gagnez *200 francs*!

## **Chapitre 9:** Voyages et transports

### En avant

Look at the opening photo in Chapter 9 of your textbook as you listen to the following conversation between Georges and Janine.

...

Now answer true or false to the following statements. You will hear the correct answer immediately after each item.

1. Georges is taking a plane to Marseille. / false
2. Janine offers to drive him to the station. / true
3. The couple leaves together in Janine's car. / false
4. Georges wants to take the subway to the train station. / true

### À l'écoute!

I. *Retour de voyage*

PHILIPPE: Alors, raconte, c'est comment, le Maroc?

ALAIN: C'est un pays fascinant. J'ai passé deux semaines merveilleuses à Marrakech. Mais toi aussi, tu es déjà allé au Maroc, non?

PHILIPPE: Non, j'ai voyagé au Sénégal et en Côte-d'Ivoire. Et qu'est-ce que tu as trouvé de différent à Marrakech?

ALAIN: Eh bien, par exemple, tout est écrit en français ou en arabe. Euh... on voit des hommes partout, mais très peu de femmes. Elles sortent rarement de chez elles.

PHILIPPE: C'est très intéressant. Et qu'est-ce que tu as mangé?

ALAIN: J'ai mangé des couscous délicieux, préparés avec de la viande ou du poisson. Et j'ai bu du thé à la menthe... formidable! Ah, voilà mes valises!

PHILIPPE: Trois valises, c'est pas possible! Mais tu es parti avec une valise seulement...

ALAIN: Oui, mais j'ai acheté beaucoup de souvenirs à Marrakech!

II. *Le pauvre Joseph*

Hier Joseph est parti de chez lui très tôt. Il a pris, comme d'habitude, l'autoroute du nord. Il a roulé pendant une heure. Puis, tout d'un coup sa voiture est tombée en panne. «C'est bizarre,»—a-t-il pensé—«je n'ai jamais eu de problèmes avec cette voiture.» Il est descendu de la voiture, il l'a tout examinée, mais il n'a rien trouvé. Heureusement, il a vu un téléphone pas trop loin. Il a appelé un garage, puis il est retourné jusqu'à la voiture pour attendre le mécanicien. Il n'a pas attendu plus de dix minutes. Quand le mécanicien est arrivé, il a inspecté la voiture. «C'est sérieux?» lui a demandé Joseph. «Pas du tout, monsieur», lui a répondu le mécanicien, «vous avez oublié de faire le plein d'essence...»

## **Chapitre 10:** Bonnes nouvelles

### En avant

Look at the opening photo in Chapter 10 of your textbook as you listen to the following conversation between Élise and Jean-Pierre.

...

Now answer the following questions. You will hear the correct answer immediately after each item.

1. Is Élise asking about a newspaper or a news magazine? / a newspaper
2. Where did Jean-Pierre read the paper that morning, in a café or in the subway? / in the subway
3. Did he read the paper thoroughly from front to back? / no

### À l'écoute!

I. *Où suis-je?*

PREMIÈRE SÉQUENCE SONORE:

—Bonjour, monsieur.

—Bonjour. Je voudrais un timbre pour envoyer une lettre aux États-Unis.

—Voici votre timbre, monsieur.

—Merci, madame. Je vous dois combien?

—4 francs, s'il vous plaît.

DEUXIÈME SÉQUENCE SONORE:

—Bonjour monsieur! *Le Figaro magazine*, s'il vous plaît.

—Le voici. Et voulez-vous autre chose, madame?

—Euh... oui, est-ce que vous avez une revue spécialisée sur le cinéma?

—Oui, bien sûr! Il y a *Première, les Cahiers du Cinéma* et *Studio*.

TROISIÈME SÉQUENCE SONORE:

—Le président des États-Unis va venir en France le mois prochain. Il va parler avec le président de la République du problème de l'exportation des produits agricoles français vers les États-Unis.

II. *Les vacances chez grand-mère*

VIVIANE: Tu te rappelles nos vacances chez grand-mère?

CATHERINE: Oui, c'était bien. Elle était très heureuse de nous voir et elle nous préparait toujours de bons goûters avec des petits gâteaux et de la limonade.

VIVIANE: Et moi, j'adorais les histoires qu'elle nous racontait. Elle n'avait pas la télé mais on ne s'ennuyait jamais.

CATHERINE: Non. Quand il faisait beau, on allait jouer dans le jardin et quand il pleuvait, elle nous lisait des livres ou elle nous montrait des photos de famille.

VIVIANE: Oui, c'était le bon temps! Parfois, elle jouait aussi du piano et nous, on chantait.

CATHERINE: En fait, j'aimerais bien encore être une petite fille. Ce n'est pas drôle d'être grande!

## **Chapitre 11:** La vie urbaine

### En avant

Look at the opening photo in Chapter 11 of your textbook as you listen to the following conversation between Madame Martin and Monsieur Dupont.

...

Now answer the following questions. You will hear the answers immediately after each item.

1. Does M. Dupont live in the city or in the suburbs? / in the suburbs
2. Does he drive to work or take public transportation? / He takes public transportation.
3. Does he live in a house or an appartment? / in a house

**À l'écoute!**

I. *Pour aller au syndicat d'initiative*

ANNE-MARIE: Pardon, monsieur. Savez-vous où est le syndicat d'initiative?
LE MONSIEUR: Oui, mademoiselle. Voulez-vous y aller à pied ou en bus?
ANNE-MARIE: À pied. Pourquoi? C'est loin d'ici?
LE MONSIEUR: Non, pas du tout. Alors, prenez la première rue à gauche et continuez tout droit jusqu'à la place de la Gare. Traversez la place et là, prenez la rue Pasteur à droite. Vous me suivez?
ANNE-MARIE: Oui, très bien.
LE MONSIEUR: Puis, descendez la rue Pasteur et tournez à gauche dans la rue... oh, j'ai oublié son nom. Mais c'est la quatrième, non, la cinquième, oui, euh... prenez la cinquième rue à gauche. Je crois qu'elle s'appelle rue de la Boétie. Ensuite, prenez à gauche de nouveau dans la première petite rue, et vous allez voir le syndicat d'initiative sur votre droite. Je ne sais pas le numéro, mais je crois qu'il est en face du commissariat, entre une boulangerie et un magasin de sport.
ANNE-MARIE: Merci beaucoup, monsieur.
LE MONSIEUR: De rien.

II. *Souvenirs de Marseille*

GEORGES: Tu connais Marseille?
LUCIEN: Oui, très bien. J'y suis allé deux fois. La première fois, c'était en 1965, j'avais 18 ans. J'y suis resté deux ans parce que j'avais trouvé un travail là-bas. J'adorais cette ville. Il faisait toujours du soleil, les gens étaient heureux, et tous les week-ends, on allait pêcher en mer.
GEORGES: Et la deuxième fois?
LUCIEN: La deuxième fois, c'était en 1992. Marseille a beaucoup changé. En fait, c'est la vie qui a changé. Je suis allé boire un pastis à la terrasse d'un café et j'ai regardé les gens. Ils ne riaient plus. J'ai cherché les petits magasins où j'allais faire mes courses autrefois mais ils n'étaient plus là. La boulangerie, la boucherie, le petit café du port, il n'y avait plus rien. J'étais triste, très triste. Alors j'ai pris le train et je suis retourné à Paris.

## Chapitre 12: La France et les arts

**En avant**

Look at the opening photo in Chapter 12 of your textbook as you listen to the following conversation.

...

Now answer true or false to the following statements. You will hear the answers immediately after each item.

1. The two travelers see a spectacular castle as they approach the town of Chartres. / false
2. The stained glass windows date from the thirteenth century. / true

**À l'écoute!**

I. *Les châteaux de la Loire*

MARC: Qu'est-ce que tu as fait ce week-end?
VIRGINIE: J'ai visité les châteaux de la Loire.
MARC: Ah bon! Et comment y es-tu allée?
VIRGINIE: En voiture avec Jeanne et Hélène.
MARC: Moi, j'adore les châteaux. Ils sont magnifiques. Je me rappelle très bien le château de Blois. J'y suis allé en 1982. C'est une merveille de la Renaissance avec son grand escalier et son immense terrasse.
VIRGINIE: Oui, mais moi j'ai préféré Azay-le-Rideau. Il a beaucoup de charme. Il se trouve sur une petite île au milieu d'une grande forêt. Et l'intérieur du château est splendide avec ses meubles d'époque, ses tableaux et ses tapisseries. Mais en fait, tous les châteaux de la Loire sont vraiment extraordinaires.
MARC: Tu as vu le château de Chinon?
VIRGINIE: Non, malheureusement. Mais j'espère y aller un jour parce qu'il date du Moyen Âge et que j'adore cette période de l'histoire.

II. *Arthur Rimbaud*

Arthur Rimbaud est né en 1854 à Charleville. Il a fait de brillantes études mais il avait déjà un caractère difficile. Il s'est révolté contre sa famille, les conventions, la religion, et est parti seul à Paris en 1870. Dans ses poèmes, il a attaqué Napoléon III, le conformisme et le catholicisme.

En 1875, Rimbaud a renoncé à la poésie et a commencé une vie de voyages et d'aventures. Il s'est engagé dans l'armée hollandaise et est allé à Java, puis il a fait du commerce en Arabie. En 1891, malade, il est rentré en France pour mourir.

Rimbaud est devenu un mythe en France. Il a écrit pendant cinq ans seulement, mais il est, pourtant, avec Baudelaire, le plus célèbre de tous les poètes français.

## **Chapitre 13:** La vie de tous les jours

### En avant

Look at the opening photo in Chapter 13 of your textbook as you listen to M. Duriez talking to Martine.

...

Now answer true or false to the following statements. You will hear the correct answer immediately after each item.

1. Martine is talking about her upcoming graduation from university. / false
2. Martine and her fiancé Alexandre are going to be married the following summer. / true
3. Martine met her fiancé in an English course. / false

### À l'écoute!

*Un rêve bizarre*

VINCENT: J'ai fait un rêve vraiment bizarre cette nuit.

GILLES: Ah bon. Vas-y, raconte!

VINCENT: Eh bien, voilà. Dans mon rêve, je me lève, comme d'habitude, à 7h30. Jusque là, tout va bien. C'est après que les catastrophes commencent. Je vais prendre ma douche, mais l'eau est toute rouge. Puis, je me brosse les dents mais le dentrifice s'est transformé en chocolat et j'ai les dents toutes noires. Ensuite, je veux me peigner: mais je me regarde dans le miroir et qu'est-ce que je vois? Je n'ai plus un seul cheveu sur la tête. Mon rasoir électrique a disparu, alors je me rase avec un grand couteau comme les cow-boys dans les westerns. Puis je me prépare le petit déjeuner mais le café est bleu et le lait est vert. Je ne comprends plus rien. Alors, je m'en vais au bureau. Dehors, tout est normal, mais les gens me regardent bizarrement. Au bureau, personne ne me dit bonjour. Ils ont peur de moi. Soudain deux policiers entrent et m'emmènent avec eux. C'est à ce moment-là que je me suis réveillé et que j'ai crié: NON!

## **Chapitre 14:** Cherchons une profession

### En avant

Look at the opening photo in Chapter 14 of your textbook as you listen to this conversation between Sylvie and Robert.

...

Now answer the following questions. You will hear the correct answer immediately after each item.

1. Where is Sylvie's summer job, in Nice or in Paris? / Nice
2. Is she going to work for a multinational corporation? / No
3. Why did she take the job with a small firm, to earn more money or to be near the beach? / to be near the beach

### À l'écoute!

*Carrières*

Et voici, comme chaque jour sur Radio France, quelques offres d'emplois.

PREMIÈRE OFFRE:

Grosse société d'ordinateurs recherche pour ses bureaux du nord de la France deux ingénieurs en informatique. Les candidats devront avoir entre 5 et 10 ans d'expérience professionnelle et une très bonne connaissance de la langue anglaise. Ils seront responsables du développement de nouveaux produits. Ils voyageront 25% du temps, surtout en Angleterre et en Hollande.

DEUXIÈME OFFRE:

Société multinationale, basée à Paris, recherche secrétaire trilingue espagnol, anglais. BTS ou niveau équivalent avec de bonnes notions de comptabilité. La personne devra être dynamique et avoir un bon sens de l'organisation. La personne travaillera en collaboration avec le responsable de gestion pour l'Europe.

TROISIÈME OFFRE:

Université africaine recherche professeur de physique-chimie pour la rentrée prochaine. Maîtrise, plus 5 ans d'expérience et de bonnes notions d'anglais souhaitées. La connaissance de l'Afrique de l'ouest sera appréciée, mais n'est pas indispensable. Le candidat travaillera à Dakar, mais donnera aussi des conférences dans les pays francophones voisins.

Si vous êtes intéressé par l'une de ces carrières, envoyez-nous votre C.V., avec une lettre à Radio France, 245 rue des Artisans, 75015 Paris.

## Chapitre 15: Vive les loisirs!

### En avant

Look at the opening photo in Chapter 15 of your textbook as you listen to the following conversation between Annick and Hervé-Louis.

...

Now answer the following questions. You will hear the correct answer immediately after each item.

1. What is Annick planning to do Saturday, play tennis or study? / play tennis
2. What does Hervé-Louis invite Annick to do on Sunday, go cycling or go to the movies? / go to the movies
3. Are they going to see a movie about Christopher Columbus or a filmed Shakespearean play? / a movie about Columbus

### À l'écoute!

*Le Tour de France*

Chers auditeurs, bonjour! Nous voici en direct de Chamonix, au cœur des Alpes pour cette douzième étape du Tour de France. Le temps est magnifique aujourd'hui et les gens sont venus très nombreux pour voir les coureurs qui arriveront ici dans un petit quart d'heure. Nous savons que le no. 52, le Français Alain Laville, qui est né ici à Chamonix, était en tête à 50 km de l'arrivée. Il a toujours 3 minutes d'avance sur 10 autres coureurs parmi lesquels on trouve 3 Français, 2 Italiens, 1 Espagnol, 2 Hollandais, 1 Belge et 1 Américain.

Attention, je vois les coureurs qui arrivent maintenant. Alain Laville est seul mais les autres se rapprochent. Plus que 200 mètres. Voilà c'est fait, Alain Laville gagne l'étape avec 40 secondes d'avance sur un autre Français, le no. 75 Gilbert Monier. L'Américain Steve Johnson, no. 142, termine 3$^{e}$ de l'étape. Au classement général du Tour, Alain Laville est maintenant 1$^{er}$ et prend le maillot jaune de leader. L'Espagnol Manuel Garcia est 2$^{e}$ et l'Italien Enzo Baggio est 3$^{e}$. Demain nous serons encore dans les Alpes, à Annecy, pour vivre avec vous la 13$^{e}$ étape de ce fantastique Tour de France. Ici Chamonix, à vous Paris.

## Chapitre 16: Opinions et points de vue

### En avant

Look at the opening photo in Chapter 16 of your textbook as you listen to the following conversation in which Christine gives her opinions about contemporary problems.

...

Now answer true or false to the following statements. You will hear the correct answer immediately after each item.

1. Christine believes corporations that pollute should police themselves more stringently. / false
2. According to Christine, acid rain is destroying the forests. / true
3. Christine claims that industrial wastes are poisoning the rivers. / true

### À l'écoute!

I. *Le candidat*

JOURNALISTE: Monsieur Deschamps, vous êtes candidat à la mairie de Lyon. À votre avis, quelles sont les qualités les plus importantes pour être le maire d'une grande ville?

M. DESCHAMPS: Pour être le maire d'une grande ville, ou d'une petite ville d'ailleurs, il faut être avant tout honnête, dynamique et responsable. Il faut aussi savoir écouter, être ouvert à toutes les suggestions et ne pas avoir peur d'agir.

JOURNALISTE: Qu'est-ce qui peut éventuellement

faire la différence entre les candidats aux yeux des électeurs?

M. DESCHAMPS: Pour être élus, la plupart des candidats promettent l'impossible. Personnellement, je pense qu'il est important de bien connaître la ville et ses problèmes pour pouvoir proposer des solutions réalistes. Il faut prouver que vous serez capable, le moment venu, de protéger les intérêts de la ville. C'est cela qui vous permettra de gagner la confiance des électeurs!

JOURNALISTE: Et pour vous, quels sont les problèmes qui exigent une attention immédiate?

M. DESCHAMPS: Ils sont nombreux, mais personnellement je crois que le chômage et la pollution sont deux problèmes très sérieux que nous devons considérer en priorité.

JOURNALISTE: Monsieur Deschamps, je vous remercie de ce court entretien et je vous souhaite bonne chance dans votre campagne électorale.

M. DESCHAMPS: C'est moi qui vous remercie.

II. *Les informations*

MARYSE: Il est midi et vous écoutez Radio Rendez-vous. C'est l'heure de notre flash d'informations. Hubert, c'est à vous!

HUBERT: Merci Maryse et bonjour à tous! L'organisation S.O.S. Racisme organisera demain à Paris à partir de 15 heures une manifestation silencieuse en hommage à Rachid Bencherif. Ce jeune Français d'origine arabe a été tué hier d'une balle de revolver par un inspecteur de police. La tragédie a eu lieu lors d'un interrogatoire au commissariat de la ville de Saffré.

M. Balladur, notre premier ministre, a annoncé ce matin les derniers chiffres du chômage: la France compte désormais plus de trois millions de chômeurs, un chiffre record. M. Balladur a précisé que le chômage devrait continuer à augmenter jusqu'à la fin de l'année 1993 mais qu'il devrait diminuer à partir de janvier 1994.

Le parti des Verts et le parti Génération Écologie qui s'étaient associés pendant les élections législatives ont décidé de se séparer.

À propos d'écologie, nous célébrons aujourd'hui «La journée de la Terre.» Le thème de cette journée sera le recyclage. Ne jetez plus vos bouteilles en verre ou en plastique: tous ces matériaux peuvent être recyclés. Le ministre de l'environnement vient d'annoncer qu'un nouveau système de ramassage des produits recyclables va être mis en place.

Pour finir, un peu de sport: Limoges a gagné hier soir la coupe d'Europe des clubs champions de basket-ball. C'est la première fois qu'un club français devient champion d'Europe. Alors, bravo Limoges.

Ce flash est maintenant terminé. Merci de votre attention et je vous retrouve ce soir à 20 heures.

## Chapitre 17: Le monde francophone

### En avant

Look at the opening photo in Chapter 17 of your textbook as you listen to the following conversation.

...

Now answer true or false to the following statements. You will hear the correct answer immediately after each item.

1. The travelers are admiring a sunset. / true
2. They are in Tahiti. / false
3. They like Raiatea because there's more night life than on Tahiti and Bora-Bora. / false

### À l'écoute!

I. *Héritage français*

Bonjour, je m'appelle Jim Bonnet et je suis américain. Pourquoi est-ce que j'ai un nom de famille français? La réponse est simple: mes ancêtres étaient français. Ils vivaient dans un petit village en Normandie et ils sont partis au Canada au XVIIème siècle. Ils y ont vécu jusqu'à l'arrivée des Anglais, et c'est alors qu'ils sont partis en Louisiane comme beaucoup d'Acadiens. Ces Acadiens sont les ancêtres des Cajuns qui habitent toujours en Louisiane. Ils se sont installés dans les bayous et ont gardé leur langue et leurs coutumes. À cette époque la Louisiane était un territoire français.

Ma famille habite maintenant La Nouvelle-Orléans. Nous ne parlons plus le français à la maison, mais nous avons gardé certaines traditions françaises. Nous fêtons, par exemple, le Mardi gras. Personnellement je suis très fier de mon héritage culturel; c'est pour cela que j'ai appris le français et que je viens regulièrement en France pour le perfectionner.

Moi, je m'appelle Louis Lafleur et je suis québécois. Mon histoire est semblable à celle de Jim; ma famille est aussi d'origine française. Elle a quitté la Bretagne il y a plus de trois siècles pour s'établir en Acadie. Puis vers 1713, je crois, l'Acadie est devenue anglaise. Comme tous les Acadiens, mes ancêtres ont eu peur parce qu'ils voulaient rester français. Je ne sais pas exactement quand, mais quelques-uns se sont exilés aux États-Unis et ils se sont installés dans l'état de Maine. Ils n'avaient qu'une seule idée en tête: retourner en Acadie. Finalement, leurs descendants ont réalisé leur rêve et sont repartis au Canada au XIX$^{\text{ème}}$ siècle. Ils se sont installés à Québec, où ma famille vit toujours. À la maison, nous parlons français. Je ne connais pas encore la France, mais je pense y aller l'année prochaine.

II. *Étudiants francophones*

RANGIRA: Kai, est-ce que l'influence française est encore visible au Viêt-Nam?

KAI: De moins en moins. Je crois qu'elle a beaucoup marqué la génération de mon père surtout à travers l'enseignement de la langue. À l'école, il a appris non seulement le français mais aussi une certaine façon de penser et de s'exprimer. Et ça, c'est surtout vrai pour les gens qui ont fait des études supérieures.

RANGIRA: Mais je croyais qu'on enseignait toujours le français comme deuxième langue.

KAI: Oui, mais on ne le parle pas dans la rue. Tu sais les Français ont quitté le Viêt-Nam il y a plus de 40 ans. C'est vrai qu'ils nous ont laissé les cafés, la mode, mais chez les jeunes, l'influence n'est que superficielle. Et dans ton pays?

RANGIRA: Au Zaïre, l'influence française est très grande.

FARAH: Mais vous étiez une colonie belge, non?

RANGIRA: Oui, mais depuis notre indépendance, nous avons aussi de très bons rapports avec la France.

KAI: Est-ce que vous apprenez le français à l'école?

RANGIRA: Oui, le français y est obligatoire. À la maison les Zaïrois parlent leur langue, mais ils ont besoin du français pour travailler. De plus, beaucoup de jeunes, comme moi, viennent finir leurs études en France. Et dans ton pays, Farah?

FARAH: Eh bien, en Algérie on parle encore français, comme dans les autres pays du Maghreb. On l'enseigne aussi à l'école. Et puis, il y a une élite qui est vraiment bilingue.

KAI: Et quelles sont les relations entre les deux pays?

FARAH: On peut dire qu'elles sont bonnes maintenant. Il y a beaucoup d'échanges commerciaux et culturels.

KAI: Bon, c'est bien tout ça, mais moi j'ai faim. Si on allait manger un couscous chez Abdel?

FARAH: Super idée! Abdel, il fait le meilleur couscous de la ville.

## Chapitre 18: La société contemporaine

### À l'écoute!

*Débat sur la publicité*

FLORENCE: À mon avis, le seul but des publicités est de vendre. Et pour vendre, le plus souvent elles jouent sur les réflexes conditionnés.

BERNARD: Je ne suis pas d'accord. Je pense que l'un des principaux objectifs de la publicité est de nous informer sur les nouveaux produits. Sans la publicité, nous continuerions toujours à utiliser les mêmes choses et nous ne pourrions pas profiter des progrès techniques, par exemple.

FLORENCE: Mais tu sais, ceux qui font les pubs font appel aux impulsions les plus basses. Prends l'exemple de cette publicité que l'on voit dans tous les magazines dernièrement. On te montre un bel homme très élégant en train de fumer une cigarette. L'objectif de cette pub est de nous faire associer cette marque de cigarette avec une image de la perfection: tout un style de vie, la beauté, l'élégance. Le message est simple: fumez cette marque et vous ressemblerez à cet homme.

BERNARD: Tu ne vois que le côté négatif de la pub. Si tu étudies la publicité pour un ordinateur que l'on passe souvent à la télé, eh bien, elle explique pas à pas, tout ce que la machine est capable de faire. Ainsi le téléspectateur peut comprendre facilement comment marche l'ordinateur et ce qu'il apporte de nouveau.

FLORENCE: Oui, mais tout ce que le fabricant veut, c'est te vendre son ordinateur! Il te racontera n'importe quoi pour essayer de te convaincre que c'est le meilleur sur le marché.

BERNARD: À mon avis, il est important de se tenir au courant. La publicité est un moyen de s'informer, c'est tout.

FLORENCE: Le problème, c'est que tout le monde ne réagit pas comme toi. Dans l'ensemble, les gens n'ont pas beaucoup de personnalité et croient tout ce qu'on leur dit. Ils sont facilement influençables.

BERNARD: Là, je crois que tu sous-estimes un peu les capacités intellectuelles du public. En fait, tu es en train de faire ce que tu reproches aux pubs.

FLORENCE: Quoi?

BERNARD: Eh bien, Florence, de te servir d'un stéréotype très négatif pour défendre ton point de vue!